New TOEIC 新制多益
聽力閱讀
全題型攻略
➕ 實戰模擬 6 回題庫大全

TOEIC Premium
6 Practice Tests + Online Audio, 10th edition

Lin Lougheed Ph.D. ──著
丁宥榆──譯

音檔使用說明

掃描 QR Code 聆聽音檔，購書讀者完成註冊、驗證與免費訂閱程序後，即可啟用音檔。音檔限本人使用，違者依法追究。

STEP 1
掃描上方 QRCode

STEP 2
快速註冊或登入 EZCourse

STEP 3
回答問題按送出

答案就在書中（需注意空格與大小寫）。

STEP 4
完成訂閱

該書右側會顯示「**已訂閱**」，表示已成功訂閱，即可點選播放本書音檔。

STEP 5
點選個人檔案

查看「**我的訂閱紀錄**」會顯示已訂閱本書，點選封面可到本書線上聆聽。

目次

多益測驗的結構 006
給教師的話 007

1 多益測驗介紹

1-1 多益測驗常見問題 012
1-2 多益讀書計畫 016
1-3 自學活動 020
1-4 考試當天 024

多益測驗解題訓練

2 聽力測驗

2-1 聽力測驗介紹與高分攻略清單 028
2-2 Part 1：照片描述 030
2-2-1 試題範例 030
2-2-2 高分攻略 031
2-3 Part 2：應答問題 046
2-3-1 試題範例 046
2-3-2 高分攻略 047
2-4 Part 3：簡短對話 061
2-4-1 試題範例 061
2-4-2 高分攻略 064
2-5 Part 4：簡短獨白 094
2-5-1 試題範例 094
2-5-2 高分攻略 096

答題訣竅總整理 122
聽力診斷測驗 124

3 閱讀測驗

3-1 閱讀測驗介紹與高分攻略清單 138
3-2 Part 5：句子填空 140
3-2-1 試題範例 140
3-2-2 高分攻略 141
3-3 Part 6：段落填空 187
3-3-1 試題範例 187
3-3-2 高分攻略 191
3-4 Part 7：閱讀測驗 240
3-4-1 試題範例 240
3-4-2 PSRA 策略 245
3-4-3 高分攻略 249
答題訣竅總整理 274
閱讀診斷測驗 276

多益實戰模擬試題

實戰模擬試題 1 304
實戰模擬試題 2 350
實戰模擬試題 3 396
實戰模擬試題 4 444
實戰模擬試題 5 488
實戰模擬試題 6 532

多益測驗的結構

多益測驗分為聽力與閱讀兩大部分,本書將針對兩大部分提供詳細說明,包含題目類型和作答策略,掌握各章內容就能從容應付考試。

多益測驗		
第一部分:聽力測驗 測驗時間:約 45 分鐘		
大題	題型	題數
Part 1	照片描述	6
Part 2	應答問題	25
Part 3	簡短對話(13)包含或不含視覺圖像	39
Part 4	簡短獨白(10)包含或不含視覺圖像	30

多益測驗		
第二部分:閱讀測驗 測驗時間:75 分鐘		
大題	題型	題數
Part 5	句子填空	30
Part 6	段落填空(4)	16
Part 7	閱讀測驗:單篇閱讀 閱讀測驗:多篇閱讀	29 25

給教師的話

為什麼需要多益備考課程

Barron's 出版的考試用書不僅適合自學，亦適合作為課堂教材使用。本書精心編排的結構能有效幫助學生提升英文程度，為多益考試做好準備。

成人學習英文多為目標導向，許多人被要求提供多益考試成績，因此取得高分是他們的目標。對學生來說，擁有一個可測量的目標是很大的學習動機。許多教師不喜歡「為考而教」，認為比起針對性的複習考試項目，培養通用英語知識對學生更有益。但學生其實喜歡「為了考試而讀書」，反而不想浪費時間學習不會考的東西。

不過教師和學生都沒有考慮到在多益備考過程中實際發生的事。在討論測驗結構、應試策略和需要培養哪些技巧的同時，學習者已經在培養通用英語知識。當他們在分析問題或延伸討論其他領域時，用的也是通用英語。幫助學生準備考試就是在提升他們的通用英語知識。

多益備考課程滿足了學習者的需求：以最簡化的方式取得考試必備知識；亦同時滿足教學者的需求：提供能確實提升學生英語能力的教學計畫。

多益備考課程之安排

課程表

所有的備考課程無不面臨同樣的兩難問題：如何將完整的複習內容壓縮到一個課表中。有的教師只安排一個下午進行多益指導，有的可能開設一週的密集班，有的則安排為期十週的課程。無論課程長短都改變不了一個事實：再長的課程都無法涵蓋所有測驗內容。

> 您可將這份計畫作為基礎，視教學時間延伸計畫。
> - 第一階段： 進行第一章的多益測驗介紹。
>   讓學生簽署多益讀書契約。
> - 第二階段： 進行模擬測驗。
>   評估學生的作答情形，決定本班的弱項。
> - 後續階段： 複習聽力部分。
>   進行診斷測驗。
>   複習閱讀部分。
>   進行診斷測驗。
>   進行額外模擬試題測驗。
> - 最後階段： 進行期末模擬試題測驗，觀察學生成績的進步情形。

當學生完成本書的即時演練、診斷測驗或模擬試題後，可利用隨附的解析本，讓他們快速核對答案並閱讀試題詳解，了解自己對及錯在哪裡。

聽力教學

多聽是增進聽力的不二法門。鼓勵學生討論聽力練習中提到的各種策略，可以兩兩一組或數人一組，讓他們有更多時間練習聽說。

只要是考試必然會要求應試者選出正確答案，因此必須有能力排除錯誤答案。測驗中有些常見陷阱，只要訓練就可以聽得出來。練習聽出陷阱的同時，聽力也會在無形中進步。

本書所提供的聽力練習是一大寶藏，善用它們來達成您的教學目標，幫助學生學會分析照片、選項、題型和語言功能。也可以利用這些內容，設計出各式各樣的交流活動。

照片描述的練習活動

照片可以協助學生累積詞彙量。讓學生挑選一張照片，兩兩一組或數人一組，說出他們在照片中看到的物品。

接著同樣以分組方式進行（也可以請學生個別回答），用剛才說出的詞彙造句。學生可以看著照片寫一段簡短的描述，如果能寫一段小故事更好。故事可以盡量發揮想像力，愈天馬行空愈好。讓學生說說看，這張照片拍下之前及之後可能發生了什麼事。

當他們能夠掌握這些詞彙後，可以讓他們做口頭報告，其他學生則必須重述該學生的報告內容，這個活動可以幫助學生評估自己的聽力。

應答問題的練習活動

這一大題會出現一個短問句和短回答，有時會是一句陳述和一個簡短的回應。讓學生根據該問題或陳述還原對話情境。說話者位於何處？他們是誰？在談論什麼？對話之前他們可能在做什麼？對話之後又可能做什麼？對話之前可能還說過哪些話？之後又可能說些什麼？

讓學生兩兩一組，創作短劇並在全班面前演出，其他學生則將兩人的對話大致描述出來。這個活動同樣可以幫助學生評估自己的聽力。

簡短對話的練習活動

前述練習也可以應用在這個題型上，而且更容易進行，因為在簡短對話當中，學生可使用的對話句子更多了。同樣讓學生看完其他小組的短劇表演，此時他們要練習造出 wh- 問句。讓學生練習預測對話中的 who（誰）、what（什麼）、when（何時）、where（何地）、why（為何）和 how（如何）等資訊。

簡短獨白的練習活動

簡短獨白的內容較有變化，可能涵蓋報導、公共服務公告和廣告等。讓學生挑選一則短獨白並加以改寫。假如是天氣預報，可把雨天改成晴天；假如是電視廣告，可改為汽車廣告。

接著如同前面的練習活動，其他學生也要針對這則改寫造出 wh- 問句，看看他們有沒有辦法問倒同學。請鼓勵學生提高獨白內容的難度。

閱讀教學

如同聽力之培訓，提升閱讀能力的不二法門亦是多讀，一讀再讀。在多益測驗中，即使是文法測驗也不離閱讀。多益要求學生理解整段文章的脈絡，不能只是讀懂其中片段。這也是為什麼文法題會放在閱讀測驗中。

閱讀測驗和聽力測驗一樣，了解一個答案之所以對或錯的原因很重要。訓練學生在閱讀時運用兩大部分提供的策略，會使他們成為更有效率的讀者。

字彙題的練習活動

學生都想提升自己的字彙量，提醒學生不要只背單字，更要知道單字用法。透過閱讀及搭配前後文學習單字，會比狂背單字表更有收穫。

學生也可創造屬於自己的單字表，每當遇到自己不懂的單字就記在筆記本上。學生必須練習將單字用於句子，甚至用於對話。讓學生用個人專屬的單字表創作短劇。

如果學生堅持要求教師提供單字表，可以讓他們看聽力和閱讀測驗各大題中的單字表。讓他們利用這些單字，學習於前後文中使用單字。

文法題的練習活動

本書所練習的文法內容涵蓋多益測驗最可能考的文法項目，也是最難的項目。可以讓學生集中分析他們在模擬試題中所犯的錯誤。

閱讀測驗的練習活動

閱讀測驗部分所提到的策略不只可以應用在多益，也可應用在所有的閱讀活動。利用課外讀物如英語新聞雜誌或報紙，讓學生不要只讀文章，要連廣告、公告、訂閱單、商品目錄等一起閱讀。事實上整本新聞雜誌都要徹底消化，小地方也不要放過，因為裡面所出現的一切，包括圖表，多益測驗都有可能會考。

學生練習聽力時已經做過 wh- 問句的造句，練習閱讀時也請如法泡製，讓他們針對自己看到的文章、圖片和表格等所有可能找到的內容，造出 wh- 問句，看能不能把其他同學問倒。如果想讓課堂交流更為熱絡，可以讓他們選一篇自己讀過的文章進行口頭報告，其他同學也以口頭方式用 wh- 問句發問。

利用實戰模擬試題作為診斷

假如學生在介系詞的測驗中犯錯較多，可以建議他們集中練習介系詞。利用本書所提供的清單，找出學生需加強練習的地方。針對問題點集中練習，學習會更有效率，且更容易取得成效。

1 多益測驗介紹

本章內容

1-1 多益測驗常見問題
1-2 多益讀書計畫
1-3 自學活動
1-4 考試當天

1-1 多益測驗常見問題

全球每年有數百萬人參加多益測驗，施行地區包括歐洲、亞洲、北美、南美和中美洲。以下是關於多益測驗的常見問題。

多益測驗的目的是什麼？

多益測驗（Test of English for International Communication, TOEIC）自 1979 年開辦至今，在國際間已經成為評估英語能力的一個標準。多益測驗是由語言學家、語言專家和誠希國際集團（Chauncey Group International）共同研發，旨在評估非英語母語人士的商務英語能力。

多益測驗考哪些能力？

多益測驗由兩大部分組成：聽力（100 題選擇題）和閱讀（100 題選擇題）。聽力部分採播放音檔方式進行。多益測驗內容不具專門性，使用到的字彙和內容都是每天用得到的日常英語。

> **TIP** 線上資源：更多資訊請見多益官方網站 www.toeic.com

誰會採用多益測驗？

政府單位、跨國企業和國際組織均採用多益測驗來評估員工和潛在員工的英語能力。多益成績常被當作衡量工作能力的一項獨立指標，有助於判斷員工是否能勝任特定語言的相關職責，或根據其來安排語言訓練課程。部分職位須具備一定的語言能力，需要一個可靠的語言標準當作晉升職員的判斷基準，多益成績就是很好的參考指標。語言訓練課程常以多益測驗來建立學習目標，評估學生整體英語能力的進步情形。

誰需要參加多益測驗？

除了前面提到的企業和組織員工之外，有些人出於個人或專業因素，需藉由多益測驗來證明自己的語言能力。

多益測驗的架構為何？

多益測驗由聽力和閱讀兩大部分組成，請參考本書〈多益測驗的結構〉中的表格，當中有聽力和閱讀測驗的架構的詳細說明。多益測驗共有 200 題，完整測驗時間（含行政作業）約為兩個半小時，聽力部分占 45 分鐘，閱讀部分占 75 分鐘。

多益測驗題目為何充滿陷阱？

多益測驗的題目是精心設計來測驗你的英語知識。題目必須有一定的難度，才能分出應試者的程度。困難的題目是用來篩選出程度高的應試者，以便與程度一般的應試者有所區別。試題和答案選項可能採用下列陷阱來測驗你的語言能力：

- 使用發音相近的單字
- 使用發音相同，但拼寫不同、意義不同的單字
- 使用相關的單字
- 省略必要字彙
- 加入不必要的字彙
- 改變正確語序

多益測驗如何計分？

聽力和閱讀分開計分，各為 5–495 分，兩項分數相加即為總分。根據答對題數的多寡，多益分數會介於 10–990 分。

多益測驗的分數代表什麼意義？

多益測驗並沒有最低通過門檻，由各組織單位憑內部規章設定要求達到的分數。

多益測驗的分數如何取得？

如果是由企業、機構或組織所贊助提供的多益測驗，由企業組織發送成績。如果是個人報名參加多益測驗，則會直接收到成績單。多益測驗成績有效時間為兩年。

哪裡可以參加考試，考試時間為何時？

多益測驗的舉辦日期、時間和地點由各地辦事處決定，請向各地辦事處洽詢考試費用、日期及時間等相關資訊。若為臺灣地區，請上 TOEIC 臺灣區官方網站（https://www.toeic.com.tw/）查詢上述資訊。

我要如何準備多益測驗？

有意參加多益考試者，應下定決心並於各種不同情境中多使用英語。
最好的準備方式就是利用本書，此書為專門設計來協助你準備多益考試的讀書計畫。本書能協助你：

- 了解特定的考試技巧
- 熟悉測驗形式
- 提高總分數

接下來的〈多益讀書計畫〉會提供更多考試建議。

我要如何才能拿高分？

假設你已經為考試做好充分準備，到了考試當天，注意下列事項才能拿到好分數。

- 仔細閱讀作答說明
- 作答速度要快
- 不可在試題本上做記號
- 不確定答案就用猜的
- 一題只可標記一個答案

1-2 多益讀書計畫

俗話說：「牽馬到河易，逼馬喝水難。」（You can lead a horse to water, but you can't make him drink.）同樣的道理，本書可以引導你完成多益測驗，卻無法強迫你去思考。學習是一種自發性的活動，只有你自己可以為多益測驗做好準備。

多益讀書契約

要學好一門外語就必須嚴守紀律，你可以和自己簽署一份契約，將承諾訴諸白紙黑字。這份契約會強制你每週投入一定的時數學英文，並持續一段時間。你必須承諾（一）研讀 New TOEIC 新制多益聽力閱讀全題型攻略＋實戰模擬 6 回題庫大全或其他備考教材，（二）安排自學活動。現在依照下列步驟簽署契約，做出你的承諾。

- 在第一行填入你的名字
- 在第五到九行填入你每週願意花多少時間學英文，務必衡量你每天和每週有多少時間可以讀書，建立一個實際可行的時間表。
- 在最後一行簽名並寫下簽署時間。
- 在每週結束之時，計算你的讀書時數。有沒有達成契約上的要求呢？有沒有閱讀本書，也做了自行規劃的學習活動呢？

多益讀書契約

我，＿＿＿＿＿＿＿＿＿＿＿＿＿＿，承諾認真準備多益測驗。我會研讀 New TOEIC 新制多益聽力閱讀全題型攻略＋實戰模擬 6 回題庫大全，並安排自己的英文學習活動。

我明白想要增進英文能力，就必須投入時間學習。

我承諾每週花 ＿＿＿＿＿＿＿ 小時學習英文。

我會每週花 ＿＿＿＿＿＿＿ 小時練習英文聽力。

我會每週花 ＿＿＿＿＿＿＿ 小時練習英文寫作。

我會每週花 ＿＿＿＿＿＿＿ 小時練習英文口說。

我會每週花 ＿＿＿＿＿＿＿ 小時練習英文閱讀。

這是我和自己的契約，我承諾達成此契約所列之一切條款。

＿＿＿＿＿＿＿＿＿＿＿＿　　　　　＿＿＿＿＿＿＿＿＿＿＿＿
立約人　　　　　　　　　　　　　　日期

多益測驗的準備技巧

1. **規律學習**。每天固定時間練習英文。假如無法建立日常規律，就不可能養成好的讀書習慣。告訴自己晚上七點半不可以滑手機，因為那是你的多益學習時間。假如有一天無法照原定時間執行也沒關係，當天找時間把進度補起來。切勿每天都在不同的時間讀書，那樣絕對學不好。

2. **一次讀一點**。告訴自己每天早上利用搭車時間讀個十分鐘，或睡前讀十分鐘。寧可用很短的時間把一個知識點弄清楚，也不要花很長的時間想通通學會。

3. **善用時間**。多益測驗是有時間限制的考試，所以也要學會限制你的讀書時間。給自己十分鐘的時間讀書，時間到就停止。你必須有效率地運用時間，請學習如何善用時間，在很短的時間內完成任務。

4. **將讀書計畫寫下**。把要做的事情寫下來，比較會認真去執行。

5. **知道目標所在**。你為什麼要考多益？假如是為了在公司取得升遷資格，就想像你已經得到那個職位。那你需要拿到多少分數才夠？以那個分數（甚至高於那個分數）為目標，鞭策自己用功。

6. **正面思考**。許多奧運選手在比賽前會閉上眼睛，想像自己從高山上滑雪而下，或沿著賽道奔跑，或游泳時全速前進，然後一馬當先抵達終點。他們會想像自己表現完美，拿下全場最高分，最後獲得金牌。這就是正面思考的力量，運動員這麼做，當然你也可以。

參加多益考試絕對需要正面思考。每天晚上睡覺之前（此時右腦處於最佳接收狀態），重複下面這個句子十次：「我英文很好，多益一定能考高分。」不要小看潛意識的力量，假如你告訴自己一定做得到，就有可能真的做到。

7. **放鬆心情**。不要為了考試而焦慮。考試前一晚好好睡覺,別念書了,只管放鬆。當你處於平靜狀態,頭腦的接收度會更好,因此考試前、考試中都要放鬆心情,考試後更是可以好好放鬆一下。

使用本書

1. **熟悉多益考題和答題方式**。看完本書提供的多益測驗結構,並詳讀聽力和閱讀測驗的說明,當中的資訊和建議對提升考試分數十分有幫助。

2. **演練實戰模擬試題**。利用本書提供的答案解析找到自己的弱項。假如介系詞的題目你答錯較多,頻率副詞答錯較少,那麼就把時間拿來加強介系詞。可參考本書提供的〈高分攻略清單〉,快速找到你最需要的練習項目。

3. **高效學習**。當時間有限,更要把時間用在刀口上,學習真正需要的東西。當時間不充裕時,就不要什麼都想學。

4. **所有可能的問題都要學會**。必須知道聽力和閱讀測驗都考些什麼題型,學會辨識錯誤答案。

5. **做本書的即時演練、診斷測驗和實戰模擬試題**。這些考題都是模擬真實多益測驗精心設計的,做這些練習不但能增進考試技巧,更能大幅提升英文能力。

6. **閱讀答案解析**。本書所有即時演練、診斷測驗和實戰模擬試題的答案均附解析。閱讀解析可增進分析試題的能力。唯有知道錯在哪裡才能避免重蹈覆轍。利用解析本提供的解答快速核對答案,找出答錯的題目,接著翻到解析部分,了解為什麼答錯、中了什麼陷阱,之後練習時便能聚焦在你最需要加強的地方。

每天讀一點

我們要不厭其煩重複這個建議。維持每天一致的讀書習慣對於準備多益測驗非常有幫助。不需要把本書全部讀過,可以選你較弱的題型加強練習。重點是每天都要讀一點!

1-3 自學活動

1. **多聽**。提升英文聽力最好的方法就是多聽。邊聽邊問自己下列問題：

   是誰在說話？
   他們在對誰說話？
   他們在談論什麼？
   他們在哪裡進行這些對話？
   他們為什麼要說這些話？

   回答上述問題的同時，梳理情境脈絡，即可提升英文理解能力。

2. **多讀**。提升閱讀理解能力最好也最容易的方式無疑就是閱讀。可以鎖定閱讀新聞週刊，不只要讀文章，就連目次、廣告、公告都要讀，不要錯過任何英文內容，包括分類廣告、火車時刻表、飯店住宿登記表等。同樣，一邊讀也要一邊問自己一些問題。

   運用本書所討論的 PSRA（Predict, Scan, Read, Answer）閱讀策略，這個策略不僅適用於多益閱讀測驗，在你平日進行任何閱讀活動時都很有幫助——即使閱讀母語讀物都用得上！

3. **多說，多寫**。練習聽力時，問自己關於對話的 who（誰）、what（什麼）、when（何時）、where（何地）、why（為何）等問題，然後大聲說出答案，並把答案寫下。

4. **準備一本單字筆記本**。純背單字的效果絕對比不上搭配前後文學習來得高。請隨時注意生活中出現的新單字，並且堅持不懈。找一些英文網頁來讀，什麼網頁都好，但建議找 CNN 或 BBC 這樣的新聞網站，可同時兼顧聽力和閱讀。很多報章雜誌、電子報和部落格都可以在網上找到，請自行搜尋感興趣的領域，你會發現網路上的資源相當豐富。

下面我們提供一些訓練英文聽說讀寫能力的方法，無論透過書報雜誌或網路，都有很多練英文的機會。勾選你感興趣的項目，並在空格內填上你自己的點子。

聽

☐ 聽播客（podcast）
☐ 聽新聞網站上的報導：CNN、BBC、NBC、ABC、CBS
☐ 看英文電影或電視節目
☐ 看網路上的英文影片
☐ 聽 CNN 和 BBC 的廣播或線上新聞
☐ 聽英文歌曲
☐ _____
☐ _____

說

☐ 把你看到的東西和正在做什麼事大聲說出來
☐ 和朋友練習對話
☐ 利用視訊聊天和朋友或同學練習說英文
☐ _____
☐ _____

寫

- ☐ 寫日記
- ☐ 寫信給英語母語人士
- ☐ 列出每日所見所聞
- ☐ 寫下對家人和朋友的描述
- ☐ 寫電子郵件給網站客服
- ☐ 寫部落格文章
- ☐ 在別人的部落格或 YouTube 底下留言
- ☐ 在聊天室裡傳訊息
- ☐ 使用臉書和 Instagram 撰寫貼文
- ☐ _____
- ☐ _____

讀

- ☐ 讀英文報章和雜誌
- ☐ 讀英文書
- ☐ 讀英文圖像小說
- ☐ 讀網路新聞和雜誌文章
- ☐ 上網搜尋感興趣的主題報導
- ☐ 追蹤感興趣的帳號
- ☐ _____
- ☐ _____

自學方法

無論是閱讀報紙或網頁文章,都可以透過一些方式來善用文章練習英文聽說讀寫。

- 閱讀關於這篇文章的資訊
- 改寫文章並寫下這篇文章在談論什麼
- 為這篇文章做一場演說或一份簡報
- 將你的簡報錄音或錄影
- 聽或看你錄製的內容
- 寫下關於這份簡報的重點事項
- 修正你在簡報中犯的錯誤
- 重新再做一遍

1-4 考試當天

現在你已做好充分準備並讀完本書，終於來到考試這天。以下建議可以幫助你考試順利：

1. **提早到考場**：考試當天不要匆匆忙忙，給自己充分時間抵達測驗中心。

2. **安頓下來**：可以的話自己選位置，找一個不容易分心的位置。不要靠門邊，以免受外面人來人往影響。靠窗的位置採光好，是不錯的選擇。可以的話盡量靠近音源播放器，萬一聽不清楚，一定要趕快告訴監考官。

3. **自備考試用品**：考場可能會提供鉛筆和橡皮擦，但保險起見，最好還是自己帶三、四支 2B 鉛筆和橡皮擦。可自帶手錶。

4. **仔細聆聽作答方式**：雖然讀完本書你已經很熟悉考試模式，還是應仔細聆聽作答方式。聽到你已經熟悉的內容可幫助你放鬆下來。

5. **所有題目都要作答**：即使不知道答案也要猜一個，盡量做合理的猜測。萬一考試時間快到了，你有題目還沒作答，切記一定要隨便塗黑一個選項──來不及看題目也要隨便塗，搞不好就幸運猜對了。

6. **核對題號**：務必確認答案卡上的題號和試題本上的題號相符。

7. **一題只能標記一個答案**：一題只能出現一個標記，如果不小心畫錯要擦掉的話，一定要擦乾淨。答案卡上不能做任何其他記號。

8. **仔細聆聽**：在聽力的第二大題中，務必把完整的題目和所有選項聽完，才開始作答。

9. **注意聆聽相關資訊**：在聽力的第三和第四大題中，先快速把題目和答案選項瀏覽一遍，然後注意聽相關線索。

10. **簡單的題目先答**：閱讀測驗可以控制作答節奏。如果無法立即判斷出答案，就先跳過去做下一題。到了測驗後段再回頭解決困難的題目，這樣可以盡可能作答更多題數。

11. **控制節奏**：聽力測驗必須跟著音源播放的速度進行，但是閱讀測驗可以自己調整作答節奏。在閱讀測驗中，每一題的作答時間不要超過 45 秒。

12. **預留時間檢查**：盡可能在考試最後留一分鐘檢查你的答案卡，確定每一題都有作答。

13. **考完慶祝一下**：恭喜你終於考完了，去慶祝一下吧！這是你應得的，做得很好！

多益測驗解題訓練

2 聽力測驗

2-1 聽力測驗介紹與高分攻略清單 Track1

多益的聽力測驗分為四個大題，作答時間約 45 分鐘。

Part 1：照片描述　　6 題
Part 2：應答問題　　25 題
Part 3：簡短對話　　39 題
Part 4：簡短獨白　　30 題

多益聽力的四個大題有特定的聆聽和分析技巧，培養這些技巧就能做好充分準備。本章所提供的高分攻略可以靈活運用於聽力的四個大題。

高分攻略清單

Part 1
照片描述

1. 假設
2. 人物
3. 物品
4. 行動
5. 大致地點
6. 具體位置

Part 2
應答問題

1. 近音字
2. 相關字
3. 同音字
4. 一字多義
5. 建議
6. 主動提出或提議
7. 請求

Part 3
簡短對話

1. 人物題
2. 職業題
3. 地點題
4. 時間題
5. 活動題
6. 看法題
7. 圖表題
8. 情境意義
9. 簡略回答

Part 4
簡短獨白

1. 活動與事實題
2. 原因題
3. 數字題
4. 主題和目的題
5. 改述題
6. 圖表題
7. 隱含意義題
8. 口音題

2-2 Part 1：照片描述

2-2-1 試題範例

> DIRECTIONS : You will see a photograph. You will hear four statements about the photograph. Choose the statement that most closely matches the photograph, and fill in the corresponding oval on your answer sheet. The statements will not be printed and will be spoken only once.
>
> 作答方式：你會看到一張照片，並聽到四個關於這張照片的陳述。選出最符合照片內容的陳述，將答案卡上對應的橢圓框塗滿。陳述部分不會印出文字，並只會朗讀一遍。

你會聽到：Look at the photo marked number 1 in your test book.
　　　　　請看試題本上標示題號 1 的照片。

Ⓐ　Ⓑ　Ⓒ　●

(A) They're waiting at the bus stop. 他們正在公車站等車。
(B) They're leaving the building. 他們正要離開大樓。
(C) They're selling tickets. 他們正在賣票。
(D) They're getting off the bus. 他們正在下公車。

最符合照片內容的陳述是 (D) They're getting off the bus.，因此要選 (D)。

2-2-2 高分攻略

高分攻略 1　假設

多益聽力測驗可能會考你關於照片內容的假設。這些假設會以照片內容為依據，你必須從聽到的四個選項中判斷哪一個正確或可能是正確的。只有一個答案選項會是正確或最有可能是正確的，那就是你要選的答案。

答題要訣　仔細聽完整個句子，再決定哪一個選項最符合照片內容。

Photo 1

Photo 2

031

》範例

下面是關於照片 1 的各種陳述。

正確的陳述：

This is a laboratory. 這是一間實驗室。	The people are wearing protective clothing. 人員身穿防護衣。
There are bottles on the shelves. 架上有瓶子。	There are at least four people in the lab. 實驗室裡至少有四個人。
There is equipment on the counter. 檯面上有設備。	Wires run from the equipment. 設備連接了一些線材。

可能正確但無法確定的陳述：

The people are lab technicians. 這些人是實驗室的技術人員。	They look like technicians, but they could be pharmacists. 他們看起來像是技術人員，但也有可能是藥劑師。
The people are students with a teacher. 這些人是學生和一位教師。	A teacher may be working with a class, or they may all be employees. 可能是一名教師和班上同學在做實驗，但也可能全都是員工。
The technicians are doing experiments. 技術人員正在做實驗。	They might be doing experiments, or they might be producing some chemical compound. 他們可能正在做實驗，也有可能正在製造化合物。

暖身練習

請看照片 2 並閱讀下列陳述。將陳述標示為正確（T）、可能正確（PT）或錯誤（F）。

A. There are five people around the table.
B. It's nighttime.
C. They're business colleagues.
D. They're smiling.
E. There is a bottle on the table.
F. There is water in the bottle.
G. They're drinking coffee.
H. They're eating something.
I. The computer is open.
J. They're reading a report.

即時演練

Track 2

選出最符合照片 1 和照片 2 的陳述。

Photo 1　Ⓐ　Ⓑ　Ⓒ　Ⓓ
Photo 2　Ⓐ　Ⓑ　Ⓒ　Ⓓ

033

高分攻略 2　人物

你可能會需要辨識照片中的人物，可能是他們的人數、性別、位置、描述、活動或職業。

> **答題要訣**　盡可能判斷照片中的人物數量、性別、位置、描述、活動和職業。

Photo 3

Photo 4

》範例

下面是關於照片 3 的陳述。

人數：There are four people in the photo. 照片中有四個人。
性別：There are two men and two women in the photo. 照片中有兩男兩女。
位置：On the left, there are two men. 左邊有兩名男子。
On the right, there are two women. 右邊有兩名女子。
描述：One of the men is wearing glasses. 其中一名男子戴眼鏡。
The woman on the right is shorter than the other woman.
最右邊的女子比另一名女子矮。
活動：The group is looking at a map. 他們正在看一張地圖。
One woman is pointing to the map. 其中一名女子指向地圖。
All four people are leaning on the table. 四個人都靠在桌子上。
職業：Their profession is unknown. They are looking at and discussing a map. We can assume they are planners of some sort.
他們的職業未知。他們正在看著地圖和討論地圖。我們可以假設他們是某一種規劃人員。

不可能所有問題都答得出來，比如你不知道他們的職業。但是可以盡量假設，假設愈多就愈容易作答。

暖身練習

根據照片 4 中的人物填入下列資訊。

人數：_____
性別：_____
位置：_____
描述：_____
活動：_____
職業：_____

即時演練

Track 3

選出最符合照片 3 和照片 4 的陳述。
Photo 3　Ⓐ　Ⓑ　Ⓒ　Ⓓ
Photo 4　Ⓐ　Ⓑ　Ⓒ　Ⓓ

高分攻略 3　物品

你可能會需要辨識照片中的物品。看照片時，試著把所有看到的物品名稱都講出來。多益測驗只會考一般的物品，不需要知道物品的專業名稱。以照片 5 為例，你只需知道鋼琴是 piano，不需知道專業名稱為 grand piano（平臺式鋼琴）。

答題要訣　利用照片中的情境幫助你辨識物品。

Photo 5

Photo 6

》範例

請在照片中找出下列物品。注意照片 5 的情境是一座私人住宅客廳。

找出下列單字代表的物品

window 窗戶	window shade 窗簾	curtain 帷幕
chair 椅子	cushion 靠墊	carpet 地毯
floor 地板	wall 牆壁	fireplace 壁爐
mantle 壁爐檯	plant 植物	piano 鋼琴
piano bench 鋼琴椅	vase 花瓶	candle 蠟燭
piano keys 琴鍵	shelf 架子	

暖身練習

列出你在照片 6 中看到的物品。

_____ _____

_____ _____

_____ _____

_____ _____

即時演練

Track 4

選出最符合照片 5 和照片 6 的陳述。

Photo 5　Ⓐ　Ⓑ　Ⓒ　Ⓓ

Photo 6　Ⓐ　Ⓑ　Ⓒ　Ⓓ

高分攻略 4　行動

你可能會需要判斷照片中出現了哪些行動。照片中出現的行動可能不只一種，即使照片中只有一個人。如果照片中有好幾個人，他們可能都在做同一件事，也可能各自在做不同的事。

答題要訣　判斷照片中的每一個人在做什麼事。

Photo 7

Photo 8

》範例

在照片 7 中辨識下列行動：

standing in the trench　站在壕溝中
standing next to the trench　站在壕溝旁
kneeling in the trench　跪在壕溝中
wearing a hard hat　戴著安全帽
holding the pipe　扶著管子
looking at the pipe　看著管子
laying the pipe　鋪設管子
leaning against the rocks　靠著岩石

暖身練習

列出你在照片 8 中看到的行動。

_____　　_____

_____　　_____

_____　　_____

_____　　_____

即時演練

選出最符合照片 7 和照片 8 的陳述。

Photo 7　Ⓐ　Ⓑ　Ⓒ　Ⓓ
Photo 8　Ⓐ　Ⓑ　Ⓒ　Ⓓ

高分攻略 5　大致地點

你可能會需要辨識照片中的大致地點。看照片時要分析當中的情境線索，用這些線索決定地點。假如你在照片裡看到一輛車、一位修車師傅、一些工具和一位客人，大概可以判斷這裡是修車廠。假如你看到男子和女子坐在辦公桌前，桌上還有電腦，大概可以判斷這裡是一間辦公室。照片中充滿了線索可以幫助你辨識大致地點。

答題要訣 利用照片中的情境幫助你判斷大致地點。

Photo 9

Photo 10

》範例

下面列出了照片 9 中的情境線索。在 Part 1 的測驗中你可能會聽到這些單字或這些字的變體，請各位注意，實際測驗中出現的單字不一定和此處列出的一樣。

情境線索

Security checkpoint 安檢站	Security officers 安檢人員
Departure information 起飛資訊	Man with mobile phone 拿著手機的男子
Gate sign 登機門標誌	Airline names 航空公司名稱
People with baggage 攜帶行李的人	Names of destinations 目的地名稱
Porter with luggage cart 推行李推車的服務員	Sign about X-ray X 光檢查標誌
Security personnel 安檢員工	Uniformed personnel 穿制服的員工

暖身練習

判斷照片 10 的大致地點，列出你所使用的情境線索。

地點 _____

_____　　_____

_____　　_____

_____　　_____

_____　　_____

即時演練　Track 6

選出最符合照片 9 和照片 10 的陳述。

Photo 9　　Ⓐ　Ⓑ　Ⓒ　Ⓓ

Photo 10　Ⓐ　Ⓑ　Ⓒ　Ⓓ

041

高分攻略 6　具體位置

你可能會需要辨識照片中人或物的具體位置。看照片時可藉由人和物之間的相對位置來分析他們的具體位置。

答題要訣　請注意聽關鍵的介系詞。

Photo 11

Photo 12

》範例

描述位置的介系詞和片語

above 在……之上	beneath 在……之下	far from 離……很遠	near 在……附近	over 在……之上
across 橫越	beside 在……旁邊	in 在……之內	next to 在……旁邊	to the left of 在……左邊
around 圍繞	between 在……之間	in back of 在……後面	on 在……上面	to the right of 在……右邊
at 在……地點	by 在……旁邊	in front of 在……前面	on top of 在……上面	under 在……下面
below 在……之下	close to 在……附近	inside 在……裡面	outside 在……外面	underneath 在……底下

下列是照片 11 中具體位置的描述。

The server is <u>next to</u> the table. 服務生在桌子旁邊。

There is a bottle <u>in front of</u> the woman. 女子的前方有一個瓶子。

The forks are <u>on</u> a plate. 叉子擺放在盤子上。

There is a plate <u>in</u> the server's hand. 服務生手上有一個盤子。

The man is sitting <u>across from</u> a woman. 男子坐在一名女子的對面。

A woman is sitting <u>next to</u> the man. 一名女子坐在男子的旁邊。

暖身練習

利用所提供的介系詞和片語,造句描述照片 12 中物品的具體位置。

A. (on) _____

B. (in front of) _____

C. (over) _____

D. (between) _____

E. (to the left of) _____

F. (on top of) _____

即時演練

Track 7

選出最符合照片 11 和照片 12 的陳述。

Photo 11　Ⓐ　Ⓑ　Ⓒ　Ⓓ

Photo 12　Ⓐ　Ⓑ　Ⓒ　Ⓓ

MEMO

2-3 Part 2：應答問題

2-3-1 試題範例

> **DIRECTIONS :** You will hear a question and three possible responses. Choose the response that most closely answers the question, and fill in the corresponding oval on your answer sheet. The statements will not be printed and will be spoken only once.
>
> 作答方式：你會聽到一個問題和三個可能的回應。選出最能回答該問題的回應，將答案卡上對應的橢圓框塗滿。題目和回答都不會印在試題本上，並只會朗讀一遍。

你會聽到： How can I get to the airport from here? 從這裡要怎麼到機場？

● Ⓑ Ⓒ

(A) Take a taxi. It's just a short ride. 搭計程車，不會很遠。
(B) No, I don't. 不，我不會。
(C) You can get on easily. 你可以很容易就上去。

「How can I get to the airport from here?」的最適當回答是 (A) Take a taxi. It's just a short ride.，因此要選 (A)。

2-3-2 高分攻略

高分攻略 1　近音字

在多益測驗中，你可能會需要辨別發音相近的單字。聆聽答案選項時要注意判斷單字意義，可以利用上下文線索幫助你理解字義，千萬不要被發音相近的單字混淆了。

> **答題要訣** 仔細聆聽陳述或問題的具體意思，再從選項中找出能真正回答該問題的答案。

》範例

下列是發音相近的單字：

母音發音不同			
bass 低音／鱸魚	car 車子	deep 深的	gun 槍
base 基礎／基座	core 核心	dip 浸、泡	gone 不見了
boots 靴子	cart 手推車	fall 落下	grass 草
boats 船	court 法院／球場	full 充滿	grease 油脂
bus 公車	drug 藥品	fun 樂趣	letter 信件
boss 老闆	drag 拖曳	phone 電話	later 後來
開頭的子音發音不同			
back 後面	core 核心	race 比賽	hair 頭髮
pack 背包	tore 撕裂（tear 的過去式）	case 箱子／案例	fair 公平的
rack 架子	sore 疼痛的	place 地方	tear 撕裂

結尾的子音發音不同			
cab 計程車	little 小的／少的	nab 突然抓住	think 想
cap 棒球帽	litter 亂丟	nap 打盹兒	thing 東西
兩個以上的單字發音和另一個單字相似			
mark it 標明、做記號	sent her 派她／傳送給她	letter 信件	in tents 在帳篷裡
market 市場	center 中心	let her 讓她	intense 強烈的
單字的發音和另一個較長單字的部分發音相同			
nation 國家	mind 頭腦／注意	give 給	intention 意圖
imagination 想像	remind 提醒	forgive 原諒	unintentional 非故意的

即時演練

Track 8

選出最適當的回答。

1. Ⓐ Ⓑ Ⓒ
2. Ⓐ Ⓑ Ⓒ
3. Ⓐ Ⓑ Ⓒ
4. Ⓐ Ⓑ Ⓒ
5. Ⓐ Ⓑ Ⓒ

高分攻略 2　相關字

在多益測驗中，你可能會需要判斷答案選項是否使用了題目中某個字的相關單字。不過請注意，包含相關字的選項未必是正確答案。

答題要訣　仔細聆聽，找出確實回答問題的選項。

》範例

下表是彼此相關的單字：

航空				
ticket 機票	pilot 機師	reservation 訂位	baggage claim 行李提領處	check-in 登機報到
seat belt 安全帶	flight attendant 空服員	ticket counter 售票櫃檯	crew 機組員	turbulence 亂流
飯店				
room 房間	pool 游泳池	floor 樓層	suite 套房	fitness center 健身房
front desk 前檯	check in/out 住宿登記／退房	bed 床	lobby 大廳	housekeeping 客房服務
餐廳				
table 桌子	server 服務生	menu 菜單	tray 托盤	waiter/waitress 服務生
dish 餐盤／菜餚	napkin 餐巾	meal 一餐	dinner 晚餐	breakfast 早餐
lunch 午餐	dessert 甜點	tip 小費	plate 盤子	bill/check 帳單

銀行				
cash 現金	deposit 存款	withdrawal 提款	teller 櫃員	officer 專員
account 帳戶	loan 貸款	savings 儲蓄	receipt 收據	check 支票
天氣				
sunny 晴朗的	cool 涼快的	rain 雨	drizzle 毛毛雨	wind 風
cold 寒冷的	sleet 冰雹／雨夾雪	rainstorm 暴風雨	mist 薄霧	breeze 微風
freezing 極冷的	warm 暖和的	hot 炎熱的	cloudy 多雲／陰天的	blizzard 暴風雪
snow 雪	humid 潮濕的	smoggy 受霧霾影響的	thunder 雷	tornado 龍捲風
chilly 寒冷的	humidity 濕度	fog 霧	lightning 閃電	hurricane 颶風

即時演練

選出最適當的回答。

1. Ⓐ Ⓑ Ⓒ
2. Ⓐ Ⓑ Ⓒ
3. Ⓐ Ⓑ Ⓒ
4. Ⓐ Ⓑ Ⓒ
5. Ⓐ Ⓑ Ⓒ

高分攻略 3　同音字

在多益測驗中，你可能會需要判斷答案選項是否含有同音字。同音字的定義為發音相同但拼寫和意義都不同的單字。

答題要訣　仔細聽這個單字在句子中的意思。

》範例

同音字（同音異形異義字）

allowed 允許 aloud 大聲地	feet 腳 feat 功績	male 男子 mail 郵件	right 右邊、對的 rite 儀式 write 書寫	tale 故事 tail 尾巴
bear 熊、承受 bare 光禿禿的	find 找到 fined 處以罰金	meat 肉 meet 遇見	sail 航行 sale 賣	threw 投擲 through 穿過
blew 吹 blue 藍色	flew 飛 flu 流行性感冒	mind 頭腦、介意 mined 採礦	seen 看見 scene 場景、現場	too 也、太 two 二 to 到、向
bough 大樹枝 bow 弓	flour 麵粉 flower 花	morning 早上 mourning 哀悼	sight 景象 site 地點	wait 等待 weight 重量
buy 買 by 由、經過	for 為了 four 四	one 一 won 贏	sowing 播種 sewing 縫紉	week 週 weak 虛弱的
do 做、從事 due 到期的 dew 露水	loan 貸款 lone 孤單的	pale 蒼白的 pail 提桶	steak 牛排 stake 賭注、椿	fare 車資 fair 公平的
made 製作 maid 少女	plane 飛機、平面 plain 樸素的、平原	steel 鋼鐵 steal 偷		

Track 10

即時演練

選出最適當的回答。

1. Ⓐ Ⓑ Ⓒ
2. Ⓐ Ⓑ Ⓒ
3. Ⓐ Ⓑ Ⓒ
4. Ⓐ Ⓑ Ⓒ
5. Ⓐ Ⓑ Ⓒ

高分攻略 4　一字多義

在多益測驗中，你可能會需要辨別發音相同、拼寫也相同，但意義不同的單字，即一字多義的情況。當你聆聽答案選項時，請注意此字到底是取其哪一個意義，一定要小心這種同一個單字有多種意義的情況。

答題要訣　仔細聆聽，從前後文判斷單字的正確意義。

》範例

一字多義

call	鳥獸叫聲 叫喊 電話、通話	file	文件夾 縱列 銼刀
class	社會階級 班級 品質等級	hard	困難的 嚴格的 堅固的
court	網球場 法庭 宮廷	note	音符 便條 紙鈔
date	棗子 約會 日期、日子	seat	座位、座椅 所在地、中心 席位
band	樂隊、樂團 帶、箍（如：絲帶、金屬環等）	park	公園 停車
bank	銀行 河岸	right	正確的 右邊 正當的、公正的
left	leave 的過去式 左邊		

即時演練

Track 11

選出最適當的回答。

1. Ⓐ Ⓑ Ⓒ
2. Ⓐ Ⓑ Ⓒ
3. Ⓐ Ⓑ Ⓒ
4. Ⓐ Ⓑ Ⓒ
5. Ⓐ Ⓑ Ⓒ

高分攻略 5　建議

Part 2 中有些問句其實是提出建議而非提問，這類問句有特定的回應方式。

答題要訣 注意聆聽表示建議的單字或句型。

》範例

假如聽到下面這樣的問句類型，就是在提出建議，要找出關於建議的回答。

建議的句型

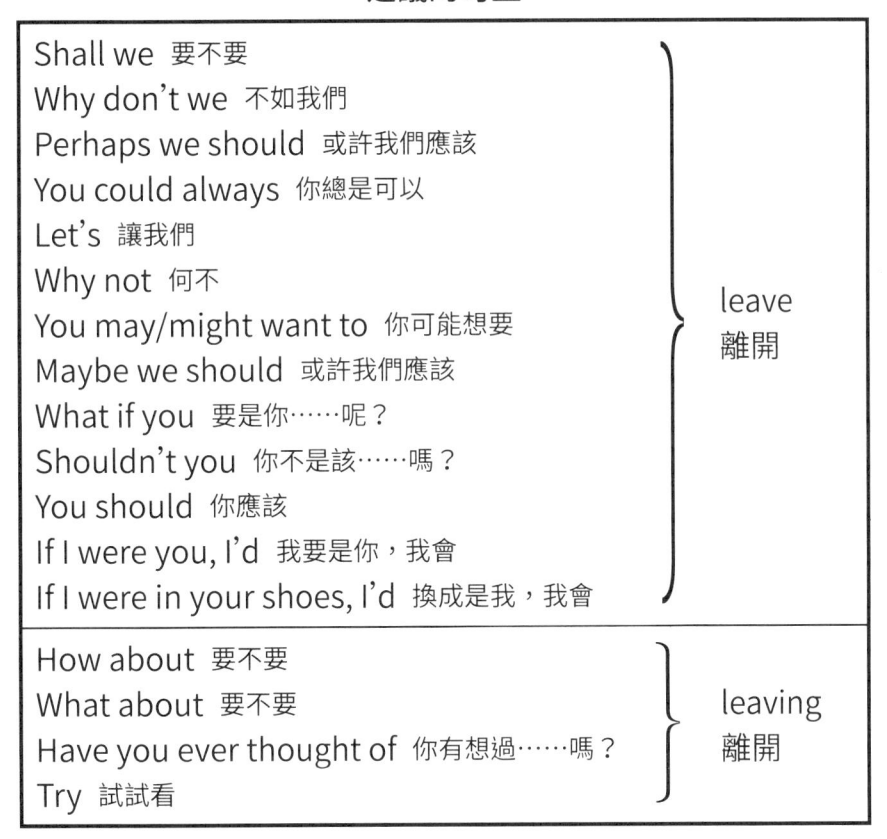

Shall we 要不要 Why don't we 不如我們 Perhaps we should 或許我們應該 You could always 你總是可以 Let's 讓我們 Why not 何不 You may/might want to 你可能想要 Maybe we should 或許我們應該 What if you 要是你……呢？ Shouldn't you 你不是該……嗎？ You should 你應該 If I were you, I'd 我要是你，我會 If I were in your shoes, I'd 換成是我，我會	leave 離開
How about 要不要 What about 要不要 Have you ever thought of 你有想過……嗎？ Try 試試看	leaving 離開

這種問句的回答通常是對別人提出的建議做出回應，可能是肯定的回應（let's go），也可能是否定的（let's not）。假如你看到或聽到接下來這樣的回答，就要注意提出建議的問句。

回答

Yes, let's. 好啊。	What a brilliant idea! 這主意太好了！
That's a good idea. 這主意不錯。	No, I haven't yet. 我還沒有。
Why not? 有何不可。	OK. 好。
Suits me. 可以。／正合我意。	Good idea. 好主意。

即時演練

Track 12

選出最適當的回答。

1. Ⓐ Ⓑ Ⓒ
2. Ⓐ Ⓑ Ⓒ
3. Ⓐ Ⓑ Ⓒ
4. Ⓐ Ⓑ Ⓒ
5. Ⓐ Ⓑ Ⓒ

高分攻略 6　主動提出或提議

Part 2 有些問句其實是主動提出願意幫忙或提議對方可以做一件事，要學會辨認表示主動提出或提議的單字、片語或句型。

答題要訣　注意聽表示主動提出或提議的單字或句型。

》範例

假如你聽到接下來這樣的問句類型，就是說話者主動提出願意幫忙或提議對方可以做一件事，要注意聽提出的內容。這種問句通常會以下列常見的句型開頭。

主動提出或提議的句型

Let me 讓我 Allow me to 讓我 Can I 我可以……嗎？ Shall I 要我……嗎？ Do you want me to 要不要我 Would you like me to 要不要我 } carry your books 幫你拿書

這種問句的回答通常是禮貌性地接受或婉拒對方提供的協助或提議自己做的事。若你看到或聽到下方這樣的回答，就要注意主動提出或提議的問句。

回答

Thank you. 謝謝。 That's very kind of you. 你人真好。 I'd appreciate that. 我很感謝。	You're too kind. 你人太好了。 No, thanks. I can manage. 不用了，謝謝，我自己可以。

057

即時演練

Track 13

選出最適當的回答。

1. Ⓐ Ⓑ Ⓒ
2. Ⓐ Ⓑ Ⓒ
3. Ⓐ Ⓑ Ⓒ
4. Ⓐ Ⓑ Ⓒ
5. Ⓐ Ⓑ Ⓒ

高分攻略 7　請求

請求是要別人做一件事的禮貌性表達，要學會辨識表達請求的問句和請求的內容。

答題要訣　注意聽表示請求的單字或句型。

》範例

若你聽到接下來這樣的句型，就是在表達請求，要注意聽請求內容是什麼。

請求

Can you May I Would you Could you Do you think you could	你可以、請你	speak louder? 說大聲一點好嗎？
How about Would you mind	麻煩你	speaking louder. 說大聲一點好嗎。

這種問句的回答通常是禮貌性回應對方的請求。假如你聽到或看到接下來這樣的回答，就要注意請求的問句。

回答

Of course. 當然可以。	I'm sorry. I can't. 不好意思，沒辦法。
Is this OK? 這樣可以嗎？	Regretfully, no. 很抱歉，不行。
No problem. 沒問題。	Not at all. I'd be glad to. 沒問題，我很樂意。
Certainly. 當然可以。	I'd be happy to. 我很樂意。

Track 14

即時演練

選出最適當的回答。

1. Ⓐ Ⓑ Ⓒ
2. Ⓐ Ⓑ Ⓒ
3. Ⓐ Ⓑ Ⓒ
4. Ⓐ Ⓑ Ⓒ
5. Ⓐ Ⓑ Ⓒ

2-4 Part 3：簡短對話

2-4-1 試題範例

> **DIRECTIONS：** You will hear a short conversation between two or more people. You will see three questions on each conversation and four possible answers. Choose the best answer to each question, and fill in the corresponding oval on your answer sheet. The conversations will not be printed and will be spoken only once.
>
> 作答方式：你會聽到兩人或多人的簡短對話。每段對話搭配三個問題，每題各有四個選項。選出每個問題的最佳答案，將答案卡上對應的橢圓框塗滿。對話內容不會印出文字，並只會朗讀一遍。

你會聽到： Man: We'll need your medical history, so take this form and fill it out, please.

Woman: Will there be a long wait for my appointment?

Man: No, the doctor is seeing patients on schedule.

Woman: That's good news. The last time I was here, I waited almost an hour.

Man: You don't have to worry about that today. I'm sure the doctor will be ready to see you in no more than five minutes.

男： 我們需要你的病歷，麻煩把這張表格填一下。

女： 我的預約會等很久嗎？

男： 不會的，醫生會照預約時間看診。

女： 太好了。我上次來等了快一個小時。

男： 今天不用擔心，醫生一定會準備好幫你看診，不會讓你等超過五分鐘。

Question 1

你會看到：Where are the speakers? 說話的人在什麼地方？

(A) At a sidewalk café　路邊的咖啡館
(B) In a history class　歷史課的教室
(C) At an airport check-in counter　機場的報到櫃檯
(D) In a physician's office　診所

Ⓐ　Ⓑ　Ⓒ　●

根據男子第一句話所提到的病歷，即可判斷對話發生地點在診所。因此「Where are the speakers?」的最適當回答是 (D) In a physician's office。

Question 2

你會看到：Who are the speakers? 說話的人是誰？

(A) A doctor and a nurse　醫師和護理師
(B) A clerk and a shopper　店員和購物的人
(C) A receptionist and a patient　櫃檯人員和病人
(D) A pilot and a passenger　機師和乘客

Ⓐ　Ⓑ　●　Ⓓ

對話中女子問男子她的預約還要等多久，男子則回應不會等太久，目前醫生有按照預約時程安排看診。從此處可得知女子為來看診的病患，男子則為櫃檯人員。因此「Who are the speakers?」的最適當回答是 (C) A receptionist and a patient。

Question 3

你會看到：How long will the woman wait? 這名女子會等多久？

(A) Five minutes or less 不到五分鐘
(B) Forty minutes 四十分鐘
(C) Over an hour 超過一小時
(D) At least two hours 至少兩小時

● Ⓑ Ⓒ Ⓓ

根據對話中最後一句男子提到不會讓女子等候超過五分鐘，即可選出正確答案，因此「How long will the woman wait?」的最適當回答是 (A) Five minutes or less。

2-4-2 高分攻略

高分攻略 1　人物題

多益測驗經常考關於人的問題，他們會要你辨識說話者或動作執行者是誰。這類問題通常以 who 開頭，但有些 what 開頭的問題也可能和人相關。

> **答題要訣** 💡　當你看到一個 who 問句，要注意聆聽關於人的資訊。

》範例

當你看到下面這些類型的問題，就要注意聽關於人的資訊。

問題

Who are the speakers? 說話者是誰？
Who is the man? 這名男子是誰？
Who will make the photocopies? 誰會去影印？
Who delivered the package? 誰寄送了這件包裹？
Who has the tickets? 誰有票？
Who is the party for? 這場派對是為誰而舉辦的？
Whose office will they use? 他們會用誰的辦公室？
Who are the speakers looking for? 說話者在找誰？

回答

專有人名	依活動或身分辨識人物	依團體辨識人物	依關係辨識人物
Mr. Tanza 譚薩先生	A tourist 觀光客	Business people 商務人士	His boss 他的老闆
Mrs. Green 格林太太	A passenger 乘客	Family members 家庭成員	Her son 她的兒子
Ms. Hu 胡小姐	A driver 司機	College students 大學生	Their teacher 他們的教師
Dr. Shapiro 夏皮羅醫師	A jogger 慢跑者		My colleague 我的同事
			The woman's friend 這名女子的朋友

即時演練

選出最適當的回答。

1. Who are the speakers?

   (A) Lifeguards at the beach
   (B) Painters
   (C) Salespeople selling coats
   (D) Bartenders

   Ⓐ Ⓑ Ⓒ Ⓓ

2. Who will prepare the wall?

   (A) The man
   (B) The woman
   (C) The boss
   (D) The helper

   Ⓐ Ⓑ Ⓒ Ⓓ

3. Who owns the house?

   (A) The man's father
   (B) The man's mother
   (C) The man's brother
   (D) The man's friend

   Ⓐ Ⓑ Ⓒ Ⓓ

4. Who is the man?

    (A) A waiter
    (B) A caterer
    (C) A pastry chef
    (D) A restaurant customer

5. Who are the women giving the dinner for?

    (A) Their boss
    (B) Their friend
    (C) Their client
    (D) Their business partner

6. Who will pay the bill?

    (A) Mary
    (B) Mary's assistant
    (C) The accountant
    (D) Everyone in the office

高分攻略 2　職業題

多益測驗很常考詢問職業的問題。作答時，先把所有答案選項看過一遍，知道可能是哪四種職業。接著想一想這四種職業有哪些相關單字，這些字會是你作答的線索。

> **答題要訣** 聆聽音檔「之前」就要先看好答案選項中出現的職業，並做一些假設，再仔細聆聽找出線索。

》範例

假如你看到下面這些類型的問題，就請注意聽關於職業的回答。

問題

What kind of job does the man have?　這名男子從事什麼樣的工作？
What is Mr. Smith's present position?　史密斯先生現在的職位是什麼？
What type of work does the woman do?　這名女子從事什麼樣的工作？
How does this man earn a living?　這名男子靠什麼維生？
What is the man's job?　這名男子的工作是什麼？
What kind of job is available?　有什麼樣的職缺？
What is the woman's occupation?　這名女子的職業是什麼？
Who can benefit from seeing this memo?　這份備忘錄對誰有幫助？
What is the man's profession?　這名男子的職業是什麼？
Who was interviewed?　接受面試的是誰？
What does this woman do?　這名女子是做什麼的？
Who would most likely use the conference hall?　誰最有可能使用會議廳？

回答

She's the director.　她是導演。	A dentist　牙醫
He's a lawyer.　他是律師。	A travel agent　旅行社職員
They're accountants.　他們是會計師。	A hotel clerk　飯店服務人員
The office manager　辦公室經理	A pilot　機師
The personnel director　人事主管	A flight attendant　空服員
The receptionist　接待員	A waiter/waitress/server　服務生
A computer programmer　程式設計師	A chef　廚師

即時演練

選出最適當的回答。

1. What is the woman's occupation?

    (A) Running coach
    (B) Baseball player
    (C) Telephone operator
    (D) Telephone installer

2. What is the man's job?

    (A) Employment counselor
    (B) Tech support specialist
    (C) Website designer
    (D) Accountant

3. Who is responsible for answering the phone?

    (A) The man only
    (B) The receptionist
    (C) Everyone at the company
    (D) The customer service specialist

4. Who is the man?

   (A) A travel agent
   (B) A tourist
   (C) A tour guide
   (D) A museum director

   Ⓐ Ⓑ Ⓒ Ⓓ

5. What is the woman's job?

   (A) Bus driver
   (B) Taxi driver
   (C) Waiter
   (D) Chef

   Ⓐ Ⓑ Ⓒ Ⓓ

6. Who will call the restaurant?

   (A) The man
   (B) The woman
   (C) The hotel manager
   (D) The front desk clerk

   Ⓐ Ⓑ Ⓒ Ⓓ

高分攻略 3　地點題

關於地點的問題多半以 where 開頭，通常會使用 in、on、at 後面接地點來回答。

> **答題要訣**　當你看到一個 where 問句，請注意聽關於地點的資訊。

》範例

假如看到接下來這些類型的問題，就要注意聽關於地點的回答。

問題

Where did the conversation probably take place? 這段對話可能發生在什麼地方？ Where did the conversation likely occur? 這段對話可能發生在什麼地方？ Where is the man? 這名男子在哪裡？ Where is the woman? 這名女子在哪裡？ Where is the speaker? 說話者在哪裡？ Where are the man and woman? 這名男子和女子在哪裡？ Where are the speakers? 說話者在哪裡？ Where is the package? 包裹在哪裡？	Where has the man/woman been? 這名男子／女子去了哪裡？ Where does the man/woman want to go? 這名男子／女子想去哪裡？ Where did the man/woman come from? 這名男子／女子從哪裡來？ Where are they going? 他們要去哪裡？ Where did the man think the woman was? 這名男子認為這名女子在哪裡？ Where should he call? 他應該打電話去哪裡？ Where did he put his coat? 他把他的外套放在哪裡了？

回答

無介系詞	有介系詞	
The train station 火車站 The store 商店 The office 辦公室 The house 房子	In the closet 在衣櫃裡 Under the desk 在桌子下 At the office 在辦公室 Next to the bank 在銀行隔壁 At the train station 在火車站 At the beach 在海灘 To the store 到商店	By the door 在門邊 In the dining room 在餐廳 At home 在家 On the bus 在公車上 At the dentist's 在牙醫診所 To the airport 到機場

即時演練

選出最適當的回答。

1. Where does this conversation take place?

    (A) In a private home
    (B) On a delivery truck
    (C) In a business office
    (D) At a shipping company

2. Where will the woman put the package?

    (A) On Jim's keyboard
    (B) On the filing cabinet
    (C) On Jim's desk
    (D) On a table

3. Where is Jim now?

    (A) At a conference
    (B) In his office
    (C) On a flight
    (D) On vacation

4. Where are the speakers?

   (A) In a taxi
   (B) On a plane
   (C) In a school
   (D) In a private home

5. Where is the woman's coat?

   (A) On a chair
   (B) On the floor
   (C) In the lobby
   (D) In the closet

6. Where is the woman going?

   (A) To her accountant's office
   (B) To the train station
   (C) To her apartment
   (D) To the bank

高分攻略 4　時間題

關於時間的問題大多以 when、how long 或 how often 開頭，通常會用表示時間的單字或片語來回答。如果是 when（何時）的問題，會回答具體時間點。如果是 how long（多久）的問題，會回答一段時間。如果是 how often（多常）的問題，會用表示頻率的詞語來回答。

答題要訣　聽音檔「之前」就要先注意答案選項中的時間線索，接著仔細聆聽音檔找出這些線索。

》範例

假如看到接下來這些類型的問題，就要注意聽關於時間的回答。請注意這類的問題會以 when 和 how 開頭。

問題

When 的問題	How long 的問題	How often 的問題
When did the conversation take place? 這段對話發生在什麼時候？ When is the man's birthday? 這名男子的生日是何時？ When is the woman's vacation date? 這名女子的度假日期是什麼時候？	How long will they be in Tokyo? 他們會在東京待多久？ How long did the meeting last? 這場會議持續了多久？ How long will it take to arrive? 要多久才會抵達？ How long do you spend on the reports? 你花了多少時間做報告？	How often do buses leave? 公車多久發車一次？ How often are the employees paid? 員工多久領一次薪水？ How often is there a conference? 會議多久舉行一次？ How often is the magazine published? 雜誌多久出刊一次？

問題

When 的問題		
When is the restaurant open? 餐廳什麼時候開？ When was the meeting? 會議是在什麼時候？ When will the increase go into effect? 這項調漲何時生效？ When did he join the firm? 他是何時加入公司的？		

回答

時間點	一段時間	頻率
11:00 a.m. 早上十一點 Noon 正午 Midnight 午夜 At 6:00 六點整 Before 5:30 五點半前 In the morning 早上 Tomorrow 明天 In the summer 夏天 Next year 明年 In April 四月 On January 3rd 一月三日	45 minutes 四十五分鐘 An hour 一小時 Two days 兩天 A week 一週 About a month 大約一個月 Less than a year 不到一年	Every hour 每小時 Every day 每天 Every other day 每隔一天 Every two weeks 每兩週 Once a month 一個月一次 Twice a year 一年兩次 Three times a week 一週三次

即時演練

聆聽對話，選出最適當的回答。

1. How much longer will the man stay?

    (A) 10 minutes
    (B) 15 minutes
    (C) 30 minutes
    (D) 60 minutes

2. When is the man's appointment?

    (A) At 9:00
    (B) Tomorrow
    (C) In a few minutes
    (D) In half an hour

3. How long will it take the man to get home?

    (A) 20 minutes
    (B) 25 minutes
    (C) 40 minutes
    (D) 45 minutes

4. How often is there a staff meeting?

   (A) Every morning
   (B) Once a week
   (C) Once a month
   (D) Twice a month

   Ⓐ Ⓑ Ⓒ Ⓓ

5. When will the meeting start?

   (A) At 1:00
   (B) At 3:00
   (C) Before lunch
   (D) In a couple of hours

   Ⓐ Ⓑ Ⓒ Ⓓ

6. How long will the meeting last?

   (A) One hour
   (B) Two hours
   (C) Three hours
   (D) Four hours

   Ⓐ Ⓑ Ⓒ Ⓓ

高分攻略 5　活動題

關於活動的問題大多以 what 開頭，部分以 how 開頭。這類問題的回答通常是短片語或完整句子。作答時應先看答案選項中的四個活動是什麼，接著思考這些活動有哪些相關的單字，以作為判斷線索。聆聽時要注意關於活動的線索，以打高爾夫球為例，音檔中可能會出現 golf club（球桿）、bag（球袋）、course（球場）、fairway（球道）、hole（球洞）、green（果嶺）等單字。

答題要訣　在聽音檔「之前」就要先看好答案選項中有哪些活動類型，並做一些相關假設，接著仔細聆聽音檔找出線索。

》範例

假如看到接下來這些類型的問題，請注意聽關於活動的回答。注意這些問題會以 what 和 how 開頭。

問題

關於「要做什麼」的問題	關於活動或事件的問題
What will the man do? 這名男子將會做什麼？ What did the woman do? 這名女子做了什麼？ What has the customer decided to do? 這位顧客決定做什麼？ What are they planning to do? 他們計劃要做什麼？ What does the woman have to do? 這名女子必須做什麼？ What is the man going to do? 這名男子要做什麼？ What is Mrs. Park supposed to do? 帕克太太應該做什麼？ What are they doing? 他們正在做什麼？	What happened? 發生了什麼事？ What occurred? 發生了什麼事？ What took place? 發生了什麼事？ What happened to the woman? 這名女子發生了什麼事？ What will happen next? 接下來會發生什麼事？
	關於「怎麼做」的問題
	How can the package be sent? 這個包裹可以怎麼寄？ How will the room be changed? 這個房間會如何改變？

回答

They are having dinner. 他們正在吃晚餐。 They will go to the store. 他們會去商店。 Seeing a movie 看電影 Playing golf 打高爾夫球 Planning a workshop 規劃工作坊 Making photocopies 影印	Mail a package 郵寄包裹 Wait on the corner 在轉角處等待 Take a Spanish course 上西班牙文課 Attend a lecture 聽講座 Take a day off 請一天假 Leave soon 很快離開 Move some furniture 移動一些家具

即時演練

聆聽對話，選出最適當的回答。

1. What are they doing?

   (A) Taking a walk
   (B) Taking a nap
   (C) Buying a map
   (D) Driving a car

   Ⓐ Ⓑ Ⓒ Ⓓ

2. What did they do earlier?

   (A) Rested
   (B) Played in the snow
   (C) Had dinner
   (D) Rented a movie

   Ⓐ Ⓑ Ⓒ Ⓓ

3. What will they do next?

   (A) Read
   (B) Go to bed
   (C) See a play
   (D) Go to the movies

   Ⓐ Ⓑ Ⓒ Ⓓ

4. What is the man trying to do?

   (A) Staple copies
   (B) Fix the machine
   (C) Make extra copies
   (D) Make the copies look darker

   Ⓐ Ⓑ Ⓒ Ⓓ

5. What does the woman suggest doing?

   (A) Add toner
   (B) Try again later
   (C) Call a repair person
   (D) Report the problem

   Ⓐ Ⓑ Ⓒ Ⓓ

6. What will the man do next?

   (A) Ask the office manager to do the job
   (B) Use another machine
   (C) Do the job tomorrow
   (D) Buy a new machine

   Ⓐ Ⓑ Ⓒ Ⓓ

高分攻略 6　看法題

詢問看法的問題多半以 what 開頭,回答時會使用簡短的句子表達看法。

答題要訣 在聽音檔「之前」就要先看好答案中出現了哪些表達看法的選項,接著仔細聆聽找出這些線索。

》範例

當你看到下面這些類型的問題,就要注意聽關於看法的回答。

問題

What 問句
What did the man think about the play? 這名男子覺得這齣戲怎麼樣?
What did the speaker think about the talk? 說話者對這段談話有什麼看法?
What did the woman say about the presentation?
這名女子對這場演講怎麼說?
What was the matter with the conference? 這場會議出了什麼問題?
What did the man like about the meal? 這名男子喜歡這頓餐點的哪一點?
What is the woman's opinion of the movie?
這名女子對這部電影有什麼看法?

回答

It's boring. 很無聊。
He's highly qualified. 他資歷很高。
The room is too dark. 房間太暗了。
It was too expensive. 太貴了。
She was very helpful. 她幫了很大的忙。
It wasn't long enough. 不夠長。

即時演練

聆聽對話，選出最適當的回答。

1. What did they like about the speaker?

   (A) His short presentation
   (B) His humor
   (C) His clothes
   (D) His folks

2. What is the man's opinion of the hotel?

   (A) The décor is nice.
   (B) The food is great.
   (C) The seats are too hard.
   (D) The room is too big.

3. What does the woman think of the hotel?

   (A) It's very expensive.
   (B) It's cheaper than she expected.
   (C) The tables are nice.
   (D) It's uncomfortable.

4. What does the man say about the meeting?

   (A) It was boring.
   (B) It was too long.
   (C) It was informative.
   (D) It was disorganized.

   Ⓐ Ⓑ Ⓒ Ⓓ

5. What is the woman's opinion of the new director?

   (A) He is not qualified for the job.
   (B) He is always busy.
   (C) He is talkative.
   (D) He is shy.

   Ⓐ Ⓑ Ⓒ Ⓓ

6. What does the man think of the cafeteria?

   (A) It has better food.
   (B) It is inexpensive.
   (C) It is too crowded.
   (D) It is quiet.

   Ⓐ Ⓑ Ⓒ Ⓓ

高分攻略 7　圖表題

Part 3 有部分對話會搭配圖表，可能是統計圖、曲線圖、議程表、時刻表或其他類似圖表。說話者可能核實圖表中的資訊，也可能反駁當中的資訊。

> **答題要訣**　快速把考題瀏覽一遍，在圖表中尋找關鍵字，接著仔細聆聽對話中的這些關鍵字。

》範例

圖表題一定以「Look at the graphic.」開頭，後面接一個 wh- 問句，例如：

Look at the graphic. Who works on Tuesday?
請看圖表，週二誰要上班？
Look at the graphic. When will the visitor arrive?
請看圖表，訪客將於何時抵達？
Look at the graphic. Where will they sit?
請看圖表，他們會坐在哪裡？

但是光看圖表無法回答問題，必須仔細聆聽對話，從中找出線索，利用這些線索從圖表中選出正確的資訊作答。

即時演練

聆聽對話，選出最適當的回答。

1. Look at the graphic. When will Sue work at the reception desk?

   (A) Monday
   (B) Tuesday
   (C) Wednesday
   (D) Thursday

   Ⓐ Ⓑ Ⓒ Ⓓ

Reception Desk Schedule	
Monday	Sue
Tuesday	Sam
Wednesday	Bill
Thursday	Jim
Friday	open

2. Look at the graphic. Which printer will the woman buy?

   (A) Model XX
   (B) Model XZ
   (C) Model Y
   (D) Model WY

   Ⓐ Ⓑ Ⓒ Ⓓ

Printer Model	Price
Model XX	$115
Model XZ	$155
Model Y	$175
Model WY	$225

3. Look at the graphic. When was Mr. Kim hired?

   (A) February
   (B) March
   (C) April
   (D) May

   Ⓐ Ⓑ Ⓒ Ⓓ

   Sales

   (line graph: January 5000, February 4500, March 3000, April 4000, May 4200; Units Sold)

4. Look at the graphic. What topic will be discussed first at the meeting?

   (A) Budget Report
   (B) Sales Update
   (C) New Ad Campaign
   (D) Hiring Update

   Ⓐ Ⓑ Ⓒ Ⓓ

   Staff Meeting
   January 12, 2:00 p.m.

   Budget Report ·············· Robert Franks
   Sales Update ·············· Maya Lopez
   New Ad Campaign ·········· Sue Lin
   Hiring Update ·············· Ben Ingram

5. Look at the graphic. Where will they meet for lunch?

   (A) Location A
   (B) Location B
   (C) Location C
   (D) Location D

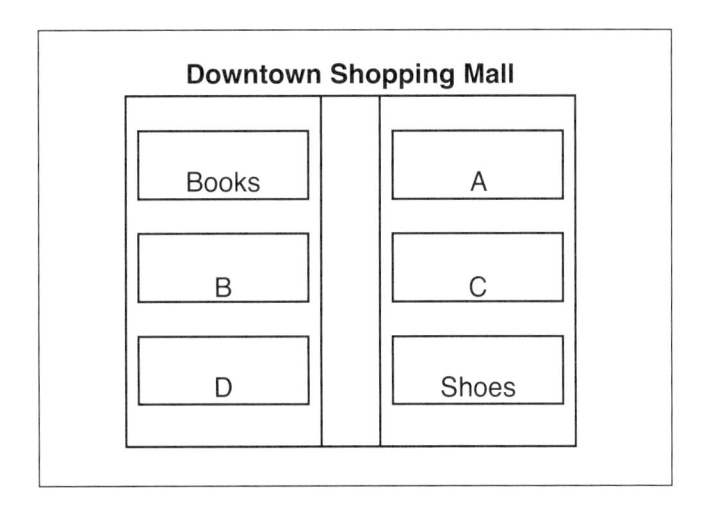

   Ⓐ Ⓑ Ⓒ Ⓓ

   Downtown Shopping Mall

Books	A
B	C
D	Shoes

高分攻略 8　　情境意義

考試會截取對話中的一個單字或片語，問你它的意思，必須知道這個單字或片語在對話情境中代表的意思。

答題要訣　必須從上下文判斷單字或片語的意義。

〉〉範例

情境意義的題型會從對話中截取一個單字或片語，例如：

What does the man mean when he says, "I got it"?
這名男子說「I got it」是什麼意思？
Why does the woman say, "Could you"?
這名女子為何要說「Could you」？

單字和片語在不同情境中的意義不同。當你看到情境意義題時，要注意聽對話內容，從上下文去了解說話者講這句話所代表的意義。

即時演練

聆聽對話，選出最適當的回答。

1. What does the woman mean when she says, "I wouldn't do it like that"?

   (A) The woman thinks the man is working inefficiently.
   (B) The woman thinks the man is working too hard.

2. What does the man mean when he says, "Things have picked up"?

   (A) He got a promotion.
   (B) He is feeling optimistic.

3. What does the man mean when he says, "that color"?

   (A) He likes the color of the carpet.
   (B) He does not like the color of the carpet.

4. What does the woman mean when she says, "I thought that meeting would never end"?

   (A) The meeting was boring.
   (B) The meeting was canceled.

5. What does the woman mean when she says, "I'm on top of it"?

   (A) The woman is aware of the work schedule.
   (B) The woman is confident she can finish the work on time.

高分攻略 9　簡略回答

在日常對話中，說話者不一定會使用完整的句子來表達，我們經常需要透過上下文來理解對方所說的話。

答題要訣　利用上下文來了解一個簡略回答的意義。

》範例

　　Are you coming to the meeting? 你會來參加會議嗎？
　　Maybe later. 也許晚點。

「Maybe later.」在這裡的意思是「Maybe I will come to the meeting later.」（也許晚點我會來參加會議），省略「I will come to the meeting」的意義可以從上下文中判斷出來。

　　I'm going out for lunch. Wanna come? 我要出去吃午餐，你要來嗎？
　　Sorry. Gotta work. 抱歉了，我要工作。

「Wanna come?」的意思是「Do you want to come?」，Do you 兩個字被省略了，want to 也縮略成 Wanna。同樣地，「Gotta work.」的意思是「I have got to work.」，主詞 I 被省略，情態動詞 have got to 縮略成 Gotta。請注意只有在口語中可以使用縮略的 wanna 和 gotta，寫作時絕對要避免。

即時演練

選出畫線部分的正確意義。

1. Woman: So, the meeting day has been changed to Friday?
   Man: <u>Right.</u>

   (A) It's on the right.　　Ⓐ Ⓑ
   (B) You are correct.

2. Man: Let's take a break now and finish this later.
   Woman: <u>Fine with me.</u>

   (A) I agree with your plan.　　Ⓐ Ⓑ
   (B) That's a bad idea.

3. Woman: Please make ten copies of this report, leave one on my desk, and send the rest to Mr. Sato.
   Man: <u>Got it.</u>

   (A) I have Mr. Sato's address.　　Ⓐ Ⓑ
   (B) I understand everything you want me to do.

4. Man: We're having lunch at Café de Oro. Will you join us?
   Woman: <u>Wish I could.</u>

   (A) I would like to join you, but I can't.　　Ⓐ Ⓑ
   (B) I have always wanted to eat at that café.

5. Woman: Ms. Chang is in a meeting and can't see you now.
   Man: <u>Too bad.</u>

   (A) The meeting is a bad idea.　　Ⓐ Ⓑ
   (B) I'm sorry she can't see me.

2-5 Part 4：簡短獨白

2-5-1 試題範例

> **DIRECTIONS :** You will hear a short talk given by a single speaker. You will see three questions on each talk, each with four possible answers. Choose the best answer to each question, and fill in the corresponding oval on your answer sheet. The talks will not be printed and will be spoken only once.
> 作答方式：你會聽到一名說話者的簡短獨白。每段獨白搭配三個問題，各有四個選項。選出每個問題的最佳回答，將答案卡上對應的橢圓框塗滿。獨白內容不會印出文字，並只會朗讀一遍。

你會聽到：OK, everyone, we expect a busy day today because of the [3]**one-day only sale** in the clothing department. Please make sure customers are aware that not everything in that department is on sale, but that [2]**sale items are clearly marked and are mostly winter items—coats, hats, boots, sweaters**—and we've included some spring jackets in the sale as well. Also, nothing in the children's department is part of the sale, so make sure customers are clear on that. [1]**All right, the store opens in five minutes, so let's get out there and sell!**

好的，各位，今天服裝部要舉辦一日特賣，預計會很忙。請確保顧客知道服裝部的商品不是全面特價，但特價商品會清楚標示，大部分是冬季商品——外套、帽子、靴子、毛衣——部分春季外套也有特價。還有，童裝部不參與特賣，一定要讓顧客清楚知道。好了，五分鐘後將開店，我們出去好好推銷一番吧！

094

Question 1

你會看到：Who is talking? 誰在說話？

   (A) A customer　顧客
   (B) A store manager　店長
   (C) A store employee　商店員工
   (D) A clothing company vendor　服飾公司的廠商

根據文中最後一句，即可得知這是店長在對其員工宣導特賣會的注意事項及請他們把握機會好好向顧客推銷，因此「Who is talking?」的最適當回答是 (B) A store manager。

Question 2

你會看到：What is on sale? 什麼東西在特價？

   (A) All clothing　所有服飾
   (B) Summer hats　夏帽
   (C) Winter clothes　冬裝
   (D) Children's boots　童靴

文中提到不是所有商品全面特價，而是大部分的冬季商品及部分春季外套。後面也提及童裝部不參與特賣，因此「What is on sale?」的最適當回答是 (C) Winter clothes。

Question 3

你會看到：How long will the sale last? 這場特賣會將持續多久？

   (A) Five minutes　五分鐘
   (B) One hour　一小時
   (C) One day　一天
   (D) Two days　兩天

根據文中第一句所提及的一日特賣，即可得知這場特賣會將持續一天，因此「How long will the sale last?」的最適當回答是 (C) One day。

2-5-2 高分攻略

高分攻略 1　活動與事實題

關於活動與事實的問題多半以 what 開頭，通常會用片語或完整句子來回答。這類問題的應答策略和前面題型差不多，請先把答案選項看過一遍，瞭解有哪些可能的活動，並做一些初步假設，接著仔細聽音檔找出相關線索。

> **答題要訣** 在聆聽音檔「之前」就要先看答案選項中出現了哪些活動或事實，接著仔細聆聽找出這些線索。

》**範例**

當你看到下面這些類型的問題，就要注意聽關於活動或事實的回答。請注意這類問題會以 what 開頭。

問題

What is the talk mainly about? 這段獨白主要在談論什麼？
What event will take place? 即將舉行什麼活動？
What will happen next week? 下週會發生什麼事？
What are the tickets for? 這是什麼活動的門票？
What will the speaker do after the meeting? 會議結束後說話者會做什麼？
What will happen after the program? 課程結束後會發生什麼事？

回答

A parade 一場遊行
A job fair 一場就業博覽會
A concert 一場演奏會
The annual banquet 年度餐會
The budget 預算
Plans for next year 明年的計畫
She will sign books. 她會簽書。
He will answer questions. 他會回答問題。
There will be a festival. 會有一場慶典。
Furniture will go on sale. 會舉辦家具特賣。

即時演練

聆聽獨白，選出最適當的回答。

1. What event will take place this weekend?

   (A) A book fair
   (B) A conference
   (C) A national celebration
   (D) An international dance

2. What will happen on Saturday evening?

   (A) A parade
   (B) A food sale
   (C) A concert
   (D) A circus performance

3. What will the mayor do on Sunday?

   (A) Sell tickets
   (B) Address the crowds
   (C) Play basketball
   (D) Buy some baskets

4. What event is the speaker celebrating?

    (A) A birthday
    (B) A graduation
    (C) A retirement
    (D) A job promotion

5. What will guests do at the celebration?

    (A) Dance
    (B) Play games
    (C) Enjoy a meal
    (D) Receive awards

6. What will the speaker do on Sunday?

    (A) Take a walk
    (B) Play tennis
    (C) Get up late
    (D) Go to work

高分攻略 2　原因題

詢問原因的問題多半以 why 開頭，有時也會以 what 開頭。這類問題的回答通常是完整句子，也可能是短片語。應答策略和其他題型是一樣的。

> **答題要訣**　在聆聽音檔「之前」就要先看答案中出現了哪些含有原因的選項，接著仔細聆聽找出這些線索。

》範例

當你看到下面這些類型的問題時，就要仔細聽關於原因的回答。注意這類題目多以 why 開頭。

問題

Why will the bus be late? 公車為何誤點？
Why has the schedule been changed? 時程表為何被更改？
Why does the speaker want to have a meeting? 說話者為何想要開會？
Why does the speaker need to change the appointment?
說話者為何要更改預約？
Why is there a sale this week? 這週為何要辦特賣活動？
Why did the speaker make the call? 說話者為何打這通電話？
What was the cause of the delay? 延誤的原因為何？

回答

The weather is bad. 天候不佳。
The director is away. 主管不在。
Traffic is heavy. 路上塞車。
She wants to discuss the project. 她想討論這個計畫。
He has to go out of town. 他必須出城一趟。
The store is closing. 商店即將打烊。
To ask for help 為了尋求協助

100

即時演練

聆聽獨白，選出最適當的回答。

1. Why is there a delay?

    (A) Workers are staging a work action.
    (B) The weather is bad.
    (C) There are flight control problems.
    (D) Passengers are boarding slowly.

2. Why should passengers get something to eat now?

    (A) The restaurants will close at midnight.
    (B) The restaurants won't be open tomorrow.
    (C) There will be no food served on the flight.
    (D) There are some restaurants close to the gate.

3. Why should passengers pay attention to the announcements?

    (A) To find out which gate their flight will leave from
    (B) To hear which restaurants are open
    (C) To keep from getting bored
    (D) To know when it is time to board the flight

4. Why does Mr. Brown have an appointment with Mr. Wilson?

   (A) To interview him for a newspaper article
   (B) To go look at an apartment for rent
   (C) To review some documents
   (D) To sign some papers

5. Why does Mr. Brown have to cancel the appointment?

   (A) He has to buy a new suit.
   (B) He has an unexpected meeting.
   (C) He has to go to the hospital emergency room.
   (D) He has not had enough time to prepare for the appointment.

6. Why doesn't Mr. Brown want the listener to call his office number today?

   (A) He is not at the office today.
   (B) His office phone is out of order.
   (C) He is too busy to answer the phone.
   (D) Mr. Wilson has only his cell phone number.

高分攻略 3　數字題

關於數字的問題會以 how many（多少）、how much（多少）、how long（多久）、what time（什麼時候）或 when（何時）開頭，你必須能夠分辨發音非常接近的數字，還有和數字發音很像甚至一樣的其他單字。

答題要訣　仔細聽朗讀內容中的數字，要能分辨數字和其他發音相近的單字。

》範例

發音相近的數字

7 和 11
13 和 30
14 和 40
15 和 50
15 和 16
16 和 60
17 和 70
18 和 80
19 和 90
50 和 60

和數字發音相近的單字

2—to, too
2 days—today, Tuesday
3—free
4—for, forget
6—picks, sick
8—ate, wait
9—fine, time
10—then, when
20—plenty

實用片語

> over 20 = more than 20　超過二十
> under 20 = fewer than 20　不到二十
> at least 20 = 20 or more　至少二十
> up to 20 = no more than 20　最多二十

即時演練

聆聽獨白，選出最適當的回答。

1. When is the workshop?

    (A) Today
    (B) In two days
    (C) On Tuesday
    (D) Wednesday

2. How many people will attend the workshop?

    (A) 13
    (B) Almost 30
    (C) Exactly 30
    (D) More than 30

3. How long does the speaker want to meet with John?

    (A) 15 minutes
    (B) 50 minutes
    (C) 30 minutes
    (D) 2 hours

4. What time is the program scheduled to start?

   (A) 2:00
   (B) 7:00
   (C) 9:00
   (D) 10:00

   Ⓐ Ⓑ Ⓒ Ⓓ

5. How many people will give presentations?

   (A) 5
   (B) 11
   (C) 13
   (D) 30

   Ⓐ Ⓑ Ⓒ Ⓓ

6. How much does admission to the program cost?

   (A) $0
   (B) $3
   (C) $4
   (D) $20

   Ⓐ Ⓑ Ⓒ Ⓓ

高分攻略 4　主題和目的題

多益經常考朗讀內容的細節，有時也會考你內容主題或說話目的。回答主題和目的問題時，必須理解整段獨白的主題或目的為何。

答題要訣　仔細聆聽可以指出說話主題或目的之語句。

》範例

當你看到下面這些類型的問題，就要注意聽說明主題或目的之回答。作答時必須在選項中找出你聽到內容的主題。題目可能問你說話者的身分、這段談話的發生情境、說話的主要目的，也可能問你關於聽眾的問題。

問題

What is this talk about?　這段談話是關於什麼？
Who is this information for?　這項資訊是要提供給誰的？
Who would be interested in this announcement?　誰會對這則公告有興趣？
What is the purpose of this message?　這則訊息的目的是什麼？
Where would you hear this talk?　你可能會在哪裡聽到這段談話？

回答

分類	例子
身分、職稱、團體	A client　客戶 A ticket clerk　售票員 The woman's colleagues　女子的同事 Airline passengers　飛機乘客
地點、情況	In an office　在辦公室 At a convention　在一場大會 During a banquet　宴會期間 At an airport　在機場

任何主題	The new machinery 新機器 Politics 政治 Environmental responsibility 環境責任 An advertising campaign 廣告活動
目的	To change an appointment 更改預約 To advertise a business 宣傳業務 To introduce a speaker 介紹講者 To change an order 更改訂單

即時演練

聆聽獨白，選出最適當的回答。

1. What changes are taking place in the company?

   (A) The Board of Directors resigned.
   (B) The managing director was fired.
   (C) The workers went on strike.
   (D) All letters will be sent by computer.

2. Who is the speaker addressing?

   (A) Some clients
   (B) His coworkers
   (C) A server
   (D) The director

3. What does the speaker plan to do soon?

   (A) Become a clothes salesman
   (B) Start a business
   (C) Go to college
   (D) Work as a restaurant manager

4. Where would you hear this announcement?

   (A) In a store
   (B) In a hotel
   (C) In a restaurant
   (D) In a train station

   Ⓐ Ⓑ Ⓒ Ⓓ

5. What is the announcement about?

   (A) A sale
   (B) How to pay
   (C) Job openings
   (D) Closing time

   Ⓐ Ⓑ Ⓒ Ⓓ

6. Who is the announcement for?

   (A) All staff
   (B) Customers
   (C) The manager
   (D) Security guards

   Ⓐ Ⓑ Ⓒ Ⓓ

高分攻略 5　改述題

有時問題的回答會是獨白內容的改述，也就是換句話說，意旨用不同的話重述同一項資訊。

答題要訣　注意可用來改述內容的同義字或類似片語。

》範例

這種題型的回答往往是將原陳述句子加以改述，也就是換句話說，例如：

陳述：Temperatures will be high today. 今天氣溫會很高。
改述：It will be a warm day. 今天會是暖和的一天。

陳述：Please remain seated. 請維持坐好。
改述：Please stay in your seats. 請留在座位上。

陳述：Mr. Johnson has written several books. 強森先生寫過幾本書。
改述：Mr. Johnson is an author. 強森先生是一名作家。

陳述：Houses in this neighborhood don't cost a great deal.
　　　這附近的房子不會很昂貴。
改述：It isn't expensive to live in this area. 住在這一區不會很花錢。

即時演練

聆聽獨白，選出最適當的回答。

1. What is the purpose of the form?

    (A) To make a complaint
    (B) To borrow money
    (C) To apply for a job
    (D) To get a license

2. How should the form be submitted?

    (A) By regular mail
    (B) By email
    (C) In person
    (D) Through a website

3. When will the listener be contacted?

    (A) In two days
    (B) In four days
    (C) In ten days
    (D) In fourteen days

4. Why did the speaker make the call?

   (A) To arrange for a delivery
   (B) To advertise products
   (C) To thank the listener
   (D) To order a table

5. What does the speaker say about the listener's address?

   (A) It is near his office.
   (B) It is difficult to find.
   (C) It is listed in his records.
   (D) It has changed recently.

6. What does the speaker ask the listener to do?

   (A) Rent a truck
   (B) Call before Friday
   (C) Go to the warehouse
   (D) Provide a phone number

高分攻略 6　　圖表題

Part 4 的部分題目會搭配圖表，可能是統計圖、議程表、時刻表或類似圖表。說話者可能核實圖表中的資訊，也可能反駁當中的資訊。

> **答題要訣**　快速把問題瀏覽一遍，然後看圖表尋找關鍵字，接著仔細聆聽獨白，找出跟關鍵字相關的描述。

》範例

Part 4 的圖表題和 Part 3 一樣，必定以「Look at the graphic.」開頭，後面接一個 wh- 問句。

　　Look at the graphic. Who will speak first?
　　請看圖表，誰會第一個發言？
　　Look at the graphic. What will they discuss first?
　　請看圖表，他們會先討論哪一個事項？
　　Look at the graphic. What time will the bus leave?
　　請看圖表，公車幾點出發？

同樣，光看圖表是無法回答問題的，必須仔細聆聽獨白內容，並利用獨白中的線索從圖表中選出正確資訊。

即時演練

聆聽獨白，選出最適當的答案。

1. Look at the graphic. Which train will Pamela take?

   (A) 30
   (B) 31
   (C) 32
   (D) 33

   Ⓐ　Ⓑ　Ⓒ　Ⓓ

   Timetable

Train No.	Lv. Ardale	Arr. Springfield
30	5:00 a.m.	7:17
31	6:45	9:02
32	8:45	11:02
33	10:30	12:47

2. Look at the graphic. Which part of the budget does the speaker want to reduce first?

   (A) Advertising
   (B) Salaries
   (C) Overhead
   (D) Materials

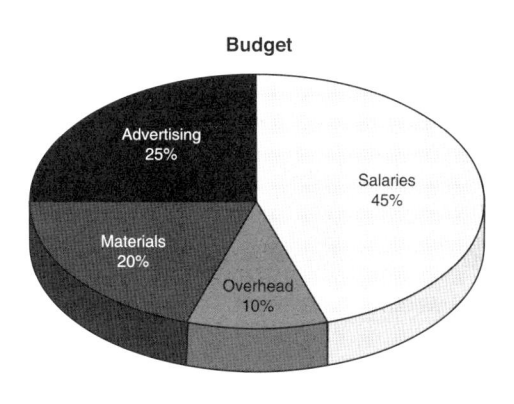

   Ⓐ　Ⓑ　Ⓒ　Ⓓ

   Budget
   - Advertising 25%
   - Salaries 45%
   - Materials 20%
   - Overhead 10%

115

3. Look at the graphic. Where will the group have lunch?

   (A) Pine Grove
   (B) Butterfly Garden
   (C) Rose Garden
   (D) Nature Center

   Ⓐ Ⓑ Ⓒ Ⓓ

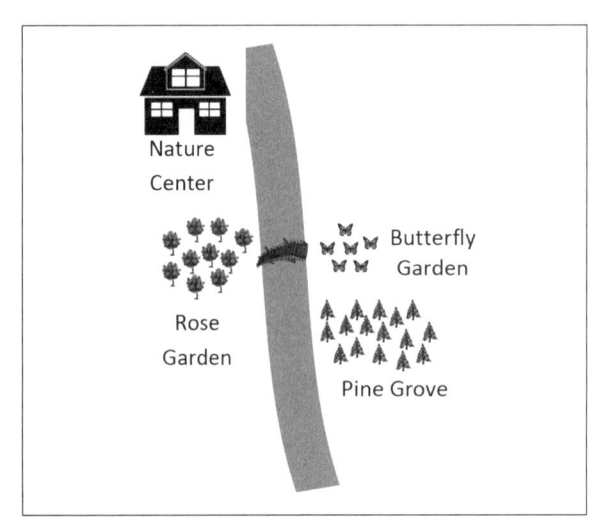

4. Look at the graphic. Which region will the speaker discuss?

   (A) Northwest
   (B) Southwest
   (C) Northeast
   (D) Southeast

   Ⓐ Ⓑ Ⓒ Ⓓ

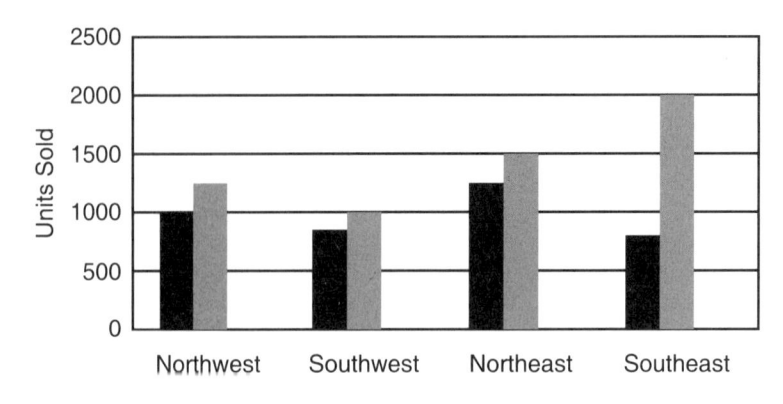

5. Look at the graphic. Which platter will the speaker probably order?

    (A) Small
    (B) Medium
    (C) Large
    (D) Extra Large

    Ⓐ Ⓑ Ⓒ Ⓓ

Kim's Catering
Cold Cuts Platter
Small .... serves 15
Medium .... serves 25
Large .... serves 50
Extra Large .... serves 75

高分攻略 7　隱含意義題

有時候說話者不一定會直接把想法說出來,而是用另一句話表達隱含意義,例如:

They were a bit disappointed by the turnout.　他們對出席人數有點失望。

隱含的意義是:

They expected more people to be there.　他們預期有更多人會來。

答題要訣　隱含意義可以從對話的上下文來判斷。

即時演練

聆聽獨白,並回答問題。

1. What does the speaker say about his appointment?

   (A) He has rescheduled this appointment several times already.
   (B) This is the first time he has rescheduled the appointment.

2. What does the speaker say about the weather?

   (A) She wishes it were warmer.
   (B) She thinks it is very nice.

3. What does the speaker say about the ticket machine?

   (A) It accepts both cash and credit cards.
   (B) The machine accepts credit cards only.

4. What does the speaker say about the celebration?

   (A) The event is more crowded than it was last year.
   (B) The stadium isn't big enough to hold the crowds.

5. What does the speaker say about the tickets?

   (A) They are discounted for members.
   (B) They are available to members only.

高分攻略 8　口音題

在國際商務的領域中，我們經常會遇到各種不同口音的英語。多益聽力測驗的說話口音可能涵蓋美國、英國、澳洲、加拿大。考試不會要你辨識口音，但你必須能夠聽懂這些口音，才能了解說話內容的意義。

答題要訣　上網找美國、英國、澳洲、加拿大的新聞廣播來聽，可以針對同一則新聞，聆聽各種不同廣播如何報導。

即時演練

聆聽獨白,並將聽到的內容寫下。

1. _____

2. _____

3. _____

4. _____

5. _____

答題訣竅總整理

Part 1：照片描述
- 仔細聽完整個句子的意思，決定哪一個選項最符合照片內容。
- 看照片時先分析當中的人物，決定他們的人數、性別、位置、職業和行動。
- 利用照片情境確認物品和它們的位置。

Part 2：應答問題
- 仔細聆聽問題或陳述的意思後作答，不要被近音字、相關字和同音字混淆。
- 注意聽表示建議、主動提議或要求的語句。

Part 3：簡短對話 & Part 4：簡短獨白
- 學習辨識不同問句類型，以及它們要問什麼，可能是詢問人物的資訊、職業、地點、時間等。
- 了解單字或片語在上下文中的意義。
- 從選項中找出對話或獨白內容的改述。
- 仔細聽出隱含的意義。
- 遇到圖表題時，先將圖表瀏覽一遍，接著注意聆聽對話或獨白中核實圖表資訊或反駁圖表資訊的內容。
- 訓練自己聽懂各國口音。

ANSWER SHEET
聽力診斷測驗答案卡

Part 1: Photographs

1. Ⓐ Ⓑ Ⓒ Ⓓ
2. Ⓐ Ⓑ Ⓒ Ⓓ
3. Ⓐ Ⓑ Ⓒ Ⓓ
4. Ⓐ Ⓑ Ⓒ Ⓓ

Part 2: Question-Response

5. Ⓐ Ⓑ Ⓒ
6. Ⓐ Ⓑ Ⓒ
7. Ⓐ Ⓑ Ⓒ
8. Ⓐ Ⓑ Ⓒ
9. Ⓐ Ⓑ Ⓒ
10. Ⓐ Ⓑ Ⓒ
11. Ⓐ Ⓑ Ⓒ
12. Ⓐ Ⓑ Ⓒ
13. Ⓐ Ⓑ Ⓒ
14. Ⓐ Ⓑ Ⓒ
15. Ⓐ Ⓑ Ⓒ
16. Ⓐ Ⓑ Ⓒ

Part 3: Conversations

17. Ⓐ Ⓑ Ⓒ Ⓓ
18. Ⓐ Ⓑ Ⓒ Ⓓ
19. Ⓐ Ⓑ Ⓒ Ⓓ
20. Ⓐ Ⓑ Ⓒ Ⓓ
21. Ⓐ Ⓑ Ⓒ Ⓓ
22. Ⓐ Ⓑ Ⓒ Ⓓ
23. Ⓐ Ⓑ Ⓒ Ⓓ
24. Ⓐ Ⓑ Ⓒ Ⓓ
25. Ⓐ Ⓑ Ⓒ Ⓓ
26. Ⓐ Ⓑ Ⓒ Ⓓ
27. Ⓐ Ⓑ Ⓒ Ⓓ
28. Ⓐ Ⓑ Ⓒ Ⓓ
29. Ⓐ Ⓑ Ⓒ Ⓓ
30. Ⓐ Ⓑ Ⓒ Ⓓ
31. Ⓐ Ⓑ Ⓒ Ⓓ
32. Ⓐ Ⓑ Ⓒ Ⓓ
33. Ⓐ Ⓑ Ⓒ Ⓓ
34. Ⓐ Ⓑ Ⓒ Ⓓ

Part 4: Talks

35. Ⓐ Ⓑ Ⓒ Ⓓ
36. Ⓐ Ⓑ Ⓒ Ⓓ
37. Ⓐ Ⓑ Ⓒ Ⓓ
38. Ⓐ Ⓑ Ⓒ Ⓓ
39. Ⓐ Ⓑ Ⓒ Ⓓ
40. Ⓐ Ⓑ Ⓒ Ⓓ
41. Ⓐ Ⓑ Ⓒ Ⓓ
42. Ⓐ Ⓑ Ⓒ Ⓓ
43. Ⓐ Ⓑ Ⓒ Ⓓ
44. Ⓐ Ⓑ Ⓒ Ⓓ
45. Ⓐ Ⓑ Ⓒ Ⓓ
46. Ⓐ Ⓑ Ⓒ Ⓓ
47. Ⓐ Ⓑ Ⓒ Ⓓ
48. Ⓐ Ⓑ Ⓒ Ⓓ
49. Ⓐ Ⓑ Ⓒ Ⓓ

聽力診斷測驗

Part 1: Photographs

> **Directions:** You will see a photograph. You will hear four statements about the photograph. Choose the statement that most closely matches the photograph, and fill in the corresponding oval on your answer sheet.
>
> Track 31

1.

2.

3.

4.

Part 2: Question-Response

> 🔊 Track 32 **Directions:** You will hear a question and three possible responses. Choose the response that most closely answers the question, and fill in the corresponding oval on your answer sheet.

5. Mark your answer on your answer sheet.

6. Mark your answer on your answer sheet.

7. Mark your answer on your answer sheet.

8. Mark your answer on your answer sheet.

9. Mark your answer on your answer sheet.

10. Mark your answer on your answer sheet.

11. Mark your answer on your answer sheet.

12. Mark your answer on your answer sheet.

13. Mark your answer on your answer sheet.

14. Mark your answer on your answer sheet.

15. Mark your answer on your answer sheet.

16. Mark your answer on your answer sheet.

Part 3: Conversations

> 🔊 **Directions:** You will hear a conversation between two or more people. You will see three questions on each conversation and four possible answers. Choose the best answer to each question, and fill in the corresponding oval on your answer sheet.
> Track 33

17. What did the woman have at the café?

   (A) Soup and a sandwich
   (B) Soup and a salad
   (C) A sandwich only
   (D) A salad only

18. What does the man imply about the café?

   (A) The food is better than the décor.
   (B) The walls are in need of repair.
   (C) Its menu isn't interesting.
   (D) It's too far from the office.

19. What will the speakers do tomorrow?

   (A) Work on a project together
   (B) Look for a new place to eat
   (C) Paint the walls
   (D) Return to the café

20. What does the man suggest the woman do?

    (A) Spend her vacation at home
    (B) Ask for more time off
    (C) Start packing soon
    (D) Go to Paris

21. How long is the woman's vacation?

    (A) One week
    (B) Two weeks
    (C) Three weeks
    (D) Four weeks

22. What will the woman do this afternoon?

    (A) Read a book
    (B) Go shopping
    (C) Walk her dog
    (D) Make trip reservations

23. What does the woman want to have printed?

- (A) Menus
- (B) Checks
- (C) Order forms
- (D) Advertisements

24. What does the man agree to do?

- (A) Print 24 copies
- (B) Forget the rush charge
- (C) Have the order ready tomorrow
- (D) Print on one side of the page only

25. What does the man want the woman to do?

- (A) Pick up the order at night
- (B) Pay ahead of time
- (C) Check the order
- (D) Use a credit card

26. What do the speakers imply about the new director?

   (A) They admire the director's professional background.
   (B) They are looking for some important documents.
   (C) They are interested in hiring a new director.
   (D) They need help writing their own résumés.

27. When did the new director begin working at this company?

   (A) Today
   (B) Two days ago
   (C) A week ago
   (D) Last Tuesday

28. What does the woman suggest?

   (A) Going to a staff meeting
   (B) Attending a social event
   (C) Getting something to eat
   (D) Calling the director at noon

Main Street Paints

Interior Paint Price List

Size	Coverage
1-liter can	……….. up to 6 sq. meters
2-liter can	……….. up to 12 sq. meters
5-liter can	……….. up to 30 sq. meters
25-liter bucket	……….. up to 150 sq. meters

29. What are they going to paint?

   (A) The closet
   (B) The office
   (C) The hallway
   (D) The stairwell

30. What color paint will they buy?

   (A) Yellow
   (B) Green
   (C) White
   (D) Blue

31. Look at the graphic. Which size paint will they probably buy?

   (A) 1-liter can
   (B) 2-liter can
   (C) 5-liter can
   (D) 25-liter bucket

Springer's Office Store

Store-wide sale

Discounts offered on most items
throughout the store!
10% off paper and pens
15% off electronics
20% off office furniture
25% off coffeemakers
This week only!

32. Look at the graphic. How much of a discount will the man get?

   (A) 10%
   (B) 15%
   (C) 20%
   (D) 25%

33. What does the woman offer to do?

   (A) Open the box
   (B) Explain the instructions
   (C) Show the man where to park
   (D) Take the purchase to the cash register

34. How will the man transport his purchase to his office?

   (A) He will ask a colleague to get it.
   (B) He will carry it with him now.
   (C) He will pick it up tomorrow.
   (D) He will have it delivered.

Part 4: Talks

> 🔊 Track 34 **Directions:** You will hear a talk given by a single speaker. You will see three questions on each talk, each with four possible answers. Choose the best answer to each question, and fill in the corresponding oval on your answer sheet.

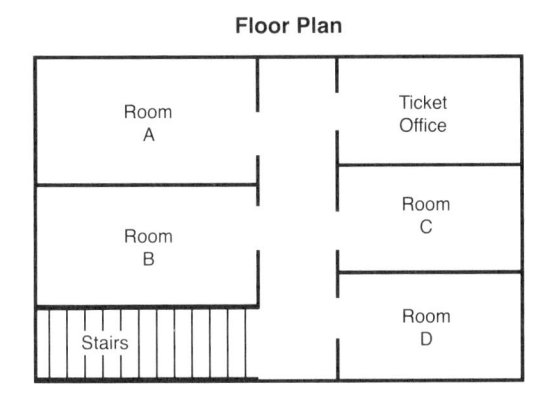

Floor Plan

```
+----------------+----+-----------------+
|                |    |   Ticket        |
|   Room A       |    |   Office        |
|                |    |                 |
+----------------+    +-----------------+
|                |    |                 |
|   Room B       |    |   Room C        |
|                |    |                 |
+--///////-------+    +-----------------+
|  Stairs        |    |   Room D        |
+----------------+----+-----------------+
```

35. Where would you hear this talk?

    (A) Shopping mall
    (B) Sports event
    (C) Museum
    (D) Theater

36. What are the listeners asked to do?

    (A) Buy a ticket
    (B) Watch a play
    (C) Choose a gift
    (D) Move their seats

37. Look at the graphic. Where is the gift shop?

   (A) Room A
   (B) Room B
   (C) Room C
   (D) Room D

---

38. Why did the speaker make the call?

   (A) To make an appointment
   (B) To solicit a new client
   (C) To ask for directions
   (D) To get information

39. What does the speaker mean when he says, "It would work better for me if you came after hours"?

   (A) He prefers the cleaners to come when the office is closed.
   (B) He thinks the work will take several hours to complete.
   (C) He's at the office just a few hours a day.
   (D) He does a better job later in the day.

40. What does the speaker want the listener to do?

   (A) Come to his office next week
   (B) Wait for another call from him
   (C) Meet him downtown
   (D) Return his call soon

41. What kind of subscription is being offered?

   (A) Movie tickets
   (B) Magazine
   (C) Cable TV
   (D) Video streaming

42. How long does a free subscription last?

   (A) Two days
   (B) Three days
   (C) One month
   (D) One year

43. How much does a one-year subscription cost?

   (A) $50
   (B) $99
   (C) $150
   (D) $100

44. What will happen tomorrow?

   (A) Software will be installed.
   (B) A new carpet will be laid.
   (C) Furniture will be delivered.
   (D) The hallway will be painted.

45. What does the speaker mean when he says, "They should be out of here by noon"?

   (A) Staff should stay out of the office all morning.
   (B) The workers will finish before 12:00.
   (C) Employees can take the afternoon off.
   (D) Office supplies are running low.

46. What are listeners asked to do?

   (A) Arrange the new furniture
   (B) Work in the front office
   (C) Use the back entrance
   (D) Arrive early

Hildamire Hotel
Directory

Ground floor
Lobby, Restaurant, Pool

First floor
Conference and Banquet Rooms

Third floor
Administrative Offices

Fourth–Tenth floors
Guest Rooms

47. What event is the listener planning?

　(A) A wedding
　(B) A conference
　(C) A training seminar
　(D) An awards banquet

48. About how many people will attend the event?

　(A) 100
　(B) 125
　(C) 200
　(D) 225

49. Look at the graphic. Where is Ms. Jones's office located?

　(A) Ground floor
　(B) First floor
　(C) Second floor
　(D) Third floor

3 閱讀測驗

3-1 閱讀測驗介紹與高分攻略清單

多益閱讀測驗共有三大題,作答時間約 75 分鐘。

  Part 5:句子填空 30 題
  Part 6:段落填空 16 題
  Part 7:閱讀測驗
  ➡ 單篇閱讀   29 題
  ➡ 多篇閱讀   25 題

閱讀測驗的準備重點在於培養字彙、文法和閱讀理解能力。在接下來的攻略清單中,第五大題的文法和字彙攻略同樣適用於第六大題,反之亦然。

高分攻略清單

Part 5
句子填空

1. 字彙家族
2. 意義相近的單字
3. 形式類似的單字
4. 主詞動詞一致與介系詞片語
5. 單數與複數主詞
6. 動詞時態
7. 介系詞
8. 動詞和形容詞的介系詞搭配
9. 對等連接詞
10. 平行結構
11. 從屬連接詞
12. 未來時間子句

Part 6
段落填空

1. 頻率副詞
2. 主要動詞後接動名詞或不定詞
3. 介系詞和形容詞後接動名詞或不定詞
4. 使役動詞
5. 真實條件句
6. 非真實條件句
7. 比較
8. 代名詞
9. 主格關係代名詞
10. 受格關係代名詞
11. 被動語態
12. 字義
13. 句子選擇

Part 7
閱讀測驗

1. 廣告
2. 表單
3. 書信
4. 備忘錄
5. 表格
6. 圖表
7. 公告
8. 通知
9. 文章
10. 時間表
11. 電子郵件
12. 網頁
13. 簡訊和線上聊天室

3-2 Part 5：句子填空

3-2-1 試題範例

> **DIRECTIONS :** You will see a sentence with a missing word. Four possible answers follow the sentence. Choose the best answer to the question, and fill in the corresponding oval on your answer sheet.
> **作答方式：**你會看到一個缺字的句子和四個可能的選項，選出最適當的答案，將答案卡上對應的橢圓框塗滿。

你會讀到：

They have decided _____ business class.
他們已經決定 _____ 商務艙。

(A) fly
(B) to fly
(C) flying
(D) flew

decide 為要搭配不定詞 (to V.) 的動詞，因此選項 (B) to fly（搭乘）最適合填入空格中完成句子。

3-2-2 高分攻略

高分攻略 1　字彙家族

字彙家族的形成是在單字後面加上字尾，藉由字尾的變化，將單字轉換成名詞、動詞、形容詞或副詞。

常見字尾

名詞	動詞	形容詞	副詞
-ance	-en	-able	-ly
-ancy	-ify	-ible	-ward
-ence	-ize	-al	-wise
-ation		-ful	
-ian		-ish	
-ism		-ive	
-ist		-ous	
-ment			
-ness			
-ship			
-or			
-er			

常見字彙家族

名詞（物）	名詞（人）	動詞	形容詞	副詞
application 應用、申請	applicant 申請人	apply 應用、申請	applicable 可應用的、適用的	
competition 競爭	competitor 競爭者	compete 競爭	competitive 競爭的	competitively 競爭地
criticism 批評、評論	critic 批評者、評論家	criticize 批評、評論	critical 批判性的	critically 批判性地
decision 決定		decide 決定	decisive 決定性的	decisively 斷然、果斷地
economy 經濟	economist 經濟學家	economize 節省、節約	economical 經濟的、節約的	economically 經濟上、節約地
finale 結尾、終曲	finalist 決賽選手	finalize 最後確定	final 最後的	finally 最後、終於
interpretation 解釋、口譯	interpreter 口譯員	interpret 解釋、口譯	interpretive 可解釋的	
maintenance 維持、維修	maintainer 維修人員	maintain 維持、維修	maintainable 可維持的、可維修的	
management 管理	manager 管理者、經理	manage 管理	managerial 管理的、管理人員的	
mechanism 機械裝置、機制	mechanic 機械工	mechanize 機械化	mechanical 機械的	mechanically 機械式地、用機械
nation 國家、民族	nationalist 國家主義者、民族主義者	nationalize 使國有化	national 國家的、民族的	nationally 全國性地

名詞				
物	人	動詞	形容詞	副詞
negotiation 談判、協商	negotiator 談判者	negotiate 談判、協商	negotiable 可協商的	
politics 政治、政治學	politician 政治家、政客	politicize 使政治化	political 政治的	politically 政治上地
production 生產、製造	producer 生產者、製造者、製作人	produce 生產、製造	productive 有成效的、多產的	productively 有成效地、高效地
prosperity 繁榮、興旺		prosper 繁榮、興旺	prosperous 繁榮的、興旺的	prosperously 繁榮地、興旺地
repetition 重複	repeater 重複者、留級生	repeat 重複	repetitious 重複的	repetitively 重複地
simplification 簡化		simplify 簡化	simple 簡單的	simply 簡單地
theory 理論	theoretician 理論家	theorize 理論化、從理論上說明	theoretical 理論的	theoretically 理論上地

答題要訣 利用字尾判斷單字的詞性。

》範例

She is a *careful* manager. 她是個細心的經理。
She read the report *carefully*. 她仔細閱讀這份報告。

careful 是形容詞，在上例中修飾 manager，告訴我們她是一位「什麼樣的」（what kind of）經理。carefully 是副詞，在上例中修飾動詞 read，告訴我們她「如何」（how）閱讀這份報告。

Mr. Kim applied for a job at our company. 金先生應徵了我們公司的工作。
His application contains a lot of information about his background.
他的求職函中包含關於他背景的豐富資訊。

applied 是一個過去式動詞，在上例中告訴我們金先生做了什麼事。application 是一個名詞，在上例中擔任句子的主詞。

即時演練

選出最適當的單字或片語完成句子。

1. The director of purchasing can _____ the best price.

    (A) negotiable
    (B) negotiate
    (C) negotiator
    (D) negotiation

2. The first day that we advertised the job on our website, there were over 700 _____ for the position.

    (A) applies
    (B) applicants
    (C) appliances
    (D) applications

3. The ability to act _____ in moments of crisis is the mark of a strong leader.

    (A) decide
    (B) decision
    (C) decisive
    (D) decisively

4. The two sample colors are so similar that it is difficult to _____ between them.

    (A) differ
    (B) difference
    (C) different
    (D) differentiate

    Ⓐ Ⓑ Ⓒ Ⓓ

5. Of all the designers in this department, Ms. Smith is considered to be the most _____ .

    (A) compete
    (B) competent
    (C) competence
    (D) competently

    Ⓐ Ⓑ Ⓒ Ⓓ

高分攻略 2　意義相近的單字

有些字的意義雖然十分接近，但是不能替換使用，因意義或用法不完全相同，也可能是文法屬性不同。

意義相近的單字

borrow 借入	lend 借出	loan 借出、貸款	lease 出租、租用
develop 發展	expand 展開、擴張	elaborate 詳盡闡述	enhance 加強
money 錢	cash 現金	currency 貨幣	coin 錢幣
obtain 獲得	earn 賺取、贏得	win 贏得、獲得	achieve 達到、達成
raise 提升、抬起	rise 上升	elevate 升高、抬起	ascend 上升、登高
say 說	tell 告訴	speak 說話	talk 談話
travel 旅行、行進	commute 通勤	go 去、移動	journey 旅行、旅程
bill 帳單	pay 薪酬	fee 費用	cost 費用、成本
down 向下、減少	decrease 減少	under 在下面、少於	descent 下降
like 相像的、如同	similar 類似的	same 同樣的	alike 相同的、相像的
soon 不久、很快地	recent 最近的	newly 新近	lately 近來、最近

》範例

Sarah *commutes* to her job in the city from the suburbs.
莎拉從郊區通勤到市區上班。
Sarah will *travel* to Tahiti on her vacation.
莎拉將前往大溪地旅遊。

commute 和 travel 的意義非常接近，然而 commute 有特定的用法，意指「每天往返於住家和工作地點」，即「通勤」，travel 的意義則較有一般概括性。

I had to *borrow* some money in order to pay for my new car.
我必須借錢來買新車。
John *lent* me the money, and I will pay him back soon.
約翰借我錢，我很快就會還他。

borrow 是從別人那裡「借入」一樣東西，借來的東西日後必須歸還給所有人。lend 表示讓別人使用你的東西，即「借出」。

They will *raise* the building in order to dig a basement underneath it.
他們會將建築抬高，以便在底下挖地下室。
Prices have continued to *rise* throughout the first half of the year.
上半年物價持續上漲。

raise 是把東西抬起或增加，為及物動詞，後面必須加受詞。在上面的例句中，raise 的受詞是 the building。rise 是上升或增加，兩個字的意義非常類似，但 rise 為不及物動詞，後面不能有受詞。

即時演練

選出最適當的單字或片語完成句子。

1. New employees _____ only a small salary during the first six months.

    (A) win
    (B) gain
    (C) reach
    (D) earn

2. Miranda has many more responsibilities at the office now because of her _____ promotion.

    (A) recent
    (B) lately
    (C) soon
    (D) newly

3. Our costs have gone down this month, but we need to _____ them even more next month.

    (A) fall
    (B) descent
    (C) decrease
    (D) under

4. A friend _____ me his car while mine was being repaired.

   (A) borrowed
   (B) leased
   (C) owed
   (D) lent

5. More and more companies are interested in investing in this region as the value of the national _____ is increasing.

   (A) money
   (B) currency
   (C) coin
   (D) cash

高分攻略 3　形式類似的單字

有些單字長得很像，意義卻截然不同。它們可能字首、字尾或字根相同，或者只是拼寫非常類似，但其實毫無關聯。

形式類似的單字

reduce 減少	produce 生產	deduce 推論	induce 引起、勸說
except 除了	expect 預期	accept 接受	accent 口音
omit 省略	emit 散發	admit 承認	permit 允許
preference 偏愛	inference 推斷	reference 提及	conference 會議
contact 接觸、聯繫	contract 契約、收縮	compact 緊密的、小型的	comport 舉止、表現
peace 和平	piece 一個、一塊	pierce 刺穿	pier 碼頭
median 中間的、中位數	medium 中等的、媒介	mediate 調停、斡旋	meditate 沉思、冥想
allusion 影射、暗示	illusion 錯覺、幻覺、假象	delusion 錯覺、妄想	elusion 規避、逃避
particle 顆粒、粒子	participant 參與者	participle 分詞	partition 隔板、隔牆

答題要訣　首先請了解句子到底是什麼意思，然後選出真正符合句意的單字。

》範例

Don't *omit* any information from the form.
不要漏掉表上的任何資訊。
We *permit* our employees to work from home occasionally.
我們允許員工偶爾在家工作。

omit 和 permit 的字根都是 mit，但兩字的意義截然不同。omit 意指「遺漏」或「刪除」，permit 意指「允許」。

Each *piece* of the report is important. 這份報告的每一部分都很重要。
She *pierced* the paper with a pin. 她用大頭針刺穿紙張。

piece 和 pierce 的拼寫幾乎一樣，但它們一點關聯都沒有，意義也完全不同。piece 是名詞，表示物品的一部分。pierce 是動詞，表示刺穿東西。

即時演練

選出最適當的單字或片語完成句子。

1. I'll need some time to read over the _____ before I sign it.

    (A) contact
    (B) contract
    (C) comport
    (D) compact

2. The room is large, but we can use _____ to divide it into smaller work areas.

    (A) partitions
    (B) participants
    (C) particles
    (D) participles

3. Because of low profits this quarter, we will have to _____ the size of our staff.

    (A) produce
    (B) induce
    (C) deduce
    (D) reduce

4. The deadline for job applications is March 1, and we will not _____ any resumes that are submitted after that date.

    (A) except
    (B) expect
    (C) accept
    (D) accent

    Ⓐ Ⓑ Ⓒ Ⓓ

5. Some people do better when working alone, while others have a _____ for working as part of a team.

    (A) preference
    (B) inference
    (C) reference
    (D) conference

    Ⓐ Ⓑ Ⓒ Ⓓ

高分攻略 4　**主詞動詞一致與介系詞片語**

一個句子的主詞與動詞必須一致，它們的「人稱」（I、we、he、they 等）和「數」（單複數）必須相符。主詞和動詞之間可能會出現介系詞片語，且介系詞片語中可能含有名詞。介系詞片語中名詞的人稱和數可以和句子主詞不同，且不影響句子主詞動詞的一致性。

> **答題要訣**　要能分辨句子的主詞和句中的其他名詞。

》範例

The order for office supplies was on my desk. 辦公用品的訂單在我桌上。

在上面這句中，主詞 order 是單數，和單數動詞 was 保持一致。主詞和動詞被一個介系詞片語分開。複數名詞 supplies 不是句子的主詞，而是介系詞片語 for office supplies 的一部分。

The workers in this factory receive many benefits.
這間工廠的工人享有很多福利。

在上面這句中，主詞 workers 是複數，和動詞 receive 保持一致。主詞和動詞被一個介系詞片語分開。單數名詞 factory 不是句子的主詞，而是介系詞片語 in this factory 的一部分。

This group of business leaders meets with the mayor every month.
這群商業領袖每個月都會和市長見面。

在上面這個句子中，主詞 group 是單數，和動詞 meets 一致。主詞和動詞被一個介系詞分開。複數名詞 leaders 不是句子的主詞，而是介系詞片語 of business leaders 的一部分。

即時演練

選出最適合的單字或片語完成句子。

1. The officers of the company _____ today at 1:00.

    (A) is meeting
    (B) meets
    (C) has met
    (D) are meeting

2. The owner of these buildings _____ his tenants a very reasonable rent.

    (A) charges
    (B) charge
    (C) are charging
    (D) have charged

3. The supplies in that closet _____ there for any staff member to use.

    (A) is
    (B) has
    (C) are
    (D) was

4. The documents in this folder _____ to be signed by both parties and returned to the attorney right away.

   (A) need
   (B) needs
   (C) needy
   (D) is needed

5. The carpets in this office _____ before we signed the lease last year.

   (A) replace
   (B) were replaced
   (C) has been replaced
   (D) was being replaced

高分攻略 5　單數與複數主詞

有些名詞看起來是複數，其實是單數。有些名詞則因複數是不規則變化，使其看起來像單數。要小心這些名詞，並注意動詞必須和主詞一致。

答題要訣 要能分辨主詞是單數還是複數。

》範例

Thirty dollars is a low price for a nice shirt like that.
這樣一件良好的襯衫只要三十美元算是低價。
Five cents is added to the price for sales tax.
價格還要加上五分美元的營業稅。

一筆錢要視為單數名詞，即使當中含有 dollars 或 cents 這樣的複數名詞，也只能算是一筆。

National Autos owns this factory.　全國汽車公司擁有這間工廠。
United Computers employs most of the workers in this town.
聯合電腦公司僱用了鎮上的大部分工人。

公司名稱可能含有複數名詞，但由於是一間公司的名稱，還是要視為單數。

Everyone wants to have lunch now.　大家現在都想吃午餐。
Nobody is ready for the meeting.　沒有人準備好開會。

以 every 或 no 開頭的單字如 everybody、everything、nobody、nothing 都是單數，就算該字代表一群人或事物，後面還是要用單數動詞。

Few people understand these laws. 很少人懂這些法律。
Children are not allowed in the office without adult supervision.
兒童在沒有大人監督的情況下不得進入辦公室。

不規則複數名詞字尾沒有 s，看起來就像單數名詞，儘管如此它們仍是複數，要使用複數動詞。

即時演練

選出最適當的單字或片語完成句子。

1. The manager from headquarters _____ this office at least twice a year.

    (A) visiting
    (B) to visit
    (C) visits
    (D) visit

2. Most people _____ that Acme, Inc. can be relied on to consistently provide high-quality products.

    (A) agree
    (B) agrees
    (C) has agreed
    (D) is agreeing

3. My assistant has assured me that everything _____ in order for the staff meeting.

    (A) have been
    (B) were
    (C) are
    (D) is

4. Although relatively young, Rheingold Consultants _____ fast becoming one of the most successful companies in the industry.

   (A) were
   (B) have
   (C) is
   (D) are

5. In the past, one thousand dollars _____ considered to be a high rent to pay for an apartment in this part of the city.

   (A) is
   (B) was
   (C) were
   (D) have been

高分攻略 6　動詞時態

句子的主要動詞一定要使用正確的時態，通常句中會有點出動詞時態的時間詞或時間表達用語。

時間詞和時間表達用語

現在簡單式	現在進行式	過去簡單式
every day 每天 every week 每週 every year 每年 always 永遠、總是 often 經常 sometimes 有時	now 現在 at this moment 此刻 currently 現在	an hour ago 一小時前 a month ago 一個月前 yesterday 昨天 last week 上週 last year 去年
現在完成式	未來式	
since last year 自去年起 since Tuesday 自週二起 for two weeks 兩週 for a long time 很久 already 已經 yet 尚未	tomorrow 明天 next month 下個月 next Friday 下週五 later this week 這週晚些時候	

答題要訣 💡 找出句中的時間詞或時間表達用語，利用這些詞語決定正確的時態。

》範例

We *hire* an accountant to audit our books at the end of *every year*.
每年年底我們都會請一位會計師審核我們的帳簿。（現在簡單式）

We cannot hold the meeting at our office as we are *currently redecorating*.
由於我們目前正在重新裝潢，不能在辦公室裡開會。（現在進行式）

Mr. Brown *traveled* to Japan *last month* in order to visit our branch office there.
布朗先生上個月到日本去拜訪我們在那裡的分公司。（過去簡單式）

Ms. Henderson *has been* a client of ours *for the last fifteen years*.
過去十五年來，韓德森小姐一直是我們的客戶。（現在完成式）

The conference room *will be* ready for use *later this afternoon*.
會議室今天下午稍晚就會準備好可供使用。（未來式）

即時演練

選出最適當的單字或片語完成句子。

1. Mr. Cho _____ the new budget at the staff meeting next Friday.

    (A) present
    (B) will present
    (C) is presenting
    (D) has presented

    Ⓐ Ⓑ Ⓒ Ⓓ

2. We are planning to repaint the office, but we _____ on a color yet.

    (A) didn't decide
    (B) don't decide
    (C) haven't decided
    (D) isn't deciding

    Ⓐ Ⓑ Ⓒ Ⓓ

3. The company _____ a picnic for all staff members at the beginning of every summer.

    (A) host
    (B) hosts
    (C) is hosting
    (D) to host

    Ⓐ Ⓑ Ⓒ Ⓓ

4. Even though they _____ on that report since last week, it still isn't finished.

   (A) have been working
   (B) will be working
   (C) will work
   (D) are working

5. After signing the contract with the new client yesterday, we all _____ to a restaurant to celebrate.

   (A) go
   (B) will go
   (C) have gone
   (D) went

高分攻略 7　介系詞

介系詞用來表示名詞／代名詞和其他詞語之間的關係，指出時間、地點和移動方向等。

答題要訣 必須掌握最常見的介系詞用法。

》範例

時間

介系詞	用法	例句
at	確切時間	They arrived at 10:30. 他們十點三十分抵達。
on	星期、日期	They arrived on Monday. 他們星期一抵達。
in	月、年	We began work in April. 我們四月開始工作。
from . . . to from . . . until	開始和結束時間	I lived there from June to December. 我從六月到十二月住在那裡。
by	不遲於某個時間	Please finish this report by noon. 請在中午前完成這份報告。

地點

介系詞	用法	例句
at	確切地址	He lives at 1267 Main Street. 他住在主街 1267 號。
on	街道	He lives on Main Street. 他住在主街。
in	城市、國家	She worked in London. 她在倫敦工作。
on	在……上面	The phone is on my desk. 電話在我桌上。
in	在……裡面	The pencil is in the drawer. 鉛筆在抽屜裡。
next to, beside, by	在……旁邊	My desk is next to the window. 我的桌子在窗邊。
across . . . from	在……對面	His house is across the street from the bank. 他家在銀行對面。

移動方向

介系詞	用法	例句
to, toward	朝某個方向	She went to the bank. 她去了銀行。
into	到……裡面	They walked into the building. 他們走進了那棟大樓。
through	從一端到另一端	Let's drive through the park. 我們開車穿過公園吧。
across	從一側到另一側	She walked across the room. 她走到房間的另一側。

即時演練

選出最適當的單字或片語完成句子。

1. Just put the packages _____ the table and I'll open them for you.

   (A) on
   (B) in
   (C) to
   (D) at

2. They realized the meeting was already in progress the minute they walked _____ the room.

   (A) on
   (B) among
   (C) until
   (D) into

3. The company cafeteria is open for lunch every day from 11:00 _____ 13:00.

   (A) at
   (B) for
   (C) until
   (D) by

4. Since the meeting is scheduled to begin _____ noon, we will provide sandwiches and snacks for attendees.

   (A) on
   (B) to
   (C) in
   (D) at

5. Their office is located on the next block, _____ the post office and the bank.

   (A) among
   (B) outside
   (C) between
   (D) through

高分攻略 8　動詞和形容詞的介系詞搭配

許多動詞和形容詞常搭配固定的介系詞。

動詞 + 介系詞

apologize for 道歉	insist on 堅持
agree to (something) 同意（某事）	object to 反對
agree with (someone) 同意（某人）	participate in 參加
ask for (something) 要求（某物）	pay for
ask to (do something) 要求（做某事）	支付……的費用、為……付出代價
believe in 相信	prepare for 準備
blame for 因……而責備	prevent from 防止、阻止
complain about 抱怨	prohibit from 禁止
decide on 考慮後決定	replace with 以……取代
depend on 依靠、取決於	result in 導致、結果是
	think about 考慮

形容詞 + 介系詞

afraid of 害怕	famous for 以……聞名
angry about (something)（對某事）生氣	good at 擅長
angry at/with (someone)（對某人）生氣	happy about 對……感到開心
aware of 意識到、知道	interested in 對……感興趣
bored with 對……感到厭倦	late for 遲到
busy with 忙於	pleased with 對……感到高興／滿意
curious about 對……感到好奇	responsible for 對……負責
different from 與……不同	serious about 認真看待
excited about 對……感到興奮	suitable for 適合
familiar with 熟悉	tired of 厭煩

答題要訣　將「動詞 + 介系詞」和「形容詞 + 介系詞」的常見組合牢記下來。

》範例

She is *thinking about* applying for a position with another company.
她正考慮應徵別家公司的職位。

Everyone in the office was able to *participate in* the training session.
辦公室每個人都可以參加培訓課程。

I'll be *busy with* some clients for the rest of the afternoon.
我下午剩下的時間都要忙於接待客戶。

This city is *famous for* its wide avenues and pretty parks.
這座城市以寬闊的街道和美麗的公園聞名。

即時演練

選出最適當的單字或片語完成句子。

1. Everyone in the office was complaining _____ the noise from the construction site across the street.

    (A) over
    (B) about
    (C) from
    (D) with

2. We replaced our old copy machine _____ a newer, more efficient model.

    (A) of
    (B) to
    (C) with
    (D) for

3. Ms. Chang is responsible _____ making sure new staff members understand their duties.

    (A) for
    (B) of
    (C) in
    (D) at

4. Many local residents objected _____ the developer's plans for building a shopping mall in their neighborhood.

   (A) about
   (B) for
   (C) on
   (D) to

5. We have rearranged the office so that we have a comfortable area that is suitable _____ meeting with clients.

   (A) on
   (B) for
   (C) from
   (D) with

高分攻略 9　對等連接詞

對等連接詞用來連接重要性相當且文法功能類似的單字、片語或子句。
譬如，對等連接詞可以連接兩個形容詞、兩個介系詞片語或兩個獨立子句。

> **答題要訣**　請注意對等連接詞的意義。

》範例

連接詞　and（和）
用法　連接類似的概念

I need some paper *and* a pencil. 我需要一些紙和一支筆。
He can both dance *and* sing. 他會唱歌跳舞。
Mary moved the table *and* John arranged the chairs.
瑪麗搬桌子，約翰擺設椅子。

連接詞　but（但是）、yet（然而、但是）
用法　連接相反的概念

He eats a lot *but* he never gets fat. 他吃很多卻不會胖。
She speaks French fluently, *yet* I never hear her use it.
她的法文說得很流暢，但我從未聽她使用過。
The room is small *but* comfortable. 房間雖小，卻很舒適。

連接詞　or（或）、either ... or（兩者任一）、neither ... nor（兩者皆不）
用法　連接可供選擇的項目

Would you like coffee *or* tea? 你要咖啡還是茶？
I can give you *either* coffee *or* tea. 我可以給你咖啡或茶。
I'm sorry but I drink *neither* coffee *nor* tea. 不好意思，我不喝咖啡也不喝茶。

即時演練

選出最適當的單字或片語完成句子。

1. Ms. Sam's work is both creative _____ accurate.

    (A) but
    (B) or
    (C) and
    (D) nor

2. George worked all night, _____ he wasn't able to finish the report on time.

    (A) yet
    (B) and
    (C) either
    (D) neither

3. We can either meet this afternoon _____ wait until later in the week if you prefer.

    (A) but
    (B) or
    (C) nor
    (D) neither

4. Neither the bus _____ the subway will get you to the airport on time.

   (A) or
   (B) and
   (C) but
   (D) nor

5. We were really interested in seeing the recent play at the National Theater, _____ the tickets sold out too quickly.

   (A) and
   (B) or
   (C) but
   (D) either

高分攻略 10　平行結構

由對等連接詞連接的兩個單字、片語或子句必須是類似的文法結構,例如:兩個名詞、兩個動詞、兩個動名詞等。

> **答題要訣** 學會判斷正確的文法形式,必須能夠分辨動名詞和不定詞、名詞和動詞、形容詞和副詞等。

》範例

Mr. Lee types *quickly* and *accurately*.　李先生打字又快又準確。
　　　　　　　副詞　　　　副詞

I enjoy both *swimming* and *sailing*.　我喜歡游泳和帆船運動。
　　　　　　動名詞　　　　動名詞

You can either *send* an email or *write* a letter.　你可以寄電子郵件或寫信。
　　　　　　原形動詞　　　　　原形動詞

Neither *the bus* nor *the subway* will take you anywhere near his office.
　　　　　名詞　　　　名詞
公車或地鐵都沒有到他公司附近。

The manager is *kind* but *strict*.　經理人很好但很嚴格。
　　　　　　　形容詞　　形容詞

即時演練

選出最適當的單字或片語完成句子。

1. Prompt and _____ customer service is a priority at our business.

    (A) friend
    (B) friendly
    (C) friendship
    (D) friendliness

2. Sharon is really good at making clients feel comfortable and _____ them interested in using our services.

    (A) get
    (B) got
    (C) gotten
    (D) getting

3. Focus on efficiency and _____ and you will get the job done right.

    (A) accurate
    (B) accurately
    (C) accuracy
    (D) accruing

4. Until the contract is signed, we can neither _____ the budget nor begin the research.

   (A) finalize
   (B) finality
   (C) finalized
   (D) final

5. In order to finish the work on time, we can stay at the office _____ today or come in to the office earlier tomorrow.

   (A) lately
   (B) lateness
   (C) later
   (D) latest

高分攻略 11　從屬連接詞

從屬連接詞用來連接文法功能不相同的子句（不能連接單字或片語）。從屬連接詞和後面接的子句合起來當作主要子句中的一個成分，我們把它稱為從屬子句。從屬子句可位於主要子句之前，也可位於主要子句之後。

答題要訣　請注意從屬連接詞的意義。

》範例

常見的從屬連接詞

- **引導一個原因**：because、as、since（因為、由於）

  I was late to the meeting *because* traffic was heavy.
  因為交通壅塞，我開會遲到。
  Since Mr. Kim is out of the office today, I will be taking all his calls.
  由於金先生今天不在辦公室，我會替他接電話。
  Ms. Roberts will be unable to meet with you *as* she has been called away on an emergency.　羅伯茲女士被緊急叫走了，因此無法與你會面。

- **引導一個矛盾事實**：though、although、even though（儘管、雖然）

  We decided to hold the conference at this hotel *even though* the rates are higher.　儘管價格較高，我們還是決定在這間飯店舉行會議。
  Although Ms. Clark is new at the company, she already knows a lot about our work.　雖然克拉克女士才剛進公司，她已經很了解我們的工作。
  Roger has agreed to be on the committee *though* his schedule is already full.　儘管行程已經排滿，羅傑還是答應加入委員會。

- **引導時間子句**：before（之前）、after（之後）、as soon as（一⋯⋯就）、when（當）、while（當⋯⋯的時候；和⋯⋯同時）、until（直到）

I met Mr. Cho *while* I was working in New York.
我在紐約工作時認識了趙先生。
As soon as the plane landed, all the passengers stood up.
飛機一降落，所有乘客就馬上起身。
We'll have a larger reception area *when* we move to our new office.
我們搬到新辦公室後，會有較大的接待區。

即時演練

選出最適當的單字或片語完成句子。

1. The usher allowed Ms. Sello into the concert hall _____ she was late.

   (A) because
   (B) yet
   (C) even though
   (D) before

2. _____ so few people showed up, we finally decided to cancel the meeting.

   (A) Since
   (B) Although
   (C) If
   (D) Until

3. Miranda will send a copy of the report to your office _____ it is ready.

   (A) but
   (B) so
   (C) as soon as
   (D) before

4. Everyone had to use the stairs _____ the elevators were out of order.

   (A) however
   (B) although
   (C) because
   (D) so

   Ⓐ Ⓑ Ⓒ Ⓓ

5. I did not get a place in the class _____ I sent my registration form in early.

   (A) as
   (B) as soon as
   (C) so
   (D) even though

   Ⓐ Ⓑ Ⓒ Ⓓ

高分攻略 12　未來時間子句

時間子句告訴我們主要子句中的動作發生於何時。時間子句由表示時間的從屬連接詞所引導，例如：when、while、before、after、until 等。在一個說明未來事件的句子中，主要子句會使用未來式（由 will 或 be going to 構成），時間子句則要用現在式，即使表示的是未來時間。

答題要訣　未來時間子句要用現在式。

》範例

I *will show* you the report as soon as I *finish* writing it.
　　　　主要子句　　　　　　　　　　時間子句
我一寫完報告就會給你看。

When the rain *stops*, *we are going to take* a walk in the park.
　　　時間子句　　　　　　　　　　主要子句
等雨停，我們就去公園散步。

He *is going to give* everyone copies of his schedule before he *leaves* on his trip.　　　主要子句　　　　　　　　　　　　　　　時間子句
他出發旅行前會把行程發給每一個人。

After they *get* to the hotel, *they'll call* us.　他們到了旅館就會打電話給我們。
　　　時間子句　　　　　　　主要子句

184

即時演練

選出最適當的單字或片語完成句子。

1. I'll let you know when the train _____ .

   (A) arrive
   (B) arrives
   (C) will arrive
   (D) arriving

2. We'll talk things over with our lawyer before we _____ the contract.

   (A) sign
   (B) to sign
   (C) will sign
   (D) signature

3. By the time the meeting _____ over, you'll know everything about our marketing plan.

   (A) will be
   (B) was
   (C) is
   (D) be

4. We will find out the decision on salary increases after the directors _____ tomorrow.

   (A) will meet
   (B) to meet
   (C) met
   (D) meet

5. They _____ ready paint the hallways next week after they finish work in the front room.

   (A) are
   (B) be
   (C) going to
   (D) will be

3-3 Part 6：段落填空

3-3-1 試題範例

> DIRECTIONS : You will see short passages, each with four blanks. Each blank has four answer options. Choose the word, phrase, or sentence that best completes the passage.
> **作答方式：**你會看到幾篇短文，每篇內含四個空格。每個空格配有四個選項，選出最適當的單字、片語或句子完成段落。

在第六大題當中，題目會考你是否理解文法、字彙和這段文字的語境。有時只要閱讀空格所在的句子就能作答，然而大多時候必須閱讀前後的句子，甚至把整段文字看完，才能選出正確答案。

本章所提供的技巧能幫助你準備第六大題的考試，第五大題所提供的答題技巧同樣可以應用在第六大題的文法和字彙題。

Dear Mr. Sanders,

I enjoyed _____ you at the conference last week. I am enclosing
            1
the brochures that you requested. I hope _____ are useful to
                                             2
you. If I can be of further assistance, please let me _____.
                                                          3

_____.
    4

Sincerely,
Bertha Smith

1. (A) met
   (B) meet
   (C) to meet
   (D) meeting

2. (A) it
   (B) they
   (C) we
   (D) its

3. (A) know
   (B) understand
   (C) realize
   (D) learn

4. (A) My assistant is, unfortunately, out of the office this week
   (B) The brochures are a good source for the information you seek
   (C) You can reach me at my office any day between 9:00 a.m. and 5:00 p.m.
   (D) The conference was interesting, and I hope to attend again next year

題目中譯

> 桑德斯先生您好：
>
> 很高興能在上週的會議中見到您，隨信附上您要的手冊，希望對您有幫助。若需要進一步的協助，請不吝告知。
>
> 您可於每天早上九點到下午五點，在辦公室聯繫到我。
>
> 敬祝順心
> 柏莎・史密斯

Question 1
(A) met　見面
(B) meet
(C) to meet
(D) meeting

解析 (D) 在「I enjoyed _____ you at the conference last week.」這個句子中，最適合填入空格的選項是 (D) meeting，動詞 enjoyed 後面必須接現在分詞 meeting，因此要選 (D)。

Question 2
(A) it　它
(B) they　他們
(C) we　我們
(D) its　它的

解析 (B) 在「I hope _____ are useful to you.」這個句子中，最適合填入空格的是選項 (B) they。回答這個問題必須看句子的前後文，有時是前文，有時是後文。以此句來說則要看前文。代名詞 they 指的是前面的複數名詞 brochures，因此要選 (B)。

Question 3

(A) know 知道

(B) understand 了解

(C) realize 意識到

(D) learn 學習

解析 **(A)** 在「If I can be of further assistance, please let me ＿＿＿＿ .」這個句子中，最適合填入空格的是選項 (A) know，這一題的四個選項意思都非常接近，但只有 know 符合段落情境，因此要選 (A)。

Question 4

(A) My assistant is, unfortunately, out of the office this week.
很不巧，我的助理本週不在辦公室。

(B) The brochures are a good source for the information you seek.
這些冊子對你在找的資料很有幫助。

(C) You can reach me at my office any day between 9:00 a.m. and 5:00 p.m. 您可於每天早上九點到下午五點，在辦公室聯繫到我。

(D) The conference was interesting, and I hope to attend again next year. 這場會議很有趣，我希望明年能再參加。

解析 **(C)** 在第四個空格中，最適合填入的是選項 (C)。前一句已表示願意提供進一步的協助，這個句子接著說明如何取得協助，因此要選 (C)。

3-3-2 高分攻略

高分攻略 1　頻率副詞

頻率副詞用來說明一件事情發生的時間或頻率。

答題要訣　請注意前後文的描述以選出正確副詞。

》範例

常見的頻率副詞

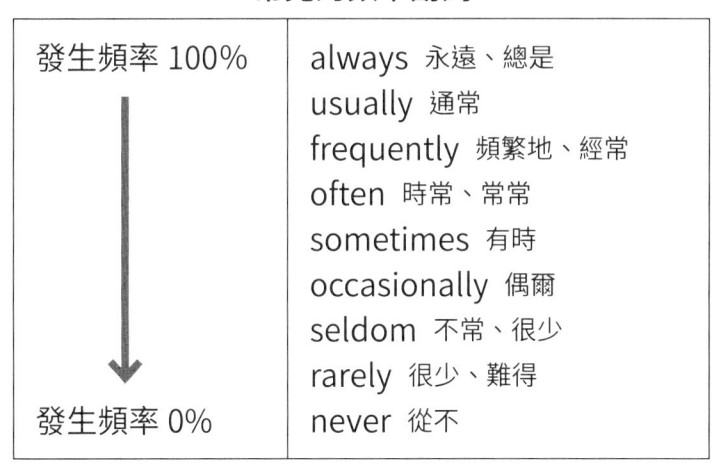

發生頻率 100% ↓ 發生頻率 0%	always 永遠、總是 usually 通常 frequently 頻繁地、經常 often 時常、常常 sometimes 有時 occasionally 偶爾 seldom 不常、很少 rarely 很少、難得 never 從不

We always eat lunch at this café because it is so close to the office.
我們一向都在這家咖啡館吃午餐，因為離辦公室很近。

I usually play golf on weekends, but last Saturday I played tennis instead. 我週末通常都打高爾夫球，但上週六我去打網球了。

The weather is usually dry in the summer, but sometimes it rains.
夏季天氣通常很乾燥，但有時也會下雨。

Sam rarely works late, although last night he stayed at the office until 8:00. 山姆很少工作到很晚，不過昨天晚上他在辦公室待到八點。

I never drink coffee at night, because it keeps me awake.
我從不在晚上喝咖啡，因為會睡不著。

即時演練

選出最適當的單字或片語完成句子。

1. We _____ hold staff meetings on weekends. In fact, I believe this is the first time we've done this, but something very important has come up.

    (A) rarely
    (B) frequently
    (C) often
    (D) sometimes

2. Please note that punctuality is very important in this company. We _____ begin our staff meetings on time and don't wait for late arrivals.

    (A) never
    (B) seldom
    (C) occasionally
    (D) always

3. Our meetings _____ last about an hour, and I expect this one will, too.

    (A) usually
    (B) sometimes
    (C) rarely
    (D) never

4. Mr. Kim will not be present at the meeting. This is unexpected, as he _____ misses meetings.

   (A) generally
   (B) seldom
   (C) frequently
   (D) occasionally

5. We _____ serve snacks when the meeting is over. However, we won't have time for that at this meeting.

   (A) rarely
   (B) never
   (C) often
   (D) seldom

高分攻略 2　主要動詞後接動名詞或不定詞

一個句子的主要動詞後面可以緊接另一個準動詞，這個準動詞可能是動名詞（-ing 形式）或不定詞（to + 原型動詞），由主要動詞決定要接何種。

答題要訣　根據句中的主要動詞決定後面要接動名詞還是不定詞。

》範例

常接動名詞的動詞

appreciate 感謝	I *appreciate* having the opportunity to speak. 很高興有這個機會發言。
avoid 避免	They *avoided* looking us in the eye. 他們避免和我們眼神接觸。
consider 考慮	We *considered* staying longer. 我們考慮停留久一點。
delay 延遲、耽擱	We *delayed* writing you until we had more information. 我們等到有更多資訊後才寫信給你。
discuss 討論	Have you *discussed* working together on this project? 你們討論過在這個案子上合作嗎？
enjoy 享受、喜歡	We *enjoyed* having you for dinner. 我們很高興你來共進晚餐。
finish 完成	They will *finish* correcting the report soon. 他們很快就會完成修正報告。
mind 介意	She didn't *mind* staying late for the meeting. 她不介意為了會議留到很晚。
miss 想念	We *miss* going to the movies with you. 我們想念和你一起去看電影。

postpone 延期、延後	Could we *postpone* leaving? 我們可以延後出發嗎？
quit 放棄、停止	He wants to *quit* smoking. 他想戒菸。
risk 冒險	They *risked* losing everything. 他們冒著失去一切的風險。
suggest 建議	We *suggest* leaving on time. 我們建議準時出發。

常接不定詞的動詞

agree 同意	He *agreed* to complete the project. 他同意完成這個計畫。
attempt 試圖、企圖	They *attempted* to climb Mt. Fuji. 他們試圖爬富士山。
claim 聲稱、主張	She *claims* to be an expert. 她自稱是專家。
decide 決定	We *decided* to hire her anyway. 我們還是決定僱用她。
demand 要求	He *demanded* to know what we were doing. 他要求知道我們在做什麼。
fail 未能、失敗	We *failed* to give a satisfactory answer. 我們未能給出一個令人滿意的答案。
hesitate 猶豫、遲疑	I *hesitated* to tell the truth. 我猶豫要不要說出真相。
hope 希望	We *hope* to leave before dawn. 我們希望在天亮前出發。
intend 打算	She *intends* to start her own club. 她打算創立自己的社團。
learn 學習	They will *learn* to swim at camp. 他們會在營隊中學習游泳。

need 需要	She *needs* to stop smoking. 她需要戒菸。
offer 主動提出、提議	They *offered* to take us home. 他們主動提出要送我們回家。
plan 計劃、打算	We *plan* to accept their offer. 我們打算接受他們的提議。
prepare 準備	She *prepared* to leave. 她準備要離開。
refuse 拒絕	He *refused* to come with us. 他拒絕和我們一起去。
seem 似乎、好像	She *seemed* to be annoyed. 她好像很惱怒。
want 想要	He didn't *want* to leave. 他不想離開。

即時演練

選出最適當的單字或片語完成句子。

1. I talked with our client, Mr. Wilson, over the phone. He has agreed _____ with us in order to discuss the contract.

   (A) met
   (B) has met
   (C) to meet
   (D) meeting

   Ⓐ Ⓑ Ⓒ Ⓓ

2. Our schedule is full this week, but Mr. Wilson doesn't mind _____ until next week for an appointment.

   (A) waits
   (B) waiting
   (C) is waiting
   (D) will wait

   Ⓐ Ⓑ Ⓒ Ⓓ

3. I've offered _____ a draft of the contract to Mr. Wilson's office. This will give him a chance to review it before our meeting.

   (A) sending
   (B) to send
   (C) can send
   (D) have sent

   Ⓐ Ⓑ Ⓒ Ⓓ

4. The contract is not complete yet. However, I should be able to finish _____ it before the end of the day.

   (A) writing
   (B) written
   (C) to write
   (D) write

5. I hope you will review the contract for me before I forward it to Mr. Wilson. I plan _____ it on your desk tomorrow morning.

   (A) putting
   (B) will put
   (C) put
   (D) to put

高分攻略 3　介系詞和形容詞後接動名詞或不定詞

動名詞和不定詞不僅可用於句子或子句的主要動詞之後，還可用於其他類型的單字或片語之後。

> **答題要訣**　必須知道哪些類型的單字或片語後面會接動名詞，哪些會接不定詞。

》範例

Harry is interested *in applying* for a position with an international company. 哈利有興趣應徵一間國際公司的職位。
Sara apologized *for arriving* at the meeting late. 莎拉為了開會遲到而道歉。

動名詞可用於介系詞之後，請參考 3-2 Part 5〈高分攻略 8〉中的「動詞 + 介系詞」和「形容詞 + 介系詞」表格，這些介系詞的後面都要接動名詞。

They will be *happy to help* you. 他們將很樂意協助你。
He was *eager to start* working on the project.
他迫不及待要開始進行這個專案。

不定詞可用於形容詞之後。

He was *hungry enough to eat* three servings of rice.
他餓到可以吃三碗飯。
They walked *too slowly to get* there in time.
他們走得太慢，無法及時到達那裡。

不定詞可以接在「形容詞／副詞 + enough」和「too+ 形容詞／副詞」這樣的片語之後。

即時演練

選出適當的單字或片語完成句子。

1. Do your employees complain about _____ frequent headaches or constant eye pain? The fault may lie with your lighting system.

    (A) have
    (B) having
    (C) to have
    (D) had

2. The bright glare of some kinds of lights is stressful on the eyes. You need a lighting system that creates soft diffused light that is easy on the eyes but still bright enough _____ by.

    (A) read
    (B) reads
    (C) to read
    (D) reading

3. With the proper lighting system in place, your employees will sit down at their desks ready _____ in ease and comfort.

    (A) to work
    (B) working
    (C) are working
    (D) have worked

4. If you are tired of _____ complaints about the lights in your workplace, it's time to make a change.

   (A) heard
   (B) to hear
   (C) should hear
   (D) hearing

5. You could start by changing the lights in just a few places. Or, you could decide on _____ a completely new lighting system in your entire office.

   (A) install
   (B) will install
   (C) installing
   (D) to install

高分攻略 4　使役動詞

使役動詞用來表示一個人讓另一個人做某件事。使役動詞後面會接原形動詞或不定詞。

答題要訣 牢記哪些使役動詞後面要接動名詞，哪些要接不定詞。

》範例

後接原形動詞的使役動詞

| have　let　make |

The manager *had* Mr. Smith *demonstrate* the product.
　　　　　　　使役動詞　　　　　　原形動詞
經理讓史密斯先生展示產品。

Our boss *lets* us *leave* early on Friday afternoons.
　　　　使役動詞 原形動詞
我們老闆讓我們週五下午提早下班。

The driver *will make* you *get* off the bus if you don't have the exact fare.
　　　　　　使役動詞　　　原形動詞
如果你不備妥剛好的車資，公車司機會要你下車。

202

後接不定詞的使役動詞

allow 允許	get 使	require 要求
cause 導致	order 命令	
force 迫使	permit 准許	

I'll *get* my assistant *to copy* those documents.　我會讓我的助理影印這些文件。
　　使役動詞　　　　　不定詞

The company never *permits* employees *to make* public statements.
　　　　　　　　使役動詞　　　　　　　不定詞
這間公司絕不允許員工發表公開聲明。

The human resources office *requires* all job applicants *to provide* three references.
　　　　　　　　　　　使役動詞　　　　　　　　　不定詞
人力資源室要求所有求職者提供三封推薦信。

203

即時演練

選出最適當的單字或片語完成句子。

1. Our newest staff member, John Greene, appears to have some confusion about ordering supplies. Please make him _____ that he must have authorization before submitting an order.

    (A) understand
    (B) understands
    (C) to understand
    (D) can understand

2. We cannot permit staff _____ anything at any time they want. That would create havoc with our budget.

    (A) order
    (B) to order
    (C) ordering
    (D) will order

3. It's time to start planning our annual holiday luncheon. Please have John Greene _____ the caterers before the end of the week.

    (A) call
    (B) calls
    (C) called
    (D) will call

4. He should get the caterers _____ several menu options. Then together we can decide which one we prefer.

   (A) provide
   (B) providing
   (C) to provide
   (D) should provide

5. Mr. Greene is a new staff member and is not familiar with the customs of this office. Therefore, I don't think we should let him _____ the menu himself.

   (A) choosing
   (B) chose
   (C) to choose
   (D) choose

高分攻略 5　真實條件句

條件句可以表達兩種條件：真實條件和非真實條件。條件句描述一個條件和一個結果，由兩個子句組成：if 子句（條件）和主要子句（結果）。真實條件句表達一件事實或確實可能發生的事。真實條件句中的 if 子句一律使用現在式，主要子句可能是現在式或未來式，也可能是命令句。

> **答題要訣**　真實條件句中的 if 子句一律使用現在式。

》範例

習慣　　*If* it rains, I drive to work.　如果下雨，我都開車去上班。
　　　　　　*if*子句　　　主要子句
　　　　　（真實條件）

未來　　*If* it rains, I will drive to work.　如果下雨，我將會開車去上班。
　　　　　　*if*子句　　　主要子句
　　　　　（真實條件）

命令　　*If* it rains, drive to work.　如果下雨，開車去上班。
　　　　　　*if*子句　　　主要子句
　　　　　（真實條件）

即時演練

選出最適當的單字或片語完成句子。

1. Class registration begins August 21 and classes begin August 29. If you _____ for a class after August 28, you will have to pay a late fee.

    (A) register
    (B) to register
    (C) will register
    (D) is going to register

2. Some classes may not have enough students. If we _____ a class due to low enrollment, we will contact you.

    (A) to cancel
    (B) cancel
    (C) canceling
    (D) will cancel

3. Please remember to provide your phone number and email address on your registration form. We _____ able to contact you if we don't have this information.

    (A) not be
    (B) aren't
    (C) won't be
    (D) weren't

4. We offer classes for working people. If you _____ time to study during the day, please check our evening class schedule.

   (A) not have
   (B) didn't have
   (C) won't have
   (D) don't have

   Ⓐ Ⓑ Ⓒ Ⓓ

5. If you bring your registration form to the school bookstore, you _____ a discount on the textbooks required for your class.

   (A) receive
   (B) to receive
   (C) will receive
   (D) have received

   Ⓐ Ⓑ Ⓒ Ⓓ

高分攻略 6　非真實條件句

非真實條件句表達一件不是事實或不可能發生的事。假如句子描述的是一個現在的情況，if 子句的動詞要用過去式，但指的依然是現在，表示與現在事實不相符，而主要子句會使用「would+ 原形動詞」的句型。假如句子描述的是一個過去的情況，if 子句的動詞要用過去完成式，主要子句會使用「would have+ 過去分詞」的句型。

> **答題要訣**　請記住 if 子句中的過去式動詞指的是一個「現在」的非真實條件。

》範例

現在情況

If George *owned* the company, he *would accept* the project.
若喬治擁有這間公司，他就會接受這個專案。

這個句子告訴我們，事實上喬治並不擁有這間公司，所以也不會接受專案。

Sarah *would get* to work on time if she *left* her house earlier every morning.
若莎拉每天早上提早出門，她就能準時上班。

這個句子告訴我們，事實上莎拉沒有提早出門，所以也沒有準時上班。

I *would eat* lunch with you if I *didn't have* so much work to do.
若我沒有那麼多工作要做，我就會跟你一起吃午餐。

這個句子告訴我們，事實上我有很多工作要做，所以我也不會跟你一起吃午餐。

過去情況

If I *had received* the promotion, I *would have bought* a new car.
若當時我有獲得升遷,我就會買新車了。

這個句子告訴我們,事實上我沒有獲得升遷,所以也沒買新車。

We *would have gone* skiing on our vacation if it *had snowed* in the mountains.
若那時山上有下雪,我們度假時就會去滑雪了。

這個句子告訴我們,事實上山上沒有下雪,所以我們沒去滑雪。

If he *hadn't been* so busy, he *would have called* you.
若他當時沒那麼忙,他就會打電話給你了。

這個句子告訴我們,事實上他當時很忙,所以沒有打電話給你。

即時演練

選出最適當的單字或片語完成句子。

1. Dear Mr. Klugman, I am terribly sorry about our misunderstanding yesterday. If I _____ that space #7 was your assigned parking space, I would never have parked there.

    (A) knew
    (B) had known
    (C) have known
    (D) could know

2. If you _____ for parking elsewhere, I would have reimbursed you. Luckily you found another free spot on the staff parking lot.

    (A) have paid
    (B) had paid
    (C) pay
    (D) will pay

3. I looked for you in the office today but found out that you are away for the day. If you _____ here today, I would apologize in person.

    (A) are
    (B) will be
    (C) were
    (D) had been

4. Parking is a big problem in this part of town. If I didn't live so far from the office, I _____ the parking problem by walking to work every day.

   (A) avoided
   (B) had avoided
   (C) would have avoided
   (D) would avoid

   Ⓐ Ⓑ Ⓒ Ⓓ

5. If I had walked to work yesterday, I _____ in your parking space.

   (A) wouldn't have parked
   (B) wouldn't park
   (C) didn't park
   (D) hadn't parked

   Ⓐ Ⓑ Ⓒ Ⓓ

高分攻略 7　比較

形容詞和副詞可用來表示人、地方、事物和動作之間的相似性和差異性。形容詞和副詞的比較有三個等級：原級、比較級（字尾 -er 或前面加 more）、最高級（字尾 -est 或前面加 most）。

單音節和以 -y 結尾的雙音節形容詞，比較級是在字尾加上 -er，最高級是在字尾加上 -est。非 -y 結尾的雙音節形容詞有一部分也採用這種形式。三音節的形容詞一律在前面加上 more 或 most 構成比較級和最高級。副詞的比較級和最高級構詞比照形容詞。

答題要訣　請注意，形容詞和副詞的最高級前面必須加 the。

》範例

字尾加 -er 或 -est 構成比較級和最高級的形容詞和副詞：

原級	比較級	最高級
pretty 漂亮的	prettier 更漂亮的	the prettiest 最漂亮的
narrow 窄的	narrower 更窄的	the narrowest 最窄的
far 遠的／遠地	farther 更遠的／更遠地	the farthest 最遠的／最遠地
soon 很快地	sooner 更快地	the soonest 最快地

I think fall is a *prettier* season *than* spring.
我認為秋天是比春天更漂亮的季節。
No one drives down that street because it is the *narrowest* in the neighborhood.　沒有人開車走那條街，因為那是這街坊附近最窄的一條。
They arrived *sooner than* we expected.　他們比我們預期的早到。
That hotel is the *farthest* from the convention center.
那家飯店是離會議中心最遠的飯店。

前面加 more 或 most 構成比較級和最高級的形容詞和副詞：

原級	比較級	最高級
popular 受歡迎的	more popular 更受歡迎的	the most popular 最受歡迎的
competent 能幹的	more competent 更能幹的	the most competent 最能幹的
efficiently 有效率地	more efficiently 更有效率地	the most efficiently 最有效率地
quickly 快速地	more quickly 更快速地	the most quickly 最快速地

That restaurant is the *most popular* one in town.
那間餐廳是鎮上最受歡迎的餐廳。
Shirley is a *more competent* accountant *than* her colleagues.
雪莉是比她同事更能幹的會計師。
She works *more efficiently than* other accountants I know.
她的工作效率比我認識的其他會計師更高。
Roger finished his presentation *the most quickly*.
羅傑最快完成報告。

不規則形容詞的比較級和最高級：

原級	比較級	最高級
good 好的	better 更好的	the best 最好的
bad 差的	worse 更差的	the worst 最差的
well 好地	better 更好地	the best 最好地
little 小、少	less 更小、更少	the least 最小、最少

This is *the worst* weather we've had all year.
這是我們整年來遇到最差的天氣。
The new copier works *better than* the old one.
新的影印機比舊的好用。

即時演練

選出最適當的單字或片語完成句子。

1. Techno Business Academy offers intensive, short-term skills training courses for office workers. We guarantee to train you _____ any other business school at a price you can afford.

    (A) faster than
    (B) nicer than
    (C) longer than
    (D) more costly than

2. Some schools charge hundreds of dollars per course. But at Techno Business Academy, we guarantee _____ prices in town.

    (A) low
    (B) lowest
    (C) lower than
    (D) the lowest

3. Our recent graduates earn _____ salaries than other office professionals with years of experience.

    (A) high
    (B) higher
    (C) highest
    (D) the highest

4. If you are looking for a _____ job than the one you have now, Techno Business Academy can help you.

    (A) the best
    (B) best
    (C) better
    (D) good

5. A certificate from Techno Business Academy will open doors for you. Employers know that _____ workers around are graduates of our program.

    (A) the highest
    (B) the most skilled
    (C) the least competent
    (D) the least expensive

高分攻略 8　代名詞

代名詞用來取代名詞。代名詞的人稱和數必須與它的先行詞（其所取代的名詞）保持一致。代名詞有好幾種類型，各有不同的文法功能。

答題要訣　找出代名詞所取代的先行詞，確保人稱和數保持一致。

主格代名詞		受格代名詞		反身代名詞	
I	we	me	us	myself	ourselves
you	you	you	you	yourself	yourselves
he/she/it	they	him/her/it	them	himself/herself/itself	themselves

所有格形容詞		所有格代名詞	
my	our	mine	ours
our	your	yours	yours
his/her/its	their	his/hers/its	theirs

》範例

Mrs. Kim was at the office yesterday, but I didn't see *her*.
金太太昨天在辦公室，但我沒看見她。

The clients will be here all day tomorrow, and *they* hope to meet with the director.
客戶明天一整天都會在這裡，他們希望與主管見面。

You should call a repair person instead of trying to fix the machine *yourself*.
你應該打電話給維修人員，而不是試圖自己修理機器。

I don't think this coat is *mine*.
我覺得這件外套不是我的。

Bob will present *his* plan at the next staff meeting.
鮑伯會在下次的員工會議提出他的計畫。

即時演練

選出最適當的單字或片語完成句子。

1. Dear Ms. Coleman, I would like thank you for the kind hospitality I received during my visit to the branch office last week. Please tell _____ staff that I very much appreciated the welcome they gave me.

    (A) yourself
    (B) yours
    (C) you
    (D) your

2. I was impressed by the friendliness and helpfulness of all the employees in the office. _____ made my work go smoothly even though I was working in an unfamiliar setting.

    (A) I
    (B) He
    (C) You
    (D) They

3. I would particularly like to mention John Malstrom, who made special efforts to make sure I had everything I needed. Please thank _____ for me.

    (A) me
    (B) him
    (C) her
    (D) them

4. Unfortunately, I left behind a folder of important documents during my visit. I think I left _____ on the table in the conference room.

   (A) it
   (B) him
   (C) them
   (D) me

5. Could you please send the forgotten item to my office? I won't have time to pick up the folder _____ .

   (A) itself
   (B) yourself
   (C) myself
   (D) themselves

高分攻略 9　主格關係代名詞

關係代名詞引導形容詞子句。形容詞子句的作用和形容詞一樣，修飾主要子句中的一個名詞。關係代名詞可以作形容詞子句的主詞或受詞。該用哪個關係代名詞取決於它修飾的名詞（先行詞），亦取決於它在子句中是作為主詞或受詞，以及這個子句是限定性還是非限定性。

> **答題要訣**　形容詞子句必然緊接在其修飾的名詞之後，可利用此線索找到先行詞。

》範例

限定性子句是辨識其修飾名詞的必要資訊，假如沒有這個限定性子句，該名詞的身分就會不明確。

主格關係代名詞──限定性子句

人	who / that
事物	which / that
所有權	whose

<u>The woman</u> <u>who</u> shares this office is very good with computers.
　　先行詞　　關係代名詞
共用這間辦公室的那個女人非常擅長使用電腦。

上面這個句子由一個主要子句（The woman is very good with computers）和一個形容詞子句（who shares this office）組成。

<u>The packages</u> <u>that</u> arrived this morning are on your desk.
　　　先行詞　　關係代名詞
今天早上送達的包裹在你桌上。

上面這個句子由一個主要子句（The packages are on your desk）和一個形容詞子句（that arrived this morning）組成。

<u>The man</u> <u>whose</u> office is next door wants to meet you.
　　先行詞　　關係代名詞
隔壁辦公室的那個男人想要見你。

上面這個句子由一個主要子句（The man wants to meet you）和一個形容詞子句（whose office is next door）組成。

非限定性子句不是辨識名詞的必要資訊，只用來補充額外資訊。假如我們把非限定性子句從句子中刪除，該名詞的身分依然明確。非限定性子句必然以逗號和句子的其他成分隔開。

主格關係代名詞──非限定性子句

人	who
事物	which
所有權	whose

<u>Mr. Maurice,</u> <u>who</u> has worked here for a long time, will retire soon.
　　先行詞　　關係代名詞
莫里斯先生在這裡工作了很長一段時間，就快要退休了。

上面這個句子由一個主要子句（Mr. Maurice will retire soon）和一個形容詞子句（who has worked here for a long time）組成。

My car, which is constantly breaking down, is at the mechanic's again today.
　　先行詞　關係代名詞
我的車子老是故障，今天又進了修車廠。

上面這個句子由一個主要子句（My car is at the mechanic's again today）和一個形容詞子句（which is constantly breaking down）組成。

My assistant, whose French is excellent, will help with the clients from France.
　　　先行詞　　　關係代名詞
我的助理法文很好，他會協助來自法國的客戶。

上面這個句子由一個主要子句（My assistant will help with the clients from France）和一個形容詞子句（whose French is excellent）組成。

即時演練

選出最適當的單字或片語完成句子。

1. Ms. McIntyre will be visiting us next week from the London offices. Staff members _____ wish to make an appointment to meet with her may contact the Human Resources office.

    (A) who
    (B) whom
    (C) whose
    (D) which

2. A luncheon for Ms. McIntyre will be held on Wednesday at the Flowers Restaurant. Everyone _____ schedule allows is welcome to attend this event.

    (A) who
    (B) their
    (C) whose
    (D) his

3. We are all looking forward to Ms. McIntyre's visit, _____ will last ten days.

    (A) who
    (B) that
    (C) whose
    (D) which

4. Ms. McIntyre will spend time in each department. If you want to know when she will be in your department, please check the schedule _____ is available on the company website.

   (A) it
   (B) that
   (C) who
   (D) whose

5. Ms. McIntyre, _____ does not often get a chance to visit overseas offices, is looking forward to the visit.

   (A) that
   (B) who
   (C) which
   (D) she

高分攻略 10　受格關係代名詞

受格關係代名詞在關係子句中作動詞或介系詞的受詞。限定性子句中的受格關係代名詞可省略，唯有 whose 是例外不可省略。

答題要訣　先確認形容詞子句的主詞，如果關係代名詞在子句中作主詞，就要用主格，如果在子句中作受詞，就要用受格。

》範例

受格關係代名詞──限定性子句

人	whom, who, that, 省略
事物	which, that, 省略
所有權	whose

The accountant whom we hired last month used to work for Ibex International.
　　先行詞　　關係代名詞
我們上個月聘請的會計師曾在艾貝克思國際公司工作過。

上面這個句子由一個主要子句（The accountant used to work for Ibex International）和一個形容詞子句（whom we hired last month）組成。

The office that we rented is very close to the subway station.
　先行詞　關係代名詞
我們租的辦公室離地鐵站非常近。

上面這個句子由一個主要子句（The office is very close to the subway station）和一個形容詞子句（that we rented）組成。

<u>The person</u> <u>whose</u> phone number you requested no longer works here.
　　　先行詞　　關係代名詞
你詢問電話號碼的那個人已經不在這裡上班了。

上面這個句子由一個主要子句（The person no longer works here）和一個形容詞子句（whose phone number you requested）組成。

受格關係代名詞——非限定性子句

人	whom, who
事物	which
所有權	whose

<u>My neighbor,</u> <u>whom</u> I have known for many years, is moving away next month.
　先行詞　　關係代名詞
我認識多年的鄰居下個月要搬走了。

上面這個句子由一個主要子句（My neighbor is moving away next month）和一個形容詞子句（whom I have known for many years）組成。

<u>The City Museum,</u> <u>which</u> I visit almost every day, has many interesting exhibits.
　　先行詞　　　關係代名詞
我幾乎天天造訪的城市博物館有很多有趣的展覽。

上面這個句子由一個主要子句（The City Museum has many interesting exhibits）和一個形容詞子句（which I visit almost every day）組成。

<u>Shirley,</u> <u>whose</u> office you were using last week, is back at work today.
　先行詞　關係代名詞
你上星期用她辦公室的雪莉今天會回來上班。

上面這個句子由一個主要子句（Shirley is back at work today）和一個形容詞子句（whose office you were using last week）組成。

> 即時演練

選出最適當的單字或片語完成句子。

1. Do you want to know more about global warming and how you can help prevent it? Dr. Herman Friedman, _____ many consider the foremost authority on the subject, will speak at Grayson Hall next Tuesday.

    (A) whose
    (B) which
    (C) whom
    (D) him

2. Dr. Freidman has written many articles and books on the subject of global warming. The gradual bleaching of the Great Barrier Reef, _____ he has been researching for several years, is the subject of his latest book.

    (A) that
    (B) which
    (C) whom
    (D) it

3. Signed copies of his book will be for sale after his talk, along with other books _____ he has written about global warming.

    (A) whose
    (B) that
    (C) them
    (D) who

4. Dr. Friedman will be accompanied by a colleague. Dr. Smythe, _____ writings on global warming are also widely known, will present slides of his research visits to coral reefs.

   (A) who
   (B) whom
   (C) that
   (D) whose

5. Those interested in understanding more about global warming will not want to miss this event. Drs. Friedman and Smythe, to _____ we owe so much of our knowledge of this subject, are both interesting and informed speakers.

   (A) whom
   (B) whose
   (C) them
   (D) which

高分攻略 11　被動語態

大部分句子使用的是主動語態，即主詞是動作執行者。然而有些句子會使用被動語態，此時主詞是動作接受者。當動作執行者（agent）不明或不重要時，就會使用被動語態。被動語態的形式是「be 動詞 + 過去分詞」。

> **答題要訣**　要辨識句子是否使用了被動語態，就要判斷主詞是動作執行者還是接受者。

》範例

在被動語態中，be 動詞負責傳達時態和否定，主要動詞一律使用過去分詞。

現在簡單式

Employees <u>are paid</u> every Friday.　員工每週五領薪水。
　　　　　　be 動詞　過去分詞

上面這個句子的主詞是 employees，動作是 pay（付薪水）。員工並沒有執行付薪水的動作，付員工薪水的另有其人，可能是老闆或公司。

Children <u>aren't allowed</u> in this office without adult supervision.
　　　　　　be 動詞　過去分詞
若無成人監督，兒童不准進入此辦公室。

這句的主詞是 children，動作是 allow（准許）。兒童並沒有執行准許這個動作，他們並非不准許自己做這件事的人。

過去簡單式

The mail <u>was delivered</u> at 10:00 this morning. 該郵件於今天上午十點送達。
　　　　be 動詞 過去分詞

上面這個句子的主詞是 mail，動作是 delivered（送達）。郵件不是動作的執行者，郵件不會自己送達，送達郵件的是句中沒有提及的郵差。

現在完成式

The annual conference <u>has been held</u> in this city every year since 2005.
　　　　　　　　　　　　be 動詞　過去分詞
自 2005 年起，這座城市每年都會舉行年度會議。

上面這個句子的主詞是 conference，動作是 held（舉行）。會議並沒有執行這個動作，會議不會自己舉行，舉行會議的是某個組織或團體。

未來式

Copies of the report <u>will be distributed</u> at tomorrow's meeting.
　　　　　　　　　　　be 動詞　　過去分詞
明天的會議上會分發這份報告的影本。

句子的主詞是 copies of the report，動作是 distributed（分發）。報告的影本不會執行這個動作，不可能自己分發。

有時句中會出現動作執行者，此時要用介系詞 by 來帶出動作執行者。

The letter was signed *by* everyone in the office.
辦公室裡的每個人都在這封信上簽了名。

All receipts are inspected *by* the accountant.
會計師檢查了所有收據。

即時演練

選出最適當的單字或片語完成句子。

1. We have just put a good deal of effort, not to mention money, into to renovating the conference room. In addition to new tables and chairs, the walls _____ painted last month.

   (A) was
   (B) are
   (C) were
   (D) have been

2. We had a problem with the carpet company, but we have worked that out, and they have promised us that the new carpet will be _____ before the end of this week.

   (A) installs
   (B) installed
   (C) installing
   (D) installation

3. The only thing in the room that isn't new is the curtains. We determined that they just needed a thorough cleaning. We sent them out to a professional cleaning facility where the stains _____ , and now they are as good as new.

   (A) remove
   (B) removed
   (C) have removed
   (D) were removed

4. Now that the conference room _____ , we hope everyone will find it to be a pleasant place to work.

   (A) has been renovated
   (B) has renovated
   (C) is renovating
   (D) renovated

5. We thank you for your patience during the renovation process. In order to celebrate the new conference room, a party _____ next month.

   (A) will give
   (B) is giving
   (C) to be given
   (D) will be given

高分攻略 12　字義

要選出正確的單字完成句子，就必須了解整段文字的語境。必須從前後的句子去了解語境，才知道哪個單字最符合這段文字的描述。

答題要訣　確實掌握語境以便選出正確單字。

》範例

1. The workshop begins at 9:00 a.m. sharp. Therefore, we ask ＿＿＿＿＿＿ to arrive early so that we can begin on time.
   工作坊於上午九點整開始，因此我們請 ＿＿＿＿＿＿ 提早到達，以便準時開始。

   (A) consultants　顧問
   (B) participants　參加者
   (C) customers　顧客
   (D) reviewers　評論家

這項資訊是針對要來參加工作坊的人，請他們提前抵達會場。參加工作坊的人通常稱為 participants（參加者），因此選項 (B) 是正確答案，其他選項都不符合此處的語境。

2. The doctor is very busy and it is difficult to get a chance to see him. I was ＿＿＿＿＿＿ to be given an appointment for two months from now.
   這位醫生很忙碌，很難有機會看到他，我很 ＿＿＿＿＿＿ 預約到兩個月後的門診。

   (A) wise　聰明的
   (B) necessary　必要的
   (C) persistent　持續的
   (D) fortunate　幸運的

題目的資訊顯示這位醫生很難預約，因此這位約到的人覺得自己很幸運 (fortunate)，選項 (D) 是正確答案，其他選項都和語境不符。

233

即時演練

選出最適合的單字或片語完成句子。

1. This is a very well-maintained building. The _____ keeps all public areas clean and recently had the hallways re-carpeted.

    (A) landlord
    (B) tenant
    (C) resident
    (D) architect

2. We had our apartment painted last year. The rooms are dark, so we _____ a light color to brighten things up.

    (A) acknowledged
    (B) possessed
    (C) selected
    (D) enjoyed

3. The building is in a great location. The subway station is just a block away, and there are many nice shops and restaurants in the neighborhood. The good location is one reason why the rent is so _____ .

    (A) reasonable
    (B) unusual
    (C) fair
    (D) high

4. Many people come to this part of the city for the _____ activities. In addition to the museums and theaters, there are concerts in the park every summer.

   (A) athletic
   (B) cultural
   (C) dramatic
   (D) performance

5. Many of the events are free for city residents. You will not be _____ an entrance fee if you can prove that you live in the city.

   (A) allowed
   (B) charged
   (C) purchased
   (D) demanded

235

高分攻略 13 句子選擇

有些題目會請你選出最符合語境的句子。語境包含這段文字的主題和目的，譬如，備忘錄的主題可能是員工會議，目的則是通知員工即將舉行會議、說明會議內容，或請大家評價一場已經舉行過的會議。

答題要訣 判斷這段文字的主題和目的。

》範例

1. There will be a meeting about our new health insurance policy next Wednesday afternoon. Attendance is not mandatory, but it is recommended. If you have any questions about this new policy, this is your opportunity to get them answered.
   _____.
   下個星期三下午將舉辦新健保政策的說明會。會議不強制參加，但建議參加。如果你對新政策有任何疑問，這是獲得解答的好機會。
   _____。

   (A) If you need a few days off work for health reasons, please inform your supervisor
   若因健康因素必須請假幾天，請通知你的主管
   (B) We hope that the new policy will save everyone some money and will be easier to understand
   希望新政策能為大家省下一點錢，也希望更好理解

這段文字宣布將舉行會議說明新的健保政策。選項 (A) 提到了 health，但這句話卻與健康保險或會議無關，因此不符合語境。選項 (B) 說明了施行新政策的出發點，符合語境，因此應該選 (B)。

2. I am sending you a draft of the new contract with the XZ Company. _____. Please review it and send me your comments as soon as possible. Your help with this matter is greatly appreciated.

我把和 XZ 公司新合約的草稿寄給您，_____，請您看過後盡快將您的意見寄給我。非常感謝您對此事的協助。

(A) The XZ Company has been our client for several years now
   XZ 公司是我們多年的客戶
(B) I would like your feedback before I meet with the client on Thursday
   希望能在週四與客戶會面之前收到您的意見

寫這封信的人正要寄出一份合約草稿，並且希望有人幫他看過後提出意見，因此選項 (B) 符合語境。選項 (A) 提到了客戶的資訊，但該資訊和要求審閱合約並無關聯。

即時演練

選出最適當的句子完成段落。

1. The elevators in this building will undergo routine maintenance during the week of September 15. _____ . When this occurs, please use another elevator or the stairs. We apologize for any inconvenience this may cause.

    (A) There are three elevators in this building, each with a capacity of 15 passengers
    (B) During this week, there may be one or two elevators out of service from time to time
    (C) Some people prefer to use the stairs because they enjoy the exercise
    (D) Each elevator is equipped with a red emergency phone

    Ⓐ Ⓑ Ⓒ Ⓓ

2. Thank you for agreeing to meet with me next week. _____ . I look forward to the opportunity to discuss my company and the services we can offer you. We have served many satisfied clients like yourself in the past, and I feel confident we can provide you with satisfactory services, as well.

    (A) I enjoy social get-togethers from time to time
    (B) I have a full schedule of meetings and little time for anything else
    (C) I will look for you at the Golden Café at 10:00
    (D) I have been unable to reach you by either phone or email

    Ⓐ Ⓑ Ⓒ Ⓓ

3. Thank you for sending your resume to us. You have exactly the kind of education and experience we are looking for. I would like you to come in for an interview soon. _____ .

   (A) Please call my office to set up a time for an appointment
   (B) There are several places in the city where you can get the training you need
   (C) We generally go through an employment agency when we need to hire new staff
   (D) Many young people are looking for a position in this field

4. Thank you for your interest in using the services of Spick and Span Office Cleaners. We have set up an appointment for you for next Monday morning. _____ . As we discussed over the phone, we expect the job will take 3–4 hours. We will vacuum and dust all rooms. Payment is due at the time of services.

   (A) We have been cleaning offices in this city for over five years
   (B) Monday is generally our busiest day of the week
   (C) Most clients hire us on a weekly basis
   (D) We will arrive at 8:00 a.m. ready to clean

3-4　Part 7：閱讀測驗

多益測驗的第七大題閱讀測驗一共有 54 題，其中 29 題為單篇閱讀，25 題為多篇閱讀。題目會問你文章的主旨、細節、字彙、語境意義，或要你插入句子。

3-4-1 試題範例

文章段落

> If you are planning a visit to Wilmington, consider staying at the Bougainvillea Inn. –[1]– This charming hotel is located in the Park View neighborhood, one of the loveliest areas of the city. –[2]– The lobby features a mural by a local artist, and each guest room is decorated with a floral theme. The staff are friendly and helpful and have many good suggestions for sights to see and places to eat. –[3]– The prices are a little higher than similar hotels in the area, but the excellent service makes it well worth the cost. –[4]–
>
> 若你計劃到威明頓一遊，可考慮入住九重葛旅館。–[1]– 這間迷人的旅館坐落於公園景觀區，是這座城市裡最美麗的地區之一。–[2]– 大廳有一幅當地藝術家所創作的壁畫，每間客房均採用一種花卉主題裝飾。員工既親切又樂於服務，也會提供很多景點和美食的好建議。–[3]– 雖然價格略高於該區類似的旅館，但良好的服務絕對有其價值。–[4]–

主旨題

Who is this article for? 這篇文章是寫給誰看的？

(A) Travel agents　旅行社職員
(B) Hotel staff　飯店員工
(C) Neighbors　鄰居
(D) Tourists　遊客

Ⓐ　Ⓑ　Ⓒ　●

這篇文章的目的是向計劃到某城市旅遊的人推薦飯店，也就是寫給「遊客」（tourists）看的，因此最適當的答案是 (D)。

細節題

What is indicated about the hotel?　關於這間飯店文中提到什麼？

(A) It is more expensive than other hotels.
　　比其他飯店貴。
(B) It is located close to downtown.　位置臨近市區。
(C) It has many guest rooms.　客房很多。
(D) It has a large lobby.　有寬敞的大廳。

●　Ⓑ　Ⓒ　Ⓓ

文章中提到「The prices are a little higher than similar hotels . . .」，因此最適當的答案是 (A)。

241

字彙題

The word "loveliest" in line 3 is closest in meaning to
第三行中的「loveliest」意思最接近於

(A) most popular　最受歡迎的
(B) most historic　最具歷史意義的
(C) prettiest　最漂亮的
(D) quietest　最安靜的

Ⓐ Ⓑ ● Ⓓ

loveliest 的意思就等於 prettiest，因此最適當的答案是 (C)。

插入句子題

In which of the following positions marked [1], [2], [3], and [4] does the following sentence best belong?
"The artistically designed interior is a delight to the eye."
下面這個句子最適合填入文中 [1][2][3][4] 哪一個位置？
「充滿藝術氣息的室內設計令人賞心悅目。」

(A) [1]
(B) [2]
(C) [3]
(D) [4]

Ⓐ ● Ⓒ Ⓓ

欲插入的此句子說明這間飯店的內部裝潢充滿藝術氣息、非常漂亮，而位置 [2] 的下一句接著舉例說明飯店內的藝術特色，因此最適當的答案是 (B)。

有些類型的段落文字，例如簡訊和線上聊天室，必定包含詢問語境意義的問題，即問你詞語在語境中是什麼意思，必須根據該單字或片語在段落中的實際用法，決定它們的意義。

文章段落

SAM SMITH	10:10
Are you at the store now?	
MARY CLARK	10:12
Yes. Why?	
SAM SMITH	10:13
Would you pick up a box of envelopes for me?	
MARY CLARK	10:15
What size do you want?	
SAM SMITH	10:16
The large ones. Business size.	
MARY CLARK	10:18
Got it.	
SAM SMITH	10:20
Thanks. Just leave them on my desk when you get back.	

山姆・史密斯	10:10
你現在在店裡嗎？	
瑪麗・克拉克	10:12
對啊，怎麼了？	
山姆・史密斯	10:13
可以幫我買一包信封嗎？	
瑪麗・克拉克	10:15
你要什麼大小的？	
山姆・史密斯	10:16
大的，商務尺寸。	
瑪麗・克拉克	10:18
了解。	
山姆・史密斯	10:20
謝謝，你回來的時候放在我桌上就行了。	

語境意義題

At 10:18, what does Ms. Clark mean when she writes, "Got it"?
在 10 點 18 分的時候，克拉克小姐寫「Got it」是什麼意思？

(A) She understands what kind of envelopes Mr. Smith wants.
她明白史密斯先生要的是哪一種信封。　● Ⓑ Ⓒ Ⓓ

(B) She already has envelopes in her office.
她的辦公室裡已經有信封了。

(C) She is almost ready to leave the store.
她已經準備要離開商店了。

(D) She knows where Mr. Smith's desk is.
她知道史密斯先生的辦公桌在哪裡。

「got it」可用來表示「我了解了」、「我明白了」。史密斯先生已說明他想要哪一種尺寸的信封，克拉克小姐用這個片語作為回應，因此最適當的答案是 (A)。

3-4-2 PSRA 策略

閱讀測驗有一個很重要的答題策略，就是用一種組織性方式處理一段文字。先對這段文字進行「預測」（prediction），接著「瀏覽」（scan），然後「閱讀」（read），最後「作答」（answer）。我們把這個策略稱為 PSRA 策略。

預測（Prediction）

在閱讀「之前」就對即將閱讀的文字進行預測，有助於建立語境，也更容易理解文章。這個步驟能提高你的閱讀測驗分數。開始閱讀一段文章之前，先把題目的說明文字看過一遍，說明文字會像這樣：

Questions 161–163 refer to the following office memo.
第 161–163 題請看下面這則辦公室備忘錄。

從題目的說明文字你會知道一共有幾題，以及文章的類型（譬如這是一則辦公室備忘錄）。文章的外觀也會給你一點暗示：電子郵件會是電子郵件的格式、手機簡訊會是手機簡訊的樣子、圖表會是圖表的樣子，從外觀就可以「預測」這段文字是關於什麼內容。

每篇文章通常配有二至三道題目，也可能多達五題。先把題目和四個選項看過一遍，大概知道應注意哪些重點，這也有助於「預測」文章內容。題目可能如下：

According to the memo, which equipment has multiple uses?
根據這則備忘錄，哪一個設備有多種用途？

(A) Desktop computers 桌上型電腦
(B) Fax machines 傳真機
(C) Answering machines 答錄機
(D) Tablet computers 平板電腦

瀏覽（Scan）

現在我們可以預測這則備忘錄和電子用品有關。當我們在「瀏覽」文章時，要設法找出題目中出現的關鍵字，不一定要一模一樣，意義類似就可以了。看題目和選項時，先想一想有哪些字的意義和其中的關鍵字差不多。以此題來說，關鍵字會是：

題目		答案選項
關鍵字	類似意義的詞語	Desktop computers 桌上型電腦
equipment 設備	electronic tools 電子工具 hardware 硬體	Fax machines 傳真機 Answering machines 答錄機
multiple uses 多用途	useful in a variety of settings 可用於多種情況	Tablet computers 平板電腦

先瀏覽文章找出文句中的關鍵字，接著在題目關鍵字的前後找找看有沒有答案關鍵字。找到答案關鍵字後，檢查看看這些字是否能回答問題，請試著作答（在心裡作答，先不要寫在答案卡上）。以下舉例說明。

> MEMORANDUM
>
> To: Lafite, Pierre
>   Purchasing Department
>
> From: Clement, Marie France
>   Personnel
>
> We need **desktop computers** for use in the office, **answering machines** for our consultants, **fax machines** for the shipping department, and **tablet computers** for everyone. This **last piece of hardware** can be used in a variety of ways.

> 備忘錄
>
> 收件者：皮耶・拉斐
>   採購部
>
> 寄件者：瑪莉・弗朗絲・克萊門特
>   人事部
>
> 我們需要辦公室用的**桌上型電腦**，顧問要用的**答錄機**，出貨部門要用的**傳真機**，還有每個人都要用的**平板電腦**。**最後這個硬體設備**可有多種用途。

According to the memo, which equipment has multiple uses?
根據這則備忘錄，哪一個設備有多種用途？

(A) Desktop computers 桌上型電腦
(B) Fax machines 傳真機
(C) Answering machines 答錄機
(D) Tablet computers 平板電腦

正確答案是 (D)。最後一句表示「This last piece of hardware can be used in a variety of ways.」（最後這個硬體設備可有多種用途），而「最後」一個提到的是平板電腦。

247

要注意的是，假如最後一個句子變成如下，答案就會不一樣：

This **first piece of hardware** can be used in a variety of ways.
第一個硬體設備可有多種用途。

只是一字之差，「first」這個字就將答案從 (D) Tablet computers 徹底變成了 (A) Desktop computers。這就是為何「不能」只靠預測和瀏覽就作答。

閱讀（Read）
你還必須「閱讀」文章。閱讀時請快速閱讀，目的是確認你的預測。你必須根據所有題目進行「預測」，並且「瀏覽」文章找出關鍵字，在心裡默默作答，然後「閱讀」文章確認你的答案後，才可以在答案卡上畫記。第一題的答案會出現在文章的第一部分，第二題會在第二部分，以此類推。題目會按照文章內容的出現順序排列。

作答（Answer）
現在準備要畫記答案卡了。簡單的題目先答，如果不知道答案，就把這個程序再執行一遍：瀏覽文章、尋找關鍵字、閱讀文章各部分。萬一還是不知道答案，就用「猜」的，無論如何都「不要」空白不作答。

3-4-3 高分攻略

高分攻略 1　廣告

多益測驗的廣告題和你在報紙、雜誌或網路上所看到的廣告非常類似，廣告內容十分多樣化，例如產品、服務、房地產、就業訊息都有可能出現。

即時演練

Questions 1–2 refer to the following advertisement. Choose the one best answer to each question.

ATTENTION MANUFACTURERS!

We introduce and distribute your products to 125,000 distributors in 155 countries, FREE!

For a FREE information kit call:

Tel: (310) 553-4434, Ext. 105; Fax (310) 553-5555

GRAND TECHNOLOGIES LIMITED

---

1. Who is the advertisement written for?

    (A) Distributors
    (B) Sales representatives
    (C) Manufacturers
    (D) Information specialists

2. How many countries are mentioned?

    (A) 125
    (B) 155
    (C) 310
    (D) 501

高分攻略 2　表單

表單是一種可以填入資料的範本，類型包括了雜誌訂閱表、採購單、預訂表、收據、申請表等。

即時演練

Questions 1–3 refer to the following form. Choose the one best answer to each question.

Journal of Business News Monthly is THE publication to keep you up to date on all national and international news affecting the world of business. Simply fill in your information below to receive a 1 year (12 issues) print & digital subscription! Or, save by ordering a two-year subscription now.

Name: Anne Kwok
Email: akwok@pharmamail.co
Company: Pharmaceutical Supply Company
Address 1: 1705 Shana Street
Address 2: New London

Payment
Card Type: Xtra Card
Card No.: 1234567

Total: $199.99 (one year)
　　　 $349.99 (two years)

1. How often is the journal published?

    (A) Once a week
    (B) Once a month
    (C) Once every six months
    (D) Once a year

    Ⓐ Ⓑ Ⓒ Ⓓ

2. How will Ms. Kwok receive the journal?

    (A) She will read it online only.
    (B) She will get a paper copy only.
    (C) She will get both an online copy and a paper copy.
    (D) She will borrow a copy from her boss.

    Ⓐ Ⓑ Ⓒ Ⓓ

3. How much does an annual subscription cost?

    (A) About $20
    (B) Just under $200
    (C) About $175
    (D) Almost $350

    Ⓐ Ⓑ Ⓒ Ⓓ

高分攻略 3 書信

書信中最重要的資訊通常位於正文，即問候語（Dear . . .）和結尾敬語（Sincerely yours）中間的這段文字當中。

即時演練

Questions 1–3 refer to the following letter. Choose the one best answer to each question.

The X-Cellent Corporation
Box 82, Plimsdale

December 3, 20—

George Hendries
Whyo, Inc.
44 Main Street
Plimsdale

Dear Mr. Hendries,

This letter will confirm our recent discussion regarding a building owned by your company in the city of Middletown. As agreed, my company will perform an appraisal of the property at 115 Bridge St. in Middletown as part of the overall valuation of assets your company is currently undertaking. We will perform a physical inspection of the building, a review of records pertaining to the ownership history of said building, and will also research other properties of similar size, location, and type. We will provide your company with a thorough report analyzing the data and methods we have used to arrive at a fair market value for your property. The report will be delivered to you before the end of next month. In order to begin the work we will need the first payment of 50% of the agreed-upon price, the remainder to be payable at the time the report is submitted. If these terms are agreeable to you, please return a signed copy of this letter to my office as soon as possible.

Sincerely,
Mark Wilson

1. What is the purpose of the letter?

   (A) To describe someone's professional background
   (B) To explain how to sell a piece of property
   (C) To accept an offer of employment
   (D) To describe work that will be done

   Ⓐ Ⓑ Ⓒ Ⓓ

2. What kind of work does the writer of the letter do?

   (A) He sells real estate.
   (B) He lends money to real estate buyers.
   (C) He determines the value of real estate.
   (D) He performs safety inspections of real estate.

   Ⓐ Ⓑ Ⓒ Ⓓ

3. What does the recipient of the letter have to do now?

   (A) Negotiate a payment
   (B) Sign a document
   (C) Submit a report
   (D) Visit a building

   Ⓐ Ⓑ Ⓒ Ⓓ

高分攻略 4　備忘錄

備忘錄（memorandum/memo）是一種內部的聯絡表單，通常由同公司的一名成員發給另一名成員。今天這些備忘錄通常以電子郵件的形式透過電腦發送，電子形式的書信或網頁有其特定的語言方式，請參考後面的〈高分攻略 11 電子郵件〉和〈高分攻略 12 網頁〉。

即時演練

Questions 1–4 refer to the following memorandum. Choose the one best answer to each question.

MEMORANDUM

To: All Employees

From:　Simon Gonzales
　　　　Personnel Officer

Date:　May 15, 20-

Sub:　Company Travel

Effective June 1 all personnel traveling on company business must use the most economical means possible. No flights under five hours can be booked in Business class. No flights regardless of duration can be booked in First class.

---

1. If a flight is over five hours, what class can be booked?

    (A) Economy
    (B) Economy Plus
    (C) Business
    (D) First

2. When will this rule go into effect?

    (A) In about two weeks
    (B) At the end of the summer
    (C) At the first of the year
    (D) In five months

3. Why was this memo written?

    (A) To save time
    (B) To save money
    (C) To reward the employees
    (D) To increase company travel

4. Who is affected by this memo?

    (A) Only the Board of Directors
    (B) Only frequent travelers
    (C) Only the personnel department
    (D) All personnel

高分攻略 5　表格

表格用來顯示彙編的數據，可使人方便進行快速比較。任何主題都有可能被做成表格。

即時演練

Questions 1–4 refer to the following table. Choose the one best answer to each question.

WORLD TEMPERATURES

January 5

	Hi (C/F)	Lo (C/F)	Weather
Amsterdam	6/41	3/37	c
Athens	13/55	8/46	sh
Bangkok	32/90	27/80	sh
Beijing	12/53	1/34	pc
Brussels	4/39	1/34	sh
Budapest	3/37	0/32	r
Frankfurt	3/37	1/34	r
Jakarta	29/84	24/75	sh
Kuala Lumpur	31/88	24/75	t
Madrid	9/48	1/34	sh
Manila	33/91	21/70	pc
Seoul	9/48	–2/29	s
Taipei	21/70	14/57	c
Tokyo	9/48	–2/29	pc

Weather: s-sunny; pc-partly cloudy; c-cloudy; sh-showers; t-thunderstorms; r-rain

1. Which two cities were cloudy on January 5?

    (A) Amsterdam and Taipei
    (B) Beijing and Manila
    (C) Athens and Tokyo
    (D) Bangkok and Seoul

2. Which city had the highest temperature?

    (A) Athens
    (B) Bangkok
    (C) Jakarta
    (D) Manila

3. Which city had the closest spread between high and low temperature?

    (A) Brussels
    (B) Frankfurt
    (C) Seoul
    (D) Tokyo

4. Kuala Lumpur had

    (A) sun
    (B) thunderstorms
    (C) rain
    (D) showers

高分攻略 6　圖表

圖表是以製圖的方式表現各種變量之間的關係。多益測驗可能出現的圖表包括折線圖、柱狀圖和圓餅圖。

即時演練

Questions 1–2 refer to the following graph. Choose the one best answer to each question.

Hotel Chain Market Share

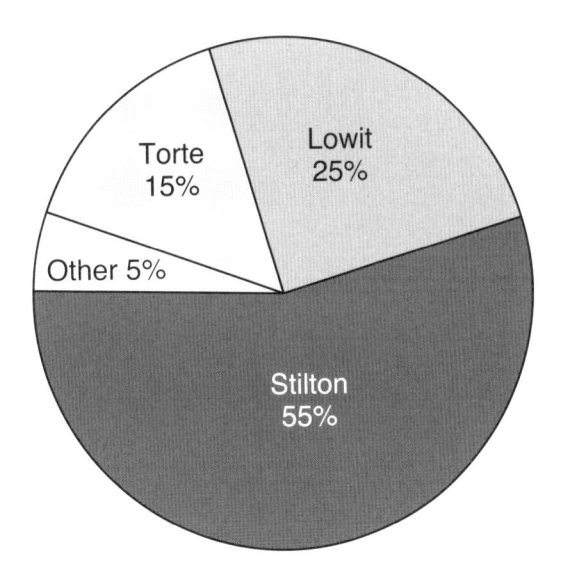

- Lowit 25%
- Torte 15%
- Other 5%
- Stilton 55%

1. Who would be most interested in reading this graph?

    (A) Tourists
    (B) Competing hotels
    (C) Landscape architects
    (D) Job hunters

    Ⓐ Ⓑ Ⓒ Ⓓ

2. According to this graph, Lowit

    (A) is the top-ranking hotel chain
    (B) is only in Latin America
    (C) has less of a share than Torte
    (D) has one-quarter of the market

    Ⓐ Ⓑ Ⓒ Ⓓ

高分攻略 7　公告

公告是向大眾宣布一項特定消息的正式聲明，內容可能關於某個人接受或辭去了一個高階職位、新建築落成、新產品上市，或關於一項特別活動。

即時演練

Questions 1–4 refer to the following announcement. Choose the one best answer to each question.

> The City Chamber of Commerce announces this year's City Job Fair, to be held on March 11 at the City Convention Center –[1]–. This is a unique opportunity to find out where the jobs are and to meet people who are hiring now. There will also be workshops on résumé writing, interview skills, resources for job hunters, and more. –[2]– There is no charge for the workshops, but pre-registration is required. –[3]– Visit the Chamber of Commerce website for more information on workshops. This event is open to the public, so come on down and get the information you need for a successful job search. –[4]–

1. How often is this event held?

    (A) One time only
    (B) Once a month
    (C) Twice a year
    (D) Once a year

2. What is indicated about the workshops?

   (A) They will be given online.
   (B) A small fee will be charged.
   (C) Participants must sign up ahead of time.
   (D) All the spaces have already been filled.

3. The word "unique" in line 3 of the passage is closest in meaning to

   (A) interesting
   (B) important
   (C) limited
   (D) rare

4. In which of the following positions marked [1], [2], [3], and [4] does the following sentence best belong?
   "Employers from all over the region and representing a variety of industries will be present."

   (A) [1]
   (B) [2]
   (C) [3]
   (D) [4]

高分攻略 8　通知

通知是寫作者認為普羅大眾或特定產品使用者必須知道的資訊，經常張貼於牆壁或公共建築上，或隨文附上產品資訊。

即時演練

Questions 1–2 refer to the following notice. Choose the one best answer to each question.

> **Corporate Policy Change**
>
> Moving Expenses. You can be reimbursed for your expenses of moving to a new home only if your new home is at least 50 miles away from your former home. In addition, expenses are limited to the costs of moving your household goods and personal effects from your former home to your new home. Meals, pre-move house-hunting expenses, and temporary-quarters expenses are no longer reimbursable.

1. Who would be most affected by this notice?

    (A) Hotel chains
    (B) Furniture rental companies
    (C) Real estate agents
    (D) New employees moving from another city

2. Which of the following will be reimbursed?

    (A) Lunch for the movers
    (B) Shipping household goods
    (C) Gas used looking for a house
    (D) Hotel expenses

高分攻略 9　文章

多益考的文章是指刊登於報章雜誌或電子報的文章，內容可能是關於當前的新聞事件，也可能是大眾普遍感興趣或特定人士感興趣的主題，要依這篇文章所出現在的刊物而定。

即時演練

Questions 1–4 refer to the following article. Choose the one best answer to each question.

　　Restaurateurs, like other business owners, are constantly seeking ways to expand their clientele and keep their restaurants filled. –[1]– Various types of advertising, networking, and discounts and special offers are all tried-and-true ways of attracting more business. Recently, many restaurant owners have had great success with offering cooking classes.

　　Customers are willing to pay to eat food prepared in your restaurant. They are also willing, it turns out, to pay to learn to prepare the meal themselves. –[2]– Cooking classes are most successful when they offer the opportunity to learn something unusual. Classes might focus on demonstrating a specialized cooking technique or showing ways to use seasonal ingredients. –[3]– Classes that explain how to prepare some unusual regional dish are the ones that tend to fill up most quickly.

　　Cooking classes can be seen as a sideline, but they are also an effective means of advertising your business. –[4]– Organizing cooking classes takes a little extra effort, but the costs are low and the return can be quite high.

1. What is this passage mainly about?

   (A) How to organize a cooking class
   (B) The costs of running a restaurant
   (C) A way for restaurants to increase business
   (D) Different methods of attracting customers

2. Which cooking classes are most popular?

   (A) The ones that cost the least
   (B) The ones about regional cooking
   (C) The ones that use seasonal ingredients
   (D) The ones that explain special techniques

3. The word "sideline" in paragraph 3, line 1, of the passage is closest in meaning to

   (A) extra activity
   (B) small task
   (C) expense
   (D) distraction

4. In which of the following positions marked [1], [2], [3], and [4] does the following sentence best belong?
   "Cooking class participants usually become loyal customers who recommend your restaurant to others."

   (A) [1]
   (B) [2]
   (C) [3]
   (D) [4]

265

高分攻略 10　時間表

時間表是列有活動舉辦或工作執行的時間或日期清單，例如火車時刻表、公車時刻表、付款時間表、課表、專案進度表等。

即時演練

Questions 1–4 refer to the following schedule. Choose the one best answer to each question.

7th & Market	East Rise P&R	Tunnel	122nd East & 16th
7:11 W	**7:21**	**7:36 T**	**8:01**
7:22 W	**7:32**	**7:47 T**	**8:12**
7:30 W	**7:41**	**7:59 T**	**8:21**
7:40	**7:51**	**8:06**	8:32
8:02 W	**8:13**	**8:25**	8:53
8:25	8:35	8:49	9:14
8:51 W	9:01	9:15	9:40
9:21	9:32	9:48	10:11
9:51 W	10:10	10:24	10:40

Key:

T = Tunnel opens at 8:00 a.m. Buses prior to this time stop on 12th and Meridian.

W = Bus departs at this time. It arrives about 5 minutes earlier.

Boldface indicates peak fare.

1. What time do off-peak fares probably start?

    (A) Before 7 a.m.
    (B) 8:25 a.m.
    (C) 8:30 a.m.
    (D) 8:51 a.m.

2. What time does the 7:30 bus arrive at 7th & Market?

    (A) 7:00
    (B) 7:22
    (C) 7:25
    (D) 7:30

3. Why doesn't the 7:30 use the tunnel?

    (A) Because it's rush hour
    (B) Bus heights exceed limits for the tunnel.
    (C) The tunnel is closed at that time.
    (D) Early buses are rarely full enough to use the tunnel.

4. How long is the trip from 7th & Market to 122nd East & 16th?

    (A) A quarter hour
    (B) A half hour
    (C) Almost an hour
    (D) An hour

高分攻略 11　電子郵件

電子郵件 email 的全稱是 electronic mail，指的是透過電腦發出的信件。電子郵件可用來傳送任何一種信函、表單或問卷，因此關於電子郵件的閱讀測驗可能涵蓋任何類型的內容。電子郵件的一大特徵是標題欄位，當中包含了寄件者、收件者和傳送資訊。另一個特徵就是電子郵件所使用的語言相較於紙本書信通常較為口語。

即時演練

Questions 1-2 refer to the following email. Choose the one best answer to each question.

From:　　Melinda Ligos
To:　　　Misha Polentesky
Subject:　Meeting in Orlando

Misha,

The meeting went better than expected. The client loved our proposal and didn't ask for any changes. They will get the necessary paperwork to us by the end of the week.

By the way, thanks for suggesting Sparazza's. I had dinner there Thursday after leaving the client's office. Loved it, and so close to my hotel.

I'll be back at the home office tomorrow. See you then.

Melinda

1. What is the purpose of the email?

   (A) To report on the results of a meeting
   (B) To ask for a signature on paperwork
   (C) To explain the contents of a proposal
   (D) To set up a new meeting with Ms. Polentesky

2. Where did the writer of the email go after the client meeting?

   (A) To another meeting
   (B) To her home office
   (C) To a restaurant
   (D) To her hotel

高分攻略 12　網頁

多益測驗的第七大題可能會出現網頁考題，可以上網探索各式各樣的網頁，讓自己熟悉網頁的版面和術語。

即時演練

Questions 1–2 refer to the following web page. Choose the one best answer to each question.

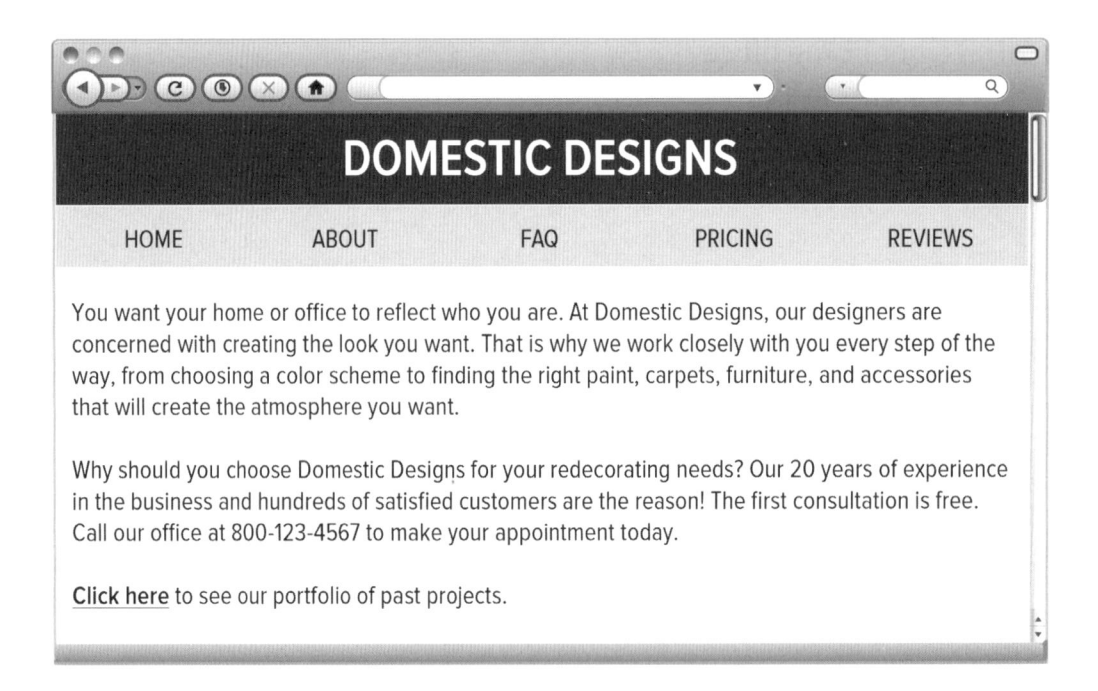

DOMESTIC DESIGNS

HOME　　ABOUT　　FAQ　　PRICING　　REVIEWS

You want your home or office to reflect who you are. At Domestic Designs, our designers are concerned with creating the look you want. That is why we work closely with you every step of the way, from choosing a color scheme to finding the right paint, carpets, furniture, and accessories that will create the atmosphere you want.

Why should you choose Domestic Designs for your redecorating needs? Our 20 years of experience in the business and hundreds of satisfied customers are the reason! The first consultation is free. Call our office at 800-123-4567 to make your appointment today.

Click here to see our portfolio of past projects.

1. What kind of business is Domestic Designs?

   (A) Architects
   (B) Furniture designer
   (C) Custom-made paints
   (D) Interior decorations

   Ⓐ Ⓑ Ⓒ Ⓓ

2. How can a customer see examples of the company's work?

   (A) Click on the link at the bottom of the page
   (B) Make an appointment with a consultant
   (C) Call past customers
   (D) Call the office

   Ⓐ Ⓑ Ⓒ Ⓓ

高分攻略 13　簡訊和線上聊天室

簡訊和線上聊天室是很常見的通訊形式，也會出現在多益測驗的第七大題。這種類型的段落必定包含語境意義的考題，要你從段落的上下文去判斷一個單字或片語的意義。

即時演練

> DIRECTIONS : Read each passage and answer the questions.
> 作答方式：閱讀每一段文字並回答問題。

Questions 1–2 refer to the following text message chain.

Lin Lee Where are you?	1:29
Jim Hart Traffic is heavy. The bus can hardly move. I'll be there in 10 – 15.	1:30
Lin Lee The client's just arriving.	1:32
Lin Lee We'll have to start without you.	1:33
Jim Hart No problem. I'll be there shortly.	1:35
Lin Lee You have the papers, right?	1:37
Jim Hart I'm sorry?	1:38
Lin Lee The work agreement for the client to sign.	1:40
Jim Hart Right, yes.	1:41

1. Why is Jim Hart late?

    (A) He missed the bus. Ⓐ Ⓑ Ⓒ Ⓓ
    (B) His bus is slow.
    (C) His client canceled.
    (D) He forgot about the meeting.

2. What does Jim Hart mean when he writes, "I'm sorry"?

    (A) He lost the papers. Ⓐ Ⓑ Ⓒ Ⓓ
    (B) He wants to apologize to the client.
    (C) He doesn't understand Lin Lee's text message.
    (D) He wishes he could get there more quickly.

答題訣竅總整理

Part 5：句子填空 & Part 6：段落填空
- 分辨意義相近或形式相近的單字
- 判斷符合語境的正確單字、片語或句子
- 辨識不同的動詞形式
- 辨識不同的形容詞和副詞形式
- 辨識單數和複數名詞
- 辨識不同類型的子句
- 了解介系詞的各種用法

Part 7：閱讀測驗
- 熟練多益測驗不同類型文章的閱讀技巧
- 熟悉多益測驗的各種閱讀題型
- 學會運用 PSRA 策略：預測（Predict）、瀏覽（Scan）、閱讀（Read）、作答（Answer）。

ANSWER SHEET
閱讀診斷測驗答案卡

Part 5: Incomplete Sentences

1. Ⓐ Ⓑ Ⓒ Ⓓ
2. Ⓐ Ⓑ Ⓒ Ⓓ
3. Ⓐ Ⓑ Ⓒ Ⓓ
4. Ⓐ Ⓑ Ⓒ Ⓓ
5. Ⓐ Ⓑ Ⓒ Ⓓ
6. Ⓐ Ⓑ Ⓒ Ⓓ
7. Ⓐ Ⓑ Ⓒ Ⓓ
8. Ⓐ Ⓑ Ⓒ Ⓓ
9. Ⓐ Ⓑ Ⓒ Ⓓ
10. Ⓐ Ⓑ Ⓒ Ⓓ
11. Ⓐ Ⓑ Ⓒ Ⓓ
12. Ⓐ Ⓑ Ⓒ Ⓓ
13. Ⓐ Ⓑ Ⓒ Ⓓ
14. Ⓐ Ⓑ Ⓒ Ⓓ
15. Ⓐ Ⓑ Ⓒ Ⓓ

Part 6: Text Completion

16. Ⓐ Ⓑ Ⓒ Ⓓ
17. Ⓐ Ⓑ Ⓒ Ⓓ
18. Ⓐ Ⓑ Ⓒ Ⓓ
19. Ⓐ Ⓑ Ⓒ Ⓓ
20. Ⓐ Ⓑ Ⓒ Ⓓ
21. Ⓐ Ⓑ Ⓒ Ⓓ
22. Ⓐ Ⓑ Ⓒ Ⓓ
23. Ⓐ Ⓑ Ⓒ Ⓓ

Part 7: Reading Comprehension

24. Ⓐ Ⓑ Ⓒ Ⓓ
25. Ⓐ Ⓑ Ⓒ Ⓓ
26. Ⓐ Ⓑ Ⓒ Ⓓ
27. Ⓐ Ⓑ Ⓒ Ⓓ
28. Ⓐ Ⓑ Ⓒ Ⓓ
29. Ⓐ Ⓑ Ⓒ Ⓓ
30. Ⓐ Ⓑ Ⓒ Ⓓ
31. Ⓐ Ⓑ Ⓒ Ⓓ
32. Ⓐ Ⓑ Ⓒ Ⓓ
33. Ⓐ Ⓑ Ⓒ Ⓓ
34. Ⓐ Ⓑ Ⓒ Ⓓ
35. Ⓐ Ⓑ Ⓒ Ⓓ
36. Ⓐ Ⓑ Ⓒ Ⓓ
37. Ⓐ Ⓑ Ⓒ Ⓓ
38. Ⓐ Ⓑ Ⓒ Ⓓ
39. Ⓐ Ⓑ Ⓒ Ⓓ
40. Ⓐ Ⓑ Ⓒ Ⓓ
41. Ⓐ Ⓑ Ⓒ Ⓓ
42. Ⓐ Ⓑ Ⓒ Ⓓ
43. Ⓐ Ⓑ Ⓒ Ⓓ
44. Ⓐ Ⓑ Ⓒ Ⓓ
45. Ⓐ Ⓑ Ⓒ Ⓓ
46. Ⓐ Ⓑ Ⓒ Ⓓ
47. Ⓐ Ⓑ Ⓒ Ⓓ

閱讀診斷測驗

Part 5: Incomplete Sentences

> **Directions:** You will see a sentence with a missing word. Four possible answers follow the sentence. Choose the best answer to the question, and fill in the corresponding oval on your answer sheet.

1. Rice Enterprises _____ some of the most talented design specialists in the field.

    (A) employ
    (B) employs
    (C) employees
    (D) have employed

2. The directors are happy to report that the advertising campaign has been _____ successful.

    (A) huge
    (B) huger
    (C) hugely
    (D) hugeness

3. Procom Industries has announced plans to _____ production by opening up a new manufacturing plant.

    (A) increase
    (B) enlarge
    (C) curtail
    (D) diminish

4. _____ the new restaurant has recently received a lot of attention from the press, business continues to be slow.

   (A) Because
   (B) Therefore
   (C) Although
   (D) Nevertheless

5. All information provided by clients will be kept entirely _____ and will never be shared with anyone outside the office.

   (A) professional
   (B) confidential
   (C) essential
   (D) intact

6. You may use the health club _____ you are employed by this company, but membership eligibility ends if you leave your position.

   (A) in the meantime
   (B) according to
   (C) in order to
   (D) as long as

7. Ms. Yamamoto is in charge of organizing the office party, so please let _____ know if you have any suggestions.

   (A) her
   (B) hers
   (C) she
   (D) herself

8. The sign posted just outside the front door _____ the history and architectural significance of the building.

   (A) recounts
   (B) explains
   (C) instructs
   (D) advises

9. The director had not expected to hear so much _____ to the proposed policy changes.

   (A) opposition
   (B) opponents
   (C) opposing
   (D) opposed

10. The manager asked everyone in the office _____ in the time sheets by noon on Friday.

    (A) turn
    (B) turns
    (C) turning
    (D) to turn

11. He received a job offer from this company, but we don't know _____ he will accept it or turn it down.

    (A) either
    (B) neither
    (C) whether
    (D) however

12. The client is considering the offer and will give us a _____ answer by the end of the week.

    (A) define
    (B) definite
    (C) definitely
    (D) definition

13. You'll notice that the new accounting system is different _____ the old one in several ways.

    (A) to
    (B) for
    (C) than
    (D) from

14. Each table must be _____ cleaned before seating the next group of diners.

    (A) thoroughly
    (B) permanently
    (C) directly
    (D) finally

15. If the client isn't completely satisfied with the terms of the contract, some _____ can be made.

    (A) introductions
    (B) developments
    (C) modifications
    (D) permissions

Part 6: Text Completion

> **Directions:** You will see two passages, each with four sets of blanks. Under each blank are four options. Choose the word or phrase that best completes the statement.

Questions 16–19 refer to the following flyer.

Stellar Professional Training

The following seminar ___(16)___ in your area on April 10: Web page Design. At this all-day seminar for business professionals, interns, and current business students, find out how you can create a web page that presents your business in the most attractive way. The price ___(17)___ lunch and materials as well as instruction. Visit us at *www.stellar.com/seminars* to sign up.

___(18)___ ends March 31. While you are there, take a look at what else we have to offer. ___(19)___ .

We look forward to seeing you at Stellar!

16. (A) offers
    (B) will offer
    (C) will be offered
    (D) will be offering

17. (A) participates
    (B) covers
    (C) accounts
    (D) charges

18. (A) Register
    (B) Registrar
    (C) Registered
    (D) Registration

19. (A) Stellar provides staff training, custom web page design, and more
    (B) You can contact us any time, day or night
    (C) The seminar lasts about seven hours
    (D) Our clients have given our seminars top ratings

Questions 20–23 refer to the following flyer.

> The Springdale Community Center offers services for all members of the Springdale community. ___(20)___ include recreational activities for children, teens, and adults, parenting workshops, arts and crafts classes, a teen drop-in center, and a daycare center. We are ___(21)___ looking for volunteers to help out with any of the above-mentioned programs. Interested people should contact our volunteer ___(22)___, Mabel Rivera (mrivera@commcenter.org), for further information. ___(23)___.

20. (A) These
    (B) There
    (C) Them
    (D) That

21. (A) lately
    (B) probably
    (C) currently
    (D) eventually

22. (A) coordinate
    (B) coordinator
    (C) coordinating
    (D) coordination

23. (A) Please indicate which program you would like to work in
    (B) All our programs are free for Springdale residents
    (C) The next workshop session begins in one week
    (D) Ms. Rivera is a long-time employee of the community center

Part 7: Reading Comprehension

> **Directions:** You will see single and multiple reading passages followed by several questions. Each question has four answer choices. Choose the best answer to the question, and fill in the corresponding oval on your answer sheet.

Questions 24–25 refer to the following email.

To: frank.knockaert@crestco.com
From: grombach@hamburgpaper.com
Subj: re: recent order

Dear Mr. Knockaert,

I sincerely regret the inconvenience caused to you by the error we made in the shipment of your recent order. The additional 1000 cases of all-purpose paper that we neglected to include in the shipment will be sent to you immediately. We will not charge you for that part of your order.

We value our relationship with your company and are very sorry for any difficulties our error may have caused you. You can be assured that this will not happen in the future.

Sincerely,
Gertrude Rombach
Customer Service Specialist
Hamburg Paper Company

24. What is the purpose of the email?
   (A) To place a new order
   (B) To give an apology
   (C) To make a complaint
   (D) To introduce new services

25. What was the problem with the shipment?
   (A) It arrived late.
   (B) It was damaged.
   (C) It was not complete.
   (D) It was sent to the wrong address.

Questions 26–27 refer to the following article.

> September 1, Zurich: RADD, A.G., the Swiss chemical company purchased the European polypropylene business of Royal Chemical Industries, P.L.C., of Britain. No price was disclosed, but RCI said the deal represented 1 to 2 percent of its net assets and would be paid in cash. Based on net assets, the price would be between $100 million and $160 million. The acquisition includes RCI production plants in England, Denmark, Norway, and Poland. The plants alone are valued at $60 million to $80 million. Polypropylene, a tough, flexible plastic, has uses that range from rope fibers to bottles.

26. What is this article mostly about?
    (A) International trade agreements
    (B) The business climate in Europe
    (C) The value of a particular company
    (D) The acquisition of one company by another

27. What does the Royal Chemical Industries company manufacture?
    (A) Different kinds of rope
    (B) Glass beverage bottles
    (C) A type of plastic
    (D) Cotton fabric

Questions 28–30 refer to the following web page.

Grey Valley Bikes

Tour the Grey Valley region by bike. Grey Valley Bikes offers group and self-guided tours of the Grey Valley region year round. We have trips for every kind of cyclist, from leisurely rides along the Grey River to challenging climbs up mountain slopes.

All tours include:

- Hotel accommodations
- Three meals a day
- Luggage transportation
- Complimentary regional map

Bring your own bike or rent one of ours.
Click here for bike rental rates.

Click here to see upcoming tours.
Click here for information about self-guided tours.

Our Top Tours

Hill and Dale Tour
Ride up and down some of the most beautiful slopes of the Grey Mountains.

Poolesville to Fitchburg
Tour the valley's charming villages.

Grey Forest
Ride through the spectacular forestlands of the Grey Valley.

EAT AND RIDE
Each day includes a lunch stop at one of the Valley's famous cafes.

28. What is NOT included in the cost of a tour?
    (A) Hotel
    (B) Food
    (C) Map
    (D) Bicycle

29. What is indicated about Grey Valley Bikes tours?
    (A) They last a week or more.
    (B) They are only for experienced cyclists.
    (C) They are for both individuals and groups.
    (D) They take place in spring and summer only.

30. Which tours are listed on this web page?
    (A) The most popular
    (B) The most difficult
    (C) The most lengthy
    (D) The most expensive

Questions 31–33 refer to the following online chat discussion.

Yoko Ota	9:15
You've ordered the fabric for the shirts, right?	
Anders Larsen	9:15
Yes. 4 bolts of printed cotton.	
Milla Colby	9:16
4 bolts? Didn't we say 6?	
Anders Larsen	9:17
We always order 4 bolts.	
Yoko Ota	9:18
We got an extra order for shirts this time. We need 6 bolts. When did you make the order?	
Anders Larsen	9:20
Yesterday afternoon. But I'm sure they haven't processed it yet. I can call them back.	
Yoko Ota	9:21
Please call them back right away. We can't wait on those extra two bolts.	
Milla Colby	9:21
I've got people lined up to start working on those shirts the minute we get the fabric. We really have to get going on this order.	
Yoko Ota	9:23
Yes. Those shirts have to be on their way by the end of the month.	

31. What kind of business are they involved in?
    (A) Clothing manufacturer
    (B) Fabric wholesaler
    (C) Shipping service
    (D) Shirt retailer

32. What does Anders have to do now?
    (A) Ship the order
    (B) Cancel the order
    (C) Add to the order
    (D) Process the order

33. What does Yoko mean when she writes at 9:23, "Those shirts have to be on their way"?
    (A) The fabric for making shirts has to be available.
    (B) The shirts have to be shipped to the customer.
    (C) The workers have to start making the shirts.
    (D) The designs for the shirts have to be ready.

Questions 34–37 refer to the following article.

> Amy Ann's Kitchen opened its doors just three months ago, but the owner is already talking about expanding. The reason? Business is booming. –[1]– Customers line up daily to buy freshly made bread, cakes, cookies, and other tasty delights at Amy Ann's. –[2]– Owner Amy Ann Anderson is pleased but surprised at the high sales volume. –[3]– In fact, she has brought in close to half that amount in the first quarter alone. –[4]– To keep up with the demand, Anderson says she will need to add at least two ovens and take on extra staff. "I am not sure I can fit all that into my current space," she says. She is looking around the neighborhood for a larger space.

34. What kind of business is Amy Ann's Kitchen?
    (A) Bakery
    (B) Restaurant
    (C) Grocery store
    (D) Kitchen supplies

35. What is indicated about the business?
    (A) It has been around for a long time.
    (B) It is very popular.
    (C) It has high prices.
    (D) Its staff is large.

36. The word "volume" in line 6 of the passage is closest in meaning to
    (A) amount
    (B) loudness
    (C) products
    (D) price

37. In which of the following positions marked [1], [2], [3], and [4] does the following sentence best belong? "She says that she originally hoped to make about $40,000 a year in profits."
    (A) [1]
    (B) [2]
    (C) [3]
    (D) [4]

Questions 38–42 refer to the following notice and memo.

Notice to tenants of South Ridge Office Complex

August 25, 20—

Reconstruction of the parking garage will begin at the end of next month and is scheduled to last three months. During this time there will be no parking for anyone in the building garage. The city has temporarily designated the parking spaces on the streets surrounding our building as all-day parking spaces for our use. A special pass is required to use these spaces. Since the number of parking spaces is limited, we will distribute four passes to each office in this building. Building tenants are asked to encourage their employees to use public transportation until the garage reconstruction is completed. There are also two public parking garages within five blocks of here where parking spaces can be rented on a daily, weekly, or monthly basis. Thank you for your cooperation.

South Ridge Office Complex Building Management Team

Memo
Parrot Communications, Inc.

To: All Office Personnel
From: Dena Degenaro
Office Manager
Date: August 28, 20—
Re: Parking

I am sure you have all seen the recent notice about the parking garage reconstruction by now. Since we have five times as many employees as allotted parking passes, we will reserve the parking passes for clients and ask our employees to make alternative plans. For your convenience, we have obtained subway passes that are valid for the entire amount of time that the garage reconstruction will last. They are available at a 25% discount to all Parrot Communications employees. Please see me before the end of this week if you are interested in getting one. Thank you.

38. When will the parking garage reconstruction begin?
(A) This week
(B) Next month
(C) In three months
(D) In August

39. How many employees work for Parrot Communications, Inc.?
(A) Four
(B) Five
(C) Twenty
(D) Twenty-five

40. Who can park next to the building during the garage reconstruction?
    (A) Parrot Communications clients
    (B) Parrot Communications employees
    (C) All South Ridge tenants
    (D) Dena Degenaro

41. Who should Parrot Communications employees contact to get a subway pass?
    (A) The city manager
    (B) Their office manager
    (C) The building manager
    (D) The subway station manager

42. How long are the subway passes valid?
    (A) One week
    (B) Three weeks
    (C) One month
    (D) Three months

Questions 43–47 refer to the following webpage, email, and article.

www.millsrealty.com

Mills Realty

Count on **Mills Realty** to help YOU find the residential or business property of your dreams.

OFFICES

1. Sunny 2nd floor office space, recently renovated, in small building across from park. Parking lot in rear. Space can be divided into waiting room + office or two smaller offices. Suitable for lawyers, accountants, therapists, health practitioners. Brightwood location. $1250/month + utilities.

2. First floor office suite, convenient downtown location, close to bus lines and subway. 150 sq. meters. Owner will remodel to suit your needs. $2,050/month includes utilities and customer parking.

3. Top floor corner office in the new Brightwood business district. One block from the planned **Brightwood Avenue subway station** Three rooms plus small kitchen. On street parking. $1,000/month, includes utilities.

4. Brightwood office, 100 sq. meters, freshly painted and carpeted. Two rooms. Just one mile from the new Brightwood subway station. On street parking. $950/month + utilities.

To: Steve Mills
From: Elsa Roper
Date: July 25
Subject: Seeking office space

Mr. Mills,

I am interested in seeing some offices advertised on your website. I run a small accounting firm and am looking for a space of about 100–125 square meters. Unfortunately, downtown is a bit out of reach for me, but I think the Brightwood neighborhood would be very suitable. Ideally, I'd like a place with its own parking lot, but if it's close enough to the new subway station, that might not be an issue. I'd like to go no higher than $1,000/month on the rent, expecting to pay utilities on top of that. I'd like to see several of your listings this week, if possible. I am busy most mornings, but I am available any day after 1:00 PM. Please let me know when you can show me these properties.

Elsa Roper, CPA

Brightwood: Up and Coming

The new Brightwood business district is fast becoming the city's hottest new neighborhood. As rapidly rising rents are driving business owners out of the popular downtown area, many are turning to much more affordable Brightwood. This neighborhood has become even more appealing since the city announced plans to extend the subway line to its center. The new Brightwood Avenue subway station is scheduled to open early next year. Already, several offices have opened their doors along Brightwood Avenue and two new restaurants catering specifically to office workers have appeared recently, as well. The beautiful Lilac Park area of the neighborhood, with its wide streets and gardens, is also a draw. Look for a new café and several boutiques to be opening there soon.

43. What is NOT true about the advertised downtown office?
    (A) The rent covers electricity and heat.
    (B) It has recently been remodeled.
    (C) It is near public transportation.
    (D) The building has a parking lot.

44. Which advertised office will Ms. Roper probably prefer?
    (A) #1
    (B) #2
    (C) #3
    (D) #4

45. When does Ms. Roper want to look at offices?
    (A) Any afternoon
    (B) Any morning
    (C) Next week
    (D) Today

46. In the article, the word driving in line 3 is closest in meaning to
    (A) operating
    (B) traveling
    (C) leading
    (D) forcing

47. What is suggested about the Brightwood neighborhood?
    (A) It is less expensive than downtown.
    (B) The streets are not attractive.
    (C) It has a bad reputation.
    (D) The rents are going up.

多益實戰模擬試題

答題訣竅總整理

Part 1：照片描述
- 仔細聽完整個句子的意思，決定哪一個選項最符合照片內容。
- 看照片時先分析當中的人物，決定他們的人數、性別、位置、職業和行動。
- 利用照片情境確認物品和它們的位置。

Part 2：應答問題
- 仔細聆聽問題或陳述的意思後作答，不要被近音字、相關字和同音字混淆。
- 注意聽表示建議、主動提議或要求的語句。

Part 3：簡短對話 & Part 4：簡短獨白
- 學習辨識不同問句類型，以及它們要問什麼，可能是詢問人物的資訊、職業、地點、時間等。
- 了解單字或片語在上下文中的意義。
- 從選項中找出對話或獨白內容的改述。
- 仔細聽出隱含的意義。
- 遇到圖表題時，先將圖表瀏覽一遍，接著注意聆聽對話或獨白中核實圖表資訊或反駁圖表資訊的內容。
- 訓練自己聽懂各國口音。

Part 5：句子填空 & Part 6：段落填空
- 分辨意義相近或形式相近的單字
- 判斷符合語境的正確單字、片語或句子
- 辨識不同的動詞形式
- 辨識不同的形容詞和副詞形式
- 辨識單數和複數名詞
- 辨識不同類型的子句
- 了解介系詞的各種用法

Part 7：閱讀測驗
- 熟練多益測驗不同類型文章的閱讀技巧
- 熟悉多益測驗的各種閱讀題型
- 學會運用 PSRA 策略：預測（Predict）、瀏覽（Scan）、閱讀（Read）、作答（Answer）。

ANSWER SHEET
實戰模擬試題1答案卡

Listening Comprehension

Part 1: Photographs

1. Ⓐ Ⓑ Ⓒ Ⓓ   3. Ⓐ Ⓑ Ⓒ Ⓓ   5. Ⓐ Ⓑ Ⓒ Ⓓ
2. Ⓐ Ⓑ Ⓒ Ⓓ   4. Ⓐ Ⓑ Ⓒ Ⓓ   6. Ⓐ Ⓑ Ⓒ Ⓓ

Part 2: Question-Response

7. Ⓐ Ⓑ Ⓒ   14. Ⓐ Ⓑ Ⓒ   21. Ⓐ Ⓑ Ⓒ   28. Ⓐ Ⓑ Ⓒ
8. Ⓐ Ⓑ Ⓒ   15. Ⓐ Ⓑ Ⓒ   22. Ⓐ Ⓑ Ⓒ   29. Ⓐ Ⓑ Ⓒ
9. Ⓐ Ⓑ Ⓒ   16. Ⓐ Ⓑ Ⓒ   23. Ⓐ Ⓑ Ⓒ   30. Ⓐ Ⓑ Ⓒ
10. Ⓐ Ⓑ Ⓒ   17. Ⓐ Ⓑ Ⓒ   24. Ⓐ Ⓑ Ⓒ   31. Ⓐ Ⓑ Ⓒ
11. Ⓐ Ⓑ Ⓒ   18. Ⓐ Ⓑ Ⓒ   25. Ⓐ Ⓑ Ⓒ
12. Ⓐ Ⓑ Ⓒ   19. Ⓐ Ⓑ Ⓒ   26. Ⓐ Ⓑ Ⓒ
13. Ⓐ Ⓑ Ⓒ   20. Ⓐ Ⓑ Ⓒ   27. Ⓐ Ⓑ Ⓒ

Part 3: Conversations

32. Ⓐ Ⓑ Ⓒ Ⓓ   42. Ⓐ Ⓑ Ⓒ Ⓓ   52. Ⓐ Ⓑ Ⓒ Ⓓ   62. Ⓐ Ⓑ Ⓒ Ⓓ
33. Ⓐ Ⓑ Ⓒ Ⓓ   43. Ⓐ Ⓑ Ⓒ Ⓓ   53. Ⓐ Ⓑ Ⓒ Ⓓ   63. Ⓐ Ⓑ Ⓒ Ⓓ
34. Ⓐ Ⓑ Ⓒ Ⓓ   44. Ⓐ Ⓑ Ⓒ Ⓓ   54. Ⓐ Ⓑ Ⓒ Ⓓ   64. Ⓐ Ⓑ Ⓒ Ⓓ
35. Ⓐ Ⓑ Ⓒ Ⓓ   45. Ⓐ Ⓑ Ⓒ Ⓓ   55. Ⓐ Ⓑ Ⓒ Ⓓ   65. Ⓐ Ⓑ Ⓒ Ⓓ
36. Ⓐ Ⓑ Ⓒ Ⓓ   46. Ⓐ Ⓑ Ⓒ Ⓓ   56. Ⓐ Ⓑ Ⓒ Ⓓ   66. Ⓐ Ⓑ Ⓒ Ⓓ
37. Ⓐ Ⓑ Ⓒ Ⓓ   47. Ⓐ Ⓑ Ⓒ Ⓓ   57. Ⓐ Ⓑ Ⓒ Ⓓ   67. Ⓐ Ⓑ Ⓒ Ⓓ
38. Ⓐ Ⓑ Ⓒ Ⓓ   48. Ⓐ Ⓑ Ⓒ Ⓓ   58. Ⓐ Ⓑ Ⓒ Ⓓ   68. Ⓐ Ⓑ Ⓒ Ⓓ
39. Ⓐ Ⓑ Ⓒ Ⓓ   49. Ⓐ Ⓑ Ⓒ Ⓓ   59. Ⓐ Ⓑ Ⓒ Ⓓ   69. Ⓐ Ⓑ Ⓒ Ⓓ
40. Ⓐ Ⓑ Ⓒ Ⓓ   50. Ⓐ Ⓑ Ⓒ Ⓓ   60. Ⓐ Ⓑ Ⓒ Ⓓ   70. Ⓐ Ⓑ Ⓒ Ⓓ
41. Ⓐ Ⓑ Ⓒ Ⓓ   51. Ⓐ Ⓑ Ⓒ Ⓓ   61. Ⓐ Ⓑ Ⓒ Ⓓ

Part 4: Talks

71. Ⓐ Ⓑ Ⓒ Ⓓ   79. Ⓐ Ⓑ Ⓒ Ⓓ   87. Ⓐ Ⓑ Ⓒ Ⓓ   95. Ⓐ Ⓑ Ⓒ Ⓓ
72. Ⓐ Ⓑ Ⓒ Ⓓ   80. Ⓐ Ⓑ Ⓒ Ⓓ   88. Ⓐ Ⓑ Ⓒ Ⓓ   96. Ⓐ Ⓑ Ⓒ Ⓓ
73. Ⓐ Ⓑ Ⓒ Ⓓ   81. Ⓐ Ⓑ Ⓒ Ⓓ   89. Ⓐ Ⓑ Ⓒ Ⓓ   97. Ⓐ Ⓑ Ⓒ Ⓓ
74. Ⓐ Ⓑ Ⓒ Ⓓ   82. Ⓐ Ⓑ Ⓒ Ⓓ   90. Ⓐ Ⓑ Ⓒ Ⓓ   98. Ⓐ Ⓑ Ⓒ Ⓓ
75. Ⓐ Ⓑ Ⓒ Ⓓ   82. Ⓐ Ⓑ Ⓒ Ⓓ   91. Ⓐ Ⓑ Ⓒ Ⓓ   99. Ⓐ Ⓑ Ⓒ Ⓓ
76. Ⓐ Ⓑ Ⓒ Ⓓ   84. Ⓐ Ⓑ Ⓒ Ⓓ   92. Ⓐ Ⓑ Ⓒ Ⓓ   100. Ⓐ Ⓑ Ⓒ Ⓓ
77. Ⓐ Ⓑ Ⓒ Ⓓ   85. Ⓐ Ⓑ Ⓒ Ⓓ   93. Ⓐ Ⓑ Ⓒ Ⓓ
78. Ⓐ Ⓑ Ⓒ Ⓓ   86. Ⓐ Ⓑ Ⓒ Ⓓ   94. Ⓐ Ⓑ Ⓒ Ⓓ

ANSWER SHEET
實戰模擬試題1答案卡

MODEL TEST 1

Reading Comprehension

Part 5: Incomplete Sentences

101. Ⓐ Ⓑ Ⓒ Ⓓ	109. Ⓐ Ⓑ Ⓒ Ⓓ	117. Ⓐ Ⓑ Ⓒ Ⓓ	125. Ⓐ Ⓑ Ⓒ Ⓓ	
102. Ⓐ Ⓑ Ⓒ Ⓓ	110. Ⓐ Ⓑ Ⓒ Ⓓ	118. Ⓐ Ⓑ Ⓒ Ⓓ	126. Ⓐ Ⓑ Ⓒ Ⓓ	
103. Ⓐ Ⓑ Ⓒ Ⓓ	111. Ⓐ Ⓑ Ⓒ Ⓓ	119. Ⓐ Ⓑ Ⓒ Ⓓ	127. Ⓐ Ⓑ Ⓒ Ⓓ	
104. Ⓐ Ⓑ Ⓒ Ⓓ	112. Ⓐ Ⓑ Ⓒ Ⓓ	120. Ⓐ Ⓑ Ⓒ Ⓓ	128. Ⓐ Ⓑ Ⓒ Ⓓ	
105. Ⓐ Ⓑ Ⓒ Ⓓ	113. Ⓐ Ⓑ Ⓒ Ⓓ	121. Ⓐ Ⓑ Ⓒ Ⓓ	129. Ⓐ Ⓑ Ⓒ Ⓓ	
106. Ⓐ Ⓑ Ⓒ Ⓓ	114. Ⓐ Ⓑ Ⓒ Ⓓ	122. Ⓐ Ⓑ Ⓒ Ⓓ	130. Ⓐ Ⓑ Ⓒ Ⓓ	
107. Ⓐ Ⓑ Ⓒ Ⓓ	115. Ⓐ Ⓑ Ⓒ Ⓓ	123. Ⓐ Ⓑ Ⓒ Ⓓ		
108. Ⓐ Ⓑ Ⓒ Ⓓ	116. Ⓐ Ⓑ Ⓒ Ⓓ	124. Ⓐ Ⓑ Ⓒ Ⓓ		

Part 6: Text Completion

131. Ⓐ Ⓑ Ⓒ Ⓓ	135. Ⓐ Ⓑ Ⓒ Ⓓ	139. Ⓐ Ⓑ Ⓒ Ⓓ	143. Ⓐ Ⓑ Ⓒ Ⓓ	
132. Ⓐ Ⓑ Ⓒ Ⓓ	136. Ⓐ Ⓑ Ⓒ Ⓓ	140. Ⓐ Ⓑ Ⓒ Ⓓ	144. Ⓐ Ⓑ Ⓒ Ⓓ	
133. Ⓐ Ⓑ Ⓒ Ⓓ	137. Ⓐ Ⓑ Ⓒ Ⓓ	141. Ⓐ Ⓑ Ⓒ Ⓓ	145. Ⓐ Ⓑ Ⓒ Ⓓ	
134. Ⓐ Ⓑ Ⓒ Ⓓ	138. Ⓐ Ⓑ Ⓒ Ⓓ	142. Ⓐ Ⓑ Ⓒ Ⓓ	146. Ⓐ Ⓑ Ⓒ Ⓓ	

Part 7: Reading Comprehension

147. Ⓐ Ⓑ Ⓒ Ⓓ	161. Ⓐ Ⓑ Ⓒ Ⓓ	175. Ⓐ Ⓑ Ⓒ Ⓓ	189. Ⓐ Ⓑ Ⓒ Ⓓ	
148. Ⓐ Ⓑ Ⓒ Ⓓ	162. Ⓐ Ⓑ Ⓒ Ⓓ	176. Ⓐ Ⓑ Ⓒ Ⓓ	190. Ⓐ Ⓑ Ⓒ Ⓓ	
149. Ⓐ Ⓑ Ⓒ Ⓓ	163. Ⓐ Ⓑ Ⓒ Ⓓ	177. Ⓐ Ⓑ Ⓒ Ⓓ	191. Ⓐ Ⓑ Ⓒ Ⓓ	
150. Ⓐ Ⓑ Ⓒ Ⓓ	164. Ⓐ Ⓑ Ⓒ Ⓓ	178. Ⓐ Ⓑ Ⓒ Ⓓ	192. Ⓐ Ⓑ Ⓒ Ⓓ	
151. Ⓐ Ⓑ Ⓒ Ⓓ	165. Ⓐ Ⓑ Ⓒ Ⓓ	179. Ⓐ Ⓑ Ⓒ Ⓓ	193. Ⓐ Ⓑ Ⓒ Ⓓ	
152. Ⓐ Ⓑ Ⓒ Ⓓ	166. Ⓐ Ⓑ Ⓒ Ⓓ	180. Ⓐ Ⓑ Ⓒ Ⓓ	194. Ⓐ Ⓑ Ⓒ Ⓓ	
153. Ⓐ Ⓑ Ⓒ Ⓓ	167. Ⓐ Ⓑ Ⓒ Ⓓ	181. Ⓐ Ⓑ Ⓒ Ⓓ	195. Ⓐ Ⓑ Ⓒ Ⓓ	
154. Ⓐ Ⓑ Ⓒ Ⓓ	168. Ⓐ Ⓑ Ⓒ Ⓓ	182. Ⓐ Ⓑ Ⓒ Ⓓ	196. Ⓐ Ⓑ Ⓒ Ⓓ	
155. Ⓐ Ⓑ Ⓒ Ⓓ	169. Ⓐ Ⓑ Ⓒ Ⓓ	183. Ⓐ Ⓑ Ⓒ Ⓓ	197. Ⓐ Ⓑ Ⓒ Ⓓ	
156. Ⓐ Ⓑ Ⓒ Ⓓ	170. Ⓐ Ⓑ Ⓒ Ⓓ	184. Ⓐ Ⓑ Ⓒ Ⓓ	198. Ⓐ Ⓑ Ⓒ Ⓓ	
157. Ⓐ Ⓑ Ⓒ Ⓓ	171. Ⓐ Ⓑ Ⓒ Ⓓ	185. Ⓐ Ⓑ Ⓒ Ⓓ	199. Ⓐ Ⓑ Ⓒ Ⓓ	
158. Ⓐ Ⓑ Ⓒ Ⓓ	172. Ⓐ Ⓑ Ⓒ Ⓓ	186. Ⓐ Ⓑ Ⓒ Ⓓ	200. Ⓐ Ⓑ Ⓒ Ⓓ	
159. Ⓐ Ⓑ Ⓒ Ⓓ	173. Ⓐ Ⓑ Ⓒ Ⓓ	187. Ⓐ Ⓑ Ⓒ Ⓓ		
160. Ⓐ Ⓑ Ⓒ Ⓓ	174. Ⓐ Ⓑ Ⓒ Ⓓ	188. Ⓐ Ⓑ Ⓒ Ⓓ		

實戰模擬試題 1

Listening Comprehension

In this section of the test, you will have the chance to show how well you understand spoken English. There are four parts to this section, with special directions for each part. You will have approximately 45 minutes to complete the Listening Comprehension sections.

Part 1: Photographs

DIRECTIONS: You will see a photograph. You will hear four statements about the photograph. Choose the statement that most closely matches the photograph, and fill in the corresponding oval on your answer sheet.

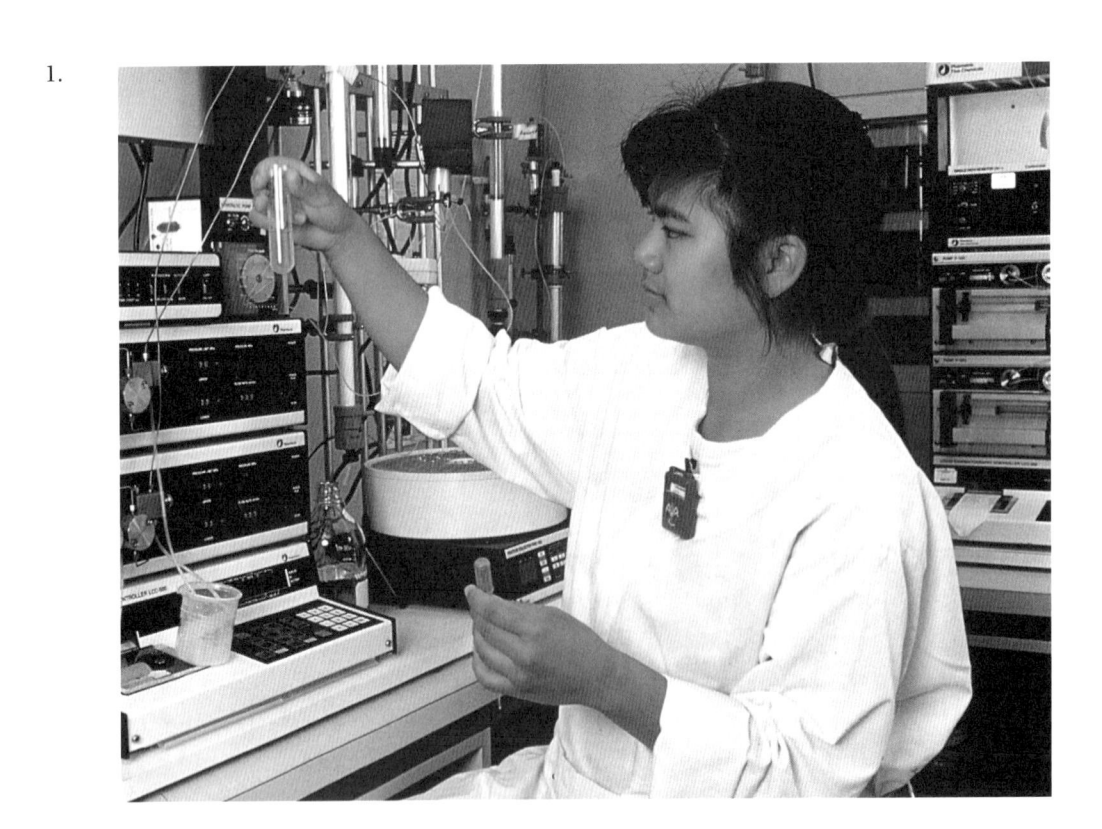

Track 35

1.

2.

3.

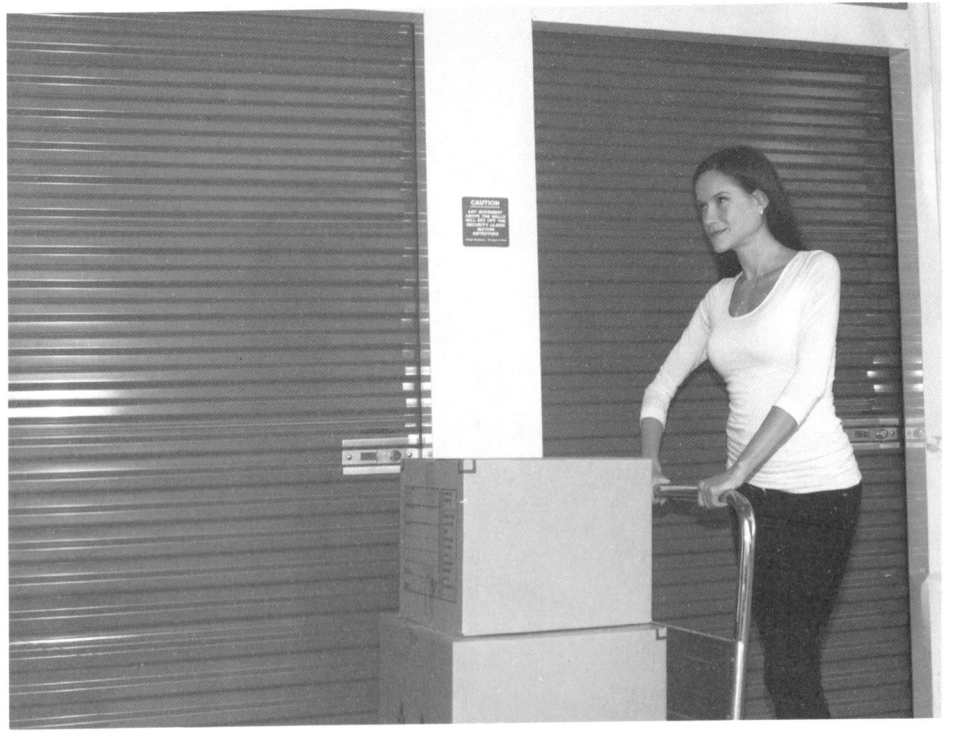

4.

5.

6.

Part 2: Question-Response

DIRECTIONS: You will hear a question and three possible responses. Choose the response that most closely answers the question, and fill in the corresponding oval on your answer sheet.

Track 36

7. Mark your answer on your answer sheet.
8. Mark your answer on your answer sheet.
9. Mark your answer on your answer sheet.
10. Mark your answer on your answer sheet.
11. Mark your answer on your answer sheet.
12. Mark your answer on your answer sheet.
13. Mark your answer on your answer sheet.
14. Mark your answer on your answer sheet.
15. Mark your answer on your answer sheet.
16. Mark your answer on your answer sheet.
17. Mark your answer on your answer sheet.
18. Mark your answer on your answer sheet.
19. Mark your answer on your answer sheet.
20. Mark your answer on your answer sheet.
21. Mark your answer on your answer sheet.
22. Mark your answer on your answer sheet.
23. Mark your answer on your answer sheet.
24. Mark your answer on your answer sheet.
25. Mark your answer on your answer sheet.
26. Mark your answer on your answer sheet.
27. Mark your answer on your answer sheet.
28. Mark your answer on your answer sheet.
29. Mark your answer on your answer sheet.
30. Mark your answer on your answer sheet.
31. Mark your answer on your answer sheet.

Part 3: Conversations

DIRECTIONS: You will hear a conversation between two or more people. You will see three questions on each conversation and four possible answers. Choose the best answer to each question, and fill in the corresponding oval on your answer sheet.

Track 37

32. When will the speakers meet?
    (A) Before lunch
    (B) At 2:00
    (C) After the conference
    (D) Tomorrow

33. Where will they meet?
    (A) At the bus stop
    (B) Downstairs
    (C) In the man's office
    (D) In the waiting room

34. What will the woman bring to the meeting?
    (A) Coffee
    (B) A letter
    (C) Photographs
    (D) Copies of a report

35. What does the man want to do?
    (A) Sell his apartment
    (B) Rent an apartment
    (C) Clean his apartment
    (D) Remodel his apartment

36. What does the woman imply about downtown apartments?
    (A) They cost more than other apartments.
    (B) There aren't many available right now.
    (C) Few people want to rent them.
    (D) They are not very large.

37. What does the woman suggest the man do?
    (A) Meet her at the library
    (B) Call back later
    (C) Look online
    (D) Visit her office

38. Where does this conversation take place?
    (A) At a store
    (B) At a hotel
    (C) At a restaurant
    (D) At the man's house

39. What does the man ask for?
    (A) Keys
    (B) More soup
    (C) A better room
    (D) Towels and soap

40. What does the woman mean when she says, "Not a bit"?
    (A) She does not mind helping the man.
    (B) She does not like her job.
    (C) She does not have what the man asked for.
    (D) She does not have time to help the man right now.

41. When did the brochures arrive?
    (A) Yesterday afternoon
    (B) Last night
    (C) This morning
    (D) This afternoon

42. What will Mary do now?
    (A) Prepare the address labels
    (B) Work on a presentation
    (C) Read the brochures
    (D) Call the printer

43. What does Jim offer to do?
    (A) Take the brochures to the post office
    (B) Drive Mary to her home
    (C) Look up some addresses
    (D) Phone customers

309

44. What kind of job is the man probably applying for?

   (A) Waiter
   (B) Chef
   (C) Newspaper editor
   (D) Advertising executive

45. What does the woman ask the man about?

   (A) His work experience
   (B) His education
   (C) His food preferences
   (D) His salary requirements

46. What does the man want to know?

   (A) The exact job title
   (B) The start date of the job
   (C) The woman's address
   (D) The name of the woman's company

47. Why can't the man play golf tomorrow?

   (A) His wife is sick.
   (B) It's going to rain.
   (C) He has to take a test.
   (D) He's feeling tired.

48. What does the man mean when he says, "What a bore"?

   (A) He does not like making phone calls.
   (B) He is looking for some entertainment.
   (C) He is sorry that he has to cancel the golf game.
   (D) He thinks golf is not an interesting game.

49. What will he do tomorrow?

   (A) Talk on the phone
   (B) Go to the movies
   (C) Move some furniture
   (D) Stay home

50. Where does the woman want to go?

   (A) To a fast food restaurant
   (B) To a parking lot
   (C) To a bank
   (D) To a park

51. Where is this place located?

   (A) On a corner
   (B) Behind a parking lot
   (C) Next door to a library
   (D) Across the street from a store

52. What does the man say about this place?

   (A) The woman will not be able to park there.
   (B) Most people are not familiar with it.
   (C) It is not very far away.
   (D) It may be difficult to find.

53. What does Jane imply about Sam?

   (A) He does not like to wait.
   (B) He is not a good driver.
   (C) He is a hard worker.
   (D) He is usually late.

54. How did Sam get to work this morning?

   (A) By bus
   (B) On foot
   (C) In a carpool
   (D) By subway

55. What will Sam do next time?

   (A) Stay home
   (B) Drive his car
   (C) Leave earlier
   (D) Take the train

56. What is probably the purpose of the woman's trip?

  (A) To visit family
  (B) To take a class
  (C) To interview for a job
  (D) To meet with business colleagues

57. What does the man say about the trip?

  (A) It is expensive.
  (B) It is too long.
  (C) It will be fun.
  (D) It will be uncomfortable.

58. How will the woman pay for the trip?

  (A) Cash
  (B) Check
  (C) Credit card
  (D) Money order

59. Where is Joe?

  (A) Away on a business trip
  (B) In the break room
  (C) In his office
  (D) At the airport

60. What does the woman want Joe to do?

  (A) Write a check
  (B) Look at a report
  (C) Meet her for lunch
  (D) Make photocopies

61. When will Joe return?

  (A) Later this afternoon
  (B) Tomorrow
  (C) At 10:00
  (D) By 12:00

62. Why doesn't the woman want to eat at the cafeteria?

  (A) She does not like the food.
  (B) She does not have time.
  (C) It is too expensive.
  (D) It is too far away.

63. What does the woman ask the man to do for her?

  (A) Bring her a sandwich
  (B) Mail a package
  (C) Pick up her mail
  (D) Go to the mall

64. What will the man do after lunch?

  (A) Take a walk
  (B) Meet with a client
  (C) Go to his apartment
  (D) Go to a doctor's appointment

Trains to Brookfield

Lv.	Arr.
10:20	12:40
11:20	1:40
11:55	2:15
1:55	4:15

65. What does the woman plan to do tomorrow morning?

  (A) Go shopping
  (B) Look for work
  (C) Plan a vacation
  (D) Attend a workshop

66. Who is George, most likely?

  (A) A travel agent
  (B) A workshop presenter
  (C) The woman's assistant
  (D) The woman's husband

67. Look at the graphic. What time will the woman take the train?

  (A) 10:20
  (B) 11:20
  (C) 11:55
  (D) 1:55

Downtown Café

Soups
Chicken and Rice
Carrot Beef
Lamb and Barley
Garden Vegetable

68. What does the man say about the café?

   (A) It is new.
   (B) It is small.
   (C) It is popular.
   (D) It is well known.

69. Look at the graphic. Which soup will the woman order?

   (A) Chicken and Rice
   (B) Carrot Beef
   (C) Lamb and Barley
   (D) Garden Vegetable

70. Where does the man want to eat his lunch?

   (A) Inside the café
   (B) On the patio
   (C) At his office
   (D) At the park

Part 4: Talks

DIRECTIONS: You will hear a talk given by a single speaker. You will see three questions on each talk, each with four possible answers. Choose the best answer to each question, and fill in the corresponding oval on your answer sheet.

Track 38

71. Where is this train located?

    (A) In an airport
    (B) In a city
    (C) Along the coast
    (D) At an amusement park

72. Where should you stand when in a train car?

    (A) By the doors
    (B) By the windows
    (C) In the center
    (D) At either end

73. When can passengers get off the train?

    (A) When they see an exit sign
    (B) Before the bell rings
    (C) After the bell rings
    (D) After the colored light goes on

74. When on Sundays is the museum open?

    (A) In the morning
    (B) In the afternoon
    (C) In the evening
    (D) All day

75. What is the lecture series probably about?

    (A) Sculpture
    (B) Museum administration
    (C) Local history
    (D) How to photograph art

76. Who doesn't have to pay to enter the museum?

    (A) Members
    (B) Adults over 65
    (C) Children under twelve
    (D) Children under five

77. What does the speaker mean when he says, "You are not alone"?

    (A) Some people work better by themselves.
    (B) Most people need help to solve problems.
    (C) Lonely people often have trouble with organization.
    (D) Many people have difficulty organizing their day.

78. What is the first step in getting organized?

    (A) Set a timeline
    (B) Get clutter out of your life
    (C) Buy a calendar
    (D) Make a list of things to be done

79. What is the last task of the day?

    (A) Review the list
    (B) Finish uncompleted tasks
    (C) Write a new list
    (D) Throw the list away

80. What is being advertised?

    (A) A new learning system
    (B) A job for professional teachers
    (C) An opportunity to help children
    (D) A special training program

81. What are listeners asked to do?

    (A) Fill out an application
    (B) Visit an office
    (C) Contact a school
    (D) Complete their schoolwork

82. What must people have to participate?

    (A) A college degree
    (B) Special training
    (C) Age of at least 18
    (D) Experience with children

83. What does the speaker imply when she says, "... it's about time"?

    (A) The weather report will be longer than usual.
    (B) The weather depends on the time of day.
    (C) The weather has been bad for a while.
    (D) The weather is nicer at this time of year.

84. What does the speaker suggest?

    (A) Stay inside
    (B) Go outdoors
    (C) Take sunglasses
    (D) Wear a sweater

85. What will the weather be like tomorrow?

    (A) Cloudy
    (B) Foggy
    (C) Rainy
    (D) Sunny

86. Why did the speaker make the call?

    (A) To inquire about ski lessons
    (B) To make a hotel reservation
    (C) To reserve a pair of rental skis
    (D) To find out the snow conditions

87. How does the speaker plan to get to the hotel?

    (A) By bus
    (B) By car
    (C) By train
    (D) By plane

88. What does the speaker imply about the hotel?

    (A) He often recommends it to his friends.
    (B) It is more expensive than other hotels.
    (C) He has never been there before.
    (D) It is in a popular area.

89. What are Greenville residents complaining about?

    (A) A new mall
    (B) The cost of living
    (C) Traffic regulations
    (D) A construction delay

90. Where are they making their complaint?

    (A) On neighborhood streets
    (B) In the newspaper
    (C) On TV
    (D) At City Hall

91. What will the mayor do later this week?

    (A) Visit the construction site
    (B) Meet with protesters
    (C) Announce new plans
    (D) Go shopping

92. When is this talk happening?

    (A) At the end of class
    (B) In the middle of class
    (C) At the beginning of class
    (D) Before class starts

93. What should be done before the next class?

    (A) Take a test
    (B) Read a chapter
    (C) Talk to Dr. Lyons
    (D) Answer a question

94. What kind of class is this, most likely?

    (A) Photography
    (B) Museum studies
    (C) Mathematics
    (D) Drawing

The Coleman Company
Prices

1 room.................................$50

2–3 rooms..........................$75

4 rooms...............................$100

5+ rooms............................$125

95. What kind of business is the Coleman Company, most likely?

   (A) House painters
   (B) Carpet installers
   (C) Furniture sales
   (D) House cleaners

96. Look at the graphic. How much will the speaker pay for Coleman's services?

   (A) $50
   (B) $75
   (C) $100
   (D) $125

97. What does the speaker plan to do with her apartment?

   (A) Sell it
   (B) Live in it
   (C) Rent it out
   (D) Redecorate it

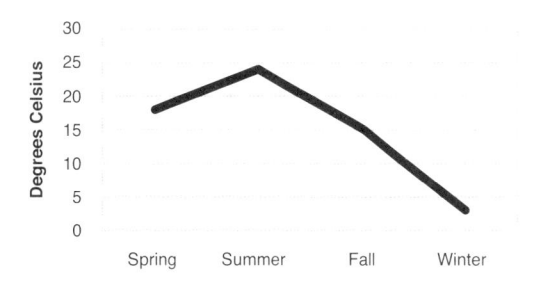

98. What kind of business is being discussed?

   (A) Hotel
   (B) Travel agency
   (C) Advertising agency
   (D) Swimming equipment

99. Look at the graphic. At what time of year is the company busiest?

   (A) Spring
   (B) Summer
   (C) Winter
   (D) Fall

100. What are listeners asked to do next?

   (A) Create a slide
   (B) Ask questions
   (C) Write something
   (D) Talk with a partner

This is the end of the Listening Comprehension portion of the test.
STOP Turn to Part 5 in your test book.

Reading Comprehension

In this section of the test, you will have the chance to show how well you understand written English. There are three parts to this section, with special directions for each part.

**YOU WILL HAVE ONE HOUR AND FIFTEEN MINUTES
TO COMPLETE PARTS 5, 6, AND 7 OF THE TEST.**

Part 5: Incomplete Sentences

> **DIRECTIONS:** You will see a sentence with a missing word. Four possible answers follow the sentence. Choose the best answer to the question, and fill in the corresponding oval on your answer sheet.

101. If the customer _____ not satisfied, please have him call the manager.
    (A) am
    (B) is
    (C) are
    (D) be

102. We _____ him to think things over carefully before agreeing to accept the new position.
    (A) recommended
    (B) suggested
    (C) proposed
    (D) advised

103. Our boss plans to _____ a party in her home for several staff members who will retire this year.
    (A) entertain
    (B) invite
    (C) host
    (D) guest

104. The seminar was canceled because the invitations were not _____ in time.
    (A) printer
    (B) printed
    (C) printing
    (D) print

105. If the waiter cannot handle your request, the captain _____ assist you.
    (A) will
    (B) has
    (C) did
    (D) is

106. Mr. Wong has been recognized by the local business community for his knowledge and _____.
    (A) leading
    (B) lead
    (C) leadership
    (D) leader

107. According to the most recent figures, our costs are expected to _____ by about five percent this year.
    (A) ascend
    (B) increase
    (C) escalate
    (D) raise

108. Any good business manager will tell you that _____ is the key to efficiency.
    (A) organized
    (B) organize
    (C) organizer
    (D) organization

316

109. They had to postpone the meeting with the client _____ Mr. Tan's plane was late.

    (A) although
    (B) while
    (C) because
    (D) with

110. Any information that a client provides us with will be kept completely _____ and not shared with anyone outside the office.

    (A) considerable
    (B) confidential
    (C) constructed
    (D) conferred

111. By the time Mr. Sato _____ in San Diego, the convention will have already begun.

    (A) arrives
    (B) arrived
    (C) has arrived
    (D) will arrive

112. Because Ms. Kimura has a long _____, she will always leave work at 5:30.

    (A) commute
    (B) commune
    (C) community
    (D) compost

113. You'll find the restaurant on the next block, _____ the bank and the bookstore.

    (A) among
    (B) outside
    (C) between
    (D) through

114. We hope to begin interviewing _____ applicants by the end of next week.

    (A) job
    (B) occupation
    (C) chore
    (D) positioning

115. When you need supplies, _____ a request with the office manager.

    (A) filling
    (B) fell
    (C) fallen
    (D) file

116. All cabin attendants must lock the cabin door _____ leaving the room.

    (A) afterwards
    (B) after
    (C) later than
    (D) late

117. _____ it was Mr. Guiton's birthday, his staff took him to lunch.

    (A) Although
    (B) During
    (C) Because
    (D) That

118. In order to respect our guests' privacy, employees at the Palms Hotel are _____ to knock before entering rooms for any reason.

    (A) requited
    (B) required
    (C) requisite
    (D) repulsed

119. The billing clerk was not able to find the invoice _____ the order.

    (A) or
    (B) and
    (C) but
    (D) though

120. Before he wrote the check, Jim visited his bank's website to find out his account _____.

    (A) size
    (B) money
    (C) supply
    (D) balance

121. Please forward a copy of the report to Mr. Maxwell as soon as it becomes _____.

    (A) avail
    (B) available
    (C) availability
    (D) availing

122. The bell captain suggested that more porters _____ hired.

    (A) are
    (B) have
    (C) be
    (D) do

123. The _____ parking spaces for company employees are located on the first level of the parking garage.

    (A) signed
    (B) assignment
    (C) assigned
    (D) significant

124. You'll find all the association members listed in the directory in _____ order.

    (A) alphabet
    (B) alphabetize
    (C) alphabetically
    (D) alphabetical

125. Raymond has been working on that account for just a few days, but he is _____ completely familiar with the client's background.

    (A) yet
    (B) since
    (C) already
    (D) soon

126. Everyone seeking entry to the premises must _____ an identification card to the security guard.

    (A) showed
    (B) showing
    (C) shows
    (D) show

127. According to several studies, _____ tasks often lead to muscular fatigue and injury.

    (A) repeat
    (B) repetitive
    (C) repetition
    (D) repetitively

128. Visitors are reminded _____ name tags at all times.

    (A) to wear
    (B) wear
    (C) be worn
    (D) is wearing

129. The position in the publicity department requires knowledge of foreign languages and _____ experience with international clients.

    (A) exciting
    (B) expectant
    (C) exquisite
    (D) extensive

130. The factory's policy is that visitors are _____ allowed to enter the manufacturing area without hard hats, for safety reasons.

    (A) rare
    (B) ever
    (C) never
    (D) no time

Part 6: Text Completion

DIRECTIONS: You will see four passages, each with four blanks. Each blank has four answer choices. For each blank, choose the word, phrase, or sentence that best completes the passage.

Questions 131–134 refer to the following notice.

International Airport Policy Regarding Security and Baggage

In accordance with international security regulations, passengers are not ___(131)___ to take the following items onto a plane, either in carry-on bags or in checked luggage: weapons of any kind, dynamite, or fireworks.

The following items may be placed in checked luggage but not in carry-on bags: Tools, including hammers, screwdrivers, and wrenches; sports equipment ___(132)___ golf clubs, baseball bats, and skis and ski poles. When you pass through the ___(133)___ line, all bags will go through our X-ray machines. ___(134)___.

Thank you for your cooperation. Have a safe and pleasant flight.

131. (A) permitted
 (B) permitting
 (C) permits
 (D) permission

132. (A) so
 (B) such as
 (C) example
 (D) instance

133. (A) ticket
 (B) arrival
 (C) security
 (D) reservations

134. (A) These machines are delicate and very costly
 (B) Check with your airline about size limits for bags
 (C) Most airlines allow just one carry-on bag per person
 (D) Some bags will be manually checked by personnel, as well

319

Questions 135–138 refer to the following magazine article.

This holiday season, computer retailers hope to increase sales of tablet computers. A heavy advertising campaign began this week, with several computer _____ placing ads on TV, radio, newspapers, and the internet. The advertising campaign will continue through the holiday season.

Tablet computers are gaining popularity because of their _____. Because they are lighter and smaller than laptops, they are much easier to carry around and are filling a growing need for mobility. _____.

The trend toward giving electronic items as holiday gifts is also growing. The old-fashioned approach to holiday celebrations is giving way to the _____ for new technology.

135. (A) manufacturers
 (B) purchasers
 (C) consumers
 (D) trainers

136. (A) fame
 (B) quantity
 (C) appearance
 (D) convenience

137. (A) Some people find them difficult to use because of the small screens
 (B) An additional benefit is that they cost less than most laptops
 (C) Laptops continue to be popular, however, in many areas
 (D) They can be connected to keyboards and printers

138. (A) enthusiast
 (B) enthusiasm
 (C) enthusiastic
 (D) enthusiastically

Questions 139–142 refer to the following email.

To: Marguerite Michelson
From: Ambar Patel
Date: September 22, 20—
Subject: Money due

I am writing in regard to _____ payment. We sent an invoice in July but still have not
                                139
received a check. _____. If we don't hear from you soon regarding this payment, we
                   140
_____ to take action. Please contact me by phone before the end of the week, so we can
141
discuss how best to resolve this matter. The details of your _____, including items and
                                                              142
prices, are attached.

---

139. (A) a remitted
     (B) an overdue
     (C) a transferrable
     (D) an enclosed

140. (A) Payment by credit card is also acceptable
     (B) We hope you were satisfied with our services
     (C) Please be sure to make the check out in the correct amount
     (D) Our phone messages inquiring about the reason for the delay have not been answered

141. (A) will have
     (B) have had
     (C) would have
     (D) going to have

142. (A) form
     (B) credit
     (C) order
     (D) rebate

Questions 143–146 refer to the following email.

From: Andrew Devon
Subject: Office Manager Position
Date: April 1
To: Richard Byron

Dear Mr. Byron,

I am contacting you in _____ to the job posted on your company's website for an office manager. _____ . I feel that I thoroughly understand the operations of an office, and that my years of experience _____ me to work as an office manager. I have good organizational and people skills, and I am familiar with most current office technology. I am also a responsible and reliable worker. I am enclosing my resume and two letters of reference.

I look forward _____ hearing from you.

Sincerely,
Andrew Devon

---

143. (A) response
 (B) repose
 (C) resort
 (D) respite

144. (A) Office managers are essential to the smooth running of an office
 (B) As part of my job search, I look at job listings on the internet almost daily
 (C) I would be interested in knowing more about the duties of an office manager at your company
 (D) I have worked as an administrative assistant at a local company for the past ten years

145. (A) qualify
 (B) qualifies
 (C) is qualifying
 (D) has qualified

146. (A) at
 (B) of
 (C) to
 (D) on

322

Part 7: Reading Comprehension

DIRECTIONS: You will see single and multiple reading passages followed by several questions. Each question has four answer choices. Choose the best answer to the question, and fill in the corresponding oval on your answer sheet.

Questions 147–148 refer to the following invoice.

```
Cooper & Allen, Architects          April 5, 20__
149 Bridge Street, Suite 107        INVOICE NUMBER  3892
Harrisville, Colorado 76521         PROJECT NAME    Headquarters-Final Design
                                    PROJECT NUMBER  925639

The Williams Corporation
5110 Falls Avenue
Thomaston, Colorado 76520

The following amounts for the period ending March 30 are due the end of
this month.
                            Current period fees   $8,200.00
                            Unpaid prior balance    $362.00
                            Total due at this time $8,562.00

We value the opportunity to service you. Your prompt payment is greatly
appreciated.
```

147. When is the payment due?

   (A) March 1
   (B) March 30
   (C) April 5
   (D) April 30

148. What is owed in addition to current fees?

   (A) Prepayment on the next project
   (B) Taxes on the current fees
   (C) Service charges on current fees
   (D) Money not paid on a previous invoice

Questions 149–150 refer to the following notice.

The company provides a pension plan covering all employees with a minimum of five years of service at the company. Payments are based on years of service and the highest salary level reached. Both the company and the employee make contributions to the plan monthly, the amount determined by government regulations. Pension payments are made bimonthly.

149. What is the notice about?

   (A) A job promotion plan
   (B) A retirement benefit
   (C) A loan program
   (D) A salary scale

150. Who is eligible to participate?

   (A) Employees with at least five years at the company
   (B) Employees earning a certain salary level
   (C) Government employees only
   (D) Any company employee

Questions 151-152 refer to the following text message chain.

SAM CHAN	9:10
Where are you? We're about to go into the meeting.	
PAT LOPEZ	9:11
Sorry. I'm stuck on the train.	
SAM CHAN	9:13
Where?	
PAT LOPEZ	9:14
I just left Middlebury. Apparently there was an accident near the bridge. All the trains are running late.	
PAT LOPEZ	1:16
I made sure to leave home early, but that didn't help.	
SAM CHAN	1:17
The client is already here.	
PAT LOPEZ	1:18
Go ahead and start without me. I should be there in 30 minutes.	
SAM CHAN	1:20
I'd rather not present the proposal alone.	
PAT LOPEZ	1:21
You'll do fine. Just start with the slide show.	
SAM CHAN	1:22
OK. But hurry. We really want to please this client. It's one of our biggest accounts.	
PAT LOPEZ	1:23
You're telling me! I'll be there soon.	

151. Why is Ms. Lopez late for the meeting?

    (A) Sam didn't remind her about the meeting.
    (B) She didn't leave home on time.
    (C) The train has been delayed.
    (D) She took the wrong train.

152. At 1:23, what does Ms. Lopez mean when she writes, "You're telling me!"?

    (A) She understands how important the client is.
    (B) She doesn't know what to say to the client.
    (C) She doesn't like Sam to give her orders.
    (D) She wants Sam to tell her what to do.

Questions 153–154 refer to the following announcement.

> We're changing our name! We are excited to announce that effective December 5, 20--, our official name will be:
>
> ### GREEN MILES WEST
>
> The substitution of "West" in our name—replacing "California"—is the result of an agreement we reached with the California Gardening Association, following a protest over the original use of "California" in our name.
>
> We hope this does not create any confusion among our loyal consumers. While this represents a change from our initial name introduction, it does not change the quality of products we offer our customers.

153. What was the original name of the company?

   (A) Miles West
   (B) Green Miles California
   (C) Green Miles West
   (D) Green California

154. According to the announcement, why was the name changed?

   (A) The corporate offices were relocated.
   (B) There was a conflict with another organization.
   (C) They did not like the initial choice.
   (D) Loyal consumers were confused.

Questions 155–157 refer to the following webpage.

---

www.palmfrondsresort.com

File   Edit   View   Favorites   Tools   Help

[HOME]   [ABOUT]   [ROOMS]   [ACTIVITIES]   [FAQ]

Palm Fronds Resort

The Palm Fronds Resort is pleased to welcome you and your entire family to a relaxing, fun-filled vacation with us. We offer spacious, comfortable rooms, fine dining, and a private beach. You can enjoy a range of beach and water sports, or just relax and enjoy the peace and quiet away from the hustle and bustle of the city.

Our all-inclusive vacation package for groups of up to four people includes

- An elegant two-room suite that sleeps four comfortably
- Breakfast and dinner daily
- Beach access
- Pool access

We offer on-site equipment rental for snorkeling, scuba diving, surfing, and tennis. **Click here** for prices.

Our world-class instructors are available for private and group lessons. **Click here** for fee schedule.

How to get here

The nearest airport is located on the mainland in Palm City. From there, you can take a shuttle or taxi to the ferry dock. **Click here** for ferry schedules.

---

155. Where is the Palm Fronds Resort probably located?

    (A) In a city
    (B) On an island
    (C) Next to an airport
    (D) On a mountain

156. What is included in the vacation package?

    (A) Transportation from the airport
    (B) Swimming lessons
    (C) Two meals a day
    (D) Sports equipment

157. Which one of the following activities can guests do at the resort?

    (A) Go fishing
    (B) Rent a bicycle
    (C) Go swimming
    (D) Take cooking lessons

Questions 158–160 refer to the following email.

From: Alan Scheider
To: All Staff
Subj: Answering your questions
Date: September 2

Everyday my inbox is full of messages concerning the transfer to the Paris office. Rather than responding to each of you individually, I am explaining the process here. Please follow the directions below and do not omit anything. And please refrain from asking me more questions. Everything you need to know is explained below.

- Pack all items in and on your desk in boxes.
- Label all boxes clearly with your name and department.
- Notify maintenance to clean your desk so it will be ready for the next occupant.
- Change the outgoing message in your voicemail to notify clients of your transfer.
- Provide the network manager with your old password and computer ID number.
- Notify clients by email of your new location and contact information.

Packing supplies are available for your use. Please ask Ms. Quimby for any supplies you need.

Thank you for your cooperation.
Alan

---

158. What is the purpose of the email?

 (A) To propose procedures for layoffs
 (B) To announce the opening of a Paris office
 (C) To give instructions for preparing to move
 (D) To suggest ways to improve workspace organization

159. What are the email recipients asked to do?

 (A) Buy their own packing supplies
 (B) Complete every one of the steps
 (C) Email their questions to Mr. Scheider
 (D) Help colleagues pack up their workspaces

160. What should each employee do for the person who will use his desk next?

 (A) Move boxes to the edge of the room
 (B) Notify clients of the new occupant
 (C) Get a computer password
 (D) Have the desk cleaned

Questions 161-163 refer to the following article.

MEETINGS

People often feel that staff meetings are a waste of time. However, by keeping the following points in mind, you can make sure your meetings run smoothly and use time well. Every meeting should have an agenda. –[1]– This seems obvious, and yet it is a detail so often overlooked. Think about what items need to be covered and how much time should be allocated to each. Make sure everyone has a copy, so they know what to expect. –[2]– As each item is discussed, keep the conversation moving. Thank each speaker for her ideas, then move on to the next speaker. –[3]– This encourages people to keep their remarks brief. When the time allocated for a specific item has passed, move the discussion on to the next item. –[4]– Your staff will feel that their time has been used well. They will return to work with fresh ideas and energy.

161. What is this article mostly about?

(A) How to run a meeting efficiently
(B) Different formats for staff meetings
(C) Reasons for having regular staff meetings
(D) Ways to make a meeting more interesting

162. What is said about speaking in a meeting?

(A) People should be allowed to comment as often as they like.
(B) Everyone should be encouraged to make comments.
(C) Comments should be about agenda items only.
(D) People should keep their comments short.

163. In which of the following positions marked [1], [2], [3], and [4] does the following sentence best belong?

"By keeping on schedule, you can ensure that the meeting will end on time."

(A) [1]
(B) [2]
(C) [3]
(D) [4]

Questions 164–167 refer to the following online chat discussion.

Silvia Prieto [1:15]
I just had a phone call from the caterers. Since we want lunch to start at 12:00, they want to start setting up at 11:00.

George Croft [1:16]
That shouldn't be a problem. They can set up in the large conference room. The trainers said the other conference room would work for them.

Marcella Lu [1:17]
Has anyone reserved the conference rooms yet?

George Croft [1:18]
Yes. I did that yesterday. It's all set.

Marcella Lu [1:19]
And the tables and chairs? The projector?

George Croft [1:21]
I've taken care of everything.

Silvia Prieto [1:22]
I also received an email from the trainers this morning with some documents attached. They want each participant to have copies for the morning session.

Marcella Lu [1:23]
I can take care of that. Do we know yet how many of the staff have signed up?

George Croft [1:25]
I have the sign up sheet. Twenty. It's full.

Marcella Lu [1:26]
Fantastic. I'll take care of those copies now. You arranged for enough chairs, right? George?

George Croft [1:27]
Relax. I have it all under control.

---

164. What kind of event are the chatters organizing, most likely?

    (A) An awards banquet
    (B) A weekly staff meeting
    (C) An association conference
    (D) A professional development workshop

165. What did Ms. Prieto do a few minutes ago?

    (A) She spoke with the caterers.
    (B) She sent an email to the trainers.
    (C) She reserved the conference rooms.
    (D) She created some documents.

166. What will Ms. Lu probably do next?

    (A) Count the participants
    (B) Go to George's office
    (C) Make photocopies
    (D) Arrange the chairs

167. At 1:27, what does Mr. Croft mean when he writes, "Relax"?

    (A) Ms. Lu should take a break.
    (B) Ms. Lu can sit in the chairs.
    (C) Ms. Lu has no need to worry.
    (D) Ms. Lu's job is not very hard.

329

Questions 168-171 refer to the following article.

-[1]- ABC Foods Corporation has reported that it is planning to raise prices by an average of 3 percent on 19 different brands of fruit cakes, pies, and other fruit-based sweets. -[2]- The company claims that this is the result of higher fruit prices resulting from the combination of a late freeze and a long drought last spring.

ABC Foods Corporation products with the higher prices will hit the supermarket shelves early next month. Other companies are expected to follow suit and raise prices on their canned fruit and vegetable products by the end of the year. -[3]- Consumers can expect to feel the effects in their pocketbooks throughout the winter.

-[4]- "We can only hope that the weather will improve in the next growing season," said Louella Pearson, president of Consumers United. "If not, and if prices continue to rise, some families will really suffer," she added.

168. On which ABC food products will prices rise?

    (A) Canned vegetables
    (B) All brands of food
    (C) Jams and jellies
    (D) Fruit desserts

169. What is the cause of the rise in price of fruit?

    (A) Poor growing conditions
    (B) Increased consumer spending
    (C) Competition from other companies
    (D) Demand for more money by farmers

170. What will probably happen before next year?

    (A) The weather will improve.
    (B) There will be more price increases.
    (C) Consumers will demand more fruit.
    (D) More varieties of canned products will be available.

171. In which of the following positions marked [1], [2], [3], and [4] does the following sentence best belong?

    "This is the second increase by ABC Foods this year."

    (A) [1]
    (B) [2]
    (C) [3]
    (D) [4]

Questions 172–175 refer to the following article.

Many hotels these days are changing their wasteful habits. For example, it is not unusual for hotel guests to find shampoo in glass dispensers instead of plastic bottles, or for hotels to encourage guests to use towels and sheets more than once before they are washed.

And it is not just the hotels. It is often the tourists themselves who seek out a "greener" way to vacation. The business of eco-tours—guided vacations with an environmental focus—is growing exponentially. Expeditions to the Amazon rainforest and similar places where participants learn about environmental issues are growing in popularity. Such trips may include lectures on the area's natural wonders, an opportunity to help scientists in the field, or a project to clean up a natural area.

Participants on these trips already have a high level of environmental awareness. A study of litter in Antarctica found that the entire collection of litter left by visitors over a two-year period could fit into one small plastic sandwich bag. Compare that amount of litter with what is usually found on the streets around most hotels.

Hotel owners and managers would be wise to pay attention to this trend. The green movement is growing everywhere. Something as simple as placing bottle recycling bins in rooms can be enough to attract the interest of environmentally conscious guests, and you'll be helping to save the planet at the same time. It's a win-win.

172. What is this article mainly about?

    (A) Ways to reduce waste
    (B) A popular type of tour
    (C) A trend in the travel industry
    (D) How to advertise a travel business

173. According to the article, what is something travelers might do on an eco-tour?

    (A) Teach a class
    (B) Build something
    (C) Assist researchers
    (D) Camp in a natural setting

174. What is indicated about travelers to Antarctica?

    (A) They enjoy collecting things.
    (B) They rarely leave behind trash.
    (C) They prefer not to use plastic bags.
    (D) They complain about the mess in their hotels.

175. What is suggested that hotel owners do?

    (A) Provide a way for guests to recycle bottles
    (B) Use glass shampoo dispensers
    (C) Paint their guest rooms green
    (D) Relocate to the rainforest

Questions 176–180 refer to the following email and graph.

To: v.goldsmith@placeco.com
From: gpmills@temppower.com
Subject: Your Career
Att: Temp Power Employment Graph

Dear Vanessa,

Thank you for attending this past week's complimentary workshop, Secretary 101 Skills, where you learned important career skills. If you're looking for a job, we want to help you. Temp Power prides itself on staffing our city's offices with top-notch administrative professionals, and we line our team up with high paying jobs and offer affordable health insurance! Many of our team go on to be hired permanently and then move up the job ladder.

Are you interested in starting your interview process? The next step is to come into our office for skills tests. You'll want to take these tests soon, while the skills you learned in our workshop tutorials are still fresh in your head.

Please click below to select a time to come to our office.

Click here to go to our Registration Page.

Please see the attached graph. We know it will convince you that you will find success as part of the Temp Power team.

Thank you,

George Mills

for Temp Power

Temp Power Workshop Participants Employment

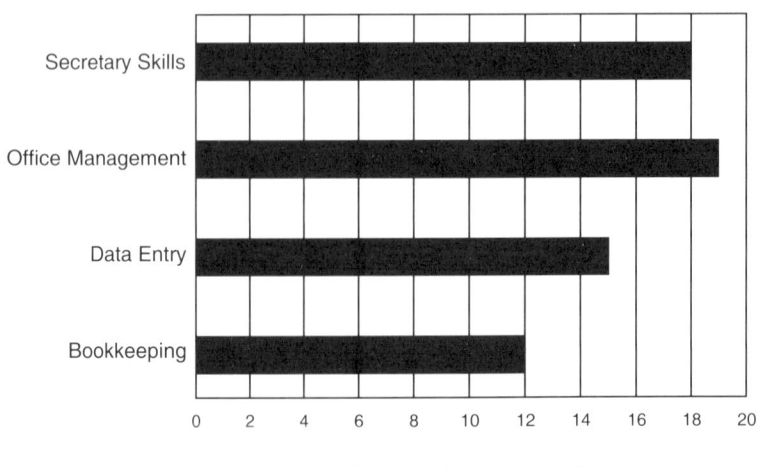

Category	Average days per month
Secretary Skills	18
Office Management	19
Data Entry	15
Bookkeeping	12

Average days per month

176. What was the ultimate purpose of the workshop?

    (A) To recruit workers
    (B) To find new clients
    (C) To introduce a college
    (D) To gather data for a graph

177. What does the message ask Vanessa to do next?

    (A) Call the company
    (B) Take a tutorial
    (C) Send test results
    (D) Sign up for a test

178. How much did Vanessa pay for the workshop?

    (A) The workshop was free.
    (B) It cost $20.
    (C) It cost $50.
    (D) The cost is unknown.

179. Which workshop led to the highest average amount of employment?

    (A) Bookkeeping
    (B) Data Entry
    (C) Office Management
    (D) Secretary Skills

180. If Vanessa signs up as a Temp Power employee, how much can she expect to work, on average?

    (A) 15 days a month
    (B) 18 days a month
    (C) 18 days a year
    (D) 12 months a year

Questions 181–185 refer to the following contract and addendum.

Contract #991YL

Hospitality Consultants Inc.

Hospitality Consultants Inc. (hereafter referred to as Contractor) agrees to perform the following duties as outlined by Cracker Barrel Winery (hereafter called the Client):

A. Statistics Analysis
1) Review the Client's wine sales over the past five years, using monthly inventory charts.
2) Review the Client's food and gift sales over the past five years.
3) Record a summary and chart for proposed sales this year, based on a five-year review.

B. Staff Review
1) Interview one staff member from each department, including the vineyards and cellar.
2) Record duties and responsibilities for each job position.
3) Suggest ways for the Client to cut staffing costs.

C. Decor
1) Meet with board members to discuss year-end renovations.
2) Research materials and costs for all indoor renovations.
3) Provide an estimate for indoor renovations by October 1st.

Any changes to this contract must be agreed upon by both parties in writing.

Contractor: *Hanson Carter*

Client: *Julia Morris*

Date: August 7th, 20—

Addendum to Contract #991YL dated August 7, 20—
between the following parties:

Contractor: **Hospitality Consultants Inc.**

Client: **Cracker Barrel Winery**

The Contractor initiates the following addendum:

1) Due to unforeseen circumstances the Contractor will be unable to provide services to Cracker Barrel Winery after October 9th, 20—. The Contractor does not expect any payment for any project work that is left incomplete as of today.

2) Before December 1st, 20— the Contractor will provide the Client with the names of three alternate consulting firms capable of completing the work set out in Contract #991YL.

3) The Contractor will submit a report of all work that has been completed, including any important data collected since August 7th 20—.

4) The Client agrees to write a reference for the Contractor, stating that Contract #991YL was broken due to illness in the family, and has no reflection on the Contractor's ability to do his job.

Date: October 9th, 20—

(Contractor) Signature: ─────────────────────────────

(Client) Signature: ─────────────────────────────

181. What type of service does this Contractor agree to provide?

(A) Labor assistance in the vineyards
(B) Consulting related to the winery's operations
(C) Inventory on glassware and dishes
(D) Taste tests of competitors' wines

182. Which is NOT an example of a person the Contractor may need to speak with to fulfill his duties?

(A) A medical professional
(B) A wine seller
(C) A board member
(D) A part-time grape picker

183. What is the reason for the addendum to the contract?

(A) The Client is not satisfied with the Contractor's work.
(B) The Contractor can't complete the job because of illness in the family.
(C) The Client wants to add to the Contractor's duties.
(D) The Contractor was able to complete the job ahead of schedule.

184. If the Contractor honored the contract up until now, what has definitely been completed?

(A) A sales chart based on a five-year review
(B) A count of all wine bottles in the cellar
(C) A calculation of proposed renovation costs
(D) An interview with at least one staff member

185. What is the Client obliged to do in the future if he signs the addendum to the contract?

(A) Rehire the Contractor when his health returns
(B) Provide a letter that states the reasons this contract was broken
(C) Write a positive reference letter about the Contractor's personality
(D) Suggest alternative companies that may hire the Contractor in the future

Questions 186–190 refer to the following parking ticket, notice, and form.

Parking Violation Notice
Springfield City Police Department

Violation:	Exceeding time limit in a 20-minute parking zone
Location:	500 block of North Main Street
Vehicle type:	Minivan
License Plate No.:	MG097
Registered owner:	Tanaka Kazuya
Date:	April 1, 20—

Amount: $75

Pay within 30 days. See reverse for payment instructions.

Reminder Notice
Springfield City Police Department

Date: April 21

You have not yet paid a parking ticket issued on April 1. Payment is due by May 1. Unpaid fines are subject to a penalty equivalent to the amount of the original ticket. You have the right to appeal. Appeals must be received by the Parking Division within 30 days of issuance of the ticket. Please use Form 25 available from the Parking Division office or online at springfieldpkingdiv.org

Form 25
Notice of Appeal

STEP 1

Reason for Appeal

Please check the legal grounds that apply. Please check ONE option only.

___ This parking violation did not occur.

___ The parking meter was out of order.

___ I am not the owner of this vehicle.

_✔_ My vehicle was stolen on the day of the violation.

STEP 2

Complete the personal information form on page two with your name and address and contact information and mail it together with this page and a photocopy of your ticket. You will hear back from the Parking Division within 20 business days. If your appeal is granted, you may have to appear in court. If your appeal is denied, you will have fifteen days from the date of denial to pay the original fine.

186. Why did Mr. Kazuya receive this ticket?

    (A) His car was parked in a spot for too long.
    (B) His car was parked in a no-parking zone.
    (C) He did not have a parking pass.
    (D) He paid for only 20 minutes.

187. Where will Mr. Kazuya find directions for paying the fine?

    (A) On the other side of the ticket
    (B) On the Parking Division website
    (C) At the police department
    (D) On Form 25

188. What happens if Mr. Kazuya fails to pay the fine or submit an appeal by May 1?

    (A) He must fill out a special form.
    (B) He must pay an additional $75.
    (C) He will lose his driver's license.
    (D) He will lose his parking privileges.

189. Why was Mr. Kazuya probably unaware of the original ticket?

    (A) The police officer forgot to leave it on his car.
    (B) The ticket was stolen from his parked car.
    (C) He thought he had parked legally.
    (D) Someone else was driving his car on April 1.

190. What does Mr. Kazuya have to include with his notice of appeal?

    (A) A check for $75
    (B) A photo of his car
    (C) A copy of his ticket
    (D) His license number

Questions 191–195 refer to the following travel itinerary, email, and shuttle schedule.

Itinerary for: Rosalind Wilson

Monday, June 1
Skyhigh Air flight 234
- Depart New York 8:20 a.m.
- Arrive Winchester 3:40 p.m.

Transportation by company car to Sunrise Hotel, Winchester

Tuesday, June 2 – Friday, June 5
At the Spring Wells, Inc. Headquarters

Saturday, June 6
Express Railways train #45
- Depart Winchester 9:00 a.m.
- Arrive Pottsburgh 1:00 p.m.

Afternoon tour of Spring Wells factory

Sunday, June 7
Skyhigh Air flight 987
- Depart Pottsburgh 7:45 a.m.
- Arrive New York 1:30 p.m.

To: Rosalind Wilson
From: Tom Lee
Subject: Your visit

Hi Rosalind,

I received your itinerary from your office. Everything looks good. The only problem is that no one from our office will be available to meet you at the airport on Monday, as we will all be in a meeting that, unfortunately, cannot be rescheduled. You have several options for getting to your hotel. The airport shuttle is very convenient and will take you to the train station, which is just half a block from your hotel. I am attaching a schedule for you. Another option would be to take a taxi, although that could cost $45 or $50, and since the shuttle is so easy, in my opinion it is not worth the cost. There are also city buses, but they are complicated if you are not familiar with them.

We look forward to seeing you next week. Have a safe flight, and call me as soon as you are settled in your room.

Tom

AIRPORT SHUTTLE SCHEDULE
To Winchester Railway Station

The Airport Shuttle is a free transportation service provided by the Winchester Transportation Authority (WTA). No tickets are required. Seating is on a first come, first served basis.

	1A	**2A**	**3A**	**4A**
Departs airport	11:20 a.m.	1:30 p.m.	4:10 p.m.	6:45 p.m.
Arrives Winchester Station	12:05 p.m.	2:15 p.m.	4:55 p.m.	7:30 p.m.

191. What will Ms. Wilson be doing on June 4?

    (A) Visiting the Spring Wells headquarters
    (B) Touring the Spring Wells factory
    (C) Returning home
    (D) Riding a train

192. Why won't Mr. Lee meet her at the airport?

    (A) He doesn't know how to get there.
    (B) He has another commitment.
    (C) He can't pay the bus fare.
    (D) He won't be working that day.

193. The word "settled" in paragraph 2, line 2, of the email is closest in meaning to

    (A) agreed
    (B) finished
    (C) decisive
    (D) comfortable

194. If Ms. Wilson takes the shuttle to her hotel, which one will she probably take?

    (A) 1A
    (B) 2A
    (C) 3A
    (D) 4A

195. How much will Ms. Wilson pay for the shuttle?

    (A) Nothing
    (B) At least $45
    (C) Between $45 and $50
    (D) $50 exactly

Questions 196–200 refer to the following notice, price list, and email.

The Hanover Business Association (HBA)
presents a lecture by

Stephanie du Bois, MBA

Ms. du Bois will discuss tips and strategies for investors in the current business climate.
Ms. du Bois received her MBA from
Pickerel University. She is the author of
Successful Investing and other popular titles.

August 18, 3:00 p.m.
Refreshments will be served

RSVP
This event is open to the public. Admission is free, but space is limited.
Please let us know if you plan to attend by calling our office at 604-0939.

Hanover Bakery Cookie Trays	
# of guests	price
up to 10	$10
up to 25	$20
up to 50	$38
up to 75	$55
Coffee and tea are also available.	
Please call us to discuss options.	

To: Carlos Vasquez
From: Serena Stanley
Subject: Refreshments for lecture

Carlos,

I'm still working on the arrangements for the lecture next week. Would you please call the bakery and order the cookies? We had only about 20 people show up at our last lecture, but Ms. du Bois is so popular, I think we can expect a much larger crowd this time. I'm still getting RSVPs, and I think we should be prepared for 40 or 50 guests. We'll make the coffee and tea here, so no need to order that. I think that's all you need to do. I've checked the room we'll be using, and everything is fine there. I think we'll have plenty of space, even for a large crowd, and there are more than enough chairs. I even tried out the sound system, and it seems to be in working order. I think that's it for now. Thanks.

Serena

196. What should people do if they want to attend the lecture?

    (A) Buy a ticket
    (B) Call the HBA office
    (C) Arrive 30 minutes early
    (D) Become a member of the HBA

197. What is indicated about Ms. du Bois?

    (A) She has written several books.
    (B) She is a university professor.
    (C) She is a member of the HBA.
    (D) She is not well known.

198. How much will Mr. Vasquez pay for the cookies?

    (A) $20
    (B) $20, plus the cost of coffee and tea
    (C) $38
    (D) $38, plus the cost of coffee and tea

199. The phrase "show up" in line 2 of the email is closest in meaning to

    (A) arrive
    (B) display
    (C) look at
    (D) guide

200. What does Ms. Stanley say about the room where the lecture will be held?

    (A) It is too small.
    (B) It is disorganized.
    (C) The chairs are very comfortable.
    (D) The sound system is in good condition.

STOP This is the end of the test. If you finish before time is called, you may go back to Parts 5, 6, and 7 and check your work.

多益測驗成績換算對照表

計算答對的題數，利用下表找到對應的分數。將聽力和閱讀分數相加，就會得到預估的多益測驗總分。逐一演練模擬試題，分數也會逐漸提升，請持續追蹤你的多益測驗預估總分。

答對題數	聽力分數	閱讀分數	答對題數	聽力分數	閱讀分數	答對題數	聽力分數	閱讀分數	答對題數	聽力分數	閱讀分數
0	5	5	26	110	65	51	255	220	76	410	370
1	5	5	27	115	70	52	260	225	77	420	380
2	5	5	28	120	80	53	270	230	78	425	385
3	5	5	29	125	85	54	275	235	79	430	390
4	5	5	30	130	90	55	280	240	80	440	395
5	5	5	31	135	95	56	290	250	81	445	400
6	5	5	32	140	100	57	295	255	82	450	405
7	10	5	33	145	110	58	300	260	83	460	410
8	15	5	34	150	115	59	310	265	84	465	415
9	20	5	35	160	120	60	315	270	85	470	420
10	25	5	36	165	125	61	320	280	86	475	425
11	30	5	37	170	130	62	325	285	87	480	430
12	35	5	38	175	140	63	330	290	88	485	435
13	40	5	39	180	145	64	340	300	89	490	445
14	45	5	40	185	150	65	345	305	90	495	450
15	50	5	41	190	160	66	350	310	91	495	455
16	55	10	42	195	165	67	360	320	92	495	465
17	60	15	43	200	170	68	365	325	93	495	470
18	65	20	44	210	175	69	370	330	94	495	480
19	70	25	45	215	180	70	380	335	95	495	485
20	75	30	46	220	190	71	385	340	96	495	490
21	80	35	47	230	195	72	390	350	97	495	495
22	85	40	48	240	200	73	395	355	98	495	495
23	90	45	49	245	210	74	400	360	99	495	495
24	95	50	50	250	215	75	405	365	100	495	495
25	100	60									

聽力測驗答對題數 ＿＿＿＿＿ ＝ 聽力測驗分數 ＿＿＿＿＿
閱讀測驗答對題數 ＿＿＿＿＿ ＝ 閱讀測驗分數 ＿＿＿＿＿
多益測驗預估總分 ＿＿＿＿＿

MEMO

ANSWER SHEET
實戰模擬試題2答案卡

Listening Comprehension

Part 1: Photographs

1. Ⓐ Ⓑ Ⓒ Ⓓ   3. Ⓐ Ⓑ Ⓒ Ⓓ   5. Ⓐ Ⓑ Ⓒ Ⓓ
2. Ⓐ Ⓑ Ⓒ Ⓓ   4. Ⓐ Ⓑ Ⓒ Ⓓ   6. Ⓐ Ⓑ Ⓒ Ⓓ

Part 2: Question-Response

7. Ⓐ Ⓑ Ⓒ   14. Ⓐ Ⓑ Ⓒ   21. Ⓐ Ⓑ Ⓒ   28. Ⓐ Ⓑ Ⓒ
8. Ⓐ Ⓑ Ⓒ   15. Ⓐ Ⓑ Ⓒ   22. Ⓐ Ⓑ Ⓒ   29. Ⓐ Ⓑ Ⓒ
9. Ⓐ Ⓑ Ⓒ   16. Ⓐ Ⓑ Ⓒ   23. Ⓐ Ⓑ Ⓒ   30. Ⓐ Ⓑ Ⓒ
10. Ⓐ Ⓑ Ⓒ   17. Ⓐ Ⓑ Ⓒ   24. Ⓐ Ⓑ Ⓒ   31. Ⓐ Ⓑ Ⓒ
11. Ⓐ Ⓑ Ⓒ   18. Ⓐ Ⓑ Ⓒ   25. Ⓐ Ⓑ Ⓒ
12. Ⓐ Ⓑ Ⓒ   19. Ⓐ Ⓑ Ⓒ   26. Ⓐ Ⓑ Ⓒ
13. Ⓐ Ⓑ Ⓒ   20. Ⓐ Ⓑ Ⓒ   27. Ⓐ Ⓑ Ⓒ

Part 3: Conversations

32. Ⓐ Ⓑ Ⓒ Ⓓ   42. Ⓐ Ⓑ Ⓒ Ⓓ   52. Ⓐ Ⓑ Ⓒ Ⓓ   62. Ⓐ Ⓑ Ⓒ Ⓓ
33. Ⓐ Ⓑ Ⓒ Ⓓ   43. Ⓐ Ⓑ Ⓒ Ⓓ   53. Ⓐ Ⓑ Ⓒ Ⓓ   63. Ⓐ Ⓑ Ⓒ Ⓓ
34. Ⓐ Ⓑ Ⓒ Ⓓ   44. Ⓐ Ⓑ Ⓒ Ⓓ   54. Ⓐ Ⓑ Ⓒ Ⓓ   64. Ⓐ Ⓑ Ⓒ Ⓓ
35. Ⓐ Ⓑ Ⓒ Ⓓ   45. Ⓐ Ⓑ Ⓒ Ⓓ   55. Ⓐ Ⓑ Ⓒ Ⓓ   65. Ⓐ Ⓑ Ⓒ Ⓓ
36. Ⓐ Ⓑ Ⓒ Ⓓ   46. Ⓐ Ⓑ Ⓒ Ⓓ   56. Ⓐ Ⓑ Ⓒ Ⓓ   66. Ⓐ Ⓑ Ⓒ Ⓓ
37. Ⓐ Ⓑ Ⓒ Ⓓ   47. Ⓐ Ⓑ Ⓒ Ⓓ   57. Ⓐ Ⓑ Ⓒ Ⓓ   67. Ⓐ Ⓑ Ⓒ Ⓓ
38. Ⓐ Ⓑ Ⓒ Ⓓ   48. Ⓐ Ⓑ Ⓒ Ⓓ   58. Ⓐ Ⓑ Ⓒ Ⓓ   68. Ⓐ Ⓑ Ⓒ Ⓓ
39. Ⓐ Ⓑ Ⓒ Ⓓ   49. Ⓐ Ⓑ Ⓒ Ⓓ   59. Ⓐ Ⓑ Ⓒ Ⓓ   69. Ⓐ Ⓑ Ⓒ Ⓓ
40. Ⓐ Ⓑ Ⓒ Ⓓ   50. Ⓐ Ⓑ Ⓒ Ⓓ   60. Ⓐ Ⓑ Ⓒ Ⓓ   70. Ⓐ Ⓑ Ⓒ Ⓓ
41. Ⓐ Ⓑ Ⓒ Ⓓ   51. Ⓐ Ⓑ Ⓒ Ⓓ   61. Ⓐ Ⓑ Ⓒ Ⓓ

Part 4: Talks

71. Ⓐ Ⓑ Ⓒ Ⓓ   79. Ⓐ Ⓑ Ⓒ Ⓓ   87. Ⓐ Ⓑ Ⓒ Ⓓ   95. Ⓐ Ⓑ Ⓒ Ⓓ
72. Ⓐ Ⓑ Ⓒ Ⓓ   80. Ⓐ Ⓑ Ⓒ Ⓓ   88. Ⓐ Ⓑ Ⓒ Ⓓ   96. Ⓐ Ⓑ Ⓒ Ⓓ
73. Ⓐ Ⓑ Ⓒ Ⓓ   81. Ⓐ Ⓑ Ⓒ Ⓓ   89. Ⓐ Ⓑ Ⓒ Ⓓ   97. Ⓐ Ⓑ Ⓒ Ⓓ
74. Ⓐ Ⓑ Ⓒ Ⓓ   82. Ⓐ Ⓑ Ⓒ Ⓓ   90. Ⓐ Ⓑ Ⓒ Ⓓ   98. Ⓐ Ⓑ Ⓒ Ⓓ
75. Ⓐ Ⓑ Ⓒ Ⓓ   82. Ⓐ Ⓑ Ⓒ Ⓓ   91. Ⓐ Ⓑ Ⓒ Ⓓ   99. Ⓐ Ⓑ Ⓒ Ⓓ
76. Ⓐ Ⓑ Ⓒ Ⓓ   84. Ⓐ Ⓑ Ⓒ Ⓓ   92. Ⓐ Ⓑ Ⓒ Ⓓ   100. Ⓐ Ⓑ Ⓒ Ⓓ
77. Ⓐ Ⓑ Ⓒ Ⓓ   85. Ⓐ Ⓑ Ⓒ Ⓓ   93. Ⓐ Ⓑ Ⓒ Ⓓ
78. Ⓐ Ⓑ Ⓒ Ⓓ   86. Ⓐ Ⓑ Ⓒ Ⓓ   94. Ⓐ Ⓑ Ⓒ Ⓓ

ANSWER SHEET
實戰模擬試題2答案卡

Reading Comprehension

Part 5: Incomplete Sentences

101. Ⓐ Ⓑ Ⓒ Ⓓ	109. Ⓐ Ⓑ Ⓒ Ⓓ	117. Ⓐ Ⓑ Ⓒ Ⓓ	125. Ⓐ Ⓑ Ⓒ Ⓓ
102. Ⓐ Ⓑ Ⓒ Ⓓ	110. Ⓐ Ⓑ Ⓒ Ⓓ	118. Ⓐ Ⓑ Ⓒ Ⓓ	126. Ⓐ Ⓑ Ⓒ Ⓓ
103. Ⓐ Ⓑ Ⓒ Ⓓ	111. Ⓐ Ⓑ Ⓒ Ⓓ	119. Ⓐ Ⓑ Ⓒ Ⓓ	127. Ⓐ Ⓑ Ⓒ Ⓓ
104. Ⓐ Ⓑ Ⓒ Ⓓ	112. Ⓐ Ⓑ Ⓒ Ⓓ	120. Ⓐ Ⓑ Ⓒ Ⓓ	128. Ⓐ Ⓑ Ⓒ Ⓓ
105. Ⓐ Ⓑ Ⓒ Ⓓ	113. Ⓐ Ⓑ Ⓒ Ⓓ	121. Ⓐ Ⓑ Ⓒ Ⓓ	129. Ⓐ Ⓑ Ⓒ Ⓓ
106. Ⓐ Ⓑ Ⓒ Ⓓ	114. Ⓐ Ⓑ Ⓒ Ⓓ	122. Ⓐ Ⓑ Ⓒ Ⓓ	130. Ⓐ Ⓑ Ⓒ Ⓓ
107. Ⓐ Ⓑ Ⓒ Ⓓ	115. Ⓐ Ⓑ Ⓒ Ⓓ	123. Ⓐ Ⓑ Ⓒ Ⓓ	
108. Ⓐ Ⓑ Ⓒ Ⓓ	116. Ⓐ Ⓑ Ⓒ Ⓓ	124. Ⓐ Ⓑ Ⓒ Ⓓ	

Part 6: Text Completion

131. Ⓐ Ⓑ Ⓒ Ⓓ	135. Ⓐ Ⓑ Ⓒ Ⓓ	139. Ⓐ Ⓑ Ⓒ Ⓓ	143. Ⓐ Ⓑ Ⓒ Ⓓ
132. Ⓐ Ⓑ Ⓒ Ⓓ	136. Ⓐ Ⓑ Ⓒ Ⓓ	140. Ⓐ Ⓑ Ⓒ Ⓓ	144. Ⓐ Ⓑ Ⓒ Ⓓ
133. Ⓐ Ⓑ Ⓒ Ⓓ	137. Ⓐ Ⓑ Ⓒ Ⓓ	141. Ⓐ Ⓑ Ⓒ Ⓓ	145. Ⓐ Ⓑ Ⓒ Ⓓ
134. Ⓐ Ⓑ Ⓒ Ⓓ	138. Ⓐ Ⓑ Ⓒ Ⓓ	142. Ⓐ Ⓑ Ⓒ Ⓓ	146. Ⓐ Ⓑ Ⓒ Ⓓ

Part 7: Reading Comprehension

147. Ⓐ Ⓑ Ⓒ Ⓓ	161. Ⓐ Ⓑ Ⓒ Ⓓ	175. Ⓐ Ⓑ Ⓒ Ⓓ	189. Ⓐ Ⓑ Ⓒ Ⓓ
148. Ⓐ Ⓑ Ⓒ Ⓓ	162. Ⓐ Ⓑ Ⓒ Ⓓ	176. Ⓐ Ⓑ Ⓒ Ⓓ	190. Ⓐ Ⓑ Ⓒ Ⓓ
149. Ⓐ Ⓑ Ⓒ Ⓓ	163. Ⓐ Ⓑ Ⓒ Ⓓ	177. Ⓐ Ⓑ Ⓒ Ⓓ	191. Ⓐ Ⓑ Ⓒ Ⓓ
150. Ⓐ Ⓑ Ⓒ Ⓓ	164. Ⓐ Ⓑ Ⓒ Ⓓ	178. Ⓐ Ⓑ Ⓒ Ⓓ	192. Ⓐ Ⓑ Ⓒ Ⓓ
151. Ⓐ Ⓑ Ⓒ Ⓓ	165. Ⓐ Ⓑ Ⓒ Ⓓ	179. Ⓐ Ⓑ Ⓒ Ⓓ	193. Ⓐ Ⓑ Ⓒ Ⓓ
152. Ⓐ Ⓑ Ⓒ Ⓓ	166. Ⓐ Ⓑ Ⓒ Ⓓ	180. Ⓐ Ⓑ Ⓒ Ⓓ	194. Ⓐ Ⓑ Ⓒ Ⓓ
153. Ⓐ Ⓑ Ⓒ Ⓓ	167. Ⓐ Ⓑ Ⓒ Ⓓ	181. Ⓐ Ⓑ Ⓒ Ⓓ	195. Ⓐ Ⓑ Ⓒ Ⓓ
154. Ⓐ Ⓑ Ⓒ Ⓓ	168. Ⓐ Ⓑ Ⓒ Ⓓ	182. Ⓐ Ⓑ Ⓒ Ⓓ	196. Ⓐ Ⓑ Ⓒ Ⓓ
155. Ⓐ Ⓑ Ⓒ Ⓓ	169. Ⓐ Ⓑ Ⓒ Ⓓ	183. Ⓐ Ⓑ Ⓒ Ⓓ	197. Ⓐ Ⓑ Ⓒ Ⓓ
156. Ⓐ Ⓑ Ⓒ Ⓓ	170. Ⓐ Ⓑ Ⓒ Ⓓ	184. Ⓐ Ⓑ Ⓒ Ⓓ	198. Ⓐ Ⓑ Ⓒ Ⓓ
157. Ⓐ Ⓑ Ⓒ Ⓓ	171. Ⓐ Ⓑ Ⓒ Ⓓ	185. Ⓐ Ⓑ Ⓒ Ⓓ	199. Ⓐ Ⓑ Ⓒ Ⓓ
158. Ⓐ Ⓑ Ⓒ Ⓓ	172. Ⓐ Ⓑ Ⓒ Ⓓ	186. Ⓐ Ⓑ Ⓒ Ⓓ	200. Ⓐ Ⓑ Ⓒ Ⓓ
159. Ⓐ Ⓑ Ⓒ Ⓓ	173. Ⓐ Ⓑ Ⓒ Ⓓ	187. Ⓐ Ⓑ Ⓒ Ⓓ	
160. Ⓐ Ⓑ Ⓒ Ⓓ	174. Ⓐ Ⓑ Ⓒ Ⓓ	188. Ⓐ Ⓑ Ⓒ Ⓓ	

MODEL TEST 2

實戰模擬試題 2

Listening Comprehension

In this section of the test, you will have the chance to show how well you understand spoken English. There are four parts to this section, with special directions for each part. You will have approximately 45 minutes to complete the Listening Comprehension sections.

Part 1: Photographs

DIRECTIONS: You will see a photograph. You will hear four statements about the photograph. Choose the statement that most closely matches the photograph, and fill in the corresponding oval on your answer sheet.

Track 39

1.

2.

3.

4.

5.

6.

Part 2: Question-Response

DIRECTIONS: You will hear a question and three possible responses. Choose the response that most closely answers the question, and fill in the corresponding oval on your answer sheet.

Track 40

7. Mark your answer on your answer sheet.

8. Mark your answer on your answer sheet.

9. Mark your answer on your answer sheet.

10. Mark your answer on your answer sheet.

11. Mark your answer on your answer sheet.

12. Mark your answer on your answer sheet.

13. Mark your answer on your answer sheet.

14. Mark your answer on your answer sheet.

15. Mark your answer on your answer sheet.

16. Mark your answer on your answer sheet.

17. Mark your answer on your answer sheet.

18. Mark your answer on your answer sheet.

19. Mark your answer on your answer sheet.

20. Mark your answer on your answer sheet.

21. Mark your answer on your answer sheet.

22. Mark your answer on your answer sheet.

23. Mark your answer on your answer sheet.

24. Mark your answer on your answer sheet.

25. Mark your answer on your answer sheet.

26. Mark your answer on your answer sheet.

27. Mark your answer on your answer sheet.

28. Mark your answer on your answer sheet.

29. Mark your answer on your answer sheet.

30. Mark your answer on your answer sheet.

31. Mark your answer on your answer sheet.

Part 3: Conversations

DIRECTIONS: You will hear a conversation between two or more people. You will see three questions on each conversation and four possible answers. Choose the best answer to each question, and fill in the corresponding oval on your answer sheet.

Track 41

32. What does the woman want to do?

    (A) Clean the coffeepot
    (B) Sit down
    (C) Wash her hands
    (D) Sweep the floor

33. Where are the speakers?

    (A) On the sixth floor
    (B) Above the sixth floor
    (C) Below the sixth floor
    (D) On the ground floor

34. What does the man want to drink?

    (A) Milk
    (B) Coffee
    (C) Cocoa
    (D) Tea

35. What does the man suggest about the shirts?

    (A) They are a popular item.
    (B) They only come in two colors.
    (C) They are good for warm weather.
    (D) They will be discounted next week.

36. How much does the woman have to pay?

    (A) $42.05
    (B) $45
    (C) $60
    (D) $245

37. How will the woman pay?

    (A) Check
    (B) Cash
    (C) Credit card
    (D) Gift certificate

38. What is the woman photocopying?

    (A) A menu
    (B) An agenda
    (C) An invitation
    (D) An address list

39. Why does the woman say, "Would you?"

    (A) To make a request
    (B) To ask for information
    (C) To make a suggestion
    (D) To accept an offer

40. What will the woman do when the copies are made?

    (A) Mail them
    (B) Read them
    (C) Show them to her boss
    (D) Take them to a meeting

41. Where does this conversation take place?

    (A) In a hotel
    (B) In a fish store
    (C) In a restaurant
    (D) In someone's house

42. What is the problem with the fish?

    (A) It is not fresh.
    (B) It is not available this evening.
    (C) It takes a long time to prepare.
    (D) It costs more than other dishes.

43. What will the man do while he waits?

    (A) Have a drink
    (B) Sit and think
    (C) Go fishing
    (D) Wash the dishes

355

44. Where does the woman most likely work?

    (A) In a dentist's office
    (B) In a surgeon's office
    (C) At a real estate agency
    (D) At a rug cleaning service

45. Where is Mr. Wu now?

    (A) In his office
    (B) Out of town
    (C) At a meeting
    (D) On a flight

46. What does the woman want Mr. Wu to do?

    (A) Make a new appointment
    (B) Visit an apartment
    (C) Check his schedule
    (D) Meet her downtown

47. Where did the woman leave her briefcase?

    (A) At a meeting
    (B) In her office
    (C) On her desk
    (D) In a cab

48. What does Jim offer to do?

    (A) Take some papers to the bank
    (B) Lend the woman his briefcase
    (C) Let the woman use his desk
    (D) Call the cab company

49. What is in the briefcase?

    (A) A cell phone
    (B) A passport
    (C) A report
    (D) A sign

50. Why does the man want to wake up early?

    (A) He has to catch an early train.
    (B) He wants to make a phone call.
    (C) He's going to take a morning plane.
    (D) He wants to hear the weather report.

51. How will the weather be tomorrow?

    (A) Snowy
    (B) Rainy
    (C) Cold
    (D) Hot

52. What does the man mean when he says, "I don't think I'll bother"?

    (A) He doesn't mind traveling on an early flight.
    (B) He is not disturbed by the other hotel guests.
    (C) He hopes he isn't causing an inconvenience.
    (D) He won't have breakfast at the hotel.

53. What does the man say about the plane trip?

    (A) It was uncomfortable.
    (B) It was expensive.
    (C) It was overnight.
    (D) It was long.

54. Why is the man annoyed?

    (A) They have to go to baggage claim.
    (B) He doesn't have enough money
    (C) The woman's bag is heavy.
    (D) They are stuck in traffic.

55. What will the man do next?

    (A) Look for a taxi
    (B) Wait for the woman
    (C) Pick up the woman's bag
    (D) Check the subway schedule

56. What did the man send the woman?

    (A) A program schedule
    (B) A personnel file
    (C) A finance report
    (D) A rent check

57. What does the woman ask the man to do?

    (A) Look in a folder
    (B) Use a different address
    (C) Explain something to her
    (D) Get some documents ready

58. What does the woman say about the man?

    (A) He is reliable.
    (B) He is often late.
    (C) He is a bit strange.
    (D) He is good with numbers.

59. What sport does the man enjoy?

    (A) Golf
    (B) Tennis
    (C) Biking
    (D) Swimming

60. Where does he practice it?

    (A) At the hotel
    (B) At the park
    (C) At the exercise club
    (D) At the community center

61. What do the women invite the man to do?

    (A) Have lunch
    (B) Walk in the park
    (C) Play a game of pool
    (D) Join the country club

62. What most likely is the man's job?

    (A) Artist
    (B) Landscaper
    (C) Tour guide
    (D) Photographer

63. What will the speakers do tomorrow?

    (A) Bike through a valley
    (B) Meet in an alley
    (C) Fish in a river
    (D) Ride on a bus

64. What should people bring?

    (A) A dress
    (B) Cold drinks
    (C) Some books
    (D) Warm clothes

Mall

Bookstore	Store A
Store B	Store C
Store D	Cafè

65. What does the man need to buy?

    (A) Another kind of paper
    (B) Notebooks and easels
    (C) Green markers
    (D) Books

66. Look at the graphic. Which is the supply store?

    (A) Store A
    (B) Store B
    (C) Store C
    (D) Store D

67. What will the woman do next?

    (A) Go to the mall
    (B) Speak with Joe
    (C) Give the man instructions
    (D) Arrange the conference room

Parking Prices
up to 1 hour.........................$5
up to 2 hours.......................$8
up to 3 hours.....................$12
over 3 hours......................$15

68. What is the man worried about?

    (A) Finding a parking space
    (B) Getting to the movie late
    (C) Waiting on line for tickets
    (D) Paying too much for parking

69. Look at the graphic. How much will the speakers probably pay for parking?

    (A) $5
    (B) $8
    (C) $12
    (D) $15

70. What does the man want to do?

    (A) Leave the theater early
    (B) Sit in the front row
    (C) Buy tickets online
    (D) Eat snacks later

Part 4: Talks

DIRECTIONS: You will hear a talk given by a single speaker. You will see three questions on each talk, each with four possible answers. Choose the best answer to each question, and fill in the corresponding oval on your answer sheet.

Track 42

71. Who is the audience for this advertisement?

    (A) Families
    (B) Businesspeople
    (C) Tourists
    (D) Students

72. What is the advertisement for?

    (A) Suitcases
    (B) Computers
    (C) Clothes
    (D) Travel agency

73. How can a customer get a discount?

    (A) By ordering online
    (B) By shopping at a retail store
    (C) By completing an application
    (D) By ordering next month

74. What best describes the weather conditions the area is facing?

    (A) Cold
    (B) Fog
    (C) Snow and ice
    (D) Wind and rain

75. What problems will this weather cause tomorrow?

    (A) People will have trouble getting to work.
    (B) People won't have enough heat.
    (C) Flights will be canceled.
    (D) People should buy plenty of food.

76. What does the speaker mean when he says, "It's not all bad news"?

    (A) The weather will improve soon.
    (B) People will enjoy a day off from work.
    (C) The news report will follow the weather report.
    (D) City officials will work to clear the roads quickly.

77. What is the first thing a receptionist should do for a visitor?

    (A) Greet her
    (B) Have her sign in
    (C) Ask for an ID card
    (D) Let her take a seat

78. Where should the visitor wait?

    (A) By the receptionist's desk
    (B) Outside the office
    (C) Next to the door
    (D) In the lobby

79. What should visitors never do?

    (A) Go upstairs
    (B) Carry books
    (C) Wait too long
    (D) Walk around alone

80. Who is Lynn?

    (A) A historian
    (B) A tour guide
    (C) A guidebook writer
    (D) A property owner

81. Where does the tour take place?

    (A) A village
    (B) A school
    (C) A city
    (D) A farm

82. What are listeners asked to do?

    (A) Carry their own suitcases
    (B) Avoid touching the displays
    (C) Purchase items in a store
    (D) Play some games

359

83. What is the purpose of this talk?
    (A) To describe library services
    (B) To introduce a tour of the library
    (C) To compare the new and old libraries
    (D) To explain how to reach each floor of the library

84. What is on the second floor?
    (A) Magazines and periodicals
    (B) Young adult books
    (C) Activity rooms
    (D) Offices

85. What does the speaker mean when he says, "It's not to be missed"?
    (A) There is nothing interesting on the sixth floor.
    (B) Everyone should visit the sixth floor.
    (C) No one is allowed on the sixth floor.
    (D) He has never visited the sixth floor.

86. What is the destination for this flight?
    (A) Dallas
    (B) Houston
    (C) Madison
    (D) Wilmington

87. What does the captain say about the flight?
    (A) It will be late.
    (B) There will be turbulence.
    (C) It will be smooth.
    (D) The flying altitude will be low.

88. What does the captain say about the final destination?
    (A) It is a popular place to visit.
    (B) The people there are friendly.
    (C) It is a good place for clothes shopping.
    (D) The weather there will be pleasant.

89. Who will give the keynote address?
    (A) The association president
    (B) A university professor
    (C) A financial expert
    (D) A journalist

90. What will take place in the Garden Room?
    (A) A wedding
    (B) A workshop
    (C) A lunch
    (D) A market

91. What is the audience asked to do?
    (A) Speak with George Williams
    (B) Leave boxes by the door
    (C) Pay for lunch
    (D) Complete a form

92. What will take place in seven days?
    (A) The voicemail system will change.
    (B) This customer will get a new telephone.
    (C) This customer will get a new telephone number.
    (D) The telephone company's web address will change.

93. How can a customer save a message?
    (A) Press two
    (B) Press four
    (C) Press seven
    (D) Press nine

94. How can a customer learn about all of the new codes?
    (A) Press ten
    (B) Press the star key
    (C) Call the company
    (D) Listen to the entire message

City Caterers Lunch Prices
15 guests $150
20 guests. $200
25 guests $250
50 guests. $450

Building Directory
Ground Floor.......... Lobby
First Floor............... City Bank
Second Floor .... Silverton Company
Third Floor ....City Sports Equipment, Inc.

95. What event is the speaker arranging?

   (A) A staff party
   (B) A training session
   (C) A client luncheon
   (D) An awards banquet

96. What does the speaker ask Evelyn to do?

   (A) Order the lunch
   (B) Count the guests
   (C) Pick up the lunch
   (D) Arrange the dining room

97. Look at the graphic. How much will the speaker pay for lunch?

   (A) $150
   (B) $200
   (C) $250
   (D) $450

98. Who is this talk for?

   (A) All building tenants
   (B) Department heads
   (C) New employees
   (D) Job applicants

99. Look at the graphic. Where is the fitness room located?

   (A) Ground Floor
   (B) First Floor
   (C) Second Floor
   (D) Third Floor

100. What will the listeners do next?

   (A) Tour the building
   (B) Break for lunch
   (C) Ask questions
   (D) View a slide

STOP This is the end of the Listening Comprehension portion of the test. Turn to Part 5 in your test book.

Reading Comprehension

In this section of the test, you will have the chance to show how well you understand written English. There are three parts to this section, with special directions for each part.

YOU WILL HAVE ONE HOUR AND FIFTEEN MINUTES
TO COMPLETE PARTS 5, 6, AND 7 OF THE TEST.

Part 5: Incomplete Sentences

> **DIRECTIONS:** You will see a sentence with a missing word. Four possible answers follow the sentence. Choose the best answer to the question, and fill in the corresponding oval on your answer sheet.

101. By Friday, twenty-five applications had been submitted _____ the position of desk clerk.
    (A) at
    (B) on
    (C) for
    (D) by

102. The deeply discounted prices offered on that line of products are sure to _____ many new customers.
    (A) offer
    (B) attract
    (C) enjoy
    (D) expect

103. Mr. Cruz needs someone to _____ him with the conference display.
    (A) assume
    (B) assign
    (C) assent
    (D) assist

104. The workshop will be repeated next week for everyone who was not able to be _____ yesterday.
    (A) resent
    (B) present
    (C) content
    (D) intent

105. One downside of living in the countryside is the long _____ to get to work.
    (A) travel
    (B) relay
    (C) commute
    (D) extension

106. The final purchase price was higher than the investors _____.
    (A) had expected
    (B) expect
    (C) are expecting
    (D) will expect

107. The new waitress made hardly any mistakes on her first day, so I imagine _____ will be hired full time.
    (A) she
    (B) him
    (C) her
    (D) they

108. The new insurance plan is especially _____ with employees who have families.
    (A) popularized
    (B) popular
    (C) populated
    (D) popularity

362

109. The provisions officer buys supplies in _____ quantities because the fishing boat is at sea for weeks at a time.

(A) largely
(B) the largest
(C) larger
(D) large

110. The airline will refund your money as _____ as your travel agent cancels your reservation.

(A) well
(B) far
(C) soon
(D) little

111. Did Mr. Fisk _____ the reference guide from the company library?

(A) loan
(B) borrow
(C) lend
(D) sent

112. _____ they were ordered, the brochures and business cards were never printed.

(A) Although
(B) Even
(C) However
(D) Despite

113. The operator does not remember receiving a message from the Madrid office _____ from the Paris office.

(A) or
(B) and
(C) either
(D) but

114. Most of our staff have not used this type of copy machine _____.

(A) before
(B) prior
(C) advance
(D) previous

115. The housekeepers will need to be paid overtime for their work over the holidays, _____ ?

(A) won't they
(B) will she
(C) aren't they
(D) they will

116. The printer in Mr. Daaka's office uses a special _____ cartridge that comes in four different colors.

(A) dye
(B) ink
(C) paper
(D) tray

117. The receptionist receives packages and _____ them until the proper department is notified.

(A) is holding
(B) held
(C) hold
(D) holds

118. The purpose of our conference is to help employees _____ our policies.

(A) understood
(B) understanding
(C) understand
(D) are understanding

119. _____ none of us were familiar with the city, Mr. Gutman drove us to the meeting.

(A) Although
(B) Because
(C) Therefore
(D) However

120. The gas station attendant suggests _____ a boat from a local to save money.

    (A) rent
    (B) rents
    (C) rented
    (D) renting

121. If this report is sent by overnight delivery, it _____ Milan by noon tomorrow.

    (A) reaches
    (B) will reach
    (C) is reaching
    (D) has reached

122. Yamamoto Sushi is across town and _____ near our hotel, so we should take a taxi.

    (A) nowhere
    (B) anywhere
    (C) somewhere
    (D) everywhere

123. Employees who _____ attending the conference can get a discount on travel arrangements.

    (A) have going
    (B) are going to
    (C) will
    (D) will be

124. Mr. Vasco has developed his _____ in electronics over many years of experience and hard work.

    (A) technician
    (B) professional
    (C) expertise
    (D) authorization

125. The city is asking for funding _____ five parks and three recreational centers.

    (A) on renovating
    (B) for renovation
    (C) by renovating
    (D) to renovate

126. The head housekeeper is going to ask Ms. Chang how much time she _____ available.

    (A) will have had
    (B) is having
    (C) have
    (D) has

127. The hotel marketing director is quite _____ about advertising in Europe.

    (A) knowing
    (B) knowledge
    (C) knowledgeable
    (D) knows

128. We _____ to know the size of the banner before we can start designing it.

    (A) must
    (B) need
    (C) could
    (D) should

129. The operator _____ Mr. Smith if she knew where to reach him.

    (A) will call
    (B) had called
    (C) called
    (D) would call

130. The trainers for the seminar had the crew _____ their equipment to the conference center.

    (A) move
    (B) moving
    (C) mover
    (D) moved

Part 6: Text Completion

DIRECTIONS: You will see four passages, each with four blanks. Each blank has four answer choices. For each blank, choose the word, phrase, or sentence that best completes the passage.

Questions 131–134 refer to the following letter.

Creek and Chung, Accountants
1040 Stone Way
Seattle, Washington 93108-2662

July 12, 20—
Mr. Hugh Ferrer
Unity Health Care
400 East Pine Street
Seattle, Washington 93129-2665

Dear Mr. Ferrer:

We are a mid-sized accounting firm. Our staff members have expressed dissatisfaction with our current insurance plan, so we are looking into other ____. The insurance company we
      131
use now has recently raised its rates, while at the same time the quality of service has gotten worse. Naturally, we are not happy about paying more and more money for poor service.
____, we are interested in learning more about Unity Health Care (UHC). Could you please
132
mail a packet of information to me? ____. First, our employees want to choose their own
                                       133
doctors. Does your program allow this? Second, do your doctors have weekend and evening hours? Our employees have busy work schedules, and it is not always ____ for them to go to
                                                                                 134
appointments during regular business hours.

Thank you for your help.

Sincerely,
Felicia Braddish
Human Resources Manager

131. (A) employees
     (B) positions
     (C) activities
     (D) options

132. (A) Therefore
     (B) However
     (C) Moreover
     (D) Nevertheless

133. (A) Most insurance plans offer a variety of options to their clients
     (B) I would also appreciate it if you could answer the following questions
     (C) We have several reasons for changing our insurance
     (D) I have outlined the most important points here

134. (A) enjoyable
     (B) difficult
     (C) convenient
     (D) interesting

365

Questions 135-138 refer to the following email.

From: Simon Yan
To: Mingmei Lee
Subject: Monday Meeting

Dear Mingmei,

I have to leave town for a business trip ___135___ there is an emergency in our Singapore office. I am sorry that I will have to miss our Monday morning meeting, especially because I am eager to see your progress on my company's new financial center. This is an important project for National Bank.

My coworker, Hugh Harrison, will ___136___ me. Hugh plans to look for you at the construction site at 9:00 a.m. ___137___. Please talk with Hugh about this. While we don't want to spend a lot of extra money on this building, it is going to be our company's headquarters and needs to look good. You have an excellent reputation as a Construction Project Manager, so I'm ___138___ that you can manage the budget and build a fantastic center for us at the same time.

I will return one week from today. You can email me until I return. Thank you.

135. (A) so
 (B) if
 (C) as
 (D) by

136. (A) escort
 (B) replace
 (C) assist
 (D) accompany

137. (A) Please be sure to arrive on time
 (B) This is a convenient time and place for both of us
 (C) Construction has been going on for quite a while now
 (D) You told me that you have some concerns about the project's budget

138. (A) doubtful
 (B) positive
 (C) wondering
 (D) concerned

Questions 139–142 refer to the following memorandum.

Memorandum

From: Belinda Beilby, Company President
To: Company Vice-Presidents
Re: Reducing electricity expenses

The electric company is _____(139)_____ its rates by 25% next month, so we need to look at ways to reduce our electricity usage. Below is a list of recommendations. Please distribute this list to the departments in your area.

Ways to Reduce Electricity Expenses

1. Lights: Turn off the lights in meeting rooms when your meeting ends. Turn off the lights in the offices before you leave for the day.

2. Computers: At the day's end, turn off your computer.

3. Photocopying: Don't photocopy and fax documents. Most documents can _____(140)_____ electronically.

4. Fans/Heaters: Using fans or heaters in the office should not be necessary. _____(141)_____. If you feel that your office is too cool or too warm, please contact the maintenance staff.

5. Home Office Option: _____(142)_____ employees to work at home one or more days a week saves money in many ways, including on electricity. Employees who are interested in this option should speak to their supervisors.

---

139. (A) cutting
 (B) increasing
 (C) dividing
 (D) improving

140. (A) send
 (B) sent
 (C) to send
 (D) be sent

141. (A) The building temperature is set at a level that most people find comfortable
 (B) However, you may bring a small space heater or fan from home if you wish
 (C) Temperatures in this region vary, depending on the time of year
 (D) Fans and heaters do not adequately control room temperature

142. (A) Allow
 (B) Allowing
 (C) To allow
 (D) Will allow

Questions 143–146 refer to the following announcement.

_____. The company announced last Friday that its president, Shirley Ocampo, will succeed Louis Freeland as chief executive officer starting in September. Ms. Ocampo will be the first female chief executive in the company's history. Sunrise Manufacturers is _____ manufacturer of farming equipment in the country. This is a sector that has been traditionally dominated by men, making Ms. Ocampo's appointment particularly _____. Mr. Freeland, who will retire from Sunrise when Ms. Ocampo takes over his position next month, _____ at the company for 25 years.

143. (A) Employees at Sunrise Manufacturers, Inc. will be getting a new boss soon
   (B) Customers of Sunrise Manufacturing, Inc. give the products high ratings
   (C) Sunrise Manufacturers, Inc. has branches in several parts of the country
   (D) Sunrise Manufacturer's, Inc. has several new positions open

144. (A) large
   (B) larger
   (C) the larger
   (D) the largest

145. (A) recent
   (B) common
   (C) significant
   (D) profitable

146. (A) works
   (B) worked
   (C) had worked
   (D) has been working

Part 7: Reading Comprehension

DIRECTIONS: You will see single and multiple reading passages followed by several questions. Each question has four answer choices. Choose the best answer to the question, and fill in the corresponding oval on your answer sheet.

Questions 147–148 refer to the following advertisement.

Data Entry/Clerk

Insurance firm seeks reliable, detail-oriented person for operations division. Responsibilities include data entry, filing, and word processing. Good salary and benefits. Pleasant atmosphere. Room to advance.

---

147. What is one responsibility of this job?

 (A) Answering the phone
 (B) Data entry
 (C) Selling insurance
 (D) Operating a division

148. What is one benefit of the position?

 (A) They'll give you your own office later.
 (B) You can work toward promotions.
 (C) Benefits apply to dependents.
 (D) You can earn commissions.

Questions 149–150 refer to the following memo.

MEMORANDUM

To: All Employees
From: Donetta Muscillo
Safety Coordinator
Date: June 5, 20—

Sub: Fire doors

Employees are reminded that doors designated as fire doors must stay closed at all times. The purpose of fire doors is to help direct smoke away from areas where people are working in case of a fire in the building. Even though the weather is hot and the repairs to the company's air conditioner are not complete, keeping the fire doors open is strictly prohibited.

---

149. What is the purpose of the memo?

    (A) To explain the function of the fire doors
    (B) To explain how to keep the fire doors closed
    (C) To explain that the fire doors should stay closed
    (D) To explain why the building is warmer than usual

150. Why were employees probably keeping the fire doors open?

    (A) To get to a higher floor
    (B) To look at the view
    (C) To go from office to office
    (D) To let in cool air

Questions 151–152 refer to the following text message chain.

MYRA LEE   4:10
Just letting you know I'll be a bit late.

HIRO MATSUO   4:11
Was your flight delayed?

MYRA LEE   4:13
No. It was early, in fact. And I got a cab right away, but I left my suitcase behind at the baggage claim.

HIRO MATSUO   4:14
What? Where?

MYRA LEE   4:16
At the airport. We were halfway to the office when I realized it. I had to make the cab driver turn around.

HIRO MATSUO   4:17
Wow. You must be tired.

MYRA LEE   4:18
It's been a long week. I hope they don't delay the staff meeting for me. Would you mind letting the boss know I'll be late? You don't have to tell him why.

HIRO MATSUO   4:20
Sure thing. See you soon.

MYRA LEE   4:21
Thanks. Expect me in 30 minutes or so.

---

151. What problem does Ms. Lee have?

(A) She lost her suitcase.
(B) She missed her flight.
(C) She couldn't find a taxi.
(D) She forgot to pick up her bag.

152. At 4:20, what does Mr. Matsuo mean when he writes, "Sure thing"?

(A) He will talk to Ms. Lee's boss.
(B) He knows Ms. Lee will arrive soon.
(C) He understands why Ms. Lee is arriving late.
(D) He is certain Ms. Lee's boss won't mind delaying the meeting.

Questions 153-154 refer to the following announcement.

ESTATE AUCTION

An auction for the estate of Raul Diega will be held on

Saturday, October 3, at 11:00 a.m.
(preview starts at 10:00 a.m.)

Location: 5667 North Hedge Lane

Some of the items to be auctioned
* 2004 Mercedes
* China and crystal
* Oriental rugs
* Jewelry
* Stamp collection

Questions? Please call Estate Planners at 778-0099 between noon and 5 p.m.

---

153. Which of the following items will be auctioned?

    (A) Chinese antiques
    (B) Rare books
    (C) Bracelets
    (D) Wall-to-wall carpeting

154. When can you start to look at things?

    (A) October 3, 11:00 a.m.
    (B) By appointment after calling 778-0099
    (C) Any day from noon to five
    (D) October 3, 10:00 a.m.

Questions 155–157 refer to the following pie chart.

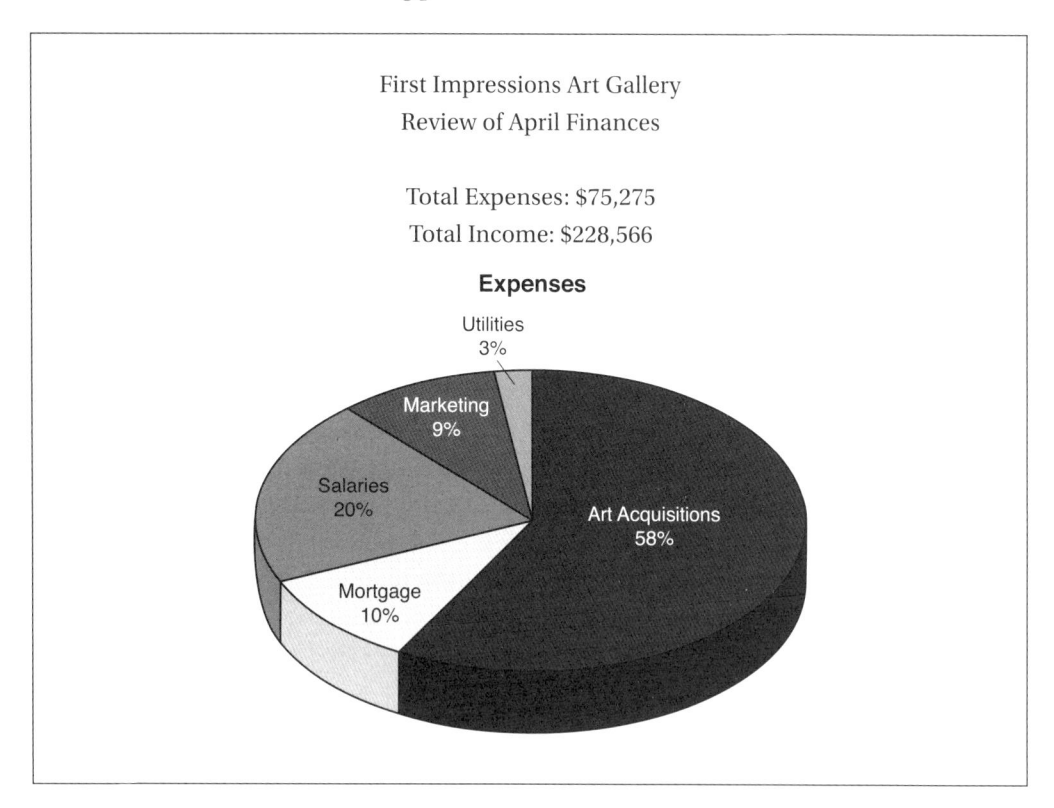

First Impressions Art Gallery
Review of April Finances

Total Expenses: $75,275
Total Income: $228,566

Expenses

- Utilities 3%
- Marketing 9%
- Salaries 20%
- Mortgage 10%
- Art Acquisitions 58%

155. When was this graph created?

   (A) Before April
   (B) After April
   (C) In early April
   (D) In late April

156. What can be said about the gallery?

   (A) It is earning about three times what it is spending.
   (B) It is spending more than it is earning.
   (C) It is spending the same amount as it is earning.
   (D) It is earning half of what it is spending.

157. What is the greatest expense for the gallery?

   (A) New inventory
   (B) Money paid to employees
   (C) Money paid to advertise
   (D) Electricity and water costs

Questions 158-160 refer to the following email.

From: Human Resources
To: Transferring Staff
Subj: Information about Transfer
Date: April 10

As you know, you are among the 60 technical and management-level employees who will be making the move to our new manufacturing plant. This is our first overseas plant, and we hope to make the transition as smooth as possible for you and your families. To this end, we are offering a series of seminars designed to help you adjust to life overseas and in a small town. The seminars will address such issues as regional customs, diet, language, and cross-cultural communication. While attendance is not mandatory, it is strongly suggested that you attend as many of these seminars as possible. I have attached a schedule. Please share it with your family members and put them on your calendar. These seminars are suitable for everyone aged 14 and over. Please contact the HR office if you have any questions or concerns.

Amanda Jones

HR officer

158. Where is the new manufacturing plant?

(A) Near the mountains
(B) In another country
(C) In a large city
(D) On the coast

159. What is the purpose of the email?

(A) To give information about a seminar series
(B) To help employees plan their move to the new plant
(C) To announce the opening of a new manufacturing plant
(D) To explain the importance of cross-cultural understanding

160. What is indicated about the seminars?

(A) They are a requirement for new employees.
(B) They are for both employees and their families.
(C) They will take place at the new plant.
(D) They will begin right away.

Questions 161–163 refer to the following announcement.

VAL D'OR CATERING SUPPLY

Val D'Or is pleased to announce its purchase of Gourmet Galore, a company focusing on specialty food products, cookware, and kitchen accessories. –[1]– Plans for Gourmet Galore include the opening of five more stores across Europe. Ten of the original sixteen stores were remodeled last year, and similar plans are in the works for the remaining six. –[2]– Gourmet Galore will also be expanding its reach with a new line of cooking schools. These schools will take advantage of the current interest in health improvement by focusing on gourmet foods that are both delicious and nutritious. –[3]– Regional specialties will also be included, and guest chefs from all over Europe will act as consultants. –[4]–

---

161. What plans does Val D'Or have for six of the Gourmet Galore stores?

   (A) Remodel them
   (B) Buy them
   (C) Sell them
   (D) Relocate them

162. What will be emphasized in the cooking classes?

   (A) Recipes from one region
   (B) Use of specialty cookware
   (C) Food from around the world
   (D) Healthful foods

163. In which of the following positions marked [1], [2], [3], and [4] does the following sentence best belong?

   "Val D'Or aims to expand the business and offerings of this already popular brand."

   (A) [1]
   (B) [2]
   (C) [3]
   (D) [4]

Questions 164–167 refer to the following online chat discussion.

Marco Silva [11:15]
I just got a call from Shipping. They have a return from a client, Sunrise, Inc.

Jane Kim [11:16]
What? Why?

Sabine Kohl [11:17]
I had an email from Sunrise this morning. They said we shipped them the wrong items. It was five bolts of dark blue cotton.

Marco Silva [11:20]
OK. I've checked the files. That's not what they ordered.

Jane Kim [11:22]
That's their usual order.

Marco Silva [11:23]
Right. But they're working on a new line of summer dresses. They wanted lighter colors for that.

Sabine Kohl [11:25]
What should I tell them?

Jane Kim [11:27]
You'll have to apologize, of course. And offer them free shipping on this order and their next order.

Sabine Kohl [11:30]
Someone should contact Shipping and find out what the story is. We can't let this happen again.

Marco Silva [11:31]
I'm on it.

Jane Kim [11:32]
Great. Let us know what you find out.

164. What kind of company do the chatters most likely work for?

(A) Shipping
(B) Clothing retail
(C) Fashion design
(D) Fabric manufacturer

165. What is indicated about the order made by the client?

(A) It was made several weeks ago.
(B) It was larger than the previous order.
(C) It was different from the client's usual order.
(D) It was changed by the client at the last minute.

166. What was the problem with the shipment?

(A) It was shipped too late.
(B) It took too long to arrive.
(C) It was sent to the wrong address.
(D) It did not contain what the client ordered.

167. At 11:31, what does Mr. Silva mean when he writes, "I'm on it"?

(A) He will let the client know what happened.
(B) He will talk with the shipping department.
(C) He is on the shipping department staff.
(D) He is good at solving problems.

Questions 168–171 refer to the following letter.

BUSINESS ASSOCIATION
FUTURE BUSINESS LEADERS EDUCATION FUND
P.O. BOX 1205, WILLIAMSTOWN

July 8, 20—
Mr. Gregory Harrison
78 North Main Street
Riverdale

Dear Mr. Harrison,

As you know, the Business Association has been supporting aspiring young professionals in our community for over 25 years through our Future Business Leaders Education Fund. In addition to our scholarship program, we offer a variety of workshops to help young business professionals acquire the skills and experience they need to advance along their career paths. Furthermore, through our awards program, we recognize young professionals in the field. This year at our annual banquet on May 1, ten young professionals from our city were the recipients of awards between $500 and $2,000 recognizing their career achievements.

As a long-time member of the Business Association, you have been a generous supporter of the Future Business Leaders Education Fund. We ask that you once again make a commitment to support our work by making a cash donation. This year, our goal is to raise $25,000 from among our membership. Your generosity, along with that of your fellow Business Association members, will allow us to continue our important work in training the business leaders of tomorrow.

Please complete the information requested on the enclosed sheet and return it, along with your check, to our office. We hope to receive all donations before the first of next month. Thank you once again for your generous support.

Sincerely,
Elisabeth Larsen
Elisabeth Larsen

168. What is the purpose of this letter?

    (A) To describe a scholarship program
    (B) To give thanks for a donation
    (C) To announce a new program
    (D) To ask for money

169. What is indicated about Mr. Harrison?

    (A) He has given money to the Education Fund in the past.
    (B) He is a new member of the Business Association.
    (C) He gives business training workshops.
    (D) He is a young business professional.

170. What happened on May 1?

    (A) A workshop was given.
    (B) There was an awards dinner.
    (C) Some scholarships were granted.
    (D) The fund received new donations.

171. What is enclosed with the letter?

    (A) A program description
    (B) A schedule
    (C) A form
    (D) A check

Questions 172-175 refer to the following article.

If you want to advance in your career, you will have to make some careful decisions, especially regarding job offers. -[1]- It is important to evaluate each offer in terms of the overall value it has for your career. -[2]- For instance, you might have to move to a new region to take a job that you feel is right for you in every other way. You may have to work late hours or even accept a decrease in salary for a job that offers you the experience you need.

-[3]- Agreeing to accept a job that is not within your career path is usually a mistake. Such a decision will not give you the training and experience you want. Moreover, you will feel frustrated because you are not working toward your goals. This will affect your colleagues, who will feel as if you are not acting as part of a team. On the other hand, if you take a position that may not be all you want in terms of salary or location but that moves you closer to your career goals, you will feel satisfied. -[4]- Study after study has shown that job satisfaction, far more than salary or other factors, results in the highest level of performance.

172. What is this advice about?

    (A) Choosing a job
    (B) Hiring staff
    (C) Getting job training
    (D) Completing a job application

173. The word "position" in paragraph 2, line 5, is closest in meaning to

    (A) opinion
    (B) location
    (C) proposition
    (D) job

174. According to the article, which workers perform best?

    (A) Those who have the right training
    (B) Those who work on a team
    (C) Those who enjoy their jobs
    (D) Those who earn the most

175. In which of the following positions marked [1], [2], [3], and [4] does the following sentence best belong?

    "You may have to make some sacrifices at first."

    (A) [1]
    (B) [2]
    (C) [3]
    (D) [4]

Questions 176–180 refer to the following agenda and email message.

HORIZON OFFICE PRODUCTS, INC.

COMMITTEE MEETING ON MARKETING

THURSDAY, JUNE 15, 20— 9:30 A.M.–11:30 A.M.

PLACE: ROOM 2

AGENDA

1. REVIEW OF CURRENT STRATEGY	BEN NGUYEN
2. GOALS FOR NEW STRATEGY	BO PARK
3. FOCUS GROUPS	MARTY TAYLOR
4. PROJECTS TO BEGIN	BARBARA SPENCER
5. PLANS FOR THE YEAR	RITA PALMER

To: Max Kohler
From: Bo Park
Subject: Committee Meeting

There were serious problems at today's meeting. We began on time, but Ben wasn't there, so we had to begin with the second agenda item. Then, thirty minutes after we began, Ben finally arrived and gave his presentation. Marty never came at all. I found out later that he's been out sick, but in any case his topic was never discussed. Barbara tried to explain her topic, but it was confusing. She did the best she could, but we really needed to hear from Marty first for her presentation to make sense. We couldn't agree on our next step, so we ended the meeting early, right after Barbara's talk. When will you return from this business trip? I know none of this would have happened if you had been here.

176. What was the topic of the June 15 meeting?

    (A) Marketing
    (B) Business trips
    (C) Work schedules
    (D) Ordering office supplies

177. What topic was discussed first?

    (A) Review of current strategy
    (B) Goals for new strategy
    (C) Focus groups
    (D) Projects to begin

178. What time did Ben start his presentation?

    (A) 9:00
    (B) 9:30
    (C) 10:00
    (D) 11:30

179. Who gave the last presentation?

    (A) Rita Palmer
    (B) Barbara Spencer
    (C) Marty Taylor
    (D) Bo Park

180. Why didn't Max attend the meeting?

    (A) He was out sick.
    (B) He wasn't invited.
    (C) He couldn't arrive on time.
    (D) He was away on a business trip.

Questions 181–185 refer to the following notice and email.

TRANSIT PASS INFORMATION
City of Springfield

Now it is easier and more affordable than ever to use the City of Springfield Public Transportation System (CSPTS). Choose the pass that best fits your needs.

C-PASSES
C-passes are good for unlimited rides anytime of day or night, Monday through Friday, except holidays.

SUBWAY C-PASS	**BUS C-PASS**	**SUBWAY/BUS C-PASS**
Two weeks: $60	Two weeks: $45	Two weeks: $75
Six months: $650	Six months: $500	Six months: $850

A-PASSES
A-passes can be used seven days a week, 24 hours a day, any day of the year.

SUBWAY A-PASS	**BUS A-PASS**	**SUBWAY/BUS A-PASS**
Two weeks: $100	Two weeks: $75	Two weeks: $125
Six months: $950	Six months: $700	Six months: $1,050

Passes are available for sale at all CSPTS subway stations, at the CSPTS downtown office, at designated banks throughout the city, and online at *www.cspts.go*.

From: Janet Jones
To: All Staff
Subj: Transit Passes
Date: November 9

In order to do our part to decrease congestion on our local roads, we are now offering all Smith Company staff members CSTPS transit passes at a reduced price. These can be used for bus and/or subway travel on all routes in the CSPTS system. To apply for the pass at the reduced price, obtain a Transit Pass Request Form from my office. After you have completed the form, have it authorized by your department head and return it to me. You can choose between a two-week and a six-month pass. Please keep in mind, however, that a new form will have to be submitted each time you need a new pass. As an added incentive to those of you who currently drive to work, we are raising the cost of parking in the company garage to $15/day starting on the first of next month.

Please let me know if you have any questions.

181. Which transit passes can be used on weekends and holidays?

   (A) Any C-pass
   (B) Any A-pass
   (C) Subway passes only
   (D) Subway/bus passes only

182. The word "good" in line 6 of the notice is closest in meaning to

   (A) nice
   (B) fresh
   (C) valid
   (D) correct

183. Who can get a discounted transit pass?

   (A) CSPTS staff
   (B) Springfield residents
   (C) Anyone who wants one
   (D) Smith Company employees

184. Where are the discounted transit passes available?

   (A) On the internet
   (B) In certain banks
   (C) At the CSPTS office
   (D) In Ms. Jones's office

185. What is the reason for the increased parking fee in the Smith Company garage?

   (A) To encourage the use of public transportation
   (B) To cover the rising cost of maintenance
   (C) To fund the expansion of the garage
   (D) To pay for the discounted passes

Questions 186-190 refer to the following notice and two emails.

Business Journalist's Convention
Accommodations

In the Convention Center neighborhood:
The *Cascade Hotel*—105 North Main St. (*www.cascadeho.com*)
The *Willowmere Inn*—12 Flower Avenue (*www.willowmereinn.com*)
Both of these hotels are within walking distance of the Convention Center.

For a more economical option, try:
Royal Hotel—234 Park Avenue (*www.parkviewho.com*)
Take the Green Line subway to the Park Avenue stop and walk east one block.

All three hotels offer a reduced rate to convention attendees. Reservations must be made before August 15 to receive this benefit.

From: Yvonne Wu
To: Royal Hotel
Subject: Room Reservation
Date: August 1

I will be attending the Business Journalist's Convention next month and would like to reserve a single room at your hotel for that time, September 15–18. I'd prefer a room on an upper floor with a queen-sized bed, if possible. Also, do you have a pool and an exercise room? I couldn't find any information about this on your website. Finally, is there a restaurant in or near the hotel?

Thank you for your help.

From: Royal Hotel
To: Yvonne Wu
Subject: re: Room Reservation
Date: August 2

Dear Ms. Wu,

We will be happy to accommodate you during your stay to attend the Business Journalist's Convention. The type of room you requested is available. With your discount, it will cost just $100 a night. However, for the first night of your stay only, we will have to give you a room with a king-sized bed, as there are no queens available that night. It costs an extra $25. I hope this will suit you. To answer your questions, our pool is currently closed for renovations, and we hope to have it reopened by the first of next year. There is a full-service restaurant located in the hotel, and our guests are entitled to a free breakfast there. Lunch and dinner are also served and can be charged to your room for your convenience. If you would like to go ahead with your reservation, please send me your credit card information. Thank you for choosing the Royal Hotel.

Bob Jimenez
Reservations Manager

186. What is indicated about the Royal Hotel?

    (A) It is the closest hotel to the Convention Center.
    (B) It costs less than the other hotels mentioned.
    (C) It has no rooms available after August 15.
    (D) It is popular among business travelers.

187. What kind of room does Ms. Wu request?

    (A) A room on the ground floor
    (B) A room with two beds
    (C) A room for one person
    (D) A room near the pool

188. Why will Ms. Wu get a discounted price on her hotel room?

    (A) She is attending the convention.
    (B) She will stay for several nights.
    (C) She is a former employee of the hotel.
    (D) She will have to change rooms after the first night.

189. What is the extra $25 charge for?

    (A) Transportation to the Convention Center
    (B) A reservation cancellation fee
    (C) A room with a larger bed
    (D) Use of the hotel pool

190. What is indicated about breakfast?

    (A) It is available at the Convention Center.
    (B) It is served all day in the hotel restaurant.
    (C) It costs extra to order it through room service.
    (D) It is included in the price of the hotel room.

Questions 191–195 refer to the following article, ad, and review.

Festival Café Reopens

The Festival Café has recently reopened following renovations that doubled its size. Located in the heart of the downtown commercial district, the café is known for its homemade ice cream. Customers have been accustomed to seeing the crowd extend along the entire length of the block on warm days, as people line up to buy this tasty frozen treat. The café is also famous for its homemade baked goods and innovative sandwiches. "Now we can accommodate many more customers at a time," said owner Bertha Maguire. "We'll have outdoor seating in warm weather as well," she added. Ms. Maguire assures loyal customers that all their old favorites are still on the menu. "We look forward to seeing old customers and new in our new space," she said.

The Festival Café
is proud to announce its
GRAND REOPENING
Come celebrate with us.
April 10, 3–8 p.m.
Free ice cream samples!
Live music! Games and prizes!
Bakery and sandwich counters
will be open.
Use the coupon below
to enjoy a free drink on us!

Festival Café
Good for
ONE COFFEE
Any size
Expires April 30

Festival Café
Good for
ONE SODA
Any size
Expires April 30

*****

by Sydney Seldman on April 12

The new Festival Café is better than ever. My family and I attended the grand reopening, and it was so much fun. The kids really loved the games and, of course, the free ice cream. The new space is nice, although I think the colors are a bit dark. But it is quite comfortable, and there is plenty of seating. The sandwiches are still fantastic, and the cake we tried was delicious and affordable. I was surprised to find that the prices had not been raised. If you are a long-time fan of the Festival, you will enjoy it as much as ever in its new space.

191. What happened at the Festival Café?

(A) The menu was changed.
(B) The space was enlarged.
(C) Old customers were lost.
(D) A new branch was opened.

192. What is implied about the Festival Café?

(A) It is very popular.
(B) It is a new business.
(C) It sells desserts only.
(D) It has several locations.

193. How can customers get a free drink?

(A) Win it as a prize
(B) Go to the grand reopening
(C) Pay for an ice cream sample
(D) Use a coupon before the end of April

194. When did Ms. Seldman go to the Festival Café?

(A) On April 10
(B) On April 12
(C) Last night
(D) Last week

195. What does Ms. Seldman say about the Festival Café?

(A) There aren't enough chairs.
(B) The prices are too high.
(C) The food is very good.
(D) The décor has improved.

Questions 196–200 refer to the following ad and two letters.

Wickford Realty Co.

For Sale

Two Retail Spaces

1. Ideal Main Street location in the heart of the downtown shopping district. Large display windows front street. Recently renovated. Near bus and subway lines. 1,500 sq ft.

2. Warren Avenue. Attractive location in the Greenwood School neighborhood. Near subway lines. Customer parking on site.

Contact Wickford Realty for more information.

The Printing Press

Dear Ms. Clark:

I have been a customer at your bank for more than ten years. I am a small business owner and have been renting a space for my operations. My company is now ready to expand, and I am looking into buying a small building.

I am interested in two buildings. The one I prefer is on Main Street. It would require a $200,000 loan, and I'm not sure if I qualify for that large a loan. There is another building that would suit my needs. The size is right, although the location is not as good. I would need to borrow only $130,000 to purchase this building.

I have a good credit record and am carrying only two debts at this time—$5,000 on my car loan and $120,000 on my house. I am hoping to get a thirty-year loan at 5% interest.

I would like to meet with you to discuss this as soon as possible. Would Tuesday, April 21 suit you? If not, I am available any other day that week. I look forward to hearing from you.

Sincerely,

Jeremiah Hernandez

Jeremiah Hernandez

FEDERAL BANK

8244 Centergate Street

San Antonio, TX 78217-0099

April 10, 20—

Jeremiah Hernandez
The Printing Press
111 Acorn Parkway
San Antonio, TX 78216-7423

Dear Mr. Hernandez:

Thank you for your interest in getting a loan from Federal Bank. We appreciate your business.

It is possible for us to lend you enough money for the cheaper building. We cannot give you a larger loan because you already have more than $100,000 in debt. We can offer you a loan at the interest rate and for the term you want.

I am happy to meet with you to discuss this. I am not available on the date you mentioned. Can we meet the following day? Please let me know.

Best Wishes,

Anneliese Clark

Anneliese Clark

196. What is indicated about the Warren Street property?

    (A) It includes a parking lot.
    (B) It is close to downtown.
    (C) It is near a bus stop.
    (D) It is very small.

197. What kind of business does Mr. Hernandez own, most likely?

    (A) A real estate office
    (B) A restaurant
    (C) A store
    (D) A school

198. Why does Mr. Hernandez prefer the Main Street Building?

    (A) It is bigger.
    (B) It is less expensive.
    (C) It is in a better location.
    (D) It is in better condition.

199. How much money will the bank lend him?

    (A) $100,000
    (B) $130,000
    (C) $200,000
    (D) $330,000

200. When does Ms. Clark want to meet with Mr. Hernandez?

    (A) April 10
    (B) April 11
    (C) April 21
    (D) April 22

STOP This is the end of the test. If you finish before time is called, you may go back to Parts 5, 6, and 7 and check your work.

多益測驗成績換算對照表

計算答對的題數,利用下表找到對應的分數。將聽力和閱讀分數相加,就會得到預估的多益測驗總分。逐一演練模擬試題,分數也會逐漸提升,請持續追蹤你的多益測驗預估總分。

答對題數	聽力分數	閱讀分數	答對題數	聽力分數	閱讀分數	答對題數	聽力分數	閱讀分數	答對題數	聽力分數	閱讀分數
0	5	5	26	110	65	51	255	220	76	410	370
1	5	5	27	115	70	52	260	225	77	420	380
2	5	5	28	120	80	53	270	230	78	425	385
3	5	5	29	125	85	54	275	235	79	430	390
4	5	5	30	130	90	55	280	240	80	440	395
5	5	5	31	135	95	56	290	250	81	445	400
6	5	5	32	140	100	57	295	255	82	450	405
7	10	5	33	145	110	58	300	260	83	460	410
8	15	5	34	150	115	59	310	265	84	465	415
9	20	5	35	160	120	60	315	270	85	470	420
10	25	5	36	165	125	61	320	280	86	475	425
11	30	5	37	170	130	62	325	285	87	480	430
12	35	5	38	175	140	63	330	290	88	485	435
13	40	5	39	180	145	64	340	300	89	490	445
14	45	5	40	185	150	65	345	305	90	495	450
15	50	5	41	190	160	66	350	310	91	495	455
16	55	10	42	195	165	67	360	320	92	495	465
17	60	15	43	200	170	68	365	325	93	495	470
18	65	20	44	210	175	69	370	330	94	495	480
19	70	25	45	215	180	70	380	335	95	495	485
20	75	30	46	220	190	71	385	340	96	495	490
21	80	35	47	230	195	72	390	350	97	495	495
22	85	40	48	240	200	73	395	355	98	495	495
23	90	45	49	245	210	74	400	360	99	495	495
24	95	50	50	250	215	75	405	365	100	495	495
25	100	60									

聽力測驗答對題數 _____ = 聽力測驗分數 _____

閱讀測驗答對題數 _____ = 閱讀測驗分數 _____

多益測驗預估總分 _____

ANSWER SHEET
實戰模擬試題3答案卡

Listening Comprehension

Part 1: Photographs

1. Ⓐ Ⓑ Ⓒ Ⓓ
2. Ⓐ Ⓑ Ⓒ Ⓓ
3. Ⓐ Ⓑ Ⓒ Ⓓ
4. Ⓐ Ⓑ Ⓒ Ⓓ
5. Ⓐ Ⓑ Ⓒ Ⓓ
6. Ⓐ Ⓑ Ⓒ Ⓓ

Part 2: Question-Response

7. Ⓐ Ⓑ Ⓒ
8. Ⓐ Ⓑ Ⓒ
9. Ⓐ Ⓑ Ⓒ
10. Ⓐ Ⓑ Ⓒ
11. Ⓐ Ⓑ Ⓒ
12. Ⓐ Ⓑ Ⓒ
13. Ⓐ Ⓑ Ⓒ
14. Ⓐ Ⓑ Ⓒ
15. Ⓐ Ⓑ Ⓒ
16. Ⓐ Ⓑ Ⓒ
17. Ⓐ Ⓑ Ⓒ
18. Ⓐ Ⓑ Ⓒ
19. Ⓐ Ⓑ Ⓒ
20. Ⓐ Ⓑ Ⓒ
21. Ⓐ Ⓑ Ⓒ
22. Ⓐ Ⓑ Ⓒ
23. Ⓐ Ⓑ Ⓒ
24. Ⓐ Ⓑ Ⓒ
25. Ⓐ Ⓑ Ⓒ
26. Ⓐ Ⓑ Ⓒ
27. Ⓐ Ⓑ Ⓒ
28. Ⓐ Ⓑ Ⓒ
29. Ⓐ Ⓑ Ⓒ
30. Ⓐ Ⓑ Ⓒ
31. Ⓐ Ⓑ Ⓒ

Part 3: Conversations

32. Ⓐ Ⓑ Ⓒ Ⓓ
33. Ⓐ Ⓑ Ⓒ Ⓓ
34. Ⓐ Ⓑ Ⓒ Ⓓ
35. Ⓐ Ⓑ Ⓒ Ⓓ
36. Ⓐ Ⓑ Ⓒ Ⓓ
37. Ⓐ Ⓑ Ⓒ Ⓓ
38. Ⓐ Ⓑ Ⓒ Ⓓ
39. Ⓐ Ⓑ Ⓒ Ⓓ
40. Ⓐ Ⓑ Ⓒ Ⓓ
41. Ⓐ Ⓑ Ⓒ Ⓓ
42. Ⓐ Ⓑ Ⓒ Ⓓ
43. Ⓐ Ⓑ Ⓒ Ⓓ
44. Ⓐ Ⓑ Ⓒ Ⓓ
45. Ⓐ Ⓑ Ⓒ Ⓓ
46. Ⓐ Ⓑ Ⓒ Ⓓ
47. Ⓐ Ⓑ Ⓒ Ⓓ
48. Ⓐ Ⓑ Ⓒ Ⓓ
49. Ⓐ Ⓑ Ⓒ Ⓓ
50. Ⓐ Ⓑ Ⓒ Ⓓ
51. Ⓐ Ⓑ Ⓒ Ⓓ
52. Ⓐ Ⓑ Ⓒ Ⓓ
53. Ⓐ Ⓑ Ⓒ Ⓓ
54. Ⓐ Ⓑ Ⓒ Ⓓ
55. Ⓐ Ⓑ Ⓒ Ⓓ
56. Ⓐ Ⓑ Ⓒ Ⓓ
57. Ⓐ Ⓑ Ⓒ Ⓓ
58. Ⓐ Ⓑ Ⓒ Ⓓ
59. Ⓐ Ⓑ Ⓒ Ⓓ
60. Ⓐ Ⓑ Ⓒ Ⓓ
61. Ⓐ Ⓑ Ⓒ Ⓓ
62. Ⓐ Ⓑ Ⓒ Ⓓ
63. Ⓐ Ⓑ Ⓒ Ⓓ
64. Ⓐ Ⓑ Ⓒ Ⓓ
65. Ⓐ Ⓑ Ⓒ Ⓓ
66. Ⓐ Ⓑ Ⓒ Ⓓ
67. Ⓐ Ⓑ Ⓒ Ⓓ
68. Ⓐ Ⓑ Ⓒ Ⓓ
69. Ⓐ Ⓑ Ⓒ Ⓓ
70. Ⓐ Ⓑ Ⓒ Ⓓ

Part 4: Talks

71. Ⓐ Ⓑ Ⓒ Ⓓ
72. Ⓐ Ⓑ Ⓒ Ⓓ
73. Ⓐ Ⓑ Ⓒ Ⓓ
74. Ⓐ Ⓑ Ⓒ Ⓓ
75. Ⓐ Ⓑ Ⓒ Ⓓ
76. Ⓐ Ⓑ Ⓒ Ⓓ
77. Ⓐ Ⓑ Ⓒ Ⓓ
78. Ⓐ Ⓑ Ⓒ Ⓓ
79. Ⓐ Ⓑ Ⓒ Ⓓ
80. Ⓐ Ⓑ Ⓒ Ⓓ
81. Ⓐ Ⓑ Ⓒ Ⓓ
82. Ⓐ Ⓑ Ⓒ Ⓓ
82. Ⓐ Ⓑ Ⓒ Ⓓ
84. Ⓐ Ⓑ Ⓒ Ⓓ
85. Ⓐ Ⓑ Ⓒ Ⓓ
86. Ⓐ Ⓑ Ⓒ Ⓓ
87. Ⓐ Ⓑ Ⓒ Ⓓ
88. Ⓐ Ⓑ Ⓒ Ⓓ
89. Ⓐ Ⓑ Ⓒ Ⓓ
90. Ⓐ Ⓑ Ⓒ Ⓓ
91. Ⓐ Ⓑ Ⓒ Ⓓ
92. Ⓐ Ⓑ Ⓒ Ⓓ
93. Ⓐ Ⓑ Ⓒ Ⓓ
94. Ⓐ Ⓑ Ⓒ Ⓓ
95. Ⓐ Ⓑ Ⓒ Ⓓ
96. Ⓐ Ⓑ Ⓒ Ⓓ
97. Ⓐ Ⓑ Ⓒ Ⓓ
98. Ⓐ Ⓑ Ⓒ Ⓓ
99. Ⓐ Ⓑ Ⓒ Ⓓ
100. Ⓐ Ⓑ Ⓒ Ⓓ

ANSWER SHEET
實戰模擬試題3答案卡

Reading Comprehension

Part 5: Incomplete Sentences

101. Ⓐ Ⓑ Ⓒ Ⓓ
102. Ⓐ Ⓑ Ⓒ Ⓓ
103. Ⓐ Ⓑ Ⓒ Ⓓ
104. Ⓐ Ⓑ Ⓒ Ⓓ
105. Ⓐ Ⓑ Ⓒ Ⓓ
106. Ⓐ Ⓑ Ⓒ Ⓓ
107. Ⓐ Ⓑ Ⓒ Ⓓ
108. Ⓐ Ⓑ Ⓒ Ⓓ
109. Ⓐ Ⓑ Ⓒ Ⓓ
110. Ⓐ Ⓑ Ⓒ Ⓓ
111. Ⓐ Ⓑ Ⓒ Ⓓ
112. Ⓐ Ⓑ Ⓒ Ⓓ
113. Ⓐ Ⓑ Ⓒ Ⓓ
114. Ⓐ Ⓑ Ⓒ Ⓓ
115. Ⓐ Ⓑ Ⓒ Ⓓ
116. Ⓐ Ⓑ Ⓒ Ⓓ
117. Ⓐ Ⓑ Ⓒ Ⓓ
118. Ⓐ Ⓑ Ⓒ Ⓓ
119. Ⓐ Ⓑ Ⓒ Ⓓ
120. Ⓐ Ⓑ Ⓒ Ⓓ
121. Ⓐ Ⓑ Ⓒ Ⓓ
122. Ⓐ Ⓑ Ⓒ Ⓓ
123. Ⓐ Ⓑ Ⓒ Ⓓ
124. Ⓐ Ⓑ Ⓒ Ⓓ
125. Ⓐ Ⓑ Ⓒ Ⓓ
126. Ⓐ Ⓑ Ⓒ Ⓓ
127. Ⓐ Ⓑ Ⓒ Ⓓ
128. Ⓐ Ⓑ Ⓒ Ⓓ
129. Ⓐ Ⓑ Ⓒ Ⓓ
130. Ⓐ Ⓑ Ⓒ Ⓓ

Part 6: Text Completion

131. Ⓐ Ⓑ Ⓒ Ⓓ
132. Ⓐ Ⓑ Ⓒ Ⓓ
133. Ⓐ Ⓑ Ⓒ Ⓓ
134. Ⓐ Ⓑ Ⓒ Ⓓ
135. Ⓐ Ⓑ Ⓒ Ⓓ
136. Ⓐ Ⓑ Ⓒ Ⓓ
137. Ⓐ Ⓑ Ⓒ Ⓓ
138. Ⓐ Ⓑ Ⓒ Ⓓ
139. Ⓐ Ⓑ Ⓒ Ⓓ
140. Ⓐ Ⓑ Ⓒ Ⓓ
141. Ⓐ Ⓑ Ⓒ Ⓓ
142. Ⓐ Ⓑ Ⓒ Ⓓ
143. Ⓐ Ⓑ Ⓒ Ⓓ
144. Ⓐ Ⓑ Ⓒ Ⓓ
145. Ⓐ Ⓑ Ⓒ Ⓓ
146. Ⓐ Ⓑ Ⓒ Ⓓ

Part 7: Reading Comprehension

147. Ⓐ Ⓑ Ⓒ Ⓓ
148. Ⓐ Ⓑ Ⓒ Ⓓ
149. Ⓐ Ⓑ Ⓒ Ⓓ
150. Ⓐ Ⓑ Ⓒ Ⓓ
151. Ⓐ Ⓑ Ⓒ Ⓓ
152. Ⓐ Ⓑ Ⓒ Ⓓ
153. Ⓐ Ⓑ Ⓒ Ⓓ
154. Ⓐ Ⓑ Ⓒ Ⓓ
155. Ⓐ Ⓑ Ⓒ Ⓓ
156. Ⓐ Ⓑ Ⓒ Ⓓ
157. Ⓐ Ⓑ Ⓒ Ⓓ
158. Ⓐ Ⓑ Ⓒ Ⓓ
159. Ⓐ Ⓑ Ⓒ Ⓓ
160. Ⓐ Ⓑ Ⓒ Ⓓ
161. Ⓐ Ⓑ Ⓒ Ⓓ
162. Ⓐ Ⓑ Ⓒ Ⓓ
163. Ⓐ Ⓑ Ⓒ Ⓓ
164. Ⓐ Ⓑ Ⓒ Ⓓ
165. Ⓐ Ⓑ Ⓒ Ⓓ
166. Ⓐ Ⓑ Ⓒ Ⓓ
167. Ⓐ Ⓑ Ⓒ Ⓓ
168. Ⓐ Ⓑ Ⓒ Ⓓ
169. Ⓐ Ⓑ Ⓒ Ⓓ
170. Ⓐ Ⓑ Ⓒ Ⓓ
171. Ⓐ Ⓑ Ⓒ Ⓓ
172. Ⓐ Ⓑ Ⓒ Ⓓ
173. Ⓐ Ⓑ Ⓒ Ⓓ
174. Ⓐ Ⓑ Ⓒ Ⓓ
175. Ⓐ Ⓑ Ⓒ Ⓓ
176. Ⓐ Ⓑ Ⓒ Ⓓ
177. Ⓐ Ⓑ Ⓒ Ⓓ
178. Ⓐ Ⓑ Ⓒ Ⓓ
179. Ⓐ Ⓑ Ⓒ Ⓓ
180. Ⓐ Ⓑ Ⓒ Ⓓ
181. Ⓐ Ⓑ Ⓒ Ⓓ
182. Ⓐ Ⓑ Ⓒ Ⓓ
183. Ⓐ Ⓑ Ⓒ Ⓓ
184. Ⓐ Ⓑ Ⓒ Ⓓ
185. Ⓐ Ⓑ Ⓒ Ⓓ
186. Ⓐ Ⓑ Ⓒ Ⓓ
187. Ⓐ Ⓑ Ⓒ Ⓓ
188. Ⓐ Ⓑ Ⓒ Ⓓ
189. Ⓐ Ⓑ Ⓒ Ⓓ
190. Ⓐ Ⓑ Ⓒ Ⓓ
191. Ⓐ Ⓑ Ⓒ Ⓓ
192. Ⓐ Ⓑ Ⓒ Ⓓ
193. Ⓐ Ⓑ Ⓒ Ⓓ
194. Ⓐ Ⓑ Ⓒ Ⓓ
195. Ⓐ Ⓑ Ⓒ Ⓓ
196. Ⓐ Ⓑ Ⓒ Ⓓ
197. Ⓐ Ⓑ Ⓒ Ⓓ
198. Ⓐ Ⓑ Ⓒ Ⓓ
199. Ⓐ Ⓑ Ⓒ Ⓓ
200. Ⓐ Ⓑ Ⓒ Ⓓ

MODEL TEST 3

實戰模擬試題 3

Listening Comprehension

In this section of the test, you will have the chance to show how well you understand spoken English. There are four parts to this section, with special directions for each part. You will have approximately 45 minutes to complete the Listening Comprehension sections.

Part 1: Photographs

DIRECTIONS: You will see a photograph. You will hear four statements about the photograph. Choose the statement that most closely matches the photograph, and fill in the corresponding oval on your answer sheet.

Track 43

1.

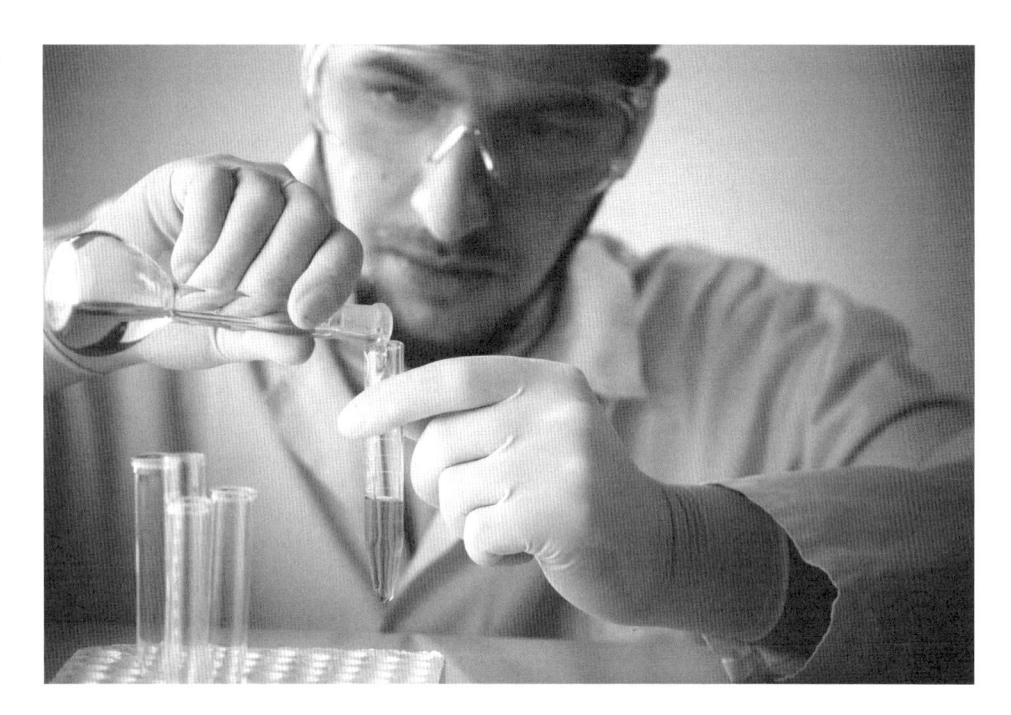

2.

3.

4.

5.

6.

Part 2: Question-Response

DIRECTIONS: You will hear a question and three possible responses. Choose the response that most closely answers the question, and fill in the corresponding oval on your answer sheet.

Track 44

7. Mark your answer on your answer sheet.
8. Mark your answer on your answer sheet.
9. Mark your answer on your answer sheet.
10. Mark your answer on your answer sheet.
11. Mark your answer on your answer sheet.
12. Mark your answer on your answer sheet.
13. Mark your answer on your answer sheet.
14. Mark your answer on your answer sheet.
15. Mark your answer on your answer sheet.
16. Mark your answer on your answer sheet.
17. Mark your answer on your answer sheet.
18. Mark your answer on your answer sheet.
19. Mark your answer on your answer sheet.
20. Mark your answer on your answer sheet.
21. Mark your answer on your answer sheet.
22. Mark your answer on your answer sheet.
23. Mark your answer on your answer sheet.
24. Mark your answer on your answer sheet.
25. Mark your answer on your answer sheet.
26. Mark your answer on your answer sheet.
27. Mark your answer on your answer sheet.
28. Mark your answer on your answer sheet.
29. Mark your answer on your answer sheet.
30. Mark your answer on your answer sheet.
31. Mark your answer on your answer sheet.

Part 3: Conversations

DIRECTIONS: You will hear a conversation between two or more people. You will see three questions on each conversation and four possible answers. Choose the best answer to each question, and fill in the corresponding oval on your answer sheet.

32. Where did the man learn about the event?

    (A) In a newspaper
    (B) On the internet
    (C) On the radio
    (D) From a friend

33. Why can't they go on Saturday?

    (A) The man promised to help someone.
    (B) The woman has plans to go to a dance.
    (C) The man has to look for a new apartment.
    (D) The woman has to work that day.

34. What does the woman want to do?

    (A) Not go
    (B) Go on Sunday
    (C) Go to next year's event
    (D) Wait until their friend can go

35. What is the appointment for?

    (A) A medical checkup
    (B) A sales meeting
    (C) A possible presentation
    (D) A job interview

36. When will the appointment take place?

    (A) On Tuesday morning
    (B) At 8:30 in the evening
    (C) Tomorrow at ten
    (D) Today at noon

37. What should the man bring?

    (A) An application
    (B) A finished test
    (C) His résumé
    (D) Nothing

38. Where is the woman?

    (A) At a department store
    (B) At a repair shop
    (C) At a hotel
    (D) At home

39. What will the man do?

    (A) Turn the TV on
    (B) Take the TV away
    (C) Have someone fix the TV
    (D) Show the woman a different TV

40. What does the woman ask the man to do?

    (A) Wait half an hour
    (B) Come back at 10:00
    (C) Send her a package
    (D) Take a picture

41. Why do the speakers need Mr. Chung?

    (A) To deliver some letters
    (B) To speak at a meeting
    (C) To announce the date
    (D) To loan them his car

42. Why is Mr. Chung late?

    (A) He lost the address.
    (B) He's stuck in traffic.
    (C) His car broke down.
    (D) He's making a phone call.

43. What will the man do next?

    (A) Look for Mr. Chung
    (B) Prepare to show a film
    (C) Take Mr. Chung's place
    (D) Start the meeting

44. What was painted?

   (A) The cafeteria
   (B) The office
   (C) The lobby
   (D) The hallways

45. What does the woman say about the elevator?

   (A) It is very messy.
   (B) It runs too slowly.
   (C) Its color makes her feel sad.
   (D) It needs a new set of lights.

46. What will the woman do next week?

   (A) Choose paint colors
   (B) Meet a new client
   (C) Eat in the cafeteria
   (D) Go away on a trip

47. What does the woman say about the man?

   (A) He's an excellent golfer.
   (B) He cooks every day.
   (C) He is often bored.
   (D) He's very busy.

48. What does the woman like to do?

   (A) Run
   (B) Eat
   (C) Cook
   (D) Read

49. What does the woman mean when she says, "That's no good"?

   (A) She can't meet the man tomorrow.
   (B) She thinks the man doesn't cook well.
   (C) She doesn't enjoy going out in the evening.
   (D) She doesn't want to have dinner with the man.

50. What is the man's problem?

   (A) He wants something to drink.
   (B) He needs to change the oil.
   (C) He has run out of gas.
   (D) He has a flat tire.

51. Where is the service station?

   (A) On the other side of the road
   (B) Several miles away
   (C) In the next town
   (D) Near a bridge

52. How will the man get to the service station?

   (A) He will walk.
   (B) He will take a bus.
   (C) He will drive his car.
   (D) He will ride with the woman.

53. What does the woman want to do?

   (A) Go on a diet
   (B) Get more exercise
   (C) Get a gym membership
   (D) Find a better place to eat lunch

54. What does the man say about the gym?

   (A) It is crowded.
   (B) It is expensive.
   (C) It is far away.
   (D) It is cold.

55. Where does the man eat his lunch?

   (A) At home
   (B) At his desk
   (C) In the park
   (D) In the cafeteria

56. What does Maria mean when she says, "I know"?

   (A) She is familiar with the offices on the fifth floor.
   (B) She agrees with what the other woman said.
   (C) She understands how to get a good office.
   (D) She has some important information.

57. What describes the man's office?

   (A) It is near a park.
   (B) It is bright and sunny.
   (C) It overlooks a vacant lot.
   (D) It has a view of the parking lot.

58. What is suggested about the man?

   (A) He is unhappy with his job.
   (B) He is worried about his work.
   (C) He has been at his job a short time.
   (D) He often works until late at night.

59. What is the woman doing?

   (A) Ordering a meal
   (B) Planning a menu
   (C) Cooking some food
   (D) Shopping for groceries

60. What time of day is it?

   (A) Morning
   (B) Noon
   (C) Afternoon
   (D) Night

61. What will the man do next?

   (A) Bring ice cream
   (B) Bring a menu
   (C) Serve coffee
   (D) Look for jelly

62. Where does this conversation take place?

   (A) On a cruise ship
   (B) On a tour bus
   (C) On a plane
   (D) On a train

63. What does the woman ask about?

   (A) The length of the trip
   (B) The cost of tickets
   (C) The arrival time
   (D) The weather

64. What does the man recommend?

   (A) Taking a guided tour
   (B) Walking around
   (C) Leaving the city
   (D) Going to a café

Conference Room Schedule

Monday	Tuesday	Wednesday	Thursday
Training Session	Staff Meeting	Job Interviews	Workshop

65. What has to be cleaned?

   (A) The furniture
   (B) The windows
   (C) The walls
   (D) The carpet

66. Look at the graphic. When will the cleaning be done?

   (A) Monday
   (B) Tuesday
   (C) Wednesday
   (D) Thursday

67. What was the problem with the previous cleaners?

   (A) They charged too much.
   (B) They always arrived late.
   (C) They never finished the job.
   (D) They were difficult to schedule.

Clark's Department Store

Don't miss our storewide sale!
School supplies......................10% off
Housewares...........................15% off
Clothing................................20% off
Books and toys......................25% off

68. Look at the graphic. How much of a discount will the woman get on her purchase?

   (A) 10%
   (B) 15%
   (C) 20%
   (D) 25%

69. What does the woman ask the man for?

   (A) Another color
   (B) A larger size
   (C) Gift wrapping
   (D) More discounts

70. What does the man say about the item the woman is purchasing?

   (A) It is very popular.
   (B) It is of high quality.
   (C) It is a new item in the store.
   (D) It is available this week only.

Part 4: Talks

DIRECTIONS: You will hear a talk given by a single speaker. You will see three questions on each talk, each with four possible answers. Choose the best answer to each question, and fill in the corresponding oval on your answer sheet.

Track 46

71. What kind of event is being announced?
    (A) A garden tour
    (B) A high school graduation
    (C) The opening of a new park
    (D) The inauguration of a new mayor

72. When will the event take place?
    (A) Next Thursday
    (B) Next week
    (C) Next weekend
    (D) Next year

73. How can you get a ticket for the ceremony?
    (A) Line up at the park
    (B) Pay three dollars
    (C) Order it online
    (D) Call City Hall

74. What kind of training does this school provide?
    (A) Computer skills
    (B) Business management
    (C) Personnel training
    (D) Teacher preparation

75. What is indicated about the school?
    (A) It is very popular.
    (B) It has many students.
    (C) It has recently opened.
    (D) It is for working people.

76. What service does the school provide?
    (A) Help finding employment
    (B) Tutoring for individuals
    (C) Free parking on site
    (D) Tuition assistance

77. Why is Mr. Robertson going to Boston?
    (A) To be a radio station guest
    (B) To attend a workshop
    (C) To meet with a client
    (D) To enjoy a vacation

78. How will Mr. Robertson get to Boston?
    (A) By train
    (B) By taxi
    (C) By plane
    (D) By car

79. What is in the email?
    (A) A travel ticket
    (B) A trip schedule
    (C) A hotel reservation
    (D) A question list

80. What kind of business most likely is Whitman's Downtown?
    (A) Delivery service
    (B) Furniture store
    (C) Interior decorator
    (D) Rug cleaning service

81. What does the speaker mean when he says, "That was taken care of"?
    (A) The order has been placed.
    (B) The invoice has been prepared.
    (C) The rug has already been paid for.
    (D) The store will handle the rug carefully.

82. What does the speaker ask the listener to do?
    (A) Call to make an appointment
    (B) Check the delivery schedule
    (C) Visit Whitman's by 5:30
    (D) Review the records

83. What is a requirement for job applicants?

   (A) A professional certificate
   (B) Availability on weekends
   (C) A high school diploma
   (D) Previous experience

84. What is mentioned as a job benefit?

   (A) Possible promotions
   (B) Regular salary raises
   (C) Paid vacation time
   (D) Insurance

85. How should you apply for these jobs?

   (A) Send a résumé
   (B) Go to the hotel
   (C) Write a letter
   (D) Make a phone call

86. Where would you hear this message?

   (A) At a bus station
   (B) At a train station
   (C) At an airport
   (D) At a subway station

87. What should the customer do first?

   (A) Insert a credit card
   (B) Check the ticket price
   (C) Enter the travel schedule
   (D) Select one-way or round trip

88. How can a customer pay cash?

   (A) Show an ID card
   (B) Go to the ticket office
   (C) Insert dollar bills in the slot
   (D) Buy the ticket from the driver

89. What is the purpose of this talk?

   (A) To compare different work methods
   (B) To describe some relaxation techniques
   (C) To explain how to organize work schedules
   (D) To give advice about relaxing during the work day

90. According to the speaker, how can you keep others from disturbing you?

   (A) Work at home
   (B) Close the door
   (C) Take a vacation
   (D) Put up a "Do not disturb" sign

91. What does the speaker mean when he says, "They don't consider that a poor use of time"?

   (A) Efficiency is a common goal.
   (B) Taking naps can be very useful.
   (C) Executives don't often have free time.
   (D) It is important to organize your time well.

92. Who are the awards for?

   (A) Professional musicians
   (B) Orchestra members
   (C) Young musicians
   (D) Music teachers

93. What kind of award is being given?

   (A) Cash
   (B) Trophy
   (C) A trip
   (D) A musical instrument

94. What are listeners asked to do?

   (A) Pay their bills
   (B) Give money
   (C) Teach music
   (D) Practice more

Highbury House

Blue Room	Red Room
Maps	Documents
Main Hall	Green Room
Paintings	History Displays

Painting Schedule

Monday	Tuesday	Wednesday	Thursday
Reception Area	Staff Break Room	Conference Room	Front Office

95. What was the original use of Highbury House?

   (A) Private family home
   (B) Office building
   (C) Museum
   (D) Hotel

96. Look at the graphic. Which exhibit will listeners be unable to see today?

   (A) Maps
   (B) Paintings
   (C) Documents
   (D) History displays

97. What does the speaker suggest listeners do?

   (A) Check the concert schedule
   (B) Visit the flower gardens
   (C) Return later in the year
   (D) Have lunch soon

98. What event will take place next week?

   (A) A luncheon
   (B) Inventory
   (C) A staff meeting
   (D) Conference registration

99. Look at the graphic. Which day will the event take place?

   (A) Monday
   (B) Tuesday
   (C) Wednesday
   (D) Thursday

100. What are listeners asked to do next?

   (A) Put the tables away
   (B) Check the schedule
   (C) Return their cups
   (D) Have some coffee

This is the end of the Listening Comprehension portion of the test.
STOP Turn to Part 5 in your test book.

Reading Comprehension

In this section of the test, you will have the chance to show how well you understand written English. There are three parts to this section, with special directions for each part.

YOU WILL HAVE ONE HOUR AND FIFTEEN MINUTES TO COMPLETE PARTS 5, 6, AND 7 OF THE TEST.

Part 5: Incomplete Sentences

> **DIRECTIONS:** You will see a sentence with a missing word. Four possible answers follow the sentence. Choose the best answer to the question, and fill in the corresponding oval on your answer sheet.

101. The office would look much better with a new coat of paint _____ a few pictures hanging on the walls.

    (A) but
    (B) and
    (C) as
    (D) though

102. Most people in the department are _____ that staffing cuts will have to be made.

    (A) aware
    (B) await
    (C) awaken
    (D) awe

103. The itinerary _____ the time and location of each meeting Dr. Richards has while he is visiting the department.

    (A) contain
    (B) contains
    (C) containing
    (D) have contained

104. Passengers can check in for the charter flight _____ 8:00 and 12:00 tomorrow.

    (A) between
    (B) with
    (C) through
    (D) from

105. The landscaper made several _____, including the installation of an automatic watering system.

    (A) recommends
    (B) recommended
    (C) recommendations
    (D) recommendable

106. Because of traffic problems, you will get there _____ by train than by car.

    (A) fast
    (B) the fastest
    (C) the faster
    (D) faster

107. You can pay your bill online, _____ you can send a check by regular mail.

    (A) so
    (B) or
    (C) but
    (D) since

108. All conference speakers need to be notified that their allowed time has been _____ from 30 minutes to 25 minutes.

    (A) heightened
    (B) lengthened
    (C) shortened
    (D) widened

109. I will ask my assistant _____ the necessary forms to you at your office.
    (A) to send
    (B) sending
    (C) will send
    (D) sends

110. Ms. Chang is very frugal and buys most of _____ business suits at large discount stores.
    (A) that
    (B) them
    (C) our
    (D) her

111. With so much light pollution in the city, it's difficult _____ many stars at night.
    (A) see
    (B) sees
    (C) to see
    (D) seeing

112. Once every three months, all stockroom employees are _____ to work overnight to do inventory.
    (A) required
    (B) suggested
    (C) preferred
    (D) appreciated

113. The variety of insurance benefits _____ very broad under this policy.
    (A) are
    (B) is
    (C) being
    (D) be

114. The purpose of the awards banquet is to _____ the many achievements of our talented staff.
    (A) acknowledge
    (B) determine
    (C) entertain
    (D) discern

115. Please leave your luggage _____ the bus for the driver to load.
    (A) among
    (B) between
    (C) from
    (D) beside

116. The hotel offers a discount for guests who stay a _____ of three nights.
    (A) podium
    (B) optimum
    (C) minimum
    (D) premium

117. If we were not certain about the safety of the product, we _____ it.
   (A) had sold
   (B) don't sell
   (C) will sell
   (D) would not sell

118. The company handbook _____ the department's policies on building customer relationships.
   (A) explains
   (B) is explaining
   (C) explain
   (D) explaining

119. Model 34 is on backorder with the _____ and probably won't be here until spring.
   (A) candidate
   (B) transportation
   (C) manufacturer
   (D) customer

120. Mr. Larsen says that he will _____ consider military veterans for the foreman position.
   (A) all
   (B) only
   (C) some
   (D) except

121. _____ we checked the budget twice, the managers found a mistake in our calculations.
   (A) Unless
   (B) However
   (C) Since
   (D) Even though

122. Everyone else left the office early, so Harry had to finish up the report by _____.
   (A) alone
   (B) just
   (C) himself
   (D) single

123. Ethel's economic predictions for the coming year _____ by her colleagues with some skepticism.
   (A) were received
   (B) were receiving
   (C) had received
   (D) received

124. Doctors _____ have recently been licensed use the medical association's website to find jobs.
   (A) what
   (B) who
   (C) whose
   (D) which

125. The only difference _____ the two flights your assistant suggested is the time of departure.

    (A) with
    (B) then
    (C) between
    (D) among

126. _____ careful planning, the caterers did not bring enough linens for the tables.

    (A) During
    (B) Because
    (C) In spite of
    (D) Although

127. The project manager is responsible for _____ every step of the project.

    (A) organization
    (B) organizing
    (C) organized
    (D) organize

128. The head of accounts _____ to sit in on the client meeting tomorrow.

    (A) decisions
    (B) are deciding
    (C) has decided
    (D) decide

129. The promotional message needs to emphasize that our product is better _____ all similar products on the market.

    (A) much
    (B) than
    (C) off
    (D) to

130. Mr. Kim spent most of the week preparing _____ his new idea to the director.

    (A) present
    (B) presented
    (C) presenting
    (D) to present

Part 6: Text Completion

DIRECTIONS: You will see four passages, each with four blanks. Each blank has four answer choices. For each blank, choose the word, phrase, or sentence that best completes the passage.

Questions 131–134 refer to the following letter.

Green Office Renovators
Da'an District, Taipei City 106-03
TAIWAN

Kao Su Mei, Vice President
377 Chiang An Road
Da'an District, Taipei City 106-03
TAIWAN

Dear Ms. Kao,

Thank you for considering Green Office Renovators for your upcoming office renovation project. I hope you will take the time to read through the enclosed brochure, which explains the materials we use and the measures we take to meet the highest standards for environmental protection. _____(131)_____ also outlines the services we provide, as well as our pricing system. Please note that Green Office Renovators _____(132)_____ a minimum deposit before work can begin on any project. The initial costs of installing energy-efficient systems can be high. _____(133)_____.

In addition, statistics show that companies that demonstrate _____(134)_____ the environment are more popular among customers.

I look forward to discussing the renovation needs of your company.

Sincerely,
Cai Mi
Cai Mi

412

131. (A) You
    (B) He
    (C) It
    (D) We

132. (A) requires
    (B) require
    (C) have required
    (D) are requiring

133. (A) Fortunately, the installation process is not overly complicated
    (B) Our workers are highly trained in all aspects of these systems
    (C) Nevertheless, these systems are used in both residences and businesses
    (D) However, they save money in the long run

134. (A) concern for
    (B) happiness about
    (C) placement in
    (D) knowledge of

Questions 135–138 refer to the following email.

To: clementinebooks@learning.org
From: rep990@gaspower.net
Subject: Equal Payment Billing Plan

Dear Sheldon Murray,

It has come to my attention that your business is still paying its gas bills using our Monthly Plan. During the past year, your _____ bill was for $400 in the month of January. However, your bills were as low as $23 in the summer months.
135

_____. We believe that you are an excellent candidate for our Equal Billing Plan. Approximately 78% of our customers have switched to this option since it became available three years ago. Though the amount of money you spend in the year will be identical, your higher bills will be _____ throughout the year. This makes it easier to budget your finances.
136   137

With the Equal Billing Plan, the amount you pay per month is based on an approximation. To do this we take an average from the bills in your previous year. After six months on the Equal Billing Plan we will adjust this amount depending on whether or not you use more or less gas than we _____. At the end of the year you will receive a debit or credit from us to balance the amount owed with the amount used.
138

135. (A) high
 (B) higher
 (C) highest
 (D) the most high

136. (A) We appreciate that you paid all of your monthly bills on time
 (B) The majority of your annual fees occurred in the four coldest months of the year
 (C) In fact, your summer bills were among the lowest of all our customers'
 (D) You may be aware that we now offer electronic billing for customers in your region

137. (A) marked down
 (B) built up
 (C) spread out
 (D) topped off

138. (A) estimated
 (B) permitted
 (C) inquired
 (D) ordered

Questions 139–142 refer to the following article.

Airport Lounge Removes Free Internet Service

By Kelly Christie

As of this Friday, passengers at Port Elizabeth Airport will no longer _____ free internet service in the business travelers' lounge. Since January of last year, free internet access has been available in the airport business lounge to travelers who have purchased a VIP card. VIP card holders enjoy numerous _____ in the business lounge in addition to internet access, including coffee, snacks, newspapers, and the use of printers. _____. Now users of the business lounge will need to purchase internet access at a cost of $5 per hour, with a two-hour _____.

139. (A) offer
 (B) offered
 (C) be offered
 (D) be offering

140. (A) utilities
 (B) furniture
 (C) benefits
 (D) functions

141. (A) Business travelers spend hours each month waiting in airports
 (B) The Airport Authority has plans to renovate the lounge next year
 (C) Prices at the airport are notoriously higher than in other parts of the city
 (D) The lounges also provide an escape from crowded waiting rooms

142. (A) minimum
 (B) minimal
 (C) minimize
 (D) minimally

Questions 143-146 refer to the following email.

From: shih-yismith@techworld.com
Subject: Technology conference
Date: October 10
To: yi-fangwu@techworld.com

Are you interested in going to that international technology conference in Taipei in December? I've never been, but everyone ___(143)___ it's the place to go to learn about the latest technology. I missed going last year because I just ___(144)___ find the time, but I know I can make it work this year. I really hope you'll be able to join me. ___(145)___. If you want to attend the conference, then we should talk to our ___(146)___ as soon as possible to make sure we can get permission. Please get back to me soon.

Shih-Yi

---

143. (A) say
(B) says
(C) are saying
(D) have said

144. (A) can't
(B) mustn't
(C) shouldn't
(D) couldn't

145. (A) I think you would get a lot out of it
(B) I like keeping up with the new technology
(C) It takes place in a different country every year
(D) You have taught me a lot about technology development

146. (A) colleagues
(B) supervisors
(C) assistants
(D) customers

Part 7: Reading Comprehension

DIRECTIONS: You will see single and multiple reading passages followed by several questions. Each question has four answer choices. Choose the best answer to the question, and fill in the corresponding oval on your answer sheet.

Questions 147–148 refer to the following advertisement.

WHY WAIT FOR A BETTER JOB?

Get a great job now!

National Air

is hiring full-time representatives for
Sales & Reservations. Talk to our employees
and discover why we're the best thing in the air.
Interviews on the spot!
Bring your résumé.

OPEN HOUSE
National Air Headquarters
Southeast Regional Airport
Thursday, June 15   7:30 P.M.

147. What is the purpose of this ad?

   (A) To advertise a job training program
   (B) To sell airline tickets
   (C) To recruit potential employees
   (D) To introduce the new headquarters

148. Where will the event be held?

   (A) At company headquarters
   (B) At a private home
   (C) On an airplane
   (D) At the company's regional office

Questions 149–150 refer to the following notice.

> ## ATTENTION RIDERS
>
> - Pay exact fare when boarding. Drivers cannot make change.
> - Upon boarding, move to the rear. Stand in the passenger area. Do not block doors.
> - Allow senior citizens and disabled riders to use the priority seating area near the front.
> - Earphones must be used when listening to music.
> - No food or open beverages. No smoking.
>
> *Thank you for riding with us!*

149. Where would you see this notice?

    (A) At a train station
    (B) On an airplane
    (C) In a taxi
    (D) On a bus

150. Which of the following is permitted?

    (A) Smoking by the door
    (B) Listening to music
    (C) Having a snack
    (D) Drinking coffee

Questions 151–152 refer to the following text message chain.

LI CHEN	11:20
They have the paper you wanted. Two packs, right?	
LINA GIAMETTI	11:21
Right. And the envelopes?	
LI CHEN	11:22
They have the size you wanted, but not in red.	
LI CHEN	11:24
They can order them for you, but it takes 5–7 days.	
LINA GIAMETTI	11:26
That's no good. The mailing has to go out by Thursday, at the latest.	
LI CHEN	11:27
The only color they have in stock in that size is ivory.	
LINA GIAMETTI	11:29
That will have to do.	
LI CHEN	11:31
OK. Do you still want me to get two boxes?	
LINA GIAMETTI	11:32
Yes. And don't forget to put it on the company credit card.	

151. Where is Mr. Chen?

　(A) At home
　(B) At a store
　(C) In his office
　(D) In the supply room

152. At 11:29, what does Ms. Giametti mean when she writes, "That will have to do"?

　(A) She will use the ivory envelopes.
　(B) She doesn't want the envelopes now.
　(C) She has to complete the mailing on time.
　(D) She wants Mr. Chen to order red envelopes.

Questions 153–154 refer to the following table.

Results of Study on Time Distribution of Tasks for Sales Managers	
Training new personnel	20%
Identifying possible clients	20%
Reviewing sales data	28%
Resolving customer problems	5%
Making sales assignments	15%
Coordinating with technical staff	7%
Administrative duties	5%

153. What do sales managers spend the most time on?

    (A) Training staff
    (B) Going over sales records
    (C) Making sales assignments
    (D) Performing administrative duties

154. What can be concluded from this information?

    (A) Too much time is spent with technical staff
    (B) Finding new customers is a low priority
    (C) There are few customer problems
    (D) Sales are going down

Questions 155–157 refer to the following advertisement.

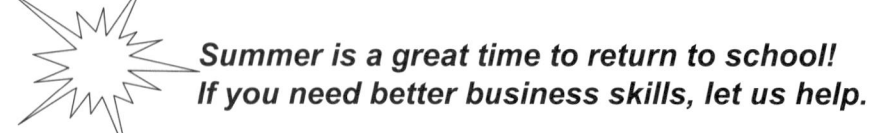

Summer is a great time to return to school!
If you need better business skills, let us help.

Each summer Claybourne University School of Business Administration offers special courses for experienced managers who want to sharpen their existing business skills or learn new ones. You will study with your peers in a week-long intensive session that simulates the world of international commerce. You will learn new theories and study the way business is conducted around the world. Students in previous sessions have reported that what they learned was immediately applicable to their own work situations.

Only one person from a company is accepted into this special program. All applications require a letter of recommendation from your current supervisor.

For more information, contact
Summer Education Center
School of Business Administration
Claybourne University
903-477-6768   admissions@suedcen.edu

155. Who is this course for?

    (A) Professional managers
    (B) College professors changing careers
    (C) Undergraduate business students
    (D) Administrative support staff

156. What is required for admission?

    (A) An entrance exam
    (B) A business degree
    (C) International experience
    (D) A reference from your boss

157. How long is the course?

    (A) All summer long
    (B) One week
    (C) Three evenings a month
    (D) Two years

Questions 158–160 refer to the following webpage.

Home   Shop   About Us   My Cart

Ginger's Botanical Designs

Our Story

For 25 years, Ginger's has been helping to beautify the homes and businesses of Burkettsville. Whatever occasion you are celebrating—from a simple birthday greeting to a lavish wedding—our bouquets, baskets, wreathes, and garlands will transform it into a beautifully memorable experience. –[1]–

Ginger's was founded by Ginger Carpenter in a small store front on Main Street. It quickly became popular and the business thrived. –[2]– It soon grew out of its small downtown space, and Ginger purchased the property on Willow Road. The company's main store and offices are now located there. The Main Street space continues as a branch store. –[3]– Our consultants are waiting to help you choose the right look and designs to celebrate your special occasion.

Ginger's is happy to deliver your order. –[4]– We charge no fee for deliveries in the local area, including most addresses in Burkettsville, Springdale, and Rosslyn. There is a mileage charge for other areas. Orders placed before 11:00 a.m. will be delivered the same day. Orders placed after 11:00 a.m. will be delivered the following day.

Click on your preferred category and start shopping!

Celebrations   Romance   Roses and Orchids

---

158. What kind of business is Ginger's?

    (A) Florist
    (B) Landscaper
    (C) Party planner
    (D) Interior designer

159. What is said about deliveries?

    (A) Deliveries usually take 24 hours or longer.
    (B) Deliveries are made only in the local area.
    (C) No deliveries are made after 11:00 a.m.
    (D) There is no charge for local deliveries.

160. In which of the following positions marked [1], [2], [3], and [4] does the following sentence best belong?

    "We are ready to serve you at either of our two locations."

    (A) [1]
    (B) [2]
    (C) [3]
    (D) [4]

Questions 161-163 refer to the following email.

From: Ravi Niazi
To: F. Omoboriowo
Subj: Re: Shipping question

Dear Mr. Omoboriowo,

Thank you for your interest in Dawn Products. I am attaching a table that shows the current prices of our most popular products for your information.

To answer your question, yes, all our products are available at wholesale prices to registered retailers and on orders of $1,000 or more. Shipping times and costs depend on your location, as well as on the size of your order. You may also be interested in knowing that all our products are manufactured here at our company facilities under the supervision of our trained managers. We do not subcontract any of our production.

Please contact me if you would like any further assistance in placing an order.

Sincerely,
Ravi Niazi
Customer Relations Manager
Dawn Products

---

161. What does the email attachment contain?

    (A) A price list
    (B) An order form
    (C) Shipping information
    (D) Staff contact information

162. What does Mr. Niazi say about shipping?

    (A) It is always done by air.
    (B) It is free on large orders.
    (C) It requires insurance.
    (D) Its price varies.

163. What kind of business does Mr. Omoboriowo probably work for?

    (A) Shipping
    (B) Retail
    (C) Advertising
    (D) Manufacturing

Questions 164–167 refer to the following memo.

> **MEMO**
>
> To: All employees
> From: K. Osafo
> Director, Personnel
>
> Date: November 23, 20—
> Subject: Charitable Leave
>
> The corporation is pleased to announce a new policy which will allow employees to take paid time off for unpaid community service. Employees may take up to eight hours of paid leave per month to volunteer for charity organizations. Employees are eligible for this program if they are full-time and have been employed here for at least one year. Charitable leave must be requested in advance; otherwise, employees will not be paid for that time. Charitable leave must also be approved by the employee's supervisor.

164. What does the new policy allow employees to do?

   (A) Take paid leave for professional training
   (B) Have more holidays
   (C) Get paid for volunteer work
   (D) Go home early

165. How much time may an employee take under this program?

   (A) One hour per week
   (B) Three hours per week
   (C) Six hours per month
   (D) Eight hours per month

166. Who can participate in the program?

   (A) Full-time employees
   (B) Part-time employees
   (C) New employees
   (D) All employees

167. What must an employee do to get paid for time off?

   (A) Complete an absence form
   (B) Have a good attendance record
   (C) Be recommended by a supervisor
   (D) Get advance supervisor approval

425

Questions 168–171 refer to the following online chat discussion.

Ruby Stone [2:10]
Has anyone noticed any problems with the carpet?

Glen Blake [2:12]
Yes. There is a big bump in the middle of my office floor. It looks like they didn't nail it down correctly.

Ruby Stone [2:13]
Right. I have the exact same problem in my office.

Kaylee O'Hara [2:14]
In the conference room, I noticed a big gap between the edge of the carpet and the wall.

Ruby Stone [2:15]
We paid a lot to get this new carpet installed. We are going to have to contact the carpet company and have them come back and do the job right.

Glen Blake [2:16]
Leave that to me. I can get to it this afternoon.

Kaylee O'Hara [2:18]
See if they can come back before the end of the week. We have the representatives from Wilson, Inc. coming for that meeting first thing Monday morning.

Ruby Stone [2:20]
I know. The new clients. We have to have everything in order before then. Why did we use this carpet company, anyway?

Glen Blake [2:23]
Don't you remember? You said it is important to give an opportunity to a business that is just starting out.

Kaylee O'Hara [2:25]
Next time I think we should give the opportunity to the business with the experience to do the job right.

168. What is the problem with the carpet?

    (A) It was installed incorrectly.
    (B) It is old and worn out.
    (C) It is the wrong color.
    (D) It needs cleaning.

169. What will happen on Monday?

    (A) Office supplies will be ordered.
    (B) There will be a staff meeting.
    (C) Clients will visit the office.
    (D) The office will be cleaned.

170. What is indicated about the carpet company?

    (A) It has relatively high fees.
    (B) It has a good reputation.
    (C) It has many employees.
    (D) It is a new business.

171. At 2:16, what does Mr. Blake mean when he writes, "Leave that to me"?

    (A) He plans to fix the carpet.
    (B) He will call the carpet company.
    (C) He will pay the bill for the carpet.
    (D) He wants to be left alone for the afternoon.

Questions 172-175 refer to the following article.

The New Target for Hackers

Is your company a sitting duck for hackers? When did you last change your passwords? How strong are your security systems?

According to the International Network Security Association, there's a new breed of hacker out there. And, there's a new target, too.

In the past, hackers gained notoriety by breaking into the networks of large companies. The bigger the company, the bigger the success in the eyes of the hackers.

-[1]- When hackers broke into Infelmax's notoriously secure system several years ago, they made headline news around the world.

The big "successes" came with a major drawback, however—international teams of investigators and serious criminal charges. Several former hackers are now sitting behind bars or working to pay off hefty fines. -[2]-

Now hackers have changed their focus. Smaller companies make an attractive target because of their less sophisticated security systems. -[3]- Also, a breached system in a smaller company may attract little attention as investigators pursue bigger problems, making the consequences less problematic for the hackers. -[4]-

172. Which is a likely victim for the new breed of hackers?

    (A) Well-known companies
    (B) Small companies
    (C) International companies
    (D) Technology companies

173. According to the article, what was one probable motive for hackers of Infelmax's network?

    (A) Money
    (B) Power
    (C) Fame
    (D) Fun

174. What has happened to some former hackers?

    (A) They have been hired by software companies.
    (B) They have been found innocent of crimes.
    (C) They are working with investigators.
    (D) They are in prison.

175. In which of the following positions marked [1], [2], [3], and [4] does the following sentence best belong?

    "They may even be lax about simple security measures, such as not changing their passwords frequently."

    (A) [1]
    (B) [2]
    (C) [3]
    (D) [4]

Questions 176–180 refer to the following advertisement and email.

MARKETING REPRESENTATIVE

New Zealand's fastest-growing women's clothing company seeks a marketing representative. Position requires travel approximately one week per month, representing the company at conferences and media events.

Required qualifications

- a degree from a four-year college or university, preferably in marketing.
- at least one year of experience in sales, preferably clothing.
- excellent communication skills, including experience giving presentations.

Send your resume and cover letter to Camilla Crowe: ccrowe@nzworld.com

---

From: Camilla Crowe
To: Akiko Sasaki
Date: March 10
Subject: Your application

Dear Ms. Sasaki:

Thank you for applying for the position of marketing representative. We appreciate your interest in NZ World.

Although your résumé shows that you have good preparation for a career in marketing, unfortunately you don't meet all our required qualifications. You have the degree we are looking for, but not the experience. Your sales experience in an electronics store is a good background, but your time there is just half of what we ask for as a minimum. In addition, you have no experience in clothing sales.

However, your résumé also shows some of your strengths. You have excellent grades and have been active in your campus' marketing club. Therefore, we would like to offer you a position as an intern.

This is a three-month, unpaid internship. Since you just graduated last month, I think this would be a great opportunity for you. It would give you some of the experience you will need to start your career. For example, your internship would give you some practice with public speaking, an important marketing skill that is lacking on your résumé.

Contact me by April 1 if you are interested in accepting this position. I look forward to hearing from you.

Sincerely,

Camilla Crowe
HR Director
NZ World

176. Which of the following is NOT a duty of the advertised job?

    (A) Recruiting new staff
    (B) Giving presentations
    (C) Traveling every month
    (D) Attending conferences

177. What field did Akiko get her degree in?

    (A) Electronics
    (B) Marketing
    (C) Communications
    (D) Clothing design

178. When did Akiko get her degree?

    (A) February
    (B) March
    (C) April
    (D) May

179. What type of work experience does Akiko have?

    (A) Clothing sales
    (B) Electronics sales
    (C) Career counselor
    (D) Marketing representative

180. What did Camilla Crowe offer Akiko?

    (A) A job
    (B) An interview
    (C) An internship
    (D) A club membership

Questions 181-185 refer to the following advertisement and email.

*This year, try something different
for your company's annual party.
Visit the Front Street Theater.*

An afternoon or evening at the Front Street Theater includes a delicious meal prepared by our Paris-trained chef, Jacques, and a show preformed by some of the region's finest actors. A tour of this historic theater is also offered before the meal. Groups of 250 or more can reserve the entire theater for their group. This option is available on Sunday afternoons only. Groups of 300-350 receive a 10% discount. Groups over 350 receive a 15% discount.

Shows are selected based on the time of the year: January-April, tragedy; May-July, drama; August-October, musical; and November-December, comedy.

Reservations are available at the following times:

Monday-Thursday:	Dinner and evening show 6-10 p.m.
Friday-Saturday	Lunch and afternoon show 12-4 p.m.
	Dinner and evening show 6-10 p.m.
Sunday	Only large groups renting the entire theater. Both lunch and dinner schedules are available. It is recommended to make large group reservations one month ahead of time.

Come to the Front Street Theater for food, entertainment, and fun. To make a reservation, email us or call us at 216-707-2268.

To: Front Street Theater, Reservations
From: Constance Hekler, Events Coordinator
Date: October 25, 20—
Subject: Holiday party

I saw your advertisement in this week's Business Journal. I am interested in renting your theater for Federal Bank's annual employee party.

We have set the date for our party on Sunday, December 20. Is the theater available then? We prefer the lunch and afternoon show. There will be 325 guests.

Please fax the menu, a description of the shows, and the price list to me. And let me know about the availability of dates in December.

Thank you.

181. What is included in a visit to the theater?

    (A) Meeting the chef
    (B) Talking with the actors
    (C) Touring the theater
    (D) Selecting shows

182. When is the theater open to individuals and small groups?

    (A) Monday through Thursday only
    (B) Friday and Saturday only
    (C) Monday through Saturday only
    (D) Sunday only

183. What time does Ms. Hekler prefer the Federal Bank party to begin?

    (A) 10 a.m.
    (B) 12 p.m.
    (C) 4 p.m.
    (D) 6 p.m.

184. What type of discount will the Federal Bank get for this party?

    (A) 0%
    (B) 10%
    (C) 15%
    (D) 20%

185. What type of show will guests at the Federal Bank party see?

    (A) Tragedy
    (B) Drama
    (C) Musical
    (D) Comedy

Questions 186–190 refer to the following notice and two emails.

Retiring Soon?

Attend a Retirement Workshop. This workshop will explain available retirement benefits and how to determine which you are eligible for.

Choose the date that is most convenient for you.

- ✓ August 1
- ✓ August 15
- ✓ August 29
- ✓ September 13

All workshops take place from 8:30–10:30 a.m. in Meeting Room F. Registration is not required. Just show up!

From: Marcus Mains
To: Jae Sun Oh
Subj: Retirement questions
Date: July 20

Mr. Oh,

I am thinking about retiring soon and have some questions about my retirement benefits. I saw the notice about retirement workshops, and I tried to attend one, but the room was empty when I showed up. That was this morning at 8:30 in Room F.

My main question is this: I am 63 years old and have been working with this company for 20 years. Since I am not yet 65, will there be a reduction in my benefits if I retire now? Also, I have some questions about taxes after I retire. Who can help me with that?

Thank you.
Marcus Mains

From: Jae Sun Oh
To: Marcus Mains
Subj: re: Retirement questions
Date: July 20

Hello Mr. Mains,

Thank you for your questions. Here is the basic information about retirement benefits:

- You can retire with full benefits if you are age 65 or over and have worked at the company for at least 20 years, or if you have worked at the company for at least 25 years, you can retire no matter what your age.

- If you are age 55-64 and have worked here for at least 20 years but less than 25 years, you can retire but with a reduction in your retirement fund. It will be reduced by 2% for each year of age under 65. For example, if you are 63, it will be reduced by 4%.

I encourage you to attend a workshop. It is led by Augusta James, who does a very good job of presenting all the possible scenarios. As far as tax issues go, I suggest you contact Fred Lee in Accounting. He is a tax specialist and should be able to answer your concerns.

Let me know if you have any more questions.

Jae Sun Oh
Human Resources Office

186. How long does each workshop last?

    (A) 1 hour
    (B) 2 hours
    (C) All morning
    (D) All day

187. How many workshops should a potential retiree attend?

    (A) 1
    (B) 2
    (C) 3
    (D) 4

188. What mistake did Mr. Mains make about the workshop?

    (A) He arrived too late.
    (B) He went to the wrong room.
    (C) He went on the wrong date.
    (D) He forgot to register ahead of time.

189. If Mr. Mains retires now, what will be the reduction in his retirement fund?

    (A) 0%
    (B) 2%
    (C) 4%
    (D) 10%

190. What does Mr. Oh suggest that Mr. Mains do about his tax questions?

    (A) Hire a tax specialist
    (B) Attend a workshop
    (C) Send them to Mr. Oh
    (D) Call the Accounting Department

Questions 191-195 refer to the following notice, course information, and email.

Professional Development Credits Update

As you know, all ABC, Inc. staff are required to earn 20 hours of professional development credits per year. You can now use coursework at the Central Technical Institute toward your required professional development credit hours. Only courses in the Office Skills category are eligible. Each course is worth 15 hours of credit. You must receive a passing grade to get credit. At the end of the course, please have your records forwarded to the Human Resources Office.

Classes offered at Central Technical Institute
CATEGORY: Office Skills

Accounting

ACTG 101	Financial Accounting, Part One
ACTG 102	Financial Accounting, Part Two*
ACTG 670	Accounting for Small Businesses

Business

BUSI 100	Introduction to Business
BUSI 200	Principles of Business

Computers

COMP 104	Introduction to Microsoft Word
COMP 207	Microsoft Excel: Basics
COMP 300	Computers in the Office**

Marketing

MARK 500	Global Marketing Strategies
MARK 600	Marketing on the internet

Classes last from January 3 until March 15. Classes at the same level are offered on the same day: 100—Monday, 200—Tuesday, 300 and 400—Wednesday, and 500 and higher—Thursday. All classes are offered from 6:00–8:00 in the evening.

The fee for each course is $300. To register, go to: *www.cti.org* and click on the "Registration" link.

*Students must take ACTG 101 and earn a grade of 75 or better before taking ACTG 102.

**This course will be offered on Tuesday evenings.

From: Amanda Minh
To: Roberto Guzman
Subj: Professional development credits

Mr. Guzman,

I have received your records from the Central Technical Institute for the Accounting 101 course you took last term. Unfortunately, we cannot count this course toward your professional development credits as your grade was too low. I see that you have signed up for Computer 207 and Business 100 this term. You can use these for professional development credits as long as you get a passing grade. Work hard! I look forward to seeing your course records at the end of this term.

Amanda Minh
HR Assistant

191. How many professional development hours can an ABC, Inc. employee earn for courses at the Central Technical Institute?

    (A) No more than 15
    (B) No more than 20
    (C) 15 per course
    (D) 20 per year

192. What time does the Accounting 102 class start?

    (A) 6:00 a.m.
    (B) 8:00 a.m.
    (C) 6:00 p.m.
    (D) 8:00 p.m.

193. How much will Roberto pay for each class he takes?

    (A) Nothing; his company will pay.
    (B) $300
    (C) $600
    (D) It depends on the level.

194. Why won't Roberto get professional development credits for the accounting course he took last term?

    (A) He did not get a passing grade.
    (B) It is not in the Office Skills category.
    (C) It was not offered at the Central Technical Institute.
    (D) He did not have his records forwarded to the HR office.

195. Which days will Roberto be in class this term?

    (A) Monday only
    (B) Monday and Tuesday
    (C) Tuesday and Wednesday
    (D) Wednesday only

Questions 196–200 refer to the following advertisement, email, and project estimate.

MITCHELL LANDSCAPERS

DESIGN • PLANT • MAINTAIN

We do it all!

* We can turn your residential or business property into a place of beauty and elegance. We will create a landscape design specifically for you and your property. Our expert gardeners will install and maintain your new garden to keep it looking beautiful.

* Are you a do-it-yourselfer? We will develop a design and help you pick plants that will give you the look you want, while at the same time being easy for you to care for.

Initial consultation is free!
Call today for an appointment,
or visit us at *www.mitchelllandscapes.com*

From: Scott Holmes
To: Shelley Silva
Subj: Landscaping Broad Street
Date: May 10

Shelley,

Do you know anything about Mitchell Landscapers? I saw their ad the other day and thought they might be able to do something for the front of our new property on Broad Street. It looks sadly neglected. The shrubbery on either side of the door needs to be replaced with some healthier-looking bushes, and it would be nice to have some sort of flowers along the walkway. There is already a nice-looking cherry tree on one side of the walkway, and I would like to add another on the other side. Find out if they could do the work for under $3,000 and have it done before the end of the month. We have that open house for prospective tenants on June 1, and I would like to have the place in shape by then.

Let me know what they say.

Scott

| MITCHELL LANDSCAPERS |
| DESIGN • PLANT • MAINTAIN |

Project estimate for: Scott Holmes Properties
Location: 156 Broad Street

Summary:
Create design for front of property, remove
shrubs, plant bushes, create flower beds along
walkway, add cherry tree

COST ESTIMATE

Design work	$500
Materials	$1,000
Labor	$650
Total	**$2,150**

Project date:
Work to begin June 2, to be completed by June 4

196. What is indicated about the landscaping business?

    (A) It works at both private homes and commercial properties.
    (B) It has worked with Mr. Holmes in the past.
    (C) It has been in business for many years.
    (D) It has several branches.

197. The word "pick" in paragraph 2, line 1, of the advertisement is closest in meaning to

    (A) harvest
    (B) choose
    (C) pull
    (D) lift

198. Who is Mr. Holmes?

    (A) An interior decorator
    (B) A real estate agent
    (C) A city planner
    (D) A landlord

199. What problem will Mr. Holmes have with the project estimate?

    (A) The project cost is too high.
    (B) It doesn't include a new tree.
    (C) The job will be completed too late.
    (D) He doesn't want shrubs to be removed.

200. How much will Mitchell Landscapers pay the workers for the Broad Street project?

    (A) $500
    (B) $650
    (C) $1,000
    (D) $2,150

STOP This is the end of the test. If you finish before time is called, you may go back to Parts 5, 6, and 7 and check your work.

多益測驗成績換算對照表

計算答對的題數,利用下表找到對應的分數。將聽力和閱讀分數相加,就會得到預估的多益測驗總分。逐一演練模擬試題,分數也會逐漸提升,請持續追蹤你的多益測驗預估總分。

答對題數	聽力分數	閱讀分數	答對題數	聽力分數	閱讀分數	答對題數	聽力分數	閱讀分數	答對題數	聽力分數	閱讀分數
0	5	5	26	110	65	51	255	220	76	410	370
1	5	5	27	115	70	52	260	225	77	420	380
2	5	5	28	120	80	53	270	230	78	425	385
3	5	5	29	125	85	54	275	235	79	430	390
4	5	5	30	130	90	55	280	240	80	440	395
5	5	5	31	135	95	56	290	250	81	445	400
6	5	5	32	140	100	57	295	255	82	450	405
7	10	5	33	145	110	58	300	260	83	460	410
8	15	5	34	150	115	59	310	265	84	465	415
9	20	5	35	160	120	60	315	270	85	470	420
10	25	5	36	165	125	61	320	280	86	475	425
11	30	5	37	170	130	62	325	285	87	480	430
12	35	5	38	175	140	63	330	290	88	485	435
13	40	5	39	180	145	64	340	300	89	490	445
14	45	5	40	185	150	65	345	305	90	495	450
15	50	5	41	190	160	66	350	310	91	495	455
16	55	10	42	195	165	67	360	320	92	495	465
17	60	15	43	200	170	68	365	325	93	495	470
18	65	20	44	210	175	69	370	330	94	495	480
19	70	25	45	215	180	70	380	335	95	495	485
20	75	30	46	220	190	71	385	340	96	495	490
21	80	35	47	230	195	72	390	350	97	495	495
22	85	40	48	240	200	73	395	355	98	495	495
23	90	45	49	245	210	74	400	360	99	495	495
24	95	50	50	250	215	75	405	365	100	495	495
25	100	60									

聽力測驗答對題數 _____ = 聽力測驗分數 _____
閱讀測驗答對題數 _____ = 閱讀測驗分數 _____
多益測驗預估總分 _____

MEMO

ANSWER SHEET
實戰模擬試題4答案卡

Listening Comprehension

Part 1: Photographs

1. Ⓐ Ⓑ Ⓒ Ⓓ   3. Ⓐ Ⓑ Ⓒ Ⓓ   5. Ⓐ Ⓑ Ⓒ Ⓓ
2. Ⓐ Ⓑ Ⓒ Ⓓ   4. Ⓐ Ⓑ Ⓒ Ⓓ   6. Ⓐ Ⓑ Ⓒ Ⓓ

Part 2: Question-Response

7. Ⓐ Ⓑ Ⓒ   14. Ⓐ Ⓑ Ⓒ   21. Ⓐ Ⓑ Ⓒ   28. Ⓐ Ⓑ Ⓒ
8. Ⓐ Ⓑ Ⓒ   15. Ⓐ Ⓑ Ⓒ   22. Ⓐ Ⓑ Ⓒ   29. Ⓐ Ⓑ Ⓒ
9. Ⓐ Ⓑ Ⓒ   16. Ⓐ Ⓑ Ⓒ   23. Ⓐ Ⓑ Ⓒ   30. Ⓐ Ⓑ Ⓒ
10. Ⓐ Ⓑ Ⓒ   17. Ⓐ Ⓑ Ⓒ   24. Ⓐ Ⓑ Ⓒ   31. Ⓐ Ⓑ Ⓒ
11. Ⓐ Ⓑ Ⓒ   18. Ⓐ Ⓑ Ⓒ   25. Ⓐ Ⓑ Ⓒ
12. Ⓐ Ⓑ Ⓒ   19. Ⓐ Ⓑ Ⓒ   26. Ⓐ Ⓑ Ⓒ
13. Ⓐ Ⓑ Ⓒ   20. Ⓐ Ⓑ Ⓒ   27. Ⓐ Ⓑ Ⓒ

Part 3: Conversations

32. Ⓐ Ⓑ Ⓒ Ⓓ   42. Ⓐ Ⓑ Ⓒ Ⓓ   52. Ⓐ Ⓑ Ⓒ Ⓓ   62. Ⓐ Ⓑ Ⓒ Ⓓ
33. Ⓐ Ⓑ Ⓒ Ⓓ   43. Ⓐ Ⓑ Ⓒ Ⓓ   53. Ⓐ Ⓑ Ⓒ Ⓓ   63. Ⓐ Ⓑ Ⓒ Ⓓ
34. Ⓐ Ⓑ Ⓒ Ⓓ   44. Ⓐ Ⓑ Ⓒ Ⓓ   54. Ⓐ Ⓑ Ⓒ Ⓓ   64. Ⓐ Ⓑ Ⓒ Ⓓ
35. Ⓐ Ⓑ Ⓒ Ⓓ   45. Ⓐ Ⓑ Ⓒ Ⓓ   55. Ⓐ Ⓑ Ⓒ Ⓓ   65. Ⓐ Ⓑ Ⓒ Ⓓ
36. Ⓐ Ⓑ Ⓒ Ⓓ   46. Ⓐ Ⓑ Ⓒ Ⓓ   56. Ⓐ Ⓑ Ⓒ Ⓓ   66. Ⓐ Ⓑ Ⓒ Ⓓ
37. Ⓐ Ⓑ Ⓒ Ⓓ   47. Ⓐ Ⓑ Ⓒ Ⓓ   57. Ⓐ Ⓑ Ⓒ Ⓓ   67. Ⓐ Ⓑ Ⓒ Ⓓ
38. Ⓐ Ⓑ Ⓒ Ⓓ   48. Ⓐ Ⓑ Ⓒ Ⓓ   58. Ⓐ Ⓑ Ⓒ Ⓓ   68. Ⓐ Ⓑ Ⓒ Ⓓ
39. Ⓐ Ⓑ Ⓒ Ⓓ   49. Ⓐ Ⓑ Ⓒ Ⓓ   59. Ⓐ Ⓑ Ⓒ Ⓓ   69. Ⓐ Ⓑ Ⓒ Ⓓ
40. Ⓐ Ⓑ Ⓒ Ⓓ   50. Ⓐ Ⓑ Ⓒ Ⓓ   60. Ⓐ Ⓑ Ⓒ Ⓓ   70. Ⓐ Ⓑ Ⓒ Ⓓ
41. Ⓐ Ⓑ Ⓒ Ⓓ   51. Ⓐ Ⓑ Ⓒ Ⓓ   61. Ⓐ Ⓑ Ⓒ Ⓓ

Part 4: Talks

71. Ⓐ Ⓑ Ⓒ Ⓓ   79. Ⓐ Ⓑ Ⓒ Ⓓ   87. Ⓐ Ⓑ Ⓒ Ⓓ   95. Ⓐ Ⓑ Ⓒ Ⓓ
72. Ⓐ Ⓑ Ⓒ Ⓓ   80. Ⓐ Ⓑ Ⓒ Ⓓ   88. Ⓐ Ⓑ Ⓒ Ⓓ   96. Ⓐ Ⓑ Ⓒ Ⓓ
73. Ⓐ Ⓑ Ⓒ Ⓓ   81. Ⓐ Ⓑ Ⓒ Ⓓ   89. Ⓐ Ⓑ Ⓒ Ⓓ   97. Ⓐ Ⓑ Ⓒ Ⓓ
74. Ⓐ Ⓑ Ⓒ Ⓓ   82. Ⓐ Ⓑ Ⓒ Ⓓ   90. Ⓐ Ⓑ Ⓒ Ⓓ   98. Ⓐ Ⓑ Ⓒ Ⓓ
75. Ⓐ Ⓑ Ⓒ Ⓓ   82. Ⓐ Ⓑ Ⓒ Ⓓ   91. Ⓐ Ⓑ Ⓒ Ⓓ   99. Ⓐ Ⓑ Ⓒ Ⓓ
76. Ⓐ Ⓑ Ⓒ Ⓓ   84. Ⓐ Ⓑ Ⓒ Ⓓ   92. Ⓐ Ⓑ Ⓒ Ⓓ   100. Ⓐ Ⓑ Ⓒ Ⓓ
77. Ⓐ Ⓑ Ⓒ Ⓓ   85. Ⓐ Ⓑ Ⓒ Ⓓ   93. Ⓐ Ⓑ Ⓒ Ⓓ
78. Ⓐ Ⓑ Ⓒ Ⓓ   86. Ⓐ Ⓑ Ⓒ Ⓓ   94. Ⓐ Ⓑ Ⓒ Ⓓ

ANSWER SHEET
實戰模擬試題4答案卡

Reading Comprehension

Part 5: Incomplete Sentences

101. Ⓐ Ⓑ Ⓒ Ⓓ   109. Ⓐ Ⓑ Ⓒ Ⓓ   117. Ⓐ Ⓑ Ⓒ Ⓓ   125. Ⓐ Ⓑ Ⓒ Ⓓ
102. Ⓐ Ⓑ Ⓒ Ⓓ   110. Ⓐ Ⓑ Ⓒ Ⓓ   118. Ⓐ Ⓑ Ⓒ Ⓓ   126. Ⓐ Ⓑ Ⓒ Ⓓ
103. Ⓐ Ⓑ Ⓒ Ⓓ   111. Ⓐ Ⓑ Ⓒ Ⓓ   119. Ⓐ Ⓑ Ⓒ Ⓓ   127. Ⓐ Ⓑ Ⓒ Ⓓ
104. Ⓐ Ⓑ Ⓒ Ⓓ   112. Ⓐ Ⓑ Ⓒ Ⓓ   120. Ⓐ Ⓑ Ⓒ Ⓓ   128. Ⓐ Ⓑ Ⓒ Ⓓ
105. Ⓐ Ⓑ Ⓒ Ⓓ   113. Ⓐ Ⓑ Ⓒ Ⓓ   121. Ⓐ Ⓑ Ⓒ Ⓓ   129. Ⓐ Ⓑ Ⓒ Ⓓ
106. Ⓐ Ⓑ Ⓒ Ⓓ   114. Ⓐ Ⓑ Ⓒ Ⓓ   122. Ⓐ Ⓑ Ⓒ Ⓓ   130. Ⓐ Ⓑ Ⓒ Ⓓ
107. Ⓐ Ⓑ Ⓒ Ⓓ   115. Ⓐ Ⓑ Ⓒ Ⓓ   123. Ⓐ Ⓑ Ⓒ Ⓓ
108. Ⓐ Ⓑ Ⓒ Ⓓ   116. Ⓐ Ⓑ Ⓒ Ⓓ   124. Ⓐ Ⓑ Ⓒ Ⓓ

Part 6: Text Completion

131. Ⓐ Ⓑ Ⓒ Ⓓ   135. Ⓐ Ⓑ Ⓒ Ⓓ   139. Ⓐ Ⓑ Ⓒ Ⓓ   143. Ⓐ Ⓑ Ⓒ Ⓓ
132. Ⓐ Ⓑ Ⓒ Ⓓ   136. Ⓐ Ⓑ Ⓒ Ⓓ   140. Ⓐ Ⓑ Ⓒ Ⓓ   144. Ⓐ Ⓑ Ⓒ Ⓓ
133. Ⓐ Ⓑ Ⓒ Ⓓ   137. Ⓐ Ⓑ Ⓒ Ⓓ   141. Ⓐ Ⓑ Ⓒ Ⓓ   145. Ⓐ Ⓑ Ⓒ Ⓓ
134. Ⓐ Ⓑ Ⓒ Ⓓ   138. Ⓐ Ⓑ Ⓒ Ⓓ   142. Ⓐ Ⓑ Ⓒ Ⓓ   146. Ⓐ Ⓑ Ⓒ Ⓓ

Part 7: Reading Comprehension

147. Ⓐ Ⓑ Ⓒ Ⓓ   161. Ⓐ Ⓑ Ⓒ Ⓓ   175. Ⓐ Ⓑ Ⓒ Ⓓ   189. Ⓐ Ⓑ Ⓒ Ⓓ
148. Ⓐ Ⓑ Ⓒ Ⓓ   162. Ⓐ Ⓑ Ⓒ Ⓓ   176. Ⓐ Ⓑ Ⓒ Ⓓ   190. Ⓐ Ⓑ Ⓒ Ⓓ
149. Ⓐ Ⓑ Ⓒ Ⓓ   163. Ⓐ Ⓑ Ⓒ Ⓓ   177. Ⓐ Ⓑ Ⓒ Ⓓ   191. Ⓐ Ⓑ Ⓒ Ⓓ
150. Ⓐ Ⓑ Ⓒ Ⓓ   164. Ⓐ Ⓑ Ⓒ Ⓓ   178. Ⓐ Ⓑ Ⓒ Ⓓ   192. Ⓐ Ⓑ Ⓒ Ⓓ
151. Ⓐ Ⓑ Ⓒ Ⓓ   165. Ⓐ Ⓑ Ⓒ Ⓓ   179. Ⓐ Ⓑ Ⓒ Ⓓ   193. Ⓐ Ⓑ Ⓒ Ⓓ
152. Ⓐ Ⓑ Ⓒ Ⓓ   166. Ⓐ Ⓑ Ⓒ Ⓓ   180. Ⓐ Ⓑ Ⓒ Ⓓ   194. Ⓐ Ⓑ Ⓒ Ⓓ
153. Ⓐ Ⓑ Ⓒ Ⓓ   167. Ⓐ Ⓑ Ⓒ Ⓓ   181. Ⓐ Ⓑ Ⓒ Ⓓ   195. Ⓐ Ⓑ Ⓒ Ⓓ
154. Ⓐ Ⓑ Ⓒ Ⓓ   168. Ⓐ Ⓑ Ⓒ Ⓓ   182. Ⓐ Ⓑ Ⓒ Ⓓ   196. Ⓐ Ⓑ Ⓒ Ⓓ
155. Ⓐ Ⓑ Ⓒ Ⓓ   169. Ⓐ Ⓑ Ⓒ Ⓓ   183. Ⓐ Ⓑ Ⓒ Ⓓ   197. Ⓐ Ⓑ Ⓒ Ⓓ
156. Ⓐ Ⓑ Ⓒ Ⓓ   170. Ⓐ Ⓑ Ⓒ Ⓓ   184. Ⓐ Ⓑ Ⓒ Ⓓ   198. Ⓐ Ⓑ Ⓒ Ⓓ
157. Ⓐ Ⓑ Ⓒ Ⓓ   171. Ⓐ Ⓑ Ⓒ Ⓓ   185. Ⓐ Ⓑ Ⓒ Ⓓ   199. Ⓐ Ⓑ Ⓒ Ⓓ
158. Ⓐ Ⓑ Ⓒ Ⓓ   172. Ⓐ Ⓑ Ⓒ Ⓓ   186. Ⓐ Ⓑ Ⓒ Ⓓ   200. Ⓐ Ⓑ Ⓒ Ⓓ
159. Ⓐ Ⓑ Ⓒ Ⓓ   173. Ⓐ Ⓑ Ⓒ Ⓓ   187. Ⓐ Ⓑ Ⓒ Ⓓ
160. Ⓐ Ⓑ Ⓒ Ⓓ   174. Ⓐ Ⓑ Ⓒ Ⓓ   188. Ⓐ Ⓑ Ⓒ Ⓓ

MODEL TEST 4

實戰模擬試題 4

Listening Comprehension

In this section of the test, you will have the chance to show how well you understand spoken English. There are four parts to this section, with special directions for each part. You will have approximately 45 minutes to complete the Listening Comprehension sections.

Part 1: Photographs

DIRECTIONS: You will see a photograph. You will hear four statements about the photograph. Choose the statement that most closely matches the photograph, and fill in the corresponding oval on your answer sheet.

Track 47

1.

2.

3.

4.

5.

6.

Part 2: Question-Response

DIRECTIONS: You will hear a question and three possible responses. Choose the response that most closely answers the question, and fill in the corresponding oval on your answer sheet.

Track 48

7. Mark your answer on your answer sheet.
8. Mark your answer on your answer sheet.
9. Mark your answer on your answer sheet.
10. Mark your answer on your answer sheet.
11. Mark your answer on your answer sheet.
12. Mark your answer on your answer sheet.
13. Mark your answer on your answer sheet.
14. Mark your answer on your answer sheet.
15. Mark your answer on your answer sheet.
16. Mark your answer on your answer sheet.
17. Mark your answer on your answer sheet.
18. Mark your answer on your answer sheet.
19. Mark your answer on your answer sheet.
20. Mark your answer on your answer sheet.
21. Mark your answer on your answer sheet.
22. Mark your answer on your answer sheet.
23. Mark your answer on your answer sheet.
24. Mark your answer on your answer sheet.
25. Mark your answer on your answer sheet.
26. Mark your answer on your answer sheet.
27. Mark your answer on your answer sheet.
28. Mark your answer on your answer sheet.
29. Mark your answer on your answer sheet.
30. Mark your answer on your answer sheet.
31. Mark your answer on your answer sheet.

Part 3: Conversations

DIRECTIONS: You will hear a conversation between two or more people. You will see three questions on each conversation and four possible answers. Choose the best answer to each question, and fill in the corresponding oval on your answer sheet.

Track 49

32. What time did the man call the woman?

   (A) 2:00
   (B) 7:00
   (C) 8:00
   (D) 10:00

33. Why didn't the woman hear the phone?

   (A) She was out.
   (B) She was singing.
   (C) She was sleeping.
   (D) She was watching TV.

34. Why did the man call the woman?

   (A) To ask her to go to a party
   (B) To ask her to see a movie
   (C) To ask her to go on a walk
   (D) To ask her to help him with work

35. What does the woman say about Room 365?

   (A) It is large.
   (B) It has two beds.
   (C) It is not available.
   (D) It has a good view.

36. What kind of room does the man ask for?

   (A) A room by the pool
   (B) A room that is quieter
   (C) A room near the garden
   (D) A room with a king-sized bed

37. What will the man do now?

   (A) Put on his sweater
   (B) Swim in the pool
   (C) Have dinner
   (D) Take a rest

38. What is the problem?

   (A) A door is locked.
   (B) A car was stolen.
   (C) An alarm went off.
   (D) A man is lost.

39. Who is Jerry?

   (A) An ambulance driver
   (B) A firefighter
   (C) A thief
   (D) A coworker

40. What will the man do?

   (A) Check the time
   (B) Fix his phone
   (C) Call Jerry
   (D) Take a break

41. What is the man's complaint?

   (A) The tour was too fast.
   (B) They didn't see any paintings.
   (C) His back hurt.
   (D) He didn't like the paintings.

42. What does the woman suggest to the man?

   (A) Take another tour
   (B) Hurry up
   (C) Return to the museum alone
   (D) Get a painting of his own

43. What does the man say about the museum?

   (A) The tour guides are knowledgeable.
   (B) The admission price is high.
   (C) There are too many rooms.
   (D) The paintings are unusual.

449

44. Why does the man take the train?

    (A) Driving is too expensive.
    (B) He sometimes needs his car.
    (C) The train is faster than driving.
    (D) He doesn't like to park in the city.

45. Where does Isabel keep her car all day?

    (A) At the park
    (B) In a garage
    (C) On the street
    (D) At the train station

46. What does the man think of Isabel's parking place?

    (A) The cost is too high.
    (B) It is always crowded.
    (C) The spaces are too small.
    (D) It is conveniently located.

47. Why is the man disappointed?

    (A) The post office is closed.
    (B) The post office isn't close.
    (C) The post office is hard to find.
    (D) The post office is underground.

48. How does the woman recommend getting to the post office?

    (A) By car
    (B) By bus
    (C) By foot
    (D) By taxi

49. What does the man mean when he says, "That's not so bad"?

    (A) He prefers walking.
    (B) He does not get lost easily.
    (C) The post office is not too far away.
    (D) The woman's directions are easy to follow.

50. Who is the woman talking to?

    (A) Her manager
    (B) Her assistant
    (C) A travel agent
    (D) A new employee

51. How often do employees at this company get paid?

    (A) Once a week
    (B) Twice a week
    (C) Once a month
    (D) Twice a month

52. What is the man excited about?

    (A) The number of insurance benefits
    (B) The length of the vacation
    (C) The size of his pay check
    (D) The type of job duties

53. Where are the speakers going?

    (A) Home
    (B) To the store
    (C) To the airport
    (D) To the train station

54. What time does the man want to leave?

    (A) At noon
    (B) At 2:00
    (C) At 3:00
    (D) At 10:00

55. Why does he want to leave at this time?

    (A) He likes to arrive early.
    (B) He doesn't like to hurry.
    (C) He's afraid traffic will be bad.
    (D) He wants to try a new way of getting there.

56. Where does this conversation take place?

    (A) Library
    (B) Bookstore
    (C) Airplane
    (D) Dentist's office

57. What does the woman want?

    (A) A video
    (B) A book
    (C) A magazine
    (D) A newspaper

58. What does the woman say she will do?

    (A) Return at 9:00
    (B) Wait for the man
    (C) Give the man 25 cents
    (D) Avoid paying a fine

59. What does the woman want to do?

    (A) Have lunch outside
    (B) Drink some coffee
    (C) Make a sandwich
    (D) Go home

60. Where are the speakers going to meet?

    (A) At a café
    (B) In the park
    (C) At the office
    (D) On the sidewalk

61. Why does the man say, "If it's not a problem"?

    (A) To make a suggestion
    (B) To explain a reason
    (C) To accept an offer
    (D) To make a request

62. How many nights did the woman stay at the hotel?

    (A) One
    (B) Two
    (C) Three
    (D) Four

63. What was the problem with her bill?

    (A) The woman misplaced the bill.
    (B) The man added the bill wrong.
    (C) The man gave her the wrong bill.
    (D) The woman read the bill incorrectly.

64. What does the woman want to do?

    (A) Cash a check
    (B) Go to the bank
    (C) Pay her bill by check
    (D) Leave her business card.

www.sportstown.com

Sports Town
Discount Coupon
Take 25% off of any purchase
of $150 or more.
Coupon good for online or
in-store purchases.
Coupon expires June 30.
Type in code: A106

Small Office Tables

One drawer	$75
Two drawers	$100
Three drawers	$115
Four drawers	$125

65. What does the woman want to buy?

    (A) Skis
    (B) Shoes
    (C) Boots
    (D) Books

66. Look at the graphic. Why did the woman have a problem with the coupon?

    (A) It has expired.
    (B) She used the wrong code.
    (C) She didn't spend enough money.
    (D) It is not valid for online purchases.

67. What does the man offer to do?

    (A) Give the woman a full refund
    (B) Take 20% off the shipping fee
    (C) Give a discount on the current order
    (D) Send a coupon for a discount on a future order

68. Which room do the speakers want to buy chairs for?

    (A) Conference room
    (B) Break room
    (C) Front office
    (D) Cafeteria

69. What do the speakers say about shipping?

    (A) The delivery is slow.
    (B) The fee is very high.
    (C) Next day delivery costs extra.
    (D) The shipping company is unreliable.

70. Look at the graphic. Which table will the speakers probably order?

    (A) One drawer
    (B) Two drawers
    (C) Three drawers
    (D) Four drawers

Part 4: Talks

DIRECTIONS: You will hear a talk given by a single speaker. You will see three questions on each talk, each with four possible answers. Choose the best answer to each question, and fill in the corresponding oval on your answer sheet.

Track 50

71. Who can get on the plane during priority boarding?
    (A) People with connecting flights
    (B) Large groups
    (C) Elderly people
    (D) Airline personnel

72. What should be given to the gate agent?
    (A) A ticket
    (B) Extra luggage
    (C) A boarding pass
    (D) Requests for assistance

73. What are other passengers asked to do?
    (A) Stand near the door
    (B) Assist the flight attendants
    (C) Make their phone calls now
    (D) Listen for their row number

74. What kind of books does this store carry?
    (A) Novels
    (B) Children's books
    (C) Professional books
    (D) Textbooks

75. If the store doesn't have the book in stock, what will it do?
    (A) Refer you to another store
    (B) Look it up in the master list
    (C) Give you a different book at a discount
    (D) Order it

76. What else does this store sell?
    (A) Newspapers
    (B) Carry-alls
    (C) Journals
    (D) CDs

77. What does the speaker mean when he says, "I've got some good news for you"?
    (A) The news report is next.
    (B) He is about to report good weather.
    (C) He has already read the newspaper.
    (D) He has been given a job promotion.

78. When will the weather change?
    (A) Today
    (B) Tonight
    (C) Tomorrow morning
    (D) Tomorrow afternoon

79. What will the weather be like on Monday?
    (A) Sunny
    (B) Cloudy
    (C) Windy
    (D) Rainy

80. Where is this train going?
    (A) Into the city
    (B) To the hospital
    (C) To the business district
    (D) To the shopping mall

81. Which subway line goes to the airport?
    (A) The gray line
    (B) The green line
    (C) The red line
    (D) The blue line

82. How often do airport trains leave?
    (A) Every two minutes
    (B) Every five minutes
    (C) Every fifteen minutes
    (D) Every sixteen minutes

83. Why are these closings taking place?

    (A) It's Sunday.
    (B) There is no transportation.
    (C) It's a federal holiday.
    (D) The weather is bad.

84. What service is the transportation system eliminating for the day?

    (A) Rush hour service
    (B) Weekend service
    (C) Service into the city
    (D) Service to recreation areas

85. Where is parking free today?

    (A) In public garages
    (B) In private garages
    (C) On downtown streets
    (D) At the bus stations

86. Who participated in this survey?

    (A) Hotel owners
    (B) Secretaries
    (C) Housekeepers
    (D) Business travelers

87. Where would travelers prefer to have hotels located?

    (A) In the business district
    (B) Close to parks and museums
    (C) Near shopping and entertainment
    (D) Beside the airport

88. What additional service should the hotels provide at night?

    (A) Access to exercise and recreation rooms
    (B) Movies in the rooms
    (C) Light snacks in the lobby
    (D) Transportation services

89. Where does this talk take place?

    (A) In an auditorium
    (B) In a museum
    (C) At a café
    (D) On a bus

90. What will listeners do after lunch?

    (A) Drive through the historic district
    (B) Visit the botanical gardens
    (C) Tour some buildings
    (D) Return to the hotel

91. What does the speaker mean when she says, "Please don't worry"?

    (A) She enjoys her job.
    (B) She knows her way around the city.
    (C) She is prepared to answer questions.
    (D) She doesn't expect any problems will occur.

92. What is the first step in packing?

    (A) Get your suitcase
    (B) Wash your clothes
    (C) Choose your outfits
    (D) Check your medicine

93. What should go into the suitcase first?

    (A) Underwear
    (B) Heavy items
    (C) Smaller items
    (D) Jeans and slacks

94. What should you use to help airport security?

    (A) Travel guides
    (B) Light items
    (C) Plastic bags
    (D) Slip-on shoes

♪♫♩♬

Kayla Sanchez

Sound Engineer

kayla@kaylas.com   456-7890

Specials

Beef Stroganoff
★ Pasta Primavera
Roast Lamb
★ Eggplant Stew

---

95. What does the speaker say about the ink color?

   (A) It is too dark.
   (B) She likes it a lot.
   (C) It looks too heavy.
   (D) She would prefer black.

96. Look at the graphic. Which information does the speaker want moved?

   (A) The logo
   (B) Her name
   (C) Her job title
   (D) The email address

97. What does the speaker ask the listener to do?

   (A) Send her the bill
   (B) Deliver the cards
   (C) Cancel the order
   (D) Return the call

98. Who is the speaker talking to?

   (A) Restaurant customers
   (B) Restaurant servers
   (C) Food wholesalers
   (D) Cooking students

99. Look at the graphic. What does the speaker say about the eggplant stew?

   (A) It is a popular dish.
   (B) It is a new dish.
   (C) It is a vegetarian dish.
   (D) It is the least expensive dish.

100. What does the speaker imply about Saturday night?

   (A) The prices are always higher.
   (B) Most restaurants close late.
   (C) There are more specials.
   (D) It is a very busy night.

STOP This is the end of the Listening Comprehension portion of the test. Turn to Part 5 in your test book.

Reading Comprehension

In this section of the test, you will have the chance to show how well you understand written English. There are three parts to this section, with special directions for each part.

**YOU WILL HAVE ONE HOUR AND FIFTEEN MINUTES
TO COMPLETE PARTS 5, 6, AND 7 OF THE TEST.**

Part 5: Incomplete Sentences

DIRECTIONS: You will see a sentence with a missing word. Four possible answers follow the sentence. Choose the best answer to the question, and fill in the corresponding oval on your answer sheet.

101. If the weather is any worse tomorrow, we _____ the client lunch.

    (A) canceled
    (B) will cancel
    (C) have canceled
    (D) are canceling

102. We cannot process the order _____ we get a copy of the purchase order.

    (A) because
    (B) that
    (C) until
    (D) when

103. Although he met many new people at the party, William was able to _____ all their names.

    (A) recall
    (B) remind
    (C) review
    (D) remark

104. After completing the questionnaire, use the _____ envelope to return it to our office.

    (A) is enclosed
    (B) enclose
    (C) enclosing
    (D) enclosed

105. When buying a home, a licensed realtor is your best source for _____.

    (A) guide
    (B) consultant
    (C) advice
    (D) lawyer

106. Check the delivery service's website to _____ out when the package will be delivered.

    (A) bring
    (B) find
    (C) get
    (D) point

107. Because of the drop in oil prices, the cost of our raw materials is expected to _____.

    (A) increase
    (B) decrease
    (C) escalate
    (D) even out

108. Using a checklist is an _____ way to make plans.

    (A) effective
    (B) effect
    (C) effectiveness
    (D) effectively

109. Lunch has been ordered, _____ the delivery person has not arrived yet.

   (A) or
   (B) since
   (C) because
   (D) but

110. It is almost impossible to schedule an appointment with Ms. Grimm at this time of year because she is busy _____ the annual report.

   (A) in
   (B) for
   (C) with
   (D) from

111. The head of operations _____ to the convention and will be away from the factory all week long.

   (A) going
   (B) are going
   (C) go
   (D) is going

112. Customers can speak with a sales _____ by calling our 1-800 number.

   (A) representation
   (B) representative
   (C) represented
   (D) represents

113. Guests can find a telephone directory and a binder with information about local attractions _____ their rooms.

   (A) around
   (B) below
   (C) in
   (D) on

114. _____ smoking nor flash photography is allowed inside the museum.

   (A) Either
   (B) Neither
   (C) But
   (D) Or

115. As part of her annual evaluation, the supervisor had Ms. Balla _____ down her job responsibilities.

   (A) to write
   (B) wrote
   (C) written
   (D) write

116. State law _____ that residents change the address on their driver's license within 30 days of moving.

   (A) submits
   (B) ignores
   (C) mandates
   (D) requests

117. Glenda _____ to arrive at work late, but she makes up the time by staying late or working over the weekend.

   (A) tends
   (B) is scheduled
   (C) is supposed
   (D) attempts

118. We hope that the new marketing _____ for the county's recycling program will encourage residents to participate.

   (A) competence
   (B) candidate
   (C) collusion
   (D) campaign

119. Mr. and Mrs. Xiao decided to stay at the hotel that _____ travel agent suggested.

   (A) their
   (B) they
   (C) them
   (D) they're

120. The YRTL-32 is our most reliable model, mostly because it is hardly ever brought in for _____.

   (A) despair
   (B) compares
   (C) impairs
   (D) repairs

121. The _____ to get into the building is 4-5-2-6.

   (A) reason
   (B) method
   (C) code
   (D) dial

122. Mr. Phelps suggested _____ a committee to research which kind of trucks we should add to our fleet.

   (A) formed
   (B) forming
   (C) form
   (D) to form

123. Human Resources asks employees _____ one months' notice when leaving their job.

   (A) to give
   (B) will give
   (C) giving
   (D) gave

124. This list of contributors is more _____ the one on the computer server.

   (A) current
   (B) currently
   (C) current than
   (D) current as

125. Stuart isn't able to use his corporate credit card _____ it was stolen along with his wallet while he was in London.

   (A) until
   (B) because
   (C) although
   (D) once

126. The ship's captain requests that all passengers _____ emergency procedures.

   (A) reviewing
   (B) reviews
   (C) review
   (D) to review

127. The person _____ lost a briefcase may claim it in the lobby.

   (A) whose
   (B) which
   (C) whom
   (D) who

128. This memo about the new schedule is _____ the one you prepared yesterday.

   (A) as confusing
   (B) confusing as
   (C) as confusing as
   (D) as confused as

129. Ms. Friel _____ about her promotion before it was announced.

   (A) knew
   (B) known
   (C) is knowing
   (D) has known

130. Please _____ me at any time if you have any questions at all about the software.

   (A) are calling
   (B) call
   (C) calls
   (D) will call

Part 6: Text Completion

DIRECTIONS: You will see four passages, each with four blanks. Each blank has four answer choices. For each blank, choose the word, phrase, or sentence that best completes the passage.

Questions 131–134 refer to the following letter.

> **Modern Tech, Inc.**
> **St. No 2, Sector H 1/6, Hunter Complex**
> **Islamabad, Pakistan**
>
> April 13th, 20—
> Vaqas Mahmood
> 21, Sharah-e-Iran, Clifton
> Karachi, Pakistan
>
> Dear Mr. Mahmood,
>
> Thank you for purchasing the XY40 USB digital speakers. _____131_____. Unfortunately, we will not be able to honor it because the rebate offer had already _____132_____ when you mailed it. Rebates must be mailed within three days of purchase. However, you sent yours in almost two weeks after your purchase was made. Please understand that we value your business, and in place of the rebate, we would like _____133_____ you a book of coupons that can be used toward other Modern Tech, Inc. products. You will find great _____134_____ on many of our products, including our new speaker phone with improved sound quality.
>
> Thank you for choosing Modern Tech, Inc. for all your technology needs.
>
> Sincerely,
> *Tarik Khan*
>
> Tarik Khan
> President

131. (A) Some items may be returned for a complete refund
     (B) Many companies offer rebates on certain products
     (C) All our products are guaranteed for one full year
     (D) We received your mail-in rebate card this week

132. (A) launched
     (B) initiated
     (C) expired
     (D) transferred

133. (A) to offer
     (B) offering
     (C) offered
     (D) will offer

134. (A) explanations
     (B) discounts
     (C) packages
     (D) instructions

Questions 135–138 refer to the following email.

To: benlivingston@accountantsgroup.ca
Copy: Kyle; Cheryl; Leslie
From: ryanedison@accountantsgroup.ca
Subject: Golf Tournament

Hi Everyone,

I'm starting the planning for the _____ company golf tournament in May. I know it's more than two months away, but I wanted to get going early this year. I'd like to get everyone's input, so I am drawing up a list of points to discuss. I will hand it _____ at our next staff meeting so we can go over it together. Last year's tournament was a great success. We _____ over $7,000 for charity. This year we are aiming for $10,000. _____.

Thanks,
Ryan

---

135. (A) daily
 (B) weekly
 (C) monthly
 (D) annual

136. (A) in
 (B) out
 (C) over
 (D) down

137. (A) spent
 (B) saved
 (C) raised
 (D) invested

138. (A) With your support, we can do it
 (B) I expect everyone to attend the staff meeting
 (C) Many other companies hold similar charity events
 (D) The golf tournament has always proved to be a popular event

Questions 139–142 refer to the following article.

Indoor Air Pollution

New studies on air quality inside office buildings show that the indoor air quality is ___(139)___ to human health than the polluted air outside. According to the Committee on the Environment, the air quality in approximately 30% of buildings ___(140)___ unsafe. The most common reason for Sick Building Syndrome, a medical condition that has been blamed on poor indoor air quality, is the ___(141)___ opening of businesses. When a building opens too early, paint fumes and cleaning products don't have enough time to disperse. ___(142)___.

139. (A) hazardous
 (B) more hazardous
 (C) most hazardous
 (D) the most hazardous

140. (A) is
 (B) are
 (C) seem
 (D) are becoming

141. (A) premeditated
 (B) premature
 (C) premium
 (D) prevented

142. (A) As a general rule, carpets should be installed after painting is finished
 (B) It is possible these days to purchase less toxic cleaning products
 (C) This is especially a problem if the space is not well ventilated
 (D) Air quality can be controlled with a good air exchange system

Questions 143–146 refer to the following email.

To: Bill O'Hara
From: Edie Saunders
Subject: Workshop

Bill,

I am trying to finalize plans for next Friday's workshop. Please let me ____ how many people you expect to attend so that I can know how much food to order. Also, how long do you expect the workshop to last? In addition to lunch, should I order afternoon coffee and snacks ____? ____. I also need to know expected numbers so I can decide which conference room to reserve. Conference Room 2 is ____ than Conference Room 1, but it might not be big enough.

Please get back to me as soon as possible because I need to take care of this soon.

Thanks,
Edie

---

143. (A) know
 (B) knows
 (C) to know
 (D) knowing

144. (A) moreover
 (B) instead
 (C) furthermore
 (D) as well

145. (A) I am also wondering if I should set up more than one table in the room
 (B) I have already ordered the pens, notepads, and other supplies you requested
 (C) I find that afternoon is not the best time for a workshop as people are often tired then
 (D) If a workshop goes all day, people usually expect some sort of midafternoon refreshment

146. (A) pleasant
 (B) more pleasant
 (C) pleasantly
 (D) the most pleasant

Part 7: Reading Comprehension

DIRECTIONS: You will see single and multiple reading passages followed by several questions. Each question has four answer choices. Choose the best answer to the question, and fill in the corresponding oval on your answer sheet.

Questions 147–148 refer to the following form.

The Griffith Hotel
Reservation Form

Name:	Charles Winston
Room type:	queen
Length of stay:	3 nights
Dates:	September 10–12
Cost:	$100/night
Total charges:	$300

A deposit equivalent to the cost of one night's stay is required to hold the reservation and must be paid 14 days prior to the reservation date. The remainder is due at check-in. Cancellation must be made 7 days prior to the check-in date in order for the deposit to be refunded.

---

147. How much must Mr. Winston pay two weeks before his arrival at the hotel?

    (A) $0
    (B) $100
    (C) $200
    (D) $300

148. What happens if Mr. Winston cancels his reservation on September 9?

    (A) He will lose his deposit.
    (B) He will receive a partial refund.
    (C) He will receive a credit to be used for a future hotel stay.
    (D) He will have to pay the entire cost of the three-night stay.

Questions 149-150 refer to the following announcement.

> Trust Line cordially invites you to attend a morning seminar to learn how you can predict the trends that will assist your clients with the success of their investments.
>
> To reserve a seat, fill out the attached card and mail it with your registration fee.
>
> Don't miss this chance to learn about the resources that drive successful fiduciary service management firms.
>
> For further information, please call 676-9980.

149. Who would be likely to attend the seminar?

    (A) A private investor
    (B) A manager in a not-for-profit organization
    (C) A stockbroker
    (D) A newspaper publisher

150. What will be discussed at the seminar?

    (A) Building client relationships
    (B) Fiduciary service management firms
    (C) How to foresee good investments
    (D) How to get new clients

Questions 151-152 refer to the following schedule.

BUS FARES

		Peak	Off Peak
Effective March 1, 20__	Any one zone	1.00	.75
Peak hours,	Between zones 1 and 2	1.35	1.00
Weekdays 5:30–9:30 A.M.	zones 1 and 3	1.70	1.35
and 3:00–7:00 P.M.	zones 2 and 3	1.35	1.00

151. When do these bus fares take effect?

    (A) Immediately
    (B) On March 1
    (C) On February 28
    (D) Next week

152. What is indicated about peak hours?

    (A) They are the same on weekends as on weekdays.
    (B) They are effective only in certain zones.
    (C) They will no longer exist after March 1.
    (D) They occur twice a day.

Questions 153–154 refer to the following text message chain.

SAMANTHA ARNAULT   1:30
Are you going to the dinner tonight?

BARRY GELLER   1:32
I wish I could. I have to finish this report, so I'll be working late.

SAMANTHA ARNAULT   1:34
Too bad. We'll miss you. I was hoping we could drive together because my car is in the shop.

BARRY GELLER   1:37
Sorry. Wish I could.

SAMANTHA ARNAULT   1:40
Do you know if Liz is going? Maybe I could ride with her.

BARRY GELLER   1:42
I'll check. Hold on.

BARRY GELLER   1:46
She says she'll pick you up at 6:30.

SAMANTHA ARNAULT   1:48
Perfect. Thanks.

---

153. Why did Ms. Arnault contact Mr. Geller?

    (A) To ask him for a ride
    (B) To give him an invitation
    (C) To check the time of the dinner
    (D) To remind him about the dinner

154. At 1:42, what does Mr. Geller mean when he writes, "Hold on"?

    (A) He thinks that riding with Liz is a bad idea.
    (B) He thinks Ms. Arnault should not go to the dinner.
    (C) He might change his mind about going to the dinner.
    (D) He is going to find the answer to Ms. Arnault's question.

Questions 155–157 refer to the following advertisement.

Leading TV-Advertising company with broadcast interests worldwide seeks a Specialist in Audience Research. The Specialist will design studies to determine consumer preferences and write reports for use within the company. Candidates must have a college degree with courses in research. Must also have experience in advertising. Outstanding oral, written, and computer skills are necessary. Downtown location. Excellent benefits.

155. What does this job involve?

   (A) Making TV commercials
   (B) Discovering what consumers like
   (C) Advertising products
   (D) Testing products

156. Who will use the reports the Specialist writes?

   (A) The consumer
   (B) The television station
   (C) The manufacturers
   (D) The TV-advertising company

157. What qualifications should the candidate have?

   (A) Education in research and experience in advertising
   (B) Experience in television audiences
   (C) Ability in accounting
   (D) A degree in broadcasting

Questions 158–160 refer to the following email.

From: O'Reilly Brokerage
Subject: Stock Alert
To: Client List

—[1]— Southern Regional Airlines earned $9.8 million in the fourth quarter, compared with a loss of $584.1 million in the previous year. —[2]— The profit was due to reduced costs and an increase in profitable routes. If the present management does not change, we assume the cost-reduction measures and their choice of routes will continue to have a positive effect on earnings. It seems likely they will continue to eliminate the less traveled routes across the Atlantic. —[3]— Thus, they should be able to focus more on the short-haul routes, where the airline has built a strong base and where most of its revenue is generated. —[4]— If there is any change in the forecast, we will advise you.

---

158. Why are airline profits up?

    (A) New marketing strategies
    (B) Lower cost and better routes
    (C) Greater ticket sales
    (D) Changes in the competition

159. Which routes have been most profitable for the airline?

    (A) Cross-Atlantic routes
    (B) International routes
    (C) Shorter routes
    (D) Freight routes

160. In which of the following positions marked [1], [2], [3], and [4] does the following sentence best belong?

    "We suggest holding on to stock in this airline at this time."

    (A) [1]
    (B) [2]
    (C) [3]
    (D) [4]

Questions 161–163 refer to the following memo.

> From: Mazola Sawarani
> Sent: Thursday, June 03, 20— 9:30 A.M.
> To: All Employees
> Sub: Vacation
>
> Supervisors must approve any and all vacation periods longer than one week. Approval is not automatic. If (1) your absence would create a heavy workload for your team, or cause your team to miss deadlines; (2) you fail to give at least one week's advance notice; (3) there are problems with your job performance; or (4) you have had other frequent absences, your request could be denied. In that case, please contact the Personnel Review Board.

161. What is said about vacations?

 (A) Only one-week vacations are allowed.
 (B) Vacations may be taken just once a year.
 (C) Approval is required for vacations over one week.
 (D) There are no paid vacations for temporary employees.

162. Why might a supervisor deny a vacation request?

 (A) The employee is a team leader.
 (B) The employee often misses work.
 (C) The employee is a hard worker.
 (D) The employee has been recently hired.

163. What can an employee do if a vacation request has been denied?

 (A) Discuss the matter with the Personnel Review Board
 (B) Request a transfer to another department
 (C) Resubmit the request after one week
 (D) Report the supervisor to the labor union

Questions 164–167 refer to the following webpage.

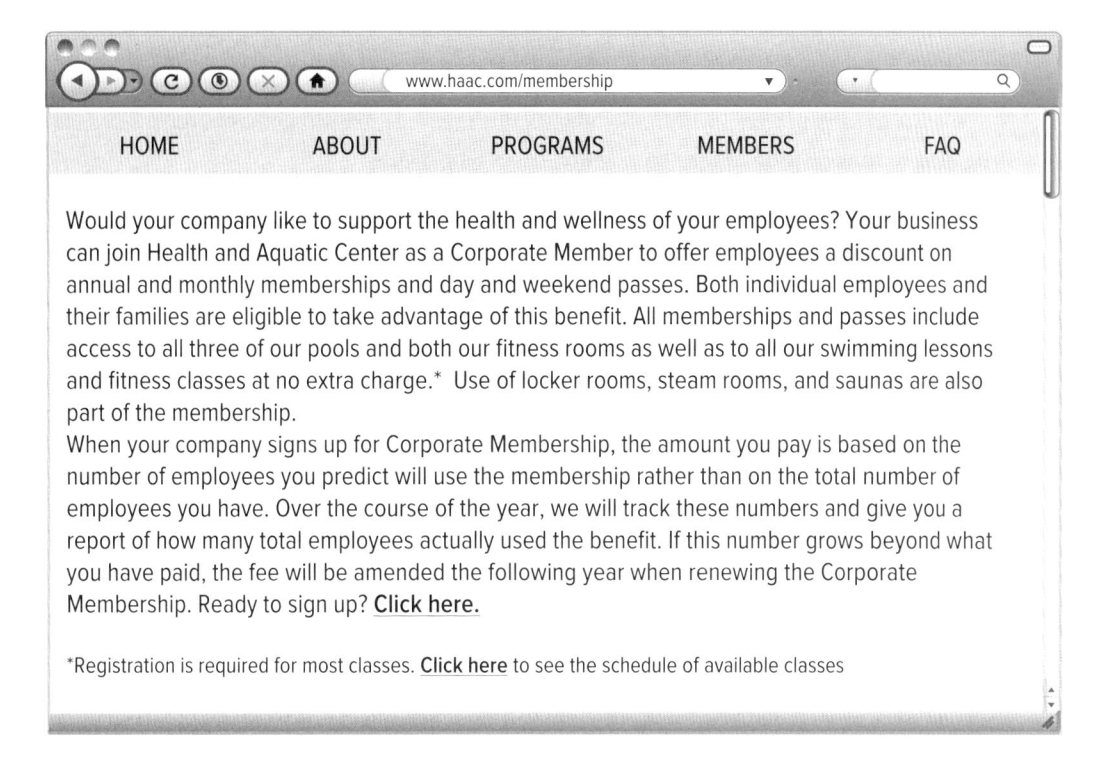

---

www.haac.com/membership

| HOME | ABOUT | PROGRAMS | MEMBERS | FAQ |

Would your company like to support the health and wellness of your employees? Your business can join Health and Aquatic Center as a Corporate Member to offer employees a discount on annual and monthly memberships and day and weekend passes. Both individual employees and their families are eligible to take advantage of this benefit. All memberships and passes include access to all three of our pools and both our fitness rooms as well as to all our swimming lessons and fitness classes at no extra charge.* Use of locker rooms, steam rooms, and saunas are also part of the membership.

When your company signs up for Corporate Membership, the amount you pay is based on the number of employees you predict will use the membership rather than on the total number of employees you have. Over the course of the year, we will track these numbers and give you a report of how many total employees actually used the benefit. If this number grows beyond what you have paid, the fee will be amended the following year when renewing the Corporate Membership. Ready to sign up? **Click here.**

*Registration is required for most classes. **Click here** to see the schedule of available classes

---

164. What is the purpose of this information?

    (A) To advertise the services of a health club
    (B) To tell how to sign up for health club membership
    (C) To describe a health and wellness program for corporate staff
    (D) To explain how businesses can get membership discounts for employees

165. What is said about the facilities at the center?

    (A) They include swimming pools and fitness rooms.
    (B) Saunas and steam rooms were recently added.
    (C) There is a separate pool for small children.
    (D) There is an outdoor pool.

166. What is said about the fitness classes?

    (A) They are for adults only.
    (B) Weekend classes cost extra.
    (C) They are a benefit of membership.
    (D) The class schedule frequently changes.

167. Why would the cost of a Corporate Membership increase?

    (A) If the number of employees using this benefit changes.
    (B) If employees' families use the membership.
    (C) If the company renews its membership late.
    (D) If the company increases its staff size.

Questions 168-171 refer to the following announcement.

NewTech Equipment Company has announced that it expects to cut 4,000 jobs at its branch in Brazil within the next six months. -[1]- NewTech has been struggling to make a profit after two years of losses worldwide.

The reduction in its labor force comes as a surprise to business analysts, who had been impressed with the performance of the company in recent months. -[2]- Although its revenues have not matched those of its first two years in business, they had been increasing steadily since June.

New competition was blamed for the loss of revenue, but sources close to the company put the blame on the lack of direction from the chairman of the company, Pierre Reinartz. Mr. Reinartz has been with the company for only three years, but he will probably resign soon. -[3]-

It is expected that Elizabeth Strube, a current company VP, will succeed him. -[4]- Ms. Strube was responsible for opening the international offices, which have been more profitable than those in Brazil. NewTech employs about 25,000 people in Brazil, another 20,000 in Asia, and 10,000 in Europe. The international office will not be affected by the staff reductions.

168. What has been happening since June?

    (A) The number of employee layoffs has been rising.
    (B) The customer base has been growing.
    (C) Earnings have been going up.
    (D) Losses have been getting worse.

169. What is the current NewTech chairman likely to do?

    (A) Sell the company
    (B) Quit his job
    (C) Increase profits
    (D) Open new offices

170. What describes the international branches of NewTech?

    (A) They earn more money than the Brazilian office.
    (B) They are less cost-effective.
    (C) They are older than the Brazilian branch.
    (D) They will be closed within six months.

171. In which of the following positions marked [1], [2], [3], and [4] does the following sentence best belong?

    "This is part of a strategy to reorganize the money-losing business."

    (A) [1]
    (B) [2]
    (C) [3]
    (D) [4]

Questions 172–175 refer to the following text message chain.

KAIA JONES	9:15
I need some help figuring out an order.	
ANN ADAMS	9:16
Sure. What's up?	
KAIA JONES	9:19
It's for the Bigelow wedding next month. They wanted chocolate-dipped strawberries, but I am not sure about our usual source for the berries. Didn't we decide not to use them anymore?	
ANN ADAMS	9:24
You mean Berry Vale Farm? Do not order from them. Last time half the berries they sent were rotten. We couldn't use them.	
ANN ADAMS	9:27
Chocolate-dipped strawberries are our specialty. We need the best berries. And we need a new source because the Smiths also want the strawberries for their party next month.	
KAIA JONES	9:29
Right. Do you think I should try Hammond Orchards?	
ANN ADAMS	9:32
Why don't you contact them and find out their prices. In the meantime, I'll ask around and see if anyone else has had experience with them.	
ANN ADAMS	9:35
How about the menu for the Wilson graduation party this weekend?	
KAIA JONES	9:38
I've ordered the meat and the vegetables, and we've already started on the cake.	
ANN ADAMS	9:41
Good. That's all set. So, let me know what you learn from Hammond Orchards.	
KAIA JONES	9:45
I'll get back to you this afternoon as soon as I've talked to them.	
ANN ADAMS	9:47
Fine.	

172. What kind of business do Ms. Jones and Ms. Adams probably work for?

　(A) A farm
　(B) A cooking school
　(C) A food wholesaler
　(D) A catering company

173. What was the problem with the last order from the strawberry supplier?

　(A) It cost too much.
　(B) It arrived too late.
　(C) The fruit was poor quality.
　(D) There was too much fruit.

174. At 9:41, what does Ms. Adams mean when she writes, "That's all set"?

　(A) The date for the party has been decided.
　(B) Everything is organized for the party.
　(C) The client has agreed to the menu.
　(D) The client has signed the contract.

175. What will Ms. Jones do this afternoon?

　(A) Find out the price of strawberries
　(B) Visit Hammond Orchards
　(C) Finish making the cake
　(D) Call the client

Questions 176–180 refer to the following email and notice.

To: Management
From: Unhappy customer
Date: Friday, February 4th

To Whom It May Concern:

I'm sending this complaint by email because I haven't been able to reach anyone at your company by telephone. I am extremely disappointed with the service that Concord's call center provides. I called yesterday at 10:30 a.m. for help with my new dishwasher. I was immediately put on hold. I listened to some annoying music for 35 minutes before I finally hung up and called again. The same person, he said his name was Kazuki, told me that he was with another caller and that my call was important to him. If my call was important, someone would have been available to help me.

The worst part is, my call really was important. I had a major flood yesterday after I turned my new dishwasher on, and I couldn't figure out how to get the water to stop running. There is a lot of damage to my kitchen floor. I would appreciate a personal phone call explaining why nobody was available to answer my call. I will not be purchasing from your store in the future.

Suzuki Kana

NOTICE

Date: February 7, 20—
For: Call center employees
Re: Weekly meetings

As of March 1, call center employees will no longer be required to attend weekly Concord staff meetings. The minutes from each meeting will be posted in the staff room for all employees to view after the Thursday morning meetings.

There are two reasons for this change:

1) Our current arrangement of using one employee to cover all ten phones during the meeting hour is not working. We have had numerous complaints from customers saying that they wait up to half an hour to have a call answered on Thursday mornings.

2) We are losing up to $300 in sales every Thursday morning because we don't have all the phones working. Call center representatives generate extra sales while handling help line calls. You are also losing money, because commission is lost when you have to take time out for meetings.

If you have any questions regarding these changes, please contact Itou Saki at manager3@concord.org.

176. Which of the following is NOT true about the caller?

(A) She recently purchased an appliance from Concord.
(B) She was calling for advice about how to clean up a flood.
(C) She was upset with the length of time she waited on the phone.
(D) She disliked the music that played while she was on hold.

177. Why are call center employees no longer required to attend weekly staff meetings?

(A) The content of the meetings is not relevant to them.
(B) They need to be available to answer the help line.
(C) They complained about the frequency of staff meetings.
(D) They are worried about the loss of sales commissions during meeting time.

178. How many people were working the phones when Suzuki called this company?

(A) None
(B) One
(C) Nine
(D) Ten

179. How will call center employees learn about what happened at the weekly meetings?

(A) A memo will be delivered two days later.
(B) There will be one call center representative taking notes.
(C) A summary will be available in the staff room.
(D) Itou Saki will send out an email with the details.

180. How did management handle this complaint?

(A) By putting the customer on hold
(B) By phoning the call center employees
(C) By changing the company procedures
(D) By sending a notice to the customer

Questions 181-185 refer to the following two emails.

To:	Operator 7, Operator 9, Operator 11
From:	Park Gi
Subject:	Recorded names and titles

I have recently discovered that a number of you have reprogrammed your telephones and changed the information on your voicemail. You have replaced the generic title, *systems operator*, with your own name, or worse for at least one of you, a nickname. Not only is this unprofessional, it is against the rules set out in your manual. The original recordings were set up with generic names and titles for a good reason. Your supervisor may ask you to change stations or departments at any time in order for you to learn a new position at the office. New interns will take your desk and the duties that go along with it.

Please refer to page 14 of your manual, which starts, "As temporary employees, you do not have the right to reprogram the telephone on your desk or the settings on your computer."

Thank you,
Park Gi

To:	parkgi@financialguide.net
From:	student7@financialguide.net
Subject:	Answering machines

Dear Mr. Park,

I want to apologize for reprogramming the voicemail for desk 12. After being referred to as Operator 7 several times by repeat customers, I decided to change the recorded name to my own. I don't believe the message I recorded was unprofessional in any way. I simply gave my full name and my title, *student intern*.

I changed the recording because I got a message from a customer who said, "It would be nice to know your name. It feels impersonal to say thank you to a number."

Would you like me to change the message back to a generic one, or do you plan to do this yourself? I know how to do it, but I don't want to break the rule again.

Finally, I didn't realize that we would be moving to other stations, but I look forward to trying new positions. I am enjoying my internship so far.

All the best,
Chong Dae

181. Who was the first email written to?

    (A) All temporary employees
    (B) Three student trainers
    (C) Selected student interns
    (D) All systems operators

182. How does Park Gi suggest interns find out the rules about voicemail?

    (A) By reading their manuals
    (B) By asking their supervisors
    (C) By emailing Park Gi
    (D) By talking with other temporary employees

183. What did Chong Dae record on her voicemail?

    (A) Her nickname
    (B) Her telephone number
    (C) Her name and job title
    (D) Her desk number

184. What excuse does Chong use to defend her actions?

    (A) Her own name is easy to pronounce.
    (B) She thought she would be offered full-time work.
    (C) A customer commented on her telephone's voicemail message.
    (D) She didn't read the training package manual.

185. What does Park Gi forget to mention in his email?

    (A) Where the rule for interns was written
    (B) If interns should change the voicemail message back
    (C) Whether or not interns are temporary employees
    (D) Why the policy was made in the first place

Questions 186–190 refer to the following advertisement, email, and form.

www.busybusinessworkers.com

It's time to take a break, relax, and enjoy some time away from the office. This month we're offering three holiday packages especially for busy business workers like you. May is the best month for travel. While students are busy with their exams, you can enjoy beaches and resorts in peace. Book a vacation this month and receive 25% off the regular price. Packages do not include tax. Cancellation insurance is recommended.

Click on any packages for full details. Prices are per person.
Package A: Twelve nights. Five-star hotel in Portugal. Includes all meals. $1,650
Package B: Five nights. Caribbean Cruise. $1,400
Package C: Angelino's Spa and Golf Getaway. From $600.
Package D: Sorry. No longer available.

Don't wait until the end of the year. Take a break now. You deserve it.

To: manager@marketpro.com
From: francogerard@marketpro.com
Subj: vacation

Hi Alain,

I recently saw an ad for a travel company that is offering some great deals on vacations, and I'd really like to take advantage of the opportunity. My wife and I have been wishing for some time to travel to the islands, and now we have a chance to do it comfortably and affordably. These trips appear to be quite popular, and early May is the soonest we can get reservations. I know that it is a busy time of year here at Market Pro; however, I only plan to be away for a week, and I am sure Stephen can cover my duties quite competently during that time. It's been some time since I last took a vacation, and I hope you will be able to approve this request. Please let me know soon, so we can finalize our reservations.

Thank you.
Franco

Reservation Form

Name:	Franco Gerard
Address:	123 Main Street, Springfield
Phone:	456-1234
Email:	francogerard@marketpro.com
Vacation:	Package B
No. of travelers:	2
Dates of trip:	May 3–May 10
Payment method:	

[X] check (mail to address below)

[ ] credit card no. _____

---

186. Who is the audience for the advertisement?

    (A) Golfers
    (B) Families
    (C) Students
    (D) Office workers

187. How can a customer get a discount on a vacation?

    (A) Make a reservation this month
    (B) Pay before the end of the year
    (C) Reserve a trip for two people
    (D) Travel in May

188. What is indicated about Package C?

    (A) It includes golf lessons.
    (B) It does not include meals.
    (C) It could cost more than $600.
    (D) It is not available at this time.

189. Why did Mr. Gerard write the email?

    (A) To ask who can cover his duties during vacation
    (B) To tell Alain about the vacation deals
    (C) To ask for vacation recommendations
    (D) To request time off from work for vacation

190. Which vacation will Mr. Gerard take?

    (A) Caribbean Cruise
    (B) Trip to Portugal
    (C) Spa and Golf Getaway
    (D) Stay in a five-star hotel

Questions 191-195 refer to the following advertisement, ticket, and email.

The North Star Center for the Performing Arts
presents its new season

October 5-30:	The City Ballet performs *Swan Lake*
November 7-21:	*Romeo and Juliet*, a play by Wm. Shakespeare
December 2-18:	The City Orchestra performs weekly concerts
January 4-30:	*Carmen*, an opera by Georges Bizet

All tickets must be bought in advance at *www.nscpa.org*. Tickets are available for individual performances, or you can subscribe to the entire season.

Ticket prices (individual performances)

Weekdays:
- Matinee: $40
- Evening: $55

Weekends:
- Matinee: $50
- Evening: $65

Print At Home Ticket

Instructions
You must print this ticket and bring it to the event.

January 4, 7:30 p.m.
North Star Center for the Performing Arts

DESCRIPTION	PRICE
Row F, seat 10	$65
Row F, seat 12	$65

All sales are final. Ticket is nonrefundable. In the event that there is a cancellation by the theater, a refund for this ticket may be issued.

To: Peter Richards
From: Amanda Osann
Subj: Tickets

Hi Pete,

Thank you so much for getting the tickets for next week. I'm really looking forward to seeing the performance. You mentioned getting dinner before the show. Unfortunately, I don't think I will be able to leave the office in time for that. We are all working late these days to get the year-end report finished. But a light supper after the show would be fun, if you're up for that. I'll have my car with me, so I can swing by your office and pick you up at around 7:00. Let me know if that works for you.

Amanda

191. How much does it cost to see a performance on a Thursday afternoon?

    (A) $40
    (B) $55
    (C) $50
    (D) $65

192. What is indicated about tickets for performances at the North Star Center?

    (A) They are available online only.
    (B) They can be picked up at the box office.
    (C) They are discounted for senior citizens.
    (D) They are no longer available for certain performances.

193. When can a customer get a refund on a ticket?

    (A) If the refund is requested before the day of the performance
    (B) If the ticket was not bought at a discount price
    (C) If the performance is canceled
    (D) Refunds are never given.

194. What kind of performance will Mr. Richards and Ms. Osann see?

    (A) Ballet
    (B) Play
    (C) Concert
    (D) Opera

195. What does Ms. Osann offer to do?

    (A) Print the tickets
    (B) Pay for supper after the show
    (C) Help Mr. Richards write a report
    (D) Give Mr. Richards a ride to the theater

Questions 196–200 refer to the following real estate listings and two emails.

To: sydneya@someplace.com
From: melissa.davenport@myjob.com
Subj: re: apartments

Hi Sydney,

I have great news. I recently accepted a position with the Sylvan Company, which means I will be moving to Winchester very soon. It will be so great to be in the same city as you. Anyhow, I was wondering if you could give me some suggestions about where to look for an apartment for my family. We'd like to live somewhere safe and quiet. We'd also like to be near a good school for our two children. We would need at least two bedrooms, although three would be better. Since we're planning to bring our car, we won't need to be near public transportation. That will give us more choices in terms of location, but we would prefer garage parking. Let me know if you have any ideas, and if you could recommend a real estate agent, that would be great.

Thanks, and I look forward to seeing you soon!

Melissa

Haskell Realty Company

Winchester Apartments

Listing A
Bright and sunny one-bedroom near Riverside Park. Small building, tenant parking lot in rear. Near schools, transportation. $1,000/month

Listing B
Charming two-bedroom apartment near university. Party room and fitness room in building. Garage parking. Near schools, stores. $1,800/month

Listing C
Spacious and affordable three-bedroom apartment on the Greenville Subway line. Street parking. Near schools, stores. $2,000/month

Listing D
Newly-renovated two-bedroom apartment close to downtown. On bus and subway lines. Near shopping, parks, museums. $1,500/month

> **To:** melissa.davenport@myjob.com
> **From:** bob@haskellrealty.com
> **Subj:** re: apartments
>
> Dear Ms. Davenport,
>
> Thank you for your email. I would be very happy to show you apartments for rent here in Winchester. We have several listings that I think would interest you. You mentioned that you will be in town next week and that your afternoons will be free. Why don't we meet on Wednesday afternoon. If you will let me know the address where you will be staying, I will pick you up at 1:30, and we can go look at apartments from there. I look forward to meeting you.
>
> Bob Haskell

196. Why is Ms. Davenport moving?

    (A) She got a new job.
    (B) She needs a bigger apartment.
    (C) She wants to be closer to her family.
    (D) She does not like her current neighborhood.

197. What is indicated about apartment Listing D?

    (A) It is close to schools.
    (B) It has a fitness room.
    (C) It has the lowest rent.
    (D) It is near public transportation.

198. Which apartment will Ms. Davenport most likely prefer?

    (A) Listing A
    (B) Listing B
    (C) Listing C
    (D) Listing D

199. Why did Mr. Haskell write the email?

    (A) To find out when Ms. Davenport is free
    (B) To recommend places to live
    (C) To make an appointment
    (D) To advertise his business

200. What does Mr. Haskell ask Ms. Davenport to do?

    (A) Meet him at his office
    (B) Give him her address
    (C) Pick him up in her car
    (D) Choose some apartments to see

STOP This is the end of the test. If you finish before time is called, you may go back to Parts 5, 6, and 7 and check your work.

多益測驗成績換算對照表

計算答對的題數，利用下表找到對應的分數。將聽力和閱讀分數相加，就會得到預估的多益測驗總分。逐一演練模擬試題，分數也會逐漸提升，請持續追蹤你的多益測驗預估總分。

答對題數	聽力分數	閱讀分數	答對題數	聽力分數	閱讀分數	答對題數	聽力分數	閱讀分數	答對題數	聽力分數	閱讀分數
0	5	5	26	110	65	51	255	220	76	410	370
1	5	5	27	115	70	52	260	225	77	420	380
2	5	5	28	120	80	53	270	230	78	425	385
3	5	5	29	125	85	54	275	235	79	430	390
4	5	5	30	130	90	55	280	240	80	440	395
5	5	5	31	135	95	56	290	250	81	445	400
6	5	5	32	140	100	57	295	255	82	450	405
7	10	5	33	145	110	58	300	260	83	460	410
8	15	5	34	150	115	59	310	265	84	465	415
9	20	5	35	160	120	60	315	270	85	470	420
10	25	5	36	165	125	61	320	280	86	475	425
11	30	5	37	170	130	62	325	285	87	480	430
12	35	5	38	175	140	63	330	290	88	485	435
13	40	5	39	180	145	64	340	300	89	490	445
14	45	5	40	185	150	65	345	305	90	495	450
15	50	5	41	190	160	66	350	310	91	495	455
16	55	10	42	195	165	67	360	320	92	495	465
17	60	15	43	200	170	68	365	325	93	495	470
18	65	20	44	210	175	69	370	330	94	495	480
19	70	25	45	215	180	70	380	335	95	495	485
20	75	30	46	220	190	71	385	340	96	495	490
21	80	35	47	230	195	72	390	350	97	495	495
22	85	40	48	240	200	73	395	355	98	495	495
23	90	45	49	245	210	74	400	360	99	495	495
24	95	50	50	250	215	75	405	365	100	495	495
25	100	60									

聽力測驗答對題數 _____ = 聽力測驗分數 _____
閱讀測驗答對題數 _____ = 閱讀測驗分數 _____
多益測驗預估總分 _____

MEMO

ANSWER SHEET
實戰模擬試題5答案卡

Listening Comprehension

Part 1: Photographs

1. Ⓐ Ⓑ Ⓒ Ⓓ
2. Ⓐ Ⓑ Ⓒ Ⓓ
3. Ⓐ Ⓑ Ⓒ Ⓓ
4. Ⓐ Ⓑ Ⓒ Ⓓ
5. Ⓐ Ⓑ Ⓒ Ⓓ
6. Ⓐ Ⓑ Ⓒ Ⓓ

Part 2: Question-Response

7. Ⓐ Ⓑ Ⓒ
8. Ⓐ Ⓑ Ⓒ
9. Ⓐ Ⓑ Ⓒ
10. Ⓐ Ⓑ Ⓒ
11. Ⓐ Ⓑ Ⓒ
12. Ⓐ Ⓑ Ⓒ
13. Ⓐ Ⓑ Ⓒ
14. Ⓐ Ⓑ Ⓒ
15. Ⓐ Ⓑ Ⓒ
16. Ⓐ Ⓑ Ⓒ
17. Ⓐ Ⓑ Ⓒ
18. Ⓐ Ⓑ Ⓒ
19. Ⓐ Ⓑ Ⓒ
20. Ⓐ Ⓑ Ⓒ
21. Ⓐ Ⓑ Ⓒ
22. Ⓐ Ⓑ Ⓒ
23. Ⓐ Ⓑ Ⓒ
24. Ⓐ Ⓑ Ⓒ
25. Ⓐ Ⓑ Ⓒ
26. Ⓐ Ⓑ Ⓒ
27. Ⓐ Ⓑ Ⓒ
28. Ⓐ Ⓑ Ⓒ
29. Ⓐ Ⓑ Ⓒ
30. Ⓐ Ⓑ Ⓒ
31. Ⓐ Ⓑ Ⓒ

Part 3: Conversations

32. Ⓐ Ⓑ Ⓒ Ⓓ
33. Ⓐ Ⓑ Ⓒ Ⓓ
34. Ⓐ Ⓑ Ⓒ Ⓓ
35. Ⓐ Ⓑ Ⓒ Ⓓ
36. Ⓐ Ⓑ Ⓒ Ⓓ
37. Ⓐ Ⓑ Ⓒ Ⓓ
38. Ⓐ Ⓑ Ⓒ Ⓓ
39. Ⓐ Ⓑ Ⓒ Ⓓ
40. Ⓐ Ⓑ Ⓒ Ⓓ
41. Ⓐ Ⓑ Ⓒ Ⓓ
42. Ⓐ Ⓑ Ⓒ Ⓓ
43. Ⓐ Ⓑ Ⓒ Ⓓ
44. Ⓐ Ⓑ Ⓒ Ⓓ
45. Ⓐ Ⓑ Ⓒ Ⓓ
46. Ⓐ Ⓑ Ⓒ Ⓓ
47. Ⓐ Ⓑ Ⓒ Ⓓ
48. Ⓐ Ⓑ Ⓒ Ⓓ
49. Ⓐ Ⓑ Ⓒ Ⓓ
50. Ⓐ Ⓑ Ⓒ Ⓓ
51. Ⓐ Ⓑ Ⓒ Ⓓ
52. Ⓐ Ⓑ Ⓒ Ⓓ
53. Ⓐ Ⓑ Ⓒ Ⓓ
54. Ⓐ Ⓑ Ⓒ Ⓓ
55. Ⓐ Ⓑ Ⓒ Ⓓ
56. Ⓐ Ⓑ Ⓒ Ⓓ
57. Ⓐ Ⓑ Ⓒ Ⓓ
58. Ⓐ Ⓑ Ⓒ Ⓓ
59. Ⓐ Ⓑ Ⓒ Ⓓ
60. Ⓐ Ⓑ Ⓒ Ⓓ
61. Ⓐ Ⓑ Ⓒ Ⓓ
62. Ⓐ Ⓑ Ⓒ Ⓓ
63. Ⓐ Ⓑ Ⓒ Ⓓ
64. Ⓐ Ⓑ Ⓒ Ⓓ
65. Ⓐ Ⓑ Ⓒ Ⓓ
66. Ⓐ Ⓑ Ⓒ Ⓓ
67. Ⓐ Ⓑ Ⓒ Ⓓ
68. Ⓐ Ⓑ Ⓒ Ⓓ
69. Ⓐ Ⓑ Ⓒ Ⓓ
70. Ⓐ Ⓑ Ⓒ Ⓓ

Part 4: Talks

71. Ⓐ Ⓑ Ⓒ Ⓓ
72. Ⓐ Ⓑ Ⓒ Ⓓ
73. Ⓐ Ⓑ Ⓒ Ⓓ
74. Ⓐ Ⓑ Ⓒ Ⓓ
75. Ⓐ Ⓑ Ⓒ Ⓓ
76. Ⓐ Ⓑ Ⓒ Ⓓ
77. Ⓐ Ⓑ Ⓒ Ⓓ
78. Ⓐ Ⓑ Ⓒ Ⓓ
79. Ⓐ Ⓑ Ⓒ Ⓓ
80. Ⓐ Ⓑ Ⓒ Ⓓ
81. Ⓐ Ⓑ Ⓒ Ⓓ
82. Ⓐ Ⓑ Ⓒ Ⓓ
82. Ⓐ Ⓑ Ⓒ Ⓓ
84. Ⓐ Ⓑ Ⓒ Ⓓ
85. Ⓐ Ⓑ Ⓒ Ⓓ
86. Ⓐ Ⓑ Ⓒ Ⓓ
87. Ⓐ Ⓑ Ⓒ Ⓓ
88. Ⓐ Ⓑ Ⓒ Ⓓ
89. Ⓐ Ⓑ Ⓒ Ⓓ
90. Ⓐ Ⓑ Ⓒ Ⓓ
91. Ⓐ Ⓑ Ⓒ Ⓓ
92. Ⓐ Ⓑ Ⓒ Ⓓ
93. Ⓐ Ⓑ Ⓒ Ⓓ
94. Ⓐ Ⓑ Ⓒ Ⓓ
95. Ⓐ Ⓑ Ⓒ Ⓓ
96. Ⓐ Ⓑ Ⓒ Ⓓ
97. Ⓐ Ⓑ Ⓒ Ⓓ
98. Ⓐ Ⓑ Ⓒ Ⓓ
99. Ⓐ Ⓑ Ⓒ Ⓓ
100. Ⓐ Ⓑ Ⓒ Ⓓ

ANSWER SHEET
實戰模擬試題5答案卡

Reading Comprehension

Part 5: Incomplete Sentences

101. Ⓐ Ⓑ Ⓒ Ⓓ
102. Ⓐ Ⓑ Ⓒ Ⓓ
103. Ⓐ Ⓑ Ⓒ Ⓓ
104. Ⓐ Ⓑ Ⓒ Ⓓ
105. Ⓐ Ⓑ Ⓒ Ⓓ
106. Ⓐ Ⓑ Ⓒ Ⓓ
107. Ⓐ Ⓑ Ⓒ Ⓓ
108. Ⓐ Ⓑ Ⓒ Ⓓ
109. Ⓐ Ⓑ Ⓒ Ⓓ
110. Ⓐ Ⓑ Ⓒ Ⓓ
111. Ⓐ Ⓑ Ⓒ Ⓓ
112. Ⓐ Ⓑ Ⓒ Ⓓ
113. Ⓐ Ⓑ Ⓒ Ⓓ
114. Ⓐ Ⓑ Ⓒ Ⓓ
115. Ⓐ Ⓑ Ⓒ Ⓓ
116. Ⓐ Ⓑ Ⓒ Ⓓ
117. Ⓐ Ⓑ Ⓒ Ⓓ
118. Ⓐ Ⓑ Ⓒ Ⓓ
119. Ⓐ Ⓑ Ⓒ Ⓓ
120. Ⓐ Ⓑ Ⓒ Ⓓ
121. Ⓐ Ⓑ Ⓒ Ⓓ
122. Ⓐ Ⓑ Ⓒ Ⓓ
123. Ⓐ Ⓑ Ⓒ Ⓓ
124. Ⓐ Ⓑ Ⓒ Ⓓ
125. Ⓐ Ⓑ Ⓒ Ⓓ
126. Ⓐ Ⓑ Ⓒ Ⓓ
127. Ⓐ Ⓑ Ⓒ Ⓓ
128. Ⓐ Ⓑ Ⓒ Ⓓ
129. Ⓐ Ⓑ Ⓒ Ⓓ
130. Ⓐ Ⓑ Ⓒ Ⓓ

Part 6: Text Completion

131. Ⓐ Ⓑ Ⓒ Ⓓ
132. Ⓐ Ⓑ Ⓒ Ⓓ
133. Ⓐ Ⓑ Ⓒ Ⓓ
134. Ⓐ Ⓑ Ⓒ Ⓓ
135. Ⓐ Ⓑ Ⓒ Ⓓ
136. Ⓐ Ⓑ Ⓒ Ⓓ
137. Ⓐ Ⓑ Ⓒ Ⓓ
138. Ⓐ Ⓑ Ⓒ Ⓓ
139. Ⓐ Ⓑ Ⓒ Ⓓ
140. Ⓐ Ⓑ Ⓒ Ⓓ
141. Ⓐ Ⓑ Ⓒ Ⓓ
142. Ⓐ Ⓑ Ⓒ Ⓓ
143. Ⓐ Ⓑ Ⓒ Ⓓ
144. Ⓐ Ⓑ Ⓒ Ⓓ
145. Ⓐ Ⓑ Ⓒ Ⓓ
146. Ⓐ Ⓑ Ⓒ Ⓓ

Part 7: Reading Comprehension

147. Ⓐ Ⓑ Ⓒ Ⓓ
148. Ⓐ Ⓑ Ⓒ Ⓓ
149. Ⓐ Ⓑ Ⓒ Ⓓ
150. Ⓐ Ⓑ Ⓒ Ⓓ
151. Ⓐ Ⓑ Ⓒ Ⓓ
152. Ⓐ Ⓑ Ⓒ Ⓓ
153. Ⓐ Ⓑ Ⓒ Ⓓ
154. Ⓐ Ⓑ Ⓒ Ⓓ
155. Ⓐ Ⓑ Ⓒ Ⓓ
156. Ⓐ Ⓑ Ⓒ Ⓓ
157. Ⓐ Ⓑ Ⓒ Ⓓ
158. Ⓐ Ⓑ Ⓒ Ⓓ
159. Ⓐ Ⓑ Ⓒ Ⓓ
160. Ⓐ Ⓑ Ⓒ Ⓓ
161. Ⓐ Ⓑ Ⓒ Ⓓ
162. Ⓐ Ⓑ Ⓒ Ⓓ
163. Ⓐ Ⓑ Ⓒ Ⓓ
164. Ⓐ Ⓑ Ⓒ Ⓓ
165. Ⓐ Ⓑ Ⓒ Ⓓ
166. Ⓐ Ⓑ Ⓒ Ⓓ
167. Ⓐ Ⓑ Ⓒ Ⓓ
168. Ⓐ Ⓑ Ⓒ Ⓓ
169. Ⓐ Ⓑ Ⓒ Ⓓ
170. Ⓐ Ⓑ Ⓒ Ⓓ
171. Ⓐ Ⓑ Ⓒ Ⓓ
172. Ⓐ Ⓑ Ⓒ Ⓓ
173. Ⓐ Ⓑ Ⓒ Ⓓ
174. Ⓐ Ⓑ Ⓒ Ⓓ
175. Ⓐ Ⓑ Ⓒ Ⓓ
176. Ⓐ Ⓑ Ⓒ Ⓓ
177. Ⓐ Ⓑ Ⓒ Ⓓ
178. Ⓐ Ⓑ Ⓒ Ⓓ
179. Ⓐ Ⓑ Ⓒ Ⓓ
180. Ⓐ Ⓑ Ⓒ Ⓓ
181. Ⓐ Ⓑ Ⓒ Ⓓ
182. Ⓐ Ⓑ Ⓒ Ⓓ
183. Ⓐ Ⓑ Ⓒ Ⓓ
184. Ⓐ Ⓑ Ⓒ Ⓓ
185. Ⓐ Ⓑ Ⓒ Ⓓ
186. Ⓐ Ⓑ Ⓒ Ⓓ
187. Ⓐ Ⓑ Ⓒ Ⓓ
188. Ⓐ Ⓑ Ⓒ Ⓓ
189. Ⓐ Ⓑ Ⓒ Ⓓ
190. Ⓐ Ⓑ Ⓒ Ⓓ
191. Ⓐ Ⓑ Ⓒ Ⓓ
192. Ⓐ Ⓑ Ⓒ Ⓓ
193. Ⓐ Ⓑ Ⓒ Ⓓ
194. Ⓐ Ⓑ Ⓒ Ⓓ
195. Ⓐ Ⓑ Ⓒ Ⓓ
196. Ⓐ Ⓑ Ⓒ Ⓓ
197. Ⓐ Ⓑ Ⓒ Ⓓ
198. Ⓐ Ⓑ Ⓒ Ⓓ
199. Ⓐ Ⓑ Ⓒ Ⓓ
200. Ⓐ Ⓑ Ⓒ Ⓓ

MODEL TEST 5

實戰模擬試題 5

Listening Comprehension

In this section of the test, you will have the chance to show how well you understand spoken English. There are four parts to this section, with special directions for each part. You will have approximately 45 minutes to complete the Listening Comprehension sections.

Part 1: Photographs

DIRECTIONS: You will see a photograph. You will hear four statements about the photograph. Choose the statement that most closely matches the photograph, and fill in the corresponding oval on your answer sheet.

Track 51

1.

2.

3.

4.

5.

6.

Part 2: Question-Response

DIRECTIONS: You will hear a question and three possible responses. Choose the response that most closely answers the question, and fill in the corresponding oval on your answer sheet.

Track 52

7. Mark your answer on your answer sheet.
8. Mark your answer on your answer sheet.
9. Mark your answer on your answer sheet.
10. Mark your answer on your answer sheet.
11. Mark your answer on your answer sheet.
12. Mark your answer on your answer sheet.
13. Mark your answer on your answer sheet.
14. Mark your answer on your answer sheet.
15. Mark your answer on your answer sheet.
16. Mark your answer on your answer sheet.
17. Mark your answer on your answer sheet.
18. Mark your answer on your answer sheet.
19. Mark your answer on your answer sheet.
20. Mark your answer on your answer sheet.
21. Mark your answer on your answer sheet.
22. Mark your answer on your answer sheet.
23. Mark your answer on your answer sheet.
24. Mark your answer on your answer sheet.
25. Mark your answer on your answer sheet.
26. Mark your answer on your answer sheet.
27. Mark your answer on your answer sheet.
28. Mark your answer on your answer sheet.
29. Mark your answer on your answer sheet.
30. Mark your answer on your answer sheet.
31. Mark your answer on your answer sheet.

Part 3: Conversations

DIRECTIONS: You will hear a conversation between two or more people. You will see three questions on each conversation and four possible answers. Choose the best answer to each question, and fill in the corresponding oval on your answer sheet.

Track 53

32. Why did the man call Mr. Wilson's office?

    (A) To make an appointment
    (B) To cancel an appointment
    (C) To ask for directions
    (D) To speak with Mr. Wilson

33. What does the woman mean when she says, "Nothing easier"?

    (A) The office isn't close to the subway station.
    (B) The streets are pleasant to walk along.
    (C) The directions are difficult to explain.
    (D) The office isn't hard to find.

34. Where is Mr. Wilson's office?

    (A) On Main Street
    (B) On Green Street
    (C) On the corner
    (D) Next to the subway station

35. What is the conversation mainly about?

    (A) An apartment
    (B) A plane ticket
    (C) A hotel room
    (D) An office

36. What is the man's problem about?

    (A) The view
    (B) The price
    (C) The size
    (D) The location

37. What does the woman suggest that the man do?

    (A) Call back later
    (B) Choose another date
    (C) Make a payment now
    (D) Look elsewhere

38. What is the purpose of the man's trip?

    (A) To take a vacation
    (B) To attend a meeting
    (C) To go to a job interview
    (D) To see a sports event

39. How is he traveling?

    (A) By plane
    (B) By train
    (C) By car
    (D) By bus

40. What does the woman imply about the man's method of travel?

    (A) It's uncomfortable.
    (B) It's expensive.
    (C) It's boring.
    (D) It's slow.

41. Where is the man going tonight?

    (A) To a dinner
    (B) To a party
    (C) To a meeting
    (D) To the office

42. Why doesn't the woman like the suit?

    (A) It isn't clean.
    (B) It is too dark.
    (C) It doesn't fit.
    (D) It has a rip in it.

43. What will the man do next?

    (A) Send the suit to the cleaner's
    (B) Ask for another opinion
    (C) Change into a new suit
    (D) Put on another tie

44. What does the woman invite the man to do?

   (A) Take a walk
   (B) Go to a play
   (C) Play golf
   (D) Have lunch

45. When does she want to do it?

   (A) Sunday
   (B) Monday
   (C) Tuesday
   (D) Saturday

46. What will the woman do tonight?

   (A) Change the meeting time
   (B) Visit her friends
   (C) Go to bed early
   (D) Call the club

Evening Bus Schedule

Lv. Winwood Street	Arr. Berksville
7:10	8:00
7:40	8:30
8:10	9:00
8:40	9:30

47. What does the man ask the woman to help with?

   (A) Finding a bus schedule
   (B) Making photocopies
   (C) Finishing a report
   (D) Reviewing a record

48. What problem does the man mention?

   (A) The photocopier needs replacement.
   (B) The office has too few employees.
   (C) The woman usually arrives late.
   (D) The bus station is too far away.

49. Look at the graphic. What time will the woman get on the bus?

   (A) 8:10
   (B) 8:30
   (C) 8:40
   (D) 9:30

50. What are the speakers discussing?

   (A) A place to meet
   (B) A time to meet
   (C) A client appointment
   (D) The weekly schedule

51. What does the woman mean when she says, "That's no good"?

   (A) She can't meet at that time.
   (B) The presentation has problems.
   (C) She doesn't like her office.
   (D) The work is too difficult.

52. What do the men imply about the presentation?

   (A) It will be well received by the client.
   (B) It will take a long time to prepare.
   (C) It is going very well so far.
   (D) It has to be finished soon.

53. What does the woman want to do?

    (A) Buy a new car
    (B) Mail a package
    (C) Order business cards
    (D) Make an appointment

54. What does the man recommend?

    (A) Increasing the order
    (B) Using only one color
    (C) Returning on Tuesday
    (D) Consulting an expert

55. What does the woman ask the man to do?

    (A) Look up an address
    (B) Pick up something
    (C) Make a delivery
    (D) Call her up

56. Who is the woman?

    (A) A bank officer
    (B) A real estate agent
    (C) A financial advisor
    (D) A business owner

57. What does the man want to do?

    (A) Buy a house
    (B) Borrow money
    (C) Start a business
    (D) Get a credit card

58. What is the man's complaint?

    (A) The forms are too long.
    (B) The situation is too risky.
    (C) He needs more information.
    (D) His accountant is not available.

59. What is the new parking policy?

    (A) Employees can't park in the garage.
    (B) Employees are charged a fee to park.
    (C) Employees must park in assigned spaces.
    (D) Employees aren't allowed to park in the lot.

60. Why do the women like the policy?

    (A) Public transportation is quicker.
    (B) The parking lot is too crowded.
    (C) Traffic is a problem in the city.
    (D) They don't like driving.

61. What does the man mean when he says, "This idea isn't going to go over"?

    (A) The parking policy won't be popular.
    (B) The parking policy won't get city approval.
    (C) The parking policy won't be in effect very long.
    (D) The parking policy won't be adopted by other companies.

Conference Room

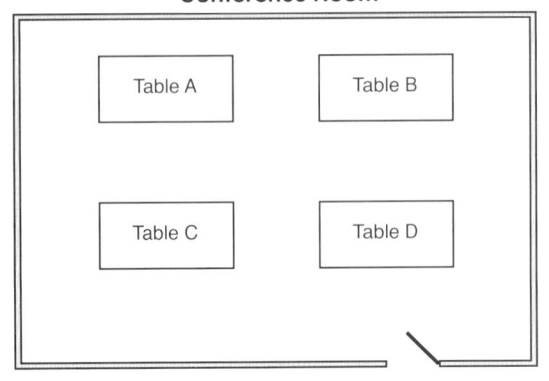

```
┌─────────────────────────────┐
│  ┌────────┐    ┌────────┐   │
│  │Table A │    │Table B │   │
│  └────────┘    └────────┘   │
│                             │
│  ┌────────┐    ┌────────┐   │
│  │Table C │    │Table D │   │
│  └────────┘    └────────┘   │
│                         ╲   │
└──────────────────────────╲──┘
```

62. What is the conversation mainly about?

    (A) A luncheon
    (B) A trip to Tokyo
    (C) A conference
    (D) A staff meeting

63. When will Ms. Yamamoto arrive?

    (A) At noon
    (B) At 4:00
    (C) Next week
    (D) In a month

64. Look at the graphic. Where will Ms. Yamamoto sit?

    (A) Table A
    (B) Table B
    (C) Table C
    (D) Table D

65. What is the woman hiring the man to do?

    (A) Rearrange furniture
    (B) Clean the office
    (C) Paint the walls
    (D) Lay a carpet

66. When will the job be done?

    (A) This afternoon
    (B) Tomorrow
    (C) Thursday
    (D) Tuesday

67. What will the woman do now?

    (A) Check her calendar
    (B) Finish her work
    (C) Greet a client
    (D) Pay the man

68. What is the man looking for?

    (A) A new job
    (B) A place to live
    (C) A business suit
    (D) An office to rent

69. What do the speakers imply about the café?

    (A) It's too noisy for conversation.
    (B) The prices are very high.
    (C) The food tastes bad.
    (D) It's too far away.

70. What does the man suggest?

    (A) Taking a walk
    (B) Going to his house
    (C) Meeting at his office
    (D) Chatting on the phone

Part 4: Talks

DIRECTIONS: You will hear a talk given by a single speaker. You will see three questions on each talk, each with four possible answers. Choose the best answer to each question, and fill in the corresponding oval on your answer sheet.

Track 54

71. What will the guest speak about?

    (A) Mountain climbing
    (B) Novel writing
    (C) Photography
    (D) Sales

72. How long will the program last?

    (A) 15 minutes
    (B) 50 minutes
    (C) One hour
    (D) One and a half hours

73. What will happen after the program?

    (A) The speaker will read from her book.
    (B) There will be a photography exhibit.
    (C) Refreshments will be served.
    (D) Signs will be removed.

74. What was the cause of the delay?

    (A) An accident
    (B) Equipment repair
    (C) Crowds on the train
    (D) Construction in the station

75. What are passengers asked to do now?

    (A) Sit in the boarding area
    (B) Travel with a group
    (C) Buy their tickets
    (D) Line up at the gate

76. Where should passengers put large suitcases?

    (A) At the luggage counter
    (B) At the gate
    (C) In the boarding area
    (D) Under their seats

77. What is the purpose of this talk?

    (A) To explain registration procedures
    (B) To announce schedule changes
    (C) To describe a workshop
    (D) To announce lunch

78. What should people interested in the Best Hiring Practices workshop do?

    (A) Wait in the Terrace Room
    (B) Check the schedule
    (C) Register now
    (D) Go to Room C

79. What does the speaker mean when she says, "I wouldn't miss that event"?

    (A) She doesn't plan to be there.
    (B) She wants to go but can't.
    (C) She recommends attending.
    (D) She expects it to be crowded.

80. Where would you hear this talk?

    (A) On a tour bus
    (B) At a theater
    (C) At a museum
    (D) In a private home

81. What is everyone asked to do now?

    (A) Save questions for later
    (B) Pay for their tickets
    (C) Stop talking
    (D) Sit down

82. What will happen at noon?

    (A) A talk will be heard.
    (B) Lunch will be served.
    (C) A tour will be given.
    (D) The schedule will be reviewed.

497

83. What is being advertised?
    (A) A school
    (B) Bank loans
    (C) An employment agency
    (D) Financial planning services

84. Who would be interested in this advertisement?
    (A) Small business owners
    (B) Bank employees
    (C) Business assistants
    (D) Police officers

85. How can someone get more information?
    (A) Make a phone call
    (B) Visit the office
    (C) Take a workshop
    (D) Read a brochure

Awards Banquet
March 17 – Winchester Hotel

Social hour	6:30–7:30
Dinner	7:30–8:30
Awards Ceremony	8:30–9:30
Music and Dancing	9:30–11:30

86. What is the purpose of this talk?
    (A) To organize an event
    (B) To choose a location
    (C) To get ideas for an event
    (D) To decide who will get awards

87. Look at the graphic. When will the speaker arrive at the banquet?
    (A) 6:30
    (B) 7:30
    (C) 8:30
    (D) 9:30

88. What will happen next?
    (A) The speaker will call the hotel.
    (B) The guests will receive invitations.
    (C) People will volunteer for different jobs.
    (D) Someone will check the sound system.

89. What does the speaker mean when he says, "Things are finally looking up"?
    (A) His predictions are based on research.
    (B) Temperatures were higher yesterday.
    (C) The condition of the sky is changing.
    (D) The bad weather is now improving.

90. What will the weather be like today?
    (A) It will be rainy.
    (B) It will cool down.
    (C) It will get warmer.
    (D) It will get cloudier.

91. What does the speaker suggest listeners do on Saturday?
    (A) Carry an umbrella in case of rain
    (B) Dress for cold temperatures
    (C) Go out to enjoy the weather
    (D) Notice the spring flowers

92. Who is Joe Roberts?
    (A) A banker
    (B) A doctor
    (C) An assistant
    (D) An accountant

93. What is the purpose of the message?
    (A) To ask for information
    (B) To explain a procedure
    (C) To make an appointment
    (D) To change an appointment

94. What does the speaker want the listener to do?

   (A) Return the call
   (B) Explain some concerns
   (C) Provide an office address
   (D) Submit a financial statement

Montrose Station Map

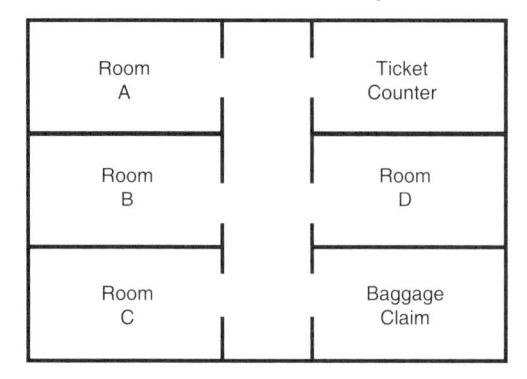

Room A	Ticket Counter
Room B	Room D
Room C	Baggage Claim

95. What has been found?

   (A) A large package
   (B) A piece of clothing
   (C) A train ticket
   (D) A blue bag

96. Where was it found?

   (A) On the track
   (B) By a door
   (C) In a waiting room
   (D) Outside the station

97. Look at the graphic. Where is the station manager's office?

   (A) Room A
   (B) Room B
   (C) Room C
   (D) Room D

98. Where would you hear this announcement?

   (A) At a farm
   (B) At a bank
   (C) At a clothing store
   (D) At a grocery store

99. How long will the special offer last?

   (A) One day
   (B) Two days
   (C) All week
   (D) Until Tuesday

100. What does the speaker suggest shoppers do?

   (A) Write a check
   (B) Return next week
   (C) Count their change
   (D) Go to the checkout counter

STOP This is the end of the Listening Comprehension portion of the test. Turn to Part 5 in your test book.

Reading Comprehension

In this section of the test, you will have the chance to show how well you understand written English. There are three parts to this section, with special directions for each part.

**YOU WILL HAVE ONE HOUR AND FIFTEEN MINUTES
TO COMPLETE PARTS 5, 6, AND 7 OF THE TEST.**

Part 5: Incomplete Sentences

> **DIRECTIONS:** You will see a sentence with a missing word. Four possible answers follow the sentence. Choose the best answer to the question, and fill in the corresponding oval on your answer sheet.

101. Registration for the computer training workshops _____ the first week of April.

    (A) begin
    (B) begins
    (C) beginning
    (D) have begun

102. ColPro, Inc. announced yesterday that Priscilla Perkins has _____ from her position as Chief Financial Officer after fifteen years with the company.

    (A) contracted
    (B) resigned
    (C) dismissed
    (D) retreated

103. It is your responsibility to let your supervisor know _____ you will be unable to attend next week's staff meeting.

    (A) if
    (B) so
    (C) then
    (D) but

104. I don't plan to _____ my contract with the company next year unless they are willing to discuss a raise.

    (A) subscribe
    (B) affirm
    (C) renew
    (D) employ

105. The agreement must _____ by both parties before work on the project can proceed.

    (A) sign
    (B) signed
    (C) to sign
    (D) be signed

106. The office manager has decided to buy a new printer for the marketing department and _____ for the front office.

    (A) either
    (B) any
    (C) another
    (D) this

107. _____ of the increasing rents in this neighborhood, Apex Market is considering relocating to another part of the city.

    (A) Because
    (B) Instead
    (C) Despite
    (D) Due

108. Staff members plan to _____ in the lobby at 5:00 for a small party in honor of Martha's retirement.

    (A) join
    (B) gather
    (C) attend
    (D) combine

109. You should always _____ your work carefully before turning it in to your supervisor.

    (A) review
    (B) reviewing
    (C) to review
    (D) reviewed

110. The directors are expecting to hear an answer _____ the client before the end of the week.

    (A) of
    (B) to
    (C) from
    (D) over

111. A sound _____ in improving manufacturing facilities now will result in increased profits over the next few years.

    (A) invest
    (B) investor
    (C) investiture
    (D) investment

112. Rising fuel costs have _____ many companies to seek alternative sources of energy for their facilities.

    (A) desired
    (B) expected
    (C) motivated
    (D) generated

113. An ad posted on the company's website resulted _____ hundreds of applicants for the vacant position.

    (A) on
    (B) in
    (C) of
    (D) about

114. The low attendance at the business conference last month was _____ due to the bad weather conditions affecting that part of the country.

    (A) largely
    (B) almost
    (C) because
    (D) usually

115. According to economic forecasters, a significant increase in transportation costs is _____ to occur in the next quarter.

    (A) like
    (B) likely
    (C) likeable
    (D) dislike

116. You should take the time to talk the matter over with your colleagues before _____ a final decision.

    (A) make
    (B) made
    (C) making
    (D) had made

117. This is a part-time position, but it requires _____ during evening hours as well as on occasional weekends.

    (A) avail
    (B) availing
    (C) available
    (D) availability

118. There is a _____ chance that the company will increase salaries this year, but it is not probable.

    (A) slight
    (B) normal
    (C) good
    (D) huge

501

119. _____ we have hired several new workers at the factory, we are still not able to meet our weekly quotas.

    (A) Since
    (B) Following
    (C) Although
    (D) Therefore

120. The board meeting had to be canceled at the last minute because so few people _____ for it.

    (A) turned in
    (B) showed up
    (C) stood by
    (D) took over

121. We will need to _____ in several areas if we want to stay within the budget.

    (A) economy
    (B) economize
    (C) economist
    (D) economics

122. We have been assured that the person _____ is giving the workshop is an expert in international finance.

    (A) who
    (B) whom
    (C) whose
    (D) which

123. If you accept a job offer from another company, please _____ the personnel director as soon as possible.

    (A) signify
    (B) testify
    (C) notify
    (D) dignify

124. Everybody _____ to find out whether an agreement about the new contract has been reached.

    (A) have waited
    (B) are waiting
    (C) is waiting
    (D) wait

125. You don't have to accept an initial salary offer because it is almost always _____.

    (A) negotiate
    (B) negotiation
    (C) negotiator
    (D) negotiable

126. I would have signed up for that workshop if I _____ it on the schedule.

    (A) saw
    (B) had seen
    (C) would see
    (D) would have seen

127. Everyone in the department _____ Mr. Hammersmith was present at last night's awards banquet.

    (A) expect
    (B) accept
    (C) except
    (D) accent

128. We chose this photocopier because it is a good deal _____ the one it is replacing.

    (A) fast
    (B) faster
    (C) the fastest
    (D) faster than

129. Ms. Soto would like you to call _____ back before 5:00 this afternoon.

    (A) her
    (B) she
    (C) hers
    (D) herself

130. We asked the designer to come up with several options so that we could _____ the best one.

    (A) select
    (B) selective
    (C) selectively
    (D) selection

Part 6: Text Completion

DIRECTIONS: You will see four passages, each with four blanks. Each blank has four answer choices. For each blank, choose the word, phrase, or sentence that best completes the passage.

Questions 131–134 refer to the following email.

To: "Stevens, Dan"
From: "Markston, Phil"
Date: June 12
Subject: Changes to Registration Form

We have a problem with our email mailing list. The problem isn't with the list ___(131)___, but with how people can sign up. Our sign up form is buried so far down on our website that it is impossible to find. We need ___(132)___ it easier for people to subscribe. ___(133)___. While we are making this change, I want to edit the form slightly. There are five questions on the form, and each must be answered to submit the form. I think these should be optional—only ___(134)___ name and email address fields should be required to subscribe.

Let's talk about this tomorrow. Come to my office when you have a moment.

Phil

131. (A) its
 (B) it's
 (C) itself
 (D) its self

132. (A) make
 (B) to make
 (C) making
 (D) will make

133. (A) One option might be to move the registration form to the home page
 (B) Most people don't mind taking a few minutes to complete the form
 (C) The number of subscribers is growing faster than we expected
 (D) Our newsletter is enjoying widespread popularity

134. (A) a
 (B) an
 (C) the
 (D) this

503

Questions 135–138 refer to the following notice.

NOTICE TO MOVERS

While picking up and lifting furniture from a client's home to the moving van is often _____ quickest option, I am asking that movers also consider pushing furniture when possible. _____. Please use hand carts to move stacks of boxes and furniture with a _____ base. Alternatively, a piece of cardboard can be placed under heavy furniture so that you can more easily slide it along the floor. _____ option you choose, remember not to track dirt into a client's home and not to damage the client's valuables.

135. (A) their
 (B) her
 (C) his
 (D) our

136. (A) Speed and efficiency are the company's top priorities
 (B) This will reduce your risk of injury and save you energy
 (C) The ability to lift heavy items is a requirement of this job
 (D) We are fully insured for any damages done to a client's property

137. (A) solid
 (B) solidly
 (C) solidify
 (D) solidity

138. (A) However
 (B) Whenever
 (C) Whichever
 (D) Whomever

Questions 139–142 refer to the following letter.

Dear Ms. Thompson,

We have received your job ____ and resume. Thank you for your interest in working
              139
with us here at the Amet Corporation. Unfortunately, we do not currently have any
____ positions for which you would be qualified. ____, we will keep your information
140   141
on file and will contact you when a suitable position becomes available. ____. In the
                                                                         142
meantime, if you have any questions, please contact Ms. Garcia, our Human Resources
Manager.

Again, thank you for your interest.

Sincerely,
Michel Boudreau

139. (A) request
     (B) solicitation
     (C) application
     (D) petition

140. (A) vacate
     (B) vacant
     (C) vacancy
     (D) vacated

141. (A) However
     (B) While
     (C) As long as
     (D) Even though

142. (A) Please call my assistant this week to make an appointment
     (B) We are looking for someone with your exact training and background
     (C) Job application forms are available on the careers page of our website
     (D) If you have not heard from us in six months, you may resubmit your résumé

Questions 143–146 refer to the following email.

> **From:** Vanessa Holden
> **To:** All department staff
> **Subject:** Away next week
> **cc:** Kyle Rogers
>
> I will be out of the office for all of next week, attending a conference in Rome. During my ____, my assistant, Kyle Rogers, will be handling all my correspondence. He will also be available ____ with any issues that may arise while I am away. I understand that some of you wish to meet with me to discuss your annual evaluation. I will be happy to do this when I ____ from the conference. ____.
>
> Vanessa Holden

143. (A) tenure
    (B) absence
    (C) pursuit
    (D) engagement

144. (A) will help
    (B) can help
    (C) to help
    (D) help

145. (A) go over
    (B) get back
    (C) come up
    (D) turn in

146. (A) The evaluations will be ready for your review next week
    (B) I plan to do some sightseeing after the conference is over
    (C) There will be many worthwhile workshops at the conference
    (D) I will be available for appointments the week after I return

Part 7: Reading Comprehension

DIRECTIONS: You will see single and multiple reading passages followed by several questions. Each question has four answer choices. Choose the best answer to the question, and fill in the corresponding oval on your answer sheet.

Questions 147–148 refer to the following advertisement.

ATTENTION JOB SEEKERS

Businesses throughout the region are hiring computer programmers every day.

You could be one of them.

Start a new career as a computer programmer by enrolling in the Computer School at City College.

Complete the program in as little as two years.

Day, evening, and weekend classes are available.

Why wait?

Call now to find out how you can become a computer programmer.

- Open to all high school graduates.
- No previous experience necessary!

147. What is being advertised?

(A) A job opening
(B) A training course
(C) An employment agency
(D) A computer programming business

148. What is a requirement?

(A) A college degree
(B) Computer training
(C) Previous experience
(D) A high school diploma

Questions 149-150 refer to the following text message chain.

Pam Spurr   10:45
I am really enjoying this conference. The exhibits are fantastic.

Kai Noda   10:46
How was your meeting with Bruce?

Pam Spurr   10:46
Great. We had coffee in the café and talked quite a while.

Pam Spurr   10:47
I'm still here, drinking my second cup. Are you still in the Finance Workshop?

Kai Noda   10:48
It's product promotion. It just finished.

Pam Spurr   10:50
Where are you going next?

Kai Noda   10:50
Sales Seminar. Should I take notes for you?

Pam Spurr   10:52
Don't bother. Just save me a seat.

Kai Noda   10:55
Will do.

---

149. Where is Ms. Spurr now?

    (A) In a meeting
    (B) In the café
    (C) In a workshop
    (D) In the exhibit hall

150. At 10:52, what does Ms. Spurr mean when she writes, "Just save me a seat"?

    (A) She is on her way to a meeting.
    (B) She will wait for her friend in the café.
    (C) She is going back to the exhibit hall.
    (D) She will attend the Sales Seminar.

Questions 151-152 refer to the following coupon.

Save $15

On your next purchase of $100 or more on select
Pennwell office products. Offer includes shipping at
no charge for purchases of ink, toner, and paper.

Coupon code: POS97865

Expires April 30

Make your selection at *www.pennwelloffice.com*
or call 800-123-4567 to place your order today.

Pennwell is the leading supplier of printers and copiers,
office furniture, and other essential office supplies.

---

151. What is the coupon good for?

   (A) Any Pennwell product
   (B) Office furniture only
   (C) A purchase of at least $100
   (D) Printers and copiers only

152. What do you have to do to get the discount?

   (A) Purchase your products by April 30
   (B) Purchase your products online
   (C) Purchase your products by phone
   (D) Purchase at least $15 worth of products

Questions 153–154 refer to the following invoice.

Invoice

SMITHFIELD KITCHEN SUPPLIES
Supplying restaurants and offices for over 50 years!

Order # 40291   Date: April 10

Your customer service representative: Pamela Jones
Thank you for your order. Please keep this invoice for your records.

Ship to:
Mark Gillman
Park House Restaurant
85 South Street
Greensboro, NH

Bill to:
The Hubert Restaurant Group
Attn: Rita Spofford
74 Belt Avenue
Hudson, MA

Product	Quantity	Price/ea.	Total
Kringle Deluxe coffeemaker	1	$250	$250
Kringle bread machine	1	$425	$425
Extended warranties	0		$0
		Shipping	$35
		Expedited shipping surcharge	$20
		Sales tax	$30
		Total due	$760

Payment due upon receipt of order.

---

153. Who will pay the invoice?

(A) Mark Gillman
(B) Pamela Jones
(C) Park House Restaurant
(D) The Hubert Restaurant Group

154. What is the $20 charge for?

(A) Holiday and weekend delivery
(B) Sending the order quickly
(C) Shipping heavy items
(D) Special packaging

Questions 155–157 refer to the following form.

Dorchester Towers
Tenant Application

Name: Howard Danes
Address: 113 Fordham Road
Winesburg, OH

Apartment type

___ studio   _X_ one-bedroom   ___ two-bedroom   ___ three-bedroom

Number of occupants   2
Desired move-in date November 15

Application fee	$100
First month's rent*	$800
Security deposit	$600
Total due on signing of lease	$1500

All apartments will be cleaned, repainted, and re-carpeted prior to move in. Return of security deposit upon termination of the lease is contingent upon an apartment inspection. Questions and repair requests should be directed by phone or email to the building manager:

Michael Lee
548-9982
michaell@redbird.com

*Rent does not include parking. A limited number of parking spaces are available in the garage for a fee. Please contact the manager for further information.

---

155. What is this purpose of this form?
    (A) To ask for repairs
    (B) To make a payment
    (C) To request an apartment
    (D) To give notification of lease termination

156. What is the monthly rent for a one-bedroom apartment?
    (A) $100
    (B) $600
    (C) $800
    (D) $1500

157. What is included with all apartments?
    (A) A parking space
    (B) A repair
    (C) A phone
    (D) A new carpet

Questions 158-160 refer to the following webpage.

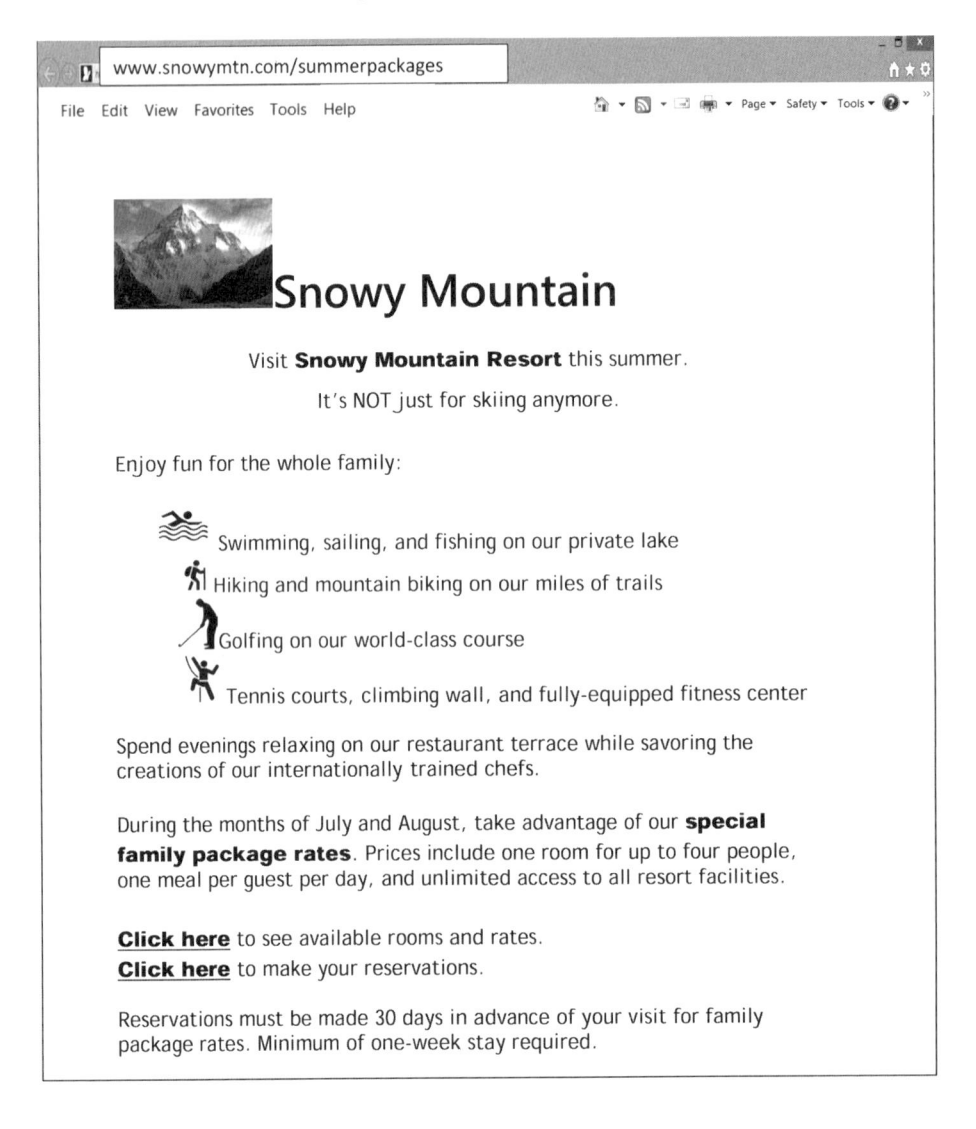

---

www.snowymtn.com/summerpackages

Snowy Mountain

Visit **Snowy Mountain Resort** this summer.

It's NOT just for skiing anymore.

Enjoy fun for the whole family:

- Swimming, sailing, and fishing on our private lake
- Hiking and mountain biking on our miles of trails
- Golfing on our world-class course
- Tennis courts, climbing wall, and fully-equipped fitness center

Spend evenings relaxing on our restaurant terrace while savoring the creations of our internationally trained chefs.

During the months of July and August, take advantage of our **special family package rates**. Prices include one room for up to four people, one meal per guest per day, and unlimited access to all resort facilities.

Click here to see available rooms and rates.
Click here to make your reservations.

Reservations must be made 30 days in advance of your visit for family package rates. Minimum of one-week stay required.

---

158. What is suggested about Snowy Mountain Resort?

    (A) It is known as a ski resort.
    (B) It is only open in the summer.
    (C) It has luxurious accommodations.
    (D) It is less expensive than other resorts.

159. Which of the following is NOT mentioned as a resort activity?

    (A) Dining
    (B) Cycling
    (C) Water sports
    (D) Horseback riding

160. When must reservations be made to get the special rate?

    (A) A week ahead of time
    (B) A month ahead of time
    (C) In July or August
    (D) Any time

Questions 161-163 refer to the following article.

Any business person who has traveled around the globe has experienced the phenomenon commonly known as jet lag. Our bodies have a "biological clock"—the sleeping and waking pattern we follow over a 24-hour period. When we travel to a different time zone, this pattern gets disrupted. During the first few days at a new destination, we may find ourselves awake in the middle of the night or falling asleep in the afternoon. Fortunately, there are things we can do to make the adjustment period more comfortable.

The process begins before leaving home. First, reserve a flight that arrives at your destination in the early evening. As soon as you board the plane, change your watch setting to reflect the time at your destination. This will help you adjust psychologically. Then, when you arrive, stay up until at least 10:00 local time. Avoid caffeine, large meals, and heavy exercise close to bedtime as these things can keep you awake no matter how tired you may be.

Finally, spend as much time as possible in the fresh air and sunshine. Exposure to the sunlight will help your biological clock adjust to the new time zone. Conversely, staying indoors will aggravate the effects of jet lag.

161. What is this article mostly about?

   (A) How to stay healthy while traveling
   (B) How to adjust to a new time zone
   (C) How to fly more comfortably
   (D) How to plan a business trip

162. What is recommended?

   (A) Get up before 10:00
   (B) Avoid eating until 10:00
   (C) Go to bed at 10:00 or later
   (D) Arrive at your destination by 10:00

163. According to the article, what will help you sleep better?

   (A) Going outside
   (B) Avoiding the sun
   (C) Getting enough exercise
   (D) Adjusting your mealtimes

Questions 164–167 refer to the following letter.

ROGERS, MILTON, & COLE, PC
17 Willow Avenue
Moltonsburgh

May 10, 20—

To Whom It May Concern:

This is a letter regarding Ms. Amelia Spark, a former employee at Rogers, Milton, & Cole, PC. Ms. Spark began with our company as an intern soon after she graduated from university. At the end of her internship, we hired her on as a full-time legal assistant. –[1]– At the same time, she continued to take classes at the university, I understand with the goal of eventually going for an advanced degree. –[2]–

As well as being reliable and hardworking, we could always count on Ms. Sparks to be pleasant and helpful to everyone in the office. –[3]– These characteristics were especially helpful in Ms. Spark's dealings with clients. In fact, clients often specifically asked to work with her. –[4]–

We were sorry to lose Ms. Spark when she left us last month, but wish her much success with her decision to move to New York and in all her future professional endeavors. We know she will be a great asset to any firm she works with. Please don't hesitate to contact me if you require any further information.

Sincerely,
Stephen Cole
Stephen Cole

---

164. What will Ms. Spark use this letter for?

    (A) To hire someone
    (B) To get a new a job
    (C) To get new clients
    (D) To apply to university

165. What profession does Ms. Spark work in?

    (A) Law
    (B) Education
    (C) Accounting
    (D) Business

166. Why did Ms. Spark leave her job?

    (A) She was fired.
    (B) She became ill.
    (C) She moved to a new city.
    (D) She returned to school.

167. In which of the following positions marked [1], [2], [3], and [4] does the following sentence best belong?

    "She worked diligently at that job, proving herself always eager to learn and willing to put in whatever time and effort a project required."

    (A) [1]
    (B) [2]
    (C) [3]
    (D) [4]

Questions 168–171 are based on the following article.

The Rockville Development Group (RDG) announced today a proposal for a mixed-use complex on the outskirts of Bingchester, close to Highway 10. The proposed complex includes 1,000 square meters of office space, 50,000 square meters of retail space, a parking garage, and several hectares of outdoor parking.

The announcement got a mixed reception. Bingchester City Council members hailed it as a boost to the local economy. "It will bring jobs. People will come here to spend money. What could be better?" proclaimed Council Member Miriam Hodges. But local business owners had a different opinion. "Its location can only hurt our businesses," said Bill Smithers, president of the Bingchester Business Owner's Association. "Look at the distance from the downtown shopping district. People driving down Highway 10 may stop at the mall, but they won't then drive the extra mile to spend money at our local shops." Environmental groups also expressed opposition to the proposal. "In addition to destroying acres of valuable agricultural land, water run-off from the pavement will dirty our local streams and rivers and damage natural habitats."

A spokesperson for RDG dismissed the opposition, saying, "This development has been five years in the planning. We have received all the necessary permits and are closely following government regulations. When it is completed, this project will be one of Bingchester's greatest assets. We expect to break ground before the end of the year." Construction will take close to two years to complete.

168. What is this article mostly about?

    (A) Local business regulations
    (B) The grand opening of a mall
    (C) A plan to build stores and offices
    (D) The revival of a downtown shopping district

169. What is a complaint about the project?

    (A) It is too big.
    (B) It harms farmland.
    (C) It is too close to downtown.
    (D) It will create parking problems.

170. Who is Miriam Hodges?

    (A) A politician
    (B) A shopper
    (C) A builder
    (D) A retailer

171. When will work on the project begin?

    (A) By December 31
    (B) Next January
    (C) In two years
    (D) In five years

Questions 172-175 refer to the following online chat.

GREG SAMSA	2:15
This is Greg in marketing. We're having a training workshop for new hires next Wednesday, and I'd like to reserve Conference Room 3. I checked the schedule online, and it's free all morning.	
BLANCA WHITE	2:20
I'm sorry. That room has been reserved for a client meeting. I'm a bit behind on updating the schedule and haven't put it up yet.	
GREG SAMSA	2:23
I don't know what to do. Room 3 is the only room big enough.	
BLANCA WHITE	2:25
How about Room 2? I believe it's available Wednesday morning.	
GREG SAMSA	2:27
The lighting in there is terrible. I can never see what I'm writing.	
BLANCA WHITE	2:29
Yes, we're going to fix that soon.	
BLANCA WHITE	2:30
How many people are you expecting?	
GREG SAMSA	2:33
At least 20.	
BLANCA WHITE	2:35
Then you could use Room 4. I'm sure you could fit 20 people in there comfortably.	
GREG SAMSA	2:39
Perhaps. But it's an all morning session, so we'll also need some room for serving refreshments during the break.	
BLANCA WHITE	2:43
The hall in that part of the building is fairly wide. I could have someone set up the refreshments just outside the door and that would leave you more space inside the room.	
GREG SAMSA	2:45
Do you think that will work?	
BLANCA WHITE	2:48
I'm sure it will. Why don't I meet you up there in 5 minutes, and I can show you where we will put the tables and how we can arrange everything.	
GREG SAMSA	2:50
Great. Thanks.	

172. What does Mr. Samsa need the room for?

(A) A luncheon
(B) A training session
(C) Meeting with a client
(D) Job applicant interviews

173. At 2:20, what does Ms. White mean when she writes, "I haven't put it up yet"?

(A) She has not yet prepared the room for the meeting.
(B) She has not yet determined which rooms are free.
(C) She has not yet created the schedule for the week.
(D) She has not yet posted the Room 3 reservation.

174. What is the problem with Room 2?

(A) It has been reserved by someone else.
(B) It is being repaired.
(C) It is very small.
(D) It is too dark.

175. What will Ms. White do next?

(A) Get some tables
(B) Update the schedule
(C) Meet Mr. Samsa by Room 4
(D) Set up the refreshments

Questions 176-180 refer to the following email and survey.

To: Elizabeth Simons
From: Rosemount Hotel
Subject: Guest Satisfaction Survey

Dear Ms. Simons,

Thank you for choosing the Rosemount Hotel during your recent visit to Springfield.

Please visit the internet link below. It will take you to our Guest Satisfaction Survey. We appreciate the time you take to fill out this survey as it enables us to provide you with the best possible experience at the Rosemount. Please follow this link to take the survey. We are sorry but we are unable to respond directly to feedback as the survey is conducted by a third party.

We hope your stay at the Rosemount was pleasant, and that we will see you here again soon. For billing or future stay assistance, please contact the following:

Billing inquiries—Mr. Perez: rperez@rosemounthotel.com

Future stay inquiries—Ms. Lee: klee@rosemounthotel.com

If you wish to opt out of future emails from the Rosemount Hotel, please follow this link to be removed from our list.

Again, thank you.

Harold Custer for the Rosemount Hotel

ROSEMOUNT HOTEL
Guest Satisfaction Survey

Please rate the hotel staff:

	Excellent	Good	Fair	Poor
Professional attitude	✗			
Professional appearance	✗			
Knowledge of local area		✗		
Speed of check in process			✗	

Please rate your room:

	Excellent	Good	Fair	Poor
Cleanliness	✗			
Comfort of bed	✗			
Lighting	✗			
Internet connection	✗			

Please rate the fitness center:*

	Excellent	Good	Fair	Poor
Cleanliness				
Selection of equipment				
Condition of equipment				

If you experienced any problems during your stay, please explain:
I had to wait several minutes before someone was available to check me in. Then, the clerk had problems with the credit card machine. One other thing, I tried to use the fitness center, but by the time I got there (10:00 p.m.), it was closed.

Comments:
I thoroughly enjoyed my stay at the Rosemount. I was here this time for a client meeting but hope to return soon with my family for some sightseeing.

Your name: Elizabeth Simons
Date of stay: April 10–11

*Please leave this section blank if you did not visit our fitness center.

---

176. What is the purpose of the email?

    (A) To ask for feedback
    (B) To explain a bill
    (C) To advertise the hotel
    (D) To confirm a reservation

177. Why should someone contact Ms. Lee?

    (A) To ask about a bill
    (B) To submit a survey
    (C) To make a hotel reservation
    (D) To be removed from the email list

178. What problem did Ms. Simons have with the hotel?

    (A) The room cost
    (B) The comfort of the bed
    (C) The cleanliness of the room
    (D) The registration process

179. Why didn't Ms. Simons use the fitness center?

    (A) It was closed.
    (B) It wasn't clean.
    (C) She never exercises.
    (D) The equipment was in poor condition.

180. What was the purpose of Ms. Simons' trip to Springfield?

    (A) A family visit
    (B) A business meeting
    (C) A sightseeing tour
    (D) A conference

Questions 181-185 refer to the following schedule and email.

BOA
TENTH ANNUAL CONFERENCE
HALISTON HOTEL

SCHEDULE

8:30-9:45	CONTINENTAL BREAKFAST (MAIN LOBBY)
10:00 - 12:00	WORKSHOP SESSION 1 A: FINANCING YOUR BUSINESS (GARDEN ROOM) B: MARKETING IN THE DIGITAL AGE (ROOM 3)
12:15-1:15	LUNCH (DINING ROOM)
1:30-3:30	WORKSHOP SESSION 2 C: SMALL BUSINESS HIRING PRACTICES (ROOM 2) D: TRAINING YOUR PERSONNEL (MEZZANINE)
4:00-5:00	SOCIAL HOUR (MAIN LOBBY)

To: Bob Schumacher
From: Anne Kemp
Date: November 10
Subject: BOA Conference

Hi Bob,

I am attaching the conference schedule as you requested. I am really looking forward to it, especially since this is the first year I will be attending without being a presenter. Without that pressure, I will really have a chance to enjoy everything the conference has to offer.

I hope we can get together sometime during the day. I'd like to take the opportunity to discuss with you a loan I hope to get for expanding my business. I would really appreciate your advice on this matter as you have so much experience in this area and with the particular lender I hope to work with. Also I know you are active in the local Finance Educators Association and could perhaps point me to further resources. I plan to attend workshops A and C. I don't know whether you will be at either one of those, but we should make another time to get together to really have a chance to talk. I have a meeting with a colleague at noon, so I won't be at the conference lunch, but what about the social hour? Let's plan to look for each other there.

Anne

181. Who is this conference for?
    (A) Marketing specialists
    (B) Business owners
    (C) Personnel managers
    (D) Money lenders

182. Why did Ms. Kemp write the email to Mr. Schumacher?
    (A) To invite him to go to the conference
    (B) To tell him about a workshop she will present
    (C) To make plans to meet with him
    (D) To suggest which workshops he should attend

183. Where will Ms. Kemp be at 1:30?
    (A) Main lobby
    (B) Dining room
    (C) Room 2
    (D) Mezzanine

184. In the email, the word *active* in paragraph 2, line 4, is closest in meaning to
    (A) busy
    (B) ready
    (C) energetic
    (D) involved

185. What does Ms. Kemp want to discuss with Mr. Schumacher?
    (A) Borrowing money
    (B) Presenting a workshop
    (C) Organizing the conference
    (D) Arranging a social hour

Questions 186–190 refer to the following schedule, newspaper announcement, and email.

Torryton 150th Annual National Day Celebration
Schedule of Events
Saturday

CRAFTS FAIR

Time: All Day   **Location: Torryton Park, Oak Walk**

Enjoy the shade of our city's famous old oak trees as you shop for hand-made items by local, national, and international crafters.

HISTORY EXHIBITS

Time: 10 am–7 pm   **Location: History Museum**

Bring the whole family to see special National Day exhibits, inside the newly renovated History Museum. Special activities for the little ones include craft making and a film.

INTERNATIONAL FOOD FESTIVAL

Time: Noon–8 pm   **Location: Main and Maple Sts.**

Sample delights from all around the world as you stroll along the sidewalks of Main and Maple Streets.

SOCCER GAME

Time: 6 pm   **Location: Torryton High School Soccer Field**

Watch local teams compete for the coveted National Day Trophy.

CONCERT

Time: 8:30 pm   **Location: Torryton Park, East Field**

Relax under the stars while listening to music from local bands.

ANNOUNCEMENT
National Day Celebration

Due to the predicted bad weather, the City Council has announced several changes to this weekend's National Day celebration. All outdoor activities have been canceled, with the exception of the evening concert. This has been moved to the Torryton Theater. Like all the weekend's events, there is no charge for the concert. However, due to limited seating, tickets must be obtained ahead of time. Contact the City Arts Council to reserve your tickets. All indoor activities will proceed as scheduled.

To: patr@ztown.com
From: timrogers@river.com
Date: June 11
Subject: Torryton trip

Hi Pat,

Thanks for recommending the Torryton National Day celebration. I had a great time despite the weather. I guess you heard about that storm. Anyhow, there were still lots of celebration events going on. I was really sorry to miss the food festival, but maybe I can catch it next year. I saw the history exhibits early in the day, then I was lucky enough to get a ticket to the concert. It was fantastic. I'll give you a full account when I see you next week.

Tim

186. What is NOT true about the celebration?

    (A) It takes place once a year.
    (B) It includes a sports event.
    (C) It costs money to attend.
    (D) It is an old tradition.

187. Which activity is especially for children?

    (A) A movie
    (B) A crafts sale
    (C) An international meal
    (D) A walk on Main Street

188. Why didn't Tim go to the food festival?

    (A) It was canceled.
    (B) He wasn't hungry.
    (C) He didn't feel well.
    (D) It was too early in the day.

189. Where was Tim in the evening?

    (A) At the park
    (B) At the theater
    (C) At the museum
    (D) At the soccer game

190. In the email, the word *account* in line 5 is closest in meaning to

    (A) bill
    (B) money
    (C) description
    (D) reason

523

Questions 191-195 refer to the following ad, review, and article.

Come to the new
Beeline Bistro
Use these coupons to take advantage of
special offers when you visit us this month.

Beeline Bistro
***** *2 for 1 Special* *****
Choose any two entrees from our dinner menu for the price of one.

Offer expires March 31
One coupon per customer

Beeline Bistro
***** *Free Dessert* *****
Enjoy one free dessert with any lunch entree.

Offer expires March 31
One coupon per customer

Beeline Bistro
*** *Sandwich Special* ***
Choose selected sandwiches from our lunch menu for just $6.99 each.

Offer expires March 31
One coupon per customer

Beeline Bistro
***** *Appetizer Tray* *****
Get 25% off our Appetizer Tray when you come in for dinner before 6:00 P.M.

Offer expires March 31
One coupon per customer

Beeline Bistro
113 Riverside Avenue
Serving 3 meals a day, seven days a week

Beeline Bistro

My husband and I tried out the new Beeline Bistro last week, and it did not disappoint! What a great dinner. It's still pricy, but we used a coupon and that made a big difference. They offer the same great selection as always. We skipped the appetizers and went straight to the entrees, and of course, couldn't pass up the great desserts. If you enjoy the old Beeline as much as we do, you're sure to like the Riverside version, too.

Penny Barlow

RIVERSIDE
Revival of a Neighborhood

The new restaurant and shopping district in the Riverside section of town is booming. Specialty clothing, book, and gift stores have popped up around the neighborhood. At the same time, numerous new eating places have appeared, and some old favorites have opened new locations there as well. The latter include the ever-popular Beeline Bistro. This is a wise move on the part of Beeline's owners, as the contemporary menu will surely appeal to the youthful residents of the neighborhood. The newcomer Café Cookie Cutter, just next door, is already the place to go for home-baked pastries.

In general, the concentration of restaurants in the area is a draw for other businesses as well, and on weekend evenings the streets are alive with shoppers, sightseers, and, most of all, people with money to spend. All in all, Riverside businesses are taking off.

191. What is suggested about the Beeline Bistro restaurant?
    (A) It is a new business.
    (B) It will be remodeled.
    (C) It has changed the menu.
    (D) It has opened a new branch.

192. Which coupon did Ms. Barlow use?
    (A) Free dessert
    (B) Appetizer tray
    (C) 2 for 1 special
    (D) Sandwich special

193. What criticism does Ms. Barlow have of the Beeline Bistro?
    (A) It is expensive.
    (B) It is too busy.
    (C) The menu is short.
    (D) The appetizers aren't good.

194. In the article, the word *concentration* in paragraph 2, line 1, is closest in meaning to
    (A) thinking
    (B) attention
    (C) crowding
    (D) shrinkage

195. What is suggested about Riverside businesses?
    (A) They are prosperous.
    (B) They are in a bad location.
    (C) They need more publicity.
    (D) They appeal only to young people.

Questions 196–200 refer to the following sign, email, and notice.

AIRPORT TRANSPORTATION
All transportation services leave from the front of the East Terminal.

	Schedule	Destinations	Cost
City Bus #46	Every hour	Downtown, Parkview, Business District	$3.50
Train Station Shuttle	Every 30 min.	Central Train Station	$5.00
Hotel Shuttles	Varies	Neighborhood hotels	None
Taxi	Varies	Any	Varies

To: m.reed@company.com
From: s.chang@company.com
Date: Friday, September 15
Subject: travel

Melinda,

Thanks for doing such a great job organizing my trip. Everything has gone smoothly so far except for one little glitch at the airport. I was all set to take the downtown bus, as you suggested, because it stops right across the street from the hotel, but unfortunately it didn't work out because of the mess at the terminal, what with all the work going on, and then, of course, Friday is such a heavy travel day. I ended up having to pay for a taxi, which cost a good deal more, and I doubt whether it saved me any time. The traffic around here is horrendous. At any rate, I'm settled into the hotel now and getting ready for tomorrow's meetings. I'll let you know how everything goes.

Sam

NOTICE to Airport Users

The following changes to airport transportation have been put in place due to renovations and repairs being carried out at the East Terminal:

- All shuttle and taxi services now leave from the front of the West Terminal.
- Service from City Bus #46 is temporarily suspended. Those desiring to connect with other City Bus lines can take a shuttle or taxi to Central Train Station, which is serviced by buses #32, #57, and #75.

Please direct any questions or concerns to the Airport Office of Public Relations.

This notice is in effect from August 30 to October 15.

196. Which type of transportation is free to use?

    (A) City Bus
    (B) Train Station Shuttle
    (C) Hotel Shuttles
    (D) Taxi

197. Why didn't Sam take the bus?

    (A) It doesn't go to his destination.
    (B) It isn't in operation right now.
    (C) It takes too long.
    (D) It costs too much.

198. What does Sam suggest about the airport?

    (A) It is crowded on Fridays.
    (B) It is not cleaned regularly.
    (C) It is far from downtown.
    (D) It is close to his hotel.

199. What is happening at the airport from August to October?

    (A) Construction of a new terminal
    (B) Changes in shuttle schedules
    (C) Reorganization of bus routes
    (D) Remodeling of a building

200. In the notice, the word *direct* in line 10 is closest in meaning to

    (A) advise
    (B) manage
    (C) express
    (D) instruct

STOP This is the end of the test. If you finish before time is called, you may go back to Parts 5, 6, and 7 and check your work.

多益測驗成績換算對照表

計算答對的題數,利用下表找到對應的分數。將聽力和閱讀分數相加,就會得到預估的多益測驗總分。逐一演練模擬試題,分數也會逐漸提升,請持續追蹤你的多益測驗預估總分。

答對題數	聽力分數	閱讀分數	答對題數	聽力分數	閱讀分數	答對題數	聽力分數	閱讀分數	答對題數	聽力分數	閱讀分數
0	5	5	26	110	65	51	255	220	76	410	370
1	5	5	27	115	70	52	260	225	77	420	380
2	5	5	28	120	80	53	270	230	78	425	385
3	5	5	29	125	85	54	275	235	79	430	390
4	5	5	30	130	90	55	280	240	80	440	395
5	5	5	31	135	95	56	290	250	81	445	400
6	5	5	32	140	100	57	295	255	82	450	405
7	10	5	33	145	110	58	300	260	83	460	410
8	15	5	34	150	115	59	310	265	84	465	415
9	20	5	35	160	120	60	315	270	85	470	420
10	25	5	36	165	125	61	320	280	86	475	425
11	30	5	37	170	130	62	325	285	87	480	430
12	35	5	38	175	140	63	330	290	88	485	435
13	40	5	39	180	145	64	340	300	89	490	445
14	45	5	40	185	150	65	345	305	90	495	450
15	50	5	41	190	160	66	350	310	91	495	455
16	55	10	42	195	165	67	360	320	92	495	465
17	60	15	43	200	170	68	365	325	93	495	470
18	65	20	44	210	175	69	370	330	94	495	480
19	70	25	45	215	180	70	380	335	95	495	485
20	75	30	46	220	190	71	385	340	96	495	490
21	80	35	47	230	195	72	390	350	97	495	495
22	85	40	48	240	200	73	395	355	98	495	495
23	90	45	49	245	210	74	400	360	99	495	495
24	95	50	50	250	215	75	405	365	100	495	495
25	100	60									

聽力測驗答對題數 _____ = 聽力測驗分數 _____
閱讀測驗答對題數 _____ = 閱讀測驗分數 _____
多益測驗預估總分 _____

MEMO

ANSWER SHEET
實戰模擬試題6答案卡

Listening Comprehension

Part 1: Photographs

1. Ⓐ Ⓑ Ⓒ Ⓓ   3. Ⓐ Ⓑ Ⓒ Ⓓ   5. Ⓐ Ⓑ Ⓒ Ⓓ
2. Ⓐ Ⓑ Ⓒ Ⓓ   4. Ⓐ Ⓑ Ⓒ Ⓓ   6. Ⓐ Ⓑ Ⓒ Ⓓ

Part 2: Question-Response

7. Ⓐ Ⓑ Ⓒ   14. Ⓐ Ⓑ Ⓒ   21. Ⓐ Ⓑ Ⓒ   28. Ⓐ Ⓑ Ⓒ
8. Ⓐ Ⓑ Ⓒ   15. Ⓐ Ⓑ Ⓒ   22. Ⓐ Ⓑ Ⓒ   29. Ⓐ Ⓑ Ⓒ
9. Ⓐ Ⓑ Ⓒ   16. Ⓐ Ⓑ Ⓒ   23. Ⓐ Ⓑ Ⓒ   30. Ⓐ Ⓑ Ⓒ
10. Ⓐ Ⓑ Ⓒ   17. Ⓐ Ⓑ Ⓒ   24. Ⓐ Ⓑ Ⓒ   31. Ⓐ Ⓑ Ⓒ
11. Ⓐ Ⓑ Ⓒ   18. Ⓐ Ⓑ Ⓒ   25. Ⓐ Ⓑ Ⓒ
12. Ⓐ Ⓑ Ⓒ   19. Ⓐ Ⓑ Ⓒ   26. Ⓐ Ⓑ Ⓒ
13. Ⓐ Ⓑ Ⓒ   20. Ⓐ Ⓑ Ⓒ   27. Ⓐ Ⓑ Ⓒ

Part 3: Conversations

32. Ⓐ Ⓑ Ⓒ Ⓓ   42. Ⓐ Ⓑ Ⓒ Ⓓ   52. Ⓐ Ⓑ Ⓒ Ⓓ   62. Ⓐ Ⓑ Ⓒ Ⓓ
33. Ⓐ Ⓑ Ⓒ Ⓓ   43. Ⓐ Ⓑ Ⓒ Ⓓ   53. Ⓐ Ⓑ Ⓒ Ⓓ   63. Ⓐ Ⓑ Ⓒ Ⓓ
34. Ⓐ Ⓑ Ⓒ Ⓓ   44. Ⓐ Ⓑ Ⓒ Ⓓ   54. Ⓐ Ⓑ Ⓒ Ⓓ   64. Ⓐ Ⓑ Ⓒ Ⓓ
35. Ⓐ Ⓑ Ⓒ Ⓓ   45. Ⓐ Ⓑ Ⓒ Ⓓ   55. Ⓐ Ⓑ Ⓒ Ⓓ   65. Ⓐ Ⓑ Ⓒ Ⓓ
36. Ⓐ Ⓑ Ⓒ Ⓓ   46. Ⓐ Ⓑ Ⓒ Ⓓ   56. Ⓐ Ⓑ Ⓒ Ⓓ   66. Ⓐ Ⓑ Ⓒ Ⓓ
37. Ⓐ Ⓑ Ⓒ Ⓓ   47. Ⓐ Ⓑ Ⓒ Ⓓ   57. Ⓐ Ⓑ Ⓒ Ⓓ   67. Ⓐ Ⓑ Ⓒ Ⓓ
38. Ⓐ Ⓑ Ⓒ Ⓓ   48. Ⓐ Ⓑ Ⓒ Ⓓ   58. Ⓐ Ⓑ Ⓒ Ⓓ   68. Ⓐ Ⓑ Ⓒ Ⓓ
39. Ⓐ Ⓑ Ⓒ Ⓓ   49. Ⓐ Ⓑ Ⓒ Ⓓ   59. Ⓐ Ⓑ Ⓒ Ⓓ   69. Ⓐ Ⓑ Ⓒ Ⓓ
40. Ⓐ Ⓑ Ⓒ Ⓓ   50. Ⓐ Ⓑ Ⓒ Ⓓ   60. Ⓐ Ⓑ Ⓒ Ⓓ   70. Ⓐ Ⓑ Ⓒ Ⓓ
41. Ⓐ Ⓑ Ⓒ Ⓓ   51. Ⓐ Ⓑ Ⓒ Ⓓ   61. Ⓐ Ⓑ Ⓒ Ⓓ

Part 4: Talks

71. Ⓐ Ⓑ Ⓒ Ⓓ   79. Ⓐ Ⓑ Ⓒ Ⓓ   87. Ⓐ Ⓑ Ⓒ Ⓓ   95. Ⓐ Ⓑ Ⓒ Ⓓ
72. Ⓐ Ⓑ Ⓒ Ⓓ   80. Ⓐ Ⓑ Ⓒ Ⓓ   88. Ⓐ Ⓑ Ⓒ Ⓓ   96. Ⓐ Ⓑ Ⓒ Ⓓ
73. Ⓐ Ⓑ Ⓒ Ⓓ   81. Ⓐ Ⓑ Ⓒ Ⓓ   89. Ⓐ Ⓑ Ⓒ Ⓓ   97. Ⓐ Ⓑ Ⓒ Ⓓ
74. Ⓐ Ⓑ Ⓒ Ⓓ   82. Ⓐ Ⓑ Ⓒ Ⓓ   90. Ⓐ Ⓑ Ⓒ Ⓓ   98. Ⓐ Ⓑ Ⓒ Ⓓ
75. Ⓐ Ⓑ Ⓒ Ⓓ   82. Ⓐ Ⓑ Ⓒ Ⓓ   91. Ⓐ Ⓑ Ⓒ Ⓓ   99. Ⓐ Ⓑ Ⓒ Ⓓ
76. Ⓐ Ⓑ Ⓒ Ⓓ   84. Ⓐ Ⓑ Ⓒ Ⓓ   92. Ⓐ Ⓑ Ⓒ Ⓓ   100. Ⓐ Ⓑ Ⓒ Ⓓ
77. Ⓐ Ⓑ Ⓒ Ⓓ   85. Ⓐ Ⓑ Ⓒ Ⓓ   93. Ⓐ Ⓑ Ⓒ Ⓓ
78. Ⓐ Ⓑ Ⓒ Ⓓ   86. Ⓐ Ⓑ Ⓒ Ⓓ   94. Ⓐ Ⓑ Ⓒ Ⓓ

ANSWER SHEET
實戰模擬試題6答案卡

Reading Comprehension

Part 5: Incomplete Sentences

101. Ⓐ Ⓑ Ⓒ Ⓓ	109. Ⓐ Ⓑ Ⓒ Ⓓ	117. Ⓐ Ⓑ Ⓒ Ⓓ	125. Ⓐ Ⓑ Ⓒ Ⓓ
102. Ⓐ Ⓑ Ⓒ Ⓓ	110. Ⓐ Ⓑ Ⓒ Ⓓ	118. Ⓐ Ⓑ Ⓒ Ⓓ	126. Ⓐ Ⓑ Ⓒ Ⓓ
103. Ⓐ Ⓑ Ⓒ Ⓓ	111. Ⓐ Ⓑ Ⓒ Ⓓ	119. Ⓐ Ⓑ Ⓒ Ⓓ	127. Ⓐ Ⓑ Ⓒ Ⓓ
104. Ⓐ Ⓑ Ⓒ Ⓓ	112. Ⓐ Ⓑ Ⓒ Ⓓ	120. Ⓐ Ⓑ Ⓒ Ⓓ	128. Ⓐ Ⓑ Ⓒ Ⓓ
105. Ⓐ Ⓑ Ⓒ Ⓓ	113. Ⓐ Ⓑ Ⓒ Ⓓ	121. Ⓐ Ⓑ Ⓒ Ⓓ	129. Ⓐ Ⓑ Ⓒ Ⓓ
106. Ⓐ Ⓑ Ⓒ Ⓓ	114. Ⓐ Ⓑ Ⓒ Ⓓ	122. Ⓐ Ⓑ Ⓒ Ⓓ	130. Ⓐ Ⓑ Ⓒ Ⓓ
107. Ⓐ Ⓑ Ⓒ Ⓓ	115. Ⓐ Ⓑ Ⓒ Ⓓ	123. Ⓐ Ⓑ Ⓒ Ⓓ	
108. Ⓐ Ⓑ Ⓒ Ⓓ	116. Ⓐ Ⓑ Ⓒ Ⓓ	124. Ⓐ Ⓑ Ⓒ Ⓓ	

Part 6: Text Completion

131. Ⓐ Ⓑ Ⓒ Ⓓ	135. Ⓐ Ⓑ Ⓒ Ⓓ	139. Ⓐ Ⓑ Ⓒ Ⓓ	143. Ⓐ Ⓑ Ⓒ Ⓓ
132. Ⓐ Ⓑ Ⓒ Ⓓ	136. Ⓐ Ⓑ Ⓒ Ⓓ	140. Ⓐ Ⓑ Ⓒ Ⓓ	144. Ⓐ Ⓑ Ⓒ Ⓓ
133. Ⓐ Ⓑ Ⓒ Ⓓ	137. Ⓐ Ⓑ Ⓒ Ⓓ	141. Ⓐ Ⓑ Ⓒ Ⓓ	145. Ⓐ Ⓑ Ⓒ Ⓓ
134. Ⓐ Ⓑ Ⓒ Ⓓ	138. Ⓐ Ⓑ Ⓒ Ⓓ	142. Ⓐ Ⓑ Ⓒ Ⓓ	146. Ⓐ Ⓑ Ⓒ Ⓓ

Part 7: Reading Comprehension

147. Ⓐ Ⓑ Ⓒ Ⓓ	161. Ⓐ Ⓑ Ⓒ Ⓓ	175. Ⓐ Ⓑ Ⓒ Ⓓ	189. Ⓐ Ⓑ Ⓒ Ⓓ
148. Ⓐ Ⓑ Ⓒ Ⓓ	162. Ⓐ Ⓑ Ⓒ Ⓓ	176. Ⓐ Ⓑ Ⓒ Ⓓ	190. Ⓐ Ⓑ Ⓒ Ⓓ
149. Ⓐ Ⓑ Ⓒ Ⓓ	163. Ⓐ Ⓑ Ⓒ Ⓓ	177. Ⓐ Ⓑ Ⓒ Ⓓ	191. Ⓐ Ⓑ Ⓒ Ⓓ
150. Ⓐ Ⓑ Ⓒ Ⓓ	164. Ⓐ Ⓑ Ⓒ Ⓓ	178. Ⓐ Ⓑ Ⓒ Ⓓ	192. Ⓐ Ⓑ Ⓒ Ⓓ
151. Ⓐ Ⓑ Ⓒ Ⓓ	165. Ⓐ Ⓑ Ⓒ Ⓓ	179. Ⓐ Ⓑ Ⓒ Ⓓ	193. Ⓐ Ⓑ Ⓒ Ⓓ
152. Ⓐ Ⓑ Ⓒ Ⓓ	166. Ⓐ Ⓑ Ⓒ Ⓓ	180. Ⓐ Ⓑ Ⓒ Ⓓ	194. Ⓐ Ⓑ Ⓒ Ⓓ
153. Ⓐ Ⓑ Ⓒ Ⓓ	167. Ⓐ Ⓑ Ⓒ Ⓓ	181. Ⓐ Ⓑ Ⓒ Ⓓ	195. Ⓐ Ⓑ Ⓒ Ⓓ
154. Ⓐ Ⓑ Ⓒ Ⓓ	168. Ⓐ Ⓑ Ⓒ Ⓓ	182. Ⓐ Ⓑ Ⓒ Ⓓ	196. Ⓐ Ⓑ Ⓒ Ⓓ
155. Ⓐ Ⓑ Ⓒ Ⓓ	169. Ⓐ Ⓑ Ⓒ Ⓓ	183. Ⓐ Ⓑ Ⓒ Ⓓ	197. Ⓐ Ⓑ Ⓒ Ⓓ
156. Ⓐ Ⓑ Ⓒ Ⓓ	170. Ⓐ Ⓑ Ⓒ Ⓓ	184. Ⓐ Ⓑ Ⓒ Ⓓ	198. Ⓐ Ⓑ Ⓒ Ⓓ
157. Ⓐ Ⓑ Ⓒ Ⓓ	171. Ⓐ Ⓑ Ⓒ Ⓓ	185. Ⓐ Ⓑ Ⓒ Ⓓ	199. Ⓐ Ⓑ Ⓒ Ⓓ
158. Ⓐ Ⓑ Ⓒ Ⓓ	172. Ⓐ Ⓑ Ⓒ Ⓓ	186. Ⓐ Ⓑ Ⓒ Ⓓ	200. Ⓐ Ⓑ Ⓒ Ⓓ
159. Ⓐ Ⓑ Ⓒ Ⓓ	173. Ⓐ Ⓑ Ⓒ Ⓓ	187. Ⓐ Ⓑ Ⓒ Ⓓ	
160. Ⓐ Ⓑ Ⓒ Ⓓ	174. Ⓐ Ⓑ Ⓒ Ⓓ	188. Ⓐ Ⓑ Ⓒ Ⓓ	

MODEL TEST 6

實戰模擬試題 6

Listening Comprehension

In this section of the test, you will have the chance to show how well you understand spoken English. There are four parts to this section, with special directions for each part. You will have approximately 45 minutes to complete the Listening Comprehension sections.

Part 1: Photographs

DIRECTIONS: You will see a photograph. You will hear four statements about the photograph. Choose the statement that most closely matches the photograph, and fill in the corresponding oval on your answer sheet.

Track 55

1.

2.

3.

4.

5.

6.

Part 2: Question-Response

DIRECTIONS: You will hear a question and three possible responses. Choose the response that most closely answers the question, and fill in the corresponding oval on your answer sheet.

Track 56

7. Mark your answer on your answer sheet.
8. Mark your answer on your answer sheet.
9. Mark your answer on your answer sheet.
10. Mark your answer on your answer sheet.
11. Mark your answer on your answer sheet.
12. Mark your answer on your answer sheet.
13. Mark your answer on your answer sheet.
14. Mark your answer on your answer sheet.
15. Mark your answer on your answer sheet.
16. Mark your answer on your answer sheet.
17. Mark your answer on your answer sheet.
18. Mark your answer on your answer sheet.
19. Mark your answer on your answer sheet.
20. Mark your answer on your answer sheet.
21. Mark your answer on your answer sheet.
22. Mark your answer on your answer sheet.
23. Mark your answer on your answer sheet.
24. Mark your answer on your answer sheet.
25. Mark your answer on your answer sheet.
26. Mark your answer on your answer sheet.
27. Mark your answer on your answer sheet.
28. Mark your answer on your answer sheet.
29. Mark your answer on your answer sheet.
30. Mark your answer on your answer sheet.
31. Mark your answer on your answer sheet.

Part 3: Conversations

DIRECTIONS: You will hear a conversation between two or more people. You will see three questions on each conversation and four possible answers. Choose the best answer to each question, and fill in the corresponding oval on your answer sheet.

Track 57

32. What does the woman ask the man to do?
    (A) Give her a ride to work
    (B) Lift something heavy
    (C) Take her shopping
    (D) Fix her car

33. Why does the man want to be at the office early?
    (A) To repair some office equipment
    (B) To get ready for a client meeting
    (C) To wrap some presents
    (D) To finish a report

34. What does the woman suggest?
    (A) Leaving later
    (B) Calling a client
    (C) Stopping at the library
    (D) Asking someone for help

35. What are the speakers discussing?
    (A) Getting the office cleaned
    (B) Renting an apartment
    (C) Buying furniture
    (D) Going out to eat

36. What problem do they have?
    (A) They lost the contact information.
    (B) They think the price is too high.
    (C) They can't find anyone to hire.
    (D) They don't like the schedule.

37. What does the man suggest they do?
    (A) Leave earlier
    (B) Offer to pay less
    (C) Meet somewhere else
    (D) Buy new furniture

38. Why is the woman talking to the man?
    (A) To invite him somewhere
    (B) To make a suggestion
    (C) To discuss a problem
    (D) To ask for advice

39. What is the man doing?
    (A) Watching sports
    (B) Writing a report
    (C) Cleaning his desk
    (D) Making a phone call

40. What does the man ask the woman to do?
    (A) Give him directions to the restaurant
    (B) Come back to talk with him later
    (C) Help him with his work
    (D) Wait for him at 7:00

41. What is the man renting?
    (A) Some furniture
    (B) An apartment
    (C) A heater
    (D) A car

42. What does the woman suggest the man do?
    (A) Request something larger
    (B) Look at other options
    (C) Rent for more time
    (D) Reread the agreement

43. What will the man do next?
    (A) Fill the tank
    (B) Sign a document
    (C) Go away for the weekend
    (D) Go to another rental agency

537

44. Why did the man make the call?

    (A) To report a problem
    (B) To make a complaint
    (C) To order a product
    (D) To ask for information

45. What costs $20?

    (A) Standard shipping
    (B) Express shipping
    (C) Special packaging
    (D) Guaranteed delivery

46. What does the man mean when he says, "That's it"?

    (A) He's decided which products to buy.
    (B) His questions have been answered.
    (C) He's chosen his shipping method.
    (D) His order is completed.

47. What best describes this conversation?

    (A) An introduction
    (B) A staff meeting
    (C) An interview
    (D) A sales pitch

48. What does the man like most about his job?

    (A) The pay
    (B) The events
    (C) The benefits
    (D) The schedule

49. What will probably happen next?

    (A) The man will answer the woman's last question.
    (B) The woman will speak with Mrs. Patterson.
    (C) The man will leave for the weekend.
    (D) The woman will go home.

50. What is likely the purpose of the man's trip?

    (A) To meet a client
    (B) To take a vacation
    (C) To take photographs
    (D) To attend a conference

51. What do the women imply about the hotel?

    (A) It is in a bad location.
    (B) It is uncomfortable.
    (C) It is too expensive.
    (D) It is very noisy.

52. What will the man do next?

    (A) Research other hotels
    (B) Reserve a room
    (C) Cancel his trip
    (D) Take a nap

53. What kind of work are they hiring contractors for?

    (A) Construction
    (B) Decorating
    (C) Transportation
    (D) Editing

54. What will happen at the meeting tomorrow?

    (A) They will write a quote for the project.
    (B) They will meet the contractor.
    (C) They will talk about the schedule.
    (D) They will review the submitted quotes.

55. What was the problem with the last contractor?

    (A) He didn't finish the work.
    (B) He left the job site a mess.
    (C) He was located too far away.
    (D) He tore up the contract.

56. Where does this conversation take place?

    (A) Clothing store
    (B) Restaurant
    (C) Paint store
    (D) Bank

57. Why is the man there?

    (A) To apply for a job
    (B) To return an item
    (C) To order something
    (D) To make a complaint

58. Why does the man say, "The selection certainly could be better"?

    (A) He wants more time to make his choice.
    (B) He doesn't like the offered choices.
    (C) He hasn't ever seen better choices.
    (D) He needs help making his choice.

59. What are the speakers discussing?

    (A) A play
    (B) A concert
    (C) A business trip
    (D) A boxing match

60. What is the woman's problem?

    (A) She has to go out of town.
    (B) She doesn't like her seat.
    (C) She is busy tomorrow.
    (D) She can't get tickets.

61. What does the second man offer to do?

    (A) Plan a trip
    (B) Call his cousin
    (C) Buy some tickets
    (D) Go to the box office

Building Directory	
1st floor:	Woolman & Fox, PC
2nd floor:	Gilchrist, Inc.
3rd floor:	Zenith Enterprises
4th floor:	HCR Company

62. Look at the graphic. What floor will the woman go to?

    (A) 1st floor
    (B) 2nd Floor
    (C) 3rd Floor
    (D) 4th Floor

63. Why is she going there?

    (A) To start a new job
    (B) For a job interview
    (C) To look at an apartment
    (D) For a doctor's appointment

64. What does the man imply about his relationship with Mr. Gill?

    (A) He works near Mr. Gill.
    (B) He is a client of Mr. Gill's.
    (C) He has never met Mr. Gill.
    (D) He wants to work for Mr. Gill.

65. What will the woman drink?

   (A) Lemonade
   (B) Coffee
   (C) Water
   (D) Tea

66. Why doesn't she want pie?

   (A) She isn't hungry.
   (B) The pie is too hot.
   (C) She doesn't like pie.
   (D) She hasn't had lunch yet.

67. What will the man do?

   (A) Have some pie
   (B) Bake some buns
   (C) Buy some bacon
   (D) Make some toast

```
           Florence Café
           Lunch Specials

1. Tuna fish salad plate.................$13
2. Mixed vegetable salad...............$12
3. Baked fish with rice...................$16
4. Sautéed vegetables with rice.....$15
```

68. Why has there been a delay?

   (A) The chef arrived late.
   (B) There aren't enough servers.
   (C) The restaurant is very crowded.
   (D) There are some new staff working.

69. What does the woman imply about the restaurant?

   (A) It has a good reputation.
   (B) It is not well known.
   (C) It is not very popular.
   (D) It always has slow service.

70. Look at the graphic. What will the woman eat?

   (A) Tuna fish salad
   (B) Vegetable salad
   (C) Baked fish
   (D) Sautéed vegetables

Part 4: Talks

DIRECTIONS: You will hear a talk given by a single speaker. You will see three questions on each talk, each with four possible answers. Choose the best answer to each question, and fill in the corresponding oval on your answer sheet.

Track 58

71. What is the purpose of this message?

    (A) To explain rules
    (B) To solve a problem
    (C) To describe a schedule
    (D) To introduce a special offer

72. What happens once a year?

    (A) The park stays open late.
    (B) There is a movie night.
    (C) A discount is offered.
    (D) A concert is performed.

73. Who can the listener talk to by pressing one?

    (A) A musician
    (B) An operator
    (C) A sales agent
    (D) A park manager

74. What is the topic of the workshop?

    (A) Budgets
    (B) Computers
    (C) Investments
    (D) Software

75. What does the speaker give each participant?

    (A) A schedule
    (B) A laptop
    (C) A snack
    (D) A chair

76. How many breaks will there be?

    (A) 1
    (B) 2
    (C) 3
    (D) 4

77. Where is this talk happening?

    (A) On a plane
    (B) On a boat
    (C) At a hotel
    (D) On a bus

78. What is the problem?

    (A) Storage compartments are full.
    (B) There are not enough seats.
    (C) There is bad weather.
    (D) Bags have been lost.

79. What has been delayed?

    (A) Serving drinks
    (B) The arrival time
    (C) Showing a movie
    (D) The departure time

80. What problem does the speaker have with the product?

    (A) It doesn't have a cover.
    (B) The fan doesn't blow.
    (C) She can't turn it on.
    (D) It doesn't heat.

81. When did the speaker buy the product?

    (A) This morning
    (B) Two days ago
    (C) Last Tuesday
    (D) Nine days ago

82. What does the speaker ask the listener to do?

    (A) Replace the product
    (B) Provide a refund
    (C) Return the call
    (D) Send a manual

83. What is the focus of the tour?

    (A) Architecture
    (B) Gardens
    (C) History
    (D) Parks

84. How will the group travel?

    (A) Bus
    (B) Van
    (C) Foot
    (D) Bike

85. What will the group do first?

    (A) Have lunch
    (B) Look at a map
    (C) Visit City Hall
    (D) Buy their tickets

86. Where will this product be used?

    (A) In an office
    (B) At a restaurant
    (C) On an airplane
    (D) In a private home

87. How many cups of coffee does the product make?

    (A) 20
    (B) 24
    (C) 28
    (D) 29

88. What are listeners asked to do?

    (A) Place an order
    (B) Try other products
    (C) Ask for a free sample
    (D) Look for information

89. What event is the speaker reporting?

    (A) Approval of bridge plans
    (B) Completion of a bridge
    (C) Repainting of an old bridge
    (D) Repair work on all city bridges

90. What are people waiting to do?

    (A) Photograph the bridge
    (B) Talk with the reporter
    (C) Cross the bridge
    (D) See the mayor

91. What does the speaker mean when she says, "It's hard to believe, but final costs came in well under budget"?

    (A) She doesn't understand the budget.
    (B) She's surprised the project cost so little.
    (C) She thinks incorrect numbers have been given.
    (D) She isn't certain what the total cost of the project is.

92. What is the book about?

    (A) History
    (B) Cooking
    (C) Travel
    (D) Memoir

93. What does the speaker mean when he says, "He jumped at the chance"?

    (A) Roger decided not to take a risk.
    (B) Roger immediately accepted a job offer.
    (C) Roger was surprised to hear about the job.
    (D) Roger looked for other work opportunities.

94. What will Roger do tomorrow?

    (A) Cook a meal
    (B) Eat at a restaurant
    (C) Read from his book
    (D) Travel to the Caribbean

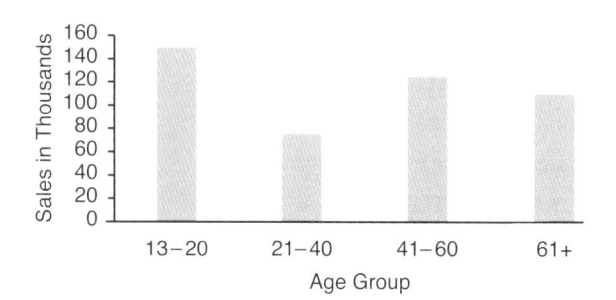

95. What type of product does this company sell?

    (A) Shoes
    (B) Clothes
    (C) Sports equipment
    (D) Construction materials

96. Look at the graphic. Which age group does the speaker want to focus on?

    (A) 13-20
    (B) 21-40
    (C) 41-60
    (D) 61+

97. What will the listeners do next?

    (A) Read a sales report
    (B) Work in groups
    (C) Have a discussion
    (D) Look at another slide

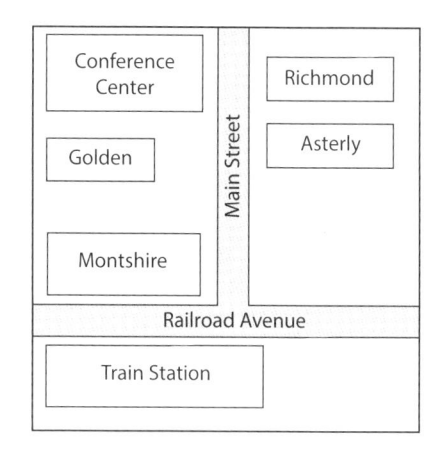

98. Who is Marc, most likely?

    (A) A ticket agent
    (B) A hotel manager
    (C) The speaker's boss
    (D) The speaker's assistant

99. Why does the speaker want to change her travel plans?

    (A) To go to a seminar
    (B) To add more meetings
    (C) To stay at a better hotel
    (D) To use a different form of transportation

100. Look at the graphic. Which hotel will the speaker prefer?

    (A) Richmond
    (B) Golden
    (C) Asterly
    (D) Montshire

This is the end of the Listening Comprehension portion of the test.

STOP Turn to Part 5 in your test book.

543

Reading Comprehension

In this section of the test, you will have the chance to show how well you understand written English. There are three parts to this section, with special directions for each part.

YOU WILL HAVE ONE HOUR AND FIFTEEN MINUTES TO COMPLETE PARTS 5, 6, AND 7 OF THE TEST.

Part 5: Incomplete Sentences

> **DIRECTIONS:** You will see a sentence with a missing word. Four possible answers follow the sentence. Choose the best answer to the question, and fill in the corresponding oval on your answer sheet.

101. Earn a good salary while building _____ job skills when you enroll in the City Tech carpentry program.

    (A) value
    (B) valued
    (C) valuably
    (D) valuable

102. The Whip cargo van can haul _____ to 5,350 pounds and comes with a rear back-up camera and security alarm.

    (A) over
    (B) up
    (C) before
    (D) in

103. The course is _____ for working professionals, so the class meets two evenings a week.

    (A) barely
    (B) rapidly
    (C) primarily
    (D) slightly

104. Greg Trist opens his art studio to the public on the first Monday of the month, which coincides _____ the city's monthly Art Walk event.

    (A) between
    (B) by
    (C) through
    (D) with

105. The executive team decided to use the pink and orange color _____ for the new laundry detergent logo.

    (A) appearance
    (B) photo
    (C) scheme
    (D) line

106. I strongly recommend _____ a contract with LL Logistics to handle our domestic deliveries.

    (A) sign
    (B) signed
    (C) signing
    (D) will sign

107. The landscaper said he _____ the hedges around the office when he comes next week.
    (A) trims
    (B) will trim
    (C) has trimmed
    (D) has been trimming

108. If you can wait a few minutes, Ms. Sato will attend _____ your problem as soon as she is free.
    (A) to
    (B) for
    (C) beside
    (D) in

109. Zasels' weekly coupon is good for 40% off items storewide _____ custom framing, furniture, and electronics.
    (A) exempt
    (B) having
    (C) without
    (D) except

110. Visitors to the factory must leave their personal _____ at the security desk and put on a protective coat and a pair of goggles.
    (A) belongings
    (B) costumes
    (C) experiences
    (D) appearances

111. While he is a team player and always on time, Daniel doesn't have the skills to do _____ job.
    (A) he
    (B) him
    (C) his
    (D) her

112. By signing this form, you _____ KM Recovery Group to act as your agent.
    (A) authorizing
    (B) authorization
    (C) authority
    (D) authorize

113. Full-time employees _____ attend the RSTLC annual conference at their department's expense with approval from their supervisor.
    (A) be
    (B) don't
    (C) can
    (D) won't

114. Unfortunately, the kitchen needs _____ repairs that have to be made by a trained plumber.
    (A) marginal
    (B) extensive
    (C) minimal
    (D) common

115. _____ budget reductions, the company will not be filling the currently available Marketing Supervisor position.
    (A) Due to
    (B) However
    (C) Because
    (D) In that

116. The remote control _____ programmed to work with the television in the lobby but not the break room.
    (A) has
    (B) be
    (C) been
    (D) is

117. The person _____ signature appears on the document is the one ultimately responsible for the deal.

   (A) who
   (B) who's
   (C) whose
   (D) whom

118. _____ until the last minute to turn in work is definitely not encouraged in this department.

   (A) Wait
   (B) Waiting
   (C) To wait
   (D) Wait for

119. You can sign up for the online training at your convenience _____ attend the next week's onsite training session in person.

   (A) or
   (B) so
   (C) if
   (D) as

120. The budget report had to be rewritten because some of the figures it contained were _____.

   (A) acceptable
   (B) inaccurate
   (C) comprehensive
   (D) calculating

121. The company has plans to _____ several neighboring properties, which will be used for expanding the manufacturing plant.

   (A) inquire
   (B) require
   (C) expire
   (D) acquire

122. _____ the client accepts the plan, the team has one month to complete the final design.

   (A) Before
   (B) After
   (C) While
   (D) Then

123. The best way to _____ approval from your supervisor is to consistently complete your projects on time.

   (A) earn
   (B) collect
   (C) grant
   (D) incur

124. When the renovations _____ complete, we will have a much more attractive and spacious office.

   (A) are
   (B) is
   (C) be
   (D) will be

125. The production team can _____ the photos if the client thinks they are too large.

   (A) size
   (B) resize
   (C) sizeable
   (D) sizing

126. _____ the shipment went out later than promised, the client decided to make another order.

   (A) Because
   (B) Therefore
   (C) Despite
   (D) Although

127. The prices quoted on the website _____ materials as well as labor, but not shipping and handling costs.

   (A) include
   (B) including
   (C) inclusive
   (D) inclusively

128. The Human Resources Department requires all applicants to provide references from their _____ employers.

   (A) before
   (B) advanced
   (C) previous
   (D) precede

129. You can choose to receive your paycheck by mail or opt for direct deposit into your bank account _____.

   (A) either
   (B) instead
   (C) alternative
   (D) in addition

130. Last quarter's sales would have been better if the company _____ more in advertising.

   (A) had invested
   (B) has invested
   (C) has been investing
   (D) would have invested

Part 6: Text Completion

DIRECTIONS: You will see four passages, each with four blanks. Each blank has four answer choices. For each blank, choose the word, phrase, or sentence that best completes the passage.

Questions 131–134 refer to the following letter.

Dear Business Owner,

We are writing to let you ___131___ about our new company, Executive Dining, which provides catering services to local businesses. We cater everything from elegant banquets to informal refreshments for meetings and workshops. We have a variety of menus from which you can choose, and we can also tailor our offerings to meet ___132___ specific needs. We do everything from set up to serving to clean up, and we can provide table settings, decorations, and chairs and tables as needed. As the company's ___133___, we have a combined 25 years of experience in food service and are both graduates of the National Culinary School. ___134___.

Sincerely,

Elaine Mayfield and Georgina Simms

131. (A) know
     (B) knows
     (C) to know
     (D) will know

132. (A) its
     (B) our
     (C) your
     (D) their

133. (A) auditors
     (B) backers
     (C) clients
     (D) founders

134. (A) We believe you will enjoy the meal we have planned for you
     (B) We hope you will contact us to discuss your catering needs
     (C) We have put your next company banquet on our schedule
     (D) We look forward to meeting you at the end of the week

Questions 135–138 refer to the following notice.

NOTICE TO RIDERS OF RED LINE BUSES

_____135_____. Therefore, Red Line service will be temporarily suspended at the Main Street stop as of June 1. Passengers can use the Oakland Avenue or River Street stops _____136_____. Please check the City Transport Services (CTS) website for schedule information for those stops. We apologize for any inconvenience this situation may cause. It is part of the mayor's initiative to _____137_____ bus service for all users. Please _____138_____ the CTS Public Relations office with any questions or comments.

135. (A) Buses are undergoing routine maintenance
 (B) Bus fares are scheduled to go up next month
 (C) The number of buses serving this line will increase
 (D) Renovations on selected bus shelters will begin soon

136. (A) also
 (B) despite
 (C) instead
 (D) nevertheless

137. (A) approve
 (B) improve
 (C) disprove
 (D) reprove

138. (A) contact
 (B) to contact
 (C) can contact
 (D) you will contact

Questions 139-142 refer to the following memo.

To: All Employees
From: Arthur Ivers
Date: February 10
Re: Annual Leave Policy

We have revised the company's annual leave policy. ___139___.

- Leave requests must ___140___ a minimum of one month in advance.
- To request time off, please complete Form 54 and make one copy for your supervisor and ___141___ for the HR office.
- You may take no more than two weeks of leave at a time. If special circumstances require that you take more, please discuss it with your supervisor.

I will be happy to answer any questions you may have ___142___ the policy revisions.

Please stop by my office any time.

---

139. (A) Revisions need approval from the HR office
 (B) Please follow the guidelines in the handbook
 (C) Annual leave can be taken at any time of year
 (D) Here is the policy as it looks with the changes

140. (A) submit
 (B) to submit
 (C) be submitted
 (D) be submitting

141. (A) another
 (B) that one
 (C) some
 (D) this

142. (A) adjusting
 (B) regarding
 (C) resuming
 (D) modifying

550

Questions 143–146 refer to the following letter.

Hotel Comar

April 3

Dear Mr. Warren,

We have received your letter describing your stay at the Hotel Comar last week. _____ 143. We pride ourselves _____ 144 our excellent customer service and strive to make all our guests feel welcome and comfortable. Unfortunately, we did not meet this goal during your _____ 145 stay. It was an unusually busy time for us as we were hosting two conferences, and it was also the height of the tourist season. However, that is not an excuse for neglecting the comfort of all our guests.

We hope you will consider _____ 146 to the Hotel Comar the next time you are in town. We offer a prime location, fully-equipped gym, and a five-star restaurant. I am enclosing a coupon for twenty percent off the cost of your next stay with us.

Sincerely,

Amalia Knight
Manager

143. (A) Thank you for choosing to stay at the Comar during your visit to this city
(B) We were very sorry to hear that you had such an unpleasant experience
(C) We regret that we have no rooms available at that time
(D) Our hotel is known as one of the finest in the city

144. (A) on
(B) in
(C) of
(D) due

145. (A) upcoming
(B) final
(C) lately
(D) recent

146. (A) return
(B) returns
(C) returning
(D) to return

Part 7: Reading Comprehension

DIRECTIONS: You will see single and multiple reading passages followed by several questions. Each question has four answer choices. Choose the best answer to the question, and fill in the corresponding oval on your answer sheet.

Questions 147–148 refer to the following webpage.

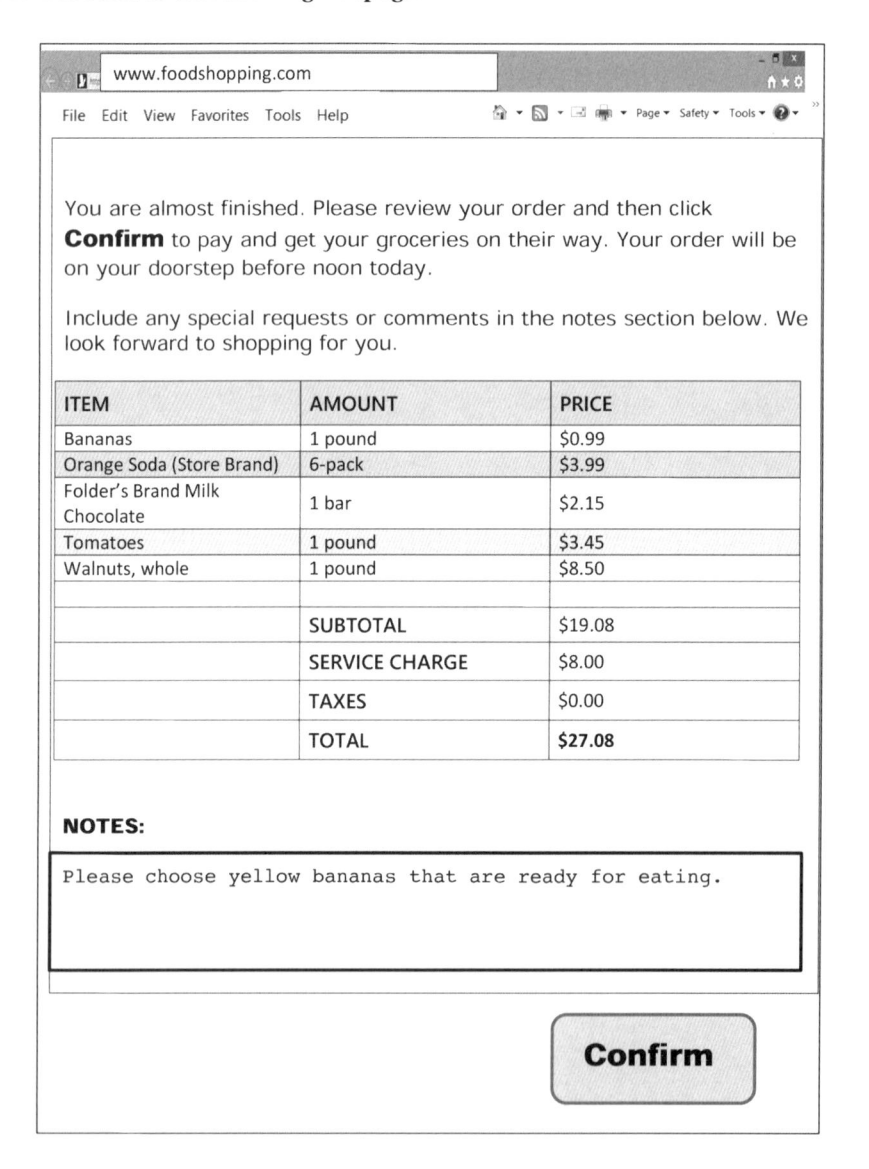

---

www.foodshopping.com

You are almost finished. Please review your order and then click **Confirm** to pay and get your groceries on their way. Your order will be on your doorstep before noon today.

Include any special requests or comments in the notes section below. We look forward to shopping for you.

ITEM	AMOUNT	PRICE
Bananas	1 pound	$0.99
Orange Soda (Store Brand)	6-pack	$3.99
Folder's Brand Milk Chocolate	1 bar	$2.15
Tomatoes	1 pound	$3.45
Walnuts, whole	1 pound	$8.50
	SUBTOTAL	$19.08
	SERVICE CHARGE	$8.00
	TAXES	$0.00
	TOTAL	$27.08

NOTES:

Please choose yellow bananas that are ready for eating.

[Confirm]

---

147. When will the order be delivered?

(A) This morning
(B) This afternoon
(C) Tomorrow morning
(D) Tomorrow afternoon

148. What does the customer request?

(A) Cold soda
(B) Yellow tomatoes
(C) Ripe bananas
(D) Chopped walnuts

Questions 149-150 refer to the following text message chain.

MILLIE WILSON   8:45
Did you see the email from the warehouse?

PAUL STONE   8:46
No. Is there a problem with the shipment?

MILLIE WILSON   8:47
It's not going out till tomorrow.

PAUL STONE   8:49
No good. Peterson is not going to like this.

MILLIE WILSON   8:51
Who?

PAUL STONE   8:52
The client. The one who paid an extra thousand dollars for overnight delivery.

MILLIE WILSON   8:54
He did? I had no idea. Let me make a few phone calls and see if I can get them to speed things up.

---

149. At 8:47, what does Ms. Wilson mean when she writes, "It's not going out till tomorrow"?

    (A) The warehouse is closed today.
    (B) The shipment will be delayed.
    (C) She will wait to email the client.
    (D) The client has not yet made an order.

150. What does Millie offer to do?

    (A) Call up the client
    (B) Make the delivery herself
    (C) Get the order sent earlier
    (D) Return the thousand dollars

Questions 151–152 refer to the following expense report.

	Asterix, Inc.			
	Expense Authorization			
	Employee: Roland Webb			
	Purpose: Wilmont office training seminar			
Category	Date	Description	Notes	Amount
Airfare	Sept. 16, Sept. 21	Round trip, business class	Seminar originally planned for week of Sept. 9. Amount includes $200 change fee.	$885
Hotel	Sept. 16–Sept. 20	$110/night x 5, at Atrium Hotel, Wilmont		$550
Car Rental	Sept. 16–Sept. 21	Zippo Rental Agency		$275

151. What fee is included in the cost of the airfare?

  (A) Special meal
  (B) Extra baggage
  (C) First class upgrade
  (D) Rescheduling charge

152. How many nights did the employee stay at the hotel?

  (A) 1
  (B) 5
  (C) 6
  (D) 10

Questions 153–154 refer to the following employment ad.

> **Part-time office assistant** needed for small accounting firm. Will be trained in all aspects of the job including computer data entry, file management, and appointment scheduling. Must have pleasant manner and ability to provide excellent customer service. Must be proficient with word processing functions and able to learn software programs used in the office. Apply in person to Estelle Fox, 110 Grayson Avenue, Suite 10. No phone calls.

153. What is a requirement of the job?

  (A) Proficiency in data entry
  (B) Ability to program computers
  (C) Knowledge of word processing
  (D) Experience with appointment scheduling

154. How can someone apply for the job?

  (A) Visit the office
  (B) Send an email
  (C) Mail a résumé
  (D) Call Ms. Fox

Questions 155–157 refer to the following article.

> Richard Wenger, director of the Metropolitan Area Public Transportation System (MPTA), has announced that as of February 1 conductors on the MPTA's commuter rail lines will start accepting e-tickets on passengers' smartphones. Passengers can go to the MPTA website to purchase single-ride and round-trip tickets as well as weekly and annual passes, which are then sent by email to the purchaser. Train conductors can scan the ticket or pass directly from the passenger's smartphones. Passengers can also choose to print their tickets, and the conductor will scan the printed copy. As an incentive to start using the new system, e-ticket purchasers will receive a 15 percent discount on all tickets and passes purchased during the month of February. Traditional paper tickets are still available for sale at ticket machines in most commuter rail stations. However, these tickets are being phased out and will no longer be available as of January 1st of next year. Mr. Wenger commented that surveys of commuter rail riders showed overwhelming enthusiasm for the new system.

155. What is this passage mostly about?

(A) A special discount
(B) A passenger survey
(C) A new kind of train ticket
(D) An increase in train fares

156. How are traditional tickets sold?

(A) On the web
(B) By machine
(C) From conductors
(D) At the MPTA office

157. The phrase *phased out* in line 11 is closest in meaning to

(A) displayed
(B) discovered
(C) distributed
(D) discontinued

Questions 158–160 refer to the following description.

> ## Professional Certification
>
> The Southeastern Interior Design Association's professional certification program offers three levels of certification for professional interior designers. The program is open to anyone who has been a member in good standing for at least one year. The Southeastern Interior Design Association's professional certificates are recognized by most interior design businesses and training programs in the country.
>
> Certificates are awarded upon successful completion of a test. To take the test for any one level of certification except Level One, you must have passed the previous level test. While no coursework is required, we do offer classes and reading materials to help you prepare for the test.
>
> Currently, certification tests are administered every six months at the association's headquarters in Savannah. A web-based test will be available by the end of next year. For information on certification levels, test preparation classes, or test registration, please request an information packet from our office: *info@sidassn.org*. Don't forget to include your member number in your message.

158. What is required to take a test?

    (A) Membership in the association
    (B) Completion of certain classes
    (C) Experience in interior design
    (D) Graduation from a training program

159. How often are the tests given?

    (A) Six times a month
    (B) Six times a year
    (C) Once a year
    (D) Twice a year

160. What should someone who wants to take the test do?

    (A) Enroll in a class
    (B) Email the office
    (C) Visit the website
    (D) Speak with an advisor

Questions 161-163 refer to the following flier.

Lightning Car Rentals

NEW: Damage Fee Waiver offer

Your standard rental agreement includes comprehensive insurance. However, if your rented vehicle is involved in an incident during your rental period, you could be responsible for a $500 damage fee that is not covered by insurance.

Renters who are aged 21 or over and haven't been involved in an accident in the past 12 months have the option to purchase a Damage Fee Waiver. These waivers are not a substitute for insurance coverage; they offer extra peace of mind against unexpected costs. The waiver must be added to the rental agreement at the time of signing.

Two Damage Fee Waivers are available.

- Half Waiver: For $10 per day of rental period, reduce your damage fee to $250
- Full Waiver: For $15 per day of rental period, reduce your damage fee to $0

Ask your rental agent to add this waiver to your rental agreement now.

---

161. Who can get a waiver?

    (A) Any agency customer
    (B) Drivers who pass a road test
    (C) Customers who rent for a week
    (D) People with a safe driving record

162. What is the waiver for?

    (A) To extend coverage to 12 months
    (B) To remove the age requirement
    (C) To reduce or eliminate a charge
    (D) To replace regular insurance

163. When should a waiver be purchased?

    (A) When signing the rental agreement
    (B) When making a reservation
    (C) When reporting an accident
    (D) When insurance is purchased

Questions 164–167 refer to the following online chat discussion.

Mija Kim [1:15]
How are the plans for Friday coming along? I haven't had an update in a while.

Jairo Perez [1:15]
I heard back from the caterers just this morning. They can accommodate my menu modifications, no problem.

Alba Jones [1:16]
At no extra charge?

Jairo Perez [1:17]
No extra charge.

Mija Kim [1:18]
That's excellent news. What about the room set up? Has anyone talked with Maintenance about that?

Alba Jones [1:20]
I did. They'll have tables and chairs for 50 all ready and arranged by 11:30, so the caterers can get in and set their stuff up. They said they want to be in there an hour ahead of time.

Mija Kim [1:21]
Fantastic! I got some more RSVPs last night. I think I've heard from just about everybody now.

Jairo Perez [1:21]
And almost everyone is coming, right?

Mija Kim [1:23]
It looks that way. So, with the caterers and the room arrangements all set, I guess that's it. We're good to go.

164. What is being planned?

 (A) A workshop
 (B) A staff meeting
 (C) A demonstration
 (D) A luncheon

165. What did Jairo change?

 (A) The menu
 (B) The schedule
 (C) The number of guests
 (D) The room arrangement

166. What did Mija receive last night?

 (A) A guest list
 (B) Invitation responses
 (C) Room arrangement plans
 (D) A message from the caterers

167. At 1:23, what does Mija mean when she writes, "We're good to go"?

 (A) The guests are happy to be invited.
 (B) It's time to set up the room.
 (C) Everything is ready.
 (D) She has to leave.

Questions 168-171 refer to the following excerpt from an article.

The question is all too common. You're new to the job market, having just finished your education. There's a lot of competition out there. How can you prepare for job interviews in a way that will help you stand out from the crowd? –[1]–

"It all boils down to one thing," says Evelyn Pritchard, former hiring manager at XQ, Inc. and now president of her own employment consulting firm, Pritchard, LLC. "Professionalism. That's the key. You've got to dress, talk, act like a professional." This may seem obvious, Pritchard explains, but many young people have a hard time grasping this concept. She offers the following advice for those setting out for their first job interviews. –[2]–

Appearance comes first. –[3]– You should dress like a professional. This means business suits for men and business suits or skirt and blouse combinations for women. Keep in mind that you don't want the color of your clothes to shout. Black, charcoal gray, or deep blue are best for job interviews.

–[4]– When you enter the room, introduce yourself with a firm handshake. Look your interviewer in the eye as you speak. Answer questions with confidence. Most important of all, keep your cell phone turned off.

168. Who would be most interested in this article?

(A) Hiring managers
(B) Employment agencies
(C) Mid-level professionals
(D) Recent college graduates

169. What does Ms. Pritchard mean in paragraph 2, line 1, when she is quoted as saying, "It all boils down to one thing"?

(A) It is important to stand out from the crowd.
(B) Her advice can be summarized in one word.
(C) People must work hard to look professional.
(D) Interviews are a key part of the hiring process.

170. What is suggested about clothes worn for job interviews?

(A) The colors should be dark.
(B) The suits should be clean.
(C) The skirts should be long.
(D) The clothes should be new.

171. In which of the positions marked [1], [2], [3], and [4] does the following sentence best belong?

"Acting like a professional is as important as looking like one."

(A) [1]
(B) [2]
(C) [3]
(D) [4]

Questions 172–175 refer to the following letter.

August 22

Stephanie Jackson
PO Box 110
Marston, NH

Dear Ms. Jackson,

I heard you speak last week when you were a guest on our local radio show, Green Energy Talk. I was very impressed with the depth of your knowledge about solar energy. I know a little bit about this subject myself. I belong to a small local organization called Sun Power that has the goal of bringing more solar power to our community. I have some familiarity with the different types of solar panels and have installed some on the roof of my house. They provide my family with most of our domestic hot water needs throughout the year.

As you are well aware, replacing fossil fuels with alternative forms of energy is crucial to our future, and I believe we need to spread the word and get more people on board with this. To that end, we are having an alternative energy fair in our community toward the end of next month. We would be very grateful if you would consider being one of our speakers. We wouldn't be able to pay you, but you would have the chance to sell your books there. If you plan to attend, I will need to hear back from you before the end of two weeks so that I can put you on the schedule. Thank you for considering my request, and I hope to see you in September.

Sincerely,

Fred Marquez

Fred Marquez

172. Why did Mr. Marquez write the letter to Ms. Jackson?

    (A) To tell her about his organization
    (B) To sell her some solar panels
    (C) To invite her to an event
    (D) To ask her for a job

173. What is indicated about Mr. Marquez?

    (A) He is the president of the Sun Power organization.
    (B) He wants to get people interested in his cause.
    (C) He makes a living installing solar panels.
    (D) He is an expert on solar energy.

174. What is suggested about Ms. Jackson?

    (A) She has written some books.
    (B) She is a friend of Mr. Marquez.
    (C) She hosts a radio show.
    (D) She travels frequently.

175. When does Mr. Marquez need to have Ms. Jackson's reply?

    (A) In one week
    (B) In two weeks
    (C) Before September
    (D) Before next month

Questions 176-180 refer to the following webpage and email.

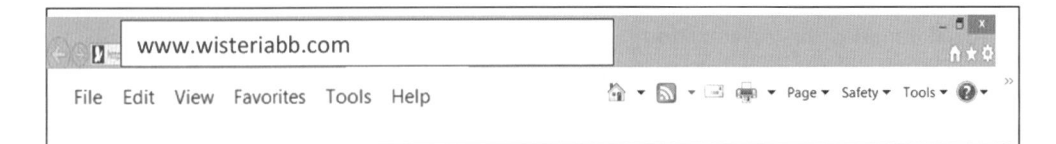

Wisteria Bed and Breakfast

Come stay with us at the Wisteria Bed and Breakfast, a historical converted farmhouse. Each one of our six guest rooms is decorated with period furnishings and artifacts. Enjoy peace and quiet while relaxing on our wisteria-covered porch with views of pastures and hills. Take a guided horseback ride through nearby wooded trails. Enjoy the many exciting cultural and sports activities available in our area.

Our spacious refurbished barn is the perfect setting for your wedding or family reunion.

Click here for information about holding your event at Wisteria Bed and Breakfast.

All rooms include breakfast of homemade pastries and seasonal dishes carefully crafted from the finest local ingredients.

Rooms start at $99/night.
Two-night minimum required for weekend stays.

Click here to see rooms and check availability.

Book your room before April 30 and receive 20% off the usual price.

From: lsimmonsherbs@simmons.com
To: info@wisteriabb.com
Subject: introducing myself
Date: April 1

Hi,

I just saw your bed and breakfast website. It looks lovely. I noticed that you include local ingredients in your breakfast dishes. I am a local grower of herbs and flowers. I sell my products at local farmer's markets and also have a number of regular customers among the area's hotels and restaurants.

I would be happy to provide your business with fresh herbs and flowers on either a regular or as-needed basis. I can supply fresh herbs for your breakfasts and floral decorations for weddings that you host. In addition, you may want to consider providing your guests with fragrant herbal bouquets in their rooms.

I can come by your place any time next week to talk it over. In the meantime, I am attaching a list of herbs and flowers I have available, by season. Prices vary but are always competitive.

I look forward to hearing from you.

Lucinda Simmons

176. What is suggested about the Wisteria?

  (A) It is a large hotel.
  (B) It is in a rural setting.
  (C) It has a flower garden.
  (D) It has a modern design.

177. What can guests do at the Wisteria?

  (A) Buy crafts
  (B) Have lunch
  (C) Host a party
  (D) Work in the barn

178. How can a guest get a discount?

  (A) Hold an event in the barn
  (B) Stay at the Wisteria in April
  (C) Stay for two weekend nights
  (D) Make a reservation before April 30

179. Why did Ms. Simmons write the email?

  (A) To offer products for sale
  (B) To make a room reservation
  (C) To ask about buying the business
  (D) To find out about holding an event

180. What kind of business does Ms. Simmons have?

  (A) Farm
  (B) Hotel
  (C) Restaurant
  (D) Event planning

Questions 181-185 refer to the following email and flier.

From: drosen@mycompany.com
To: customerservice@marvelclean.com
Subject: cleaning
Date: December 15

Dear Marvel Cleaning Service,

I am interested in finding out about your cleaning services. I am currently located at the Octagon Towers, but plan to be leaving next month. According to the terms of the lease here, tenants must leave everything in good condition or be charged a penalty by the landlord. So, I need a service to come in and clean up after I have left, and a colleague at work suggested I contact you. I am contacting several services at this time, so that I can compare costs. Could you let me know how much you would charge to clean my place? Would you need to visit it first, or can you tell me the price based on size? It is an efficiency apartment, so it consists of just one large room.

Thank you.
David Rosen

Marvel Cleaning Service

"Big or small, we clean it all."

Leave the housekeeping to us. Whether you live in a palatial mansion or an efficiency apartment, we will make your home sparkle and shine.

Up to 3 rooms	$75
4–5 rooms	$125
6–7 rooms	$175
8 rooms	$200
Over 8 rooms	Contact us

If your space is larger than 8 rooms, a customer service representative will discuss your needs with you and provide you with an estimate. We guarantee that our prices are always competitive.
Call us when you need us, or arrange for regular weekly or monthly service.

Book your cleaning today.
customerservice@marvelclean.com
303-555-1212

181. Why does Mr. Rosen need to have his apartment cleaned?

   (A) He is looking for a tenant.
   (B) He is expecting visitors.
   (C) He is moving away.
   (D) He is hosting a party.

182. How did Mr. Rosen hear about Marvel?

   (A) A co-worker recommended it.
   (B) He found it on the internet.
   (C) His landlord suggested it.
   (D) He saw the flier.

183. How much will it cost to clean Mr. Rosen's apartment?

   (A) $75
   (B) $125
   (C) $175
   (D) $200

184. What is suggested about Marvel Cleaning Service?

   (A) It charges more than other cleaners.
   (B) It cleans residences only.
   (C) It doesn't serve one-time customers.
   (D) It rarely cleans spaces larger than 8 rooms.

185. In the flier, the word *estimate* in paragraph 2, line 3, is closest in meaning to

   (A) guess
   (B) value
   (C) analysis
   (D) approximation

Questions 186–190 refer to the following webpage, email, and review.

LANNON'S OFFICE SUPPLY

✱Special Promotions✱

E-Z Folding Table

Need extra work space? Holding a large meeting or luncheon? Desk too small? The E-Z Folding Table expands your space in just seconds. It quickly unfolds to accommodate up to 8 people. When you no longer need it, it folds back up to a compact size that fits easily in most closets. Black table top with chrome legs.

Buy now and save!

Small (seats 4)	$65
Medium (seats 6)	$85
Large (seats 8)	$110
Set of 3 (1 of each size)	$230

(Prices good through March 30.)

First-time customer? Use coupon code **Z54** at checkout for a 15% discount.

Click here to calculate shipping costs.

Free shipping on all orders of $100 or more.

From: noreply@lannon.com
To: miker@trex.com
Subject: your order

The following item(s) shipped today.

Item	Quantity	Price
E-Z Folding Table	1	$110.00
Tax		$6.50
Shipping		$0
Total		$116.50

Tracking no. 1205039299919111
You can track your order at *www.lannons.com/tracking* September 15–19

★★★★★

By Mike Rivera on June 14, 2016

I received my Lannon's E-Z Folding Table last week. Everything was great until I went to put it away. It unfolds easily and is very sturdy and also attractive, but when I first folded it up to put away, I realized the clips were missing. These are needed because without them the table doesn't stay folded and you can't store it. I originally gave this product 3 stars because of this. However, I contacted customer service and they sent me the clips right away. The customer service person was very polite, and now that I have the clips, the table perfectly suits my needs. We use it in our office for our weekly staff meetings and everybody says it is very comfortable and convenient to use. Highly recommended.

186. What is suggested about the folding table?

   (A) It is currently on sale.
   (B) It is available only in March.
   (C) It comes in a variety of colors.
   (D) It is the website's most popular item.

187. Which table did Mr. Rivera order?

   (A) Small
   (B) Medium
   (C) Large
   (D) Set of 3

188. Why didn't Mr. Rivera pay shipping costs?

   (A) He had a coupon for free shipping.
   (B) His order cost more than $100.
   (C) The company never charges for shipping.
   (D) He forgot to include this on his order form.

189. Why did Mr. Rivera order the table?

   (A) For client consultations
   (B) For extra desk space
   (C) For guests at a lunch
   (D) For use at meetings

190. Why did Mr. Rivera change his original product rating?

   (A) His use of the product changed.
   (B) His co-workers liked the product.
   (C) The company corrected a mistake.
   (D) He listened to other reviewers' opinions.

Questions 191–195 refer to the following flier and emails.

Stoneybrook Dinner Theater

presents

Romeo and Juliet

by William Shakespeare

June 12, 13, 14, 19, 20, and 21

Enjoy a three-course meal followed by our own specially choreographed version of Shakespeare's classic tale.

Reserve your place now! Visit us online at *www.stoneybrookdt.com* or call us at 493-555-2121.

	Show only	Dinner and Show
Per person	$50	$80
Per couple	$90	$135

Dinner begins at 6:30, show begins at 8:00.
Three-course meal includes:
- Choice of soup or salad
- Entrée—beef, chicken, or vegetarian
- Dessert

From: estherwilson@acme.com
To: bobcharles@workplace.com
Subject: dinner theater
Date: June 12

Bob,

Are you interested in seeing *Romeo and Juliet*? My sister gave me some tickets that she can't use. They're for that Stoneybrook Dinner Theater place, so we'd have dinner first and then see the play. I've heard the food there is only mediocre, but the play got fantastic reviews.

The tickets are for June 21st. I won't be able to leave the office that day until a little after 6:00, and I really don't want to be late for the dinner, so I think the best plan would be for me to take a cab and meet you there. I hope you can come. I know it will be fun.

Esther

From: bobcharles@workplace.com
To: estherwilson@acme.com
Subject: re: dinner theater
Date: June 12

Hi Esther,

Yes, I would love to join you at the dinner theater. It sounds like a lot of fun, and it will be my first time seeing this particular play. I'll have my car with me, so I'll plan to pick you up. Then you won't have to worry about a cab. It only takes 15 minutes to get to the dinner theater from your office, so I think we'll make it just in time.

I know what you mean about the food. I've actually eaten there before. I suppose we could just skip the dinner and see the show only, but you already have the tickets, so we might as well enjoy it as much as we can. And I am really looking forward to seeing the play.

See you June 21st.

Bob

---

191. What is suggested about the meal at the dinner theater?

    (A) It is served after the show.
    (B) It includes dishes without meat.
    (C) It can be bought apart from show tickets.
    (D) It is highly rated by restaurant reviewers.

192. How much did Esther pay for the dinner theater tickets?

    (A) $0
    (B) $80
    (C) $90
    (D) $135

193. How will Esther probably get to the dinner theater?

    (A) She will drive.
    (B) She will take a cab.
    (C) She will ride the bus.
    (D) She will get a ride with Bob.

194. What is suggested about Bob?

    (A) He doesn't like to see plays.
    (B) He has never seen *Romeo and Juliet*.
    (C) He thinks the play won't be very good.
    (D) He has not been to the dinner theater before.

195. In the second email, the word *skip* in paragraph 2, line 2, is closest in meaning to

    (A) consume
    (B) improve
    (C) omit
    (D) jump

Questions 196–200 refer to the following itinerary, flier, and email.

HR Manufacturers
Itinerary for: Siri Hakim
Wiltshire/Montague trip
April 10–April 15

Sunday, April 10	lv. 2:30 p.m. Breezeways Flight 23
	arr. Wiltshire 8:30 p.m. Rivera Hotel, Wiltshire
Monday, April 11	10 a.m.–5 p.m. Meetings with Product Development Team
Tuesday, April 12	8:00 a.m. Train to Montague
	Tour of HR Manufacturers Plant, Hotel Pine, Montague
Wednesday, April 13	9:15 a.m. Train to Wiltshire
	2:00 p.m. Meeting with Marketing Department,
	Riviera Hotel, Wiltshire
Thursday, April 14	8:00 a.m. Breakfast meeting with John Andrews
	10:00 a.m. Tour of Wiltshire
	1:30 p.m. Presentation to Wiltshire staff
Friday, April 15	lv. 9:45 a.m. Breezeways Flight 567

Don't miss the 3rd annual Wiltshire
Business Expo!

Exhibits by businesses from all over the region
✔ See new products and innovations.
✔ Find out about current best business practices.

Workshops by renowned business experts
✔ Learn from some of the country's most respected business professionals.
(See other side for a list of workshop topics and a complete schedule.)

Bring your résumé!
✔ Recruiters from major companies will be available to meet with job seekers and discuss employment opportunities.

Wiltshire Conference Center
April 15–17

From: shakim@hrmanufacturersinc
To: kkato@hrmanufacturersinc
Subject: April trip
Date: March 29

Ken,

Thanks for putting together the itinerary for my trip next month. It all looks great. I'm really looking forward to finally having the chance to meet the Wiltshire team. Just one thing. I've learned that there will be a business expo in Wiltshire that weekend, and I'd like to take the opportunity to see it. It would be a chance to meet up with some former colleagues and possibly make some valuable connections. So if you could just change my return date to Saturday, that would be great. I guess that'll mean another night at the hotel as well as rescheduling the flight.

Thanks.

Siri

196. When will Ms. Hakim visit a factory?

    (A) April 10
    (B) April 11
    (C) April 12
    (D) April 13

197. What can people do at the business expo?

    (A) Buy products
    (B) Interview for jobs
    (C) Learn to write résumés
    (D) Find out about business loans

198. In the flier, the word *renowned* in line 6 is closest in meaning to

    (A) trained
    (B) famous
    (C) experienced
    (D) knowledgeable

199. What change does Ms. Hakim want to make to her itinerary?

    (A) Add a day to her trip
    (B) Move to a different hotel
    (C) Have another staff meeting
    (D) Stay in Wiltshire for the weekend

200. What is suggested about Ms. Hakim?

    (A) She has never been to the Wiltshire office.
    (B) She takes frequent business trips.
    (C) She is looking for people to hire.
    (D) She used to work in Wiltshire.

STOP This is the end of the test. If you finish before time is called, you may go back to Parts 5, 6, and 7 and check your work.

多益測驗成績換算對照表

計算答對的題數，利用下表找到對應的分數。將聽力和閱讀分數相加，就會得到預估的多益測驗總分。逐一演練模擬試題，分數也會逐漸提升，請持續追蹤你的多益測驗預估總分。

答對題數	聽力分數	閱讀分數	答對題數	聽力分數	閱讀分數	答對題數	聽力分數	閱讀分數	答對題數	聽力分數	閱讀分數
0	5	5	26	110	65	51	255	220	76	410	370
1	5	5	27	115	70	52	260	225	77	420	380
2	5	5	28	120	80	53	270	230	78	425	385
3	5	5	29	125	85	54	275	235	79	430	390
4	5	5	30	130	90	55	280	240	80	440	395
5	5	5	31	135	95	56	290	250	81	445	400
6	5	5	32	140	100	57	295	255	82	450	405
7	10	5	33	145	110	58	300	260	83	460	410
8	15	5	34	150	115	59	310	265	84	465	415
9	20	5	35	160	120	60	315	270	85	470	420
10	25	5	36	165	125	61	320	280	86	475	425
11	30	5	37	170	130	62	325	285	87	480	430
12	35	5	38	175	140	63	330	290	88	485	435
13	40	5	39	180	145	64	340	300	89	490	445
14	45	5	40	185	150	65	345	305	90	495	450
15	50	5	41	190	160	66	350	310	91	495	455
16	55	10	42	195	165	67	360	320	92	495	465
17	60	15	43	200	170	68	365	325	93	495	470
18	65	20	44	210	175	69	370	330	94	495	480
19	70	25	45	215	180	70	380	335	95	495	485
20	75	30	46	220	190	71	385	340	96	495	490
21	80	35	47	230	195	72	390	350	97	495	495
22	85	40	48	240	200	73	395	355	98	495	495
23	90	45	49	245	210	74	400	360	99	495	495
24	95	50	50	250	215	75	405	365	100	495	495
25	100	60									

聽力測驗答對題數 ＿＿＿＿＿＿ ＝ 聽力測驗分數 ＿＿＿＿＿＿

閱讀測驗答對題數 ＿＿＿＿＿＿ ＝ 閱讀測驗分數 ＿＿＿＿＿＿

多益測驗預估總分 ＿＿＿＿＿＿

MEMO

MEMO

MEMO

EZ TALK

New TOEIC 新制多益聽力閱讀全題型攻略＋實戰模擬 6 回題庫大全

TOEIC Premium: 6 Practice Tests + Online Audio, 10th edition

作　　者	Lin Lougheed Ph.D.
譯　　者	丁宥榆
主　　編	潘亭軒
責任編輯	鄭雅方
審　　訂	Judd Piggott、洪欣
封面設計	兒日設計
版型設計	洪伊珊
內頁排版	簡單瑛設
行銷企劃	張爾芸

發 行 人	洪祺祥
副總經理	洪偉傑
副總編輯	曹仲堯
法律顧問	建大法律事務所
財務顧問	高威會計師事務所

出　　版	日月文化出版股份有限公司
製　　作	EZ 叢書館
地　　址	臺北市信義路三段 151 號 8 樓
電　　話	(02)2708-5509
傳　　真	(02)2708-6157
客服信箱	service@heliopolis.com.tw
網　　址	www.heliopolis.com.tw
郵撥帳號	19716071 日月文化出版股份有限公司

總 經 銷	聯合發行股份有限公司
電　　話	(02)2917-8022
傳　　真	(02)2915-7212
印　　刷	中原造像股份有限公司
初　　版	2025 年 8 月
定　　價	899 元
I S B N	978-626-7641-75-0

New TOEIC 新制多益聽力閱讀全題型攻略 + 實戰模擬 6 回題庫大全 = TOEIC premium : 6 practice tests + online audio/Lin Lougheed 著；丁宥榆譯. -- 初版. -- 臺北市：日月文化出版股份有限公司, 2025.08
1264 面；　19x25.7 公分 . -- (EZ talk)
譯自：TOEIC premium : 6 practice tests + online audio, 10th ed.
ISBN 978-626-7641-75-0 (平裝)
1.CST: 多益測驗

805.1895　　　　　　　　　　114007746

This edition arranged with Barron's Educational Series in association with Biagi Literary Management through Andrew Nurnberg Associates International Limited.
Traditional Chinese copyright © 2025 by HELIOPOLIS CULTURE GROUP

◎版權所有 翻印必究
◎本書如有缺頁、破損、裝訂錯誤，請寄回本公司更換

本書所附音檔由 EZ Course 平台（https://ezcourse.com.tw）提供。購書讀者使用音檔，須註冊 EZ Course 會員，並同意平台服務條款及隱私權與安全政策，完成信箱認證後，前往「書籍音頻」頁面啟動免費訂閱程序。訂閱過程中，購書讀者需完成簡易書籍問答驗證，以確認購書資格與使用權限。完成後，即可免費線上收聽本書專屬音檔。

音檔為授權數位內容，僅限購書讀者本人使用。請勿擅自轉載、重製、散布或提供他人，違反使用規範者將依法追究。購書即表示購書讀者已了解並同意上述條件。詳細操作方式請見書中說明，或至 EZ Course 網站「書籍音頻操作指引」常見問答頁面查詢。

New TOEIC 新制多益
聽力閱讀
全題型攻略
➕ 實戰模擬 6 回題庫大全

TOEIC Premium
6 Practice Tests + Online Audio, 10th edition

解析本

Lin Lougheed Ph.D.——著

丁宥榆——譯

聽力暖身練習&即時演練解答

Part 1 照片描述

高分攻略 1　假設

暖身練習

A. T　B. F　C. PT　D. T　E. T　F. PT　G. F　H. F　I. T　J. PT

中譯

A. 桌邊共有五個人。
B. 時間是晚上。
C. 他們是公司同事。
D. 他們面帶微笑。
E. 桌上有一個瓶子。
F. 瓶子裡裝了水。
G. 他們正在喝咖啡。
H. 他們正在吃東西。
I. 電腦開著。
J. 他們正在看報告。

即時演練

Photo 1：B　Photo 2：C

高分攻略 2　人物

暖身練習

人數：There are two people in the photo. 照片中有兩個人。
性別：There is one man and one woman. 照片中有一男一女。
位置：The man is on the right, and the woman is on the left. 男子在右邊，女子在左邊。
描述：They are elderly. They have short hair. The man has a mustache.
　　　他們都上了年紀，且都是短髮，男子留了小鬍子。
活動：They are looking at a computer. The man is pointing at the computer screen. They are sitting on a bench. 他們正看著一臺電腦，男子指著電腦螢幕，兩人都坐在長椅上。
職業：They may be retired. They look like tourists.
　　　他們可能是退休人士，看起來像是觀光客。

即時演練

Photo 3：A　Photo 4：B

高分攻略 3　物品

暖身練習

table（桌子）、chairs（椅子）、glasses（玻璃杯）、plates（盤子）、napkins（餐巾）、forks（叉子）、vase（花瓶）、flower（花）

即時演練

Photo 5：A　Photo 6：C

高分攻略 4　行動

暖身練習（答案僅供參考）

shopping（購物）、holding the fruit（拿著水果）、picking up the fruit（拿起水果）、looking at the fruit（看著水果）、pushing the cart（推手推車）、choosing fruit（挑選水果）、standing in the aisle（站在走道上）

即時演練

Photo 7：D　Photo 8：D

高分攻略 5　大致地點

暖身練習

地點：Park（公園）

線索：benches（長椅）、grass（草地）、trees（樹）、bushes（灌木叢）、walking path（步道）、fence（圍欄）、lamppost（路燈）

即時演練

Photo 9：B　Photo 10：D

高分攻略 6　具體位置

暖身練習（答案僅供參考）

A: The pen is on the notebook. 筆在筆記本上。

B: The notebook is in front of the computer. 筆記本在電腦前面。

C: The lamp is over the table. 燈在桌子上方。

D: The computer is between the two speakers. 電腦在兩個喇叭中間。

E: The books are to the left of the speaker. 書在喇叭的左邊。

F: The plant is on top of the bookshelf. 植物在書架上面。

即時演練

Photo 11：A　Photo 12：C

003

Part 2 應答問題

高分攻略 1	近音字	1. A	2. C	3. A	4. B	5. B
高分攻略 2	相關字	1. A	2. B	3. C	4. C	5. A
高分攻略 3	同音字	1. A	2. B	3. A	4. A	5. A
高分攻略 4	一字多義	1. B	2. C	3. B	4. C	5. B
高分攻略 5	建議	1. C	2. A	3. C	4. B	5. A
高分攻略 6	主動提出或提議	1. C	2. A	3. B	4. A	5. B
高分攻略 7	請求	1. A	2. B	3. C	4. B	5. C

Part 3 簡短對話

高分攻略 1	人物題	1. B	2. B	3. A	4. B	5. A	6. B
高分攻略 2	職業題	1. D	2. D	3. C	4. C	5. A	6. D
高分攻略 3	地點題	1. C	2. A	3. D	4. C	5. D	6. B
高分攻略 4	時間題	1. C	2. B	3. D	4. C	5. A	6. B
高分攻略 5	活動題	1. D	2. C	3. D	4. A	5. D	6. B
高分攻略 6	看法題	1. B	2. B	3. A	4. C	5. D	6. C
高分攻略 7	圖表題	1. D	2. A	3. B	4. B	5. A
高分攻略 8	情境意義	1. A	2. B	3. B	4. A	5. B
高分攻略 9	簡略回答	1. B	2. A	3. B	4. A	5. B

Part 4 簡短獨白

高分攻略 1	活動與事實題	1. C	2. C	3. C	4. B	5. C	6. B
高分攻略 2	原因題	1. A	2. A	3. D	4. C	5. B	6. A
高分攻略 3	數字題	1. B	2. D	3. A	4. B	5. A	6. A
高分攻略 4	主題和目的題	1. B	2. B	3. B	4. A	5. D	6. B
高分攻略 5	改述題	1. B	2. A	3. D	4. A	5. C	6. B
高分攻略 6	圖表題	1. C	2. B	3. C	4. D	5. A
高分攻略 7	隱含意義題	1. A	2. B	3. B	4. A	5. B
高分攻略 8	口音題

1. Good evening and welcome to tonight's presentation. We are very excited to have with us tonight a world-famous journalist. I am sure

you will enjoy his talk very much.
2. Here is the weather outlook for the weekend. We will have cloudy skies all day Saturday. Expect rain to begin late Saturday evening and continue through Sunday morning. The rain will clear up on Sunday afternoon.
3. Thank you for calling the Acme Company. We value your call. To check your order status, press one. For shipping information, press two. To speak with a customer service representative, press three. To repeat this menu, press four.
4. Attention shoppers. We will be closing the store in ten minutes. Please take your purchases to the checkout area at this time. If you are purchasing ten items or fewer, you may use the express checkout lane
5. The tour will begin in just a few minutes. Please line up by the main entrance. If you don't have a ticket, you can purchase one in the gift shop.

聽力暖身練習與即時演練解析&錄音稿

Part 1 照片描述

高分攻略 1 假設

Photo 1
(A) The pharmacist serves his customers.
(B) The technicians are conducting experiments.
(C) The laboratory animals are in a cage.
(D) The shelves are empty.
(A) 藥師服務他的客人。
(B) 技術人員正在做實驗。
(C) 實驗動物被關在籠子裡。
(D) 架上是空的。

解析 (B) 選項(B)根據照片情境假設身穿白袍的是技術人員，他們可能正在做實驗。選項(A)不正確，照片中這些人雖然可能是藥師，但並沒有類似客人的人。選項(C)不正確，照片中並沒有看到實驗動物。選項(D)不正確，因為架上有瓶瓶罐罐等用品。

Photo 2
(A) They're washing the bottle.
(B) They're buying a computer.
(C) They're having a business meeting.
(D) They're eating dinner.
(A) 他們正在洗瓶子。
(B) 他們正在買電腦。
(C) 他們正在開商務會議。
(D) 他們正在吃晚餐。

解析 (C) 照片中的人物穿著就像商務人士，他們似乎在討論一些文件，因此可以假設他們是商務人士正在開會。選項(A)正確部分為提到瓶子，但並沒有人在洗瓶子。選項(B)提到電腦也沒錯，但這裡不是商店，沒人在買東西。選項(D)與他們圍坐桌邊有關聯，但照片中並沒有食物，反而是一些商務會議會看到的物品，例如文件和電腦，所以不正確。

高分攻略 2 人物

Photo 3
(A) Four people are looking at a map.
(B) The men are wearing suits.
(C) Both women are taller than the men.
(D) The man with glasses is pointing to a chart.
(A) 四個人正在看一張地圖。
(B) 男子都穿西裝。
(C) 兩名女子都比男子高。
(D) 戴眼鏡的男子正指向一張圖表。

解析 (A) 選項(A)正確指出人數和他們的活動。選項(B)不正確，男子都穿短袖。選項(C)不正確，其中一名女子沒有比男子高。選項(D)不正確，應是其中一名女子正指向地圖。

Photo 4
(A) The man and woman are looking for a bench.
(B) Two tourists are using a computer.
(C) The woman's hair is very long.
(D) The man is carrying the suitcases.
(A) 這名男子和女子正在找一張長椅。
(B) 兩位觀光客正在使用電腦。
(C) 這名女子的頭髮很長。
(D) 這名男子正提著行李箱。

解析 (B) 選項(B)正確描述了人物和活動。選項(A)不正確，錯誤描述這名男子和女子正在找一張長椅，事實上他們已經坐在長椅上。選項(C)對女子頭髮的描述並不正確。選項(D)錯誤因為並沒有人提著行李箱。

高分攻略 3 物品

Photo 5
(A) The candles are on the mantle.
(B) A man is playing the piano.
(C) They are sitting on the chairs.
(D) The cushions are on the floor.
(A) 蠟燭在壁爐檯上。
(B) 一位男子正在彈鋼琴。
(C) 他們正坐在椅子上。
(D) 靠墊在地上。

解析 (A) 選項(A)正確指出蠟燭和蠟燭的位置——在壁爐檯上。選項(B)正確指出鋼琴，但照片中沒有人。選項(C)正確指出椅子，但沒有人坐在椅子上。選項(D)正確指出靠墊，但靠墊的位置不正確。

Photo 6
(A) The flowers are in the garden.
(B) The forks are on the plates.
(C) The vase is next to the glass.
(D) The food is on the table.
(A) 花在花園裡。
(B) 叉子在盤子上。
(C) 花瓶在玻璃杯旁。
(D) 食物在桌上。

解析 (C) 選項(C)正確指出了花瓶和花瓶的位置。選項(A)正確指出了花，但是位置錯誤，花在花瓶內，不在花園裡。選項(B)對叉子的位置描述錯誤，叉子在餐巾上，不在盤子上。選項(D)正確指出了桌子，但桌上並沒有食物。

高分攻略 4 行動

Photo 7
(A) The men are smoking pipes.
(B) The earth is planted with crops.
(C) The trench is being dug.
(D) The workers are laying pipeline.
(A) 這些男人在抽菸斗。
(B) 地上種了農作物。
(C) 壕溝正在被開挖。
(D) 工人正在鋪設管線。

解析 (D) 選項(D)正確描述了照片人物（工人）正在做什麼事（鋪設管線）。選項(A)不正確，這些人是在鋪設管線，不是在抽菸斗。選項(B)所描述的情境不正確。選項(C)描述的行動發生在鋪設管線前。

Photo 8
(A) The fruit is being washed.
(B) She's looking for a cart.
(C) They're packing the oranges in boxes.
(D) She's shopping for fruit.

(A) 水果正被清洗。
(B) 她正在找手推車。
(C) 他們正在把橘子裝箱。
(D) 她正在買水果。

解析 (D) 選項(D)正確描述了女子在做的事。選項(A)正確指出了水果,但並沒有人在洗水果。選項(B)不正確,這名女子正在推手推車而不是找手推車。選項(C)正確指出了橘子和箱子,但沒有人在進行裝箱的動作。

高分攻略 5 大致地點

Photo 9
(A) Some shoppers want to buy new luggage.
(B) Passengers are passing through airport security.
(C) The police guard the bank.
(D) The flight attendant seats the passengers.
(A) 有幾位消費者想買新的行李箱。
(B) 乘客正通過機場安檢站。
(C) 警察看守銀行。
(D) 空服員引導乘客入座。

解析 (B) 選項(B)正確描述這些人是乘客,正要通過安檢站。選項(A)把場景錯認為商店。選項(C)把場景錯認為銀行。選項(D)描述的行動發生在飛機上,不會發生在機場的安檢站。

Photo 10
(A) The bus stop is empty.
(B) Cars are parked along the street.
(C) The lamppost is in front of the bank.
(D) Benches line the path through the park.
(A) 公車站空無一人。
(B) 車輛沿著街道停放。
(C) 路燈位於銀行前面。
(D) 長椅沿著穿過公園的小徑排列。

解析 (D) 選項(D)正確指出地點為公園,對長椅的描述也無誤。選項(A)對地點的假設錯誤,公車站的確會有長椅,但照片中的其他特徵均顯示這是一座公園。選項(B)把park這個字的字義搞錯。選項(C)正確指出路燈,但路燈位置描述錯誤,照片中並沒有看到銀行。

高分攻略 6　**具體位置**

Photo 11

(A) There are two glasses on the table.
(B) They are sitting beside a window.
(C) The napkins are in a box.
(D) The server is standing behind the man.

(A) 桌上有兩個玻璃杯。
(B) 他們坐在窗邊。
(C) 餐巾放在一個盒子裡。
(D) 服務生站在男子身後。

解析 (A) 選項(A)正確指出了玻璃杯和它們的具體位置。選項(B)正確指出了人物的活動，但對於位置的描述不正確，照片中沒有窗戶。選項(C)正確指出了餐巾，但對餐巾的位置描述錯誤，餐巾在叉子下方。選項(D)正確指出了服務生的活動，但是對她的位置描述錯誤，她並不在靠近男子的位置。

Photo 12

(A) The plant is on the desk.
(B) The pen is in the cup.
(C) There is a small clock on the shelf.
(D) There are two speakers behind the computer.

(A) 植物在書桌上。
(B) 筆在杯子裡。
(C) 架上有一個小時鐘。
(D) 電腦後方有兩個喇叭。

解析 (C) 選項(C)正確指出了小時鐘的位置。選項(A)不正確，植物位於書架上方，不在書桌上。選項(B)不正確，筆在筆記本上，不在杯子裡。選項(D)不正確，喇叭在電腦旁邊，或在電腦的兩側，不在後面。

Part 2 應答問題

高分攻略 1 近音字

1. Was the letter delivered today?
    (A) Yes, it came this morning.
    (B) The ladder was on the delivery truck.
    (C) He was late on Tuesday.
    信今天寄達了嗎？
    (A) 是的，今天早上到了。
    (B) 梯子放在貨車上。
    (C) 他星期二遲到。

解析 (A) 選項(A)以Yes回答了題目的yes-no問句。選項(B)使用了delivered的相關字delivery和truck，以及近音字letter/ladder、delivered/delivery。選項(C)使用了近音字today/Tuesday、Was the letter/was late。聆聽時要聽出完整意思，同時善用文法線索，例如題目是以be動詞was開頭的yes-no問句，這會影響回答方式。

2. Where can I find the nearest post office?
    (A) I think this one's the softest.
    (B) He was fined for parking in a no-parking zone.
    (C) There's one on the next block.
    最近的郵局在哪裡？
    (A) 我覺得這是最軟的。
    (B) 他因在禁止停車區停車而被罰款。
    (C) 下一個街區就有一間。

解析 (C) 選項(C)以一個地點（on the next block）回答了題目的Where問句。選項(A)使用了近音字office/softest。選項(B)使用了近音字find/fined。

3. Mary Ann is a very nice person, isn't she?
    (A) Yes, she gets along well with everyone.
    (B) Yes, she eats rice at every meal.
    (C) No, I don't believe that's her purse.
    瑪麗・安是一個很好的人，對不對？
    (A) 對，她和每個人都相處愉快。
    (B) 對，她每餐都吃米飯。
    (C) 不，我不認為那是她的錢包。

解析 **(A)** 附加問句 isn't she 的作用是徵求同意，題目表示瑪莉・安是一個好人（nice person），選項(A)以 she gets along well 附和了題目的想法，與 nice person 是同樣的意思。選項(B)使用了近音字 nice/rice。選項(C)使用了近音字 person/purse。

4. Did anyone pay this bill?
   (A) Yes, I know how to play.
   (B) Yes, I sent a check yesterday.
   (C) Yes, I think he will.
   有人付了帳單嗎？
   (A) 是的，我知道怎麼玩。
   (B) 是的，我昨天寄出一張支票。
   (C) 是的，我想他會。

解析 **(B)** 選項(B)中的 I sent a check 是對帳單支付問題的合理回應。選項(A)混淆了近音字 pay 和 play。選項(C)混淆了近音字 bill 和 will。

5. Could you make copies of this report for me?
   (A) You should use this form.
   (B) Of course. Right away.
   (C) I enjoy watching sports.
   可以幫我影印這份報告嗎？
   (A) 你應該用這張表格。
   (B) 當然可以，我馬上幫你弄。
   (C) 我喜歡觀看體育比賽。

解析 **(B)** 選項(B)是對一個禮貌請求的適當回應。選項(A)混淆了近音字 for me 和 form。選項(C)混淆了近音字 report 和 sports。

高分攻略 2　相關字

1. How long have you been married?
   (A) Almost ten years.
   (B) About five feet.
   (C) The bride is my cousin.
   你結婚多久了？
   (A) 快要十年了。
   (B) 大概五英尺。
   (C) 新娘是我表妹。

解析 **(A)** 聆聽時要仔細聽出完整的意思，注意 How long 和動詞 married 的文法線索都暗示了題目與時間長度有關。選項(A)提出了 how long 問題的適當回答（ten years）。選項(B) 使用了相關字 long/five feet，但題目問的是時間，不是距離。選項(C) 使用了相關字 married/bride。

2. When does your flight leave?
   (A) It's a first-class ticket.
   (B) At ten tomorrow morning.
   (C) I made the reservation last week.
   你的班機何時起飛？
   (A) 這是頭等艙的機票。
   (B) 明天早上十點。
   (C) 我上週就訂票了。

解析 **(B)** When 的考題就是在問時間，選項(B)以一個時間「ten tomorrow morning」回答了問題。選項(A)使用了相關字 flight/ticket。選項(C)使用了相關字 flight/reservation。

3. Where would you like to eat dinner tonight?
   (A) Choose anything you like from the menu.
   (B) It's my favorite meal of the day.
   (C) There's a nice restaurant near my office.
   今晚你想去哪裡吃飯？
   (A) 從菜單上挑你愛吃的。
   (B) 這是我今天最喜歡的一餐。
   (C) 我公司附近有一間不錯的餐廳。

解析 **(C)** Where 的考題就是在問地點，選項(C)以 restaurant 回答了吃飯地點的問題。選項(A)使用了相關字 dinner/menu，並且重複了問題中的 like 這個字。選項(B)使用了相關字 dinner/meal。

4. Do you know what time the bus leaves?
   (A) I think he's the driver.
   (B) You need a ticket.
   (C) At half past two.
   你知道公車幾點出發嗎？
   (A) 我認為他是司機。
   (B) 你要有車票。
   (C) 兩點半。

013

解析 (C)「At half past two」是 What time 問題的合理回答。選項 (A) 和 (B) 分別使用了 bus 的相關字 driver 和 ticket。

5. Whose office is this?
  (A) It's mine.
  (B) On my desk.
  (C) I work here.
  這是誰的辦公室？
  (A) 我的。
  (B) 在我桌上。
  (C) 我在這裡上班。

解析 (A)「It's mine」是 Whose 問題的合理回答。選項 (B) 和 (C) 分別使用了 office 的相關字 desk 和 work。

高分攻略 3　同音字

1. He leaves next week, doesn't he?
  (A) No, he's going tomorrow.
  (B) Yes, he's very weak.
  (C) The leaves are turning yellow.
  他下週離開，對嗎？
  (A) 不，他明天就要走了。
  (B) 是的，他很虛弱。
  (C) 葉子正在轉黃。

解析 (A) 附加問句 doesn't he 必須以 yes 或 no 來回答。選項 (A) 以 No 回答了問題，並且補充說明離開的時間。選項 (B) 使用了同音字 week/weak。選項 (C) 使用了一字多義的 leaves，動詞表示離開，名詞表示葉子。

2. Do you think we should use blue paint on the waiting room walls?
  (A) Yes, the wind blew for a long time last night.
  (B) Yes, it's a very calming color.
  (C) Yes, I have put on a little bit of weight.
  你覺得我們要不要把等候室的牆壁漆成藍色？
  (A) 是的，昨晚風吹了很久。
  (B) 好啊，那是讓人感到很平靜的顏色。
  (C) 是的，我的體重增加了一點。

解析 (B) 題目問的是油漆顏色。選項(B)以一個與顏色相關的評論回答了問題。選項(A)使用了同音字blue/blew。選項(C)使用了同音字wait (waiting room)/weight。

3. Do you know who won the employee of the month award?
   (A) It was Mr. Cho in the accounting department.
   (B) There's only one left.
   (C) I think it's due tomorrow.
   你知道誰獲得本月最佳員工獎嗎？
   (A) 是會計部門的趙先生。
   (B) 只剩下一個了。
   (C) 我認為明天會到期。

解析 (A) 內嵌的who問句顯示問題和人有關。選項(A)以一個人名Mr. Cho回答了問題。選項(B)使用了同音字won/one。選項(C)使用了近音字do/due。

4. How many computers did he buy?
   (A) Only one.
   (B) He said goodbye.
   (C) Yes, the one by the door.
   他買了幾臺電腦？
   (A) 只有一臺。
   (B) 他說了再見。
   (C) 是的，門邊的那一個。

解析 (A) 選項(A)以Only one回答了How many的問題。選項(B)混淆了同音字buy和bye。選項(C)混淆了同音字buy和by。

5. Would you rather meet this week or next?
   (A) Next week is more convenient.
   (B) I feel a bit weak.
   (C) The sound on this one is weak.
   你想這週見面還是下週？
   (A) 下週比較方便。
   (B) 我感覺有點虛弱。
   (C) 這個的聲音有點弱。

解析 (A) 選項(A)回答了題目關於見面時間的偏好。選項(B)和(C)混淆了同音字week和weak。

高分攻略 4　一字多義

1. Is this bed too hard?
   (A) Yes, it's very difficult.
   (B) Not for me. I like it firm.
   (C) The flower bed needs water.
   這張床太硬了嗎？
   (A) 是的，非常困難。
   (B) 我覺得不會，我喜歡硬的。
   (C) 花壇需要澆水。

   解析 (B) 選項(B)中的片語 Not for me 即代表 No，回答了題目的 yes-no 問句，意思是「No, the bed is not too hard for me.」，而 a hard bed 就等於 a firm bed。選項(A)誤把題目中的 hard 理解為「困難的」(difficult)。選項(C)中的 bed 指的是花壇。

2. There's not enough light in this room.
   (A) It's really quite heavy.
   (B) There's enough room for everyone to sit.
   (C) I'll open the curtains.
   這個房間的光線不足。
   (A) 真的很重。
   (B) 空間足夠讓每個人都有位子坐。
   (C) 我去把窗簾拉開。

   解析 (C) 題目在抱怨室內的光線不足，選項(C)是合理的回應。選項(A)誤把 light 理解為「很輕」(not heavy)。選項(B)誤把 room 理解為「空間」。

3. Can you call me right after the meeting?
   (A) I believe that answer was correct.
   (B) Sure, I'll phone you as soon as it's over.
   (C) Take a right at the next corner.
   開完會立刻打電話給我好嗎？
   (A) 我認為那個答案是對的。
   (B) 沒問題，一結束我就打給你。
   (C) 下一個轉角右轉。

   解析 (B) 選項(B)中的「I'll phone you」是對請求回電的合理回應。選項(A)誤把 right 理解為「正確的」(correct)。選項(C)誤把 right 理解為「右邊」。

4. Do you know when John will be back?
   (A) He put it in the back room.
   (B) Because his back hurts.
   (C) At around six o'clock, I think.
   你知道約翰幾點回來嗎？
   (A) 他把它放在後面房間。
   (B) 因為他背痛。
   (C) 六點左右吧，我想。

解析 (C) 選項(C)以six o'clock回答了when的間接問句。題目中的back意指「回來」，而選項(A)中的back意指「後面的」，選項(B)中的back意指「背部」。

5. We're running out of paper for the printer.
   (A) The printer is running well.
   (B) The machine is not running well.
   (C) Yes, I know how to run this equipment.
   印表機快沒紙了。
   (A) 印表機運作良好。
   (B) 這臺機器運作不是很好。
   (C) 是的，我知道如何操作這個設備。

解析 (B) 選項(B)是對印表機快沒紙的合理回應，而題目「running out of paper」的run out是「用完」的意思。選項(A)使用了run的「運作」之意。選項(C)使用了run的另一個意思「操作」。

高分攻略 5　建議

1. Shouldn't we leave more time to get there?
   (A) I left my watch at home.
   (B) I don't drive anymore.
   (C) Yes, let's leave earlier.
   我們是不是該多留些時間到那邊？
   (A) 我把手錶忘在家裡了。
   (B) 我已經不開車了。
   (C) 是的，我們早點出發吧。

解析 (C) 題目是建議句，選項(C)以Yes回答了問題，並且提出一個出發時間。選項(A)使用近音字混合相關字的片語leave more time/left my watch。選項(B)混淆了近音字more和anymore。

2. Why don't we meet at three tomorrow afternoon?
    (A) OK, I'll see you then.
    (B) Because I stopped eating meat.
    (C) I don't think three chairs are enough.
    不如我們明天下午三點碰面？
    (A) 好啊，到時候見。
    (B) 因為我不吃肉了。
    (C) 我覺得三張椅子不夠。

解析 (A) 選項(A)以OK回答了Why don't we的建議句，對這個建議表示同意。選項(B)混淆了同音字meet/meat。選項(C)重複了題目中的three這個字。

3. Let's talk this over with Mr. Sato before we make a decision.
    (A) It was over earlier than expected.
    (B) He did it with such precision.
    (C) Good idea. We'll discuss it with him.
    我們做決定前先和佐藤先生討論一下吧。
    (A) 比預期的還要早結束。
    (B) 他如此精準地完成了。
    (C) 好主意，我們和他討論吧。

解析 (C) 選項(C)以Good idea回答了Let's的建議句，並換了一句話複述該建議。選項(A)重複了題目中的over這個字。選項(B)混淆了近音字decision/precision。

4. Why don't we use the big conference room for the meeting?
    (A) Thanks, but I never eat meat.
    (B) That's a good idea.
    (C) He's reading it now.
    我們何不使用那間大會議室開會？
    (A) 謝謝，但我不吃肉。
    (B) 好主意。
    (C) 他正在讀。

解析 (B) 題目建議使用大會議室，「That's a good idea.」是對這個建議的合理回應。選項(A)混淆了同音字meet/meat。選項(C)混淆了近音字meeting/reading。

5. Let's take a break and finish this work later.
   (A) Yes, let's.
   (B) It works fine.
   (C) No, it didn't break.
   我們休息一下，待會再完成這份工作。
   (A) 好啊，休息一下。
   (B) 它運作良好。
   (C) 不，它沒有壞掉。

   解析 (A)「Yes, lets.」是對建議休息的合理回應。選項(B)使用了 work 的另一個意思。選項(C)使用了 break 的另一個意思。

高分攻略 6　主動提出或提議

1. We're going out for coffee if you want to join us.
   (A) I'll have a tea with milk and sugar.
   (B) The café around the corner.
   (C) Thanks, but I'm too busy right now.
   我們要去喝咖啡，如果你要一起來的話也可以。
   (A) 我要一杯奶茶加糖。
   (B) 轉角那間咖啡廳。
   (C) 謝謝，但我現在太忙了。

   解析 (C) 除了(C)以外的其他選項都沒有回應到和他們一起去喝咖啡的提議。選項(A)使用了與 coffee 有關聯的單字 milk 和 sugar。選項(B)說的是喝咖啡的地點（café）。

2. Shall I let you know when the visitors arrive?
   (A) Yes, I'd appreciate that.
   (B) No, I don't like the way he drives.
   (C) Yes, they visited her last week.
   要不要訪客抵達時我跟你說一聲？
   (A) 好啊，非常感謝。
   (B) 不，我不喜歡他開車的方式。
   (C) 是的，他們上週去拜訪她了。

   解析 (A) 選項(A)是對方主動提出願意幫忙時的適切回應。選項(B)混淆了近音字 arrives/drives。選項(C)混淆了相關字 visitors/visited。

3. Do you want me to help you get ready for tomorrow's meeting?
    (A) I haven't read that one yet.
    (B) Thank you. You could copy these agendas for me.
    (C) Yes, I look forward to meeting them.
    要不要我幫你準備明天的會議？
    (A) 我還沒讀過那一份。
    (B) 謝謝，你可以幫我影印這些議程表。
    (C) 是的，我很期待見到他們。

解析 (B) 選項(B)先是感謝說話者願意提供協助，接著表達自己需要何種協助。選項(A)混淆了近音字 ready/read。選項(C)搞錯了 meeting 這個字的意義。

4. Would you like to sit here while you wait?
    (A) Yes, thank you.
    (B) It's about a 15-minute wait.
    (C) I'm waiting for Dr. Kim.
    你要不要坐在這裡等？
    (A) 好的，謝謝。
    (B) 大約要等十五分鐘。
    (C) 我在等金醫師。

解析 (A) 選項(A)是對此禮貌提議的適切回應。選項(B)和(C)重複問句中的 wait 這個字。

5. Let me carry that package for you.
    (A) It came in the mail this morning.
    (B) No thanks. I can manage.
    (C) I packed it myself.
    我幫你拿那個包裹。
    (A) 它早上寄來了。
    (B) 不用了，謝謝，我自己可以。
    (C) 我自己打包的。

解析 (B) 選項(B)是對這個禮貌提議的適切回應。選項(A)使用了相關字 package/mail。選項(C)混淆了近音字 package/packed。

高分攻略 7　請求

1. Would you mind opening the window?
    (A) Not at all. It is warm in here.
    (B) I opened the door.
    (C) The curtains are new.
    麻煩你開一下窗好嗎？
    (A) 沒問題，這裡挺暖和的。
    (B) 我開了門。
    (C) 窗簾是新的。

    解析 (A)　除了 (A) 以外的其他選項都沒有回應題目中的請求。選項(B) 使用了相關字 window/door。選項(C) 使用了相關字 window/curtains。

2. Could you ship this package before lunch today?
    (A) I already packed it.
    (B) Of course. I'll do it right now.
    (C) In the cafeteria across the street.
    你能在今天午餐前寄出這個包裹嗎？
    (A) 我已經打包好了。
    (B) 當然可以，我現在就去寄。
    (C) 在對街的自助餐廳。

    解析 (B)　選項(B)是對這個請求的適切回應。選項(A)混淆了近音字 package/packed it。選項(C) 使用了相關字 lunch/cafeteria。

3. Would you collect my mail for me while I'm out of town?
    (A) I don't recollect his name.
    (B) He lives in another town.
    (C) I'd be happy to.
    我不在城裡的時候，你可以幫我收一下郵件嗎？
    (A) 我不記得他的名字了。
    (B) 他住在另一個城鎮。
    (C) 我很樂意。

    解析 (C)　選項(C)是對一項請求的適切回應。選項(A)混淆了近音字 collect/recollect。選項(B)重複了問句中的 town 這個字。

021

4. Do you think you could lock that door for me?
   (A) I used my own key.
   (B) Of course.
   (C) Just put it on the floor.
   你可以幫我鎖那扇門嗎？
   (A) 我用了自己的鑰匙。
   (B) 當然可以。
   (C) 放在地上就好。

解析 (B) 選項(B)是對鎖門這個禮貌請求的適切回應。選項(A)使用了相關字lock/key。選項(C)混淆了近音字door/floor。

5. Can you pour me another cup of coffee?
   (A) He's still coughing.
   (B) Just a little cream and sugar.
   (C) Certainly.
   可以再幫我倒一杯咖啡嗎？
   (A) 他還在咳嗽。
   (B) 一點奶油和糖就好。
   (C) 沒問題。

解析 (C) 選項(C)是對再倒一杯咖啡這個禮貌請求的適切回應。選項(A)混淆了近音字coffee和coughing。選項(B)使用了coffee的相關字cream和sugar。

Part 3 簡短對話

高分攻略 1　人物題

Man: Sand this wall until it's smooth. Don't forget to sand all the way down to the end of the room.
Woman: Then it'll be ready for the first coat of paint. We're using semi-gloss, right?
Man: Actually we're using this other kind of paint. My father says he prefers flat. I'll help you mix the color.
Woman: Thanks. This is a lot of work. I sure hope your father likes his new house once we're finished with it.

男： 用砂紙把牆面打磨光滑，別忘了房間整面牆要一路打磨到底。
女： 接著就可以上第一層漆了。我們要用半平光漆對嗎？
男： 事實上我們要用另一種油漆，我父親說他比較喜歡平光的，我會幫你調色。
女： 謝謝，這要費不少功夫。等我們漆好，希望你父親會喜歡他的新家。

1. Who are the speakers? 說話者是誰？
   (A) Lifeguards at the beach 海灘救生員
   (B) Painters 油漆師傅
   (C) Salespeople selling coats 外套銷售員
   (D) Bartenders 調酒師

   解析 **(B)** 注意對話中的上下文線索，如：sand、wall、first coat of paint、mix the color。選項(A)使用了相關字lifeguards，是誤把sand理解為sand at the beach（海灘上的沙），而不是對話中的動詞用法sand a wall（打磨牆壁）。選項(C)使用了一字多義的coat，題目中的coat指油漆塗層，選項中的coat指外套。選項(D)使用了相關的概念，油漆師傅調油漆（mix paints），調酒師調酒（mix drinks）。

2. Who will prepare the wall? 誰負責處理牆面？
   (A) The man 這名男子
   (B) The woman 這名女子
   (C) The boss 老闆
   (D) The helper 協助者

   解析 **(B)** 對話中這名男子要這名女子打磨牆壁。選項(A)不正確，因為男子是叫女子去做這件事。選項(C)使用了gloss的近音字boss。選項(D)混淆了I'll help you和helper。

3. Who owns the house? 這間房子是誰的？
   (A) The man's father 男子父親的
   (B) The man's mother 男子母親的
   (C) The man's brother 男子哥哥的
   (D) The man's friend 男子朋友的

   解析 (A) 說話者談到父親喜歡的油漆類型，女子則回應等房子漆好，希望他的父親會滿意新家，由此可見房子是這位男子父親的。選項(B)和(C)的mother和brother是和對話中的近音字other有所混淆。選項(D)使用了end的近音字friend。

Man:　　　So you want a buffet dinner for twenty-five people?
Woman 1：Yes, with both meat and vegetarian options.
Man:　　　Of course. And for dessert, would you like an assortment of pastries?
Woman 2：Actually, we thought a large cake would be nice. It's our boss's retirement party. He deserves something special.
Man:　　　We can do that. My partner is very good at decorating cakes. I'll have her call you to discuss ideas.
Woman 1：That sounds perfect.
Man:　　　Also, we require a deposit before we start any job.
Woman 2：Of course. Mary, can you handle that?
Woman 1：Just send the bill to my assistant. She'll take care of it. She handles everything regarding the expense account.

男：　您要二十五人份的自助式晚餐是嗎？
女1：是的，葷食與素食的餐點都要有。
男：　當然。甜點的部分，您要各式糕點嗎？
女2：其實我們覺得大蛋糕會比較好。這是我們老闆的退休派對，他值得特別一點的餐點。
男：　我們可以安排。我的夥伴很擅長裝飾蛋糕，我會請她打電話跟您討論想法。
女1：太好了。
男：　另外，我們開始進行任何工作前需要先收訂金。
女2：沒問題。瑪麗，交給你處理可以嗎？
女1：請把帳單寄給我的助理，她會處理。報銷帳戶的相關事務都是她在處理的。

4. Who is the man? 這名男子是誰？
   (A) A waiter 服務生
   (B) A caterer 宴席承辦人
   (C) A pastry chef 糕點師傅

(D) A restaurant customer 餐廳客人

解析 (B) 這些女子請男子為一場退休派對安排自助晚餐和蛋糕，由此可知這名男子是宴席承辦人。選項(A)(C)(D)都是和飲食相關的職業或身分。

5. Who are the women giving the dinner for? 這些女子為誰辦晚宴？
   (A) Their boss 她們的老闆
   (B) Their friend 她們的朋友
   (C) Their client 她們的客戶
   (D) Their business partner 她們的商業夥伴

解析 (A) 其中一名女子說「It's our boss's retirement party.」，所以是為老闆辦的。選項(B)和(C)是有可能，但對話中沒有提到。選項(D)是因為男子提到他的夥伴很擅長裝飾蛋糕，因此可能造成誤解。

6. Who will pay the bill? 誰會付帳單？
   (A) Mary 瑪麗
   (B) Mary's assistant 瑪麗的助理
   (C) The accountant 會計師
   (D) Everyone in the office 辦公室裡的每一個人

解析 (B) 瑪麗說「Just send the bill to my assistant.」，所以是她的助理。選項(A)重複了對話中的Mary這個名字。選項(C)使用了account的相關字accountant。選項(D)在對話中並未提及。

高分攻略 2　職業題

Man:　　　I'd like you to put one in each room.
Woman:　　I'll have to run wires along the baseboard to do that.
Man:　　　No problem. I'll need one on each employee's desk. We're all responsible for answering the phone here.
Woman:　　Right. Good customer service is important for every business.
Man:　　　Yes, and I want to start this new business out right. Our website has brought in a lot of new clients already, and we need to be sure there is always at least one person here ready to answer questions and provide support.
Woman:　　I'm sure the business will do well. Lots of people need accounting services.
男：　　　我想請你每個房間都裝一個。
女：　　　我得讓電線沿著護壁板走才有辦法。
男：　　　沒問題。每個員工桌上也都要一個，我們這裡所有人都要負責接電話。

025

女： 是的。好的客服對每個企業都很重要。

男： 沒錯,我希望這項新事業有個好的開始。我們的網站已經帶來很多新客戶,因此必須確保隨時至少有一個人可以回答問題並提供支援。

女： 我相信這項事業一定會成功,很多人需要會計服務。

1. What is the woman's occupation? 這名女子的職業是什麼?
    (A) Running coach 跑步教練
    (B) Baseball player 棒球員
    (C) Telephone operator 接線生
    (D) Telephone installer 電話安裝人員

解析 (D) 注意對話中的上下文線索,像是 put one in each room(每個房間放一個)、wires along the baseboard(沿著護壁板的電線)以及 phone(電話)。選項(A)混淆了 run wires(安裝電線)和 running(跑步)的意義。選項(B)使用了 baseboard 的近音字 baseball。選項(C)使用了 phone 的相關字 telephone operator。

2. What is the man's job? 這名男子的工作是什麼?
    (A) Employment counselor 職業諮詢師
    (B) Tech support specialist 技術支援專員
    (C) Website designer 網頁設計師
    (D) Accountant 會計師

解析 (D) 女子評論男子的事業時,說了「Lots of people need accounting services.」,因此我們知道這名男子正在經營會計事業。選項(A)中的 employment 是 employee 的相關字。選項(B)重複了對話中 support。選項(C)重複了對話中的 website。

3. Who is responsible for answering the phone? 誰負責接電話?
    (A) The man only 只有這名男子
    (B) The receptionist 接待員
    (C) Everyone at the company 公司裡的每一個人
    (D) The customer service specialist 客服專員

解析 (C) 這名男子說了「We're all responsible for answering the phone here.」,因此答案為所有人。選項(A)不正確,因為人人都要接電話。選項(B)在對話中並未提及。選項(D)重複了對話中的片語 customer service。

Man:	I've asked everyone to be on the bus by eight forty-five. That way we'll be able to start the tour at nine sharp.
Woman:	OK. So you want me to take you to the museum first, right?
Man:	Right. And drive through the historic district so I can point out some of the old mansions.
Woman:	All right. That's easy enough. Then after the museum, do you still want me to drive the group to the Chalet Restaurant for lunch?
Man:	Yes. I spoke with the manager last week to make the reservation, and I've asked the front desk clerk here at the hotel to call the restaurant this morning to confirm it.
男：	我已經要求大家八點四十五分前上遊覽車，這樣才能準時九點開始遊覽。
女：	好。所以你要我先載你們到博物館是嗎？
男：	對。麻煩開車經過歷史區，我可以指出一些老舊住宅給大家看。
女：	沒問題，那很簡單。參觀完博物館，你還是要我載大家到夏萊餐廳吃午餐嗎？
男：	對。我上週已經和經理訂位了，也已經請飯店前檯服務人員早上打電話給餐廳確認訂位了。

4． Who is the man? 這名男子是誰？
(A) A travel agent 旅行社職員
(B) A tourist 觀光客
(C) A tour guide 導遊
(D) A museum director 博物館館長

解析 **(C)** 這名男子正在討論早上要進行的遊覽活動，他要帶大家去看博物館和歷史區，由此可知他是導遊。選項 (A) 和 (B) 都和對話主題有關，但都不是正確答案。選項 (D) 重複了對話中的 museum 這個字。

5． What is the woman's job? 這名女子的工作是什麼？
(A) Bus driver 遊覽車司機
(B) Taxi driver 計程車司機
(C) Waiter 服務生
(D) Chef 廚師

解析 **(A)** 男子提到了遊覽車（bus），女子也多次提到她會「載送」（drive）這個團體，因此可知她是遊覽車司機。選項 (B) 不正確，說話者討論的是遊覽車，不是計程車。選項 (C) 和 (D) 與對話中提到餐廳有關。

6. Who will call the restaurant? 誰會打電話給餐廳？
   (A) The man 男子
   (B) The woman 女子
   (C) The hotel manager 飯店經理
   (D) The front desk clerk 前檯服務人員

解析 (D) 這名男子說「I've asked the front desk clerk here at the hotel to call the restaurant」，因此知道打電話的會是前檯服務人員。選項 (A) 和 (B) 不正確，因為男子已經請別人做這件事了。選項 (C) 重複了對話中的 hotel 和 manager 兩字。

高分攻略 3　地點題

Woman:　A package was delivered for Jim today. I told them to put it on the table in the conference room.
Man:　He'll never see it there. Put it somewhere in his office.
Woman:　I don't want to leave it on his desk. It's all covered with papers—mail, file folders, magazines. He won't see it in all that mess.
Man:　Then put it on his computer keyboard. He won't miss it there.
Woman:　Good idea. I'll do that. By the way, when is Jim due back here?
Man:　He's returning from vacation tomorrow night, so he should be in first thing the following morning.

女：　今天來了一個吉姆的包裹，我叫他們放在會議室桌上。
男：　放在那裡他會看不到，放到他辦公室的某處。
女：　我不想放他桌上，他的桌上全都是文件資料——信、文件夾、雜誌啊。桌上亂七八糟的，他不會看到的。
男：　不然放在他的鍵盤上，他絕不可能沒看到。
女：　好主意，就這麼辦。對了，吉姆什麼時候回來？
男：　他明天晚上結束度假回來，應該隔天一大早就會進辦公室。

1. Where does this conversation take place? 這段對話發生在什麼地方？
   (A) In a private home 在私人住宅
   (B) On a delivery truck 在送貨車上
   (C) In a business office 在商務辦公室
   (D) At a shipping company 在貨運公司

解析 (C) 說話者談論要把包裹放在會議室（conference room）和放在桌上（desk），還提到放在辦公室（office），因此他們應該是在一間商務辦公室裡。選項 (A) 在對話中並未提及。選項 (B) 和 (D) 使用了 package 的相關字 delivery 和 shipping。

028

2. Where will the woman put the package? 這名女子會將包裹放在哪裡？
    (A) On Jim's keyboard 吉姆的鍵盤上
    (B) On the filing cabinet 檔案櫃上
    (C) On Jim's desk 吉姆的辦公桌上
    (D) On a table 桌子上

解析 (A) 選項(A)是男子建議放包裹的地方，女子也同意了。選項(B)使用了 file folders 的相關字 filing cabinet。選項(C)是女子不想放置包裹的地方。選項(D)是包裹目前的所在位置。

3. Where is Jim now? 吉姆現在人在哪裡？
    (A) At a conference 在研討會
    (B) In his office 在辦公室
    (C) On a flight 在飛機上
    (D) On vacation 度假中

解析 (D) 男子說到「He's returning from vacation tomorrow night」，可見他目前正在度假中。選項(A)因為對話提到會議室而會混淆作答。選項(B)重複了對話中的 office 這個字。選項(C)混淆了近音字 flight 和 night。

Woman: Excuse me, have you seen my coat? I thought I'd left it here in the teacher's break room.
Man: You did. It was on that chair, but it was about to fall on the floor, so I hung it in the closet.
Woman: You mean in the lobby?
Man: No, right out there, in the hall.
Woman: Oh. Thanks. Well, I've got to run. I've got to get to the station to catch a five o'clock train.
Man: I'll go with you. We can share a taxi. I'm headed to that part of town, too, for an appointment with my accountant. Just wait a sec while I get my things out of my classroom.

女： 不好意思，請問你有看到我的外套嗎？我好像把它忘在教師休息室裡了。
男： 你的確忘在這裡了，它原本在椅子上但快掉到地上，所以我把它掛在衣櫃裡了。
女： 你是說在大廳嗎？
男： 不是，就在外面走廊上。
女： 喔，謝謝。啊，我要走了，我要到車站趕五點的火車。
男： 我跟你一起走，我們可以共乘計程車，我也要去那一帶，我跟會計師有約。等我一下，我回教室收東西。

029

4. Where are the speakers? 說話者在什麼地方？
   (A) In a taxi 計程車上
   (B) On a plane 飛機上
   (C) In a school 學校裡
   (D) In a private home 私人住宅裡

   解析 **(C)** 女子提到teacher's break room，男子提到my classroom，由此可知他們在學校裡。選項(A)重複了對話中的taxi這個字，說話者表示他們要搭計程車前往下一個目的地。選項(B)混淆了近音字plane和train。選項(D)是同樣擁有hall（門廳）和closet（衣櫃）的地方。

5. Where is the woman's coat? 這名女子的外套在哪裡？
   (A) On a chair 椅子上
   (B) On the floor 地上
   (C) In the lobby 大廳裡
   (D) In the closet 衣櫃裡

   解析 **(D)** 這名男子談論外套時說「I hung it in the closet」，所以外套最後到了衣櫃裡。選項(A)是女子最初遺留外套的地方。選項(B)是男子不希望外套出現的地方。選項(C)是女子原本以為男子放外套的地方。

6. Where is the woman going? 這名女子正要去哪裡？
   (A) To her accountant's office 她會計師的辦公室
   (B) To the train station 火車站
   (C) To her apartment 她的公寓
   (D) To the bank 銀行

   解析 **(B)** 女子說「I've got to get to the station to catch a five o'clock train.」，所以是火車站。選項(A)是男子要去的地方。選項(C)混淆了近音字apartment和appointment。選項(D)使用了accountant的相關字bank。

高分攻略 4　時間題

Man:　　　It's getting late, and I have an early appointment tomorrow. I need to go in about ten minutes.
Woman:　Your appointment isn't until eight thirty. You can stay for another hour, can't you?
Man:　　　Let's compromise. I'll leave in half an hour.
Woman:　Good. That will leave you plenty of time to get home and get to sleep early. You can get to your house from here in forty-five minutes easily.

男：　有點晚了，我明天一早還有預約，再過大約十分鐘我就得走了。
女：　你的預約是八點半，可以再待一個小時吧？
男：　不然我們折衷，我半小時後離開。
女：　太好了。那樣你有充分的時間回到家早點睡。你從這裡出發，四十五分鐘內就可以到家。

1． How much longer will the man stay? 這名男子會再待多久？
　　(A) 10 minutes 十分鐘
　　(B) 15 minutes 十五分鐘
　　(C) 30 minutes 三十分鐘
　　(D) 60 minutes 六十分鐘

解析 (C) 半小時（half an hour）就是三十分鐘。關於時間的問題，有時需在小時和分鐘之間轉換，例如，one and half hours（一個半小時）就等於 90 minutes（九十分鐘）。選項 (A) 是男子原本預計離開的時間。選項 (B) 在對話中並未提及。選項 (D) 是女子希望男子多待的時間。

2． When is the man's appointment? 這名男子的預約是什麼時候？
　　(A) At 9:00 九點
　　(B) Tomorrow 明天
　　(C) In a few minutes 幾分鐘後
　　(D) In half an hour 半小時後

解析 (B) 男子說「I have an early appointment tomorrow」，所以是明天。選項 (A) 混淆了近音字 nine 和 time。選項 (C) 在對話中並未提及。選項 (D) 是最終男子會離開的時間。

031

3. How long will it take the man to get home? 這名男子回到家要花多久時間？
   (A) 20 minutes 二十分鐘
   (B) 25 minutes 二十五分鐘
   (C) 40 minutes 四十分鐘
   (D) 45 minutes 四十五分鐘

解析 (D) 女子說男子可以在四十五分鐘內到家。選項(A)和(B)都混淆了近音字 twenty 和 plenty。選項(C)則是和正確答案的發音相近。

Woman: Don't forget the monthly staff meeting is tomorrow.
Man 1: Already? It seems like we just had one last week. We'll be finished before lunch, I hope.
Man 2: Didn't you get the memo? It's in the afternoon this time.
Woman: The boss has to see a client in the morning, so he changed the meeting to after lunch.
Man 1: What time, exactly?
Woman: One. It should only last a couple of hours, though. Then we'll be free.

女： 別忘了明天是每月一次的員工會議。
男1： 這麼快？好像我們上週才開過會似的。希望午餐前能結束。
男2： 你沒收到通知嗎？這次會議是在下午。
女： 老闆早上要見客戶，所以把會議改到午餐後。
男1： 確切時間是幾點？
女： 一點。不過應該只會進行兩小時，然後我們就解脫了。

4. How often is there a staff meeting? 員工會議多久舉辦一次？
   (A) Every morning 每天早上
   (B) Once a week 一週一次
   (C) Once a month 一個月一次
   (D) Twice a month 一個月兩次

解析 (C) 女子提到「the monthly staff meeting」，可知是一個月一次。選項(A)重複了對話中的 morning 這個字。選項(B)重複了 week。選項(D)重複了 month。

5. When will the meeting start? 會議什麼時候開始？
   (A) At 1:00 一點
   (B) At 3:00 三點
   (C) Before lunch 午餐前
   (D) In a couple of hours 兩小時後

解析 (A) 其中一名男子詢問會議幾點開始，女子回答 one，所以是一點。選項 (B) 混淆了近音字 three 和 free。選項 (C) 是其中一名男子希望會議結束的時間。選項 (D) 重複了對話中的 a couple of hours，是會議的持續時間。

6. How long will the meeting last? 會議會持續多久？
   (A) One hour 一小時
   (B) Two hours 兩小時
   (C) Three hours 三小時
   (D) Four hours 四小時

解析 (B) 女子說「It should only last a couple of hours」，就是兩小時。選項 (A) 是和會議的開始時間有所混淆。選項 (C) 混淆了近音字 three 和 free。選項 (D) 混淆了近音字 before 和 four。

高分攻略 5　活動題

Man:　　　Turn left here. I think the movie theater is just up this street.
Woman:　　I can't turn left. This is a one-way street. I knew we should have brought a map. Now we'll get there after the show has started.
Man:　　　We don't need a map. I can find the theater. Just make a left up ahead. We shouldn't have spent so much time in the restaurant.
Woman:　　What did you want me to do? Skip dinner? I was starving.
男：　　　在這裡左轉，我想電影院就在這條街上。
女：　　　這裡是單行道不能左轉。早知道就該帶地圖，這下我們到的時候電影已經開演了。
男：　　　我們不需要地圖，我找得到電影院。前面左轉就對了，剛剛我們不應該在餐廳停留那麼多時間。
女：　　　那你要我怎麼樣？不吃晚餐嗎？我都快餓死了。

1. What are they doing? 他們正在做什麼？
   (A) Taking a walk 散步
   (B) Taking a nap 小睡一會兒
   (C) Buying a map 買地圖
   (D) Driving a car 開車

解析 (D) 請注意像是 turn left（左轉）、one-way street（單行道）、map（地圖）這樣的上下文線索，從這些線索可以判斷是在開車。選項 (A) 和 one-way street 的線索相衝突。選項 (B) 使用了 map 的近音字 nap。選項 (C) 和 should have brought a map（早知道就該帶

地圖）的線索相衝突。

2. What did they do earlier? 他們剛才在做什麼？
(A) Rested 休息
(B) Played in the snow 玩雪
(C) Had dinner 吃晚餐
(D) Rented a movie 租借電影

解析 (C) 男子提到餐廳，女子提到晚餐，由此可知他們剛才吃了晚餐。選項(A)使用了 restaurant 的近音字 rested。選項(B)使用了 show 的近音字 snow。選項(D)使用了 spent 的近音字 rent，並且重複了 movie 這個字。

3. What will they do next? 他們接下來要做什麼？
(A) Read 讀書
(B) Go to bed 睡覺
(C) See a play 看戲劇演出
(D) Go to the movies 看電影

解析 (D) 他們正在尋找電影院，所以是要看電影。選項(A)使用了 need 的近音字 read。選項(B)使用了 ahead 的近音字 bed。選項(C)使用了 theater 的相關字 play。

Man:	I can't get this machine to work.
Woman:	What's the matter? The copies aren't dark enough?
Man:	No, the copies look fine. I just added toner. But the machine is supposed to staple, too. But, look, the copies are all coming out without staples.
Woman:	Oh, how annoying.
Man:	It certainly is. A repair person was in here just last week so everything should be working fine.
Woman:	You should probably report it to the office manager.
Man:	Yes, I suppose I should. I'll have to do it later though, because I think he's out until tomorrow.
Woman:	Oh, too bad.
Man:	That's OK. There's another machine down on the third floor. I'll just go use that one.
男：	我沒辦法讓這臺機器開始運作。
女：	怎麼了？印出來不夠黑嗎？
男：	不是，印出來還好，我剛才加了碳粉。可是這臺機器應該可以自動裝訂，但

	你看，印出來的都沒有裝訂。
女：	噢，這樣真煩。
男：	就是啊。上週才有維修人員來整修過，應該要可以用才對。
女：	你可能要跟辦公室經理報告這件事。
男：	我也認為如此，但要晚點才能報告，因為我想他好像明天才會進辦公室。
女：	真糟糕。
男：	沒關係，三樓還有一臺機器，我去那邊印就好了。

4. What is the man trying to do? 這名男子正嘗試做什麼事？
   (A) Staple copies 裝訂影印文件
   (B) Fix the machine 修理機器
   (C) Make extra copies 多印幾份文件
   (D) Make the copies look darker 讓印出來的文件看起來黑一點

解析 (A) 男子操作機器時發生問題，並說了「But the machine is supposed to staple, too. But, look, the copies are all coming out without staples.」，可見是裝訂上的問題。由於機器運作有問題，選項(B)的確合乎邏輯，但對話中並未提及。選項(C)重複了對話中的copies這個字。選項(D)是女子認為男子想做的事。

5. What does the woman suggest doing? 這名女子建議做什麼？
   (A) Add toner 添加碳粉
   (B) Try again later 等一下再嘗試列印
   (C) Call a repair person 打電話給維修人員
   (D) Report the problem 報告這個問題

解析 (D) 女子說「You should probably report it to the office manager.」，建議呈報問題。選項(A)是男子已經做過的事。選項(B)重複了對話中的later。選項(C)是上週已經做過的事。

6. What will the man do next? 這名男子接下來會做什麼？
   (A) Ask the office manager to do the job 找辦公室經理來做這份工作
   (B) Use another machine 使用另一臺機器
   (C) Do the job tomorrow 明天再做
   (D) Buy a new machine 買一臺新機器

解析 (B) 男子提到還有另外一臺機器，並說「I'll just go use that one.」，所以他會去使用另一臺機器。選項(A)重複了對話中的office manager。選項(C)重複了tomorrow這個字。選項(D)是有此可能，但對話中並未提及。

高分攻略 6 看法題

Man: That speaker was really funny. I've never laughed so hard.
Woman: I know. Where did he get those jokes?
Man: And this hotel is such a great place for a banquet. The food they gave us to eat was fantastic, and I couldn't believe how big the portions were.
Woman: You're right about the food, and the décor is so lovely. But, you know, it's a bit on the expensive side. I'd expected it to be cheaper. I was uncomfortable when I found out the price.

男： 那位講者真有趣，我從沒笑得這麼厲害過。
女： 我知道。他從哪裡找來那些笑話的？
男： 而且這間飯店真是辦宴會的好地方，他們供應的食物太好吃了，我真不敢相信分量這麼大。
女： 沒錯食物好吃，裝潢也很美觀。可是，你知道，這裡的價位有點高，我原本以為會便宜一點，因此看到價錢讓我有點不適應。

1. What did they like about the speaker? 他們喜歡講者哪一點？
    (A) His short presentation 他的簡短演講
    (B) His humor 他的幽默
    (C) His clothes 他的服裝
    (D) His folks 他的親屬

解析 (B) 上下文線索全都指向幽默：funny（有趣）、laughed（大笑）、jokes（玩笑）。但要注意「I've never laughed so hard.」的意思是「我從來沒笑得這麼厲害過」，表示非常好笑而非不好笑。選項(A)使用了speaker的相關字presentation。選項(C)在對話中並未提及。選項(D)混淆了近音字jokes和folks。

2. What is the man's opinion of the hotel? 這名男子對飯店有什麼看法？
    (A) The décor is nice. 裝潢漂亮。
    (B) The food is great. 食物好吃。
    (C) The seats are too hard. 座椅太硬。
    (D) The room is too big. 房間太大。

解析 (B) 男子說了「The food they gave us to eat was fantastic」，表示食物很好吃。選項(A)是女子的看法。選項(C)使用了eat的近音字seats，同時也搞錯了hard的意思。選項(D)不正確，大的是食物分量而不是房間。

3. What does the woman think of the hotel? 這名女子覺得這間飯店如何？
   (A) It's very expensive. 非常昂貴。
   (B) It's cheaper than she expected. 比她想的便宜。
   (C) The tables are nice. 桌子不錯。
   (D) It's uncomfortable. 不舒服。

解析 (A) 女子說「it's a bit on the expensive side」，表示偏貴了。選項(B)搞錯了「I'd expected it to be cheaper.」這句話的意思。選項(C)使用了兩個近音字tables/uncomfortable和nice/price。選項(D)是女子對價位的感受，不是對飯店的感受。

Woman 1: Well, that meeting certainly wasn't too long.
Woman 2: No, it wasn't. The new director definitely knows how to run a meeting. Everything was so well organized.
Man: Yes, we got a lot of information in a short time. By the way, have either of you had a chance to talk with the new director individually?
Woman 1: Not yet. He's a bit timid, hard to talk to.
Woman 2: He is the quiet type, but seems smart and well-qualified. So, are we all headed to the cafeteria for lunch?
Man: Let's not go there. It's always full of people at lunch time. Let's try that café across the street.
Woman 1: Yes, it's quieter there. It's just as cheap and the food is better.

女1： 嗯，那場會議確實不會太長。
女2： 對，不會。新來的主管非常了解如何主持會議，一切都井井有條。
男： 是的，我們在短時間內獲得很多資訊。對了，你們有機會單獨和新主管說話了嗎？
女1： 還沒。他有點羞怯，跟他講話很難。
女2： 他是比較安靜的類型，不過看起來很聰明，也有充分的資格。所以我們現在要去自助餐廳吃午餐嗎？
男： 我們別去那裡，它午餐時間人都好多。我們去對面的咖啡廳吃吃看。
女1： 對啊，那裡比較安靜。價格一樣便宜，而且食物更棒。

4. What does the man say about the meeting? 這名男子對這場會議有什麼看法？
   (A) It was boring. 很無聊。
   (B) It was too long. 太長了。
   (C) It was informative. 資訊豐富。
   (D) It was disorganized. 雜亂無章。

解析 (C) 男子說「we got a lot of information in a short time」，表示獲得了大量資訊。選項(A)是有可能，但並未提及。選項(B)和(D)和說話者的陳述相反。

5. What is the woman's opinion of the new director? 女子對新主管有什麼看法？
   (A) He is not qualified for the job. 他不夠資格勝任這份工作。
   (B) He is always busy. 他總是很忙。
   (C) He is talkative. 他很健談。
   (D) He is shy. 他很害羞。

解析 (D) 女子們說「He's a bit timid, hard to talk to.」，還說「He is the quiet type」，都可以判斷新主管個性比較害羞。選項(A)和(C)與她們所說的恰好相反。選項(B)是有可能，但並未提及。

6. What does the man think of the cafeteria? 這名男子覺得自助餐廳怎麼樣？
   (A) It has better food. 食物比較好。
   (B) It is inexpensive. 不太貴。
   (C) It is too crowded. 人太多。
   (D) It is quiet. 很安靜。

解析 (C) 男子評論自助餐廳時說「It's always full of people at lunch time.」，可見他覺得那邊人太多。選項(A)(B)(D)是女子對咖啡廳的看法。

高分攻略 7　圖表題

Number 1

Woman:　Today's Monday, isn't it?
Man:　　Yes. Why?
Woman:　Because Jim's at the reception desk. I'm looking at the schedule, and it says that Sue should be covering reception today.
Man:　　Right. But she was needed to help out with setting up for this afternoon's meeting, so she asked Jim to cover the desk for her.
Woman:　Oh. So, then Sue will work the reception desk on Jim's scheduled day?
Man:　　Right.

Look at the graphic. When will Sue work at the reception desk?

女　　今天是星期一，對嗎？
男　　對啊，為何這樣問？
女　　因為吉姆在接待櫃檯。我看班表上寫今天應該是蘇負責接待櫃檯。

男	沒錯,但是今天下午的會議需要她幫忙布置,所以她請吉姆幫她顧櫃檯。
女	喔。所以,吉姆的值班日就換成蘇去顧接待櫃檯嗎?
男	沒錯。

請看圖表,蘇會在何時負責接待櫃檯的工作?

(A) Monday 星期一
(B) Tuesday 星期二
(C) Wednesday 星期三
(D) Thursday 星期四

接待櫃檯排班表	
星期一	蘇
星期二	山姆
星期三	比爾
星期四	吉姆
星期五	未定

解析 (D) 從對話中可判斷蘇會在吉姆的值班日負責接待櫃檯的工作,吉姆的值班日是星期四。選項(A)是蘇原定的值班日,但吉姆已替她值班了。選項(B)和(C)都是別人的值班日。

Number 2

Woman: We need a new printer. The one we have has completely stopped working.
Man: I'm sorry, but we're already over budget for office supplies.
Woman: I know. But we can't do anything without a printer. We have to have one that works.
Man: Of course, you're right. I guess we could come up with a little money. So, OK, get the new printer, but I can only authorize a hundred fifty dollars. Don't spend any more than that.

Look at the graphic. Which printer will the woman buy?

女	我們需要一臺新的印表機,現在這臺已經完全不能用了。
男	很抱歉,但我們辦公用品的預算已經超支了。
女	我知道,可是沒有印表機,我們什麼都不能做,一定要有一臺能用的。
男	當然,你說得對。我想應該可以挪出一點錢來。好吧,可以買新印表機,但是我

只能核准一百五十美元,不能花超過這個數目。

請看圖表,這名女子會買哪一臺印表機?

(A) Model XX 型號 XX
(B) Model XZ 型號 XZ
(C) Model Y 型號 Y
(D) Model WY 型號 WY

印表機型號	售價
型號 XX	$115
型號 XZ	$155
型號 Y	$175
型號 WY	$225

解析 **(A)** 男子說不可以花超過一百五十美金,選項 (A) 是唯一低於這個價錢的型號。選項 (B)(C)(D) 都超過了男子核准的預算。

Number 3

Man: We really made the right decision when we hired Mr. Kim to be the new marketing manager.

Woman: Oh, yes. He's really turned things around.

Man: And so fast. The month after we hired him, sales were up for the first time all year.

Woman: I know. It's truly amazing. And the new advertising campaign he plans to launch next month should be very effective, too.

Look at the graphic. When was Mr. Kim hired?

男　　我們聘請金先生擔任新的行銷經理真是正確的決定。
女　　喔,沒錯。他真的扭轉了局面。
男　　而且十分快速。我們聘請他才一個月,銷售量於全年首度上升。
女　　我知道,真是太神奇了。他計劃下個月推出的新廣告活動應該也會非常有效。

請看圖表,金先生是何時被聘用的?

(A) February 二月

(B) March 三月
(C) April 四月
(D) May 五月

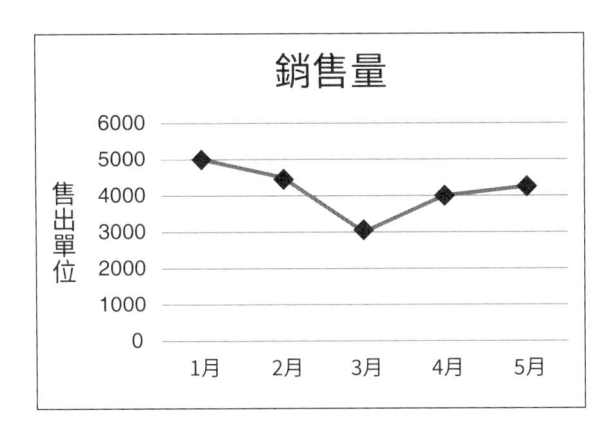

銷售量

月份	售出單位
1月	5000
2月	4500
3月	3000
4月	4000
5月	4300

解析 **(B)** 男子說「The month after we hired him, sales were up for the first time all year.」，表示聘請金先生一個月後銷售量首度上升，從圖表可看出四月銷售開始上升，而四月的前一個月就是三月。選項(A)(C)(D)都和男子的陳述不符。

Number 4

Man: Here's the agenda for this afternoon's meeting.
Woman: Great. Oh, there's a problem.
Man: Really? What?
Woman: Robert's going to be a bit late, so we'll need to put his presentation last and start the meeting off with Maya's report. Can you fix that?
Man: Sure. No problem. I'll change that and then make copies for everyone.

Look at the graphic. What topic will be discussed first at the meeting?

男　　這是下午會議的議程表。
女　　好。噢，有個問題。
男　　真的嗎？什麼問題？
女　　羅伯特會晚一點到，所以我們需要把他的報告排在最後，讓瑪雅的報告做會議開場。你可以改一下嗎？
男　　當然，沒問題。我會修改好後印給大家。

請看圖表，這場會議會先討論哪一個主題？

(A) Budget Report 預算報告

041

(B) Sales Update 銷售情況更新
(C) New Ad Campaign 新廣告活動
(D) Hiring Update 招聘進度更新

```
            員工會議
         1月12日下午2點

   預算報告 ............ 羅伯特・法蘭克斯
   銷售情況更新 ........ 瑪雅・羅培茲
   新廣告活動 .......... 蘇・林
   招聘進度更新 ........ 班・英葛倫
```

解析 (B) 女子要男子調整議程表，將羅伯特的報告排在最後，讓瑪雅第一個報告，表中顯示瑪雅的報告主題是 Sales update。選項 (A) 是議程表上原定第一個報告的主題。選項 (C) 和 (D) 是安排在 Sales update 之後的報告主題。

Number 5

Woman: Do you want to meet for lunch tomorrow?
Man: Sure. How about that new place at the Downtown Shopping Mall?
Woman: Do you mean the Garden Café? The one next to the shoe store?
Man: Yes, the Garden Café, but it's not by the shoe store. It's across from the bookstore.
Woman: I know the place. I'll meet you there at twelve thirty.

Look at the graphic. Where will they meet for lunch?

女　　你明天要一起吃午餐嗎？
男　　好啊。去市區購物中心那間新開的餐廳如何？
女　　你是說花園咖啡館嗎？鞋店旁邊那家？
男　　對，花園咖啡館，但是它不在鞋店旁邊，是在書店對面。
女　　我知道那個地方，我們十二點半在那裡碰面。

請看圖表，他們會在哪裡碰面吃午餐？

(A) Location A 位置 A
(B) Location B 位置 B
(C) Location C 位置 C
(D) Location D 位置 D

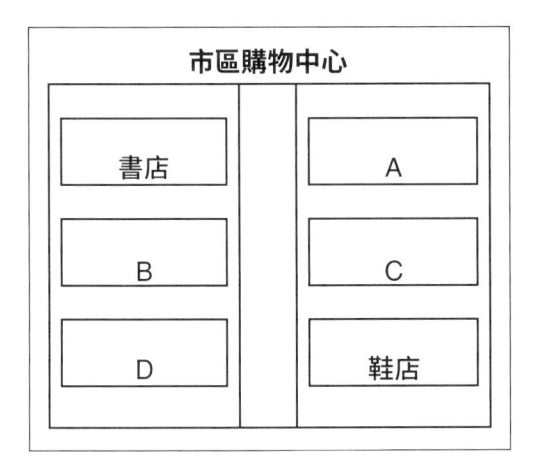

```
┌─────────────────────────────┐
│        市區購物中心          │
│  ┌───────┐   ┌───────┐      │
│  │ 書店  │   │   A   │      │
│  └───────┘   └───────┘      │
│  ┌───────┐   ┌───────┐      │
│  │   B   │   │   C   │      │
│  └───────┘   └───────┘      │
│  ┌───────┐   ┌───────┐      │
│  │   D   │   │ 鞋店  │      │
│  └───────┘   └───────┘      │
└─────────────────────────────┘
```

解析 (A) 男子說咖啡館位在書店對面，所以是 A 的位置。選項 (B)(C)(D) 都不符合男子的描述。

高分攻略 8　情境意義

Number 1

Woman:　　Why are you at the office so late?
Man:　　　I have to have this project finished soon.
Woman:　　I wouldn't do it like that. It will take you forever to finish.
女：　　　這麼晚了你怎麼還在辦公室？
男：　　　我必須趕快把這個計畫完成。
女：　　　我不會用那種方式做，這樣永遠做不完的。

1. What does the woman mean when she says, "I wouldn't do it like that"?
   這名女子說「I wouldn't do it like that.」是什麼意思？
   (A) The woman thinks the man is working inefficiently.
   這名女子認為男子工作沒效率。
   (B) The woman thinks the man is working too hard.
   這名女子認為男子工作太認真。

043

解析 (A) 女子批評男子的工作方式，認為會花更長的時間完成工作，也就是說他工作沒效率。

Number 2

Woman:	How's your job hunt going? I heard it was very slow for a while.
Man:	Yes, but things have picked up. In fact, I have a job interview tomorrow.
Woman:	Oh, I'm glad to hear that.
女：	你工作找得如何了？聽說有一段時間進度很慢。
男：	對啊，但情況已經好轉了。事實上，我明天有個工作面試。
女：	喔，太好了。

2. What does the man mean when he says, "Things have picked up"?
   這名男子說「Things have picked up.」是什麼意思？
   (A) He got a promotion. 他升職了。
   (B) He is feeling optimistic. 他感到樂觀。

解析 (B) 男子說「things have picked up」，意思是事情正在好轉，此外他也排定了一次工作面試，所以他必定感到非常樂觀。

Number 3

Woman:	They're almost done with the redecorating. What do you think of the new look?
Man:	Well, I wonder who chose that new carpet in the front office. I mean, that color!
Woman:	I know. It's certainly not one that would be at the top of my list.
女：	他們快要重新裝潢好了，你覺得新的樣貌如何？
男：	嗯，不知道前面辦公室的地毯是誰選的，我的意思是，看看那個顏色！
女：	我知道。那個顏色肯定不是我的首選。

3. What does the man mean when he says, "that color"?
   這名男子說「that color」是什麼意思？
   (A) He likes the color of the carpet. 他喜歡地毯的顏色。
   (B) He does not like the color of the carpet. 他不喜歡地毯的顏色。

解析 (B) 男子先是質疑到底誰選的地毯，接著又說「I mean, that color!」，暗示了他不滿意地毯的顏色。而女子回應說這個顏色「not one that would be at the top of my list」，表示不會是她的首選。由於女子並不喜歡這個顏色，不僅不是首選，或說不定根本不會考慮。從女子的附和也可判斷男子不喜歡地毯顏色。

Number 4

Woman: I thought that meeting would never end.
Man: I know what you mean. I almost fell asleep in the middle of it.
Woman: Looks like it's time for a coffee break!
女： 我以為那場會議會開到天荒地老。
男： 我懂你的意思，會議到一半我就快睡著了。
女： 看來該去喝杯咖啡休息了！

4. What does the woman mean when she says, "I thought that meeting would never end"?
   這名女子說「I thought that meeting would never end」是什麼意思？
   (A) The meeting was boring. 會議很無聊。
   (B) The meeting was canceled. 會議被取消了。

解析 (A) 從女子的陳述可判斷會議太過無聊以至於感覺十分漫長，而從男子的陳述也可看出他無聊到快睡著了。

Number 5

Man: This report is going to need a lot of editing, and we need it ready for the meeting tomorrow.
Woman: Don't worry. I'm on top of it.
Man: OK. I'm counting on you.
男： 這份報告還有很多地方要修改，而且明天早上開會就要準備好。
女： 別擔心，一切都在我的掌握之中。
男： 好，我就靠你了。

5. What does the woman mean when she says, "I'm on top of it"?
   這名女子說「I'm on top of it.」是什麼意思？
   (A) The woman is aware of the work schedule. 女子知道工作進度。
   (B) The woman is confident she can finish the work on time. 女子有信心準時完成工作。

解析 (B)「to be on top of something」意思是「掌握了某件事」，表示女子認為她可以在僅有的時間內完成工作。

045

高分攻略 9　簡略回答

1. Woman: So, the meeting day has been changed to Friday?
   Man: Right.
   女：所以說，開會日改到星期五了？
   男：對。

   (A) It's on the right. 在右邊。
   (B) You are correct. 你說得沒錯。

   解析 (B)「Right.」在這裡意指「正確的」，男子確認女子正確理解他前面說的話。

2. Man: Let's take a break now and finish this later.
   Woman: Fine with me.
   男：我們休息一下，待會再完成吧。
   女：我可以啊。

   (A) I agree with your plan. 我同意你的計畫。
   (B) That's a bad idea. 這個想法很糟糕。

   解析 (A) 這句的完整回應是「It's fine with me.」，fine 在這裡意指「可以、好」。

3. Woman: Please make ten copies of this report, leave one on my desk, and send the rest to Mr. Sato.
   Man: Got it.
   女：請把這份報告印十份，一份放我桌上，剩下的送去給佐藤先生。
   男：知道了。

   (A) I have Mr. Sato's address. 我有佐藤先生的地址。
   (B) I understand everything you want me to do. 我明白你要我做的事。

   解析 (B) get 在這裡的意思是「理解、知道」。男子對女子確認自己明白了，並已記下她的要求。

4. Man: We're having lunch at Café de Oro. Will you join us?
   Woman: Wish I could.
   男：我們要去金色咖啡館吃午餐，你要一起嗎？
   女：我也想啊。

   (A) I would like to join you, but I can't. 我想跟你們一起去，但我不能。
   (B) I have always wanted to eat at that café. 我一直想去那間咖啡館吃飯。

   解析 **(A)**「Wish I could.」的完整說法是「I wish I could join you.」，意指我也想跟你們去，但我無法。

5. Woman: Ms. Chang is in a meeting and can't see you now.
   Man: Too bad.
   女：張小姐正在開會，現在沒辦法見你。
   男：好可惜。

   (A) The meeting is a bad idea. 開這個會議是壞主意。
   (B) I'm sorry she can't see me. 可惜她不能見我。

   解析 **(B)**「Too bad.」的完整說法是「That's too bad.」，常用來表達遺憾。這名男子對於張小姐正在忙而無法接見他感到遺憾。

047

Part 4 簡短獨白

高分攻略 1　活動與事實題

Everyone in town is getting ready for the big event of the year—our annual celebration of National Day is this weekend, with activities for everyone Friday through Sunday. The event kicks off with a parade downtown on Friday evening. All day Saturday, the Main Street Food Fair will give you a chance to taste international cuisine from all over the world, and there will be a circus at City Park in the afternoon. Large crowds are expected to show up for the concert at City Conference Center on Saturday evening. Tickets are selling fast, so buy yours now. At the same time, you can book seats for Sunday's basketball tournament at City Arena. This is an event you do not want to miss as our own city mayor will be participating. So come on out and celebrate. A good time is guaranteed to be had by all.

城裡的每個人都已經準備好迎接這場年度盛會——一年一度的國慶慶祝活動即將在本週末登場，從週五到週日會舉辦各種活動，人人都可參加。這場盛會將在週五晚間以市區遊行揭開序幕。週六一整天，主街美食博覽會讓您得以一嘗來自世界各地的各國佳餚，而下午在城市公園則有一場馬戲表演。週六晚間在城市會議中心的演奏會預期將吸引大批人潮，門票熱賣中，請即刻購票。同時，週日在城市體育館舉行的籃球錦標賽也可以訂票選位了，我們市長會親自參與千萬不要錯過。大家一起出來慶祝，保證人人都可以玩得開心。

1. What event will take place this weekend? 這個週末將舉辦什麼活動？
   (A) A book fair 書展
   (B) A conference 會議
   (C) A national celebration 國慶慶祝活動
   (D) An international dance 國際舞蹈節

   解析 (C) 說話者提到「our annual celebration of National Day is this weekend」，故知將舉辦國慶祝活動。選項(A)誤解了book的意思，獨白中的book意指「預訂」（如：book your ticket 訂票），而不是書籍，同時也重複使用fair這個字（獨白中是food fair）。選項(B)被獨白中提到City Conference Center給誤導了。選項(D)重複使用international這個字（獨白中為international cuisine），同時也混淆了近音字dance和chance。

048

2. What will happen on Saturday evening? 週六晚間有什麼活動？
   (A) A parade 遊行
   (B) A food sale 美食特賣
   (C) A concert 演奏會
   (D) A circus performance 馬戲表演

   解析 (C) 說話者提到週六晚上在城市會議中心有一場演奏會。選項(A)不正確，因為遊行是在週五晚間舉行。選項(B)和(D)不正確，兩個活動雖然都是週六舉行，卻是在白天，不是晚上。

3. What will the mayor do on Sunday? 週日市長會做什麼？
   (A) Sell tickets 賣票
   (B) Address the crowds 向群眾發表演說
   (C) Play basketball 打籃球
   (D) Buy some baskets 買一些籃子

   解析 (C) 市長會參與週日晚上的籃球錦標賽，所以是打籃球。選項(A)重複了對話中的 tickets。選項(B)重複了 crowds。選項(D)混淆了 basketball 和 baskets 兩個近音字。

Hi, it's Sarah. I'm having a small get-together on Saturday, and I hope you can come. It's to celebrate my nephew's graduation from high school. He graduated top of his class and won some awards, and we're all so proud of him. He has, however, insisted on a quiet gathering, so we'll just have dinner and conversation, and it won't be a late evening because my nephew is starting his summer job the next morning. And speaking of that, I'll be at the club Sunday morning playing tennis with some friends, and I hope you can join us. It's been a long time since we've seen you there. OK, talk to you later.

嗨，我是莎拉，週六我要舉辦一場小型聚會，希望各位能共襄盛舉。這場聚會是為了慶祝我姪子高中畢業，他以全班第一名的成績畢業，也得了一些獎項，我們都以他為榮。不過他堅持要低調聚會，所們我們就只會吃個飯、聊聊天不會到太晚，因為他隔天早上就要開始暑期打工。說到這個，我週日早上會跟一些朋友到俱樂部打網球，希望大家一起來，我們好久沒在那裡碰面了。好的，之後再聊。

049

4．What event is the speaker celebrating? 說話者要慶祝什麼？
(A) A birthday 生日
(B) A graduation 畢業
(C) A retirement 退休
(D) A job promotion 升職

解析 **(B)** 說話者表示她要「celebrate my nephew's graduation from high school」，慶祝姪子高中畢業。選項(A)和(C)也是人們經常慶祝的事，但獨白中並未提及。選項(D)重複使用了獨白中的job這個字。

5．What will guests do at the celebration? 賓客在慶祝會上要做什麼？
(A) Dance 跳舞
(B) Play games 玩遊戲
(C) Enjoy a meal 用餐
(D) Receive awards 領獎

解析 **(C)** 說話者提到dinner，可以知道他們會用餐。選項(B)重複了獨白中的play。選項(D)重複了awards這個字。

6．What will the speaker do on Sunday? 說話者週日要做什麼？
(A) Take a walk 散步
(B) Play tennis 打網球
(C) Get up late 晚點起床
(D) Go to work 上班

解析 **(B)** 說話者講了「I'll be at the club Sunday morning playing tennis」，所以是打網球。選項(A)混淆了近音字walk和talk。選項(C)重複了獨白中的late這個字。選項(D)使用了job的相關字work。

高分攻略 2 原因題

Because of a work slowdown, all flights will be delayed. We apologize to our passengers for the inconvenience and hope to have them on their way as soon as possible. In the meantime, there are several restaurants in the airport if you would like some refreshments while waiting for your flight. We suggest that you take advantage of them now, as all airport restaurants will close at midnight and won't reopen until tomorrow morning at six. At this time we are unable to say when each flight will leave. If you leave the gate area, please pay careful attention to the announcements so that you can hear when your flight is ready for boarding.

由於怠工問題，所有航班都將延誤。造成乘客不便，我們深表歉意，並期待員工盡快返回工作崗位。在此期間，等待航班的同時若您需要享用茶點，機場有數間餐廳提供服務。由於機場餐廳只營業到晚間十二點，直到明天早上六點才會開始營業，我們建議您利用現在這段時間前往用餐。此刻我們無法提供各航班的起飛時間，若您離開登機口區域，請留意機場廣播，以便得知您的班機何時可以登機。

1. Why is there a delay? 為何發生延誤？
    (A) Workers are staging a work action. 員工正發起勞工抗議行動。
    (B) The weather is bad. 天候不佳。
    (C) There are flight control problems. 航班管制出現問題。
    (D) Passengers are boarding slowly. 乘客登機速度緩慢。

解析 (A) 怠工（work slowdown）是一種勞工抗議行動，類似於罷工，唯獨員工仍現身職場，只是降低工作速度。選項(B)(C)(D)都沒有在獨白中提及。

2. Why should passengers get something to eat now? 為何乘客應該現在就去用餐？
    (A) The restaurants will close at midnight. 餐廳將於晚間十二點打烊。
    (B) The restaurants won't be open tomorrow. 餐廳明天不會營業。
    (C) There will be no food served on the flight. 班機上不提供餐飲。
    (D) There are some restaurants close to the gate. 登機口附近有幾間餐廳。

解析 (A) 播報員建議大家即刻去用餐，因為餐廳半夜十二點就會打烊。選項(B)是搞錯了「won't reopen until tomorrow morning」的意思。選項(C)重複使用了獨白中的flight，但獨白中並未提及飛機上是否供餐。選項(D)混淆了一字多義的close（靠近）和close（關閉）。

3. Why should passengers pay attention to the announcements? 為何乘客要留意機場廣播？
   (A) To find out which gate their flight will leave from 以便得知班機從哪一個登機口起飛
   (B) To hear which restaurants are open 以便聽到哪些餐廳有營業
   (C) To keep from getting bored 以免感到無聊
   (D) To know when it is time to board the flight 以便知道何時可以登機

解析 **(D)** 播報員建議大家仔細聽廣播，才不會錯過班機的登機時間。選項(A)重複了廣播中的gate。選項(B)重複了restaurants。選項(C)使用了board的近音字bored。

Hi. This is Tom Brown calling. I have a two o'clock appointment this afternoon with Mr. Wilson to go over some papers but, unfortunately, I won't be able to make it, as I have an emergency meeting. I'm sorry, as I know Mr. Wilson has done a lot of preparation for this and I hope we can reschedule soon. I am free any afternoon this week, so please call and let me know what day best suits Mr. Wilson. Don't call me at the office today, as I won't be there. Call my cell phone instead. Thanks.

嗨，我是湯姆·布朗，今天下午兩點和威爾森先生約了一起審閱文件，但不巧的是我有個緊急會議要開，沒辦法過去了。真的很抱歉，我知道威爾森先生為了這次會面做了很多準備，希望我們可以盡快重約時間。這週下午我都有空，麻煩來電告訴我威爾森先生哪一天方便。請不要打我的辦公室電話，我今天不會在那裡，請打我的手機，謝謝！

4. Why does Mr. Brown have an appointment with Mr. Wilson? 布朗先生為何和威爾森先生有約？
   (A) To interview him for a newspaper article 為了寫一篇報導需要採訪他
   (B) To go look at an apartment for rent 為了去看一間出租公寓
   (C) To review some documents 為了審閱一些文件
   (D) To sign some papers 為了簽訂一些文件

解析 **(C)** 布朗先生說他和威爾森先生約了要「go over some papers」，一起看一些文件。選項(A)混淆了近音字newspaper和papers。選項(B)混淆了近音字apartment和appointment。選項(D)重複了留言中的papers這個字。

5. Why does Mr. Brown have to cancel the appointment? 布朗先生為何要取消約會？
   (A) He has to buy a new suit. 他要去買一套新的西裝。
   (B) He has an unexpected meeting. 他突然要開會。
   (C) He has to go to the hospital emergency room. 他要去掛急診。
   (D) He has not had enough time to prepare for the appointment. 他不夠時間準備這次的會面。

解析 (B) 布朗先生說了「I have an emergency meeting」，他有緊急會議要開。選項 (A) 重複使用了 suit 這個字，但取其另一個意義。選項 (C) 重複了 emergency 這個字。選項 (D) 使用了 preparation 的相關字 prepare。

6. Why doesn't Mr. Brown want the listener to call his office number today? 布朗先生為何要聽者今天別打他的辦公室電話？
   (A) He is not at the office today. 他今天不在辦公室。
   (B) His office phone is out of order. 他辦公室的電話壞了。
   (C) He is too busy to answer the phone. 他太忙無法接電話。
   (D) Mr. Wilson has only his cell phone number. 威爾森先生只有他的手機號碼。

解析 (A) 布朗先生說「Don't call me at the office today, as I won't be there.」，所以他不會在辦公室。選項 (B) 和 (C) 雖然有可能，但獨白中並未提及。選項 (D) 重複了獨白中的 cell phone。

高分攻略 3　數字題

Hi John. This is Lee calling. We need to get together soon to make the final plans for the workshop. We only have two days left. Have you seen all the registration forms? I think there will be over thirty participants. That's a lot more than we expected. We'll need to find a larger room, and more tables, too. Do you have time to get together this afternoon to talk over the plans with me? It'll only take fifteen minutes or so, just to decide what each of us needs to do. Call me back and let me know when's a good time for you.

嗨，約翰，我是李。我們需要盡快見面完成工作坊的最終計畫，只剩兩天了。你看過全部的報名表了嗎？我想大約會有超過三十名參加者，比我們預期的還多很多。我們需要找一個更大的地方，桌子也需要增加。你今天下午有沒有空跟我會面，討論這個計畫？只需十五分鐘左右，決定我們彼此的分工就行了。請給我回電，讓我知道你什麼時候方便。

1. When is the workshop? 工作坊是什麼時候？
    (A) Today 今天
    (B) In two days 兩天後
    (C) On Tuesday 週二
    (D) Wednesday 週三

解析 (B) 說話者說「We only have two days left.」，表示距離工作坊只剩兩天。選項(A)和(C)和正確答案的發音相近。選項(D)混淆了近音字Wednesday和when's。

2. How many people will attend the workshop? 有多少人會來參加工作坊？
    (A) 13 十三人
    (B) Almost 30 將近三十人
    (C) Exactly 30 剛好三十人
    (D) More than 30 超過三十人

解析 (D) 說話者說「there will be over thirty participants」，over就等於more than。選項(A)和正確答案的發音相近。選項(B)和(C)都搞錯了over的意思。

3. How long does the speaker want to meet with John? 說話者希望和約翰見面多久？
    (A) 15 minutes 十五分鐘
    (B) 50 minutes 五十分鐘
    (C) 30 minutes 三十分鐘
    (D) 2 hours 兩小時

解析 (A) 說話者先提議和約翰見面，接著說「It'll only take fifteen minutes」，所以是十五分鐘。選項(B)和正確答案的發音相近。選項(C)把工作坊的參加人數誤解成時間了。選項(D)混淆了近音字two和to。

Good evening and welcome to our program. We will be ready to begin in just a few minutes. Tonight's topic is preserving the rainforests and the program is scheduled to go from seven o'clock until nine thirty. In that time, we will have a presentation from each of our five speakers, who will then take questions after all of them have had a chance to talk. So please hold your questions until then, there will be plenty of time to ask them. Next month's program will focus on the environmental impact of mountaineering. Remember, all our programs are free of charge, but we do accept donations. You can leave your donations in the box by the door.

各位晚安，歡迎參加我們的講座。講座將於幾分鐘後開始，今晚的主題是保育雨林，本講座預計從七點進行到九點半。期間將由五位講者分別發表演說，所有講者都發言過後，會

接受大家的提問。請各位先保留問題，屆時會有充分時間可以發問。下個月的講座重點是登山活動造成的環境影響。請記住，我們的講座全部都免費參加，但有接受捐款，大家可以將捐款投入門口的箱子內。

4. What time is the program scheduled to start? 講座預計幾點開始？
   (A) 2:00 兩點
   (B) 7:00 七點
   (C) 9:00 九點
   (D) 10:00 十點

解析 (B) 說話者說「the program is scheduled to go from seven o'clock until nine thirty」，所以是七點開始。選項(A)混淆了近音字two和獨白中的few（in just a few minutes）。選項(C)的發音和9:30相近。選項(D)混淆了近音字ten和獨白中的then。

5. How many people will give presentations? 有多少人會進行演講？
   (A) 5 五人
   (B) 11 十一人
   (C) 13 十三人
   (D) 30 三十人

解析 (A) 說話者說「we will have a presentation from each of our five speakers」，所以是五人。選項(B)混淆了近音字eleven和seven。選項(C)混淆了近音字thirteen和thirty。選項(D)重複使用了thirty這個字。

6. How much does admission to the program cost? 這個講座的入場費是多少？
   (A) $0 零元
   (B) $3 三元
   (C) $4 四元
   (D) $20 二十元

解析 (A) 說話者說「all our programs are free of charge」，也就是免費。選項(B)混淆了近音字three和free。選項(C)混淆了近音字four和獨白中的door。選項(D)混淆了近音字twenty和獨白中的plenty。

高分攻略 4　　主題和目的題

I regret to announce that as of this afternoon I will no longer serve as your Managing Director. The Board of Directors asked me to submit my letter of resignation and I have done so. They told me to leave by the close of business today. I want to thank you for the privilege of having worked with you all. I would also like to express my heartfelt gratitude for the support that many of you have given me during this difficult time, and for all your expressions of concern. I plan to take the next few weeks to rest, then I am hoping to open up a consulting business, as several of my colleagues have encouraged me to do.

很遺憾要向大家宣布一件事，今天下午我將不再擔任各位的總經理。董事會要求我提出辭呈，我也這麼做了。他們要我今天下班前離開。我要向各位致上謝意，很榮幸能與各位共事。在這段困難時期你們許多人給予我支持與關心，我要表示衷心感謝。接下來這幾個星期我打算休息一下，然後希望能開一間諮商公司，因一些同事也鼓勵我這麼做。

1. What changes are taking place in the company? 這間公司正歷經什麼改變？
    (A) The Board of Directors resigned. 董事會請辭。
    (B) The managing director was fired. 總經理被解僱。
    (C) The workers went on strike. 員工進行罷工。
    (D) All letters will be sent by computer. 所有信件將由電腦寄出。

解析 (B) 片語「asked me to submit my letter of resignation」（要我提辭呈）和「told me to leave by the close of business today」（要我下班前離開）都指出這位總經理被公司解僱了。選項(A)重複了獨白中的 Board of Directors，亦使用 resignation 的相關字 resigned。選項(C)並未被提及。選項(D)重複了獨白中的 letter 這個字。

2. Who is the speaker addressing? 說話者在對誰說話？
    (A) Some clients 一些客戶
    (B) His coworkers 他的同事
    (C) A server 一位服務生
    (D) The director 主管

解析 (B) 說話者說「I will no longer serve as your Managing Director」，可以知道他正在對他的下屬說話。選項(A)使用了 business 的相關字 clients。選項(C)搞錯了 serve 的意思。選項(D)是說話者自己的職位。

3. What does the speaker plan to do soon? 說話者不久後打算做什麼？
   (A) Become a clothes salesman 成為服裝銷售員
   (B) Start a business 展開新業務
   (C) Go to college 上大學
   (D) Work as a restaurant manager 擔任餐廳經理

解析 **(B)** 說話者說他希望開啟一個諮詢事業，所以是展開新業務。選項(A)使用了close的同音字clothes。選項(C)使用了colleague的近音字college。選項(D)使用了rest的近音字restaurant，以及managing的相關字manager。

May I have your attention, please? We will be closing in fifteen minutes. Please take your items to be purchased to a cashier now. If you are purchasing ten items or fewer, you may use one of the express checkout lanes. Cash, check, and credit cards are all accepted in the express checkout lanes. As a reminder, our sale continues all week, with manager's specials throughout the store, so see you tomorrow! And thank you for shopping with us.

各位來賓請注意，我們即將於十五分鐘後結束營業，請立即攜帶欲購買之商品前往結帳櫃檯。若您購買的商品在十件以下，請利用快速結帳通道，快速結帳通道接受現金、支票和信用卡支付。在此提醒，我們的特賣活動將持續一整週，全店有多款店長推薦的特惠商品，那麼明天見！感謝您蒞臨購物。

4. Where would you hear this announcement? 你會在哪裡聽到這則廣播？
   (A) In a store 商店
   (B) In a hotel 飯店
   (C) In a restaurant 餐廳
   (D) In a train station 火車站

解析 **(A)** 說話者提到items to be purchased（欲購買之物品）和「manager's specials throughout the store」（店長推薦特惠商品），由此可知這裡是商店。選項(B)使用了checkout的相關字hotel。選項(C)在廣播中並未提及。選項(D)使用了express的相關字train。

5. What is the announcement about? 這則廣播是關於什麼？
   (A) A sale 特賣活動
   (B) How to pay 付款方式
   (C) Job openings 職缺
   (D) Closing time 營業結束時間

解析 (D) 說話者在廣播的一開始就提到「We will be closing in fifteen minutes.」（十五分鐘後將打烊），接著請顧客盡快結帳，所以是在說本日營業結束時間。選項(A)和(B)雖然在廣播中都有提及，但並非廣播的主旨。選項(C)則未被提及。

6. Who is the announcement for? 這段廣播的聽眾是誰？
   (A) All staff 全體職員
   (B) Customers 顧客
   (C) The manager 經理
   (D) Security guards 警衛

解析 (B) 這段廣播是在告訴顧客盡快結帳，因為商店即將打烊。選項(A)和(D)在廣播中並未提及。選項(C)重複了 manager 這個字。

高分攻略 5　改述題

When completing the loan application form, it is important to use black ink, as blue and other colors do not copy well on our machine. We will make four copies, which will be distributed to the departments that will track your loan application. After you have completed the form, please submit it through the postal service. We do not accept e-mailed applications. You will be contacted by each department head individually after they have reviewed your case within two weeks of receipt of the form.

填寫貸款申請表時務必使用黑色墨水，藍色與其他顏色用我們的機器影印效果不好。我們會影印四份，分送給負責追蹤貸款申請的部門。申請表填妥後，請以郵寄方式提交，我們不接受電子郵件申請。各部門主管會在收到申請表後兩週內審查你的案件情況，並個別與你聯繫。

1. What is the purpose of the form? 這份申請表的作用為何？
    (A) To make a complaint 提出客訴
    (B) To borrow money 借錢
    (C) To apply for a job 應徵工作
    (D) To get a license 取得執照

解析 (B) 獨白中說了這份表格是申請貸款之用。選項(A)(C)(D)在獨白中均未提及。

2. How should the form be submitted? 申請表要如何提交？
    (A) By regular mail 以普通郵件寄出
    (B) By email 以電子郵件寄出
    (C) In person 親送
    (D) Through a website 透過網站提交

解析 (A) 說話者說「please submit it through the postal service」，要求以郵寄的方式提交。選項(B)不正確，說話者有提到「We do not accept e-mailed applications.」（不接受電子郵件申請）。選項(C)和(D)雖然有可能，但並未提及。

3. When will the listener be contacted? 聽者何時會被聯繫？
    (A) In two days 兩天內
    (B) In four days 四天內
    (C) In ten days 十天內
    (D) In fourteen days 十四天內

解析 (D) 說話者表示聽者會在兩週內（within two weeks）接到聯繫，兩週就是十四天。選項(A)重複了獨白中的 two。選項(B)的數字是申請表的影印份數。選項(C)使用了 then 的近音字 ten。

Hello. I'm calling from Springfield Furniture Company. The table you ordered has arrived in our warehouse. Our truck will be in your neighborhood on Wednesday and Friday of next week and can drop off the table at your office on either one of those days. We have your address on file, so all you need to do is let me know which day you prefer and whether morning or afternoon is best. Please contact me by phone before Friday, so I can put you on next week's schedule. Thank you for shopping with us.

您好，這裡是春田家具公司，您訂的桌子已經到倉庫了。我們的貨車會在下週三和五經過鄰近您的地區，可以在這兩天的其中一天送桌子到您的辦公室。我們有將您的地址建檔，您只需要讓我知道希望哪一天送貨，以及上午還是下午方便。請於週五前與我電話聯繫，讓我可以將您的出貨排入下週行程表。感謝您的購買。

4． Why did the speaker make the call? 說話者為何打這通電話？
   (A) To arrange for a delivery 安排送貨
   (B) To advertise products 宣傳產品
   (C) To thank the listener 感謝聽者
   (D) To order a table 訂購桌子

   解析 (A) 說話者通知聽者訂購的桌子已經到倉庫了，並表示他們的貨車可以「drop off the table at your office」（送去您的辦公室），drop off 就等於 deliver。選項(B)雖然有可能，但並未提及。選項(C)是說話者在留言結尾時說的話，但並非這通電話的主要目的。選項(D)是聽者已經做的事。

5． What does the speaker say about the listener's address? 說話者提到關於聽者地址的什麼事？
   (A) It is near his office. 很靠近他的辦公室。
   (B) It is difficult to find. 很難找到。
   (C) It is listed in his records. 已列入他的資料紀錄。
   (D) It has changed recently. 最近有變更。

   解析 (C) 說話者說「We have your address on file」，意思就是資料有建檔。選項(A)重複了留言中的 office。選項(B)和(D)都有可能，但並未提及。

6． What does the speaker ask the listener to do? 說話者要聽者做什麼？
   (A) Rent a truck 租貨車
   (B) Call before Friday 週五前回電
   (C) Go to the warehouse 前往倉庫
   (D) Provide a phone number 提供電話號碼

   解析 (B) 說話者說「contact me by phone before Friday」，表示要聽者週五前回電。選項(A)重複了留言中的 truck。選項(C)重複了 warehouse。選項(D)重複了 phone。

高分攻略 6　圖表題

Number 1

Hi, this is Pamela Chang calling to let you know I've finalized the details of my trip. I'll be arriving tomorrow morning by train, and if I could get a ride from the station, that'd be great. My train gets into Springfield Station at just after eleven o'clock. Let me know if you can meet me there. Otherwise, I'll take a cab to your office. I'm looking forward to meeting you. See you tomorrow.

Look at the graphic. Which train will Pamela take?

嗨，我是潘蜜拉・張，我打電話是要告訴你我已經敲定了旅行的細節。我明天早上坐火車到那邊，假如能從車站搭便車就太好了。我的火車會在十一點出頭抵達春田車站。請讓我知道你能否來那裡接我？不然的話，我就搭計程車到你的辦公室。期待與你相會，我們明天見。

請看圖表，潘蜜拉會搭哪一班火車？

(A) 30
(B) 31
(C) 32
(D) 33

火車時刻表

火車編號	自阿爾戴爾發車時間	抵達春田時間
30	5:00 a.m.	7:17
31	6:45	9:02
32	8:45	11:02
33	10:30	12:47

解析　**(C)** 說話者說她的火車「gets into Springfield Station at just after eleven」（十一點出頭到站），表中預定於11:02到站的32號列車符合她的陳述。選項 (A)(B)(D) 中的列車都不在她說的時間抵達。

Number 2

Thank you all for being here at today's meeting. As you know, we need to take a close look at our budget and discuss where we can start cutting back. If you'll look at the chart, you'll see how our dollars were allocated across different categories in the past year. In my view, as we make our plans for the next quarter, the most logical place to start cutting is in the category where the largest percentage of our budget has been spent.

Look at the graphic. Which part of the budget does the speaker want to reduce first?

感謝各位參與今天的會議。如各位所知，我們需要仔細審視我們的預算，討論從哪裡開始削減。從這張圖表可看到過去一年我們的美元分配在不同項目的情況。依我看，制定下一季的計畫時，從預算占比最大的部分開始削減是最合理的。

請看圖表，說話者想從哪一部分的預算開始削減？

(A) Advertising 廣告
(B) Salaries 薪資
(C) Overhead 間接成本
(D) Materials 材料

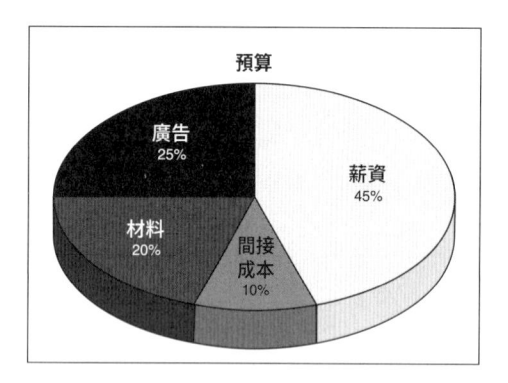

預算
- 廣告 25%
- 薪資 45%
- 材料 20%
- 間接成本 10%

解析 (B) 說話者說「the most logical place to start cutting is in the category where the largest percentage of our budget has been spent」，他想從占比最大的部分開始削減，對照圖表就是 salaries（薪資）這塊，占了所有預算的百分之四十五。選項 (A)(C)(D) 都不符合他的陳述。

Number 3

Welcome to the Hyattsville Public Gardens tour. We'll begin our tour with a stroll through the pine grove, and then continue along the river to the footbridge. After crossing the bridge, we'll stop for lunch just on the other side. Then we will continue our walk along the river and end at the nature center. Please remember to stay with the group at all times. Are there any questions?

Look at the graphic. Where will the group have lunch?

歡迎參加海耶茲維爾公共花園遊覽，我們會先從松林漫步開始，然後沿著河畔走到人行橋，過橋後在對岸吃午餐。接著繼續沿著河畔散步，最後在自然中心結束行程。請大家全程不要脫隊。有沒有任何問題呢？

請看圖表，這群人會在哪裡吃午餐？

(A) Pine Grove 松林
(B) Butterfly Garden 蝶園
(C) Rose Garden 玫瑰花園
(D) Nature Center 自然中心

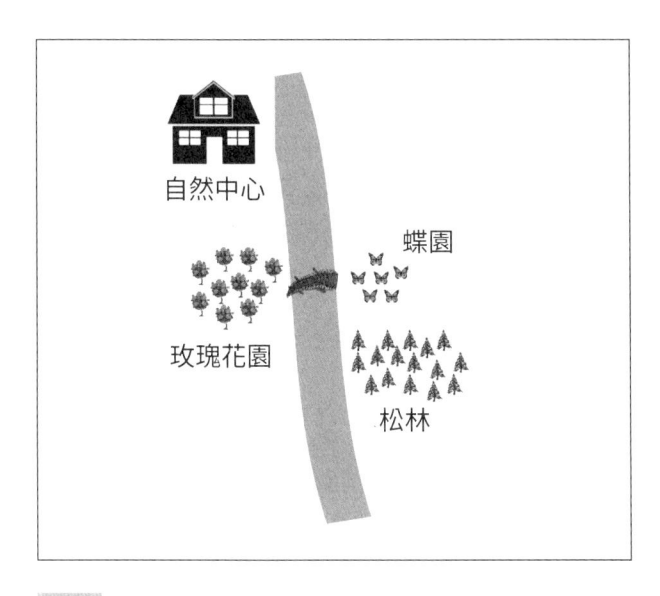

解析 **(C)** 遊覽活動從位於右岸的松園（Pine Grove）出發，說話者說他們過了橋就會停下來吃午餐，看圖就是玫瑰園（Rose Garden）的位置。選項(A)(B)(D)都不在過橋後的位置。

Number 4

Let's take a look at the graph, which shows sales in June and December. As you can see, there was a significant increase in sales in one part of the country. That's exactly the region where we launched our new ad campaign. Now, was this increase a result of the ad campaign only? Or were other factors involved? That is what I want to go over with you today.

Look at the graphic. Which region will the speaker discuss?

請看這張圖表，上面顯示了六月和十二月的銷售情況。大家可以看到國內有一區的銷售大幅增加，正是我們推出新廣告活動的地區。那麼，銷售上升是否僅是廣告活動造成的？還是有受到其他因素影響呢？這是我今天要和大家討論的問題。

請看圖表，說話者將討論的是哪一個地區？

(A) Northwest 西北區
(B) Southwest 西南區
(C) Northeast 東北區
(D) Southeast 東南區

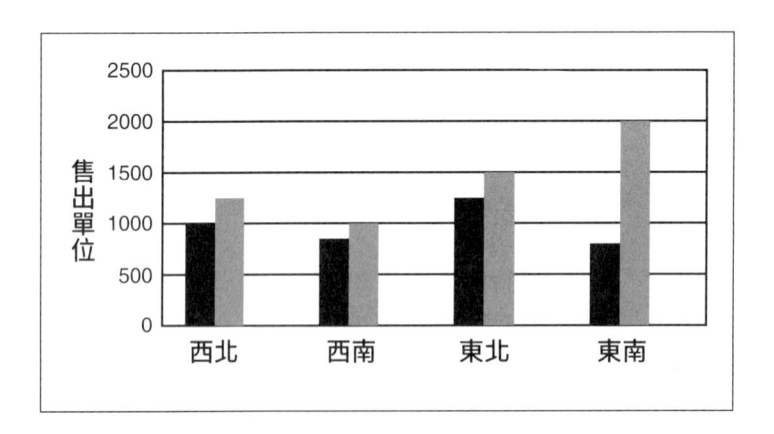

售出單位	西北	西南	東北	東南
六月	1000	850	1250	800
十二月	1250	1000	1500	2000

解析 (D) 說話者提到「a significant increase in sales in one part of the country」，而從圖表中可以看到唯一銷售大幅增加的地區是東南區（Southeast）。選項(A)(B)(C)所指區域都只有小幅增加。

Number 5

Hi, I'm calling about ordering lunch for a workshop we'll be hosting at our office. It's not a large group of people. We're expecting probably ten or twelve people, and certainly no more than fifteen. I'm interested in ordering the cold cuts platter and some sort of simple dessert. We'll provide the tea and coffee ourselves. Please call me back and let me know how much this would cost. Thanks.

Look at the graphic. Which platter will the speaker probably order?

嗨，因為我們要在辦公室舉辦工作坊，所以我打電話來訂午餐。人數不多，大概會有十或十二人，且絕不會超過十五人。我想訂冷盤和一些簡單的甜點。我們自己會提供茶和咖啡。請回電給我，讓我知道要花費多少錢，謝謝！

請看圖表，說話者可能會訂哪一種冷盤？

(A) Small 小
(B) Medium 中
(C) Large 大
(D) Extra Large 特大

金之餐飲
冷盤
小......................十五人份 中......................二十五人份 大......................五十人份 特大...................七十五人份

解析 (A) 說話者預計人數不會超過十五人（no more than fifteen），小份的冷盤剛好可以滿足需求。選項(B)(C)(D)都比較適合更多人享用。

高分攻略 7　**隱含意義題**

Number 1
Hi. This is Timmy Cho. I'm calling to reschedule my appointment yet again. I'm sorry about this, but things just keep coming up. Would next Tuesday at two o'clock be OK?
嗨，我是提米・趙，我打電話來是要再次更改約定時間。很抱歉，可是事情一直出現。請問下週二的兩點鐘可以嗎？

1. What does the speaker say about his appointment?
   關於他的約定，說話者有何表示？

   (A) He has rescheduled this appointment several times already.
      他已經改約好幾次了。
   (B) This is the first time he has rescheduled the appointment.
      這是他第一次改約時間。

解析 (A) 說話者表示他又要「再次」（yet again）改約時間，由此可知他已經不只一次更改時間。

Number 2
This is Marge Smith with the morning weather report. Today we're looking at a high of around twenty-four degrees Celsius, with clear skies and plenty of lovely, warm sunshine. Could we ask for a better day? I don't think so!
我是瑪姬・史密斯，為您帶來晨間氣象報告。本日氣溫最高約攝氏 24 度，晴朗無雲，陽光溫暖普照。還能有比這更好的天氣嗎？我不認為！

2. What does the speaker say about the weather?
   關於天氣，說話者有何表示？

   (A) She wishes it were warmer. 她希望天氣更暖和一些。
   (B) She thinks it is very nice. 她認為天氣非常好。

解析 (B) 說話者說「Could we ask for a better day? I don't think so!」，就是表示天氣好到不得了。

Number 3

To purchase your ticket, first insert your credit card, and then select your destination on the screen. Paying cash? Please approach the ticket office on the other side of the station.
如欲購票,請先插入您的信用卡,接著在螢幕上選擇目的地。想用現金支付?請到車站另一邊的售票處辦理。

3. What does the speaker say about the ticket machine?
   關於售票機,說話者有何表示?

   (A) It accepts both cash and credit cards. 售票機接受付現和刷卡。
   (B) The machine accepts credit cards only. 售票機只接受刷卡。

解析 (B) 說話者建議付現的人到售票處,暗示了售票機不收現金。

Number 4

This is Rita Edwards reporting live from the National Day Celebration at City Stadium. It's only ten a.m. and the place is already mobbed. It looks like we're going to have a huge turnout, certainly much more than we had a year ago.
我是莉塔‧愛德華茲,在城市體育場的國慶慶典進行現場報導。現在才上午十點,現場已經人滿為患。看來這次的出席人數極高,肯定比去年人潮還多很多。

4. What does the speaker say about the celebration?
   關於這場慶典,說話者有何表示?

   (A) The event is more crowded than it was last year.
       這場活動比去年人潮更擁擠。
   (B) The stadium isn't big enough to hold the crowds.
       這座體育場不夠大,不足以容納人潮。

解析 (A) 說話者說到「It looks like we're going to have a huge turnout」,a huge turnout 意思就是人潮眾多、出席人數極高。

Number 5

The ticket booth is now open. Please line up over here to buy tickets. Please have your membership card ready to show the ticket seller. We regret that tickets cannot be sold to non-cardholders.
售票亭現已開放,請到這裡排隊購票。請準備好您的會員卡,向售票人員出示卡片。很抱歉,無持卡者無法購票。

5. What does the speaker say about the tickets?
   關於門票,說話者有何表示?

   (A) They are discounted for members. 會員享有優惠。
   (B) They are available to members only. 僅販售給會員。

解析 (B) 說話者表示排隊者應向售票人員出示會員卡,接著說「tickets cannot be sold to non-cardholders」(不販售給無持卡者),意思就是不販售給非會員。

高分攻略 8　口音題

Number 1

Good evening and welcome to tonight's presentation. We are very excited to have with us tonight a world-famous journalist. I am sure you will enjoy his talk very much.
晚安,歡迎各蒞臨今晚的演講。今晚,我們很高興請到世界知名記者為我們演講,相信各位一定會非常喜歡他的演講。

Number 2

Here is the weather outlook for the weekend. We will have cloudy skies all day Saturday. Expect rain to begin late Saturday evening and continue through Sunday morning. The rain will clear up on Sunday afternoon.
以下是週末氣象預報。週六整日多雲,預計深夜開始下雨並持續至週日早上,週日下午天氣將會放晴。

Number 3

Thank you for calling the Acme Company. We value your call. To check your order status, press one. For shipping information, press two. To speak with a customer service representative, press three. To repeat this menu, press four.
感謝您致電艾克美公司,我們十分重視您的來電。查詢訂單狀態請按1,出貨資訊請按2,欲和客服人員對話請按3,重聽請按4。

Number 4

Attention shoppers. We will be closing the store in ten minutes. Please take your purchases to the checkout area at this time. If you are purchasing ten items or fewer, you may use the express checkout lane.

各位顧客請注意,本店營業時間將於十分鐘後結束。請即刻帶著您的採購物品至結帳區,若您購買的物品在十件以下可利用快速結帳通道。

Number 5

The tour will begin in just a few minutes. Please line up by the main entrance. If you don't have a ticket, you can purchase one in the gift shop.

再過幾分鐘導覽即將開始,請在主入口處排隊。若您還沒有門票,可至禮品店購買。

聽力診斷測驗解答

Part 1 照片描述

1. **B**   2. **C**   3. **A**   4. **D**

Part 2 應答問題

5. **B**   8. **C**   11. **A**   14. **C**
6. **A**   9. **B**   12. **C**   15. **B**
7. **A**   10. **b**   13. **A**   16. **A**

Part 3 簡短對話

17. **C**   22. **B**   27. **C**   32. **C**
18. **A**   23. **A**   28. **B**   33. **D**
19. **D**   24. **C**   29. **B**   34. **B**
20. **A**   25. **D**   30. **D**
21. **B**   26. **A**   31. **C**

Part 4 簡短獨白

35. **C**   39. **A**   43. **C**   47. **C**
36. **A**   40. **B**   44. **B**   48. **B**
37. **C**   41. **D**   45. **B**   49. **A**
38. **D**   42. **C**   46. **C**

聽力診斷測驗解析&錄音稿

Mini-Test for Listening Comprehension 聽力診斷測驗

Part 1 : Photographs 照片描述

> DIRECTIONS : You will see a photograph. You will hear four statements about the photograph. Choose the statement that most closely matches the photograph, and fill in the corresponding oval on your answer sheet.
> 作答方式：你會看到一張照片，並聽到四個關於這張照片的陳述。選出最符合照片內容的陳述，將答案卡上對應的橢圓框塗滿。

1. Look at the photo marked number 1 in your test book.
   (A) The doctor is hanging up his coat.
   (B) The pharmacist is speaking with a customer.
   (C) The cook is opening a bottle.
   (D) The farmer is selling his products.
   請看試題本上標示為1的照片。
   (A) 醫師正在掛他的外套。
   (B) 藥師正在和一位客人說話。
   (C) 廚師正在打開一個瓶子。
   (D) 農夫正在販售他的產品。

   解析 (B) 照片中，一名身穿白袍、手裡拿著藥罐的藥師正在和客人說話。選項(A)不正確，這名男子的外套穿在身上，不是正在掛外套。選項(C)正確提到了瓶子，但男子並沒有開瓶的動作，且他看起來也不像廚師。選項(D)混淆了近音字 pharmacist 和 farmer。

2. Look at the photo marked number 2 in your test book.
   (A) The eggs are on the stove.
   (B) The pencil is in the drawer.
   (C) The book is between the bowls.
   (D) The flowers are in the bowl.
   請看試題本上標示為2的照片。
   (A) 蛋在火爐上。
   (B) 鉛筆在抽屜裡。
   (C) 書在碗的中間。
   (D) 花在碗裡。

   解析 (C) 選項(C)正確描述了書本位置。選項(A)正確指出了蛋，但是蛋的位置錯誤。選項(B)正確指出了鉛筆，但鉛筆的位置錯誤。選項(D)正確指出了花，但花的位置錯誤。

071

3. Look at the photo marked number 3 in your test book.
   (A) The gardener is trimming bushes.
   (B) The barber is cutting hair.
   (C) The man is mowing the lawn.
   (D) The florist is arranging flowers.
   請看試題本上標示為3的照片。
   (A) 園丁正在修剪灌木。
   (B) 理髮師正在剪頭髮。
   (C) 男子正在為草坪除草。
   (D) 花藝師正在插花。

解析 (A) 照片中可以看到一名男子正在花園裡修剪灌木。選項(B)的動詞對男子動作的描述正確，cutting = trimming，都是修剪，但照片中剪的不是頭髮。選項(C)將mowing和cutting聯想在一起。選項(D)將flowers和garden聯想在一起。

4. Look at the photo marked number 4 in your test book.
   (A) She's reading a book.
   (B) She's putting on her glasses.
   (C) She's buying a computer.
   (D) She's looking at her phone.
   請看試題本上標示為4的照片。
   (A) 她正在看書。
   (B) 她正在戴眼鏡。
   (C) 她正在買電腦。
   (D) 她正在看手機。

解析 (D) 照片中可以看到一名女子正在看手上拿的手機。選項(A)正確指出女子的動作，但她看的是手機螢幕，不是書。選項(B)正確指出女子的眼鏡，但她沒有正在戴眼鏡。選項(C)正確指出女子腿上的電腦，但她不是正在買電腦。

Part 2: Question-Response 應答問題

> DIRECTIONS : You will hear a question and three possible responses. Choose the response that most closely answers the question, and fill in the corresponding oval on your answer sheet.
>
> 作答方式：你會聽到一個問題和三個可能的回應。選出最能夠回答該問題的回應，將答案卡上對應的橢圓框塗滿。

5. How long did you stay in Vancouver?
    (A) I enjoyed it very much.
    (B) Only two days.
    (C) About ten kilometers.
    你在溫哥華待了多久？
    (A) 我非常喜歡。
    (B) 兩天而已。
    (C) 大約十公里。

解析 (B) 選項(B)以 two days 回答了 How long 的時間問題。選項(A)會回答「How did you like . . . ?」的問題。選項(C)會回答 How long 的距離問題。

6. Would you mind helping me move this desk?
    (A) Not at all.
    (B) Yes, I would.
    (C) It's not his desk.
    你介不介意幫我搬一下書桌？
    (A) 完全不介意。
    (B) 是的，我會。
    (C) 這不是他的書桌。

解析 (A)「Not at all.」是回應請求幫助的禮貌用語。選項(B)會回答 yes-no 問句。選項(C)重複使用了題目中的 desk 這個字。

7. Whose package is that by the door?
    (A) It's mine.
    (B) Put it in the mail.
    (C) Yes, it's by the door.
    門口的包裹是誰的？
    (A) 我的。
    (B) 把它郵寄出去。
    (C) 是的，就在門口。

解析 (A)「It's mine.」是詢問所有權的適當回應。選項(B)將mail和package聯想在一起。選項(C)重複了題目中的door這個字。

8. Do you know how many people work here?
    (A) No, he doesn't work here.
    (B) I'm sorry, I didn't hear.
    (C) There are about twenty-five employees.
    你知道有多少人在這裡工作嗎？
    (A) 不，他不在這裡工作。
    (B) 很抱歉，我沒聽到。
    (C) 大概有二十五名員工。

解析 (C)「twenty-five employees」回答了How many的問題。選項(A)重複了題目中的work here。選項(B)混淆了同音字here和hear。

9. What time does the restaurant close?
    (A) It's across the street.
    (B) At ten o'clock.
    (C) I closed the door.
    餐廳幾點打烊？
    (A) 就在對街。
    (B) 十點鐘。
    (C) 我關了門。

解析 (B)「ten o'clock」回答了What time的問題。選項(A)會用來回答Where的問題。選項(C)重複了題目中的close這個字。

10. I'd like to make an appointment with Dr. Jones.
    (A) This is his apartment.
    (B) Of course. Are you available on Friday?
    (C) I like him, too.
    我想跟瓊斯醫師預約。
    (A) 這是他的公寓。
    (B) 沒問題，星期五可以嗎？
    (C) 我也喜歡他。

解析 (B) 選項(B)是對請求預約的適當回應。選項(A)混淆了近音字 appointment 和 apartment。選項(C)混淆了 like 在對話情境中的意義。

11. Where did you meet with the client?
    (A) At his office downtown.
    (B) About a month ago.
    (C) I enjoy meeting people.
    你和客戶是在哪裡見面的？
    (A) 在他的市區辦公室。
    (B) 大約一個月前。
    (C) 我喜歡結識朋友。

解析 (A) 「At his office」回答了 Where 的問題。選項(B)會用來回答 When 的問題。選項(C)重複了題目中的 meet 這個字。

12. It's dark in here, isn't it?
    (A) No, I parked over there.
    (B) They arrived after dark.
    (C) Yes. I'll turn on the light.
    這裡好黑喔，對吧？
    (A) 不，我把車停在那邊。
    (B) 他們天黑後抵達的。
    (C) 好的，我去開燈。

解析 (C) 選項(C)是對評論房間太黑的適當回應。選項(A)混淆了近音字 dark 和 park。選項(B)重複了題目中的 dark 這個字。

13. How much paper should I buy?
    (A) Two boxes should be enough.
    (B) Yes, you can buy paper there.
    (C) It's over by the door.
    我應該買多少紙？
    (A) 兩盒應該夠。
    (B) 是的，你可以在那裡買紙。
    (C) 就在門邊。

解析 (A)「Two boxes」回答了 How much 的問題。選項(B)重複使用題目中的 paper 這個字。選項(C)混淆了同音字 buy 和 by。

14. When is the report due?
    (A) About fifteen pages.
    (B) Bob and Sally are doing it.
    (C) By the end of the week.
    報告何時要繳交？
    (A) 大約十五頁。
    (B) 鮑伯和莎莉正在做。
    (C) 這週結束前。

解析 (C)「By the end of the week.」回答了 When 的問題。選項(A)會用來回答 How many 的問題。選項(B)會回答 Who 的問題。

15. Would you rather wait or come back later?
    (A) In the lobby.
    (B) I think I'll wait.
    (C) That one is our waiter.
    您要稍等還是晚點再過來？
    (A) 在大廳。
    (B) 我等一下好了。
    (C) 那一位是我們的服務生。

解析 (B) 選項(B)是對偏好問題的合理回應。選項(A)會用來回答 Where 的問題。選項(C)混淆了近音字 later 和 waiter。

16. Was John at yesterday's meeting?
    (A) Yes, he was there.
    (B) He's reading it now.
    (C) It was yesterday.
    約翰有參加昨天的會議嗎？
    (A) 有，他有參加。
    (B) 他正在讀。
    (C) 是在昨天。

解析 (A) 選項(A)以「Yes」回答了題目的yes-no問句。選項(B)混淆了近音字meeting和reading。選項(C)重複題目中的yesterday。

Part 3: Conversations 簡短對話

> **DIRECTIONS :** You will hear a conversation between two or more people. You will see three questions on each conversation and four possible answers. Choose the best answer to each question, and fill in the corresponding oval on your answer sheet.
>
> **作答方式：**你會聽到兩人或多人的對話。每段對話搭配三個問題，各有四個選項。選出每個問題的最佳答案，將答案卡上對應的橢圓框塗滿。

Questions 17 through 19 refer to the following conversation.

Man: I finally had a chance to try that new café down the street.

Woman: And?

Man: After I got past those wild colors they've painted on the walls, I actually enjoyed my lunch. Great soup, and the salad was really fresh.

Woman: Oh, I'd like to try the soup next time. I had the sandwich of the day and it wasn't bad at all.

Man: Yeah, at least they've got the food part right. But those walls! Hey, would you want to give the place another try? Tomorrow maybe?

Woman: Sure, tomorrow works for me.

第 17 到 19 題請聽下面這段對話。

男　　我終於有機會去試街上那家新開的咖啡館了。

女　　然後呢？

男　　在我好不容易才適應了他們牆壁漆的狂野色彩後，我其實對午餐還挺滿意的。湯很好喝，沙拉也非常新鮮。

女　　哦，那我下次也要喝喝看他們的湯。我之前吃過本日三明治，還不錯。

男　　對啊，至少食物還不錯。但那個牆壁！嘿，你想再去那邊吃一次嗎？或許明天可以？

女　　好啊，我明天可以。

17. What did the woman have at the café? 這名女子在咖啡館吃了什麼？
    (A) Soup and a sandwich 湯和三明治
    (B) Soup and a salad 湯和沙拉
    (C) A sandwich only 只吃了三明治
    (D) A salad only 只吃了沙拉

解析 (C) 這名女子提到她吃了本日三明治，所以答案是 (C)。選項 (A) 不正確，女子說「I'd like to try the soup next time.」，暗示她沒喝過湯。選項 (B) 是男子吃的。選項 (D) 重複了對話中的 salad 這個字。

18. What did the man imply about the café? 這名男子對咖啡館有何暗示？
    (A) The food is better than the décor. 食物優於裝潢。
    (B) The walls are in need of repair. 牆壁需要整修。
    (C) Its menu isn't interesting. 菜單不吸引人。
    (D) It's too far from the office. 離辦公室太遠。

解析 (A) 男子說「After I got past those wild colors they've painted on the walls, I actually enjoyed my lunch.」以及「But those walls!」，暗示了他不喜歡牆壁的顏色。不過他也提到湯很好喝，沙拉很新鮮，而且他還說「at least they've got the food part right」，都暗示了他對食物很滿意。選項 (B) 重複了對話中的 walls 這個字，但對話中並未提到整修的事。選項 (C) 不正確，男子對食物讚譽有加。選項 (D) 不正確，咖啡館就在同一條街上（down the street），意即就在附近而已。

19. What will the speakers do tomorrow? 說話者明天要做什麼？
    (A) Work on a project together 一起做專案計畫
    (B) Look for a new place to eat 找一間新的餐廳吃飯
    (C) Paint the walls 油漆牆壁
    (D) Return to the café 回到那間咖啡館

解析 (D) 男子問女子想不想再去那個地方（咖啡館）吃一次，女子回答「tomorrow works for me」，表示明天有空可以去。選項 (A) 混淆了 work 在對話情境中的意義。選項 (B) 重複對話中的 place。選項 (C) 反映了男子不喜歡牆壁顏色的事實，但對話中並無提到要油漆牆壁。

Questions 20 through 22 refer to the following conversation.

Woman: My vacation is coming up in just one more week. I sure can't wait to have some free time. I am just so tired.

Man: What are you planning to do during your time off?

Woman: I've booked a trip to Paris. And I'd better start getting ready. I have to plan what to take and arrange for someone to take care of my dog, and a thousand other things.

Man: That sounds exhausting. You might be better off staying home. It would be more relaxing.

Woman: You're kidding, right? I can relax quite nicely during my two weeks in Paris. For now, I think I'll take the afternoon off and buy some things for my trip.

第 20 到 22 題請聽下面這段對話。

女　　再過一週就是我的假期，我已經等不及要享受一些空閒時間了，我真的好疲憊。
男　　休假期間你打算做什麼？
女　　我已經訂了去巴黎的旅行，我最好開始做準備。我需要計劃要帶的東西，和找人照顧我的狗，而且還有一大堆事情要做。
男　　聽起來很累，你倒不如待在家裡還能放鬆一些。
女　　你在開玩笑吧？我在巴黎有兩週的時間可以好好放鬆。現在，我想下午請假去買一些旅行用品。

20. What does the man suggest the woman do? 這名男子建議女子做什麼？
    (A) Spend her vacation at home 在家休假
    (B) Ask for more time off 要求更多休假時間
    (C) Start packing soon 趕快開始打包行李
    (D) Go to Paris 去巴黎

解析 (A) 女子把一切的行前準備事項解釋完後，男子說「You might be better off staying home.」，認為她倒不如待在家。選項(B)重複了對話中的 time off 這個片語。選項(C)雖然有可能，但對話中並未提及。選項(D)是這名女子打算做的事。

21. How long is the woman's vacation? 這名女子要休假多久？
    (A) One week 一週
    (B) Two weeks 兩週
    (C) Three weeks 三週
    (D) Four weeks 四週

解析 (B) 女子提到「my two weeks in Paris」，所以是兩週。選項(A)是距離她的假期還有多少時間。選項(C)混淆了近音字 three 和 free。選項(D)混淆了同音字 four 和 for。

22. What will the woman do this afternoon? 這名女子今天下午要做什麼？
    (A) Read a book 看書
    (B) Go shopping 購物
    (C) Walk her dog 遛狗
    (D) Make trip reservations 預訂旅行

解析 (B) 這名女子說「I think I'll take the afternoon off and buy some things for my trip.」，表示她下午要去採買旅行用品。選項(A)混淆了 book 這個字的意義，女子說「booked a trip to Paris」，book 是預訂而不是書。選項(C)是被女子提到她需要找人照顧狗給混淆了。選項(D)是女子早就做好的事。

Questions 23 through 25 refer to the following conversation.

Woman: Look. This is the new menu for my restaurant. It's two colors and I need it printed on both sides of the page. Forty copies. Can you have it done by tomorrow morning?
Man: Sure thing.
Woman: Great. I see you charge a rush fee for twenty-four-hour service.
Man: That's right. Fifteen percent.
Woman: I guess that's reasonable. Should I write a check for the total now?
Man: No, you can pay when you pick up the order, but we prefer credit cards.

第23到25題請聽下面這段對話。
女　　　你看一下。這是我餐廳的新菜單，是雙色的，我想要雙面列印，一共四十份，明天早上能完成嗎？
男　　　沒問題。
女　　　太好了。我知道二十四小時急件你會加收費用。
男　　　沒錯，加收百分之十五。
女　　　還算合理。我需要現在就開支票付清嗎？
男　　　不需要，來拿的時候再付就好了，不過我們比較偏好刷卡。

23. What does the woman want to have printed? 這名女子想列印什麼？
    (A) Menus 菜單
    (B) Checks 支票
    (C) Order forms 訂購單
    (D) Advertisements 廣告

解析 (A) 這名女子提到「This is the new menu for my restaurant.」，所以是菜單。選項(B)重複了對話中的check這個字，是女子希望的付款方式。選項(C)重複了對話中的order。選項(D)雖然有可能，但並未提及。

24. What does the man agree to do? 這名男子答應做什麼事？
    (A) Print 24 copies 列印二十四份
    (B) Forget the rush charge 不收急件費
    (C) Have the order ready tomorrow 明天把訂單準備好
    (D) Print on one side of the page only 單面列印

解析 (C) 女子詢問她的訂單明天早上能不能完成（by tomorrow morning），男子則回覆「Sure thing」，等於yes。選項(A)重複了對話中的24這個數字（二十四小時急件費）。選項(B)雖然提到急件費，但男子表示會收急件費百分之十五。選項(D)不正確，女子要求雙

081

面列印，男子也並未表示不行。

25. What does the man want the woman to do? 這名男子希望女子做什麼？
    (A) Pick up the order at night 晚上來取件
    (B) Pay ahead of time 先付款
    (C) Check the order 檢查訂單
    (D) Use a credit card 刷卡

解析 **(D)** 女子表示要開支票，男子回覆說「we prefer credit cards」，所以男子希望女子刷卡。選項(A)重複了對話中的 pick up 這個動詞片語。選項(B)是女子想做的事。選項(C)混淆了 check 的意義，同時也重複對話中的 order 這個字。

Questions 26 through 28 refer to the following conversation.
Woman:　Have you met the new director yet?
Man 1:　Today makes a week since he started here, and I still haven't seen him.
Man 2:　I talked with him a few days ago. He seems nice.
Woman:　Sure, but that's not what matters most. Have you seen his résumé? It's very impressive.
Man 2:　Oh, yes. He's been in the industry for years. And he did great things at his last company.
Man 1:　I hear he's a graduate of a top university.
Woman:　You know, George, there's a social hour with him this afternoon. That would be your chance to finally meet him. We should all go.
Man 1:　Great idea.

第 26 到 28 題請聽下面這段對話。
女　　　你們見過新主管了沒？
男1　　他來這裡至今日滿一星期，而我還沒見過他。
男2　　我幾天前跟他說過話，他看起來人挺好的。
女　　　當然，但那不是最重要的。你們看過他的履歷嗎？真的非常出色。
男2　　喔，對。他在業界很多年了，在前公司也做得不錯。
男1　　我聽說他是頂大畢業的。
女　　　你知道嗎，喬治，今天下午有一場能與他認識的社交活動。你終於有機會見到他了，我們都應該去。
男1　　好主意。

26. What do the speakers imply about the new director?
    說話者們對這名新主管有何暗示？
    (A) They admire the director's professional background.
        他們很欽佩這位主管的專業背景。
    (B) They are looking for some important documents.
        他們正在尋找一些重要文件。
    (C) They are interested in hiring a new director.
        他們有興趣聘請新主管。
    (D) They need help writing their own résumés.
        他們需要人幫忙寫他們的履歷。

解析 (A) 女子在對話中提到「It's very impressive.」（極為出色），男子表示同意，並且補充了主管的豐富職業背景，由此可見他們十分欽佩主管。選項(B)(C)(D)都不符合對話內容。

27. When did the new director begin working at this company?
    這名新主管何時開始在這家公司工作？
    (A) Today 今天
    (B) Two days ago 兩天前
    (C) A week ago 一週前
    (D) Last Tuesday 上週二

解析 (C) 第一名男子說「Today makes a week since he started here」（今天滿一週），可見是一週前。選項(A)重複了對話中的today。選項(B)和(D)都使用了發音和today相近的詞語。

28. What does the woman suggest? 這名女子建議什麼？
    (A) Going to a staff meeting 參加一場員工會議
    (B) Attending a social event 參加一場社交活動
    (C) Getting something to eat 吃點東西
    (D) Calling the director at noon 中午打電話給主管

解析 (B) 女子提到有一場社交活動，還說「We should all go.」，由此可知她建議一起參加這場社交活動。選項(A)使用了meet的相關字meeting。選項(C)混淆了近音字meet和eat。選項(D)混淆了近音字afternoon和noon。

Questions 29 through 31 refer to the following conversation and price list.

Woman: The office is looking very drab.

Man: Yeah, we should paint it. Do we have any leftover paint from when we did the hallway?

Woman: You could check the closet. But I wanna try a different color this time. Look. There are a lot of choices here on the paint store website.

Man: Hmmm. That yellow is nice.

Woman: But it seems a bit bright, don't you think? What about this blue?

Man: Sure. Get it, but make sure you get the right amount. We need to cover about twenty or twenty-five square meters.

第 29 到 31 題請聽下面這段對話並參考價格表。

女　　這間辦公室看起來好單調。

男　　對啊，我們應該把它漆一漆。上次漆走廊的油漆還有剩嗎？

女　　你可以去壁櫥裡查看。不過這次我想換一種不同的顏色。你看，油漆行的網站上有好多選擇。

男　　嗯，那個黃色不錯。

女　　但好像有點太明亮了，你不覺得嗎？這個藍色如何？

男　　不錯，就買吧，但你要確保算好正確用量。我們需要覆蓋二十或二十五平方公尺左右的面積。

```
              大街油漆行
             室內油漆售價

   容量                  覆蓋面積
   一公升罐裝    ……………  最大六平方公尺
   兩公升罐裝    ……………  最大十二平方公尺
   五公升罐裝    ……………  最大三十平方公尺
   二十五公升桶裝 …………  最大一百五十平方公尺
```

29. What are they going to paint? 他們要油漆哪裡？
    (A) The closet 壁櫥
    (B) The office 辦公室
    (C) The hallway 走廊
    (D) The stairwell 樓梯間

解析 (B) 女子提到 this office，所以是辦公室。選項(A)是他們上次漆走廊剩下的油漆放置地方。選項(C)是他們已經油漆過的地方。選項(D)雖然有可能，但並未提及。

30. What color paint will they buy? 他們會買什麼顏色的油漆？
    (A) Yellow 黃色
    (B) Green 綠色
    (C) White 白色
    (D) Blue 藍色

解析 (D) 女子建議藍色，男子回覆說「Sure. Get it.」，表示同意。選項(A)是男子原先的建議。選項(B)混淆了近音字 seem 和 green。選項(C)混淆了近音字 bright 和 white。

31. Look at the graphic. Which size paint will they buy?
    請看圖表，他們會買哪一種容量的油漆？
    (A) 1-liter can 一公升罐裝
    (B) 2-liter can 兩公升罐裝
    (C) 5-liter can 五公升罐裝
    (D) 25-liter bucket 二十五公升桶裝

解析 (C) 男子說「We need to cover about twenty or twenty-five square meters.」，而五公升罐裝可以覆蓋這個面積再多一點。選項(A)和(B)的容量不夠用。選項(D)超過需求太多。

Questions 32 through 34 refer to the following conversation and advertisement.
Man: I'm looking for a computer table for my office.
Woman: Yes, we have a wide selection. Let me show you.
Man: Hmm. I see. OK, I think that brown one will do. Does it come assembled?
Woman: Unfortunately, no. But it's very easy to put together. Just follow the instructions in the box.
Man: All right. I'll take it.
Woman: Very good. Do you want it delivered? We offer free delivery within a ten-block radius.

Man: Thanks, but I'll just take it back to the office in my car. It'll fit in the trunk easily.
Woman: OK. I'll take it up front for you so you can pay.

第32到34題請聽下面這段對話，並參考廣告圖表。
男　　我想替我的辦公室找一張電腦桌。
女　　好的，我們有很多選擇，我帶您看一下。
男　　嗯，我看看。好，我覺得那張咖啡色的可以。會組裝好才送來嗎？
女　　不好意思，不含組裝。但自己組裝十分容易，依照箱子裡附的說明書組裝即可。
男　　好吧，那就這張了。
女　　好的。您需要我們幫忙配送嗎？十個街區的範圍內免運。
男　　謝謝，我自己開車載回辦公室就可以了，它很容易可以放到後車廂。
女　　好的，我幫您拿到前面去結帳。

```
史普林格辦公用品店

全面特賣
全店多數商品折扣優惠中！

紙筆類九折
電子用品八五折
辦公家具八折
咖啡機七五折
僅限本週！
```

32. Look at the graphic. How much of a discount will the man get?
請看圖表，這名男子會獲得幾折優惠？
(A) 10％ 九折
(B) 15％ 八五折
(C) 20％ 八折
(D) 25％ 七五折

解析 (C) 男子要買的電腦桌屬於辦公家具，所以是八折。選項(A)(B)(D)的折扣商品都不是他要買的。

33. What does the woman offer to do? 這名女子表示願意提供什麼服務？
    (A) Open the box 打開箱子
    (B) Explain the instructions 解釋使用說明
    (C) Show the man where to park 指示男子哪裡可以停車
    (D) Take the purchase to the cash register 拿採購物品到收銀檯

解析 (D) 女子說「I'll take it up front for you so you can pay.」，表示會幫男子把電腦桌拿到前面去。選項(A)重複了對話中的box這個字，但女子並未表示要打開箱子。選項(B)重複了對話中的instructions，女子表示使用說明很簡單，但並未表示要為他解釋。選項(C)從男子提到car而聯想到park。

34. How will the man transport his purchase to his office?
    這名男子會如何將採購物品運送到辦公室？
    (A) He will ask a colleague to get it. 他會請同事來拿。
    (B) He will carry it with him now. 他現在就會自己帶回去。
    (C) He will pick it up tomorrow. 他明天再來拿。
    (D) He will have it delivered. 他會使用配送服務。

解析 (B) 男子說「I'll just take it back to the office in my car」，表示他打算自己開車載回。選項(A)和(C)是有這種可能，但對話中並未提及。選項(D)是女子提出的建議。

Part 4: Talks 簡短獨白

> DIRECTIONS : You will hear a talk given by a single speaker. You will see three questions on each talk, each with four possible answers. Choose the best answer to each question, and fill in the corresponding oval on your answer sheet.
> 作答方式：你會聽到一名說話者的獨白。每段獨白搭配三個問題，各有四個選項。選出每個問題的最佳回答，將答案卡上對應的橢圓框塗滿。

Questions 35 through 37 refer to the following talk and floor plan.
第35到37題請聽下面這段獨白，並參考樓層平面圖。

Welcome to the tour. If you haven't purchased a tour ticket yet, please do so now before we move away from the ticket counter. OK, it looks like everyone is ready, so let's get going. We'll start our tour in the gallery just across the hall where we'll view nineteenth-century paintings and prints. Then, it's on to the sculpture gallery, where we have some magnificent pieces on display. We'll go upstairs to look at our collection of modern works, then we'll come back down and end right next door to where we are now, at the gift shop. That'll give you the chance to do a little shopping, if you like.

歡迎各位參加本次導覽。假如您尚未購買導覽票，請在我們離開售票櫃檯前，現在先去購票。好的，看來大家都準備好了，我們出發吧。我們的導覽會從走廊對面的展廳開始，在那裡欣賞十九世紀的繪畫和版畫。接著我們會來到雕塑展廳，那裡正展出一些非常精美的作品。然後我們會上樓看現代藝術的收藏品，再下樓到我們目前所在位置的隔壁，也就是禮品店，並在那裡結束本次導覽。如果各位想要的話，屆時會有機會可以購物。

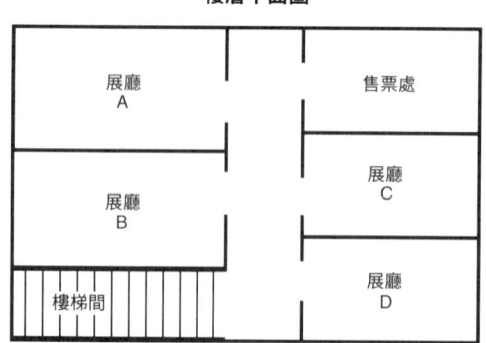

樓層平面圖

展廳 A	售票處
展廳 B	展廳 C
樓梯間	展廳 D

35. Where would you hear this talk? 你會在哪裡聽到這段獨白？
    (A) Shopping mall 購物中心
    (B) Sports event 體育活動
    (C) Museum 博物館
    (D) Theater 戲劇院

    解析 (C) 從 gallery（展廳）、painting（繪畫）、prints（版畫）、sculpture（雕塑）這些字可判斷出這裡是博物館。選項(A)和說話者提到禮品店購物有關。選項(B)和(D)則和獨白中提到tickets有關。

36. What are the listeners asked to do? 聽者被要求做什麼？
    (A) Buy a ticket 購票
    (B) Watch a play 看劇
    (C) Choose a gift 選禮物
    (D) Move their seats 換座位

    解析 (A) 說話者說「If you haven't purchased a tour ticket yet, please do so now」，要求聽者立刻去購票。選項(B)是被近音字display給混淆了。選項(C)重複了獨白中的gift。選項(D)重複了move。

37. Look at the graphic. Where is the gift shop? 請看圖表，禮品店在哪裡？
    (A) Room A 展廳A
    (B) Room B 展廳B
    (C) Room C 展廳C
    (D) Room D 展廳D

    解析 (C) 在獨白一開始，說話者就指出他們正站在售票櫃檯的旁邊，獨白結束時，她又說他們會在「right next door to where we are now, at the gift shop」的位置結束導覽，由此可知禮品店在他們目前所在位置即售票櫃檯的隔壁，唯一位於售票櫃檯隔壁的就是展廳C。選項(A)(B)(D)的位置都不符合描述。

Questions 38 through 40 refer to the following phone message.
第38到40題請聽下面這段電話留言。

Hi, this is Pete Merola. A colleague suggested I call you because I need a cleaning service for my office, and you are located just down the street. I was wondering if I could find out about prices. It's not a large office, and I'd only need it cleaned once a week. So, I'd like to know how much that would cost, and also if you are available evenings, since it would work better for me if you came after hours. I'm going out of town for a few days, so I'll give you a ring when I get back early next week and we can discuss. Thanks.

嗨，我是彼特・梅洛拉。我的辦公室需要清潔服務，我同事建議我打電話給您，而且您剛好也在這條街上。我想知道您的報價。我的辦公室不大，只需要一週打掃一次，我想知道這樣的收費會是多少，且您晚上是否可以配合。因為您於下班時間過來的話，我會比較方便。我會出城幾天，下週初回來再打電話跟您討論，謝謝。

38. Why did the speaker make the call? 說話者為何要打這通電話？
    (A) To make an appointment 預約時間
    (B) To solicit a new client 招攬新客戶
    (C) To ask for directions 問路
    (D) To get information 取得資訊

解析 (D) 說話者想要找人打掃他的辦公室，因此打電話詢問價格和時間。選項(A)(B)(C)都是打電話的合理原因，但在這裡都不正確。

39. What does the speaker mean when he says, "It would work better for me if you came after hours"？說話者說「因為您於下班時間過來的話，我會比較方便」是什麼意思？
    (A) He prefers the cleaners to come when the office is closed.
        他希望清潔員在辦公室關門後再過來。
    (B) He thinks the work will take several hours to complete.
        他認為這份工作需要幾個小時才能完成。
    (C) He's at the office just a few hours a day.
        他一天只有幾個小時會在辦公室。
    (D) He does a better job later in the day.
        他在一天較晚的時候工作效率較高。

解析 (A) 片語「it would work better for me」表示偏好，「after hours」是下班時間，所以說話者偏好對方在辦公室的上班時間結束關門後過來。選項(B)(C)(D)都使用了這句話中的某些字，但意思都不對，不符合獨白內容。

090

40. What does the speaker want the listener to do? 說話者希望聽者做什麼？
    (A) Come to his office next week 下週來他的辦公室
    (B) Wait for another call from him 等他的另一通電話
    (C) Meet him downtown 在市區與他會面
    (D) Return his call soon 儘速回電

解析 (B) 說話者說「I'll give you a ring when I get back early next week」，意思是等他行程結束回來會再打一次電話。選項(A)重複了 next week 這個片語。選項(C)混淆了 out of town 和 downtown。選項(D)雖然與電話這個主題有關，但不是正確答案。

Questions 41 through 43 refer to the following advertisement.
第41到43題請聽下面這段廣告。

Movie Time video streaming service allows you to watch all your favorite movies and TV shows when you want to watch them in the comfort of your own living room. A subscription to Movie Time lets you watch your movie or show at the click of a button. It's easy! Just visit our website and sign up today to enjoy the widest selection of movies and shows available anywhere. We invite you to try our service at no cost. The first month is free. That's right, free. After that, enjoy a monthly or yearly subscription at a cost so low, you can't afford not to sign up! Subscriptions start at one hundred fifty dollars, annually.
所有您最愛的電影和電視節目都在電影時光影音串流服務，可以讓你在自家客廳就能舒適地觀看。訂閱電影時光即可一鍵觀賞電影或電視節目，操作非常簡單！今日至我們的官網註冊登錄，即可隨處享受最豐富的電影和電視節目。誠摯邀請您免費體驗我們的服務，首月免費，沒錯！就是免費！次月開始即可以超低價格選擇月訂或年訂方案，如此好的優惠怎能錯過！訂閱方案每年一百五十美元起。

41. What kind of subscription is being offered? 廣告宣傳的是何種訂閱服務？
    (A) Movie tickets 電影票
    (B) Magazine 雜誌
    (C) Cable TV 有線電視
    (D) Video streaming 影音串流

解析 (D) 這段獨白是宣傳電影時光影音串流服務的廣告，所以答案是(D)。選項(A)是因為獨白中提到電影而產生聯想。選項(B)也是一種可訂閱的東西，但在獨白中並未提及。選項(C)是因為獨白中提到了電視節目而產生的聯想。

091

42. How long does a free subscription last? 免費訂閱時間持續多久？
    (A) Two days 兩天
    (B) Three days 三天
    (C) One month 一個月
    (D) One year 一年

解析 (C) 說話者提到「The first month is free.」，所以免費時間是一個月。選項(A)是和近音字today產生了混淆。選項(B)混淆了近音字free和three。選項(D)是被獨白中提到年訂方案給混淆了，年訂方案並不是免費的。

43. How much does a one-year subscription cost? 訂閱一年的價格是多少？
    (A) $50 五十美元
    (B) $99 九十九美元
    (C) $150 一百五十美元
    (D) $100 一百美元

解析 (C) 說話者說「Subscriptions start at one hundred fifty dollars, annually.」，表示一百五十美元起。選項(A)和(D)都和正確答案的發音相似。選項(B)則和sign的發音相似。

Questions 44 through 46 refer to the following announcement.
第44到46題請聽下面這段公告。

One final announcement. You will be happy to hear that the renovation project is almost complete. As you know, the new furniture was delivered last week, and now all that's left to be done is finish up the floors. A team will be in tomorrow morning to install the carpet in the hallway and front office. They'll arrive early and should be out of here by noon, so the disruption will be minimal. They have requested that you enter the building through the rear doorway while they're working. Thank you. Your cooperation is appreciated.

最後一項公告。各位一定很高興聽到翻修計畫即將完成。如各位所知，新家具上週已經送達，現在只剩地板工程需要完成。明天早上會有一組人進來鋪設走廊和前辦公室的地毯，他們會早到，中午前應該就離開了，所以影響會降至最小。他們要求施工期間請大家從後門進入大樓。謝謝，感謝各位的配合。

44. What will happen tomorrow? 明天會發生什麼事？
    (A) Software will be installed. 安裝軟體。
    (B) A new carpet will be laid. 鋪設新地毯。
    (C) Furniture will be delivered. 送達家具。
    (D) The hallway will be painted. 油漆走廊。

解析 (B) 說話者說「A team will be in tomorrow morning to install the carpet in the hallway and front office.」，可知會有人來鋪地毯。選項(A)重複了install這個字。選項(C)是上週發生的事。選項(D)重複了hallway這個字。

45. What does the speaker mean when he says, "They should be out of here by noon"? 說話者說「他們中午前應該就離開了」是什麼意思？
    (A) Staff should stay out of the office all morning.
        職員早上都不能進辦公室。
    (B) The workers will finish before 12：00.
        工人會在十二點前完工。
    (C) Employees can take the afternoon off.
        員工下午可以休假。
    (D) Office supplies are running low.
        辦公用品快用完了。

解析 (B) 說話者是在描述那些會來鋪地毯的工人，「should be out of here by noon」意思是中午前他們「也許已經離開」。選項(A)(C)(D)都不符合獨白內容，也不是說話者講這句話的意思。

46. What are listeners asked to do? 聽者被要求做什麼事？
    (A) Arrange the new furniture 擺放新家具
    (B) Work in the front office 在前辦公室工作
    (C) Use the back entrance 使用後門
    (D) Arrive early 早點到

解析 (C) 說話者表示工人要求他們從後門進入大樓（requested that you enter the building through the rear doorway），所以答案是(C)。選項(A)重複了獨白中的new furniture這個片語。選項(B)重複了front office這個片語。選項(D)是工人會做的事。

Questions 47 through 49 refer to the following phone message and building directory.
第47到49題請聽下面這段電話留言，並參考樓層簡介。

Hello. This is Martha Jones from the Hildamire Hotel, returning your call. You asked about renting a space for a training seminar on April fifth. We have several rooms you could consider. The East Banquet Room is a possibility, although it might be a bit large for your purposes as it can accommodate up to two hundred people. The Terrace Conference Room is also available. It has seating for one hundred and twenty-five people, which is just the number you are expecting, I believe. We also have a couple of larger rooms. I would be happy to show you all our facilities and discuss arrangements in person. You can drop by the hotel any morning. You'll find my office just behind the front desk in the lobby.

哈囉，我是希爾德邁爾飯店的瑪莎‧瓊斯，在這裡給您回電。您詢問了四月五日要租用場地舉辦培訓研討會，我們有幾個場地給您參考。一個是東宴會廳，可容納多達兩百人，不過以您的用途來說可能稍大了些。還有一個是露臺會議室，可以坐一百二十五人，我想剛好是您預計的人數。我們還有幾個較大的場地，我很樂意親自帶您參觀所有設施並討論安排事宜。您可於任何一天早上過來飯店一趟，我的辦公室就在大廳服務櫃檯後方。

希爾德邁爾飯店	
樓層簡介	
地面樓	大廳 餐廳 游泳池
一樓	會議室 宴會廳
三樓	行政辦公室
四至十樓	客房

47. What event is the listener planning? 聽者正在規劃什麼活動？

  (A) A wedding 婚禮
  (B) A conference 會議
  (C) A training seminar 培訓研討會
  (D) An awards banquet 頒獎宴會

解析 (C) 說話者提到「You asked about renting a space for a training seminar」，由此可知聽者要辦培訓研討會。選項 (A) 雖然有可能，但並未提及。選項 (B) 重複了 conference room 中的 conference。選項 (D) 重複了 banquet room 中的 banquet。會議室（conference room）和宴會廳（banquet room）是說話者提到可以考慮的活動場所。

48. About how many people will attend the event? 大約多少人會參加這場活動？
  (A) 100 一百人
  (B) 125 一百二十五人
  (C) 200 兩百人
  (D) 225 兩百二十五人

解析 (B) 說話者提到其中一個場所「has seating for one hundred and twenty-five people, which is just the number you are expecting」（可坐一百二十五人，正好符合預計人數），由此可知大約有一百二十五人參加。選項 (A) 和 (D) 都和正確答案發音相近。選項 (C) 是東宴會廳可以容納的人數。

49. Look at the graphic. Where is Ms. Jones's office located?
  請看圖表，瓊斯小姐的辦公室在哪裡？
  (A) Ground floor 地面樓
  (B) First floor 一樓
  (C) Second floor 二樓
  (D) Third floor 三樓

解析 (A) 說話者表示「You'll find my office just behind the front desk in the lobby.」，即辦公室在大廳服務櫃檯後方，從樓層圖可看出大廳位於地面樓。選項 (B)(C)(D) 是其他設施的所在位置。

閱讀即時演練解答

Part 5 句子填空

高分攻略	主題	1	2	3	4	5
高分攻略 1	字彙家族	1. B	2. B	3. D	4. D	5. B
高分攻略 2	意義相近的單字	1. D	2. A	3. C	4. D	5. B
高分攻略 3	形式類似的單字	1. B	2. A	3. D	4. C	5. A
高分攻略 4	主詞動詞一致與介系詞片語	1. D	2. A	3. C	4. A	5. B
高分攻略 5	單數與複數主詞	1. C	2. A	3. D	4. C	5. B
高分攻略 6	動詞時態	1. B	2. C	3. B	4. A	5. D
高分攻略 7	介系詞	1. A	2. D	3. C	4. D	5. C
高分攻略 8	動詞和形容詞的介系詞搭配	1. B	2. C	3. A	4. D	5. B
高分攻略 9	對等連接詞	1. C	2. A	3. B	4. D	5. C
高分攻略10	平行結構	1. B	2. D	3. C	4. A	5. C
高分攻略11	從屬連接詞	1. C	2. A	3. C	4. C	5. D
高分攻略12	未來時間子句	1. B	2. A	3. C	4. D	5. D

Part 6 段落填空

高分攻略	主題	1	2	3	4	5
高分攻略 1	頻率副詞	1. A	2. D	3. A	4. B	5. C
高分攻略 2	主要動詞後接動名詞或不定詞	1. C	2. B	3. B	4. A	5. D
高分攻略 3	介系詞和形容詞後接動名詞或不定詞	1. B	2. C	3. A	4. D	5. C
高分攻略 4	使役動詞	1. A	2. B	3. A	4. C	5. D
高分攻略 5	真實條件句	1. A	2. B	3. C	4. D	5. C
高分攻略 6	非真實條件句	1. B	2. B	3. C	4. D	5. A
高分攻略 7	比較	1. A	2. D	3. B	4. C	5. B
高分攻略 8	代名詞	1. D	2. D	3. B	4. A	5. C
高分攻略 9	主格關係代名詞	1. A	2. C	3. D	4. B	5. B
高分攻略10	受格關係代名詞	1. C	2. B	3. B	4. D	5. A
高分攻略11	被動語態	1. C	2. B	3. D	4. A	5. D
高分攻略12	字義	1. A	2. C	3. D	4. B	5. B
高分攻略13	句子選擇	1. B	2. C	3. A	4. D	

Part 7 閱讀測驗

高分攻略 1	廣告	1. C	2. B		
高分攻略 2	表單	1. B	2. C	3. B	
高分攻略 3	書信	1. D	2. C	3. B	
高分攻略 4	備忘錄	1. C	2. A	3. B	4. D
高分攻略 5	表格	1. A	2. D	3. B	4. B
高分攻略 6	圖表	1. B	2. D		
高分攻略 7	公告	1. D	2. C	3. D	4. A
高分攻略 8	通知	1. D	2. B		
高分攻略 9	文章	1. C	2. B	3. A	4. D
高分攻略10	時間表	1. C	2. C	3. C	4. C
高分攻略11	電子郵件	1. A	2. C		
高分攻略12	網頁	1. D	2. A		
高分攻略13	簡訊和線上聊天室	1. B	2. C		

閱讀即時演練解析

Part 5 句子填空

高分攻略 1　字彙家族

1. 採購主管能協商出最好的價錢。
   (A) 可協商的
   (B) 協商 (v.)
   (C) 協商者
   (D) 協商 (n.)

   解析 (B) negotiate是動詞，符合題目需求。選項(A)是形容詞。選項(C)和(D)是名詞。

2. 我們在網站上刊登招聘廣告的第一天，就有超過七百人應徵此職位。
   (A) 申請 (v.)
   (B) 申請者、應徵者
   (C) 器具、家用電器
   (D) 申請 (n.)

   解析 (B) applicants是名詞，指人。選項(A)是動詞。選項(C)是名詞，雖然長得很像字彙家族的一員，但是意義完全不同。選項(D)是名詞，但不用於指人。

3. 於危機時刻能果斷行動的能力是強大領導者的標誌特質。
   (A) 決定 (v.)
   (B) 決定 (n.)
   (C) 決定性的
   (D) 果斷地

   解析 (D) decisively是一個情狀副詞（又稱方式副詞），修飾動詞act。選項(A)是動詞。選項(B)是名詞。選項(C)是形容詞。

4. 這兩個樣本顏色太接近了，很難區別它們。
   (A) 不同於、相異、有區別
   (B) 區別 (n.)
   (C) 有區別的、不同的
   (D) 區別 (v.)

   解析 (D) differentiate是動詞，意思是「區別」。選項(A)是動詞，意思是「有區別、不同於」。選項(B)是名詞。選項(C)是形容詞。

098

5. 這個部門的所有設計師當中,史密斯小姐被認為是最有能力的。
   (A) 競爭
   (B) 有能力的
   (C) 能力
   (D) 有能力地

解析 (B) competent是形容詞,作為主詞補語用來修飾主詞史密斯小姐。選項(A)是動詞,且意義完全不同。選項(C)是名詞。選項(D)是副詞。

高分攻略 2　意義相近的單字

1. 新進員工前六個月只能賺取微薄的薪水。
   (A) 贏得
   (B) 獲得
   (C) 到達
   (D) 賺取

解析 (D) earn常用來表示透過工作獲得金錢。選項(A)表示在比賽中獲勝,得到第一名。選項(B)代表得到或獲得某物。選項(C)代表抵達某地點。

2. 由於她最近獲得升遷,現在米蘭達在公司的責任更多了。
   (A) 最近的
   (B) 近來
   (C) 不久
   (D) 新近

解析 (A) recent是形容詞,描述不久前才剛發生的事。在這個句子中,recent修飾名詞promotion。選項(B)、(C)和(D)都是副詞,不能修飾名詞。

3. 我們的成本這個月降低了,但下個月我們需要讓成本降低更多。
   (A) 落下
   (B) 下降
   (C) 降低
   (D) 低於

解析 (C) decrease意指「減少」或「縮減」,這個句子相當於「We will make our costs smaller.」。選項(A)和(B)意指「下降」,在這裡不能用是因為它們都是不及物動詞。選項(D)是一個介系詞,但這個句子需要的是一個及物動詞。

4. 我的車子在維修時，一位朋友把他的車借給我。
   (A) 借入
   (B) 租用
   (C) 欠
   (D) 借出

解析 **(D)** lend 是讓別人使用你的東西。選項(A)是使用別人的東西。選項(B)涉及簽約並付費使用不屬於你的東西，為一種商業交易行為。選項(C)表示有義務還錢或人情。

5. 由於本國貨幣升值，愈來愈多公司對投資這個地區感興趣。
   (A) 錢
   (B) 貨幣
   (C) 硬幣
   (D) 現金

解析 **(B)** currency 是一個國家使用的金錢系統，也就是貨幣。選項(A)是一個統稱，一般不會用來指一個特定國家的貨幣。選項(C)是金屬製圓形貨幣。選項(D)包括硬幣和紙鈔。

高分攻略 3　形式類似的單字

1. 我需要一點時間把合約讀過再簽核。
   (A) 聯繫
   (B) 合約
   (C) 舉止
   (D) 緊密的

解析 **(B)** contract 是一種法律文件。選項(A)指「與某人通訊、聯繫」。選項(C)是「舉止、表現」。選項(D)意指「小型的」或「緊密的」。

2. 這個房間很大，不過我們可以用隔板把它分成較小的工作區域。
   (A) 隔板
   (B) 參加者
   (C) 顆粒、微粒
   (D) 分詞

解析 **(A)** partitions 是用來將一個房間分成不同區域的隔牆或隔板。選項(B)是參加某個活動的人。選項(C)是極小的粒狀物。選項(D)是一種動詞形式。

3. 由於本季利潤較低，我們將不得不縮減員工規模。
   (A) 生產

(B) 勸說
(C) 推斷
(D) 縮減

解析 (D) reduce 是「減少」或「減小」的意思。選項(A)是「製造」或「生產」東西。選項(B)是「勸說、引起」之意。選項(C)意指「做出邏輯推斷」。

4. 工作申請的截止日期是 3 月 1 日，在那天後提交的履歷我們不會接受。
   (A) 除了……之外
   (B) 預期
   (C) 接受
   (D) 口音

解析 (C) accept 是「接受」。選項(A)是「除了……之外」。選項(B)意指「相信某件事會發生」。選項(D)指發音腔調。

5. 有些人獨立作業的效率較高，有些人則更偏好團隊工作。
   (A) 偏好
   (B) 推斷、推論
   (C) 提及
   (D) 會議

解析 (A) have a preference 意指喜歡其中一個勝過其他選擇。選項(B)指一個結論或暗示。選項(C)意指「提及」。選項(D)是正式會議的一種。

高分攻略 4　主詞動詞一致與介系詞片語

1. 公司的高階主管今天下午一點開會。
   (A)(B)(C)(D) 開會

解析 (D) 複數動詞 are meeting 和句子的複數主詞 officers 一致。選項(A)(B)(C)都是單數動詞。

2. 這些建築物的所有人向租戶收取非常合理的房租。
   (A)(B)(C)(D) 收費

解析 (A) 單數動詞 charges 和單數主詞 owner 一致。選項(B)(C)(D)都是複數動詞。

3. 那個櫃子裡的用品是提供給所有員工使用的。

解析 (C) 複數動詞 are 和複數主詞 supplies 一致。選項(A)(B)(D)都是單數動詞。

4. 這個文件夾裡的文件需要雙方簽署，並立即交還給律師。
   (A)(B)(D) 需要 (C) 貧窮的、需要多關懷的

解析 **(A)** 複數動詞 need 與複數主詞 documents 一致。選項 (B) 和 (D) 和主詞不一致。選項 (C) 是一個形容詞。

5. 這間辦公室的地毯在去年我們簽訂租約之前更換過了。
   (A)(B)(C)(D) 更換

解析 **(B)** 複數動詞 were replaced 和複數主詞 carpets 一致。選項 (A)(C)(D) 都和主詞不一致。

高分攻略 5　單數與複數主詞

1. 總公司經理每年至少造訪這間辦公室兩次。
   (A)(B)(C)(D) 拜訪、造訪

解析 **(C)** 單數動詞 visits 和單數主詞 manager 一致。選項 (A) 是動名詞。選項 (B) 是不定詞。選項 (D) 用於複數主詞。

2. 多數人都同意艾克美公司能持續提供高品質的產品，值得信賴。
   (A)(B)(C)(D) 同意

解析 **(A)** 複數動詞 agree 和複數主詞 people 一致。選項 (B)(C)(D) 都是單數動詞。

3. 我的助理向我保證員工會議一切都已準備就緒。

解析 **(D)** 單數動詞 is 和單數主詞 everything 一致。選項 (A)(B)(C) 都是複數動詞。

4. 儘管成立時間相對較短，萊茵金顧問公司正迅速成為業界最成功的公司之一。

解析 **(C)** Rheingold Consultants 是公司名稱，視為單數，要用單數動詞。選項 (A)(B)(D) 都是複數動詞。

5. 過去在城市的這一區，一間公寓租一千美元算是很高的租金。

解析 **(B)** one thousand dollars 是一筆錢的數量，要視為單數名詞。選項 (A) 雖然是單數，卻是現在式動詞，但此句需要的是過去式動詞。選項 (C) 和 (D) 都是複數動詞。

高分攻略 6　動詞時態

1. 趙先生會在下週五的員工會議上提出新的預算。
   (A)(B)(C)(D) 提出

解析 **(B)** 時間表達用語 next Friday 說明了這裡必須使用未來式動詞。選項 (A) 是現在簡單式。選項 (C) 是現在進行式。選項 (D) 是現在完成式。

2. 我們正打算重新粉刷辦公室，但我們還沒決定顏色。
   (A)(B)(C)(D) 尚未決定

解析 **(C)** 時間詞 yet 用於現在完成式，因此這裡需要一個現在完成式的動詞。選項 (A) 是過去簡單式。選項 (B) 是現在簡單式。選項 (D) 是現在進行式，同時也和複數主詞不一致。

3. 該公司每年夏初都會為所有員工舉辦野餐活動。
   (A)(B)(C)(D) 舉辦

解析 **(B)** 時間表達用語 every summer 說明了這裡需要一個現在簡單式的動詞。選項 (A) 雖然是現在簡單式，但和單數主詞不一致。選項 (C) 是現在進行式。選項 (D) 是不定詞，不定詞不可當作主要動詞使用。

4. 雖然他們從上星期起就在趕製那份報告，但仍尚未完成。
   (A)(B)(C)(D) 從事、忙於

解析 **(A)** 現在完成進行式用來表示從過去某一時刻開始，到現在仍在進行的動作。選項 (B) 和 (C) 是未來式。選項 (D) 是現在進行式。

5. 昨天和新客戶簽約後，我們全都去餐廳慶祝了。

解析 **(D)** 時間詞 yesterday 點出動作發生在昨天，動詞要用過去簡單式。選項 (A) 是現在簡單式。選項 (B) 是未來式。選項 (C) 是現在完成式。

高分攻略 7 　介系詞

1. 把包裹放在桌上就好，我會幫你打開。
   (A) 在……上面
   (B) 在……裡面
   (C) 到……地點
   (D) 在……地點

   解析 (A) on 是地方介系詞，意思是「在……上」。選項 (B)(C)(D) 放到句中意思都不通。

2. 他們一走進房間，馬上意識到會議已在進行中。
   (A) 在……上面
   (B) 在……之中
   (C) 直到……的時候
   (D) 到……裡面

   解析 (D) into 表示往某物的內部移動。選項 (A)(B)(C) 放到句中意思都不通。

3. 公司餐廳每天中午十一點開到下午一點。
   (A) 在……時候
   (B) 花費多久時間
   (C) 直到……的時候
   (D) 在……之前

   解析 (C) 在這個句子中，until 搭配 from（from . . . until），點出一個動作的開始和結束時間。選項 (A)(B)(D) 放入句中意思都不通。

4. 由於會議定於正午開始，我們將為參加者提供三明治和點心。
   (A) 在……的時候
   (B) 到……的時候
   (C) 在……期間
   (D) 在……的時候

   解析 (D) at 用來指出一個特定的時間點，例如 at noon（正午）。選項 (A)(B)(C) 都不用於一個特定的時間點。

5. 他們的辦公室位於下一個街區，就在郵局和銀行之間。
   (A) 在……之中
   (B) 在……之外
   (C) 在……之間
   (D) 穿過

解析 **(C)** between 表示物體所在位置兩側都有東西，在本句中一側是郵局，另一側是銀行。選項(A)用於三個以上的參考點。選項(B)不正確，辦公室通常不會在室外。選項(D)表示移動方向，不表示位置。

高分攻略 8　動詞和形容詞的介系詞搭配

1. 辦公室每個人都在抱怨對街工地傳來的噪音。

解析 **(B)** 動詞 complain 搭配的正確介系詞是 about。選項(A)(C)(D)的介系詞一般不和 complain 搭配使用。

2. 我們把舊的影印機換成了更新、更高效的型號。

解析 **(C)** 動詞 replace 搭配的正確介系詞是 with，replace 和 with 的中間可以有受詞（our old copy machine）。選項(A)(B)(D)的介系詞一般不和 replace 搭配使用。

3. 張小姐負責確保新進員工了解自己的職責。

解析 **(A)** 形容詞 responsible 搭配的正確介系詞是 for。選項(B)(C)(D)的介系詞一般不和 responsible 搭配使用。

4. 許多當地居民反對開發商在他們社區興建購物中心的計畫。

解析 **(D)** 動詞 object 後面要使用介系詞 to。選項(A)(B)(C)的介系詞一般不和 object 搭配使用。

5. 我們重新佈置了辦公室，好讓我們有一個適合接待客戶的舒適空間。

解析 **(B)** 形容詞 suitable 後面要接介系詞 for。選項(A)(C)(D)的介系詞一般不和 suitable 搭配使用。

高分攻略 9 對等連接詞

1. 薩姆女士的作品既有創意又精準。
    (A) 但是
    (B) 或者
    (C) 和
    (D) 也不

解析 (C) and 用來連接兩個類似的概念：creative 和 accurate，兩個字都是對薩姆女士作品的正面描述。選項 (A) 用來連接兩個相反的概念。選項 (B) 用來連接兩個供選擇的項目。選項 (D) 必須搭配 neither 使用。

2. 喬治工作了一整晚，卻還是沒能準時完成報告。
    (A) 但是
    (B) 和
    (C) 兩者任一
    (D) 兩者皆不

解析 (A) yet 用來連接兩個相反的概念，在這個句子中，我們預期喬治工作了一整晚應已完成報告，實際上卻沒有。選項 (B) 用來連接兩個類似的概念。選項 (C) 表示可能的選擇，但必須和 or 一起使用。選項 (D) 表示沒有選擇，且必須和 nor 一起使用。

3. 我們可以今天下午見面，或者如果你希望的話，可以等這週晚些時候再見。
    (A) 但是
    (B) 或者
    (C) 也不
    (D) 兩者都不

解析 (B) or 搭配 either 表示可能的選擇，這裡是在兩個見面時間當中選擇。選項 (A) 用來連接兩個相反的概念。選項 (C) 必須搭配 neither 使用，表示沒有選擇。選項 (D) 必須搭配 nor 使用。

4. 無論你搭公車或地鐵都無法準時到達機場。
    (A) 或者
    (B) 和
    (C) 但是
    (D) 也不

解析 (D) nor 是搭配 neither 的正確介系詞。選項 (A)(B)(C) 都不能和 neither 搭配使用。

5. 我們真的很想去看國家戲劇院最近上演的那部戲劇，但門票太快就賣光了。
    (A) 和
    (B) 或者
    (C) 但是
    (D) 兩者任一

解析 (C) but用來連接兩個相反的概念，在這裡連接的概念是「想看戲劇」和「買不到票」（沒看成）。選項(A)用來連接兩個類似的概念。選項(B)用來連接兩個供選擇的項目。選項(D)也用來連接兩個選擇項目，但必須和or一起使用。

高分攻略 10　平行結構

1. 及時、親切的客戶服務是本公司的優先考量。
    (A) 朋友
    (B) 友善的、親切的
    (C) 友誼
    (D) 友善、親切

解析 (B) friendly是形容詞，和另一個形容詞prompt形成平行結構。選項(A)(C)(D)都是名詞。

2. 雪倫很擅長讓客戶感到自在，並讓他們對使用我們的服務產生興趣。
    (A)(B)(C)(D) 使、讓

解析 (D) 動名詞getting和動名詞making平行。這個句子告訴我們雪倫擅長兩件事：「making clients feel comfortable」和「getting them interested in using our services」。選項(A)是原形動詞。選項(B)是過去式動詞。選項(C)是過去分詞。

3. 注重效率和準確性就能把工作做好。
    (A) 準確的
    (B) 準確地
    (C) 準確性
    (D) 累積、增加

解析 (C) 名詞accuracy和名詞efficiency平行。選項(A)是形容詞。選項(B)是副詞。選項(D)是動名詞，雖然長得和正確答案或其他選項很相似，但意義上完全不同。

4. 在合約簽好之前，我們無法確定最終預算，也不能開始研究。
   (A) 最後確定、定案
   (B) 終結、定局
   (C) 最後確定、定案 (ved)
   (D) 最後的、決定性的、決賽

   解析 (A) 現在式動詞 finalize 和現在式動詞 begin 平行。選項 (B) 是名詞。選項 (C) 是過去式動詞。選項 (D) 是形容詞及名詞。

5. 為了準時完成工作，我們可以今天在辦公室留晚一點，也可以明天早一點進辦公室。
   (A) 近來
   (B) 遲、晚
   (C) 晚些時候的
   (D) 最新的

   解析 (C) 比較級形容詞 later 和比較級形容詞 earlier 平行。選項 (A) 是副詞。選項 (B) 是名詞。選項 (D) 是形容詞最高級。

高分攻略 11　從屬連接詞

1. 儘管賽洛女士遲到，引座員還是讓她進入演奏廳。
   (A) 因為
   (B) 然而
   (C) 儘管
   (D) 在……之前

   解析 (C) 一般而言，演奏開始後就不得進場，因此這個子句描述的情況和一般的預期相違背，要使用表達矛盾關係的從屬連接詞。選項 (A) 用來引導一個原因。選項 (B) 是對等連接詞，不用來引導從屬子句。選項 (D) 用來引導時間子句。

2. 由於到場的人太少，我們最終決定取消這場會議。
   (A) 由於
   (B) 雖然
   (C) 如果
   (D) 直到

   解析 (A) since 用來引導一個原因，這個子句描述了會議取消的原因。選項 (B) 用來引導一個矛盾事實。選項 (C) 用來引導條件子句。選項 (D) 用來引導時間子句。

3. 報告一準備好，米蘭達就會寄一份到你的辦公室。
   (A) 但是
   (B) 因此
   (C) 一……就
   (D) 在……之前

解析 (C) as soon as 引導一個時間子句，意思是「……之後馬上」。這個子句陳述了米蘭達何時會把報告寄出去。選項(A)是連接兩個相反概念的對等連接詞。選項(B)用來引導一個結果。選項(D)引導的雖然也是時間子句，但放入句中不合邏輯，不可能在報告準備好之前就寄出去。

4. 因為電梯故障，所有人都要走樓梯。
   (A) 然而
   (B) 儘管
   (C) 因為
   (D) 所以

解析 (C) because 引導一個原因或理由。選項(A)和(B)引導一個矛盾事實。選項(D)引導一個結果。

5. 儘管我很早就送出報名表，還是沒搶到課堂名額。
   (A) 因為
   (B) 一……就
   (C) 因此
   (D) 即使

解析 (D) even though 引導一個矛盾事實，提早報名的預期結果是搶到課堂名額，沒搶到就是一種矛盾事實。選項(A)引導一個原因。選項(B)引導一個時間子句。選項(C)引導一個結果。

高分攻略 12　未來時間子句

1. 我會讓你知道火車抵達的時間。
   (A)(B)(C)(D) 抵達

解析 (B) arrives 是現在式動詞，用於未來時間子句，並和子句的主詞 train 一致。選項(A)雖然是現在式，卻和主詞不一致。選項(C)是未來式。選項(D)是動名詞。

2. 簽約之前我們會先和律師討論過。
    (A)(B)(C) 簽名 (v.)
    (D) 簽名 (n.)

解析 **(A)** 主要子句的動詞是未來式，因此時間子句要用現在式。選項(B)是不定詞，不能當作子句的主要動詞。選項(C)是未來式。選項(D)是名詞。

3. 會議結束時，你們就會完全了解我們的行銷計畫。

解析 **(C)** 主要子句的動詞是未來式，因此時間子句要用現在式。選項(A)是未來式。選項(B)是過去式。選項(D)是原形動詞。

4. 等明天主管們開完會，我們就會知道加薪方面的決定。
    (A)(B)(C)(D) 開會

解析 **(D)** 未來時間子句的動詞必須使用現在式。選項(A)是未來式。選項(B)是不定詞。選項(C)是過去式。

5. 他們完成前面房間的工程後，下週就會準備粉刷走廊。

解析 **(D)** 這是一個描述未來事件（next week）的句子，空格所在之處為主要子句，要用未來式。選項(A)是現在式。選項(B)是原形動詞。選項(C)是一個不完整的未來式，完整應為 are going to be。

Part 6 段落填空

高分攻略 1　頻率副詞

1. 我們很少在週末舉行員工會議。事實上，我想這是第一次我們這樣做，不過突然有很重要的事情被提出了。
   (A) 很少
   (B) 經常
   (C) 時常
   (D) 有時

   解析 (A) rarely 的意思是「幾乎從不」，從句中的資訊可看到這是第一次在週末開會，因此選項(A)符合前後文的描述。選項(B)(C)(D)所描述的頻率較高。

2. 請注意，嚴守時間在本公司非常重要。我們一向準時開始員工會議，不會等遲到的人。
   (A) 從未
   (B) 很少
   (C) 偶爾
   (D) 總是

   解析 (D) always 的意思是「總是、一向」，從前後文可清楚知道會議一向準時開始。選項(A)(B)(C)所描述的頻率較低。

3. 我們的會議通常進行一小時左右，我預計這次也是一樣。
   (A) 通常
   (B) 有時
   (C) 很少
   (D) 從未

   解析 (A) usually 的意思是「大多時候」，前後語意連貫。選項(B)(C)(D)所描述的頻率都較低。

4. 金先生不會出席本次會議，這在大家的意料之外，因為他很少缺席會議。
   (A) 通常
   (B) 很少
   (C) 經常
   (D) 偶爾

   解析 (B) seldom 的意思是「幾乎從不」，從前後文可看出金先生的缺席是「意料之外」，暗示了他幾乎從不缺席會議。選項(A)(C)(D)所描述的頻率較高。

5. 會議結束後我們經常提供點心，然而這次會議我們沒有時間那樣做。
   (A) 很少
   (B) 從未
   (C) 經常
   (D) 很少

   解析 (C) however 所引導的資訊顯示這次不會提供點心，暗示了以前常常提供點心，often 就是「常常、經常」。選項 (A)(B)(D) 所描述的頻率較低。

高分攻略 2　主要動詞後接動名詞或不定詞

1. 我和我們的客戶威爾森先生在電話上談過了，他同意和我們見面討論這份合約。
   (A)(B)(C)(D) 見面

   解析 (C) agree 後面要接不定詞。選項 (A)(B)(D) 都不是不定詞。

2. 我們這週的行程已經滿了，但威爾森先生不介意等到下週再預約。
   (A)(B)(C)(D) 等待

   解析 (B) mind 後面要接動名詞。選項 (A)(C)(D) 都不是動名詞。

3. 我已提出可以寄一份合約草稿到威爾森先生的辦公室，讓他有機會在會議前先看過。
   (A)(B)(C)(D) 寄

   解析 (B) offer 後面要接不定詞。選項 (A)(C)(D) 都不是不定詞。

4. 這份合約尚未完成，不過今天結束之前我應該可以寫好。
   (A)(B)(C)(D) 寫

   解析 (A) finish 後面要接動名詞。選項 (B)(C)(D) 都不是動名詞。

5. 在我將合約寄給威爾森先生之前，希望你先幫我看過一遍。我打算明天早上放在你的辦公桌上。
   (A)(B)(C)(D) 放

   解析 (D) plan 後面要接不定詞。選項 (A)(B)(C) 都不是不定詞。

高分攻略 3 　介系詞和形容詞後接動名詞或不定詞

1. 你的員工是否抱怨經常頭痛或持續眼睛痛呢？問題可能出在你的照明系統。
   (A)(B)(C)(D) 患有

   解析 (B) about是介系詞，後面要接動名詞。選項(A)(C)(D)都不是動名詞。

2. 有些類型的燈光會發出刺眼強光，給眼睛帶來壓力，你需要的是能產生柔和散光的照明系統，既不傷眼睛，又足夠明亮可供閱讀。
   (A)(B)(C)(D) 閱讀

   解析 (C) bright enough使用的是「形容詞+enough」的句型，後面要接不定詞。選項(A)(B)(D)都不是不定詞。

3. 有了適當的照明系統，員工就能輕鬆舒適地坐在辦公桌前準備開始工作。
   (A)(B)(C)(D) 工作

   解析 (A) ready是形容詞，後面要接不定詞。選項(B)(C)(D)都不是不定詞。

4. 如果你已經厭倦了在工作場所聽到關於燈光的抱怨，現在是時候做出改變了。
   (A)(B)(C)(D) 聽到

   解析 (D) of是介系詞，後面要接動名詞。選項(A)(B)(C)都不是動名詞。

5. 你可先從改變幾個地方的燈光開始，或可決定在整間辦公室安裝全新的照明系統。
   (A)(B)(C)(D) 安裝

   解析 (C) on是介系詞，後面要接動名詞。選項(A)(B)(D)都不是動名詞。

高分攻略 4 　使役動詞

1. 我們新來的員工約翰‧格林似乎對訂購辦公用品有點疑惑，請讓他明白送出訂單前必須取得核准。
   (A)(B)(C)(D) 明白、了解

   解析 (A) 使役動詞make後面要接原形動詞。選項(B)(C)(D)都不是原形動詞。

113

2. 我們無法允許員工隨時訂購任何用品,這樣會造成預算混亂。
   (A)(B)(C)(D) 訂購

   解析 **(B)** 使役動詞permit後面要接不定詞。選項(A)(C)(D)都不是不定詞。

3. 是時候開始規劃我們的年度假期午餐會了。請讓約翰・格林在本週結束前打電話給餐飲承辦商。
   (A)(B)(C)(D) 打電話

   解析 **(A)** 使役動詞have後面要接原形動詞。選項(B)(C)(D)都不是原形動詞。

4. 他應該讓餐飲承辦商提供幾種菜單選擇,然後我們可以一起決定想要哪一種。
   (A)(B)(C)(D) 提供

   解析 **(C)** 使役動詞get後面要接不定詞。選項(A)(B)(D)都不是不定詞。

5. 格林先生是新進員工,還不熟悉公司的習慣,所以我覺得我們不應該讓他自己選菜單。
   (A)(B)(C)(D) 選擇

   解析 **(D)** 使役動詞let後面要接原形動詞。選項(A)(B)(C)都不是原形動詞。

高分攻略 5　真實條件句

1. 8月21日開始選課登記,8月29日開始上課。如果你在8月28日之後才選課,必須繳交逾期費。
   (A)(B)(C)(D) 報名、註冊

   解析 **(A)** 真實條件句中的if子句必須使用現在式。選項(B)是不定詞。選項(C)和(D)是未來式。

2. 部分課程可能學生不足。如因人數太少而取消課程,我們會與你聯繫。
   (A)(B)(C)(D) 取消

   解析 **(B)** 真實條件句中的if子句必須使用現在式。選項(A)是不定詞。選項(C)是動名詞。選項(D)是未來式。

3. 請記得在報名表上提供你的電話和電子郵件地址,如果沒有這些資訊,我們將無法與你聯繫。

   解析 **(C)** 真實條件句中的主要子句必須使用未來式。選項(A)是原形動詞。選項(B)是現在式。選項(D)是過去式。

4. 我們為在職人士提供課程。如果你白天沒時間上課，請參考我們的夜間課程表。
   (A)(B)(C)(D) 沒有

   解析 **(D)** 真實條件句中的if子句必須使用現在式。選項(A)是原形動詞。選項(B)是過去式。選項(C)是未來式。

5. 若你攜帶報名表至學校書店，購買課程所需之教科書可享優惠。
   (A)(B)(C)(D) 得到、收到

   解析 **(C)** 真實條件句中的主要子句必須使用未來式。選項(A)是現在式或原形動詞。選項(B)是不定詞。選項(D)是現在完成式。

高分攻略 6　非真實條件句

1. 克魯格曼先生您好，關於昨日發生的誤會，我感到十分抱歉。要是我知道七號車位是您的指定車位，我絕不會把車停在那裡。
   (A)(B)(C)(D) 知道

   解析 **(B)** 描述過去情況的非真實條件句，if子句要用過去完成式。選項(A)是過去簡單式。選項(C)是現在完成式。選項(D)如果用在描述現在情況的非真實條件句，就會是正確答案。

2. 若您在別的地方付費停車，我一定賠償這些費用。幸好您在員工停車場有找到免費車位了。
   (A)(B)(C)(D) 支付

   解析 **(B)** 描述過去情況的非真實條件句，if子句要用過去完成式。選項(A)是現在完成式。選項(C)是現在式。選項(D)是未來式。

3. 我今天在辦公室找您，發現您今天不在。假如您今天在的話，我一定會當面向您道歉。

   解析 **(C)** 描述現在情況的非真實條件句，if子句要用過去式。選項(A)是現在式。選項(B)是未來式。選項(D)是過去完成式。

4. 停車在這一帶是個嚴重問題。若我住得沒離辦公室那麼遠，我每天走路上班就能避免停車問題了。
   (A)(B)(C)(D) 避免

   解析 **(D)** 描述現在情況的非真實條件句，主要子句要用「would+原形動詞」。選項(A)是過去式。選項(B)是過去完成式。選項(C)是描述過去情況的非真實條件句。

5. 假如我昨天走路去上班的話，就不會把車停到您的車位了。
   (A)(B)(C)(D) 不會停車

解析 (A) 描述過去情況的非真實條件句，主要子句要用「would have+過去分詞」的句型。選項(B)是描述現在情況的非真實條件句。選項(C)是過去式。選項(D)是過去完成式。

高分攻略 7　比較

1. 泰克諾商業學院為上班族提供短期密集的技能培訓課程。我們保證會以您能負擔的價格，提供比其他商業學院更快速的培訓。
   (A) 更快速
   (B) 更好
   (C) 更長
   (D) 更昂貴

解析 (A)「faster than」使用了「字尾-er + than」的比較級句型，是正確用法，同時符合情境意義。選項(B)不符合商業培訓的情境。選項(C)不正確，該課程為短期而非長期。選項(D)不正確，該課程是「您能負擔的價格」，也就是說不貴。

2. 有些學校每項課程會收取數百美金的費用，但在泰克諾商業學院，我們保證是全鎮最低價。
   (A) 低的
   (B) 最低的
   (C) 低於
   (D) 最低的

解析 (D)「the lowest」使用了「the + 字尾-est」的最高級句型，是正確用法。選項(A)是形容詞，卻沒有使用最高級。選項(B)是形容詞最高級，但忘了加the。選項(C)是比較級，不是最高級。

3. 我們應屆畢業生得到的薪資高於其他擁有多年經驗的辦公室專業人士。
   (A) 高的
   (B) 高於
   (C) 最高的
   (D) 最高的

解析 (B) higher是形容詞比較級，句中已出現了than，因此正確答案應填入higher。選項(A)(C)(D)都不能和than搭配使用。

4. 如果你正在找一個比現在更好的工作，泰克諾商業學院可以幫助你。
   (A) 最好的
   (B) 最好的
   (C) 更好的
   (D) 好的

   解析 (C) better 和句中的 than 可以搭配構成比較級。選項(A)和(B)是最高級，但(B)忘了加 the。選項(D)是原級。

5. 泰克諾商業學院所頒發的證書會為你開啟就業大門，雇主知道技術能力最強的員工都是我們課程的畢業生。
   (A) 最高的
   (B) 技術能力最強的
   (C) 最不能勝任的
   (D) 最便宜的

   解析 (B) 雇主最有可能在找技術能力最強的員工。選項(A)不會用來描述員工。選項(C)和(D)所描述的特質不會是雇主想要的。

高分攻略 8　代名詞

1. 柯爾曼女士您好，上週拜訪分公司時，承蒙您的熱情款待，十分感謝。請告訴您的員工，我非常感激他們對我的歡迎。
   (A) 你自己
   (B) 你的（東西）
   (C) 你
   (D) 你的

   解析 (D) your 是所有格形容詞，修飾名詞 staff，其先行詞為 you（指柯爾曼女士）。選項(A)是反身代名詞。選項(B)是所有格代名詞。選項(C)是主格或受格代名詞。

2. 辦公室所有員工友善和樂於助人的態度讓我留下深刻印象。即使我在一個不熟悉的環境中工作，他們仍讓我的工作進行得非常順利。
   (A) 我
   (B) 他
   (C) 你
   (D) 他們

解析 **(D)** 這裡的先行詞是第三人稱複數名詞employees，因此代名詞也要用第三人稱複數they。選項(A)是第一人稱單數。選項(B)是第三人稱單數。選項(C)是第二人稱單數或複數。

3. 我要特別提及約翰‧馬爾斯壯，他特別努力確保我需要的一切都有齊全，請代我向他致謝。
    (A) 我
    (B) 他
    (C) 她／她的
    (D) 他們

解析 **(B)** 這裡的先行詞是第三人稱單數名詞John Malstrom，因此代名詞也要用第三人稱單數him。選項(A)是第一人稱單數。選項(C)是第三人稱單數，但用於女性而非男性，John是男性的名字。選項(D)是第三人稱複數。

4. 不幸的是，我在拜訪期間把一個裝有重要文件的資料夾遺留在那裡。我想我把它放在會議室桌上。
    (A) 它
    (B) 他
    (C) 他們
    (D) 我

解析 **(A)** 先行詞folder是第三人稱單數名詞且指物品。選項(B)雖然也是第三人稱單數，但用來指人。選項(C)是第三人稱複數。選項(D)是第一人稱單數。

5. 能否煩請您將我遺忘的物品寄到我辦公室呢？我沒有時間自己過去拿資料夾。
    (A) 它自己
    (B) 你自己
    (C) 我自己
    (D) 他們自己

解析 **(C)** 這裡的先行詞是I，因此要用第一人稱的反身代名詞myself。選項(A)(B)(D)都不是第一人稱。

高分攻略 9　主格關係代名詞

1. 麥金泰爾女士下週會從倫敦辦公室過來拜訪我們。想預約與她見面的職員可聯繫人力資源室。

   解析 (A) 先行詞 staff members 是一群人，且這裡需要一個主格關係代名詞，因此要選 who。選項(B)是受格關係代名詞。選項(C)指代的是所有格。選項(D)指代的是事物。

2. 週三將在繁花餐廳為麥金泰爾女士舉辦午餐宴，行程安排允許的人都歡迎參加此活動。

   解析 (C) whose 是所有格關係代名詞，指代的是 everyone's，即「everyone's schedule」。選項(A)用來指代人，不指代所有格。選項(B)和(D)都不是關係代名詞。

3. 我們都期待麥金泰爾女士的來訪，這次造訪將持續十天。

   解析 (D) 先行詞 visit 是事物，因此要選 which。選項(A)用來指代人。選項(B)指代的是人或物，但不能用於非限定性子句。選項(C)用於指代所有格。

4. 麥金泰爾女士會在各部門停留一些時間。假如你想知道她何時會到你的部門，請查看公司網站提供的行程表。

   解析 (B) that 引導一個限定性子句，先行詞是 schedule。選項(A)不是關係代名詞。選項(C)用來指代人而非物。選項(D)用來指代所有格。

5. 麥金泰爾女士難得有機會造訪海外辦公室，她十分期待這次的造訪。

   解析 (B) 關係代名詞 who 用來指代人，在這裡指代的是 Ms. McIntyre。選項(A)只能用於限定性子句，但此處為非限定性子句。選項(C)用來指代事物。選項(D)不是關係代名詞。

高分攻略 10　受格關係代名詞

1. 你想更了解全球暖化以及如何為防止全球暖化盡一分心力嗎？赫曼·弗烈德曼博士是許多人公認該主題的最高權威，下週二將於葛雷森廳演講。

   解析 (C) 先行詞 Dr. Herman Friedman 是人，要用指人的關係代名詞。選項(A)指代所有格。選項(B)指事物。選項(D)不是關係代名詞。

2. 弗烈德曼博士寫過許多關於全球暖化主題的文章和書籍。他多年研究大堡礁逐漸白化的現象，這也是他最新一本書的主題。

解析 (B) 先行詞the gradual bleaching of the Great Barrier Reef為事物，要用指事物的關係代名詞。選項(A)雖也可指代事物，但只能用於限定性子句，這裡是非限定性子句。選項(C)指人。選項(D)不是關係代名詞。

3. 演講結束後，他的簽名書和其他全球暖化相關著作將會販售。

解析 (B) 先行詞books是物，且此為限定性子句因此要用that。選項(A)用於指代所有格。選項(C)不是關係代名詞。選項(D)指人。

4. 弗烈德曼博士將由一名同事陪同。史邁斯博士的全球暖化著作亦廣為人知，他將展示研究考察珊瑚礁的投影片。

解析 (D) whose是所有格關係代名詞，在這裡指代Dr. Smythe's，表示Dr. Smythe's writings。選項(A)(B)(C)都不是所有格。

5. 想進一步了解全球暖化現象的人，千萬別錯過這場活動。弗烈德曼博士和史邁斯博士都是風趣且知識淵博的講者，他們在此主題知識上的貢獻令我們受惠良多。

解析 (A) 這裡的先行詞是兩個人：Drs. Friedman and Smythe，因此要用whom。選項(B)用於指代所有格。選項(C)不是關係代名詞。選項(D)用於指事物。

高分攻略 11　被動語態

1. 我們才剛投入大量心力整修會議室，更不必說金錢了。除了添購新桌椅，牆壁上個月也進行了粉刷。

解析 (C) 這個句子是過去式（last month）的被動語態，主詞是複數的walls，因此be動詞要用were。選項(A)是單數。選項(B)是現在式。選項(D)是現在完成式。

2. 我們和地毯公司的合作出了點狀況，但已經解決，他們答應在這週結束前鋪好新地毯。
   (A)(B)(C)(D) 安裝、鋪設

解析 (B) 這裡要用被動語態，主詞carpet（地毯）不可能自己鋪設，be動詞後面要用過去分詞（installed）。選項(A)是主動語態。選項(C)是動名詞。選項(D)是名詞。

3. 會議室裡唯一沒換新的是窗簾。我們決定窗簾只需徹底清潔。我們把窗簾送到一家專業的清潔機構，將汙漬去除，現在它們就跟新的一樣。
   (A)(B)(C)(D) 去除

解析 (D) 這裡要用被動語態，主詞stains（汙漬）不可能自己去除。選項(A)(B)(C)都是主動語態。

4. 現在會議室已經整修完成，希望大家會覺得那裡是個令人感到愉悅的工作空間。
   (A)(B)(C)(D) 整修

解析 **(A)** 這裡要用被動語態，主詞 conference room 不會自己整修。選項 (B)(C)(D) 都是主動語態。

5. 整修期間感謝大家的耐心等待。為慶祝新的會議室啟用，下個月將舉辦一場派對。
   (A)(B)(C)(D) 舉辦

解析 **(D)** 這裡要用被動語態，主詞 party 不會自己舉辦，而這個動作發生在未來（next month），所以要用未來式的被動語態 will be given。選項 (A) 和 (B) 是主動語態。選項 (C) 是不定詞，不是未來式。

高分攻略 12　字義

1. 這棟大樓維護得非常好，房東將所有公共區域維持清潔，最近還重新鋪設了走廊地毯。
   (A) 房東
   (B) 房客
   (C) 居民
   (D) 建築師

解析 **(A)** landlord 指的是建物的持有者，也是能夠維持大樓清潔和重新鋪設走廊地毯的合理人選。選項 (B)(C)(D) 不會負責這些事情。

2. 我們去年粉刷了公寓，房間很暗，所以我們選了一個淺色讓空間變得明亮。
   (A) 承認
   (B) 擁有
   (C) 選擇
   (D) 享受

解析 **(C)** selected 是「選擇」的意思。選項 (A)(B)(D) 都不適用於這個句子。

3. 這棟大樓的地理位置很好，距離一個街區就是地鐵站，附近也有許多不錯的商店和餐廳。優越的地理位置是租金如此高的一個原因。
   (A) 合理的
   (B) 不尋常的
   (C) 公平的
   (D) 高的

解析 **(D)** 如果大樓的位置非常理想，通常租金會很高（high rent）。選項 (A)(B)(C) 都不符合這裡的語境。

4. 許多人到城市這一區從事文化活動。這裡除了有博物館和戲院,每年夏天公園都會舉辦演奏會。
   (A) 體育的
   (B) 文化的
   (C) 戲劇的
   (D) 表演

解析 (B) 與藝術、音樂、戲院等相關的活動會叫文化活動（cultural activities）。選項(A)(C)(D)均不符合這裡的語境。

5. 許多活動免費開放市民參加,只要證明你住在本市,就不會向你收取入場費。
   (A) 允許
   (B) 收費
   (C) 購買
   (D) 要求

解析 (B) charged 的意思是「向……收費」。選項(A)(C)(D)都不適用於這個句子。

高分攻略 13　句子選擇

1. 本大樓電梯將於9月15日當週進行例行維修,_____,出現這種情況時,請利用另一部電梯或走樓梯。造成您的不便,我們深表歉意。
   (A) 本大樓共有三部電梯,各可容納十五名乘客
   (B) 在這週,不時會有一或兩部電梯暫停服務
   (C) 有些人因為喜歡運動,所以傾向於走樓梯
   (D) 每部電梯都配有紅色緊急電話

解析 (B) 這段文字是在通知住戶預定進行的電梯維修工程,以及可能造成使用上的不便。從邏輯上來看,選項(B)適合填入這個段落,選項(A)(C)(D)都不符合這裡的語境。

2. 感謝您同意下週與我見面,_____。我非常期待有機會與您討論我的公司和我們能為您提供的服務。過去我們已服務過許多像您這樣的客戶,他們都表示滿意,我相信我們也能提供令您滿意的服務。
   (A) 我喜歡時不時的社交聚會
   (B) 我的會議行程很滿,沒什麼時間安排其他事情
   (C) 我會在十點的時候到金色咖啡館找您
   (D) 我一直無法透過電話或電子郵件聯繫到您

解析 (C) 前面的句子提到兩人約定見面,選項(C)的句子進一步描述見面的時間和地點,邏輯上前後連貫。選項(A)(B)(D)都不符合這裡的語境。

3. 感謝您將履歷寄給我們，您的教育背景和經驗正是我們在找的，我想請您盡快過來面試，_____。
   (A) 請打電話到我辦公室約時間
   (B) 市內有幾個地方可以提供您所需的培訓
   (C) 我們需要僱用新員工時，通常透過職業介紹所
   (D) 很多年輕人在找這個領域的職位

解析 (A) 前一句請求職者過來面試，選項(A)進一步說明約時間的方法，邏輯上前後連貫。選項(B)(C)(D)都不符合這裡的語境。

4. 感謝您有興趣使用潔塵辦公室清潔公司的服務，我們已經為您預約下週一早上的服務時間，_____。如同我們在電話中討論過的，我們預計這項工作會進行三到四小時。我們會將所有房間用吸塵器吸過並且除塵。費用於服務時支付。
   (A) 我們在本市從事辦公室清潔已有五年以上的時間
   (B) 週一通常是我們一週中最忙碌的一天
   (C) 大部分客戶每週固定找我們清潔一次
   (D) 我們會在上午八點抵達，準備開始打掃

解析 (D) 前面的句子說明預約的日子，選項(D)說明預約的確切時間，邏輯上前後連貫。選項(A)(B)(C)都不符合這裡的語境。

Part 7 閱讀測驗

高分攻略 1 廣告

第1–2題請看下面這則廣告。選出最適當的答案回答問題。

製造業者請注意！

我們可以將您的產品介紹並分銷到155個國家的125,000個經銷商，而且免費！

索取免費資料包請撥打：

電話：(310) 553-4434 分機105
傳真：(310) 553-5555
宏大科技有限公司

---

1. 這則廣告是寫給誰看的？
   (A) 經銷商
   (B) 業務
   (C) 製造商
   (D) 資訊專員

解析 (C) 標題「Attention Manufacturers」指出作者希望製造業者來看這則廣告。選項(A)把廣告的作者和讀者混淆了。選項(B)和(D)在廣告中均未提及。

2. 廣告中提到幾個國家？
   (A) 125個
   (B) 155個
   (C) 310個
   (D) 501個

解析 (B) 廣告中提到他們可將產品分銷到155個國家。選項(A)少於提及的數量。選項(C)和(D)均多於提及的數量。

高分攻略 2　表單

第 1–3 題請看下面這張表單。選出最適當的答案回答問題。

《商業新聞月刊》是讓您了解影響國內與國際商務世界最新消息的首選刊物。只要在下方填入您的資訊，就能訂閱一年（十二期）的紙本和電子雜誌！或現在一次訂閱兩年可以省更多。

姓名：郭安妮
電子郵件：akwok@pharmamail.co
公司：藥品供應公司
地址 1：夏那街 1705 號
地址 2：新倫敦

付款資訊
卡別：Xtra Card
卡號：1234567

總計：$199.99（一年）
　　　$349.99（兩年）

---

1. 這份刊物多久出刊一次？
    (A) 一週一次
    (B) 一個月一次
    (C) 半年一次
    (D) 一年一次

解析 (B) 表單中提到一年十二期，可見是一個月出刊一次。選項 (A) 的出刊頻率比描述的高，選項 (C) 和 (D) 則比描述的低。

2. 郭小姐會以何種形式收到月刊？
    (A) 她只能線上閱讀。
    (B) 她只會收到紙本。
    (C) 她會同時收到線上版和紙本。
    (D) 她會跟上司借一本來看。

解析 (C) 這份表單訂閱的是紙本加電子雜誌，訂閱者會同時收到紙本和線上版。選項 (A) 和 (B) 不正確，兩種她都會收到，不會只收到其中一種。選項 (D) 並未被提及。

3. 訂閱一年的費用是多少？
   (A) 大約20美元
   (B) 略低於200美元
   (C) 大約175美元
   (D) 將近350美元

解析 (B) 訂閱一年的費用是199.99美元，略低於200美元。選項(A)和(C)未被提及。選項(D)是接近訂閱兩年的費用。

高分攻略 3　書信

第1–3題請看下面這封信。選出最適當的答案回答問題。

X-Cellent 公司
普林斯戴爾82號信箱

20—年12月3日

喬治·韓德利斯
Whyo 公司
主街44號
普林斯戴爾

韓德利斯先生，您好：

此信是對我們近日關於貴公司於米道敦市所持有大樓的討論進行確認。按協定，本公司將對位於米道敦市橋街115號之房產進行評估，作為貴公司目前正在進行之整體資產評估的一部分。我們會對該大樓進行實體檢查，並審核該大樓所有權歷史的相關紀錄，同時針對其他大小、地點和類型相當的房產進行研究。我們會向貴公司提供一份詳細報告，分析我們用於得出貴公司房產之公平市場價值的數據和方法。這份報告將於下個月底前交付給您。為了開始上述工作之進行，我們需要商定價格的50％作為首款，餘款則待報告提交時再支付。若您同意上述條款，請盡快將簽字的信件副本寄到我的辦公室。

祝好，
馬克·威爾森

1. 這封信的目的是什麼？
    (A) 描述某人的專業背景
    (B) 說明如何販售一處房產
    (C) 接受一份工作邀約
    (D) 描述將會進行的工作

解析 (D) 這封信描述了威爾森先生的公司將會進行的工作，包括檢查大樓、審核紀錄、研究其他房產。選項(A)和(C)把公司將進行的工作，和某人有資格做的工作、某人將受僱做的工作混為一談了。選項(B)則是被信中關於房產和市值的討論給混淆了，但信中並沒有提到販售之事。

2. 這封信的撰寫人從事何種職業？
    (A) 他是賣房地產的。
    (B) 他借錢給房地產買家。
    (C) 他決定房地產的價值。
    (D) 他對房地產進行安全檢查。

解析 (C) 這封信提到他的公司會「對房產進行評估」(perform an appraisal of the property)，意思就是說，他會決定房地產的價值。選項(A)(B)(D)是與房地產銷售有關的工作，但不是本信撰寫人所從事的職業。

3. 這封信的收件者現在必須做什麼？
    (A) 協商付款事宜
    (B) 簽署文件
    (C) 提交報告
    (D) 造訪大樓

解析 (B) 這封信的最後一句話說「若您同意上述條款，請盡快將簽字的信件副本寄到我的辦公室」，所以收件者現在要做的是簽署文件。選項(A)不正確，這封信提到已有商定價格，也說明了付款方式，不需再協商。選項(C)和(D)則是寄件者要做的事。

高分攻略 4 備忘錄

第1–4題請看下面這則備忘錄。選出最適當的答案回答問題。

備忘錄

收件人：全體員工
發布人：賽門・岡薩雷斯
　　　　人事專員
日期：20─年5月15日
主旨：出差

自6月1日起，所有因公出差的員工必須盡可能使用最經濟的交通方式。五小時以內的飛行時間不得訂商務艙，無論飛行時間多長一律不得訂頭等艙。

---

1. 飛行時間超過五小時可以訂何種艙等？
    (A) 經濟艙
    (B) 豪華經濟艙
    (C) 商務艙
    (D) 頭等艙

解析 (C) 文中提到「五小時以內的飛行時間不得訂商務艙」，這就表示五小時以上可以。選項(A)和(B)或許也可以，但文中並未提及。選項(D)和文中「無論飛行時間多長一律不得訂頭等艙」的描述相矛盾。

2. 這項規定何時生效？
    (A) 約兩週後
    (B) 夏末
    (C) 年初
    (D) 五個月後

解析 (A) 這份備忘錄的撰寫日期是5月15日，生效日期是6月1日，那就是兩週後生效。選項(B)和(C)都和6月1日的時間不符。選項(D)把文中的五小時（five hours）混淆成五個月。

3. 為什麼要寫這份備忘錄？
    (A) 省時
    (B) 省錢
    (C) 獎勵員工
    (D) 增加出差量

解析 (B) 這份備忘錄要求大家使用經濟的方式出差，也就是為了省錢。選項(A)(C)(D)均未被提及。

4. 誰會受這份備忘錄影響？
    (A) 只有董事會
    (B) 只有經常出差的人
    (C) 只有人事部
    (D) 全體員工

解析 (D) 受這份備忘錄影響的人，也就是收件人，是 all employees，和 all personnel 的意思一樣，都指全體員工。選項(A)(B)(C)都和全體員工相抵觸。

高分攻略 5 **表格**

第 1–4 題請看下面這個表格。選出最適當的答案回答問題。

全球氣溫
1月5日

	高溫（攝氏／華氏）	低溫（攝氏／華氏）	天氣狀況
阿姆斯特丹	6／41	3／37	多雲
雅典	13／55	8／46	陣雨
曼谷	32／90	27／80	陣雨
北京	12／53	1／34	晴時多雲
布魯塞爾	4／39	1／34	陣雨
布達佩斯	3／37	0／32	雨
法蘭克福	3／37	1／34	雨
雅加達	29／84	24／75	陣雨
吉隆坡	31／88	24／75	雷雨
馬德里	9／48	1／34	陣雨
馬尼拉	33／91	21／70	晴時多雲
首爾	9／48	−2／29	晴
臺北	21／70	14／57	多雲
東京	9／48	−2／29	晴時多雲

天氣狀況：s 晴、pc 晴時多雲、c 多雲、sh 陣雨、t 雷雨、r 雨

1. 哪兩座城市在1月5日是多雲的天氣？
    (A) 阿姆斯特丹和臺北
    (B) 北京和馬尼拉
    (C) 雅典和東京
    (D) 曼谷和首爾

解析 (A) 阿姆斯特丹和臺北都標示為c，代表cloudy（多雲）。選項(B)中的兩座城市都是晴時多雲。選項(C)和(D)中的城市天氣不同，且都不是多雲。

2. 哪座城市的氣溫最高？
    (A) 雅典
    (B) 曼谷
    (C) 雅加達
    (D) 馬尼拉

解析 (D) 馬尼拉的高溫達到攝氏33度（華氏91度），為最高的。選項(A)(B)(C)的溫度都沒有馬尼拉高。

3. 哪座城市的溫差最小？
    (A) 布魯塞爾
    (B) 法蘭克福
    (C) 首爾
    (D) 東京

解析 (B) 法蘭克福的最高溫為攝氏3度，最低溫為攝氏1度，溫差為2度是最小的。選項(A)(C)(D)的溫差都比法蘭克福大。

4. 吉隆坡的天氣狀況為
    (A) 晴
    (B) 雷雨
    (C) 雨
    (D) 陣雨

解析 (B) 吉隆坡的標示為t，代表thunderstorms（雷雨）。選項(A)(C)(D)都與這座城市的天氣標示不符。

高分攻略 6　　圖表

第 1–2 題請看下面這張圖表。選出最適當的答案回答問題。

連鎖飯店市占率

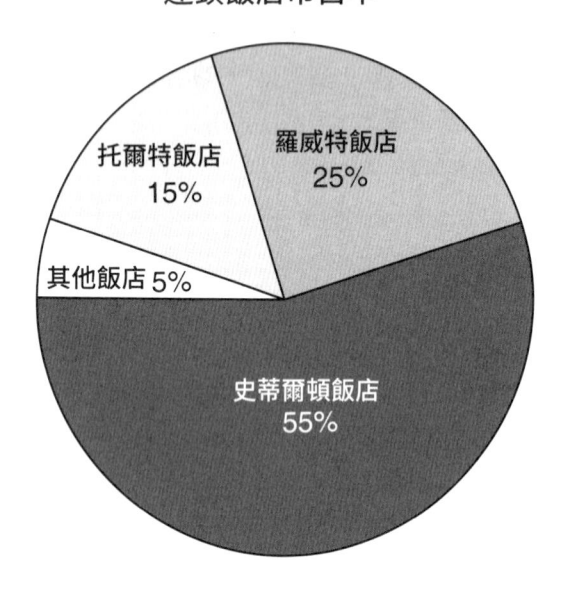

- 羅威特飯店 25%
- 托爾特飯店 15%
- 其他飯店 5%
- 史蒂爾頓飯店 55%

1. 誰對閱讀這張圖表最感興趣？
    (A) 觀光客
    (B) 競爭飯店
    (C) 景觀設計師
    (D) 求職者

解析 (B) 對市占率最感興趣的應為競爭飯店。選項 (A)(C)(D) 不太可能對這項資訊感興趣。

2. 根據這張圖表，羅威特飯店
    (A) 是市占率最高的連鎖飯店
    (B) 只開在拉丁美洲
    (C) 市占率不如托爾特飯店
    (D) 占有四分之一的市場

解析 (D) 羅威特占有 25%，也就是四分之一的市場。選項 (A) 不正確，最高的是史蒂爾頓飯店。選項 (B) 不正確，圖表中並未提供地點資訊。選項 (C) 不正確，托爾特飯店的市占率只有 15%，低於羅威特飯店。

高分攻略 7　公告

第 1–4 題請看下面這則公告。選出最適當的答案回答問題。

> 城市商會宣布今年的城市就業博覽會將於 3 月 11 日在城市會議中心舉行，–[1]– 這是了解哪裡有職缺並認識招聘方的難得機會，同時還有關於履歷撰寫、面試技巧、求職資源等的工作坊。–[2]– 工作坊為免費參加，但須事先報名。–[3]– 更多關於工作坊的資訊請見商會官網。本活動開放大眾參加，快來這裡取得求職成功所需的資訊。–[4]–

1. 這項活動多久舉辦一次？
    (A) 僅此一次
    (B) 一個月一次
    (C) 一年兩次
    (D) 一年一次

解析 (D) 這項活動被描述為「this year's City Job Fair」，片語 this year's 暗示了這項活動每年都會舉辦。選項(A)(B)(C)都不是這個片語的意思。

2. 關於工作坊有何說明？
    (A) 會採線上方式進行。
    (B) 會收取小額費用。
    (C) 參加者必須事先報名。
    (D) 已經額滿。

解析 (C) 這段文字中提到「pre-registration is required」（須事先報名）。選項(A)是被文中提到可上官網獲得更多資訊給混淆了。選項(B)不正確，文中提到工作坊為免費參加。選項(D)也許有可能，但文中並未提及。

3. 第三行中的「unique」與下列何者意義最接近？
    (A) 有趣的
    (B) 重要的
    (C) 有限的
    (D) 稀有的

解析 (D) unique 為獨特的、珍奇的，和 rare（稀有的、罕見的）意思相近。選項(A)(B)(C)都不是這個字的意義。

4. 下面這個句子最適合填入文中 [1][2][3][4] 哪一個位置？
「來自各地區代表各行業的雇主都將出席。」
   (A) [1]
   (B) [2]
   (C) [3]
   (D) [4]

解析 (A) 第一句陳述了即將舉辦一場就業博覽會，選項(A)的句子進一步提到會有哪些人參加，大致說明了博覽會的性質，後面內容都在詳述博覽會的細節，因此選項(B)(C)(D)的位置都不適合插入這個句子。

高分攻略 8　通知

第 1–2 題請看下面這則通知。選出最適當的答案回答問題。

公司政策調整

搬家費。新家與舊家距離五十英里以上才可報銷搬家費用。此外，報銷費用僅限於將家居用品和個人財產從舊家搬至新家的費用。餐費、搬家前找房子的支出和臨時住宿費均不再提供報銷。

---

1. 誰受這項通知的影響最大？
   (A) 連鎖飯店
   (B) 家具出租公司
   (C) 房地產經紀人
   (D) 從其他城市搬來的新員工

解析 (D) 這項通知的內容是關於搬家費用報銷的調整，因此從其他城市搬來的新員工受影響最大。選項(A)(B)(C)都不受這些調整影響。

2. 下列哪個項目可以報銷？
   (A) 搬家工人的午餐
   (B) 家居用品的運送
   (C) 找房子的油錢
   (D) 飯店住宿

解析 (B) 文中提到「moving household goods」（搬運家居用品）可以報銷。選項(A)(C)(D)已經不再可以報銷了。

高分攻略 9 文章

第 1-4 題請看下面這篇文章。選出最適當的答案回答問題。

餐廳經營者和其他企業經營者一樣，總是在不斷尋找擴大客源和讓餐廳滿座的方法。-[1]- 各式各樣的廣告、社交活動、折扣和特別優惠都是能招攬更多生意的有效方法。近來許多餐廳經營者推出烹飪課程，結果非常成功。

客人願意付錢吃你餐廳準備的食物，事實證明他們也願意花錢學習，讓自己可以親自下廚做飯。-[2]- 提供機會讓民眾學習特殊料理的烹飪課程最為成功。課程可能主要示範一種專門烹飪技術，或展示如何運用當季食材。-[3]- 講解如何料理罕見地方菜的課程往往是最快額滿的。

烹飪課可以當作一項副業，但同時也是替餐廳打廣告的有效方法。-[4]- 舉辦烹飪課需多花一點心力，但成本很低，報酬可能很高。

---

1. 這篇文章主要在講什麼？
    (A) 如何舉辦烹飪課
    (B) 經營餐廳的成本
    (C) 餐廳拓展生意的一種方式
    (D) 吸引顧客的不同方式

解析 (C) 這篇文章講述開設烹飪課程是餐廳吸引顧客進而增加生意的一種方式。選項(A)和(B)雖與主題有關，但在文中並未討論。選項(D)有被提及，但不是文章主旨。

2. 哪一種烹飪課程最受歡迎？
    (A) 學費最低的
    (B) 料理地方菜的
    (C) 運用當季食材的
    (D) 講解特殊技術的

解析 (B) 第二段提到料理地方菜的烹飪課「最快額滿」(fill up most quickly)，也就是說很多人想參加、很受歡迎。選項(A)並未提及。選項(C)和(D)雖被提及，但不是因為最受歡迎才被提及的。

3. 第三段第一行中的「sideline」與下列何者意義最接近？
   (A) 額外的活動
   (B) 小任務
   (C) 費用
   (D) 分心

解析 **(A)** sideline是本業以外的其他活動或工作，即副業。選項(B)(C)(D)都不是sideline的意義。

4. 下面這個句子最適合填入文中[1][2][3][4]哪一個位置？
   「來上烹飪課的人通常會成為忠實顧客，並向別人推薦你的餐廳。」
   (A) [1]
   (B) [2]
   (C) [3]
   (D) [4]

解析 **(D)** 前一個句子說明舉辦烹飪課可有效替餐廳打廣告，接著選項(D)的句子進一步說明細節，講述是如何達到廣告效果的，語意連貫。選項(A)(B)(C)插入這個句子後語意邏輯不通。

高分攻略 10　時間表

第1-4題請看下面這個時刻表。選出最適當的答案回答問題。

第七街與市場街	東升轉運站	隧道站	東122街與十六街
7:11 W	7:21	7:36 T	8:01
7:22 W	7:32	7:47 T	8:12
7:30 W	7:41	7:59 T	8:21
7:40	7:51	8:06	8:32
8:02 W	8:13	8:25	8:53
8:25	8:35	8:49	9:14
8:51 W	9:01	9:15	9:40
9:21	9:32	9:48	10:11
9:51 W	10:10	10:24	10:40

標示說明：

T：隧道上午八點開放，在此時間之前，公車將停靠於十二街與梅瑞迪恩街。

W：公車於此時間發車，將提前約五分鐘抵達本站。

粗體表示尖峰時段票價。

1. 離峰時段票價大概從什麼時間開始？
    (A) 上午7點前
    (B) 上午8點25分
    (C) 上午8點30分
    (D) 上午8點51分

解析 (C) 離峰時段票價大概始於8點25分之後，因此8點30分是合理猜測。選項(A)在表中完全沒有出現。選項(B)和(D)有出現在表中，只是都不是離峰時段票價的開始時間。

2. 7點30分的公車何時抵達第七街和市場街？
    (A) 7點整
    (B) 7點22分
    (C) 7點25分
    (D) 7點30分

解析 (C) 標示說明中提到標示W的公車將提前五分鐘進站，所以7點30分的公車25分就會進站。選項(A)和(B)沒有出現在表中。選項(D)是公車的發車時間。

3. 7點30分的公車為何不能使用隧道？
    (A) 那時是尖峰時段。
    (B) 公車高度超過隧道限高。
    (C) 隧道該時間關閉。
    (D) 早班車的載客量很少足以使用隧道。

解析 (C) 隧道八點才開放。選項(A)雖然可能是事實，但表中沒有提到。選項(B)和(D)都沒有被提到。

4. 從第七街和市場街站到東122街和十六街站要多久時間？
    (A) 十五分鐘
    (B) 半個小時
    (C) 將近一小時
    (D) 一小時整

解析 (C) 一趟大約五十分鐘，也就是將近一小時。這一題需要快速進行數學運算才能作答。選項(A)是十五分鐘。選項(B)是三十分鐘。選項(D)不正確。

高分攻略 11 電子郵件

第1–2題請看下面這封電子郵件。選出最適當的答案回答問題。

寄件者：梅琳達・里格斯
收件者：蜜莎・波蘭泰斯基
主旨：　奧蘭多會議

蜜莎：

這次會議進行得比預期順利。客戶很滿意我們的提案，並未提出任何修改要求。本週結束前他們會將必要的文件準備好給我們。

對了，謝謝你推薦史派樂薩餐廳。我週四離開客戶的辦公室後去那邊吃晚餐。很喜歡，且離我飯店又近。

我明天就會回總公司，到時候見。

梅琳達

---

1. 這封電子郵件的目的是什麼？
    (A) 報告一場會議的結果
    (B) 要求對方在文件上簽名
    (C) 說明一項提案的內容
    (D) 安排和波蘭泰斯基女士的下一次會議

解析 **(A)** 主旨列寫明「Meeting in Orlando」（奧蘭多會議），正文的第一段也說明和客戶開會的結果。選項(B)重複使用文中的paperwork這個字。選項(C)重複使用proposal這個字。選項(D)指的是這封信的收件者，但信中並未提到要與她開會。

2. 這封電子郵件的撰寫者和客戶開完會之後去了哪裡？
    (A) 另一場會議
    (B) 她的總公司
    (C) 一間餐廳
    (D) 她的飯店

解析 **(C)** 撰寫者提到她和客戶開會後去了一間餐廳吃飯。選項(A)也許有可能，但信中並未提及。選項(B)是她明天要去的地方。選項(D)雖有被提及，但不是她開完會之後去的地方。

> **高分攻略 12**　網頁

第 1–2 題請看下面這個網頁。選出最適當的答案回答問題。

家內設計				
首頁	關於	常見問題	價格	評論

您一定希望自己的家或辦公室能展現個人風格。在家內設計，我們設計師在意的是打造出您想要的室內樣貌。正因如此，從選擇色彩主題，到尋找能創造您想要氛圍的合適油漆、地毯、家具、飾品，每一個環節我們都與您密切合作。

為什麼您應選擇家內設計來滿足您的裝潢需求呢？我們擁有二十年的裝潢經驗，數百名滿意我們服務的客戶，這就是最好的理由！首次諮詢完全免費，即刻撥打 800-123-4567 聯繫我們的辦公室進行預約。

點此觀看過去合作案件作品集

1. 家內設計是一間什麼樣的公司？
    (A) 建築師
    (B) 家具設計師
    (C) 客製化油漆
    (D) 室內裝潢

解析 (D) 這間公司替住家和辦公室挑選色彩、地毯和家具，還說可以幫客戶滿足「裝潢」（redecorating）需求，這些都是室內裝潢的工作範圍。選項(A)也是相關工作，但著重於室外的建築設計而非室內。選項(B)重複使用文中的 furniture 這個字。選項(C)重複使用 paint 這個字。

2. 客戶要如何看到這間公司的作品集？
    (A) 點擊網頁底部的連結
    (B) 和顧問預約
    (C) 打電話給過往的客戶
    (D) 致電辦公室

解析 (A) 文中請客戶點擊一個連結以觀看公司作品集（portfolio）。選項(B)也是文中請客戶做的事，但應該是要討論裝潢需求。選項(C)和(D)都是被文中建議大家打電話聯繫辦公室給誤導，打電話的目的是諮詢裝潢需求，不是觀看作品集。

高分攻略 13 簡訊和線上聊天室

第 1–2 題請看下面這段簡訊對話串。

琳・李 你在哪裡？	1:29
吉姆・哈特 現在塞車，公車根本動不了。 我再過十到十五分鐘到。	1:30
琳・李 客戶剛到。	1:32
琳・李 我們要先開始了，不等你了。	1:33
吉姆・哈特 好，我馬上就到。	1:35
琳・李 你有帶文件吧？	1:37
吉姆・哈特 什麼？	1:38
琳・李 要給客戶簽的工作合約。	1:40
吉姆・哈特 是的，有帶。	1:41

1. 吉姆・哈特為什麼遲到？
   (A) 他沒趕上公車。
   (B) 他的公車行進緩慢。
   (C) 他的客戶取消會面。
   (D) 他忘記要開會。

解析 **(B)** 吉姆・哈特說因為塞車導致「公車動彈不得」(the bus can hardly move)。選項(A)(C)(D)邏輯上雖然可能導致遲到，但都不是正確原因。

2. 吉姆・哈特說「I'm sorry?」是什麼意思？
   (A) 他把文件弄丟了。
   (B) 他想向客戶道歉。
   (C) 他不懂琳・李的訊息是什麼意思。
   (D) 他希望能快點趕到那裡。

解析 **(C)** 「I'm sorry?」以問句形式說出或寫出時，是「I'm sorry, but I don't understand.」（抱歉，我不懂你的意思）的縮略。從琳・李的回應可看到她補充說明是什麼文件，可見吉姆・哈特是要請她解釋。選項(A)和訊息中提到的文件有關，但並未提及他弄丟了。選項(B)是「I'm sorry」的另一種詮釋方法，但不是此處的用法。選項(D)是因為遲到，想表達歉意的另一種方法。

141

閱讀診斷測驗解答

Part 5 句子填空

1. **B**	5. **B**	9. **A**	13. **D**
2. **C**	6. **D**	10. **D**	14. **A**
3. **A**	7. **A**	11. **C**	15. **C**
4. **C**	8. **B**	12. **B**	

Part 6 段落填空

16. **C**	18. **D**	20. **A**	22. **B**
17. **B**	19. **A**	21. **C**	23. **A**

Part 7 閱讀測驗

24. **B**	30. **A**	36. **A**	42. **D**
25. **C**	31. **A**	37. **C**	43. **B**
26. **D**	32. **C**	38. **B**	44. **C**
27. **C**	33. **B**	39. **C**	45. **A**
28. **D**	34. **A**	40. **A**	46. **D**
29. **C**	35. **B**	41. **B**	47. **A**

閱讀診斷測驗解析

Mini-Test for Reading Comprehension 閱讀診斷測驗

Part 5：句子填空

> 作答方式：你會看到一個缺字的句子和四個可能的選項，選出最適當的答案，將答案卡上對應的橢圓框塗滿。

1. 萊斯企業僱用了此領域最具才華的設計專家。
   (A)(B)(D) 僱用 (C) 員工

   解析 (B) 第三人稱單數動詞 employs 和單數主詞 Rice Enterprises 一致，Rice Enterprises 是公司名稱，視為單數。選項(A)和(D)也是動詞，但是它們的數（單複數）和主詞不一致。選項(C)是名詞，但此處需要的是動詞。

2. 主管們很高興報告這次的宣傳活動大獲成功。
   (A) 巨大的
   (B) 更巨大的
   (C) 巨大地、非常地
   (D) 巨大

   解析 (C) hugely 是副詞，修飾形容詞 successful。選項(A)和(B)是形容詞，選項(D)是名詞，都不能用來修飾形容詞。

3. 普洛康工業公司宣布將藉由設立新製造廠來增加產量的計畫。
   (A) 增加
   (B) 擴大
   (C) 縮減、縮短
   (D) 減少

   解析 (A) increase 的意思是「增加」，從句中可看到公司要「設立新製造廠」，就是計劃增加產量。選項(B)也是擴大的意思，但只用於大小，不用於「產量」或「數量」。選項(C)和(D)都是減少的意思。

4. 雖然這間新開的餐廳最近獲得很多媒體關注，生意還是很冷清。
   (A) 因為
   (B) 因此
   (C) 雖然
   (D) 然而

143

解析 **(C)** although 引導一個矛盾的原因，我們通常預期媒體關注會使生意更好，但此處的事實卻非如此。選項(A)用來引導一個原因或理由。選項(B)用來引導一個結果。選項(D)引導一個矛盾的結果，但 nevertheless 為副詞不能用來連接句子，但可放在句首、句中或句尾來使用。

5. 客戶提供的所有資訊將受到完全保密，絕不與辦公室外的人分享。
   (A) 專業的
   (B) 機密的
   (C) 必要的
   (D) 完好的

解析 **(B)** confidential 的意思是「祕密的、機密的」。選項(A)(C)(D)都與文意不符。

6. 只要您在本公司任職都可以使用健康俱樂部，但若您離職，會員資格則會終止。
   (A) 同時
   (B) 根據
   (C) 為了
   (D) 只要

解析 **(D)** as long as 的意思是「只要」。選項(A)(B)(C)都與文意不符。

7. 山本女士負責舉辦公司聚會，有任何建議都可以告訴她。
   (A) 她（受格）
   (B) 她的
   (C) 她（主格）
   (D) 她自己

解析 **(A)** her 是受格代名詞，用於動詞之後，指代女子 Ms. Yamamoto。選項(B)是所有格代名詞。選項(C)是主格代名詞。選項(D)是反身代名詞。

8. 前門外張貼的告示說明了這棟建築物的歷史和建築學上的意義。
   (A) 敘述
   (B) 說明
   (C) 指示
   (D) 建議、勸告

解析 **(B)** 在此句中，explains 表示提供關於某件事物的相關資訊。選項(A)(C)(D)都與文意不符。

9. 主管沒預料會聽到這麼多對提議政策改變的反對聲浪。
    (A) 反對 (n.)
    (B) 對手
    (C) 反對的
    (D) 反對 (v.)

解析 (A) 這裡需要一個名詞當作動詞 hear 的受詞，且前面還有形容詞 much 修飾。選項 (B) 是名詞，但指人而非指一種情況，此外 opponents 是複數名詞，不能被 much 修飾。選項 (C) 是動名詞或現在分詞。選項 (D) 是動詞過去式或過去分詞。

10. 經理要求辦公室所有人在週五中午前提交工時表。
    (A)(B)(C)(D) 提交（turn in）

解析 (D) 主要動詞 asked 後面要接不定詞。選項 (A) 是原形動詞或現在式動詞。選項 (B) 是現在式動詞。選項 (C) 是動名詞或現在分詞。

11. 他收到這間公司的工作邀約，但我們不知道他會接受還是拒絕。
    (A) 兩者任一
    (B) 兩者皆不
    (C) 是⋯⋯還是
    (D) 然而

解析 (C) whether 用來引導可能的選擇。選項 (A) 也用來表達選擇，但必須放在子句的主詞後面。選項 (B) 具有否定意義，會把句子變成否定敘述。選項 (D) 則用來引導一個矛盾的事實。

12. 客戶正在考慮這個提議，並會在本週結束前給我們明確的答覆。
    (A) 定義 (v.)
    (B) 明確的
    (C) 明確地
    (D) 定義 (n.)

解析 (B) definite 是形容詞，修飾名詞 answer。選項 (A) 是動詞。選項 (C) 是副詞。選項 (D) 是名詞。

13. 你會注意到新會計系統和過去的在一些方面有所不同。

解析 (D) different 搭配的正確介系詞是 from。選項 (A)(B)(C) 通常不是 different 會搭配的介系詞。

145

14. 安排下一組用餐者入座前，每張桌子必須徹底清潔。
    (A) 徹底地
    (B) 永久地
    (C) 直接地
    (D) 最後地

    解析 **(A)** thoroughly 的意思是「完全地、徹底地」。選項(B)(C)(D)都與文意不符。

15. 如果客戶對合約條款並不完全滿意，可做一些修改。
    (A) 介紹
    (B) 發展
    (C) 修改
    (D) 允許

    解析 **(C)** modifications 的意思是「改變、修改」。選項(A)(B)(D)都與文意不符。

Part 6：段落填空

作答方式：你會看到兩篇短文，各含四個空格，每個空格配有四個選項，選出最適當的單字或片語完成這段敘述。

第 16–19 題請看下面這張傳單。

恆星專業培訓

4月10日將於您的所在地區提供下列研討會：網頁設計。在這場為商務專業人士、實習者和商學院在學學生所舉辦的全天研討會上，您將了解如何創建網頁，以最吸引人的方式呈現你的公司業務。費用包含午餐、教材和指導費。報名請至 www.stellar.com/seminars，截止日期為3月31日。在研討會期間，您也可以參考我們的其他服務，恆星公司提供員工培訓、客製化網頁設計等多項服務。

期待與您在恆星相見！

---

16. (A) 提供
    (B) 將提供
    (C) 將被提供
    (D) 將提供

解析 (C) seminar（研討會）不會主動提供，而是由恆星公司所提供，因此這裡要用被動語態。選項(A)(B)(D) 都是主動語態。

17. (A) 參與
    (B) 包含
    (C) 說明、描述
    (D) 索價、收費

解析 (B) covers 在這裡意指「包含」，表示報名者支付的費用涵蓋研討會本身以及午餐和教材。選項(A)(C)(D) 都與文意不符。

147

18. (A) 報名 (v.)
    (B) 報名承辦人員
    (C) 報名 (ved)
    (D) 報名 (n.)

解析 (D) 此處需要一個名詞當作句子的主詞。選項(A)和(C)都是動詞。選項(B)是名詞，但指人而非程序，這裡要填入的意義是報名程序。

19. (A) 恆星公司提供員工培訓、客製化網頁設計等多項服務
    (B) 您可以隨時與我們聯繫，無分日夜
    (C) 這場研討會將進行約七小時
    (D) 客戶對我們的研討會均給予最高評價

解析 (A) 前一個句子說「可以參考我們的其他服務」，接著選項(A)的句子詳細說明提供了哪些服務，語意連貫。選項(B)(C)(D)都與文意不符。

第20–23題請看下面這張傳單。

史普林戴爾社區活動中心為史普林戴爾社區的所有民眾提供服務，服務內容包含適合兒童、青少年和成人的休閒活動、親職教育工作坊、手工藝課程、青少年活動中心和日照中心。目前我們正在尋找志工協助上述活動，意者請聯繫我們的志工協調員梅博・里維拉（mrivera@commcenter.org）取得進一步資訊，並請說明您想要參與哪一項活動。

20. (A) 這些
    (B) 那裡
    (C) 它們
    (D) 那個

解析 (A) these是代名詞，指代複數名詞services，並且作句子的主詞。選項(B)不是代名詞。選項(C)是受格代名詞。選項(D)是單數。

21. (A) 近來
　　(B) 或許、大概
　　(C) 目前
　　(D) 最終

　解析 **(C)** currently 的意思是「現在、目前」。選項(A)的意思是「最近」，表示過去時間。選項(B)的意思是「大概、或許」。選項(D)的意思是「最終、終於」，可用來表示未來的某個時間。

22. (A) 協調 (v.)
　　(B) 協調員
　　(C) 協調 (ving)
　　(D) 協調 (n.)

　解析 **(B)** coordinator 是名詞，指人。選項(A)是動詞。選項(C)是動名詞或現在分詞。選項(D)是名詞，但不指人。

23. (A) 請說明您想要參與哪一項活動
　　(B) 我們的所有活動均免費開放史普林戴爾社區居民參加
　　(C) 下一期的工作坊將於一週後開始
　　(D) 里維拉女士是本社區活動中心的資深員工

　解析 **(A)** 前一個句子建議意者聯繫某個人，以取得志工活動的相關資訊，選項(A)的句子進一步告訴大家，參與志工活動需要提供的特定資訊，語意是連貫的。選項(B)(C)(D)都和社區活動中心有關，但都與如何成為中心的志工無關。

Part 7：閱讀測驗

作答方式：你會看到單篇文章或多篇文章的題組，文章後面配有幾個題目，各含四個選項。選出最適當的答案回答問題，將答案卡上對應的橢圓框塗滿。

第24–25題請看下面這封電子郵件。

收件者：frank.knockaert@crestco.com
寄件者：grombach@hamburgpaper.com
主旨：　關於：最近的訂單

諾卡爾先生您好：

我們在您最近訂單的出貨上發生了錯誤，造成您的不便，我們深表歉意。我們會將貨件中遺漏的另外一千箱萬用紙立刻補寄給您，同時該部分訂單不會向您收費。

我們非常重視與貴公司的合作關係，對於我們的錯誤可能給您帶來的任何困擾，我們深感抱歉。請放心未來不會再有這種事情發生。

謹祝 順心
葛楚德・隆巴赫
客服專員
漢堡紙業公司

---

24. 這封電子郵件的目的是什麼？
    (A) 下新訂單
    (B) 道歉
    (C) 客訴
    (D) 介紹新服務

解析 (B) 這間公司在出貨上發生錯誤，郵件的撰寫者提到「regrets the inconvenience caused to you」（造成不便，深表歉意）還有「are very sorry for any difficulties our error may have caused you」（對可能造成的困擾深感抱歉），可以知道這封電子郵件之目的是為了道歉。選項(A)和(C)是收件者已經做的事。選項(D)並未被提及。

150

25. 貨件發生了什麼問題？
    (A) 延遲送達
    (B) 受損
    (C) 不完整
    (D) 送錯地址

解析 (C) 這批貨件少了一千箱萬用紙，所以是不完整的。選項(A)(B)(D)是貨件可能發生的問題，但在文中並未提及。

第26–27題請看下面這篇文章。

> 9月1日蘇黎世：瑞士化學RADD股份公司收購了英國皇家化學工業公眾有限公司的歐洲地區聚丙烯業務，交易價格並未公開，但皇家化學工業表示該筆交易相當於其淨資產之百分之一到二，並將以現金支付。根據淨資產的計算，交易價格會介於一億到一億六千萬美元之間。此次收購包含皇家化學工業在英格蘭、丹麥、挪威和波蘭的工廠，這些工廠本身就價值六千萬到八千萬美元。聚丙烯是一種強韌的彈性塑料，用途涵蓋繩纖維到瓶子等的製造。

26. 這篇文章主要是關於什麼？
    (A) 國際貿易協定
    (B) 歐洲的商業環境
    (C) 一間特定公司的價值
    (D) 一間公司被另一間公司收購

解析 (D) 這篇文章說明一間瑞士公司收購了皇家化學工業公司的聚丙烯業務。選項(A)指的是文中提到了許多國家，但並沒有提到貿易協定。選項(B)是因為文中出現了好幾個歐洲國家的名字。選項(C)則是被文中關於收購價格和工廠價值的討論給混淆，但這些都不是文章的主題。

27. 皇家化學工業製造的是什麼？
    (A) 各種繩子
    (B) 玻璃飲料瓶
    (C) 一種塑膠
    (D) 棉布

解析 (C) 這間公司製造聚丙烯，文中描述聚丙烯為「一種強韌的彈性塑料」（a tough, flexible plastic）。選項(A)和(B)是被文中提到這種塑膠可以製造的產品所混淆。選項(D)完全沒被提到。

第 28–30 題請看下面這個網頁。

---

www.greyvalleybikes.com

檔案　編輯　檢視　收藏項目　工具　說明　　　　　頁面▼　安全性▼　工具▼

灰谷自行車

騎著單車一遊灰谷地區。灰谷自行車全年提供灰谷地區的跟團或自助旅行。我們有適合各類自行車騎士的行程，從悠哉地沿著灰河騎乘，到沿山坡而上的高難度攀登都有。

所有行程均含：
▶ 飯店住宿
▶ 一日三餐
▶ 行李托運
▶ 免費地區地圖

可攜帶自己的自行車或向我們租借。
點此查詢租車費用

點此查詢近期行程
點此查詢自由行資訊

熱門行程

山丘谷地單車行
沿著灰山最美麗的山坡上下騎行。

普爾斯威爾到斐茲堡單車遊
一遊谷中最迷人的村莊。

灰森林單車之旅
騎單車穿越灰谷最壯觀的林地。

吃飽再出發
每日行程包含中午在谷中其中一間知名咖啡館用餐。

28. 行程費用未包含哪一項目？
    (A) 飯店
    (B) 飲食
    (C) 地圖
    (D) 自行車

解析 (D) 網站中提到「Bring your own bike or rent one of ours」，接著提供了一個租車費用的連結，所以費用不含自行車。選項(A)(B)(C)都包含在行程之內。

29. 哪一項是關於灰谷自行車的行程說明？
    (A) 為期一週或一週以上。
    (B) 只適合有經驗的單車騎士參加。
    (C) 適合個人和團體參加。
    (D) 只有春夏兩季的行程。

解析 (C) 文中提到有提供跟團（group）和自助旅行（self-guided 就是沒有導遊的自助旅行或自由行，一個人即可參加）。選項(A)不正確，文中並沒有提到行程的時間長短。選項(B)不正確，有「適合各類自行車騎士」（for every kind of cyclist）的行程。選項(D)不正確，行程全年（year round）都有。

30. 這個網頁列出了哪一種行程？
    (A) 最熱門的
    (B) 難度最高的
    (C) 時間最長的
    (D) 最昂貴的

解析 (A) 網頁底下列出了「Our Top Tours」，就是最熱門的行程。選項(B)(C)(D)都不是 top 的意思。

第31–33題請看下面這則線上聊天室的討論串。

太田洋子	9:15
你有訂購襯衫要用的布料吧?	
安德斯・拉森	9:15
有,四匹印花棉布。	
蜜拉・寇比	9:16
四匹?我們不是說六匹嗎?	
安德斯・拉森	9:17
我們一直都是訂四匹。	
太田洋子	9:18
我們這次的襯衫有多一筆訂單,需要六匹。你什麼時候訂購的?	
安德斯・拉森	9:20
昨天下午。但是我確定他們還沒處理,我可以再打電話給他們。	
太田洋子	9:21
請馬上打電話給他們。我們沒時間等那兩匹布料。	
蜜拉・寇比	9:21
我已經安排好人手了,一收到布料就會馬上開始製作襯衫。我們真的要趕快開始處理這筆訂單。	
太田洋子	9:23
沒錯,這批襯衫月底前就要出貨。	

31. 他們是在哪一種公司工作？
　　(A) 服飾製造商
　　(B) 布料批發商
　　(C) 貨運服務
　　(D) 襯衫零售商

解析 (A) 他們正在討論訂購布料來製造襯衫的事，所以是在服飾製造商工作。選項(B)是他們買布料的地方。選項(C)和他們討論下單有關。選項(D)使用了對話中出現過的shirt這個字。

32. 安德斯現在必須做什麼？
　　(A) 出貨
　　(B) 取消訂單
　　(C) 追加訂單
　　(D) 處理訂單

解析 (C) 安德斯訂了四匹布，但他們需要六匹，所以他主動說會再打電話給廠商（call them back），告知要追加兩匹布。選項(A)(B)(D)和下單的情境有關聯，但不是正確答案。

33. 洋子在9點23分時說「Those shirts have to be on their way」是什麼意思？
　　(A) 必須取得製作襯衫的布料
　　(B) 必須將襯衫出貨給客戶
　　(C) 工人必須開始製作襯衫
　　(D) 襯衫的樣式必須設計好

解析 (B) 蜜拉提到他們要盡快完成訂單，所以洋子提到接下來就要出貨。on their way 的意思是送往一個特定地方。選項(A)(C)(D)都不是這句話的意思。

第 34-37 題請看下面這篇文章。

> 艾美安廚房三個月前才剛開幕，但老闆已經在談論擴展店舖的事。原因呢？生意太好了！–[1]– 顧客每天都到艾美安排隊購買新鮮出爐的麵包、蛋糕、餅乾和其他美味點心。–[2]– 高銷售量讓老闆艾美・安・安德森既開心又驚訝。–[3]– 事實上，光是第一季她已經賺得接近該數字的一半。–[4]– 為了滿足消費者需求，安德森說她必須添購至少兩臺烤箱，並多請員工。「我不確定目前空間是否可把這些全部安排進來。」她說。她正在附近尋找更大的空間。

34. 艾美安廚房是一間什麼樣的店？
    (A) 麵包店
    (B) 餐廳
    (C) 雜貨店
    (D) 廚具店

解析 (A) 文中提到顧客到艾美安廚房購買「新鮮出爐的麵包、蛋糕、餅乾和其他美味點心」(freshly made bread, cakes, cookies, and other tasty delights)，所以是麵包店。選項(B)(C)(D)是飲食相關店家，但不是正確答案。

35. 關於這家店有何說明？
    (A) 已經開很久了。
    (B) 很受歡迎。
    (C) 價格很高。
    (D) 員工很多。

解析 (B) 文章中提到「顧客每天排隊」(customers line up daily)，表示顧客多到必須排隊才能購買，這家店一定是很受歡迎了。選項(A)不正確，這家店三個月前才開幕。選項(C)並未被提及。選項(D)不大可能，因老闆提到他們需要多請人手才能滿足顧客對產品的需求。

36. 第六行中的「volume」與下列何者意義最接近？
    (A) 數量
    (B) 音量
    (C) 產品
    (D) 價格

解析 (A) volume在這裡指銷售量，文中提到其超乎老闆的預期。選項(B)是volume的另一個意思，但在文中不是這個意思。選項(C)和(D)都不會是volume的意思。

37. 下面這個句子最適合填入文中 [1][2][3][4] 哪一個位置？
「她說她原本希望一年可以有大約四萬美元的盈利。」
(A) [1]
(B) [2]
(C) [3]
(D) [4]

解析 (C) 編號 [3] 後面的句子說已經賺得「接近該數字的一半」（close to half that amount），該數字指的就是插入句所提到的四萬美元，因此插入這個位置會使語意連貫。選項(A)(B)(D)放入這個句子語意都不連貫。

第 38–42 題請看下面的通知和備忘錄。

南脊辦公大樓租戶通知
20―年 8 月 25 日

停車場整建工程將於下個月底動工，預計進行三個月。施工期間，任何人均不得於大樓停車場內停車。市政府臨時在大樓周圍街道指定車位供我們全天候使用，使用時必須出示特別停車證。由於車位數量有限，我們會發給本大樓每間辦公室四張停車證。在停車場整建工程完工前，大樓租戶應鼓勵員工多加利用大眾交通工具。離此五個街區內還有兩座公共停車場，提供日租、週租或月租車位。感謝您的配合。

南脊辦公大樓管理處

備忘錄
鸚鵡通訊公司

收件人：全體辦公人員
發布人：狄娜・德杰納羅
　　　　辦公室經理
日期：20―年 8 月 28 日
關於：停車

相信此刻你們都已看到最近停車場整建工程的通知。由於我們的員工人數是分配到停車證的五倍，我們會將停車證保留給客戶使用，並請員工另做其他安排。為了大家方便，我們已經準備了地鐵通行證，在整個停車場整建期間皆可使用，鸚鵡通訊公司員工可享七五折優惠。有興趣的人，請在本週結束前來找我，謝謝。

38. 停車場整建工程何時動工？
    (A) 本週
    (B) 下個月
    (C) 三個月後
    (D) 八月

解析 (B) 通知單上面說工程會在下個月底（at the end of next month）動工。選項(A)是員工應索取地鐵通行證的時間。選項(C)是工程預計進行的時間。選項(D)是這個月。

39. 鸚鵡通訊公司一共有多少員工？
    (A) 四名
    (B) 五名
    (C) 二十名
    (D) 二十五名

解析 (C) 大樓中的每間辦公室會分到四張停車證，而備忘錄中提到鸚鵡通訊公司的員工數是停車證的五倍，所以是二十名。選項(A)是停車證的數量。選項(B)是被五倍的員工數給混淆了。選項(D)是被地鐵通行證的優惠折數給混淆。

40. 停車場整建工程期間，誰可以在大樓周邊停車？
    (A) 鸚鵡通訊公司的客戶
    (B) 鸚鵡通訊公司的員工
    (C) 南脊辦公大樓的所有租戶
    (D) 狄娜‧德杰納羅

解析 (A) 持有停車證就可以在大樓周邊的街道停車，而鸚鵡通訊公司決定將停車證保留給客戶使用。選項(B)不正確，鸚鵡通訊公司的員工無法取得停車證。選項(C)不正確，每間辦公室只有四張停車證，不是人人都有。選項(D)不正確，狄娜‧德杰納羅也是鸚鵡通訊公司的員工，因此她也拿不到停車證。

41. 鸚鵡通訊公司的員工如果要取得地鐵通行證，要去找誰？
    (A) 城市管理者
    (B) 他們的辦公室經理
    (C) 大樓管理者
    (D) 地鐵站站長

解析 (B) 備忘錄是辦公室經理寄出的，提出讓員工來「找我」（see me）拿地鐵通行證。選項(A)之所以混淆，是因為分配部分車位給大樓租戶的是市政府。選項(C)是張貼通知的人，不是發地鐵通行證的人。選項(D)是取得地鐵通行證的合理邏輯推論，但在通知單和備忘錄中均未提及。

42. 地鐵通行證的效期有多長？
    (A) 一週
    (B) 三週
    (C) 一個月
    (D) 三個月

解析 (D) 地鐵通行證在整個施工期間皆可使用，施工要進行三個月，所以效期是三個月。選項(A)(B)(C)均未被提及。

第43–47題請看下面的網頁、電子郵件和文章。

---

www.millscrealty.com

| 檔案 | 編輯 | 檢視 | 收藏項目 | 工具 | 說明 | 頁面▼ | 安全性▼ | 工具▼ |

米爾斯不動產公司

尋找理想的住宅或商用不動產，就交給米爾斯不動產公司。

辦公室

1. 日照充足的二樓辦公空間，近期裝修完畢，位於公園對面的小型建築內。後方有停車場。可隔成接待室加辦公室或兩間小辦公室。適合律師、會計師、治療師、健康從業人員使用。位於布萊特伍德。月租1250美元，水電另計。

2. 一樓辦公套房，位於市中心交通便利，鄰近公車路線和地鐵站。面積150平方公尺。屋主可依需求重新裝修。月租2050美元含水電和客戶停車位。

3. 新興布萊特伍德商業區頂樓角落辦公室，距離規劃中的布萊特伍德大道地鐵站僅一個街區。三房外加一間小型廚房。有路邊停車位。月租1000美元，含水電。

4. 布萊特伍德辦公室，面積100平方公尺，全新粉刷及鋪設地毯。兩房。距離新布萊特伍德地鐵站一英里。有路邊停車位。月租950美元，水電另計。

收件者：史蒂夫‧米爾斯
寄件者：愛爾莎‧洛培
日期： 7月25日
主旨： 尋找辦公空間

米爾斯先生：

我對您網站上廣告的幾間辦公室有興趣。我經營小型會計師事務所，正在尋找100–125平方公尺的空間。不幸的是，市中心對我來說有點難以負擔，但布萊特伍德地區就非常適合。理想的話，我想找附有停車位的地方，但如果離新地鐵站夠近，倒也不成問題。我希望月租不要超過1000美元，水電我可以另付。可以的話，我想這週去看看你們清單上的幾個出租物件。我早上通常很忙，但每天下午一點後都有空，請告訴我何時方便帶我去看房子。

愛爾莎‧洛培
註冊會計師

布萊特伍德：前景看好

新興的布萊特伍德商業區正迅速成為全市最炙手可熱的新地區。房租飆漲使得許多企業經營者被迫離開熱門的市中心，轉而選擇較為經濟實惠的布萊特伍德地區。市政府宣布將地鐵路線延伸至此區中心的計畫後，該區更是魅力大增。全新規劃的布萊特伍德大道地鐵站預計明年初開始營運。目前布萊特伍德大道已有多間辦公室進駐，近期還有兩家鎖定上班族的餐廳出現。區內的紫丁香公園區域擁有寬敞的街道和花園，景色優美怡人，也是一大亮點。預計不久將有一間新咖啡館和數間精品店陸續開幕。

43. 關於廣告中的市中心辦公室，下列敘述何者為非？
　　(A) 租金包含電費和暖氣費。
　　(B) 近期才剛裝修。
　　(C) 鄰近大眾交通系統。
　　(D) 大樓附設停車場。

解析 (B) 廣告中說「屋主可依需求重新裝修」（Owner will remodel to suit your needs），因此可假設近期沒有裝修過。選項(A)為事實，因為租金有含水電。選項(C)為事實，辦公室鄰近公車路線和地鐵站。選項(D)為事實，因為租金有含車位。

44. 洛培女士可能選擇廣告中的哪一間辦公室？
   (A) 第一間
   (B) 第二間
   (C) 第三間
   (D) 第四間

解析 (C) 洛培女士期望的月租是1000美元，水電可以另付。她還希望附帶車位，但如果靠近地鐵站的話，沒有也無妨。第三間辦公室的月租是1000美元且含水電，距離地鐵站一個街區，符合她的條件。選項(A)和(B)的租金太貴了。選項(D)沒有車位也不靠近地鐵站。

45. 洛培女士希望什麼時候去看辦公室？
   (A) 任何一個下午
   (B) 任何一個早上
   (C) 下週
   (D) 今天

解析 (A) 洛培女士「每天下午一點後」（any day after 1:00 PM）都有空，也就是任何一個下午都可以。選項(B)不正確，她說她早上都很忙。選項(C)不正確，她說希望這週去看。選項(D)並未被提及。

46. 在最後這篇文章裡，第三行中的「driving」意義與下列何者最接近？
   (A) 操作
   (B) 旅行
   (C) 引領
   (D) 迫使

解析 (D) 這句在說因為租金漲得太高，企業被迫離開市中心區。選項(A)(B)(C)是driving的其他用法，於此處不是正確答案。

47. 關於布萊特伍德地區文中有何暗示？
   (A) 租金比市中心便宜。
   (B) 街道沒有吸引力。
   (C) 名聲不好。
   (D) 租金正在上漲。

解析 (A) 文章中先是提到企業因高租金而離開市中心，然後描述布萊特伍德地區為「affordable」，就是可負擔的、不貴的。另外在電子郵件中，洛培女士說市中心有點「out of reach」，就是價格超出她所能負擔的範圍，接著又說布萊特伍德地區比較適合。選項(B)不正確，文章提到街道寬敞，有花園及公園，都是吸引人的地方。選項(C)不正確，從文章描述看來，此地區已經開始熱門起來了。選項(D)對市中心來說為事實，對布萊特伍德地區則不是。

161

實戰模擬試題1
解答

聽力測驗

Part 1 照片描述

1. **B**
2. **B**
3. **B**
4. **A**
5. **D**
6. **A**

Part 2 應答問題

7. **A**
8. **A**
9. **C**
10. **B**
11. **C**
12. **B**
13. **A**
14. **C**
15. **B**
16. **C**
17. **A**
18. **A**
19. **B**
20. **C**
21. **C**
22. **B**
23. **A**
24. **B**
25. **B**
26. **A**
27. **C**
28. **C**
29. **B**
30. **C**
31. **A**

Part 3 簡短對話

32. **C**
33. **C**
34. **D**
35. **B**
36. **A**
37. **D**
38. **B**
39. **D**
40. **A**
41. **C**
42. **A**
43. **A**
44. **B**
45. **A**
46. **C**
47. **B**
48. **C**
49. **D**
50. **C**
51. **A**
52. **C**
53. **D**
54. **A**
55. **B**
56. **A**
57. **A**
58. **C**
59. **D**
60. **B**
61. **D**
62. **A**
63. **C**
64. **B**
65. **D**
66. **C**
67. **B**
68. **B**
69. **D**
70. **C**

Part 4 簡短獨白

71. **A**
72. **C**
73. **C**
74. **B**
75. **C**
76. **D**
77. **D**
78. **D**
79. **A**
80. **C**
81. **A**
82. **C**
82. **C**
84. **B**
85. **D**
86. **A**
87. **D**
88. **C**
89. **A**
90. **D**
91. **B**
92. **A**
93. **B**
94. **B**
95. **D**
96. **B**
97. **C**
98. **A**
99. **B**
100. **C**

實戰模擬試題1 解答

閱讀測驗

Part 5 句子填空

101.	**B**	109.	**C**	117.	**C**	125.	**C**
102.	**D**	110.	**B**	118.	**B**	126.	**D**
103.	**C**	111.	**A**	119.	**A**	127.	**B**
104.	**B**	112.	**A**	120.	**D**	128.	**A**
105.	**A**	113.	**C**	121.	**B**	129.	**D**
106.	**C**	114.	**A**	122.	**C**	130.	**C**
107.	**B**	115.	**D**	123.	**C**		
108.	**D**	116.	**B**	124.	**D**		

Part 6 段落填空

131.	**A**	135.	**A**	139.	**B**	143.	**A**
132.	**B**	136.	**D**	140.	**D**	144.	**D**
133.	**C**	137.	**B**	141.	**A**	145.	**A**
134.	**D**	138.	**B**	142.	**C**	146.	**C**

Part 7 閱讀測驗

147.	**D**	161.	**A**	175.	**A**	189.	**D**
148.	**D**	162.	**D**	176.	**A**	190.	**C**
149.	**B**	163.	**D**	177.	**D**	191.	**A**
150.	**A**	164.	**D**	178.	**A**	192.	**B**
151.	**C**	165.	**A**	179.	**C**	193.	**D**
152.	**A**	166.	**C**	180.	**B**	194.	**C**
153.	**B**	167.	**C**	181.	**B**	195.	**A**
154.	**B**	168.	**D**	182.	**A**	196.	**B**
155.	**B**	169.	**A**	183.	**B**	197.	**A**
156.	**C**	170.	**B**	184.	**C**	198.	**C**
157.	**C**	171.	**B**	185.	**B**	199.	**A**
158.	**C**	172.	**C**	186.	**A**	200.	**D**
159.	**B**	173.	**C**	187.	**A**		
160.	**D**	174.	**B**	188.	**B**		

Model Test 1 實戰模擬試題1題目中譯&解析

聽力測驗

在本段測驗當中,你將有機會展現自己對口說英語的理解能力。聽力測驗共有四個大題,每一大題均有作答說明。你有大約45分鐘時間完成聽力測驗。

Part 1：照片描述

> 作答方式：你會看到一張照片,並聽到四個關於這張照片的陳述。選出最符合照片內容的陳述,將答案卡上對應的橢圓框塗滿。

1. Look at the photo marked number 1 in your test book.
   (A) A doctor is examining a patient.
   (B) A scientist is looking at a test tube.
   (C) A cook is preparing dinner.
   (D) A woman is watching a film.

   請看試題本標示為1的照片。
   (A) 一名醫生正在檢查病人。
   (B) 一名科學家正看著一支試管。
   (C) 一名廚師正在準備晚餐。
   (D) 一名女子正在看影片。

   解析 (B) 這位科學家手裡正拿著一支試管。選項(A)使用了looking的相關字examining,但照片中沒有病人。選項(C)使用了和照片內容（preparing an experiment 準備實驗）有關的單字preparing。選項(D)使用了looking的相關字watching。

2. Look at the photo marked number 2 in your test book.
   (A) The men are shaking hands.
   (B) The speaker is explaining the chart.
   (C) The workers are enjoying a quick meal.
   (D) The trainees are watching TV.

   請看試題本標示為2的照片。
   (A) 這些男人正在握手。
   (B) 這名講者正在說明圖表。
   (C) 這些員工正簡單快速地吃一頓飯。
   (D) 這些受訓人員正在看電視。

解析 (B) 選項(B)正確指出了講者說明圖表的動作。選項(A)將男子伸出手的動作誤認成握手。選項(C)誤把桌上的咖啡杯當成一頓飯。選項(D)誤把白板當成電視。

3. Look at the photo marked number 3 in your test book.
   (A) Some farmers are harvesting fruit.
   (B) Some men are loading a truck.
   (C) Some shoppers are buying socks.
   (D) Some workers are standing in the rain.

   請看試題本標示為3的照片。
   (A) 一些農夫正在收成水果。
   (B) 一些男人正把貨物裝上卡車。
   (C) 一些購物者正在買襪子。
   (D) 一些工人正站在雨中。

解析 (B) 照片中是一些農場工人正在把農產品裝車的畫面。選項(A)正確指出了照片中的水果，但是對男人們的動作描述不正確。選項(C)混淆了近音字box和socks。選項(D)不正確，工人們站在陽光下而非雨中。

4. Look at the photo marked number 4 in your test book.
   (A) There are stairs leading up to the flagpole.
   (B) A soldier's standing on the roof.
   (C) The courtyard is full of tourists.
   (D) The building is ten stories tall.

   請看試題本標示為4的照片。
   (A) 有樓梯通往旗杆。
   (B) 一名士兵正站在屋頂上。
   (C) 中庭擠滿了遊客。
   (D) 這棟建築有十層樓高。

解析 (A) 照片前方顯示一座樓梯通往旗杆。選項(B)正確指出了屋頂，但照片中沒有士兵。選項(C)正確指出了中庭，但照片中沒有遊客。選項(D)不正確，照片中並沒有十層樓高的建築物。

5. Look at the photo marked number 5 in your test book.
   (A) Some gates are being opened.
   (B) A driver is parking her car.
   (C) Some boxes are on the shelf.
   (D) A woman is pushing a cart.

   請看試題本標示為5的照片。
   (A) 一些大門正被打開。
   (B) 一名司機正在停車。
   (C) 架上有一些箱子。
   (D) 一名女子正推著一部推車。

   解析 (D) 照片中的女子正推著一部推車，推車上有一些箱子。選項(A)正確指出了照片中的大門，但沒人在開門。選項(B)混淆了近音字cart和car。選項(C)對箱子的位置描述不正確。

6. Look at the photo marked number 6 in your test book.
   (A) A man is cleaning the floor.
   (B) A plant is being trimmed.
   (C) A pot is on the stove.
   (D) A gardener is mowing the lawn.

   請看試題本標示為6的照片。
   (A) 一名男子正在清理地板。
   (B) 一棵植物正在被修剪。
   (C) 火爐上有一個鍋子。
   (D) 一名園丁正在修剪草坪。

   解析 (A) 選項(A)正確描述了這名男子的動作。選項(B)正確指出了植物，但沒人在修剪植物。選項(C)把花盆和鍋子搞混了，兩者都可稱為pot。選項(D)為從plant聯想到gardener的誘答。

Part 2：應答問題

作答方式：你會聽到一個問題和三個可能的回應。選出最適合回答該問題的回應，將答案卡上對應的橢圓框塗滿。

7. What did you order for dinner?
   (A) We're having steak.
   (B) My wife and her mother.
   (C) After I get home.

   你晚餐點了什麼？
   (A) 我們要吃牛排。
   (B) 我太太和她媽媽。
   (C) 等我到家之後。

   解析 (A) 選項(A)是對食物問題的合理回應。選項(B)回答的是誰會來吃晚餐（Who's coming to dinner?）的問題。選項(C)回答的是何時吃晚餐（When is dinner?）的問題。

8. You weren't around at all last week. Where were you?
   (A) I was on vacation.
   (B) This weekend I'm at home.
   (C) The event will last a week.

   妳上星期完全不見人影，妳去哪裡了？
   (A) 我去度假了。
   (B) 這週末我在家。
   (C) 這場活動會持續進行一週。

   解析 (A) 選項(A)是對地點問題的合理回應。選項(B)混淆了時間，一個是this weekend（現在式表未來時間），一個是last week（過去時間）。選項(C)混淆了will last a week（持續時間）和last week（過去時間）。

9. How often do you play golf?
   (A) The play will be over at ten.
   (B) Get off the golf course.
   (C) Almost every Sunday.

你多久打一次高爾夫球？
(A) 這齣戲十點結束。
(B) 請離開高爾夫球場。
(C) 幾乎每個星期天。

解析 **(C)** 選項(C)是對頻率問題的合理回應。選項(A)混淆了一字多義的play，這個字可作動詞指「打球」，亦可作名詞指「戲劇」。選項(B)混淆了發音相似的off和often。

10. Please let me pay for dinner. It'd be my pleasure.
    (A) She looks much thinner.
    (B) Thank you. That's very generous.
    (C) Pay day is next Friday.

　　這頓晚餐讓我請客吧，這是我的榮幸。
    (A) 她看起來瘦多了。
    (B) 謝謝，妳真大方。
    (C) 發薪日是下週五。

解析 **(B)** 第二位說話者感謝第一位說話者大方請客，為合理的回應。選項(A)混淆了近音字thinner和dinner。選項(C)重複使用了pay這個字。

11. Did anyone leave any messages while I was out?
    (A) The massage room is over there.
    (B) Any of us could do it.
    (C) Your brother called three times.

　　我不在的時候有人留言給我嗎？
    (A) 按摩室就在那邊。
    (B) 這件事我們誰都能做。
    (C) 妳哥哥打了三通電話。

解析 **(C)** 選項(C)是對留言問題的合理回應。選項(A)混淆了近音字massage（按摩）和message（訊息）。

12. What did you buy at the mall?
    (A) Upstairs, in the jewelry store.
    (B) Just a pair of gloves.
    (C) Yes, I told him goodbye.

你在購物中心買了什麼？
(A) 在樓上，珠寶店裡。
(B) 就一副手套而已。
(C) 是的，我跟他道了再見。

解析 (B) 選項(B)回答了「What」（什麼）的問題。選項(A)是用來回答「Where」（哪裡）的問題。選項(C)混淆了近音字 buy 和 goodbye。

13. How many copies of the handout do we need?
    (A) Ten should be enough.
    (B) We'll hand them out first thing.
    (C) About forty-five dollars.

    我們需要幾份講義？
    (A) 十份應該夠。
    (B) 我們會先把它們發出去。
    (C) 大約四十五美元。

解析 (A)「ten」回答了「How many」（多少）的問題。選項(B)重複使用了 handout 這個字，但用的是動詞 hand out（分發）的概念。選項(C)誤解了問題，題目問的是數量（how many），而不是價格（how much）。

14. When is the plane expected to leave?
    (A) At the airport.
    (B) Before we take off.
    (C) In about forty-five minutes.

    飛機預計何時起飛？
    (A) 在機場。
    (B) 在我們起飛前。
    (C) 約四十五分鐘後。

解析 (C) 選項(C)是對時間問題的合理回應。選項(A)提到的地點（機場）正確，但沒有回答時間。選項(B)使用了相關片語 take off（起飛），但沒有回答何時起飛。

169

15. Why don't you take a coffee break?
    (A) The cup was broken.
    (B) I have too much work.
    (C) The car brakes won't work.

    何不休息一下喝杯咖啡呢？
    (A) 杯子破了。
    (B) 我的工作太多了。
    (C) 車子的煞車失靈了。

    解析 **(B)** 選項(B)是對提議休息的合理回應。選項(A)把 coffee break（咖啡休息時間）誤解為 broken (coffee) cup（破掉的咖啡杯）。選項(C)一方面在發音上將 break 誤解成 brake（煞車），一方面在意義上將 break 誤解成 won't work（壞掉）。

16. What's left to do to make the cake?
    (A) Thanks. It looks delicious.
    (B) It's a white cake with chocolate filling.
    (C) Nothing; it's in the oven right now.

    還剩下什麼要做才能完成蛋糕？
    (A) 謝謝，看起來很好吃。
    (B) 這是含巧克力餡的白色蛋糕。
    (C) 沒了，蛋糕現在已經在烤箱裡了。

    解析 **(C)** 選項(C)是被詢問還有什麼需要做時的合理回應。選項(A)是對方請吃蛋糕時的合理回應。選項(B)用來回答「What kind」（哪一種）的問題。

17. Where is the hotel you booked for Dr. Hartford?
    (A) It's across from the park.
    (B) Rooms are two hundred dollars a night.
    (C) The elevator is around the corner.

    妳幫哈特福德博士訂的飯店在哪裡？
    (A) 在公園對面。
    (B) 房價是一晚兩百美元。
    (C) 電梯就在轉角處。

    解析 **(A)** 選項(A)是對地點問題的合理回應。選項(B)回答的是房價，不是飯店的地點。

18. Mr. Kim called while you were out.
    (A) Did he leave a message?
    (B) Yes, it's very cold out.
    (C) His file is on my desk.

    你不在的時候，金先生有打電話來。
    (A) 他有留言嗎？
    (B) 是的，外面很冷。
    (C) 他的檔案在我桌上。

解析 (A) 第一個說話者說有一通來電，所以第二個說話者想知道來電者是否有留言。選項 (B) 不僅把 cold 和近音字 called 搞混，還重複使用 out 這個字。選項 (C) 混淆了近音字 file 和 while。

19. Which desk do you want me to use?
    (A) The hours are very long.
    (B) The one by the window.
    (C) Have a seat please.

    你要我使用哪一張桌子？
    (A) 工時很長。
    (B) 窗戶旁邊那張。
    (C) 請坐。

解析 (B) 選項(B)是對「Which」（哪一個）問題的合理回應。選項(A)混淆了同音字 hours 和 ours（you 的所有格代名詞）。選項(C)使用了相關字 seat（座位），但沒有回答到「Which」的問題。

20. It's very cold in here.
    (A) I like the winter.
    (B) I sold it last year.
    (C) I'll close the window.

    這裡非常冷。
    (A) 我喜歡冬天。
    (B) 我去年把它賣掉了。
    (C) 我去關窗戶。

解析 (C) 第一個說話者覺得冷，所以第二個說話者主動表示要去關窗戶。選項(A)從 cold 聯想到 winter。選項(B)把近音字 sold 和 cold、year 和 here 搞混了。

171

21. Is your office anywhere near here?
    (A) My earache is better.
    (B) My office is closed today.
    (C) It's only a few blocks from here.

    妳的辦公室離這裡近嗎？
    (A) 我的耳痛好多了。
    (B) 我的辦公室今天沒開。
    (C) 離這裡幾個街區而已。

解析 (C) 選項(C)是對地點問題的合理回應。選項(A)混淆了近音字 ear 和 here。選項(B)誤把 near 解釋成 closed，near 相當於 close（近的），而不是 closed（關閉的）。

22. Has the meeting with Mr. Stuartson begun?
    (A) Yes, it's on the agenda.
    (B) Yes, about five minutes ago.
    (C) Yes, I'm still reading it.

    和史都華森先生的會議開始了嗎？
    (A) 是的，已經列入議程。
    (B) 是的，大約五分鐘前開始了。
    (C) 是的，我還在讀。

解析 (B) 選項(B)是被問及會議開始時間的合理回應。選項(A)從 meeting 聯想到 agenda，卻沒有回答問題。選項(C)混淆了近音字 meeting 和 reading。

23. Can you do me a favor and lower the volume of your music?
    (A) OK, sorry. I didn't realize it was so loud.
    (B) Sure. I'll get the party favors this weekend.
    (C) Because my father likes pop music.

    能不能請妳幫個忙，把音樂關小聲一點？
    (A) 好，對不起。我不知道這麼大聲。
    (B) 沒問題，這個週末我會去買派對小禮物。
    (C) 因為我爸喜歡聽流行音樂。

解析 (A) 選項(A)是對方請求幫忙時的合理回應。選項(B)搞錯了 favor 這個字的用法，題目的 favor 指幫忙。選項(C)重複使用了 music 這個字。

24. Is there a place where I can leave my coat?
    (A) I live on Fourteenth Street.
    (B) Just hang it in the hall closet.
    (C) You can leave your card with me.

    有地方可以讓我放外套嗎？
    (A) 我住在第十四街。
    (B) 掛在玄關的櫃子裡就好。
    (C) 你可以留名片給我。

解析 (B) 選項(B)是被詢問哪裡可以掛外套時的合理回應。選項(A)混淆了近音字 leave 和 live。選項(C)重複使用了 leave 這個字。

25. Did you meet up with anyone important at the conference?
    (A) It runs from Tuesday until Saturday.
    (B) No one noteworthy; just the usual.
    (C) We can go to a workshop when we're there.

    你在會議上有見到什麼重要人物嗎？
    (A) 從週二到週六。
    (B) 沒什麼值得注意的人，都是平常那些人。
    (C) 我們到那裡後，可以去參加工作坊。

解析 (B) 選項(B)是被問及會議參加者類型時的合理回應。選項(A)用來回答關於會議日期的問題。選項(C)使用了 conference 的相關字 workshop。

26. Shouldn't we ask your father to join us at the theater?
    (A) He'd rather not come.
    (B) It's not that far.
    (C) The task was not finished.

    我們是否應該找你爸一起去電影院？
    (A) 他不太想去。
    (B) 沒那麼遠。
    (C) 任務尚未完成。

解析 (A) 選項(A)是被問及要不要找你爸一起去時的合理回應。選項(B)混淆了近音字 far 和 father。選項(C)混淆了近音字 ask 和 task。

27. Do you prefer to work alone or as part of a team?
    (A) So it would seem.
    (B) Yes, if given the choice.
    (C) I'd rather work by myself.

    你比較喜歡獨立作業還是團隊合作呢？
    (A) 看來是。
    (B) 是的，如果可以選擇的話。
    (C) 我寧可自己工作。

解析 (C) 選項(C)是被問到工作偏好時的合理回應，by myself 就是 alone。選項(A)混淆了近音字 team 和 seem。選項(B)用來回答「yes-no」問句，但這是一個「or」問句，需要對方做選擇。

28. There's a nice restaurant on the corner.
    (A) I need a rest.
    (B) I don't like ice cream.
    (C) Let's eat there.

    轉角有一家不錯的餐廳。
    (A) 我需要休息。
    (B) 我不喜歡吃冰淇淋。
    (C) 我們去那裡吃飯吧。

解析 (C) 第二個說話者同意到第一個說話者建議的餐廳去吃飯。選項(A)混淆了近音字 rest 和 restaurant。選項(B)混淆了近音字 ice 和 nice。

29. What does the chart on page 8 of the report show?
    (A) I really like that part.
    (B) That we're seeing a decline in sales.
    (C) Yes, it's on page 8.

    報告第八頁的圖表顯示什麼？
    (A) 我真的很喜歡那部分。
    (B) 我們看到銷售下降。
    (C) 是的，在第八頁。

解析 (B) 選項(B)是對圖表內容問題的合理回應。選項(A)混淆了近音字 chart 和 part。選項(C)重複使用了 page 8 這個詞。

30. Which department does Fred work in?
    (A) It's not a large apartment.
    (B) I saw him on the elevator.
    (C) He's in research and development.

    弗列德在哪個部門工作？
    (A) 那不是一間很大的公寓。
    (B) 我在電梯裡看到他。
    (C) 他在研發部工作。

    解析 (C) research and development（研發部）回答了哪一個部門的問題。選項(A)混淆了近音字 department 和 apartment。選項(B)用來回答「Where」的問題。

31. How much do we have left in our account?
    (A) Over three thousand dollars.
    (B) I can withdraw the money.
    (C) Here's a check.

    我們帳戶裡還剩多少錢？
    (A) 超過三千美元。
    (B) 我可以提款。
    (C) 這裡有一張支票。

    解析 (A) 選項(A)回答了「How much」（多少）的問題。選項(B)和(C)使用了 account 的相關字 money 和 check。

Part 3：簡短對話

> **作答方式**：你會聽到兩人或多人之間的對話。每段對話搭配三個問題，各有四個選項。選出最適當的答案回答問題，將答案卡上對應的橢圓框塗滿。

> 複習要訣：閱讀 Part 3 和 Part 4 的錄音稿時，可在每題之間停約 8 秒鐘。

Questions 32 through 34 refer to the following conversation.

Man: I have a lunch meeting downstairs today until about two. Can we meet then? Or would later be better for you?

Woman: It'll have to be later. I have a, uh, I'll be in a conference until five.

Man: OK. Let's meet then because I'd rather not put it off until tomorrow. I'll wait for you in my office.

Woman: Sounds good. I'll bring those photocopies of the budget report.

第 32–34 題請聽下面這段對話。
男：我今天在樓下有個午餐聚會，要到兩點左右。那時候見面可以嗎？還是晚一點比較方便呢？
女：要晚一點。我有一個，呃，我要參加一個會議到五點。
男：好，我們那時候見，我不想拖到明天。我會在我的辦公室等你。
女：很好。我會帶預算報告的影本過去。

32. When will the speakers meet? 說話者會在什麼時候見面？
    (A) Before lunch 午餐前
    (B) At 2:00 兩點鐘
    (C) After the conference 會議後
    (D) Tomorrow 明天

解析 (C) 女子說「I'll be in a conference until five」，男子便提議「那時」(then) 見面，也就是五點會議結束時。選項(A)重複了對話中的 lunch 這個字，是男子在見面之前要做的事。選項(B)是男子有空的時候。選項(D)是男子不想見面的時間。

33. Where will they meet? 他們會在哪裡見面？
    (A) At the bus stop 公車站
    (B) Downstairs 樓下
    (C) In the man's office 男子的辦公室
    (D) In the waiting room 等候室

176

解析 (C) 男子說「I'll wait for you in my office」，所以是約在辦公室見面。選項(A)混淆了 bus stop 和發音相近的 budget。選項(B)是男子更早時會在的地方。選項(D)把 I'll wait for you 混淆成 waiting room。

34. What will the woman bring to the meeting? 見面時女子會帶什麼過去？
    (A) Coffee 咖啡
    (B) A letter 一封信
    (C) Photographs 照片
    (D) Copies of a report 報告影本

解析 (D) 女子說她會帶預算報告的影本過去。選項(A)混淆了近音字 coffee 和 copy。選項(B)混淆了近音字 letter 和 better。選項(C)混淆了 photographs 和 photocopies。

Questions 35 through 37 refer to the following conversation.
Woman: City Wide Realtors. How may I help you?
Man: Yes, I'd like to rent, um, I'm looking for an apartment, preferably downtown. I'd like to sign a lease this month, if possible.
Woman: Certainly. We have several vacancies listed. Could you tell me your price range? Because you know that neighborhood isn't the cheapest.
Man: Yes, I'm aware of that. I've seen your listings online. I'm wondering if you could, you know, show me a few today or tomorrow. Some one-bedroom models, or larger.
Woman: Certainly. Why don't you stop by my office later today? It's right by the library. Do you know where that is?

第35–37題請聽下面這段對話。
女：全市房仲公司您好，請問有什麼可以為您服務的？
男：是的，我想要租房，嗯，我在找公寓，最好在市中心。可以的話，希望這個月就能簽約。
女：沒問題，我們列有幾個空出的公寓。請問您的預算空間是多少？因為您也知道那一帶不是最便宜的。
男：是的，我知道。我有在網路上看過你們刊登的物件。我在想你能不能，就是，今天或明天帶我去看幾間。一些一房的房型，或大一點也可以。
女：當然可以。您要不要今天稍晚來我辦公室一趟？就在圖書館旁邊，您知道在哪裡嗎？

35. What does the man want to do? 這名男子想做什麼？
    (A) Sell his apartment 賣公寓
    (B) Rent an apartment 租公寓
    (C) Clean his apartment 清潔公寓
    (D) Remodel his apartment 整修公寓

解析 (B) 男子說他正在找一間公寓，並想簽訂租約。選項(A)(C)(D)都重複使用了apartment這個字，卻都不是男子想做的事。

36. What does the woman imply about downtown apartments? 關於市中心的公寓，女子有何暗示？
    (A) They cost more than other apartments. 它們比其他公寓貴。
    (B) There aren't many available right now. 目前沒有太多空出的公寓。
    (C) Few people want to rent them. 很少人想租它們。
    (D) They are not very large. 它們不是很大。

解析 (A) 男子說他想要一間位於市中心的公寓，女子回答說「you know that neighborhood isn't the cheapest」（那一帶不是最便宜的），表示比其他地方的貴。選項(B)不正確，女子說有幾個空出的公寓。選項(C)重複了對話中的few這個字，男子表示他想看幾間（a few）公寓。選項(D)重複了對話中的large這個字，男子表示他想要一房或更大（larger）的公寓。

37. What does the woman suggest the man do? 女子建議男子做什麼？
    (A) Meet her at the library 到圖書館與她碰面
    (B) Call back later 稍後回電
    (C) Look online 上網查看
    (D) Visit her office 到她的辦公室

解析 (D) 女子說「Why don't you stop by my office later today?」，所以是請男子過去她的辦公室。選項(A)重複使用了library這個字，圖書館在女子辦公室的旁邊。選項(B)重複了later這個字。選項(C)重複了online這個字，是男子提到的。

Questions 38 through 40 refer to the following conversation.

Woman: Front desk. Amanda speaking. How may I help you?
Man: Yes, uh, we seem to be missing some towels in Room six-oh-three. Could you send up two, please? As soon as possible.
Woman: Of course. I'll have a housekeeper get them to you right away. Six-oh-three you said, right?
Man: Right. And if we could get some soap, too, that would be great. I hope it's not too much trouble.
Woman: Not a bit. It's my job.

第 38–40 題請聽下面這段對話。
女：服務臺您好，我是雅曼達，請問有什麼需要為您服務的嗎？
男：是的，呃，這裡是603房，我們好像少了幾條毛巾。可以請你送兩條過來嗎？越快越好。
女：沒問題，我現在就請房務員給您送過去。您說603房，對嗎？
男：對。還有如果可以給我們一些肥皂，那就太好了，希望不會太麻煩。
女：一點也不麻煩，這是我該做的。

38. Where does this conversation take place? 這段對話發生在什麼地方？
    (A) At a store 商店
    (B) At a hotel 飯店
    (C) At a restaurant 餐廳
    (D) At the man's house 男子家

解析 (B) 男子正在索取毛巾和肥皂，並請對方送到他房間，所以應該是飯店。選項(A)和(C)也是會需要索取東西的地方，但都不是正確答案。選項(D)不正確，如果是在家裡，房間不太可能有號碼。

39. What does the man ask for? 這名男子要求的是什麼東西？
    (A) Keys 鑰匙
    (B) More soup 再來點湯
    (C) A better room 好一點的房間
    (D) Towels and soap 毛巾和肥皂

解析 (D) 男子索取的是毛巾和肥皂。選項(A)混淆了近音字keys和please。選項(B)混淆了近音字soup和soap。選項(C)重複使用了對話中的room這個字。

179

40. What does the woman mean when she says, "Not a bit"？女子說「Not a bit」是什麼意思？

　　(A) She does not mind helping the man. 她不介意幫助這名男子。
　　(B) She does not like her job. 她不喜歡她的工作。
　　(C) She does not have what the man asked for. 她沒有這名男子要的東西。
　　(D) She does not have time to help the man right now. 她現在沒時間幫助這名男子。

解析 (A) 男子說希望他的要求不會太麻煩，女子回應「Not a bit」，意思是「It is not a bit of trouble.」（一點也不麻煩）。選項(B)重複了job這個字。選項(C)和(D)都搞錯了這個用語的意思。

Questions 41 through 43 refer to the following conversation with three speakers.
Woman:　The brochures arrived from the printers this morning.
Man 1:　That's great, Mary. They came much sooner than we expected.
Man 2:　Uh huh. And if we can get them in the mail right away, our customers will have them before the end of the week.
Woman:　Yes, well, I still have to get the address labels on them. I'll go print those out right now.
Man 1:　I wish I could help you, but I have that presentation I have to work on.
Man 2:　I'm tied up all day, too. But if you want, after you get those addresses done, I could drive them down to the post office for you.
Woman:　Thanks, Jim. That would be very helpful.

第 41–43 題請聽下面這段三人之間的對話。
女：　印刷廠今天早上把手冊送來了。
男1：太好了，瑪麗。比我們預期的還早送來。
男2：對啊，而且如果我們可以立刻把它們寄出，客戶在本週結束前就可以收到了。
女：　沒錯，但我還要貼地址標籤，我現在就去把它們印出來。
男1：我很想幫你，但是我還要做那份簡報。
男2：我也整天都要忙，但如果你想的話，等你把地址弄好，我可以開車幫你把它們送去郵局。
女：　謝了，吉姆。那會有很大的幫助。

41. When did the brochures arrive? 手冊何時送到的？
　　(A) Yesterday afternoon 昨天下午
　　(B) Last night 昨天晚上
　　(C) This morning 今天早上
　　(D) This afternoon 今天下午

180

解析 **(C)** 女子說手冊今天早上送來了。選項(A)和(D)混淆了近音字afternoon和soon。選項(B)在對話中並未提及。

42. What will Mary do now? 瑪麗現在要做什麼？
    (A) Prepare the address labels 準備地址標籤
    (B) Work on a presentation 處理一份簡報
    (C) Read the brochures 閱讀手冊
    (D) Call the printer 打電話給印刷廠

解析 **(A)** 瑪麗提到了地址標籤，並說「I'll go print those out right now.」（我現在就去印出來）。選項(B)是其中一名男子要做的事。選項(C)重複了對話中的brochures這個字，但對話中沒提到要閱讀這些手冊。選項(D)使用了print的相關字printer。

43. What does Jim offer to do? 吉姆表示要幫忙做什麼事？
    (A) Take the brochures to the post office 把手冊送去郵局
    (B) Drive Mary to her home 開車送瑪麗回家
    (C) Look up some addresses 查詢一些地址
    (D) Phone customers 打電話給客戶

解析 **(A)** 吉姆說「I could drive them down to the post office for you」（我可以開車幫你把它們送去郵局）。選項(B)重複了對話中的drive這個字。選項(C)重複了addresses這個字。選項(D)重複了customers這個字。

Questions 44 through 46 refer to the following conversation.

Man: Hello. Yes. I'm interested in applying for the job you advertised in today's newspaper.
Woman: Thank you for calling. You know, we're a big catering company. Have you ever had a job in the food industry before?
Man: Uh huh. After I graduated from the National Culinary Institute, I worked for five years as an assistant cook at Bob's Restaurant.
Woman: That sounds excellent. You may have just the experience we're looking for. Could you come in for an interview some time tomorrow?
Man: Wait a minute while I check my calendar. Yes, I can be there by two. Can you tell me exactly where you're located?

第 44–46 題請聽下面這段對話。

男：你好，是的。我想應徵你們今天在報紙上刊登的工作。

女：感謝你的來電。你知道的，我們是一間大型餐飲承辦公司。你以前曾經在食品業工作過嗎？

男：有的。我從國家烹飪學院畢業後，在鮑伯餐廳當了五年的助理廚師。

女：聽起來很不錯。你的經驗可能正是我們需要的，明天有空過來面試嗎？

男：請稍等，讓我看一下我的行程。沒問題，我可以兩點過去。請告訴我你們的確切位置好嗎？

44. What kind of job is the man probably applying for? 這名男子可能在應徵何種工作？
    (A) Waiter 服務生
    (B) Chef 廚師
    (C) Newspaper editor 報紙編輯
    (D) Advertising executive 廣告業務

解析 (B) 這名男子應徵的是餐飲承辦公司的工作，而且他曾經做過助理廚師，因此很有可能是在應徵廚師的職位。選項(A)混淆了相關字 wait 和 waiter。選項(C)重複使用對話中的 newspaper 這個字，男子是在報紙上看到徵才廣告的。選項(D)混淆了相關字 advertised 和 advertising。

45. What does the woman ask the man about? 這名女子詢問男子哪方面的事情？
    (A) His work experience 他的工作經驗
    (B) His education 他的學歷
    (C) His food preferences 他的飲食偏好
    (D) His salary requirements 他的希望待遇

解析 (A) 女子說「Have you ever had a job in the food industry before?」，問的是有沒有在食品業的工作經驗。選項(B)是男子自己提的，但女子沒有問。選項(C)重複使用對話中 food 這個字。選項(D)和求職主題有關，但在對話中並未提及。

46. What does the man want to know? 這名男子想知道什麼？
    (A) The exact job title 確切的職稱
    (B) The start date of the job 工作的開始時間
    (C) The woman's address 女子的公司地址
    (D) The name of the woman's company 女子的公司名稱

解析 (C) 男子說「Can you tell me exactly where you're located?」，為詢問女子公司的確切地點。選項(A)(B)(D)都與主題有關，但在對話中均未提及。

Questions 47 through 49 refer to the following conversation.

Woman: Look at all this rain. I'm really getting tired of it, and more rain is predicted tomorrow.

Man: Really? Then it looks like I'll have to call my friends and cancel our nine o'clock golf game. What a bore.

Woman: If you're not going to play golf, why don't you go to the movies with me? We haven't been in a while.

Man: Sorry, but if I'm not playing golf, I'm not going anywhere. I'll just stay home and take a nice rest.

第 47–49 題請聽下面這段對話。

女：你看，雨下個不停，我真的快受不了了，而且氣象預報說明天還會繼續下雨。
男：真的嗎？那看來我只好打電話給朋友取消九點的高爾夫球活動了，真令人厭煩。
女：你不去打高爾夫球的話，不如和我去看電影如何？我們好久沒看電影了。
男：抱歉，如果不去打高爾夫球，那我哪裡也不去，我要在家好好休息。

47. Why can't the man play golf tomorrow? 男子明天為何不能打高爾夫球？
    (A) His wife is sick. 他太太生病了。
    (B) It's going to rain. 將會下雨。
    (C) He has to take a test. 他要參加考試。
    (D) He's feeling tired. 他覺得很累。

解析 (B) 因為天氣預測會下雨，所以他不能打高爾夫球。選項(A)混淆了近音字 sick 和 predict。選項(C)混淆了近音字 test 和 rest。選項(D)使用了對話中的 tired 這個字。

48. What does the man mean when he says, "What a bore"? 這名男子說「What a bore」是什麼意思？
    (A) He does not like making phone calls. 他不喜歡打電話。
    (B) He is looking for some entertainment. 他需要一些娛樂活動。
    (C) He is sorry that he has to cancel the golf game. 他對必須取消高爾夫球活動感到遺憾。
    (D) He thinks golf is not an interesting game. 他覺得高爾夫球不有趣。

解析 (C) 「What a bore」可用來表示某個人很不想做的事，在此對話中，男子很不想取消高爾夫球活動，卻不得不取消。選項(A)是男子取消高爾夫球活動的方式。選項(B)和(D)用 bore 的字面意義「無趣、無聊的事」去理解「What a bore」，但都是不正確的。

183

49. What will he do tomorrow? 他明天要做什麼？
    (A) Talk on the phone 打電話聊天
    (B) Go to the movies 看電影
    (C) Move some furniture 搬動一些家具
    (D) Stay home 待在家裡

解析 (D) 男子明天不能去打高爾夫球，所以他說要待在家裡好好休息（stay home and take a nice rest）。選項(A)混淆了近音字 phone 和 home。選項(B)是女子希望男子做的事。選項(C)混淆了近音字 move 和 movies。

Questions 50 through 52 refer to the following conversation.
Man: Drive past the park and turn right and you'll see a bank on the next corner. It's a small brick building just across the street from the library.
Woman: Does it have a drive-in window? So I won't have to, you know, get out of the car.
Man: Yes, and there's also a parking lot next door, too, just in case. It's not hard to find. It's just five minutes from here.

第50–52題請聽下面這段對話。
男：你開車過了公園右轉，到了下個轉角會看到一間銀行，是一棟小小的紅磚建築，就在圖書館對面。
女：那裡有免下車服務窗口嗎？這樣我就不用，你知道的，不用下車。
男：有的，而且隔壁也有停車場，萬一需要停車的話可以使用。不會很難找，從這裡過去五分鐘就到了。

50. Where does the woman want to go? 這名女子想去哪裡？
    (A) To a fast food restaurant 速食店
    (B) To a parking lot 停車場
    (C) To a bank 銀行
    (D) To a park 公園

解析 (C) 男子正在告訴這名女子銀行怎麼去。選項(A)是從 drive-in window（免下車窗口）聯想到速食店。選項(B)位於銀行旁邊。選項(D)是女子前往銀行途中會經過的地方。

51. Where is this place located? 這個地方位於哪裡？
    (A) On a corner 一個轉角處
    (B) Behind a parking lot 一座停車場後面
    (C) Next door to a library 一間圖書館隔壁
    (D) Across the street from a store 一家商店對面

解析 (A) 男子提到銀行位於一個轉角處。選項(B)把「a parking lot next door」（隔壁的停車場）誤解成在停車場後面。選項(C)和(D)把「across the street from the library」（圖書館對面）分別誤解成在圖書館隔壁和在商店對面。

52. What does the man say about this place? 關於這個地方男子有何說明？
    (A) The woman will not be able to park there. 女子不能在那裡停車。
    (B) Most people are not familiar with it. 大部分的人對那裡不熟。
    (C) It is not very far away. 那裡不會很遠。
    (D) It may be difficult to find. 可能很難找。

解析 (C) 男子說「It's just five minutes from here.」（距離這裡五分鐘路程而已），所以不遠。選項(A)不正確，男子說旁邊有停車場。選項(B)並未被提及。選項(D)和男子所說的恰好相反。

Questions 53 through 55 refer to the following conversation with three speakers.
Woman 1: Hey, Sam. Do you know what time it is? Nine thirty. You're fifteen minutes late. Why can't you ever arrive on time?
Man: Sorry. The bus was delayed. Traffic was bad all over the city this morning, you know, with all this rain.
Woman 2: He's right, Jane. Didn't you see how hard it was coming down?
Woman 1: Right, but we all know that buses are late when it rains. We have to leave home earlier in bad weather.
Man: I'll just drive next time. It's faster.
Woman 2: You'll still run into heavy traffic, even in your own car.

第53–55題請聽下面這段三人之間的對話。
女1：喂！山姆，你知道現在幾點了嗎？9點30分，你遲到了十五分鐘。你為什麼就不能準時到呢？
男： 對不起，公車延誤了，今天早上全市到處都塞車，你知道的啊，雨下這麼大。
女2：他說得沒錯，珍。你沒看到雨下得這麼大嗎？
女1：好吧，可是我們都知道下雨天公車會遲到啊，天氣不好就應該提早出門。
男： 下次我會開車，那樣比較快。
女2：就算自己開車，你還是會遇上交通堵塞的情況。

53. What does Jane imply about Sam? 對於山姆，珍有何暗示？
    (A) He does not like to wait. 他不喜歡等待。
    (B) He is not a good driver. 他開車技術不好。
    (C) He is a hard worker. 他工作很認真。
    (D) He is usually late. 他老是遲到。

解析 (D) 珍抱怨山姆遲到，並且說「Why can't you ever arrive on time?」（你為什麼就不能準時到）。選項(A)混淆了近音字 late 和 wait。選項(B)混淆了近音字 arrive 和 driver。選項(C)重複使用了 hard 這個字。

54. How did Sam get to work this morning? 山姆今天早上怎麼去上班的？
    (A) By bus 搭公車
    (B) On foot 走路
    (C) In a carpool 共乘
    (D) By subway 搭地鐵

解析 (A) 山姆說他遲到是因為公車延誤，所以可得知他搭公車。選項(B)和(D)雖然有可能，但對話中並未提及。選項(C)重複使用了 car 這個字。

55. What will Sam do next time? 山姆下次會怎麼做？
    (A) Stay home 待在家
    (B) Drive his car 自己開車
    (C) Leave earlier 提早出門
    (D) Take the train 搭火車

解析 (B) 男子說他會自己開車，因為那樣比較快。選項(A)重複了對話中的 home 這個字。選項(C)是其中一名女子給他的建議。選項(D)混淆了近音字 train 和 rain。

Questions 56 through 58 refer to the following conversation.

Man: Have you got everything in order for your trip next Sunday?

Woman: Just about. I've found a flight that's leaving at noon. I've decided to go first class. It's more comfortable than business class.

Man: Wow. That's a bit pricy, isn't it? The flight is only an hour long.

Woman: That's true. But I checked the prices, and decided I could afford it, especially since I'll put it on my credit card. So I can take the rest of the year to pay for it if I want.

Man: Well, it's up to you, of course. Will your cousins meet you at the airport?

Woman: Yes, I can't wait to see them.

第 56–58 題請聽下面這段對話。

男：你下週日旅行要帶的東西都準備好了嗎？
女：差不多了。我找到一班中午起飛的航班，我決定搭頭等艙，比商務艙還舒適。
男：哇！那有點貴不是嗎？飛行時間也才一小時。
女：是沒錯，但我查過價格了，我覺得負擔得起，尤其我打算刷卡，所以如果我想的話，可以用今年剩下的時間慢慢付。
男：嗯當然，由你自己決定。你表姐妹們會到機場接你嗎？
女：會啊，我等不及見到她們了。

56. What is probably the purpose of the woman's trip? 女子此行的目的可能是什麼？
    (A) To visit family 探望親人
    (B) To take a class 上課
    (C) To interview for a job 面試工作
    (D) To meet with business colleagues 和公司同事見面

解析 (A) 男子問說「Will your cousins meet you at the airport?」，可知是探望親人。選項(B)誤解了 class 的意義。選項(C)雖然有可能，但對話中並未提及。選項(D)重複使用了 business 這個字。

57. What does the man say about the trip? 關於這趟旅程，男子說了什麼？
    (A) It is expensive. 花費很高。
    (B) It is too long. 時程很長。
    (C) It will be fun. 會很好玩。
    (D) It will be uncomfortable. 會很不舒服。

解析 (A) 女子說她要搭頭等艙，男子回應「That's a bit pricy, isn't it?」（有點貴不是嗎）。選項(B)重複使用了 long 這個字。選項(C)雖然有可能，但對話中並未提及。選項(D)和相關字 comfortable 互相混淆了，女子說的是頭等艙很舒適。

58. How will the woman pay for the trip? 女子會用什麼方式支付這趟旅程？
    (A) Cash 現金
    (B) Check 支票
    (C) Credit card 信用卡
    (D) Money order 匯票

解析 (C) 女子說她打算刷卡（put it on my credit card）。選項(A)並未被提及。選項(B)混淆了 check 的意思。選項(D)混淆了 order 的意思。

Questions 59 through 61 refer to the following conversation.

Woman: Have you seen Joe? He's not in his office. He's not even in the break room. I can't find him anywhere.

Man: He's gone to pick up Evelyn at the airport. She's coming in on a ten o'clock flight.

Woman: Oh, right. I forgot. I wanted to ask him, uh, I need him to check my figures on the monthly report, but I guess it can wait.

Man: He'll be back before noon. I know because we have a lunch date then.

Woman: That'll be plenty of time. I don't need to make the final copies until tomorrow.

第 59–61 題請聽下面這段對話。
女：你有看到喬嗎？他不在他的辦公室，也不在休息室，到處都找不到他。
男：他去機場接伊芙琳了，她搭十點的飛機過來。
女：喔對，我都忘了。我是要問他，嗯，我需要他幫我檢查每月報告上的數字，不過不急。
男：他中午前就會回來，我知道是因為我跟他約了吃午餐。
女：那時間還很充裕，我明天才要製作最後的影本。

59. Where is Joe? 喬在哪裡？
    (A) Away on a business trip 出差去了
    (B) In the break room 在休息室
    (C) In his office 在他的辦公室
    (D) At the airport 在機場

解析 (D) 男子說喬去機場接伊芙琳（gone to pick up Evelyn at the airport）。選項(A)從 airport 和 flight 聯想到 business trip。選項(B)和(C)是女子已經找過的地方，但喬不在那裡。

60. What does the woman want Joe to do? 這名女子要喬做什麼事？
    (A) Write a check 開支票
    (B) Look at a report 查看報告
    (C) Meet her for lunch 一起吃午餐
    (D) Make photocopies 影印文件

解析 (B) 女子說「I need him to check my figures on the monthly report」（需要他幫忙看每月報告上的數字）。選項(A)誤解了 check 的意思。選項(C)搞混了人物，和喬約吃午餐的是男子。選項(D)是女子等喬看完報告後要做的事。

188

61. When will Joe return? 喬什麼時候回來？
    (A) Later this afternoon 今天下午晚點的時候
    (B) Tomorrow 明天
    (C) At 10：00 十點
    (D) By 12：00 十二點前

解析 (D) 男子說喬中午前會回來（He'll be back before noon）。選項(A)混淆了近音字 noon 和 afternoon。選項(B)是女子要把報告影本準備好的時間。選項(C)是伊芙琳班機抵達的時間。

Questions 62 through 64 refer to the following conversation.
Man: I'm going down to the cafeteria for a quick lunch. Will you join me?
Woman: No, thanks. I don't really care for the food there. I brought a sandwich from home. But while you're down there, could you get my mail from the mail room? I'm expecting a package.
Man: Sorry, but I won't be coming back right away. I've got an appointment with a client at two. It's all the way downtown and I plan to take the bus, so I'll be gone for a while.
Woman: Oh, OK, then. Never mind. I'll get it myself.

第 62–64 題請聽下面這段對話。
男：我要到樓下自助餐廳快速吃個午餐，要一起嗎？
女：不了，謝謝，我不是很喜歡那邊的食物。我自己從家裡帶了三明治。不過你下去的時候，可以幫我到郵件室拿郵件嗎？我在等一個包裹。
男：不好意思，我沒有馬上要回來，我兩點和一位客戶有約，地點在老遠的市中心，我打算搭公車去，所以會離開一陣子。
女：喔，那好吧，沒關係，我自己去拿。

62. Why doesn't the woman want to eat at the cafeteria? 這名女子為何不想去自助餐廳吃飯？
    (A) She does not like the food. 她不喜歡那裡的食物。
    (B) She does not have time. 她沒有時間。
    (C) It is too expensive. 太貴了。
    (D) It is too far away. 太遠了。

解析 (A) 女子說「I don't really care for the food there」，care for 是「喜歡」，所以她不喜歡那裡的食物。選項(B)和(C)雖然都有可能，但對話中並未提及。選項(D)被男子說他要到老遠的市中心給混淆了。

189

63. What does the woman ask the man to do for her? 這名女子要求男子替她做什麼事？
    (A) Bring her a sandwich 幫她帶一個三明治
    (B) Mail a package 寄一個包裹
    (C) Pick up her mail 取她的郵件
    (D) Go to the mall 去購物中心

解析 (C) 女子說「could you get my mail from the mail room」，就是要男子替她取郵件。選項(A)錯誤因為女子已從自己家裡帶三明治來了。選項(B)重複使用了package 和mail這兩個字。選項(D)混淆了近音字mail和mall。

64. What will the man do after lunch? 男子吃完午餐要做什麼？
    (A) Take a walk 散步
    (B) Meet with a client 和客戶見面
    (C) Go to his apartment 去他的公寓
    (D) Go to a doctor's appointment 去看醫生

解析 (B) 男子說「I've got an appointment with a client at two」（兩點和客戶有約）。選項(A)重複使用了take這個字。選項(C)混淆了近音字appointment和apartment。選項(D)重複使用了appointment這個字。

Questions 65 through 67 refer to the following conversation and train schedule.

Woman: George, would you check the train schedule, please? I'd like to leave for the Brookfield office as soon as tomorrow morning's workshop is over.

Man: OK. I know there are several trains a day. Around what time would you want to leave?

Woman: As soon after eleven as possible. And I'd like to arrive in Brookfield by two.

Man: Got it. I'll let you know as soon as I've made the reservation. And I'll let the Brookfield staff know when to expect you.

Woman: Perfect. And please arrange for a car to take me to the station.

第65–67題請聽下面這段對話，並參考火車時刻表。

女：喬治，你可以查一下火車時刻表嗎？我想明天早上工作坊一結束就前往布魯克菲爾德辦公室。

男：好的。我知道一天有好幾班火車，你大概想要幾點出發？

女：十一點過後越快越好，而且我希望兩點前抵達布魯克菲爾德。

男：了解，我訂好馬上告知你。我也會通知布魯克菲爾德辦公室的職員你什麼時候會抵達。

女：很好，還有順便安排一輛車送我到車站。

往布魯克菲爾德的列車

出發時間	抵達時間
10:20	12:40
11:20	1:40
11:55	2:15
1:55	4:15

65. What does the woman plan to do tomorrow morning? 這名女子明天早上計劃要做什麼？
    (A) Go shopping 購物
    (B) Look for work 找工作
    (C) Plan a vacation 規劃度假
    (D) Attend a workshop 參加工作坊

解析 (D) 女子說她想明天早上工作坊一結束（as soon as tomorrow morning's workshop is over）就前往布魯克菲爾德，所以她明天早上有個工作坊要參加。選項(A)和(B)分別把workshop誤解成shopping和work。選項(C)不正確，女子是要去辦公，不是度假。

66. Who is George, most likely? 喬治最有可能是什麼人？
    (A) A travel agent 旅行代辦人
    (B) A workshop presenter 工作坊講者
    (C) The woman's assistant 女子的助理
    (D) The woman's husband 女子的先生

解析 (C) 喬治正在幫這名女子規劃商務旅行，最有可能是她的助理。選項(A)不正確，因為除了安排旅行事宜，喬治還會通知辦公室員工，旅行代辦人不太可能會做這件事。選項(B)重復使用了workshop這個字。選項(D)不正確，喬治是幫女子安排工作事宜，不是安排私人生活。

67. Look at the graphic. What time will the woman take the train? 請看圖表，女子會搭幾點的火車？
    (A) 10:20
    (B) 11:20
    (C) 11:55
    (D) 1:55

解析 (B) 女子十一點後才能出發，並希望兩點前抵達，選項(B)是唯一符合要求的列車。選項(A)(C)(D)都不符合女子的行程安排。

Questions 68 through 70 refer to the following conversation and menu.

Woman: This place looks wonderful. Why haven't I ever been here before?
Man: I don't know. It's been here for quite a while. Anyhow, even though it isn't large, this café has the best lunch menu around.
Woman: I'm in the mood for soup. What do you recommend?
Man: The carrot beef is good. Oh, but you're a vegetarian.
Woman: Right. But here's a soup I can try. I'll take that. Do you want to sit on the patio? The view of the park looks nice.
Man: It's getting late. I think we'd better just take our food back to work and eat at our desks.

第68-70題請聽下面這段對話，並參考菜單。

女：這個地方看起來真棒，我以前怎麼都沒來過？
男：不知道，這間咖啡廳已經在這裡開很久了。不管怎樣，咖啡廳雖然不大，午餐菜單可是這附近最棒的。
女：我想喝湯，你推薦什麼？
男：胡蘿蔔牛肉湯不錯，啊，但你是素食主義者。
女：對，但這裡有一道湯我能喝，我就點這個。你要不要坐在戶外用餐區？公園的景色挺不錯的。
男：時間有點晚了，我看我們還是外帶回公司，在座位上吃就好了。

```
市中心咖啡廳

      湯類
    雞肉米湯
   胡蘿蔔牛肉湯
   羊肉大麥湯
   田園蔬菜湯
```

68. What does the man say about the café? 這名男子對咖啡廳有何描述？
    (A) It is new. 它是新開的。
    (B) It is small. 它空間很小。
    (C) It is popular. 它很受歡迎。
    (D) It is well known. 它很知名。

解析 (B) 男子說了「... it isn't large」（不大）。選項(A)不正確，男子說「It's been here for quite a while」（開很久了）。選項(C)有可能，但對話中沒有提到。選項(D)重複使用了 know 的近音字。

69. Look at the graphic. Which soup will the woman order? 請看圖表，這名女子會點哪一道湯？
    (A) Chicken and Rice 雞肉米湯
    (B) Carrot Beef 胡蘿蔔牛肉湯
    (C) Lamb and Barley 羊肉大麥湯
    (D) Garden Vegetable 田園蔬菜湯

解析 (D) 男子提到女子吃素，田園蔬菜湯是唯一沒有肉的湯。選項(A)(B)(C)都有肉。

70. Where does the man want to eat his lunch? 這名男子想在哪裡吃午餐？
    (A) Inside the café 咖啡廳內
    (B) On the patio 戶外用餐區
    (C) At his office 他的辦公室
    (D) At the park 公園裡

解析 (C) 男子說「I think we'd better just take our food back to work and eat at our desks」，表示他想外帶回公司座位上吃。選項(A)合乎邏輯，但對話中沒有提到。選項(B)是女子建議用餐的地方。選項(D)重複使用了park這個字。

Part 4：簡短獨白

> 作答方式：你會聽到一名說話者的獨白。每段獨白搭配三個問題，各有四個選項。選出最適當的答案回答問題，並將答案卡上對應的橢圓框塗滿。

Questions 71 through 73 refer to the following announcement.

Attention, please. This is the Blue Line train, providing service to all arrival and departure gates, baggage claims, and ticketing areas. The train does not, I repeat, does not, provide service to any of the parking lots. Color-coded maps of the terminal and signs are posted within each car. Please move to the center of the car and away from the doors. Please do not attempt to exit the train until it has come to a complete stop, the doors are fully opened, and the exit bell rings. Thank you.

第71–73題請聽下面這段廣播。

各位旅客請注意，這裡是藍線列車，為您提供前往所有到達門與登機門、行李提領區和售票區的服務。本列車不提供，再重複一次，不提供前往任何停車場的服務。各節車廂內均貼有航廈的彩色標示地圖和標誌。請往車廂中央移動，並遠離車門。列車尚未停妥、車門未完全打開以及下車鈴未響起之前，請勿嘗試下車。謝謝。

71. Where is this train located? 這班列車位在哪裡？
    (A) In an airport 機場
    (B) In a city 城市
    (C) Along the coast 沿岸地區
    (D) At an amusement park 遊樂園

解析 (A) 從到達門和登機門、行李提領區和售票區可以判斷出這裡是機場。選項(B)和(C)的地點都不夠具體。選項(D)不正確，遊樂園中的列車通常不會停靠行李提領區。

72. Where should you stand when in a train car? 在車廂內你應該站在什麼位置？
    (A) By the doors 門邊
    (B) By the windows 窗邊
    (C) In the center 中央
    (D) At either end 兩端

解析 (C) 列車的廣播請大家往「車廂中央」（center of the car）移動。選項(A)和「遠離車門」（away from the doors）的指示相抵觸。選項(B)不正確，廣播中並未提到窗戶。選項(D)和「車廂中央」（to the center）的指示相矛盾。

73. When can passengers get off the train? 乘客何時可以下車？
    (A) When they see an exit sign 看到下車指示燈亮起時
    (B) Before the bell rings 下車鈴響起之前
    (C) After the bell rings 下車鈴響起之後
    (D) After the colored light goes on 彩色指示燈亮起之後

解析 (C) 乘客被要求聽到下車鈴響起才可以下車。選項(A)重複使用了sign這個字。選項(B)和正確答案恰好相反。選項(D)重複使用了color這個字。

Questions 74 through 76 refer to the following recording.

Thank you for calling the City Museum. Our hours are ten a.m. to six p.m. Monday through Saturday and one to five p.m. Sunday. This month we have a special exhibit of paintings depicting the early history of our city, as well as a Monday afternoon lecture series in conjunction with this exhibit. Please visit our website for further information as well as for a complete schedule of painting, photography, and sculpture classes for people of all ages. Admission to the museum costs fifteen dollars for adults and ten dollars for children ages five to twelve, with no charge for children under five. Museum members receive a twenty-five percent discount.

第74–76題請聽下面這段電話語音。

感謝您來電城市博物館，本館開放時間為週一至週六上午十點到下午六點，週日下午一點至五點。本月我們有一場特展，展出描繪我們城市早期歷史的繪畫，並配合特展於週一下午舉辦一系列講座。請至我們的官網了解更多資訊，上面也有我們為所有年齡層舉辦的繪畫、攝影、雕塑課程的詳細時間表。博物館入場費為成人十五美元，五到十二歲兒童十美元，五歲以下兒童免費入場。博物館會員可享七五折優惠。

74. When on Sundays is the museum open? 博物館週日的開放時間為何？
    (A) In the morning 上午
    (B) In the afternoon 下午
    (C) In the evening 夜間
    (D) All day 全日

解析 (B) 博物館週日的開放時間是一點到五點，也就是下午。選項(A)和(C)都沒有被提到。選項(D)與一點開放至五點的事實相矛盾。

75. What is the lecture series probably about? 系列講座的內容可能為何？
    (A) Sculpture 雕塑
    (B) Museum administration 博物館管理
    (C) Local history 當地歷史
    (D) How to photograph art 如何拍攝藝術品

解析 (C) 這系列的講座是為了配合（in conjunction with）特展而舉辦，該特展展出的是描繪我們城市早期歷史（the early history of our city）的畫作。選項(A)和(D)是博物館舉辦的課程主題，不是講座內容。選項(B)重複使用了 museum 這個字。

76. Who doesn't have to pay to enter the museum? 誰可以免費進入博物館？
    (A) Members 會員
    (B) Adults over 65 六十五歲以上成人
    (C) Children under twelve 十二歲以下兒童
    (D) Children under five 五歲以下兒童

解析 (D) 根據語音內容，五歲以下兒童免費入場（no charge for children under five）。選項(A)是可享七五折優惠的人。選項(B)是必須付十五美元入場費的人。選項(C)是必須付十美元入場費的人。

Questions 77 through 79 refer to the following information.

Do you have trouble organizing your work day? You are not alone! While this problem isn't uncommon, it also isn't difficult to solve. Start every morning by making a list of things you need to accomplish during the day. Next, rank each task on the list according to its importance. Work on the most important task first, and stay with it until it is completed. Then, move on to the next task. At the end of the day, look over your task list. Have you completed everything on your list? If so, very good. If not, save the uncompleted items for your next day's list.

第 77–79 題請聽下面這段資訊。

你在安排一天的工作上有困難嗎？你並不孤單！這個問題雖然並不罕見，卻也不難解決。從每天早上列出當天需要完成的事項開始，接著將清單上的任務依重要程度排列。從最重要的事項開始做，堅持下去直到完成，然後再進行下一項任務。在一天結束之時把任務清單看過一遍，你是否完成了清單上的所有事項呢？如果是，非常好。如果沒有，把未完成的事項留到明天的清單上。

77. What does the speaker mean when he says, "You are not alone"? 說話者說「You are not alone」是什麼意思？
    (A) Some people work better by themselves. 有些人獨立作業的效率更高。
    (B) Most people need help to solve problems. 大多數人都需要別人幫助解決問題。
    (C) Lonely people often have trouble with organization. 孤單的人在組織生活上往往有困難。
    (D) Many people have difficulty organizing their day. 許多人對於安排一天的工作有困難。

解析 (D) 說話者提到了安排一天工作的困難，然後說「You are not alone」，意思是「不是只有你有這個問題」。選項(A)重複使用了work這個字。選項(B)重複了problems這個字。選項(C)使用了alone的相關字lonely。

78. What is the first step in getting organized? 若要規劃好自己的工作，第一步要做什麼事？
    (A) Set a timeline 制定一個時間表
    (B) Get clutter out of your life 把生活中的雜亂清除
    (C) Buy a calendar 買一個日曆
    (D) Make a list of things to be done 列出待辦事項

解析 (D) 這段敘述中提到「Start every morning by making a list」（從每天列出清單開始）。選項(A)(B)(C)都沒有被提到。

79. What is the last task of the day? 一天的最後一項任務是什麼？
    (A) Review the list 回顧清單
    (B) Finish uncompleted tasks 將未完成的任務做完
    (C) Write a new list 寫一份新的清單
    (D) Throw the list away 把清單丟掉

解析 (A) 根據這段敘述，一天結束之時應該回顧任務清單。選項(B)不正確，聽者被告知應將未完成的事項留到隔天再做。選項(C)重複了list這個字，但這段敘述中沒有提到要寫新的清單。選項(D)把away和近音字day搞混了。

實戰模擬試題 1

197

Questions 80 through 82 refer to the following advertisement.

Are you successful? Pass some of that success along to a new generation by serving as a volunteer tutor. If you have just two hours a week to spare, you can help a child with his schoolwork and share your love of learning. Children of all ages are waiting for your help. Please visit the Office of City Schools website and complete the volunteer application there. No college degree or special training? No worries! The only requirement is a desire to help children. That's all you need! You must be eighteen or older to participate.

第 80–82 題請聽下面這則廣告。

你的人生成功嗎？藉由擔任志工導師，把成功經驗傳給新的一代。一週只要騰出兩小時，就能幫助一個孩子完成學校作業，並分享你對學習的愛。各年齡層的孩子都在等待你的幫助。請至城市學校辦事處的網站填寫志工申請表。沒有大學學位也沒受過特殊訓練？不用擔心！只要有一顆願意幫助孩子的心就已足夠！這是我們唯一的要求條件。報名者須年滿十八歲。

80. What is being advertised? 這則廣告在宣傳什麼？
    (A) A new learning system 一套新的學習系統
    (B) A job for professional teachers 一份專業教師的工作
    (C) An opportunity to help children 一個幫助孩子的機會
    (D) A special training program 一個特殊的訓練課程

解析 **(C)** 這則廣告在徵求可以幫助學童的志工。選項(A)重複使用了 learning 這個字。選項(B)不正確，廣告在找的是志工。選項(D)重複使用了 special training 這個片語。

81. What are listeners asked to do? 聽者被要求做什麼？
    (A) Fill out an application 填寫申請表
    (B) Visit an office 造訪辦公室
    (C) Contact a school 聯絡學校
    (D) Complete their schoolwork 完成學校作業

解析 **(A)** 聽者被要求到一個網站上填寫申請表。選項(B)重複使用了 visit 和 office 這兩個字。選項(C)重複了 school 這個字。選項(D)重複了 complete 和 schoolwork 這兩個字。

82. What must people have to participate? 想報名的人必須擁有什麼？
    (A) A college degree 大學學位
    (B) Special training 特殊訓練
    (C) Age of at least 18 年滿十八歲
    (D) Experience with children 和孩子相處的經驗

解析 (C) 廣告中提到報名者須年滿十八歲。選項(A)和(B)雖有被提及,但不是必要條件。選項(D)重複使用了 children 這個字,但廣告中並無提到要有和孩子相處的經驗。

Questions 83 through 85 refer to the following weather report.

Good Morning. This is Amanda Smithers with the early morning weather report. I'm happy to report that we've finally got some nice weather coming in today, and I'd say it's about time, wouldn't you? Temperatures will be in the low seventies with breezes of ten to fifteen miles per hour. The sun will shine all day with no clouds expected, so it looks like a great day to spend some time outdoors. The same great weather conditions will continue tomorrow and till the end of the week. Fog will roll in late Friday and heavy rainstorms are expected on Saturday. So enjoy the nice weather while you can.

第83–85題請聽下面這段氣象報告。

早安,我是雅曼達・史密特斯,為您帶來晨間氣象報告。很高興告訴大家今天終於迎來了好天氣,我想也該是時候了,您不覺得嗎?氣溫大約在華氏七十度出頭,吹微風,風速每小時十到十五英里。預計一整天都是陽光普照、萬里無雲的天氣,看來是個適合到戶外走走的好日子。同樣的好天氣會持續到明天,一直到本週結束。週五稍晚將有霧氣籠罩,週六預計會有劇烈暴風雨。所以請趁現在把握好天氣!

83. What does the speaker imply when she says, ". . . it's about time"? 說話者說「. . . it's about time」是什麼意思?
    (A) The weather report will be longer than usual. 這段氣象報告會比平常還要長。
    (B) The weather depends on the time of day. 天氣會隨一天不同時段而有變化。
    (C) The weather has been bad for a while. 壞天氣已經持續一段時間了。
    (D) The weather is nicer at this time of year. 每年這個時候天氣都比較好。

解析 (C) 說話者先是說「we've finally got some nice weather coming in today」(今天終於有好天氣了),接著又說「it's about time」(也該是時候了),暗示已經有好一段時間大家都在等天氣變好。選項(A)(B)(D)都和文意不符。

84. What does the speaker suggest? 這名說話者建議什麼?
    (A) Stay inside 待在室內
    (B) Go outdoors 去戶外
    (C) Take sunglasses 攜帶太陽眼鏡
    (D) Wear a sweater 穿毛衣

解析 (B) 這位氣象學家建議大家到戶外走走(spend some time outdoors)。選項(A)和去戶外的建議正好相反。選項(C)和(D)都有可能,但並未提及。

85. What will the weather be like tomorrow? 明天天氣將會如何？
    (A) Cloudy 多雲
    (B) Foggy 有霧
    (C) Rainy 有雨
    (D) Sunny 晴天

解析 (D) 氣象報告說明天的天氣會和今天一樣，也就是晴天。選項(A)(B)(C)都是本週稍後的天氣。

Questions 86 through 88 refer to the following phone message.

Hi. Yes. I'm calling about, uh, I have reservations at your hotel for next weekend, and I wanted to know about ski lessons. I'll be flying in around noon Friday, so I could start that afternoon, and also I'd like to be in a class Saturday morning, if there's space in an intermediate level group. I'll be bringing my own skis, so that won't be a problem, I mean, I won't need any rentals. So, anyhow, if it's not too late to sign up for classes, that would be great. I'm sure the snow conditions will be great next weekend. I'm really looking forward to seeing the hotel. All my friends recommend it as the most comfortable place in the area.

第86–88題請聽下面這段電話留言。

嗨，是的，我打電話來是為了，呃，我下週末訂了你們的飯店，我想知道關於滑雪課程的事。我會在週五中午左右飛抵，那天下午就可以開始上課，另外，如果中級班還有名額，我也想參加週六早上的課程。我會自己帶滑雪板，裝備不是問題，我的意思是，我不需要租裝備。總之，如果還來得及報名課程，那就太好了。我相信下週末的雪況會很棒，很期待看到你們的飯店，我所有的朋友都推薦你們飯店，說是那個地區最舒適的地方。

86. Why did the speaker make the call? 說話者打電話的目的為何？
    (A) To inquire about ski lessons 詢問滑雪課程
    (B) To make a hotel reservation 預訂飯店
    (C) To reserve a pair of rental skis 預訂一組出租的滑雪板
    (D) To find out the snow conditions 詢問雪況

解析 (A) 說話者說「I wanted to know about ski lessons」，接著談到他想要的上課時間和他的程度。選項(B)不正確，他說他已經預訂飯店了。選項(C)是他說要自備所以不需租借的東西。選項(D)不正確，他已經知道雪況了。

87. How does the speaker plan to get to the hotel? 說話者打算如何到達飯店？
    (A) By bus 搭公車
    (B) By car 開車
    (C) By train 搭火車
    (D) By plane 搭飛機

解析 (D) 說話者提到「I'll be flying in」（飛抵），故知為搭飛機。選項(A)(B)(C)都沒有被提到。

88. What does the speaker imply about the hotel? 說話者對這間飯店有何暗示？
    (A) He often recommends it to his friends. 他常向朋友推薦。
    (B) It is more expensive than other hotels. 比其他飯店來得貴。
    (C) He has never been there before. 他還沒有來過。
    (D) It is in a popular area. 位於熱門地區。

解析 (C) 說話者表示「I'm really looking forward to seeing the hotel. All my friends recommend it …」，暗示他還沒來過這家飯店，是朋友推薦他來的。選項(A)說反了，是朋友向他推薦，不是他向朋友推薦。選項(B)並未被提及。選項(D)重複使用area這個字。

Questions 89 through 91 refer to the following news item.

Construction of the much-discussed shopping mall in the Greenville district, due to begin next month, has been delayed. Residents of the area filed a complaint with City Hall this morning protesting the project. They are concerned that it will bring traffic and noise to quiet neighborhood streets, and that it is in violation of city zoning regulations. The mayor has agreed to meet with protestors to discuss their concerns later on this week. She said that most citizens support the project because it will bring jobs to the city as well as expand shopping options. But she is open to hearing the concerns of those who have expressed opposition to the construction plans.

第89–91題請聽下面這段新聞報導。

引發熱議的格林維爾區購物中心原定於下個月動工，目前已將工程延後。該區居民今早向市政府提出投訴，抗議這項計畫。他們擔心購物中心會為寧靜的住宅區街道帶來交通和噪音問題，且也違反了城市分區法規。市長同意於本週稍後與抗議者見面，針對他們的顧慮進行討論。她表示多數市民支持這項計畫，認為不僅能為本市帶來就業機會，也能增加購物選擇。不過她也願意聽取反對建設計畫者的擔憂。

201

89. What are Greenville residents complaining about? 格林維爾區的居民針對什麼提出投訴？
    (A) A new mall 新的購物中心
    (B) The cost of living 生活費
    (C) Traffic regulations 交通法規
    (D) A construction delay 工程延期

解析 (A) 格林維爾區的居民向市政府提出投訴，抗議一座購物中心的建設。選項(B)並未被提及。選項(C)重複使用了traffic這個字，居民擔心的是購物中心會帶來交通問題。選項(D)是因格林維爾區居民抗議所導致的事。

90. Where are they making their complaint? 他們在哪裡提出投訴？
    (A) On neighborhood streets 住宅區街道上
    (B) In the newspaper 報紙上
    (C) On TV 電視上
    (D) At City Hall 市政府

解析 (D) 新聞中提到格林維爾區居民向市政府提出投訴（filed a complaint with City Hall）。選項(A)是指居民抱怨購物中心會為住宅區街道帶來噪音。選項(B)和(C)均未在新聞中被提及。

91. What will the mayor do later this week? 市長本週稍後將會做什麼？
    (A) Visit the construction site 造訪施工地點
    (B) Meet with protesters 和抗議者見面
    (C) Announce new plans 宣布新計畫
    (D) Go shopping 購物

解析 (B) 說話者提到「The mayor has agreed to meet with protestors to discuss their concerns later on this week」。選項(A)重複使用了construction這個字。選項(C)重複了plans這個字。選項(D)重複了shopping這個字。

Questions 92 through 94 refer to the following talk.

Before you go, I'd like to remind everyone about Friday's class. We'll be meeting at the city's new art museum, so please be there by three thirty sharp. I've arranged a tour with the museum's manager, Dr. Jeffrey Lyons. Please be sure to read Chapter ten in your textbooks ahead of time. It's on museum management. I hope you'll use our time with Dr. Lyons to fully understand what it takes to do his job. Come up with a few questions to ask him, especially those of you who are graduating and will be looking for a job soon. One last thing: Photography isn't allowed inside the museum, so you might want to bring a sketchpad and pencil. See you all next week.

第 92–94 題請聽下面這段談話。

在各位離開之前，我要提醒大家關於週五的課。我們會在本市新開的美術館集合，請準時三點半抵達。我已經和館長傑弗瑞‧萊恩斯安排了一場導覽，請務必提前把課本第十章讀過，那一章是在講述博物館管理。希望大家能好好利用這次和萊恩斯博士相處的時間，充分了解他的工作需具備哪些條件。可以想一些問題問他，尤其是那些即將畢業、就快要找工作的人。最後一件事：館內禁止攝影，所以你可能會需要帶素描本和鉛筆。那麼我們下週見囉！

92. When is this talk happening? 這段談話發生在何時？
    (A) At the end of class 準備下課的時候
    (B) In the middle of class 上課到一半的時候
    (C) At the beginning of class 開始上課的時候
    (D) Before class starts 上課之前

解析 (A) 說話者說了「Before you go」，表示學生已經準備離開教室，但說話者還想交代一些事。選項 (B)(C)(D) 都和正確答案相抵觸。

93. What should be done before the next class? 下次上課前，大家應該做好什麼事？
    (A) Take a test 參加考試
    (B) Read a chapter 閱讀一個章節
    (C) Talk to Dr. Lyons 和萊恩斯博士談話
    (D) Answer a question 回答一個問題

解析 (B) 說話者要大家提前（ahead of time）閱讀課本第十章。選項 (A) 並沒有被提及。選項 (C) 是下次校外教學要做的事。選項 (D) 把這段談話中的「Come up with a few questions to ask him」搞混了。

94. What kind of class is this, most likely? 這門課最有可能是什麼課？
    (A) Photography 攝影課
    (B) Museum studies 博物館研究
    (C) Mathematics 數學課
    (D) Drawing 繪畫課

解析 **(B)** 下一堂課要到美術館和館長對談，同時聽者被要求閱讀關於博物館管理的課文。選項(A)被談話中提到的館內請勿攝影給混淆了。選項(C)並未被提及。選項(D)則是被說話者建議帶素描本給誤導。

Questions 95 through 97 refer to the following phone message and price list.

Hello, this is Pat Wilson calling. I spoke to you earlier about working in my apartment, and I was wondering if you'd be available early next week. The painters will be finishing up by the weekend, and I'd like you to come after that, but before the carpet installers who will be in the following Thursday. So if you could come clean Monday or Tuesday, that would be best. I hope to have it ready to show to prospective tenants as soon as possible. The apartment is only three rooms, so it shouldn't take long and since there's no furniture in it yet, vacuuming the floors should be easy. OK, let me know what you can do. Thanks.

第95-97題請聽下面這段電話留言，並參考價目表。

你好，我是佩特‧威爾森。我之前和你談過到我公寓工作的事，不知道你下週前幾天有沒有空。油漆工這週末會把工作完成，我希望你接著來做，但要在下週四地毯鋪設員來之前完成，所以如果你能在週一或週二過來打掃是最理想的。我希望盡快把房子準備好展示給潛在租戶看。這間公寓只有三個房間，應該不會花太多時間，而且目前裡面還沒有家具，用吸塵器清潔地板應該很容易。好，你看看能怎麼做再跟我說。謝謝！

```
           柯爾曼公司
            價目表
  一房 .............................. $50
  二至三房 ........................ $75
  四房 ............................. $100
  五房以上 ....................... $125
```

95. What kind of business is the Coleman Company, most likely? 柯爾曼公司最有可能從事哪方面的業務？
    (A) House painters 房屋油漆師傅
    (B) Carpet installers 地毯鋪設人員
    (C) Furniture sales 家具銷售員
    (D) House cleaners 居家清潔員

解析 (D) 說話者說「if you could come clean」（如果你能過來打掃），並提到用吸塵器清潔地板（vacuuming the floors），所以很有可能是居家清潔公司。選項(A)和(B)都有被提及，但都不是說話者在留言中要求的服務。選項(C)重複使用了 furniture 這個字。

96. Look at the graphic. How much will the speaker pay for Coleman's services? 請看圖表，說話者需要付給柯爾曼公司多少錢？
    (A) $50
    (B) $75
    (C) $100
    (D) $125

解析 (B) 說話者提到她的公寓有三個房間，而二到三房顯示的價格是 75 美元。選項(A)(C)(D)是其他大小公寓的價格。

97. What does the speaker plan to do with her apartment? 說話者計劃如何處理她的公寓呢？
    (A) Sell it 賣掉
    (B) Live in it 入住
    (C) Rent it out 出租
    (D) Redecorate it 重新裝潢

解析 (C) 說話者提到「I hope to have it ready to show to prospective tenants」（準備好展示給潛在租戶看），所以是要出租。選項(A)(B)(D)都有可能，但並未提及。

Questions 98 through 100 refer to the following talk and graph.

This slide shows, uh, the average temperatures throughout the year, and right here, when temperatures are highest, well, that also happens to be our company's busy season, obviously. I mean, who doesn't like a beach vacation when it's warm, right? Swimming, sunbathing, all that. But the problem is here, the cold months of the year, we have a lot of empty rooms then. So what I want to talk about is, what can we do to attract more guests to stay with us during the winter? How should we advertise ourselves? I'd like you now to pick up a pen and jot down a few ideas to answer this question: What activities do people enjoy in the winter?

第 98–100 題請聽下面這段談話，並參考圖表。

這張投影片顯示，呃，全年的平均溫度，然後這裡，溫度最高的時候，嗯，顯然也是我們公司的旺季。我的意思是，天氣一熱誰不喜歡到海邊度假呢？享受游泳、做日光浴這類的活動。但問題在這裡，一年中的寒冷月份，我們出現大量空房。所以我想討論的是，冬季時我們可以做些什麼來吸引更多住客？我們應該如何自我宣傳？現在我想請各位拿起筆，寫下一些想法回答這個問題：人們冬天喜歡從事哪些活動？

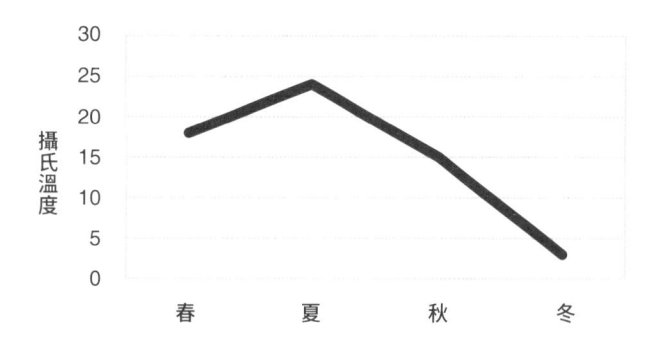

98. What kind of business is being discussed? 哪一種行業正在被討論？
    (A) Hotel 飯店
    (B) Travel agency 旅行社
    (C) Advertising agency 廣告公司
    (D) Swimming equipment 泳具

解析 **(A)** 說話者提到空房（empty rooms）和需要吸引更多住客（attract more guests），由此可知是一間飯店。選項 (B) 使用與 beach vacation 有關的 travel。選項 (C) 使用了與題目 advertise 相關的 advertising 這個字。選項 (D) 重複使用 swimming 這個字。

206

99. Look at the graphic. At what time of year is the company busiest? 請看圖表，哪一個季節是這間公司最忙的時候？
    (A) Spring 春季
    (B) Summer 夏季
    (C) Winter 冬季
    (D) Fall 秋季

解析 (B) 說話者提到公司的旺季是氣溫最高的時候，而氣溫最高的是夏季。選項(A)(C)(D)都與描述不符。

100. What are listeners asked to do next? 聽者被要求接下來做什麼？
    (A) Create a slide 製作一張投影片
    (B) Ask questions 提出問題
    (C) Write something 寫些東西
    (D) Talk with a partner 和一名合夥人談話

解析 (C) 說話者說「I'd like you now to pick up a pen and jot down a few ideas」（我想請各位拿起筆寫下一些想法）。選項(A)重複使用了slide這個字。選項(B)不正確，因為聽者被要求回答一個問題，而不是提出問題。選項(D)並未被提及。

STOP 本測驗之聽力測驗到此結束，請翻頁進行Part 5的測驗。

閱讀測驗

在本段測驗當中，你將有機會展現自己對書面英語的理解能力。閱讀測驗共有三個大題，每一大題均有作答說明。

你有 75 分鐘時間完成本測驗的第五到第七大題。

Part 5：句子填空

作答方式： 你會看到一個缺字的句子和四個可能的選項，選出最適當的答案，將答案卡上對應的橢圓框塗滿。

101. 如果顧客不滿意，請他打電話給經理。

解析 (B) customer是單數且為第三人稱，因此要用第三人稱單數動詞is。選項(A)雖然是單數，但是第一人稱。選項(C)是複數。選項(D)是be動詞的原形。

102. 我們建議他在同意接受新職位之前好好考慮清楚。
　　　(A) 推薦
　　　(B) 建議
　　　(C) 提議
　　　(D) 建議

解析 (D) 四個選項的意義都非常類似，但只有(D) advised符合句子的文法要求。選項(A)(B)(C)必須使用另一種句型：「We _____ that he think things over . . .」。

103. 我們老闆打算在她家為幾名今年要退休的員工舉辦一場派對。
　　　(A) 招待
　　　(B) 邀請
　　　(C) 主辦
　　　(D) 客人

解析 (C) host的意思是主辦一場社交活動。選項(A)和(B)用來描述對客人所做的事：招待（entertain）客人和邀請（invite）客人。選項(D)是受邀參加聚會的人，不符合這個句子的要求，且guest是名詞，這裡需要的是動詞。

104. 由於邀請函沒有及時印好，研討會被取消了。
　　　(A) 印表機
　　　(B) 印製 (ved)
　　　(C) 印製 (ving)
　　　(D) 印製 (v.)

解析 (B) were not後面需接一個過去分詞來完成動詞片語。選項(A)是名詞。選項(C)是進行式動詞。選項(D)是原形動詞。

105. 如果服務員無法處理您的要求，領班會協助您。

解析 **(A)** if子句使用了現在式，主要子句（後面的子句）要用未來式，will 可以搭配 assist 構成一個完整的動詞。選項(B)是現在完成式的助動詞，且後面必須接過去分詞，不符合句子的結構。選項(C)是過去式。選項(D)是現在式，且後面必須接現在分詞或動詞的進行式，不符合句子的結構。

106. 王先生的知識和領導力獲得當地商界的認可。
(A) 領導 (ving)
(B) 領導 (v.)
(C) 領導力
(D) 領導者

解析 **(C)** 名詞 knowledge 後面用了對等連接詞 and，因此要連接另一個名詞。選項(A)是動名詞，選項(B)是動詞。選項(D)雖然是名詞，但指人而非事物。

107. 根據最新數據，今年我們的成本預計將增加約百分之五。
(A) 上升
(B) 增加
(C) 升高、加劇
(D) 提高

解析 **(B)** costs（成本）最常用 increase 來表示「上升、增加」。選項(A)(C)(D)也是「上升、增加」的意思，但不用於和百分比相關的名詞。

108. 好的業務經理會告訴你組織能力是提高效率的關鍵。
(A) 組織 (ved)
(B) 組織 (v.)
(C) 組織者
(D) 組織 (n.)

解析 **(D)** 空格是子句的主詞位置，因此需要一個名詞。選項(A)和(B)是動詞。選項(C)是名詞，可指人或物，但用在本句意思不通。

109. 由於譚先生的飛機誤點，他們不得不延後和客戶的會議。
(A) 雖然
(B) 當……的時候
(C) 因為
(D) 有……的、與……一起

解析 (C) because建立兩個事件之間的邏輯因果關係。選項(A)用來說明對比關係，在這個句子中除非飛機準時，否則使用although就不合邏輯。選項(B)暗示兩個事件同時發生，但這不可能，一定是飛機先誤點了才會延後會議。選項(D)是一個介系詞，不能用來連接子句。

110. 客戶提供給我們的任何資料將受到完全保密，不會與辦公室外的人分享。
　　 (A) 相當大的
　　 (B) 祕密的、機密的
　　 (C) 建造
　　 (D) 授予、協商

解析 (B) confidential的意思是「祕密的、機密的」，符合語意要求。選項(A)(C)(D)都不符合語意要求。

111. 當佐藤先生抵達聖地牙哥時，大會將已經開始。
　　 (A) 抵達 (v.)
　　 (B) 抵達 (ved)
　　 (C) 已經抵達
　　 (D) 將抵達

解析 (A) 空格所在的子句是一個未來時間子句，動詞要用現在式。選項(B)是過去式。選項(C)是現在完成式。選項(D)是未來式。

112. 木村女士因為通勤路程很長，總是五點半就下班。
　　 (A) 通勤
　　 (B) 公社
　　 (C) 社區
　　 (D) 堆肥

解析 (A) commute意指往返於住家和工作場所之間，即「通勤」。選項(B)(C)(D)都不適用於這個句子。

113. 你在下一個街區可以找到這家餐廳，就在銀行和書店中間。
　　 (A) 在……之中
　　 (B) 在……之外
　　 (C) 在……之間
　　 (D) 穿過

211

解析 (C) between 表示一個物體的兩側各有其他物體。選項(A)通常用於一個難以計算的團體或事物，例如：among the paper clips（在這些迴紋針之中）、among the office equipment（在辦公室設備之中）。選項(B)和(D)放入句中都不合邏輯。

114. 我們希望能在本週結束前開始面試工作應徵者。
　　(A) 工作
　　(B) 職業
　　(C) 雜務、苦差事
　　(D) 位置、立場

解析 (A) job 在這裡指個別的職位。選項(B)比較偏向專業身分而非個別職位，例如：In his career (occupation) as an insurance investigator, he held jobs with several companies.（在他從事保險調查員的職業生涯中，曾任職於數家公司）。選項(C)暗示比個別職位還要瑣碎的苦差事，例如：I like my job as a secretary, but it's a chore to sort the boss's mail.（我喜歡祕書這份工作，但整理老闆的郵件是件苦差事）。選項(D)使用了相關字 position，但放入句中語意邏輯不通。

115. 你需要辦公用品時，請向辦公室經理提出申請。
　　(A) 填充
　　(B) 落下 (ved)
　　(C) 落下 (ven)
　　(D) 提出

解析 (D) file 在這裡的意思等同於 submit（提出）。選項(A)是動詞 fill 的動名詞形式。選項(B)和(C)是動詞 fall 的過去式及過去分詞形式。

116. 所有空服員在離開房間之後必須鎖上艙門。
　　(A) 之後
　　(B) 在……之後
　　(C) 遲於
　　(D) 遲的

解析 (B) after 建立兩個事件之間的邏輯時間關係。選項(A)是副詞不能用來連接句子，表示特定事件之後的一段時間。選項(C)表示比較，例如：His fax arrived later than mine.（他的傳真比我的晚到）。選項(D)是形容詞，不能用來連接子句。

117. 因為那天是吉頓先生的生日，他的員工帶他去吃午餐。
    (A) 雖然、儘管
    (B) 在……期間
    (C) 因為
    (D) 那個

解析 (C) because 指出了兩個事件之間的因果關係。選項(A)用來表達對比關係。選項(B) during 後面不能接句子。選項(D)放入句中意思不通。

118. 為尊重客人隱私，棕櫚飯店員工在出於任何原因要進入房間之前，都必須先敲門。
    (A) 報答
    (B) 必須的
    (C) 必要的
    (D) 擊退、驅逐

解析 (B) required 的意思是「必須」。選項(A)(C)(D)都不符合語意要求。

119. 帳務人員找不到請款單或訂單。
    (A) 或
    (B) 和
    (C) 但是
    (D) 儘管

解析 (A) 這裡使用 or 合乎邏輯，且 or 可以連接兩個名詞。選項(B)通常不用於表達否定意義。選項(C)和(D)放入句中都不合邏輯。

120. 吉姆開支票前先到銀行網站上查詢他的帳戶餘額。
    (A) 尺寸
    (B) 金錢
    (C) 供應
    (D) 餘額

解析 (D) balance 指的是銀行帳戶裡所剩的錢。選項(A)(B)(C)通常不會用在這種情況。

121. 報告出來後，請馬上轉寄一份給麥斯威爾先生。
    (A) 有用、利用 (v.)
    (B) 可得到的
    (C) 可得性
    (D) 有用、利用 (ving)

213

解析 **(B)** 空格需要填入一個形容詞，選項中只有 available 是形容詞。選項(A)和(D)是動詞和動詞的進行式。選項(C)是名詞。

122. 行李服務領班建議多請幾位行李員。

解析 **(C)** 動詞 suggest 後面要用原形動詞。選項(A)是 be 動詞的複數形。選項(B)和(D)雖然也是原形動詞，但用在這裡都不合語意邏輯。

123. 公司員工的指定停車位位於停車場一樓。
    (A) 已簽署的
    (B) 任務、工作
    (C) 分配的、指定的
    (D) 重要的、重大的

解析 **(C)** 空格處需要一個形容詞來修飾 spaces。選項(A)和(D)也是形容詞，但意思上不合邏輯。選項(B)是名詞。

124. 你會在通訊錄上看到所有協會成員的名字按照字母順序排列。
    (A) 字母表
    (B) 按字母順序排列
    (C) 按字母順序地
    (D) 按字母順序的

解析 **(D)** order 前面需要一個形容詞來修飾它。選項(A)是名詞。選項(B)是動詞。選項(C)是副詞。

125. 雷蒙處理那個帳戶才幾天時間而已，就已經完全熟悉客戶的背景。
    (A) 尚未
    (B) 自……以來
    (C) 已經
    (D) 很快

解析 **(C)** already 可用來表示比預期還早發生的事。在這個句子中，雷蒙在很短的時間內就掌握了客戶的背景。選項(A)(B)(D)放入句中都沒有意義。

126. 要進入該場所的人都必須向保全人員出示身分證。
    (A)(B)(C)(D) 出示

解析 **(D)** must 後面要接原形動詞。選項(A)是過去式動詞。選項(B)是進行式。選項(C)是第三人稱單數。

127. 根據幾項研究，重複性的工作經常導致肌肉疲勞和損傷。
    (A) 重複 (v.)
    (B) 重複的
    (C) 重複 (n.)
    (D) 重複地

解析 (B) tasks需要用形容詞修飾。選項(A)是動詞。選項(C)是名詞。選項(D)是副詞。

128. 遊客被提醒要隨時佩戴名牌。
    (A)(B)(C)(D) 佩戴

解析 (A) reminded後面要接不定詞。選項(B)是原形動詞。選項(C)是過去分詞。選項(D)是進行式。

129. 宣傳部的這個職位需要外語知識和與國際客戶交流的廣泛豐富經驗。
    (A) 令人興奮的
    (B) 期待的
    (C) 精美的
    (D) 廣泛的、大量的

解析 (D) extensive的意思是「廣泛的」或「大量的」。選項(A)(B)(C)都不符合語意要求。

130. 基於安全考量，工廠政策規定訪客如未戴安全帽不得進入製造區。
    (A) 很少
    (B) 從來
    (C) 絕不
    (D) 沒有時間

解析 (C) never可用於be動詞和動詞之間。選項(A)是形容詞，不符合此處的要求。選項(B)的意思不通。選項(D)如果是at no time（任何時候皆不）就可以使用。

Part 6：段落填空

> 作答方式：你會看到四篇短文，各含四個空格，每個空格配有四個選項，選出最適當的單字、片語或句子完成這段敘述。

第 131–134 題請看下面這份通知。

國際機場之安全與行李相關政策

依國際安全法規，乘客不得攜帶下列物品上機，無論置於手提行李或托運行李：任何形式之武器、炸藥或煙火。

下列物品可置於托運行李，但不可置於手提行李：工具，包括鐵鎚、螺絲起子和扳手；運動裝備，如高爾夫球桿、棒球棒、滑雪板和滑雪杖。當你通過安檢時，所有行李都將通過X光機進行檢查。部分行李也將由安檢人員手動檢查。

感謝您的配合，祝您有一個安全又愉悅的航程。

---

131. (A)(B)(C)(D) 允許

   解析 (A) 主詞 passengers 不是執行動作的人，這裡需要使用過去分詞來構成被動語態。選項(B)是現在分詞或動名詞。選項(C)是主動語態。選項(D)是名詞。

132. (A) 因此
     (B) 例如
     (C) 例子
     (D) 例子

   解析 (B) such as 可用來舉出一系列的例子。選項(A)為連接詞且不能用在這種情況。選項(C)和(D)前面要加上for構成for example、for instance，並在片語前後加上逗號才能用於此句。

133. (A) 售票（區）
     (B) 入境檢查（區）
     (C) 安檢（區）
     (D) 訂位（區）

   解析 (C) 乘客需要通過安檢，檢查行李是否內含禁帶物品。選項(A)(B)(D)都是乘客可能會通過的區域，但不符合此處的語境。

134. (A) 這些機器非常精密且造價昂貴。
(B) 請向您的航空公司確認行李尺寸限制。
(C) 大部分航空公司僅允許每人攜帶一件手提行李。
(D) 部分行李也將由安檢人員手動檢查。

解析 (D) 前一個句子提到行李通過安檢時需要接受何種檢查，選項(D)的句子繼續說明其他的檢查方式。選項(A)(B)(C)都不符合此處的語境。

第 135–138 題請看下面這篇雜誌文章。

電腦零售業者希望利用這次假期提高平板電腦的銷售量。大規模宣傳活動於本週展開，多家電腦製造商在電視、廣播、報紙和網路播放或刊登廣告。於假期期間，廣告活動將持續進行。

平板電腦的便利性使其越來越受歡迎。由於它們比筆記型電腦更輕、更小，因此更好攜帶，滿足了與日俱增的移動需求。另一個好處是它們比大部分的筆記型電腦便宜。

把電子產品當作佳節禮物贈送也是日益增長的趨勢，慶祝節日的傳統方法正被人們對新科技的熱衷所取代。

135. (A) 製造商
(B) 採購者
(C) 消費者
(D) 訓練員

解析 (A) computer manufacturers 是製造和販售電腦的公司。選項(B)和(C)都是買家。選項(D)是可能使用電腦的人，但應該不會販售電腦。

136. (A) 名聲
(B) 數量
(C) 外觀
(D) 方便

解析 (D) 平板電腦很容易隨身攜帶，因此非常方便。選項(A)(B)(C)都與文意不符。

217

137. (A) 有些人覺得螢幕太小所以很難使用。
(B) 另一個好處是它們比大部分的筆記型電腦便宜。
(C) 然而在某些領域，筆記型電腦還是很受歡迎。
(D) 它們能夠連接鍵盤和印表機。

解析 (B) 這段文字已討論了平板電腦的一個好處——便利性，而選項(B)則又補充了另一個好處。選項(A)(C)(D)都與文意不符。

138. (A) 熱衷於……的人
(B) 熱情、熱衷
(C) 熱情的、熱衷的
(D) 滿腔熱情地、熱衷地

解析 (B) 定冠詞the後面需要一個名詞。選項(A)也是名詞，但指人。選項(C)是形容詞。選項(D)是副詞。

第139-142題請看下面這封電子郵件。

收件者：瑪格麗特・邁克森
寄件者：安巴爾・派特爾
日期：　20—年9月22日
主旨：　應付款項

茲就逾期付款一事，特此來信。我們已在七月寄出請款單，但至今仍未收到支票。我們於電話留言中要求說明延遲理由，卻未得到回應。就此付款一事，若未能盡快獲得您的回應，我們將會採取行動。請在本週結束前與我電話聯繫，討論如何最好地解決此事宜。隨信附上您的訂單細節，包含採購項目與價格。

---

139. (A) 匯出的、匯款的
(B) 逾期的
(C) 可轉移的
(D) 封閉的

解析 (B) 請款單在七月寄出，郵件日期顯示現在是九月，又提到留言詢問延遲一事，可知付款逾期（overdue）了。選項(A)(C)(D)都與文意不符。

140. (A) 亦接受信用卡付款。
(B) 希望您滿意我們的服務。
(C) 請務必開立金額正確的支票。
(D) 我們於電話留言中要求說明延遲理由，卻未得到回應。

解析 **(D)** 這封電子郵件是關於一份尚未支付的請款單，選項(D)描述了寄件者試圖與欠款人溝通卻未獲得回應，下一句接著表示如果再沒有獲得回應將採取行動，語意連貫。選項(A)(B)(C)的語意都不通。

141. (A)(B)(C)(D) 必須

解析 **(A)** 空格所在子句是一個未來真實條件句的主要子句，動詞要用未來式。選項(B)是現在完成式。選項(C)是非真實條件句的句型。選項(D)是一個不完整的未來式，少了are（are going to have）。

142. (A) 表格
(B) 信用
(C) 訂單
(D) 退款

解析 **(C)** order是訂單，當中會包含項目和價格，符合電子郵件的描述。其他選項都與下訂單有關，但皆非正確答案。

第143–146題請看下面這封電子郵件。

寄件者：安德魯・戴文
主旨：　辦公室經理職位
日期：　4月1日
收件者：理查・拜倫

拜倫先生您好：

我聯繫您是為了貴公司網站上所發布徵求辦公室經理的資訊。過去十年我一直在本地的一家公司擔任行政助理，且自認為非常了解一間辦公室的營運，多年的經驗也讓我足以勝任辦公室經理一職。我擁有良好的組織能力和人際溝通技巧，也對大多數現在使用的辦公室技術十分熟悉。本人也是負責任又可靠的工作者。隨信附上我的履歷和兩封推薦信。

期待收到您的回覆。

敬祝 順心
安德魯・戴文

143. (A) 回應
    (B) 休息
    (C) 訴諸
    (D) 暫緩

解析 **(A)** response 的意思是「回應」，這封信是要回應一則徵才訊息。選項 (B)(C)(D) 長得和正確答案很像，但意義大不相同。

144. (A) 辦公室經理對於辦公室的順利運作非常重要。
    (B) 作為我求職的一部分，我幾乎每天都會上網查看職缺資訊。
    (C) 我有興趣進一步了解貴公司的辦公室經理職務。
    (D) 過去十年我一直在本地的一家公司擔任行政助理。

解析 **(D)** 選項(D)描述了寄件者的工作經驗，他在下一句所指的經驗就是這個。其他選項放入文中語意都不通順。

145. (A)(B)(C)(D) 具備資格

解析 **(A)** 現在式動詞 qualify 和複數主詞 years 一致。選項(B)(C)(D)都必須搭配單數主詞。

146.

解析 **(C)** look forward to 意指「期待」或「希望」。選項(A)(B)(D)都不是這個片語該用的介系詞。

Part 7：閱讀測驗

作答方式：你會看到單篇或多篇文章的題組，文章後面配有幾道題目，各含四個選項。選出最適當的答案回答問題，並將答案卡上對應的橢圓框塗滿。

第 147–148 題請看下面這份請款單。

庫柏與艾倫建築師事務所
科羅拉多州哈瑞斯維爾橋街 149 號 107 室
郵遞區號：76521

20—年 4 月 5 日
請款單編號：3892
專案名稱：總部——最終設計
專案編號：925639

威廉斯公司
科羅拉多州托瑪斯頓瀑布大道 5110 號
郵遞區號：76520

以下截至 3 月 30 日之款項應於本月底支付。

本期費用	$8,200.00
前期未付餘額	$362.00
本次應付總額	$8,562.00

我們重視為您服務的機會，感謝您及時付款。

---

147. 何時應該付款？
　　(A) 3 月 1 日
　　(B) 3 月 30 日
　　(C) 4 月 5 日
　　(D) 4 月 30 日

解析 (D) 請款單中提到「at the end of this month」（本月底），且請款單開立的月份為 4 月，因此是 4 月 30 日。選項 (A) 未被提及。選項 (B) 是款項計算的截至日期。選項 (C) 是請款單的開立日期。

148. 除了本期費用之外還需支付什麼費用？
    (A) 下一個專案的預付款
    (B) 本期費用的稅金
    (C) 本期費用的服務費
    (D) 前次請款未付的款項

解析 (D) 請款單上列出了「unpaid prior balance」，指的是上次請款未付的金額。選項(A)未被提及。選項(B)和(C)不正確，款項並未細分稅金和其他費用。

第149–150題請看下面這則通知。

本公司為於公司服務五年以上之所有員工提供退休金計畫，支付款項依據年資及最高薪資等級而定。公司與員工雙方每月共同繳納計畫款項，金額依政府規定。退休金每兩個月發放一次。

---

149. 這則通知是關於什麼？
    (A) 一個升職計畫
    (B) 一項退休福利
    (C) 一個貸款方案
    (D) 一個薪資等級

解析 (B) 這則通知是關於一個退休金計畫（pension plan），是發給退休員工的款項。選項(A)使用了employees的相關字job。選項(C)使用了payments的相關字loan。選項(D)重複使用了文中的salary這個字。

150. 誰有資格參與這個計畫？
    (A) 年資達五年以上的員工
    (B) 達到一定薪水等級的員工
    (C) 僅限政府員工
    (D) 公司所有員工

解析 (A) 這項計畫適用於服務五年以上的員工（employees with a minimum of five years of service）。選項(B)重複使用了salary這個字。選項(C)重複使用了government這個字。選項(D)不正確，服務未滿五年之員工不符合條件。

第 151–152 題請看下面這則簡訊對話串。

山姆・陳 你在哪裡？我們要去開會了。	9:10
佩特・羅培茲 對不起，我還在火車上。	9:11
山姆・陳 哪裡？	9:13
佩特・羅培茲 我剛離開米道博里，橋樑那邊好似發生了事故，所有列車都延誤了。	9:14
佩特・羅培茲 我已經提早出門了，但還是沒用。	1:16
山姆・陳 客戶已經到了。	1:17
佩特・羅培茲 你們先開始吧，不用等我。我應該三十分鐘後就到。	1:18
山姆・陳 我可不想一個人報告提案。	1:20
佩特・羅培茲 你沒問題的，就先播放投影片。	1:21
山姆・陳 好吧，那你趕快來。我們真的必須討好這位客戶，他是我們的大客戶之一。	1:22
佩特・羅培茲 這還用你說！我很快就到。	1:23

151. 羅培茲女士為何開會遲到？
    (A) 山姆沒有提醒她要開會。
    (B) 她沒有準時出門。
    (C) 火車延誤。
    (D) 她搭錯列車。

解析 **(C)** 羅培茲女士解釋說，因為發生事故，所有列車都延誤了。選項(A)在對話中並未提及。選項(B)不正確，她說她已經提早出門了。選項(D)並未被提及。

223

152. 在 1:23 時，羅培茲女士說「You're telling me!」是什麼意思？
    (A) 她知道這位客戶有多重要。
    (B) 她不知道該對客戶說什麼。
    (C) 她不喜歡山姆對她發號施令。
    (D) 她希望山姆告訴她該怎麼做。

解析 **(A)**「You're telling me!」用來表示「你不需要告訴我，因為我已經知道了」的語境。山姆說這位客戶是大客戶，他們要討好他，羅培茲女士用這句話回覆說她當然知道。選項(B)(C)(D)都錯誤解讀了這句話的意思。

第 153–154 題請看下面這則公告。

我們改名了！很高興宣布從 20—年 12 月 5 日起，我們的正式名稱將是：

綠色里程西方

我們原先名稱使用的「加州」一詞因遭到抗議，在與加州園藝協會達成協議後，我們以「西方」取代名稱中的「加州」。

希望這次改名不會造成忠實客戶的困惑。雖然這代表我們原本的名稱有所改變，但我們為客戶提供的產品品質依舊不變。

---

153. 這間公司的原名是什麼？
    (A) 里程西方
    (B) 綠色里程加州
    (C) 綠色里程西方
    (D) 綠色加州

解析 **(B)** 這間公司的原名是 Green Miles California，公告中說明 California 被取代為 West。選項 (A) 和 (D) 把公司名稱拆開來並重新排列組合，因此不正確。選項 (C) 是新的公司名稱。

154. 根據這則公告，這間公司為何要改名？
    (A) 公司的辦公室搬遷了。
    (B) 他們的名稱與另一個機構有所衝突。
    (C) 他們不喜歡最初的選擇。
    (D) 忠實客戶感到困惑。

解析 **(B)** 加州園藝協會（California Gardening Association）抗議兩公司的名稱雷同。選項(A)把offices和brands（品牌）搞混了，有所變更的是品牌名稱，而非辦公室地點。選項(C)重複使用了initial這個字。選項(D)把文中說他們希望客戶不要感到困惑誤解為公司改名的原因。

第155–157題請看下面這個網頁。

---

www.palmfrondsresort.com

| 檔案 | 編輯 | 檢視 | 收藏項目 | 工具 | 說明 | 頁面▼ | 安全性▼ | 工具▼ |

首頁　　關於　　客房　　活動　　常見問題

棕櫚葉度假村

棕櫚葉度假村竭誠歡迎您闔家光臨，與我們共度一個放鬆、歡樂的假期。我們提供寬敞舒適的客房、精緻的餐飲和一座私人海灘。您可以享受各種海灘和水上運動，或只是放鬆身心，享受遠離城市喧囂的平靜。

四人以下全包式假期內含：
❖ 雅緻兩室套房，可舒適入住四人
❖ 每日早餐與晚餐
❖ 可使用海灘設施
❖ 可使用游泳池

現場提供浮潛、水肺潛水、衝浪和網球裝備之租借服務。點此查看價目表。
我們有世界級的教練開設私人和團體課程，點此查看收費標準。

交通方式

最近的機場位於棕櫚市本島，可自機場搭乘接駁車或計程車至渡輪碼頭。點此查看渡輪時刻表。

155. 棕櫚葉度假村可能位在那裡？
    (A) 城市裡
    (B) 小島上
    (C) 機場旁
    (D) 山上

解析 **(B)** 度假村緊鄰海灘，且最近的機場被描述為位於本島，遊客還需搭乘渡輪才能到達度假村，所以位於小島上是合理的推論。選項(A)和(C)都有被提到，但是位於本島。選項(D)未被提及。

156. 下列哪一項包含在假期套裝行程中？
    (A) 機場到度假村接駁
    (B) 游泳課
    (C) 一日兩餐
    (D) 運動裝備

解析 **(C)** 網頁中段列出了全包式假期的內含項目，其中包括了每天的早餐與晚餐。選項(A)雖有被提及，但不包含在假期套裝行程中。選項(B)指的是可使用海灘和游泳池的服務，網頁中也提到私人和團體的教練課程，但課程需額外付費。選項(D)是提供租借的物品，所以也是要額外付費。

157. 下列哪一項是客人可以在度假村中從事的活動？
    (A) 釣魚
    (B) 租腳踏車
    (C) 游泳
    (D) 上烹飪課

解析 **(C)** 網頁中提到可使用海灘和游泳池，因此可以合理推斷客人可以去游泳。選項(A)(B)(D)雖然都有可能，但並未提及。

第158–160題請看下面這封電子郵件。

寄件者：艾倫・施埃德
收件者：全體員工
主旨：　回覆各位問題
日期：　9月2日

每天我的信箱都會湧入關於搬遷到巴黎辦公室的訊息。我在這裡統一說明搬遷流程，不再個別一一回覆。請按照下列指示進行，不要遺漏任何步驟。請大家不要再問我更多問題，你們所需知道的事項都在下方說明了。

- 將桌上、桌內所有物品裝箱。
- 在所有箱子上清楚標示姓名和部門。
- 通知維護人員清理你的桌子，準備好給下一位使用者。
- 更改語音信箱的提示訊息，通知客戶你即將搬遷。
- 將你的舊密碼和電腦編號提供給網路管理員。
- 以電子郵件通知客戶你的新地點和聯絡方式。

我們有提供打包用品，如有需要請找昆貝女士索取。

感謝各位的配合。
艾倫

158. 這封電子郵件的目的是什麼？
　　(A) 提出裁員程序
　　(B) 宣布巴黎辦公室啟用
　　(C) 提供搬遷指引
　　(D) 提出改善工作空間規畫的方法

解析 (C) 這封電子郵件是關於搬遷（transfer）到巴黎辦公室的事情。選項(A)和(D)描述的是公司員工也可能需要收拾辦公桌的情況。選項(B)重複使用了Paris這個字。

159. 這封電子郵件的收件者被要求做什麼？
　　(A) 自行購買打包用品
　　(B) 完成所有步驟
　　(C) 將問題寄給施埃德先生
　　(D) 協助同事收拾工作空間

解析 (B) 郵件中提到「Please follow the directions below and do not omit anything.」，要員工遵循指示不要遺漏任何步驟。選項(A)不正確，郵件中有提到會提供打包用品（Packing supplies are available）。選項(C)不正確，郵件中要大家不要再問更多問題（please refrain from asking me more questions）。選項(D)並未被提及。

160. 每位員工應為下一位使用辦公桌的人做些什麼？
　　(A) 把箱子搬到房間邊緣
　　(B) 通知客戶新的使用者是誰
　　(C) 取得一組電腦密碼
　　(D) 把桌子收拾乾淨

解析 (D) 郵件中提到「Notify maintenance to clean your desk so it will be ready for the next occupant.」，表示要大家把桌子收拾乾淨留給下一位使用者。選項(A)和(C)都使用了郵件中出現過的單字，但皆未正確解讀郵件訊息。選項(B)雖然有被提及，但不是為下一個使用者所做的事。

第161–163題請看下面這篇文章。

會議

人們經常覺得員工會議是浪費時間。然而只要記住下列幾點，就能確保會議順利進行，時間有被妥善利用。每次會議都該建立議程，–[1]– 這一點看似理所當然，卻是時常被忽略的細節。先想好哪些事項需要討論，每個事項又該分配多少時間。務必讓每個人都拿到一份議程表，他們才知道將會進行哪些討論。–[2]– 討論每個事項時，保持對話持續進行。感謝每位發言者提出自己的想法，接著請下一位發言。–[3]– 這種方式能讓每個人的發言保持簡潔有力。一個事項所分配的時間到時，就進行下一個事項的討論。–[4]– 你的員工將會覺得自己的時間有被妥善利用，並帶著滿滿的新點子和活力回去工作。

161. 這篇文章主要在討論什麼？
　　(A) 如何有效率地開會
　　(B) 員工會議的各種形式
　　(C) 定期召開員工會議的原因
　　(D) 讓會議更有趣的方法

解析 (A) 第二句說「. . . you can make sure your meetings run smoothly and use time well」，可見這篇文章是在說明如何充分運用會議時間而不白白浪費，換句話說就是要有效率。選項(B)(C)(D)都和員工會議這個主題有關，但不是這篇文章主要討論的事。

162. 關於會議中的發言，文中有何說明？
　　(A) 應該允許大家盡情多多發言。
　　(B) 應該鼓勵每個人都發言。
　　(C) 只能針對議程所列事項發言。
　　(D) 大家發言應力求簡潔。

解析 (D) 文章提到發言應力求簡潔（keep their remarks brief），remarks 就是 comments，brief 就是 short。選項(A)(B)(C)都未被提及。

163. 下面這個句子最適合放入文中[1][2][3][4]哪一個位置？
　　「只要按照時間表進行，就能確保會議準時結束。」
　　(A) [1]
　　(B) [2]
　　(C) [3]
　　(D) [4]

解析 (D) 編號[4]前面的句子表示按照分配時間進行很重要，而插入的句子進一步說明為什麼很重要，支持了前一句。選項(A)(B)(C)的位置插入此句語意都不通順。

第 164–167 題請看下面這段線上聊天室的討論串。

希薇雅・普里耶托 [1:15]
我剛接到宴會承辦商的電話，因為我們希望午餐十二點開始，他們想要十一點就開始準備。

喬治・克洛夫特 [1:16]
應該沒問題，他們可以在大會議室準備。培訓師說他們可以用其他會議室。

瑪賽拉・盧 [1:17]
有人預約會議室了嗎？

喬治・克洛夫特 [1:18]
有，我昨天預約了，流程都已完成。

瑪賽拉・盧 [1:19]
桌椅呢？投影機呢？

喬治・克洛夫特 [1:21]
我全都準備好了。

希薇雅・普里耶托 [1:22]
我今天早上還收到培訓師的電子郵件，附加了一些文件，早上的課他們希望每位參加者都有拿到文件影本。

瑪賽拉・盧 [1:23]
我可以處理。我們已經知道有多少員工報名了嗎？

喬治・克洛夫特 [1:25]
我有報名表。二十個，已額滿了。

瑪賽拉・盧 [1:26]
太好了，我現在就去印那些文件。喬治，你準備的椅子夠吧？

喬治・克洛夫特 [1:27]
放心，一切都在我的掌握之中。

164. 這些聊天者最有可能正在籌備何種活動？
    (A) 頒獎宴會
    (B) 員工週會
    (C) 協會會議
    (D) 專業培訓工作坊

解析 (D) 這個活動是由培訓師所主持，對象是員工，因此很有可能是一個專業培訓工作坊。選項(A)從對話中提到午餐才會聯想到宴會（banquet）。選項(B)不正確，員工週會不太可能需要勞師動眾，還請人來準備午餐。選項(C)也不大可能，因為這場活動的參加者只有公司員工。

165. 普里耶托女士幾分鐘前做了什麼事？
    (A) 她和宴會承辦商說過話。
    (B) 她寄了一封電子郵件給培訓師。
    (C) 她預約了會議室。
    (D) 她製作了一些文件。

解析 (A) 普里耶托女士在聊天室裡說「I just had a phone call from the caterers.」（我剛接到宴會承辦商的電話）。選項(B)被她收到來自培訓師的電子郵件給混淆了。選項(C)是喬治做的事。選項(D)不正確，文件是培訓師寄給她的，不是她製作的。

166. 盧女士接下來可能會做什麼？
    (A) 計算參加者人數
    (B) 到喬治的辦公室
    (C) 影印文件
    (D) 擺設椅子

解析 (C) 盧女士寫說「I'll take care of those copies now」，表示她會去影印培訓師要求的文件。選項(A)是她詢問的問題，但喬治已經幫她算好了。選項(B)並未提及。選項(D)是喬治的工作。

167. 在1:27時，克洛夫特先生說「Relax」是什麼意思？
    (A) 盧女士應該休息一下。
    (B) 盧女士可以坐在椅子上。
    (C) 盧女士不用擔心。
    (D) 盧女士的工作不會很困難。

解析 (C) relax 經常用來表示「不用擔心」。選項(A)(B)(D)都不是 relax 在這裡的意思。

231

第168-171題請看下面這篇文章。

–[1]– ABC食品公司報告說,該公司計劃提高十九個不同品牌之水果蛋糕、餡餅和其他水果甜點的價格,平均漲幅百分之三。–[2]– 該公司聲稱此為去年春季晚霜及長期乾旱導致水果價格上漲的結果。

ABC食品公司價格調漲之產品將於下個月初在各大超市上架,其他公司預計年底將跟進提高水果罐頭和蔬菜罐頭的價格。–[3]– 消費者可預見整個冬天都將會感受到荷包壓力。

–[4]–「我們只能希望明年生長季的天氣能夠好轉。」消費者聯合會會長盧艾拉·皮爾森表示。「否則,如果價格持續上漲,一些家庭會受到極大的影響。」她補充說道。

168. 下列哪項ABC食品公司的產品會漲價?
　　(A) 蔬菜罐頭
　　(B) 所有品牌的食品
　　(C) 果醬和果凍
　　(D) 水果甜點

解析 (D) ABC食品公司將調漲水果蛋糕、餡餅和其他水果甜點的價格。選項(A)是其他公司不久後會提高價格的產品。選項(B)重複使用了brands這個字。選項(C)也是水果製品,但文中並未特別提到。

169. 水果價格提高的原因是什麼?
　　(A) 生長條件不佳
　　(B) 消費支出增加
　　(C) 來自其他公司的競爭
　　(D) 農民要求更多的金錢

解析 (A) 文中提到價格提高是因為晚霜和長期乾旱之故。選項(B)(C)(D)都有可能,但並未提及。

170. 明年之前可能會發生何事?
　　(A) 天氣會好轉。
　　(B) 會有更多價格調漲行為。
　　(C) 消費者會需要更多水果。
　　(D) 會有更多種類的罐裝產品上市。

解析 (B) 文中提到其他公司年底會跟進漲價。選項(A)(C)(D)都有可能,但文中並未提及。

171. 下面這個句子最適合放入文中 [1][2][3][4] 哪一個位置？
    「這是ABC食品公司今年第二次調漲價格。」
    (A) [1]
    (B) [2]
    (C) [3]
    (D) [4]

解析 (B) 編號 [2] 的前一句提到要調漲價格，這一句接著補充此為第二次調漲，語意連貫。選項 (A)(C)(D) 放入這個句子意思都不通。

第 172–175 題請看下面這篇文章。

現在很多飯店正在改變浪費的習慣，譬如，飯店客人會發現洗髮精用玻璃製而非塑膠製的壓按瓶裝，或者飯店會鼓勵客人毛巾和床單可重複使用，不要一次就洗，這些情況已並不罕見。

不只飯店，遊客往往會主動尋找「更環保」的度假方式。生態旅遊──以環境為主題的導覽假期──這門行業正在快速成長。到亞馬遜雨林或類似地方讓參與者認識環保議題的探險之旅越來越受歡迎，行程可能包含說明該地區自然奇觀的講座、協助科學家進行實地研究的機會，或清理自然環境的活動。

參與這些行程的人本身已具備高度的環保意識。一項南極洲的垃圾研究發現，觀光客在兩年期間所留下的垃圾量可以裝進一個小型三明治塑膠袋，和多數飯店週邊街道常見的垃圾量可說是天壤之別。

世界各地的綠色環保運動正在不斷成長，飯店經營者和管理者最好關注這個趨勢。在客房內簡單放一個瓶罐回收桶，就足以引起注重環保客人的興趣，還可以同時為拯救地球盡一分力，是個雙贏的局面。

172. 這篇文章主要在講什麼？
    (A) 減少浪費的方法
    (B) 一種熱門的旅遊類型
    (C) 旅遊業的一個趨勢
    (D) 如何宣傳旅遊業務

解析 (C) 這篇文章描述飯店和遊客對環境友善的做法越來越感興趣。選項 (A) 和 (B) 是文章的細節，而不是主旨。選項 (D) 和主題有關，但並未提及。

173. 根據這篇文章，下列哪一項是參加生態旅遊的遊客可能會做的事？
    (A) 教課
    (B) 建造物品
    (C) 協助研究者
    (D) 在自然環境中露營

解析 (C) 其中一個行程活動的描述是「an opportunity to help scientists in the field」（協助科學家進行實地研究）。選項(A)(B)(D)並非不可能，但未提及。

174. 關於南極洲的遊客文中有何說明？
    (A) 他們喜歡收集東西。
    (B) 他們很少留下垃圾。
    (C) 他們傾向不使用塑膠袋。
    (D) 他們抱怨飯店亂七八糟。

解析 (B) 文中提到一項研究，當中發現南極洲遊客所留下的垃圾量可裝進一個小型三明治塑膠袋（could fit into one small plastic sandwich bag）。選項(A)使用了collected的相關字collecting。選項(C)重複使用了plastic bag。選項(D)是被文中提到飯店週邊的垃圾給混淆了。

175. 文章建議飯店經營者做何事？
    (A) 提供客人回收瓶罐的方法
    (B) 使用玻璃瓶裝洗髮精
    (C) 把客房漆成綠色
    (D) 搬遷到雨林地帶

解析 (A) 文章建議飯店經營者在客房內放置瓶罐回收桶。選項(B)是被文中提到現在飯店經常使用玻璃壓按瓶來裝洗髮精給混淆了。選項(C)混淆了green的用法，文中此字為環保之意。選項(D)重複使用了rainforest這個字，文中提到雨林是熱門觀光景點。

第176–180題請看下面這封電子郵件和圖表。

收件者：v.goldsmith@placeco.com
寄件者：gpmills@temppower.com
主旨： 你的職業生涯
附件： 臨時力就業圖

凡妮莎，您好：

感謝您參加過去一週基礎祕書技能的免費工作坊，學習重要的職業生涯技能。如果您正在尋找工作，我們希望能助您一臂之力。臨時力公司以為本市辦公室提供頂尖的行政專員自豪，我們不僅為團隊成員爭取高薪工作，更提供可負擔的健康保險！許多成員後來皆受僱成為正式員工，一步一步往上晉升。

您有興趣進入面試流程嗎？下一步是來我們辦公室接受能力測驗。您一定會想趁著在工作坊學到的技能還記憶猶新時，趕快參加測驗。

請點擊下方連結選擇來訪時段。

點此進入登錄頁面。

請參考隨附的圖表，相信一定能說服您，加入臨時力團隊就能成功。

謝謝！

喬治・米爾斯

臨時力公司

臨時力工作坊參加者就業情形

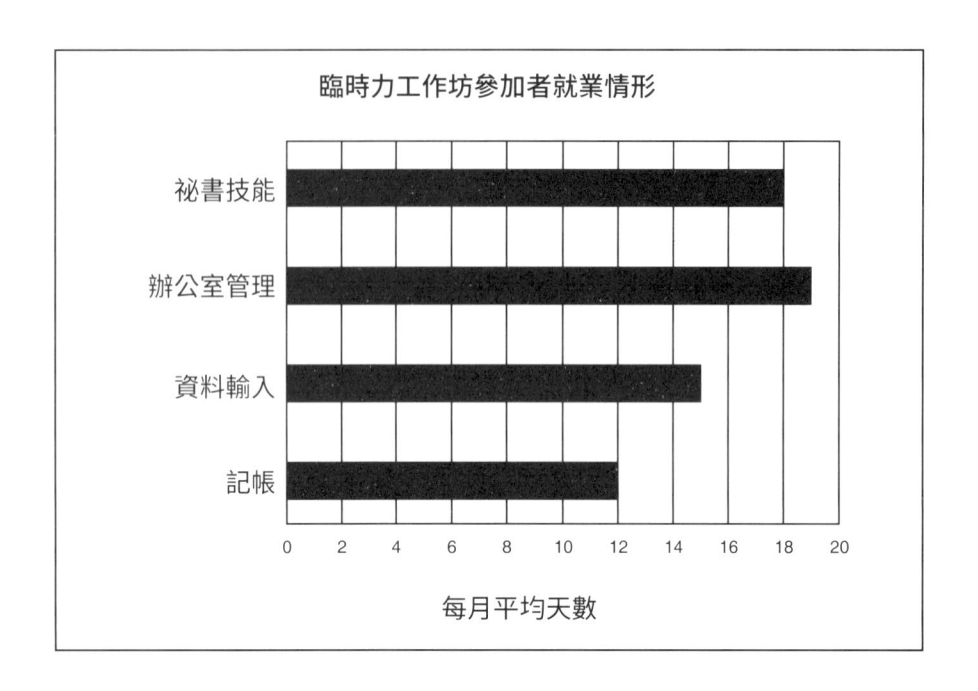

類別	每月平均天數
祕書技能	18
辦公室管理	19
資料輸入	15
記帳	12

176. 這個工作坊的最終目的為何？
    (A) 招募員工
    (B) 發掘新客戶
    (C) 介紹一所大學
    (D) 收集資料以製作圖表

解析 (A) 這封電子郵件鼓勵工作坊的參加者凡妮莎進一步成為員工。選項(B)和(C)都未被提及。選項(D)的圖表有被提及，但圖表的作用是鼓勵凡妮莎成為員工。

177. 這則訊息要求凡妮莎接下來做何事？
    (A) 致電公司
    (B) 參加輔導課程
    (C) 寄出測試結果
    (D) 報名參加測驗

解析 (D) 電子郵件中提到「The next step is to come into our office for skills tests.」（下一步是參加能力測驗）。選項(A)不正確，凡妮莎被要求透過官網聯繫公司，而不是打電話。選項(B)是凡妮莎已經做過的事。選項(C)重複使用了 test 這個字。

178. 凡妮莎參加工作坊的費用是多少？
    (A) 工作坊免費
    (B) 花費二十美元
    (C) 花費五十美元
    (D) 費用未知

解析 (A) 電子郵件中使用了complimentary workshop，complimentary為「贈送的」之意，等同於free，所以就是免費。選項(B)(C)(D)都和正確答案相衝突。

179. 哪一個工作坊的平均就業天數最高？
    (A) 記帳
    (B) 資料輸入
    (C) 辦公室管理
    (D) 祕書技能

解析 (C) 辦公室管理工作坊的參加者平均就業天數是每月十九天，選項(A)(B)(D)的平均工作天數都少於十九天。

180. 如果凡妮莎登錄成為臨時力的員工，她可以預期平均工作幾天？
    (A) 每月十五天
    (B) 每月十八天
    (C) 一年十八天
    (D) 一年十二個月

解析 (B) 凡妮莎參加的是祕書技能工作坊，根據圖表會是平均每月工作十八天。選項(A)是資料輸入工作坊的工作天數。選項(C)和(D)都不正確，圖表內的單位是每個月，不是一年幾天或一年幾個月。

第181–185題請看下面這份合約和補充協議。

合約書 編號：991YL
款待顧問公司

款待顧問公司（以下簡稱承包方）同意履行下列由餅乾桶酒莊（以下簡稱委託方）所概述之職責：

A. 統計分析
1) 審視委託方過去五年之葡萄酒銷售，並使用每月存貨表。
2) 審視委託方過去五年內之食品和禮品銷售。
3) 根據五年的審視結果，記錄今年預期銷售之摘要和圖表。

B. 員工審視
1) 訪談包含葡萄園及酒窖在內之各部門的一名員工。
2) 記錄各職位之職責和責任。
3) 向委託方提出削減人事費用之方法。

C. 裝潢
1) 與董事會成員會面討論年終整修事宜。
2) 研究所有室內整修之材料與成本。
3) 於10月1日前提出室內整修之預算評估。

本契約之修改須經雙方書面同意。

承包方：　韓森・卡特
委託方：　茱莉亞・莫里斯
日　　期：20—年8月7日

合約編號991YL 補充協議書　日期：20─年8月7日

以下為立協議書人：

承包方：款待顧問公司

委託方：餅乾桶酒莊

承包方提出以下補充協議：

一、由於不可預見之情況，承包方無法於20─年10月9日之後為餅乾桶酒莊提供服務。截至今日尚未完成之專案工作，承包方不會要求支付任何款項。

二、承包方將於20─年12月1日前提供三個有能力完成合約編號991YL內容之替代顧問公司名稱給委託方。

三、承包方將提交所有已完成工作之報告，包含自20─年8月7日起收集之所有重要資料。

四、委託方同意為承包方撰寫推薦信，說明合約編號991YL乃因家人生病而中止，無關承包方完成工作之能力。

日期：20─年10月9日
（承包方）簽名：
（委託方）簽名：

181. 承包方同意提供哪一種服務？
　　(A) 葡萄園的勞動協助
　　(B) 酒莊營運相關的顧問服務
　　(C) 玻璃器皿和餐盤的存貨盤點
　　(D) 競爭酒莊的葡萄酒品嚐測試

解析 (B) 承包方會針對該酒莊的各方面營運提供顧問服務。選項(A)(C)(D)都和酒莊這個行業有關，但契約中並未提及。

182. 下列何者不是承包方為履行職責需要與之交談的人？
　　(A) 醫療專業人員
　　(B) 葡萄酒銷售人員
　　(C) 董事會成員
　　(D) 兼職採葡萄工

解析 (A) 這份合約最終因緊急醫療情況而未能履行，但合約中所概述的職責均不涉及任何醫療相關的人事物。選項(B)和(D)都是酒莊的工作人員，合約指明要訪談他們。選項(C)是承包方會與之交談的人，在合約中的 C 條款有提到。

183. 訂立補充協議的原因是什麼？
    (A) 委託方不滿意承包方的工作。
    (B) 承包方因家人生病無法完成工作。
    (C) 委託方想增加承包方的職責。
    (D) 承包方可在預定時間前完成工作。

解析 (B) 補充協議書第一條說明承包方無法於某特定日期後提供服務，第四條則說明原因是家人生病。選項(A)(C)(D)雖然也是立補充協議書的可能原因，但不是這裡的答案。

184. 如果承包方至今都有遵守合約，下列哪一項必定已經完成？
    (A) 基於五年審視結果之銷售圖表
    (B) 酒窖中所有酒瓶之清點
    (C) 建議裝修費用之計算
    (D) 至少一位工作人員之訪談

解析 (C) 合約中明定於 10 月 1 日前必須完成整修費用的預算評估，而補充協議書的立約時間是 10 月 9 日，因此整修費用之計算必定已經完成（若有遵守合約的話）。選項(A)(B)(D)的工作並沒有指定具體完成日期。

185. 若委託方簽署了補充協議書，未來必須做什麼事？
    (A) 當承包方恢復健康後，必須重新僱用他。
    (B) 提供一份信函，說明這份合約未能履行的原因。
    (C) 寫一封推薦信，對承包方之性格予以正面描述。
    (D) 提出未來可聘用承包方的替代公司。

解析 (B) 選項(B)即補充協議書第四條所明定之事項。選項(A)並未被提及。選項(C)乍看之下很像正確答案，但補充協議書並沒有提到要描述承包方的性格。選項(D)不正確，提出替代公司是承包方要做的事。

第186–190題請看下面的停車罰單、通知和表格。

違規停車通知單
史普林菲爾德市警察局

違規事實：於限時二十分鐘停車區超時停車
違規地點：北主街500街區
車輛種類：廂型休旅車
車牌號碼：MG 097
登記車主：田中和也
違規日期：20—年4月1日

罰鍰：75美元

限三十日內繳納，繳款方式見背面說明。

催繳通知
史普林菲爾德市警察局

日期：4月21日

您有一筆4月1日開立之違規停車罰單尚未繳納，繳款期限為5月1日。逾期未繳罰款將處以原罰單金額之相同罰鍰。您有申訴之權利。申訴應於罰單開立之日起三十日內送抵停車管理處。請使用停車管理處辦公室所提供的表25，或至springfieldpkingdiv.org線上填寫。

表25
申訴通知

步驟一
申訴理由
請勾選適用之法律依據，只能勾選一項。
___ 本次違規停車之事實不存在。
___ 停車計時器故障。
___ 本人並非此車輛之車主。
✓ 本人之車輛於違規事發當日遭竊。

步驟二
完成第2頁之個人資料表，填上您的姓名、地址和聯絡資料，連同此頁及違規停車通知單影本一起寄出。您將於二十個工作天內收到來自停車管理處之回覆。若申訴獲准，您可能需要出庭。若申訴被駁回，您有自駁回日起十五天的時間繳清原罰鍰金額。

186. 和也先生為什麼會收到這張罰單？
    (A) 他的車子停在一個位置太久。
    (B) 他的車子停在禁止停車區。
    (C) 他沒有停車證。
    (D) 他只付了二十分鐘的停車費。

解析 (A) 罰單上寫的違規事實為「Exceeding time limit in a 20-minute parking zone」（在限時二十分鐘的停車區超時停車）。選項(B)(C)(D)都是被開罰單的可能原因，但在這裡都不是正確答案。

187. 和也先生可以在哪裡找到罰款繳納方式的說明？
    (A) 罰單背面
    (B) 停車管理處的網站
    (C) 警察局
    (D) 表25

解析 (A) 罰單上寫「See reverse for payment instructions」，所以是看背面。選項(B)(C)(D)重複使用了單據和表格中的單字或片語，但都不是正確答案。

188. 假如和也先生未能於5月1日前繳清罰款或提出申訴，會怎麼樣？
    (A) 他必須填寫一張特殊表格。
    (B) 他必須多繳七十五美元。
    (C) 他會被吊銷駕照。
    (D) 他會喪失停車權利。

解析 (B) 催繳通知中說「Unpaid fines are subject to a penalty equivalent to the amount of the original ticket.」，表示會被處以原罰單金額相同的罰鍰，而原罰單金額是七十五美元。選項(A)是提出申訴必須做的事。選項(C)和(D)雖然都有可能，但文中並未提及。

189. 和也先生為什麼似乎沒注意到原始罰單？
    (A) 警察忘了放在他的車上。
    (B) 罰單被人從他停放的車上偷走。
    (C) 他認為自己有依法停車。
    (D) 4月1日那天別人開了他的車。

解析 (D) 申訴通知書上被勾選的申訴理由為「My vehicle was stolen on the day of the violation」，可知他的車那天被偷了，不是他本人開車。選項(A)(B)(C)重複使用了單據和表格中的單字或片語，但都不是正確答案。

190．和也先生必須在申訴書之外附加什麼？
　　(A) 一張七十五美元的支票
　　(B) 一張車輛照片
　　(C) 一張罰單影本
　　(D) 他的駕照號碼

解析 **(C)** 表格的步驟二提到必須連同違規停車通知單影本一起寄出。選項(A)(B)(D)重複使用了單據和表格中的單字或片語，但都不是正確答案。

第191–195題請看下面的旅遊行程表、電子郵件和接駁時刻表。

行程：羅莎琳德・威爾森

6月1日星期一
擎天航空234號航班
● 上午8:20自紐約出發
● 下午3:40抵達溫徹斯特
搭乘公司專車前往溫徹斯特日出酒店

6月2日星期二至6月5日星期五
春井公司總部

6月6日星期六
高鐵45號列車
● 上午9:00自溫徹斯特出發
● 下午1:00抵達博茲堡
下午參觀春井公司的工廠

6月7日星期日
擎天航空987號航班
● 上午7:45自博茲堡出發
● 下午1:30抵達紐約

收件者：羅莎琳德・威爾森
寄件者：湯姆・李
主旨： 你的來訪

嗨，羅莎琳德：

我已收到你公司傳來的行程，一切看起來都沒問題。唯一的問題是，週一當天我們公司沒有人有空去接機，因為我們全部都要開會，很不幸的是此會議也無法改期。你有幾個方法可以前往飯店。你可以搭機場接駁車，十分方便，它會送你到火車站，距離你的飯店只有半個街區。我把接駁時刻表附上給你。另一個選擇是搭計程車，不過可能要花45到50美元，況且接駁車很方便，我覺得不值得花這個費用。還有市區公車可以搭乘，但若你對這裡的公車不熟悉的話，會有點複雜。

期待下週與你見面，祝你旅途平安，到飯店安頓好之後請盡快給我打電話。

湯姆

機場接駁時刻表
往溫徹斯特火車站

機場接駁是由溫徹斯特交通運輸管理局（WTA）所提供的免費交通運輸服務。無需購票，座位採先到先坐之方式。

	1A	2A	3A	4A
自機場出發	11:20 a.m.	1:30 p.m.	4:10 p.m.	6:45 p.m.
抵達溫徹斯特車站	12:05 p.m.	2:15 p.m.	4:55 p.m.	7:30 p.m.

191. 威爾森女士6月4日要做什麼？
　　(A) 造訪春井公司總部
　　(B) 參觀春井公司工廠
　　(C) 返家
　　(D) 坐火車

解析 **(A)** 根據行程說明，6月2日至6月5日威爾森女士會在該公司的總部停留，因此6月4日她會在公司總部。選項(B)和(D)是她6月6日要做的事。選項(C)則是她6月7日要做的事。

192. 李先生為何不能去機場接她？
    (A) 他不知道怎麼去機場。
    (B) 他另有要事。
    (C) 他無法付公車錢。
    (D) 他那天不上班。

解析 (B) 李先生在信中解釋說「no one from our office will be available to meet you at the airport on Monday, as we will all be in a meeting」，表示所有人都要開會無法去接機。選項(A)和(C)均未被提及。選項(D)不正確，那天他要開會，所以會上班。

193. 電子郵件正文第二段第二行中的「settled」這個字，意義與下列何者最為接近？
    (A) 同意
    (B) 完成
    (C) 決定的
    (D) 舒適的

解析 (D) settled 在這裡表示已經到達飯店房間，把一切都安頓好，讓自己覺得舒適自在了。選項(A)(B)(C)都不是這個字在此處的意思。

194. 假如威爾森女士選擇搭接駁車前往飯店，她可能會搭哪一班車？
    (A) 1 A
    (B) 2 A
    (C) 3 A
    (D) 4 A

解析 (C) 威爾森女士的班機3:40抵達，3A是在她抵達後最早出發的一班接駁車。選項(A)和(B)太早出發了，選項(D)太晚出發了。

195. 威爾森女士若搭接駁車要付多少車資？
    (A) 不用付
    (B) 至少四十五美元
    (C) 四十五到五十美元
    (D) 五十美元整

解析 (A) 接駁時刻表上面說這是一項免費服務。選項(B)(C)(D)都被電子郵件中關於計程車費用的討論給混淆了。

第196–200題請看下面的通知、價目表和電子郵件。

漢諾威商業協會（HBA）
邀請下列主講人進行講座：

史蒂芬妮・杜波伊斯，工管碩士

杜波伊斯女士將討論投資者於當前商業環境之投資祕訣和策略。
杜波伊斯女士於匹克瑞爾大學取得工商管理碩士，
著有《成功投資學》等暢銷作品。

8月18日下午3點
現場提供茶點

敬請回覆
本活動開放民眾參加，免入場費，但名額有限，
請打 604-0939 到我們的辦公室，告知是否參加。

漢諾威麵包店
餅乾拼盤

賓客人數	價格
十人以下	$10
二十五人以下	$20
五十人以下	$38
七十五人以下	$55

亦可提供咖啡與茶。
請來電討論選擇。

收件者：卡洛斯・瓦斯奎茲
寄件者：賽琳娜・史丹利
主旨：　講座茶點

卡洛斯：

我還在忙著安排下週的講座，可以請你打電話到麵包店訂餅乾嗎？我們上次辦的講座只有二十人左右到場，可是杜波伊斯女士如此受歡迎，我覺得這次應該會有更多人出席。我還在陸續收到回覆，且我覺得應該準備四十到五十人份。我們這裡可以準備咖啡和茶，所以不需要訂。我想這就是全部要麻煩你的事了。我已查看過到時會使用的房間，一切都沒問題。我想我們的空間會非常充足，很多人來也沒問題，椅子數量也十分足夠。我還試過音響設備，看起來也是正常運作的狀態。我想目前就先這樣了，謝謝！

賽琳娜

196. 想參加講座的人要做什麼事？
　　(A) 購票
　　(B) 致電漢諾威商業協會辦公室
　　(C) 提前三十分鐘到
　　(D) 成為漢諾威商業協會的會員

解析 (B) 通知裡面提到「Please let us know if you plan to attend by calling our office...」。選項(A)不正確，通知裡說免費入場（Admission is free）。選項(C)和(D)均未提及。

197. 關於杜波伊斯女士有何說明？
　　(A) 她寫了幾本書。
　　(B) 她是大學教授。
　　(C) 她是漢諾威商業協會的會員。
　　(D) 她不是很有名。

解析 (A) 通知中提到杜波伊斯女士是《成功投資學》和一些暢銷書的作者。選項(B)是因通知中提到杜波伊斯女士擁有碩士學位而有所混淆。選項(C)並未提及。選項(D)不正確，因為史丹利女士在電子郵件中提到杜波伊斯女士非常受歡迎。

198. 瓦斯奎茲先生訂購餅乾需要花多少錢？
    (A) 二十美元
    (B) 二十美元，外加咖啡和茶的費用
    (C) 三十八美元
    (D) 三十八美元，外加咖啡和茶的費用

解析 (C) 史丹利女士在電子郵件中說她預計會有四十到五十名客人，價目表中顯示三十八元的餅乾拼盤可供應最多五十人。選項(A)和(B)價位的餅乾拼盤只夠最多二十五個人吃。選項(D)不正確，史丹利女士跟瓦斯奎茲先生說不用訂咖啡和茶。

199. 電子郵件第二行的「show up」一詞，意義與下列何者最接近？
    (A) 到達
    (B) 展示
    (C) 觀看
    (D) 引導

解析 (A)「show up」在這裡意指「到達、到來」，史丹利女士在電子郵件中提到上次到場參加講座的人數。選項(B)(C)(D)都不是這個片語的意思。

200. 關於舉辦講座的房間，史丹利女士說了什麼？
    (A) 它太小。
    (B) 它雜亂無章。
    (C) 椅子非常舒適。
    (D) 音響設備的狀況良好。

解析 (D) 史丹利女士在電子郵件中說，音響設備處於正常運作狀態（in working order）。選項(A)不正確，史丹利女士說空間非常足夠。選項(B)不正確，史丹利女士說房間一切都沒問題（everything is fine）。選項(C)不正確，史丹利女士提到椅子時，只說了數量十分充足。

STOP 本測驗到此結束。如果你在時間結束前作答完畢，可以回頭檢查 Part 5、6、7 的答案。

實戰模擬試題1

實戰模擬試題2
解答

聽力測驗

Part 1 照片描述

1. **C**
2. **A**
3. **B**
4. **C**
5. **D**
6. **A**

Part 2 應答問題

7. **A**
8. **C**
9. **A**
10. **A**
11. **C**
12. **A**
13. **B**
14. **A**
15. **B**
16. **A**
17. **B**
18. **C**
19. **A**
20. **C**
21. **B**
22. **A**
23. **B**
24. **A**
25. **A**
26. **B**
27. **B**
28. **C**
29. **A**
30. **B**
31. **A**

Part 3 簡短對話

32. **A**
33. **B**
34. **C**
35. **A**
36. **B**
37. **D**
38. **C**
39. **D**
40. **A**
41. **C**
42. **C**
43. **A**
44. **A**
45. **C**
46. **A**
47. **D**
48. **D**
49. **B**
50. **C**
51. **B**
52. **D**
53. **D**
54. **A**
55. **B**
56. **C**
57. **B**
58. **A**
59. **B**
60. **D**
61. **A**
62. **C**
63. **D**
64. **D**
65. **C**
66. **A**
67. **D**
68. **B**
69. **C**
70. **B**

Part 4 簡短獨白

71. **B**
72. **A**
73. **A**
74. **C**
75. **A**
76. **A**
77. **A**
78. **D**
79. **D**
80. **B**
81. **D**
82. **B**
82. **B**
84. **C**
85. **B**
86. **B**
87. **B**
88. **D**
89. **C**
90. **A**
91. **D**
92. **A**
93. **D**
94. **B**
95. **B**
96. **A**
97. **C**
98. **C**
99. **B**
100. **D**

實戰模擬試題2 解答

閱讀測驗

Part 5 句子填空

101.	**C**	109.	**D**	117.	**D**	125.	**D**
102.	**B**	110.	**C**	118.	**C**	126.	**D**
103.	**D**	111.	**B**	119.	**B**	127.	**C**
104.	**B**	112.	**A**	120.	**D**	128.	**B**
105.	**C**	113.	**A**	121.	**B**	129.	**D**
106.	**A**	114.	**A**	122.	**A**	130.	**A**
107.	**A**	115.	**A**	123.	**D**		
108.	**B**	116.	**B**	124.	**C**		

Part 6 段落填空

131.	**D**	135.	**C**	139.	**B**	143.	**A**
132.	**A**	136.	**B**	140.	**D**	144.	**D**
133.	**B**	137.	**D**	141.	**A**	145.	**C**
134.	**C**	138.	**B**	142.	**B**	146.	**D**

Part 7 閱讀測驗

147.	**B**	161.	**A**	175.	**B**	189.	**C**
148.	**B**	162.	**D**	176.	**A**	190.	**D**
149.	**C**	163.	**A**	177.	**B**	191.	**B**
150.	**D**	164.	**D**	178.	**C**	192.	**A**
151.	**D**	165.	**C**	179.	**B**	193.	**D**
152.	**A**	166.	**D**	180.	**D**	194.	**A**
153.	**C**	167.	**B**	181.	**B**	195.	**C**
154.	**D**	168.	**D**	182.	**C**	196.	**A**
155.	**B**	169.	**A**	183.	**D**	197.	**C**
156.	**A**	170.	**B**	184.	**D**	198.	**C**
157.	**A**	171.	**C**	185.	**A**	199.	**B**
158.	**B**	172.	**A**	186.	**B**	200.	**D**
159.	**A**	173.	**D**	187.	**C**		
160.	**B**	174.	**C**	188.	**A**		

Model Test 2 實戰模擬試題2題目中譯&解析

聽力測驗

在本段測驗當中，你將有機會展現自己對口說英語的理解能力。聽力測驗共有四個大題，每一大題均有作答說明。你有大約45分鐘時間完成聽力測驗。

Part 1：照片描述

作答方式：你會看到一張照片，並聽到四個關於這張照片的陳述。選出最符合照片內容的陳述，將答案卡上對應的橢圓框塗滿。

複習要訣：閱讀Part 1和Part 2的錄音稿時，可在每題之間停5秒鐘。

1. Look at the photo marked number 1 in your test book.
   (A) Passengers are boarding the plane.
   (B) The concourse is empty.
   (C) Some passengers are waiting at the airport.
   (D) Some bags are on a truck.

   請看試題本標示為1的照片。
   (A) 乘客正在登機。
   (B) 大廳空無一人。
   (C) 一些乘客正在機場等候。
   (D) 一些行李放置在貨車上。

   解析 (C) 選項(C)假設了照片地點是機場，正在等候的人是乘客。選項(A)誤認了乘客所在地點，他們在機場，而非在飛機上。選項(B)說空無一人與照片內容矛盾，從照片中可看到大廳內人潮眾多。選項(D)對行李的位置描述不正確，行李在地上，不在貨車上。

2. Look at the photo marked number 2 in your test book.
   (A) They're looking at their laptop outdoors.
   (B) They're making coffee for two.
   (C) They're pointing to each other.
   (D) They're waiting for a table.

請看試題本標示為2的照片。
(A) 他們正在戶外看自己的筆電。
(B) 他們正在煮兩人份的咖啡。
(C) 他們正指著對方。
(D) 他們正在候位。

解析 **(A)** 選項(A)正確描述了人物的動作,他們正看著筆電,而從背景可判斷他們人在戶外。選項(B)搞錯了動作,照片中的確有兩個人,桌上也有一個咖啡杯,但他們沒有在煮咖啡。選項(C)不正確,照片中看不到兩人的手。選項(D)不正確,他們已經坐在桌子前了。

3. Look at the photo marked number 3 in your test book.
    (A) Cranes are standing in the water.
    (B) The trains are passing on a bridge.
    (C) Narrow carts are going through the tunnel.
    (D) Pedestrians are crossing the bridge.

    請看試題本標示為3的照片。
    (A) 幾隻鶴站在水中。
    (B) 火車正行駛過一座橋樑。
    (C) 狹窄的小車正通過隧道。
    (D) 行人正在過橋。

解析 **(B)** 選項(B)正確指出了火車的具體位置。選項(A)混淆了發音相近的train和crane,還使用了和bridge有關的單字water。選項(C)使用了train的相關字tunnel(隧道),但並沒有正確描述照片內容,同時也把train car說成發音相近的cart。選項(D)不正確,過橋的是火車,不是行人。

4. Look at the photo marked number 4 in your test book.
    (A) He's talking on the telephone.
    (B) He's walking toward his home.
    (C) He's holding a microphone.
    (D) He's waving his hand.

    請看試題本標示為4的照片。
    (A) 他正在講電話。
    (B) 他正往家的方向走去。
    (C) 他正拿著一支麥克風。
    (D) 他正在揮手。

解析 **(C)** 一名男子正拿著一支麥克風說話。選項(A)混淆了近音字microphone和telephone。選項(B)混淆了近音字talking和walking。選項(D)提到男子的手是正確的，但他沒有在揮手。

5. Look at the photo marked number 5 in your test book.
   (A) The waiter is setting the table.
   (B) The painters are painting the chairs.
   (C) The salesclerk is selling ties.
   (D) The businessmen are wearing nametags.

   請看試題本標示為5的照片。
   (A) 服務生正在擺設桌子。
   (B) 油漆師傅正在粉刷椅子。
   (C) 銷售人員正在賣領帶。
   (D) 商務人士佩戴著名牌。

解析 **(D)** 照片中有兩名身穿西裝、配戴名牌的男子。選項(A)正確指出了桌子，但照片中沒有看到服務生。選項(B)正確指出椅子，但沒人在粉刷椅子。選項(C)正確指出了男子配戴的領帶，但沒有銷售人員在賣東西。

6. Look at the photo marked number 6 in your test book.
   (A) A pharmacist is holding some medicine.
   (B) A customer is counting the pills.
   (C) A farmer is opening the bottle.
   (D) A clerk is stocking the shelves.

   請看試題本編號為6的照片
   (A) 一名藥師正拿著一些藥品。
   (B) 一名顧客正在數藥片。
   (C) 一名農夫正在開瓶。
   (D) 一名店員正在上架。

解析 **(A)** 一名藥師手裡拿著一個藥罐子，即藥品（medicine），並和顧客說話。選項(B)對顧客的動作描述錯誤，他正在和藥師交談，也許眼睛正看著藥片，但藥片仍裝在藥罐裡，顧客並沒有在數藥片。選項(C)混淆了近音字pharmacist和farmer。選項(D)提到了照片中的商品架，但沒有人在把東西上架。

Part 2：應答問題

> 作答方式：你會聽到一個問題和三個可能的回應。選出最適合回答該問題的回應，將答案卡上對應的橢圓框塗滿。

7. Could you recommend a good hotel in Los Angeles?
   (A) I always stay at the Royal Palm Inn.
   (B) The manager's name is Carlos.
   (C) Yes, it's a very nice place.

   你能不能推薦洛杉磯不錯的飯店？
   (A) 我都是住皇家棕櫚酒店。
   (B) 經理的名字是卡洛斯。
   (A) 是的，那是很不錯的地方。

   解析 (A) 選項(A)是對飯店推薦問題的合理回應。選項(B)使用了hotel的相關字manager。選項(C)使用了Los Angeles的相關字place。

8. Where is your family from?
   (A) All her books made her famous.
   (B) My children are at school.
   (C) My parents were born here.

   你們家是來自哪裡？
   (A) 她出版的所有書籍使她出名。
   (B) 我的小孩在學校。
   (C) 我父母在這裡出生的。

   解析 (C) 選項(C)是對家族來源問題的合理回應。選項(A)混淆了近音字family和famous。選項(B)使用了family的相關字children，回答的卻是「Where」（在哪裡）的問題：在學校。

9. How soon will you be ready for our meeting?
	(A) In about ten minutes.
	(B) Her son left early.
	(C) We said we wanted red.

	你多久可以準備好跟我們開會？
	(A) 大概再十分鐘。
	(B) 她的兒子提早離開。
	(C) 我們說了要紅色。

解析 (A) 選項(A)是對「How soon」（多久、多快）問題的合理回應。選項(B)混淆了近音字soon和son。選項(C)混淆了近音字ready和red。

10. I think the food at Marcello's is excellent.
	(A) I agree. It's the best restaurant in town.
	(B) Yes, he's in an excellent mood.
	(C) Sorry, I don't know how to spell it.

	我覺得馬切洛餐廳的食物非常好吃。
	(A) 我同意，那是城裡最好的餐廳。
	(B) 是的，他的心情非常好。
	(C) 不好意思，我不知道那個字怎麼拼。

解析 (A) 選項(A)表示同意對方對餐廳的想法。選項(B)重複使用了excellent這個字。

11. The train leaves at four, doesn't it?
	(A) It stopped raining at four.
	(B) This time let's take the train.
	(C) Yes, it departs every hour on the hour.

	火車四點出發，對嗎？
	(A) 四點時雨停了。
	(B) 我們這次搭火車吧。
	(C) 是的，每小時整點發車。

解析 (C) 選項(C)是詢問火車出發時間的合理回應。選項(A)使用了train的相關字stopped，以及train的近音字rain。選項(B)使用了train的相關字time，並重複使用了train這個字。

12. Thank you for calling. Will you hold, please?
    (A) No, I'll call back later.
    (B) I'll hold that bag for you.
    (C) She's not very old.

    感謝您的來電,請稍候好嗎?
    (A) 不了,我晚點再打
    (B) 我幫你拿包包。
    (C) 她沒有很老。

    解析 (A) 此處的對話情境是一通電話,來電者被要求「稍候」(hold),但她選擇晚點再打。選項(B)使用的是hold的另一個意思「拿著」。選項(C)混淆了近音字hold和old。

13. Who's working the night shift this week?
    (A) It's too heavy for me to lift.
    (B) The schedule says Jeffrey is.
    (C) I don't like walking at night.

    這週上晚班的是誰?
    (A) 太重了,我抬不動。
    (B) 班表上寫是傑弗瑞。
    (C) 我不喜歡晚上走路。

    解析 (B) 選項(B)是對「Who」(誰)問題的合理回應。選項(A)混淆了近音字shift和lift。選項(C)混淆了近音字working和walking,還重複使用了night這個字。

14. Do you remember when the invoice was sent?
    (A) Two weeks ago.
    (B) My voice is very soft.
    (C) We went in March.

    你還記得請款單是何時寄出的嗎?
    (A) 兩週前。
    (B) 我的聲音很輕柔。
    (C) 我們是三月去的。

    解析 (A) 選項(A)是對「何時寄出」此問題的合理回應。選項(B)混淆了近音字invoice和voice。選項(C)混淆了近音字sent和went,還附上了月份(in March),但沒有回答「請款單」是何時寄出的問題。

257

15. I can't find my cell phone.
    (A) I'll call you tonight.
    (B) I think I saw it on your desk.
    (C) His home is near the park.

    我找不到我的手機。
    (A) 我晚上打給你。
    (B) 我好像看到在你桌上。
    (C) 他家在公園附近。

解析 (B) 第一個說話者遺失手機，第二個說話者說在桌上，是合理的回應。(A) 為從 phone 聯想到 call 的混淆選項。選項(C)混淆了近音字 home 和 phone。

16. Why don't you come over tonight?
    (A) Thank you. I'd like to.
    (B) His pants are too tight.
    (C) There's more light over here.

    不如你今晚過來吧？
    (A) 謝謝，我很樂意。
    (B) 他的褲子太緊了。
    (C) 這邊比較亮。

解析 (A) 選項(A)是回應對方邀請的合理方式。選項(B)和(C)分別使用了 tonight 的近音字 tight 和 light。

17. Which team is your favorite?
    (A) I prefer tea with milk.
    (B) I like them both.
    (C) Your fee seems right.

    你最喜歡哪一隊？
    (A) 我比較喜歡喝奶茶。
    (B) 我兩隊都喜歡。
    (C) 你的費用似乎正確。

解析 (B) 選項(B)是對偏好問題的合理回應。選項(A)混淆了近音字 team 和 tea。選項(C)混淆了近音字 team 和 seem。

18. The traffic was very heavy today.
    (A) That's too heavy to lift.
    (B) There's a traffic light on the corner.
    (C) The traffic's always bad when it rains.

    今天路上很塞車。
    (A) 那個太重了抬不動。
    (B) 轉角處有紅綠燈。
    (A) 下雨時交通都很差。

    解析 (C) 第一個說話者提到路上很塞車，第二個說話者回應說下雨是交通狀況不好的原因。選項(A)重複使用了 heavy 這個字，但用的是另一個意思「沈重的」。選項(B)重複使用了 traffic 這個字。

19. This office has a fax machine, doesn't it?
    (A) It does. It's next to the copier.
    (B) They always charge a tax.
    (C) We need to hear all the facts.

    這間辦公室有傳真機，不是嗎？
    (A) 有的，在影印機旁邊。
    (B) 他們每次都要收稅。
    (C) 我們需要聽過所有事實。

    解析 (A) 選項(A)是對方詢問傳真機是否存在時的合理回應。選項(B)和(C)分別把 fax 和發音相近的 tax、facts 互相混淆。

20. What day is Marissa scheduled to see the dentist?
    (A) It only left a scratch, not a dent.
    (B) His name is Dr. Harris.
    (C) Tuesday morning, I think.

    瑪麗莎預定星期幾要看牙醫？
    (A) 只有擦到而已，沒有凹痕。
    (B) 他的名字是哈里斯醫師。
    (C) 我想應該是星期二早上。

    解析 (C) Tuesday 回答了「What day」（星期幾）的問題。選項(A)混淆了近音字 dent 和 dentist。選項(B)用來回答「Who」的問題。

259

21. Are you sure we need a reservation?
    (A) We're a party of six.
    (B) Definitely. You won't get a table without one.
    (C) Yes, I will read it.

    你確定我們需要預約嗎？
    (A) 我們有六個人。
    (B) 一定要的，不預約沒有位子。
    (C) 好的，我會閱讀它。

> **解析 (B)** 選項(B)是對方詢問是否需要預約時的合理回應。選項(A)表示預約人數。選項(C)混淆了近音字 need 和 read。

22. Where do we sign the contract?
    (A) On page 4.
    (B) Just your initials.
    (C) To make it official.

    我們要在合約哪裡簽字？
    (A) 第四頁。
    (B) 只要簽姓名首字母。
    (C) 這樣才能成為正式合約。

> **解析 (A)** 選項(A)回答了「Where」的問題。選項(B)用來回答「How」的問題。選項(C)用來回答「Why」的問題。

23. What's the deadline for the Blue Ridge project?
    (A) Yes, it's filed under "B".
    (B) We need to finish it by Thursday.
    (C) The contract was signed yesterday.

    藍嶺專案的截止時間為何時？
    (A) 是的，被歸檔在「B」的類別下。
    (B) 我們需在星期四前完成。
    (C) 合約是昨天簽的。

> **解析 (B)** 問題問的是時間（deadline 是截止時間），選項(B)也以一個時間——星期四前（by Thursday）——回答了問題。選項(A)會用來回答專案文件被放在哪裡（Where）的問題。選項(C)混淆了近音字 deadline 和 signed。

24. I read this book in just three days.
    (A) You're a fast reader.
    (B) I like having free days.
    (C) Red is a nice color.

    我三天就把這本書讀完了。
    (A) 你的閱讀速度好快。
    (B) 我喜歡有空閒時間的日子。
    (C) 紅色是個好顏色。

    解析 (A) 第二個說話者認為第一個說話者的閱讀速度很快，竟然三天就把一本書讀完了。選項(B)混淆了發音相近的片語 free days 和 three days。選項(C)混淆了近音字 red 和 read。

25. Who's that standing outside our front door?
    (A) That's a client of mine.
    (B) He's sanding the chair.
    (C) Sorry. I'll close the door.

    站在我們前門外的那個人是誰？
    (A) 那是我的客戶。
    (B) 他正在打磨椅子。
    (C) 對不起，我去關門。

    解析 (A)「a client」（客戶）回答了「Who」的問題。選項(B)混淆了近音字 standing 和 sanding。選項(C)重複使用了 door 這個字。

26. There's a package for you on your desk.
    (A) He packed last night.
    (B) It must be the new jacket I ordered.
    (C) There's a post office on the next block.

    你桌上有一個你的包裹。
    (A) 他昨晚打包了。
    (B) 一定是我買的新夾克。
    (C) 下一個街區有一間郵局。

    解析 (B) 第二個說話者認為那個包裹裡有他訂購的東西。選項(A)混淆了近音字 package 和 packed。選項(C)把 package 和 post office 聯想在一起。

27. Do you know where I can get my pants pressed?
    (A) Don't be depressed.
    (B) Send them to the cleaners.
    (C) I got a new pair last week.

    你知道哪裡可以熨燙我的褲子嗎？
    (A) 不要沮喪。
    (B) 把它們送去洗衣店。
    (C) 我上個禮拜買了一件新的。

解析 (B) 選項(B)是詢問洗衣相關服務的合理回答。選項(A)混淆了近音字pressed和depressed。選項(C)使用了相關字pants和pair。

28. When are you going to start exercising?
    (A) I start my day with a healthful breakfast.
    (B) The exercises are at the end of the book.
    (C) I'll start when I have more free time.

    你什麼時候要開始運動？
    (A) 我以健康的早餐開始我的一天。
    (B) 練習題在書本最後面。
    (C) 等我比較有空就會開始。

解析 (C) 選項(C)是對時間問題的合理回應。選項(A)使用了exercise的相關字healthful。選項(B)混淆了exercise的動詞和名詞用法，意思也不相同，一個指運動，一個指練習題。

29. Did you reach your sales goals for the month?
    (A) Yes, but just barely.
    (B) We go to the beach next month.
    (C) No, I'm not tall enough.

    妳這個月有達成銷售目標嗎？
    (A) 有的，勉強達標。
    (B) 我們下個月去海邊。
    (C) 不，我不夠高。

解析 (A) 選項(A)回答了題目中的yes-no問句。選項(B)混淆了近音字reach和beach，同時重複使用了month這個字。選項(C)混淆了reach的字義用法。

30. Have you seen the article in this month's journal?
    (A) Yes, it's the green one.
    (B) No, but I plan to read it soon.
    (C) It's a well-regarded journal.

    你有看過本月期刊裡的那篇文章嗎？
    (A) 有，是綠色的。
    (B) 沒有，但我打算盡快去讀。
    (C) 那是一本備受推崇的期刊。

解析 (B) 選項(B)是被問到一篇期刊文章問題時的合理回應。選項(A)混淆了近音字 seen 和 green。選項(C)重複使用了 journal 這個字。

31. Where would you recommend I go?
    (A) At this time of year, I would go south.
    (B) I'll go sometime soon.
    (C) You should comment on this memo.

    你會建議我去哪裡？
    (A) 每年這個時候我都會到南方去。
    (B) 我很快就會去了。
    (C) 你應對這份備忘錄發表意見。

解析 (A) 選項(A)是詢問地點的合理回應。選項(B)重複使用了 go 這個字，但回答的是「When」的問題。選項(C)混淆了近音字 recommend 和 comment。

Part 3：簡短對話

> 作答方式：你會聽到兩人或多人之間的對話。每段對話搭配三個問題，各有四個選項。選出最適當的答案回答問題，將答案卡上對應的橢圓框塗滿。

> 複習要訣：閱讀 Part 3 和 Part 4 的錄音稿時，可在每題之間停 8 秒鐘。

Questions 32 through 34 refer to the following conversation.

Woman: I can't believe how filthy this coffeepot is. And the coffee's probably been sitting in it since yesterday. Is there somewhere I could wash it out?

Man: There's a kitchen down on the sixth floor you could use.

Woman: OK. While I'm down there I might as well make some fresh coffee. Would you like me to bring you a cup?

Man: Um, well, I think I'd prefer cocoa, if you wouldn't mind. I'm pretty sure there's some milk down there you can make it with.

第 32–34 題請聽下面這段對話。

女：真不敢相信這個咖啡壺這麼髒，裡面的咖啡大概從昨天就放到今天了，哪裡可以讓我洗一下？

男：下面六樓有一個廚房妳可以用。

女：好，我下去的時候順便現煮一些咖啡，要不要拿一杯給你？

男：嗯……如果不麻煩的話，我比較想喝可可。我確定樓下有牛奶可以泡可可。

32. What does the woman want to do? 這名女子想做什麼？
    (A) Clean the coffeepot 洗咖啡壺
    (B) Sit down 坐下
    (C) Wash her hands 洗手
    (D) Sweep the floor 掃地

解析 (A) 女子說咖啡壺很髒（filthy），她想拿去洗一下（wash it out）。選項 (B) 重複使用了 down 這個字。選項 (C) 不正確，女子想要洗的是咖啡壺，而不是手。選項 (D) 重複使用了 floor 這個字。

33. Where are the speakers? 說話者所在的位置是哪裡？
    (A) On the sixth floor 六樓
    (B) Above the sixth floor 六樓之上
    (C) Below the sixth floor 六樓之下
    (D) On the ground floor 地面樓

解析 (B) 男子說下面六樓（down on the sixth floor）有廚房，暗示了說話者位於六樓之上。選項 (A)(C)(D) 都和正確答案相抵觸。

34. What does the man want to drink? 這名男子想喝什麼？
    (A) Milk 牛奶
    (B) Coffee 咖啡
    (C) Cocoa 可可
    (D) Tea 茶

解析 (C) 男子說「I think I'd prefer cocoa」，所以是可可。選項 (A) 是用來泡可可的。選項 (B) 是女子要喝的。選項 (D) 也有可能，但並未提及。

Questions 35 through 37 refer to the following conversation.

Woman: These shirts are just lovely, and they look so warm. I'll take two—a blue one and a checked one. Size sixteen, please. I can't believe how inexpensive they are!

Man: Yes, everything in the store is discounted this week, and these shirts are just flying off the shelves. So, two shirts comes to forty-five dollars. Will that be cash, or shall I put it on your credit card?

Woman: Actually, I have a gift certificate.

第 35–37 題請聽下面這段對話。

女：這些襯衫真好看，看起來很保暖。我要兩件，一件藍的，一件格紋的，尺寸16號。真不敢相信它們這麼便宜！

男：是的，店裡所有商品本週都有折扣，這些襯衫賣得很快。那麼，兩件襯衫一共四十五美元，請問您要付現還是刷卡？

女：其實我有一張禮券。

35. What does the man suggest about the shirts? 關於襯衫，男子有何暗示？
    (A) They are a popular item. 它們是人氣商品。
    (B) They only come in two colors. 它們只有兩個顏色。
    (C) They are good for warm weather. 它們在溫暖天氣時穿很適合。
    (D) They will be discounted next week. 它們下週會打折。

解析 (A) 男子說「these shirts are just flying off the shelves」，意思就是賣得很快，十分受消費者歡迎。選項(B)不正確，對話中並沒有提到襯衫只有兩個顏色。選項(C)重複使用了warm這個字。選項(D)搞錯了男子說的話，男子說的是本週（this week）全店商品都有折扣。

36. How much does the woman have to pay? 這名女子一共要付多少錢？
    (A) $42.05
    (B) $45
    (C) $60
    (D) $245

解析 (B) 男子說兩件襯衫總共四十五美元。選項(A)和(D)的發音和正確答案非常接近。選項(C)混淆了近音字sixty和sixteen，16號是女子要求的襯衫尺寸。

37. How will the woman pay? 女子要用什麼方式付款？
    (A) Check 支票
    (B) Cash 現金
    (C) Credit card 信用卡
    (D) Gift certificate 禮券

解析 (D) 女子說她有禮券（gift certificate）。選項(A)使用了對話中的check這個字，但取用的意義不同。選項(B)和(C)是男子詢問的付款方式。

Questions 38 through 40 refer to the following conversation.

Man: Oh. Were you going to use the copier?
Woman: Yes, if you don't mind. It's a bit urgent. The banquet, you know.
Man: Right. The invitations. You go ahead, and if you want, I can help you with the address labels after.
Woman: Would you? That would be fantastic. I have to have them ready right away. My boss wants me to get them to the post office this morning.
Man: Happy to help. I can copy this meeting agenda later. It won't be needed till this afternoon.

第 38–40 題請聽下面這段對話。
男：哦，你要用影印機嗎？
女：對啊，如果你不介意的話。這件事有點急迫，宴會的事情，你知道的。
男：對，邀請函。你先用吧，需要的話，等你印好後我可以幫你做地址標籤。
女：可以嗎？那就太好了。我必須馬上把它們準備好，老闆要我今天早上就送去郵局。
男：樂意之至。我可以晚點再印會議議程，反正這個下午才要用。

38. What is the woman photocopying? 這名女子正要影印什麼？
    (A) A menu 菜單
    (B) An agenda 議程
    (C) An invitation 邀請函
    (D) An address list 地址列表

解析 (C) 女子說她正要印宴會要用的東西，而男子回應「Right. The invitations.」，可知女子要印的是邀請函。選項(A)使用了 banquet 的相關字 menu。選項(B)是男子要影印的東西。選項(D)是被男子提到地址標籤給混淆了。

39. Why does the woman say, "Would you?" 女子為何要說「Would you?」？
    (A) To make a request 為了提出要求
    (B) To ask for information 為了請對方提供資訊
    (C) To make a suggestion 為了提出建議
    (D) To accept an offer 為了接受對方提議

解析 (D) 男子提議要幫女子處理地址標籤，女子用這個片語作為回應，表示接受男子的提議。選項(A)(B)(C)都不符合此處的語境。

40. What will the woman do when the copies are made? 邀請函影印好之後，女子會做什麼？
    (A) Mail them 把它們郵寄出去
    (B) Read them 閱讀它們
    (C) Show them to her boss 把它們拿給老闆看
    (D) Take them to a meeting 把它們拿到會議上

解析 (A) 女子說她要把影印好的東西送去郵局，也就是郵寄出去。選項(B)混淆了近音字 read 和 ready。選項(C)重複使用了 boss 這個字。選項(D)是男子要對其影印的議程所做之事。

Questions 41 through 43 refer to the following conversation.

Woman: Thank you for dining with us this evening. Would you like to hear about our house specialties?

Man: Uh, well, I'm really in the mood for some seafood. So, something with fish would be great.

Woman: We have a grilled salmon with mushrooms that is very popular. But I have to tell you that it's cooked fresh, so there would be a twenty-minute wait.

Man: Oh, I don't mind. It sounds delicious, and a nice piece of fish is always worth the wait. I'll just order a drink to have meanwhile.

第41–43題請聽下面這段對話。
女：感謝您今晚蒞臨用餐，需要向您介紹我們的招牌菜嗎？
男：嗯……我很想吃海鮮，如果有魚類料理就太好了。
女：我們的蘑菇烤鮭魚很受歡迎，不過必須告訴您，由於是現烤，需要等二十分鐘。
男：喔沒關係，聽起來很美味，上好的魚排總是值得等待。我先點飲料，邊等邊喝就行。

41. Where does this conversation take place? 這段對話發生何處？
    (A) In a hotel 飯店
    (B) In a fish store 魚店
    (C) In a restaurant 餐廳
    (D) In someone's house 某人的家

解析 (C) 這名男子正在和服務生點餐，所以地點是餐廳。選項(A)在對話中沒有提及。選項(B)重複使用了fish這個字。選項(D)使用了對話中的house這個字，但取用的意義並不相同。

42. What is the problem with the fish? 這條魚有什麼問題？
    (A) It is not fresh. 不新鮮。
    (B) It is not available this evening. 今晚沒有供應。
    (C) It takes a long time to prepare. 準備時間很長。
    (D) It costs more than other dishes. 比其他料理貴。

解析 (C) 女子告訴男子說，這條魚的烹煮時間需要二十分鐘。選項(A)不正確，女子說魚很新鮮。選項(B)不正確，女子向男子推薦了這道料理，所以一定有提供。選項(D)所說的餐點價格沒有被提及。

43. What will the man do while he waits? 男子等待的時候會做什麼？
    (A) Have a drink 喝飲料
    (B) Sit and think 坐著想事情
    (C) Go fishing 去釣魚
    (D) Wash the dishes 洗碗

解析 (A) 男子說他要一邊喝飲料一邊等待。選項 (B) 混淆了近音字 think 和 drink。選項 (C) 從 fish（魚）聯想到 fishing（釣魚）。選項 (D) 混淆了近音字 dish 和 fish。

Questions 44 through 46 refer to the following conversation.

Woman:　Hello. Yes, I'm calling from Dr. Soto's office. May I speak with Mr. Wu, please?
Man:　　I'm afraid Mr. Wu is out of the office right now. He's at a meeting downtown. Would you like to leave a message?
Woman:　I would. Mr. Wu has an appointment tomorrow to have his teeth cleaned, but, unfortunately, Dr. Soto has an emergency and has to cancel.
Man:　　I'm sorry to hear that. I'll let Mr. Wu know.
Woman:　Thank you. And please have him call our office to reschedule. We have several openings next week.

第 44–46 題請聽下面這段對話。
女：您好，我這裡是索托醫師的診所，請問吳先生在嗎？
男：吳先生現在不在辦公室，他到市區開會了，請問您要留言嗎？
女：是的，吳先生明天預約了洗牙，但是不巧索托醫師臨時有事必須取消。
男：很遺憾聽到這個消息，我會轉告吳先生的。
女：謝謝，另外要請他打電話到我們診所重新預約，我們下週有好幾個空檔。

44. Where does the woman most likely work? 這名女子最有可能在哪裡工作？
    (A) In a dentist's office 牙醫診所
    (B) In a surgeon's office 外科醫師辦公室
    (C) At a real estate agency 房地產仲介公司
    (D) At a rug cleaning service 地毯清潔服務公司

解析 (A) 女子替索托醫師工作，打電話來說明吳先生預約洗牙取消一事，所以應是在牙醫診所工作。選項 (B) 使用了與 dentist 相關的單字 surgeon。選項 (C) 在對話中並未提及。選項 (D) 重複使用了 clean 這個字。

45. Where is Mr. Wu now? 吳先生現在在哪裡？
    (A) In his office 他的辦公室
    (B) Out of town 出城了
    (C) At a meeting 會議上
    (D) On a flight 飛機上

解析 **(C)** 男子說吳先生在開會。選項(A)搞錯了，對話中說的是 out of the office。選項(B)也搞錯了，對話中說的是 downtown（市區），不是 out of town。選項(D)混淆了近音字 flight 和 right。

46. What does the woman want Mr. Wu to do? 這名女子要吳先生做什麼？
    (A) Make a new appointment 重新預約
    (B) Visit an apartment 造訪一間公寓
    (C) Check his schedule 查看他的時間表
    (D) Meet her downtown 和她在市區見面

解析 **(A)** 女子要男子請吳先生打電話到診所重新預約（have him call our office to reschedule）。選項(B)混淆了近音字 appointment 和 apartment。選項(C)重複使用了 schedule 這個字。選項(D)重複使用了 downtown 這個字。

Questions 47 through 49 refer to the following conversation with three speakers.

Woman: Oh, no! Where's my briefcase?
Man 1: You came by cab, didn't you? You must have left it there.
Woman: That's exactly what I did. Now what am I going to do?
Man 2: The cab company probably has a lost and found. I could phone them for you. I have the number right here on my desk.
Woman: Thanks, Jim, I appreciate it. I hope they have it.
Man 1: Was there anything important in it?
Woman: You know those papers I got signed at the bank meeting this morning? They're in there. And my passport, too.
Man 2: You'll have to report that as lost if you can't find it.
Woman: I know.

第 47–49 題請聽下面這段三人之間的對話。
女： 噢，不！我的公事包呢？
男 1：你是搭計程車來的對不對？一定是忘在計程車上了。
女： 就是那樣，現在我該怎麼辦？
男 2：計程車公司可能有失物招領處，我可以幫你打電話給他們，我桌上有他們的電話。

270

女： 謝了，吉姆，感激不盡。希望公事包有在他們那裡。
男1：裡面有重要物品嗎？
女： 今天早上到銀行開會簽的文件，你知道的吧？它們在公事包裡，我的護照也在裡面。
男2：萬一沒找回來一定要去申報掛失。
女： 我知道。

47. Where did the woman leave her briefcase? 女子把她的公事包遺留在哪裡了？
    (A) At a meeting 會議上
    (B) In her office 她的辦公室裡
    (C) On her desk 她的辦公桌上
    (D) In a cab 計程車上

解析 (D) 女子提到她把公事包忘在計程車上。

48. What does Jim offer to do? 吉姆主動說要幫什麼忙？
    (A) Take some papers to the bank 帶一些文件去銀行
    (B) Lend the woman his briefcase 把他的公事包借給女子
    (C) Let the woman use his desk 讓女子使用他的辦公桌
    (D) Call the cab company 打電話給計程車公司

解析 (D) 吉姆提到了計程車公司，然後說「I could phone them for you」，表示可以幫她打電話。選項(A)是女子已經做過的事。選項(B)重複使用了 briefcase 這個字，但對話中沒有提到要出借公事包。選項(C)重複使用了 desk 這個字，但對話中男子沒有提到要讓女子使用他的辦公桌。

49. What is in the briefcase? 公事包裡有什麼？
    (A) A cell phone 手機
    (B) A passport 護照
    (C) A report 報告
    (D) A sign 標牌

解析 (B) 女子說除了一些文件外，她的護照也在公事包裡。選項(A)重複使用了 phone 這個字。選項(C)重複使用了 report 這個字，但用的是名詞用法，而不是對話中的動詞用法（report the loss 掛失）。選項(D)混淆了 sign 的意義，女子帶了文件去「簽署」(got the papers signed)，而不是帶了「標牌」(carry a sign)。

Questions 50 through 52 refer to the following conversation.

Man: I'll need a wake-up call at six tomorrow morning. I have to catch an eight o'clock flight.

Woman: You might want to get up earlier. It's going to rain tomorrow and bad weather always makes traffic slower, especially to the airport.

Man: Oh, I didn't know that. All right, then, I'd like a five thirty wake-up call.

Woman: Certainly. You also might like to know that we offer an early bird buffet-style breakfast in the hotel restaurant starting at five. Many of our guests leave on early flights.

Man: Thanks, but I don't think I'll bother. I'll just get something to eat at the airport.

第 50–52 題請聽下面這段對話。

男：我需要明天早上六點的晨喚服務，我要趕八點的班機。

女：您或許可以考慮早點起床，明天會下雨，天氣不好一定會塞車，尤其是去機場的路上。

男：啊，我都不知道。好吧，那我要五點半的晨喚服務。

女：沒問題。您或許會想知道，我們飯店餐廳有提供自助式的早起早餐，五點就開始供應，我們很多客人都要搭早班飛機。

男：謝謝，我想我就不用了，我到機場再找點東西吃。

50. Why does the man want to wake up early? 這名男子為何想早起？
    (A) He has to catch an early train. 他要趕早班火車。
    (B) He wants to make a phone call. 他想打一通電話。
    (C) He's going to take a morning plane. 他要搭早上的飛機。
    (D) He wants to hear the weather report. 他想聽氣象報告。

解析 (C) 男子說他必須趕早上八點的飛機。選項 (A) 混淆了近音字 train 和 rain。選項 (B) 重複使用了 call 這個字。選項 (D) 重複使用了 weather 這個字。

51. How will the weather be tomorrow? 明天的天氣如何？
    (A) Snowy 下雪的
    (B) Rainy 下雨的
    (C) Cold 寒冷的
    (D) Hot 炎熱的

解析 (B) 女子說明天會下雨。選項 (A) 混淆了近音字 snow 和 know。選項 (C) 混淆了近音字 cold 和 call。選項 (D) 未被提及。

52. What does the man mean when he says, "I don't think I'll bother"? 男子說「I don't think I'll bother」是什麼意思？
    (A) He doesn't mind traveling on an early flight. 他不介意搭乘早班飛機。
    (B) He is not disturbed by the other hotel guests. 他沒有被飯店其他客人打擾。
    (C) He hopes he isn't causing an inconvenience. 他希望沒有造成任何不便。
    (D) He won't have breakfast at the hotel. 他不會在飯店裡用早餐。

解析 (D) 女子提到飯店很早就會供應早餐，男子回覆這句話，意思是他不會在飯店裡用早餐，到機場再吃比較方便。選項(A)(B)(C)都不是這句話在此處的意思。

Questions 53 through 55 refer to the following conversation.
Woman: I am so glad finally to be off that plane.
Man: I know. I thought that flight would never end. So, do you want to catch a taxi? Or should we save some money and take the subway?
Woman: Before we decide that, I have to pick up my suitcase at baggage claim.
Man: That means we'll be stuck here forever. I don't know why you didn't just bring a carry-on bag, like me.
Woman: Relax. It'll only take a few minutes. You stay here while I get the bag. I'll be back before you know it.

第53–55題請聽下面這段對話。
女：謝天謝地，終於下飛機了。
男：我懂，我還以為要飛到天荒地老了。所以你要叫計程車嗎？還是我們省點錢搭地鐵就好？
女：在我們做決定前，我要先去行李提領區拿我的行李箱。
男：那就等於我們要永遠困在這裡了。我不懂，你為什麼不像我一樣帶個手提行李就好。
女：放輕鬆點，只要幾分鐘而已。你在這邊等，我去拿行李，馬上回來。

53. What does the man say about the plane trip? 男子對於這趟飛行旅程有何說法？
    (A) It was uncomfortable. 很不舒服。
    (B) It was expensive. 很昂貴。
    (C) It was overnight. 飛了一整夜。
    (D) It was long. 飛行時間很長。

解析 (D) 男子說「I thought that flight would never end」，意思是很漫長，好像永遠不會結束。選項(A)(B)(C)也是有可能，但並未提及。

54. Why is the man annoyed? 男子為何生氣？
    (A) They have to go to baggage claim. 他們要去行李提領區。
    (B) He doesn't have enough money. 他身上的錢不夠。
    (C) The woman's bag is heavy. 女子的行李太重。
    (D) They are stuck in traffic. 他們被塞在車陣中。

解析 (A) 女子說她要先去行李提領區拿她的行李，男子回應說「That means we'll be stuck here forever」，意思是他預期他們要等很久才能領到行李，因此他才會生氣。選項(B)重複使用了money這個字，男子是說他們可以搭地鐵省錢，並未說他身上的錢帶得夠不夠。選項(C)提到了女子的行李，但對話中沒有提到行李重不重。選項(D)重複使用了stuck這個字，但他們還在機場內，因此不可能塞在車陣中。

55. What will the man do next? 男子接下來會做什麼？
    (A) Look for a taxi 尋找計程車
    (B) Wait for the woman 等女子
    (C) Pick up the woman's bag 去領女子的行李
    (D) Check the subway schedule 查看地鐵時刻表

解析 (B) 女子對男子說「You stay here while I get the bag」，所以我們可推測他會待在原地等女子。選項(A)重複使用了taxi這個字，但他們還沒決定要用哪種交通方式。選項(C)是女子要做的事。選項(D)重複使用了subway這個字，但對話中沒有提及時刻表。

Questions 56 through 58 refer to the following conversation.

Woman: Didn't you say you'd send me that, you know, that finance report? It's getting late and I really need to see it.
Man: I e-mailed it last week. You didn't get it?
Woman: No.
Man: Hmmm. My e-mail program shows it as sent. I don't know why it didn't go through. Maybe because I had an attachment? Can you check your spam folder?
Woman: Let's see. No, I don't see it at all. You'd better resend it. This time try my personal e-mail address.
Man: OK. I'll do it right now.
Woman: Thanks. I thought it was a bit strange that I hadn't received it already. I know I can always count on you to do what you say you will.

第 56–58 題請聽下面這段對話。

女：你不是說已經寄給我了嗎？就是那個啊，財務報告。時間已經很晚了，我真的必須看到它。

男：我上個禮拜就寄了，你沒收到嗎？

女：沒有。

男：嗯，我的電子郵件程式顯示已經寄出，不知道為什麼沒傳過去。也許是我加了附件的關係？你可以檢查一下垃圾郵件夾嗎？

女：我看一下。沒有，我完全沒看到。你最好重寄，這次寄到我的私人電子郵件信箱看看。

男：好，我馬上寄。

女：謝謝。我就覺得奇怪，怎麼會還沒收到。我知道你說到做到，一向很可靠。

56. What did the man send the woman? 男子寄了什麼給女子？
    (A) A program schedule 節目表
    (B) A personnel file 人事檔案
    (C) A finance report 財務報告
    (D) A rent check 房租支票

解析 (C) 男子寄了一封電子郵件給女子，附加了一份財務報告的檔案。選項 (A) 搞錯了 program 這個字的字義用法。選項 (B) 混淆了近音字 personal 和 personnel。選項 (D) 搞錯了 check 這個字的用法，同時還混淆了近音字 sent 和 rent。

57. What does the woman ask the man to do? 女子要求男子做什麼？
    (A) Look in a folder 查看一個郵件夾
    (B) Use a different address 使用不同的郵件地址
    (C) Explain something to her 向她說明一些事情
    (D) Get some documents ready 準備好一些文件

解析 (B) 女子要求男子重寄文件，並說「This time try my personal e-mail address」，改寄到另一個郵件地址。選項 (A) 是男子要求女子做的事。選項 (C) 未被提及。選項 (D) 混淆了近音字 already 和 ready。

58. What does the woman say about the man? 關於男子，女子有何說法？
    (A) He is reliable. 他很可靠。
    (B) He is often late. 他經常遲到。
    (C) He is a bit strange. 他有點奇怪。
    (D) He is good with numbers. 他很會算數。

解析 (A) 女子說「I know I can always count on you」，表示永遠可以相信這名男子會完成任務。選項(B)重複使用了 late 這個字，但 late 在對話中並不是描述這名男子。選項(C)重複使用了 a bit strange，但女子指的是沒收到檔案的情況很奇怪。選項(D)搞錯了 count 的意思。

Questions 59 through 61 refer to the following conversation with three speakers.
Woman 1: I never see you at the country club. I thought you played golf there.
Man: Not me. I don't like it. Tennis is my sport.
Woman 2: I used to take tennis lessons at the park, but I was never any good at it.
Man: You have to practice a lot. I'm on the courts five days a week. I play with a group at the community center.
Woman 1: How do you feel about swimming? Shirley and I are going over to the hotel pool on Saturday.
Woman 2: And we're going out for a bite to eat with some friends after. There's a great lunch place at the hotel. Join us?
Man: Thank you. That sounds like fun.

第59–61題請聽下面這段三人之間的對話。
女1：我從來沒在鄉村俱樂部見過你，我以為你在那裡打高爾夫球。
男：沒有，我不喜歡打高爾夫球，網球才是我的運動。
女2：我以前在公園上過網球課，但一直打不好。
男：你要多加練習。我一個星期有五天在球場上練習，我在社區中心和一群人一起打球。
女1：你覺得游泳如何？我和雪莉星期六要去飯店的游泳池。
女2：之後我們要跟幾個朋友去外面吃點東西，飯店那邊有個不錯的地方可以吃午餐。要不要一起來？
男：謝謝，聽起來很好玩。

59. What sport does the man enjoy? 這名男子喜歡從事什麼運動？
    (A) Golf 高爾夫球
    (B) Tennis 網球
    (C) Biking 自行車
    (D) Swimming 游泳

解析 (B) 男子說「Tennis is my sport」，網球是他的運動。選項(A)是女子問他的運動。選項(C)混淆了發音相近的 biking 和 like。選項(D)是女子喜歡的運動。

60. Where does he practice it? 他都在哪裡練習打網球？
    (A) At the hotel 飯店
    (B) At the park 公園
    (C) At the exercise club 健身俱樂部
    (D) At the community center 社區中心

解析 (D) 男子都在社區中心和一群人打網球。選項(A)是女子游泳的地方。選項(B)是其中一名女子過去打網球的地方。選項(C)重複使用了club這個字。

61. What do the women invite the man to do? 女子們邀請男子去做什麼？
    (A) Have lunch 吃午餐
    (B) Walk in the park 公園散步
    (C) Play a game of pool 打撞球
    (D) Join the country club 加入鄉村俱樂部

解析 (A) 女子們邀請男子加入（join）她們，一起去吃點東西，接著提到一個很棒的午餐地點。選項(B)重複使用了park這個字，公園是其中一名女子以前上網球課的地方。選項(C)搞錯了pool這個字的意義，對話中提到的是游泳池。選項(D)不正確，女子是要男子加入她們，和她們一起吃午餐，不是加入鄉村俱樂部。

Questions 62 through 64 refer to the following conversation.
Man: I hope everybody's ready for an early start tomorrow. We have a spectacular drive through the river valley planned, with several stops along the way.
Woman: Sounds great.
Man: I'll need everybody to be at the bus by eight a.m. sharp.
Woman: Should we bring anything special with us?
Man: Just remember to dress warmly. It'll be a cold day, and we'll be getting out of the bus often to look at the views. It will be a great opportunity for any landscape photographers in the group.
Woman: Oh, then I'm sorry I didn't bring a good camera.

第62-64題請聽下面這段對話。
男：希望大家準備好明天要早點出發了。我們計劃開車穿過河谷，沿路會停靠幾個地方，景色十分壯觀。
女：聽起來好棒。
男：我需要大家早上八點準時到遊覽車集合。
女：我們需要帶什麼特別的東西嗎？
男：記得穿暖一點就好了，明天會很冷，而且我們常要下車欣賞風景。我們這團若有風景

277

攝影師的話，可要把握這個好機會。

女：噢，那我很遺憾沒帶好相機來了。

62. What most likely is the man's job? 這名男子最有可能從事什麼工作？
    (A) Artist 藝術家
    (B) Landscaper 景觀設計師
    (C) Tour guide 導遊
    (D) Photographer 攝影師

解析 (C) 這名男子正在說明遊覽車的觀光行程，告訴大家做哪些準備，所以他是導遊。選項(A)和(B)都和對話中提到遊覽途中會看到的景觀（landscape）有關。選項(D)重複使用了 photographer 這個字，對話裡指的是有些團員可能是風景攝影師。

63. What will the speakers do tomorrow? 這些說話者明天要做什麼？
    (A) Bike through a valley 騎自行車穿過山谷
    (B) Meet in an alley 在一個小巷子集合
    (C) Fish in a river 在河中釣魚
    (D) Ride on a bus 搭乘遊覽車

解析 (D) 男子說每個人都要在早上八點準時到遊覽車集合，所以他們要搭乘遊覽車。選項(A)重複使用了 valley 這個字，但他們會搭遊覽車而不是騎自行車。選項(B)混淆了近音字 valley 和 alley。選項(C)重複使用了 river 這個字，但對話中沒有提到釣魚。

64. What should people bring? 大家要帶什麼東西？
    (A) A dress 洋裝
    (B) Cold drinks 冷飲
    (C) Some books 幾本書
    (D) Warm clothes 保暖衣物

解析 (D) 男子說「Just remember to dress warmly」，要大家穿暖一點。選項(A)搞錯了 dress 的用法。選項(B)重複使用了 cold 這個字，cold 在對話中用來描述天氣，而非飲料。選項(C)未被提及。

Questions 65 through 67 refer to the following conversation and map.

Man: I knew we shouldn't have waited till the last minute.

Woman: What's the matter?

Man: We're all out of, uh, we need markers for this afternoon's presentation. Joe specifically said he needed green markers. There's no time to order them now.

Woman: Relax. You can get them at the mall. You know, that new office supply store that just opened up there.

Man: Oh, right. Where is that exactly?

Woman: Just across the corridor from the bookstore. They've got all kinds of paper, too, and easels and notebooks, just about everything.

Man: We've already got all that. It's just the markers. I'll go pick some up now.

Woman: OK. I'll start getting the conference room set up. I have Joe's instructions about how he wants it done.

第 65–67 題請聽下面這段對話，並參考地圖。

男：我就知道不該等到最後一刻。

女：怎麼了？

男：我們的麥克筆一支也不……呃，我們需要麥克筆，下午簡報要用。喬還特別交代他要綠色的麥克筆，現在已經來不及訂購了。

女：別緊張，你可以去購物中心買，你知道那家吧，就那裡新開的辦公用品店。

男：喔，對。確切位置在哪裡？

女：就在書店隔著走廊對面。他們也有各種紙類，還有白板架和筆記本，什麼都有。

男：那些我們已經有了，只缺麥克筆，我現在就去買。

女：好，我先開始布置會議室，喬有交代我要怎麼做。

購物中心

書店	商店 A
商店 B	商店 C
商店 D	咖啡館

279

65. What does the man need to buy? 這名男子需要買什麼？
    (A) Another kind of paper 另一種紙
    (B) Notebooks and easels 筆記本和白板架
    (C) Green markers 綠色麥克筆
    (D) Books 書本

解析 (C) 男子說他需要買綠色麥克筆，下午簡報要用。選項(A)和(B)是女子說在辦公用品店能買到的東西。選項(D)是被對話中提到書店（bookstore）給混淆。

66. Look at the graphic. Which is the supply store? 請看圖表，哪一間是辦公用品店？
    (A) Store A 商店A
    (B) Store B 商店B
    (C) Store C 商店C
    (D) Store D 商店D

解析 (A) 女子說辦公用品店在書店隔著走廊的對面，所以是商店A。選項(B)(C)(D)都不符合描述。

67. What will the woman do next? 女子接下來會做什麼？
    (A) Go to the mall 前往購物中心
    (B) Speak with Joe 和喬說話
    (C) Give the man instructions 給男子指示
    (D) Arrange the conference room 布置會議室

解析 (D) 女子說「I'll start getting the conference room set up」，所以是布置會議室。選項(A)是男子要做的事。選項(B)重複使用了Joe這個名字，對話中提到Joe兩次，但完全沒提到要和他說話。選項(C)重複使用了instructions這個字，女子說她收到喬的指示。

Questions 68 through 70 refer to the following conversation and sign.

Man: Here's a place. Hurry and park. I'm afraid we're not going to get to the movie on time.
Woman: Relax. The movie doesn't start for another fifteen minutes, and I already bought the tickets online, so we just have to go in and sit down.
Man: OK, OK. Oh, here are the parking prices.
Woman: Hmmm, not bad. We'll only be here three hours, or maybe a little less, so it won't cost us much.
Man: Did you bring the snacks?
Woman: No. I'd rather get something to eat at the theater. I know it's expensive, but I like the selection.

Man: That's fine with me. Come on, hurry. I want to make sure we get front row seats.

第68–70題請聽下面這段對話，並參考告示牌。
男：這裡有車位，趕快停好！我怕我們趕不上電影。
女：放輕鬆好不好？電影還有十五分鐘才開演，我已經上網買好票了，我們只需要進去坐下就好。
男：好啦，好啦。哦，這裡有停車收費表。
女：嗯，還行。我們只會在這裡停留三小時，或許還不到三小時，所以不會花太多錢。
男：你有帶零食嗎？
女：沒有。我想到電影院再買東西來吃，我知道很貴，但我喜歡那裡的餐點選擇。
男：我沒意見。快點啦！我一定要搶到前排的位子。

```
停車費
一小時以下 …….$ 5
兩小時以下 …….$ 8
三小時以下 …….$ 12
超過三小時 …….$ 15
```

68. What is the man worried about? 這名男子在擔心什麼？
    (A) Finding a parking space 找停車位
    (B) Getting to the movie late 看電影遲到
    (C) Waiting on line for tickets 排隊買票
    (D) Paying too much for parking 付太多停車費

解析 (B) 男子說「I'm afraid we're not going to get to the movie on time」，他怕無法準時看電影。選項(A)不正確，他們才剛找到一個停車位。選項(C)不正確，女子已經買好票了。選項(D)不正確，對話中唯一提到停車費的地方，是女子表示停車不會花太多錢。

69. Look at the graphic. How much will the speakers probably pay for parking? 請看圖表，說話者可能要付多少停車費？
    (A) $ 5
    (B) $ 8
    (C) $ 12
    (D) $ 15

解析 (C) 女子說他們最多停留三小時，也許更少，而三小時以下的停車費是十二美元。選項(A)(B)(D)都不是這個時間的停車費。

281

70. What does the man want to do? 這名男子想要做什麼？
    (A) Leave the theater early 提早離開電影院
    (B) Sit in the front row 坐在前排
    (C) Buy tickets online 上網購票
    (D) Eat snacks later 晚點再吃零食

解析 (B) 男子說了「I want to make sure we get front row seats.」，可以知道他想坐前排。選項(A)並未被提及。選項(C)是女子已經做的事。選項(D)不正確，雖然男子有提到零食，但沒有說他想什麼時候吃。

Part 4：簡短獨白

作答方式：你會聽到一名說話者的獨白。每段獨白搭配三個問題，各有四個選項。選出最適當的答案回答問題，並將答案卡上對應的橢圓框塗滿。

Questions 71 through 73 refer to the following advertisement.

Nothing adds to your professional look more than a set of Legerton's luggage. Legerton's provides you with everything you need from computer carriers and small overnight cases to large garment bags. All our products are carefully manufactured from imported leather and other fine materials. Legerton's products are available in most fine retail stores. Or, visit our website at www dot legertons dot com to order your Legerton's products today. Place your order before the end of the month and receive a fifteen percent discount. Offer good only on orders made through our website. Some restrictions may apply.

第71–73題請聽下面這則廣告。

沒有什麼比一套萊格頓的行李箱更能增添您的專業形象了。萊格頓為您提供一切所需，從電腦包、小型過夜行李箱到大型衣物袋，應有盡有。我們所有產品均採用進口皮革和上等材料精心製造，在大多數高級零售店均有販售。也可以現在就到我們的網站訂購您的萊格頓商品，網址是www.legertons.com。月底前下單可享八五折優惠。本優惠為官網限定，部分商品不適用。

71．Who is the audience for this advertisement? 這則廣告的目標客群是誰？
　　(A) Families 家庭
　　(B) Businesspeople 商務人士
　　(C) Tourists 觀光客
　　(D) Students 學生

　解析 **(B)** 這則廣告的目標客群是在意自己專業形象（professional look）的人。選項(A)(C)(D)都是會使用行李箱的人，但不會被認為需要看起來很有專業風範。

72．What is the advertisement for? 這則廣告是要銷售什麼？
　　(A) Suitcases 行李箱
　　(B) Computers 電腦
　　(C) Clothes 衣服
　　(D) Travel agency 旅行社

283

解析 **(A)** 說話者表示這則廣告是要推銷萊格頓行李箱（Legerton's luggage），luggage 就是 suitcase。當中還提到了過夜箱、電腦包、衣物袋等各式各樣的行李箱。選項(B)重複使用了 computers 這個字。選項(C)是 garment 的同義字。選項(D)是從各種旅行用品聯想而來的。

73. How can a customer get a discount? 購物者要如何享有優惠？
    (A) By ordering online 上網訂購
    (B) By shopping at a retail store 到零售店購買
    (C) By completing an application 填寫申請表
    (D) By ordering next month 下個月再訂購

解析 **(A)** 廣告最後有提到優惠是官網限定。選項(B)是有販售商品的地方，但店面購買沒有折扣。選項(C)使用了 apply 的名詞形式 application。選項(D)誤解了「before the end of the month」（本月底）的意思，本月底是折扣活動截止的時候。

Questions 74 through 76 refer to the following weather report.

A winter storm warning is in effect for this area through midnight tonight. Heavy rain is expected early, turning to snow by late this afternoon. This will create ice hazards tonight as the rain and snow freeze over. This means dangerous icy conditions for rush hour tomorrow, and city officials recommend staying home if you possibly can. It's not all bad news, however. Warmer temperatures tomorrow afternoon should melt most of the ice and clear the roads by the evening rush hour. Strong sunshine will help keep temperatures above freezing most of the afternoon.

第 74–76 題請聽下面這則氣象報告。

本地區的冬季風暴警報將持續發布至今晚十二點。本日清晨會有大雨，下午稍晚將轉為降雪。今晚隨著雨雪凍結，將造成結冰危險。明日的尖峰時刻會出現路面結冰的情況，非常危險，市府呼籲民眾盡可能留在家中。不過也不全是壞消息。明天下午氣溫回升，應能融化大部分的結冰，並在晚間尖峰時刻來臨之前恢復路況。下午大部分時間日照強烈，將有助於維持氣溫在冰點以上。

74. What best describes the weather conditions the area is facing? 下列何者最能描述本地區的天氣狀況？
    (A) Cold 寒冷
    (B) Fog 有霧
    (C) Snow and ice 下雪結冰
    (D) Wind and rain 颳風下雨

解析 (C) 氣象報告說「rain . . . turning to snow . . . will create ice hazards」，可見先是下雨，然後降雪，最後造成結冰危險。選項(A)沒有錯，但是並不完整。選項(B)並未被提及。選項(D)不正確，氣象報告中沒有提到會颳風。

75. What problems will this weather cause tomorrow? 這樣的天氣會導致明天發生什麼問題？
    (A) People will have trouble getting to work. 民眾上班會有困難。
    (B) People won't have enough heat. 民眾將沒有足夠的暖氣。
    (C) Flights will be canceled. 航班將被取消。
    (D) People should buy plenty of food. 民眾應採買大量食物。

解析 (A) 氣象報告中提到尖峰時刻（rush hour），就是指民眾上下班的時間。選項(B)(C)(D) 均未提及。

76. What does the speaker mean when he says, "It's not all bad news"? 說話者說「It's not all bad news」是什麼意思？
    (A) The weather will improve soon. 天氣很快就會好轉。
    (B) People will enjoy a day off from work. 民眾可以放假一天。
    (C) The news report will follow the weather report. 氣象報告之後將播放新聞報告。
    (D) City officials will work to clear the roads quickly. 市府官員會盡快恢復路況。

解析 (A) 通常在提出了一些壞消息或令人不悅的訊息後，會用「It's not all bad news」引出一則好消息。以此處來說，先是描述了冰冷的天氣狀況，接著用這句話作為轉折，表示下午就會回暖。選項(B)(C)(D)都不是這個句子在此處的意思。

Questions 77 through 79 refer to the following excerpt from a training session.

Your job as receptionists is a very important one. You are the first face a visitor sees when entering the building, so it's important that you make a good first impression and follow procedures correctly. As soon as a visitor comes through the door, say "hello" and then ask for her name and the name of the person she's here to see. Have the visitor sign the guest book and then invite her to take a seat. Then call the person she's visiting. Make sure the visitor stays in the lobby until someone comes to escort her upstairs. Remember, visitors should never be allowed to wander around the building unaccompanied.

第 77–79 題請聽下面這段培訓課程的節錄談話。

接待員的工作非常重要。訪客進入大樓後，第一個見到的人就是你，因此給人留下好的第一印象，並正確遵守流程非常重要。在訪客進入大門後，立刻說「您好」，並詢問對方姓名和要找的人。請訪客在登記簿上簽名，並請她稍坐一會。然後打電話給她要找的人，同時確保訪客留在大廳之內，直到有人來陪同她上樓。請記住，絕不能讓訪客在無人陪伴下於大樓內四處遊蕩。

77. What is the first thing a receptionist should do for a visitor? 接待員見到訪客後，第一件事要做什麼？
    (A) Greet her 和她打招呼
    (B) Have her sign in 請她登記
    (C) Ask for an ID card 請她出示身分證
    (D) Let her take a seat 請她坐下

解析 (A) 說話者提到「As soon as a visitor comes through the door, say "hello"」，建議接待員看到訪客進來要馬上說「您好」。選項(B)和(D)都是建議要做的事，但不是第一件事。選項(C)並沒有被提及。

78. Where should the visitor wait? 訪客應在哪裡等候？
    (A) By the receptionist's desk 接待櫃檯旁
    (B) Outside the office 辦公室外
    (C) Next to the door 門邊
    (D) In the lobby 大廳內

解析 (D) 說話者說「Make sure the visitor stays in the lobby」，所以是大廳內。選項(A)(B)(C)都使用了這段談話中的單字，但這些地方都沒有被提及。

79. What should visitors never do? 訪客禁止做什麼事？
    (A) Go upstairs 上樓
    (B) Carry books 攜帶書籍
    (C) Wait too long 等待太久
    (D) Walk around alone 單獨四處走動

解析 (D) 說話者說「Remember, visitors should never be allowed to wander around the building unaccompanied.」（訪客不得在無人陪伴下四處遊蕩）。選項(A)(B)(C)都使用了這段談話中的單字，但這些事都沒有被提及。

Questions 80 through 82 refer to the following talk.

Good morning, everyone. My name is Lynn, and I am pleased to welcome you to the Janteck Homestead. Let's begin with a little history of the place. Mr. and Mrs. Janteck arrived in this area in the eighteen-fifties and bought a small farm outside of the city. As the family grew, so did the number of structures on the property. Today, we'll visit six of the ten buildings on the property, including three small houses, a grain storehouse, a barn, and a root cellar. Our historians have restored these buildings to exactly how they were during the Janteck's time. As we tour the property, please be mindful of our rules: pick up your trash and keep your hands away from the display cases.

第 80–82 題請聽下面這段談話。

各位早安，我叫琳，非常歡迎各位來到詹特克農莊。我先簡單介紹一下這裡的歷史。詹特克夫婦在 1850 年代來到這個地區，在城市外買下了一座小農場。隨著家族不斷擴大，農莊內的建築也越來越多。今天我們會參觀農莊十座建築物的其中六座，包括三間小房子、一間穀倉、一個牲口棚和一個根菜貯藏窖。我們的歷史學家已經把這些建築修復成詹特克家族時期的原貌，參觀時請遵守我們的規定：撿起你的垃圾，且請勿碰觸展示櫃。

80. Who is Lynn? 琳是什麼人？
　　(A) A historian 歷史學家
　　(B) A tour guide 導遊
　　(C) A guidebook writer 旅遊指南的作者
　　(D) A property owner 房地產持有人

解析 (B) 說話者，也就是琳，正在帶領詹特克農莊的導覽行程，所以她是導遊。選項 (A) 重複使用了 historian 這個字，是修復農莊的人。選項 (C) 和這段說話的導覽語境有關。選項 (D) 重複使用了 property 這個字。

81. Where does the tour take place? 這個導覽活動發生在哪裡？
　　(A) A village 一個村莊
　　(B) A school 一所學校
　　(C) A city 一座城市
　　(D) A farm 一座農場

解析 (D) 說話者提到詹特克家族在城市外買了一座農場，homestead 就是一種農場。選項 (A) 也是導覽行程可能會去的地方，也涉及參觀好幾棟建築物，和這裡的行程非常類似因此會讓人混淆。選項 (B) 混淆了近音字 rule 和 school。選項 (C) 重複使用了 city 這個字。

287

82. What are listeners asked to do? 聽者被要求做什麼？
    (A) Carry their own suitcases 拿著自己的行李箱
    (B) Avoid touching the displays 避免碰觸展示品
    (C) Purchase items in a store 在一家店裡購物
    (D) Play some games 玩一些遊戲

解析 (B) 說話者提到「keep your hands away from the display cases」（不要碰觸展示櫃）。選項(A)混淆了display cases和suitcases。選項(C)混淆了restored和store。選項(D)混淆了display和play。

Questions 83 through 85 refer to the following talk.

Welcome to the city's new Central Library. I look forward to showing you around this evening as part of our grand opening. We're proud to say that the new library is twice the size of the old one, so that, uh, gives us plenty of opportunity to expand our collection. We'll begin our visit on the second floor. We will see the children's room and activity rooms. From there we'll move to the young adult section on the third floor. On the fourth floor, we'll see the adult collection, as well as magazines and periodicals. We'll skip the fifth floor, which is mainly offices, and go right up to enjoy the view from the sixth floor. It's not to be missed.

第83–85題請聽下面這段談話。

歡迎蒞臨本市全新的中央圖書館。今晚在我們盛大的開幕活動中，我非常期待帶各位四處參觀。我們可以很自豪地說，新圖書館是舊圖書館的兩倍大，給了我們，呃，充分的機會擴增館藏。參觀活動會從二樓開始，我們會看到兒童圖書室和活動室。接著來到三樓的青少年閱覽區，四樓則包括了成人館藏和雜誌期刊的閱覽區。我們會跳過五樓，該樓層主要是辦公室，接著直接前往六樓欣賞風景，千萬不要錯過。

83. What is the purpose of this talk? 這段談話的目的是什麼？
    (A) To describe library services 描述圖書館的服務
    (B) To introduce a tour of the library 介紹圖書館的導覽活動
    (C) To compare the new and old libraries 比較新舊圖書館
    (D) To explain how to reach each floor of the library 說明如何前往圖書館各個樓層

解析 (B) 說話者提到「I look forward to showing you around this evening as part of our grand opening」，所以他準備帶領聽者進行圖書館導覽活動。選項(A)未被提及。選項(C)只是稍微提了一下，說話者比較了兩座圖書館的大小，但不是這段談話的主要目的。選項(D)被談話中描述各個樓層的配置給混淆了。

288

84. What is on the second floor? 二樓有什麼？
    (A) Magazines and periodicals 雜誌和期刊
    (B) Young adult books 青少年圖書
    (C) Activity rooms 活動室
    (D) Offices 辦公室

    解析 (C) 說話者提到二樓有兒童圖書室和活動室。選項(A)(B)(D)位於其他樓層。

85. What does the speaker mean when he says, "It's not to be missed"? 說話者說「It's not to be missed」是什麼意思？
    (A) There is nothing interesting on the sixth floor. 六樓沒有什麼有趣的。
    (B) Everyone should visit the sixth floor. 每個人都應該到六樓參觀一下。
    (C) No one is allowed on the sixth floor. 六樓禁止進入。
    (D) He has never visited the sixth floor. 他從來沒到過六樓。

    解析 (B) 「It's not to be missed」表示說話者認為必看、必體驗的事物。選項(A)(C)(D)都不是這句話在這裡的意思。

Questions 86 through 88 refer to the following announcement.

Welcome aboard Flight six-two-seven to Houston. We'll be flying today at a cruising altitude of thirty-five thousand feet. Our flying time will be two hours and forty minutes, putting us at our gate on time, at four forty-seven Houston time. We have had some reports of turbulence on this route today, so we ask that you remain seated with your seat belt on. But once you get to Houston, the skies will be clear and the sun bright. In fact you'll have cloudless, sunny skies all week, if Houston is your final destination. Thank you for flying with us.

第86–88題請聽下面這則廣播。

歡迎搭乘627航班前往休士頓。本日的飛行高度是三萬五千英尺，飛行時間是兩小時四十分鐘，預計於休士頓時間4點47分準時停靠登機門。我們收到本航線今日將有亂流的報告，請留在您的座位上，並繫好安全帶。但抵達休士頓後天氣晴朗，陽光普照。事實上，若您的最終目的地是休士頓，整週都會是無雲、晴空萬里的好天氣。感謝您的搭乘。

86. What is the destination for this flight? 這班飛機的目的地是哪裡？
    (A) Dallas 達拉斯
    (B) Houston 休士頓
    (C) Madison 麥迪遜
    (D) Wilmington 威明頓

289

解析 (B) 廣播第一句就說明這班飛機飛往休士頓。選項(A)(C)(D)都沒有被提到。

87. What does the captain say about the flight? 關於這次飛行，機長說了什麼？
    (A) It will be late. 會延遲抵達。
    (B) There will be turbulence. 會遭遇亂流。
    (C) It will be smooth. 會很平穩。
    (D) The flying altitude will be low. 飛行高度很低。

解析 (B) 機長說有收到亂流報告（reports of turbulence），請乘客留在座位上並繫好安全帶，可以推斷飛行會很顛簸。選項(A)不正確，機長預計會準時停靠登機門。選項(C)不正確，機長預期會遭遇亂流，不會很平穩。選項(D)不正確，機長提到飛行高度是三萬五千英尺，屬於高空而非低空。

88. What does the captain say about the final destination? 關於最終目的地，機長有何說明？
    (A) It is a popular place to visit. 是熱門的旅遊勝地。
    (B) The people there are friendly. 當地人民十分友善。
    (C) It is a good place for clothes shopping. 是買衣服的好地方。
    (D) The weather there will be pleasant. 當地天氣舒適宜人。

解析 (D) 機長對休士頓（也就是最終目的地）的描述為「. . . the skies will be clear and the sun bright. In fact you'll have cloudless, sunny skies all week」，可見天氣舒適宜人。選項(A)(B)(C)都有可能是事實，但機長沒有提到。

Questions 89 through 91 refer to the following announcement.

Welcome to the twenty-fifth annual convention of the National Business Association. I am Priscilla Prescott, your president. We are honored to have as our keynote speaker today, George Williams, one of our country's top financial experts. But before we begin our program, I have a few housekeeping announcements. Because of a scheduling mix up, the Garden Room has been reserved for a wedding, so this morning's workshop on marketing has been moved to the Patio Room. Lunch will be served at noon instead of at twelve thirty, but still in the Rooftop Restaurant, as originally planned. Finally, you will find a conference evaluation form in your packets. Please fill it out before you go home tonight, and leave it in the box by the door.

第 89–91 題請聽下面這段宣布內容。

歡迎各位參加全國商業學會的第二十五屆年度大會，我是普莉希拉・普萊斯考特，你們的會長。今天很榮幸邀請到國內頂尖的金融專家之一，喬治・威廉斯作為我們的主講人。但活動開始之前，我有幾件注意事項要宣布。由於行程安排出了差錯，花園廳已被預訂作為婚禮場地，因此今天早上的行銷工作坊改到露臺廳進行。午餐改於十二點鐘提供，而非原定的十二點半，地點則不變，依然在頂樓餐廳。最後，各位會在資料袋裡找到一份會議評估表，請在今晚回家之前填好，並放入門邊的箱子。

89. Who will give the keynote address? 誰會進行主題演講？
    (A) The association president 協會會長
    (B) A university professor 一位大學教授
    (C) A financial expert 一位金融專家
    (D) A journalist 一位記者

解析 (C) 說話者提到本次主講人時的描述為「George Williams, one of our country's top financial experts」（國內頂尖金融專家之一）。選項(A)是宣布這些事情的人。選項(B)和(D)也有可能，但並未提及。

90. What will take place in the Garden Room? 花園廳會進行什麼活動？
    (A) A wedding 婚禮
    (B) A workshop 工作坊
    (C) A lunch 午餐
    (D) A market 市集

解析 (A) 說話者提到花園廳已經被預訂作為婚禮場地。選項(B)是花園廳原定要進行的活動。選項(C)會在頂樓餐廳進行。選項(D)是被工作坊的主題 marketing（行銷）給混淆了。

91. What is the audience asked to do? 聽眾被要求做什麼事？
    (A) Speak with George Williams 與喬治・威廉斯交談
    (B) Leave boxes by the door 把箱子放在門邊
    (C) Pay for lunch 支付午餐費用
    (D) Complete a form 填寫一份表格

解析 (D) 說話者要聽者填寫資料袋裡的評估表。選項(A)被喬治・威廉斯是主講人(keynote speaker)這件事混淆了，並沒有要與他交談。選項(B)搞混了，聽者被要求把填好的表格「放入門邊的箱子」，而不是把箱子放在門邊。選項(C)重複使用了 lunch 這個字，但內容中沒有提到要付餐費。

Questions 92 through 94 refer to the following telephone message.

Hello. This is your Veriphone voicemail system. Please listen carefully to the following information. We are changing your voicemail system in seven days. On August first, some of the codes will change. You will control your voicemail with new numbers. For example, you will press "seven" to delete a message, and you will press "nine" to save a message. You can press the star key now to hear all ten of the new codes, or you can go to our website, at www dot veriphone dot com, and read the entire message. Thank you.

第92–94題請聽下面這段電話留言。

您好，這是您的維力豐語音信箱系統，請仔細聆聽以下訊息。我們將於七天後變更您的語音信箱系統。自8月1日起，部分代碼有所調整，您將使用新的號碼控制您的語音信箱。例如，按「7」刪除留言，按「9」保存留言。您可立即按米字鍵聽取全部十個新代碼，或至本公司網站www.veriphone.com閱讀完整訊息，謝謝。

92. What will take place in seven days? 七天後會發生什麼事？
    (A) The voicemail system will change. 語音信箱系統將有所變更。
    (B) This customer will get a new telephone. 這名顧客將會收到一支新電話。
    (C) This customer will get a new telephone number. 這名顧客將會收到一組新的電話號碼。
    (D) The telephone company's web address will change. 這家電信公司的網址將會改變。

解析 (A) 這通留言是關於電信公司語音信箱系統變更的事。選項(B)把telephone和voicemail聯想在一起。選項(C)重複使用了new number這個詞。選項(D)是從website聯想過來的。

93. How can a customer save a message? 顧客要如何保存留言？
    (A) Press two 按2
    (B) Press four 按4
    (C) Press seven 按7
    (D) Press nine 按9

解析 (D) 這通留言中提到保存留言要按9。選項(A)混淆了two和發音相近的new。選項(B)混淆了four和發音相近的or。選項(C)是刪除留言。

94. How can a customer learn about all of the new codes? 顧客要如何才能知道全部的新代碼？
    (A) Press ten 按 10
    (B) Press the star key 按米字鍵
    (C) Call the company 打電話給公司
    (D) Listen to the entire message 聽取完整訊息

解析 (B) 留言中指示聽者按米字鍵聽取新的代碼。選項 (A) 是新代碼的數量。選項 (C) 重複使用了 call 這個字，但留言中並未提到要打電話給電信公司。選項 (D) 把留言中提到閱讀完整訊息（read the entire message）誤解成聽取。

Questions 95 through 97 refer to the following telephone message and price list.

Hi, Evelyn. I need a little bit of help with the arrangements for next week's professional development session, uh, with the food. We'll be serving lunch, you know, in the big dining room, and I'd like to get it from the same caterers we used last time. So could you call them and arrange it? Last time we got the lunch for fifty people, but it was way too much, so I think this time the one that serves twenty-five should be plenty. So ask for that and tell them we'll need it by noon on Friday. They deliver, so you won't need to pick it up. OK, thanks, and let me know how it goes.

第 95–97 題請聽下面這段電話留言，並參考價目表。

嗨，伊芙琳。下週的專業發展課程安排，我需要你幫我個忙，呃，是食物的部分。你知道的，我們會在大餐廳供應午餐，我想跟我們上次找的那家餐飲承辦商訂購。你能不能打電話安排一下？上次我們訂了五十人份的午餐，結果太多了，這次我想訂二十五人份的應該就夠了。你去訂一下，跟他們說週五中午前需準備好。請他們外送，這樣你就不用自己去拿。好了，謝謝你，再告訴我事情進行得如何。

```
        城市餐飲承辦商
          午餐價目表

    十五位賓客 ........ $150
    二十位賓客 ........ $200
    二十五位賓客 ..... $250
    五十位賓客 ........ $450
```

95. What event is the speaker arranging? 說話者正在安排何種活動？
    (A) A staff party 員工聚會
    (B) A training session 培訓課程
    (C) A client luncheon 客戶午餐會
    (D) An awards banquet 頒獎宴會

    解析 **(B)** 說話者他正在安排下週的專業發展課程（professional development session）。選項(A)(C)(D)都是有可能包含午餐的活動，但留言中都未提到這些活動。

96. What does the speaker ask Evelyn to do? 說話者請伊芙琳做什麼事。
    (A) Order the lunch 訂午餐
    (B) Count the guests 清點賓客人數
    (C) Pick up the lunch 去取午餐
    (D) Arrange the dining room 布置餐廳

    解析 **(A)** 說話者說明他想向哪一家餐飲承辦商訂餐，然後說「could you call them and arrange it?」，表示請求伊芙琳打電話安排這件事。選項(B)被留言中提到他們該訂多少人份的午餐給誤導。選項(C)不正確，說話者建議外送而不是自取。選項(D)重複使用了dining room這個字，但留言中沒有提到要布置。

97. Look at the graphic. How much will the speaker pay for lunch? 請看圖表，說話者需要支付多少的午餐費用？
    (A) $150
    (B) $200
    (C) $250
    (D) $450

    解析 **(C)** 說話者要求訂購二十五人份的午餐，對照價目表就是250美元。選項(A)(B)(D)都不符合人數。

Questions 98 through 100 refer to the following talk and building directory.

Most of you have been with us here at Silverton for less than a week, and the purpose of today's meeting is to familiarize you with some of the procedures and processes of our company. Your department heads are available at all times, of course, to help you with any specific concerns or questions. OK, let's start with the benefits. As a Silverton employee you are entitled to use the fitness room that is available to all building tenants. It is located just below our offices, across the hall from the bank. You can use it on your lunch break or at any other time you like. Now, if you'll just look at this slide here, we'll go over some other company benefits.

第 98–100 題請聽下面這段談話，並參考樓層介紹表。

你們大多數人來希爾威登公司還不到一星期，而今天開會的目的是讓你們熟悉公司的一些作業程序和流程。當然，如果你有任何具體的關注事項或問題，你的部門主管隨時都可以為你解答。好了，我們就從福利開始。身為希爾威登公司的員工，你有權使用開放給大樓全體租戶使用的健身房，就在我們辦公室樓下，銀行穿過大廳的對面。你可以利用午休時間或其他你方便的時間去使用。現在請大家看這張投影片，我們來看一下公司的其他福利。

```
           樓層介紹

地面樓 …… 大廳
一樓 ……… 城市銀行
二樓 ……… 希爾威登公司
三樓 ……… 城市體育器材公司
```

98. Who is this talk for? 這段談話針對的對象是誰？
    (A) All building tenants 大樓全體租戶
    (B) Department heads 部門主管
    (C) New employees 新進員工
    (D) Job applicants 工作應徵者

解析 (C) 說話者正在對剛進公司不到一星期的新人說話，也就是新進員工。選項(A)是可以使用健身房的人。選項(B)是可以為新進員工解答關切事項和問題的人。選項(D)有可能但未提及。

99．Look at the graphic. Where is the fitness room located? 請看圖表，健身房位於哪裡呢？
    (A) Ground Floor 地面樓
    (B) First Floor 一樓
    (C) Second Floor 二樓
    (D) Third Floor 三樓

解析 (B) 說話者表示健身房就在公司樓下、銀行對面（is located just below our offices, across the hall from the bank），符合描述的是一樓。選項(A)(C)(D)都與描述不符。

100．What will the listeners do next? 聽者接下來要做什麼？
    (A) Tour the building 參觀大樓
    (B) Break for lunch 午休用餐
    (C) Ask questions 發問
    (D) View a slide 觀看投影片

解析 (D) 說話者最後說「Now, if you'll just look at this slide here」，表示請大家看投影片。選項(A)被談話中關於健身房位置的說明給混淆了。選項(B)被員工可以利用午休時間使用健身房的建議給混淆。選項(C)被說話者建議大家可以找部門主管詢問問題給混淆。

本測驗之聽力測驗到此結束，請翻頁進行 Part 5 的測驗。

閱讀測驗

在本段測驗當中,你將有機會展現自己對書面英語的理解能力。閱讀測驗共有三個大題,每一大題均有作答說明。

你有 75 分鐘時間完成本測驗的第五到第七大題。

Part 5：句子填空

> 作答方式：你會看到一個缺字的句子和四個可能的選項，選出最適當的答案，將答案卡上對應的橢圓框塗滿。

101. 截至週五，已有二十五份應徵櫃檯人員職位的申請書被提交了。

解析 (C) for在這裡的意思是「關於」。選項(A)和(B)如果放在這裡會變成說明位置，不合邏輯。選項(D)的意思是「藉由……的方式」。

102. 該系列產品下殺的超低折扣價肯定會吸引許多新顧客。
    (A) 提供
    (B) 吸引
    (C) 享受
    (D) 期待

解析 (B) attract的意思是「吸引」。選項(A)(C)(D)都不符合語意要求。

103. 克魯茲先生需要有人協助他處理會議展示的事情。
    (A) 假定、假設
    (B) 分配、指派
    (C) 同意、贊成
    (D) 協助、幫助

解析 (D) assist是「協助」的意思。選項(A)是「猜測、假定」。選項(B)是把一份工作或職責分配給某個人。選項(C)表示「同意」或「贊成」。

104. 對於昨天無法到場的人，下週還會再舉辦一次工作坊。
    (A) 怨恨、討厭
    (B) 出席的、在場的
    (C) 滿足的
    (D) 熱切的、專心致志的

解析 (B) present用來表示出現在某個特定地點。選項(A)(C)(D)都與文意不符。

105. 住在鄉下的一個缺點就是通勤時間很長。
(A) 旅行
(B) 接替
(C) 通勤
(D) 延長

解析 (C) commute 的意思是固定往返於住家和工作場所之間，即「通勤」。選項(A)雖然意義上有關聯，但通常不用於此情況。選項(B)和(D)不符合語意的要求。

106. 最終的成交價超過投資者的預期。
(A)(B)(C)(D) 預期

解析 (A) 句子前面的 was higher 已經用了過去式，因此要表達比過去更早的時間點，必須使用過去完成式 had expected。選項(B)是原形動詞。選項(C)是現在進行式。選項(D)是未來式。

107. 新來的服務生第一天上班幾乎沒有犯錯，我想她應該會被僱用為全職員工。
(A) 她
(B) 他
(C) 她／她的
(D) 他們

解析 (A) she 是用於女性的單數主格代名詞，waitress 是女服務生，且為單數，因此要用 she。選項(B)是用於男性的受格代名詞。選項(C)是所有格形容詞或受格代名詞。選項(D)是複數主格代名詞。

108. 新的保險計畫特別受有家庭的員工歡迎。
(A) 使受歡迎
(B) 受歡迎的
(C) 居住於
(D) 流行、普及

解析 (B) 形容詞 popular 可以修飾名詞 plan，又可以被副詞 especially 修飾。選項(A)和(C)是動詞。選項(D)是名詞。

109. 漁船每次出海就是好幾個星期，因此補給人員會大量採購補給品。
    (A) 大量地
    (B) 最大量的
    (C) 更大量的
    (D) 大量的

解析 **(D)** 這裡需要一個形容詞原級來修飾名詞 quantities。選項(A)是副詞。選項(B)和(C)是形容詞的最高級和比較級，但這裡並沒有可以比較的事物。

110. 你的旅行社業務員取消預訂之後，航空公司會立刻退款給你。
    (A) 和、還有（as well as）
    (B) 遠至、就……（as far as）
    (C) 一……就（as soon as）
    (D) 低至、只要（as little as）

解析 **(C)** as soon as 的意思是「一……就／馬上做某事」。選項(A)(B)(D)放到這個句子意思都不通。

111. 斐斯克先生的參考指南是向公司圖書館借的嗎？
    (A) 借出物
    (B) 借入
    (C) 借給
    (D) 送出

解析 **(B)** borrow 用於向別人借東西。選項(A)是你借用的東西（例如 reference guide 就可以用 loan 來表示）。選項(C)是把東西借給別人。選項(D)是「送出、寄送」。

112. 雖然已經訂購，但手冊和名片卻始終沒有印製。
    (A) 雖然
    (B) 甚至
    (C) 然而
    (D) 儘管

解析 **(A)** although 是從屬連接詞，可用來連接後面的子句，表示雖然已經做了某件事（訂購），但另一件事（印製）卻沒有發生。選項(B)(C)(D)都不適用於這個句子。

113. 接線生不記得有收到來自馬德里辦公室或巴黎辦公室的留言。
    (A) 或
    (B) 和
    (C) 兩者其一
    (D) 但

解析 (A) or 用來表示在列舉的選項之間作選擇。選項(B)表示「兩者都」。選項(C)必須和 or 一起使用。選項(D)用來表示對比關係。

114. 我們大多數員工以前都沒有使用過這種影印機。
    (A) 以前
    (B) 在……之前
    (C) 預先的
    (D) 先前的

解析 (A) before 是副詞，說明沒用過影印機的時間。選項(B)(C)(D)都不適用於這個句子。

115. 房務人員假日工作應該要有加班費的，不是嗎？

解析 (A) 這個句子是未來式的肯定句，要用否定附加問句 won't they。選項(B)用於第三人稱單數主詞的否定句。選項(C)不是未來式。選項(D)不是附加問句。

116. 達卡先生辦公室的印表機使用一種特殊的墨水匣，一共有四種顏色。
    (A) 染料
    (B) 墨水
    (C) 紙張
    (D) 托盤

解析 (B) 印表機的墨水叫做 ink，會有不同顏色。選項(A)也有各種不同顏色，但不用來指印表機的墨水。選項(C)和(D)都和印表機有關，但不符合這裡的文意。

117. 接待員收到包裹，並於通知相關部門之前暫時保管。
    (A)(B)(C)(D) 保管

解析 (D) holds 和 receives 用 and 連接，格式上要彼此一致。選項(A)是現在進行式。選項(B)是過去式。選項(C)是現在簡單式，但和主詞不一致。

118. 我們會議的目的是協助員工了解公司政策。
    (A)(B)(C)(D) 了解

解析 (C) 表示某一人或物（the conference）協助另一人或物（employees）做某事時，help 後面要用原形動詞或不定詞。選項(A)是過去式動詞。選項(B)是動名詞。選項(D)是現在進行式。

119. 由於我們對這個城市都不熟，古特曼先生開車送我們去開會。
    (A) 雖然
    (B) 由於
    (C) 因此
    (D) 然而

解析 (B) because建立了兩個事件之間的因果邏輯關係。選項(A)和(D)放入空格中不合邏輯，因為兩個事件不是對比關係。如果句子改成「Although we knew the city …」或「We knew the city, however, …」就會正確。選項(C)用於結果子句，要改成「… therefore, Mr. Gutman drove …」。

120. 加油站的服務員建議跟當地人租船，如此可以省錢。
    (A)(B)(C)(D) 租借

解析 (D) 動詞suggest後面要用動名詞。選項(A)是原形動詞或現在式。選項(B)是第三人稱單數現在式。選項(C)是過去式。

121. 假如用隔夜快遞寄出這份報告，明天中午就能到達米蘭。
    (A)(B)(C)(D) 到達

解析 (B) 在真實條件句中，如果if子句使用了現在式，主要子句必須使用未來式。選項(A)是現在式。選項(C)是現在進行式。選項(D)是現在完成式。

122. 山本壽司在城鎮的另一邊，離我們飯店很遠，應該要搭計程車。
    (A) 不在任何地方
    (B) 在任何地方
    (C) 在某個地方
    (D) 在所有地方

解析 (A) nowhere的意思是「不在任何地方」，片語nowhere near表示「不在很近的地方」、「離……很遠」。選項(B)用於否定句或疑問句。選項(C)的意思是「在某個地方」，但如果他們的目的地在「靠近飯店的某個地方」（somewhere near the hotel），就沒必要搭計程車。選項(D)的意思是「在所有地方、到處」。

123. 將參加會議的員工可享有旅行安排上的折扣。

解析 (D) attending 前面加上 will be 構成了未來進行式（will be attending）。選項 (A)(B)(C) 後接 attending 都不構成合理的時態及文法結構。

124. 瓦斯科先生憑藉著多年的經驗和努力工作，累積了電子方面的專業知識。
    (A) 技術人員
    (B) 專家
    (C) 專業知識
    (D) 授權

解析 (C) expertise 和 expert（專家）這個字有關，這句話的意思是說，瓦斯科先生在電子領域的能力很強。選項 (A)(B)(D) 都不適合用在這個句子。

125. 該市正在為五座停車場和三座休閒活動中心的翻修工程尋求經費。
    (A)(B)(C)(D) 翻修

解析 (D) to renovate 是表目的之不定詞，這個句子是在說明尋求經費的目的。選項 (A)(B)(C) 都不適合用在這個句子。

126. 房務主管要去詢問張小姐她有多少時間可用。
    (A)(B)(C)(D) 有

解析 (D) 這裡可以用現在式或未來簡單式，選項中有兩個現在式可選，而 Ms. Chang 是第三人稱單數，要用 has。選項 (A) 是未來完成式。選項 (B) 是現在進行式。選項 (C) 是複數。

127. 飯店的行銷總監對於歐洲地區的廣告宣傳很在行。
    (A) 知道 (ving)
    (B) 知識
    (C) 知識豐富的
    (D) 知道 (v.)

解析 (C) 形容詞 knowledgeable 修飾名詞 director，同時又被副詞 quite 修飾。選項 (A) 是動名詞。選項 (B) 是名詞。選項 (D) 是動詞。

128. 我們需要知道橫幅的大小才能開始設計。
    (A) 必須
    (B) 需要
    (C) 能夠
    (D) 應該

解析 (B) 只有 need 後面可以接不定詞，選項(A)(C)(D)全都是助動詞，後面必須接原形動詞才可以。

129. 若接線生知道哪裡可以聯絡到史密斯先生，就會打電話給他了。
    (A)(B)(C)(D) 打電話

解析 (D) 這是一個非真實條件句，if子句使用了過去式，則主要子句必須使用「would + 原形動詞」的句型。選項(A)是未來式。選項(B)是過去完成式。選項(C)是過去式。

130. 研討會的培訓師要工作人員將他們的設備搬到會議中心。
    (A) 搬動 (v.)
    (B) 搬動 (ving)
    (C) 搬運人員
    (D) 搬動 (ved)

解析 (A) 表示某人（trainers）要另一人（crew）做某事時，have後面要用原形動詞。選項(B)是動名詞。選項(C)是名詞。選項(D)是過去式。

Part 6：段落填空

作答方式：你會看到四篇短文，各含四個空格，每個空格配有四個選項，選出最適當的單字、片語或句子完成這段敘述。

第 131–134 題請看下面這封信。

克里克與鍾會計師事務所
華盛頓州西雅圖市石頭路 1040 號
郵遞區號：93108-2662

20—年 7 月 12 日
修・斐瑞先生
聯合醫療保健公司
華盛頓州西雅圖市東松街 400 號
郵遞區號：93129-2665

斐瑞先生，您好：

我們是一間中型的會計師事務所。我們的職員對目前的保險計畫不甚滿意，所以我們正在考慮其他選擇方案。我們目前合作的保險公司最近一方面提高保費，另一方面服務品質卻越來越差。付了更多錢卻得到更差的服務，我們自然感到不滿。因此，我們想進一步了解聯合醫療保健公司。能不能請您寄一份資料給我？若您能回答以下問題，我將感激不盡。第一，我們員工希望能自己選擇醫師，你們的方案允許此點嗎？第二，你們的醫師有週末和夜間門診嗎？我們的員工工作時程很忙，平常上班時間不一定方便去看診。

感謝您的協助。

敬祝 商祺

妃莉西雅・布拉迪許
人力資源經理

131. (A) 員工
    (B) 職位
    (C) 活動
    (D) 選擇

解析 (D) 這間公司不滿意目前的保險計畫，因此想換一個不同的選擇。選項(A)雖然在信中有提到，但這間公司並不是在找新員工。選項(B)和(C)都和會計師事務所的工作有關，但信中都沒有提到。

132. (A) 因此
    (B) 然而
    (C) 此外
    (D) 然而

解析 (A) therefore帶出了一個結果，表示想進一步了解聯合醫療保健公司是對當前保險計畫不滿的結果。選項(B)和(D)的意思和「但是」接近，用來帶出一個和前句矛盾的想法。選項(C)的意思是「此外」。

133. (A) 大多數的保險計畫會提供客戶各種選擇。
    (B) 若您能回答以下問題，我將感激不盡。
    (C) 我們想改變保險計畫有幾個原因。
    (D) 我已經大致說明了最重要的幾點。

解析 (B) 選項(B)的句子帶出了後面的問題，也就是寫信者要問保險公司的一些問題。選項(A)(C)(D)都和文意不符。

134. (A) 令人愉快的、享受的
    (B) 困難的
    (C) 方便的
    (D) 有趣的

解析 (C) 文中說「it is not easy」就是「it is not convenient」的意思，表示員工不方便在上班時間去看醫生。選項(A)和(D)一般不會用來描述看醫生這件事。選項(B)和正確答案恰好相反。

第 135–138 題請看下面這封電子郵件。

寄件者：賽門・嚴
收件者：明美・李
主旨：　週一的會議

親愛的明美：

因為我們的新加坡辦公室臨時有急事，我需要出差一趟。很遺憾無法參加週一早上的會議，尤其我迫不及待想看你在公司新金融中心方面的進度如何了，這是國家銀行的一個重要計畫。

我的同事修・哈里森會取代我去開會，他打算早上九點去工地找你。你跟我說過有點擔心這項計畫的預算，請和修討論此事。雖然我們不想在這棟大樓上額外花太多錢，但畢竟是我們公司總部，還是要氣派才行。你作為營建專案經理向來備受推崇，我確信你能妥善管理預算，同時為我們建造出一座出色的金融中心。

我一週後回來，在我回來之前，你可以用電子郵件與我聯繫。謝謝。

135. (A) 因此
　　　(B) 如果
　　　(C) 因為、由於
　　　(D) 藉由

解析 **(C)** as 的意思是「因為、由於」，在這裡引導一個原因子句。選項(A)用來引導結果子句。選項(B)用來引導條件子句。選項(D)是介系詞，不能用來引導子句。

136. (A) 陪同
　　　(B) 取代
　　　(C) 協助
　　　(D) 陪同

解析 **(B)** 賽門無法去開會，因此修會取代他去開會。選項(A)和(D)都是「陪同」的意思。選項(C)意指「協助」。

307

137. (A) 請務必準時到。
(B) 這個時間和地點對我們雙方都方便。
(C) 營建工程已經進行了好一段時間。
(D) 你跟我說過有點擔心這項計畫的預算。

解析 (D) 寫信者在空格後面接著說「Please talk with Hugh about this」（請和修討論此事），然後提到了錢的事。選項(D)是邏輯上唯一可以和修討論的主題，也是唯一提到金錢方面擔憂的句子。選項(A)(B)(C)都與文意不符。

138. (A) 懷疑的
(B) 確信的
(C) 疑惑的
(D) 擔心的

解析 (B) positive 的意思是「確信的、肯定的」。嚴先生非常肯定明美可以勝任這份工作，因為她的名聲很好。選項(A)(C)(D)都會讓句子變成相反的意義。

第139-142請看下面這則備忘錄。

備忘錄

寄件者：貝琳達‧倍爾比，公司總裁
收件者：公司副總裁
關於：　減少電費支出

下個月電力公司要調漲費率25％，所以我們必須設法減少用電。以下是一些建議，請把這個列表分發給你負責區域的部門。

減少電費支出的方法

1. 燈光：會議結束時，請將會議室的燈關掉。下班時，請將辦公室的燈關掉。
2. 電腦：一天工作結束時，請關閉電腦。
3. 影印：不要影印和傳真文件，大部分文件可以電子方式傳送。
4. 電風扇／電暖器：在辦公室使用電風扇或電暖器應非必要，大樓的溫度設定在多數人覺得舒適的度數。如果覺得辦公室太冷或太熱，請與維修人員聯絡。
5. 居家辦公選擇：允許員工一週在家工作一天或多天，很多方面都能省下費用，包括電費。對此選擇有興趣的員工，請找主管討論。

139. (A) 減少
    (B) 增加
    (C) 分配
    (D) 改善

解析 (B) 因為成本提高，所以總裁想要減少用電。選項(A)和(C)會讓句子意思和正確答案相反。選項(D)放在這個句子中語意不通。

140. (A)(B)(C)(D) 傳送

解析 (D) 由於句子的主詞不是動作執行者，必須使用被動語態。選項(A)(B)(C)都是主動語態。

141. (A) 大樓的溫度設定在多數人覺得舒適的度數。
    (B) 然而，如果想要的話，你可以從家裡帶一個小型電暖器或電風扇。
    (C) 這個地區的溫度會隨季節變化。
    (D) 電風扇和電暖器無法充分調節室內溫度。

解析 (A) 選項(A)進一步說明前一個句子的想法──為什麼不需要電風扇或電暖器。選項(B)(C)(D)都和文意不符。

142. (A)(B)(C)(D) 允許

解析 (B) Allowing是動名詞，整句Allowing employees to work at home one or more days a week作為句子的主詞。選項(A)(D)都是動詞的一種形式，不能放在句子的主詞位置。選項(C)為不定詞表目的，放入句中不符合語意邏輯。

第143–146題請看下面這則公告。

旭日製造公司的員工即將迎來新老闆。公司上週五宣布自九月起，總裁雪莉・奧坎波將接替路易・費里蘭擔任執行長一職。奧坎波女士將是公司有史以來首位女性執行長。旭日製造公司是國內最大的農業設備製造公司，這個行業傳統上一直由男性主導，使得奧坎波女士的任命格外具重大意義。費里蘭先生在本公司已經服務了二十五年，下個月奧坎波女士接替他的職位後，他將自旭日公司退休。

143. (A) 旭日製造公司的員工即將迎來新老闆。
    (B) 旭日製造公司的顧客給予產品高度評價。
    (C) 旭日製造公司在國內幾個地區都有分公司。
    (D) 旭日製造公司有幾個新的職缺。

解析 **(A)** 選項(A)是整段敘述的主旨，說明公司將有新的執行長，或者說老闆。選項(B)(C)(D)都與文意不符。

144. (A) 大的
     (B) 更大的
     (C) 更大的
     (D) 最大的

解析 **(D)** the largest是形容詞的最高級，用來比較這間公司和國內的其他公司。選項(A)是形容詞，但不是最高級。選項(B)和(C)都是比較級，但此處需要最高級。

145. (A) 最近的
     (B) 常見的
     (C) 有意義的、重要的
     (D) 可獲利的

解析 **(C)** significant的意思是「有意義的」或「重要的」。這個句子指出，在一個傳統上只有男性擔任過執行長職位的領域裡，出現了一位女性執行長的重要性。選項(A)(B)(D)都與文意不符。

146. (A)(B)(C)(D) 工作

解析 **(D)** has been working是現在完成進行式，描述一個從過去（二十五年前）開始並持續到現在的動作。選項(A)是現在式。選項(B)是過去簡單式。選項(C)是過去完成式。(B)和(C)描述的都是已經完成、結束的事。

Part 7：閱讀測驗

作答方式：你會看到單篇或多篇文章的題組，文章後面配有幾道題目，各含四個選項。選出最適當的答案回答問題，並將答案卡上對應的橢圓框塗滿。

第 147–148 題請看下面這則廣告。

資料輸入／職員

保險公司營運部尋找可靠、注重細節的員工。職責包含資料輸入、歸檔和文字處理。薪資優渥、福利佳，工作氣氛良好，有升遷空間。

---

147. 這份工作的其中一個職責是什麼？
　　(A) 接電話
　　(B) 資料輸入
　　(C) 賣保險
　　(D) 負責一個部門的營運

解析 (B) 廣告中具體提到了資料輸入這個職責。選項(A)(C)(D)都沒有被提及。

148. 這個職位的其中一個福利是什麼？
　　(A) 之後會給你個人專用辦公室。
　　(B) 你可以努力爭取升遷。
　　(C) 家屬亦享有福利。
　　(D) 你可以賺取佣金。

解析 (B) 廣告中的 Room to advance 是「有升遷機會」的意思。選項(A)(C)(D)都是福利的一種，但不是這個職位會有的福利。

第 149-150 題請看下面這則備忘錄。

備忘錄

收件人：全體員工
發布人：朵內塔‧穆希洛　安全協調員
日　期：20- 年 6 月 5 日
主　旨：防火門

員工請注意，指定為防火門的門必須隨時保持關閉。防火門的目的是一旦建築物發生火災，可將煙霧阻擋於工作區域之外。即使天氣炎熱，公司空調也尚未維修完成，仍嚴禁開啟防火門。

---

149. 這則備忘錄的目的是什麼？
　　(A) 說明防火門的功能
　　(B) 說明如何保持防火門關閉
　　(C) 說明防火門應保持關閉
　　(D) 說明大樓為何比平常熱

解析 (C) 備忘錄的開頭和結尾都說防火門應保持關閉，不能開著。其他內容則為這個主旨提供了支持論點，說明為何要這樣做。選項(A)和(D)是備忘錄中的細節而不是主旨。選項(B)則未被提及。

150. 員工為何有可能把門開著？
　　(A) 為了走到更高的樓層
　　(B) 為了欣賞風景
　　(C) 為了在辦公室之間移動
　　(D) 為了讓涼風進來

解析 (D) 文中提到若天氣炎熱，空調又沒修好，員工很可能會打開防火門讓涼風進來。選項(A)(B)(C)都是打開門的作用，但和消防安全無關。

第 151–152 題請看下面這段簡訊對話串。

麥拉・李	4:10
我會晚點到，跟你說一下。	
松尾博	4:11
你的班機誤點了嗎？	
麥拉・李	4:13
沒有，事實上還早到了。我也馬上叫了計程車，但我把行李箱忘在提領區了。	
松尾博	4:14
什麼？哪裡？	
麥拉・李	4:16
在機場。我在前往辦公室的半路上才發現，只好請計程車司機掉頭。	
松尾博	4:17
哇，你一定累了。	
麥拉・李	4:18
這週過得很漫長。希望他們沒有因為我而把員工會議延後。你可以跟老闆說我會晚到嗎？不用告訴他原因。	
松尾博	4:20
沒問題，一會見。	
麥拉・李	4:21
謝了，我大概三十分鐘左右會到。	

151. 李小姐出了什麼問題？
 (A) 她遺失了行李箱。
 (B) 她錯過了她的班機。
 (C) 她找不到計程車。
 (D) 她忘了去拿行李。

解析 (D) 李小姐寫說「I left my suitcase behind at the baggage claim」，表示把行李箱忘在提領區了。選項(A)不正確，她知道行李箱在提領區，沒有遺失。選項(B)不正確，她有坐上飛機，而且班機還早到了。選項(C)不正確，她說她馬上就叫到計程車了。

313

152. 在4:20時，松尾先生說「Sure thing」是什麼意思？
    (A) 他會告訴李小姐的老闆。
    (B) 他知道李小姐很快就會到。
    (C) 他瞭解李小姐為何遲到。
    (D) 他很確定李小姐的老闆不會介意延後會議。

解析 (A)「Sure thing」的意思是李小姐可以信賴松尾先生，因松尾先生會按照她的交代去做，告訴她的老闆她會晚到。選項(B)(C)(D)都不是這個片語在此處的意思。

第153–154題請看下面這則公告。

遺產拍賣會

保羅．迪亞加之遺產拍賣會將於下列時間舉行：
10月3日星期六，上午11點
（預展自上午10點開始）
地點：北樹籬巷5667號

拍賣物品：
* 2004年賓士
* 瓷器和水晶
* 東方風格地毯
* 珠寶
* 郵票收藏

如有疑問，請於中午12點至下午5點間撥打778-0099聯繫遺產規劃師。

---

153. 下列哪一項物品會被拍賣？
    (A) 中國古董
    (B) 珍稀書本
    (C) 手鍊
    (D) 全鋪式地毯

解析 (C) 拍賣物品中有一樣是珠寶，當中應會有手鍊。選項(A)把China（瓷器）誤解成Chinese antiques（中國古董）。選項(B)在公告中並未提及，但會使人覺得stamp和rare books有關。選項(D)把wall-to-wall carpeting和oriental rugs互相混淆了。

154. 什麼時候可以開始參觀拍賣物品？
    (A) 10月3日上午11點
    (B) 打778-0099電話預約時間
    (C) 每天中午12點至下午5點
    (D) 10月3日上午10點

解析 (D) 預展從10月3日星期六的上午10點開始。選項(A)是拍賣會開始的時間。選項(B)未被提及。選項(C)是可以打電話聯絡遺產規劃師詢問的時間。

第155–157題請看下面這張圓餅圖。

第一印象美術館
四月財務檢視

總支出：$75,275
總收入：$228,566

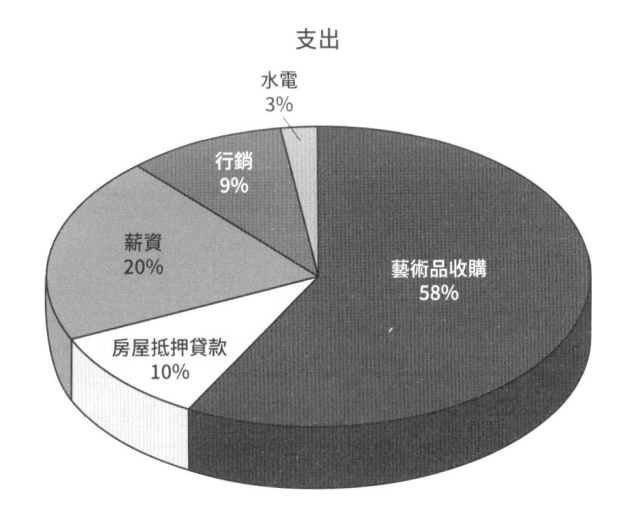

支出

- 水電 3%
- 行銷 9%
- 薪資 20%
- 房屋抵押貸款 10%
- 藝術品收購 58%

155. 這張圖表是何時製作的？
    (A) 四月前
    (B) 四月後
    (C) 四月初
    (D) 四月末

解析 (B) 這張圖表是在檢視四月份的支出，必須過了四月才有可能製作。選項(A)(C)(D)都不可能。

156. 關於這座美術館，下列敘述何者正確？
    (A) 收入約為支出的三倍。
    (B) 支出高於收入。
    (C) 支出等於收入。
    (D) 收入是支出的一半。

解析 (A) 美術館的總收入是＄228,566，總支出是＄75,275，收入是高於支出的，因此選項(B)(C)(D)都不正確。

157. 美術館支出最高的項目是什麼？
    (A) 新增收藏品庫存
    (B) 支付給員工的費用
    (C) 支付的廣告費用
    (D) 電費和水費的成本

解析 (A) 四月份有58％的支出用於art acquisitions，這些是美術館收購並用於販售的藝術品，因此屬於庫存（inventory）。選項(B)指的是薪資（salaries），占總支出的20％。選項(C)指的是行銷（marketing），占總支出的9％。選項(D)即水電費（utilities），占總支出的3％。

第158-160題請看下面這封電子郵件。

寄件者：人力資源部
收件者：調派工作人員
主旨：　調派資訊
日期：　4月10日

如您所知，您是即將調到新製造廠的六十名技術人員和管理人員之一。這是我們首座位於海外的製造廠，我們希望您和您的家人在過渡時期都能順利。因此，我們將舉辦一系列研討會，幫助您適應海外和小鎮生活。研討會將討論地方風俗、飲食、語言以及跨文化交流等議題。研討會並不強制參加，但強烈建議盡可能多參加幾場。我附上了研討會的日程表，請分享給您的家人，並記在您的行事曆上。研討會適合年滿十四歲者參加。如有任何疑問或疑慮，請聯繫人力資源辦公室。

雅曼達・瓊斯

人力資源專員

158. 新的製造廠位在哪裡？
(A) 靠近山區
(B) 別的國家
(C) 大城市裡
(D) 沿海地區

解析 (B) 新的製造廠位於海外（overseas），也就是在別的國家。選項(A)沒有被提及。選項(C)不正確，信中提到工廠位於小鎮（small town）。選項(D)把overseas和coast互相混淆了。

159. 這封電子郵件的目的是什麼？
(A) 提供一系列研討會的資訊
(B) 幫助員工規劃搬遷至新廠事宜
(C) 宣布一座新製造廠的啟用
(D) 說明跨文化理解的重要性

解析 (A) 這封電子郵件旨在說明研討會主題和舉辦的原因。選項(B)是研討會的目的而不是郵件的目的。選項(C)不正確，我們可推斷這件事情已經發生了。選項(D)是研討會的內容之一。

160. 關於研討會有何說明？
(A) 新進員工必須參加。
(B) 對象是員工和員工的家人。
(C) 將於新的製造廠中舉行。
(D) 將會即刻展開。

解析 (B) 研討會旨在協助員工和員工的家人適應新環境。選項(A)不正確，信中表示研討會不是強制參加。選項(C)和(D)不正確，信中沒有提到研討會的時間和地點。

第 161–163 題請看下面這則公告。

瓦爾多爾餐飲用品公司

瓦爾多爾公司很高興宣布將收購美食匯公司，該公司專營特色食品、炊具和廚房用品。–[1]– 美食匯公司的計畫包含在歐洲各地開設五間分店。原有的十六間店有十間已在去年進行翻修，其餘六間也有類似計畫正在進行。–[2]– 美食匯公司也將開設烹飪學校，拓展業務版圖。這些學校將藉助當前注重養生的潮流，以料理美味與營養兼備的美食為主，–[3]– 地方特色菜也將包含在內，並邀請歐洲各地的客座主廚擔任顧問。–[4]–

---

161. 瓦爾多爾公司對於美食匯公司的六間店面有何種計畫？
    (A) 翻修它們
    (B) 收購它們
    (C) 販售它們
    (D) 搬遷它們

解析 (A) 文中指出十間店已在去年進行翻修，其餘六間店也有類似計畫正在進行中。選項(B)是已經完成的事。選項(C)和(D)均未提及。

162. 烹飪課程將以什麼為主？
    (A) 一個地區的烹飪方式
    (B) 專門炊具的使用
    (C) 世界各地的食物
    (D) 健康的食物

解析 (D) 文中指出烹飪課程將以美味與營養兼備的食物為主。選項(A)不正確，來自歐洲不同地區的廚師都會參與課程。選項(B)被該公司所販售的其中一種商品給混淆了。選項(C)不正確，文中只有提到歐洲。

163. 下面這個句子最適合放入文中 [1] [2] [3] [4] 哪一個位置？
    「瓦爾多爾公司把目標放在拓展這個已經很受歡迎品牌的業務和服務項目。」
    (A) [1]
    (B) [2]
    (C) [3]
    (D) [4]

解析 (A) 編號[1]的位置後面提供了進一步的訊息，描述這間公司將如何拓展這個品牌。選項(B)(C)(D)的位置放入後語意都不連貫。

第 164–167 題請看下面這段網路聊天室的討論。

馬可・席爾瓦 [11:15]
我剛接到出貨部的來電，他們收到一個客戶的退貨，是日昇公司。

珍・金 [11:16]
什麼？怎麼會這樣？

莎賓・柯爾 [11:17]
日昇公司早上寄了一封電子郵件給我，說我們的出貨品項錯誤，我們出了五匹深藍色的棉布給他們。

馬可・席爾瓦 [11:20]
好，我查過檔案了，那不是他們訂的貨。

珍・金 [11:22]
那是他們平常的訂貨。

馬可・席爾瓦 [11:23]
對，但他們正在做新的夏裝系列，想要用比較淺的顏色。

莎賓・柯爾 [11:25]
我要怎麼跟他們說啊？

珍・金 [11:27]
妳只能道歉了，然後提供他們這單和下次訂單免運。

莎賓・柯爾 [11:30]
應該要有人聯絡一下出貨部，搞清楚發生了什麼事。我們不能再讓這種情況發生了。

馬可・席爾瓦 [11:31]
我來聯絡。

珍・金 [11:32]
太好了，結果怎麼樣再告訴我們。

164. 聊天者最有可能服務於哪一類型的公司？
    (A) 貨運
    (B) 服飾零售
    (C) 時裝設計
    (D) 布料製造

解析 **(D)** 他們公司在賣棉布，所以是布料製造商。選項(A)不是正確答案，貨運只是該公司的一個部門，不是公司的主要業務。選項(B)和(C)是客戶的業務範圍，他們的客戶可能是服飾零售商或服裝設計師。

165. 關於客戶訂的貨品有何說明？
    (A) 是前幾週訂的。
    (B) 貨量比前一次的訂單大。
    (C) 和客戶平常的訂單不同。
    (D) 客戶在最後一刻改單。

解析 **(C)** 客戶平常都是訂深藍色的棉布，但這次訂的是較淺的顏色。選項(A)(B)(D)均未提及。

166. 貨物出了什麼問題？
    (A) 太晚出貨。
    (B) 到貨時間太久。
    (C) 被送到錯誤的地址。
    (D) 不是客戶所訂的東西。

解析 **(D)** 柯爾女士說貨物因「出貨品項錯誤」（shipped them the wrong items）而被退了。選項(A)(B)(C)也是貨物可能出的問題，但對話中並未提及。

167. 在11:31時，席爾瓦先生說「I'm on it」是什麼意思？
    (A) 他會讓客戶知道發生了什麼事。
    (B) 他會和出貨部門談話。
    (C) 他是出貨部門的員工。
    (D) 他很擅長解決問題。

解析 **(B)** 柯爾女士說應該要有人找出貨部的員工談話，了解到底發生了什麼事。而席爾瓦先生回覆「I'm on it」，意思是他準備要做柯爾女士建議的事。選項(A)(C)(D)都不是這句話在這裡的意思。

第168-171題請看下面這封信。

商業協會
未來商業領袖教育基金
威廉斯頓第1205號郵政信箱

20—年7月8日
葛雷格里・哈里森先生
瑞文戴爾北主街78號

哈里森先生,您好:

如您所知,透過我們的未來商業領袖教育基金,商業協會為社區內年輕有志的專業人士提供支持已有二十五年以上的時間。除了獎學金計畫外,我們還舉辦各式各樣的工作坊,協助年輕的商業專業人士取得職業發展道路所需的技能和經驗。此外,我們亦藉由獎勵計畫肯定業界的年輕專業人才。今年在我們5月1日舉行的年度盛宴上,十位來自本市的專業青年獲頒500到2000美元不等的獎項,以表彰他們的職業成就。

作為商業協會的長期會員,您一直慷慨支持未來商業領袖教育基金。我們懇請您再次透過現金捐款,承諾支持我們的工作。我們今年的目標是向會員籌募25,000美元。您與其他會員的慷慨解囊,將使我們培育明日商業領袖的重要工作能持續進行。

請將附件表格要求的資料填寫完畢,連同您的支票寄回我們辦公室。我們希望能在下個月1號之前收到捐款。再次感謝您慷慨的支持。

謹祝 安康

伊莉莎白・拉森
伊莉莎白・拉森

---

168. 這封信的目的是什麼?
    (A) 描述一個獎學金計畫
    (B) 為一筆捐款表達感謝
    (C) 宣布一項新計畫
    (D) 請求捐款

解析 (D) 信中指出收件人過去一直是該基金的支持者,請求他持續支持,並指出目標募款金額為25,000美元,所以是為了請求捐款而來信。選項(A)是該基金募款的目的。選項(B)和請求捐款的主題有關。選項(C)不正確,信中提到的計畫都不是新的。

169. 關於哈里森先生，信中有何說明？
    (A) 他過去曾捐款給教育基金。
    (B) 他是商業協會的新會員。
    (C) 他舉辦商業培訓工作坊。
    (D) 他是年輕的商務專業人士。

解析 **(A)** 信中提到「As a long-time member of the Business Association, you have been a generous supporter of the Future Business Leaders Education Fund.」，表示收件人（哈里森先生）是商業協會的長期會員，並且一直慷慨支持教育基金，可見他過去曾經捐款過。選項(B)不正確，哈里森先生是長期會員。選項(C)提到工作坊，但信中沒有指出哈里森先生曾舉辦工作坊。選項(D)不正確，哈里森先生被要求支持年輕專業人士，不太可能他自己也是其中一員。除此之外，他加入協會已有很長一段時間，暗示了他可能是年長、經驗豐富的專業人士。

170. 5月1日發生了什麼事？
    (A) 舉辦了一個工作坊。
    (B) 有一個頒獎晚宴。
    (C) 發放了一些獎學金。
    (D) 該基金收到了新捐款。

解析 **(B)** 信中指出十位專業青年在5月1日的年度盛宴上領獎。選項(A)(C)(D)是信中提到的其他細節，但都不是發生在5月1日。

171. 這封信內含什麼附件？
    (A) 一份計畫說明書
    (B) 一份日程表
    (C) 一張表格
    (D) 一張支票

解析 **(C)** 信中要求收信人填妥隨附表格（complete the information requested on the enclosed sheet）。選項(A)和(B)與信中提到的其他細節有關。選項(D)是必須連同表格一起寄回的東西。

第 172–175 題請看下面這篇文章。

如果你想在職業生涯中有所發展，做決定就必須謹慎，尤其是關於工作機會的決定。–[1]– 評估每個工作機會時，務必衡量它們對你職業發展的整體價值。–[2]– 譬如，一份工作也許各方面都很適合你，但你可能必須為了這份工作搬到新的地區。一份工作可以讓你累積所需的經驗，但你可能必須加班甚至接受減薪。

–[3]– 同意接受一份不在你職業規畫中的工作，通常會是一個錯誤。這樣的決定無法為你帶來想要的訓練和經驗。此外，你會因為沒有努力朝自己的目標前進而感到沮喪。你的同事也會連帶受到影響，覺得你沒有把自己當作團隊的一分子。另一方面，如果你接受一份薪水和工作地點不完全如你意、但能讓你朝職業目標更靠近一步的職位，你會感到滿足。–[4]– 研究一再顯示比起薪水或其他因素，工作滿足感更能提升工作表現。

172. 這篇文章是關於哪方面的建議？
    (A) 選擇工作
    (B) 聘僱員工
    (C) 接受職業訓練
    (D) 填寫求職申請表

解析 (A) 文章的第一句已經點題：「. . . you will have to make some careful decisions, especially regarding job offers」，可知文章在講如何決定接受哪一份工作。選項(B)(C)(D)都是工作或職業的相關主題，但不是本篇文章的主旨。

173. 第二段第五行的「position」這個字，和下列何者意義最接近？
    (A) 看法
    (B) 位置
    (C) 提議
    (D) 工作

解析 (D) 這句的 take a position 意思就等於 accept a job。

174. 根據這篇文章的說法，哪一種員工的工作表現最佳？
    (A) 受過正確訓練的員工
    (B) 團隊合作的員工
    (C) 樂在工作的員工
    (D) 薪水最高的員工

解析 (C) 文章最後一句指出比起薪水或其他因素，工作滿足感更能提升工作表現。選項(A)(B)(D)是文章提到的其他細節，但不會帶來最好的工作表現。

175. 下面這個句子最適合放入文中 [1][2][3][4] 哪一個位置？

「一開始你可能必須做出犧牲。」

(A) [1]
(B) [2]
(C) [3]
(D) [4]

解析 (B) 編號 [2] 後面的句子提供做出犧牲的具體例子。選項 (A)(C)(D) 都不適合插入這個句子。

第 176–180 題請看下面的議程表和電子郵件。

地平線辦公用品公司
行銷委員會議
20―年 6 月 15 日星期四，上午 9：30–11：30
地點：第二會議室

議程

1. 現行策略檢視　　　班・阮
2. 新策略之目標　　　朴寶
3. 焦點小組　　　　　馬提・泰勒
4. 即將展開的計畫　　芭芭拉・史賓塞
5. 年度計畫　　　　　麗塔・帕爾瑪

收件者：馬克斯・寇勒
寄件者：朴寶
主旨：　委員會議

今天的會議發生了嚴重問題。我們準時開始，班卻不在現場，我們只好從第二個議程項目開始討論。然後，我們已經開始三十分鐘了，班才姍姍來遲並開始報告。馬提則根本沒來，我後來才知道他請病假，但無論如何，他負責的主題從沒討論到。芭芭拉試著解釋她的主題，但我們聽得一頭霧水。她已經盡力了，但我們真的需要先聽馬提的報告，再聽她的報告才能清楚瞭解。對於下一步該做什麼，我們也無法達成共識，只好在芭芭拉講完後提早結束會議。你這次出差何時回來？要是你在，就不會發生這些事情了。

176. 6月15日的會議主題是什麼？
    (A) 行銷
    (B) 差旅
    (C) 工作行程
    (D) 辦公用品訂購

解析 (A) 議程的標題指出會議主題是行銷。選項(B)被馬克斯出差給混淆。選項(C)把會議行程（meeting schedule）混淆成工作行程。選項(D)被公司名稱給誤導。

177. 哪一個主題最先被討論？
    (A) 現行策略檢視
    (B) 新策略之目標
    (C) 焦點小組
    (D) 即將展開的計畫

解析 (B) 由於負責第一個項目的報告者沒有準時出現，最先討論的是第二個項目。選項(A)是原定第一個討論的項目。選項(C)和(D)都是排在後面的項目。

178. 班在幾點的時候開始報告？
    (A) 9：00
    (B) 9：30
    (C) 10：00
    (D) 11：30

解析 (C) 會議九點半開始，班在會議開始三十分鐘後才到，所以是十點開始報告。選項(A)是會議開始前三十分鐘。選項(B)是會議開始時間。選項(D)是會議原定結束時間。

179. 誰最後一個報告？
    (A) 麗塔・帕爾瑪
    (B) 芭芭拉・史賓塞
    (C) 馬提・泰勒
    (D) 朴寶

解析 (B) 會議在芭芭拉報告完就提早結束。選項(A)是原定最後一個報告的人。選項(C)和(D)是排在前面報告的人。

325

180. 馬克斯為何缺席會議？
    (A) 他請病假。
    (B) 他沒被邀請。
    (C) 他無法準時到達。
    (D) 他出差去了。

解析 **(D)** 電子郵件中提到馬克斯去出差了。選項(A)是馬提缺席會議的原因。選項(B)也有可能，但並未提及。選項(C)是指班，不是麥克斯。

第181–185題請看下面這份通知和電子郵件。

交通票證資訊
史普林菲爾德市

現在使用史普林菲爾德市交通運輸系統（CSPTS）將更容易也更便宜，請選擇最符合個人需求的交通票證。

C-PASSES
C-pass 交通卡可於週一至週五（假日除外）白天和晚上任何時間無限次數搭乘。

地鐵 C-PASS	公車 C-PASS	地鐵／公車 C-PASS
兩週：$60	兩週：$45	兩週：$75
六個月：$650	六個月：$500	六個月：$850

A-PASSES
A-PASS 交通卡可於全年任何一天，一週七天，一天二十四小時使用。

地鐵 A-PASS	公車 A-PASS	地鐵／公車 A-PASS
兩週：$100	兩週：$75	兩週：$125
六個月：$950	六個月：$700	六個月：$1,050

交通卡於史普林菲爾德市交通運輸系統各地鐵站均有販售，亦可至史普林菲爾德市交通運輸系統的市區辦公室、市內指定銀行或 www.cspts.go 網站購買。

寄件者：珍妮特・瓊斯
收件者：全體職員
主旨：　交通票證
日期：　11月9日

為了替減少本地道路壅塞盡一份力，我們為史密斯公司全體職員提供優惠價之史普林菲爾德市交通運輸系統交通票證，可用於史普林菲爾德市交通運輸系統所有路線之公車和／或地鐵搭乘。如欲申請優惠價之票證，請到我的辦公室領取交通票證申請表，填寫完畢並經部門主管核准後交回給我。你有兩週和六個月的交通卡可選。然而請記住，每次需要更換新卡時，都要重新提交表格。為了進一步鼓勵目前開車上班的員工改乘大眾交通運輸工具，我們將從下個月1日起，將公司停車場的停車費調高為每日十五美元。

若有任何問題，敬請告知。

181. 哪一種交通卡可用於週末和假日？
　　(A) 任何一種C-PASS交通卡
　　(B) 任何一種A-PASS交通卡
　　(C) 只有地鐵交通卡
　　(D) 只有地鐵／公車交通卡

解析 (B) 通知裡提到A-PASS可用於全年任何一天，一週七天，一天二十四小時。選項(A)不正確，C-PASS只適用於週一到週五，且假日除外。選項(C)和(D)不正確，所有的A-PASS交通卡都能在週末和假日使用。

182. 通知單第六行的「good」這個字，與下列何者意義最接近？
　　(A) 好的
　　(B) 新鮮的
　　(C) 有效的
　　(D) 正確的

解析 (C) 這個句子的意思是說，交通卡是有效的，即能按照描述的方式使用。選項(A)(B)(D)是good的其他意義，但在這裡都不適用。

183. 誰可以取得優惠的交通票證？
    (A) 史普林菲爾德市交通運輸系統的員工
    (B) 史普林菲爾德市的市民
    (C) 任何想要的人
    (D) 史密斯公司的員工

解析 (D) 電子郵件中說明了史密斯公司的員工可以優惠價（reduced price）購買票證。選項(A)(B)(C)都是可以取得票證的人，但信中沒有提到他們可享優惠。

184. 哪裡可以購買優惠的交通票證？
    (A) 網路上
    (B) 部分銀行
    (C) 史普林菲爾德市交通運輸系統辦公室
    (D) 瓊斯女士的辦公室

解析 (D) 電子郵件的寄件者瓊斯女士說她的辦公室有提供交通票證申請表，填妥後交給她，即可以優惠價購買交通票證。選項(A)(B)(C)都沒有被提到有優惠價。

185. 史密斯公司停車場為何調高停車費？
    (A) 為了鼓勵員工使用大眾交通工具
    (B) 為了填補增加的維修成本
    (C) 為了資助停車場擴建工程
    (D) 為了支付優惠的交通票證

解析 (A) 電子郵件中有說明，提供優惠票證的目的是鼓勵員工使用大眾交通工具，而停車費的調漲則是「進一步的鼓勵」（as an added incentive）。選項(B)(C)(D)都有可能，但未被提及。

第 186–190 題請看下面的通知和兩封電子郵件。

商業記者大會
住宿

會議中心周邊住宿：
瀑布飯店──北主街 105 號（www.cascadeho.com）
威洛梅爾酒店──繁花大道 12 號（www.willowmereinn.com）
兩間飯店都在會議中心的步行距離內。

更加經濟實惠的住宿選擇：
皇家飯店──公園大道 234 號（www.parkviewho.com）
搭乘地鐵綠線到公園大道站後，往東走一個街區即可到達。

三間飯店都為大會參加者提供優惠價格，須於 8 月 15 日前訂房才能享有優惠。

寄件者：依芳・吳
收件者：皇家飯店
主旨：　客房預訂
日期：　8 月 1 日

我會參加下個月的商業記者大會，想在你們飯店訂一間單人房，時間是 9 月 15 至 18 日。如果可以，我想要高樓層的大床房。另外想請問，你們有游泳池和健身房嗎？我在你們網站上找不到相關資訊。最後，你們飯店裡或飯店附近有餐廳嗎？

感謝你的協助。

寄件者：皇家飯店
收件者：依芳‧吳
主旨：　關於房間預訂
日期：　8月2日

吳小姐，您好：

我們很樂意在您參加商業記者大會期間為您提供住宿服務。您所要求的房型有空房，您的優惠價格是每晚100美元。然而，在您住宿的第一晚，由於當晚大床房已滿，我們必須為您安排一間特大床房，需要加收25美元。希望這能符合您的需求。關於您的問題，我們的游泳池目前正關閉進行整修，預計於明年1月1日前重新開放。飯店設有一間全包式服務餐廳，住客可在那裡享用免費早餐。午晚餐亦有供應，為了方便可記在您房間的帳上。如果您要繼續訂房，請將您的信用卡資訊傳送給我。感謝您選擇皇家飯店。

鮑伯‧希曼尼斯
訂房經理

186. 關於皇家飯店有何說明？
    (A) 是離會議中心最近的飯店。
    (B) 比其他提及的飯店便宜。
    (C) 8月15日後沒有空房。
    (D) 很受商務旅客歡迎。

解析 (B) 皇家飯店被描述為更加經濟實惠的選擇（a more economical option）。選項(A)不正確，它是唯一一間不在會議中心步行距離內的飯店。選項(C)是享有住房優惠的最後一天。選項(D)並未被提及。

187. 吳小姐要求什麼樣的房間？
    (A) 位於地面樓的房間
    (B) 有兩張床的房間
    (C) 給一個人住的房間
    (D) 靠近游泳池的房間

解析 (C) 吳小姐要求要一間單人房（single room）。選項(A)不正確，她要求高樓層的房間。選項(B)不正確，她要的是一張大床。選項(D)重複使用了郵件中的pool這個字，但吳小姐只問了飯店是否有游泳池，沒有要求房間要靠近游泳池。

188. 吳小姐為何能以優惠價格訂房？
(A) 她將會參加大會。
(B) 她會住好幾晚。
(C) 她是飯店的前員工。
(D) 她在第一晚之後必須換房。

解析 (A) 通知單上指出大會的參加者住飯店可享優惠價（reduced rate）。選項(B)和(C)也是可能的原因，但並未被提及。選項(D)是吳小姐必須接受的事，但她沒有因此獲得折扣，事實上還被加收了費用。

189. 額外加收的二十五美元是什麼費用？
(A) 前往會議中心的交通費
(B) 訂房取消的費用
(C) 更大床型的房間費用
(D) 使用飯店游泳池的費用

解析 (C) 訂房經理在信中寫說，其中一晚他會替吳小姐安排一間特大床房，而不是吳小姐原本要求的大床房，而這樣要多收二十五美元。選項(A)和(B)均未提及。選項(D)不可能，因為飯店的游泳池正在整修關閉當中。

190. 關於早餐有何說明？
(A) 會議中心有提供早餐。
(B) 飯店餐廳全天候供應早餐。
(C) 透過客房服務點餐需加收費用。
(D) 房價已含早餐。

解析 (D) 訂房經理提到了飯店附設餐廳，然後說「our guests are entitled to a free breakfast there」，表示住客享用早餐是免費的。選項(A)(B)(C)都有可能，但都未被提及。

第 191–195 題請看下面的文章、廣告和評論。

節慶咖啡館重新開幕

節慶咖啡館完成整修工程將規模擴大為原來的兩倍後，已於近日重新開幕。咖啡館位於市中心商業區的中心地帶，以其自製的冰淇淋聞名。天氣一熱，人群沿著整個街區大排長龍的景象，顧客們早就習以為常，大家都在排隊購買這個美味冰品。這間咖啡館也以自製的烘焙食品和創意三明治而聞名。「現在我們可以一次招待更多顧客了。」老闆柏莎・馬奎爾說。「天氣溫暖的時候，我們也會開放戶外座位區。」她補充說道。馬奎爾女士向忠實顧客保證，他們過去最愛的品項都還在菜單上。「我們期待在新的空間看到老熟客和新客人。」她說道。

節慶咖啡館
很高興宣布
盛大重新開幕
歡迎一起來慶祝！
4月10日下午3點到晚上8點
冰淇淋免費試吃！
現場音樂演奏！玩遊戲，拿獎品！
麵包和三明治櫃檯將會開放。
出示以下優惠券
免費招待飲料一杯！

節慶咖啡館 憑此券兌換 一杯咖啡 不限容量 使用期限：4月30日	節慶咖啡館 憑此券兌換 一杯汽水 不限容量 使用期限：4月30日

★★★★★
席妮・賽爾德曼
4月12日

新的節慶咖啡館比以前還要棒。我和家人參加了盛大重新開幕活動,真的非常好玩。孩子們玩遊戲玩得很開心,當然,他們也很喜歡免費冰淇淋。新的空間很棒,不過我覺得顏色有點暗沉,但是相當舒適,座位也很多。三明治還是一樣讚,我們吃的蛋糕很美味,價格又親民。我很驚訝竟然沒有漲價。如果你是節慶咖啡館的老粉絲,新的空間一定能讓你一如既往地享受。

191. 節慶咖啡館發生了什麼事?
(A) 菜單換了。
(B) 空間擴大了。
(C) 老顧客流失了。
(D) 新的分店開幕了。

解析 (B) 文章提到咖啡館進行了整修,規模擴大為原來的兩倍(doubled its size)。選項(A)不正確,文章引用了咖啡館老闆的話,提到「their old favorites are still on the menu」(他們最愛的品項都還在菜單上),所以代表沒換菜單。選項(C)重複使用了文章中的customers這個字,但文中沒有提到有顧客流失。選項(D)完全未被提及。

192. 關於節慶咖啡館,文中有何暗示?
(A) 它很受歡迎。
(B) 它是新開的店。
(C) 它只賣甜點。
(D) 有好幾家分店。

解析 (A) 文章中指出顧客大排長龍只為了買冰淇淋,咖啡館還擴店以便容納更多客人,暗示了這是個很受歡迎的地方。選項(B)不正確,咖啡館被整修過,不是新開的。選項(C)不正確,除了賣冰淇淋和烘焙食品,也有賣三明治。選項(D)沒有被提及。

193. 顧客要如何獲得免費飲料？
　　　(A) 贏得獎品
　　　(B) 去參加盛大重新開幕活動
　　　(C) 花錢試吃冰淇淋
　　　(D) 在四月底前使用優惠券

解析 **(D)** 廣告傳單上面附了一杯免費咖啡和一杯免費汽水的優惠券，使用期限到 4 月 30 日。選項 (A) 是被廣告提到重新開幕活動中可以玩遊戲拿獎品給混淆。選項 (B) 和 (C) 整個搞混資訊了，參加開幕活動可以免費試吃冰淇淋，但不能免費喝飲料（要有優惠券）。

194. 賽爾德曼女士是什麼時候去節慶咖啡館的？
　　　(A) 4 月 10 日
　　　(B) 4 月 12 日
　　　(C) 昨天晚上
　　　(D) 上個星期

解析 **(A)** 賽爾德曼女士寫說她去參加了盛大重新開幕活動，而廣告上寫開幕日期是 4 月 10 日。選項 (B) 是賽爾德曼女士寫評論的日期。選項 (C) 和 (D) 都沒有被提及。

195. 賽爾德曼女士覺得節慶咖啡館如何？
　　　(A) 椅子不夠。
　　　(B) 價格太高。
　　　(C) 食物很好吃。
　　　(D) 裝潢有改善。

解析 **(C)** 賽爾德曼女士寫說「The sandwiches are still fantastic, and the cake we tried was delicious and affordable」，表示她覺得咖啡館的東西很好吃。選項 (A) 不正確，她說座位很充足。選項 (B) 不正確，她說價格很親民（affordable），她還很驚訝竟然沒漲價。選項 (D) 不正確，她並沒有比較整修前和整修後的裝潢，只提到店內顏色有點暗沉。

第 196–200 題請看下面的廣告和兩封信。

威克弗德房地產公司
待售
兩個零售空間

1. 位於市中心購物區中心地帶，坐落主街，地理位置優越。面街大型展示窗，近期完成翻修。近公車和地鐵路線。面積 1,500 平方英尺。

2. 華倫大道。位於格林伍德學校社區，位置理想。近地鐵路線。顧客可現場停車。

欲取得進一步資訊請洽威克弗德房地產公司。

印刷社

克拉克女士，您好：

我是你們銀行客戶已經超過十年。我是小企業老闆，一直租用空間作為營運之用。現在我的公司準備擴大營運，我正在考慮買一棟小型建築。

我對兩棟建築有興趣，我比較中意在主街上的，需要二十萬美元的貸款，但我不確定我是否有資格申請如此大額的一筆貸款。還有另外一棟符合我的需求，大小剛好，不過地點沒那麼理想。如果買那一棟，我只需要貸款十三萬。

我的信用紀錄良好，目前只有背負兩筆債務——車貸五千，房貸十二萬。我希望能貸到三十年期、利率百分之五的貸款。

我希望能盡快與你見面討論此事。不知道 4 月 21 日星期二你方不方便？如果不方便，那週其他任一天我都可以。期待你的回覆。

敬祝 順心

傑瑞邁亞・赫南德茲
傑瑞邁亞・赫南德茲

> 聯邦銀行
> 德州聖安東尼奧中門街8244號
> 郵遞區號：78217-0099

20—年4月10日

傑瑞邁亞・赫南德茲
印刷社
德州聖安東尼奧橡實公園大道111號
郵遞區號：78216-7423

赫南德茲先生，您好：

感謝您有興趣向聯邦銀行申請貸款。我們感謝您的業務支持。

我們有可能提供您足夠金額購買較低價的那棟建築。由於您已經負債超過十萬美元，我們無法提供您更大額度的貸款。我們可依您的希望利率和期限提供貸款。

我非常樂意與您見面討論此事。您提的日期我無法抽出時間，我們隔天見面可以嗎？再請告訴我您的想法。

謹祝 安好

安娜麗絲・克拉克
安娜麗絲・克拉克

196. 關於華倫大街的房產有何說明？
    (A) 設有停車場。
    (B) 靠近市中心。
    (C) 靠近公車站。
    (D) 非常小。

解析 (A) 房地產廣告中說「Customer parking on site」，表示現場有地方可以停車。選項(B)和位於市中心的主街房產互相混淆了。選項(C)描述的是位於主街的房產。選項(D)不正確，廣告中沒有提到這座房產的面積。

197. 赫南德茲先生最有可能是哪一種企業的老闆？
    (A) 房地產公司
    (B) 餐廳
    (C) 商店
    (D) 學校

解析 (C) 赫南德茲先生看的房地產在廣告中被描述為零售空間（retail space），可見他經營的是商店。選項(A)是刊登廣告的公司。選項(B)未被提及。選項(D)是社區名稱的一部分（Greenwood School neighborhood）。

198. 赫南德茲先生為何比較中意位於主街的建築？
　　(A) 比較大。
　　(B) 比較便宜。
　　(C) 位置較理想。
　　(D) 屋況較好。

解析 (C) 赫南德茲先生說另一棟建築的位置沒有主街這棟理想（the location is not as good）。選項(A)不正確，他說另一棟建築的大小剛剛好。選項(B)不正確，主街的這棟建築比較貴，因赫南德茲先生需要二十萬美元的貸款才能購買此建築。選項(D)有可能，但並未提及。

199. 銀行會借他多少錢？
　　(A) 十萬美元
　　(B) 十三萬美元
　　(C) 二十萬美元
　　(D) 三十三萬美元

解析 (B) 銀行會借給赫南德茲先生足夠購買較低價建築的金額，而赫南德茲先生提到比較便宜的那棟需借貸十三萬。選項(A)是被信中提到赫南德茲先生目前負債已超過十萬給混淆。選項(C)是他買主街建築需要的貸款金額。選項(D)是兩棟建築加起來所需的貸款費用。

200. 克拉克女士希望哪一天和赫南德茲先生見面？
　　(A) 4月10日
　　(B) 4月11日
　　(C) 4月21日
　　(D) 4月22日

解析 (D) 赫南德茲先生建議4月21日見面，而克拉克女士說她希望隔天見面（meet the following day）。選項(A)是克拉克女士的回信日。選項(B)是克拉克女士回信日的隔日。選項(C)是赫南德茲先生提議的見面日期。

STOP 本測驗到此結束。如果你在時間結束前作答完畢，可以回頭檢查 Part 5、6、7 的答案。

實戰模擬試題3
解答

聽力測驗

Part 1 照片描述

1. C
2. D
3. A
4. B
5. B
6. C

Part 2 應答問題

7. C
8. A
9. C
10. A
11. C
12. C
13. B
14. B
15. C
16. C
17. B
18. C
19. A
20. A
21. A
22. C
23. B
24. A
25. C
26. B
27. A
28. B
29. C
30. A
31. A

Part 3 簡短對話

32. C
33. A
34. B
35. D
36. A
37. D
38. C
39. C
40. A
41. B
42. B
43. B
44. C
45. C
46. D
47. D
48. B
49. A
50. C
51. D
52. D
53. B
54. A
55. B
56. B
57. D
58. C
59. A
60. A
61. C
62. A
63. C
64. B
65. D
66. B
67. B
68. C
69. A
70. A

Part 4 簡短獨白

71. C
72. C
73. D
74. A
75. D
76. A
77. B
78. A
79. B
80. B
81. C
82. C
82. B
84. A
85. B
86. A
87. C
88. B
89. D
90. B
91. B
92. C
93. A
94. B
95. A
96. D
97. B
98. A
99. D
100. C

實戰模擬試題3 解答

閱讀測驗

Part 5 句子填空

101.	**B**	109.	**A**	117.	**D**	125.	**C**
102.	**A**	110.	**D**	118.	**A**	126.	**C**
103.	**B**	111.	**C**	119.	**C**	127.	**B**
104.	**A**	112.	**A**	120.	**B**	128.	**C**
105.	**C**	113.	**B**	121.	**D**	129.	**B**
106.	**D**	114.	**A**	122.	**C**	130.	**D**
107.	**B**	115.	**D**	123.	**A**		
108.	**C**	116.	**C**	124.	**B**		

Part 6 段落填空

131.	**C**	135.	**C**	139.	**C**	143.	**B**
132.	**A**	136.	**B**	140.	**C**	144.	**D**
133.	**D**	137.	**C**	141.	**D**	145.	**A**
134.	**A**	138.	**A**	142.	**A**	146.	**B**

Part 7 閱讀測驗

147.	**C**	161.	**A**	175.	**C**	189.	**C**
148.	**A**	162.	**D**	176.	**A**	190.	**D**
149.	**D**	163.	**B**	177.	**B**	191.	**C**
150.	**B**	164.	**C**	178.	**A**	192.	**C**
151.	**B**	165.	**D**	179.	**B**	193.	**B**
152.	**A**	166.	**A**	180.	**C**	194.	**A**
153.	**B**	167.	**D**	181.	**C**	195.	**B**
154.	**C**	168.	**A**	182.	**C**	196.	**A**
155.	**A**	169.	**C**	183.	**B**	197.	**B**
156.	**D**	170.	**D**	184.	**B**	198.	**D**
157.	**B**	171.	**B**	185.	**D**	199.	**C**
158.	**A**	172.	**B**	186.	**B**	200.	**B**
159.	**D**	173.	**C**	187.	**A**		
160.	**C**	174.	**D**	188.	**C**		

Model Test 3 實戰模擬試題3題目中譯&解析

聽力測驗

在本段測驗當中,你將有機會展現自己對口說英語的理解能力。聽力測驗共有四個大題,每一大題均有作答說明。你有大約45分鐘時間完成聽力測驗。

> 複習要訣:閱讀Part 1和Part 2的錄音稿時,可在每題之間停5秒鐘。

Part 1:照片描述

> **作答方式**:你會看到一張照片,並聽到四個關於這張照片的陳述。選出最符合照片內容的陳述,將答案卡上對應的橢圓框塗滿。

1. Look at the photo marked number 1 in your test book.
   (A) All the plates are empty.
   (B) The waiter's taking an order.
   (C) Customers are enjoying their meal.
   (D) The menu is on the table.

   請看試題本標示為1的照片。
   (A) 所有盤子都是空的。
   (B) 服務生正在點餐。
   (C) 顧客正在享用餐點。
   (D) 菜單在桌上。

   解析 (C) 選項(C)正確指出了餐廳裡的顧客和他們的動作:享用餐點。選項(A)不正確,盤子上有食物。選項(B)對服務生的動作描述錯誤,他正在上菜而不是點餐。選項(D)從餐廳的場景聯想到菜單,但照片中沒有出現菜單。

2. Look at the photo marked number 2 in your test book.
   (A) He's washing the test tube.
   (B) He's putting on his coat.
   (C) He's pouring himself a drink.
   (D) He's wearing gloves.

請看試題本標示為 2 的照片。
(A) 他正在清洗試管。
(B) 他正在穿外套。
(C) 他正在替自己倒一杯飲料。
(D) 他戴著手套。

解析 (D) 這位科學家工作時戴著手套保護雙手。選項(A)正確指出了試管，但是他正在倒東西進試管，而不是在清洗試管。選項(B)正確指出了外套，但他已經穿在身上。選項(C)對「倒」的動作描述正確，但是他正在倒東西進試管，而不是倒進裝飲料用的杯子。

3. Look at the photo marked number 3 in your test book.
    (A) The road is filled with traffic.
    (B) The cars are in the garage.
    (C) The parking lot is empty.
    (D) The bridge goes across the river.

    請看試題本標示為 3 的照片。
    (A) 這條馬路十分壅塞。
    (B) 這些車停在車庫裡。
    (C) 這座停車場空蕩蕩的。
    (D) 這座橋樑橫跨了河流。

解析 (A) 從照片中可以看到一條馬路被車子擠得水洩不通。選項(B)正確辨識出車子，但對位置的描述不正確。選項(C)把cars和parking lot聯想在一起。選項(D)正確辨識出橋樑，但橋橫跨的是馬路而不是河流。

4. Look at the photo marked number 4 in your test book.
    (A) The people are standing in the rain.
    (B) The passengers are ready to board.
    (C) The plane is taking off.
    (D) The grain is being harvested.

    請看試題本標示為 4 的照片。
    (A) 人們正站在雨中。
    (B) 乘客們正準備上車。
    (C) 飛機準備起飛。
    (D) 穀物正在被收割。

解析 (B) 選項(B)正確辨識出照片中的乘客和他們準備上火車的動作。選項(A)混淆了近音字rain和train。選項(C)混淆了近音字plane和train。選項(D)混淆了近音字grain和train。

5. Look at the photo marked number 5 in your test book.
   (A) The ducks are on the pond.
   (B) The trucks are at the loading dock.
   (C) The ship is being loaded.
   (D) The shoppers are in the aisle.

   請看試題本標示為5的照片。
   (A) 這些鴨子在池塘裡。
   (B) 這些卡車停在裝卸區。
   (C) 這艘船正在裝貨。
   (D) 這些購物者在走道上。

解析 (B) 照片中有多輛卡車停靠在一間大型倉庫的裝卸區。選項(A)混淆了近音字duck和truck。選項(C)使用了shipping的相關字ship，shipping意指「運貨、運送」，以陸運來說是用卡車運送貨物，ship作名詞則指「船」。選項(D)使用了shoppers這個字，但照片中沒有購物者，也看不到有走道。

6. Look at the photo marked number 6 in your test book.
   (A) The students are in the hallway.
   (B) The classroom is empty.
   (C) The men are by the blackboard.
   (D) The professor is in her office.

   請看試題本標示為6的照片。
   (A) 這些學生在走廊上。
   (B) 教室空無一人。
   (C) 這些男子在黑板旁邊。
   (D) 這名教授在她的辦公室。

解析 (C) 教室前方的黑板旁邊有兩名男子。選項(A)(B)(D)都使用了和學校有關的單字——students、classroom、professor——但是對情境的描述都不正確。

Part 2：應答問題

> 作答方式：你會聽到一個問題和三個可能的回應。選出最適合回答該問題的回應，將答案卡上對應的橢圓框塗滿。

7. What's the book you're reading about?
   (A) The book is on the shelf.
   (B) It costs about five dollars.
   (C) It's a war story.

   你在讀什麼書？
   (A) 書在書架上。
   (B) 花費大約五美元。
   (C) 是戰爭故事。

   解析 (C) 選項(C)是對主題問題的合理回應。選項(A)回答的是書的位置而不是主題。選項(B)回答的是價錢。

8. City Hall is closed over the weekend.
   (A) Then let's go on Monday.
   (B) I prefer the countryside.
   (C) That's where my sister works.

   市政府週末關閉。
   (A) 那我們週一去。
   (B) 我比較喜歡鄉下。
   (C) 我妹在那裡上班。

   解析 (A) 建議週一再去是對市政府「週末關閉」的合理回應。選項(B)使用了city的相關字countryside。選項(C)暗示說話者的妹妹在市政府上班，但用這句話回應題目的陳述不合邏輯。

9. Which train should we take to get to Hampstead?
   (A) It won't rain today.
   (B) They teach a good class at the local college.
   (C) Let's take the express.

   我們應該搭哪一班火車到漢普斯特德？
   (A) 今天不會下雨。
   (B) 他們在當地大學的課教得很棒。
   (C) 我們搭快車吧。

   解析 (C) 選項(C)是被問及哪一班車（which train）時的合理回應。選項(A)混淆了近音字 train 和 rain。選項(B)回答的則是「Which class should I take?」（我該上哪一門課）的問題。

10. Why isn't our permit ready yet?
    (A) Because our application had problems.
    (B) No, we aren't allowed to.
    (C) I already read it.

    我們的許可證為什麼還沒好？
    (A) 因為我們的申請資料有問題。
    (B) 不行，我們不被允許這樣做。
    (C) 我已經讀過了。

    解析 (A) 選項(A)回答了「Why」的問題。選項(B)搞錯了 permit 這個字的意義。選項(C)混淆了近音字 ready 和 already。

11. He's expected to arrive before noon, isn't he?
    (A) For a month.
    (B) She waited too long.
    (C) No, around two p.m.

    他預計中午前會抵達，對嗎？
    (A) 為期一個月。
    (B) 她等太久了。
    (C) 不對，是下午兩點左右。

    解析 (C) 選項(C)是對「When」問題的合理回應。選項(A)回答的是「How long」的問題而不是「When」。

12. Could I ask how much your hotel bill was?
    (A) I paid with a credit card.
    (B) Over thirty stories.
    (C) Just under five hundred dollars.

    我可以問一下你的飯店帳單是多少嗎？
    (A) 我是用信用卡付款的。
    (B) 超過三十層樓。
    (C) 不到五百美元。

解析 (C) 選項(C)是對「How much」（多少錢）問題的合理回應。選項(A)回答的是「How」的問題（How you paid? 如何付款）。選項(B)回答的是「How many」的問題（How many stories the hotel had? 飯店有幾層樓）。

13. The rent is going up again next month.
    (A) I already lent you one.
    (B) Maybe we should look for a cheaper apartment.
    (C) This elevator's going up.

    下個月房租又要漲了。
    (A) 我已經借你一個了。
    (B) 也許我們應該找間便宜一點的公寓。
    (C) 這部電梯是要上樓的。

解析 (B) 由於房租調漲，第二個說話者建議找個便宜一點的地方居住。選項(A)混淆了近音字 lent 和 rent。選項(C)重複使用了 going up 這個片語。

14. Whose handwriting is this?
    (A) She writes in cursive.
    (B) It looks like Robert's.
    (C) I can sign it.

    這是誰的筆跡？
    (A) 她使用草寫。
    (B) 看起來像是羅伯特的。
    (C) 我可以簽字。

解析 (B) 所有格「Robert's」回答了「Whose」的所有格疑問句。選項(A)使用了和 handwriting 有關的 cursive（草寫字）。選項(C)使用了和 handwriting 有關的單字 sign（簽字）。

345

15. The meeting is about to start.
    (A) I left it in the conference room.
    (B) I enjoyed meeting you, too.
    (C) I'll be there in a minute.

    會議快要開始了。
    (A) 我把它留在會議室了。
    (B) 我也很高興見到你。
    (C) 我馬上就到。

解析 (C) 第二個說話者回覆他馬上就會抵達會議現場。選項 (A) 從 meeting 聯想到 conference room。選項 (B) 重複使用了 meeting 這個字，但用了動詞的意義，因此不符合語境。

16. Who won the tennis match?
    (A) I don't smoke.
    (B) No, there were nine not ten.
    (C) The game was canceled.

    誰贏了網球比賽？
    (A) 我不抽菸。
    (B) 不，有九個而不是十個。
    (C) 比賽取消了。

解析 (C) 選項 (C) 是被問及「誰贏了網球賽」時的合理回應。選項 (A) 使用了 match 另一個意義（火柴）的相關字 smoke。選項 (B) 混淆了近音字 ten 和 tennis。

17. Could you tell me the purpose of Mark's visit?
    (A) The visitors left early.
    (B) He just wanted to say hello.
    (C) The proposal was on the list.

    能否告訴我馬克來訪的目的？
    (A) 訪客們很早就離開了。
    (B) 他只是想要打聲招呼。
    (C) 那個提案有在清單上。

解析 (B) 選項 (B) 是被問及來訪目的時的合理回應。選項 (A) 使用了 visit 的相關字 visitors。選項 (C) 混淆了 proposal 和 purpose，以及 list 和 visit。

18. I love winter. Which season do you prefer?
    (A) Just a little salt and pepper.
    (B) I can refer you to someone.
    (C) Summer's my favorite.

    我喜歡冬天,你喜歡哪個季節?
    (A) 一點鹽和胡椒就好。
    (B) 我可以介紹一個人給你。
    (C) 夏天是我的最愛。

解析 (C) 選項(C)是對季節偏好問題的合理回應。選項(A)把season(季節)和seasoning(調味料)搞混了。選項(B)混淆了近音字refer和prefer。

19. I saw Jim at the party last night.
    (A) Really? How is he doing?
    (B) I like dancing.
    (C) This part is yours.

    我昨晚在派對上有看到吉姆。
    (A) 真的嗎?他過得如何?
    (B) 我喜歡跳舞。
    (C) 這部分是你的。

解析 (A) 第一個說話者提到在派對上看到吉姆,所以第二個說話者就問吉姆現在過得如何。選項(B)把party和dancing聯想在一起。選項(C)混淆了近音字part和party。

20. When does the mail come?
    (A) Every morning at eleven.
    (B) They're always welcome here.
    (C) You're welcome.

    郵件什麼時候送來?
    (A) 每天早上十一點。
    (B) 這裡隨時歡迎他們來。
    (C) 不客氣。

解析 (A) 選項(A)是對郵件何時送來問題的合理回應。選項(B)和(C)都混淆了發音相近的welcome和come。

21. Do you know where the nearest bank is?
    (A) There's one in the shopping center.
    (B) I agree. It's nowhere.
    (C) I'd rather wear the brown one.

    你知道最近的銀行在哪裡嗎？
    (A) 購物中心裡有一家。
    (B) 我同意，到處都找不到。
    (C) 我寧可穿咖啡色的那件。

解析 (A) 選項(A)是被問及銀行在哪裡時的合理回應。選項(B)混淆了近音字where和nowhere。選項(C)混淆了近音字where和wear。

22. Do you think it's going to rain today?
    (A) He's going tomorrow.
    (B) Why don't you complain?
    (C) I don't think so. The sky is clear.

    你覺得今天會下雨嗎？
    (A) 他明天要去。
    (B) 你為什麼不抱怨？
    (C) 我覺得不會，天空很晴朗。

解析 (C) 選項(C)是對天氣問題的合理回應。選項(A)使用了和問句非常類似的動詞is going，以及today的相關字tomorrow。選項(B)混淆了近音字rain和complain。

23. How much should I tip the waiter?
    (A) I tipped the boat over.
    (B) Fifteen percent is sufficient.
    (C) Ten children waded in the water.

    我該給服務生多少小費？
    (A) 我把船弄翻了。
    (B) 百分之十五就足夠了。
    (C) 十個孩子正在涉水。

解析 (B) 選項(B)是被問及小費金額時的合理回應。選項(A)重複使用了tip這個字，但用的是另一個意義（使傾斜），tip over是「使翻覆」，而題目中的tip是「給小費」。選項(C)把題目中的waiter和近音字waded和water給混淆了，而且回答的是「How many」而不是「How much」的問題。

24. Who designed your house?
   (A) The same architect that did our office building.
   (B) I resigned this morning.
   (C) I use a mouse with my computer.

   你的房子是誰設計的？
   (A) 設計我們辦公大樓的同一位建築師。
   (B) 我今天早上辭職了。
   (C) 我用滑鼠操作電腦。

   解析 (A) 選項(A)是被問及設計師是誰的合理回應。選項(B)混淆了近音字 resign 和 design。選項(C)混淆了近音字 house 和 mouse。

25. Ken eats meat, doesn't he?
   (A) The steak, please.
   (B) It's not very neat.
   (C) No, he's vegetarian.

   肯恩吃肉對吧？
   (A) 牛排，謝謝。
   (B) 不是很整齊。
   (C) 不，他吃素。

   解析 (C) 選項(C)是被問及某人吃不吃肉並使用了附加問句時的合理回應。選項(A)使用了 meat 的相關字 steak。選項(B)混淆了近音字 meat 和 neat。

26. What is this shirt made of?
   (A) It was made in Hong Kong.
   (B) It's made of cotton.
   (C) It's my favorite dessert.

   這件襯衫是什麼材質？
   (A) 是香港製的。
   (B) 是棉質的。
   (C) 那是我最愛的甜點。

   解析 (B) 選項(B)是被問及襯衫布料時的合理回應。選項(A)把介系詞從 made of 改成了 made in，意義就不同了，變成回答製造地。選項(C)把發音相近的 this shirt 和 dessert 互相混淆了。

27. Isn't this a beautiful view?
    (A) Yes, it's very nice.
    (B) Yes, he told me too.
    (C) Yes, we already knew.

    這景色是不是很美?
    (A) 對啊,真美。
    (B) 沒錯,他也跟我說了。
    (C) 是的,我們早就知道了。

解析 (A) 題目是關於景色的否定疑問句,否定疑問句常用來表達讚歎並期待附和,而選項 (A) 是對這類問題的合理回應。選項 (B) 混淆了近音字 view 和 too。選項 (C) 混淆了近音字 view 和 knew。

28. Where did you study English?
    (A) The students are not going to England.
    (B) I studied it at school.
    (C) For six years.

    你是在哪裡學英文的?
    (A) 這些學生不會去英格蘭。
    (B) 我在學校學的。
    (C) 六年了。

解析 (B) 選項 (B) 是被問及在哪裡學英文時的合理回應。選項 (A) 使用了 study 的相關字 students,以及 English 的相關字 England。選項 (C) 回答的是「How long」的問題。

29. Which sweater do you think fits me better?
    (A) These sweat pants are too large for you.
    (B) The weather is better in the south.
    (C) The wool one fits you perfectly.

    你覺得哪一件毛衣比較適合我?
    (A) 這件運動褲對你來說太大了。
    (B) 南部的天氣比較好。
    (C) 羊毛的那件太適合你了。

解析 (C) 選項 (C) 是被問及哪一件毛衣更適合時的合理回應。選項 (A) 把 sweater 混淆成 sweat pants,文不對題,也把 fit 的概念和 too large 混淆。選項 (B) 混淆了近音字 sweater 和 weather。

30. What time do you have?
    (A) It's almost half past one.
    (B) I have both yours and mine.
    (C) In about twenty minutes.

    現在幾點了？
    (A) 快要一點半了。
    (B) 我有你的和我的。
    (C) 大約二十分鐘後。

解析 **(A)** 選項(A)是對詢問時間問題的合理回應。選項(B)回答的是另一種「do you have」（你有沒有……）的問題。選項(C)回答的問題會類似「What time do you have to leave?」（你什麼時候要離開？）。

31. Would you close the window please?
    (A) Of course. Are you cold?
    (B) Yes, just pack these clothes.
    (C) All teller windows are open.

    麻煩你關一下窗戶好嗎？
    (A) 當然好，你會冷嗎？
    (B) 是的，打包這些衣物就好。
    (C) 所有的櫃員窗口都有開放。

解析 **(A)** 選項(A)是對方請求關窗時的合理回應。選項(B)混淆了近音字 close 和 clothes。選項(C)使用了 close 的相關字 open。

Part 3：簡短對話

> **作答方式**：你會聽到兩人或多人之間的對話。每段對話搭配三個問題，各有四個選項。選出最適當的答案回答問題，將答案卡上對應的橢圓框塗滿。

複習要訣：閱讀 Part 3 和 Part 4 的錄音稿時，可在每題之間停 8 秒鐘。

Questions 32 through 34 refer to the following conversation.

Man: I was listening to that radio program, you know, the one about cultural events? They were saying that the annual art show, Art in the Park, is coming up soon, this weekend, in fact.

Woman: That sounds like fun. We can go on Saturday.

Man: That won't work. I already promised Fred I would help him move to his new apartment. That's going to take all day, I bet. He has a lot of stuff.

Woman: OK. Let's go on Sunday, then. There won't be another chance until next year.

第 32–34 題請聽下面這段對話。

男：我之前聽那個廣播節目，你知道吧，關於文化活動的那個？他們說年度藝術大展《公園裡的藝術》即將開展，事實上就是這個週末。

女：聽起來很有趣，我們可以星期六去。

男：星期六不行，我已經答應弗列德要幫他搬家，我想一定會用掉一整天，他東西超多的。

女：好吧，那我們星期天去。明年之前不會再有這樣的機會了。

32. Where did the man learn about the event? 男子是從哪裡得知這項活動的？
    (A) In a newspaper 報紙
    (B) On the internet 網路
    (C) On the radio 廣播
    (D) From a friend 朋友

解析 (C) 男子說他是在廣播上聽到的。選項 (A) 沒有被提及。選項 (B) 混淆了 internet 和發音相近的 I bet。選項 (D) 混淆了 friend 和發音相近的 Fred，Fred 是男子要去幫忙的人。

352

33. Why can't they go on Saturday? 他們星期六為什麼不能去？
    (A) The man promised to help someone. 男子答應要去幫別人的忙。
    (B) The woman has plans to go to a dance. 女子已經計劃要去跳舞。
    (C) The man has to look for a new apartment. 男子須要找一間新公寓。
    (D) The woman has to work that day. 女子那天要上班。

解析 (A) 男子已經答應要幫弗列德搬家。選項(B)混淆了近音字chance和dance。選項(C)重複使用了apartment這個字。選項(D)並未被提及。

34. What does the woman want to do? 這名女子想做什麼？
    (A) Not go 不去
    (B) Go on Sunday 星期天去
    (C) Go to next year's event 明年活動再去
    (D) Wait until their friend can go 等到他們朋友能去的時候

解析 (B) 女子說「Let's go on Sunday」，所以她想星期天去。選項(A)不正確，女子想去。選項(C)重複使用了next year這個片語。選項(D)混淆了近音字Fred和friend。

Questions 35 through 37 refer to the following conversation.
Woman: I read through your résumé, Mark, and I think we have a position that suits you. I'd like to schedule an interview with you.
Man: That would be fine. When should we meet?
Woman: I'd like to do it soon. How about next Tuesday at, let's say, eight thirty a.m.? Could you come to our office on Oak Avenue?
Man: Of course. I can be there then. Should I bring anything with me?
Woman: No. We have a test we give to all our applicants. Just come prepared to show us your computer skills.

第35–37題請聽下面這段對話。
女：馬克，我看過你的履歷了，我想我們有一個適合你的職位，我想和你約時間面試。
男：好的，我們應該何時見面呢？
女：我想盡快，比方說下週二早上八點半如何？你可以過來我們橡樹大道的辦公室嗎？
男：沒問題，我那個時間可以到。我需要帶些什麼嗎？
女：不用，我們會給所有應徵者做個考試，只要準備好展現你的電腦技能給我們看就行了。

35. What is the appointment for? 為何要約時間會面？
    (A) A medical checkup 做健康檢查
    (B) A sales meeting 開銷售會議
    (C) A possible presentation 一場可能進行的簡報
    (D) A job interview 進行工作面試

解析 (D) 從對話中的 résumé（履歷）和 position（職位）可以看出是要進行工作面試。選項(A)(B)(C)都是需要透過預約時間來安排的事情，但都不會涉及履歷。

36. When will the appointment take place? 排定的面試是何時？
    (A) On Tuesday morning 週二早上
    (B) At 8:30 in the evening 晚上八點半
    (C) Tomorrow at ten 明天十點
    (D) Today at noon 今天中午

解析 (A) 女子提出週二早上八點半進行面試，男子也同意。選項(B)不正確，女子說的是早上（a.m.）而不是晚上（p.m.）。選項(C)混淆了近音字 ten 和 then。選項(D)混淆了近音字 noon 和 soon。

37. What should the man bring? 男子應該帶什麼東西？
    (A) An application 申請表
    (B) A finished test 完成的考卷
    (C) His résumé 他的履歷
    (D) Nothing 什麼都不用帶

解析 (D) 對話中男子問是否需帶些什麼，女子回答不用。選項(A)和女子在對話中提到的 applicant（應徵者、申請者）有關。選項(B)不正確，男子到了面試現場才要接受考試。選項(C)不正確，女子說她已經看過他的履歷了。

Questions 38 through 40 refer to the following conversation.

Man: Front desk. How may I help you?
Woman: Yes, I'm in Room six-twenty-four. I'm having problems with the TV in here. I can't get it to, uh, it doesn't have a picture.
Man: You've checked that the power is on, right?
Woman: Of course.
Man: I'm sorry you're having this problem. I'll send someone up right away.
Woman: Great, but I'm getting ready to take a shower. I'll be going out in about half an hour. Could you send someone then?
Man: Certainly.

第 38–40 題請聽下面這段對話。

男：服務臺，您好，請問需要什麼服務？
女：是的，這裡是 624 號房，房間裡的電視有點問題，我無法，呃，它沒有畫面。
男：您檢查過電源有打開了，對嗎？
女：當然。
男：很抱歉讓您遇到這個問題，我馬上派人過去。
女：很好，可是我正準備要洗澡，大概半小時後要外出，可以那時候再派人過來嗎？
男：沒問題。

38. Where is the woman? 女子人在哪裡？
    (A) At a department store 百貨公司
    (B) At a repair shop 維修店
    (C) At a hotel 飯店
    (D) At home 家中

解析 (C) 男子接起電話時說「front desk」（即為飯店前檯），並為「Room 624」的住客提供協助，所以這裡很有可能是一間飯店。選項 (A) 和 (B) 都和對話中討論的電視有關聯。選項 (D) 不正確，家中不會有前檯，房間也不會有號碼。

39. What will the man do? 男子將會做什麼？
    (A) Turn the TV on 打開電視
    (B) Take the TV away 把電視帶走
    (C) Have someone fix the TV 派人去修電視
    (D) Show the woman a different TV 給女子看另一臺電視

解析 (C) 女子描述了電視的問題後，男子說「I'll send someone up right away」（我馬上派人過去）。選項 (A) 不正確，女子說她已經試過打開電視了。選項 (B) 把對話中提到的片語 right away 混淆成 take away。選項 (D) 如果對話發生在百貨公司或商店就有可能。

40. What does the woman ask the man to do? 女子要求男子做什麼事？
    (A) Wait half an hour 等半個小時
    (B) Come back at 10:00 十點時再過來一趟
    (C) Send her a package 寄一個包裹給她
    (D) Take a picture 拍照

解析 (A) 女子說「I'll be going out in about half an hour. Could you send someone then?」，要男子過半小時再派人過來。選項 (B) 混淆了近音字 ten 和 then。選項 (C) 未被提及。選項 (D) 被女子對電視故障的描述給混淆了，女子說的是電視沒有「畫面」（picture）。

Questions 41 through 43 refer to the following conversation.

Woman: Does anyone know where Mr. Chung is? He's due to address the meeting this morning.

Man: He called from his car to say he'll be late. He's stuck in traffic.

Woman: Oh, great. Now what will we do?

Man: Well, we could show the film first, while we're waiting for him.

Woman: That's not a bad idea. That would probably give him enough time to get here.

Man: All right. I can have it ready to go in ten minutes. We'll be able to start the meeting right on time.

第 41–43 題請聽下面這段對話。

女：有誰知道鍾先生在哪裡？他預定今天早上要在會議上發言。

男：他從車上打電話來說會遲到，他被塞在路上了。

女：喔，這下可好了，現在我們該怎麼辦？

男：我們可以先放影片，一邊等他。

女：這個點子不錯，那他應該有足夠時間可以趕到這裡。

男：好，我十分鐘內就可以準備好，我們能準時開會。

41. Why do the speakers need Mr. Chung? 這些說話者為什麼需要鍾先生？
    (A) To deliver some letters 需要他送一些信
    (B) To speak at a meeting 需要他在會議中發言
    (C) To announce the date 需要他宣布日期
    (D) To loan them his car 需要他把車借給他們

解析 (B) 女子說他要找鍾先生是因為早上會議預定他要發言（He's due to address the meeting this morning）。選項(A)搞錯了 address 的意思。選項(C)在對話中並未提及。選項(D)是因為對話中提到鍾先生從車上打電話來而有所混淆。

42. Why is Mr. Chung late? 鍾先生為何遲到？
    (A) He lost the address. 他把地址搞丟了。
    (B) He's stuck in traffic. 他在路上塞車了。
    (C) His car broke down. 他的車子拋錨了。
    (D) He's making a phone call. 他正在打電話。

解析 (B) 鍾先生打電話來說他被塞在路上、困在車陣中了。選項(A)重複使用了 address 這個字，但用的不是對話語境中的意義。選項(C)重複使用了 car 這個字，並從交通（traffic）聯想到汽車拋錨。選項(D)是因為他遲到要打電話告知同事，而不是原因。

43. What will the man do next? 這名男子接下來會做什麼事？
    (A) Look for Mr. Chung 尋找鍾先生
    (B) Prepare to show a film 準備播放影片
    (C) Take Mr. Chung's place 替代鍾先生
    (D) Start the meeting 開始開會

解析 (B) 兩名說話者同意在等待鍾先生時先播放影片，然後男子說「I can have it ready to go in ten minutes」，表示他十分鐘內會把影片準備好。選項(A)不正確，說話者知道鍾先生在哪裡。選項(C)不正確，說話者提到他們要等鍾先生，而不是替代他。選項(D)不正確，男子必須先準備好影片才能開始開會。

Questions 44 through 46 refer to the following conversation with three speakers.
Man 1: I like the way the lobby looks now. It's important to have a nice entrance to an office building.
Woman: Yes, it's a lot brighter since they painted it white.
Man 2: I know. It never had enough light before.
Man 1: A nice, bright lobby will make a good impression on our clients. But I wish they would do something about these drab hallways.
Woman: Or the elevator. The color is really depressing.
Man 2: Actually, I think the cafeteria's next. Painting is due to start there next week.
Woman: Oh. Good thing I'll be out of town then. I mean, I'm glad it'll be painted but I don't like to be around the mess.

第 44-46 題請聽下面這段三人之間的對話。
男1：我喜歡大廳現在的樣子，辦公大樓的入口美觀很重要。
女　：沒錯，他們把大廳漆成白色之後明亮多了。
男2：對啊，這裡以前一直光線不足。
男1：一個漂亮又明亮的大廳能給客戶留下好印象，但我真希望他們處理一下這些死氣沉沉的走廊。
女　：電梯也是，顏色讓人很鬱悶。
男2：事實上，我想下一個應該是自助餐廳，那裡下週就要開始粉刷了。
女　：喔，還好那時候我不在城裡。我是說，要重新粉刷我很高興，但到時候會很混亂，我不想待在這裡。

44. What was painted? 哪裡進行了粉刷工程？
    (A) The cafeteria 自助餐廳
    (B) The office 辦公室
    (C) The lobby 大廳
    (D) The hallways 走廊

解析 (C) 第一個說話者說他喜歡大廳現在的樣子（I like the way the lobby looks now），接著第二個說話者提到大廳被漆成白色（they painted it white），可見大廳進行了粉刷工程。選項(A)是未來要進行粉刷的地方。選項(B)和(D)是對話中提到的其他地方，但還沒有進行粉刷。

45. What does the woman say about the elevator? 女子提到電梯的什麼？
    (A) It is very messy. 很雜亂。
    (B) It runs too slowly. 移動速度太慢。
    (C) Its color makes her feel sad. 顏色讓她心情不好。
    (D) It needs a new set of lights. 需要換一組新的燈。

解析 (C) 女子評論電梯說「The color is really depressing」，表示顏色讓人鬱悶、心情不好。選項(A)是被對話中提到的 mess（混亂）給誤導，對話中是說自助餐廳進行粉刷時會一片混亂，不是在講電梯。選項(B)或許有可能，但對話中並未提及。選項(D)混淆了對話中關於大廳的討論，他們抱怨大廳粉刷之前看起來很暗，而不是電梯。

46. What will the woman do next week? 這名女子下週要做什麼？
    (A) Choose paint colors 選油漆顏色
    (B) Meet a new client 見一個新客戶
    (C) Eat in the cafeteria 到自助餐廳吃飯
    (D) Go away on a trip 去旅行

解析 (D) 其中一名男子說自助餐廳下禮拜要進行粉刷，女子說那時她不在城裡（out of town then），因此很有可能是去旅行。選項(A)和對話中討論了大廳和電梯的油漆顏色有關，但並沒有提到女子要選油漆顏色。選項(B)重複使用了對話中的 client 這個字。選項(C)重複使用了對話中的 cafeteria 這個字。

Questions 47 to 49 refer to the following conversation.

Woman: Your job must keep your days well occupied. You probably don't have a lot of free time for sports or hobbies.

Man: No, but I definitely take advantage of the free time I do have. I really enjoy cooking when I have the time, and I try to play golf every Saturday.

Woman: I have to say I never thought playing golf was much fun, but I certainly love eating.

Man: Why don't you come over sometime soon and I'll make dinner for you? Actually, I'm free tomorrow evening.

Woman: Sorry, that's no good. What about Friday?

Man: Friday it is.

第 47–49 題請聽下面這段對話。

女：你的工作一定把你每天的行程都塞滿了，大概不會有太多時間從事運動或培養嗜好吧。

男：對啊，但我一定會充分利用僅有的空閒時間。我有時間時喜歡下廚，每週六也會盡量去打高爾夫球。

女：不得不說我以前從不覺得高爾夫球有什麼好玩的，但我真的很愛吃。

男：要不要哪天過來我做晚餐給你吃？事實上，我明天晚上沒事。

女：真抱歉，明天晚上不行，星期五如何？

男：那就星期五囉。

47. What does the woman say about the man? 女子如何描述這名男子？

(A) He's an excellent golfer. 他很會打高爾夫球。

(B) He cooks every day. 他每天下廚。

(C) He is often bored. 他經常感到無聊。

(D) He's very busy. 他非常忙碌。

解析 (D) 女子說男子的工作滿檔，把時間都占據了（well occupied），以至於他可能沒有什麼空閒時間。選項 (A) 跟男子說他喜歡打高爾夫球有關，但對話中並未提到他打得有多好。選項 (B) 不正確，男子說他有時間時（when I have time）喜歡下廚，暗示了他不一定有時間。選項 (C) 不大可能，男子既要忙工作，又至少有兩項嗜好 ── 打高爾夫球和做飯，不會感到無聊。

48. What does the woman like to do? 這名女子喜歡做什麼？
    (A) Run 跑步
    (B) Eat 吃東西
    (C) Cook 做飯
    (D) Read 閱讀

解析 (B) 女子說「I certainly love eating」，表示她很愛吃東西。選項(A)和(D)並沒有被提及。選項(C)是男子喜歡做的事。

49. What does the woman mean when she says, "That's no good"? 女子說「That's no good」是什麼意思？
    (A) She can't meet the man tomorrow. 她明天不能和男子見面。
    (B) She thinks the man doesn't cook well. 她覺得男子做飯不好吃。
    (C) She doesn't enjoy going out in the evening. 她不喜歡晚上出門。
    (D) She doesn't want to have dinner with the man. 她不想和男子共進晚餐。

解析 (A) 男子邀請她明天見面，說要做飯給她吃，女子回說「That's no good」並提出了另一個時間，表示男子提議的時間（明天）和她的行程衝突，她不能和男子見面。選項(B)(C)(D)都不符合對話的語境。

Questions 50 through 52 refer to the following conversation.

Woman: Do you need help? Is it a flat tire? I can help you change it.
Man: Thanks, but that's not it. You probably won't believe this, but my gas tank is empty. Is there a service station nearby?
Woman: There's one down the road, just this side of the bridge. It's about a mile or so from here, I think.
Man: Thank you. That's not too far to walk, I guess.
Woman: Yes, it is, especially in this heat. I'll drive you.

第 50–52 題請聽下面這段對話。
女：需要幫忙嗎？爆胎了是不是？我可以幫你換輪胎。
男：謝了，但不是這個問題。你大概不會相信，我的油箱沒油了。這附近有加油站嗎？
女：這條路上有一家，就在橋的這一側。從這裡過去大概一英里左右吧，我想。
男：謝謝，我想走路應該不算太遠。
女：很遠的，尤其在這麼熱的天氣下，我載你吧。

50. What is the man's problem? 男子遇到了什麼問題？
    (A) He wants something to drink. 他想喝點東西。
    (B) He needs to change the oil. 他需要換機油。
    (C) He has run out of gas. 他的汽油沒了。
    (D) He has a flat tire. 他的車子爆胎了。

解析 (C) 男子說「my gas tank is empty」，意指他的油箱空了、沒油了。選項(A)未被提及。選項(B)重複使用了change這個字，女子是說要幫他換輪胎不是換機油。選項(D)是女子以為男子遇到的問題。

51. Where is the service station? 加油站在哪裡？
    (A) On the other side of the road 馬路的另一側
    (B) Several miles away 數英里之外
    (C) In the next town 下一個鎮上
    (D) Near a bridge 靠近橋的地方

解析 (D) 女子說加油站就在橋的這一側（just this side of the bridge）。選項(A)重複使用了side和road這兩個字。選項(B)不正確，女子說加油站距離這裡大概一英里左右。選項(C)雖然有可能，但對話中並未提及。

52. How will the man get to the service station? 男子會怎麼去加油站？
    (A) He will walk. 他會走路去。
    (B) He will take a bus. 他會搭公車去。
    (C) He will drive his car. 他會開自己的車去。
    (D) He will ride with the woman. 他會坐女子的車去。

解析 (D) 女子最後說「I'll drive you」（我載你去），所以他會坐女子的車去。選項(A)指的是女子還沒提議要載他去之前，男子原本打算用走的。選項(B)在對話中並未提及。選項(C)不正確，因為男子的車已經沒油了。

Questions 53 through 55 refer to the following conversation.

Woman: I wish I had more time to exercise. I just can't ever fit it into my day.

Man: You could exercise during your lunch break. There's a gym downstairs, you know. And it's free for company staff.

Woman: Uh huh. But I like to spend my lunch hour in the cafeteria eating my lunch. I mean, that's why they call it lunch hour, right?

Man: Yeah, and there usually are a lot of people using the gym at lunch time, anyway. What I do is, I spend my lunch hour walking in the park. That's good exercise.

Woman: But what about lunch? Don't you eat?

Man: Sure. I have a quick bite at my desk before heading out to the park.

第 53–55 題請聽下面這段對話。

女：真希望我有更多時間可以運動，我實在排不出時間啊。

男：你可以利用午休時間運動啊，樓下就有健身房，你知道的。而且公司員工可以免費使用。

女：我知道啊。可是午休時間我想在自助餐廳吃飯，我是說，不然為何要叫午休時間，對吧？

男：也是啦，反正午休時間通常很多人在使用健身房。我自己是利用午休時間到公園走路，這樣運動也不錯。

女：那午餐怎麼辦？你都不用吃嗎？

男：當然要吃，我會在辦公桌前快速吃點東西再去公園。

53. What does the woman want to do? 這名女子想做什麼？
    (A) Go on a diet 節食
    (B) Get more exercise 多運動
    (C) Get a gym membership 辦健身房會員
    (D) Find a better place to eat lunch 找個更好的地方吃午餐

解析 (B) 女子說「I wish I had more time to exercise」，表示她希望有更多時間可以運動。選項 (A) 和對話主題有關，但女子未提到要節食。選項 (C) 和使用健身房有關，但對話中未提到要辦會員。選項 (D) 和午餐的討論有關，但同樣沒說要找更好的地方吃午餐。

54. What does the man say about the gym? 男子對健身房有何描述？
    (A) It is crowded. 人很多。
    (B) It is expensive. 很貴。
    (C) It is far away. 很遠。
    (D) It is cold. 很冷。

解析 (A) 男子說午餐時間通常很多人使用健身房。選項(B)不正確，公司員工可以免費使用健身房。選項(C)和(D)在對話中都沒有提到。

55. Where does the man eat his lunch? 男子都在哪裡吃午餐？
    (A) At home 家裡
    (B) At his desk 他的辦公桌前
    (C) In the park 公園裡
    (D) In the cafeteria 自助餐廳裡

解析 (B) 男子說「I have a quick bite at my desk」，他都在辦公桌前快速吃一吃。選項(A)未被提及。選項(C)是他散步的地方。選項(D)是女子吃午餐的地方。

Questions 56 through 58 refer to the following conversation with three speakers.
Woman 1: I just moved to a new office on the fifth floor. It's bright and sunny and it overlooks the park.
Woman 2: Yeah, there's a great view from that office. You were really fortunate to get it, Maria.
Woman 1: I know. I mean, the fifth floor offices are especially nice.
Man: My office faces the parking lot.
Woman 2: Oh, don't feel bad. You've been at the company only a few months.
Woman 1: Yeah, you'll probably get a better office after a while.
Man: You're right. I shouldn't worry, especially since I like everything else about my job.

第56–58題請聽下面這段三人之間的對話。
女1：我剛搬到五樓的新辦公室，那裡很明亮且陽光充足，還可以看到公園。
女2：對啊，那間辦公室看出去景色很棒。你能得到那間真的非常幸運，瑪麗亞。
女1：我知道。我是說，五樓辦公室特別好。
男： 我的辦公室面向停車場。
女2：噢，別難過啦，你才到公司幾個月而已。
女1：對啊，過一陣子你或許就有機會換到更好的辦公室了。
男： 你說得對，我不該擔心的，尤其這份工作的其他各方面我都很喜歡。

363

56. What does Maria mean when she says, "I know"？瑪麗亞說「I know」是什麼意思？
    (A) She is familiar with the offices on the fifth floor. 她很熟悉五樓辦公室。
    (B) She agrees with what the other woman said. 她同意另一名女子所說的。
    (C) She understands how to get a good office. 她知道如何得到一間好辦公室。
    (D) She has some important information. 她知道一些重要資訊。

解析 (B) 另一名女子說瑪麗亞很幸運可以得到這麼好的辦公室，瑪麗亞說「I know」表示同意。選項(A)(C)(D)都不符合這裡的語境。

57. What describes the man's office? 下列哪一句話可以描述男子的辦公室？
    (A) It is near a park. 靠近公園。
    (B) It is bright and sunny. 明亮又充滿陽光。
    (C) It overlooks a vacant lot. 俯瞰一片空地。
    (D) It has a view of the parking lot. 看出去是停車場。

解析 (D) 男子說「My office faces the parking lot」，表示他的辦公室面向停車場。選項(A)和(B)描述的是瑪麗亞的辦公室。選項(C)重複使用了 lot 這個字。

58. What is suggested about the man? 關於這名男子，對話中有何暗示？
    (A) He is unhappy with his job. 他不滿意自己的工作。
    (B) He is worried about his work. 他很擔心自己的工作。
    (C) He has been at his job a short time. 他才剛做這份工作沒多久。
    (D) He often works until late at night. 他時常加班到很晚。

解析 (C) 其中一名女子對男子說「You've been at the company only a few months」（你才到公司幾個月），而另一名女子又補充說「you'll probably get a better office after a while」（過一陣子你或許有機會換到更好的辦公室），兩句話都說明了男子才剛做這份工作沒多久。選項(A)和(B)不正確是因為男子說他喜歡這份工作。選項(D)在對話中沒有提及。

Questions 59 through 61 refer to the following conversation.

Woman: Mmm, everything on the menu looks so good. You're still serving breakfast, right?

Man: Uh huh. We serve it all day. You can have breakfast morning, noon, or night.

Woman: Oh. Lovely. But it's still not noon yet, and that's the best time for breakfast as far as I'm concerned. So, anyhow, I'll have, let's see, bring me the number two with whole wheat toast and a cup of coffee. Cream and sugar in the coffee, please. Oh, and some grape jelly for the toast.

Man: Number two, whole wheat toast, grape jelly, got it. Be right back with your beverage.

第59–61題請聽下面這段對話。

女：嗯，菜單上每樣看起來都好好吃喔。早餐還有供應對吧？

男：有的，全日供應，早、中、晚都可以吃早餐。

女：喔，太好了。現在還不到中午，對我來說是吃早餐的最佳時間。總之我要，我看看……我要二號餐配全麥吐司，還要一杯咖啡，加奶油和糖，謝謝。喔，還要葡萄果醬，抹在吐司上的。

男：二號餐，全麥吐司，葡萄果醬，好的。馬上幫您送上飲料。

59. What is the woman doing? 這名女子正在做什麼？
　　(A) Ordering a meal 點餐
　　(B) Planning a menu 規劃菜單
　　(C) Cooking some food 做飯
　　(D) Shopping for groceries 購買食品雜貨

解析 (A) 女子正在看菜單，並請男子幫她送一點食物過來，所以是在餐廳點餐。選項(B)(C)(D)都和餐飲的主題有關，但都不是正確答案。

60. What time of day is it? 現在是一天的什麼時候？
　　(A) Morning 早上
　　(B) Noon 中午
　　(C) Afternoon 下午
　　(D) Night 晚上

解析 (A) 女子說「it's still not noon yet」（還不到中午），所以是早上。選項(B)(C)(D)的時間都與這句描述不符。

61. What will the man do next? 這名男子接下來會做什麼？
    (A) Bring ice cream 拿冰淇淋過來
    (B) Bring a menu 拿菜單過來
    (C) Serve coffee 上咖啡
    (D) Look for jelly 尋找果醬

解析 (C) 男子說「Be right back with your beverage」（馬上幫您送上飲料），而女子點的飲料是咖啡。選項(A)是被女子咖啡要加的奶油（cream）給搞混了。選項(B)不正確，女子已經有菜單了。選項(D)重複使用了jelly這個字，女子要了果醬來配吐司，但不是男子說要馬上送來的東西。

Questions 62 through 64 refer to the following conversation.
Woman: Excuse me. Can you tell me when we're due in Boston?
Man: Very shortly. I heard a crew member say we'll be docking at one thirty, and then we can go ashore right away.
Woman: Wonderful. I'm really looking forward to seeing the city. We couldn't have better weather for sightseeing. There's a guided tour for passengers, isn't there?
Man: Yes, I believe a bus will be leaving the dock at two o'clock.
Woman: That sounds fun.
Man: Uh huh. But, personally I think it'd be more fun to just walk around. Most of the famous sights are close to the harbor.
Woman: Maybe that isn't a bad idea. It might even be interesting to just sit in a café for a bit and watch the people go by.

第62–64題請聽下面這段對話。
女：不好意思，請問我們預計什麼時候會到波士頓？
男：很快，我聽到一個船員說一點三十分會靠港，那時我們可以立刻上岸。
女：太棒了，好期待看看這座城市，今天天氣很好，最適合觀光了。聽說有個導覽行程給乘客參加，對嗎？
男：對，有一輛遊覽車應該兩點時會從碼頭出發。
女：好像很有趣。
男：是啊，不過我個人覺得四處走走更有意思，大部分知名景點都在港口附近。
女：那或許是個不錯的想法。說不定只是在咖啡館坐一下，看著人來人往都很有趣。

62. Where does this conversation take place? 這段對話發生在什麼地方？
    (A) On a cruise ship 遊輪上
    (B) On a tour bus 觀光巴士上
    (C) On a plane 飛機上
    (D) On a train 火車上

解析 (A) 男子提到了靠港（docking）和上岸（go ashore），所以他們是在一艘遊輪上。選項(B)被乘客上岸後要參加的城市觀光巴士遊覽行程給誤導了。選項(C)和(D)也是會有乘客的地方，但不符合這裡的語境。

63. What does the woman ask about? 這名女子詢問了什麼？
    (A) The length of the trip 行程長度
    (B) The cost of tickets 票價
    (C) The arrival time 抵達時間
    (D) The weather 天氣

解析 (C) 女子問說「Can you tell me when we're due in Boston?」，due 就是「預定抵達」的意思。選項(A)和這裡的旅行語境有關，但對話中並未提及。選項(B)是從語境相關的 ships（船）和 tour buses（觀光巴士）聯想到 tickets，但對話中並沒有提到票價的事。選項(D)是因為女子提到天氣而有所混淆，女子是說天氣很好，不是詢問天氣如何。

64. What does the man recommend? 男子建議做什麼？
    (A) Taking a guided tour 參加導覽行程
    (B) Walking around 四處走走
    (C) Leaving the city 離開這座城市
    (D) Going to a café 去一間咖啡館

解析 (B) 男子說「I think it'd be more fun to just walk around」，表示他只想四處走走看看。選項(A)和(D)是女子的想法。選項(C)重複使用了 city 這個字，但對話中沒有提到要離開城市。

Questions 65 through 67 refer to the following conversation and schedule.

Man: We have to finish cleaning the conference room. The walls and windows are done but the carpet still needs shampooing.
Woman: Right. It should be done soon, but I've checked the schedule and it looks like that room's being used for something every day next week.
Man: Let me see. Oh, here, the staff meeting. That only takes the morning, so the room will be free in the afternoon.
Woman: All right. I'll schedule the cleaning for then. It's a good thing we were able to book this company. They're so reliable. It's worth the extra cost.
Man: I know. Those cleaners at that old company were terrible. They never showed up on time and then always had to hurry to finish the job.

第65–67題請聽下面這段對話，並參考時間表。
男：我們必須把會議室打掃完畢，牆壁和窗戶已經清潔好了，但地毯還要洗。
女：對，這件事要趕快做好。但我查了會議室的時間表，下週好像每天都排了活動。
男：我看看。哦，這裡，員工會議。員工會議只有早上，會議室下午就空了。
女：好，我就排定這個時間清洗。我們能預約到這家公司真好，他們很可靠，價格貴一點是值得的。
男：我知道。之前那家公司的清潔人員好糟糕，從來不準時到，每次都只能匆匆忙忙把事情做完。

會議室使用時間表

星期一	星期二	星期三	星期四
培訓課程	員工會議	工作面試	工作坊

65. What has to be cleaned? 什麼必須要清洗？
    (A) The furniture 家具
    (B) The windows 窗戶
    (C) The walls 牆壁
    (D) The carpet 地毯

解析 (D) 男子說「the carpet still needs shampooing」，shampooing 就是「洗（地毯）」的意思。選項(A)未被提及。選項(B)和(C)已經清洗好了。

66. Look at the graphic. When will the cleaning be done? 請看圖表，清潔工作將於哪一天完成？
    (A) Monday 星期一
    (B) Tuesday 星期二
    (C) Wednesday 星期三
    (D) Thursday 星期四

解析 (B) 男子建議把清潔工作排在員工會議那天，根據圖表，員工會議是星期二。選項(A)(C)(D)排定的是其他活動。

67. What was the problem with the previous cleaners? 之前的清潔人員有什麼問題？
    (A) They charged too much. 收費過高。
    (B) They always arrived late. 總是遲到。
    (C) They never finished the job. 從未把工作做完。
    (D) They were difficult to schedule. 很難預約時間。

解析 (B) 男子說「They never showed up on time」（從未準時出現），就是遲到的意思。選項(A)不大可能，因為女子說新的清潔人員「價錢貴一點是值得的」（worth the extra cost），這就表示之前的比較便宜。選項(C)和(D)分別使用了對話中的詞語 finish the job 和 schedule，但描述的內容均和對話不符。

Questions 68 through 70 refer to the following conversation and advertisement.

Woman: I'd like to pay for this shirt, please.
Man: Certainly. And you're in luck! There's a discount on all clothing this week.
Woman: Oh. I wasn't aware. In that case, I'd like another one. Do you have them in green?
Man: We do. Same size?
Woman: Yes. I'll keep this blue one for me, and the green one will be a gift for my sister, and she's the same size as me.
Man: I'll have someone get it for you. Your sister will like it. These shirts are selling fast. Everyone seems to want one.

第68–70題請聽下面這段對話，並參考廣告標示。
女：我要結帳這件襯衫，謝謝。
男：好的。你很幸運！這週所有服飾都有折扣。
女：哦，我都不知道。這樣的話，我還要再買一件，有綠色的嗎？
男：有的，同樣尺寸嗎？
女：對，藍色的我自己要，綠色的送我姐姐，她的尺寸和我一樣。
男：我請人幫你拿。你姐姐一定會喜歡的，這些襯衫賣得很快，似乎大家都想要一件。

```
克拉克百貨公司
全店特賣，千萬別錯過！

學校用品 ..................... 九折
居家用品 ..................... 八五折
服飾 ........................... 八折
圖書與玩具 ................. 七五折
```

68. Look at the graphic. How much of a discount will the woman get on her purchase? 請看圖表，女子買的東西可以打幾折？
    (A) 10％ 九折
    (B) 15％ 八五折
    (C) 20％ 八折
    (D) 25％ 七五折

解析 (C) 女子買的是襯衫，屬於服飾類，廣告標示服飾打八折。選項 (A)(B)(D) 是其他商品的折扣。

69. What does the woman ask the man for? 女子要男子給她什麼？
    (A) Another color 另一個顏色
    (B) A larger size 大一點的尺寸
    (C) Gift wrapping 禮物包裝
    (D) More discounts 更多折扣

解析 (A) 女子問說「Do you have them in green?」，所以她要了另一個顏色。選項 (B) 不正確，女子買了兩件同尺寸的襯衫。選項 (C) 指的是其中一件襯衫要送給姐姐當禮物，但女子沒有提出要包裝。選項 (D) 不正確，女子看起來對目前的折扣很滿意，還因為打折而多買了一件。

70. What does the man say about the item the woman is purchasing? 對於女子所購買的物品，男子有何描述？
    (A) It is very popular. 很熱賣。
    (B) It is of high quality. 品質很好。
    (C) It is a new item in the store. 是店裡的新品。
    (D) It is available this week only. 只有本週才買得到。

解析 (A) 男子說「These shirts are selling fast. Everyone seems to want one.」（這些襯衫賣很快，大家都想要），可見很多人都喜歡。選項 (B) 和 (C) 雖然也有可能，但對話中並沒有提到。選項 (D) 不正確，只限本週的是折扣而不是襯衫。

Part 4：簡短獨白

> 作答方式：你會聽到一名說話者的獨白。每段獨白搭配三個問題，各有四個選項。選出最適當的答案回答問題，並將答案卡上對應的橢圓框塗滿。

Questions 71 through 73 refer to the following announcement.

The moment you've been waiting for has finally arrived. I'm talking about the event that's been years in the planning and months in the making. That's right, it's the inauguration of the new City Garden Park. We'll be celebrating all next weekend with activities for the whole family, so come on down to City Garden Park and join in the fun. The weather promises to be fine, and you'll enjoy barbecues, games and rides, a concert by our own City High School band, not to mention speeches by Mayor Green and other city officials. Attendance at the concert and speech ceremony is free, but tickets are required as seating is limited. Get yours by phoning City Hall before Thursday evening.

第 71–73 題請聽下面這則公告。

各位等待已久的一刻終於來臨。我說的是歷經多年計劃和數個月籌備的盛事，沒錯！就是新的城市花園公園的開幕典禮。下週末我們會舉辦適合全家大小的慶祝活動，歡迎前來城市花園公園共襄盛舉。下週末預期會是好天氣，現場有烤肉可以享用，有遊戲攤位和遊樂設施，還有由我們城市高中樂隊所帶來的演奏會，更不用說格林市長和其他市府官員將蒞臨致詞。演奏會與致詞典禮皆為免費參加，但由於座位有限，必須事先索取門票，有需要請在週四晚上前打電話到市政府索取。

71. What kind of event is being announced? 宣布了何種活動？
    (A) A garden tour 花園參觀活動
    (B) A high school graduation 高中畢業典禮
    (C) The opening of a new park 新公園開幕典禮
    (D) The inauguration of a new mayor 新市長就職典禮

解析 (C) 說話者說「it's the inauguration of the new City Garden Park」，所以是新公園的開幕典禮。選項(A)重複使用了 garden 這個字。選項(B)重複使用了 high school 這個片語。選項(D)重複使用了 inauguration 和 mayor 這兩個字。

72. When will the event take place? 這場活動將在何時舉行？
    (A) Next Thursday 下週四
    (B) Next week 下週
    (C) Next weekend 下週末
    (D) Next year 明年

解析 (C) 說話者說「We'll be celebrating all next weekend」，所以是下週末。選項(A)是索票的截止日。選項(B)的發音和正確答案十分接近。選項(D)重複使用了year這個字，敘述中講的是該活動在舉辦之前歷經了多年計劃（years in the planning）。

73. How can you get a ticket for the ceremony? 要如何取得慶祝活動的門票？
    (A) Line up at the park 到公園排隊
    (B) Pay three dollars 付三塊錢
    (C) Order it online 上網訂票
    (D) Call City Hall 打電話到市政府

解析 (D) 說話者請有需要的人打電話到市政府索取門票。選項(A)混淆了近音字fine和line，並重複使用了park這個字。選項(B)混淆了近音字free和three，而且門票不用錢，所以也不正確。選項(C)混淆了近音字fine和online。

Questions 74 through 76 refer to the following advertisement.

Are you bored with your current job? With the right training, you can start a new career in business. Our computer school can train you in just six months on the most popular business software. Learn word processing, spread sheets, data management, and more. Job placement assistance is available at the end of the course. Are you currently working during the daytime? Don't worry! All our classes are taught evenings and weekends to accommodate the busy schedules of working people like you. Call now to register.

第74–76題請聽下面這則廣告。

你厭倦了現在的工作嗎？只要接受正確的訓練，就能在商業領域展開全新的職業生涯。我們的電腦學校能在短短六個月內訓練你使用大部分的熱門商業軟體，你將學到文字處理、試算表、資料管理等各項技能。課程結束時，我們也會提供就業安置協助。你目前白天要上班嗎？別擔心！為了配合像你這樣行程忙碌的上班族，我們所有課程都安排在夜間或週末。現在立即打電話報名。

74. What kind of training does this school provide? 這所學校提供何種培訓？
    (A) Computer skills 電腦技能
    (B) Business management 商業管理
    (C) Personnel training 人員培訓
    (D) Teacher preparation 師資培育

> **解析 (A)** 從廣告內容可得知這是一所電腦學校（computer school），提供的當然是電腦技能方面的訓練。選項(B)不正確，這所學校的目的是訓練學生使用商業軟體（business software），而不是商業管理（business management）。選項(D)不正確，這所學校是在教學（teaches），不是培育師資（train teachers）。

75. What is indicated about the school? 廣告中對這所學校有何說明？
    (A) It is very popular. 很熱門。
    (B) It has many students. 學生很多。
    (C) It has recently opened. 最近才剛開辦。
    (D) It is for working people. 專為上班族設立。

> **解析 (D)** 說話者先是問「你是否厭倦現在的工作」（Are you bored with your current job?），然後提到該校的課程表是專為「像你這樣的上班族」（working people like you）而制定的，所以這所學校是為了目前有工作的上班族而設立。選項(A)重複使用了 popular 這個字，廣告中的 popular 描述的是商業軟體。選項(B)和(C)不是沒有可能，只是廣告中並未提及。

76. What service does the school provide? 這所學校有提供什麼服務？
    (A) Help finding employment 協助就業
    (B) Tutoring for individuals 個人輔導
    (C) Free parking on site 免費現場停車
    (D) Tuition assistance 學費援助

> **解析 (A)** 說話者提到「Job placement assistance is available」，表示有提供就業輔導的協助。選項(B)(C)(D)都有可能，但並未提及。

Questions 77 through 79 refer to the following message.

This message is for Zach Robertson. This is Ken, Dr. Phillips' assistant, calling. I've arranged your travel to Boston for this weekend's workshop. Please take Train three-four-two-five, leaving your city at four forty-five p.m. on Friday. You'll arrive in Boston at seven twenty-five p.m. I'll be waiting for you at the station, and I'll take you by taxi to the hotel. You're scheduled to return home Monday morning. Dr. Phillips wants to take you to breakfast that morning, and she'll drive you to the station in time for your train. Please check your e-mail for your complete itinerary and my contact information, in case you have any questions. We're looking forward to meeting you.

第 77–79 題請聽下面這段留言。

這通留言是給札克・羅伯森。我是肯恩，菲利普斯博士的助理。我已經幫您安排好前來波士頓的交通方式，以便參加週末的工作坊。請搭乘週五下午4點45分從您城市出發的3425號列車，接著您將於晚上7點25分抵達波士頓。我會在車站等您，再一起坐計程車到飯店。您預定週一早上回家，當天早上菲利普斯博士想帶您去吃早餐，接著會開車送您到車站，讓您準時搭上火車。請查看您的電子郵件，內含您的完整行程和我的聯絡方式，萬一您有問題可以參考。我們期待與您見面。

77. Why is Mr. Robertson going to Boston? 羅伯森先生為什麼要到波士頓？
    (A) To be a radio station guest 擔任廣播電臺嘉賓
    (B) To attend a workshop 參加工作坊
    (C) To meet with a client 和客戶會面
    (D) To enjoy a vacation 度假

解析 (B) 說話者說「I've arranged your travel to Boston for this weekend's workshop」，可知他要來參加工作坊。選項(A)搞錯了station的意義，留言中指的是火車站（train station），而不是廣播電臺（radio station）。選項(C)和(D)也是人們會前往某個地方的原因，但此處沒有提到這兩件事。

78. How will Mr. Robertson get to Boston? 羅伯森先生會使用哪種交通方式前往波士頓？
    (A) By train 搭火車
    (B) By taxi 搭計程車
    (C) By plane 搭飛機
    (D) By car 開車

解析 (A) 說話者說到「take Train 3425」，可知是搭火車。選項(B)是羅伯森先生抵達波士頓後，接著會使用的交通方式。選項(C)的發音和正確答案十分接近。選項(D)和留言中的drive這個字有關，是羅伯森先生要返家當天前往火車站的交通方式。

79. What is in the e-mail? 電子郵件當中含有什麼？
    (A) A travel ticket 交通票券
    (B) A trip schedule 行程表
    (C) A hotel reservation 飯店訂房紀錄
    (D) A question list 問題列表

解析 (B) 說話者說「Please check your e-mail for your complete itinerary」，表示附上了完整的行程表。選項(A)和留言的主題有關，但留言中沒有提到任何交通票券。選項(C)重複使用了hotel這個字。選項(D)重複使用了question這個字。

Questions 80 through 82 refer to the following voice mail message.

Hello. This is Steve Jones calling from Whitman's Downtown just to let you know that the new rug you ordered for your office is here. It came in on last night's delivery. The desk and chairs you ordered should be in next week. So, uh, according to our records, no payment is due on the rug as that was taken care of when you placed the order. So all you need to do is come down and get the rug. You can come by any time that's convenient for you. Someone will be here all day until five thirty. Call back if you have any questions.

第80–82題請聽下面這段語音信箱留言。

您好，這裡是惠特曼市中心店，我是史蒂夫・瓊斯。要通知您，您訂購辦公室要用的地毯已經到店了，昨晚到貨的。您訂購的桌椅大概下個禮拜會到貨。所以，呃，根據我們的紀錄，地毯不需要付款，您下單時已經付清了，所以您只需過來取貨地毯即可。您方便的時候隨時可以過來，我們這裡到五點半前全天都有人在。有任何問題都可以打電話過來。

80. What kind of business most likely is Whitman's Downtown? 惠特曼市中心店最有可能從事哪方面的生意？
    (A) Delivery service 送貨服務
    (B) Furniture store 家具行
    (C) Interior decorator 室內設計
    (D) Rug cleaning service 地毯清洗服務

解析 (B) 說話者是從惠特曼市中心店打電話過來的，從留言中可得知他賣了一張地毯、一個桌子和幾張椅子給聽者，所以很有可能是經營家具行的。選項(A)是被留言中提到地毯昨天到貨給混淆了。選項(C)是從新家具聯想到室內設計。選項(D)重複使用了rug這個字，但留言中說的顯然是地毯銷售而不是清洗。

375

81. What does the speaker mean when he says, "that was taken care of"? 說話者說「that was taken care of」是什麼意思？
   (A) The order has been placed. 訂單已經下好了。
   (B) The invoice has been prepared. 請款單已經準備好了。
   (C) The rug has already been paid for. 地毯的錢已經付了。
   (D) The store will handle the rug carefully. 店家會小心處理這張地毯。

解析 (C) 說話者說「no payment is due on the rug as that was taken care of when you placed the order」，「was taken care of」是「已經處理好了」，意思是顧客已經把地毯的錢付清了。選項(A)重複使用了order和placed兩個字。選項(B)使用了payment的相關字invoice。選項(D)是有可能的，但留言中並未提及。

82. What does the speaker ask the listener to do? 說話者要求聽者做什麼事？
   (A) Call to make an appointment 打電話約時間
   (B) Check the delivery schedule 查看配送時程表
   (C) Visit Whitman's by 5：30 五點半前到惠特曼商店
   (D) Review the records 查看紀錄

解析 (C) 說話者說顧客可以過來拿地毯，接著又說「Someone will be here all day until five thirty」，暗示五點半關門，因此顧客應在那個時間之前來店內取貨。選項(A)重複使用了call這個字。選項(B)重複使用了delivery這個字。選項(D)重複使用了records這個字。

Questions 83 through 85 refer to the following announcement.

The Royal Hotel is currently accepting applications for a variety of jobs. We have positions open for front desk clerks, waiters, food prep assistants, and housekeepers. None of these positions require experience because we train all new employees. All you need is a desire to learn. You must be over eighteen and willing to work weekends. We offer competitive wages and opportunity for advancement. Interested parties should apply in person to the hotel manager.

第83-85題請聽下面這則公告。

皇家飯店目前有多項職位開放應徵，我們的職缺包括前檯接待員、服務生、備餐助理和房務員。所有職位均無經驗要求，因我們會為所有新進員工提供培訓，你只要肯學習就好。應徵者須年滿十八歲，且願意週末上班。我們提供有競爭力的薪資和升遷機會。意者請親自找飯店經理應徵職位。

83. What is a requirement for job applicants? 工作應徵者的要求條件是什麼？
   (A) A professional certificate 專業證照
   (B) Availability on weekends 週末可上班
   (C) A high school diploma 高中文憑
   (D) Previous experience 過去經驗

解析 (B) 說話者說「You must be over eighteen and willing to work weekends」，可知應徵者必須可以週末上班。選項(A)(C)(D)是常見的工作要求，但在這裡並未提及。

84. What is mentioned as a job benefit? 下列哪一項是工作福利之一？
   (A) Possible promotions 升遷機會
   (B) Regular salary raises 定期加薪
   (C) Paid vacation time 有薪假
   (D) Insurance 保險

解析 (A) 說話者提到他們提供升遷機會（opportunity for advancement）。選項(B)(C)(D)都是常見的工作福利，但在這裡都沒有提及。

85. How should you apply for these jobs? 你要如何應徵這些職位？
   (A) Send a résumé 寄送履歷
   (B) Go to the hotel 前往飯店
   (C) Write a letter 寫信
   (D) Make a phone call 打電話

解析 (B) 說話者提到「apply in person」（親自應徵），意思就是要本人前往飯店。選項(A)(C)(D)都是常見的應徵方式，但在這裡都沒有提及。

Questions 86 through 88 refer to the following instructions.

Welcome to the new automated ticket system of City Bus Service. Please follow these instructions to purchase your ticket. To begin, enter the date and time of your travel, then select one-way or round trip. When the ticket price appears on the screen, insert your credit card into the upper slot. Retrieve your printed ticket from the bottom slot. This machine does not accept cash. Please approach the ticket office if you wish to pay cash. Please buy your ticket before boarding, as drivers cannot issue tickets.

第 86–88 題請聽下面這段指示。

歡迎使用城市公車服務的全新自動購票系統，請依下列指示購票。首先，輸入行程日期和時間，接著選擇單程或來回。當螢幕顯示票價時，將您的信用卡插入上方插槽，並自下方

插槽取出票券。本機器不接受現金，欲以現金購票者請洽售票處。請在上車前完成購票，因駕駛員無法出票。

86. Where would you hear this message? 你會在哪裡聽到這段訊息？
    (A) At a bus station 公車站
    (B) At a train station 火車站
    (C) At an airport 機場
    (D) At a subway station 地鐵站

解析 (A) 說話者提到城市公車服務（City Bus Service），隨後又提到駕駛員（driver），可以判斷是公車站。選項(B)(C)(D)都是需要買票的地點，但在這裡不是正確答案。

87. What should the customer do first? 顧客首先要做什麼事？
    (A) Insert a credit card 插入信用卡
    (B) Check the ticket price 查看票價
    (C) Enter the travel schedule 輸入行程資訊
    (D) Select one-way or round trip 選擇單程或來回

解析 (C) 說話者說「To begin, enter the date and time of your travel」（首先，輸入行程日期和時間），指的就是行程資訊（travel schedule）。選項(A)(B)(D)都是後面的步驟。

88. How can a customer pay cash? 顧客要如何才能付現？
    (A) Show an ID card 出示身分證
    (B) Go to the ticket office 前往售票處
    (C) Insert dollar bills in the slot 將美元鈔票插入插槽
    (D) Buy the ticket from the driver 向駕駛員購票

解析 (B) 說話者說「Please approach the ticket office if you wish to pay cash」，所以是到售票處才能付現。選項(A)把credit card（信用卡）和ID card（身分證）搞混了。選項(C)不正確，指示中提到機器不接受現金。選項(D)不正確，指示中說駕駛員無法出票。

Questions 89 through 91 refer to the following talk.

Even though you are a busy executive, you need to take breaks regularly, so set aside some time during the workday for yourself. The amount doesn't matter so much—an hour, half hour, fifteen minutes—whatever works for you. Close your office door and tell your assistant to hold all calls. Walk away from your computer and put down your mobile phone. Use this time for relaxing your mind. Use whatever techniques suit you best, such as meditation, deep breathing, or reading. Some executives even take a nap, and they don't consider that a poor use of time. A relaxed mind is ready to take on difficult tasks once the break is over.

第 89–91 題請聽下面這段談話。

即使你是忙碌的主管，也需要定時休息，請在工作日留一點時間給自己。時間長短不重要——一小時、半小時、十五分鐘——看你方便就好。將辦公室的門關上，並告知助理暫時別把電話轉接進來。離開電腦，放下手機。利用這段時間放鬆你的大腦，用任何適合你的方式，例如：冥想、深呼吸或閱讀。有些主管甚至會小睡一會，且他們不覺得這樣是浪費時間。大腦放鬆了，才能在休息結束後迎接困難的任務。

89. What is the purpose of this talk? 這段談話的目的是什麼？
    (A) To compare different work methods 比較不同的工作方式
    (B) To describe some relaxation techniques 描述一些放鬆的技巧
    (C) To explain how to organize work schedules 說明如何安排工作時程
    (D) To give advice about relaxing during the work day 提供在工作日放鬆的建議

解析 (D) 這段談話旨在強調工作日也要定時休息的重要性，並且建議可以怎麼做。選項 (A)(B)(C) 都不是這段談話的目的。

90. According to the speaker, how can you keep others from disturbing you? 根據說話者的說法，怎樣可以不讓別人打擾你？
    (A) Work at home 在家工作
    (B) Close the door 關門
    (C) Take a vacation 度假
    (D) Put up a "Do not disturb" sign 掛上「請勿打擾」的牌子

解析 (B) 說話者的建議是把門關上。選項 (A) 和這段談話的主題有關，但沒有被提及。選項 (C) 把 take a break 的意思混淆了，break 雖然也有「假期」的意思，但在這裡指「休息」。且談話中只有建議休息一下，並無提及去度假。選項 (D) 不無可能，但並未提及。

91. What does the speaker mean when he says, "They don't consider that a poor use of time"? 說話者說「They don't consider that a poor use of time」是什麼意思？
    (A) Efficiency is a common goal. 效率是共同的目標。
    (B) Taking naps can be very useful. 小睡一會非常有用。
    (C) Executives don't often have free time. 主管通常沒有空閒時間。
    (D) It is important to organize your time well. 妥善安排自己的時間很重要。

解析 (B) 這句話是用來說明前面小睡一會的建議，強調這項活動其實是善用時間的好方法。選項 (A)(C)(D) 都不符合這段談話的語境，也不是這句話的意思。

Questions 92 through 94 refer to the following announcement.

Thank you for joining us this afternoon at the third annual International Music Awards Ceremony. We support the musicians of the future by honoring teenage musicians who show special promise. The money we award today is intended to help these fine young people on their journeys toward a professional career in music. Each honoree will receive five thousand dollars, which may be used for private music lessons, tuition to music school, or attendance at special educational programs. Without the generous support of people like you, we wouldn't be able to honor our fine young musicians. Please continue to give generously. You can make a donation today by placing it in one of the red boxes in this room.

第 92–94 題請聽下面這段公告。

感謝各位今天下午來參加第三屆的年度國際音樂大獎頒獎典禮。我們藉由表彰那些展現非凡潛力的青少年音樂家，來支持音樂界的明日之星。我們今天所要頒發的獎金，旨在幫助這些優秀的年輕人踏上專業音樂生涯的旅程。每位受獎人將可獲得五千美元，可用來上私人音樂課、支付音樂學校的學費，或拿來參加特殊教育課程。沒有各位的慷慨支持，我們就無法表彰這些優秀的年輕音樂家。懇請各位繼續慷慨解囊，今天就可以捐款，請將款項投入室內任一個紅色捐款箱。

92. Who are the awards for? 這個獎項是頒給誰的？
    (A) Professional musicians 專業音樂家
    (B) Orchestra members 管弦樂團團員
    (C) Young musicians 年輕音樂家
    (D) Music teachers 音樂老師

解析 (C) 說話者分別提到「honoring teenage musicians」和「honor our fine young musicians」由此可知受獎人是年輕音樂家。選項 (A)(B)(D) 都是以音樂為職業的人，但不是正確答案。

93. What kind of award is being given? 獎品是什麼形式？
    (A) Cash 現金
    (B) Trophy 獎杯
    (C) A trip 旅遊
    (D) A musical instrument 樂器

解析 (A) 說話者分別提到「The money we award today」和「Each honoree will receive five thousand dollars」，可知是頒發獎金五千美元。選項 (B)(C)(D) 是其他形式的獎品，但這裡沒有提到。

94. What are listeners asked to do? 聽者被要求做什麼？
    (A) Pay their bills 付帳單
    (B) Give money 給錢
    (C) Teach music 教音樂
    (D) Practice more 多練習

解析 (B) 聽者被要求捐款，未來才能繼續頒發這個獎項。選項(A)(C)(D)是得獎者拿到錢之後可能做的事。

Questions 95 through 97 refer to the following talk and map.

Welcome to the Highbury House tour. As you know, this building was first constructed as a residence for the Highbury family and has since been used as a hotel and office building, until it became the history museum you see today. We're standing now in the Main Hall. After we enjoy the paintings in here, we'll move on to the exhibits in the other rooms. Unfortunately, the Green Room is closed today for cleaning, but the rest of the rooms are open. After the tour, you may want to look at the gardens on your own. The flowers are lovely this time of year, and I believe there is a lunchtime concert scheduled there today.

第 95–97 題請聽下面這段談話，並參考地圖。

歡迎各位來參觀海伯里大宅。大家都知道，這棟建築最早是海伯里家族的宅邸，後來改作飯店和辦公大樓，直到今日成為各位眼前的歷史博物館。我們現在所在位置是主廳，我們會先在這裡欣賞畫作，再去參觀其他房間的展品。不巧的是，綠廳今天正在進行清潔，所以沒有開放，但其他展廳都有開放。參觀完畢後，你們可以自行到花園逛一逛。這個季節正好繁花盛開，且我記得那裡今天的午餐時間有一場音樂會。

海伯里大宅

藍廳	紅廳
地圖	文件
主廳	綠廳
繪畫	歷史展品

95. What was the original use of Highbury House? 海伯里大宅最早是作為什麼之用？
    (A) Private family home 私宅
    (B) Office building 辦公大樓
    (C) Museum 博物館
    (D) Hotel 飯店

    解析 (A) 說話者描述這棟建築時說「this building was first constructed as a residence for the Highbury family」，由此可知建造之初是作為一個家族的私人住宅。選項(B)(C)(D)是這棟建築後來的用途。

96. Look at the graphic. Which exhibit will listeners be unable to see today? 請看圖表，聽者今天將無法欣賞到哪一項展品？
    (A) Maps 地圖
    (B) Paintings 繪畫
    (C) Documents 文件
    (D) History displays 歷史展品

    解析 (D) 說話者說「the Green Room is closed today」（綠廳今天關閉），從圖中可以看到綠廳展示的是歷史展品。選項(A)(B)(C)是其他展廳的展品，今天都有開放。

97. What does the speaker suggest listeners do? 說話者建議聽者做什麼事？
    (A) Check the concert schedule 查看音樂會的時間表
    (B) Visit the flower gardens 參觀花園
    (C) Return later in the year 今年晚些時候再來
    (D) Have lunch soon 盡快去吃午餐

    解析 (B) 說話者提到「After the tour, you may want to look at the gardens on your own」，建議聽者自己到花園逛一逛。選項(A)是被花園今天有音樂演奏給混淆了。選項(C)重複使用了 year 這個字。選項(D)是被談話中提到的 lunchtime 給誤導，說話者是說午餐時間會有音樂會，不是叫大家去吃午餐。

Questions 98 through 100 refer to the following meeting excerpt and schedule.

Before we end our meeting today, I have a couple of housekeeping items. First, in order to thank you all for the fantastic job you did during inventory last week, you are invited to a special staff luncheon next week. Unfortunately, the offices are scheduled for painting then, too, and since this conference room is the only one large enough, we'll have to wait till they've finished painting it. So we've scheduled the luncheon for the very next day. I hope you all can come. OK, I think that's it for today. If you would just put your coffee cups back on the snack table before you leave, that would be helpful. Thanks.

第 98–100 題請聽下面這段會議節錄，並參考時程表。

今天會議結束之前，我有幾件小事項要提醒大家。首先，為了感謝各位在上週盤點期間表現出色，下週要邀請大家參加特別舉辦的員工午餐會。可惜的是，辦公室已經預定了下週要進行粉刷，而且只有這間會議室夠大，所以我們只能等到他們粉刷完畢再來聚餐。所以我們就把午餐會定在粉刷結束的隔天，希望大家都能來參加。好了，今天就到這裡結束，麻煩請大家離開之前，隨手把咖啡杯放回點心桌上，謝謝大家。

粉刷時程表

星期一	星期二	星期三	星期四
接待區	員工休息室	會議室	前辦公室

98. What event will take place next week? 下週會舉辦什麼活動？
    (A) A luncheon 午餐會
    (B) Inventory 盤點、清點
    (C) A staff meeting 員工會議
    (D) Conference registration 會議登記

解析 (A) 說話者說「you are invited to a special staff luncheon next week」，所以會舉辦一場員工午餐會。選項 (B)(C)(D) 都重複使用了談話中的單字，但都不是正確答案。

383

99. Look at the graphic. Which day will the event take place? 請看圖表，這項活動會在哪一天舉辦？
    (A) Monday 星期一
    (B) Tuesday 星期二
    (C) Wednesday 星期三
    (D) Thursday 星期四

解析 (D) 說話者說午餐會預定在會議室完成粉刷後的隔天舉辦，會議室的粉刷日是星期三，所以午餐會是在星期四舉辦。選項(A)(B)(C)都與說話者的描述不符。

100. What are listeners asked to do next? 聽者被要求接下來做什麼？
    (A) Put the tables away 把桌子收好
    (B) Check the schedule 查看時程表
    (C) Return their cups 把杯子放回去
    (D) Have some coffee 喝點咖啡

解析 (C) 說話者要聽者在離開前把咖啡杯放回點心桌上（put your coffee cups back on the snack table before you leave）。選項(A)(B)(D)都重複使用了談話中的單字，但都不是正確答案。

本測驗之聽力測驗到此結束，請翻頁進行 Part 5 的測驗。

閱讀測驗

在本段測驗當中,你將有機會展現自己對書面英語的理解能力。閱讀測驗共有三個大題,每一大題均有作答說明。

你有 75 分鐘時間完成本測驗的第五到第七大題。

Part 5：句子填空

> **作答方式**：你會看到一個缺字的句子和四個可能的選項，選出最適當的答案，將答案卡上對應的橢圓框塗滿。

101. 只要上一層新的油漆，牆上再掛幾幅畫，這間辦公室就會美觀許多。
　　(A) 但是
　　(B) 和
　　(C) 隨著、因為
　　(D) 雖然、因為

解析 (B) paint 和 pictures 是對等的物品，可以用 and 連接。選項 (A)(C)(D) 只用來連接子句，不能連接兩個名詞。

102. 部門裡大多數人都知道公司必須裁員。
　　(A) 知道的、察覺的
　　(B) 等待
　　(C) 醒、喚醒
　　(D) 敬畏

解析 (A) 題目的 be 動詞後面需要一個形容詞，aware 是選項中唯一的形容詞。選項 (B)(C)(D) 都不符合句子的要求。

103. 行程表內含理查茲博士造訪部門時，各場會議的時間和地點。
　　(A)(B)(C)(D) 包含

解析 (B) 動詞 contains 和第三人稱單數主詞 itinerary 一致。選項 (A) 和 (D) 不是單數形式。選項 (C) 是動名詞，不能當作主要動詞。

104. 乘客可於明天上午八點到十二點間辦理包機報到手續。
　　(A) 在……之間
　　(B) 和……一起、以……方式
　　(C) 穿過
　　(D) 來自

解析 (A) between 可和 and 連用，表達一件事情的開始和結束時間。選項 (B) 的意思是「和……一起」或「以……方式／工具」。選項 (C) 表示穿過某樣東西或某處。選項 (D) 用來說明來源。

105. 景觀設計師提出了幾個建議，其中包括安裝一個自動灑水系統。
    (A) 推薦、建議 (v.)
    (B) 推薦、建議 (ved)
    (C) 推薦、建議 (n.)
    (D) 值得推薦的

解析 (C) recommendations是名詞，在這個句子作動詞made的受詞。選項(A)和(B)是動詞。選項(D)是形容詞。

106. 因為交通狀況，你坐火車會比開車去更快。
    (A) 快的
    (B) 最快的
    (C) 更快的
    (D) 更快的

解析 (D) than需要搭配一個比較級，faster是正確的比較級形式。選項(A)是原級。選項(B)是最高級。選項(C)多了不必要的定冠詞the。

107. 你可以上網繳帳單，或用普通郵件寄出支票。
    (A) 所以
    (B) 或
    (C) 但是
    (D) 既然、自從

解析 (B) or用於兩個事物之間的選擇，以這個句子來說，是在兩種繳帳單的方式之間選擇。選項(A)用來引出一個結果。選項(C)用來引出一個矛盾事實。選項(D)可用來引導一個原因或一個時間。

108. 所有會議發言人都需要被通知發言時間已從三十分鐘縮短為二十五分鐘。
    (A) 加高
    (B) 加長
    (C) 縮短
    (D) 加寬

解析 (C) 從句中可以知道時間被縮短了，被縮短可以用「made shorter」或「shortened」來表示。選項(A)是加高（make higher）。選項(B)是加長（make longer）。選項(D)是加寬（make wider）。

387

109. 我會請助理把必要的表格寄到你的辦公室。
    (A)(B)(C)(D) 寄、送

解析 **(A)** 使役動詞ask後面要用不定詞。選項(B)是動名詞。選項(C)是未來式。選項(D)是現在式。

110. 張小姐十分節儉，她的商務套裝大多是在大型折扣商店買的。
    (A) 那個
    (B) 它們
    (C) 我們的
    (D) 她的

解析 **(D)** her是女性的第三人稱單數所有格形容詞，和先行詞Ms. Chang一致，並且修飾了名詞business suits。選項(A)和(B)都不是所有格形容詞。選項(C)的人稱數量和先行詞不一致。

111. 都市光害嚴重，夜晚很難看到滿天星斗。
    (A)(B)(C)(D) 看到

解析 **(C)** 形容詞difficult後面要接不定詞。選項(A)和(B)是現在式動詞。選項(D)則是動名詞。

112. 所有倉庫員工每三個月都被要求加班進行盤點。
    (A) 要求
    (B) 建議
    (C) 偏好
    (D) 感謝

解析 **(A)** 這個句子是一個被動使役結構，選項(B)(C)(D)都不能當作使役動詞使用。

113. 這份保單涵蓋的保險給付項目十分廣泛。

解析 **(B)** 這個句子的主詞是variety，因此要用單數動詞is。選項(A)是複數動詞。選項(C)是動名詞。選項(D)是原形動詞。

114. 這場頒獎宴會是為了肯定我們優秀員工所達成的眾多成就。
    (A) 肯定
    (B) 決定
    (C) 娛樂
    (D) 分辨

解析 (A) acknowledge 在這裡是「肯定、認可」（= recognize）的意思。選項 (B)(C)(D) 都不符合語意上的要求。

115. 請將行李放在遊覽車旁邊，司機會負責裝車。
    (A) 在……之中
    (B) 在……之間
    (C) 從……起
    (D) 在……旁邊

解析 (D) beside 的意思是「在……旁邊」，符合這裡的語境。選項 (A) 和 (B) 需要兩輛以上的遊覽車當作參考點。選項 (C) 表示「從……起」，語意邏輯不通。

116. 飯店提供住三晚以上的住客優惠價格。
    (A) 講臺
    (B) 最佳狀態／條件
    (C) 最低限度
    (D) 獎金、加價、津貼

解析 (C) 「a minimum of」的意思是「至少」，符合語意要求。選項 (A)(B)(D) 都不符合語意要求。

117. 如果我們不確定產品的安全性，就不會販售。
    (A) 已售出
    (B) 不販售
    (C) 將販售
    (D) 不會販售

解析 (D) 這是一個非真實條件句，表示與現在事實相反，非 if 開頭的子句要用 would。選項 (A) 的時態錯誤。選項 (B) 和 (C) 都沒有用 would。

118. 公司手冊說明了該部門在建立顧客關係方面的政策。
    (A)(B)(C)(D) 說明

解析 **(A)** 習慣性的動作必須使用現在簡單式，而主詞 handbook 是第三人稱單數，因此動詞要用 explains。選項(B)是現在進行式。選項(C)是原形動詞，不能用於第三人稱單數。選項(D)是動名詞。

119. 型號34目前製造商那邊缺貨待補，大概要到春天才會到貨。
    (A) 候選人
    (B) 運輸
    (C) 製造商
    (D) 顧客

解析 **(C)** 這個句子的意思是這項產品（型號34）的製造商要到春天才會補貨並完成訂單。選項(A)(B)(D)都不是可以訂購商品的地方。

120. 拉森先生說他只會考慮用退伍軍人擔任工頭的職位。
    (A) 完全
    (B) 只
    (C) 一些
    (D) 除了

解析 **(B)** only是副詞，修飾動詞consider，這裡的意思是拉森先生只考慮僱用退伍軍人而不考慮其他人。選項(A)(C)(D)都不能放在句子的助動詞和主要動詞之間。

121. 儘管我們已經把預算檢查了兩遍，經理們還是在我們的計算中發現一個錯誤。
    (A) 除非
    (B) 然而
    (C) 既然
    (D) 儘管

解析 **(D)** even though建立了兩個子句之間轉折的邏輯關係。選項(A)(B)(C)放入句中都不合邏輯。

122. 其他人都早早離開辦公室了，所以哈利只好一個人完成報告。
    (A) 單獨的
    (B) 只是
    (C) 他自己
    (D) 單人的

解析 (C) by himself 相當於 alone，意思是「獨自、一個人」，沒有其他人的幫助。選項 (A)(B)(D) 都不能和 by 一起使用。

123. 艾瑟兒對下一年所做的經濟預測遭到同事們的質疑。
    (A)(B)(C)(D) 收到、受到

解析 (A) 句子的主詞 predictions 不是動作（receive）的執行者，因此動詞要用被動語態。選項 (B)(C)(D) 都是主動語態。

124. 最近剛取得證照的醫師利用該醫療協會的網站尋找工作。
    (A) 什麼
    (B) ……的人
    (C) 那個／那些人的
    (D) 那個／那些

解析 (B) who 在這個句子中作主格關係代名詞，先行詞是 doctors。選項 (A) 不能當作關係代名詞。選項 (C) 是所有格。選項 (D) 指物，不指人。

125. 你助理建議的兩個班機之間，唯一的差別是起飛時間。
    (A) 和……一起
    (B) 那時、然後
    (C) 在……之間
    (D) 在……之中

解析 (C) 兩樣事物（two flights）之間的比較要用 between。選項 (A) 的意思是「和……一起」。選項 (B) 用來指出時間。選項 (D) 用於三樣以上的事物。

126. 儘管已經做了周密計畫，餐飲承辦商還是沒有帶足桌巾。
    (A) 在……期間
    (B) 因為
    (C) 儘管
    (D) 雖然

解析 (C) in spite of 的意思是「儘管」，是一個介系詞片語，後面必須接名詞或動名詞。選項 (A) 放在這個句子裡意思不通。選項 (B) 和 (D) 後面只能接子句。

127. 專案經理負責組織專案的每個環節。
    (A) 組織 (n.)
    (B) 組織 (ving)
    (C) 組織 (ved)
    (D) 組織 (v.)

解析 (B) organizing 是動名詞，在這裡作介系詞 for 的受詞。選項 (A) 是名詞。選項 (C) 和 (D) 是動詞。

128. 會計部主管決定明天旁聽客戶會議。
    (A) 決定 (n.)
    (B)(C)(D) 決定 (v.)

解析 (C) 第三人稱單數動詞 has decided 和主詞 The head of accounts 一致。選項 (A) 是名詞，不是動詞。選項 (B) 和 (D) 是複數動詞，和主詞不一致。

129. 促銷訊息必須強調我們的產品比市面上的類似產品好。
    (A) 許多
    (B) 比
    (C) 離、離開
    (D) 到、往

解析 (B) than 搭配 better 構成完整的形容詞比較級。選項 (A) 可作副詞放在形容詞之前，但不能放在形容詞之後。選項 (C) 和 (D) 不能用來構成比較級。

130. 金先生把一週大部分時間都用在準備向主管提出他的新想法。
    (A)(B)(C)(D) 提出、呈現

解析 (D) prepare 後面要接不定詞。選項 (A) 是原形動詞或現在式動詞。選項 (B) 是過去式。選項 (C) 是動名詞。

Part 6：段落填空

作答方式：你會看到四篇短文，各含四個空格，每個空格配有四個選項，選出最適當的單字、片語或句子完成這段敘述。

第 131–134 題請看下面這封信。

格林辦公室裝修公司
臺灣臺北市大安區
郵遞區號：106-03

高素梅，副總經理
臺灣臺北市大安區蔣安路 377 號
郵遞區號：106-03

高女士，您好：

感謝您考慮選擇格林辦公室裝修公司承辦即將進行的辦公室整修計畫。希望您能抽空看一下隨信附上的手冊，裡面說明了我們為符合最高環保標準所使用的材料和採取的方法，它也概述了我們提供的服務和定價制度。請注意，任何專案動工之前，格林辦公室裝修公司需要先收取訂金。初期安裝節能系統的成本可能很高，但長期下來可以省很多錢。

此外，統計資料顯示重視環境問題的公司更受消費者青睞。

期待與您討論貴公司的整修需求。

順頌 商祺

蔡米
蔡米

---

131. (A) 你
　　 (B) 他
　　 (C) 它
　　 (D) 我們

解析 (C) 代名詞 it 和動詞 outlines 一致，它的先行詞是 brochure。選項 (A) 和 (D) 都和動詞不一致。選項 (B) 指人，不指物。

132. (A)(B)(C)(D) 要求

解析 **(A)** 動詞 requires 和單數主詞 Green Office Renovators 一致，Green Office Renovators 雖然含有複數名詞，但由於是一間公司的名稱，必須視為單數。選項 (B)(C)(D) 都和主詞不一致。

133. (A) 幸好，安裝程序不會太過複雜。
　　(B) 我們的工人在這些系統的各方面都受過高度訓練。
　　(C) 儘管如此，住宅和商業場所都有使用這些系統。
　　(D) 但長期下來可以省很多錢。

解析 **(D)** 前一個句子提到初期成本很高，這個句子接著說明長期來看，成本其實沒有表面上那麼高。選項 (A)(B)(C) 都與前面句子語意不連貫。

134. (A) 對……的關心／重視
　　(B) 因……而感到幸福
　　(C) 放置於
　　(D) ……的知識

解析 **(A)** 「demonstrate concern for something」的意思是「表現出對某件事的關心或重視」。選項 (B)(C)(D) 都不符合語意要求。

第 135–138 題請看下面這封電子郵件。

收件者：clementinebooks@learning.org
寄件者：rep990@gaspower.net
主旨：　等額繳費計畫

薛爾登‧莫瑞，您好：

我注意到貴公司仍採用我們的月繳方案支付瓦斯費。去年期間，您的最高額帳單落在一月，是四百美元。然而到了夏季月份，您的帳單有時低至二十三美元。您的年費大部分落在最冷的四個月份。我們認為您很適合採用我們的等額繳費計畫。這個計畫自三年前推出以來，大約有 78% 的客戶已經轉換成此方案。雖然全年支付的金額相同，但較高額的帳單可以分攤到各個月份，讓您更容易管理財務。

等額繳費計畫是以預估方式計算您每月繳納的金額，我們會以您前一年的帳單作為基準，計算出一個平均值。計畫執行六個月後，我們會根據您實際使用的瓦斯量是否高於或低於預估來調整金額。年底我們會根據應付金額和實際使用金額的差額，從您的帳戶進行扣款或退款。

135. (A) 高的
     (B) 更高的
     (C) 最高的
     (D) 最高的

解析 (C) 此需填入一個最高級形容詞，high是單音節形容詞，正確的最高級形式是highest。選項(A)是原級。選項(B)是比較級。選項(D)不是單音節形容詞正確的最高級形式。

136. (A) 感謝您準時繳納每月帳單。
     (B) 您的年費大部分集中在一年中最冷的四個月份。
     (C) 事實上，您的夏季帳單算是我們客戶當中最低的。
     (D) 您可能知道我們現在對您所在地區的客戶提供電子帳單。

解析 (B) 這個句子總結了這段敘述的重點，即該顧客的帳單在一年的某個特定時段特別高。選項(A)(C)(D)都與文意不符。

137. (A) 減價
     (B) 增加
     (C) 分攤、分配
     (D) 添加

解析 (C) spread out有「分攤、分配」的意思，客戶不需在一年中的某個時段支費高額費用，而是把費用分成小額分散於全年支付。選項(A)的意思是「減價」。選項(B)的意思是「增加」。選項(D)的意思是「添加」。

138. (A) 估算
     (B) 允許
     (C) 詢問
     (D) 訂購

解析 (A) 這家公司會根據客戶前一年的瓦斯用量，估算（estimate）或者說推測客戶一年會使用多少瓦斯。選項(B)的意思是「允許」。選項(C)的意思是「詢問」。選項(D)的意思是「訂購」。

第 139–142 題請看下面這篇文章。

> 機場休息室取消免費網路服務
> 文／凱莉・克里斯蒂
>
> 自本週五起，伊莉莎白港機場的旅客將不再享有商務旅客休息室的免費網路服務。自去年一月起，已購買貴賓卡的旅客可在機場的商務休息室免費上網。持有貴賓卡的旅客享有商務休息室的各項福利，除了可以免費上網，還能享用咖啡點心、看報紙和使用印表機。休息室也讓旅客有機會逃離擁擠的候機室。現在商務休息室的使用者必須另外購買上網服務，每小時是五美元，最少需購買兩小時。

139. (A)(B)(C)(D) 提供

解析 (C) 這裡必須使用被動語態，因為主詞 passengers 不是執行動作的人，而是機場提供網路服務。選項 (A)(B)(D) 都是主動語態。

140. (A) 公共設施
    (B) 家具
    (C) 福利
    (D) 功能

解析 (C) 持有貴賓卡的人可以享有福利（benefits），意思就是說，因為他們購買了貴賓卡，所以可以享有特殊優待或好處。選項 (A)(B)(D) 的語意都不通。

141. (A) 商務旅客每個月都要花好幾小時在機場等候。
    (B) 機場當局計劃於明年翻修休息室。
    (C) 機場的價格是出了名的高於城市其他地方。
    (D) 休息室也讓旅客有機會逃離擁擠的候機室。

解析 (D) 前一個句子列舉了使用休息室的各種好處，而這個句子又再補充了一個好處。選項 (A)(B)(C) 填入後語意都不通。

142. (A) 最小量、最低限度
    (B) 最小的、最低限度的
    (C) 減到最小／最低
    (D) 最小地、最低限度地

解析 (A) 這裡需要填入一個名詞，因此要選 minimum。選項 (B) 是形容詞。選項 (C) 是動詞。選項 (D) 是副詞。

第 143–146 題請看下面這封電子郵件。

寄件者：shih-yismith@techworld.com
主旨：　科技會議
日期：　10 月 10 日
收件者：yi-fangwu@techworld.com

你有興趣參加十二月在臺北舉辦的國際科技會議嗎？我沒去過，可是大家都說那是可以學習到最新科技的地方。我去年實在抽不出時間所以錯過了，但我知道今年一定去得成，希望你能跟我一起去，我相信你一定能從中獲益良多。如果你想參加會議的話，我們就要盡快與主管洽談，才能確保取得同意。請盡快與我聯絡。

世宜

143. (A)(B)(C)(D) 說

解析 (B) everyone 必須使用單數動詞 says。選項 (A)(C)(D) 都是複數動詞。

144. (A) 不能
　　 (B) 不可
　　 (C) 不應
　　 (D) 不能

解析 (D) 這裡要用過去式 couldn't，意思是無法做某件事。選項 (A) 是現在式，時態不正確。選項 (B) 和 (C) 的語意不通。

145. (A) 我相信你一定能從中獲益良多。
　　 (B) 我喜歡跟上新科技。
　　 (C) 每年都在不同的國家舉辦。
　　 (D) 你教過我很多關於科技發展的事。

解析 (A) 這個句子承接前一個句子，說明寄件者為什麼認為朋友應該去參加會議。選項 (B)(C)(D) 都與前後文的意思不連貫。

146. (A) 同事
　　 (B) 主管
　　 (C) 助理
　　 (D) 客戶

解析 (B) 只有 supervisors（主管）有權力批准他們參加會議。選項 (A)(C)(D) 放入這個句子都不合理。

Part 7：閱讀測驗

> **作答方式**：你會看到單篇或多篇文章的題組，文章後面配有幾個題目，各含四個選項。選出最適當的答案回答問題，將答案卡上對應的橢圓框塗滿。

第 147–148 題請看下面這則廣告。

何必苦苦等待更好的工作出現？
現在就取得一份好工作！

國家航空公司
誠徵全職銷售與訂票專員。
來和我們的員工聊一聊，就知道我們
為何是航空界的最佳團隊。
現場面試！
請攜帶履歷。

現場招募會
國家航空公司總部
東南地區機場
6月15日星期四，晚上7點30分

---

147. 這則廣告的目的是什麼？
 (A) 宣傳職業培訓計畫
 (B) 銷售機票
 (C) 招募潛在員工
 (D) 介紹新的總部

解析 (C) 廣告中說現在就可以得到一份好工作（get a great job now），並提到公司正在招募人員（hiring），還要大家帶履歷（bring your résumé），由此可知是在招募員工。選項(A)和廣告的主題有關，但不是正確答案。選項(B)和航空公司總部所在地點（機場）有關，從機場聯想到機票，但也不是正確答案。選項(D)重複使用了 headquarters 這個字，但廣告中並沒有介紹新的總部。

148. 招募會將在哪裡舉辦？
    (A) 公司總部
    (B) 私人住宅
    (C) 飛機上
    (D) 公司的地區辦事處

解析 (A) 廣告中提到了國家航空公司總部（National Air Headquarters），接著給出日期和時間，可以判斷總部是招募會的舉辦地點。選項(B)完全沒被提及。選項(C)不是舉辦招募會的合理地點。選項(D)是被Southeast Regional Airport給混淆，廣告中提到的是東南地區機場，不是地區辦事處。

第149–150題請看下面這張告示。

乘客請注意

- 上車請備妥正確車資，司機不找零。
- 上車時請往後方移動，並站立於乘客區，勿擋住車門。
- 請將前排博愛座禮讓給老人和行動不便的乘客。
- 聽音樂請配戴耳機。
- 請勿攜帶食物或開封飲料。禁止吸菸。

感謝您的搭乘！

---

149. 你會在哪裡看到這張告示？
    (A) 火車站
    (B) 飛機上
    (C) 計程車上
    (D) 公車上

解析 (D) 這張告示出現的地方，應該是乘客可以站立，並且會有司機的地方，公車是唯一符合這些條件的選項。選項(A)(B)(C)都有乘客，但是其他條件都不符合。

150. 下列哪一項是被允許的？
    (A) 在門邊抽菸
    (B) 聽音樂
    (C) 吃零食
    (D) 喝咖啡

解析 (B) 聽音樂是允許的，只是必須戴耳機。選項(A)不正確，告示上面說禁止吸菸（No smoking）。選項(C)和(D)不正確，告示上說請勿攜帶食物或開封飲料（No food or open beverages）。

第 151-152 題請看下面這段簡訊討論串。

陳立	11:20
他們有你要的紙。兩包對嗎？	
麗娜・賈梅堤	11:21
對。有信封嗎？	
陳立	11:22
他們有你要的大小，但沒有紅色的。	
陳立	11:24
他們可以幫你訂，但是要五到七天。	
麗娜・賈梅堤	11:26
那可不行，這批郵件最晚星期四要寄出。	
陳立	11:27
那個尺寸有貨的只有象牙白色。	
麗娜・賈梅堤	11:29
也只好那樣了。	
陳立	11:31
好，這樣你還要我買兩盒嗎？	
麗娜・賈梅堤	11:32
是的。還有別忘了刷公司的信用卡。	

151. 陳先生人在哪裡？
　　(A) 家裡
　　(B) 商店
　　(C) 他的辦公室
　　(D) 儲藏室

解析 (B) 陳先生打算買信封，還會使用信用卡，所以應該是在商店裡。選項 (A)(C)(D) 也是會有紙和信封的地方，但不符合對話中的描述。

152. 在 11:29 時，賈梅堤小姐說「That will have to do」是什麼意思？
　　(A) 她會使用象牙白色的信封。
　　(B) 她現在不要信封了。

400

(C) 她必須準時把郵件寄出。
(D) 她希望陳先生幫她訂紅色信封。

解析 (A) 這句話的意思是說，賈梅堤小姐決定使用象牙白色的信封，因為她想要的顏色目前缺貨。選項(B)(C)(D)既不是這句話的意思，也和前後的對話邏輯不連貫。

第153–154題請看下面這張表格。

業務經理任務時間分配研究結果	
培訓新進員工	20％
發掘潛在客戶	20％
檢視銷售數據	28％
解決客戶問題	5％
分配銷售任務	15％
與技術人員進行協調	7％
行政職責	5％

153. 業務經理把最多時間花在哪裡？
 (A) 培訓員工
 (B) 檢視銷售紀錄
 (C) 分配銷售任務
 (D) 履行行政職責

解析 (B) 檢視銷售紀錄占據了28％的時間，是所有列出任務中花最多時間的一項。選項(A)(C)(D)花費的時間都比較少。

154. 這份資訊可以推導出什麼結論？
 (A) 花在技術人員身上的時間太多了。
 (B) 尋找新客戶的優先順序較低。
 (C) 客戶的問題很少。
 (D) 銷售正在下滑。

解析 (C) 解決客戶問題所花的時間非常少，只占5％的時間，可見問題很少。選項(A)和技術人員協調只占7％的時間，不太可能推斷出這樣的結論。選項(B)發掘新客戶占去20％的時間，相對於其他任務算是很多時間，不能說是低優先順序。選項(D)不正確，表格中完全沒有提供銷售資訊。

第 155–157 題請看下面這則廣告。

暑期正是返校學習的好時候！
若你需要提升商務技能，請讓我們協助你！

每年夏天，克萊柏恩大學商業管理學院都為資深經理人開設特殊課程，協助他們精進現有商務技能，或學習新的商務技能。在為期一週、模擬國際商業世界的密集課程中，你將和同儕一起學習。你會學到新理論，並研究世界各地的商業經營模式。曾經參與課程的學員都回饋提到，他們所學的知識能馬上應用在自己的工作上。

每家公司僅限一人可參加本特殊課程，所有申請者須附現任主管的推薦信。

更多資訊請洽
暑期教育中心
商業管理學院
克萊柏恩大學
903-477-6768 admissions@suedcen.edu

---

155. 這個課程是為誰開設的？
　　(A) 專業經理人
　　(B) 轉換職業跑道的大學教授
　　(C) 大學部商學院學生
　　(D) 行政支援人員

解析 (A) 廣告中提到「offers special courses for experienced managers」（為資深、有經驗的經理人所開設），experienced managers 就是 professional managers。選項(B)(C)(D)都沒有被提到。

156. 申請入學有什麼條件？
　　(A) 入學考試
　　(B) 商學院學位
　　(C) 國際經驗
　　(D) 老闆的推薦信

解析 (D) 廣告中指出「All applications require a letter of recommendation from your current supervisor」，所有申請者都要附上現任主管的推薦信才可以。選項(A)(B)(C)都沒有被提到。

157. 這個課程為期多久？
    (A) 整個夏天
    (B) 一週
    (C) 一個月的三個晚上
    (D) 兩年

解析 (B) 這個課程是為期一週（week-long）的密集班。其他選項的時間都沒有被提到。

第 158–160 題請看下面這個網頁。

| 首頁 | 商店 | 關於我們 | 購物車 |

金潔植感設計公司

品牌故事

二十五年以來，金潔植感設計公司一直致力於美化柏克茲維爾的住家和企業空間。無論是何種慶祝場合──從簡單的生日祝賀到奢華的婚禮──我們的花束、花籃、花環和花串都能讓它化為一段美好難忘的經驗。–[1]–

金潔公司是由金潔・卡本特所創建，當時只是位於主街的一間小店面，而後迅速累積人氣，生意蒸蒸日上。–[2]– 隨著生意越做越好，市中心的小空間很快就不敷使用，金潔便買下位於楊柳路的房子，目前是該公司本店和辦公室的所在地，主街的空間則持續作為分店營運。–[3]– 我們的顧問正等著協助您挑選適合的外觀和設計，慶祝這對您意義非凡的日子。

金潔公司樂意為您提供配送服務。–[4]– 本地配送不收取費用，範圍涵蓋柏克茲維爾、史普林戴爾和羅斯林，其他地區按里程收費。上午十一點前下單當日送達，十一點後下單隔日送達。

請選擇您感興趣的類別，開始購物吧！

慶祝活動　　　　　浪漫時刻　　　　　玫瑰與蘭花

403

158. 金潔公司是做哪方面的生意？
    (A) 花藝
    (B) 景觀設計
    (C) 派對規劃
    (D) 室內設計

解析 (A) 金潔公司販售的項目包含花束、花籃、花環和花串（bouquets, baskets, wreathes, and garlands），都是花飾品，由此可知應是從事花藝方面的生意。選項(B)雖然也和花有關，但以販售服務為主，並不是專賣花飾品的。選項(C)和文中提到慶祝特殊場合有關。選項(D)因文中提到設計而有所混淆，文中指的是花藝設計，而不是室內設計。

159. 關於配送，文中有何說明？
    (A) 配送時間通常需要二十四小時或以上。
    (B) 僅提供本地配送服務。
    (C) 上午十一點後不進行配送。
    (D) 本地配送免運。

解析 (D) 文中提到本地配送是不收取費用的（no fee for deliveries in the local area）。選項(A)不正確，上午下單當天就送達了。選項(B)不正確，其他地區也提供配送服務，只是需要收費。選項(C)是若想要當日送達的下單截止時間，不是不進行配送。

160. 下面這個句子最適合放入文中[1][2][3][4]哪一個位置？
    「兩家分店隨時可以為您服務。」
    (A) [1]
    (B) [2]
    (C) [3]
    (D) [4]

解析 (C) 編號[3]的空格前面兩句描述了該公司的兩家店面，這個句子則承接了前面兩個句子，語意連貫。選項(A)(B)(D)放入這個句子語意都不通順。

第 161–163 題請看下面這封電子郵件。

寄件者：拉維・尼亞茲
收件者：F. 奧莫波里沃
主旨：　關於：出貨問題

奧莫波里沃先生，您好：

感謝您對黎明製品有興趣。隨信附上一份表格，當中有我們最熱門產品的現行價格，提供給您參考。

關於您的問題，是的，登記零售商和一千美元以上的訂單都能以批發價購買我們所有的產品，運送時間和運費視您的所在地點和訂購量而定。您可能也有興趣知道，我們所有產品都是在自家工廠製造，並由受過專業訓練的管理人員全程監督，生產作業完全不外包。

如果需要進一步協助訂購，請與我聯絡。

敬祝 順心
拉維・尼亞茲
客戶關係經理
黎明製品

---

161. 電子郵件的附件中含有什麼？
   (A) 一份價目表
   (B) 一張訂購單
   (C) 運送資訊
   (D) 員工聯絡資訊

解析 (A) 尼亞茲先生在信中寫到「I am attaching a table that shows the current prices …」，由此可知是價目表。選項(B)和(C)與電子郵件的其他內容有關。選項(D)未被提及。

162. 尼亞茲先生對運送服務有何說明？
   (A) 一律採用空運。
   (B) 大筆訂單免運。
   (C) 需要辦理保險。
   (D) 價格會變動。

解析 (D) 尼亞茲寫到「Shipping times and costs depend on your location, as well as on the size of your order」，運費會依據地點和訂購量而有所不同。選項(A)(B)(C)也許有可能，但並未提及。

163. 奧莫波里沃先生有可能服務於哪一行業？
    (A) 貨運
    (B) 零售
    (C) 廣告
    (D) 製造

解析 (B) 電子郵件中特別提到登記零售商（registered retailers）可享批發價，可見這封郵件的收件者，即奧莫波里沃先生應該是零售業者。選項(A)和(D)和信中提到的其他主題有關。選項(C)完全沒被提及。

第164–167題請看下面這則備忘錄。

備忘錄

收件人：全體員工
發布人：K. 奧薩佛
　　　　人事主管
日　期：20—年11月23日
主　旨：慈善假

本公司很高興宣布一項新政策，員工參與無償社區服務將可請有薪假。員工每月可請最多八小時的有薪假，來參與慈善機構的志工服務。在本公司服務滿一年的全職員工有資格參加本計畫。慈善假必須事先提出，否則請假期間將不予支薪。慈善假也必須經過主管批准。

---

164. 新政策允許員工做什麼？
    (A) 請有薪假接受職業培訓
    (B) 享有更多假期
    (C) 領薪水參與志工服務
    (D) 提早下班回家

解析 (C) 備忘錄中提到「allow employees to take paid time off for unpaid community service」（允許員工帶薪參與無償社區服務），以及「up to eight hours of paid leave per month to volunteer . . .」（每月最多八小時帶薪參與志工服務），所以答案是(C)。選項(A)(B)(D)則是其他形式的休假（time off）。

165. 根據這項計畫，員工可以請多久的慈善假？
    (A) 每週一小時
    (B) 每週三小時
    (C) 每月六小時
    (D) 每月八小時

解析 (D) 備忘錄中說「up to eight hours of paid leave per month」，所以每月有至多八小時的有薪慈善假。選項(A)和(C)低於允許的時間。選項(B)高於允許的時間。

166. 誰可以參加這項計畫？
    (A) 全職員工
    (B) 兼職員工
    (C) 新進員工
    (D) 全體員工

解析 (A) 備忘錄中說有資格參加計畫的員工，必須是全職且在公司服務滿一年。選項(B)(C)(D)都和這項描述有所衝突。

167. 欲請有薪假的員工必須做什麼？
    (A) 填妥請假單
    (B) 擁有良好出勤紀錄
    (C) 經主管推薦
    (D) 事先取得主管批准

解析 (D) 根據備忘錄內容，要擔任志工的人必須事先提出（requested in advance）和經主管批准（approved by the employee's supervisor）。選項(A)(B)(C)都沒有被提到。

第168-171題請看下面這段線上聊天室討論串。

> 露比・史東 [2:10]
> 有人發現地毯有什麼問題嗎？
>
> 葛倫・布萊克 [2:12]
> 有，我辦公室的地毯中間隆起了一大塊，看起來像是他們沒有把它釘好。
>
> 露比・史東 [2:13]
> 對，我辦公室也有相同的問題。
>
> 凱莉・奧哈拉 [2:14]
> 在會議室裡，我發現地毯邊緣和牆壁之間有很大的空隙。
>
> 露比・史東 [2:15]
> 我們請人鋪新地毯花了很多錢，必須連絡地毯公司，叫他們回來把事情做好。
>
> 葛倫・布萊克 [2:16]
> 交給我，我今天下午就處理。
>
> 凱莉・奧哈拉 [2:18]
> 看他們能不能這週結束前就來處理，下週一一早威爾森公司的代表就要來開會。
>
> 露比・史東 [2:20]
> 我知道，是新客戶。我們必須在那之前把一切準備就緒。到底為什麼要找這家地毯公司呢？
>
> 葛倫・布萊克 [2:23]
> 你不記得了嗎？是你自己說要給剛起步的公司一個機會的。
>
> 凱莉・奧哈拉 [2:25]
> 下次我認為應該把機會留給有經驗、能把工作做好的公司。

168. 地毯有什麼問題？
    (A) 沒有鋪好。
    (B) 十分破舊。
    (C) 顏色不對。
    (D) 需要清洗。

解析 (A) 對話中提到地毯隆起一塊（bump）又有空隙（gap），史東女士寫說「We paid a lot to get this new carpet installed」（花了很多錢請人鋪設新地毯），並且要求地毯公司回來重做，都可以看出地毯沒有鋪好。選項(B)(C)(D) 也都是地毯可能出現的問題，但對話中沒有提及。

169. 週一會發生什麼事情？
    (A) 將訂購辦公用品。
    (B) 將召開員工會議。
    (C) 客戶將造訪公司。
    (D) 辦公室將進行清潔。

解析 (C) 奧哈拉女士提到週一早上有訪客，史東女士則描述他們是新客戶（the new clients）。選項(A)(B)(D) 都使用了對話中的單字，但都不是正確答案。

170. 文中提到關於地毯公司的什麼？
    (A) 收費相對較高。
    (B) 名聲很好。
    (C) 員工很多。
    (D) 是新公司。

解析 (D) 布萊克先生描述這家公司為「just starting out」，意思是新成立、才剛起步，而奧哈拉女士的回應暗示該公司沒經驗。選項(A)(B)(C) 都有可能是事實，但對話中並未提及。

171. 在2:16時，布萊克先生說「Leave that to me」是什麼意思？
    (A) 他打算修好地毯。
    (B) 他會打電話給地毯公司。
    (C) 他會支付地毯的帳單。
    (D) 他下午不想被打擾。

解析 (B) 史東女士表示必須有人聯絡地毯公司，布萊克先生回說「Leave that to me」，意思是他會負責做這件事。選項(A)(C)(D) 都不是這句話的意思。

第172–175題請看下面這篇文章。

駭客鎖定新目標

你的公司是否已成為駭客好下手的目標？你上次變更密碼是什麼時候？你的安全系統有多強？

根據國際網路安全協會，現在外面已經出現了一種新型態的駭客，而且也出現了新的下手目標。

過去駭客以駭入大企業網路系統而惡名昭彰。在駭客眼中，公司規模越大，就代表他們能獲得的成功越大。

–[1]– 數年前，駭客成功入侵英菲爾麥克斯公司出了名的安全系統，因而登上全球頭條新聞。

然而重大的「成功」卻伴隨著重大的不利——國際調查小組介入和嚴重刑事指控。多名前駭客現在不是在監獄中，就是在努力償還高額罰款。–[2]–

現在駭客已經轉移注意力。小公司由於安全系統沒那麼複雜，而成為非常誘人的目標。–[3]– 此外，由於調查人員喜歡追查大案子，小公司的安全系統遭駭比較不會引起太多注意，駭客所要面臨的後果也就沒那麼嚴重。–[4]–

---

172. 誰容易成為新型駭客的下手目標？
 (A) 知名公司
 (B) 小公司
 (C) 國際公司
 (D) 科技公司

解析 (B) 文章中討論了過去駭客以大企業為目標，如今則將注意力轉向小型公司。選項(A)(C)(D)雖然都有可能，但文中並未提及。

173. 根據這篇文章，哪一項是駭客入侵英菲爾麥克斯公司網路的可能動機？
 (A) 金錢
 (B) 權力
 (C) 名聲
 (D) 好玩

解析 (C) 文章中說他們駭入大企業可以「gain notoriety」，notoriety 就是 fame，只不過

帶有負面意義,指惡名或臭名。選項(A)(B)(D)也是駭客入侵的可能動機,不過在本文當中並未被提及。

174. 一些前駭客發生了什麼事?
(A) 他們被軟體公司僱用。
(B) 他們被判無罪。
(C) 他們與調查人員合作。
(D) 他們正在坐牢。

解析 (D) 文章中以「sitting behind bars」描述多名前駭客,意思就是坐牢、被關監獄,等同於 in prison。選項(A)是從安全系統(security systems)聯想而來。選項(B)是從刑事指控(criminal charges)聯想而來。選項(C)重複使用了 investigators 這個字,但他們是被調查,而不是與調查人員合作。

175. 下面這個句子最適合放入文中[1][2][3][4]哪一個位置?
「他們可能連簡單的安全措施都疏忽大意,例如不經常變更密碼。」
(A) [1]
(B) [2]
(C) [3]
(D) [4]

解析 (C) 編號[3]前面的句子指出小公司的安全系統較不複雜,而這個句子進一步補充細節,提到可能連簡單措施都輕忽了。選項(A)(B)(D)的前後文都和這句話語意不連貫。

第176-180題請看下面的廣告和電子郵件。

行銷代表

紐西蘭成長最快速的女裝公司誠徵行銷代表。
本職位要求每月出差一週,並代表公司參加會議和媒體活動。

資格要求
● 四年制學院或大學學位,行銷相關科系佳
● 一年以上銷售經驗,服飾銷售經驗佳
● 良好溝通技巧,包含具備簡報經驗

請將履歷和求職信寄給卡蜜拉・柯洛:ccrowe@nzworld.com

寄件者：卡蜜拉‧柯洛
收件者：佐佐木明子
日期：　三月十日
主旨：　您的工作應徵

佐佐木小姐，你好：

感謝你應徵行銷代表一職，也感謝你對 NZ 世界有興趣。

雖然你的履歷顯示你在發展行銷事業上已做了充分準備，很遺憾你不符合我們要求的全部資格。你的學位符合我們的徵才條件，但經驗卻不符。你有電子產品商店的銷售經驗，是個相當不錯的背景，但你在那裡的工作時間只達到我們最低要求的一半。除此之外，你沒有服飾銷售的相關經驗。

不過你的履歷也展現了你的一些優勢。你的學業成績優異，也活躍於學校的行銷社團，因此我們想提供你一個實習生的職位。

這是為期三個月的無薪實習。由於你上個月才剛畢業，我認為這對你來說是個很好的機會，可以給你開啟職業生涯所需的部分經驗。舉例來說，透過本次實習，你有機會練習公開演說，此為你履歷上所缺乏的一項重要行銷技能。

如果你有意願接受這個職位，請在 4 月 1 日前與我聯繫。期待收到你的回覆。

敬祝 順心

卡蜜拉‧柯洛
人力資源主管
NZ 世界

176. 下列哪一項「不是」該廣告職位的職責？
　　(A) 招聘新員工
　　(B) 進行簡報
　　(C) 每月出差
　　(D) 參加會議

解析 (A) 選項(A)是這則廣告的目的（徵才），而不是該職位的其中一項職責。選項(B)(C)(D) 都是廣告提到的職責之一。

177. 明子拿到的是哪一領域的學位？
    (A) 電子
    (B) 行銷
    (C) 傳播
    (D) 服裝設計

解析 (B) 卡蜜拉提到明子的學位符合條件，根據廣告中的說明，他們要求的學位是行銷相關科系。選項(A)是被明子打工過的商店給混淆了。選項(C)是被廣告要求具備溝通技巧（communication skills）給混淆。選項(D)是被該公司販售女裝給混淆。

178. 明子是何時拿到學位的？
    (A) 二月
    (B) 三月
    (C) 四月
    (D) 五月

解析 (A) 卡蜜拉提到明子上個月才剛畢業，而這封信的日期是三月，因此上個月是二月。選項(B)是信件的撰寫的月份。選項(C)是明子最晚必須回覆卡蜜拉願不願意實習的月份（4月1日）。選項(D)完全沒被提到。

179. 明子有哪方面的工作經驗？
    (A) 服飾銷售員
    (B) 電子產品銷售員
    (C) 職業諮詢師
    (D) 行銷代表

解析 (B) 電子郵件中提到明子有電子產品商店的銷售經驗（sales experience in an electronics store）。選項(A)是公司要求的工作經驗。選項(C)未被提及。選項(D)是明子應徵的職位。

180. 卡蜜拉・柯洛提供了什麼給明子？
    (A) 一份工作
    (B) 一次面試機會
    (C) 一個實習機會
    (D) 一個俱樂部會員資格

解析 (C) 卡蜜拉提供明子三個月的無薪實習（a three-month unpaid internship）。選項(A)指的是明子應徵的工作，但是卡蜜拉認為她經驗不足，沒有給她這份工作。選項(B)和應徵工作有關，但未被提及。選項(D)被明子參加的行銷社團（Marketing Club）給混淆了（club可指社團也可指俱樂部）。

第181–185題請看下面的廣告和電子郵件。

今年,給公司年度聚會來點不一樣的體驗。
歡迎蒞臨前街劇院

在前街劇院度過一個美好午後或夜晚,享用我們巴黎受訓主廚雅克為您準備的美味佳餚,並欣賞本地區最優秀演員的精彩演出。用餐之前,亦可參加本歷史劇院的參觀導覽行程。250人以上團體提供劇院包場服務,僅限週日下午。300–350人之團體享九折優惠,350人以上團體享八五折優惠。

節目依時節安排:一月到四月──悲劇;五月到七月──戲劇;八月到十月──音樂劇;十一月到十二月──喜劇。

開放預約時段:

週一至週四	晚餐及晚間表演 晚上6–10點
週五至週六	午餐及午間表演 中午12點到下午4點
	晚餐及晚間表演 晚上6–10點
週日	僅限大型團體包場預約。午餐和晚餐時段皆開放。大型團體建議提前一個月預約。

歡迎蒞臨前街劇院享受美食、娛樂表演和歡樂時光。預約請以電子郵件或來電216-707-2268洽詢。

收件者：前街劇院，預約部
寄件者：康思坦絲・海克勒，活動統籌
日期： 20—年10月25日
主旨： 假日聚會

我在本週的商業週刊上看到你們的廣告，我有興趣租用你們劇院作為聯邦銀行年度員工聚會的場地。

我們的聚會定在12月20日星期日，那天劇院可以預約嗎？我們傾向午餐和午間表演的時段，總共會有325位賓客。

請將你們的菜單、表演說明和價目表傳真給我，並告訴我十二月可預約的日期。

謝謝！

181. 劇院的體驗內容包括下列哪一項？
(A) 見到主廚
(B) 和演員對談
(C) 參觀劇院
(D) 選擇表演節目

解析 (C) 廣告中有提到可參加參觀導覽行程。選項(A)是因廣告提到法國受訓主廚而有所混淆。選項(B)是因廣告提到本地區優秀演員而有所混淆。選項(D)是由劇院決定，來賓無法自行選擇。

182. 劇院何時開放給個人和小型團體？
(A) 僅週一至週四
(B) 僅週五和週六
(C) 僅週一至週六
(D) 僅週日

解析 (C) 週日僅開放大型團體預約，因此可推斷其他日子開放給個人和小型團體。選項(A)是僅提供晚間表演的日子。選項(B)是同時提供午間和晚間表演的日子。選項(D)是保留給大型團體的日子。

183. 海克勒女士希望聯邦銀行的聚會從幾點開始？
    (A) 上午十點
    (B) 中午十二點
    (C) 下午四點
    (D) 晚上六點

解析 (B) 海克勒女士在電子郵件中說，她希望預約午餐和午間表演的時段，對照廣告上的說明是中午十二點到下午四點。選項(A)未被提及。選項(C)是午間活動的結束時間。選項(D)是晚間活動的開始時間。

184. 聯邦銀行舉辦這次聚會可享多少折扣？
    (A) 沒有折扣
    (B) 九折
    (C) 八五折
    (D) 八折

解析 (B) 聯邦銀行一共有325人要來參加，而廣告中說300–350人之團體享九折優惠。選項(A)適用於不到300人的團體。選項(C)適用於350人以上的團體。選項(D) 20是海克勒女士提到想預約的聚會日期，與折扣無關。

185. 聯邦銀行聚會的賓客將可欣賞到哪一類型的表演？
    (A) 悲劇
    (B) 戲劇
    (C) 音樂劇
    (D) 喜劇

解析 (D) 聯邦銀行的聚會是在十二月，而劇院排定十二月的演出是喜劇。選項(A)是一月到四月的演出類型。選項(B)是五月到七月的演出類型。選項(C)是八月到十月的演出類型。

第 186–190 題請看下面這則通知和兩封電子郵件。

即將退休？

歡迎參加退休工作坊。本工作坊將說明有哪些退休福利，以及如何確認自己符合哪些申請資格。

請選擇自己最方便的日期。

✓ 8月1日
✓ 8月15日
✓ 8月29日
✓ 9月13日

所有工作坊時間皆為上午8點30分到10點30分，在F會議室舉行。無需報名，直接到場即可！

寄件者：馬庫斯・梅恩斯
收件者：吳載善
主旨：　退休問題
日期：　7月20日

吳先生：

我正在考慮近期退休，有一些關於退休福利的問題。我看到通知說有舉辦退休工作坊，我嘗試參加其中一場，可到場時卻空無一人，就是今天早上八點半在F會議室。

我的主要問題是：我今年六十三歲，在這間公司已經服務二十年了。由於我還未滿六十五歲，如果現在退休的話，福利會減少嗎？還有，我有一些關於退休後的稅務問題，可以找誰請教呢？

謝謝！
馬庫斯・梅恩斯

寄件者：吳載善
收件者：馬庫斯・梅恩斯
主旨：　關於：退休問題
日期：　7月20日

嗨，梅恩斯先生：

感謝您來信詢問。以下是退休福利的基本資訊：

● 年滿65歲並於本公司服務20年以上，退休後享有全部福利。或於本公司服務25年以上，不分年齡均可退休且同享福利。

● 年齡介於55到64歲，並於本公司服務滿20年但未滿25年者，仍可退休，但退休金會予以扣減。65歲以下每少一歲，退休金扣減2%。舉例來說，如果您是63歲，將被扣減4%。

我會鼓勵您參加工作坊，工作坊是由奧古斯塔・詹姆斯主講，他會把所有可能的情況都講述得很清楚。至於稅務問題，我建議您聯繫會計部的弗列德・李，他是稅務專家，應該可以解答您的問題。

有其他問題再跟我聯繫。

吳載善
人力資源辦公室

186. 每場工作坊會進行多久？
　　(A) 一小時
　　(B) 兩小時
　　(C) 整個早上
　　(D) 全天

解析 (B) 工作坊預計從上午8點30分進行到10點30分，一共是兩個小時。選項(A)(C)(D)都不正確。

187. 有退休打算的人應參加幾場工作坊？
　　(A) 一場
　　(B) 兩場
　　(C) 三場
　　(D) 四場

解析 (A) 通知上有提到「Choose the date that is most convenient for you」，選擇自己最方便的日期就好，可見每場工作坊的內容是一樣的。選項(B)和(C)都沒有被提及。選項(D)是工作坊總共的場數。

188. 關於工作坊，梅恩斯先生犯了什麼錯誤？
    (A) 他太晚到了。
    (B) 他走錯會議室。
    (C) 他去錯了日期。
    (D) 他忘了事先報名。

解析 **(C)** 梅恩斯先生在電子郵件中說他今天早上（this morning）試圖參加工作坊，從郵件日期可知今天是 7 月 20 日，並沒有舉行任何工作坊，首場工作坊是 8 月 1 日。選項(A)和(B)不正確，他早上八點半到了 F 會議室，時間和地點都和通知所提到的吻合。選項(D)不正確，通知上說無需報名。

189. 假如梅恩斯先生現在退休，他的退休金將被扣多少？
    (A) 0％
    (B) 2％
    (C) 4％
    (D) 10％

解析 **(C)** 梅恩斯先生說他今年 63 歲，吳先生在信中寫到「if you are 63, it will be reduced by 4%」，這裡的 it 就是指退休金，會被扣減 4％。選項(A)和(D)未被提及。選項(B)是 65 歲以下每少一歲會被扣除的量。

190. 關於稅務問題，吳先生建議梅恩斯先生做什麼？
    (A) 聘請一名稅務專家。
    (B) 參加一場工作坊。
    (C) 把問題傳給吳先生。
    (D) 打電話到會計部。

解析 **(D)** 吳先生在信中寫到「As far as tax issues go, I suggest you contact Fred Lee in Accounting」，所以是建議他聯繫會計部的同事。選項(A)重複使用了 tax specialist 這個詞，是吳先生對弗列德‧李的描述。選項(B)也是吳先生的建議，但不是為了解答稅務問題。選項(C)則未被提及。

第191–195題請看下面的通知、課程資訊和電子郵件。

專業進修時數最新消息

如你所知，ABC公司的全體員工每年都必須取得二十小時的專業進修時數。現在，你在中央技術學院完成的課程作業也可計入必須的專業進修時數，只限辦公室技能類的課程。每一課程可獲得十五小時的進修時數，必須達到及格分數方能取得時數。課程結束時，請將成績轉交人力資源辦公室。

中央技術學院課程資訊
類別：辦公室技能

會計學
會計學101　　　　　　財務會計（一）
會計學102　　　　　　財務會計（二）*
會計學670　　　　　　中小企業會計實務

商學
商學100　　　　　　　商業概論
商學200　　　　　　　商業原理

電腦科學
電腦科學104　　　　　微軟Word入門
電腦科學207　　　　　微軟Excel：基礎技能
電腦科學300　　　　　辦公室電腦應用**

行銷學
行銷學500　　　　　　全球行銷策略
行銷學600　　　　　　網路行銷

課程自1月3日至3月15日，同級之課程均在每星期同一天授課：100──週一，200──週二，300和400──週三，500和500以上──週四。所有課程均為晚上6點到8點授課。

每一課程學費為300美元，報名請至www.cti.org，並點擊「報名」連結。

* 學生必須修過會計學101並取得75分（含）以上分數，方得修習會計學102。
** 本課程將於週二晚間授課。

寄件者：亞曼達・明
收件者：羅伯托・古茲曼
主旨： 專業進修時數

古茲曼先生：

我已收到你上一期在中央技術學院修習會計學101的成績了。很可惜，因為你的成績太低了，我們不能把此課程計入你的專業進修時數。我看到你這一期報了電腦科學207和商學100，只要你成績有及格，還是可以把它們計入專業進修時數的。再努力加油喔！期待這期結束看到你的課程成績。

亞曼達・明
人力資源助理

191. ABC公司員工參加中央技術學院開設的課程，可以獲得多少專業進修時數？
　　(A) 低於十五小時
　　(B) 低於二十小時
　　(C) 每課程十五小時
　　(D) 每年二十小時

解析 (C) 通知提到「Each course is worth 15 hours of credit」，每一課程可獲得十五小時的時數。選項(A)和(B)不正確，並沒有限制可以取得多少時數。選項(D)是員工每年必須取得的時數。

192. 會計學102幾點開始上課？
　　(A) 早上6點
　　(B) 早上8點
　　(C) 晚上6點
　　(D) 晚上8點

解析 (C) 課程資訊中提到所有課程都是晚上6點到8點授課。選項(A)和(B)不正確，課程都在晚上，不在早上。選項(D)是下課時間。

193. 羅伯托參加每一門課要花多少錢？
　　(A) 免費，他的公司會支付。
　　(B) 300美元
　　(C) 600美元
　　(D) 要看課程級數。

解析 (B) 課程資訊中提到學費是每一課程300美元。選項(A)和(D)均未提及。選項(C)是他這一期報名兩門課程加起來的學費。

194. 羅伯托上一期修的會計學課程為何無法取得專業進修時數？
　　(A) 他的分數不及格。
　　(B) 這門課不屬於辦公室技能類。
　　(C) 這不是中央技術學院開設的課程。
　　(D) 他沒有把成績轉交給人力資源辦公室。

解析 **(A)** 通知中提到「You must receive a passing grade to get credit」（必須達到及格分數才能取得時數），然後在電子郵件中，明小姐寫到「we cannot count this course toward your professional development credits as your grade was too low」（不能計入時數因為分數太低），由此可知他的分數沒有及格。選項(B)(C)(D)的描述都不正確。

195. 這一期，羅伯托星期幾要上課？
　　(A) 只有星期一
　　(B) 星期一和星期二
　　(C) 星期二和星期三
　　(D) 只有星期三

解析 **(B)** 根據電子郵件的描述，羅伯托這期會上一門100級的課，和一門200級的課，對照課程資訊，兩門課分別是星期一和星期二上課。選項(A)(C)(D)都不是羅伯托選擇課程的上課時間。

第196–200題請看下面的廣告、電子郵件和專案估價單。

米切爾景觀設計公司
設計．種植．維護
我們全部包辦！

＊我們能將您的住宅或商業房地產變成一個美麗又雅緻的場所。我們會為您和您的房地產量身打造景觀設計。我們的專業園藝師會為您建置新的花園，並提供維護服務，讓您的花園永保美麗。

＊您喜歡自己動手做嗎？我們可以為您規劃設計，並協助挑選能達到您理想外觀又好照顧的植栽。

首次諮詢免費！
現在就打電話預約，
或造訪我們的網站：www.mitchelllandscapes.com

寄件者：史考特・霍爾姆斯
收件者：雪麗・席爾瓦
主旨：　闊街景觀設計
日期：　5月10日

雪麗：

你知道米切爾景觀設計公司嗎？我前幾天看到他們的廣告，覺得我們在闊街上的新房子正面也許可以找他們來做些點設計，目前看起來十分疏於維護。大門兩邊的灌木叢需要換成健康一點的灌木，而且若沿人行道種點花應該會很美。人行道的一邊已經有棵漂亮的櫻桃樹了，我想在另一邊也種一棵。去詢問一下這樣三千元以下能否做好，還有是否可在月底前完成。我們6月1日要舉辦看屋日，讓潛在租客過來參觀房子，我想在那之前把這個地方整理好。

再告訴我他們怎麼說。

史考特

米切爾景觀設計公司
設計・種植・維護

估價專案名稱：史考特・霍爾姆斯的房地產
地點：闊街156號

概述：
房子正面規劃設計，移除灌木叢，
種植新灌木，沿人行道鋪設花壇，
增加一棵櫻桃樹

成本預估

設計費	$500
材料費	$1,000
人工費	$650
總計	$2,150

專案日期：
預計6月2日動工，6月4日以前完工。

196. 關於這間景觀設計公司有何說明？
    (A) 承接私人住宅和商用建築的案子。
    (B) 過去曾和霍爾姆斯先生合作過。
    (C) 已經營多年了。
    (D) 有數間分公司。

解析 **(A)** 廣告中提到residential（= private home）和business（= commercial）兩種房地產。選項(B)不正確，霍爾姆斯先生在郵件的一開頭就問「Do you know anything about Mitchell Landscapers?」，暗示他對這間公司不熟悉。選項(C)和(D)都沒有被提及。

197. 廣告第二段第一行的「pick」這個字，意義與下列何者最接近？
    (A) 收割
    (B) 選擇
    (C) 拉
    (D) 抬起

解析 **(B)** 廣告中說該公司會協助客戶挑選合適的植栽。選項(A)(C)(D)是pick的其他意義，但不是pick在此處的意思。

198. 霍爾姆斯先生是什麼人？
    (A) 室內裝潢師
    (B) 房屋仲介
    (C) 城市規劃師
    (D) 房東

解析 **(D)** 霍爾姆斯先生擁有闊街上的房子，正打算舉辦看屋日（open house），讓潛在房客（prospective tenants）過來參觀房子，由此可知他是房東。選項(A)和設計（design）的主題產生聯想。選項(B)和房地產（property）的主題產生聯想。選項(C)未被提及。

199. 對於這份專案估價單，霍爾姆斯先生可能會有什麼問題？
    (A) 專案成本過高。
    (B) 沒有把種新的樹算進去。
    (C) 完工日太晚。
    (D) 他不想移除灌木叢。

解析 **(C)** 霍爾姆斯先生在電子郵件中提到他希望6月1日前完工，而專案估價單上面顯示施工時間是6月2-4日，對他來說太晚了。選項(A)不正確，他的預算是3000美元，而估價低於這個數字。選項(B)不正確，估價單上面有提到多種一棵櫻桃樹。選項(D)不正確，霍爾姆斯先生寫說他想把灌木叢移除。

200. 米切爾景觀設計公司要付多少錢給闊街專案的工人？
    (A) $500
    (B) $650
    (C) $1,000
    (D) $2,150

解析 (B) 估價單上的人工費（labor）是650美元。選項(A)是設計費。選項(C)是材料費。選項(D)是總計費用。

STOP 本測驗到此結束。如果你在時間結束前作答完畢，可以回頭檢查 Part 5、6、7 的答案。

實戰模擬試題4
解答

聽力測驗

Part 1 照片描述

1. **C**
2. **A**
3. **C**
4. **D**
5. **C**
6. **C**

Part 2 應答問題

7. **B**
8. **A**
9. **C**
10. **C**
11. **A**
12. **B**
13. **B**
14. **A**
15. **B**
16. **A**
17. **C**
18. **A**
19. **C**
20. **A**
21. **A**
22. **C**
23. **B**
24. **A**
25. **B**
26. **A**
27. **C**
28. **B**
29. **A**
30. **A**
31. **C**

Part 3 簡短對話

32. **B**
33. **D**
34. **A**
35. **A**
36. **B**
37. **D**
38. **C**
39. **D**
40. **C**
41. **A**
42. **C**
43. **B**
44. **D**
45. **B**
46. **A**
47. **B**
48. **B**
49. **C**
50. **D**
51. **D**
52. **B**
53. **C**
54. **C**
55. **C**
56. **A**
57. **B**
58. **D**
59. **A**
60. **B**
61. **C**
62. **A**
63. **C**
64. **C**
65. **C**
66. **A**
67. **D**
68. **A**
69. **B**
70. **A**

Part 4 簡短獨白

71. **C**
72. **B**
73. **D**
74. **C**
75. **D**
76. **C**
77. **B**
78. **D**
79. **A**
80. **D**
81. **A**
82. **C**
82. **C**
84. **A**
85. **C**
86. **D**
87. **C**
88. **A**
89. **D**
90. **B**
91. **C**
92. **C**
93. **B**
94. **C**
95. **B**
96. **C**
97. **A**
98. **B**
99. **C**
100. **D**

實戰模擬試題4
解答

閱讀測驗

Part 5 句子填空

101. **B**	109. **D**	117. **A**	125. **B**
102. **C**	110. **C**	118. **D**	126. **C**
103. **A**	111. **D**	119. **A**	127. **D**
104. **D**	112. **B**	120. **D**	128. **C**
105. **C**	113. **C**	121. **C**	129. **A**
106. **B**	114. **B**	122. **B**	130. **B**
107. **B**	115. **D**	123. **A**	
108. **A**	116. **C**	124. **C**	

Part 6 段落填空

131. **D**	135. **D**	139. **B**	143. **A**
132. **C**	136. **B**	140. **A**	144. **D**
133. **A**	137. **C**	141. **B**	145. **D**
134. **B**	138. **A**	142. **C**	146. **B**

Part 7 閱讀測驗

147. **B**	161. **C**	175. **A**	189. **D**
148. **A**	162. **B**	176. **B**	190. **A**
149. **C**	163. **A**	177. **B**	191. **A**
150. **C**	164. **D**	178. **B**	192. **A**
151. **B**	165. **A**	179. **C**	193. **C**
152. **D**	166. **C**	180. **C**	194. **D**
153. **A**	167. **A**	181. **C**	195. **D**
154. **D**	168. **C**	182. **A**	196. **A**
155. **B**	169. **B**	183. **C**	197. **D**
156. **D**	170. **A**	184. **C**	198. **B**
157. **A**	171. **A**	185. **B**	199. **C**
158. **B**	172. **D**	186. **D**	200. **B**
159. **C**	173. **C**	187. **A**	
160. **D**	174. **B**	188. **C**	

Model Test 4 實戰模擬試題4 題目中譯&解析

聽力測驗

在本段測驗當中，你將有機會展現自己對口說英語的理解能力。聽力測驗共有四個大題，每一大題均有作答說明。你有大約45分鐘時間完成聽力測驗。

> 複習要訣：閱讀 Part 1 和 Part 2 的錄音稿時，可在每題之間停5秒鐘。

Part 1：照片描述

> **作答方式**：你會看到一張照片，並聽到四個關於這張照片的陳述。選出最符合照片內容的陳述，將答案卡上對應的橢圓框塗滿。

1. Look at the photo marked number 1 in your test book.
   (A) The lamps are on the table.
   (B) The picture is on the wall.
   (C) The table is between the beds.
   (D) The pillow is next to the bed.

   請看試題本標示為1的照片。
   (A) 燈在桌子上。
   (B) 畫在牆上。
   (C) 桌子在兩張床中間。
   (D) 枕頭在床旁邊。

   解析 (C) 選項(C)正確指出了桌子的位置。選項(A)不正確，因為燈在牆上。選項(B)不正確，因為牆上沒有畫。選項(D)不正確，兩個枕頭都在床上，不在床旁邊。

2. Look at the photo marked number 2 in your test book.
   (A) The customer is ordering a meal.
   (B) They are learning to read.
   (C) The waiter is approaching the customer.
   (D) The guests are waiting to order.

   請看試題本標示為2的照片。
   (A) 客人正在點餐。
   (B) 他們正在學習閱讀。
   (C) 服務生正走向客人。
   (D) 客人們正等著點餐。

解析 (A) 選項(A)對照片情境做了合理的推測：此圖看起來像一間餐廳，客人手上拿的應為菜單，他正在點餐。選項(B)把看菜單的動作誤解為學習閱讀。選項(C)不正確，服務生已經站在客人身邊了。選項(D)不正確，客人已經在點餐了，而不是在等待點餐。

3. Look at the photo marked number 3 in your test book.
    (A) She's at the luggage store.
    (B) She's looking for her bag.
    (C) She's putting her suitcase in the car.
    (D) She's checking her baggage at the airport.

    請看試題本標示為 3 的照片。
    (A) 她正在賣行李箱的店裡。
    (B) 她正在找她的包包。
    (C) 她正在把她的行李箱放到車上。
    (D) 她正在機場辦理行李托運。

解析 (C) 選項(C)正確指出了照片中的動作：一名女子正在把行李箱放入車子的後車廂。選項(A)正確指出行李，但對女子所在位置描述不正確。選項(B)和(D)正確指出照片中的包包和行李箱，但對女子的動作描述不正確。

4. Look at the photo marked number 4 in your test book.
    (A) A car is driving through the gate.
    (B) The lamps are on the ground.
    (C) A man is opening the lock.
    (D) The gate doors are shut.

    請看試題本標示為 4 的照片。
    (A) 一輛車正駛過大門。
    (B) 燈在地上。
    (C) 一名男子正在開鎖。
    (D) 大門緊閉。

解析 (D) 選項(D)正確指出大門的狀態——照片中所有的門都是關閉的。選項(A)正確指出了大門，但是照片中沒有車子。選項(B)正確指出了燈，但對燈的位置描述不正確。選項(C)從大門聯想到鎖，但照片中沒有人。

5. Look at the photo marked number 5 in your test book.
    (A) He's opening the boxes.
    (B) He's washing the glass.
    (C) He's knocking on the door.
    (D) He's delivering a hat.

    請看試題本標示為 5 的照片。
    (A) 他正在打開箱子。
    (B) 他正在清洗玻璃。
    (C) 他正在敲門。
    (D) 他正在遞送一頂帽子。

解析 **(C)** 照片中有一名送貨員正在敲門，他要遞送包裹。選項(A)正確指出了箱子，但男子並沒有打開它們。選項(B)正確指出了門上的玻璃，但男子並沒有在清洗玻璃。選項(D)正確指出了男子的動作，但對他遞送的物品辨識錯誤，他遞送的是幾個箱子或包裹，而不是帽子。

6. Look at the photo marked number 6 in your test book.
    (A) The shopping bags are large.
    (B) The pillows are stuffed with cotton.
    (C) The cargo is being unloaded.
    (D) The ship is going through customs.

    請看試題本標示為 6 的照片。
    (A) 這些購物袋很大。
    (B) 這些枕頭裡塞滿了棉花。
    (C) 這些貨物正被卸下。
    (D) 這艘船正在過海關。

解析 **(C)** 選項(C)正確指出卸下貨物的動作。選項(A)和(B)誤把貨物辨識成購物袋和枕頭。選項(D)與照片情境不符。

Part 2：應答問題

> 作答方式：你會聽到一個問題和三個可能的回應。選出最適合回答該問題的回應，將答案卡上對應的橢圓框塗滿。

7. Did you pack everything we need for the camping trip?
   (A) I don't know how to light a fire.
   (B) Yes. I used a checklist to be sure.
   (C) Your backpack is heavier than mine.

   我們露營旅遊需要的東西你都打包好了嗎？
   (A) 我不知道如何生火。
   (B) 好了，我用清單確認過了。
   (C) 你的後背包比我的重。

   解析 (B) 選項(B)是被問及打包露營用品時的合理回應。選項(A)使用了和camping trip（露營旅遊）有關的light a fire（生火）。選項(C)使用了和camping trip（露營旅遊）有關的backpack（後背包）。

8. How was the weather during your vacation?
   (A) It rained every day.
   (B) She was wearing a hat.
   (C) The clothes are still wet.

   你度假期間的天氣如何？
   (A) 每天都在下雨。
   (B) 她戴著一頂帽子。
   (C) 衣服還是濕的。

   解析 (A) 選項(A)是對天氣問題的合理回應。選項(B)使用了同樣的動詞was，內容可能也和天氣有關（因天氣不好，所以有人戴了帽子），但沒有明確回答天氣如何的問題，同時也使用了weather的近音字wearing。選項(C)使用了weather的近音字wet。

9. Do you take milk in your coffee?
   (A) Yes, I have a cough.
   (B) The fee was quite high.
   (C) No. Just sugar.

   你喝咖啡會加牛奶嗎？
   (A) 對，我咳嗽。
   (B) 費用挺高的。
   (C) 不會，只加糖。

解析 (C) 選項(C)是對咖啡問題的合理回應。選項(A)混淆了近音字coffee和cough。選項(B)混淆了近音字coffee和fee。

10. Do you know if the utility bill was paid this month?
    (A) I opened it by mistake.
    (B) The pain is in my back.
    (C) Yes. I took care of it.

    你是否知道這個月的水電費繳了沒？
    (A) 我不小心打開它了。
    (B) 我的背在痛。
    (C) 有，我繳了。

解析 (C) 題目是詢問帳單繳了沒的「yes-no」問句，選項(C)是合理的回應，「I took care of it」的意思是「我處理好了」，在這裡表示「I paid it」。選項(A)中的「I opened it」是收到帳單時會做的動作。選項(B)混淆了近音字paid和pain。

11. No cake for me, thanks. I'm on a diet.
    (A) Perhaps you'd like some fruit instead.
    (B) Baking is my hobby.
    (C) Yes, I think you should buy it.

    我不要蛋糕，謝謝。我在節食。
    (A) 那你也許會想吃點水果。
    (B) 烘焙是我的興趣。
    (C) 對，我覺得你應該買它。

解析 (A) 第一個說話者說他不要蛋糕，第二個說話者就改給他水果，是合理的回應。選項(B)把cake和baking聯想在一起。選項(C)把diet和發音相近的片語buy it互相混淆了。

12. Which time is better for you—morning or afternoon?
    (A) This watch is better.
    (B) I'm free after lunch.
    (C) It's time to get up.

    哪時候你比較方便，早上還是下午？
    (A) 這隻手錶比較好。
    (B) 我午餐後有空。
    (C) 該起床了。

    解析 (B) 選項(B)是對時間問題的合理回應。選項(A)混淆了相關字 time 和 watch。選項(C)混淆了相關字 morning 和 get up。

13. Could you tell me how long the train ride is?
    (A) The bride is very tall.
    (B) It's very short—only two hours.
    (C) There are ten cars on the train.

    你可以告訴我火車要坐多久嗎？
    (A) 新娘子很高。
    (B) 很短，兩小時而已。
    (C) 火車有十節車廂。

    解析 (B) 選項(B)是對時間長度問題的合理回應。選項(A)混淆了近音字 ride 和 bride，同時也混淆了相關字 long 和 tall。選項(C)描述的是火車有多長（十節車廂），而不是車程有多長（兩小時）。

14. Would you mind telling me your occupation?
    (A) I'm an accountant.
    (B) I'll pay close attention.
    (C) The room is occupied.

    你介不介意告訴我你的職業？
    (A) 我是會計師。
    (B) 我會密切注意。
    (C) 這個房間有人。

    解析 (A) 選項(A)是對職業問題的合理回應。選項(B)混淆了近音字 occupation 和 attention。選項(C)混淆了近音字 occupied 和 occupation。

15．Are you coming to the party tomorrow or not?
　　(A) He is not coming.
　　(B) Yes, but I'll be late.
　　(C) They didn't come last night.

　　你會不會去明天的派對？
　　(A) 他不會來。
　　(B) 會，但我會晚點到。
　　(C) 他們昨晚沒來。

解析 (B) 選項(B)是被問及會不會來時的合理回應。選項(A)用not coming來回答問題，但主詞不對，問的是you，答的卻是he。選項(C)用didn't come來回答問題，但主詞不對，問的是you，回答的是they，時態也不對，問的是明天（未來式），回答的卻是昨天（過去式）。

16．What seat are you sitting in?
　　(A) I'm in seat twenty-seven J.
　　(B) In New York City.
　　(C) She's a reliable babysitter.

　　你坐在哪個位子？
　　(A) 我坐在27 J。
　　(B) 在紐約市。
　　(C) 她是位可靠的保姆。

解析 (A) 選項(A)是對座位問題的合理回應。選項(B)混淆了近音字sitting和city。選項(C)混淆了近音字sitting和sitter。

17．It's a lovely day for a walk.
　　(A) You shouldn't work so hard.
　　(B) He really likes to talk.
　　(C) Let's go to the park and walk there.

　　今天天氣真好，很適合散步。
　　(A) 你不該這麼努力工作的。
　　(B) 他真的很愛說話。
　　(C) 我們去公園散步吧。

解析 (C) 第一個說話者想去散步，第二個說話者就提議到公園去。選項(A)混淆了近音字work和walk。選項(B)混淆了近音字talk和walk。

18. Jack is your brother, isn't he?
    (A) No, he's my cousin.
    (B) You really shouldn't bother.
    (C) Yes, we're all very busy.

    傑克是你哥哥，對不對？
    (A) 不是，他是我表哥。
    (B) 你真的不用麻煩了。
    (C) 是的，我們都很忙。

    解析 (A) 選項(A)是對親戚關係問題的合理回應。選項(B)混淆了近音字 brother 和 bother。

19. Wasn't the staff meeting rather long?
    (A) Yes, there was plenty of seating.
    (B) Yes, he'd rather go tomorrow.
    (C) Yes, I thought it would never be over.

    那場員工會議是不是開太久了？
    (A) 是的，座位很多。
    (B) 是的，他寧可明天去。
    (C) 沒錯，我還以為永遠都不會結束。

    解析 (C) 題目是關於會議時間的否定疑問句，選項(C)是對此問題的合理回應。選項(A)混淆了近音字 meeting 和 seating。選項(B)用的是 rather 的另一個意義。

20. We have to be at the airport by seven.
    (A) Then we should leave here at six.
    (B) These plane tickets weren't cheap.
    (C) Court opens at eleven.

    我們七點前必須到機場。
    (A) 那我們六點就要從這裡出發。
    (B) 這些機票不便宜。
    (C) 法庭十一點開庭。

    解析 (A) 第二個說話者建議六點出發才能準時到機場。選項(B)從 airport 聯想到 plane tickets。選項(C)把發音相近的 court 和 airport 彼此混淆了。

21. What color do you think we should paint the hall?
    (A) Let's leave it white.
    (B) He's over six feet tall.
    (C) The painting hangs on the wall.

    你覺得我們應該把大廳漆成什麼顏色？
    (A) 就維持白色吧。
    (B) 他身高超過六英尺。
    (C) 這幅畫掛在牆上。

解析 (A) 選項(A)是對顏色問題的合理回應。選項(B)混淆了近音字 hall 和 tall。選項(C)混淆了相關字 paint 和 painting，以及近音字 hall 和 wall。

22. Which tie should I wear with my gray suit?
    (A) I always get migraines at work.
    (B) I tried, but I couldn't do it.
    (C) Either the red or the blue one.

    我該戴哪一條領帶來配我的灰色西裝？
    (A) 我工作時老是偏頭痛。
    (B) 我試過了，但做不到。
    (C) 紅色或藍色那條。

解析 (C) 選項(C)是對「Which」問題的合理回應。選項(A)混淆了發音相近的 my gray 和 migraine。選項(B)混淆了發音相近的 tie 和 tried。

23. How did you get a visitor's badge?
    (A) We frequently get visitors.
    (B) The security guard gave it to me.
    (C) Yes, I got one.

    你怎麼拿到訪客證的？
    (A) 我們經常有訪客。
    (B) 警衛給我的。
    (C) 是的，我有一個。

解析 (B) 選項(B)是對「How」問題的合理回應。選項(A)重複使用了 visitor 這個字。選項(C)用來回答「yes-no」問句。

24. When do you think you'll be finished?
    (A) In about an hour.
    (B) They finished after me.
    (C) I thought about it yesterday.

    你覺得你大概什麼時候會完成？
    (A) 大概一小時後。
    (B) 他們在我之後完成。
    (C) 我昨天想過這件事。

解析 (A) 選項(A)是對「When」問題的合理回應。選項(B)不正確，finished（過去式）和題目中的 will be finished（未來式）時態不一致。選項(C)不正確，thought（過去式）和題目中的 think（現在式）時態不一致。

25. Why aren't you coming with us?
    (A) We won't go with you.
    (B) I don't feel well.
    (C) I didn't come with you.

    你為什麼不跟我們一起去？
    (A) 我們不會跟你一起去。
    (B) 我身體不舒服。
    (C) 我沒有跟你一起去。

解析 (B) 選項(B)是被問及為何不一起去時的合理回應。選項(A)使用了 come 的相關字 go，但沒有回答「Why」的問題。選項(C)不正確，didn't come（過去式）和題目中的 aren't coming（未來式）時態不一致。

26. You have a key to the office, don't you?
    (A) Yes. I was given one when I started.
    (B) The answer key is at the end.
    (C) You can use mine.

    你有辦公室的鑰匙，對不對？
    (A) 有，我開始上班時公司給了我一把。
    (B) 答案在最後。
    (C) 你可以用我的。

解析 (A) 選項(A)回答了詢問有沒有鑰匙的附加問句。選項(B)用的是 key 的另一個意義。選項(C)是對方說「我沒有鑰匙」時的回應。

27. Which page of the newspaper is the article on?
    (A) It's on Wednesday.
    (B) Did you look under the bed?
    (C) It's on page two at the bottom of the page.

    這篇文章在報紙的哪一頁？
    (A) 在星期三。
    (B) 床下你看過了嗎？
    (C) 在第二頁的最底下。

解析 (C) 選項(C)是回答哪一頁（Which page）問題的合理回應。選項(A)回答的是「When」，而不是「Which page」。選項(B)把 on 誤解成 under，也沒回答「Which page」的問題。

28. Where should I wait for you?
    (A) You weigh too much already.
    (B) Wait for me on the corner.
    (C) I waited for an hour for you.

    我應該在哪裡等你？
    (A) 你已經太重了。
    (B) 在轉角處等我。
    (C) 我等你等了一個小時。

解析 (B) 選項(B)是對「Where」問題的合理回應。選項(A)混淆了近音字 wait 和 weigh。選項(C)不正確，waited（過去式）和 should wait（表未來的現在式）的時態不一致，而且回答的是「How long」的問題（一小時），而不是「Where」的問題。

29. How long a cord do you need?
    (A) About five to six feet long.
    (B) Three hundred cards, at the very minimum.
    (C) I need it tomorrow morning.

    你需要多長的繩子？
    (A) 大概五到六英尺長。
    (B) 最少要三百張卡片。
    (C) 我明天早上需要。

解析 (A) 選項(A)回答了「How long」的問題。選項(B)把近音字 cord 和 card 搞混了。選項(C)回答的是「When」的問題。

30. Has this memo been sent to all departments?
    (A) Yes, it was sent by e-mail.
    (B) The shipping department is on the first floor.
    (C) No, the department store is closed.

    這份備忘錄已經發給所有部門了嗎？
    (A) 是的，用電子郵件發出去了。
    (B) 出貨部在一樓。
    (C) 不，百貨公司打烊了。

解析 (A) 選項(A)是被問及發送備忘錄時的合理回應。選項(B)把sent和shipping department聯想在一起，但任何部門都可以收發備忘錄。選項(C)把departments和相關用語department store混為一談。

31. I don't have enough change for the bus.
    (A) You don't need to rush.
    (B) People never change.
    (C) I can lend you some.

    我身上零錢不夠，沒辦法坐公車。
    (A) 你不用著急。
    (B) 人們不會改變。
    (C) 我可以借你一些錢。

解析 (C) 第二名說話者表示願意借第一名說話者一些錢搭公車。選項(A)把rush和發音相近的bus搞混。選項(B)使用了change的另一個意義。

Part 3：簡短對話

> 作答方式：你會聽到兩人或多人之間的對話。每段對話搭配三個問題，各有四個選項。選出最適當的答案回答問題，將答案卡上對應的橢圓框塗滿。

Questions 32 through 34 refer to the following conversation.
Man: Did you go out last night? I called around seven, but there was no answer.
Woman: I guess I didn't hear the phone ringing because I had the TV on. I was watching a scary movie.
Man: Too bad I missed you. I wanted to invite you to a party. I had a great time and didn't get home till after two.
Woman: I couldn't have gone anyway. I went to sleep before ten because I had to get up early for work today.

第32-34題請聽下面這段對話。
男：妳昨晚出去了嗎？我大約七點時打電話但沒人接。
女：可能是因為我開著電視，所以沒聽到電話響。我正在看恐怖片。
男：太可惜了，沒聯絡到妳。我是想邀妳去參加派對。我玩得很開心，兩點以後才回家。
女：反正我也不能去。我十點以前就睡了，因為今天要早起工作。

32. What time did the man call the woman? 男子幾點打電話給女子？
    (A) 兩點
    (B) 七點
    (C) 八點
    (D) 十點

解析 (B) 男子在對話中提到他七點左右（around seven）打電話給女子。選項(A)是男子回到家的時間。選項(C)把近音字eight和great搞混了。選項(D)是女子睡覺的時間。

33. Why didn't the woman hear the phone? 女子為什麼沒聽到電話聲？
    (A) She was out. 她出去了。
    (B) She was singing. 她在唱歌。
    (C) She was sleeping. 她在睡覺。
    (D) She was watching TV. 她在看電視。

解析 (D) 女子說她沒聽到電話聲是因為她開了電視。選項(A)是男子的猜測。選項(B)混淆了近音字singing和ringing。選項(C)是女子晚一點做的事。

34. Why did the man call the woman? 男子為什麼要打電話給女子？
    (A) To ask her to go to a party 邀她去參加派對
    (B) To ask her to see a movie 邀她去看電影
    (C) To ask her to go on a walk 邀她去散步
    (D) To ask her to help him with work 請她幫他處理工作上的事

解析 (A) 男子說他想邀請女子去參加派對。選項(B)是女子正在看恐怖電影的混淆選項。選項(C)把近音字walk和work搞混了。選項(D)重複使用了對話中的work這個字。

Questions 35 through 37 refer to the following conversation.

Woman: I'm putting you in Room three-sixty-five. It's quite spacious with a king-sized bed, and it overlooks the pool. Here's your key.
Man: I imagine the pool area gets crowded during the day. Could you give me something less noisy?
Woman: Room two-seventeen is available. It's a bit smaller but has a view of the garden and is very relaxing. How does that sound?
Man: Much better. I am sure I'll be quite comfortable there. In fact, I'd like to go right up and get some rest before dinner.

第35–37題請聽下面這段對話。
女：我給您安排了365號房，那間非常寬敞，有一張特大床，還可以俯瞰游泳池。這是您的鑰匙。
男：我想游泳池白天人應該很多，能不能給我一間不那麼吵的房間？
女：217號房是空的，稍微小一點，但可觀賞花園景致，令人很放鬆。這間如何？
男：好多了，我想我在那邊應該會住得很舒服。其實我想在晚餐前先上去休息一下。

35. What does the woman say about Room 365? 女子對365號房有何描述？
    (A) It is large. 很大。
    (B) It has two beds. 有兩張床。
    (C) It is not available. 已經有人使用。
    (D) It has a good view. 景觀很好。

解析 (A) 女子說那個房間很寬敞（quite spacious）。選項(B)不正確，女子說那個房間是一張特大床。選項(C)被對話中提到的available給混淆了，對話中的available是用來描述217號房。選項(D)也是對217號房的描述。

36. What kind of room does the man ask for? 男子要求一間怎麼樣的房間？
   (A) A room by the pool 游泳池旁的房間
   (B) A room that is quieter 安靜一點的房間
   (C) A room near the garden 靠近花園的房間
   (D) A room with a king-sized bed 有一張特大床的房間

解析 **(B)** 男子擔心游泳池的人潮眾多，並說「Could you give me something less noisy?」，可見他想要安靜一點的房間。選項(A)是他不想要的房間。選項(C)和(D)都是女子描述過的房間特徵。

37. What will the man do now? 男子現在要做什麼？
   (A) Put on his sweater 穿上他的毛衣
   (B) Swim in the pool 到游泳池裡游泳
   (C) Have dinner 吃晚餐
   (D) Take a rest 休息

解析 **(D)** 男子說他想先上去休息一下。選項(A)把sweater和近音字better搞混了。選項(B)重複使用了pool這個字。選項(C)是他晚一點才要做的事。

Questions 38 through 40 refer to the following conversation.
Man: Someone opened the emergency exit door by accident in Hall C. I need someone to turn off the alarm.
Woman: I don't have the code for Hall C. Jerry does, I think, but he's on break right now.
Man: I'll see if I can contact him on his cell phone. He can take a longer break later to make up for the time.

第38–40題請聽下面這段對話。
男：有人不小心打開了C廳的逃生門，我需要有人把警報器關掉。
女：我沒有C廳的密碼。我想傑瑞有，可是他現在正在休息。
男：我打他手機看看能不能聯絡上他，他可以之後再休息久一點，把時間補回來。

38. What is the problem? 出了什麼問題？
   (A) A door is locked. 有一道門被鎖上了。
   (B) A car was stolen. 有一輛車被偷了。
   (C) An alarm went off. 有一個警報器響了。
   (D) A man is lost. 有一名男子走失了。

解析 (C) 男子說他需要有人把逃生門上的警報器關掉。選項(A)不正確，門被打開而不是被鎖上。選項(B)和 alarm（警報器）有關。選項(D)被他們正在尋找傑瑞的事給混淆了，傑瑞是去休息，並沒有走失。

39. Who is Jerry? 傑瑞是什麼人？
    (A) An ambulance driver 救護車駕駛
    (B) A firefighter 消防員
    (C) A thief 小偷
    (D) A coworker 同事

解析 (D) 對話者需要把警報器關掉，而傑瑞可以協助他們處理這件事，肯定是一起工作的同事。選項(A)和(B)都和 accident（意外）和 emergency（緊急事件）有關。選項(C)可能造成警報響起，但不是此處警報響起的原因。

40. What will the man do? 這名男子將會做什麼事？
    (A) Check the time 查看時間
    (B) Fix his phone 修裡他的手機
    (C) Call Jerry 打電話給傑瑞
    (D) Take a break 休息

解析 (C) 男子說他會試著打傑瑞的手機聯絡他。選項(A)重複使用了 time 這個字。選項(B)重複使用了 phone 這個字。選項(D)是傑瑞正在做的事。

Questions 41 through 43 refer to the following conversation.
Woman:　I enjoyed this afternoon's museum tour so much. Didn't you?
Man:　　Yes, parts of it were quite interesting. But the tour guide was in such a hurry, I didn't get to see all the paintings I was interested in.
Woman:　Maybe you can go back on your own. You've got time. We aren't leaving the city until next weekend.
Man:　　That's true, but it costs so much to get in, I don't think, I mean, I'm not sure how I feel about paying it again.

第 41–43 題請聽下面這段對話。
女：下午的博物館導覽活動真是太棒了，你不覺得嗎？
男：是的，有一部分非常有趣。但導覽員太趕了，我感興趣的畫作都沒辦法全部看完。
女：也許你可以自己再去一次，你還有時間，我們下週末才會離開這座城市。
男：是沒錯，但入場費那麼貴，我不認為，我是說，我不確定我會還想再付一次。

41. What is the man's complaint? 男子在抱怨什麼？
    (A) The tour was too fast. 導覽活動進行太快。
    (B) They didn't see any paintings. 他們什麼畫作也沒看到。
    (C) His back hurt. 他背痛。
    (D) He didn't like the paintings. 他不喜歡這些畫作。

解析 (A) 男子抱怨導覽員太趕了（in such a hurry）。選項(B)混淆了近音字any和many。選項(C)使用了back的另一個意義。選項(D)重複使用了paintings這個字。

42. What does the woman suggest to the man? 女子建議男子做什麼？
    (A) Take another tour 參加另一場導覽活動
    (B) Hurry up 動作快一點
    (C) Return to the museum alone 自己回去博物館
    (D) Get a painting of his own 取得一幅屬於自己的畫作

解析 (C) 女子建議男子自己回去博物館，再參觀一次。選項(A)重複使用了tour這個字。選項(B)重複使用了hurry這個字。選項(D)使用了own的另一個意義，on one's own是「獨自做一件事」，of one's own是「屬於自己的」。

43. What does the man say about the museum? 男子對博物館有何說法？
    (A) The tour guides are knowledgeable. 導覽員知識淵博。
    (B) The admission price is high. 入場費很貴。
    (C) There are too many rooms. 展廳太多了。
    (D) The paintings are unusual. 畫作非常特別。

解析 (B) 男子說「it costs so much to get in」，表示進去要花很多錢。選項(A)和(D)都重複使用了對話中的單字。選項(C)未被提及。

Questions 44 through 46 refer to the following conversation with three speakers.
Woman 1: Do you drive to work?
Man: No, I take the commuter train. I don't like to park in the city. It's impossible to find a place.
Woman 2: I always drive. I like having my car nearby in case I need it.
Man: Really? But where do you park? I can never find anything on the street.
Woman 1: Me neither. Where do you keep your car all day, Isabel?
Woman 2: In the garage downstairs. It costs eleven dollars a day, but it's certainly worth it, and it's right in the building.
Man: Eleven dollars a day? Who can afford that?
Woman 1: Not very many people, I'm sure.

第 44–46 題請聽下面這段三人之間的對話。
女1：你開車上班嗎？
男： 沒有，我都搭通勤火車。我不喜歡在城市裡停車，根本找不到車位。
女2：我一向自己開車，我喜歡車子就在附近，以防萬一我需要用車。
男： 真假？你都停在哪裡？我在街上永遠找不到停車位。
女1：我也是。伊莎貝兒，你一整天都把車停在哪裡？
女2：樓下的停車場啊，一天十一美元，可是絕對值得，而且就在大樓裡面。
男： 一天十一美元？誰付得起啊？
女1：我想應該沒多少人付得起。

44. Why does the man take the train? 男子為何要搭火車？
    (A) Driving is too expensive. 開車太花錢了。
    (B) He sometimes needs his car. 他有時會需要用車。
    (C) The train is faster than driving. 搭火車比開車快。
    (D) He doesn't like to park in the city. 他不喜歡在城市裡停車。

解析 (D) 男子有提到他不喜歡在城市裡停車。選項(A)和其中一名女子為了停車花很多錢有關，但不是男子不開車的原因。選項(B)是其中一名女子開車的原因。選項(C)重複使用了 train 這個字。

45. Where does Isabel keep her car all day? 伊莎貝兒一整天把車子停在哪裡？
    (A) At the park 公園裡
    (B) In a garage 停車場內
    (C) On the street 街上
    (D) At the train station 火車站

解析 (B) 伊莎貝兒說她把車子停在樓下的停車場。選項(A)使用了 park 的另一個意義。選項(C)是男子的猜測。選項(D)重複使用了 train 這個字。

46. What does the man think of Isabel's parking place? 男子對伊莎貝兒停車的地方有什麼看法？
    (A) The cost is too high. 收費太高。
    (B) It is always crowded. 總是停滿了車。
    (C) The spaces are too small. 停車格太小。
    (D) It is conveniently located. 地點很方便。

解析 (A) 男子說「Who can afford that?」（誰付得起），認為對大多數人來說太貴了。選項(B)(C)(D)雖然都有可能，但男子並無提及。

Questions 47 through 49 refer to the following conversation.

Man: Excuse me. Can you tell me, uh, is there a post office anywhere around here?

Woman: Yes, the main post office is not too far. Take the number forty-six bus two stops, then cross the street and there you are. You can't miss it.

Man: I know where that one is. I was hoping there was one closer that I could walk to.

Woman: Oh, it takes hardly any time to get there. It's just a five-minute bus ride.

Man: I guess that's not so bad. And the bus stop is right here.

第47–49題請聽下面這段對話。

男：不好意思，請問，呃，這附近有郵局嗎？
女：有，主郵局不遠。搭46號公車，坐兩站下車，過馬路就到了，你不會找不到的。
男：我知道那間在哪裡，我是希望近一點、走路就可以到的。
女：喔，到那邊不會花什麼時間的，坐公車五分鐘就到了。
男：好像也還行，而且公車站就在這裡。

47. Why is the man disappointed? 男子為何感到失望？
    (A) The post office is closed. 郵局關門了。
    (B) The post office isn't close. 郵局沒有很近。
    (C) The post office is hard to find. 郵局很難找。
    (D) The post office is underground. 郵局位於地下樓層。

解析 (B) 這名男子正在尋找近一點、走路可到達的郵局，所以對於郵局無法步行抵達有點失望。選項(A)混淆了近音字closed和close。選項(C)不正確是因為女子說不會找不到（You can't missed it）。選項(D)混淆了近音字underground和around。

48. How does the woman recommend getting to the post office? 女子建議用什麼方式前往郵局？
    (A) By car 搭車
    (B) By bus 搭公車
    (C) By foot 走路
    (D) By taxi 搭計程車

解析 (B) 女子建議男子搭公車去。選項(A)混淆了近音字car和far。選項(C)是男子希望的方式。選項(D)未被提及。

49. What does the man mean when he says, "That's not so bad"?
    男子說「That's not so bad」是什麼意思？
    (A) He prefers walking. 他比較想要走路。
    (B) He does not get lost easily. 他不容易迷路。
    (C) The post office is not too far away. 郵局不會太遠。
    (D) The woman's directions are easy to follow. 女子的指示很好懂。

解析 (C) 女子說搭公車到郵局只要五分鐘，男子用這句話回應，表示路程好像很短、很容易到達。選項(A)(B)(D)都不符合這裡的語境。

Questions 50 through 52 refer to the following conversation.
Woman: Welcome to our company. Let's go over some basic information. The first thing most people want to know is when will they get paid, so I'll tell you right off, paychecks are issued every two weeks.
Man: Actually, your assistant already explained that part to me. That's better than once a month, like at my old job.
Woman: Good. Also, you'll get health insurance, disability insurance, and life insurance. And you get three weeks paid vacation, as well as one personal day a month.
Man: Three weeks vacation? Fantastic. My manager didn't tell me about that.

第50–52題請聽下面這段對話。
女：歡迎來到我們公司，我們來了解一下基本資訊。大多數人最想知道的第一件事是何時領薪水，我就直接告訴你了，每兩個星期發一次薪水。
男：其實，你的助理已經跟我說明過此部分了，這種方式比我以前的工作一個月發薪一次來得好。
女：很好。還有，你會有健康保險、失能保險和人壽保險。還有三週的有薪假，以及一個月一天的事假。
男：三週的假？太棒了，我的經理沒告訴我這件事。

50. Who is the woman talking to? 這名女子正在和誰說話？
    (A) Her manager 她的經理
    (B) Her assistant 她的助理
    (C) A travel agent 旅行社業務員
    (D) A new employee 新來的員工

解析 (D) 這名女子正在向新來的員工說明公司福利。選項(A)重複使用了manager這個字。選項(B)重複使用了assistant這個字。選項(C)從vacation聯想到travel agent。

51. How often do employees at this company get paid?
    這間公司的員工多久領一次薪水？
    (A) Once a week 一週一次
    (B) Twice a week 一週兩次
    (C) Once a month 一個月一次
    (D) Twice a month 一個月兩次

解析 (D) 員工每兩週（every two weeks）領一次薪水，所以就是一個月兩次。選項(A)重複使用了 once 這個字。選項(B)把(every) two weeks 誤解為 twice a week。選項(C)是男子比較不喜歡的發薪方式。

52. What is the man excited about? 男子對何事感到興奮？
    (A) The number of insurance benefits 保險福利的數量
    (B) The length of the vacation 假期的長度
    (C) The size of his pay check 薪水的多寡
    (D) The type of job duties 職務的類型

解析 (B) 女子說男子可享有三週的有薪假，男子回應「Three weeks vacation? Fantastic.」，可見他對三週假期感到興奮。選項(A)是女子提到的資訊，但男子對這項資訊並無反應。選項(C)不正確，對話中唯一提到薪資的部分，只說了多久會發薪一次。選項(D)在對話中並未提及。

Questions 53 through 55 refer to the following conversation.
Man: I'd like to leave for the airport by three o'clock, if you don't mind.
Woman: We'll arrive way too soon if we leave home then.
Man: Yes, but we'll avoid heavy traffic that way. And it'll be worse today because of the rain.
Woman: All right, but I really don't think you need to worry. We'll have more than enough time to get there if we leave that early. And then we'll be waiting at the airport for hours.
Man: That's OK. I'd rather do that than arrive at the last minute.

第 53-55 題請聽下面這段對話。
男：如果你不介意，我想在三點前出發到機場。
女：那時候出發會太早到。
男：對，但那樣才能避開塞車。而且今天下雨，路上會更塞。
女：好吧，但我真的覺得你不用擔心。我們那麼早出發，到機場的時間綽綽有餘，然後我們就會在機場等好幾個小時。
男：沒關係，我寧可早到，也不要趕在最後一分鐘到。

53. Where are the speakers going? 說話者要去哪裡？
    (A) Home 家
    (B) To the store 商店
    (C) To the airport 機場
    (D) To the train station 火車站

解析 (C) 男子說他們要出發到機場（leave for the airport）。選項(A)是他們的出發地。選項(B)混淆了近音字store和more。選項(D)混淆了近音字train和rain。

54. What time does the man want to leave? 男子希望幾點出發？
    (A) At noon 正午
    (B) At 2:00 兩點
    (C) At 3:00 三點
    (D) At 10:00 十點

解析 (C) 男子說他想要三點出發。選項(A)混淆了近音字noon和soon。選項(B)混淆了同音字two和too。選項(D)混淆了近音字ten和then。

55. Why does he want to leave at this time? 他為何想在那個時間出發？
    (A) He likes to arrive early. 他喜歡早點到。
    (B) He doesn't like to hurry. 他不喜歡匆匆忙忙。
    (C) He's afraid traffic will be bad. 他擔心交通狀況不好。
    (D) He wants to try a new way of getting there. 他想嘗試用新的交通方式到那邊。

解析 (C) 男子提到他想避開塞車（heavy traffic 交通壅塞）。選項(A)重複使用了early這個字。選項(B)混淆了近音字hurry和worry。選項(D)使用了對話中的way這個字，但用的是另一個意義。

Questions 56 through 58 refer to the following conversation.
Man: You can borrow books and videos for three weeks, and you can renew once for three more weeks. We generally don't allow people to take magazines and newspapers home, but you are welcome to read them here.
Woman: Thanks, that's good to know, but I just want to take this one novel for now. So, uh, what happens if I bring it back late?
Man: We charge a fine of twenty-five cents a day for each day it's overdue.
Woman: I'll be sure to return it on time, then!

449

第 56–58 題請聽下面這段對話。

男：書籍和影片可以借三個禮拜，之後可以續借一次，也是三個禮拜。我們一般不讓大家把雜誌和報紙帶回家，但歡迎在這邊閱讀。

女：謝謝，這樣很不錯，但我這次只想借這本小說。所以，呃，要是我太晚還書會怎樣？

男：逾期一天要罰二十五分美金。

女：那我到時一定會準時還書！

56. Where does this conversation take place? 這段對話發生在什麼地方？
    (A) Library 圖書館
    (B) Bookstore 書店
    (C) Airplane 飛機
    (D) Dentist's office 牙醫診所

解析 (A) 對話者正在討論借書和影片，還有閱讀雜誌和報紙的事情，並說逾期要罰錢，所以是在圖書館。選項(B)不正確，你會在書店買書而不是借書。選項(C)和(D)都是有可能閱讀雜誌和報紙的地方。

57. What does the woman want? 這名女子想要什麼？
    (A) A video 一支影片
    (B) A book 一本書
    (C) A magazine 一本雜誌
    (D) A newspaper 一份報紙

解析 (B) 女子說她要借一本小說，小說是一種圖書類型。選項(A)(C)(D)是對話中提到的其他讀物類型。

58. What does the woman say she will do? 女子說她會做什麼？
    (A) Return at 9:00 九點回來
    (B) Wait for the man 等男子
    (C) Give the man 25 cents 給男子二十五分美金
    (D) Avoid paying a fine 避免被罰錢

解析 (D) 男子提到逾期未還書要繳的罰款後，女子就說「I'll be sure to return it on time, then!」（我到時會準時還書），如果她準時還書，就不用被罰錢。選項(A)混淆了近音字 nine 和 fine。選項(B)未被提及。選項(C)是女子要避免支付的罰款金額。

Questions 59 through 61 refer to the following conversation.

Woman: What a beautiful day! You wanna have lunch at that sidewalk café? We could sit outside, and they have the best salads.

Man: Actually, I brought a sandwich from home and was planning to take it to the park and eat there.

Woman: Oh, that's a better idea. I'll pick up a sandwich and a cookie at the café and meet you there. Should I bring you a cookie, too?

Man: Sure, if it's not a problem. I'll wait for you by the fountain. But don't be long. I have to be back at the office by one.

第 59–61 題請聽下面這段對話。

女：今天天氣真好！你要不要去路邊那家咖啡館吃午餐？我們可以坐在戶外，而且他們的沙拉超好吃的。

男：其實我從家裡帶了三明治，並打算到公園去吃。

女：喔，那樣更好。我去咖啡館買三明治和餅乾，然後到公園和你碰面。要不要幫你也買份餅乾？

男：好啊，不麻煩的話。我在噴水池旁等你，但別太久喔，我一點前要回辦公室。

59. What does the woman want to do? 這名女子想做什麼？
    (A) Have lunch outside 在戶外吃午餐
    (B) Drink some coffee 喝點咖啡
    (C) Make a sandwich 做三明治
    (D) Go home 回家

解析 (A) 女子建議到路邊的一家咖啡館吃午餐，還說「We could sit outside」，所以她想在戶外吃午餐。選項(B)從café聯想到coffee。選項(C)指的是男子自己帶三明治當午餐。選項(D)重複使用了home這個字。

60. Where are the speakers going to meet? 說話者打算在哪裡碰面？
    (A) At a café 咖啡館
    (B) In the park 公園
    (C) At the office 辦公室
    (D) On the sidewalk 路邊

解析 (B) 男子說他打算到公園吃午餐，女子同意在那邊與他碰面。選項(A)是女子原先的建議。選項(C)是他們吃完午餐要回去的地方。選項(D)是對咖啡館的描述。

61. Why does the man say, "If it's not a problem"?
    男子為何要說「If it's not a problem」？
    (A) To make a suggestion 為了提出建議
    (B) To explain a reason 為了解釋原因
    (C) To accept an offer 為了接受提議
    (D) To make a request 為了提出要求

解析 (C) 這是男子對女子的提議「Should I bring you a cookie, too?」所作的回應。選項(A)(B)(D) 都不符合此處的語境。

Questions 62 through 64 refer to the following conversation.
Woman: Look. There's a problem with my hotel bill. I was charged for three nights, but I stayed only one.
Man: Let's see.
Woman: It really isn't right. I don't owe this much.
Man: Give me a minute. My poor addition could account for the problem. Oh, I see. I'm terribly sorry. I gave you another guest's bill by mistake. This one's yours.
Woman: Uh, yes, this looks right. Thank you. Will you take a personal check? It's on a local bank, actually.
Man: I'm sorry, but we can't accept checks or cash. I'll need to put it on your credit card.

第 62 – 64 題請聽下面這段對話。
女：你看，我的飯店帳單有個問題。我被收了三晚的錢，但我只住了一晚。
男：讓我看看。
女：這真的不對，我不應該付這麼多。
男：給我一點時間，可能是我蹩腳的加法造成這個問題的。哦，我明白了。真的很抱歉，我給錯帳單了，這是另一位客人的帳單，這張才是您的。
女：啊，這才對，謝謝。你們收個人支票嗎？其實是本地銀行的支票。
男：很抱歉，我們不接受支票或現金，我必須刷您的信用卡。

62. How many nights did the woman stay at the hotel? 這名女子在飯店住了幾晚？
    (A) One 一晚
    (B) Two 兩晚
    (C) Three 三晚
    (D) Four 四晚

解析 (A) 女子說「I was charged for three nights, but I stayed only one.」，所以她只住了一晚。選項(B)和(D)沒有被提及。選項(C)是她被收費的住宿天數。

63. What was the problem with her bill? 她的帳單出了問題？
    (A) The woman misplaced the bill. 女子把帳單放錯地方了。
    (B) The man added the bill wrong. 男子把帳單金額加錯了。
    (C) The man gave her the wrong bill. 男子給了她錯誤的帳單。
    (D) The woman read the bill incorrectly. 女子看錯帳單金額。

解析 (C) 男子說「I gave you another guest's bill by mistake」，他把別人的帳單給她了。選項(A)和(D)未被提及。選項(B)是男子原本以為的問題。

64. What does the woman want to do? 這名女子想做什麼？
    (A) Cash a check 兌現支票
    (B) Go to the bank 去銀行
    (C) Pay her bill by check 以支票支付帳單
    (D) Leave her business card 留下她的名片

解析 (C) 女子問說「Will you take a personal check?」，表示她想用個人支票付款。選項(A)是被對話中提到check和cash給混淆。選項(B)重複使用了bank這個字。選項(D)把business card（名片）和credit card（信用卡）搞混了。

Questions 65 through 67 refer to the following conversation and coupon.
Woman: I'm calling because I had a problem ordering some ski boots from your website.
Man: Could you describe what happened?
Woman: I had a coupon for twenty-five percent off, but it didn't show on the total. The order form said I owe the full hundred and seventy-five dollars.
Man: We frequently have coupons for discounts on various items. Could you read me the code at the bottom of the coupon?
Woman: The number at the bottom? A one-oh-six.
Man: (pause) Ah, I see your problem. Look at the date. Today's July third. I'll tell you what. I'll e-mail you a coupon for twenty percent off your next order.
Woman: Thank you.

453

第 65-67 題請聽下面這段對話，並參考優惠券。

女：我打電話來是因為我在你們官網訂購滑雪靴時出了一個問題。

男：可以請您描述發生了什麼問題嗎？

女：我有一張七五折券，可是總計沒有顯示出來，訂單上說我要付全額175美元。

男：我們經常針對不同商品提供折價券，可以麻煩您將折價券底下的折扣碼唸給我嗎？

女：底下的號碼嗎？A106。

男：（停頓了一會兒）啊，我知道您的問題了，請看一下日期，今天是7月3日。這樣吧，我用電子郵件寄一張八折券給您，下次訂單可使用。

女：謝謝。

```
www.sportstown.com

體育小鎮
折價券
不限商品購物滿$150可享75折
適用於網路商店或實體門市
有效期限：6月30日
使用時請輸入折扣碼：A106
```

65. What does the woman want to buy? 這名女子想買什麼東西？
    (A) Skis 滑雪板
    (B) Shoes 鞋子
    (C) Boots 靴子
    (D) Books 書

解析 **(C)** 女子說她打算要買滑雪靴（ski boots）。選項(A)混淆了skies和ski boots。選項(B)未被提及。選項(D)混淆了近音字books和boots。

66. Look at the graphic. Why did the woman have a problem with the coupon? 請看圖表，女子的折價券有什麼問題？
    (A) It has expired. 折價券過期了。
    (B) She used the wrong code. 她輸入了錯誤的折扣碼。
    (C) She didn't spend enough money. 她購買的金額不足。
    (D) It is not valid for online purchases. 折價券不適用於網路購物。

解析 **(A)** 折價券的有效期限是 6 月 30 日，而男子說今天是 7 月 3 日，所以折價券已經過期了。選項 (B) 不正確，女子報給男子的折扣碼和折價券上的數字一模一樣。選項 (C) 不正確，訂單是 175 美元，而滿 150 美元就可以使用折價券。選項 (D) 不正確，折價券上說網路購物也適用。

67. What does the man offer to do? 男子表示願意做什麼？
    (A) Give the woman a full refund 給女子全額退款
    (B) Take 20% off the shipping fee 運費打八折
    (C) Give a discount on the current order 提供當前訂單優惠
    (D) Send a coupon for a discount on a future order
        寄折價券給女子，未來訂單可打折

解析 **(D)** 男子說「I'll e-mail you a coupon for twenty percent off your next order」，表示會提供八折優惠券，可在下一筆訂單使用。選項 (A) 不正確，對話中沒有提到退款。選項 (B) 不正確，對話中沒有提到運費。選項 (C) 是女子原本以為當前這筆訂單應有優惠。

Questions 68 through 70 refer to the following conversation and price list.

Man: Look at this website. They have those chairs we've been wanting to order. You know, for the conference room.
Woman: Hm. Their prices seem good, but look how much they charge for shipping.
Man: It is more than most companies charge, but they have next day delivery and we'd still come in under budget. And we'd still have enough to order something else, like one of these tables. It would go great in the front office.
Woman: Right. I see. And it wouldn't add to the shipping charges. But we couldn't spend more than seventy-five dollars on it.
Man: That's all right. We can get a nice one for that price.

第 68–70 題請聽下面這段對話，並參考價目表。
男：你看這個網站，他們有我們一直想訂的椅子，你知道吧，會議室要用的。
女：嗯，他們的價錢看起來不錯，可是你看運費。
男：比大多數公司的運費還要高，但是他們有隔日送達，而且最後算起來還是落在我們的預算之內，剩下的錢還夠買別的東西，像是這些桌子，放在前辦公室很適合。
女：是的，我明白，而且不用多加運費，但桌子就不能花超過 75 美元。
男：沒關係，那個價錢已經可以買到很好的。

小型辦公桌

一個抽屜	$75
兩個抽屜	$100
三個抽屜	$115
四個抽屜	$125

68. Which room do the speakers want to buy chairs for? 說話者要為哪個房間訂購椅子？
    (A) Conference room 會議室
    (B) Break room 休息室
    (C) Front office 前辦公室
    (D) Cafeteria 自助餐廳

解析 **(A)** 男子說椅子是要給會議室用的。選項(B)和(D)未被提及。選項(C)是他們要放桌子的地方。

69. What do the speakers say about shipping? 說話者提到關於運費的什麼？
    (A) The delivery is slow. 配送很慢。
    (B) The fee is very high. 費用很高。
    (C) Next day delivery costs extra. 隔日送達需要加價。
    (D) The shipping company is unreliable. 這家貨運公司很不可靠。

解析 **(B)** 女子說「look how much they charge for shipping」（你看他們的運費），然後男子回應說「It is more than most companies charge」（比大多數公司的收費還高），可見運費很貴。選項(A)不正確，他們有隔日送達服務。選項(C)不正確，對話中沒有提到隔日送達要加價。選項(D)未被提及。

70. Look at the graphic. Which table will the speakers probably order? 請看圖表，說話者大概會訂購哪一種桌子？
    (A) One drawer 一個抽屜
    (B) Two drawers 兩個抽屜
    (C) Three drawers 三個抽屜
    (D) Four drawers 四個抽屜

解析 **(A)** 女子說桌子不可以超過75美元，所以只能買一個抽屜的桌子。選項(B)(C)(D)都超過他們的預算。

Part 4：簡短獨白

> 作答方式：你會聽到一名說話者的獨白。每段獨白搭配三個問題，各有四個選項。選出最適當的答案回答問題，並將答案卡上對應的橢圓框塗滿。

Questions 71 through 73 refer to the following announcement.

This is the first call for priority boarding for flight two-nine-four to Minneapolis. Persons with disabilities, senior citizens, and persons traveling with small children are invited to board at this time. Anyone needing extra help may request assistance from a flight attendant. As a reminder, all passengers are allowed one carry-on bag only. Please give any extra bags to the gate agent before boarding the plane. I repeat, we are now beginning priority boarding. All other passengers, please stay away from the door until you hear your row number called. Thank you for your cooperation.

第 71–73 題請聽下面這段廣播。

這是飛往明尼亞波利斯294航班的優先登機第一次廣播。行動不便、年長及攜帶幼童的旅客請於此時登機。需要額外幫助的旅客可向空服員請求協助。提醒您，所有旅客僅能攜帶一件手提行李，登機前請將多餘行李交給登機門服務人員。再重複一遍，現在開始優先登機，其他旅客請先遠離入口，等待叫到您的排號。感謝您的配合。

71. Who can get on the plane during priority boarding? 誰可以在優先登機期間登機？
    (A) People with connecting flights 轉機的旅客
    (B) Large groups 大型團體
    (C) Elderly people 老年人
    (D) Airline personnel 航空公司人員

解析 (C) 廣播中的 senior citizens 就等於 elderly people。選項(A)(B)(D)都沒有被提及。

72. What should be given to the gate agent? 什麼東西必須交給登機門的服務人員？
    (A) A ticket 機票
    (B) Extra luggage 多餘行李
    (C) A boarding pass 登機證
    (D) Requests for assistance 協助請求

解析 (B) 說話者提醒旅客每人只能攜帶一件手提行李，接著說「Please give any extra bags to the gate agent」，要將多餘行李交給登機門服務人員。選項(A)和(C)也是可能交給登機門服務人員的東西，但在這段敘述中並未提及。選項(D)則必須向空服員提出。

457

73. What are other passengers asked to do? 其他旅客被要求做什麼？
    (A) Stand near the door 站在靠近入口處
    (B) Assist the flight attendants 協助空服員
    (C) Make their phone calls now 現在打電話
    (D) Listen for their row number 注意聽自己的排號

解析 (D) 其他旅客被要求遠離登機門的入口，直到聽到自己的座位排號。選項(A)與廣播要求恰好相反。選項(B)應該是向空服員請求協助，而不是協助空服員。選項(C)使用了 call 的另一個意義。

Questions 74 through 76 refer to the following advertisement.

Can't find the information you need? Come see our wide selection of technical and professional books. We cover a variety of topic areas in over fifty fields, including computer science, psychology, economics, and international law. If it's not in stock, we'll order it for you! We also carry all the major scientific and technical journals, containing the newest information on important research. Keep abreast of what's happening in your field. Visit us today.

第74–76題請聽下面這段廣告。

找不到你要的資訊嗎？我們有各式各樣的技術和專業書籍，歡迎過來查看。我們的書籍涵蓋超過五十個領域的各種主題，包括電腦科學、心理學、經濟學和國際法。如果您要的書籍缺貨，我們也能替您訂書！我們也有各大科學和技術期刊，內含重要研究的最新資訊。掌握您專業領域的最新情況，今天就來店參觀選購。

74. What kind of books does this store carry? 這家店賣的是哪一種類型的書？
    (A) Novels 小說
    (B) Children's books 童書
    (C) Professional books 專業書籍
    (D) Textbooks 教科書

解析 (C) 廣告中提到了「professional books」（專業書籍）。選項(A)和(B)不會在這種店販售。選項(D)不正確，教科書是給還未成為專業人士的學生看的。

75. If the store doesn't have the book in stock, what will it do? 假如書店沒有你要的書，他們會怎麼做？
    (A) Refer you to another store 介紹你到別家書店
    (B) Look it up in the master list 查看圖書總表
    (C) Give you a different book at a discount 以折扣價給你另一本書
    (D) Order it 訂書

解析 (D) 廣告中提到他們會幫你訂書（we'll order it for you）。選項(A)沒有必要，因為他們可以訂書。選項(B)無助於取得書籍。選項(C)在廣告中並無提及。

76. What else does this store sell? 這家店還有賣什麼？
    (A) Newspapers 報紙
    (B) Carry-alls 大型手提袋
    (C) Journals 期刊
    (D) CDs 光碟片

解析 (C) 書店還有販售科學和技術期刊（scientific and technical journals）。選項(A)把newspapers和發音相近的newest搞混了。選項(B)把廣告中的carry all（全部都有）誤解成carry-all（大手提袋）。選項(D)未被提及。

Questions 77 through 79 refer to the following report.

Good morning. This is Sam Smith with the weather update. Listeners, I've got some good news for you. The fantastic weather we've been enjoying all week will continue for a while longer. Today will be warm and sunny, so get out there and enjoy it. Tomorrow morning will be the same, but by early afternoon we'll have cloudy skies and scattered rain showers, with more steady rain arriving overnight. Rainy weather will continue throughout the weekend, but by Monday the clouds should be gone and the skies should be clear and sunny once more.

第77–79題請聽下面這段報告。

早安，我是山姆‧史密斯，為您帶來最新氣象消息。各位聽眾，我有好消息要告訴你們，本週的大好天氣還會持續一段時間。今日天氣暖和，陽光普照，不妨出去走走，享受好天氣！明天上午的天氣狀況維持不變，但到了下午稍早時，天空將轉為多雲，並有零星陣雨，入夜時將會持續降雨。有雨的天氣會持續整個週末，但預計週一雲層就會消散，將再次回到萬里無雲、陽光普照的好天氣。

77. What does the speaker mean when he says, "I've got some good news for you"?
說話者說「I've got some good news for you」是什麼意思？
(A) The news report is next. 接下來將播放新聞報告。
(B) He is about to report good weather. 他準備向大家報告好天氣。
(C) He has already read the newspaper. 他已經看過報紙了。
(D) He has been given a job promotion. 他升職了。

解析 (B) 說話者是氣象播報員，在這句話之後，他接著報告了好天氣：「The fantastic weather we've been enjoying all week will continue for a while longer」，因此是要預報好天氣。選項(A)(C)(D)都不符合這裡的語境。

78. When will the weather change? 什麼時候將開始變天？
(A) Today 今天
(B) Tonight 今晚
(C) Tomorrow morning 明天早上
(D) Tomorrow afternoon 明天下午

解析 (D) 說話者表示今天天氣晴朗又暖和，接著說「Tomorrow morning will be the same, but by early afternoon we'll have cloudy skies and scattered rain showers」，所以是明天下午開始變天。選項(A)重複使用了today這個字。選項(B)混淆了近音字tonight和overnight。選項(C)是天氣維持不變的時候。

79. What will the weather be like on Monday? 週一的天氣如何？
(A) Sunny 晴朗
(B) Cloudy 多雲
(C) Windy 颱風
(D) Rainy 下雨

解析 (A) 說話者對週一的描述是「the skies should be clear and sunny once more」，表示會放晴。選項(B)和(D)是明天下午到週一之前的天氣。選項(C)未被提及。

Questions 80 through 82 refer to the following announcement.

Attention passengers. You are on the green line train to the northern suburbs with stops at University Park, the shopping mall, and points in between. If you are trying to get to the airport, you are on the wrong train. I repeat, this train does not go to the airport. Passengers for the airport need to disembark at this station and take the gray line train. Airport trains leave every fifteen minutes. The next one is due to depart this station at two-oh-five.

第 80–82 題請聽下面這段廣播。

各位乘客請注意,您現在搭乘的是前往北郊的綠線列車,本列車停靠大學公園和購物中心及中間各站。如果您欲前往機場,您搭錯車了。重複一遍,本列車沒有到機場,欲前往機場的乘客請在本站下車,並改搭灰線列車。機場列車每十五分鐘一班,下一班預計2點05分自本站發車。

80. Where is this train going? 這班列車開往哪裡?
    (A) Into the city 城市裡
    (B) To the hospital 醫院
    (C) To the business district 商業區
    (D) To the shopping mall 購物中心

解析 (D) 這班列車開往北部郊區(to the northern suburbs)和購物中心(shopping mall)。選項(A)和(C)和北部郊區相抵觸。選項(B)未被提及。

81. Which subway line goes to the airport? 哪一線列車會開往機場?
    (A) The gray line 灰線
    (B) The green line 綠線
    (C) The red line 紅線
    (D) The blue line 藍線

解析 (A) 廣播中請欲前往機場的乘客在本站下車並改搭灰線列車(disembark at this station and take the gray line train)。選項(B)是乘客目前所在的列車。選項(C)和(D)都未被提及。

82. How often do airport trains leave? 機場列車多久一班?
    (A) Every two minutes 每兩分鐘
    (B) Every five minutes 每五分鐘
    (C) Every fifteen minutes 每十五分鐘
    (D) Every sixteen minutes 每十六分鐘

解析 (C) 廣播員提到機場列車每十五分鐘會有一班。選項(A)和(B)都被下一班列車預計2點05分發車的描述給混淆了。選項(D)和正確答案的發音接近。

Questions 83 through 85 refer to the following announcement.

Because of the federal holiday, all government offices will be closed on Monday. Schools, banks, and libraries will also be closed. Buses, subways, and other public transportation will operate on a weekend schedule, with no additional buses or trains for rush hour service. Street parking in downtown metered spaces will be free today, though city-operated public parking garages will be closed. Many private garages will be charging weekend rates.

第83–85題請聽下面這段公告。

為配合聯邦假日，所有政府機關週一停止辦公，學校、銀行和圖書館也將關閉。公車、地鐵和其他公共運輸系統依週末行車時刻正常營運，公車和地鐵尖峰時段不加開班次。市中心的路邊計時停車位本日停車免費，但市營公共停車場將暫停服務，許多私人停車場則按週末費率計費。

83. Why are these closings taking place? 為何發生這些關閉事件？
    (A) It's Sunday. 今天是星期天。
    (B) There is no transportation. 今天沒有交通運輸服務。
    (C) It's a federal holiday. 今天是聯邦假日。
    (D) The weather is bad. 天氣不好。

解析 (C) 所有機關都暫停服務是為了配合聯邦假日。選項(A)是被公告中的weekend schedule（週末行車時刻）給混淆。選項(B)和各大公共運輸系統將正常營運（public transportation will operate）的描述相抵觸。選項(D)未被提及。

84. What service is the transportation system eliminating for the day? 這一天交通運輸系統的哪一項服務會取消？
    (A) Rush hour service 尖峰時段服務
    (B) Weekend service 週末服務
    (C) Service into the city 開往城市的服務
    (D) Service to recreation areas 開往休閒區的服務

解析 (A) 公告中說「no additional buses or trains for rush hour service」，尖峰時段不會加開班次。選項(B)把依週末行車時刻營運（operate on a weekend schedule）的描述搞混了。選項(C)和(D)都不大可能，畢竟交通運輸系統還是會依照週末的服務方式營運。

85. Where is parking free today? 本日哪裡停車免費？
    (A) In public garages 公共停車場
    (B) In private garages 私人停車場
    (C) On downtown streets 市中心街道
    (D) At the bus stations 公車站

解析 (C) 公告中提到市中心的路邊計時停車位本日可免費停車（Street parking in downtown metered spaces will be free today）。選項(A)不正確是因為公共停車場本日暫停服務。選項(B)不正確是因為許多私人停車場會按週末費率收費。選項(D)則是被公告中提到的 buses 給混淆了。

Questions 86 through 88 refer to the following news item.

The latest survey shows that business travelers have some suggestions for improving hotel service. Most travelers would like hotels to be located closer to shopping and entertainment facilities, rather than in the business district. They also suggest that the hotel restaurants include lighter meals, such as fresh salads and vegetable plates. They request that exercise and recreation facilities at the hotels be open at night as well as during the day, to accommodate business travelers' hectic schedules.

第86–88題請聽下面這段新聞報導。

最新調查顯示，商務旅客對於改善飯店服務提出了一些建議。大部分旅客希望飯店設在靠近購物和娛樂設施的地點，而不是位於商業區內。他們也建議飯店的餐廳可以加入一些輕食，例如新鮮沙拉和蔬菜盤。他們要求飯店內的健身和休閒設施除了白天開放外，夜晚也能開放，以配合商務旅客繁忙的行程。

86. Who participated in this survey? 誰參與了這份調查？
    (A) Hotel owners 飯店所有人
    (B) Secretaries 祕書
    (C) Housekeepers 房務員
    (D) Business travelers 商務旅客

解析 (D) 報導中說「The latest survey shows that business travelers . . .」，所以是針對商務旅客所做的調查。

87. Where would travelers prefer to have hotels located? 旅客希望飯店位於什麼地點？
    (A) In the business district 商業區內
    (B) Close to parks and museums 靠近公園和博物館
    (C) Near shopping and entertainment 鄰近購物和娛樂設施
    (D) Beside the airport 機場旁邊

    解析 **(C)** 報導中提到他們希望飯店設在鄰近購物和娛樂設施的地點。選項 (A) 是他們不希望飯店開設的地點。選項 (B) 和 (D) 都沒有被提及。

88. What additional service should the hotels provide at night? 飯店晚上應提供什麼附加服務？
    (A) Access to exercise and recreation rooms 可使用健身房和休閒室
    (B) Movies in the rooms 客房內提供電影
    (C) Light snacks in the lobby 大廳提供小點心
    (D) Transportation services 交通運輸服務

    解析 **(A)** 報導中提到旅客要求飯店的健身和休閒設施晚上也能開放，「(provide) access to . . .」就等於「. . . (should) be open」。選項 (B) 未被提及。選項 (C) 把 light snacks 和旅客建議飯店供應的 lighter meals 搞混了。選項 (D) 未被提及。

Questions 89 through 91 refer to the following talk.

Good morning, everyone. It looks like everyone is here and has found a seat, so we'll get going in just a few minutes, as soon as our driver is ready. Our first stop will be the City History Museum. On the way, we'll drive through the historic district, and I'll point out some of the more interesting buildings. Then, at the museum we'll have a chance to learn more about some of these buildings. Lunch will be at the museum café, and then we'll head over to the botanical gardens. If there's anything along the way that you'd like to find out more about, please don't worry. I'm happy to explain anything you want to know.

第 89–91 題請聽下面這段談話。

大家早安，看來所有人都到了，也都找好座位了，那再過幾分鐘，等司機一準備好我們就出發。我們的第一站是城市歷史博物館，途中會經過歷史區，我會指出一些比較有趣的建築。接著到了博物館，我們會有機會深入了解這些建築。午餐安排在博物館的咖啡廳，然後我們就會前往植物園。行程中如果各位有什麼想了解更多的，請放心，任何想知道的我都很樂意為各位說明。

89. Where does this talk take place? 這段談話發生在什麼地方？
    (A) In an auditorium 禮堂內
    (B) In a museum 博物館內
    (C) At a café 咖啡廳內
    (D) On a bus 遊覽車上

    解析 (D) 說話者是一名導遊，正在向旅行團的團員說話，她提到聽者已經找好座位，還說等司機一準備好，遊覽行程就會開始（we'll get going . . . as soon as our driver is ready），可見他們在一輛遊覽車上。選項(A)是從seats（座位）聯想而來。選項(B)和(C)是他們等一下要去的地方。

90. What will listeners do after lunch? 聽者吃完午餐要做什麼？
    (A) Drive through the historic district 搭車穿過歷史區
    (B) Visit the botanical gardens 參觀植物園
    (C) Tour some buildings 參觀一些建築
    (D) Return to the hotel 返回飯店

    解析 (B) 說話者先說明他們用餐的地點，接著說「then we'll head over to the botanical gardens」，所以他們要去參觀植物園。選項(A)是他們更早時要做的事。選項(C)重複使用了buildings這個字。選項(D)也有可能，但並未提及。

91. What does the speaker mean when she says, "Please don't worry"?
    說話者說「Please don't worry」是什麼意思？
    (A) She enjoys her job. 她樂在工作。
    (B) She knows her way around the city. 她對這座城市熟門熟路。
    (C) She is prepared to answer questions. 她準備好回答問題。
    (D) She doesn't expect any problems will occur. 她預計不會出什麼問題。

    解析 (C) 在說出這句話之前，說話者提到聽者可能對某件事物會想了解更多，在這句話之後，她又說「I'm happy to explain anything you want to know」，表示她很樂意回答大家的問題。選項(A)(B)(D)都和語境不符。

實戰模擬試題 4

465

Questions 92 through 94 refer to the following talk.

This evening's talk focuses on how to pack for your next flight. First, select the clothes that you will take. Lay out everything that you need, including medicine, travel guides, and shoes. Then it's time to start packing. Place the heavier items, such as shoes, at the bottom of the suitcase. Next, add jeans and slacks followed by sweaters and shirts. Place the lightest items on top. I recommend putting smaller items, such as socks and underwear, in clear plastic bags. This helps airport security, who can easily see what you've packed. It also helps you to keep your suitcase tidy. Are there any questions?

第 92–94 題請聽下面這段談話。

今晚的談話重點是如何為你下一次的航程打包行李。首先，挑好要帶的衣服，將所有需要的東西擺出來，包括藥品、旅遊指南和鞋子。接著就開始打包。先將鞋子等較重的物品放在行李箱底部，然後放入牛仔褲和長褲，接著是毛衣和襯衫，最輕的物品要放在最上方。我建議將襪子和內衣褲等較小的物品用透明塑膠袋裝，不但方便機場安檢人員看到裡面裝了什麼，也有助於維持行李箱的整潔。有沒有其他問題？

92. What is the first step in packing? 打包行李的第一步是什麼？
　　(A) Get your suitcase 取得行李箱
　　(B) Wash your clothes 洗衣服
　　(C) Choose your outfits 挑選要穿的衣服
　　(D) Check your medicine 檢查藥品

解析 **(C)** 說話者說「First, select the clothes」，所以第一步是挑衣服。選項(A)重複使用了suitcase這個字。選項(B)重複使用了clothes這個字。選項(D)重複使用了medicine這個字。

93. What should go into the suitcase first? 哪樣東西應該先放入行李箱內？
　　(A) Underwear 內衣褲
　　(B) Heavy items 重的物品
　　(C) Smaller items 較小的物品
　　(D) Jeans and slacks 牛仔褲和長褲

解析 **(B)** 說話者建議把較重的物品放在最底下，也就是先放。選項(A)(C)(D)是說話者提到的其他物品，但會放在比較上方，所以是後放。

94. What should you use to help airport security? 你應該使用哪樣物品方便機場安檢人員檢查？
    (A) Travel guides 旅遊指南
    (B) Light items 輕的物品
    (C) Plastic bags 塑膠袋
    (D) Slip-on shoes 好穿脫的鞋子

解析 (C) 說話者建議使用透明塑膠袋，讓安檢人員可以看到裡面的東西。選項 (A) 和 (B) 是說話者提到的其他物品，但和安檢人員無關。選項 (D) 中的 shoes 有出現在談話內容，slip-on shoes 則沒有。

Questions 95 through 97 refer to the following voicemail message and business card.

Hi. This is Kayla Sanchez calling about the design for my business card. I love the way it's turned out. You were right about the ink color. The dark blue looks great, so much less heavy than the black. And I love what you did with the logo. There's just one little change I'd like to make. I think it would look better if you dragged the words that are under my name just a bit lower, so that there's a little more space there. Otherwise the design is perfect, so please print five hundred and send the invoice to my e-mail address. Oh, and let me know when I can pick up the finished cards. Thanks.

第95–97題請聽下面這段語音信箱留言，並參考名片。

嗨，我是凱拉・桑切斯，打電話來是要談論我的名片設計。我很喜歡它最後呈現出來的樣子。關於墨水的顏色你是對的，深藍色看起來效果很好，也沒有黑色那麼沉重，而且我喜歡你的標誌設計。只有一個小地方我想改一下，我覺得名字下方的文字如果能夠下移一點，留出多一點空間會更好看。除了這個部分外，其他設計都很完美。請幫我印五百張，將請款單寄到我的電子郵件地址。喔，順便告訴我何時可去取完成的名片。謝謝！

♪♫♩♬
凱拉・桑切斯
音效工程師
kayla@kaylas.com　456-7890

95. What does the speaker say about the ink color? 說話者對墨水顏色有什麼看法？
    (A) It is too dark. 太深了。
    (B) She likes it a lot. 她很喜歡。
    (C) It looks too heavy. 看起來太沉重了。
    (D) She would prefer black. 她比較喜歡黑色。

解析 (B) 說話者評論墨水顏色時說「The dark blue looks great」，可見她很喜歡。選項(A)重複使用了 dark 這個字。選項(C)是女子對黑色墨水的看法，也是之所以她喜歡深藍色的原因。選項(D)是她比較不喜歡的墨水顏色。

96. Look at the graphic. Which information does the speaker want moved? 請看圖表，說話者希望移動的是哪一項資訊？
    (A) The logo 標誌
    (B) Her name 她的名字
    (C) Her job title 她的職稱
    (D) The email address 電子郵件地址

解析 (C) 說話者說「I think it would look better if you dragged the words that are under my name just a bit lower」（名字下方的文字如果能下移一點會更好看），而名字下方是她的職稱「sound engineer」。選項(A)(B)(D)是名片上的其他資訊，但說話者並無提出要移動位置。

97. What does the speaker ask the listener to do? 說話者要求聽者做什麼？
    (A) Send her the bill 把帳單寄給她
    (B) Deliver the cards 把名片送來
    (C) Cancel the order 取消訂單
    (D) Return the call 回電

解析 (A) 說話者說「send the invoice to my e-mail address」，invoice 就是「請款單、帳單」。選項(B)(C)(D)在留言中並未提及。

Questions 98 through 100 refer to the following talk and menu.

This evening's specials are, as usual, listed on the specials board, but tonight we've added a new feature. You'll notice that some of the items are starred. Those are the vegetarian dishes, so be sure to point that out to your customers. This evening's specials also include roast lamb, one of our more popular dishes. We've had to raise the price a little, but I think it'll sell well. OK, it's Saturday, and that means we can expect the biggest crowd of the week, so be ready to work hard.

第 98–100 題請聽下面這段談話,並參考菜單。

今晚的特餐照常列在特餐告示牌上,但今晚我們增加了一個新特色。你會發現有些餐點前面標示了星號,那些是素食料理,所以務必要向顧客說明這一點。今晚的特餐當中有一道是烤羊肉,是我們的人氣料理之一。我們必須稍微提高價格,不過我想應該還是會賣得很好。好了,今天是星期六,也就是說今天會是本週客人最多的一天,所以請大家準備好努力工作吧。

```
         特餐
      俄羅斯酸奶牛肉
    ★ 蔬菜義大利麵
       烤羊肉
    ★ 燉茄子
```

98. Who is the speaker talking to? 說話者正在對誰說話?
    (A) Restaurant customers 餐廳的客人
    (B) Restaurant servers 餐廳的服務生
    (C) Food wholesalers 食品批發商
    (D) Cooking students 烹飪課的學生

解析 (B) 說話者應該是餐廳的管理者或主廚,正在向服務生說明晚上的特餐。選項(A)(C)(D)都和餐廳餐點的主題有關,但在談話中均未提及。

99. Look at the graphic. What does the speaker say about the eggplant stew? 請看圖表,說話者對燉茄子有何描述?
    (A) It is a popular dish. 是一道人氣料理。
    (B) It is a new dish. 是新菜色。
    (C) It is a vegetarian dish. 是素食料理。
    (D) It is the least expensive dish. 是最便宜的一道菜。

解析 (C) 說話者說菜單上的部分餐點標示了星號,並說「Those are the vegetarian dishes」,而燉茄子有星號,所以是素食料理。選項(A)(B)(D)都有可能用來描述菜單上的餐點,只是談話中都沒有提到。

100. What does the speaker imply about Saturday night?
    對於星期六晚上，說話者有何暗示？
    (A) The prices are always higher. 價格向來較高。
    (B) Most restaurants close late. 大多數餐廳營業到很晚。
    (C) There are more specials. 會推出更多特餐。
    (D) It is a very busy night. 晚上生意會很好。

解析 (D) 說話者提到「it's Saturday, and that means we can expect the biggest crowd of the week」，表示星期六是整個星期客人最多的一天。選項(A)(B)(C)都有可能，但沒有特別提及。

本測驗之聽力測驗到此結束，請翻頁進行 Part 5 的測驗。

閱讀測驗

在本段測驗當中，你將有機會展現自己對書面英語的理解能力。閱讀測驗共有三個大題，每一大題均有作答說明。

你有 75 分鐘時間完成本測驗的第五到第七大題。

Part 5：句子填空

> 作答方式：你會看到一個缺字的句子和四個可能的選項，選出最適當的答案，將答案卡上對應的橢圓框塗滿。

101. 如果明天天氣變得更差，我們就會取消和客戶吃午飯。
　　(A)(B)(C)(D) 取消

解析 (B) 這是一個真實條件句，if子句用了現在式，主要子句要用未來式。選項(A)是過去式。選項(C)是現在完成式。選項(D)是現在進行式。

102. 直到我們收到採購單後，才能開始訂購流程。
　　(A) 因為
　　(B) 引導名詞字句（that作為連接詞）
　　(C) 直到
　　(D) 當……時

解析 (C) until可連接兩個子句，語意上也合乎邏輯。選項(A)和(D)放入句子語意不合邏輯。選項(B)用來引導關係子句或名詞子句。

103. 雖然威廉在聚會上認識很多新的人，他卻都記得他們的名字。
　　(A) 記得、回想
　　(B) 提醒
　　(C) 檢查、回顧
　　(D) 評論、談到

解析 (A) recall是「記得」的意思。選項(B)(C)(D)的意義都與文意不符。

104. 完成問卷之後，請用隨附的信封裝好，寄回我們辦公室。
　　(A)(B)(C)(D) 放入信封

解析 (D) enclose是「隨信附上」的意思，有人隨信附上了這個信封，而信封是被附上的，若要表達「隨附的」就要用過去分詞enclosed來修飾envelope。選項(A)多了一個不必要的is，變成動詞。選項(B)是原形動詞。選項(C)是現在分詞。

105. 買房時，持有證照的房仲是你最好的諮詢對象。
    (A) 導遊
    (B) 顧問
    (C) 建議
    (D) 律師

解析 (C) 房仲（realtor，協助民眾買賣房子的專業經理人）能夠提供的是建議或諮詢（advice）。選項(A)(B)(D)都指人，但都不能提供買房的建議。

106. 查一下配送服務的網站，看看包裹何時送達。
    (A) 拿出（bring out）
    (B) 了解（find out）
    (C) 取出（get out）
    (D) 指出（point out）

解析 (B) 片語動詞 find out 的意思是「了解、發現」，符合這裡的語意要求。選項(A)(C)(D)都可以和 out 構成片語動詞，但不符合這個句子的語意要求。

107. 由於油價下跌，我們的原物料成本預計會降低。
    (A) 增加、提高
    (B) 減少、降低
    (C) 上升、升級
    (D) 變平坦、變均衡

解析 (B) decrease 的意思是「減少、降低」，放在這個句子很合理，因為油價下跌，整體原物料成本自然也會跟著降低。選項(A)和(C)的意思是「增加」。選項(D)的意思是「變平坦」或「變均衡」，都不符合此句的語意邏輯。

108. 使用清單是一種有效的計劃方式。
    (A) 有效的
    (B) 效果
    (C) 有效
    (D) 有效地

解析 (A) 形容詞 effective 修飾名詞 way。選項(B)和(C)是名詞。選項(D)是副詞。

109. 午餐已經訂好了，但外送員還沒送到。
    (A) 或者
    (B) 由於、自從
    (C) 因為
    (D) 但是

解析 (D) 連接兩個對比子句要用 but。選項 (A)(B)(C) 用在這裡語意都不合邏輯。

110. 每年這個時候要和格林小姐約時間幾乎是不可能的，因為她正忙著處理年度報告。

解析 (C) 形容詞 busy 一般搭配的介系詞是 with。選項 (A)(B)(D) 都是介系詞，只是一般不與 busy 搭配使用。

111. 營運主管要去參加大會，整個禮拜都不會在工廠裡。
    (A)(B)(C)(D) 到、去

解析 (D) 主詞 head of operations 是單數，要用單數動詞 is going。選項 (A) 是動名詞。選項 (B) 是複數動詞。選項 (C) 是原形動詞。

112. 顧客可撥打我們的 1-800 專線和業務專員交談。
    (A) 代表 (n.)
    (B) 代表（n. 指人）
    (C) 代表 (ved)
    (D) 代表 (v.)

解析 (B) representative 是指「人」的名詞。選項 (A) 是名詞，但不指人。選項 (C) 和 (D) 都是動詞。

113. 住客可在房內找到一本電話簿和一個內含當地景點資訊的活頁夾。
    (A) 在……四處
    (B) 在……之下
    (C) 在……之中
    (D) 在……之上

解析 (C) in 的意思是「在……之中」，in their rooms 就是在他們房內。選項 (A)(B)(D) 放入句中意思都不通。

474

114. 博物館內禁止吸菸和使用閃光燈拍照。
    (A) 兩者之一
    (B) 兩者皆不
    (C) 但是
    (D) 或者

解析 (B) neither 搭配 nor 表示否定選擇（兩者都不可以）。選項 (A)(C)(D) 都不能和 nor 搭配使用。

115. 主管要芭拉女士寫下她的工作職責，以列入她的年度考核。
    (A)(B)(C)(D) 寫

解析 (D) 使役動詞 had 後面要用原形動詞。選項 (A) 是不定詞。選項 (B) 是過去式。選項 (C) 是過去分詞。

116. 州法規定居民須於搬家後三十天內變更駕照地址。
    (A) 提交
    (B) 忽視
    (C) 要求
    (D) 請求

解析 (C) mandate 的意思是「要求、規定」，常用來談論法律。選項 (A)(B)(D) 都不適用於這裡的法律語境。

117. 葛蘭達經常上班遲到，但她會晚點下班或週末加班把時間補回來。
    (A) 常常、傾向於（tend to）
    (B) 排定於（is scheduled to）
    (C) 應當（is supposed to）
    (D) 企圖、試圖（attempts to）

解析 (A) tend to 意指「有……的習慣」，在這裡表示習慣性遲到、常常遲到。選項 (B)(C)(D) 都不符合語意要求。

118. 我們希望本郡回收計畫的新行銷活動能鼓勵居民踴躍參與。
    (A) 能力
    (B) 候選人
    (C) 共謀、勾結
    (D) 活動

解析 (D) marketing campaign（行銷活動）是一個規劃好的行動方案，目的是銷售商品。選項 (A)(B)(C) 放入句子意思都不通。

119. 蕭先生和蕭太太決定住在他們旅行社業務員建議的飯店。
    (A) 他們的
    (B) 他們（主格）
    (C) 他們（受格）
    (D) 他們是／要

解析 **(A)** their是所有格形容詞，指代先行詞Mr. and Mrs. Xiao，修飾後面的名詞travel agent。選項(B)是主格代名詞。選項(C)是受格代名詞。選項(D)是主格代名詞「they are」的縮寫形式。

120. YRTL-32是我們最可靠的一個型號，主要是因為它很少送修。
    (A) 絕望
    (B) 比較
    (C) 削弱
    (D) 修理

解析 **(D)** repair是「修理」的意思，其他選項放入句子意思都不通。

121. 進入這棟大樓的密碼是4526。
    (A) 理由
    (B) 方法
    (C) 密碼
    (D) 撥號

解析 **(C)** code在這裡指用來解鎖的一組數字，即為密碼。選項(A)(B)(D)放入句中意思都不通。

122. 菲爾普斯先生建議組成委員會，研究我們車隊該增加哪一種卡車。
    (A)(B)(C)(D) 形成、構成

解析 **(B)** 使役動詞suggest後面要接動名詞。選項(A)是過去式。選項(C)是現在式。選項(D)是不定詞。

123. 人力資源部要求員工離職時須提前一個月通知。
    (A)(B)(C)(D) 提出

解析 **(A)** 主要動詞ask後面要用不定詞。選項(B)是未來式。選項(C)是動名詞。選項(D)是過去式。

124. 這份貢獻者名單比電腦伺服器上面的那份還新。
    (A) 當前的
    (B) 目前
    (C) 比……更新
    (D) 和……一樣新

解析 (C) 比較級 more 後面要接形容詞和 than。選項(A)少了 than。選項(B)是副詞。選項(D)是「as . . . as」的比較句型，但也不完整，因少了一個 as。

125. 斯圖亞特無法使用他的公司信用卡，因為在倫敦時他的信用卡和皮夾一同被偷了。
    (A) 直到
    (B) 因為
    (C) 雖然
    (D) 曾經

解析 (B) because 建立了兩個句子之間的因果關係。選項(A)(C)(D)放入句子都不合邏輯。

126. 船長要求所有乘客閱讀緊急應變處理程序。
    (A)(B)(C)(D) 檢視、查看

解析 (C) 使役動詞 request 後面要用原形動詞。選項(A)是動名詞。選項(B)是現在式單數動詞。選項(D)是不定詞。

127. 遺失公事包的人可到大廳認領。
    (A) 他／她／它（們）的
    (B) 這個、這些
    (C) 他／她（們）、……的人（受格）
    (D) 他／她（們）、……的人（主格）

解析 (D) 主格關係代名詞 who 是子句的主詞，指代前面的 person。選項(A)是所有格。選項(B)指物，不用於指人。選項(C)是受格，不能當主詞。

128. 這份關於新時間表的備忘錄和你昨天準備的那份一樣令人困惑。
    (A)(B)(C)(D) 令人困惑

解析 (C) 同等比較會使用「as + 形容詞 + as」的句型，表示「和……一樣」。這裡的主詞 memo 是讓人產生困惑的主動者，因此形容詞要用現在分詞。選項(A)少了第二個 as。選項(B)少了第一個 as。選項(D)使用了過去分詞。

129. 弗瑞爾女士在她升職的消息公布之前就已經知道了。
    (A)(B)(C)(D) 知道

解析 **(A)** 由於「知道」與「公布」（was announced）都是發生在過去的事情，因此必須使用過去式。選項(B)是過去分詞。選項(C)是現在進行式。選項(D)是現在完成式。

130. 關於軟體有任何疑問都可以隨時打電話給我。
    (A)(B)(C)(D) 打電話

解析 **(B)** 這個句子是祈使句，要用原形動詞。選項(A)是現在進行式。選項(C)是現在式單數動詞。選項(D)是未來式。

Part 6：段落填空

作答方式：你會看到四篇短文，各含四個空格，每個空格配有四個選項，選出最適當的單字、片語或句子完成這段敘述。

第 131–134 題請看下面這封信件。

現代科技公司
杭特綜合園區 H 1/6 區第二街
巴基斯坦伊斯蘭馬巴德

20—年 4 月 13 日
瓦卡斯・馬哈穆德
克里夫頓區薩拉伊朗大道 21 號
巴基斯坦喀拉蚩

馬哈穆德先生，您好：

感謝您購買型號 XY 40 的 USB 數位喇叭。我們本週已經收到您寄來的回饋卡，很可惜我們無法兌換這張卡片，因為在您寄出卡片時，這項回饋優惠已經過期了。回饋申請必須在購買後三天內寄出，然而您的回饋卡是在購物完成後快兩週才寄出的。請您理解我們非常重視您的惠顧，為了彌補這次回饋，我們會送您一本優惠券，可用於購買現代科技公司的其他產品。您可以非常優惠的折扣購買我們許多產品，包括我們提升了音質的最新免持電話。

感謝您選擇現代科技公司來滿足您的科技需求。

敬祝 順心

塔里克・汗
塔里克・汗
總裁

131. (A) 部分商品可退回並獲得全額退款。
　　 (B) 很多公司都針對特定商品提供回饋。
　　 (C) 我們所有產品均提供一年保固。
　　 (D) 我們本週已經收到您寄來的回饋卡。

解析 (D) 這封信是關於一件商品的回饋申請，空格後面的句子說明由於寄出時間太晚，公司無法兌換這張回饋卡（honor it 的 it 即 rebate card），因此選項(D)的句子說已經收到了，在語意上是連貫的。選項(A)(B)(C)都與前後句子不連貫。

132. (A) 推出
　　 (B) 開始
　　 (C) 到期
　　 (D) 轉換

解析 (C) expired 的意思是這張回饋卡的使用期限已經過了。選項(A)(B)(D)代入句中都與文意不符。

133. (A)(B)(C)(D) 提供

解析 (A) would like 後面要接不定詞。選項(B)是動名詞。選項(C)是過去式。選項(D)是未來式。

134. (A) 說明
　　 (B) 折扣
　　 (C) 套組
　　 (D) 指示

解析 (B) 這家公司打算寄一本優惠券（coupons）給這名顧客，coupons 就是一種 discount（折扣）的形式。

第135–138題請看下面這封電子郵件。

> 收件者：benlivingston@accountantsgroup.ca
> 副本：　凱爾、雪柔、萊斯利
> 寄件者：ryanedison@accountantsgroup.ca
> 主旨：　高爾夫球賽
>
> 大家好：
>
> 我要開始規劃五月的公司年度高爾夫球賽了。我知道現在離五月還有兩個多月，但今年我想早點開始準備。我想聽聽大家的意見，所以列了幾個討論事項，下次員工會議時會發給大家，這樣我們就能一起討論。去年的比賽辦得很成功，一共募得超過七千美元的慈善款項。今年的目標是一萬美元，有你們的支持，我們一定可以辦到。
>
> 謝謝！
> 萊恩

135. (A) 每日的
 (B) 每週一次的
 (C) 每月一次的
 (D) 每年一次的

解析 (D) 萊恩在郵件中提到「wanted to get going early this year」（今年想早點開始準備）、「Last year's tournament」（去年的比賽），可推斷這場比賽為一年舉辦一次。也由於比賽距離現在還有兩個多月（more than two months away），因此選項(A)(B)(C)都不太可能。

136. (A) 提交、繳交（hand in）
 (B) 分發（hand out）
 (C) 交出（hand over）
 (D) 傳下去（hand down）

解析 (B) hand out 的意思是「分發」，符合這裡的語境。選項(A)會變成另一個片語 hand in，意指「提交」。選項(C)會變成另一個片語 hand over，表示「交出控制權或所有權」。選項(D)會變成另一個片語 hand down，意指「傳給下一代或別人使用」。

137. (A) 花費
 (B) 節省
 (C) 募集
 (D) 投資

解析 (C) raised 的意思是「募集、籌集」，這句話的意思是公司在比賽期間募集要捐給慈善機構的款項。選項(A)(B)(D)都是和錢有關的單字，但不適用於這個句子。

138. (A) 有你們的支持，我們一定可以辦到。
 (B) 我希望每個人都能參加員工會議。
 (C) 很多其他公司都會舉辦類似的慈善活動。
 (D) 高爾夫球賽一直是很受歡迎的活動。

解析 (A) 這封電子郵件的目的是請員工協助規劃一場慈善募款活動，選項(A)的句子作為郵件的結語非常適合，同時也承接了前面立下募款目標的句子。選項(B)(C)(D)在語意上都與前一句不連貫。

第 139–142 題請看下面這篇文章。

室內空汙

辦公大樓室內空氣品質的最新研究顯示，比起室外被汙染的空氣，室內空氣品質對人體健康的危害更大。根據環境委員會的資料，約有百分之三十的建築物內空氣品質不安全。

病態建築症候群是室內空氣品質不良所造成的病症，而商家過早開始營業是造成這種病症的最常見原因。建築物過早開放時，油漆味和殘留的清潔劑沒有足夠的時間消散。假如空間的通風不良，這個問題就會更加嚴重。

---

139. (A) 有害的
　　 (B) 更有害的
　　 (C) 最有害的
　　 (D) 最有害的

解析 (B) 這是一個比較句，由於句中含有 than，必須搭配一個形容詞的比較級，hazardous 的比較級是 more hazardous。選項(A)是形容詞的原級，不是比較級。選項(C)是缺少 the 的最高級形容詞。選項(D)是最高級形容詞，不能和 than 一起使用。

140. (A) 第三人稱單數 be 動詞
　　 (B) 複數 be 動詞
　　 (C) 似乎
　　 (D) 正變得、正成為

解析 (A) 這裡的主詞是 air quality，動詞必須使用單數以維持一致。選項(B)(C)(D)都用於複數主詞。

141. (A) 預謀的
　　 (B) 過早的
　　 (C) 優質的
　　 (D) 阻止

解析 (B) premature 的意思是「過早的」，等於下一句的 too early。這句話的意思是大樓工程的油漆味和殘留的清潔劑都還沒散盡，就過早讓商家進駐營業，導致人體吸入有害氣體。選項(A)(C)(D)長得和正確答案相似，但意義不同，放入這個句子語意不通。

142. (A) 一般而言，地毯應在油漆完成後才進行鋪設。
 (B) 如今已經有可能買到毒性較弱的清潔劑。
 (C) 假如空間的通風不良，這個問題就會更加嚴重。
 (D) 空氣品質可以透過好的換氣系統加以控制。

解析 (C) 前一個句子提到剛粉刷好的油漆和剛使用的清潔劑會造成空氣品質不良，選項(C)的句子進一步補充說明，表示需要良好的通風才能幫助這些殘留氣體消散。選項(A)(B)(D)放入這個位置語意都不連貫。

第143–146題請看下面這封電子郵件。

收件者：比爾‧奧哈拉
寄件者：艾迪‧桑德斯
主旨：　工作坊

比爾：

我正在努力為下週五的工作坊規畫做最後確認。請告訴我你預計會有多少人來參加，我才知道該訂多少食物。還有，你預計工作坊會進行多久呢？除了午餐外，我是不是也該訂下午的咖啡和點心？如果工作坊進行一整天，大家通常預期會有下午茶點可享用。我也需要知道預計人數才能決定要預約哪間會議室。2號會議室比1號會議室舒適，但可能不夠大。

請盡快回覆我，因為我需要趕快處理這件事。

謝謝！
艾迪

---

143. (A)(B)(C)(D) 知道

解析 (A) 動詞 let 後面要接原形動詞。選項(B)是現在簡單式。選項(C)是不定詞。選項(D)是動名詞。

144. (A) 此外
 (B) 反而、卻
 (C) 此外
 (D) 也

解析 (D) as well 的意思是「也」。選項(A)和(C)用來為一段文字補充資訊。選項(B)的意思是「反而、卻」。

145. (A) 我也在想要不要在會議室裡多設置幾張桌子。
(B) 我已經把你要求的筆、記事本和其他用品都訂購好了。
(C) 我發現下午不是最適合舉辦工作坊的時候，因為那時大家通常都很累。
(D) 如果工作坊進行一整天，大家通常預期會有下午茶點可享用。

解析 (D) 前一個句子寫信者問該不該訂下午的咖啡和點心，這個句子接著解釋為什麼要這麼做。選項(A)(B)(C)都和前後句子不連貫。

146. (A) 舒適的
(B) 更舒適的
(C) 舒適地
(D) 最舒適的

解析 (B) 這個句子比較了2號會議室和1號會議室，所以要用形容詞的比較級。選項(A)是形容詞的原級。選項(C)是副詞。選項(D)是形容詞的最高級。

Part 7：閱讀測驗

作答方式：你會看到單篇或多篇文章的題組，文章後面配有幾個題目，各含四個選項。選出最適當的答案回答問題，將答案卡上對應的橢圓框塗滿。

第 147–148 題請看下面這張表單。

格瑞菲斯大飯店
訂房單

姓名： 查爾斯・溫斯頓
房型： 大床房
住宿時長：三晚
住宿日期：9 月 10–12 日
房價： 100 美元／晚
總計： 300 美元

如欲保留訂房，須預付一晚房價作為訂金，並於預定入住日的十四天前完成支付，餘款則於入住時支付。如欲取消，必須在入住日的七天前辦理，才能退還訂金。

---

147. 溫斯頓先生抵達飯店的兩週之前，必須先付多少費用？
 (A) $ 0
 (B) $ 100
 (C) $ 200
 (D) $ 300

解析 (B) 訂房資訊裡面提到「A deposit equivalent to the cost of one night's stay is required to hold the reservation and must be paid 14 days prior to the reservation date」，表示預定入住日的十四天前（也就是兩週前）要付一晚房價的訂金，而一晚的房價是 100 美元。選項(A)不正確，必須要付訂金。選項(C)未被提及。選項(D)是三晚的費用。

148. 如果溫斯頓先生9月9日取消訂房會怎麼樣？
    (A) 他會失去訂金。
    (B) 他會收到部分退款。
    (C) 他會獲得一筆抵用金，下次住宿可以使用。
    (D) 他會需要支付住宿三晚的全額房價。

解析 (A) 訂房資訊裡說「Cancellation must be made 7 days prior to the check-in date in order for the deposit to be refunded」，七天前取消可退訂金，但是9月9日是入住日的前一天，已經不能退訂金了。選項(B)(C)(D)在實際生活中有可能，但此處沒有提及。

第149–150題請看下面這則公告。

信託線誠摯邀您參加晨間研討會，了解如何預測趨勢，協助客戶投資成功。

如欲預訂座位請填寫附件之卡片，並連同報名費寄回。

不要錯過這個好機會，了解能推動信託服務管理公司成功發展的重要資源。

欲了解更多資訊，請來電676-9980。

---

149. 誰有可能參加這場研討會？
    (A) 私人投資者
    (B) 非營利組織的管理者
    (C) 證券業務員
    (D) 報紙出版商

解析 (C) 會想了解如何協助客戶投資的是證券業務員。選項(A)和client（客戶）的描述矛盾。選項(B)混淆了manager和文中的management firm。選項(D)不太可能參加這樣的研討會。

150. 研討會將討論什麼主題？
    (A) 建立客戶關係
    (B) 信託服務管理公司
    (C) 如何預測好的投資
    (D) 如何開發新客戶

解析 (C) 這場研討會是要協助參加者了解如何預測趨勢，以便投資成功。選項(A)和(B)雖然都有被提到，但不是研討會要討論的主題。選項(D)重複使用了clients這個字。

第151–152題請看下面這張資費表。

公車資費		尖峰時段	離峰時段
自20—年3月1日起生效 尖峰時段： 平日上午5:30–9:30及 下午3:00–7:00	單區搭乘 第1區與第2區之間搭乘 第1區與第3區之間搭乘 第2區與第3區之間搭乘	1.00 1.35 1.70 1.35	.75 1.00 1.35 1.00

151. 表中所述的資費何時生效？
　　(A) 即刻
　　(B) 3月1日
　　(C) 2月28日
　　(D) 下週

解析 (B) 資費表上面寫「effective March 1」，就是自3月1日起生效的意思。選項(A)(C)(D)都沒有出現在表中。

152. 表中對尖峰時段有何說明？
　　(A) 週末和平日的尖峰時段是一樣的。
　　(B) 僅特定區域實施尖峰時段費率。
　　(C) 自3月1日後便不再區分尖峰時段。
　　(D) 一天有兩個尖峰時段。

解析 (D) 表中描述尖峰時段為「平日上午5:30–9:30及下午3:00–7:00」，因此一天有兩個時段。選項(A)不正確，表中只提到平日的尖峰時段，並無提到週末的尖峰時段。選項(B)重複使用了zones這個字，但表中有提到Any one zone（單區搭乘）的尖峰費率，因此不是特定區域才實施。選項(C)重複使用了March 1這個日期，但表中提到的是三月一日起生效，與此選項的描述相矛盾。

第 153–154 題請看下面這段簡訊對話串。

珊曼莎・阿爾諾 你今天晚上有要去聚餐嗎？	1:30
貝瑞・蓋勒 我能去就好了。我必須完成這份報告，所以要加班到很晚。	1:32
珊曼莎・阿爾諾 太可惜了，我們會想你的。我還想說可以一起開車去因為我的車還在修車廠。	1:34
貝瑞・蓋勒 抱歉了，我也希望可以。	1:37
珊曼莎・阿爾諾 你知道麗姿會去嗎？也許我可以坐她的車。	1:40
貝瑞・蓋勒 我問一下，等等。	1:42
貝瑞・蓋勒 她說她六點半會去接你。	1:46
珊曼莎・阿爾諾 太棒了，謝啦！	1:48

153. 阿爾諾小姐為何聯絡蓋勒先生？
    (A) 問他能不能讓她搭便車
    (B) 拿邀請函給他
    (C) 詢問晚上聚餐時間
    (D) 提醒他晚上聚餐的事

解析 (A) 阿爾諾小姐想搭便車去晚上的聚餐，因為她的車還在修車廠。蓋勒先生表示幫不上忙，所以她就決定改搭麗姿的車。選項 (B)(C)(D) 都和聚餐的主題有關，但對話中都沒有提到。

154. 在1:42時,蓋勒先生說「Hold on」是什麼意思?
(A) 他認為坐麗姿的車是個壞主意。
(B) 他認為阿爾諾小姐不應該去聚餐。
(C) 他可能會改變心意去晚上的聚餐。
(D) 他會替阿爾諾小姐的問題找到答案。

解析 (D) hold on 的意思是「等一下、稍等」,蓋勒先生要阿爾諾小姐等一下,他去詢問麗姿再來回答阿爾諾小姐的問題「Do you know if Liz is going?」。選項(A)(B)(C)都不是這個片語在這裡的意思。

第155–157題請看下面這則廣告。

> 業界領先的電視廣告公司,廣播業務遍及全球,現誠徵一名觀眾調查專員。須負責設計研究以了解消費者偏好,並撰寫公司內部使用之報告。應徵者須擁有大學學位,並修過研究相關課程,亦須擁有廣告相關經驗。須具備卓越之口語表達和寫作能力,及優異的電腦操作技能。工作地點位於市中心,福利佳。

155. 這份工作內容涵蓋什麼?
(A) 製作電視廣告
(B) 了解消費者喜好
(C) 宣傳產品
(D) 測試產品

解析 (B) 廣告中的 consumer preferences 就等於 what consumers like。選項(A)和(C)是了解消費者喜好後,可能把這些資訊拿來做的事,但不是這名專員的職責。選項(D)不正確,產品測試確實是了解消費者喜好的一種方式,但廣告中並未提及。

156. 誰會使用這名專員所撰寫的報告?
(A) 消費者
(B) 電視臺
(C) 製造商
(D) 這家電視廣告公司

解析 (D) 廣告中提到專員所撰寫的報告是供公司內部使用的(for use within the company)。選項(A)不正確,這份報告是「關於」消費者,而不是供消費者使用。選項(B)和(C)都和公司內部的描述相抵觸。

157. 應徵者須具備何種資格？
    (A) 研究相關教育和廣告相關經驗
    (B) 應對電視觀眾的經驗
    (C) 會計能力
    (D) 廣播電視相關科系學位

解析 (A) 廣告中提到的資格要求是「a college degree with courses in research」和「experience in advertising」。選項(B)與選項(C)未被提及。選項(D)和廣告的主題有關，但不是必備條件。

第158-160題請看下面這封電子郵件。

寄件者：歐萊禮證券
主旨： 個股訊息通知
收件者：客戶名單

–[1]– 南方地區航空公司第四季獲利980萬美元，而去前同期虧損5億8410萬美元。–[2]– 獲利來自於成本降低和獲利航線增加。如果當前管理階層維持不變，我們可以假設其降低成本措施和航線選擇會持續對獲利產生正面影響。他們很有可能繼續取消跨大西洋的冷門航線。–[3]– 因此，他們應能更專注經營短程航線，該航空公司已在這些航線上建立紮實基礎，且為該公司的主要營收來源。–[4]– 如果預測有所變化，我們會另行通知。

---

158. 為何這家航空公司的獲利提升了？
    (A) 新的行銷策略
    (B) 較低的成本和較佳的航線
    (C) 機票銷售量提升
    (D) 競爭出現變化

解析 (B) 文中所說的reduced costs就等於lower costs，而航空公司的獲利航線 (profitable routes) 數量也增加了。選項(A)(C)(D)都沒有被提及。

159. 這家航空公司最賺錢的是哪一種航線？
    (A) 跨大西洋航線
    (B) 國際航線
    (C) 短程航線
    (D) 貨運航線

解析 (C) 電子郵件中描述到「the short-haul routes, where the airline has built a strong base and where most of its revenue is generated」，表示這家航空公司已在短程航線上累積了廣大客源，且為主要營收來源。選項(A)是航空公司打算停掉的航線。選項(B)和(D)沒有被提及。

160. 下面這個句子最適合放入文中［1］［2］［3］［4］哪一個位置？
「我們建議此時繼續持有這家航空公司的股票。」
　　(A)［1］
　　(B)［2］
　　(C)［3］
　　(D)［4］

解析 (D) 這則通知描述了股票的預測分析，且為正面描述，而這個句子建議投資者繼續持有這張股票，做為結論是合乎邏輯的。選項(A)(B)(C)放入這個句子都不合邏輯。

第161–163題請看下面這份備忘錄。

發布人：墨佐拉・薩瓦拉尼
發送日期：20—年6月3日星期四，上午9:30
收件人：全體員工
主旨：休假

超過一週的休假須經主管核准，提出請求不代表自動核准。若（一）你的缺勤會造成團隊工作繁重，或導致團隊無法如期完成工作；（二）你沒有至少提前一週通知；（三）你的工作績效不佳；或（四）你有太過頻繁的缺勤紀錄，可能不予准假。此情況下，請聯繫人事審查委員會。

---

161. 備忘錄中對休假有何說明？
　　(A) 只准請一週的假。
　　(B) 一年只能休假一次。
　　(C) 休假超過一週須經主管核准。
　　(D) 臨時員工沒有支薪假。

解析 (C) 備忘錄中提到「Supervisors must approve any and all vacation periods longer than one week」，因此只要超過一週的休假都要經過主管核准。選項(A)不正確，可以休更長的假，只是需要經過核准。選項(B)和(D)實際上也許可能，但備忘錄中並未提及。

162. 為何主管有可能拒絕休假請求？
    (A) 該名員工是團隊領導者。
    (B) 該名員工經常沒來上班。
    (C) 該名員工認真工作。
    (D) 該名員工最近才剛被僱用。

解析 (B) 備忘錄中提到不予准假的其中一個理由是「you have had other frequent absences」（有太過頻繁的缺勤紀錄）。選項(A)重複使用了team這個字。選項(C)混淆了hard worker和heavy workload這兩個片語。選項(D)雖然不無可能，但在備忘錄中並未提及。

163. 如果休假請求被駁回，員工可以怎麼做？
    (A) 和人事審查委員會討論這件事
    (B) 請求調到其他部門
    (C) 一週後重新提出請求
    (D) 向工會舉報這名主管

解析 (A) 備忘錄中提到如果主管不予准假，請員工聯繫人事審查委員會（please contact the Personnel Review Board）。選項(B)(C)(D)也許有可能，但備忘錄中並未提及。

第164–167題請看下面這個網頁。

首頁	關於我們	方案	會員	常見問題

您的公司是否願意支持員工的身心健康呢？您的公司可以加入健康與水上活動中心，成為我們的企業會員，員工便能享有年繳會員、月繳會員、單日通行券和週末通行券的折扣。員工本人和家人都能享此優惠。持有任何會員資格或通行券，皆可使用我們的三座游泳池、兩間健身房，並可參加我們所有的游泳課和健身課，無需額外付費。*使用更衣室、蒸氣室和三溫暖也包含在會員資格內。

您的公司申辦企業會員所需支付的金額，是依據您預測會使用會員資格的員工人數，而非公司實際的員工總人數。在一年期間，我們會追蹤這些數字，提供您一份報告說明實際使用福利的員工人數。如果數字超過您所支付的會費，下一年續約企業會員時將調整費用。準備好申辦會員了嗎？點此。

*大部分課程須報名才可參加。點此查看課程表。

164. 這項資訊的目的是什麼？
    (A) 宣傳一家健康俱樂部的服務
    (B) 說明如何辦理健康俱樂部的會員
    (C) 描述提供給企業員工的健康方案
    (D) 說明企業如何為員工取得會員折扣

解析 (D) 這項資訊說明一間公司可以成為該中心的企業會員，以便提供員工各種會員折扣（to offer employees a discount on annual and monthly memberships and day and weekend passes）。選項(A)不正確，這不是一則廣告。選項(B)過於廣泛，這項資訊只有說明其中一種會員形式。選項(C)不正確，這項資訊是在說明企業會員資格，並沒有提供某一種健康方案的具體細節。

165. 關於該中心的設施有何說明？
    (A) 他們有游泳池和健身房。
    (B) 最近新增了三溫暖和蒸氣室。
    (C) 小孩有專用游泳池。
    (D) 有一座室外游泳池。

解析 (A) 會員資格的描述中提到「all three of our pools and both our fitness rooms」，由此可知該中心有游泳池和健身房。選項(B)指的是文中提到的蒸氣室和三溫暖，但並沒有說是什麼時候增加的設施。選項(C)和(D)都不正確，文中並沒有具體說明游泳池的地點和使用對象。

166. 關於健身課有何說明？
    (A) 僅限成人參加。
    (B) 週末課程須額外付費。
    (C) 屬於會員福利。
    (D) 課程表經常更換。

解析 (C) 會員資格的描述中提到「swimming lessons and fitness classes at no extra charge」，表示健身課是不需額外付費的。選項(A)和(B)都沒有被提及。選項(D)指的是最後補充的課程表連結，但沒有提到是否會更換課表或多久更換一次。

167. 企業會員的會費為什麼會增加？
    (A) 如果使用福利的員工人數有所變動。
    (B) 如果員工的家人也使用了會員資格。
    (C) 如果公司太晚續約。
    (D) 如果公司員工人數增加。

解析 **(A)** 這項資訊中說明企業會員的會費是依據使用會員資格的人數而定，而不是公司的員工總人數，並說「If this number grows beyond what you have paid, the fee will be amended the following year」，表示如果使用會員資格的員工人數增加就會調整會費。選項(B)不正確是因為員工本人和家人都可以使用會員資格。選項(C)未被提及。選項(D)誤解了文中所說的人數增加，這裡所說的人數增加是使用會員資格的員工人數，而不是全體員工人數。

第168–171題請看下面這則公告。

新科技設備公司宣布，預計在未來的六個月內，其巴西分公司將裁員四千人。–[1]– 歷經了兩年的全球財務虧損後，新科技公司至今仍難以獲利。

商業分析師對此裁員之舉感到十分意外，他們對該公司過去幾個月來的表現一直印象深刻。–[2]– 儘管該公司的營收不如成立頭兩年亮眼，但自六月以來一直穩定成長。

新的競爭出現被認為是營收減少的主要原因，但與該公司關係密切的消息人士則將責任歸咎於公司董事長皮耶·雷納茨缺乏領導方針。雷納茨先生加入公司僅三年，大概不久後就會辭職。–[3]–

現任副董事長伊莉莎白·施特魯布可望接替他的位置。–[4]– 施特魯布女士負責開設國際分公司，這些分公司的獲利都比巴西分公司來得高。新科技公司在巴西一共僱用了兩萬五千名員工，亞洲有兩萬名員工，歐洲也有一萬名員工。其他國際分公司將不受這次裁員影響。

---

168. 自六月以來發生了什麼事？
    (A) 裁員人數不斷增加。
    (B) 顧客群不斷擴展。
    (C) 營收不斷增加。
    (D) 虧損日益嚴重。

解析 **(C)** 文中指出「Although its revenues have not matched those of its first two years in business, they had been increasing steadily since June.」，表示營收自六月以來一直穩定成長，revenue就是earnings，increase就是going up。選項(A)(B)(D)都和文章主題有關，但文中並未提及。

169. 新科技公司的現任董事長很有可能會做什麼事？
    (A) 把公司賣掉
    (B) 辭去他的職位
    (C) 增加利潤
    (D) 開設新分公司

解析 (B) 文中指出董事長雷納茨先生大概不久後會辭職（will probably resign soon）。選項(A)不太可能發生，文中已經說了裁員，並有可能換新董事長。選項(C)正是這位董事長一直做不到的事。選項(D)把現任副董事長開設國際分公司的描述搞混了。

170. 下列哪一句話描述了新科技公司的國際分公司？
    (A) 它們賺的錢比巴西分公司多。
    (B) 它們的成本效益較低。
    (C) 它們比巴西分公司成立得早。
    (D) 它們將在六個月內關閉。

解析 (A) 在施特魯布女士的管理下，國際分公司的獲利高於巴西分公司。選項(B)(C)(D)都沒有被提及。

171. 下面這個句子最適合放入文中[1][2][3][4]哪一個位置？
    「這是該公司重組虧損業務的策略之一。」
    (A) [1]
    (B) [2]
    (C) [3]
    (D) [4]

解析 (A) 這裡的this指的是編號[1]前面句子的裁員一事，該公司試圖以裁員來解決業務虧損的情況。選項(B)(C)(D)放入這個句子後語意都不通。

第172-175題請看下面這段簡訊對話串。

凱雅・瓊斯	9:15
我需要妳幫我弄清楚一份訂單。	
安・亞當斯	9:16
好啊,怎麼了?	
凱雅・瓊斯	9:19
就是下個月畢格羅夫婦的婚禮,他們希望有巧克力草莓,但我不確定是否要用我們平常合作的莓果供應商,我們不是已經決定不再用他們家了嗎?	
安・亞當斯	9:24
妳是說莓谷農場嗎?不要跟他們訂。上次他們送來的草莓有一半是腐爛的,我們根本不能用。	
安・亞當斯	9:27
巧克力草莓是我們的特色,我們需要品質最好的草莓。我們需要找一家新的供應商,因為下個月史密斯家的派對也要用草莓。	
凱雅・瓊斯	9:29
好,那妳覺得要不要嘗試找哈蒙德果園?	
安・亞當斯	9:32
不如你跟他們聯絡看看,了解一下價格。同時,我也會打聽一下有沒有人跟他們合作過。	
安・亞當斯	9:35
那這個週末威爾森家的畢業派對,菜單怎麼辦?	
凱雅・瓊斯	9:38
我已經把肉和蔬菜都訂好了,蛋糕也開始準備了。	
安・亞當斯	9:41
很好,那就都安排好了。妳看哈蒙德果園怎麼說,再告訴我。	
凱雅・瓊斯	9:45
我和他們一談完,下午就回覆妳。	
安・亞當斯	9:47
好。	

172. 瓊斯女士和亞當斯女士可能在哪一種類型的公司工作？
(A) 農場
(B) 烹飪學校
(C) 食品批發商
(D) 外燴公司

解析 (D) 瓊斯女士和亞當斯女士正在討論婚禮和派對的食物，所以很有可能是做外燴的。選項(A)是他們合作的供應商。選項(B)和(C)是與食品主題有關的其他行業。

173. 上一次他們跟草莓供應商訂的草莓出了什麼問題？
(A) 太貴了。
(B) 太慢送到。
(C) 水果品質很差。
(D) 水果太多了。

解析 (C) 亞當斯女士寫說「Last time half the berries they sent were rotten」（上次的草莓有一半腐爛了）。選項(A)(B)(D)雖然也有可能，但並未提及。

174. 在9:41時，亞當斯女士寫說「That's all set」是什麼意思？
(A) 派對的時間已經決定好了。
(B) 派對的一切都安排好了。
(C) 客戶已經同意使用這份菜單。
(D) 客戶已經簽約了。

解析 (B)「all set」的意思是「都安排好、準備就緒了」，瓊斯女士說她已訂好威爾森家派對要用的食物，而亞當斯女士就以這句話來回應。選項(A)(C)(D)都不符合這裡的語境。

175. 瓊斯女士下午會做什麼？
(A) 查詢草莓價格
(B) 造訪哈蒙德果園
(C) 把蛋糕做好
(D) 打電話給客戶

解析 (A) 亞當斯女士要瓊斯女士聯絡果園，詢問草莓的價格，後面幾句說到果園時，瓊斯女士則寫說「I'll get back to you this afternoon as soon as I've talked to them」（我和他們談完下午就回覆妳），可見她下午會去做這件事。選項(B)不正確，她只說要聯絡果園，沒有說要親自造訪。選項(C)指的是威爾森家派對要用的蛋糕，但對話中沒有提到何時要做好。選項(D)完全沒有被提及。

第176-180題請看下面的電子郵件和通知。

收件者：管理層
寄件者：不滿的顧客
日期： 2月4日星期五

敬啟者：

我之所以透過電子郵件提出客訴，是因為我打電話到貴公司找不到任何人。康科德公司電話客服中心的服務真的令人很失望。我昨天上午10點30分打電話，因為我新買的洗碗機有點問題需要協助。電話那邊馬上要我等候，我聽了那煩人的音樂三十五分鐘，才掛斷重打一次。結果又是同一個人接，他說他叫和樹，並告訴我他正在處理另一位來電的客人，還說我的來電對他很重要。如果我的來電很重要，就應該有人來協助我才對。

最糟糕的是，我的來電真的很重要。昨天我啟動新洗碗機後，廚房就大淹水了，我完全不知道該怎麼讓水停下來，我的廚房地板嚴重受損。希望有人親自打電話來解釋一下，為什麼沒人可以接聽我的電話。以後我再也不會跟你們店買東西了。

鈴木香奈

通知

日期：20—年2月7日
致：電話客服中心員工
關於：每週會議

自3月1日起，電話客服中心的員工將不再需要參加每週舉行的康科德公司員工會議。週四早上開完會後，每次的會議紀錄都會張貼在員工休息室，供所有員工查看。

這項改變的原因有兩個：

（一）公司現行的安排，是讓一位員工負責接聽開會期間的所有十支電話，但這樣的安排已經行不通了，很多客戶抱怨週四早上要等上半小時才有人接電話。

（二）每到週四早上，我們的銷售損失高達300美元，就因為電話無法被全面接聽。電話客服中心的專員在處理這些求助專線的來電時，也能創造額外的銷售額。而你們因為必須花時間去開會，損失了接電話的抽成獎金，導致收入也變少了。

對於上述調整如有任何疑問，請寫信到manager3@concord.org和伊藤咲聯絡。

176. 關於這名來電者，下列敘述何者錯誤？
　　(A) 她最近向康科德公司買了一樣家電。
　　(B) 她打電話來詢問如何清理淹水。
　　(C) 她對來電等待時間太長感到不滿。
　　(D) 她不喜歡電話等待時播放的音樂。

解析 (B) 來電者想知道如何把水關掉，以便停止淹水，而不是想詢問如何清理淹水。選項(A)是對的，她新買的洗碗機有問題，才會打這通電話。選項(C)和(D)都是讓她感到不滿的事情。

177. 電話客服中心的員工為何不需要再參加每週的員工會議？
　　(A) 會議內容與他們無關。
　　(B) 他們需要有空接聽求助電話。
　　(C) 他們抱怨員工會議召開得過於頻繁。
　　(D) 他們擔心會議期間會損失銷售的抽成獎金。

解析 (B) 開會政策改變是因為需要有人處理求助專線的來電。選項(A)不是事實，每次會議紀錄都會公布，可推斷為所有員工都需知道的事項。選項(C)也不是事實，文中提到顧客

抱怨求助時等太久，但沒提到員工有所抱怨。選項(D)在通知中被描述為參加會議的一個缺點，但提出這點的是管理層，不是員工本人；同時也只是作為附帶的損失一提，不是政策改變的主要原因。

178. 鈴木小姐打電話到這間公司時，有幾個人在負責接聽電話？
    (A) 沒有人
    (B) 一個人
    (C) 九個人
    (D) 十個人

解析 **(B)** 她是星期四早上打的電話，根據通知內容，當時正在召開員工會議，只留下一位員工負責接電話。選項(A)不是事實，的確有人接了電話。選項(C)是無人接聽的電話數量。選項(D)是全面運作時的電話數量。

179. 電話客服中心的員工要如何得知每週會議的討論內容？
    (A) 兩天後會發送備忘錄。
    (B) 會有一位客服中心的代表員工去做筆記。
    (C) 員工休息室可以看到會議摘要。
    (D) 伊藤咲會傳電子郵件告知會議詳情。

解析 **(C)** 通知中說會議紀錄會公布在員工休息室。選項(A)(B)(D)都沒有被提到。

180. 管理層如何處理這件客訴？
    (A) 讓顧客來電時等待
    (B) 打電話給電話客服中心的員工
    (C) 改變公司的作業程序
    (D) 發一份通知給顧客

解析 **(C)** 這間公司處理這個問題的方法，是讓電話客服中心的員工不用參加每週會議，這樣就有足夠的人手接聽電話。選項(A)是顧客抱怨的事。選項(B)使用的都是文中的單字，但文中沒有提到管理層要打電話給員工。選項(D)把給員工的通知誤解成給顧客的通知。

第181–185題請看下面這兩封電子郵件。

收件者：7號操作員、9號操作員、11號操作員
寄件者：朴基
主旨：　錄音名稱和職稱

我最近發現你們當中有不少人重設了自己的電話，還更改了語音信箱的訊息。你們把「系統操作員」的通用職稱改成自己的名字，更糟糕的是，其中至少一個人還用綽號。這種行為不僅很不專業，還違反了你們員工手冊裡的規定。原本的錄音設定為通用名稱和職稱是有原因的。你們的主管隨時有可能要你們調換工作崗位或部門，讓你們在公司內學習新職務。新的實習生會接手你的辦公桌和相關職務。

請看你們的手冊第14頁，上面寫說：「身為臨時員工，你無權重設桌上的電話或電腦上的設定。」

謝謝！
朴基

收件者：parkgi@financialguide.net
寄件者：student7@financialguide.net
主旨：　電話答錄機

朴先生，您好：

我要為重設12號辦公桌的語音信箱道歉。因為好幾次被老顧客叫7號操作員，我就決定把錄音改成我的名字。我不認為我錄製的訊息有任何不專業之處，我只不過錄了我的全名和職稱「實習生」而已。

我會更改錄音是因為有一位顧客留言給我，說：「如果能知道你的名字就好了，對一個編號說謝謝，感覺好沒人情味。」

您希望我把訊息改回原來通用的嗎？還是您要自己處理？我知道怎麼重設，但我不想再次違反規定。

最後，我之前沒想到會被調到其他工作崗位，我很期待嘗試新的職務。到目前為止的實習工作我做得很開心。

敬祝 順心
鍾黛

實戰模擬試題4

181. 第一封郵件是寫給誰的？
    (A) 所有的臨時員工
    (B) 三位學生的培訓師
    (C) 特定的實習生
    (D) 所有的系統操作員

解析 **(C)** 從郵件內容可判斷收件的這幾位操作員全都是實習生。選項(A)不正確，這封電子郵件只發給三個人。選項(B)不正確，這些操作員是實習生或受訓者，不是培訓師。選項(D)不正確，這封電子郵件只發給三位系統操作員。

182. 朴基建議實習生用什麼方式查看語音信箱的使用規則？
    (A) 閱讀他們的手冊
    (B) 向他們的主管詢問
    (C) 寄電子郵件給朴基
    (D) 和其他臨時員工交談

解析 **(A)** 朴基要實習生看手冊中某一頁上的相關規則。選項(B)(C)(D)都是郵件中提到的人物，但朴基沒有要實習生去找他們。

183. 鍾黛在她的語音信箱中錄製了什麼訊息？
    (A) 她的暱稱
    (B) 她的電話號碼
    (C) 她的名字和職稱
    (D) 她的桌號

解析 **(C)** 鍾黛說她把語音留言改成她的名字和職稱。選項(A)是其他實習生在語音留言中錄製的資訊。選項(B)未被提及。選項(D)在她的郵件中有提及，但她沒有把這項資訊放入語音留言中。

184. 鍾黛以什麼理由為自己的行為辯護？
    (A) 她自己的名字比較好發音。
    (B) 她以為她會被僱為全職員工。
    (C) 一名顧客對她的語音留言發表了意見。
    (D) 她沒有看培訓資料中的手冊。

解析 **(C)** 一名顧客說，用編號稱呼一個人而不用名字很沒人情味，所以她才改了錄音。選項(A)(B)(D)都和主題有關，但郵件中都沒有提到。

185．朴基在電子郵件中沒有提到哪件事？
　　(A) 給實習生的規定寫在哪裡
　　(B) 實習生是否該把語音留言改回來
　　(C) 實習生算不算臨時員工
　　(D) 這項政策制定的初衷

解析 (B) 鍾黛說她沒有把語音留言改回原樣，因為她不確定這樣做是否被允許，而朴基在電子郵件中也沒提到這件事。選項(A)有提到規定在手冊的第14頁。選項(C)可從手冊規則的用詞As temporary employees得到推論，表示實習生為臨時員工。選項(D)有提到，他說實習生隨時可能被調到其他部門，電話和語音信箱將由別人接手，所以才有這條規定。

第 186–190 題請看下面的廣告、電子郵件和表單。

---

www.busybusinessworkers.com

是時候放鬆休息一下、享受遠離辦公室的美好時光了！這個月，我們特別為像您這樣的忙碌商務人士準備了三種假期套裝行程。五月是最適合旅遊的月份，當學生們忙著考試時，您可以清靜地享受海灘和度假中心。本月預訂行程可享原價七五折優惠。套裝價格不含稅。建議購買旅程取消保險。

點擊下面的套裝行程查看詳細說明。價格為每人之費用。
套裝行程A：十二晚。葡萄牙五星級飯店。含所有餐食。1650美元。
套裝行程B：五晚。加勒比海遊輪。1400美元。
套裝行程C：安潔利諾水療與高爾夫球假期。600美元起。
套裝行程D：抱歉，本行程已無法預訂。

別再等到年底，現在就給自己放個小假，您值得好好享受！

實戰模擬試題 4

收件者：manager@marketpro.com
寄件者：francogerard@marketpro.com
主旨： 假期

嗨，亞蘭：

我最近看到一個旅行社的廣告，他們提供了一些很棒的度假行程優惠，我很想把握這個機會。我老婆和我一直希望有時間去小島旅行，現在剛好有這個機會，可以舒適地遊玩，又不用花太多錢。這些行程看來很熱門，我們最快可以訂到五月初的時間。我知道那是我們市場專家公司一年中正忙碌的時候，但我只會離開一個禮拜，且我相信那段時間史蒂分有能力可以代理我的職務。距離我上次休假已經有一段時間了，希望你可以准假。請盡快回覆，我們才能確認預訂行程的事。

謝謝！
法蘭科

預訂表

姓名： 　　法蘭科・杰拉德
地址： 　　史普林菲爾德市主街123號
電話： 　　456-1234
電子郵件： francogerard@marketpro.com
假期方案： 套裝行程B
旅行人數： 2
旅行日期： 5月3–10日
付款方式：
☒ 支票（請寄至下列地址）
☐ 信用卡卡號

---

186. 這則廣告的受眾是誰？
　　(A) 打高爾夫球的人
　　(B) 家庭
　　(C) 學生
　　(D) 上班族

解析 (D) 廣告中提到「away from the office」（遠離辦公室）和「busy business workers like you」（像你這樣的忙碌商務人士），由此可知是上班族。選項 (A) 是被廣告中提到的高爾夫球假期給混淆了，但度假行程不僅限於高爾夫球，還有其他種類的度假行程。選項 (B) 未被提及。選項 (C) 重複使用了廣告中的 students 這個字。

187. 顧客要如何享有度假行程優惠？
    (A) 於本月預訂行程
    (B) 於年底前付款
    (C) 預訂雙人行程
    (D) 五月時去旅行

解析 **(A)** 廣告中說「Book a vacation this month and receive 25％ off the regular price」，所以這個月預訂可以打七五折。選項(B)重複使用了廣告中的片語the end of the year。選項(C)也可能有優惠，但廣告中沒有提到。選項(D)是建議的旅行時間，但和折扣無關。

188. 關於套裝行程C有何說明？
    (A) 內含高爾夫球課程。
    (B) 不含餐食。
    (C) 費用可能高於600美元。
    (D) 目前無法預訂。

解析 **(C)** 廣告資訊裡面寫「from $600」，就是「600美元起」，實際金額要看顧客選擇的內容而定。選項(A)重複使用了golf這個字，但廣告中沒有提到課程，因此無法確定是否包含在內。選項(B)不正確，廣告中沒有提到餐食，因此無法確定是否包含在內。選項(D)是套裝行程D的描述。

189. 杰拉德先生為什麼要寫這封電子郵件？
    (A) 詢問誰能在他休假期間代理職務
    (B) 告知亞蘭有這個度假行程優惠
    (C) 請對方推薦度假行程
    (D) 請求休假

解析 **(D)** 杰拉德先生解釋他為何希望在五月時休假，並寫說「I hope you will be able to approve this request」（希望准假），所以他是要請求休假。選項(A)不正確，杰拉德在信中寫他已經知道誰能代理他的職務。選項(B)在信中確實有提到，不過不是寫這封信的目的。選項(C)不正確，因杰拉德先生心中已有想要的度假行程。

190. 杰拉德先生會參加哪一個度假行程？
    (A) 加勒比海遊輪
    (B) 葡萄牙之旅
    (C) 水療與高爾夫球假期
    (D) 五星級飯店住宿

505

解析 **(A)** 從預訂表可以看出杰拉德先生選擇了套裝行程B，而根據廣告內容，套裝行程B是加勒比海遊輪之旅。選項(B)(C)(D)是廣告中提到的其他行程。

第191–195題請看下面的廣告、門票和電子郵件。

北極星表演藝術中心
最新一季節目資訊

10月5–30日　　城市芭蕾舞團演出《天鵝湖》
11月7–21日　　《羅密歐與茱麗葉》，莎士比亞戲劇
12月2–18日　　城市管弦樂團演出每週演奏會
1月4–30日　　《卡門》，喬治・比才歌劇

所有門票須預先至www.nscpa.org購買。可購買單場演出門票，亦可購買全季套票。

票價（單場）

平日：
．日場：40美元
．晚場：55美元

週末：
．日場：50美元
．晚場：65美元

自行列印門票
使用說明
請自行列印此門票，並攜至會場。

1月4日晚上7點30分
北極星表演藝術中心

座位詳情　　　　　　票價
F排10號　　　　　　65美元
F排12號　　　　　　65美元

門票售出，概不退費。如遇劇院取消演出，本票可辦理退費。

> 收件者：彼德・理查茲
> 寄件者：雅曼達・奧桑
> 主旨：　門票
>
> 嗨，彼德：
>
> 非常感謝你幫我買到下週的票，我好期待去看這場演出。你提到表演之前一起吃晚餐，可惜的是，我覺得我應該沒辦法準時下班去吃飯。這幾天為了完成年終報告，我們都要加班。不過若你願意的話，看完表演去吃點晚餐倒是不錯。我有開車，大概七點左右可以順道去你的辦公室接你。再告訴我這樣的安排你行不行。
>
> 雅曼達

191. 如果要看週四下午的演出場次，要花多少錢？
    (A) $40
    (B) $55
    (C) $50
    (D) $65

解析 (A) 廣告裡寫說平日的日場（日場就是下午場次）票價是40美元。選項(B)(C)(D)是其他場次的票價。

192. 關於北極星表演藝術中心節目的門票有何說明？
    (A) 只開放網路購票。
    (B) 可至售票處取票。
    (C) 年長者可享優惠。
    (D) 部分表演場次門票已售罄。

解析 (A) 廣告中寫說「All tickets must be bought in advance at www.nscpa.org」，就是只能網路購票的意思。選項(B)不正確，所有門票都必須透過網站購買，並且要自行列印。選項(C)和(D)的確有可能，只不過廣告中都沒有提到。

193. 什麼情況下顧客可以拿到退費？
    (A) 如果在演出當日前辦理退費
    (B) 如果票券不是以優惠價購入
    (C) 如果演出取消
    (D) 概不退費

解析 **(C)** 門票上的資訊寫說「All sales are final. Ticket is nonrefundable. In the event that there is a cancellation by the theater, a refund for this ticket may be issued.」，意思是原則上不可退費，但如果演出被劇院方取消，則可辦理退費。選項(A)和(B)也有可能是條件之一，但文中沒有特別說明。選項(D)不正確，儘管票券上寫著nonrefundable（不可退費），後面還是提出了補充條件，如果演出取消可以退費。

194. 理查茲先生和奧桑小姐要去看哪一類的表演？
　　(A) 芭蕾舞
　　(B) 戲劇
　　(C) 演奏會
　　(D) 歌劇

解析 **(D)** 票券日期是1月4日，根據廣告上的節目資訊，當天演出的是歌劇。選項(A)(B)(C)是其他日期的演出。

195. 奧桑小姐主動提議做什麼？
　　(A) 列印門票
　　(B) 演出結束後請吃晚餐
　　(C) 幫理查茲先生寫報告
　　(D) 載理查茲先生去劇院

解析 **(D)** 奧桑小姐寫說「I'll have my car with me, so I can swing by your office and pick you up」，表示她可以開車去接理查茲先生。選項(A)和門票的討論有關，但她沒提到要列印門票。選項(B)重複使用了文中的單字supper，但奧桑小姐只有提議吃晚餐，沒說要請客。選項(C)搞錯了人物，要寫報告的是奧桑小姐，不是理查茲先生。

第 196–200 題請看下面的房地產物件清單和兩封電子郵件。

收件者：sydneya@someplace.com
寄件者：melissa.davenport@myjob.com
主旨：　關於：公寓

嗨，席妮：

我有好消息要告訴你。我最近接受了希爾文公司的職位，這就表示說我很快就會搬到溫徹斯特去了。可以跟你住在同一個城市，真是太棒了。總之，我想請你給我一點建議，哪裡可以找到適合我們家住的公寓。我們希望是比較安全、安靜的地方，最好在好學校附近，方便兩個孩子上學。我們需要至少兩個房間，但三個房間會更好。因為我們打算把車開過去，所以不用靠近大眾交通運輸系統，這樣地點的選擇會比較多，但最好有車庫。如果你有什麼想法請告訴我，如果可以推薦一位房仲，那就太好了。

謝謝！期待很快見到你！

梅麗莎

赫斯克爾房地產公司
溫徹斯特公寓

物件 A
明亮、陽光充足，一房，近河濱公園。小型建築，後方附設租戶停車場。近學校和交通運輸系統。1000 美元／月。

物件 B
大學周邊迷人的兩房公寓。大樓附設派對空間和健身房。有車庫。附近有學校、商店。1800 美元／月。

物件 C
空間寬敞、經濟實惠的三房公寓，位於格林威爾地鐵線上。可路邊停車。附近有學校、商店。2000 美元／月。

物件 D
全新裝修兩房公寓，近市中心。位於公車和地鐵線上。附近有購物商圈、公園和博物館。1500 美元／月。

```
收件者：melissa.davenport@myjob.com
寄件者：bob@haskellrealty.com
主旨：　關於：公寓

戴文波特女士，您好：

非常感謝您的來信，我非常樂意帶您看看溫徹斯特這一帶的出租公寓。我們有幾個房
屋物件我覺得您會感興趣。您提到下週會到城裡來，並且下午都有空。不如我們就約
週三的下午見面。如果您方便告訴我留宿處的地址，我一點半會去接您，然後再一起
去看公寓。期待與您見面。

鮑伯‧赫斯克爾
```

196. 戴文波特女士為什麼要搬家？
　　(A) 她找到一份新工作。
　　(B) 她需要大一點的公寓。
　　(C) 她想住得離家人近一點。
　　(D) 她不喜歡現在住的社區。

解析 (A) 戴文波特女士在信中寫說「I recently accepted a position with the Sylvan Company, which means I will be moving to Winchester」，所以她是為了新工作而搬家。選項(B)和(D)雖然也有可能，但並未提及。選項(C)重複使用了family這個字。

197. 關於物件D的公寓有何說明？
　　(A) 離學校很近。
　　(B) 有健身房。
　　(C) 租金是最低的。
　　(D) 靠近大眾運輸系統。

解析 (D) 物件描述中說「On bus and subway lines」，所以表示它靠近大眾交通運輸系統。選項(A)和(B)是其他物件的描述。選項(C)不正確，租金最低的是物件A。

198. 戴文波特女士最有可能選擇哪一間公寓？
　　(A) 物件A
　　(B) 物件B
　　(C) 物件C
　　(D) 物件D

解析 (B) 戴文波特女士在信中說她想要兩至三房的公寓,最好有車庫並在學校附近,符合全部條件的只有物件 B。選項 (A)(C)(D) 都只符合部分條件。

199. 赫斯克爾先生為什麼要寫這封電子郵件?
　　(A) 詢問戴文波特女士何時有空
　　(B) 推薦居住的地方
　　(C) 約時間會面
　　(D) 宣傳他的業務

解析 (C) 赫斯克爾先生回應了戴文波特女士的請求,答應帶她去看幾間公寓,並提出了一個時間。選項 (A) 不正確,從信中可以看出他已經知道她何時有空。選項 (B) 在信中沒有提到,且應該是他們碰面後才要做的事。選項 (D) 不正確,他會回信就表示對方已知道他是從事何種行業。

200. 赫斯克爾先生要戴文波特女士做什麼?
　　(A) 到他辦公室和他碰面
　　(B) 把她的地址給他
　　(C) 開車來接他
　　(D) 挑幾間公寓來看

解析 (B) 赫斯克爾先生寫說「If you will let me know the address where you will be staying, I will pick you up」,所以是向她要地址。選項 (A) 不正確,他提議到她留宿的地方碰面。選項 (C) 不正確,是赫斯克爾先生要開車去接她。選項 (D) 未被提及,但他說有幾個物件對方會感興趣,想必是替她挑好幾間符合她條件的公寓了。

STOP 本測驗到此結束。如果你在時間結束前作答完畢,可以回頭檢查 Part 5、6、7 的答案。

實戰模擬試題5
解答

聽力測驗

Part 1 照片描述

1. **A**
2. **D**
3. **C**
4. **A**
5. **B**
6. **C**

Part 2 應答問題

7. **B**	14. **C**	21. **C**	28. **A**
8. **B**	15. **A**	22. **A**	29. **B**
9. **C**	16. **B**	23. **B**	30. **C**
10. **A**	17. **C**	24. **C**	31. **B**
11. **A**	18. **A**	25. **C**	
12. **C**	19. **C**	26. **A**	
13. **B**	20. **B**	27. **B**	

Part 3 簡短對話

32. **C**	42. **B**	52. **D**	62. **A**
33. **D**	43. **D**	53. **C**	63. **C**
34. **A**	44. **C**	54. **A**	64. **D**
35. **C**	45. **D**	55. **D**	65. **B**
36. **B**	46. **A**	56. **A**	66. **B**
37. **C**	47. **C**	57. **B**	67. **D**
38. **A**	48. **B**	58. **A**	68. **B**
39. **B**	49. **C**	59. **B**	69. **A**
40. **D**	50. **B**	60. **C**	70. **C**
41. **B**	51. **A**	61. **A**	

Part 4 簡短獨白

71. **A**	79. **C**	87. **C**	95. **B**
72. **D**	80. **A**	88. **C**	96. **C**
73. **C**	81. **D**	89. **D**	97. **A**
74. **B**	82. **B**	90. **C**	98. **D**
75. **D**	82. **B**	91. **A**	99. **A**
76. **A**	84. **A**	92. **D**	100. **B**
77. **B**	85. **C**	93. **C**	
78. **C**	86. **A**	94. **A**	

實戰模擬試題5
解答

閱讀測驗

Part 5 句子填空

101.	B	109.	A	117.	D	125.	D
102.	B	110.	C	118.	A	126.	B
103.	A	111.	D	119.	C	127.	C
104.	C	112.	C	120.	B	128.	D
105.	D	113.	B	121.	B	129.	A
106.	C	114.	A	122.	A	130.	A
107.	A	115.	B	123.	C		
108.	B	116.	C	124.	C		

Part 6 段落填空

131.	C	135.	D	139.	C	143.	B
132.	B	136.	B	140.	B	144.	C
133.	A	137.	A	141.	A	145.	B
134.	C	138.	C	142.	D	146.	D

Part 7 閱讀測驗

147.	B	161.	B	175.	C	189.	B
148.	D	162.	C	176.	A	190.	C
149.	B	163.	A	177.	C	191.	D
150.	D	164.	B	178.	D	192.	C
151.	C	165.	A	179.	A	193.	A
152.	A	166.	C	180.	B	194.	C
153.	D	167.	A	181.	B	195.	A
154.	B	168.	C	182.	C	196.	C
155.	C	169.	B	183.	C	197.	B
156.	C	170.	A	184.	D	198.	A
157.	D	171.	A	185.	A	199.	D
158.	A	172.	B	186.	C	200.	C
159.	D	173.	D	187.	A		
160.	B	174.	D	188.	A		

Model Test 5 實戰模擬試題5 題目中譯&解析

聽力測驗

在本段測驗當中，你將有機會展現自己對口說英語的理解能力。聽力測驗共有四個大題，每一大題均有作答說明。你有大約45分鐘時間完成聽力測驗。

Part 1：照片描述

> 作答方式：你會看到一張照片，並聽到四個關於這張照片的陳述。選出最符合照片內容的陳述，將答案卡上對應的橢圓框塗滿。

1. Look at the photo marked number 1 in your test book.
   (A) She's checking her watch.
   (B) She's watching the bus.
   (C) She's planting a tree.
   (D) She's riding the bus.

   請看試題本標示為1的照片。
   (A) 她正在查看手錶。
   (B) 她正看著公車。
   (C) 她正在種樹。
   (D) 她正在搭公車。

   解析 (A) 照片中可以看到一名女子正看著她的腕錶。選項(B)和(D)正確指出了背景中的公車，但女子沒有在看公車，也沒有在搭公車。選項(C)正確指出了背景中的樹，但女子沒有在種樹。

2. Look at the photo marked number 2 in your test book.
   (A) The doors are open.
   (B) The people are sitting on benches.
   (C) The table is set for lunch.
   (D) The tables are in front of the houses.

   請看試題本標示為2的照片。
   (A) 門開著。
   (B) 人們坐在長椅上。
   (C) 午餐餐桌已經擺設好了。
   (D) 這些桌子位於房子前面。

解析 **(D)** 照片中可以看到房子前面有幾張空的桌椅。選項(A)不正確,門是關著的。選項(B)正確指出了長椅,但沒有人坐在椅子上。選項(C)不正確,桌上空無一物。

3. Look at the photo marked number 3 in your test book.
   (A) He's opening a jar.
   (B) He's cooking food.
   (C) He's reading a label.
   (D) He's cleaning the shelves.

   請看試題本標示為3的照片。
   (A) 他正在開罐。
   (B) 他正在煮飯。
   (C) 他正在讀標籤。
   (D) 他正在清理貨架。

解析 **(C)** 一名男子正站在超市的走道上,讀著罐子上的標籤。選項(A)正確指出了罐子,但對男子的動作描述不正確。選項(B)把grocery store和food聯想在一起了。選項(D)正確指出了貨架,但對男子的動作描述不正確。

4. Look at the photo marked number 4 in your test book.
   (A) The train is in the station.
   (B) The passengers are boarding now.
   (C) Crowds fill the platform.
   (D) It's starting to rain.

   請看試題本標示為4的照片。
   (A) 火車停在車站內。
   (B) 乘客們正在上車。
   (C) 月臺上人潮擁擠。
   (D) 開始下雨了。

解析 **(A)** 照片中可以看到一列火車停在火車站內。選項(B)不正確,照片中沒有看到乘客。選項(C)不正確,月臺上空無一人。選項(D)混淆了近音字train和rain。

5. Look at the photo marked number 5 in your test book.
   (A) The man is wearing a tie.
   (B) The woman is wearing glasses.
   (C) The shelves are empty.
   (D) The coffee is in the pot.

   請看試題本標示為5的照片。
   (A) 男子打了領帶。
   (B) 女子戴著眼鏡。
   (C) 書架是空的。
   (D) 咖啡壺中有咖啡。

   解析 (B) 照片中可以看到女子戴著眼鏡。選項(A)不正確，男子沒有打領帶。選項(C)不正確，書架上擺滿了書。選項(D)混淆了 coffee cup 和 coffee pot。

6. Look at the photo marked number 6 in your test book.
   (A) The man is eating chicken.
   (B) The vegetables are in the garden.
   (C) The chef is in the kitchen.
   (D) The plates are in the dishwasher.

   請看試題本標示為6的照片。
   (A) 男子正在吃雞肉。
   (B) 蔬菜在花園裡。
   (C) 廚師在廚房裡。
   (D) 盤子在洗碗機裡。

   解析 (C) 照片中可以看到一名廚師站在廚房裡。選項(A)混淆了近音字 kitchen 和 chicken。選項(B)正確指出了照片中的蔬菜，但對蔬菜所在的位置描述不正確。選項(D)正確指出了照片中的盤子，但對盤子所在的位置描述不正確。

Part 2：應答問題

> 作答方式：你會聽到一個問題和三個可能的回應。選出最適合回答該問題的回應，將答案卡上對應的橢圓框塗滿。

7． Do you know which house they live in?
   (A) Yes, they lived there last year.
   (B) The large one on the corner.
   (C) I wish I had one.

   你知道他們住在哪一棟房子嗎？
   (A) 是的，他們去年住在那裡。
   (B) 轉角很大的那間。
   (C) 真希望我有一個。

   解析 (B) 選項(B)回答了「Which house」的問題。選項(A)重複使用了live這個字。選項(C)混淆了近音字which和wish。

8． Did you make an appointment to see the dentist?
   (A) It was quite disappointing.
   (B) Yes, it's next Wednesday at two o'clock.
   (C) You left your calendar on the desk.

   你預約看牙醫了嗎？
   (A) 這件事相當令人失望。
   (B) 預約了，下星期三的兩點。
   (C) 你把行事曆留在桌上了。

   解析 (B) 選項(B)回答了題目的「yes-no」問句，並補充說明了預約的時間。選項(A)混淆了近音字appointment和disappointing。選項(C)把appointment和calendar聯想在一起了。

9． Who took this phone message from Mr. Jenkins?
   (A) Yes, it was Mr. Jenkins.
   (B) I always take my phone with me.
   (C) Susan took it.

詹金斯先生的電話留言是誰記錄的？
(A) 是的，是詹金斯先生。
(B) 我一向都帶著手機。
(C) 是蘇珊記錄的。

解析 (C)「Susan」回答了「Who」的問題。選項(A)重複使用了 Mr. Jenkins 這個名字。選項(B)重複使用了 phone 這個字。

10. When did you start working here?
    (A) Just about two months ago.
    (B) No, he didn't hear.
    (C) Yes, it's right here.

    你是從什麼時候開始在這裡工作的？
    (A) 大概兩個月前。
    (B) 不，他沒聽到。
    (C) 是的，就在這裡。

解析 (A)「two months ago」回答了「When」的問題。選項(B)混淆了同音字 here 和 hear。選項(C)重複使用了 here 這個字。

11. You were at last month's conference, weren't you?
    (A) No, I wasn't able to attend it.
    (B) They are conferring about it right now.
    (C) Yes, it lasted just about a month.

    你有參加上個月的會議，不是嗎？
    (A) 沒有，我沒辦法參加。
    (B) 他們現在正在協商這件事。
    (C) 是的，持續了大約一個月。

解析 (A) 選項(A)回答了有沒有參加會議的「yes-no」問句。選項(B)使用了 conference 的相關字 conferring（商談、協商）。選項(C)使用了 last 的另一個意義，並重複使用了 month 這個字。

12. Would you like a cup of coffee while you wait?
    (A) They charge based on the weight.
    (B) Please excuse my coughing.
    (C) Yes, thank you very much.

你等待的時候，要不要喝杯咖啡？
(A) 他們按重量收費。
(B) 我咳嗽，請見諒。
(C) 好的，非常感謝你。

解析 (C) 選項(C)是對方提供咖啡時的適當回應。選項(A)混淆了同音字 wait 和 weight。選項(B)混淆了近音字 coffee 和 coughing。

13. Would you mind carrying this box for me?
    (A) Yes, I do.
    (B) Of course. I'd be glad to.
    (C) There's a box over there.

    你介不介意幫我拿這個箱子？
    (A) 是的，我會。
    (B) 沒問題，我很樂意幫忙。
    (C) 那裡有一個箱子。

解析 (B) 選項(B)是對方請求幫忙拿東西時的適當回應。選項(A)用來回答非請求性的「yes-no」問句。選項(C)重複使用了 box 這個字。

14. Have the visitors arrived yet?
    (A) We enjoyed our visit very much.
    (B) Yes, it's in the front hall.
    (C) No, we expect them later today.

    訪客到了嗎？
    (A) 我們這次拜訪非常開心。
    (B) 是的，它在前門廳。
    (C) 還沒，我們預計他們今天晚點才會到。

解析 (C) 選項(C)回答了關於客人到了沒的「yes-no」問句。選項(A)使用了 visitors 的相關字 visit。選項(B)回答的是某樣東西（it）到了沒，而不是人到了沒。

15. Would you rather take the bus or the train?
    (A) I'd prefer the train.
    (B) It looks like rain.
    (C) He's very well trained.

你比較想坐公車還是火車？
(A) 我比較想坐火車。
(B) 看起來快下雨了。
(C) 他訓練有素。

解析 (A) 選項(A)回答了關於偏好的問題。選項(B)混淆了近音字train和rain。選項(C)使用了train的另一個意義。

16. How long do you think the meeting will last?
    (A) Here's the agenda.
    (B) No more than an hour.
    (C) It's about three meters long.

    你覺得這場會議將持續多久？
    (A) 這是議程。
    (B) 不超過一小時。
    (C) 大約三公尺長。

解析 (B) 選項(B)回答了「How long」的時間問題。選項(A)使用了meeting的相關字agenda。選項(C)回答的是「How long」的長度問題。

17. Whose coat is that in the closet?
    (A) He's the closest one.
    (B) They're mine.
    (C) I think it belongs to Tom.

    櫃子裡的那件外套是誰的？
    (A) 他是最近的人。
    (B) 它們是我的。
    (C) 我想應該是湯姆的。

解析 (C) 從belongs這個字可以判斷這個句子正確回答了「Whose」的所有權問題。選項(A)混淆了近音字closet和closest。選項(B)使用了複數代名詞they，但題目問的是單數名詞coat。

18. Why did you take the bus to work today?
    (A) My car broke down.
    (B) The fares are going up.
    (C) Yes, I have to work today.

520

你今天怎麼會搭公車上班？
(A) 我的車壞了。
(B) 車資要上漲了。
(C) 是的，我今天要上班。

解析 (A) 選項(A)提供了一個合理的理由回答「Why」的問題。選項(B)使用了bus的相關字fares。選項(C)重複使用了work這個字。

19. Are you interested in a game of tennis?
    (A) I have a new racket.
    (B) There will be ten of us.
    (C) Sure. I'm free on Saturday.

你有沒有興趣打一場網球？
(A) 我有一支新球拍。
(B) 我們會有十個人。
(C) 好啊，我星期六有空。

解析 (C) 選項(C)是對方邀約打網球時的合理回應。選項(A)使用了tennis的相關字racket。選項(B)混淆了發音相近的tennis和ten of us。

20. What did you do last weekend?
    (A) It's weakened quite a bit.
    (B) I just relaxed at home.
    (C) Yes, it was due last week.

你上週末做了什麼？
(A) 它已經減弱了很多。
(B) 我就在家放鬆而已。
(C) 是的，上週到期了。

解析 (B) 選項(B)回答了「What」的問題。選項(A)和(C)分別把weekend和發音相近的weakened、week搞混了。

21. This cord is too short to reach the outlet.
    (A) Yes, it's a power cord.
    (B) I'm not really bored.
    (C) I'll look for a longer one.

521

這條電線太短了，碰不到插座。
(A) 是的，那是電源線。
(B) 我其實不覺得無聊。
(C) 我去找一條長一點的。

解析 (C) 選項(C)是對方說電線太短時的合理回應。選項(A)重複使用了cord這個字。選項(B)混淆了近音字cord和bored。

22. Is that your car parked out front?
    (A) Yes, it's mine.
    (B) It's the red one.
    (C) In the garage.

    門口停的是你的車嗎？
    (A) 對，是我的。
    (B) 是紅色的那一個。
    (C) 在車庫裡。

解析 (A) 選項(A)回答了關於車子所有權的「yes-no」問句。選項(B)回答的是「Which」的問題。選項(C)回答的是「Where」的問題。

23. When did Mr. Smith's bus arrive?
    (A) He's always on time.
    (B) At around noon, I think.
    (C) At the station.

    史密斯先生的公車是什麼時候到的？
    (A) 他一向都很準時。
    (B) 中午左右吧，我想。
    (C) 在車站。

解析 (B) 「noon」回答了「When」的問題。選項(A)使用了arrive的相關詞on time，但並沒有回答問題。選項(C)用來回答「Where」的問題。

24. I really enjoyed the play last night.
    (A) Please play that song again.
    (B) The play opens next week.
    (C) I did too. It was great.

我真的很喜歡昨晚那齣劇。
(A) 請再放一遍那首歌。
(B) 這齣劇下週開演。
(C) 我也是，它很好看。

解析 (C) 第一個說話者表示喜歡那齣戲劇，第二個說話者表示同意。選項(A)搞錯了 play 的意義。選項(B)重複使用了 play 這個字，但沒有回答問題。

25. Where can I leave my bags?
    (A) Just some books and papers.
    (B) He left before lunch.
    (C) Put them behind my desk.

我可以把包包放在哪裡？
(A) 只是一些書和文件。
(B) 他午餐之前就離開了。
(C) 放在我的桌子後面。

解析 (C)「behind my desk」回答了「Where」的問題。選項(A)回答的是「What」的問題。選項(B)使用了 leave 的過去式 left，但用的是另一個意義。

26. Was John at the party last night?
    (A) No, I didn't see him there.
    (B) Yes, he'll go.
    (C) I don't enjoy parties.

昨晚約翰有去派對嗎？
(A) 沒有，我在那裡沒看到他。
(B) 是的，他會去。
(C) 我不喜歡派對。

解析 (A) 選項(A)回答了約翰有沒有出現在派對上的「yes-no」問句。選項(B)是未來式，但題目問的是過去的事。選項(C)不能用來回答「yes-no」問句。

27. How many people can fit in the conference room?
    (A) There were many people there.
    (B) At least fifteen, I'm sure.
    (C) Yes, we can sit there.

這間會議室可以容納多少人？
(A) 那裡有很多人。
(B) 至少十五人，我可以確定。
(C) 是的，我們可以坐在那裡。

解析 (B)　「fifteen」回答了「How many」的問題。選項(A)重複使用了many這個字。選項(C)混淆了近音字fit和sit。

28. Don't you have a key to the office?
    (A) No, I've never had one.
    (B) We always lock the door.
    (C) Yes, I can sing on key.

你沒有辦公室的鑰匙嗎？
(A) 沒有，我從來都沒有過一把。
(B) 我們一向會鎖門。
(C) 是的，我唱歌音很準。

解析 (A)　選項(A)回答了關於鑰匙的否定「yes-no」問句。選項(B)使用了key的相關字lock。選項(C)搞錯了key的意義。

29. What are they talking about?
    (A) They're walking in the park.
    (B) They're discussing their plans for the week.
    (C) They're talking in the conference room.

他們在談論什麼？
(A) 他們正在公園裡散步。
(B) 他們正在討論這週的計畫。
(C) 他們正在會議室裡交談。

解析 (B)　選項(B)回答了「What」的問題。選項(A)混淆了近音字talking和walking。選項(C)重複使用了talking這個字，但回答的卻是「Where」的問題。

30. Which office is Sam's?
    (A) He's in his office.
    (B) No, it's not his.
    (C) The one on the left.

    山姆的辦公室是哪一間？
    (A) 他在他的辦公室。
    (B) 不，這不是他的。
    (C) 左邊那間。

解析 (C) 選項(C)回答了「Which」的問題。選項(A)重複使用了 office 這個字。選項(B)回答的是「yes-no」的問題。

31. Why don't we take a walk?
    (A) I'll take two, thanks.
    (B) Great idea. I'll get my coat.
    (C) I'll make it.

    不如我們去散步一下？
    (A) 我要兩個，謝謝。
    (B) 好主意，我去拿外套。
    (C) 我來得及／我做得到。

解析 (B) 選項(B)是對方提議散步時的合理回應。選項(A)重複使用了 take 這個字。選項(C)混淆了近音字 take 和 make。

Part 3：簡短對話

作答方式：你會聽到兩人或多人之間的對話。每段對話搭配三個問題，各有四個選項。選出最適當的答案回答問題，將答案卡上對應的橢圓框塗滿。

Questions 32 through 34 refer to the following conversation.

Man: Good morning. This is Jim Morgan calling about my appointment with Mr. Wilson tomorrow.

Woman: Yes, it's on his calendar for three in the afternoon. Did you want to cancel?

Man: Oh, no. I just wanted to find out how to get there from the subway.

Woman: Nothing easier. Get off at the Green Street station, walk down to the corner, and take a left on Main Street. Our building is on the right, about halfway down the block.

第 32–34 題請聽下面這段對話。

男：早安，我是吉姆・摩根，打電話來是要說明天與威爾森先生預約會面的事。

女：是的，他的行事曆上有寫下午三點，你是想要取消嗎？

男：喔，不是。我只是想問從地鐵站要怎麼到那裡？

女：非常容易的。你在格林街站下車，走到轉角，接著左轉到主街上，我們大樓在右手邊，走到約街區的中段就是了。

32. Why did the man call Mr. Wilson's office? 這名男子為何要打電話到威爾森先生的辦公室？
    (A) To make an appointment 預約會面
    (B) To cancel an appointment 取消會面
    (C) To ask for directions 問路
    (D) To speak with Mr. Wilson 和威爾森先生交談

解析 (C) 男子說他打電話來是要問從地鐵站到辦公室怎麼走。選項 (A) 不正確，男子和威爾森先生已經約好會面了。選項 (B) 是女子問的問題。選項 (D) 重複使用了 Mr. Wilson 這個人名。

33. What does the woman mean when she says, "Nothing easier"? 女子說「Nothing easier」是什麼意思？
   (A) The office isn't close to the subway station. 辦公室離地鐵站沒有很近。
   (B) The streets are pleasant to walk along. 街道走起來很舒適。
   (C) The directions are difficult to explain. 路線方向很難解釋。
   (D) The office isn't hard to find. 辦公室不會很難找。

解析 (D)「Nothing easier」在這裡的意思是「Nothing easier than finding the office」（沒有比找到辦公室更容易的事了），表示它很好找。選項(A)(B)(C)都不是這句話的意思。

34. Where is Mr. Wilson's office? 威爾森先生的辦公室在哪裡？
   (A) On Main Street 主街上
   (B) On Green Street 格林街上
   (C) On the corner 轉角處
   (D) Next to the subway station 地鐵站旁

解析 (A) 根據女子的指示，男子左轉到主街上就會看到辦公室的大樓，所以辦公室在主街上。選項(B)和(C)是女子說明路線時提到的其他地點。選項(D)不正確，男子出了地鐵站還需要走到另一條街上，才會看到辦公室。

Questions 35 through 37 refer to the following conversation.
Woman: We have a very nice room available on the top floor with a wonderful view of the city. It's only three hundred and fifty dollars a night.
Man: Hmm. That's more than I expected to pay. Don't you have anything that would cost a little less? Maybe a smaller room?
Woman: I'm sorry, I don't have anything else available on that date. If you want this one, you should put a deposit down now instead of waiting until later.

第35–37題請聽下面這段對話。
女：我們頂樓有一間很好的房間，可以眺望城市美景，每晚只要350美元。
男：嗯，比我預期的還要高，有沒有便宜一點的？或許小一點的房間？
女：很抱歉，我們那天已經沒有其他空房了。如果您要這間的話，現在就要付訂金了，再晚些就沒了。

35. What is the conversation mainly about? 這段對話主要在談論什麼？
   (A) An apartment 一間公寓
   (B) A plane ticket 一張機票
   (C) A hotel room 一間飯店房間
   (D) An office 一間辦公室

解析 (C) 男子和女子都提到一間房間，女子還說了每晚的價錢，所以應該是在談論飯店的房間。選項(A)(B)(D)都可能需要支付訂金，但比較不會以每晚多少來計算。

36. What is the man's problem about? 男子在意的是什麼問題？
    (A) The view 景觀
    (B) The price 價格
    (C) The size 大小
    (D) The location 位置

解析 (B) 男子說「That's more than I expected to pay」，並問有沒有便宜一點的房間，所以表示他在意的是價格。選項(A)(C)(D)在對話中都有提到，但男子並沒有表達他覺得有什麼問題。

37. What does the woman suggest that the man do? 女子建議男子做什麼？
    (A) Call back later 晚一點再打電話來
    (B) Choose another date 選擇另一天
    (C) Make a payment now 現在就付款
    (D) Look elsewhere 到別的地方去找

解析 (C) 女子建議男子現在就付訂金（put a deposit down now）。選項(A)重複使用了later這個字。選項(B)重複使用了date這個字。選項(D)也有可能，但對話中並沒有提到。

Questions 38 through 40 refer to the following conversation.

Man:　　　I just got my train ticket for my trip next week. I am so looking forward to getting away from it all—the meetings, the reports—and just relaxing.

Woman:　You're not flying? It'll take you forever to get there.

Man:　　　Oh, I don't mind. I'll be on vacation. There's no hurry. And I'm not going far, anyhow.

Woman:　Even so, I wouldn't have the patience.

Man:　　　Well, I like it. The seats are comfortable, and it costs a lot less than flying.

第38-40題請聽下面這段對話。
男：我剛拿到下週旅行的火車票了，真期待擺脫這一切——會議啊，報告啊——然後好好放鬆。
女：你不坐飛機嗎？坐火車到那裡要很久。
男：喔，我不介意，我是要去度假，沒什麼好急的，而且我又沒有要去很遠的地方。
女：就算是這樣，我可沒那個耐心。
男：嗯，我就是喜歡坐火車。座位舒適，而且比坐飛機便宜很多。

38. What is the purpose of the man's trip? 男子這趟旅行的目的是什麼？
    (A) To take a vacation 度假
    (B) To attend a meeting 開會
    (C) To go to a job interview 參加工作面試
    (D) To see a sports event 觀看體育賽事

解析 (A) 男子說他要去度假（I'll be on vacation）。選項(B)重複使用了 meeting 這個字。選項(C)未被提及。選項(D)有可能，但對話中並未提及。

39. How is he traveling? 他會使用何種交通方式？
    (A) By plane 搭飛機
    (B) By train 坐火車
    (C) By car 開車
    (D) By bus 搭公車

解析 (B) 男子說他買了火車票，所以是搭火車。選項(A)混淆了近音字 train 和 plane，同時也被女子提到搭飛機（flying）給混淆。選項(C)混淆了近音字 far 和 car。選項(D)未被提及。

40. What does the woman imply about the man's method of travel? 女子對男子選擇的交通方式有何暗示？
    (A) It's uncomfortable. 不舒適。
    (B) It's expensive. 很昂貴。
    (C) It's boring. 很無聊。
    (D) It's slow. 很慢。

解析 (D) 女子說「It'll take you forever to get there」（要花很長的時間），並且說「I wouldn't have the patience」（我可沒那個耐心），可見她覺得火車很慢。選項(A)和(B)與男子的看法有關但正好相反，他覺得坐火車既舒適又經濟實惠。選項(C)和慢的概念有關，但對話中沒有提到無聊。

Questions 41 through 43 refer to the following conversation.
Woman: You're not wearing that suit tonight, are you?
Man: What's the matter with it? It just came back from the cleaner's, and I think it looks great. Is the fit not right?
Woman: The fit is fine. It's just that it's so serious looking. You're going to a party. You should wear a lighter color, something more cheerful.
Man: I don't agree with your opinion. I like the color, and it makes me look thinner. I think I'll change my tie, though.

第 41–43 題請聽下面這段對話。

女：你晚上該不會要穿那套西裝吧？
男：那套西裝怎麼了嗎？它才剛送洗回來，而且我覺得很好看。是因為不合身嗎？
女：不是不合身，只是看起來好嚴肅，你是要去參加派對，應該穿淺一點的顏色，活潑一點的。
男：我不同意你的看法。我喜歡這個顏色，而且它讓我顯瘦。但我會換條領帶就是了。

41. Where is the man going tonight? 這名男子今晚要去哪裡？
    (A) To a dinner 晚餐聚會
    (B) To a party 派對
    (C) To a meeting 會議
    (D) To the office 辦公室

解析 **(B)** 女子提到男子要去參加派對。選項(A)混淆了近音字 thinner 和 dinner。選項(C)使用了和 suit 有關的 meeting。選項(D)使用了和 suit 有關的 office。

42. Why doesn't the woman like the suit? 女子為什麼不喜歡這套西裝？
    (A) It isn't clean. 不乾淨。
    (B) It is too dark. 顏色太深。
    (C) It doesn't fit. 不合身。
    (D) It has a rip in it. 上面有一道裂縫。

解析 **(B)** 女子說「You should wear a lighter color」，可見她覺得顏色太深。選項(A)使用了 cleaner's 的相關字 clean。選項(C)重複使用了 fit 這個字。選項(D)混淆了近音字 fit 和 rip。

43. What will the man do next? 男子接下來會做什麼？
    (A) Send the suit to the cleaner's 將西裝送洗
    (B) Ask for another opinion 詢問別人的看法
    (C) Change into a new suit 換一套新西裝
    (D) Put on another tie 換一條領帶

解析 **(D)** 男子說「I think I'll change my tie」，所以是換領帶。選項(A)是男子已經做好的事。選項(B)重複使用了 opinion 這個字。選項(C)是女子希望男子做的事，但男子並不願意換西裝。

Questions 44 through 46 refer to the following conversation.

Woman: Some friends and I are playing golf on Saturday morning. You wanna join us? Come on, it'll be fun.
Man: Sorry, I'm working that morning. But I'll be free after lunch.
Woman: Hmmm, we planned to meet at seven, but I don't see why we couldn't play later. I'll call my friends tonight and tell them to meet at two instead.
Man: Thanks. That'd be great. I'll get my clubs out.

第 44–46 題請聽下面這段對話。
女：星期六早上我和幾位朋友要去打高爾夫球，要不要一起來？來嘛！會很好玩的。
男：抱歉，我那天早上要工作，不過午餐過後就有空了。
女：嗯，我們原本計劃七點見面，但晚一點也沒什麼不行。我今晚會打電話給我朋友，跟他們改約下午兩點。
男：謝謝，那就太好了，我去把我的球桿拿出來。

44. What does the woman invite the man to do? 女子邀男子去做什麼？
    (A) Take a walk 散步
    (B) Go to a play 去觀看戲劇
    (C) Play golf 打高爾夫球
    (D) Have lunch 吃午餐

解析 (C) 女子和幾位朋友要去打高爾夫球，邀男子加入他們。選項(A)混淆了近音字 work 和 walk。選項(B)搞錯了 play 的意義。選項(D)重複使用了 lunch 這個字。

45. When does she want to do it? 她想什麼時候去打高爾夫球？
    (A) Sunday 星期天
    (B) Monday 星期一
    (C) Tuesday 星期二
    (D) Saturday 星期六

解析 (D) 女子說星期六早上要去打高爾夫球（. . . are playing golf on Saturday morning）。

46. What will the woman do tonight? 女子今天晚上會做什麼事？
    (A) Change the meeting time 更改見面時間
    (B) Visit her friends 拜訪她的朋友
    (C) Go to bed early 早點睡
    (D) Call the club 打電話到俱樂部

解析 **(A)** 女子今晚會打電話給她朋友，把原定早上七點見面改成下午兩點。選項(B)不正確，因為她會打電話而不是直接拜訪朋友。選項(C)在對話中沒有提及。選項(D)重複使用了call這個字，同時也搞錯了club的意義，男子說的(golf) club是指高爾夫球桿，而不是指俱樂部。

Questions 47 through 49 refer to the following conversation and schedule.

Man: Can you stay late tonight and help me get this report done?
Woman: Sure, but not too late. I have to catch a bus home. How late were you thinking?
Man: I'd say eight thirty at the latest. My assistant can make the copies first thing tomorrow morning.
Woman: OK, that'll give me time to make the last bus leaving from Winwood Street.
Man: Thanks. I wouldn't have to ask you to do this if this office weren't so short staffed.
Woman: That's OK.

第47–49題請聽下面這段對話，並參考時刻表。
男：你今晚能不能留晚一點，幫我完成這份報告。
女：可以啊，但不能太晚，我要趕公車回家。你覺得會到多晚？
男：我想最晚八點半吧，我助理明天一早可以製作影本。
女：好，那樣我還有時間趕上從溫伍德街發車的最後一班車。
男：謝謝。要不是辦公室人手不足，我也不會拜託你做這件事。
女：沒關係。

夜間公車時刻表

溫伍德街發車	到達柏克斯維爾
7:10	8:00
7:40	8:30
8:10	9:00
8:40	9:30

47. What does the man ask the woman to help with? 男子拜託女子幫忙做什麼事？
    (A) Finding a bus schedule 找一份公車時刻表
    (B) Making photocopies 影印
    (C) Finishing a report 完成一份報告
    (D) Reviewing a record 檢視一份紀錄

解析 (C) 男子請女子幫他完成報告（help me get this report done）。選項(A)和女子要趕搭末班車的討論有關。選項(B)不正確，因為男子的助理會負責影印。選項(D)混淆了近音字 report 和 record。

48. What problem does the man mention? 男子提到了什麼問題？
    (A) The photocopier needs replacement. 影印機需要換新。
    (B) The office has too few employees. 辦公室的員工太少。
    (C) The woman usually arrives late. 女子通常都遲到。
    (D) The bus station is too far away. 公車站太遠。

解析 (B) 男子提到辦公室人手不足（short staffed）。選項(A)使用了 copies 的相關字 photocopier。選項(C)重複使用了 late 這個字，對話中是希望女子晚點離開，而不是說她通常都遲到。選項(D)和公車時刻表的討論有關。

49. Look at the graphic. What time will the woman get on the bus? 請看圖表，女子幾點會搭上公車？
    (A) 8：10
    (B) 8：30
    (C) 8：40
    (D) 9：30

解析 (C) 女子說她可以趕上從溫伍德街發車的末班車，根據圖表，末班車是 8：40。選項(A)是倒數第二班車的發車時間。選項(B)是其中一班車抵達柏克斯維爾的時間。選項(D)是末班車抵達目的地柏克斯維爾的時間。

Questions 50 through 52 refer to the following conversation.
Man 1:　　We need to get together to work on the presentation for the Rothman project.
Man 2:　　Right. How about we meet at my office tomorrow at two?
Woman:　　That's no good. I have an appointment then. What about Wednesday morning at nine?
Man 2:　　I can do that. How about you, George? We really have to get going on this.
Man 1:　　Uh huh. Monday's coming up soon. So, yeah, Wednesday morning's fine with me.
Woman:　　All right. Wednesday it is, then.

第 50–52 題請聽下面這段對話。

男1： 我們須要聚在一起討論羅斯曼專案的簡報。
男2： 好，明天下午兩點在我辦公室見面如何？
女： 我不行，我那時有約。星期三早上九點可以嗎？
男2： 我可以，那喬治呢？我們真的要趕快開始進行才行。
男1： 對，星期一快到了。那好吧，星期三早上我也可以。
女： 好，那就星期三了。

50. What are the speakers discussing? 說話者在討論什麼事？
　　(A) A place to meet 見面地點
　　(B) A time to meet 見面時間
　　(C) A client appointment 客戶之約
　　(D) The weekly schedule 每週計畫

解析 (B) 第一個男子說「We need to get together to work on the presentation」，接著他們就開始討論哪一天的幾點來做這件事。選項(A)不正確，說話者很快就對地點達成共識，需要討論的是時間。選項(C)重複使用了appointment這個字，在對話中，女子因為已經有約而無法同意最初提出的時間。選項(D)和各種時間、星期幾的討論有關，但不是討論的重點。

51. What does the woman mean when she says, "That's no good"？女子說「That's no good」是什麼意思？
　　(A) She can't meet at that time. 她無法在那個時間見面。
　　(B) The presentation has problems. 這份簡報有問題。
　　(C) She doesn't like her office. 她不喜歡她的辦公室。
　　(D) The work is too difficult. 這份工作太困難了。

解析 (A)「That's no good」在這裡的意思是「I can't do that」（我辦不到、我不行），女子用這句話回應最初提出的見面時間她無法配合。選項(B)(C)(D)都不是這句話在這裡的意思。

52. What do the men imply about the presentation? 男子們對這份簡報有何暗示？
　　(A) It will be well received by the client. 會獲得客戶的好評。
　　(B) It will take a long time to prepare. 需要很長的時間準備。
　　(C) It is going very well so far. 到目前為止進行順利。
　　(D) It has to be finished soon. 必須盡快完成。

解析 (D) 一名男子說「We really have to get going on this」，意思是「我們要趕快開始做這件事」，另一男子表示同意，並提出完成期限：「Monday's coming up soon」。選項(A)(B)(C)在對話中都沒有提到。

Questions 53 through 55 refer to the following conversation.

Woman: I'd like to get some business cards made for my consulting business—about two hundred and fifty should be enough. Here's my name and address, and can you put this logo on them?

Man: Of course. It's only one color, so that'll be easy. But I should tell you that it'll cost you much less per card if you order five hundred at a time.

Woman: Oh, yes. That makes sense. OK, so five hundred, and I'd like them by Tuesday if at all possible. Please phone me when they're ready for pickup.

第 53–55 題請聽下面這段對話。

女：我想為我的顧問事業製作一些名片——大概兩百五十張就夠了。這是我的名字和地址，你可以在上面放這個標誌嗎？

男：當然可以，因為是單色印刷，所以還滿容易的。但我必須跟您說一下，一次訂購五百張的話，單張成本會比較低。

女：喔，對，那很合理。好吧，那就五百張。如果可以的話，我希望週二之前可以拿到。可取貨時，麻煩打電話通知我一聲。

53. What does the woman want to do? 這名女子想做什麼？
    (A) Buy a new car 買新車
    (B) Mail a package 寄包裹
    (C) Order business cards 訂購名片
    (D) Make an appointment 預約時間

解析 (C) 女子一開始就說「I'd like to get some business cards」，所以是要訂購名片。選項 (A) 混淆了近音字 card 和 car。選項 (B) 使用了 address（女子名片上要放的資訊）的相關字 mail。選項 (D) 使用了 Tuesday（女子希望拿到名片的時間）的相關字 appointment。

54. What does the man recommend? 男子提出什麼建議？
    (A) Increasing the order 增加訂量
    (B) Using only one color 使用單色印刷
    (C) Returning on Tuesday 週二再過來
    (D) Consulting an expert 向專家諮詢

解析 (A) 女子原本想訂兩百五十張，但男子說一次五百張比較省錢。選項 (B) 指的是女子希望在名片上放的標誌，男子描述為單色印刷。選項 (C) 重複使用了 Tuesday 這個字。選項 (D) 和女子的顧問事業有關。

55. What does the woman ask the man to do? 女子要求男子做什麼事？
   (A) Look up an address 查詢一個地址
   (B) Pick up something 取貨
   (C) Make a delivery 送貨
   (D) Call her up 打電話通知她

解析 **(D)** 女子要求男子，當名片可取貨時打電話通知她。選項(A)重複使用了address這個字。選項(B)重複使用了pick up這個片語。選項(C)使用了address的相關字delivery。

Questions 56 through 58 refer to the following conversation.
Man: I'm interested in taking out a loan so I can expand my business. How can I apply?
Woman: OK. So the first thing you need to do is provide some financial information. You can start by filling out these forms.
Man: Wow. That's a lot of paper. Do I really need to complete all those pages? I've had an account here for years, my credit history is excellent, I own my own house. I promise you, I'm a good risk.
Woman: And the information you provide on the forms will show all that.

第56-58題請聽下面這段對話。
男：我有興趣申請貸款，擴展事業用的，我要怎麼申請呢？
女：好的。首先您需要提供一些財務資訊，您可以先填寫這些表格。
男：哇，這表格也太多了。這麼多頁我真的全部都要填寫完嗎？我在這裡開戶很多年了，信用歷史良好，房子也是自有的。我向你保證，貸款給我的風險不大。
女：那麼，您在表格上所提供的資訊，將可以證明一切。

56. Who is the woman? 這名女子是什麼人？
   (A) A bank officer 銀行職員
   (B) A real estate agent 房仲
   (C) A financial advisor 理財顧問
   (D) A business owner 企業老闆

解析 **(A)** 男子想要申請貸款，所以這名女子應該是銀行職員。選項(B)使用了house的相關用語real estate。選項(C)重複使用了financial這個字。選項(D)是男子的身分。

57. What does the man want to do? 這名男子想要做什麼？
    (A) Buy a house 買房
    (B) Borrow money 借錢
    (C) Start a business 創業
    (D) Get a credit card 辦信用卡

解析 (B) 男子說他想申請貸款（taking out a loan），就是借錢。選項(A)重複使用了house這個字。選項(C)不正確，男子已經擁有自己的事業，只是想要擴展事業。選項(D)重複使用了credit這個字。

58. What is the man's complaint? 男子抱怨什麼事？
    (A) The forms are too long. 表格太長。
    (B) The situation is too risky. 情況太有風險。
    (C) He needs more information. 他需要更多資訊。
    (D) His accountant is not available. 他的會計師沒空。

解析 (A) 男子說「That's a lot of paper. Do I really need to complete all those pages?」，抱怨表格太多，不想全部都填完。選項(B)使用了risk的相關字risky，男子說貸款給他的風險很低（I'm a good risk），意思就是他保證會還款。選項(C)重複使用了information這個字。選項(D)使用了account的相關字accountant。

Questions 59 through 61 refer to the following conversation.

Woman 1: What do you think of the company's new parking policy?
Man: You mean the one where we employees will lose our assigned parking spaces and have to pay to park in the lot? I think it's terrible.
Woman 2: Well, I think it's a great idea. It'll encourage more people to use public transportation.
Woman 1: I agree. Traffic in this city just crawls. We need fewer drivers, not more.
Man: Perhaps, but this idea isn't gonna go over with most of the staff. Most people prefer driving their own cars.
Woman 2: Unfortunately, you may be right.

第59–61題請聽下面這段對話。
女1：你覺得公司新的停車政策怎麼樣？
男： 你是說員工不再有指定車位，還得付費停在停車場的政策嗎？我覺得很糟糕。
女2：嗯，我覺得這個想法很好，可以鼓勵更多人使用大眾交通運輸。
女1：我同意。這座城市的交通簡直是龜速，我們需要的是少一點人開車，而不是多一點。
男： 也許吧。但大部分員工應該無法接受這個想法，大多數人還是寧願自己開車。
女2：不幸的是，你可能說對了。

59. What is the new parking policy? 新的停車政策是什麼？
    (A) Employees can't park in the garage. 員工不能把車停在車庫。
    (B) Employees are charged a fee to park. 員工要支付停車費。
    (C) Employees must park in assigned spaces. 員工必須把車停在指定車位。
    (D) Employees aren't allowed to park in the lot. 員工不被允許把車停在停車場。

解析 (B) 男子對停車政策的描述是「the one . . . have to pay to park in the lot」，也就是員工必須付費使用停車場。選項(A)未被提及。選項(C)不正確，該政策取消了員工的指定車位。選項(D)和正確答案相矛盾。

60. Why do the women like the policy? 女子們為何喜歡這個政策？
    (A) Public transportation is quicker. 大眾交通運輸比較快。
    (B) The parking lot is too crowded. 停車場太多車子了。
    (C) Traffic is a problem in the city. 交通是這座城市的一個問題。
    (D) They don't like driving. 她們不喜歡開車。

解析 (C) 兩名女子都同意應該鼓勵大家使用大眾交通運輸，避免開車，因為城市的交通已經慢到龜速的地步了。選項(A)重複使用了 public transportation 這個片語，但對話中沒有提到其是否較快。選項(B)未被提及。選項(D)和停車及開車的討論有關，但對話中沒有提到她們喜不喜歡開車。

61. What does the man mean when he says, "This idea isn't going to go over"? 男子說「This idea isn't going to go over」是什麼意思？
    (A) The parking policy won't be popular. 停車政策不會受到歡迎。
    (B) The parking policy won't get city approval. 停車政策不會獲得市政府核准。
    (C) The parking policy won't be in effect very long. 停車政策不會實施很久。
    (D) The parking policy won't be adopted by other companies. 停車政策不會被其他公司採納。

解析 (A) 一個計畫不會「go over」，就表示不會被喜歡或接受。選項(B)(C)(D)都不是這句話在對話中的意思。

Questions 62 through 64 refer to the following conversation and chart.

Woman: I'm working on next week's luncheon for Ms. Yamamoto.
Man: The rep from the Tokyo office?
Woman: Yes, her visit's really soon. We've decided to use the conference room to serve lunch. It's big enough.
Man: Is this the seating chart? I think you should put Ms. Yamamoto near the door. That way it'll be easier for people to greet her individually.
Woman: I see what you mean. OK, I'll do that.

第 62-64 題請聽下面這段對話,並參考圖表。

女:我正在準備下週為山本女士舉辦的午餐會。

男:東京分公司的代表嗎?

女:對,她很快就要過來參訪。我們決定在會議室供應午餐,那裡空間夠大。

男:這是座位表嗎?我認為你應該把山本女士安排在靠近門的位置,這樣大家比較方便個別和她打招呼。

女:我懂你的意思,好,我會那樣做。

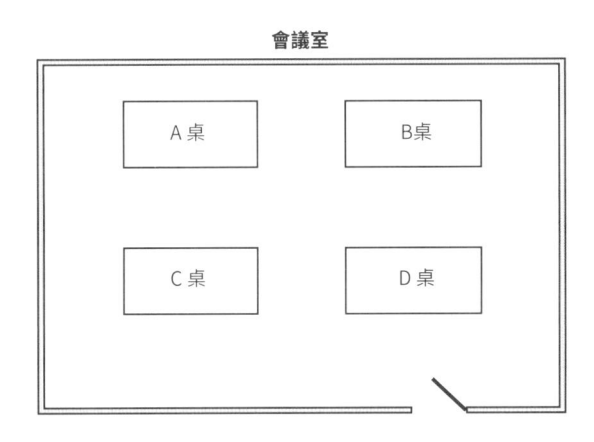

```
            會議室
    ┌──────────────────┐
    │  ┌────┐  ┌────┐  │
    │  │ A桌│  │ B桌│  │
    │  └────┘  └────┘  │
    │                  │
    │  ┌────┐  ┌────┐  │
    │  │ C桌│  │ D桌│  │
    │  └────┘  └────┘  │
    │              ╱   │
    └──────────────────┘
```

62. What is the conversation mainly about? 這段對話主要是關於什麼?
    (A) A luncheon 一場午餐會
    (B) A trip to Tokyo 一趟東京之旅
    (C) A conference 一場會議
    (D) A staff meeting 一場員工會議

解析 (A) 說話者正在討論為東京分公司代表舉辦午餐會的計畫。選項(B)重複使用了Tokyo這個字。選項(C)是被對話中提到的conference room給混淆,會議室是舉辦午餐會的地點。選項(D)混淆了近音字seating和meeting。

63. When will Ms. Yamamoto arrive? 山本女士何時抵達?
    (A) At noon 中午
    (B) At 4:00 四點
    (C) Next week 下週
    (D) In a month 一個月後

解析 (C) 女子提到她正在準備下週為山本女士舉辦的午餐會。選項(A)混淆了近音字soon和noon。選項(B)混淆了近音字door和four。選項(D)未被提及。

539

64. Look at the graphic. Where will Ms. Yamamoto sit?
    請看圖表，山本女士將會坐在哪裡？
    (A) Table A　A桌
    (B) Table B　B桌
    (C) Table C　C桌
    (D) Table D　D桌

解析 (D) 說話者都同意山本女士應坐在靠近門的位置，根據圖表，靠近門的是D桌。選項(A)(B)(C)都不是靠近門的位置。

Questions 65 through 67 refer to the following conversation.
Woman:　So, the carpets in all these rooms should be shampooed, and all the walls need washing.
Man:　　Got it. And the furniture? Do you want us to polish anything?
Woman:　Yes. Please do all the desks and tables. And as far as the hallway goes, just vacuum the carpet.
Man:　　OK. We can have it all done by tomorrow afternoon at five. Will that do?
Woman:　Perfect. We have a big client meeting Thursday morning, so that works perfectly. If you can wait a minute, I'll write you a check for the deposit.

第65–67題請聽下面這段對話。
女：那麼，所有房間的地毯都要清洗，所有牆壁也都要洗。
男：了解。那家具呢？有沒有什麼要我們擦亮的？
女：有的，所有辦公桌和桌子都擦一下。至於走廊，用吸塵器吸一下地毯就好。
男：好的。明天下午五點之前我們可以全部弄好，這樣可以嗎？
女：很完美。我們週四早上有個重要的客戶會議，所以這樣安排很好。請你等一下，我開張訂金支票給你。

65. What is the woman hiring the man to do? 女子僱用男子做什麼事？
    (A) Rearrange furniture 重新擺放家具
    (B) Clean the office 打掃辦公室
    (C) Paint the walls 粉刷牆壁
    (D) Lay a carpet 鋪設地毯

解析 (B) 女子要男子清洗地毯，還要洗牆壁、擦亮桌子，可見是打掃辦公室。選項(A)重複使用了furniture這個字。選項(C)重複使用了walls這個字。選項(D)重複使用了carpet這個字。

66. When will the job be done? 這份工作何時會完成？
   (A) This afternoon 今天下午
   (B) Tomorrow 明天
   (C) Thursday 週四
   (D) Tuesday 週二

解析 (B) 男子說「We can have it all done by tomorrow afternoon at five」，所以是明天。選項(A)重複使用了afternoon這個字。選項(C)是女子要和客戶開會的日子。選項(D)未被提及。

67. What will the woman do now? 這名女子現在要做什麼？
   (A) Check her calendar 查看她的行事曆
   (B) Finish her work 完成她的工作
   (C) Greet a client 迎接一名客戶
   (D) Pay the man 付錢給這名男子

解析 (D) 女子說她要開張支票給男子當作訂金。選項(A)使用了check的另一個意義。選項(B)重複使用了work這個字。選項(C)重複使用了client這個字。

Questions 68 through 70 refer to the following conversation.

Woman: I was wondering how your house hunting was going because I have some ideas for you.
Man: Oh, great! We should get together and talk about it. How about we meet for lunch at the corner café? It's not expensive.
Woman: I don't know. The food there's not bad, but I think some place quieter would be better.
Man: Yeah, you're right. It's not really suited for talking. So why don't you come to my office around noon tomorrow, and I'll order in some food. Then we can eat and chat.

第68–70題請聽下面這段對話。
女：我想知道你房子找得如何了，因為我想給你一些建議。
男：喔，太好了！我們應該聚一聚，好好聊一聊。不如我們去轉角那間咖啡館吃個午餐，怎麼樣？那裡不貴。
女：我不知道。那裡的食物是不難吃，但我覺得找個安靜一點的地方比較好。
男：嗯，你說得對，那裡確實不太適合交談。不然你明天中午到我辦公室，我叫一些外送，然後我們可以邊吃邊聊。

68. What is the man looking for? 這名男子正在找什麼？
    (A) A new job 新工作
    (B) A place to live 住處
    (C) A business suit 商務西裝
    (D) An office to rent 出租辦公室

解析 (B) 女子問男子找房子的事（house hunting），所以他正在找要住的房子。選項(A)和(D)和對話中提及的office有關。選項(C)混淆了suit的意義。

69. What do the speakers imply about the café? 對於那間咖啡館，說話者們有何暗示？
    (A) It's too noisy for conversation. 太吵雜不適合交談。
    (B) The prices are very high. 價格非常高昂。
    (C) The food tastes bad. 食物很難吃。
    (D) It's too far away. 太遠了。

解析 (A) 男子提議去咖啡館時，女子說她想找個比較安靜的地方（some place quieter），而男子也同意，並說「It's not really suited for talking」，可見其不夠安靜，不適合交談。選項(B)不正確，男子說那間咖啡館不貴（It's not expensive）。選項(C)不正確，女子說那裡的食物不難吃（The food there's not bad）。選項(D)在對話中並未提及。

70. What does the man suggest? 男子有什麼建議？
    (A) Taking a walk 去散步
    (B) Going to his house 去他家
    (C) Meeting at his office 在他辦公室見面
    (D) Chatting on the phone 電話上聊

解析 (C) 男子說「So why don't you come to my office around noon tomorrow」，他建議明天中午到他辦公室。選項(A)混淆了近音字talk和walk。選項(B)重複使用了house和going兩個字。選項(D)不正確，男子建議到他辦公室聊，而不是電話上聊。

Part 4：簡短獨白

> 作答方式：你會聽到一名說話者的獨白。每段獨白搭配三個問題，各有四個選項。選出最適當的答案回答問題，並將答案卡上對應的橢圓框塗滿。

Questions 71 through 73 refer to the following introduction.

Good evening. I'm pleased to introduce our special guest, Elizabeth Hines. While Ms. Hines's talents as a novelist are well known, few are aware that she is also an avid world traveler and amateur photographer. Tonight she will speak to us about her recent trip climbing in the Andes Mountains, a setting which has been featured in several of her novels. As part of the program, Ms. Hines will show a fifteen-minute movie which she filmed while in the Andes. This will make our program a little longer than usual, about an hour and a half total, but it will be well worth it, especially as Ms. Hines has assured us that her program includes a book signing at the end. As usual, following the program, coffee, tea, and snacks will be available in the lobby.

第71–73題請聽下面這段介紹。

晚安，很高興向大家介紹我們的特別來賓伊莉莎白・海因斯。海因斯女士作為小說家的才華眾所皆知，但很少人知道她也是熱愛環遊世界的旅行家和業餘攝影師。今晚她要和我們分享最近的安地斯山脈攀登之旅，這座山脈曾是她多部小說的故事背景。在這個活動當中，海因斯女士會播放拍攝於安地斯山脈的十五分鐘影片，因此會比平常略長，總共進行一個半小時左右，但絕對非常值得，特別是海因斯女士向我們保證，活動最後一定會有簽書會。和往常一樣，活動結束後，大廳會供應咖啡、茶和小點心。

71. What will the guest speak about? 這位來賓將談論什麼主題？
    (A) Mountain climbing 登山
    (B) Novel writing 小說寫作
    (C) Photography 攝影
    (D) Sales 銷售

解析 (A) 這位來賓將談論安地斯山脈的攀登之旅。選項(B)和(C)都是她喜愛的事，但不是這次談話的主題。選項(D)未被提及。

72. How long will the program last? 這場活動將會進行多久？
    (A) 15 minutes 十五分鐘
    (B) 50 minutes 五十分鐘
    (C) One hour 一小時
    (D) One and a half hours 一個半小時

解析 **(D)** 說話者提到這場活動總共會進行大約一個半小時（about an hour and a half total）。選項(A)是要播放的影片長度。選項(B)和 15 minutes 的發音相近。選項(C)和正確答案的發音相近。

73. What will happen after the program? 活動後會發生什麼事？
    (A) The speaker will read from her book. 講者會朗讀自己的書。
    (B) There will be a photography exhibit. 會有一場攝影展。
    (C) Refreshments will be served. 會供應茶點。
    (D) Signs will be removed. 會移除告示牌。

解析 **(C)** 說話者說「coffee, tea, and snacks will be available in the lobby」，大廳會供應茶點。選項(A)搞錯了 book signing（簽書）的意思。選項(B)是被來賓的攝影愛好給混淆了。選項(D)混淆了 sign 這個字的意義。

Questions 74 through 76 refer to the following announcement.

Attention all passengers for the six o'clock train to London. We apologize for the short delay in our departure time due to emergency maintenance work on the engine. The train is now ready for boarding. Please approach Gate nine and line up single file. Because of construction in the station, there is no seating in the boarding area. We apologize for the inconvenience. Please have your ticket ready to show the gate agent. Passengers traveling with a group are asked to remain together with their group members during boarding. Tonight's train is very crowded, and there will be no room for extra luggage. Please check any large suitcases at the luggage counter before boarding. Thank you for your cooperation.

第 74-76 題請聽下面這段廣播。

欲搭乘六點整開往倫敦列車的旅客請注意，由於引擎緊急維修，發車時間略有延誤，敬請見諒。本列車現在準備開始登車，請往九號閘門移動，並排成一列。由於車站正在施工，登車區不提供座椅，造成您的不便，敬請見諒。請準備好您的車票，向閘門服務人員出示。團體旅客上車時務必團體行動。本晚列車十分擁擠，沒有空間放置多餘的行李，請在登車前將大型行李箱拿到行李櫃檯辦理托運。感謝您的配合。

74. What was the cause of the delay? 何者是火車延誤的原因？
    (A) An accident 意外事故
    (B) Equipment repair 設備維修
    (C) Crowds on the train 車上人多擁擠
    (D) Construction in the station 車站施工

解析 **(B)** 說話者為火車延誤致歉，且說明是因為引擎緊急維修之故。選項(A)和 emergency 有關。選項(C)和(D)雖然有被提到，但不是造成延誤的原因。

75. What are passengers asked to do now? 乘客被要求現在做什麼？
    (A) Sit in the boarding area 坐在登車區
    (B) Travel with a group 跟團行動
    (C) Buy their tickets 購票
    (D) Line up at the gate 在閘門口排隊

解析 (D) 說話者說「Please approach Gate nine and line up single file」，所以是到閘門口排成一列。選項(A)不可能，登車區正在施工中，不會有座椅。選項(B)和(C)雖然有被提到，但不是乘客被要求做的事。

76. Where should passengers put large suitcases? 乘客應將大型行李箱放在哪裡？
    (A) At the luggage counter 行李櫃檯
    (B) At the gate 閘門口
    (C) In the boarding area 登車區
    (D) Under their seats 座位底下

解析 (A) 說話者要乘客在登車前把大型行李箱拿到行李櫃檯托運。選項(B)(C)(D)雖然都有被提到，但不是放置行李的地方。

Questions 77 through 79 refer to the following talk.

Good afternoon. I hope you all enjoyed that delicious lunch as much as I did. Before we proceed with this afternoon's workshops, you need to be aware of a few minor adjustments to the schedule. The Technology in the Workplace workshop will start at one o'clock instead of one thirty. The Employee Motivation workshop has been postponed until tomorrow morning. Finally, the Best Hiring Practices workshop has been moved from Room C to Room D. There is still room in that workshop, so anyone interested in attending it should visit the registration desk now. And don't forget, this evening's social hour will begin at five thirty in the Terrace Room, as originally scheduled. I wouldn't miss that event. It promises to be a really good time.

第77–79題請聽下面這段談話。

午安，希望大家都和我一樣享受那頓美味的午餐。在我們繼續進行下午的工作坊之前，有幾個時程安排上的小調整要讓大家知道。工作場所技術工作坊將於1點開始，而不是原定的1點30分。員工激勵工作坊將延至明天早上舉行。最後，最佳招聘實務工作坊將從C廳改至D廳舉行。這個工作坊尚有名額，有興趣參加的人請即刻前往報名處。還有別忘了，今晚的社交時間將照原定計畫於5點30分在露臺廳舉行，我不會想錯過這場活動，它一定會是一段美好的時光。

77. What is the purpose of this talk? 這段談話的目的是什麼？
    (A) To explain registration procedures 說明報名程序
    (B) To announce schedule changes 宣布時程上的調整
    (C) To describe a workshop 描述一個工作坊
    (D) To announce lunch 宣布午餐時間

解析 (B) 說話者先是提到「you need to be aware of a few minor adjustments」，接下來的談話幾乎都在描述時程上的調整。選項(A)被談話中提到其中一個工作坊還可以報名給混淆。選項(C)重複使用了 workshop 這個字，但談話中所有的工作坊都只提到名稱，沒有針對細節提供進一步的描述。選項(D)不正確，談話開頭說「I hope you all enjoyed that delicious lunch as much as I did」，表示午餐時間已經結束了。

78. What should people interested in the Best Hiring Practices workshop do? 對最佳招聘實務工作坊有興趣的人，應該做什麼事？
    (A) Wait in the Terrace Room 在露臺廳等候
    (B) Check the schedule 查看時程表
    (C) Register now 即刻報名
    (D) Go to Room C 前往 C 廳

解析 (C) 說話者提到這場工作坊時，說「anyone interested in attending it should visit the registration desk now」，所以是即刻報名。選項(A)是社交時間的舉行地點。選項(B)重複使用了 schedule 這個字。選項(D)不正確，因為這場工作坊已經從 C 廳改到 D 廳了。

79. What does the speaker mean when she says, "I wouldn't miss that event"? 說話者說「I wouldn't miss that event」是什麼意思？
    (A) She doesn't plan to be there. 她不打算出席。
    (B) She wants to go but can't. 她想去但不能去。
    (C) She recommends attending. 她建議大家參加。
    (D) She expects it to be crowded. 她預計會有很多人參加。

解析 (C) 「I wouldn't miss that」常用來推薦某件事、某個活動，表示這件事或活動實在太棒、太精彩了，絕對不能錯過。在這段談話中，說話者建議聽者一定要參加社交時間。選項(A)(B)(D)都不符合這裡的語境。

Questions 80 through 82 refer to the following talk.

Welcome everybody. We will be starting in just a minute so please take your seats now, as no standing is allowed once we get moving. We will pay a brief visit to some historical buildings today before we reach our final destination, the City Art Museum, where you can enjoy a special exhibit on local architecture. Our first stop will be a historical building, which today houses Logan Department store, but which was originally built as a private home. There have been questions regarding who the original designer of the house was, and we will discuss that further as we view the building. We will make one more stop before noon, when we are scheduled for lunch at the Blue Moon Restaurant. Following that, it's on to the museum for a special talk on architecture in the city.

第 80–82 題請聽下面這段談話。

歡迎大家！我們馬上就要開始了，請大家趕快就座，一旦車子開動就不允許站著了。今天，我們會先短暫參觀幾座歷史建築，然後抵達最終目的地城市藝術博物館，在那裡可以欣賞當地建築特展。我們的第一站是一座歷史建築，那裡現在是羅根百貨公司，但最初是建造作為私宅之用。關於這棟房子原本的設計師到底是誰，一直存在疑問，待會在參觀建築時，我們再深入討論。中午之前我們還會再停留一站，中午則安排在藍月餐廳用餐。用餐完畢後，我們就前往博物館，聽一場關於本市建築的特別演講。

80. Where would you hear this talk? 你會在哪裡聽到這段談話？
    (A) On a tour bus 遊覽車上
    (B) At a theater 劇院裡
    (C) At a museum 博物館內
    (D) In a private home 私宅內

解析 (A) 說話者正在向車上的遊客說明遊覽車會載大家到哪些地方。選項 (B) 未被提及。選項 (C) 和 (D) 是他們要參觀的地方。

81. What is everyone asked to do now? 所有人被要求現在做什麼？
    (A) Save questions for later 把問題留到待會再問
    (B) Pay for their tickets 付車票錢
    (C) Stop talking 停止說話
    (D) Sit down 坐下

解析 (D) 說話者說「please take your seats now」，請大家趕快就座。選項 (A) 重複使用了 questions 這個字。選項 (B) 符合談話情境，但並沒有特別提到。選項 (C) 重複使用了談話中的 stop 和 talk 這兩個字。

82. What will happen at noon? 中午會進行什麼事？
   (A) A talk will be heard. 聽一場演講。
   (B) Lunch will be served. 供應午餐。
   (C) A tour will be given. 進行導覽。
   (D) The schedule will be reviewed. 檢視行程。

解析 (B) 說話者說中午安排在藍月餐廳用餐（we are scheduled for lunch at the Blue Moon Restaurant）。選項(A)會在中午午餐過後進行。選項(C)是整段談話的內容。選項(D)是說話者正在做的事。

Questions 83 through 85 refer to the following advertisement.

If you're thinking about starting your own business or are planning to expand an existing business, we at the City National Bank are here to help you. We believe in supporting local businesses and the employment opportunities they provide to our community. Because we want you to be successful, we have established a special Small Business Assistance Program to provide financial assistance to qualifying small businesses. Our officers are ready to help you determine the best type of loan to suit your situation and to get you the money you need to start or grow your business. Find out more about what we have to offer by attending one of our monthly workshops.

第83-85題請聽下面這段廣告。

如果您正在考慮自己創業，或打算擴展既有業務，城市國家銀行竭誠為您服務。我們堅信支持在地企業和其為社區提供之就業機會的價值。我們希望您成功發展，因此建立了一個特別的小型企業援助計畫，為符合條件的小型企業提供財務援助。我們的專員隨時可以協助您決定您的情況最適合哪一種貸款，讓您取得創業或擴展業務所需的資金。歡迎參加我們每月舉辦的工作坊，進一步了解我們所提供的服務。

83. What is being advertised? 這份廣告所要宣傳的是什麼？
   (A) A school 一所學校
   (B) Bank loans 銀行貸款
   (C) An employment agency 一間就業服務機構
   (D) Financial planning services 財務規劃服務

解析 (B) 說話者提到「financial assistance」（財務援助）、「loans」（貸款）、「the money you need to start or grow your business」（創業或擴展業務所需資金），可知宣傳的是銀行貸款。選項(A)是因為廣告中提到workshop（工作坊）而有所混淆。選項(C)重複使用了employment這個字。選項(D)和廣告主題有關，但不是廣告所要宣傳的服務。

84. Who would be interested in this advertisement? 誰會對這則廣告有興趣？
    (A) Small business owners 小企業老闆
    (B) Bank employees 銀行職員
    (C) Business assistants 業務助理
    (D) Police officers 警察

解析 (A) 貸款計畫名為「Small Business Assistance Program」（小型企業援助計畫），此外說話者也提到「We believe in supporting local businesses」（支持在地企業），因此小企業老闆是這則廣告的受眾。選項(B)(C)(D)都重複使用了廣告中的單字。

85. How can someone get more information? 要如何了解更多資訊？
    (A) Make a phone call 打電話
    (B) Visit the office 造訪辦公室
    (C) Take a workshop 參加工作坊
    (D) Read a brochure 閱讀手冊

解析 (C) 說話者提到「Find out more about what we have to offer by attending one of our monthly workshops」，所以是參加工作坊。選項(A)(B)(D)都是可能的方式，但廣告中並未提及。

Questions 86 through 88 refer to the following talk and graphic.

Let's go over the plans for the awards banquet on Saturday. I am especially concerned that we get everything arranged ahead of time because, unfortunately, I will have to miss the dinner part of the evening, and won't arrive until the ceremony begins. So, let's begin by deciding who will be responsible for what. We need a couple of people to arrive at the hotel early, say four o'clock, to check the sound system and make sure the tables and everything are all set up properly. Then, we'll need one or two people to greet guests as they arrive and hand out the programs. OK, let's start with those tasks. Who would like to do what?

第86–88題請聽下面這段談話，並參考圖表。

我們來討論一下週六頒獎宴會的計畫。我特別擔心能不能提前把一切安排好，因為很遺憾，我無法參加當晚的晚餐部分，典禮開始我才會到。那麼，我們就先決定誰負責哪件事開始吧。我們需要幾個人提早到飯店，比方說四點，檢查音響系統和確認桌子和所有物品都擺設妥當。然後，需要有一兩個人在賓客抵達時負責接待，並且發放流程表。好，就先從決定這些任務開始。誰要負責哪個部分？

頒獎宴會
3月17日 —— 溫徹斯特大飯店

社交時間	6：30 - 7：30
晚餐	7：30 - 8：30
頒獎典禮	8：30 - 9：30
音樂與舞蹈時間	9：30 - 11：30

86. What is the purpose of this talk? 這段談話的目的是什麼？
    (A) To organize an event 組織一場活動
    (B) To choose a location 選擇一個地點
    (C) To get ideas for an event 為一個活動蒐集點子
    (D) To decide who will get awards 決定誰能得獎

解析 **(A)** 說話者一開始便說「Let's go over the plans」，接著整段談話都在談有哪些事需要做、由誰來做。選項(B)和(C)不正確，從談話內容我們可判斷這兩件事已經完成了。選項(D)使用了awards這個字，但談話中沒有提到誰會得獎。

87. Look at the graphic. When will the speaker arrive at the banquet? 請看圖表，說話者將於何時抵達宴會？
    (A) 6：30
    (B) 7：30
    (C) 8：30
    (D) 9：30

解析 **(C)** 說話者說她要到典禮開始才會抵達現場，根據流程表，典禮開始的時間是8：30。選項(A)(B)(D)是其他活動的進行時間。

88. What will happen next? 接下來會發生什麼事？
    (A) The speaker will call the hotel. 說話者會打電話到飯店。
    (B) The guests will receive invitations. 賓客會收到邀請函。
    (C) People will volunteer for different jobs. 大家會主動負責不同工作。
    (D) Someone will check the sound system. 有人會檢查音響系統。

解析 **(C)** 說話者描述了需要完成的任務，並以這句話當作結語：「Who would like to do what?」，要大家自己說想負責哪一項工作。選項(A)重複使用了hotel這個字，但談話中沒有提到要打電話到飯店。選項(B)重複使用了guests這個字，但談話中沒有提到要寄邀請函給賓客。選項(D)是其中一項任務，但不是接下來要做的事。

Questions 89 through 91 refer to the following weather report.

Good morning. This is Sam Chen with your morning weather update. I'm happy to report that after these last few days, things are finally looking up. Cloudy skies this morning will clear up by early afternoon with rising temperatures throughout the day. We'll enjoy sunny weather for the rest of the week. Temperatures will remain pleasant through the weekend, but don't forget to bring along that umbrella if you venture out on Saturday as occasional showers are expected in the afternoon and evening. Sunday will be clear, but colder.

第89–91題請聽下面這段氣象報告。

早安，我是山姆・陳，為您帶來最新晨間氣象報告。很高興告訴大家，經過了這幾天，天氣終於要好轉了。今天早上的多雲天空到了下午稍早就會放晴，全天氣溫將逐漸回升。本週接下來幾天都是晴朗的好天氣。週末依舊維持舒適宜人的氣溫，不過週六下午和晚上有短暫陣雨，外出別忘了帶雨傘。週日天氣晴朗，氣溫則略低。

89. What does the speaker mean when he says, "Things are finally looking up"？說話者說「Things are finally looking up」是什麼意思？
    (A) His predictions are based on research. 他的預測是根據研究所做出的。
    (B) Temperatures were higher yesterday. 昨天的氣溫較高。
    (C) The condition of the sky is changing. 天空狀況正在改變。
    (D) The bad weather is now improving. 壞天氣現在有所好轉。

解析 (D)「things are looking up」的意思是「事情有所好轉」。說話者說完這句話，接著描述天空放晴、氣溫回升，都是天氣好轉的描述。選項(A)使用了look up的另一個意義「研究」。選項(B)和(C)從up聯想到higher和sky。

90. What will the weather be like today? 今天天氣如何？
    (A) It will be rainy. 會下雨。
    (B) It will cool down. 會降溫。
    (C) It will get warmer. 會回暖。
    (D) It will get cloudier. 雲層更厚。

解析 (C) 說話者說氣溫會回升（rising temperatures）。選項(A)是週六的天氣。選項(B)是週日的天氣。選項(D)和說話者的描述恰好相反，他說多雲的天空會放晴（Cloudy skies this morning will clear up）。

91. What does the speaker suggest listeners do on Saturday? 說話者建議聽者星期六做什麼？
    (A) Carry an umbrella in case of rain 攜帶雨傘以防下雨
    (B) Dress for cold temperatures 穿著適合低溫天氣的衣服
    (C) Go out to enjoy the weather 出門享受好天氣
    (D) Notice the spring flowers 注意欣賞春天的花朵

解析 (A) 說話者說「bring along that umbrella if you venture out on Saturday as occasional showers are expected」，所以是提醒大家帶傘，因為會有短暫陣雨。選項(B)是被週日的低溫描述給混淆了。選項(C)重複使用了 enjoy 和 out 兩個字。選項(D)混淆了近音字 showers 和 flowers。

Questions 92 through 94 refer to the following telephone message.

Good afternoon. This is Rosa Merton calling, assistant to your accountant, Joe Roberts. Mr. Roberts wants you to know that he has finished reviewing the financial statement you provided and has some ideas and concerns he'd like to discuss with you this week, if possible. He's free Thursday afternoon, if you could come to his office at three o'clock. If that time doesn't suit you, please suggest a time this week or next when you could meet with Mr. Roberts. My number at the office is four-oh-five-two-three-four-nine. Thank you. We look forward to working with you.

第 92–94 題請聽下面這段電話留言。

午安，我是羅莎・墨頓，您的會計師喬・羅伯茲的助理。羅伯茲先生想讓您知道，他已經看完您所提供的財務報表，如果可以的話，他有些想法和顧慮希望能在本週與您討論。他星期四下午有空，如果您能在三點到他辦公室的話。如果那個時間您不方便，可以提出這週或下週方便與羅伯茲先生見面的時間。我的辦公室電話是 405-2349，謝謝，我們期待與您合作。

92. Who is Joe Roberts? 喬・羅伯茲是誰？
    (A) A banker 一名銀行家
    (B) A doctor 一名醫生
    (C) An assistant 一名助理
    (D) An accountant 一名會計師

解析 (D) 說話者表示自己是會計師喬・羅伯茲的助理，因此喬・羅伯茲是會計師。選項(A)和留言中提到 financial statement（財務報表）有關。選項(B)和約時間的主題有關。選項(C)是說話者本人的身分。

552

93. What is the purpose of the message? 這通留言的目的是什麼？
    (A) To ask for information 詢問資訊
    (B) To explain a procedure 說明流程
    (C) To make an appointment 約見面時間
    (D) To change an appointment 更改約定時間

   解析 (C) 說話者表示羅伯茲先生想和聽者見面，並提出了一個日子和時間。選項(A)和(B)雖然也有可能，但在留言中並未提及。選項(D)不可能，因為留言中沒有提到之前已有預約會面時間。

94. What does the speaker want the listener to do? 說話者希望聽者做什麼？
    (A) Return the call 回電
    (B) Explain some concerns 說明一些顧慮
    (C) Provide an office address 提供一個辦公室地址
    (D) Submit a financial statement 繳交一份財務報表

   解析 (A) 說話者想知道聽者何時方便和羅伯茲先生見面，並留下了自己的電話號碼，等待對方回電。選項(B)是羅伯茲先生約見面的目的。選項(C)重複使用了office這個字。選項(D)是已經做過的事。

Questions 95 through 97 refer to the following announcement and graphic.

May I have your attention please? A blue, woolen lady's jacket has been found on the floor in the Track ten waiting area. If you believe this item belongs to you, please come to the station manager's office to identify and claim it. The office is located across from the ticket counter. We remind passengers that we cannot be responsible for personal property. Please keep an eye on your belongings at all times. Any found items can be turned into the manager's office at any time. Thank you for your cooperation.

第95–97題請聽下面這段廣播，並參考圖表。

各位旅客請注意，有民眾在第十月臺候車區地上拾獲一件藍色的羊毛女用外套，如果這是您所遺失的物品，請至站長室認領。站長室位於售票櫃檯對面。提醒旅客，我們不對個人財產負責，請隨時留意個人物品。如有拾獲物品，可隨時交到站長室。謝謝您的合作。

蒙特羅斯車站平面圖

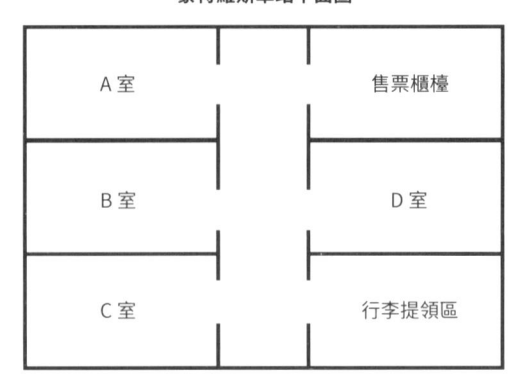

A 室		售票櫃檯
B 室		D 室
C 室		行李提領區

95. What has been found? 什麼物品被拾獲？
    (A) A large package 一個大包裹
    (B) A piece of clothing 一件衣服
    (C) A train ticket 一張火車票
    (D) A blue bag 一個藍色袋子

解析 (B) 被拾獲的物品是一件外套，也就是衣服。選項(A)混淆了近音字 jacket 和 package。選項(C)重複使用了 ticket 這個字。選項(D)重複使用了 blue 這個字。

96. Where was it found? 物品是在哪裡拾獲的？
    (A) On the track 軌道上
    (B) By a door 門邊
    (C) In a waiting room 候車區內
    (D) Outside the station 車站外

解析 (C) 說話者說物品是在第十月臺的候車區（Track ten waiting area）拾獲的。選項(A)重複使用了 track 這個字。選項(B)混淆了近音字 floor 和 door。選項(D)不正確，我們可以合理推斷候車區位於站內，而不是站外。

97. Look at the graphic. Where is the station manager's office? 請看圖表，站長室位於哪裡？
    (A) Room A A室
    (B) Room B B室
    (C) Room C C室
    (D) Room D D室

解析 (A) 說話者提到站長室位於售票櫃檯的對面，對照圖表是 A 室。選項(B)(C)(D)都與描述不符。

554

Questions 98 through 100 refer to the following announcement.

Attention shoppers. Don't miss today's special discount in the produce section. All fruit is being offered at twenty percent off. That's right. For today only you can save twenty percent on apples, bananas, oranges, on all fruit in our produce section. So check it out. You can't beat savings like that. Take advantage while you can because the sale ends at closing time this evening, and we'll change back to regular prices tomorrow. We offer special sales every Friday, so don't forget to come back next week to take advantage of our special weekly discount.

第 98–100 題請聽下面這段廣播。

各位顧客請注意！農產品區本日進行特價活動，千萬不要錯過。水果全面八折。是的！購買蔬果區的所有水果，蘋果、香蕉、柳橙等等，全面享有八折優惠，只限今日！趕快過去看看，沒有如此好康的優惠了。促銷只到今晚營業時間結束，明天就會調回原價，趁現在把握機會。我們每逢週五就會推出促銷活動，別忘了下週回來以享有每週一次的特價優惠！

98. Where would you hear this announcement? 你會在哪裡聽到這段廣播？
    (A) At a farm 一座農場
    (B) At a bank 一間銀行
    (C) At a clothing store 一間服飾店
    (D) At a grocery store 一間超市

解析 (D) 促銷活動區域是「蔬果區」（produce section，農產品區就包含蔬菜水果區），所以這裡是超市。選項(A)把fruit和farm聯想在一起了。選項(B)把savings和bank聯想在一起了。選項(C)混淆了近音字closing和clothing。

99. How long will the special offer last? 特價活動將持續多久？
    (A) One day 一天
    (B) Two days 兩天
    (C) All week 整週
    (D) Until Tuesday 直到星期二

解析 (A) 廣播中說促銷活動僅限今日（For today only）。選項(B)和(D)把today和發音相近的two days、Tuesday互相混淆了。選項(C)重複使用了week這個字。

555

100. What does the speaker suggest shoppers do? 說話者建議購物者做什麼事？
    (A) Write a check 開支票
    (B) Return next week 下週再來
    (C) Count their change 數一下找錢
    (D) Go to the checkout counter 前往結帳櫃檯

解析 (B) 說話者要大家下週回來（come back next week）才能享有每週一次的促銷活動。選項(A)搞錯了check的意義。選項(C)搞錯了change的意義。選項(D)搞錯了checkout的意義。

STOP 本測驗之聽力測驗到此結束，請翻頁進行Part 5的測驗。

閱讀測驗

在本段測驗當中，你將有機會展現自己對書面英語的理解能力。閱讀測驗共有三個大題，每一大題均有作答說明。

你有 75 分鐘時間完成本測驗的第五到第七大題。

Part 5：句子填空

> 作答方式：你會看到一個缺字的句子和四個可能的選項，選出最適當的答案，將答案卡上對應的橢圓框塗滿。

101. 電腦培訓工作坊將於四月的第一週開始報名。
    (A)(B)(C)(D) 開始

解析 (B) begins是第三人稱單數現在式，和主詞registration一致。選項(A)和(D)與主詞不一致。選項(C)是動名詞或現在分詞，不能當作句子的動詞。

102. 科普羅公司昨日宣布，於該公司服務十五年後，普莉希拉‧柏金斯已辭去財務長一職。
    (A) 承包、承辦
    (B) 辭職
    (C) 解散、解僱
    (D) 撤退

解析 (B) resign是「辭職」的意思。選項(A)(C)(D)帶入句中都與文意不符。

103. 如果你無法參加下週的員工會議，你有責任告知你的主管。
    (A) 如果
    (B) 所以
    (C) 然後、於是
    (D) 但是

解析 (A) if用來帶出一個條件。選項(B)帶出一個結果。選項(C)用來表示時間順序，或帶出某個條件之下的結果。選項(D)帶出一個矛盾事實。

104. 除非公司願意討論加薪事宜，否則明年我不打算和公司續約。
    (A) 訂閱
    (B) 申明、堅稱、證實
    (C) 續（約／期／訂）
    (D) 僱用

解析 (C) renew有「繼續、延展」的意思，renew a contract就是「續約」。選項(A)(B)(D)都與文意不符。

105. 雙方必須簽署協議，專案才能繼續進行。
    (A)(B)(C)(D) 簽署

解析 (D) 主詞 agreement 是動作的承受者，不是執行者，因此要用被動語態。選項(A)(B)是主動語態。選項(C)是不定詞。

106. 辦公室經理決定買一臺新的印表機給行銷部使用，另外再買一臺給前辦公室使用。
    (A) 兩者任一
    (B) 任一
    (C) 另一個
    (D) 這個

解析 (C) another 在句中作代名詞，指 another printer。空格處需要一個名詞或代名詞，當作動詞 buy 的受詞。選項(A)和(B)不是代名詞。選項(D)可作代名詞，但放入此處意思不通。

107. 由於這一帶的租金日益高漲，巔峰超市考慮搬到城市的另一區。
    (A) 由於
    (B) 反而
    (C) 儘管
    (D) 因為

解析 (A) because of 帶出一個原因。選項(B)用來帶出一個替代做法。選項(C)用來帶出一個矛盾事實，且不能與 of 搭配使用。選項(D)用來帶出一個原因，但不能與 of 搭配使用，需使用介系詞 to 才可以。

108. 員工計劃五點時在大廳集合，辦一場小型派對來慶祝瑪莎退休。
    (A) 加入
    (B) 聚集
    (C) 參加
    (D) 結合

解析 (B) gather 是「聚集」的意思，可作不及物動詞（後面不加受詞，如這句的用法）。選項(A)和(C)是及物動詞，後面必須要有受詞。選項(D)放入後與文意不符。

109. 把工作交給主管之前，每次都應該仔細檢查。
    (A)(B)(C)(D) 檢查

解析 (A) 情態動詞 should 後面要接原形動詞 review。選項(B)(C)(D)都不是原形動詞。

110. 董事們期望能在本週結束前收到客戶的回覆。

解析 (C) 介系詞 from 可表示某個事物「從……來、來自……」，在這裡表示來自客戶的回覆（answer from the client）。

111. 現在若能穩健投資於改善生產設備，未來幾年將能看到利潤成長。
(A) 投資 (v.)
(B) 投資者
(C) 授予、授職儀式
(D) 投資 (n.)

解析 (D) investment 是名詞，指付出金錢以求未來獲利。選項(A)是動詞。選項(B)是名詞，但指人。選項(C)是名詞，但意義完全不同，不適用於這個句子。

112. 燃料成本上漲促使許多公司為其設備尋找替代能源。
(A) 渴望
(B) 預期
(C) 促使
(D) 產生

解析 (C) motivate 的意思是促使某人想要做某事。選項(A)(B)(D)都與文意不符。

113. 公司網站刊登的一則廣告，吸引了數百人應徵這個職缺。

解析 (B) result 搭配的介系詞是 in，形成動詞片語 result in，表示導致某一個結果。選項(A)和(D)都不能接在 result 的後面使用。選項(C)所構成的 result of 意思為戰績、比賽結果，與此句文意不符。

114. 上個月的商務會議出席率偏低，主要是因為該地區天候不佳所致。
(A) 主要地
(B) 幾乎
(C) 因為
(D) 通常

解析 (A) largely 的意思是「主要地」（= mostly）。選項(B)(C)(D)都與文意不符。

115. 根據經濟預測專家的說法，下一季運輸成本可能大幅增加。
(A) 喜歡 (v.)、相像的 (adj.)
(B) 很可能的
(C) 可愛的
(D) 不喜歡

解析 (B) likely 是形容詞，意思是「很可能的」。選項(A)作形容詞時指「相像的」。選項(C)的意思是「可愛的」或「討人喜歡的」。選項(D)是動詞。

116. 做最終決定之前，你應該花時間和同事討論這個問題。
    (A)(B)(C)(D) 做出（某個舉動）

解析 (C) before 的後面要接動名詞。選項(A)(B)(D)都不是動名詞。

117. 這是一個兼職職位，但需要能上晚班，偶爾週末也要能加班。
    (A) 利用、有用、有益
    (B) 利用 (ving)
    (C) 有空的、可用的
    (D) 有空、可用性

解析 (D) availability 是名詞，在這個句子中當作動詞 requires 的受詞。選項(A)是動詞。選項(B)是動名詞。選項(C)是形容詞。

118. 今年公司有一絲微小的機會加薪，但可能性不大。
    (A) 微小的
    (B) 正常的
    (C) 好的
    (D) 巨大的

解析 (A) slight 的意思是「非常小」。選項(B)(C)(D)都與文意不符。

119. 雖然我們已經在工廠僱用了幾名新的工人，還是無法達成每週的配額。
    (A) 由於
    (B) 在……之後
    (C) 雖然
    (D) 因此

解析 (C) although 用來帶出一個矛盾事實。選項(A)用來帶出一個原因。選項(B)用來描述接下來的事件。選項(D)帶出一個結果。

120. 由於太少人出席，董事會議被迫在最後一刻取消。
    (A) 繳交
    (B) 出現、出席
    (C) 支持、待命
    (D) 接管

解析 (B) show up 的意思是「出現、出席」。選項(A)(C)(D)都與文意不符。

121. 若我們想控制在預算之內，就需要在幾個方面節省開銷。
　　(A) 經濟
　　(B) 節省、節約
　　(C) 經濟學家
　　(D) 經濟學

解析 (B) economize是動詞，在這個句子中搭配to構成不定詞，接在主要動詞need的後面。選項(A)(C)(D)都是名詞。

122. 有人向我們保證，工作坊的主講人絕對是國際金融方面的專家。
　　(A) 他／她（們）、……的人（主格）
　　(B) 他／她（們）、……的人（受格）
　　(C) 他／她／它（們）的
　　(D) 這個、這些

解析 (A) who是主格關係代名詞，其先行詞為person。選項(B)是受格關係代名詞。選項(C)是所有格。選項(D)作關係代名詞時，指物不指人。

123. 如果你接受了其他公司的工作，請盡快通知人事主管。
　　(A) 表示、表明
　　(B) 作證
　　(C) 通知
　　(D) 使……有尊嚴

解析 (C) notify的意思是「通知」。選項(A)(B)(D)都與文意不符。

124. 大家都在等著知道新合約是否已經達成協議。
　　(A)(B)(C)(D) 等待

解析 (C) 主詞everybody是單數，要用單數動詞is waiting以維持一致。選項(A)(B)(D)都必須搭配複數主詞。

125. 你不需要接受最初開出的薪資條件，因為幾乎都是可以協商的。
　　(A) 談判、協商 (v.)
　　(B) 談判、協商 (n.)
　　(C) 談判者、協商者
　　(D) 可談判的、可協商的

解析 (D) negotiable是形容詞，修飾名詞offer。選項(A)是動詞。選項(B)和(C)都是名詞。

126. 如果我有在時程表上看到那個工作坊，我就會報名參加了。
　　　(A)(B)(C)(D) 看到

解析 (B) 這是一個與過去事實相反的非真實條件句，if子句要用過去完成式。選項(A)是過去簡單式。選項(C)是與現在事實相反條件句的主要子句句型。選項(D)可用於與過去事實相反的條件句，但必須用於主要子句。

127. 該部門除了漢默史密斯先生以外，全都出席了昨晚的頒獎宴會。
　　　(A) 期待、預期
　　　(B) 接受
　　　(C) 除了……以外
　　　(D) 口音

解析 (C) except的意思是「除了……以外」。選項(A)(B)(D)都與文意不符。

128. 我們選擇這臺影印機，是因為它比要換掉的那臺快得多。
　　　(A) 快的
　　　(B) 更快的
　　　(C) 最快的
　　　(D) 比……更快

解析 (D) faster than是形容詞的比較級用法，這裡是兩臺影印機互相比較，因此要用比較級。選項(A)不是比較級。選項(B)少了than。選項(C)是最高級。

129. 索托女士希望你今天下午五點之前給她回電。
　　　(A) 她（受格）
　　　(B) 她（主格）
　　　(C) 她的
　　　(D) 她自己

解析 (A) her是受格代名詞，在這個句子作動詞call的受詞。選項(B)是主格代名詞。選項(C)是所有格代名詞。選項(D)是反身代名詞。

130. 我們要求設計師提供幾個選項，好讓我們選出最適合的一個。
　　　(A) 選擇 (v.)
　　　(B) 有選擇的
　　　(C) 有選擇地
　　　(D) 選擇、選項

解析 (A) 情態動詞could後面要用原形動詞select。選項(B)是形容詞。選項(C)是副詞。選項(D)是名詞。

Part 6：段落填空

作答方式：你會看到四篇短文，各含四個空格，每個空格配有四個選項，選出最適當的單字、片語或句子完成這段敘述。

第131–134題請看下面這封電子郵件。

收件者：「史蒂文斯・丹」
寄件者：「馬克斯頓・菲爾」
日期：　6月12日
主旨：　訂閱單變更

我們的電子郵件發送名單有問題，問題不在名單本身，而是人們要如何才能加入訂閱。我們的訂閱單被埋在網頁最底下，根本不可能找到。我們必須讓大家更容易訂閱，其中一個做法是把訂閱單移至首頁。進行這項變更的同時，我想稍微編輯一下表單。表單上有五個問題，必須全部回答才能送出。我覺得這個應改成選擇性──只有姓名和電子郵件欄位必填。

我們明天討論一下這個問題，你有空到我辦公室來一趟。

菲爾

131. (A) 它的
　　　(B) 它是
　　　(C) 它本身
　　　(D) 它的自我

解析 (C) itself是反身代名詞，用來強調其先行詞list。選項(A)是所有格代名詞或所有格形容詞。選項(B)是 it is 的縮寫。選項(D)是分開的兩個字，不是正確的反身代名詞形式。

132. (A)(B)(C)(D) 讓、使

解析 (B) 動詞 need 後面要接不定詞。選項(A)是原形動詞。選項(C)是動名詞。選項(D)是未來式動詞。

133. (A) 其中一個做法是把訂閱單移至首頁。
    (B) 大多數人不介意花幾分鐘完成表單。
    (C) 訂閱人數增加的速度超乎我們預期。
    (D) 我們的電子報廣受歡迎。

解析 (A) 前一個句子表示需要讓訂閱變得容易，選項(A)的句子接著提出一個可能的做法。選項(B)(C)(D)都和加入電子郵件名單的主題有關，但不適合放在此處。

134. (A) 一個
    (B) 一個
    (C) 這個
    (D) 這個

解析 (C) 定冠詞the用來表示已經確定的事物，讀者知道這裡的姓名和電子郵件欄位是指訂閱單上的姓名和電子郵件欄位。選項(A)和(B)是不定冠詞，且只能用於單數名詞。選項(D)也只能用於單數名詞。

第135–138題請看下面這則通知。

搬家工人須知

雖然將家具從客戶家抬起搬到搬家貨車上，通常是我們最快的做法，我要請搬家工人盡可能也考慮以推的方式移動家具，這樣可以降低你的受傷風險並節省體力。請使用手推車來搬運成堆的箱子和底座牢固的家具，或在重型家具底下墊一張硬紙板，方便在地上滑動。無論你選擇哪一種方式，請記得不要把泥土踩進客戶家裡，也不可損壞客戶的貴重物品。

---

135. (A) 他們的
    (B) 她的
    (C) 他的
    (D) 我們的

解析 (D) our指在這家搬家公司上班的人，包括這張通知的撰寫人。選項(A)(B)(C)所指的團體或個人，要麼不包括本通知的撰寫人，要麼不包括讀件人。

136. (A) 速度和效率是本公司的優先考量。
　　 (B) 這樣可以降低你的受傷風險並節省體力。
　　 (C) 這份工作要求具備抬重物的能力。
　　 (D) 我們對造成客戶財產任何損害均有完整保險。

解析 (B) 這句話合理解釋為何要搬家工人用推的而不要用抬的搬動家具。選項(A)(C)(D)都與前後文語意不連貫。

137. (A) 牢固的、堅固的
　　 (B) 牢固地、堅固地
　　 (C) 鞏固、凝固
　　 (D) 堅固、堅硬

解析 (A) solid是形容詞，修飾名詞base。選項(B)是副詞。選項(C)是動詞。選項(D)是名詞。

138. (A) 無論如何、不管用什麼方法
　　 (B) 無論什麼時候
　　 (C) 無論哪個／哪些
　　 (D) 無論誰

解析 (C) whichever表示在兩個或多個事物中選擇一個，在這個句子中，是在不同的方式當中選擇一個方式。選項(A)指做事情的方式。選項(B)指時間。選項(D)指人。

第139–142題請看下面這封信。

湯普森女士，您好：

我們已經收到您的求職申請和履歷，感謝您有興趣加入艾密特公司與我們一起工作。很遺憾，我們目前沒有適合您條件的職缺。不過，我們會將您的資料存檔，一旦有合適的職位，我們會和您聯絡。若六個月內沒收到我們的通知，請重新送出履歷。在此期間，若您有任何疑問，請聯繫我們的人力資源經理賈西亞女士。

再次感謝您對本公司的興趣。

敬祝 順利
米歇爾‧布德羅

---

139. (A) 要求
    (B) 請求
    (C) 申請
    (D) 請願

解析 (C) job application（求職申請）是藉由提交個人資料來求職的過程。選項(A)(B)(D)的意義都和索討東西有關，但用在這裡並不正確。

140. (A) 空出
    (B) 空缺的
    (C) 空缺
    (D) 空出 (ved)

解析 (B) vacant是形容詞，修飾名詞positions。選項(A)和(D)是動詞。選項(C)是名詞。

141. (A) 然而、不過
    (B) 當……的時候
    (C) 只要
    (D) 即使

解析 (A) however用來帶出一個對比事實，意義和用法類似於but——目前沒有職缺，但是（but）他們會將應徵者的資料保留。選項(B)(C)(D)都不適用於這個句子。

142. (A) 請在本週打電話給我的助理約時間。
    (B) 我們正在尋找具備和您相同受訓經歷和背景的人。
    (C) 求職申請表可在我們網站的徵才頁面上找到。
    (D) 若六個月內沒收到我們的通知，請重新送出履歷。

解析 (D) 前面說明了目前沒有職缺，接著以這個句子邀請應徵者過一段時間後重新申請。選項(A)不合邏輯，既然目前沒有職缺，就沒有理由約時間。選項(B)和前面的敘述互相矛盾。選項(C)和這封信毫無關聯，因為求職申請的動作已經完成了。

第 143–146 題請看下面這封電子郵件。

寄件者：凡妮莎・霍爾登
收件者：部門全體員工
主旨：　下週不在辦公室
副本：　凱爾・羅傑斯

下週我要到羅馬開會，一整週都不在辦公室。我不在時，我的助理凱爾・羅傑斯會負責處理我的所有信件。任何我不在時可能產生的問題，他也可以協助處理。我知道你們有些人想和我見面討論年度考核的事，等我開完會回來，我很樂意和你們討論。我回來後的那週就會有空，可以約時間會面。

凡妮莎・霍爾登

143. (A) 任期
　　 (B) 不在、缺席
　　 (C) 追求
　　 (D) 訂婚

解析 (B) absence 指不在一個地方，在這封郵件中，撰寫者表示她下週不在辦公室。選項(A)(C)(D) 都與文意不符。

144. (A)(B)(C)(D) 幫助

解析 (C) 形容詞 available 後面要接不定詞。選項(A)是未來式。選項(B)是「助動詞 + 動詞」的結構。選項(D)是原形動詞。

145. (A) 查看
　　 (B) 回來
　　 (C) 發現、出現
　　 (D) 繳交

解析 (B) get back 的意思是「回來」。其他選項放入句中意思都不通。

568

146. (A) 考核結果下週就會準備好供你們查閱。
    (B) 開完會後我打算去觀光一下。
    (C) 會議上將有許多值得參加的工作坊。
    (D) 我回來後的那週就會有空,可以約時間會面。

解析 (D) 在前一個句子中,電子郵件的寫作者提到大家可能會想和她見面,這個句子接著說有空、可以約時間,語意是連貫且合乎邏輯的。選項(A)(B)(C)和郵件中提到的其他事情有關,如開會、考核,但都不適合放在這個位置。

Part 7：閱讀測驗

> **作答方式**：你會看到單篇或多篇文章的題組，文章後面配有幾個題目，各含四個選項。選出最適當的答案回答問題，將答案卡上對應的橢圓框塗滿。

第 147–148 題請看下面這則廣告。

求職者請注意

本地區各大企業每天都在聘用電腦程式設計師。

你也可能成為其中一員。

報名城市大學電腦學院，
展開電腦程式設計師的嶄新職涯。

短短兩年就能完成課程。

有日間、夜間和週末班可供選擇。

還在等什麼？

現在就打電話詢問
如何成為電腦程式設計師。

● 高中畢業生皆可報名參加。
● 無需過往經驗！

---

147. 這則廣告宣傳的是什麼？
    (A) 一個職缺
    (B) 一個培訓課程
    (C) 一間職業介紹所
    (D) 一家電腦程式設計公司

解析 (B) 這則廣告宣傳的是大學裡的電腦程式設計培訓課程。選項 (A) 和 (C) 是被廣告標題中的 job seekers（求職者）給混淆了。選項 (D) 被電腦程式設計的培訓課程給誤導，但廣告明顯是在講學校而不是公司。

148. 哪一項是要求條件?
　　(A) 大學學位
　　(B) 電腦培訓
　　(C) 過往經驗
　　(D) 高中文憑

解析 (D) 廣告中提到該課程開放給高中畢業生。選項(A)被課程的開設地點——城市大學——給混淆了。選項(B)是課程內容。選項(C)是廣告明言不需要的條件。

第149–150題請看下面這段簡訊對話串。

潘・斯柏 我真的很喜歡這場會議,展示的內容太精彩了。	10:45
凱・諾達 你和布魯斯見面談得如何?	10:46
潘・斯柏 還不錯,我們在咖啡館喝咖啡,聊了好一會。	10:46
潘・斯柏 我還沒離開,而且正在喝第二杯咖啡了。你還在財務工作坊嗎?	10:47
凱・諾達 是產品推廣工作坊,才剛結束。	10:48
潘・斯柏 你接下來要去哪裡?	10:50
凱・諾達 銷售研討會。要幫你做筆記嗎?	10:50
潘・斯柏 不用,幫我占位子就好。	10:52
凱・諾達 我會的。	10:55

實戰模擬試題 5

149. 斯柏女士現在人在哪裡？
    (A) 一場會議
    (B) 一間咖啡館
    (C) 一個工作坊
    (D) 一個展場

解析 **(B)** 斯柏女士描述她和別人在咖啡館談事情，接著寫說「I'm still here」，所以她人還在咖啡館。選項(A)和(C)是對話中提到的地方。

150. 在 10：52 時，斯柏女士說「Just save me a seat」是什麼意思？
    (A) 她正在前往會議途中。
    (B) 她會在咖啡館等朋友。
    (C) 她正要回到展場。
    (D) 她會參加銷售研討會。

解析 **(D)** 諾達先生接下來要參加銷售研討會，斯柏女士表示要去那裡找他，請他幫忙占位子。選項(A)(B)(C)都和語境不符。

第 151–152 題請看下面這張優惠券。

折價 15 美元
下次購買潘威爾公司的指定辦公用品
滿 100 美元可享此優惠。
購買墨水、碳粉、紙張另享免運。

優惠碼：POS 97865

使用期限：4 月 30 日

今天就到 www.pennwelloffice.com 參觀選購
或來電 800-123-4567 訂購。

潘威爾公司是印表機、影印機、辦公家具
及其他必備辦公用品之領導供應商。

---

151. 這張優惠券適用於哪些產品？
    (A) 潘威爾公司的任何產品
    (B) 僅限辦公家具
    (C) 100美元以上的購物
    (D) 僅限印表機和影印機

解析 (C) 優惠券上寫說「purchase of $100 or more」，所以是消費滿 100 美元可使用。選項 (A) 不正確，優惠券有提到指定商品（select products）才能使用，select 的意思是「指定的」(= designated)。選項 (B) 和 (D) 不正確，優惠券上面還提到了其他產品，如墨水、紙張等。

152. 要怎樣做才能享有折扣優惠？
    (A) 於 4 月 30 日前購物
    (B) 網路購物
    (C) 電話購物
    (D) 購買至少 15 美元的產品

解析 (A) 這張優惠券的使用期限是 4 月 30 日。選項 (B) 和 (C) 混淆了優惠券上的聯絡資訊。選項 (D) 是可折抵的金額。

第 153–154 題請看下面這張發貨單。

發貨單

史密斯菲爾德廚房用品
為餐廳及辦公室提供用品超過五十年！

訂單編號：40291　　　　　　　　　　　　　　　　訂單日期：4 月 10 日

您的客服代表：潘蜜拉・瓊斯
感謝您的訂購，請保留此發貨單以備查核。

收貨地址：	帳單地址：
馬克・吉爾曼	修伯特餐飲集團
園屋餐廳	收件人：麗塔・史波福德
新罕布夏州格林斯伯勒南街 85 號	麻薩諸塞州哈德遜貝爾特大道 74 號

產品	數量	單價	總價
克林格豪華咖啡機	1	$250	$250
克林格麵包機	1	$425	$425
延長保固	0		$0
		運費	$35
		快速到貨加收運費	$20
		營業稅	$30
		合計	$760

訂單收到後請立即付款。

153. 誰會付款這筆發貨單？
　　　(A) 馬克・吉爾曼
　　　(B) 潘蜜拉・瓊斯
　　　(C) 園屋餐廳
　　　(D) 修伯特餐飲集團

解析 (D) 帳單地址寫的是修伯特餐飲集團（Hubert Restaurant Group）。選項(A)是收貨人。選項(B)是客服代表。選項(C)是這批貨要送去的地方。

154. 發貨單上有一筆20美元是什麼費用？
　　　(A) 假日及週末配送
　　　(B) 快速到貨
　　　(C) 重型物品運送
　　　(D) 特殊包裝

解析 (B) 這筆費用是快速（expedited）運送的費用。選項(A)(C)(D)也有可能加收費用，但不是此處的情況。

第 155–157 題請看下面這張表單。

多徹斯特塔
承租申請書

姓名　霍華德・丹恩斯
地址　俄亥俄州溫斯堡福德漢路 113 號

公寓類型

_____ 工作室　　× 一房　　_____ 兩房　　_____ 三房

入住人數　2
希望入住日期　11 月 15 日

申請費　　　　　　　　　　　　　　$100
首月租金＊　　　　　　　　　　　　$800
押金　　　　　　　　　　　　　　　$600

簽訂租約時應付總額　　　　　　　　$1500

所有公寓皆於入住前進行清潔、重新粉刷和鋪設新地毯。租約終止時，將視公寓檢查情況決定是否退還押金。如有疑問或修繕要求，請以電話或電子郵件聯繫大樓管理者：

麥可・李
548-9982
michaell@redbird.com

＊租金不含停車費。車庫提供少量收費車位，詳情請洽管理者。

---

155. 這張表單的目的是什麼？
　　(A) 請求修繕
　　(B) 付款
　　(C) 申請一間公寓
　　(D) 告知租約終止

解析 **(C)** 這張申請表提到了入住日期（move-in date）、租金（rent）、租約（lease）等，所以是申請一間公寓的表單。選項 (A)(B)(D) 都使用了表單中的單字，但皆不是這張表單的目的。

156. 一房的公寓月租是多少？
    (A) $100
    (B) $600
    (C) $800
    (D) $1500

解析 **(C)** 表單上顯示申請人第一個月的租金是$800，此即月租費。選項(A)是申請費。選項(B)是押金。選項(D)是簽約時總共要付的金額。

157. 所有公寓都附有什麼？
    (A) 車位
    (B) 修繕服務
    (C) 電話
    (D) 新地毯

解析 **(D)** 表中指出所有公寓都會在入住之前鋪設新地毯。選項(A)和(B)是承租人可以提出的要求。選項(C)混淆了表中可以聯絡大樓管理者的方式之一。

158–160題請看下面這個網頁。

www.snowymtn.com/summerpackages
檔案　編輯　檢視　收藏項目　工具　說明　　頁面▼　安全性▼　工具▼
雪山 今夏歡迎前來雪山度假村 不再只是來滑雪而已 歡迎闔家同遊，體驗趣味活動： 在我們的私人湖泊中游泳、駕帆船、釣魚 在我們綿延數英里的步道上健行、騎登山自行車 在我們世界級的球道上打高爾夫球 使用網球場、攀岩牆及設備完善的健身中心 在我們的餐廳露臺上享受放鬆的夜晚，大啖國際受訓主廚為您準備的美味佳餚。 七月和八月期間，歡迎利用我們的家庭套裝行程特惠方案。價格包含一房（最多入住四人）、一日每人一餐，並可無限次數使用度假村所有設施。 點此查看可訂房型及房價。 點此預訂。 須於來訪前三十天預訂，才能享有家庭套裝行程優惠，且須至少住宿一週。

158. 關於雪山度假村,文中有何暗示?
    (A) 素來以滑雪勝地聞名。
    (B) 只有夏天開放。
    (C) 擁有豪華住宿設施。
    (D) 比其他度假村便宜。

解析 (A) 文中提到「It's not just for skiing anymore」,表示不再只是來滑雪而已了,可見大多數人都把這裡視為滑雪勝地,而現在他們要推出新的活動了。選項(B)不正確,既然這裡是滑雪勝地,冬天肯定會開放。選項(C)不正確,文中沒有提到住宿設施的品質。選項(D)不正確,文中沒有和其他度假村比較價格。

159. 下列哪一項「不是」度假村提供的活動?
    (A) 用餐
    (B) 騎自行車
    (C) 水上運動
    (D) 騎馬

解析 (D) 文中完全沒提到騎馬活動。選項(A)指的是文中提到的餐廳和主廚製作的佳餚。選項(B)是文中提到的騎登山自行車。選項(C)指的是游泳、駕帆船和釣魚活動。

160. 什麼時候預訂才能享有特惠?
    (A) 一週前
    (B) 一個月前
    (C) 七月或八月
    (D) 任何時候

解析 (B) 文中表示「Reservations must be made 30 days in advance of your visit」,必須在三十天前預訂,即一個月前。選項(A)是最少的住宿時長。選項(C)是可享有特惠的月份。選項(D)和正確答案相抵觸。

第 161–163 題請看下面這篇文章。

> 經常全球旅行的商務人士一定都經歷過俗稱時差的現象。人體有「生理時鐘」——以二十四小時為週期所遵循的睡眠與甦醒模式。當我們到了不同的時區，這個模式會被打亂。到新地方的前幾天，我們可能發現自己半夜還醒著，或者下午卻睡著了。幸好，有些做法可以讓我們在適應期過得更舒適一些。
>
> 這個過程從出發前就開始了。首先，預訂傍晚抵達目的地的航班。一上飛機馬上把手錶調成目的地的時間，這可以幫助你心理上更快調適。抵達後，至少撐到當地時間十點以後再睡覺。睡前避免攝取咖啡因、大量進食或劇烈運動，因這些活動會讓你無論多累都睡不著。
>
> 最後，盡可能多到戶外呼吸新鮮空氣、多曬太陽，接觸陽光可以幫助你的生理時鐘調整到新時區。反之，待在室內則會加劇時差的影響。

161. 這篇文章主要在談論什麼？
 (A) 旅行中如何維持健康
 (B) 如何適應新時區
 (C) 如何讓搭機更加舒適
 (D) 如何規劃商務旅行

解析 (B) 這篇文章談論如何調整睡眠模式以適應新時區。選項(A)指的是文中提到的大量進食、運動、攝取咖啡因這些事，但談論這些的目的只是為了管理睡眠，而不是維持整體健康。選項(C)與時差和搭飛機等描述有關。選項(D)指的是這篇文章的語境——商務旅行，但文中關於旅行的規劃也只談到管理睡眠模式而已。

162. 文中建議做哪件事？
 (A) 十點前起床
 (B) 十點前避免進食
 (C) 十點或更晚上床睡覺
 (D) 十點前抵達目的地

解析 (C) 這篇文章建議至少撐到當地時間十點再上床睡覺（stay up until at least 10:00 local time）。選項(A)(B)(D)雖然都提到十點，但文中沒有建議做這些事。

163. 根據這篇文章,哪一項活動可以幫助你睡得更好?
    (A) 到戶外去
    (B) 避免曬太陽
    (C) 充足的運動量
    (D) 調整用餐時間

解析 (A) 這篇文章建議多到戶外呼吸新鮮空氣、多曬太陽(spend as much time as possible in the fresh air and sunshine)。選項(B)和建議做法恰好相反。選項(C)混淆了避免睡前劇烈運動的描述。選項(D)混淆了避免睡前大量進食的描述。

第164–167題請看下面這封信。

羅傑斯、米爾頓與柯爾律師事務所
莫頓斯伯格柳樹大道17號

20—年5月10日

敬啟者:

這封信是關於艾蜜莉雅・史帕克小姐,她是羅傑斯、米爾頓與柯爾律師事務所的前員工。史帕克小姐大學畢業不久便在本公司擔任實習生,並於實習結束後獲聘為全職法律助理。–[1]– 同時她也繼續在大學修課,據我了解,她的目的是將來攻讀更高學位。–[2]–

史帕克小姐不僅為人可靠、工作勤奮,在辦公室也總是待人親切、樂於助人。–[3]– 這些特質在史帕克小姐與客戶打交道時格外有幫助。事實上,客戶經常特別指定要與她合作。–[4]–

上個月史帕克小姐離開本公司,失去史帕克小姐,我們雖然深感遺憾,但也祝她搬到紐約的決定和未來事業發展均圓滿成功。我們知道無論她到哪一間公司,都會是該公司的重要人才資產。若需了解更多資訊,請隨時與我聯繫。

順頌商祺
史蒂分・柯爾
史蒂分・柯爾

164. 史帕克女士將使用這封信來做什麼？
    (A) 僱用某個人
    (B) 應徵新工作
    (C) 爭取新客戶
    (D) 申請大學

解析 (B) 這是一封推薦信，所以是用來應徵工作的。選項(A)是收信者會利用這封信來做的事。選項(C)和(D)重複使用了信中出現過的單字。

165. 史帕克女士從事何種職業？
    (A) 法律
    (B) 教育
    (C) 會計
    (D) 商業

解析 (A) 史帕克女士的前一個職位是法律助理（legal assistant），因此她從事的是法律相關職業。選項(B)和信中提到大學（university）有關。選項(C)和(D)未被提及。

166. 史帕克女士為何離職？
    (A) 她被解僱。
    (B) 她生病。
    (C) 她搬到新城市。
    (D) 她重返校園。

解析 (C) 最後一段提到史帕克女士搬到紐約的決定（her decision to move to New York），可見是搬到新城市。選項(A)和(B)都是離職的可能原因，但信中沒有提到。選項(D)不正確，史帕克女士已從大學畢業，文中只提到她在工作的同時仍有持續修課。

167. 下面這個句子最適合放入文中[1][2][3][4]哪一個位置？
    「她在這個職位上工作認真，證明自己總是渴望學習，願意付出一切時間和努力完成專案。」
    (A) [1]
    (B) [2]
    (C) [3]
    (D) [4]

解析 (A) that job 指的是前一句提到的 legal assistant。選項(B)(C)(D)放入這個句子語意都不通。

第 168–171 題請看下面這篇文章。

洛克威爾開發集團今日宣布一項提案，將在賓徹斯特外郊靠近十號公路處建造一座複合式建築。提案中的建築包含一千平方公尺的辦公空間、五萬平方公尺的零售空間、一座室內停車場，以及數公頃的戶外停車場。

外界對這項宣布的反應不一。賓徹斯特市議員稱其為推動地方經濟的一大助力。「這項建設會帶來工作機會，人們會到這裡來消費，還有什麼比這更好的？」市議員蜜莉安・霍吉斯表示。然而地方商家卻不這麼認為。「它的地點只會打擊我們的生意。」賓徹斯特企業持有人協會會長比爾・史密瑟斯說。「你看它和市中心商圈的距離，大家開車沿十號公路過來，可能會在購物中心停留，但是就不會多開幾英里到我們這些在地店家消費了。」環保團體也對這項提案表示反對。「除了摧毀好幾英畝的寶貴農地之外，從人行道溢流的水會汙染當地溪流，破壞自然棲地。」

洛克威爾開發集團的發言人駁斥了這些反對意見，表示：「這項開發計畫已經規劃了五年，我們取得了所有必要的許可，也嚴格遵守政府規定。一旦完工，這項計畫將成為賓徹斯特最大的資產。我們預計在年底之前動工。」建設工程將耗時近兩年。

168. 這篇文章主要在談論什麼？
(A) 地方商業法規
(B) 一間購物中心的盛大開幕
(C) 商店和辦公室的建造計畫
(D) 市中心商圈的復甦

解析 (C) 這篇文章談論建造一座複合式建築的提案（a proposal for a mixed-use complex），這座建築會包含辦公室（office）和零售（retail）空間。選項(A)和文章主題有關，但不是主題。選項(B)的mall和文中的retail space有關，但沒有盛大開幕這件事，因為還沒開始建造。選項(D)和文中提到的downtown shopping district有關，但沒有提到復甦的事。

169. 哪一項是外界對這項計畫的抱怨？
(A) 規模太大。
(B) 會破壞農地。
(C) 太靠近市中心。
(D) 會產生停車問題。

解析 (B) 環保團體反對這項計畫，認為會摧毀數英畝的寶貴農地（destroying acres of valuable agricultural land）。選項(A)和文中對計畫規模的描述有關，但沒有人對此提出抱怨。選項(C)和商家的擔憂正好相反，他們認為新建築距離他們商店太遠，很難把生意帶過來。選項(D)和文中提到停車有關，但沒有說會產生問題。

581

170. 蜜莉安・霍吉斯是誰？
    (A) 一名政治人物
    (B) 一位購物者
    (B) 一名建商
    (C) 一個零售商

解析 (A) 霍吉斯女士是市議會的議員（City Council member），所以是政治人物。選項(B)和(D)和文中提到零售空間（retail space）有關。選項(C)指的是洛克威爾開發集團。

171. 這項計畫何時動工？
    (A) 12月31日前
    (B) 明年一月
    (C) 兩年後
    (D) 五年後

解析 (A) 洛克威爾開發集團的發言人表示他們會在年底之前動工（break ground before the end of the year），break ground 就是「動工」。選項(B)是明年初。選項(C)是建設工程所需的總時間。選項(D)是該計畫所耗費的規劃時間。

第 172–175 題請看下面這段線上聊天對話串。

葛雷格・山薩 我是行銷部的葛雷格，我們下個星期三要為新聘員工舉辦一個培訓工作坊，我想預訂3號會議室。我上網查了使用時間表，那天整個早上都沒人使用。	2:15
布蘭卡・懷特 抱歉，那間會議室已經預定給一個客戶會議了。我有點落後沒更新時間表，所以還沒放上去。	2:20
葛雷格・山薩 我不知道該怎麼辦了，只有3號會議室夠大。	2:23
布蘭卡・懷特 2號會議室呢？我記得星期三早上沒有人使用。	2:25
葛雷格・山薩 那間的燈光很差，我都看不清楚自己在寫什麼。	2:27
布蘭卡・懷特 對，我們很快就會處理。	2:29
布蘭卡・懷特 你預計會有多少人參加？	2:30
葛雷格・山薩 至少二十人。	2:33
布蘭卡・懷特 那你可以用4號會議室，我相信那裡可以輕鬆容納二十個人。	2:35
葛雷格・山薩 也許吧。但工作坊會進行一整個上午，休息時間會需要一些空間供應茶點。	2:39
布蘭卡・懷特 大樓那一區的大廳很寬敞，我可以請人把茶點擺在門外，這樣你們裡面就會有更多空間。	2:43
葛雷格・山薩 那樣行得通嗎？	2:45
布蘭卡・懷特 我覺得肯定可以。要不我們五分鐘後那裡見，我讓你看一下我們會把桌子擺在哪裡，還有我們可以怎麼安排一切。	2:48
葛雷格・山薩 太好了，謝謝！	2:50

172. 山薩先生要用這間會議室來做什麼？
    (A) 辦午餐會
    (B) 辦培訓課程
    (C) 和客戶開會
    (D) 面試應徵者

解析 **(B)** 山薩先生要預訂一間會議室，為新聘員工舉辦培訓工作坊。選項(A)被茶點的描述混淆。選項(C)是別人預訂這間會議室的用途。選項(D)混淆了job applicants（應徵者）和new hires（新聘員工）。

173. 在2:20時，懷特女士說「I haven't put it up yet」是什麼意思？
    (A) 她還沒把那間會議室準備好供開會之用。
    (B) 她還沒確定哪些會議室是空的。
    (C) 她還沒製作那週的使用時間表。
    (D) 她還沒把3號會議室已被預訂的訊息放上去。

解析 **(D)** 懷特女士還沒把3號會議室已被預訂的訊息放到網路的時間表上，以至於山薩先生不知道會議室已被預訂。選項(A)(B)(C)都和對話的內容不符。

174. 2號會議室有什麼問題？
    (A) 已被別人預訂。
    (B) 正在修繕中。
    (C) 太小。
    (D) 太暗。

解析 **(D)** 山薩先生描述2號會議室說「The lighting in there is terrible. I can never see what I'm writing.」（燈光太差，寫什麼都看不清楚）。選項(A)不正確，因為懷特女士建議山薩先生預訂這一間，所以不可能已被預訂。選項(B)是懷特女士表示之後會做的事。選項(C)和山薩先生擔心會議室不夠大有關，但對話中沒有提到2號會議室的大小。

175. 懷特女士接下來會做什麼？
    (A) 去找一些桌子
    (B) 更新使用時間表
    (C) 和山薩先生在4號會議室碰面
    (D) 準備茶點

解析 **(C)** 懷特女士提議五分鐘後和山薩先生碰面，讓他看一下4號會議室的茶點桌會怎麼安排。選項(A)(B)(D)是未來某個時間點懷特女士可能會去做的事，但她沒說現在就要做。

第 176–180 題請看下面的電子郵件和調查表。

收件者：伊莉莎白・西蒙斯
寄件者：羅斯蒙特飯店
主旨：　住客滿意度調查

西蒙斯女士，您好：

感謝您於到訪史普林菲爾德市期間，選擇入住羅斯蒙特飯店。

請自以下連結進入我們的住客滿意度調查表。我們誠邀您撥冗填寫調查表，這將使我們能為您提供在羅斯蒙特飯店的最佳住宿體驗。請點此連結填寫調查表。由於此調查乃由第三方機構進行，我們無法直接回覆您的意見回饋，敬請見諒。

希望您在羅斯蒙特飯店的住宿愉快，我們期待很快再次與您相見。如有帳單或未來住宿需求協助，請與以下負責人員聯繫：

帳單查詢——裴瑞茲先生：rperez@rosemounthotel.com
未來住宿查詢——李小姐：klee@rosemounthotel.com

如不希望繼續收到羅斯蒙特飯店的電子郵件，請點此連結取消訂閱。

再次感謝您！

哈洛德・克斯特　羅斯蒙特飯店

羅斯蒙特飯店
住客滿意度調查

請評價飯店工作人員：

	非常好	好	普通	差
專業態度	×			
專業形象	×			
當地知識		×		
住宿辦理速度			×	

請評價您的房間：

	非常好	好	普通	差
清潔度	×			
床的舒適度	×			
燈光	×			
網路連線	×			

請評價健身中心＊：

	非常好	好	普通	差
清潔度				
設備選擇				
設備狀況				

如果您在住宿期間遇到任何問題，請描述於此：
我等了好幾分鐘才有人來為我辦理住宿手續。然後那位服務員操作刷卡機時又出了問題。還有一件事，我想使用健身中心，但我到那邊時（晚上十點），已經關門了。

意見：
我對羅斯蒙特飯店的住宿非常滿意，這次來是為了和客戶開會，但希望很快可以帶家人來這裡觀光。

您的姓名：伊莉莎白・西蒙斯
住宿日期：4月10–11日

＊如未使用健身房，此項可不填。

176. 這封電子郵件的目的是什麼？
　　(A) 要求回饋意見
　　(B) 說明一張帳單
　　(C) 宣傳這間飯店
　　(D) 確認訂房

解析 (A) 這封電子郵件要求飯店住客填寫一份住客滿意度調查表（Guest Satisfaction Survey）。選項(B)(C)(D)都和飯店的業務有關，但不是這封郵件的目的。

177. 什麼事情需要聯絡李小姐？
    (A) 詢問帳單事宜
    (B) 提交調查表
    (C) 預訂飯店
    (D) 取消訂閱

解析 (C) 電子郵件中說，未來住宿查詢（future stay inquiries）可以聯絡李小姐，future stay inquiries 指的就是未來規劃入住飯店。選項(A)必須聯絡裴瑞茲先生。選項(B)和(D)要點擊網路連結來辦理。

178. 西蒙斯女士覺得飯店哪方面有問題？
    (A) 房價
    (B) 床的舒適度
    (C) 房間的清潔度
    (D) 住宿手續

解析 (D) 在調查表中，西蒙斯女士描述了辦理住宿手續時的問題，check in 就等於 registration。選項(A)未被提及。選項(B)和(C)都被她評價為「非常好」（Excellent）。

179. 西蒙斯女士為什麼沒有使用健身中心？
    (A) 關門了。
    (B) 不乾淨。
    (C) 她從不運動。
    (D) 設備狀況很差。

解析 (A) 西蒙斯女士描述「but by the time I got there (10：00 p.m.), it was closed」，她到健身中心時已經關門了。選項(B)和(D)是她沒有評價的項目，因為她沒使用。選項(C)不正確，她說了她想使用健身中心。

180. 西蒙斯女士此次前來史普林菲爾德市的目的是什麼？
    (A) 家庭旅行
    (B) 商務會議
    (C) 觀光之旅
    (D) 一場會議

解析 (B) 西蒙斯女士指出此行的目的是一場客戶會議（client meeting）。選項(A)和(C)是她未來的打算。選項(D)未被提及。

587

第181-185題請看下面的時程表和電子郵件。

企業持有人協會
第十屆年會
豪力斯頓大飯店

會議時程表

8:30-9:45　　　　　歐陸式早餐（主大廳）

10:00-12:00　　　　工作坊（第一場）
　　　　　　　　　A：籌措企業資金（花園廳）
　　　　　　　　　B：數位時代行銷（第3廳）

12:15-1:15　　　　　午餐（餐廳）

1:30-3:30　　　　　工作坊（第二場）
　　　　　　　　　C：小型企業招聘實務（第2廳）
　　　　　　　　　D：人員培訓（中層樓）

4:00-5:00　　　　　社交時間（主大廳）

收件者：鮑伯・舒馬赫
寄件者：安妮・坎普
日期：　11月10日
主旨：　企業持有人協會會議

嗨，鮑伯：

我附上你要求的會議時程表了。我真的非常期待，尤其這是我第一年以非講者的身分參加。少了那個壓力，我終於有機會可以好好享受會議的精彩內容。

我希望那天可以找時間聚一聚，我想利用這個機會和你討論一筆擴展業務用的貸款。如果這件事你能給我一些建議，我會非常感謝，畢竟你在這方面的經驗豐富，對我想合作的貸款機構也有經驗。同時我知道你活躍於當地的財務教育工作者協會，也許可以幫我引介更多資源。我打算參加A場和C場的工作坊，不知道這兩場你有沒有要參加其中哪一場，但我們應該另外找時間聚聚，才有機會好好聊一下。我中午要和一位同事開會，不會參加大會安排的午餐。但社交時間如何呢？我們約好在那裡見面吧。

安妮

181. 這場會議是為誰而舉辦的？
    (A) 行銷專家
    (B) 企業持有人
    (C) 人事經理
    (D) 放款人

解析 (B) 會議時程表的標題為 BOA，即為 Business Owner's Association（企業持有人協會），且工作坊各場次的主題都和企業經營有關。選項(A)(C)(D)是特定工作坊的主題，但不是整場會議的主題。

182. 坎普女士為什麼要寫信給舒馬赫先生？
    (A) 邀請他參加會議
    (B) 告訴他由她主講的一場工作坊
    (C) 約時間和他見面
    (D) 建議他參加哪些工作坊

解析 (C) 在電子郵件第二段的開頭，坎普女士寫說「I hope we can get together sometime during the day」，表示想找時間聚一聚，接下來的內容都在討論如何安排這件事。選項(A)不正確，舒馬赫先生早就計劃要參加會議。選項(B)不正確，第一段她就提到自己不是以講者的身分出席。選項(D)不正確，坎普女士有提到自己要參加的工作坊，但她沒有給舒馬赫先生建議。

183. 1點30分時，坎普女士會在哪裡？
    (A) 主大廳
    (B) 餐廳
    (C) 第2廳
    (D) 中層樓

解析 (C) 坎普女士說她會參加C場工作坊，而C場的時間是1:30在第2廳。選項(A)(B)(D)是其他場工作坊的舉辦地點。

184. 電子郵件第二段第四行的active這個字，意義與下列何者最接近？
    (A) 忙碌的
    (B) 準備好的
    (C) 精力充沛的
    (D) 參與在內的

解析 (D) 由於舒馬赫先生參與了當地的財務教育工作者協會，坎普女士認為他可能知道一些對她貸款有幫助的資源。選項(A)(B)(C)是active的其他意義，但都不是這個字在這裡的意義。

589

185. 坎普女士想和舒馬赫先生討論什麼事？
　　(A) 借錢一事
　　(B) 主講一場工作坊
　　(C) 組織這場會議
　　(D) 安排社交時間

解析 **(A)** 電子郵件中坎普女士提到想與舒馬赫先生討論一筆貸款事宜。選項(B)(C)(D)都重複使用了電子郵件中的單字，但不是正確答案。

第186-190題請看下面的時程表、報紙公告和電子郵件。

朵萊頓150週年國慶慶祝活動
活動時程表
週六

手工藝博覽會
時間：全日　　　　　　　　　　　　　　　　地點：朵萊頓公園，橡樹步道
一邊享受本市著名老橡樹的林蔭，一邊採購出自地方、國內與國際工匠的手工製品。

歷史展覽
時間：上午10點至晚上7點　　　　　　　　地點：歷史博物館
帶著全家一起來參觀國慶特展，地點就在全新整修的歷史博物館。還有特別為小朋友舉辦的手作活動和電影欣賞。

國際美食節
時間：中午至晚上8點　　　　　　　　　　地點：主街和楓樹街
漫步於主街和楓樹街的街道，品嘗來自世界各地的美饌佳餚。

足球賽
時間：晚上6點　　　　　　　　　　　　　　地點：朵萊頓高中足球場
觀賞地方球隊爭奪夢寐以求的國慶獎杯。

音樂會
時間：晚上8點30分　　　　　　　　　　　地點：朵萊頓公園，東側草地
在星光下放鬆身心，欣賞地方樂團帶來的音樂演出。

公告
國慶慶祝活動

由於天氣預報不佳，市議會宣布本週末的國慶慶祝活動將有幾項變更。所有戶外活動全部取消，除夜間音樂會照常舉行，地點改為朵萊頓劇院。如同其他週末活動，音樂會為免費參加，然而座位有限，須事先取得門票。預約門票請洽城市藝術委員會。所有室內活動照常舉行。

收件者：patr@ztown.com
寄件者：timrogers@river.com
日期：　6月11日
主旨：　朵萊頓之行

嗨，派特：

謝謝你推薦我去參加朵萊頓國慶慶祝活動，雖然天氣不好，我還是玩得很開心。我想你應該有聽說那場暴風雨。總之，還是有很多慶祝活動順利進行了。錯過美食節我實在太遺憾了，不過也許明年還有機會。那天早些時候我看了歷史展覽，然後還很幸運拿到音樂會的票，實在太精彩了。下星期見面我會再詳細跟你說。

提姆

186. 關於這場慶祝活動，哪一項敘述「不」正確？
(A) 一年舉辦一次。
(B) 內含體育活動。
(C) 須付費參加。
(D) 是個歷史悠久的傳統。

解析 (C) 公告中提到「Like all the weekend's events, there is no charge for the concert」，表示所有活動都是免費。選項(A)是正確描述，活動時程表描述這場慶祝活動為「annual」，即「一年一度的」。選項(B)是正確描述，因為時程表上有一項活動是足球賽。選項(D)是正確描述，因為這是150週年的慶祝活動了。

187. 哪一項活動是專門為小孩子舉辦的？
　　　(A) 電影播放
　　　(B) 手工藝品販售
　　　(C) 國際美食
　　　(D) 主街散步

解析 **(A)** 根據活動時程表，歷史展覽的說明中提到有給小朋友（little ones = children）看的電影（film = movie）。選項(B)(C)(D)都是慶祝活動，但沒有提到是特別為小朋友舉辦的。

188. 提姆為什麼沒有參加美食節？
　　　(A) 美食節被取消了。
　　　(B) 他不餓。
　　　(C) 他身體不舒服。
　　　(D) 那天時間還太早。

解析 **(A)** 提姆想參加這個活動，但根據公告內容，大部分的戶外活動都因天候不佳而取消，對照活動時程表可以知道美食節屬於戶外活動，因此被取消。選項(B)(C)(D)雖然都有可能導致他沒參加活動，但都不是此處的正確原因。

189. 提姆晚上在什麼地方？
　　　(A) 公園
　　　(B) 劇院
　　　(C) 博物館
　　　(D) 足球賽

解析 **(B)** 提姆參加了晚上舉行的音樂會，地點從原本的戶外改至劇院。選項(A)是音樂會原定舉行的地方。選項(C)是提姆那天早些時候（early in the day）所在的地方。選項(D)不正確，因為所有戶外活動都取消了。

190. 電子郵件第五行的 account 這個字，意義與下列何者最為接近？
　　　(A) 帳單
　　　(B) 金錢
　　　(C) 描述
　　　(D) 原因

解析 **(C)** 提姆的意思是他們見面時，他會詳細跟派特描述當天的慶祝活動。選項(A)(B)(D)是 account 的其他意義，但都不是這個字在此處的意義。

第 191–195 題請看下面的廣告、評論和文章。

歡迎蒞臨新開的
直奔餐酒館
本月來店出示優惠券可享優惠。

直奔餐酒館 ***** 買一送一優惠 ***** 晚餐菜單任選兩道主菜，只收一道的價格。 優惠期限：3月31日 每人限用一張	直奔餐酒館 ***** 免費甜點 ***** 午餐任選一道主菜，即贈一份甜點。 優惠期限：3月31日 每人限用一張
直奔餐酒館 ***** 三明治優惠 ***** 午餐菜單指定三明治，每份只要 $6.99。 優惠期限：3月31日 每人限用一張	直奔餐酒館 ***** 開胃菜拼盤 ***** 6點前入內享用晚餐，點開胃菜拼盤可享75折優惠。 優惠期限：3月31日 每人限用一張

直奔餐酒館
河濱大道113號
每日供應三餐，天天營業

直奔餐酒館

上週我和先生去吃了新開的直奔餐酒館，果然沒讓人失望！晚餐太好吃了！價格還是貴了點，但我們有用優惠券所以差很多。他們還是如往常一樣，提供同樣豐富美味的菜色。我們跳過開胃菜，直接點主菜，當然也沒有錯過好吃的甜點。如果你和我們一樣喜愛直奔餐酒館的老店，你一定也會喜歡河濱店。

潘妮・巴羅

河濱
一個地區的復甦

河濱地區新興的餐飲購物區正蓬勃發展，服飾、書籍、禮品特色商店紛紛進駐社區。同時也出現了許多新的用餐地點，一些人氣老店也在這裡開設分店，後者包括向來熱門的直奔餐酒館。這對直奔餐酒館的老闆來說確實是明智之舉，他們的現代風格菜單絕對能吸引該區的年輕人，而隔壁新開的餅乾模咖啡館，已經成為品嚐自製糕點的好地方了。

整體來說，該區餐廳聚集，也吸引了其他商家進駐。每到週末夜晚，街上熙熙攘攘，滿是購物者和觀光客，且更重要的是那些有消費能力的人。總而言之，河濱商圈正在起飛。

191. 關於直奔餐酒館，文中有何暗示？
    (A) 是新開的店。
    (B) 將進行整修。
    (C) 更換了菜單。
    (D) 開了新分店。

解析 (D) 雖然評論中以「new」來描述這間餐酒館，但文章清楚說明了這是老店的新分店，而不是新創的店，因此選項(A)是錯的。選項(B)未被提及。選項(C)不正確，因為評論提到「the same great selection」(＝the same great menu)，表示菜色或菜單是沒變的。

192. 巴羅女士使用了哪一張優惠券？
    (A) 免費甜點
    (B) 開胃菜拼盤
    (C) 買二送一優惠
    (D) 三明治優惠

解析 (C) 她在評論中提到吃的是晚餐，因此午餐限定的選項(A)和(D)就被排除了。她又說他們沒點開胃菜，所以選項(B)也被排除。

193. 哪一項是巴羅女士對直奔餐酒館的批評？
    (A) 價格昂貴。
    (B) 人太多。
    (C) 菜色不多。
    (D) 開胃菜不好吃。

解析 (A) 她形容這家餐廳「pricy」，就是價格昂貴。選項(B)未被提及。選項(C)不正確，她形容菜色豐富又美味。選項(D)不正確，她沒有吃開胃菜，因此也沒有發表任何評論。

194. 文章第二段第一行的concentration這個字，意義與下列何者最為接近？
    (A) 思考
    (B) 注意
    (C) 聚集
    (D) 收縮、減低

解析 (C) 文章描述該區開了很多家新餐廳，從前後文可以判斷concentration指的是「聚集」。選項(A)(B)(D)是concentration的其他意義，但不是這個字在此篇文章中的意思。

195. 關於河濱商圈，文中有何暗示？
    (A) 非常繁榮。
    (B) 地點不佳。
    (C) 需要更多宣傳。
    (D) 只對年輕人有吸引力。

解析 (A) 文章中提到該商圈正蓬勃發展（booming）和起飛（taking off），都是快速繁榮起來的意思。選項(D)有所混淆，文中說的是餐酒館的菜單能吸引年輕人。

第196–200題請看下面的告示、電子郵件和通知。

| 機場交通運輸 |||||
| 所有交通運輸服務皆從東航廈前方發車。 |||||

	時程	目的地	車資
市公車46號	每小時	市中心、公園景觀區、商業區	$3.50
火車站接駁車	每30分鐘	中央火車站	$5.00
飯店接駁車	不定	附近飯店	無
計程車	不定	任何地點	不定

收件者：m.reed@company.com
寄件者：s.chang@company.com
日期： 9月15日星期五
主旨： 旅行

梅琳達：

謝謝妳幫我把行程安排得這麼好，到目前為止，每件事都進展順利，只有在機場發生了一個小問題。聽妳的建議，我本來準備好要搭往市中心的公車，因為它就停在飯店對街。結果不幸沒搭成，因為航廈那邊一團亂，一方面在施工，再加上星期五本來就人潮眾多，最後我只好花錢搭計程車，還花了很多錢，而且我懷疑根本沒有省下任何時間，這附近的交通超級恐怖。無論如何，我現在總算入住飯店了，準備參加明天的會議。我再跟妳說事情進展如何。

山姆

機場旅客須知

由於東航廈正在進行整修及修繕工程，機場交通運輸將進行以下調整：
● 所有接駁車和計程車服務改由西航廈前方發車。
● 市公車46號暫停服務，欲轉乘其他市公車的旅客，可搭乘接駁車或計程車到中央火車站，該站有32號、57號和75號公車提供服務。

如有任何疑問和顧慮，請洽機場公共關係處。

本通知有效時間為8月30日至10月15日。

196．哪一種交通運輸可免費使用？
　　(A) 市公車
　　(B) 火車站接駁車
　　(C) 飯店接駁車
　　(D) 計程車

解析 **(C)** 飯店接駁車的車資標示為「無」（none）。選項(A)(B)(D)都有價錢。

197. 山姆為何沒搭公車？
    (A) 公車沒有到他的目的地。
    (B) 公車目前停駛。
    (C) 公車太慢。
    (D) 公車太貴。

解析 (B) 根據機場通知，由於正在進行整修工程，開往機場的公車暫停服務 (temporarily suspended)。山姆也提到他沒搭公車，因為機場航廈一團亂（the mess at the terminal），部分原因是受到整修工程的干擾。選項(A)(C)(D)都是不搭公車的可能原因，但都不是正確答案。

198. 山姆暗示了關於機場的什麼？
    (A) 星期五人很多。
    (B) 沒有定期清理。
    (C) 離市區很遠。
    (D) 離他的飯店很近。

解析 (A) 山姆說「Friday is such a heavy travel day」，暗示了這天機場有很多旅客。選項(B)誤解了mess在文中的意義。選項(C)和(D)都未被提及。

199. 八月到十月期間，機場正發生什麼事？
    (A) 新航廈施工
    (B) 接駁車時刻表變更
    (C) 公車路線重新規劃
    (D) 一座建築重新整修

解析 (D) 通知中提到「renovations and repairs being carried out at the East Terminal」，表示東航廈正在進行整修和修繕工程。選項(A)和正確答案有所混淆，正在施工的是已經存在的建築，不是正在蓋新的建築。選項(B)有所混淆，變更的是接駁車的發車地點，不是時刻表。選項(C)指通知中提到之中央火車站的好幾個公車路線，但沒提到要重新規劃。

200. 通知第七行的「direct」這個字,意義與下列何者最為接近?
    (A) 建議
    (B) 管理
    (C) 表達
    (D) 指示

解析 **(C)** 這裡的意思是,民眾可以向公共關係處表達(express)或談論(talk about)他們的疑問和顧慮。選項(A)(B)(D)是direct的其他意義,但不符合這裡的語境。

本測驗到此結束。如果你在時間結束前作答完畢,可以回頭檢查Part 5、6、7的答案。

實戰模擬試題5

實戰模擬試題6 解答

聽力測驗

Part 1 照片描述

1. **C**
2. **A**
3. **D**
4. **A**
5. **B**
6. **D**

Part 2 應答問題

7. **B**
8. **A**
9. **C**
10. **A**
11. **C**
12. **A**
13. **B**
14. **B**
15. **A**
16. **C**
17. **C**
18. **B**
19. **A**
20. **B**
21. **B**
22. **A**
23. **C**
24. **C**
25. **B**
26. **A**
27. **A**
28. **C**
29. **B**
30. **A**
31. **A**

Part 3 簡短對話

32. **A**
33. **B**
34. **A**
35. **A**
36. **D**
37. **C**
38. **A**
39. **B**
40. **C**
41. **D**
42. **C**
43. **B**
44. **D**
45. **B**
46. **B**
47. **C**
48. **D**
49. **B**
50. **D**
51. **B**
52. **A**
53. **A**
54. **D**
55. **C**
56. **D**
57. **C**
58. **B**
59. **A**
60. **D**
61. **B**
62. **C**
63. **B**
64. **A**
65. **D**
66. **A**
67. **A**
68. **B**
69. **A**
70. **B**

Part 4 簡短獨白

71. **D**
72. **A**
73. **C**
74. **C**
75. **A**
76. **B**
77. **A**
78. **C**
79. **A**
80. **D**
81. **B**
82. **C**
82. **A**
84. **C**
85. **B**
86. **A**
87. **B**
88. **D**
89. **B**
90. **C**
91. **B**
92. **B**
93. **B**
94. **C**
95. **A**
96. **B**
97. **C**
98. **D**
99. **A**
100. **D**

實戰模擬試題6 解答

閱讀測驗

Part 5 句子填空

101.	**D**	109.	**D**	117.	**C**	125.	**B**
102.	**B**	110.	**A**	118.	**B**	126.	**D**
103.	**C**	111.	**C**	119.	**A**	127.	**A**
104.	**D**	112.	**D**	120.	**B**	128.	**C**
105.	**C**	113.	**C**	121.	**D**	129.	**B**
106.	**C**	114.	**B**	122.	**B**	130.	**A**
107.	**B**	115.	**A**	123.	**A**		
108.	**A**	116.	**D**	124.	**A**		

Part 6 段落填空

131.	**A**	135.	**D**	139.	**D**	143.	**B**
132.	**C**	136.	**C**	140.	**C**	144.	**A**
133.	**D**	137.	**B**	141.	**A**	145.	**D**
134.	**B**	138.	**A**	142.	**B**	146.	**C**

Part 7 閱讀測驗

147.	**A**	161.	**D**	175.	**B**	189.	**D**
148.	**C**	162.	**C**	176.	**B**	190.	**C**
149.	**B**	163.	**A**	177.	**C**	191.	**B**
150.	**C**	164.	**D**	178.	**D**	192.	**A**
151.	**D**	165.	**A**	179.	**A**	193.	**D**
152.	**B**	166.	**B**	180.	**A**	194.	**B**
153.	**C**	167.	**C**	181.	**C**	195.	**C**
154.	**A**	168.	**D**	182.	**A**	196.	**C**
155.	**C**	169.	**B**	183.	**A**	197.	**B**
156.	**B**	170.	**A**	184.	**B**	198.	**B**
157.	**D**	171.	**D**	185.	**D**	199.	**A**
158.	**A**	172.	**C**	186.	**A**	200.	**A**
159.	**D**	173.	**B**	187.	**C**		
160.	**B**	174.	**A**	188.	**B**		

Model Test 6 實戰模擬試題6 題目中譯&解析

聽力測驗

在本段測驗當中，你將有機會展現自己對口說英語的理解能力。聽力測驗共有四個大題，每一大題均有作答說明。你有大約45分鐘時間完成聽力測驗。

Part 1：照片描述

> 作答方式：你會看到一張照片，並聽到四個關於這張照片的陳述。選出最符合照片內容的陳述，將答案卡上對應的橢圓框塗滿。

1. Look at the photo marked number 1 in your test book.
   (A) She's talking on her cell phone.
   (B) She's standing in front of the door.
   (C) She's speaking into the microphone.
   (D) She's shaking hands with her boss.

   請看試題本標示為1的照片。
   (A) 她正在講手機。
   (B) 她正站在門前面。
   (C) 她正對著麥克風說話。
   (D) 她正和她的老闆握手。

   解析 (C) 照片中一名女子正站在講桌前，對著一支麥克風說話。選項(A)混淆了發音相近的 microphone 和 cell phone。選項(B)正確指出了站立的動作，但照片中沒有門。選項(D)指的是女子的手，照片中可以看到她的手，但她沒有在和任何人握手。

2. Look at the photo marked number 2 in your test book.
   (A) The businessman is writing something down.
   (B) The waiter is bringing a glass of water.
   (C) The salesman is showing the customer a computer.
   (D) The teacher is reading from a book.

   請看試題本標示為2的照片。
   (A) 這位商務人士正在寫一些東西。
   (B) 這位服務生正端來一杯水。
   (C) 這位銷售員正在向顧客展示一臺電腦。
   (D) 這位老師正在讀一本書的內容。

解析 (A) 照片中一名身穿西裝的男子正看著電腦，並拿著一支筆寫筆記。選項(B)正確指出了桌上的水杯，但照片中沒有服務生。選項(C)正確指出了電腦，但照片中沒有銷售員，場景也不像是商店。選項(D)不正確，男子正看著電腦的內容，不是一本書的內容。

3. Look at the photo marked number 3 in your test book.
   (A) The dishes are on the kitchen counter.
   (B) The flowers have been placed on the table.
   (C) The teapot is sitting by the stove.
   (D) The teacups have been set on a tray.

   請看試題本標示為3的照片。
   (A) 盤子在廚房檯面上。
   (B) 花朵被擺在桌上。
   (C) 茶壺放在火爐旁邊。
   (D) 茶杯被擺在托盤上。

解析 (D) 照片中可以看到托盤上有兩個茶杯、一個茶壺和一瓶花。選項(A)(B)(C)都正確指出了照片中的一樣物品，但對位置的描述都不正確。

4. Look at the photo marked number 4 in your test book.
   (A) Some shoppers are at a hardware store.
   (B) A man is raking leaves.
   (C) A woman is paying for her purchases.
   (D) A janitor is sweeping with a broom.

   請看試題本標示為4的照片。
   (A) 一些顧客正在一家五金行。
   (B) 一名男子正在用耙子耙樹葉。
   (C) 一名女子正在結帳。
   (D) 一名清潔工正在用掃把掃地。

解析 (A) 照片中顯示一名男子和一名女子正在一間店裡挑東西，從商品的類型看來應為五金行。選項(B)指的是男子手上拿的耙子，但他沒有在耙任何東西。選項(C)指的是照片場景的所在地點（商店），但是對女子的動作描述不正確。選項(D)正確指出了照片中的掃把，但沒有人在掃地。

5. Look at the photo marked number 5 in your test book.
   (A) The customers are ordering coffee.
   (B) Two men are crossing the street.
   (C) The inspector is opening the suitcase.
   (D) Some policemen are directing traffic.

   請看試題本標示為5的照片。
   (A) 顧客們正在點咖啡。
   (B) 兩名男子正在過馬路。
   (C) 檢查員正在打開行李箱。
   (D) 幾名警察正在指揮交通。

   解析 **(B)** 照片中可看到兩名男子正在過馬路。選項(A)指的是其中一名男子手上的咖啡杯，但沒有人在點咖啡。選項(C)把suitcase（行李箱、手提箱）和其中一名男子手上的briefcase（公事包）互相混淆了。選項(D)從街道場景聯想到交通（traffic），但照片中沒有警察。

6. Look at the photo marked number 6 in your test book.
   (A) The river flows through the city.
   (B) The conductor is taking tickets.
   (C) The railroad bridge is closed.
   (D) The freight train is moving through the countryside.

   請看試題本標示為6的照片。
   (A) 這條河流經城市。
   (B) 這位車掌正在驗票。
   (C) 這座鐵路橋樑已關閉。
   (D) 這列貨運火車正在駛過鄉間。

   解析 **(D)** 照片中可以看到一列貨運火車，背景則是鄉間。選項(A)指的是照片中的水域，但場景並不是城市。選項(B)使用了train的相關字conductor。選項(C)使用了train的相關字railroad。

Part 2：應答問題

> 作答方式：你會聽到一個問題和三個可能的回應。選出最適合回答該問題的回應，將答案卡上對應的橢圓框塗滿。

7. Has Sam arrived yet?
    (A) It's all set.
    (B) Yes, he got here at ten.
    (C) His name is Sam.

    山姆到了嗎？
    (A) 一切都準備好了。
    (B) 到了，他十點時到的。
    (C) 他的名字叫山姆。

解析 (B) 選項(B)回答了詢問山姆到了沒的「yes-no」問句。選項(A)混淆了近音字yet和set。選項(C)重複使用了Sam這個名字。

8. Where can I get some coffee?
    (A) There's a shop right across the street.
    (B) Please wash your cup.
    (C) No thanks, none for me.

    哪裡可以買到咖啡？
    (A) 對街就有一家店。
    (B) 請清洗你的杯子。
    (C) 不用了謝謝，我不喝。

解析 (A) 「a shop right across the street」回答了「Where」的問題。選項(B)把coffee和cup聯想在一起。選項(C)是對方提議幫你倒咖啡時的回應。

9. Could you show me how to use this printer?
    (A) I saw the show last night.
    (B) Please print two copies.
    (C) Sure. It's very easy.

    可以教我怎麼用這臺印表機嗎？
    (A) 我昨晚看了表演。
    (B) 請列印兩份。
    (C) 當然可以，很簡單的。

解析 (C) 選項(C)是對方請求協助時的適當回應。選項(A)混淆了 show 的意思。選項(B)混淆了相關字 printer 和 print。

10. Why did you eat lunch at your desk?
    (A) I had some work to finish.
    (B) Just a sandwich.
    (C) No, that isn't my desk.

    你為什麼要在辦公桌上吃午餐？
    (A) 我有工作要完成。
    (B) 只是一個三明治。
    (C) 不，那不是我的辦公桌。

解析 (A) 選項(A)以一個合理的可能原因回答了「Why」的問題。選項(B)從 lunch 聯想到 sandwich。選項(C)重複使用了 desk 這個字。

11. How many chairs will we need for the dinner?
    (A) He's the winner.
    (B) Tomorrow at two thirty.
    (C) I think fifteen will be enough.

    我們晚餐需要幾張椅子？
    (A) 他是贏家。
    (B) 明天下午兩點半。
    (C) 我想十五張應該夠。

解析 (C)「fifteen」回答了「How many」的問題。選項(A)混淆了近音字 dinner 和 winner。選項(B)回答的是「When」的問題。

12. This lamp isn't working.
    (A) I'll get a new bulb.
    (B) Because he isn't feeling well.
    (C) The room's a bit damp.

    這盞燈不會亮。
    (A) 我去拿一個新燈泡。
    (B) 因為他身體不舒服。
    (C) 這個房間有點潮濕。

解析 (A) 選項(A)是對方說燈不亮時的合理回應。選項(B)用來回答「Why」的問題。選項(C)混淆了近音字 lamp 和 damp。

13. When did the meeting start?
    (A) It's on the agenda.
    (B) About half an hour ago.
    (C) Start right here.

    會議是何時開始的？
    (A) 此事已列入議程。
    (B) 大約半小時前。
    (C) 就從這裡開始。

解析 (B) 「half an hour ago」回答了「When」的問題。選項(A)使用了meeting的相關字agenda。選項(C)重複使用了start這個字。

14. You live in the neighborhood, don't you?
    (A) It's a pleasant neighborhood.
    (B) Yes, just down the street.
    (C) No, it doesn't taste good.

    你住在這附近，不是嗎？
    (A) 這是一個宜人的社區。
    (B) 對，就在這條街上。
    (C) 不，它不好吃。

解析 (B) 題目是關於是否住附近的「yes-no」問句，而選項(B)是合理的回應。選項(A)重複使用了neighborhood這個字。選項(C)混淆了近音字neighborhood和good。

15. What are your plans for the weekend?
    (A) I just want to relax at home.
    (B) The plants need watering.
    (C) I'll be back after the weekend.

    你週末有什麼計畫？
    (A) 我只想在家放鬆。
    (B) 這些植物需要澆水。
    (B) 週末過後我就會回來。

解析 (A) 選項(A)是對週末計畫問題的合理回應。選項(B)混淆了近音字plans和plants。選項(C)重複使用了weekend這個字。

16. How much time do we have left?
    (A) I left it over there.
    (B) It's lunchtime now.
    (C) Only fifteen minutes.

    我們還剩多少時間？
    (A) 我把它留在那裡了。
    (B) 現在是午餐時間。
    (C) 只剩十五分鐘。

    解析 (C)「fifteen minutes」回答了「How much time」的問題。選項(A)搞錯了 left 的意思。選項(B)混淆了發音相近的 much time 和 lunchtime。

17. Do you know why this window is open?
    (A) I opened it.
    (B) Yes, it's open.
    (C) It was hot in here earlier.

    你知道這扇窗為何開著嗎？
    (A) 我打開的。
    (B) 是的，它是開著的。
    (C) 剛才這裡很熱。

    解析 (C) 選項(C)以一個可能的原因回答了「Why」的間接問句。選項(A)和(B)都重複使用了 open 這個字。

18. Would you like me to answer the phone for you?
    (A) I left a message yesterday.
    (B) Thank you, that would be helpful.
    (C) We had a lot of fun.

    要我幫你接電話嗎？
    (A) 我昨天有留言。
    (B) 謝謝，那樣會很有幫助。
    (C) 我們玩得很開心。

    解析 (B) 選項(B)是對方提供幫助時的合理回應。選項(A)使用了 phone 的相關字 message。選項(C)混淆了近音字 phone 和 fun。

19. The museum opens at ten in the morning.
   (A) Really? I thought it opened at nine.
   (B) There are only seven left.
   (C) Use a can opener.

   博物館上午十點開門。
   (A) 是嗎？我以為它九點開門。
   (B) 只剩下七個。
   (C) 使用開罐器。

解析 (A) 選項(A)是談論開門時間時的合理回應。選項(B)使用了一個數字，但不是在談論時間。選項(C)使用了open的相關字opener。

20. Have you decided which sofa to buy?
   (A) They would like one.
   (B) Yes. The leather one.
   (C) That's my decision.

   你決定好要買哪一張沙發了嗎？
   (A) 他們想要一個。
   (B) 是的，皮的那張。
   (C) 那是我的決定。

解析 (B)「The leather one」回答了「Which」的問題。選項(C)使用了decide的相關字decision。

21. What are you reading?
   (A) A salad with ranch dressing.
   (B) It's a biography about a war hero.
   (C) Nothing. I don't need anything.

   你在閱讀什麼？
   (A) 一份沙拉配田園沙拉醬。
   (B) 一本關於戰爭英雄的傳記。
   (C) 不用，我不需要任何東西。

解析 (B)「a biography」回答了關於讀物的問題。選項(A)用來回答關於食物的問題。選項(C)混淆了近音字read和need。

22. Where was your credit card issued?

(A) In England.

(B) About five years ago.

(C) I have good credit.

你的信用卡是哪裡核發的？

(A) 英格蘭。

(B) 大約五年前。

(C) 我的信用良好。

解析 (A)「In England」回答了「Where」的問題。選項(B)回答的是「When」的問題。選項(C)重複使用了credit這個字。

23. Are you working today?

(A) Thursday and Sunday.

(B) Only when it's snowing.

(C) No. Today's my day off.

你今天要工作嗎？

(A) 星期四和星期日。

(B) 只有下雪的時候。

(C) 不用，今天我休息。

解析 (C) 選項(C)回答了題目的「yes-no」問句。選項(A)和(B)則是用來回答「When」的問題。

24. Would you like to sign up for a class?

(A) One glass is enough.

(B) It's a very nice sign.

(C) Yes, I would.

你想要報名上課嗎？

(A) 一杯就夠了。

(B) 那是個很漂亮的招牌。

(C) 是的，我想要。

解析 (C) 選項(C)回答了題目的「yes-no」問句。選項(A)混淆了近音字class和glass。選項(B)用的是sign的另一個意義。

25. How much would a new air conditioner cost?
    (A) 74 degrees.
    (B) Around two thousand dollars.
    (C) Two or three, probably.

    新的冷氣機要多少錢？
    (A) 74度。
    (B) 大約兩千美元。
    (C) 大概兩三個吧。

解析 (B)「two thousand dollars」回答了「How much」的費用問題。選項(A)使用了air conditioner的相關字degrees。選項(C)回答的是「How many」的問題。

26. When will you be leaving to go to the dentist?
    (A) Probably in about fifteen minutes.
    (B) Because I have a toothache.
    (C) My appointment is at four thirty this afternoon.

    你什麼時候要出門去看牙醫？
    (A) 大概十五分鐘後。
    (B) 因為我牙齒痛。
    (C) 我預約的時間是下午4點30分。

解析 (A) 選項(A)回答了「When will you be leaving」（何時出發／出門）的問題。選項(B)用來回答「Why」的問題。選項(C)回答的問題會是「When is your appointment?」（你的預約是何時？）。

27. Do you want to watch a movie?
    (A) No, I'd prefer to go on a walk.
    (B) I don't wear a watch.
    (C) You're very welcome.

    你想看電影嗎？
    (A) 不想，我比較想去散步。
    (B) 我不戴手錶。
    (C) 不客氣。

解析 (A) 選項(A)回答了題目的「yes-no」問句。選項(B)使用了watch的另一個意義。選項(C)會用來回應「Thank you」這句話。

28. Someone left the office lights on last night.
    (A) I can turn them on, too.
    (B) The electrician can fix that.
    (C) I think it was Henry.

    昨天晚上有人沒關辦公室的燈。
    (A) 我也可以打開它們。
    (B) 電工可以把那個修好。
    (C) 我想應該是亨利。

解析 (C) 題目的句子說有人沒關燈，選項(C)以「Henry」回應了可能是誰。選項(A)從lights 聯想到turn on。選項(B)從lights 聯想到electrician。

29. What are Bill and Leslie talking about?
    (A) They're in the conference room.
    (B) The Clinton project, I'm pretty sure.
    (C) Yeah, they don't sound very happy.

    比爾和萊斯利在談論什麼？
    (A) 他們在會議室。
    (B) 我很確定是在談論柯林頓專案。
    (C) 對，他們聽起來不是很開心。

解析 (B) 「Clinton project」回答了「What」的問題。選項(A)用來回答「Where」的問題。選項(C)從talking 聯想到sound。

30. You look nervous.
    (A) I am. I have a job interview this morning.
    (B) I've looked for it everywhere.
    (C) I think the service here is excellent.

    你看起來很緊張。
    (A) 對啊，我今天早上有個工作面試。
    (B) 我到處都找過了。
    (C) 我覺得這裡的服務很棒。

解析 (A) 選項(A)以一個理由回應了「You look nervous」的評論。選項(B)使用了look 的另一個意義。選項(C)混淆了近音字nervous 和service。

31. Do I have your phone number?
    (A) No, but I can give it to you.
    (B) Yes, that is my cell phone.
    (C) There are five.

    我有你的電話號碼嗎?
    (A) 沒有,但我可以給你。
    (B) 是的,那是我的手機。
    (C) 有五個。

解析 (A) 選項(A)合理回應了關於電話號碼的「yes-no」問句。選項(B)重複使用了phone這個字。選項(C)使用了number的相關字five。

Part 3：簡短對話

作答方式：你會聽到兩人或多人之間的對話。每段對話搭配三個問題，各有四個選項。選出最適當的答案回答問題，將答案卡上對應的橢圓框塗滿。

Questions 32 through 34 refer to the following conversation.

Woman: Can you give me a lift tomorrow? My car's been giving me some trouble and now it's in the shop.

Man: Sure. Wait for me in front of the library at seven o'clock.

Woman: So early?

Man: I have to give a presentation to a client at ten thirty. I want to get to the office before eight, so I'll have time to finish preparing.

Woman: I could help you with that. I know the client. Why don't you pick me up at eight, and I'll help you put the presentation together when we get to the office.

第 32–34 題請聽下面這段對話。

女：你明天可以載我嗎？我的車子有點問題，目前在修車廠。
男：當然可以，七點在圖書館前面等我。
女：那麼早？
男：我十點半要向一位客戶做簡報。我想在八點前到辦公室，才有時間完成準備工作。
女：我可以幫你，我認識那位客戶。你八點來接我，到了辦公室，我幫你把簡報整理一下。

32. What does the woman ask the man to do? 這名女子要求男子做什麼？

    (A) Give her a ride to work 載她去上班
    (B) Lift something heavy 抬重物
    (C) Take her shopping 帶她去逛街
    (D) Fix her car 修理她的車

解析 (A) 女子要求男子載她一程（a lift = a ride），而男子說要早點到辦公室，可知是載她去上班。選項 (B) 搞錯了 lift 的意義。選項 (C) 搞錯了 shop 的意義，對話中的 shop 指修車廠。選項 (D) 不正確，女子提到她的車已經在修車廠了。

33. Why does the man want to be at the office early? 男子為什麼想早點到辦公室？
    (A) To repair some office equipment 為了修理一些辦公設備
    (B) To get ready for a client meeting 為了準備和客戶開會
    (C) To wrap some presents 為了包裝一些禮物
    (D) To finish a report 為了完成一份報告

解析 (B) 男子說他要向一位客戶做簡報，需要時間準備。選項(A)混淆了近音字prepare和repair。選項(C)混淆了近音字presentation和present。選項(D)重複使用了finish這個字。

34. What does the woman suggest? 這名女子提出什麼建議？
    (A) Leaving later 晚點出發
    (B) Calling a client 打電話給一位客戶
    (C) Stopping at the library 在圖書館停一下
    (D) Asking someone for help 請別人幫忙

解析 (A) 男子希望七點出發，女子則說「Why don't you pick me up at eight」（八點來接我），所以她建議晚點出發。選項(B)重複使用了client這個字。選項(C)重複使用了library這個字，圖書館是他們碰面的地點。選項(D)重複使用了help這個字，女子表示可以幫忙男子，但沒有說要請別人幫忙。

Questions 35 through 37 refer to the following conversation.
Woman: I was finally able to contact the cleaning company. They'll be here next Monday.
Man: Next Monday? I was hoping they could come before that. We have that client meeting on Thursday, and this place is a wreck.
Woman: I know, but they can't come earlier. And they do such a good job, not only on the floors and windows, but they really make the furniture shine.
Man: You're right, of course, and their prices are really reasonable. Why don't we plan to meet the clients at a restaurant instead of here? Then, we won't have to worry about getting the cleaning done on time.

第35-37題請聽下面這段對話。
女：我終於連絡上清潔公司了，他們下星期一會過來。
男：下星期一？我還希望他們在那之前來。我們星期四有個客戶會議，這裡卻亂成一團。
女：我知道，但他們就是沒辦法早點過來。而且他們做得那麼好，不只地板和窗戶，連家具都擦得亮晶晶的。
男：當然，你說得沒錯，而且他們的收費也很合理。不如我們和客戶約在餐廳見面，不要在這裡？這樣我們就不用擔心一定要準時打掃完畢。

615

35. What are the speakers discussing? 說話者在討論什麼？
    (A) Getting the office cleaned 清潔辦公室
    (B) Renting an apartment 承租公寓
    (C) Buying furniture 購買家具
    (D) Going out to eat 外出用餐

    解析 (A) 女子說她聯絡了清潔公司，接著還提到他們把地板、窗戶和家具都清理得很乾淨，可知他們是在討論辦公室的清潔工作。選項(B)和對話中提到地板、窗戶、家具有關。選項(C)重複使用了furniture這個字。選項(D)和對話中提到restaurant有關。

36. What problem do they have? 他們遇到了什麼問題？
    (A) They lost the contact information. 他們把聯絡資訊弄丟了。
    (B) They think the price is too high. 他們認為費用太高。
    (C) They can't find anyone to hire. 他們僱用不到人。
    (D) They don't like the schedule. 他們對時間安排不滿意。

    解析 (D) 男子希望在客戶會議之前把辦公室清潔好，但清潔公司要下星期一才會來，已經是會議之後了。選項(A)不正確，女子說她已經聯絡了清潔公司。選項(B)不正確，他們說價格合理。選項(C)不正確，他們正在僱用這家清潔公司。

37. What does the man suggest they do? 男子建議他們做什麼？
    (A) Leave earlier 早點離開
    (B) Offer to pay less 提出少付一點
    (C) Meet somewhere else 改到其他地方見面
    (D) Buy new furniture 購買新家具

    解析 (C) 男子說「Why don't we plan to meet the clients at a restaurant instead of here?」，建議他們改到餐廳見面。選項(A)重複使用了earlier這個字。選項(B)使用了price的相關字pay。選項(D)重複使用了furniture這個字。

Questions 38 through 40 refer to the following conversation.

Woman: A group of us are going out to eat after work. Wanna come? We're gonna try that new restaurant on State Street.
Man: Maybe. I'm not sure. I still have this report to finish, and it has to be all done and on the boss's desk before I leave.
Woman: We're not leaving till seven. That'd give you enough time, wouldn't it?
Man: I guess so. It would, if you'd work on the last part of it with me.

第 38–40 題請聽下面這段對話。

女：我們一群人下班後要去吃飯，要一起來嗎？我們要去吃史泰特街上新開的那家餐廳。
男：也許吧，我不太確定。我還有這份報告要完成，下班前必須全部做好放在老闆桌上。
女：我們七點才要走，那樣你時間應該夠吧？
男：我想應該可以吧，如果你願意和我一起做最後那部分的話。

38. Why is the woman talking to the man? 這名女子為何要跟男子說話？
    (A) To invite him somewhere 為了邀請他去一個地方
    (B) To make a suggestion 為了提出一個建議
    (C) To discuss a problem 為了討論一個問題
    (D) To ask for advice 為了徵求建議

解析 (A) 這名女子正要和一群朋友到餐廳吃飯，問男子要不要一起去。選項(B)(C)(D)都是交談的可能原因，但不是這裡的情況。

39. What is the man doing? 這名男子正在做什麼？
    (A) Watching sports 看體育比賽
    (B) Writing a report 撰寫報告
    (C) Cleaning his desk 清潔他的辦公桌
    (D) Making a phone call 打電話

解析 (B) 男子說「I still have this report to finish」，所以他正在撰寫報告。選項(A)混淆了近音字 report 和 sports。選項(C)重複使用了 desk 這個字。選項(D)混淆了近音字 all 和 call。

40. What does the man ask the woman to do? 男子要求女子做什麼？
    (A) Give him directions to the restaurant 告訴他如何去餐廳
    (B) Come back to talk with him later 晚點再過來和他說話
    (C) Help him with his work 幫他完成工作
    (D) Wait for him at 7:00 七點的時候等他

解析 (C) 男子說「if you'd work on the last part of it with me」，it 指的就是 report，男子要求女子和他一起處理報告的最後部分，這樣他就可以準時完成工作，和他們一起去吃飯。選項(A)重複使用了 restaurant 這個字。選項(B)未被提及。選項(D)是他們要去餐廳的時間。

Questions 41 through 43 refer to the following conversation.

Woman: Here's the rental agreement. I think you'll like this vehicle. It's quite large and has lots of leg room, as you requested.

Man: OK, let's see . . . GPS, air conditioning, heated seats . . . It all looks good. Oh, and I see I have to bring it back with a full tank of gas.

Woman: Yes, that's standard. The agreement says one week, but you can keep it over the weekend, if you want it for a little longer. Bring it back by Sunday evening, and we'll only charge for one extra day.

Man: Great. Do you have a pen?

第 41–43 題請聽下面這段對話。

女：這是租賃協議，我想你一定會喜歡這輛車的，它很大，腿部空間也很寬敞，就像你所要求的那樣。

男：好的，我來看看……導航系統、空調、加熱座椅……一切看起來都很好。喔，我看到還車時必須加滿油。

女：是的，這是標準規定。協議上是寫一週，不過如果你希望租久一點的話，週末可以繼續使用。週日晚上之前還車的話，只會加收一天的費用。

男：太好了。你有筆嗎？

41. What is the man renting? 這名男子正在租什麼？
    (A) Some furniture 一些家具
    (B) An apartment 一間公寓
    (C) A heater 一臺暖氣
    (D) A car 一部車

解析 (D) 女子提到 vehicle（交通工具），男子又提到 GPS（導航／定位系統）、tank of gas（油箱），所以是在談論汽車。選項 (A) 和對話中提到 seats 有關。選項 (B) 不正確，如果是公寓，不會提到要 bring back（帶回來）。選項 (C) 和對話中提到 heated seats（加熱座椅）有關。

42. What does the woman suggest the man do? 這名女子建議男子做什麼？
    (A) Request something larger 要求更大一點的
    (B) Look at other options 查看其他選擇
    (C) Rent for more time 租久一點
    (D) Reread the agreement 重讀一遍協議

解析 (C) 女子說「you can keep it over the weekend, if you want it for a little longer」，建議他有需要的話可以租久一點。選項 (A) 和男子要求大一點的車型有關。選項 (B) 也有可能，但對話中並未提及。選項 (D) 重複使用了 agreement 這個字。

43. What will the man do next? 這名男子接下來會做什麼？
    (A) Fill the tank 加滿油
    (B) Sign a document 簽一份文件
    (C) Go away for the weekend 週末出去玩
    (D) Go to another rental agency 到另一家租車公司

解析 (B) 女子給男子看了租賃協議，然後男子要了一支筆，表示準備簽字。選項(A)是還車時才要做的事。選項(C)重複使用了 weekend 這個字。選項(D)和租車的主題有關，但對話中並未提及。

Questions 44 through 46 refer to the following conversation.
Man: I wonder if you could tell me about your shipping options.
Woman: Certainly. Our products are sold by individual sellers, but they all must follow our shipping standards.
Man: Yes?
Woman: Let me explain. The seller must package and ship each order within twenty-four hours of the purchase. Buyers can choose either standard or express shipping. And all packages are given a tracking number.
Man: I see. And how much do you generally charge for shipping?
Woman: Standard shipping is ten dollars with a seven-day delivery guarantee, and there is a twenty-dollar surcharge for express shipping. Is there anything else?
Man: That's it.

第 44–46 題請聽下面這段對話。
男：我想知道你們有哪些運送方式。
女：好的。我們的產品經由個人賣家銷售，不過他們都必須遵守我們的運送標準。
男：然後呢？
女：讓我解釋一下。賣家必須在收到訂單後二十四小時內打包出貨。買家可以選擇標準運送或快速運送，所有包裹都會附上追蹤號碼。
男：了解。那你們的運費一般是多少？
女：標準運送是十美元，保證七天送達。快速運送是二十美元。還有其他問題嗎？
男：就這樣。

44. Why did the man make the call? 男子為何打這通電話？
    (A) To report a problem 為了回報一個問題
    (B) To make a complaint 為了提出客訴
    (C) To order a product 為了訂購一項產品
    (D) To ask for information 為了詢問資訊

解析 **(D)** 男子打電話詢問運送方式。選項(A)(B)(C)都是打電話的可能原因，但不是這裡的情況。

45. What costs ＄20？哪個項目要收二十美元？
    (A) Standard shipping 標準運送
    (B) Express shipping 快速運送
    (C) Special packaging 特殊包裝
    (D) Guaranteed delivery 保證送達

解析 **(B)** 女子說「there is a twenty-dollar surcharge for express shipping」，所以是快速運送。選項(A)的費用是十美元。選項(C)未被提及。選項(D)是標準運送的一部分。

46. What does the man mean when he says, "That's it"？
    男子說「That's it」是什麼意思？
    (A) He's decided which products to buy. 他已經決定好要買哪些產品。
    (B) His questions have been answered. 他的問題已經獲得解答。
    (C) He's chosen his shipping method. 他已經選定運送方式。
    (D) His order is completed. 他的訂單已經完成了。

解析 **(B)** 女子說「Is there anything else?」，完整的問句是「Is there anything else you want to know?」（你還有什麼想知道的嗎？），而男子回答「That's it.」，表示沒有其他問題了。選項(A)(C)(D)在購物的語境中雖然是有可能的，但不是這裡的正確答案。

Questions 47 through 49 refer to the following conversation.
Man: Before we conclude, do you have any questions?
Woman: Yes, one or two. First, what do you like most about working at this company?
Man: Good question. I have to say that the hours are great. We work an extra half-hour Monday through Thursday, so we can get out of work at three on Fridays. It's a great way to start the weekend.
Woman: If I'm hired, do you know how long until my benefits kick in?
Man: Mrs. Patterson is the person to answer that. I'll bring you back to her office and she can answer that and any similar questions you might have.

第 47–49 題請聽下面這段對話。

男：在我們結束之前，你還有什麼問題嗎？
女：有，我有一兩個問題。第一個問題是，在這家公司工作，你最喜歡的是哪一點？
男：好問題。我不得不說，這裡的工作時間安排很棒，週一到週四多上半個小時的班，週五下午三點就可以下班，用這種方式展開週末很棒。
女：如果我被錄用，多久可以開始享有福利？
男：這個問題要問派特森女士。我帶妳回到她的辦公室，她可以為妳解答這個問題和其他類似問題。

47. What best describes this conversation? 下列何者最能描述這段對話？
    (A) An introduction 一段介紹
    (B) A staff meeting 一場員工會議
    (C) An interview 一場面試
    (D) A sales pitch 一段產品推銷

解析 (C) 女子問到工作和福利（benefits）的事，並且說「If I'm hired . . .」（如果我被錄用），可知這是一場工作面試。選項 (A)(B)(D) 都有可能作為對話內容，但不適合描述這段對話。

48. What does the man like most about his job? 這名男子最喜歡他工作的哪一點？
    (A) The pay 薪資
    (B) The events 活動
    (C) The benefits 福利
    (D) The schedule 工時安排

解析 (D) 男子說「the hours are great」，表示他很喜歡工作時間的安排。選項 (A)(B)(C) 是大家可能喜歡一份工作的原因，但不是這名男子的情況。

49. What will probably happen next? 接下來可能會發生什麼事？
    (A) The man will answer the woman's last question.
       男子會回答女子的最後一個問題。
    (B) The woman will speak with Mrs. Patterson. 女子會和派特森女士交談。
    (C) The man will leave for the weekend. 男子會離開去度過週末。
    (D) The woman will go home. 女子會回家。

解析 (B) 女子詢問了關於福利的問題，而男子說他會帶她去見派特森女士，由派特森女士來回答這個問題。選項 (A) 不正確，男子說派特森女士才能回答這個問題。選項 (C) 重複使用了 weekend 這個字，對話中是在說明工作時間的安排時提到這個字。選項 (D) 和正確答案相抵觸。

Questions 50 through 52 refer to the following conversation.

Woman 1: Are you planning to stay at the Sun Hotel on your trip next week?
Man: I'm thinking about it. The photos on the website look good, and it's right next to the conference center.
Woman 2: I stayed there last year.
Woman 1: Me too, and I won't stay there again.
Man: What's the matter with it? It's reasonably priced.
Woman 1: Yes, and well located, but the beds . . . I didn't sleep a wink.
Woman 2: I know what you mean about the beds. And the rooms are so tiny.
Man: Hmmm. I guess I'll look into some other possibilities.

第 50–52 題請聽下面這段對話。
女1：你下週旅行打算住在日光飯店嗎？
男： 我正在考慮。網站上的照片看起來好棒，而且就在會議中心旁邊。
女2：我去年住過。
女1：我也是，但我不會再住第二次了。
男： 那家飯店怎麼了嗎？它的價格挺合理的。
女1：是的，地點也很好，但那張床……我整晚都沒睡著。
女2：我知道你說的床的問題，而且房間超小。
男： 嗯，我再查看別間飯店好了。

50. What is likely the purpose of the man's trip? 男子此行的目的最有可能是什麼？
    (A) To meet a client 和一位客戶見面
    (B) To take a vacation 度假
    (C) To take photographs 拍照
    (D) To attend a conference 參加一場會議

解析 (D) 男子說他打算住的飯店就在會議中心旁邊，所以應該是去參加會議。選項(A)和(B)是有可能，但未被提及。選項(C)被男子提到飯店網站上的照片給混淆了。

51. What do the women imply about the hotel? 女子對這間飯店有何暗示？
    (A) It is in a bad location. 地點很差。
    (B) It is uncomfortable. 很不舒適。
    (C) It is too expensive. 太貴。
    (D) It is very noisy. 太吵。

解析 (B) 其中一名女子說因為床的關係,她都睡不著,另一名女子表示同意,還補充說房間很小,這都說明了這是一間很不舒適的飯店。選項(A)不正確,他們說飯店的地點很好(well located)。選項(C)不正確,所有說話者都同意價格是合理的(reasonably priced)。選項(D)是睡不著的可能原因,但對話中並未提及。

52. What will the man do next? 這名男子接下來會做什麼?
    (A) Research other hotels 研究其他飯店
    (B) Reserve a room 預訂房間
    (C) Cancel his trip 取消他的行程
    (D) Take a nap 小睡一會

解析 (A) 男子說「I'll look into some other possibilities」,意思就是他要研究看看有沒有別間飯店可以住。選項(B)和正確答案相抵觸。選項(C)就旅行的語境本身是有可能,但這裡是要去參加會議,不大可能因為飯店不舒適而取消。選項(D)使用了sleep的相關字nap。

Questions 53 through 55 refer to the following conversation.
Man: What's the status on the West Park renovation project?
Woman: It looks like we're on schedule. Three contractors have submitted quotes, and the team is meeting tomorrow to review them. Are you coming to the meeting?
Man: No, you can handle it. Just remember that we need a contractor that's based within thirty miles of the job site. I don't want a repeat of the Lake Keely project problem.
Woman: Yeah, I heard about that. The contractor complained about the distance and wanted to charge us for wear and tear to his crew's trucks.

第53–55題請聽下面這段對話。
男:西方公園的整建計畫進行得如何了?
女:看起來有按計畫進行。三個承包商已提供了報價,且小組明天會開會審核。你會來開會嗎?
男:不會,你可以處理。只是要記得,我們需要一個位於工地三十英里範圍內的承包商,我不想讓基利湖計畫的問題重演。
女:是,我聽說了。那個承包商抱怨距離太遠,想跟我們收取工班卡車的磨損費。

53. What kind of work are they hiring contractors for? 他們僱用承包商來進行什麼樣的工作？
    (A) Construction 建設
    (B) Decorating 裝潢
    (C) Transportation 運輸
    (D) Editing 編輯

解析 (A) 說話者正在討論一項整建計畫（renovation project），並提到承包商的卡車。選項(B)和整建（renovation）有關。選項(C)和卡車（trucks）有關。選項(D)和承包商（contractors）有關，是承包商（或者說外包人員）可能受僱來做的事。

54. What will happen at the meeting tomorrow? 明天的會議上會發生什麼事？
    (A) They will write a quote for the project. 他們會為該計畫寫一份報價。
    (B) They will meet the contractor. 他們會和承包商見面。
    (C) They will talk about the schedule. 他們會討論時程安排。
    (D) They will review the submitted quotes. 他們會審核提出的報價。

解析 (D) 女子說「Three contractors have submitted quotes, and the team is meeting tomorrow to review them」，三個承包商提了報價，而他們明天要開會審核報價。選項(A)重複使用了quote這個字。選項(B)重複使用了contractor這個字。選項(C)重複使用了schedule這個字。

55. What was the problem with the last contractor? 上一個承包商出了什麼問題？
    (A) He didn't finish the work. 他沒有完成工作。
    (B) He left the job site a mess. 他把工地搞得一團亂。
    (C) He was located too far away. 他的所在位置太遠。
    (D) He tore up the contract. 他撕毀了合約。

解析 (C) 男子說「we need a contractor that's based within thirty miles of the job site」（位於工地三十英里內的承包商），而女子則回應說，她聽說上一個承包商抱怨距離太遠（complained about the distance）。選項(A)(B)(D)在外包工程的語境中都有可能發生，但不是這裡的情況。

Questions 56 through 58 refer to the following conversation.

Man: I need to get some more checks. I'm almost out.

Woman: Do you have an account with us?

Man: Yes. Here, let me show you the kind of check I already have. I'd like more of the same.

Woman: I'm sorry, we don't carry that style anymore. Let me show you a catalogue of the styles and colors you can order.

Man: Wow. The selection certainly could be better. There's really not a whole lot here.

Woman: Let me know when you've made your choice and I'll place the order, then you should have your new checks in about two weeks.

第56–58題請聽下面這段對話。

男：我需要再領一些支票，我的快用完了。

女：您在我們這裡有帳戶嗎？

男：有的。在這裡，這是我已經在使用的支票類型，我想再領同樣的支票。

女：很抱歉，我們已經沒有這種款式了。讓我拿目錄給您看，裡面有現在可以訂的樣式和顏色。

男：哇！選擇還可以更多的，這裡真的沒什麼可選的。

女：您選好了告訴我，我再幫您下訂，大概兩個禮拜就可以拿到新支票。

56. Where does this conversation take place? 這段對話發生在何處？
(A) Clothing store 服飾店
(B) Restaurant 餐廳
(C) Paint store 油漆行
(D) Bank 銀行

解析 **(D)** 男子正在一個他有帳戶（account）的地方訂支票（check），所以是銀行。選項(A)和(C)和對話中提到style（樣式）和color（顏色）有關。選項(B)和對話中提到order（訂購）和check（支票）有關，但意義卻不同，餐廳語境下的order是「點餐」，check則是「帳單」。

57. Why is the man there? 男子為什麼在那裡？
(A) To apply for a job 應徵工作
(B) To return an item 歸還商品
(C) To order something 訂購東西
(D) To make a complaint 客訴

解析 (C) 男子說他想要更多支票，女子則拿可訂的樣式和顏色給他挑，並說兩個禮拜可以拿到，可見男子正在訂支票。選項(A)(B)(D)都不是正確答案。

58. Why does the man say, "The selection certainly could be better"? 男子為什麼說「The selection certainly could be better」？
    (A) He wants more time to make his choice. 他需要更多時間才能做好選擇。
    (B) He doesn't like the offered choices. 他不滿意所提供的選擇。
    (C) He hasn't ever seen better choices. 他沒看過這麼好的選擇。
    (D) He needs help making his choice. 他需要有人幫他選擇。

解析 (B) selection指的是可選擇的種類，如果形容為「could be better」，就表示種類不夠多、不夠好。選項(A)(C)(D)不僅和對話語境不符，也不是這句話的意思。

Questions 59 through 61 refer to the following conversation.
Man 1:　　Have you seen the show at City Theater yet?
Man 2:　　I was there last night. Great acting.
Man 1:　　The best.
Woman:　You both are lucky. By the time I got around to calling the box office, the show was all sold out.
Man 2:　　You know, my cousin got seats for tomorrow, but it turns out he has to go out of town on a business trip. Want me to call him for you? He might not have given them away yet.
Woman:　Thanks, yes. That'd be great.

第59–61題請聽下面這段對話。
男1：你去看城市劇院的那場表演了嗎？
男2：我昨晚去了，演得很棒。
男1：超讚的。
女：　你們兩個真幸運，等我終於有空打電話到售票處時，門票已經賣光了。
男2：你知道嗎，我表弟買了明天的票，結果他因為出差要出城去。要不要我幫你打電話給他？他可能還沒把票給出去。
女：　好啊，謝謝，那太好了。

59. What are the speakers discussing? 說話者在討論什麼？
    (A) A play 一齣戲劇
    (B) A concert 一場音樂會
    (C) A business trip 一趟商務旅行
    (D) A boxing match 一場拳擊賽

解析 (A) 他們正在討論劇院的一場表演，這場表演不僅演得很精彩（great acting），而且需要門票，所以是一齣戲劇。選項(B)也是可能在劇院舉行的活動，也需要門票，但不會「演」得很精彩。選項(C)和(D)都是需要購票的活動。

60. What is the woman's problem? 女子的問題是什麼？
    (A) She has to go out of town. 她須要出城去。
    (B) She doesn't like her seat. 她不滿意她的座位。
    (C) She is busy tomorrow. 她明天很忙。
    (D) She can't get tickets. 她買不到票。

解析 (D) 女子打電話到售票處，卻發現票已經賣光了（sold out）。選項(A)是其中一名男子的表弟要做的事。選項(B)重複使用了seat這個字。選項(C)重複使用了tomorrow這個字，明天是其中一名男子表弟要出城的日子。

61. What does the second man offer to do? 第二名男子表示可以幫什麼忙？
    (A) Plan a trip 規劃旅行
    (B) Call his cousin 打電話給他表弟
    (C) Buy some tickets 買幾張票
    (D) Go to the box office 前往售票處

解析 (B) 男子表示可以打電話給表弟，詢問能不能把票讓給這名女子。選項(A)重複使用了trip這個字，但對話中沒提到規劃一事。選項(C)不正確，他只說要幫忙問還有沒有票，沒說要幫忙買票。選項(D)重複使用了box office此片語，是女子打電話去買票的地方。

Questions 62 through 64 refer to the following conversation and directory.
Woman: Can you help me? I have an appointment with Mr. Gill at Zenith Enterprises, but I'm not sure where his office is.
Man: I can show you myself. It's right on the way to my office at HCR. So I guess you don't work with Mr. Gill, then? I've never seen you around here.
Woman: I don't work with him yet, but I hope to. I'm here to interview for a job. Wish me luck!

第62–64題請聽下面這段對話，並參考樓層簡介。
女：可以幫我一下嗎？我和吉爾先生約在澤尼斯企業，但我不確定他的辦公室在哪裡。
男：我帶你去，就在我到HCR辦公室的路上。我猜你不是吉爾先生的同事囉？我沒在這附近見過你。
女：我還沒成為他的同事，但我希望可以。我是來面試的，祝我好運吧！

樓層簡介	
一樓	伍爾曼與福克斯專業公司
二樓	吉爾克里斯特股份有限公司
三樓	澤尼斯企業
四樓	HCR公司

62. Look at the graphic. What floor will the woman go to? 請看圖表，這名女子將會到幾樓？
    (A) 1st floor 一樓
    (B) 2nd Floor 二樓
    (C) 3rd Floor 三樓
    (D) 4th Floor 四樓

解析 (C) 女子要到澤尼斯企業去見吉爾先生，而澤尼斯企業在三樓。選項(A)(B)(D)是其他公司的所在樓層。

63. Why is she going there? 她為什麼要去那裡？
    (A) To start a new job 開始新工作
    (B) For a job interview 參加工作面試
    (C) To look at an apartment 看一間公寓
    (D) For a doctor's appointment 看醫生

解析 (B) 女子說她希望能和吉爾先生一起工作，就是成為他的同事，因此現在要和他會面，進行工作面試。選項(A)和他們聊到工作有關。選項(C)混淆了近音字 appointment 和 apartment。選項(D)重複使用了對話中的 appointment 這個字。

64. What does the man imply about his relationship with Mr. Gill? 男子暗示他和吉爾先生是什麼樣的關係？
    (A) He works near Mr. Gill. 他工作的地方在吉爾先生附近。
    (B) He is a client of Mr. Gill's. 他是吉爾先生的客戶。
    (C) He has never met Mr. Gill. 他從來沒見過吉爾先生。
    (D) He wants to work for Mr. Gill. 他想為吉爾先生工作。

解析 (A) 男子說吉爾先生的辦公室就在他到自己辦公室的路上，又說他沒見過這名女子，都暗示了他工作的地方就在吉爾先生附近。選項(B)(C)(D)都和正確答案相抵觸。

Questions 65 through 67 refer to the following conversation.
Woman:　No coffee for me thanks. I'd prefer a cup of hot tea with lemon.

Man: All right. I'll boil some water. I just baked a pie. Would you like a piece?
Woman: Oh, no thank you. I had a big lunch and couldn't eat another bite.
Man: Well, if you don't mind, I'll have one. I haven't eaten anything all day except a piece of toast at breakfast.

第 65–67 題請聽下面這段對話。
女：我不要咖啡，謝謝。我比較想喝一杯熱茶加檸檬。
男：好啊，我來燒水。我剛烤了一個派，要來一塊嗎？
女：喔，不了謝謝。我中午吃了一頓大餐，已經吃不下了。
男：那你不介意的話，我就來一塊囉。我一整天都沒吃東西，只有早餐吃了一片吐司而已。

65. What will the woman drink? 這名女子會喝什麼？
　　(A) Lemonade 檸檬水
　　(B) Coffee 咖啡
　　(C) Water 水
　　(D) Tea 茶

解析 (D) 女子說她比較想喝熱茶。選項(A)是從 lemon 想到 lemonade。選項(B)是女子不想喝的。選項(C)是男子要用來泡茶的。

66. Why doesn't she want pie? 她為什麼不想吃派？
　　(A) She isn't hungry. 她不餓。
　　(B) The pie is too hot. 派太燙了。
　　(C) She doesn't like pie. 她不愛吃派。
　　(D) She hasn't had lunch yet. 她還沒吃午餐。

解析 (A) 女子說她午餐吃很飽，已經吃不下任何東西了。選項(B)重複使用了 hot 這個字。選項(C)未被提及。選項(D)錯誤因女子說她中午已經吃一頓大餐了。

67. What will the man do? 這名男子將會做什麼？
　　(A) Have some pie 吃一點派
　　(B) Bake some buns 烤一些麵包
　　(C) Buy some bacon 買一些培根
　　(D) Make some toast 做一些吐司

解析 (A) 男子說他要吃一塊派（have one = have a piece of pie）。選項(B)重複使用了 bake 這個字。選項(C)混淆了近音字 bacon 和 baked。選項(D)重複使用了 toast 這個字。

Questions 68 through 70 refer to the following conversation and menu.

629

Man: Good afternoon. I'm sorry you had to wait so long. We're a bit understaffed today.

Woman: That's OK. I don't mind. Everybody knows the food here's worth waiting for. So, what do you recommend?

Man: Here's a list of the chef's daily lunch specials. The tuna fish salad is very nice and quite popular.

Woman: Well, I am in the mood for something cold, but I don't think I particularly care for fish. Let's see, something with vegetables. Hmm. I think I'll try the number two. And I'll have a glass of soda with that.

第68-70題請聽下面這段對話，並參考菜單。

男：午安，抱歉讓您久等，我們今天人手不足。
女：沒關係，我不介意，大家都知道這裡的食物值得等待。那麼，你推薦哪一道呢？
男：這張單子上有主廚的每日午間特餐，鮪魚沙拉很不錯而且很受歡迎。
女：嗯，我想吃點冷的，但我不是特別愛吃魚。讓我看看，來點有蔬菜的。好，我試試二號餐，再配一杯蘇打水。

```
佛羅倫斯咖啡館
午間特餐

1. 鮪魚沙拉盤 ………… $13
2. 綜合蔬菜沙拉 ……… $12
3. 烤魚飯 ……………… $16
4. 清炒時蔬佐米飯 …… $15
```

68. Why has there been a delay? 為什麼發生延誤？
    (A) The chef arrived late. 廚師遲到。
    (B) There aren't enough servers. 服務生不夠。
    (C) The restaurant is very crowded. 餐廳人太多。
    (D) There are some new staff working. 有一些新員工在上班。

解析 (B) 男子說「We're a bit understaffed today」，意思是今天來上班的員工數不足。既然說話者人在餐廳，就表示服務生不夠。選項(A)重複使用了chef這個字。選項(C)也可能造成延誤，但對話中並未提及。選項(D)使用了understaffed的相關字staff。

69. What does the woman imply about the restaurant? 女子對這家餐廳有何暗示？
    (A) It has a good reputation. 口碑很好。
    (B) It is not well known. 不是很有名。
    (C) It is not very popular. 人氣不高。
    (D) It always has slow service. 服務一直都很慢。

解析 (A) 女子說「Everybody knows the food here's worth waiting for」，表示大多數人對這家餐廳的評價都很好，知道食物好吃到值得等待。選項(B)未被提及。選項(C)重複使用了popular這個字。選項(D)和今天發生延誤有關。

70. Look at the graphic. What will the woman eat? 請看圖表，女子會吃哪道菜？
    (A) Tuna fish salad 鮪魚沙拉
    (B) Vegetable salad 蔬菜沙拉
    (C) Baked fish 烤魚
    (D) Sautéed vegetables 清炒時蔬

解析 (B) 女子說「I'll try the number two」，對照菜單，二號餐是綜合蔬菜沙拉。選項(A)和(C)都有魚，女子說她不愛吃魚。選項(D)雖然有蔬菜，但她有提到想吃點冷的，而不是熱炒菜。

Part 4：簡短獨白

作答方式：你會聽到一名說話者的獨白。每段獨白搭配三個問題，各有四個選項。選出最適當的答案回答問題，並將答案卡上對應的橢圓框塗滿。

Questions 71 through 73 refer to the following recorded message.

Thank you for calling Weston Water Park. We are happy to announce a new deal for state residents. Show us your proof of residence and get fifteen percent off the regular price of an annual pass. Your pass allows you entry to the park seven days a week for a full year. You will also be able to attend events at the park, such as concerts and movie nights, at no extra charge, and you will be invited to the annual Evening Extravaganza, our summer event exclusively for pass holders, when we stay open until midnight. Please press one to talk to a representative about purchasing annual passes for your entire family.

第 71–73 題請聽下面這段錄音留言。

感謝您來電韋斯頓水上樂園。我們很高興宣布一項本州居民獨享的新優惠。出示您的居住證明，購買年票可享原價八五折優惠。持有此票，全年每日皆可入園。您也可以參加園內舉辦的活動，例如音樂會和電影之夜，無須額外付費。您將受邀參加我們每年專為持票者舉辦的夏日活動——夜間盛會，當日開放時間將延長至午夜。請按1與服務專員通話，了解如何為全家購買年票。

71. What is the purpose of this message? 這則留言的目的是什麼？
    (A) To explain rules 說明規則
    (B) To solve a problem 解決一個問題
    (C) To describe a schedule 描述一個時間表
    (D) To introduce a special offer 介紹一個優惠活動

解析 (D) 這則留言提出一項年票優惠，並說明持有年票可享有哪些好處。選項 (A) 和 (B) 也是留言的可能目的，但在這則留言中並未提到。選項 (C) 和樂園中舉辦的各種活動之描述有關。

72. What happens once a year? 下列何者一年發生一次？
    (A) The park stays open late. 園區開放到很晚。
    (B) There is a movie night. 有電影之夜。
    (C) A discount is offered. 提供優惠。
    (D) A concert is performed. 舉辦音樂會。

解析 (A) 說話者提到夜間盛會（Evening Extravaganza），並說當日園區會開放到午夜。選項 (B) 和 (D) 是留言中提到的活動，但沒說多久會舉辦一次。選項 (C) 是這則留言的主題，但留言中沒提到多久會提供一次優惠。

73. Who can the listener talk to by pressing one? 聽者可按1和誰通話？
    (A) A musician 音樂家
    (B) An operator 接線生
    (C) A sales agent 銷售專員
    (D) A park manager 樂園經理

解析 (C) 留言中說「press one to talk to a representative about purchasing annual passes」，按1可和專員通話了解購買年票事宜，所以這位專員會負責銷售。選項 (A) 和留言中提到的音樂會有關。選項 (B) 和留言中提到和專員通話有關。選項 (D) 和樂園這個主題有關。

Questions 74 through 76 refer to the following talk.

Welcome to this morning's workshop. Please, everyone, take a seat now. I see you've all brought your laptops as requested, good. We'll need them a little later when we try out some software. OK, as you can see on the schedule I'm passing out, we'll begin with an overview of stocks and bonds—what are they and how they help your money grow. Then we'll look at some other places you can put your money, such as real estate, banks, etc. We'll take one break after the first hour and then another at around eleven. That'll give you a chance to stretch your legs and get some coffee and a snack.

第74–76題請聽下面這段談話。

歡迎各位參加今天早上的工作坊，大家請坐。我看到你們都按照要求帶了筆電，很好。待會試用一些軟體時會用到。好的，如同大家在我發下去的時程表上所看到的，我們首先會大致介紹股票和債券──它們是什麼，以及它們如何幫助你的資金增值。接著我們會談論還可以把錢放到哪裡，像是房地產、銀行等。第一個小時後會有一次休息時間，十一點左右還會有一次休息。你們可以利用時間活動一下筋骨，喝點咖啡、吃些點心。

74. What is the topic of the workshop? 這個工作坊的主題是什麼？
    (A) Budgets 預算
    (B) Computers 電腦
    (C) Investments 投資
    (D) Software 軟體

解析 (C) 工作坊會談論股票和債券（stocks and bonds）、如何幫助資金增值（how they help your money grow）、把錢放到哪裡（places you can put your money），所以是投資。選項(A)使用了 money 的相關字 budgets。選項(B)使用了 laptops 的相關字 computers。選項(D)重複使用了 software 這個字。

75. What does the speaker give each participant? 說話者發給每位參加者什麼東西？
    (A) A schedule 一份時程表
    (B) A laptop 一臺筆記型電腦
    (C) A snack 一份點心
    (D) A chair 一張椅子

解析 (A) 說話者提到「the schedule I'm passing out」，所以是時程表。選項(B)是參加者被要求攜帶的物品。選項(C)是參加者在休息時間可能會吃的東西。選項(D)使用了 seat 的相關字 chair。

76. How many breaks will there be? 一共會有幾次休息時間？
    (A) 1
    (B) 2
    (C) 3
    (D) 4

解析 (B) 說話者描述「We'll take one break after the first hour and then another at around eleven」，所以一共會有兩次休息。選項(A)被描述中的 one break 給誤導。選項(C)和(D)未被提及。

Questions 77 through 79 refer to the following announcement.

May I have your attention, please. The captain has just told us that we will be entering a small storm. We cannot fly over or around it, unfortunately. Please return to your seats as soon as possible and fasten your seat belts. Please stow all bags under your seats or in the overhead storage compartment. Unfortunately, this means our next beverage service will be suspended until further notice. We are very sorry for this inconvenience, but it is for our safety. I'll let you know when we have more information to share. Thank you.

第 77–79 題請聽下面這段廣播。

各位旅客請注意。機長剛才通知，我們即將進入一個小型風暴區，很不幸，我們無法飛越或繞行。請盡快回到您的座位，並繫好安全帶。請將所有行李置於座位下方或頭頂置物櫃。很遺憾，這表示我們下一次的飲料服務也將因此暫停，直到有進一步通知。很抱歉造成您的不便，但這是為了大家的安全。如果有更多資訊，我會告知各位。謝謝。

77. Where is this talk happening? 這段談話發生在什麼地方？
    (A) On a plane 飛機上
    (B) On a boat 船上
    (C) At a hotel 飯店裡
    (D) On a bus 公車上

解析 (A) 說話者正在對乘客說話，提到有一場風暴，並說無法飛越或繞行（We cannot fly over or around it），既然講「fly」，一定是在飛機上。選項(B)也會有乘客（passenger）和船長（機長和船長都叫captain），但船不能飛。選項(C)和廣播中提到bags有關。選項(D)也有乘客，但同樣不能飛。

78. What is the problem? 發生了什麼問題？
    (A) Storage compartments are full. 置物櫃已滿。
    (B) There are not enough seats. 座位不夠。
    (C) There is bad weather. 天氣狀況不佳。
    (D) Bags have been lost. 行李遺失。

解析 (C) 他們遇上一個風暴（storm），所以是天氣問題。選項(A)重複使用了storage compartments這個片語。選項(B)重複使用了seats這個字。選項(D)重複使用了bags這個字。

79. What has been delayed? 下列何者被延後了？
    (A) Serving drinks 供應飲料
    (B) The arrival time 抵達時間
    (C) Showing a movie 播放電影
    (D) The departure time 起飛時間

解析 (A) 說話者提到「beverage service will be suspended until further notice」，表示飲料服務將暫停直到有進一步通知。選項(B)(C)(D)是搭機情境中可能延後的事，但此處並未提及。

Questions 80 through 82 refer to the following telephone message.

Hi. I'm having a problem with the HR 10 space heater I recently bought. The first time I used it, it worked fine, but now it doesn't. When I turn it on, I hear the fan blowing, but it just blows cold air. I've had the heater for two days now, and I haven't been able to get it to heat again. I've read the manual cover to cover, but I can't find an answer there. I know I could take it back to the store for a refund, but I'd rather try to fix the problem first. Please let me know if there is any way to do this. You can phone me any morning before noon. Thank you.

第80–82題請聽下面這段電話留言。

嗨，我最近購買的HR 10空間加熱器出了一點問題。第一次使用時還運作良好，現在卻不行了。我啟動時，有聽到風扇在吹，但只吹出冷風。這臺加熱器我買來已經兩天了，一直沒辦法再次加熱。我把使用手冊從頭到尾都看過一遍了，就是找不到解決方式。我知道可以拿回店裡退貨，但我想先試著解決問題，請告訴我有沒有什麼辦法可以處理此問題。每天早上到中午以前都可以打電話給我，謝謝。

80. What problem does the speaker have with the product? 說話者使用這個產品時出了什麼問題？
    (A) It doesn't have a cover. 它沒有蓋子。
    (B) The fan doesn't blow. 風扇吹不動。
    (C) She can't turn it on. 她無法啟動。
    (D) It doesn't heat. 它無法加熱。

解析 (D) 這項產品是一個加熱器，說話者說「I haven't been able to get it to heat again」，表示無法再次加熱。選項(A)和使用手冊的封面（cover）產生了混淆，cover to cover字面上是從封面到封面，意思就是「從頭到尾」。選項(B)不正確，女子說她有聽到風扇在吹。選項(C)不正確，女子說她可以啟動，而且啟動後風扇有在吹。

81. When did the speaker buy the product? 說話者是何時購買這項產品的？
    (A) This morning 今天早上
    (B) Two days ago 兩天前
    (C) Last Tuesday 上個星期二
    (D) Nine days ago 九天前

解析 (B) 說話者說「I've had the heater for two days」，她已經買兩天了。選項(A)重複使用了morning這個字。選項(C)的發音和正確答案相近。選項(D)混淆了近音字fine和nine。

636

82. What does the speaker ask the listener to do? 說話者要求聽者做什麼事？
    (A) Replace the product 更換產品
    (B) Provide a refund 提供退款
    (C) Return the call 回電
    (D) Send a manual 寄送使用手冊

解析 (C) 說話者請聽者回電（phone me），告訴她是否有辦法修好加熱器。選項(A)就此語境來說是有可能，但留言中並未提及。選項(B)是說話者不想做的事。選項(D)不正確，說話者已經有使用手冊，而且也看完了。

Questions 83 through 85 refer to the following talk.

Welcome to Old City Tours. This morning we will take a stroll through the city's historic district to view some of the neighborhood's most notable buildings. We'll start with the old City Hall, notable for its Greek Revival style, then take a look at a private home built to resemble a castle, and view several other places representing a range of building styles popular in the nineteenth century. We'll also take a quick walk through Atwell Park and the flower gardens there, and end with lunch at the Atwell Café. I already have everyone's ticket, so if you'll all gather around here, I'll show you on a map all the places we'll be seeing.

第 83–85 題請聽下面這段談話。

歡迎參加古城區之旅。今天早上我們會漫步穿越城市的歷史區，欣賞那一帶最著名的建築。我們會從以希臘復興式建築風格聞名的舊市政廳開始，接著參觀一座仿城堡建築的私人宅邸，然後看幾座代表十九世紀不同建築風格的建築物。我們也會到艾特威爾公園和那裡的花園快速走一下，最後在艾特威爾咖啡館享用午餐。大家的票都在我這裡，請大家靠過來，我在地圖上指出全部要參觀的地方給你們看。

83. What is the focus of the tour? 這個行程的重點是什麼？
    (A) Architecture 建築
    (B) Gardens 花園
    (C) History 歷史
    (D) Parks 公園

解析 (A) 說話者提到參觀建築和欣賞不同的建築風格。選項(B)和(D)是他們在行程中會看到的地方，但不是此行程的重點。選項(C)和歷史區（historic district）有關，是他們要參觀的城區，但行程重點並不在於歷史。

637

84. How will the group travel? 此團將採用何種交通方式？
(A) Bus 公車
(B) Van 廂型車
(C) Foot 步行
(D) Bike 自行車

解析 (C) 說話者分別提到 take a stroll 和 take a quick walk，都是步行的意思。選項(A)(B)(D)在參觀導覽的語境中雖有可能，但並非此處的正確答案。

85. What will the group do first? 此團將會先做哪件事？
(A) Have lunch 享用午餐
(B) Look at a map 看地圖
(C) Visit City Hall 參觀市政廳
(D) Buy their tickets 購票

解析 (B) 說話者要大家靠過來，他要先讓大家看一下地圖，這件事做完了才會開始參觀行程。選項(A)是行程最後才要做的事。選項(C)是參觀行程的第一站，但是看完地圖才會出發到市政廳。選項(D)是已經完成的事，說話者提到他手上已經有大家的票了。

Questions 86 through 88 refer to the following advertisement.

Tired of old, burnt coffee? With the new Stenson's Executive Coffeemaker in your break room, you and your colleagues can enjoy fresh, delicious coffee all day long. It's so easy to use. Just fill the container with water. Then, insert a premeasured Stenson's coffee packet, press the button, and that's it. Fresh coffee will be ready for you in just a few minutes. There's no mess and no measuring. With Stenson's patented warming system, your coffee stays at just the right temperature without burning for up to eight hours. The Stenson's Executive Coffeemaker can make twenty-four cups at a time. Visit us at www dot stensons dot com to find out about this and other fine Stenson's products.

第 86–88 題請聽下面這段廣告。

厭倦了放久又焦苦的咖啡嗎？茶水間有了全新的史坦森高級咖啡機，您和同事就能全天享用新鮮香醇的咖啡。使用方法非常簡單，只要將容器加滿水，然後放入預先量好的史坦森咖啡包，按下按鈕，就完成了。只要幾分鐘，新鮮的咖啡就會為您準備好。無須弄得亂七八糟，也無須自己量取。史坦森的專利保溫系統，能讓咖啡維持適宜溫度達八小時，絕不產生焦苦味。史坦森高級咖啡機一次可沖煮二十四杯咖啡。請上官網www.stensons.com，了解這款咖啡機及更多史坦森的優質產品。

86. Where will this product be used? 這項產品會用在什麼地方？
　　(A) In an office 辦公室
　　(B) At a restaurant 餐廳
　　(C) On an airplane 飛機上
　　(D) In a private home 私人住宅

解析 (A) 說話者提到這項產品會放在茶水間（break room），並且和同事（colleagues）一起享用，所以它的行銷對象是辦公室的員工。選項(B)(C)(D)都是可以放咖啡機的地方，但不是正確答案。

87. How many cups of coffee does the product make? 這項產品可沖煮幾杯咖啡？
　　(A) 20
　　(B) 24
　　(C) 28
　　(D) 29

解析 (B) 說話者說這款咖啡機一次可沖煮二十四杯（can make twenty-four cups at a time）。選項(A)與正確答案發音相近。選項(C)被咖啡的保溫時間（eight hours）給混淆。選項(D)混淆了近音字 time 和 nine。

88. What are listeners asked to do? 聽者被要求做什麼？
　　(A) Place an order 下訂單
　　(B) Try other products 試試其他產品
　　(C) Ask for a free sample 索取免費試用品
　　(D) Look for information 尋找資訊

解析 (D) 說話者要聽者到公司網站了解這款咖啡機及更多史坦森的優質產品（to find out about this and other fine Stenson's products），就是尋找資訊的意思。選項(A)和(C)是顧客上網也可能做的事。選項(B)重複使用了 products 這個字。

Questions 89 through 91 refer to the following news report.

This is Rosa Mendez for Channel five news. I'm here on the new Swift River Bridge as the opening ceremony is about to begin. It's a beautiful day for the ceremony, with a deep blue sky and a warm breeze. Mayor Johnson will be arriving any minute now to cut the ribbon, and there is a long line of drivers waiting to be among the first to go across the new bridge. This project has been popular from the start. Initial plans met with loud approval from city residents, who were tired of traffic congestion on the two other bridges crossing the Swift. And, the construction costs have been kept very low. It's hard to believe, but final costs came in well under budget. All in all, the bridge project has been a huge success.

第 89-91 題請聽下面這段新聞報導。

我是羅莎‧曼德茲,第五頻道新聞報導。我現在正在新建的斯威夫特河大橋上,開幕儀式即將開始。今日天氣很好,天空湛藍,暖風輕拂,非常適合開幕。強森市長馬上就會抵達現場進行剪綵,而這裡已有長長的隊伍等著成為第一批通過新橋的駕駛者。這項計畫從一開始就受到歡迎,初始計畫獲得市民熱烈支持,他們早已厭倦斯威特河另外兩座橋的交通堵塞。同時,建造工程的成本控制得非常低。實在難以置信,最後成本竟然遠低於預算。總而言之,這項橋樑計畫非常成功。

89. What event is the speaker reporting? 說話者正在報導何種活動?
　　(A) Approval of bridge plans 橋樑計畫的核准
　　(B) Completion of a bridge 橋樑竣工
　　(C) Repainting of an old bridge 舊橋重新粉刷
　　(D) Repair work on all city bridges 所有市內橋樑的維修工程

解析 (B) 說話者正在談論一座新橋的開幕儀式。選項(A)混淆了談話中的 loud approval,說話者是說橋樑計畫獲得市民的熱烈支持(met with loud approval)。選項(C)和(D)是此語境下可能進行的活動,但報導中並未提及。

90. What are people waiting to do? 人們正等待做什麼事?
　　(A) Photograph the bridge 拍攝橋樑
　　(B) Talk with the reporter 和記者談話
　　(C) Cross the bridge 過橋
　　(D) See the mayor 見市長

解析 (C) 說話者說「there is a long line of drivers waiting to be among the first to go across the new bridge」,所以人們正排隊等待過橋。選項(A)和(B)也有可能,但並未提及。選項(D)重複了 mayor 這個字。

91. What does the speaker mean when she says, "It's hard to believe, but final costs came in well under budget"?
說話者說「It's hard to believe, but final costs came in well under budget」是什麼意思?
　　(A) She doesn't understand the budget. 她不了解預算。
　　(B) She's surprised the project cost so little. 她很驚訝這項計畫的成本竟然這麼低。
　　(C) She thinks incorrect numbers have been given. 她認為提供的數字不正確。
　　(D) She isn't certain what the total cost of the project is. 她不確定這項計畫的總成本是多少。

解析 (B) 片語「It's hard to believe」用來表示對一件事情感到驚訝。選項 (A)(C)(D) 都沒有正確解釋這句話的意思。

Questions 92 through 94 refer to the following announcement.

Welcome to Talk Radio. Our guest tonight is Roger Maguire, author of Island Cuisine. Roger started out as a cook in Chicago. When he was offered a position as head chef at a restaurant in Jamaica, he jumped at the chance. Since then, he has worked at restaurants around the Caribbean, learning not only about local food traditions but also about how the cuisine is intimately connected with the culture and history of the region. In his book, he shares with us the recipes he has developed based on his island experiences. You can meet Roger in person tomorrow at the Palm Restaurant, where he will share excerpts from his book.

第 92–94 題請聽下面這段廣播。

歡迎收聽《談話廣播》。今晚的來賓是《島嶼美食》的作者羅傑・麥奎爾。羅傑最初在芝加哥當廚師。當他收到牙買加一家餐廳的主廚職位邀約時，他馬上抓住了機會。從那時開始，他就在加勒比海地區各大餐廳工作，不僅學習了當地飲食傳統，也認識到美食與地區文化和歷史是如何密不可分的。他在書中和我們分享了根據島嶼生活經驗所研發的食譜。各位明天可以在棕櫚餐廳親自見到他，他也會分享書中的一些內容。

92. What is the book about? 這本書在講什麼？
    (A) History 歷史
    (B) Cooking 烹飪
    (C) Travel 旅行
    (D) Memoir 回憶錄

解析 (B) 書名包含了 cuisine（料理、美食）這個字，羅傑又是一名廚師（chef），書中還會分享食譜（recipes），所以是一本談論烹飪的書。選項 (A) 和 (C) 是廣播中提到的細節。選項 (D) 在此語境中雖然有可能，但不是正確答案。

93. What does the speaker mean when he says, "He jumped at the chance"? 說話者說「He jumped at the chance」是什麼意思？
    (A) Roger decided not to take a risk. 羅傑決定不要冒險。
    (B) Roger immediately accepted a job offer. 羅傑馬上接受了一個工作邀約。
    (C) Roger was surprised to hear about the job. 羅傑聽到這份工作的消息時很驚訝。
    (D) Roger looked for other work opportunities. 羅傑尋找了其他工作機會。

解析 (B)「jump at the chance」這個片語的意思是「立刻把握住機會」。羅傑受邀擔任主廚的職位，而他馬上接受了。選項 (A)(C)(D) 都和語境不符，也不是這句話的意思。

94. What will Roger do tomorrow? 羅傑明天會做什麼？
    (A) Cook a meal 煮一頓飯
    (B) Eat at a restaurant 在一間餐廳用餐
    (C) Read from his book 讀他書中的內容
    (D) Travel to the Caribbean 前往加勒比海地區

解析 **(C)** 說話者說羅傑明天會在一間餐廳分享書中的內容（share excerpts from his book）。選項(A)和(B)與羅傑明天會在的地方有關。選項(D)是羅傑過去所做的事。

Questions 95 through 97 refer to the following excerpt from a meeting and graph.

Let's take a look at this first slide, which shows the last quarter's sales for our new footwear line. These are the reported sales for all our retail outlets, both brick-and-mortar stores and online sales. You'll notice that there were noticeably lower sales among this age group here. So that's who we're going to need to pay the most attention to as we move forward. Whether it's sandals, slippers, or running shoes, that's the age group we've got to target our advertising at. So before we look at the rest of the figures, I'd like to take a few minutes to talk over any ideas you might have about how best to reach this group.

第95-97題請聽下面這段會議節錄，並參考圖表。

先看第一張投影片，上面顯示我們新鞋類產品系列上一季的銷售額。這是我們所有零售點回報的銷售額，包含實體店和網路銷售。你會注意到這個年齡層的銷售額明顯偏低，所以在我們未來的工作中，最需要關注的就是這個族群。無論是涼鞋、拖鞋還是跑鞋，我們的廣告必須鎖定這個目標年齡層。所以，在我們看其他數字之前，我想花幾分鐘談談，你們對觸及這個族群有什麼想法。

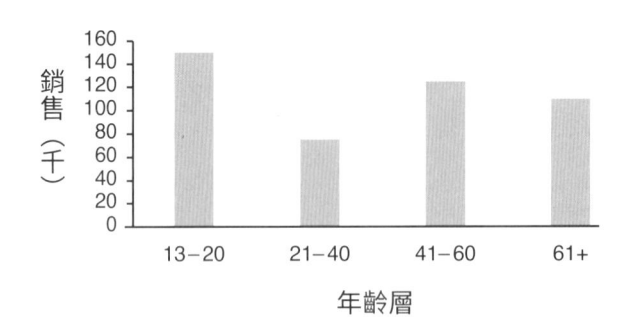

95. What type of product does this company sell? 這家公司販賣哪一類商品？
    (A) Shoes 鞋類
    (B) Clothes 服飾
    (C) Sports equipment 運動用品
    (D) Construction materials 建材

解析 (A) 說話者提到 footwear，是鞋類的總稱，並提到 sandals（涼鞋）、slippers（拖鞋）和 running shoes（跑鞋），都是鞋的類型。選項 (B) 和 footwear 是相關字。選項 (C) 和 running shoes 有關。選項 (D) 被 brick-and-mortar stores 給混淆，這個用語指的是相對於網路商店的「實體店」。

96. Look at the graphic. Which age group does the speaker want to focus on?
    請看圖表，說話者想特別關注的是哪個年齡層？
    (A) 13–20
    (B) 21–40
    (C) 41–60
    (D) 61+

解析 (B) 說話者在意的是銷售額明顯偏低（noticeably lower sales）的那個年齡層，對照圖表，明顯偏低的是 21–40 的年齡層。選項 (A)(C)(D) 的銷售額都較高，且三者之間沒有顯著差距。

97. What will the listeners do next? 聽者接下來會做什麼？
    (A) Read a sales report 閱讀一份銷售報告
    (B) Work in groups 分組工作
    (C) Have a discussion 進行討論
    (D) Look at another slide 看另一張投影片

解析 (C) 說話者說「I'd like to take a few minutes to talk over any ideas you might have」，所以是要他們討論彼此的想法。選項 (A) 使用了 reported 的相關字 report。選項 (B) 重複使用了 groups 這個字。選項 (D) 重複使用了 slide 這個字。

Questions 98 through 100 refer to the following telephone message and map.

Hi, Marc. I'm going over the trip itinerary you made, and it all looks great—the meetings schedule, the transportation, everything. There's just one thing I'd like to change. I'd want to add a couple of days to the trip because Professor Obard will be giving a seminar at the conference center in Millington, and I'd really like to attend it, especially since it's just a short train ride from where I'll be. So please get me a ticket to Millington for the fourteenth. Also, I'll need a hotel room for two nights. I'd like to be as close to the train station as possible, so I don't have to worry about taxis. Thanks.

第 98–100 題請聽下面這段電話留言，並參考地圖。

嗨，馬克。我正在看你安排的行程，一切看起來都很棒──會議日程、交通安排，全部都很好。只有一個地方我想改一下，我想把行程增加幾天，因為歐巴德教授會在密靈頓的會議中心開研討會，我真的很想參加，尤其那裡從我所在的地方搭火車一下就能到達。所以要請你幫我買十四號到密靈頓的車票，還要訂兩晚的飯店。我希望住的地方盡可能靠近火車站，才不用煩惱還要搭計程車，謝謝。

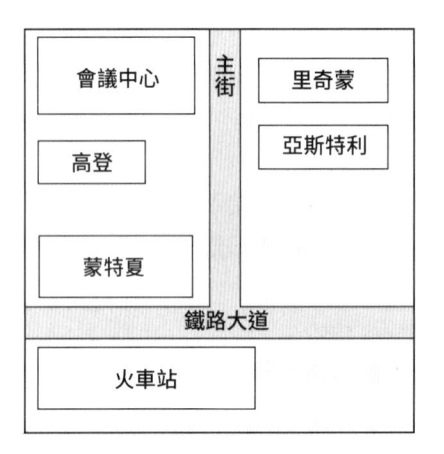

會議中心	里奇蒙
高登	亞斯特利
蒙特夏	

主街 / 鐵路大道 / 火車站

98. Who is Marc, most likely? 馬克最有可能是什麼人？
    (A) A ticket agent 售票員
    (B) A hotel manager 飯店經理
    (C) The speaker's boss 說話者的老闆
    (D) The speaker's assistant 說話者的助理

解析 (D) 馬克正在安排說話者的行程細節，應該是她的助理。選項 (A) 和 (B) 不正確，因為馬克負責安排的不是只有火車票或飯店業務，他還要安排會議日程。選項 (C) 和這裡的語境有關，但不太可能由老闆來安排行程細節。

99. Why does the speaker want to change her travel plans? 說話者為何想更改她的旅行計畫？
    (A) To go to a seminar 為了參加研討會
    (B) To add more meetings 為了加入更多場會議
    (C) To stay at a better hotel 為了住更好的飯店
    (D) To use a different form of transportation 為了使用另一種交通方式

解析 (A) 說話者想增加行程時間，以便參加歐巴德教授的研討會。選項(B)重複使用了meetings這個字，但留言中沒有提到要加入一些會議。選項(C)重複使用了hotel這個字，但留言中沒有提到要住更好的飯店。選項(D)重複使用了transportation這個字，留言中也沒有提到要更換交通方式。

100. Look at the graphic. Which hotel will the speaker prefer? 請看圖表，說話者會想住哪一間飯店？
    (A) Richmond 里奇蒙
    (B) Golden 高登
    (C) Asterly 亞斯特利
    (D) Montshire 蒙特夏

解析 (D) 說話者提到她想住盡可能靠近火車站的飯店，對照圖表，最近的是蒙特夏飯店（Montshire）。選項(A)(B)(C)距離火車站都比蒙特夏飯店還遠。

STOP 本測驗之聽力測驗到此結束，請翻頁進行 Part 5 的測驗。

閱讀測驗

在本段測驗當中，你將有機會展現自己對書面英語的理解能力。閱讀測驗共有三個大題，每一大題均有作答說明。

你有 75 分鐘時間完成本測驗的第五到第七大題。

Part 5：句子填空

作答方式：你會看到一個缺字的句子和四個可能的選項，選出最適當的答案，將答案卡上對應的橢圓框塗滿。

101. 報名城市技術學院木工課程，培養寶貴工作技能，同時賺取好薪水。
    (A) 價值 (n.)、重視 (v.)
    (B) 重視 (ved)
    (C) 有價值地
    (D) 有價值的、寶貴的

解析 (D) valuable是形容詞，修飾名詞skills。選項(A)是動詞或名詞。選項(B)是過去式或過去分詞。選項(C)是副詞。

102. 惠普廂型貨車可承載高達5350磅重的貨物，並配備倒車攝影機和安全警示系統。
    (A) 在……之上
    (B) 向上、上升
    (C) 在……之前
    (D) 在……之內

解析 (B) up to的意思是「高達、多達」。選項(A)(C)(D)放入句中意思都不通。

103. 這個課程主要是為職場專業人士開設，因此每週兩個晚上會上課。
    (A) 幾乎沒有
    (B) 迅速地
    (C) 主要地
    (D) 稍微地

解析 (C) primarily的意思是「主要地」(= mainly)。選項(A)(B)(D)都與文意不符。

104. 葛雷格・崔斯特每月的第一個星期一對外開放他的藝術工作室，和城市每月舉行的藝術漫步活動同一天。

解析 (D) 動詞coincide固定搭配的介系詞是with。選項(A)(B)(C)的介系詞通常不與coincide連用。

105. 管理團隊決定新的洗衣精標誌將採用粉橘配色。
    (A) 外表
    (B) 照片
    (C) 組合
    (D) 線條

解析 **(C)** color scheme 指的是顏色的組合或配置。選項 (A)(B)(D) 都與文意不符。

106. 我強烈建議與 LL 物流公司簽約，來處理我們的國內配送。
    (A)(B)(C)(D) 簽約

解析 **(C)** 主要動詞 recommend 後面要接動名詞。選項 (A) 是現在式或原形動詞。選項 (B) 是過去式。選項 (D) 是未來式。

107. 園藝師說他下禮拜過來時會把辦公室周圍的樹籬修剪一下。
    (A)(B)(C)(D) 修剪

解析 **(B)** 句中出現了時間用語 next week，因此動詞要用未來式。選項 (A) 是現在式。選項 (C) 是現在完成式。選項 (D) 是現在完成進行式。

108. 若你能等幾分鐘，佐藤女士一有空就會處理你的問題。

解析 **(A)** 動詞 attend 搭配介系詞 to，表示「處理、照料」。選項 (B)(C)(D) 的介系詞通常不與 attend 連用。

109. 札賽爾每週優惠券可享全店商品六折，除訂製相框、家具及電子產品不適用。
    (A) 免除、豁免
    (B) 擁有
    (C) 無、沒有
    (D) 除了……之外

解析 **(D)** except 是介系詞，意指「除了……之外、不含」。選項 (A) 和 (B) 不是介系詞。選項 (C) 帶入句中語意邏輯不通。

110. 工廠訪客必須將個人物品留在警衛櫃檯，並穿上防護衣、戴上護目鏡。
    (A) 所有物、財物
    (B) 戲服、道具服
    (C) 經驗
    (D) 外觀、出現

解析 **(A)** belongings 意指「所有物、財物」，這句話的意思是，訪客不得將個人物品帶進工廠。選項 (B)(C)(D) 放入句子語意都不通。

111. 丹尼爾雖然有團隊精神,也一向準時,卻沒有勝任這份工作的能力。
    (A) 他(主格)
    (B) 他(受格)
    (C) 他的
    (D) 她的

解析 (C) his是所有格形容詞,在這個句子中指Daniel's,並修飾名詞job。選項(A)是主格代名詞。選項(B)是受格代名詞。選項(D)用於女性。

112. 簽署這份表格,即表示您授權KM索償處理公司作為您的代理人。
    (A) 授權 (ving)
    (B) 授權 (n.)
    (C) 權力、權威人士
    (D) 授權 (v.)

解析 (D) 這裡需要一個動詞當作子句的主要動詞。選項(A)是動名詞或現在分詞。選項(B)和(C)是名詞。

113. 全職員工經主管核准,可由部門承擔費用,參加RSTLC年度會議。
    (A) be動詞
    (B) 不
    (C) 能、可以
    (D) 不會、不能

解析 (C) can是情態動詞,在這個句子中,can放在原形動詞attend的前面,表示「可以、允許」。選項(A)文法不正確。選項(B)和(D)放入句中意思不通。

114. 很不幸的是廚房需要大規模整修,必須由受訓過的水電工來進行。
    (A) 邊緣的
    (B) 大規模的
    (C) 最小的
    (D) 常見的

解析 (B) extensive在這裡指「大規模的、大量的」。選項(A)(C)(D)都不符合這裡的語意要求。

115. 由於預算消減，該公司將不會填補目前空缺的行銷主管一職。
    (A) 因為、由於
    (B) 然而
    (C) 因為
    (D) 因為、在……方面

解析 **(A)** due to 在這裡引導一個名詞片語。選項(B)用來表達對比，同時也不能引導名詞片語。選項(C)和(D)只能引導子句，不能引導片語。

116. 這支遙控器被設定和大廳的電視配對，而不是休息室的。

解析 **(D)** 這個句子是被動語態，動詞結構為「現在式 be 動詞 + 主要動詞的過去分詞」。選項(A)不是 be 動詞。選項(B)和(C)是 be 動詞，但未表現出時態。

117. 文件上簽名的人是最終要為這筆交易負責的人。
    (A) 他／她（們）、……的人（主格）
    (B) who is 或 who has 的縮寫
    (C) 他／她／它（們）的
    (D) 他／她（們）、……的人（受格）

解析 **(C)** whose 是所有格關係代名詞，在這個句子中，whose signature 代表 the person's signature。選項(A)和(D)可以作關係代名詞，但不是所有格。選項(B)是 who is 或 who has 的縮寫。

118. 本部門絕不鼓勵最後一刻才交付工作。
    (A)(B)(C)(D) 等待

解析 **(B)** waiting 是動名詞，在句中擔任主詞。選項(A)和(D)是原形動詞或現在式。選項(C)是不定詞。

119. 你可在你方便時報名參加線上培訓課程，或親自參加下週的實體培訓課程。
    (A) 或者
    (B) 所以
    (C) 如果
    (D) 隨著、像……一樣

解析 **(A)** or 用來帶出一個選擇。選項(B)帶出一個結果。選項(C)帶出一個條件。選項(D)引導一個子句或進行比較。

120. 這份預算報告必須重寫,因當中有些數字不正確。
    (A) 可接受的
    (B) 不正確的
    (C) 全面的
    (D) 計算的

解析 (B) inaccurate 的意思是「不正確的、不精確的」,inaccurate figures(不正確的數字)是重寫預算報告的合理原因。選項(A)(C)(D)放入句子都不合理。

121. 該公司計劃買下鄰近的幾塊地,以用來擴建製造廠。
    (A) 詢問
    (B) 要求、需要
    (C) 到期
    (D) 取得、購得

解析 (D) acquire 的意思是「取得、購得」。選項(A)(B)(C)放入句子意思都不通。

122. 客戶接受方案之後,團隊有一個月的時間來完成最後設計。
    (A) 在……之前
    (B) 在……之後
    (C) 當……之時
    (D) 當時、然後

解析 (B) after 引導的時間子句描述的是發生在前的動作,在這個句子中,客戶先接受方案,團隊才有一個時間來完成設計。選項(A)和(D)用來引導發生在後的動作。選項(C)引導一個同時發生的動作。

123. 獲得主管認可的最好方式,是始終準時完成專案。
    (A) 贏得、獲得
    (B) 收集
    (C) 同意、給予
    (D) 招致

解析 (A) to earn approval 用來表達因某個行動而獲得認可,這裡的 earn 等同於 get。選項(B)(C)(D)都與文意不符。

124. 等整修工作完成,我們就會擁有一間更漂亮、更寬敞的辦公室。

解析 (A) 這是一個未來時間子句,要用現在式代替未來式。選項(B)是現在式,但與複數主詞 renovations 不一致。選項(C)是原形動詞。選項(D)是未來式。

651

125. 若客戶認為照片太大，製作團隊可以調整大小。
    (A) 尺寸、大小
    (B) 調整……的大小
    (C) 相當大的
    (D) 調整大小

解析 (B) resize是動詞，在句中接在情態動詞can的後面。選項(A)是名詞。選項(C)是形容詞。選項(D)是名詞或動名詞。

126. 雖然貨物比承諾的時間晚寄出，客戶還是決定再次下單。
    (A) 因為、由於
    (B) 因此
    (C) 儘管
    (D) 雖然

解析 (D) although引導一個描述矛盾事實的從屬子句。選項(A)用來帶出一個原因。選項(B)帶出一個結果。選項(C)是介系詞，不能引導子句。

127. 網站上的報價包含了材料費和人工費，但不含運費和處理費。
    (A) 包含 (v.)
    (B) 包含 (ving)
    (C) 包含的、包括的
    (D) 包含地、包括地

解析 (A) include在這個句子中當主要動詞。選項(B)是動名詞或現在分詞。選項(C)是形容詞。選項(D)是副詞。

128. 人力資源部要求所有應徵者提供前雇主所寫的推薦信。
    (A) 在……之前
    (B) 在前面的
    (C) 以前的、先前的
    (D) 位於……之前、先於

解析 (C) previous是形容詞，描述先前的人或事物，在此句中描述的是先前的雇主 (employers)。選項(A)是介系詞，不是形容詞。選項(B)指位於前方或領先的東西。選項(D)是動詞，不是形容詞。

129. 你可以選擇以郵寄方式收取薪資支票，或選擇直接存入你的銀行帳號。
    (A) 兩者任一
    (B) 作為替代
    (C) 兩者擇一
    (D) 此外

解析 (B) instead是副詞，表示「作為替代」。選項(A)必須用於or前面的子句。選項(C)不是副詞。選項(D)的意義不適用於這個句子。

130. 如果公司投資更多在廣告上，上一季的銷售會更好。
    (A)(B)(C)(D) 投資

解析 (A) 這是一個與過去事實相反的假設（非真實條件句），if子句的動詞要用過去完成式。選項(B)是現在完成式。選項(C)是現在完成進行式。選項(D)是主要子句的句型，不用在if子句。

Part 6：段落填空

> **作答方式**：你會看到四篇短文，各含四個空格，每個空格配有四個選項，選出最適當的單字、片語或句子完成這段敘述。

第 131–134 題請看下面這封信。

> 企業老闆，您好：
>
> 我們寫信是要向您介紹我們的新公司行政餐飲公司，專為本地企業提供外燴服務，從雅緻的宴會到會議和工作坊的非正式茶點都有。我們有各式各樣的菜單供您選擇，還可以根據您的特殊需求提供客製化服務。從場地布置、餐飲服務到清潔善後，我們全部一手包辦，也可依需要提供餐具、擺飾和桌椅。身為公司創辦人，我們擁有加起來二十五年的餐飲服務經驗，且都畢業於國家烹飪學校。希望您能與我們聯絡，討論您的外燴需求。
>
> 伊蓮・梅菲爾德和喬吉娜・席姆斯
> 敬上

131. (A)(B)(C)(D) 知道

    解析 (A) let 後面必須使用原形動詞。選項 (B) 是現在式。選項 (C) 是不定詞。選項 (D) 是未來式。

132. (A) 它的
     (B) 我們的
     (C) 你的、你們的
     (D) 他們的

    解析 (C) 所有格形容詞 your 修飾名詞 needs，這裡指的是這封信的收信人，因此要用第二人稱。選項 (A) 和 (D) 是第三人稱。選項 (B) 是第一人稱。

133. (A) 稽核員
     (B) 支持者
     (C) 客戶
     (D) 創辦人

    解析 (D) founder 是創辦公司的人，這裡寫信介紹新公司的即該公司的創辦人。選項 (A)(B)(C) 放入句子意思都不通。

654

134. (A) 相信您一定會滿意我們為您安排的餐點。
    (B) 希望您能與我們聯絡,討論您的外燴需求。
    (C) 我們已將您下次的公司宴會排入行程。
    (D) 我們期待本週最後一天與您見面。

解析 (B) 這封信的主題是介紹一家新公司,而以這句話作為此類信件的結語非常合理。選項(A)(C)(D)都暗示了寫信者和收信者已經簽約、談好合作了,既然這是一封介紹公司服務的信,這三個選項自然都不合邏輯。

第135–138題請看下面這則通知。

紅線公車乘客須知

部分指定候車亭即將展開整修,因此自6月1日起,紅線的主街站將暫停服務,乘客可改利用奧克蘭大道站或河街站,請至城市交通服務處(CTS)網站查詢這些站點之時刻資訊。對此造成不便,我們深表歉意。這是市長為所有乘客改善公車服務的計畫一環。若有任何疑問或意見,請洽城市交通服務處之公共關係辦公室。

---

135. (A) 公車正在進行例行維修。
    (B) 公車票價預定下個月調漲。
    (C) 行駛這條路線的公車數量會增加。
    (D) 部分指定候車亭即將展開整修。

解析 (D) 選項(D)的描述是公車站暫停服務的合理原因。選項(A)(B)(C)都與公車有關,但不符合這裡的文意。

136. (A) 也
    (B) 儘管
    (C) 代替、反而
    (D) 儘管如此

解析 (C) instead 的意思是「代替、反而」,這裡表示乘客可以使用這些車站來代替主街站。選項(A)(B)(D)放在這裡意思都不通。

137. (A) 同意、批准
　　 (B) 改善
　　 (C) 證明……不實、反駁
　　 (D) 責備、指責

解析 (B) improve 的意思是「改善」，整修候車亭是改善公車服務的一個方式。選項(A)(C)(D)放入句子意思都不通。

138. (A) 聯絡
　　 (B) 聯絡 (to V)
　　 (C) 可以聯絡
　　 (D) 你將聯絡

解析 (A) contact 在這裡作祈使語氣動詞，用來建議讀者可以做什麼事。選項(B)是不定詞。選項(C)必須搭配主詞。選項(D)表達命令，不適合用於此類通知。

第 139–142 題請看下面這則備忘錄。

收件人：全體員工
發布人：亞瑟・艾維斯
日期：2月10日
關於：年假政策

我們修改了公司的年假政策。

以下是修改後之政策內容。

● 年假申請須至少提前一個月提交。
● 欲申請休假，請填寫表 54，一份交給主管，一份交至人力資源辦公室。
● 一次休假勿超過兩週。如有特殊情況必須請假超過兩週，請與你的主管討論。

關於政策修改如有任何問題，我很樂意為你回答。

請隨時到我的辦公室。

139. (A) 修改須經人力資源辦公室核准。
(B) 請遵守手冊中的準則。
(C) 一年當中任何時候皆可請年假。
(D) 以下是修改後之政策內容。

解析 (D) 這個句子用來引出下面的條列項目。選項 (A)(B)(C) 都和公司政策的主題有關，但不適合放在這個位置。

140. (A)(B)(C)(D) 提交

解析 (C) 句子的主詞 requests 不會主動執行動作，申請不會自己提交出去，因此這裡要用被動語態動詞。選項 (A)(B)(D) 都是主動語態形式。

141. (A) 另一個
(B) 那一個
(C) 一些
(D) 這個

解析 (A) another 在這個句子中作代名詞，表示 another copy（另一份），這個句子的意思是「one copy for your supervisor and one copy for the HR office」（一份給主管，一份給人力資源辦公室）。選項 (B) 和 (D) 不符合這個句子的意思。選項 (C) 不正確是因為 some 指代複數名詞，這裡需要一個單數代名詞。

142. (A) 調整
(B) 關於
(C) 重新開始、繼續
(D) 更改、修改

解析 (B) regarding 在這裡指「關於」（= about）。選項 (A)(C)(D) 帶入句中都不合語意。

第 143–146 題請看下面這封信。

> 寇瑪爾飯店
> 4月3日
>
> 華倫先生，您好：
>
> 我們已收到您關於上週入住寇瑪爾飯店的來信，對於您如此不愉快的住宿體驗，我們深感遺憾。我們以卓越的客戶服務自豪，並致力於讓住客感到賓至如歸且住得舒適。很遺憾，在您最近一次住宿期間，我們未能達成此目標。由於當時飯店承辦兩場會議，且正值旅遊旺季的高峰，對我們而言是格外忙碌的時期。然而，這不能作為我們疏忽賓客舒適感受的藉口。
>
> 希望下次您到城內時，願意考慮再次入住寇瑪爾飯店。我們飯店的地理位置優越，配有設備完善的健身房和五星級餐廳。我隨信附上一張優惠券，下次入住時可享八折優惠。
>
> 阿瑪莉雅‧奈特
> 經理
> 敬上

143. (A) 感謝您造訪本市期間選擇入住寇瑪爾飯店。
 (B) 對於您如此不愉快的住宿體驗，我們深感遺憾。
 (C) 很遺憾我們那個時間沒有空房。
 (D) 我們飯店名列本市最優良的飯店之一。

解析 (B) 這封信的目的是向一名住客道歉，讓他有這麼不好的住宿經驗，選項 (B) 表達了這個想法。選項 (A)(C)(D) 都和飯店主題有關，但不符合此處的語境。

144. (A) on
 (B) in
 (C) of
 (D) due

解析 (A) pride oneself on something 為固定用法，正確的介系詞是 on。選項 (B)(C)(D) 都不能用在這個片語。

145．(A) 即將來臨的
(B) 最後的
(C) 近來、最近
(D) 最近的

解析 (D) recent用來表示不久前剛發生的事，這封信的第一個句子告訴我們，這名客人入住飯店是上星期才發生的事。選項(A)用來描述不久的未來即將發生的事。選項(B)的意思是「最後的」。選項(C)是副詞，不能修飾名詞。

146．(A)(B)(C)(D) 返回

解析 (C) 動詞consider後面要接動名詞。選項(A)是現在式或原形動詞。選項(B)是現在式。選項(D)是不定詞。

Part 7：閱讀測驗

作答方式：你會看到單篇或多篇文章的題組，文章後面配有幾個題目，各含四個選項。選出最適當的答案回答問題，將答案卡上對應的橢圓框塗滿。

第 147–148 題請看下面這個網頁。

---

www.foodshopping.com

檔案　編輯　檢視　收藏項目　工具　說明　　　頁面▼　安全性▼　工具▼

即將完成，請檢查您的訂單，並按下「確認結帳」進行付款，您的生鮮雜貨會立即安排出貨。您訂購的商品將於今日中午前送達。

如有任何特殊要求或意見，請在下方備註欄中說明。我們期待下次為您採購。

品名	數量	價格
香蕉	1磅	$0.99
橘子汽水（自有品牌）	6罐裝	$3.99
佛奧德牌牛奶巧克力	1條	$2.15
番茄	1磅	$3.45
整顆核桃	1磅	$8.50
	小計	$19.08
	服務費	$8.00
	稅金	$0.00
	總計	$27.08

備註：

請挑黃香蕉，馬上可以食用的。

確認結帳

147. 這筆訂單將於何時送達？
    (A) 今天早上
    (B) 今天下午
    (C) 明天早上
    (D) 明天下午

解析 (A) 網頁上描述這筆訂單將於今天中午前（before noon today）送達，也就是今天早上。選項(B)(C)(D)都與描述不符。

148. 顧客要求什麼？
    (A) 冰的汽水
    (B) 黃的番茄
    (C) 熟的香蕉
    (D) 切碎的核桃

解析 (C) 顧客在備註欄中寫著「yellow bananas that are ready for eating」（黃一點、馬上能食用的），也就是成熟的香蕉。選項(A)不正確，顧客沒有指定汽水的溫度。選項(B)重複使用了yellow這個字，但是和番茄無關。選項(D)不正確，顧客已經指定要買完整的核桃（whole walnuts）。

第149–150題請看下面這段簡訊對話串。

米莉・威爾森 你有看到倉庫寄來的電子郵件嗎？	8:45
保羅・史東 沒有。出貨有問題嗎？	8:46
米莉・威爾森 明天才會出貨。	8:47
保羅・史東 不行啊，彼德森會不高興的。	8:49
米莉・威爾森 誰？	8:51
保羅・史東 客戶，多付一千美金要求隔日到貨的那位。	8:52
米莉・威爾森 是嗎？我都不知道。我來打幾通電話，看看他們能不能加快速度。	8:54

149. 在 8：47 時，威爾森女士寫「It's not going out till tomorrow」是什麼意思？
    (A) 倉庫今天已經關閉。
    (B) 出貨會延遲。
    (C) 她會等一下再寫信給客戶。
    (D) 客戶還沒下訂單。

解析 (B) 史東先生問是不是出貨有問題，威爾森女士用這句話回覆，表示出貨會延遲，語意連貫。選項 (A)(B)(C) 的語意都不連貫。

150. 米莉表示要幫忙做什麼？
    (A) 打電話給客戶
    (B) 親自送貨
    (C) 讓訂單早點出貨
    (D) 退還一千元

解析 (C) 米莉寫說她會嘗試讓他們加快速度（get them to speed things up），意思就是讓這批貨早點送出。選項 (A) 指的是米莉要打電話，但她是要打去倉庫，不是打給客戶。選項 (B) 在對話中未被提及。選項 (D) 指的是客戶支付的隔日到貨運費，但對話中沒有提到要退還。

第 151-152 題請看下面這張費用報告。

艾斯特力克斯公司
費用核准單

員工姓名：羅蘭・韋伯
用途：威爾蒙特辦公室培訓研討會

類別	日期	描述	備註	金額
機票	9月16日至9月21日	來回票，商務艙	研討會原定於9月9日當週舉行，金額包含$200的更改費。	$885
飯店	9月16日至9月20日	威爾蒙特市雅翠恩飯店 $110／晚，共五晚		$550
租車	9月16日至9月21日	奇寶租車公司		$275

151. 機票費內含什麼費用？
    (A) 特殊餐點
    (B) 超額行李
    (C) 升等至頭等艙
    (D) 重新安排費用

解析 (D) 備註欄位提到一筆更改費（change fee），因為行程時間從9月9日改為9月16日，更改機票時產生了這筆費用。選項(A)(B)(C)都是產生額外費用的可能原因，但並非此處的正確答案。

152. 這名員工在飯店住了幾晚？
    (A) 1
    (B) 5
    (C) 6
    (D) 10

解析 (B) 飯店費用的描述中寫「$110/night x 5」，意思就是每晚110美元的費用被收取了五次，所以代表他住了五晚。選項(A)(C)(D)都與描述不符。

第153-154題請看下面這則徵才廣告。

> 小型會計師事務所誠徵兼職辦公室助理，將接受全方位工作訓練，包含電腦資料輸入、檔案管理和預約安排。須態度親切並能提供良好客戶服務。須熟練文書處理功能，並能學習辦公室常用軟體程式。請親自前往格雷森大道110號10室，找艾絲泰兒・福克斯應徵。請勿來電。

153. 這份工作的其中一項要求條件是什麼？
    (A) 熟練資料輸入
    (B) 會寫電腦程式
    (C) 懂文書處理
    (D) 有預約安排經驗

解析 (C) 廣告中提到「Must be proficient with word processing functions」，所以要懂文書處理。選項(A)和(D)是錄取後要接受的培訓項目。選項(B)重複使用了program和computers這兩個字，但廣告中沒提到要編寫電腦程式。

154. 要如何應徵這個職位？
    (A) 前往辦公室
    (B) 寄電子郵件
    (C) 寄出履歷
    (D) 打電話給福克斯女士

解析 **(A)** 廣告中說要親自應徵（Apply in person），並提供了辦公室的地址。選項(B)和(C)未被提及。選項(D)不正確，廣告中明確指出不要打電話（No phone calls）。

第155–157題請看下面這篇文章。

> 大都會區大眾運輸系統（MPTA）主管理查・溫格宣布，自2月1日起MPTA通勤鐵路線的列車長，將接受乘客出示智慧手機上的電子票證。乘客可至MPTA官網購買單程票、來回票，以及週票和年票，票證將以電子郵件寄送給購買者。列車長可直接掃描乘客智慧手機上的票證。乘客也可選擇自行列印票證，列車長將掃描列印之票證。為鼓勵民眾使用新系統，在二月期間購買所有電子票證可享八五折優惠。傳統紙本票仍可於多數通勤鐵路車站之售票機購買，不過此類票證將逐步淘汰，並自明年1月1日起停止販售。溫格先生表示，通勤鐵路之乘客調查顯示，他們對新系統的反應相當熱烈。

155. 這篇文章主要在講什麼？
    (A) 一個特別折扣
    (B) 一項乘客調查
    (C) 一種新型火車票
    (D) 火車資費調漲

解析 **(C)** 這篇文章講述通勤列車將逐步淘汰紙本票，改採用電子票證。選項(A)和(B)雖然有被提及，但不是文章的主旨。選項(D)未被提及。

156. 傳統票以何種方式販售？
    (A) 網路
    (B) 機器
    (C) 列車長
    (D) MPTA辦公室

解析 **(B)** 文中指出傳統票證由售票機販售。選項(A)是購買電子票證的方式。選項(C)雖然有被提及，但不是購票方式。選項(D)未被提及。

157. 第11行的片語 phased out，意義與下列何者最為接近？
    (A) 展示
    (B) 發現
    (C) 分配
    (D) 停止、中斷

解析 (D) phased out 的意思是「停止」，在這裡表示由於推出電子車票，傳統的紙本票不久後就會停止販售。選項 (A)(B)(C) 都不是這個片語的意思。

第 158–160 題請看下面這段描述。

專業認證

東南室內設計協會的專業認證計畫，為專業室內設計師提供三種等級的資格認證。本計畫開放給維持資格完備至少一年的會員參加。東南室內設計協會所發放的專業證書，受到國內大部分室內設計公司及培訓計畫的認可。

通過考試會獲頒證書。除了一級認證之外，任一級的考試都必須通過前一級考試才能參加。本計畫不需要課程作業，但我們會提供課程和閱讀材料，幫助你準備考試。

目前，認證考試每六個月舉行一次，地點在協會位於薩瓦納的總部。明年底前將推出網路測驗。想了解認證級別、備試課程或考試報名的相關資訊，請向我們的辦事處索取資料包：info@sidassn.org。請記得在郵件中註明你的會員編號。

---

158. 何者是參加考試的條件？
    (A) 協會會員資格
    (B) 完成特定課程
    (C) 室內設計經驗
    (D) 培訓計畫畢業

解析 (A) 文中寫到「The program is open to anyone who has been a member in good standing for at least one year」，所以必須是協會會員。選項 (B) 是協會提供的備試課程，可自由選擇參加，但不是必要條件。選項 (C) 就語境來說是有可能，但此處並未提及。選項 (D) 重複使用了 training program 這個片語，在文中指的是認可這項證書的培訓計畫或公司機構。

159. 考試多久舉行一次？
　　(A) 一個月6次
　　(B) 一年6次
　　(C) 一年一次
　　(D) 一年兩次

解析 **(D)** 文中提到考試每六個月（every six months）舉行一次，也就是一年兩次。選項(A)和(B)重複使用了 six 這個字。選項(C)誤解了 every six months 的意思。

160. 想參加考試的人應該做什麼？
　　(A) 報名上課
　　(B) 寄電子郵件到辦事處
　　(C) 造訪網站
　　(D) 與顧問交談

解析 **(B)** 文中提供了一個電子郵件地址，讓大家索取考試報名的相關資料。選項(A)是準備考試可以選擇做的事。選項(C)和(D)就語境來說是有可能，但此處並未提及。

第161–163題請看下面這張傳單。

閃電租車

最新消息：推出車損免責方案

您的標準租賃協議包含綜合保險。但若在租賃期間，您租用的車輛發生事故，您可能必須支付500美元的車損費，這筆費用不在保險範圍內。

年滿21歲、過去十二個月未曾發生事故的承租人，可選擇購買車損免責方案。免責方案不能取代保險，但能在意外費用發生時給您多一份安心。免責方案須於簽約時加入租賃協議。

我們提供兩種車損免責方案：
● 部分免責方案：租賃期間每日10美元，車損自負額降至250美元。
● 全額免責方案：租賃期間每日15美元，車損自負額降至0元。

現在就詢問您的租車專員，將此免責方案加入租賃協議。

161. 誰可以申請免責方案？
    (A) 租車公司的任何顧客
    (B) 通過路考的駕駛人
    (C) 租用一個禮拜的顧客
    (D) 擁有安全駕駛紀錄的人

解析 (D) 購買免責方案的條件是必須年滿21歲，且在過去十二個月內無事故紀錄（haven't been involved in an accident in the past 12 months）。選項(A)和標準答案相抵觸。選項(B)和(C)就語境而言是有可能，但未被提及。

162. 這個免責方案的目的是什麼？
    (A) 將保險期限延長為十二個月
    (B) 取消年齡要求
    (C) 減少或免除一筆費用
    (D) 取代常規保險

解析 (C) 免責方案可將車損自負額從500美元減至250美元或0元。選項(A)重複使用了12 months這個片語。選項(B)指的是購買免責方案的年齡要求，但沒有取消。選項(D)與傳單內容相抵觸，傳單上寫「These waivers are not a substitute for insurance coverage」，代表不可取代保險。

163. 免責方案須於何時購買？
    (A) 簽署租賃協議時
    (B) 預約時
    (C) 通報交通事故時
    (D) 購買保險時

解析 (A) 傳單上寫「The waiver must be added to the rental agreement at the time of signing」，所以是簽約時就要加入。選項(B)(C)(D)都和租車主題有關，但不是正確答案。

第 164–167 題請看下面這段網路聊天室討論串。

> 米哈・金 [1:15]
> 星期五的計畫進行得如何了？我好一陣子沒收到更新進度了。
>
> 海洛・裴瑞茲 [1:15]
> 我今天早上剛收到外燴公司的回覆，他們可以配合我的菜單調整，沒問題。
>
> 艾芭・瓊斯 [1:16]
> 不用多收費嗎？
>
> 海洛・裴瑞茲 [1:17]
> 不用。
>
> 米哈・金 [1:18]
> 真是好消息。場地布置呢？有人和維修部講過這件事嗎？
>
> 艾芭・瓊斯 [1:20]
> 我講了。他們會在11點30分以前把五十人用的桌椅準備完成並擺設好，外燴公司就可以進來布置他們的東西，他們說希望能提前一小時到場。
>
> 米哈・金 [1:21]
> 太棒了！昨晚我又收到了一些回覆，我想差不多所有人都回我了。
>
> 海洛・裴瑞茲 [1:21]
> 幾乎所有人都會來，對嗎？
>
> 米哈・金 [1:23]
> 看起來是。所以，外燴和場地布置都安排好了，我想應該就這樣了，我們都準備好了。

164. 他們正在規劃什麼？
    (A) 一場工作坊
    (B) 一場員工會議
    (C) 一場實物示範
    (D) 一場午餐會

解析 **(D)** 對話中出現了 caterers（外燴公司）、menu（菜單）、tables and chairs（桌椅），都暗示著會有餐飲服務，選項(D)是唯一和飲食有關的活動。選項(A)(B)(C)是同事間有可能一起討論的活動，但不是正確答案。

165．海洛修改了什麼？
    (A) 菜單
    (B) 時程
    (C) 賓客人數
    (D) 會場布置

解析 (A) 海洛提到「my menu modifications」，所以他修改了菜單。選項(B)(C)(D)在對話中都有提到，但不是海洛修改的事項。

166．米哈昨晚收到了什麼？
    (A) 一份賓客名單
    (B) 邀請函的回覆
    (C) 會場布置計畫
    (D) 外燴業者傳來的訊息

解析 (B) 米哈寫說她收到了一些RSVP。RSVP是法文répondez s'il vous plaît的縮寫，意思是「敬請回覆」，常用於邀請函，請求對方回覆要不要參加。在這句話之後，米哈和海洛又繼續討論是不是所有人都會來，指的就是所有受邀的人。選項(A)和對話主題有關，但對話中並未提及。選項(C)是對話討論的內容，但不是米哈收到的東西。選項(D)是海洛今天早上收到的訊息。

167．在1:23時，米哈寫「We're good to go」是什麼意思？
    (A) 賓客們很高興受到邀請。
    (B) 是時候布置會場了。
    (C) 一切準備就緒。
    (D) 她必須離開。

解析 (C) 「We're good to go」這個用語意指「我們準備好可以開始了」，米哈的意思是事情（外燴和場地）都安排好了、可以開始了。選項(A)(B)(D)都不是這句話的意思，放入對話中語意也不通。

第 168–171 題請看下面這段文章節錄。

這個問題十分常見。你剛完成學業，成為職場新鮮人。外面的競爭激烈，你要如何準備面試，才能在眾多競爭者中脫穎而出？–[1]–

「歸根究柢，就只有一件事。」伊芙琳・普立查說。她是XQ公司的前用人主管，現在則是自己創立之就業顧問公司──普立查有限責任公司──的總裁。「專業。這就是關鍵。你的衣著、談吐、舉止都要像個專業人士。」普立查解釋說，這一點看似顯而易見，但很多年輕人都掌握不了這個概念。她對準備展開初次面試的人提供了以下建議。–[2]–

外表優先。–[3]– 你必須穿得像個專業人士。男士請著西裝，女士可著西裝或襯衫搭配裙子的套裝。請記住衣服顏色不要太顯眼，黑色、深灰或深藍色都很適合面試。

–[4]– 進入面試房間時，以堅定的握手搭配自我介紹。說話時眼睛看著面試官，回答問題時要充滿自信。最重要的一點是手機一定要保持關機。

168. 誰會對這篇文章感興趣？
 (A) 用人主管
 (B) 就業機構
 (C) 中階專業人士
 (D) 應屆大學畢業生

解析 (D) 這篇文章的目標讀者被描述為「new to the job market, having just finished your education」和「young people」，所以是應屆畢業生。選項(A)和(B)不正確，這篇文章是寫給求職者看的，不是寫給招聘方看的。選項(C)不正確，這篇文章的目標讀者不是有經驗的人。

169. 文章的第二段第一行引用普立查女士的話：「It all boils down to one thing」，這句話是什麼意思？
 (A) 自人群中脫穎而出很重要。
 (B) 她的建議可以總結為一個字。
 (C) 人們必須努力讓自己看起來很專業。
 (D) 面試是聘僱過程中關鍵的一環。

解析 (B) 「It all boils down to . . .」就等於「It can be summarized as . . .」，表示「可以總結為……」，隨後馬上提出了一個字──professionalism（專業態度、專業精神）──來總結普立查女士的建議。選項(A)(C)(D)既非這句話的意思，也不符合此段落的文意。

170. 文中對面試衣著有何建議？
    (A) 顏色應採深色系。
    (B) 西裝要乾淨。
    (C) 裙子要長。
    (D) 服裝要是新的。

解析 (A) 文中指出「Keep in mind that you don't want the color of your clothes to shout. Black, charcoal gray, or deep blue are best for job interviews.」，代表顏色不要顯眼，並以深色系為主。選項(B)(C)(D)就面試語境來說是有可能，但文中並未提及。

171. 下面這個句子最適合放入文中[1][2][3][4]哪一個位置？
    「舉止表現得像個專業人士和外表像個專業人士一樣重要。」
    (A) [1]
    (B) [2]
    (C) [3]
    (D) [4]

解析 (D) 這句話點出這段文字的主題——行為舉止如何像個專業人士。選項(A)(B)(C)的位置並不適合放入此句。

第172-175題請看下面這封信。

8月22日

史蒂芬妮・傑克遜
新罕布夏州馬爾斯頓
郵政信箱第110號

傑克遜女士，您好：

我聽了您上週上本地廣播節目《綠能談話》的演講，您對太陽能的了解之深令我印象深刻。我自己對此主題也是略懂。我加入了一個名叫太陽能源的小型地方組織，該組織旨在引進更多太陽能到我們社區。我對各種太陽能板都有一點了解，我家屋頂也有裝一些，家中全年的熱水絕大多數都靠這些太陽能板提供。

如您所知，以替代能源來取代化石燃料攸關著我們的未來。我認為我們必須把觀念宣導出去，讓更多人加入我們。為了達到此目的，我們下個月底要在社區舉辦一場替代能源博覽會。如果您願意成為我們的演講嘉賓，我們將不勝感激。我們無法支付酬勞，但您可以利用此機會賣書。如果您打算參加，我需要在兩週內收到您的回覆，好將您排入日程。感謝您考慮我的請求，期待九月與您見面。

弗列德・馬奎茲
弗列德・馬奎茲
敬上

172. 馬奎茲先生為何寫這封信給傑克遜女士？
　　(A) 為了向她介紹他的組織
　　(B) 為了向她兜售太陽能板
　　(C) 為了邀請她參加一個活動
　　(D) 為了向她討個職位

解析 **(C)** 馬奎茲先生寫這封信是為了請傑克遜女士到替代能源博覽會上演講，也就是邀她參加一個活動。選項(A)是信中的部分內容，但不是主旨。選項(B)不正確，信中沒有要她買東西。選項(D)是寫信的可能原因，但不是這裡的情況。

173. 關於馬奎茲先生,文中有何說明?
　　(A) 他是太陽能源組織的主席。
　　(B) 他想讓更多人對他的理念感興趣。
　　(C) 他靠安裝太陽能板為生。
　　(D) 他是太陽能專家。

解析 (B) 馬奎茲先生描述替代能源時寫道:「I believe we need to spread the word and get more people on board with this」,就表示他想告訴大家、說服大家認同他的觀點。選項(A)是馬奎茲先生參與的組織,但沒提到他是不是主席。選項(C)不正確,他只有裝在自己家的屋頂。選項(D)描述的是傑克遜女士,馬奎茲先生提到他也略懂,但應該不到專家的程度。

174. 關於傑克遜女士,文中有何暗示?
　　(A) 她寫了一些書。
　　(B) 她是馬奎茲先生的朋友。
　　(C) 她主持一個廣播節目。
　　(D) 她經常旅行。

解析 (A) 馬奎茲先生在信中告訴傑克遜女士,她可以在博覽會上賣書,可見她有寫書。選項(B)不正確,信中可以看出馬奎茲先生並沒有見過傑克遜女士,只聽過她上廣播節目。選項(C)不正確,她只是節目來賓,不是主持人。選項(D)雖然可能是事實,但信中沒有任何一處有所暗示。

175. 馬奎茲先生何時必須收到傑克遜女士的回覆?
　　(A) 一週內
　　(B) 兩週內
　　(C) 九月前
　　(D) 下個月前

解析 (B) 馬奎茲先生寫道:「I will need to hear back from you before the end of two weeks」,兩週結束前就是兩週內。

第 176–180 題請看下面的網頁和電子郵件。

---

www.wisteriabb.com

檔案　編輯　檢視　收藏項目　工具　說明　　　頁面▼　安全性▼　工具▼

紫藤花民宿

紫藤花民宿是由一座歷史悠久的農舍改建而成，歡迎大家前來體驗住宿。我們一共有六間客房，每個房間都以具有時代特色的家具和文物作為裝飾。在布滿紫藤花的門廊放鬆身心，欣賞牧場和山丘景色，享受一片祥和與寧靜。參加導遊帶領的騎馬活動，穿越附近林間小徑。參與本地區所提供之多種精彩刺激的文化和體育活動。

我們寬敞的穀倉經過重新裝修，非常適合當作婚禮或家庭聚會場地。

欲了解如何在紫藤花民宿舉辦活動，請點此。

所有房型均附早餐，內含自製糕點和以當地嚴選食材精心製作的時令菜餚。

房價每晚 99 美元起。
週末期間，最少須住宿兩晚。

房型與空房查詢，請點此。

4 月 30 日前訂房可享原價八折優惠。

寄件者：lsimmonsherbs@simmons.com
收件者：info@wisteriabb.com
主旨：　自我介紹
日期：　4月1日

嗨，

我剛看到你們的民宿網站，看起來好漂亮！我注意到你們早餐使用的是當地食材。我自己是種植香草花卉的在地小農，平常都在地方的農夫市集賣我的產品，這一帶的飯店和餐廳很多都是我的常客。

我很樂意為你的民宿供應新鮮香草和花卉，可定期供應，也可依需求供應。我可以為你的早餐供應新鮮香草，和為你承辦的婚禮供應花飾。除此之外，你也可以考慮為客人在房內放一些芬芳的草本花束。

我下週隨時都可以過去詳談。同時，我也附上手上可提供的香草和花卉清單，按季節分類。價格會視情況調整，但總是很有競爭力。

期待您的回覆。

露辛達‧西蒙斯

176. 關於紫藤花民宿，文中有何暗示？
　　　(A) 是一間大飯店。
　　　(B) 位於鄉村地區。
　　　(C) 擁有一座花園。
　　　(D) 採用現代設計。

解析 (B) 紫藤花民宿是一座改造過的農舍，可以看到牧場和山丘景色，附近又有小徑可以騎馬穿越樹林，所以位於鄉村地區。選項(A)不正確，因只有六間客房，所以是一間民宿。選項(C)雖然有可能，但並未提及。選項(D)不正確，這間民宿位於一座歷史悠久的農舍。

177. 住客在紫藤花民宿可以做什麼？
　　　(A) 買手工藝品
　　　(B) 吃午餐
　　　(C) 舉辦聚會
　　　(D) 在穀倉工作

解析 (C) 網頁中提到住客可以租用穀倉舉辦婚禮或家庭聚會。選項(A)混淆了craft這個字的用法。選項(B)不正確，網頁中只有提到早餐。選項(D)重複使用了barn這個字，但網頁中只有說其是婚禮或聚會場地，沒有說是工作場所。

178. 住客要如何享有優惠？
　　(A) 在穀倉辦活動
　　(B) 4月入住紫藤花民宿
　　(C) 週末住宿兩晚
　　(D) 4月30日前訂房

解析 (D) 網頁上的資訊寫說「Book your room before April 30 and receive 20% off」，所以4月30日前訂房就可以打折。選項(A)雖然有被提到，但是和折扣無關。選項(B)是必須訂房的時間，不是入住時間。選項(C)雖然有被提及，但和折扣無關。

179. 西蒙斯女士為何寫這封電子郵件？
　　(A) 為了販售產品
　　(B) 為了訂房
　　(C) 為了詢問能不能買下這間民宿
　　(D) 為了詢問舉辦活動的事

解析 (A) 西蒙斯女士寫說「I would be happy to provide your business with fresh herbs and flowers」，所以她是要販售自家產品。選項(B)也是聯絡紫藤花民宿的可能原因，但不是這封信的目的。選項(C)重複使用了business這個字。

180. 西蒙斯女士是做哪一種生意？
　　(A) 農場
　　(B) 飯店
　　(C) 餐廳
　　(D) 活動規劃

解析 (A) 西蒙斯女士在種植香草和花卉，所以她是農夫，經營農場。選項(B)和(C)是和西蒙斯女士有生意往來的客戶類型。選項(D)和網頁中提到在穀倉辦活動有關。

第181–185題請看下面的電子郵件和傳單。

寄件者：drosen@mycompany.com
收件者：customerservice@marvelclean.com
主旨：　清潔
日期：　12月15日

驚奇清潔服務公司，您好：

我有興趣了解貴公司的清潔服務。我目前位於八角大樓，但計劃下個月搬走。根據這裡的租約條款，租戶必須將一切維持良好狀態，否則會被房東罰款。所以我需要請人在我離開後進來打掃，我同事建議我和您聯絡。我目前正在聯絡幾家清潔公司，這樣我才能比價。請問如果請您來打掃我的住處，要多少錢呢？您需要先到現場看一下嗎？還是可以根據房子的大小報價？它是小套房，所以裡面就只有一個大房間而已。

謝謝！
大衛・羅森

驚奇清潔服務公司
無論房子大小，我們通通打掃。

清潔事宜，交給我們。無論是富麗堂皇的豪宅，還是精巧簡約的套房，我們會讓您的家變得閃閃發亮。

三房以下	………	$75
四到五房	………	$125
六到七房	………	$175
八房	………	$200
多於八房	………	聯繫我們

如果您的場地超過八房，客服專員會和您討論您的需求，並提供報價單給您。我們保證價格絕對具有競爭力。可以在有需要時打電話給我們，也可以安排每週或每月定期打掃。

今天就預約清潔服務。
customerservice@marvelclean.com
303-555-1212

181. 羅森先生為何需要請人打掃他的公寓？
    (A) 他正在尋找房客。
    (B) 他有客人要來。
    (C) 他要搬走了。
    (D) 他要舉辦派對。

解析 **(C)** 羅森先生在信中提到他下個月要搬走（leaving next month），必須把房子恢復到良好狀態才不會被罰款。選項(A)重複使用了tenants這個字。選項(B)把信中的visit混淆成visitors，信中羅森先生是問對方要不要先來看一下（visit）房子。選項(D)是找人來打掃房子的可能原因，但不是此處的情況。

182. 羅森先生是怎麼知道驚奇清潔公司的？
    (A) 同事推薦的。
    (B) 他上網找到的。
    (C) 他的房東介紹的。
    (D) 他看到傳單。

解析 **(A)** 羅森先生寫說「a colleague at work suggested I contact you」，所以是同事推薦的。選項(B)雖然有可能，但不是正確答案。選項(C)重複使用了landlord這個字。選項(D)不正確，羅森先生問的資訊（價格），傳單上都有寫，所以不太可能看過傳單。

183. 清潔羅森先生的公寓會花費多少錢？
    (A) $75
    (B) $125
    (C) $175
    (D) $200

解析 **(A)** 羅森先生說他的公寓就只有一個房間，對照傳單上的價目表，三房以下是75美元。選項(B)(C)(D)是房間更多的清潔費。

184. 關於驚奇清潔服務公司，文中有何暗示？
    (A) 收費高於其他清潔公司。
    (B) 只做住宅清潔。
    (C) 不接單次顧客。
    (D) 很少清潔多於八個房間的場所。

解析 **(B)** 傳單上提到mansion（豪宅）、apartment（公寓）、home（家），都是住宅，且沒有提到其他類型的場所。選項(A)不正確，傳單上說價格很有競爭力（competitive），就表示他們的價格和競爭對手差不多。選項(C)不正確，傳單上寫說「Call us when you need us, or arrange for regular weekly or monthly service.」，表示歡迎顧客單次預約，或定期安排打掃。選項(D)不正確，傳單上有此類場所的報價，代表常接到這種案子。

185. 傳單第二段第三行的 estimate 這個字，意義與下列何者最為接近？
　　(A) 猜測
　　(B) 價值
　　(C) 分析
　　(D) 近似額

解析 (D) estimate 在傳單中指一個預估的價錢，或者說是一個接近的價格。選項 (A)(B)(C) 都和此處的語境不符。

第 186–190 題請看下面的網頁、電子郵件和評論。

```
www.lannons.com
```

| 檔案 | 編輯 | 檢視 | 收藏項目 | 工具 | 說明 | 頁面▼ | 安全性▼ | 工具▼ |

藍儂辦公用品

◆特別促銷◆

E-Z 折疊桌

需要額外的辦公空間嗎？要辦大型會議或午餐會嗎？辦公桌太小了嗎？只需幾秒，E-Z 摺疊桌就能擴大你的空間。這款桌子可快速展開，最多可坐八人。不需要使用時，可摺疊成小巧尺寸，即可輕鬆放入大多數櫥櫃。黑色桌面搭配鍍鉻桌腳。

馬上下單，即享優惠！

小（可坐四人）	$65
中（可坐六人）	$85
大（可坐八人）	$110
三件組（大中小各一）	$230

（價格有效至 3 月 30 日）

是首購客嗎？結帳輸入優惠碼 Z54，可享八五折。

點此計算運費。

購物滿 100 美元免運。

實戰模擬試題 6

寄件者：noreply@lannon.com
收件者：miker@trex.com
主旨： 您的訂單

以下商品已於今日出貨。

訂購商品	數量	價格
E-Z 摺疊桌	1	$110.00
稅金		$6.50
運費		$0
總金額		$116.50

貨物追蹤號碼：1205039299919111
您可於9月15–19日至www.lannons.com/tracking追蹤您的訂單

★★★★★

麥可・里維拉　2016年6月14日

上週我收到了藍儂的E-Z摺疊桌，使用上一切都很順利，直到我要收納它的時候。它展開容易，非常堅固，而且好看，但是我第一次要把它摺起來收納時，才發現找不到桌腳的固定扣。一定要有固定扣，如果沒有，桌子就無法維持折疊狀態且你收納不了。因為此原因，我原本給這項產品三顆星。不過，我聯繫了客服，他們馬上就寄送固定扣給我了。客服人員非常客氣，有了固定扣，這張桌子完全符合我的需求。我們在辦公室開每週員工會議時使用，大家都說用起來很舒適又方便。非常推薦！

186. 關於這款折疊桌，文中有何暗示？
　　(A) 目前正在特價。
　　(B) 是三月限定商品。
　　(C) 有各種顏色。
　　(D) 是網站上最熱門的商品。

解析 **(A)** 這項產品被放在網站的特別促銷（special promotions）頁面，而列出的價格底下標注了優惠價格有效至3月30日（good through March 30），表示過了這個時間就會更改價格。選項(B)不正確，是目前的價格於三月期間有效，而不是產品。選項(C)不正確，網頁中只提到一種配色。選項(D)未被提及。

680

187. 里維拉先生訂了哪一款桌子？
　　　(A) 小的
　　　(B) 中的
　　　(C) 大的
　　　(D) 三件組

解析 (C) 根據電子郵件，里維拉先生付了110美元的商品費用，對照網頁上的價目表，是大型桌子的價格。選項(A)(B)(D)都不是這個價格。

188. 里維拉先生為什麼不用付運費？
　　　(A) 他有免運優惠券。
　　　(B) 他的訂單超過100美元。
　　　(C) 這家公司從不收運費。
　　　(D) 他忘記把這筆費用加入訂購單。

解析 (B) 網頁上說「Free shipping on all orders of $100 or more」，表示超過100美元就免運，而里維拉先生買的桌子是110美元，已達到免運門檻。選項(A)是被網頁上提到的首購優惠給混淆。選項(C)不正確，網頁上有給計算運費的連結。選項(D)不正確，他的訂單本來就免運了，不需要加入這筆費用。

189. 里維拉先生為什麼要訂購桌子？
　　　(A) 客戶諮詢用
　　　(B) 擴大辦公桌空間
　　　(C) 午餐時給客人用
　　　(D) 開會用

解析 (D) 里維拉先生在評論中說，他會在每週員工會議時使用這張桌子。選項(A)未被提及。選項(B)和(C)是網頁建議的使用方式。

190. 里維拉先生為什麼要修改原本的產品評分？
　　　(A) 他使用產品的方式改變。
　　　(B) 他的同事喜歡這項產品。
　　　(C) 這家公司修正了一個錯誤。
　　　(D) 他聽了其他評論者的意見。

解析 (C) 里維拉先生說他的桌子少了零件（固定扣），因為這樣原本給三顆星，後來公司補寄了零件給他，所以現在他對產品十分滿意。選項(A)和(D)也有可能，但並未提及。選項(B)在他的評論中有提到，但不是改評分的原因。

第 191–195 題請看下面的傳單和電子郵件。

史東尼布魯克晚餐劇場
為您呈現
《羅密歐與茱麗葉》
威廉・莎士比亞劇作
6月 12／13／14／19／20／21日

享用三道菜套餐，餐後欣賞我們精心編排的莎士比亞經典故事。
立即訂位！請上網造訪 www.stoneybrookdt.com，或來電 493-555-2121。

	僅表演	晚餐加表演
每人	$50	$80
雙人	$90	$135

晚餐 6:30 開始，表演 8:00 開始。
三道菜套餐內含：
- 湯或沙拉（擇一）
- 主菜——牛肉／雞肉／素食
- 甜點

寄件者：estherwilson@acme.com
收件者：bobcharles@workplace.com
主旨：　晚餐劇場
日期：　6月12日

鮑伯：

你有興趣看《羅密歐與茱麗葉》嗎？我妹給了我一些票，她用不到。它們是史東尼布魯克晚餐劇場的票，所以會先吃晚餐，然後看戲劇。我聽說那裡的餐點普通，但是戲劇的評價都很高。

票是6月21日的，那天我要6點出頭才能離開辦公室，我實在不想吃晚餐遲到，所以我想最好的辦法是我搭計程車到那邊和你碰面。希望你能來，我知道會很有趣的。

艾絲特

寄件者：bobcharles@workplace.com
收件者：estherwilson@acme.com
主旨：　關於：晚餐劇場
日期：　6月12日

嗨，艾絲特：

好的，我很樂意和妳一起去。聽起來很有趣，我還是第一次去看這齣戲劇呢！我會開車，所以我打算去接妳，妳就不用擔心要搭計程車。從妳辦公室到晚餐劇場只要十五分鐘，我想我們應該可以及時抵達。

我知道妳說關於食物的部分是什麼意思。其實我以前去那裡吃過，我覺得我們可以直接跳過晚餐，看表演就好。不過既然妳已經有票了，我們就盡可能好好享用吧。我非常期待看劇呢。

6月21日見。

鮑伯

191. 關於晚餐劇場供應的餐點，文中有何暗示？
　　(A) 會在表演結束後上菜。
　　(B) 包含無肉料理。
　　(C) 可以和表演的票分開買。
　　(D) 餐廳評論者給予很高的評價。

解析 (B) 菜單的描述中出現了vegetarian（素食）這個字，是其中一道主菜。選項(A)不正確，傳單上說表演在晚餐之後開始（meal followed by ...）。選項(C)不正確，價目表中有「僅表演」(show only)，但沒有「僅晚餐」(dinner only)。選項(D)不正確，艾絲特寫說食物普通，鮑伯也表示同意，而獲得很高評價的是戲劇。

192. 艾絲特花了多少錢購買晚餐劇場的票？
　　(A) $ 0
　　(B) $ 80
　　(C) $ 90
　　(D) $ 135

解析 (A) 艾絲特沒有付任何錢買票，票是她妹妹給她的。選項(B)(C)(D)是傳單上所列的價格。

193. 艾絲特大概會怎麼去晚餐劇場？
    (A) 她會自己開車。
    (B) 她會搭計程車。
    (C) 她會搭公車。
    (D) 她會搭鮑伯的車。

解析 (D) 鮑伯在電子郵件中提議開車去接艾絲特，所以艾絲特會搭他的車去劇場。選項(A)不正確，開車的是鮑伯，而不是艾絲特。選項(B)是艾絲特原本的打算。選項(C)在文中未被提及。

194. 關於鮑伯，文中有何暗示？
    (A) 他不愛看戲劇。
    (B) 他沒看過《羅密歐與茱麗葉》。
    (C) 他不認為這齣劇會很好看。
    (D) 他沒去過晚餐劇場。

解析 (B) 鮑伯在信中寫說「it will be my first time seeing this particular play」，表示他沒看過《羅密歐與茱麗葉》的戲劇演出。選項(A)和(C)不正確，鮑伯寫說「I am really looking forward to seeing the play」，表示他很期待看劇。選項(D)不正確，鮑伯寫說「I've actually eaten there before」，表示他曾經去過。

195. 第二封電子郵件的第二段第二行，skip 這個字的意義與下列何者最為接近？
    (A) 吃、喝
    (B) 改善
    (C) 省略
    (D) 跳躍

解析 (C) 鮑伯的意思是他們可以省略晚餐不吃，因為可能不好吃。選項(A)(B)(D)都與文意不符。

第196–200題請看下面的行程、傳單和電子郵件。

```
HR製造商
行程表：希莉・哈金
威爾特郡／蒙太古之行
4月10–15日

4月10日星期日            2:30 p.m. 搭乘微風航空23號航班離開
                        8:30 p.m. 抵達威爾特郡 威爾特郡里維拉飯店
4月11日星期一            10 a.m.–5 p.m. 和產品研發小組開會
4月12日星期二            8:00 a.m. 搭火車前往蒙太古
                        參觀HR製造商工廠 蒙太古松林飯店
4月13日星期三            9:15 a.m. 搭火車前往威爾特郡
                        2:00 p.m. 和行銷部開會
                        威爾特郡里維拉飯店
4月14日星期四            8:00 a.m. 和約翰・安德魯斯共進早餐
                        10:00 a.m. 威爾特郡遊覽
                        1:30 p.m. 向威爾特郡員工進行簡報
4月15日星期五            9:45 a.m. 搭乘微風航空567號航班離開
```

```
                不要錯過第三屆威爾特郡
                     商務博覽會！
由本地區各企業擺設的展示攤位
✓ 來看新產品和創新成果。
✓ 了解當前最好的商業實務。

由知名商業專家開設的工作坊
✓ 向國內最受尊崇的商業專家學習。
（請見另一面的工作坊主題列表和完整時程表。）

攜帶你的履歷！
✓ 各大企業的招募人員會在這裡與求職者會面，並討論就業機會。

                  威爾特郡會議中心
                     4月15–17日
```

實戰模擬試題6

寄件者：shakim@hrmanufacturersinc
收件者：kkato@hrmanufacturersinc
主旨：　四月之行
日期：　3月29日

肯：

謝謝你幫我安排好下個月的行程，一切看起來很好。終於有機會和威爾特郡的團隊見面，我非常期待。只有一件事。我得知那個週末威爾特郡會有一場商業博覽會，我想藉此機會去看看。這會是和前同事見面的好機會，說不定還可以建立一些寶貴的人脈關係。所以，如果你能把我回程的日期改為星期六，那就太好了。我想，這代表飯店要多住一天，航班時間也要重新安排。

謝謝！

希莉

196. 哈金女士何時會參觀工廠？
　　(A) 4月10日
　　(B) 4月11日
　　(C) 4月12日
　　(D) 4月13日

解析 (C) 根據行程表，哈金女士會在4月12日參觀HR製造商工廠。選項(A)(B)(D)的日期安排的是其他活動。

197. 民眾在商業博覽會上可以做什麼？
　　(A) 購買產品
　　(B) 面試工作
　　(C) 學習撰寫履歷
　　(D) 了解商業貸款

解析 (B) 傳單上有一條資訊寫說「Recruiters from major companies will be available to meet with job seekers and discuss employment opportunities」，招募者會和求職者見面討論就業機會。選項(A)指的是展示攤位的產品，但沒有提到販售之事。選項(C)重複使用了 résumé 這個字，傳單中建議民眾攜帶履歷。選項(D)未被提及。

198. 傳單第六行的 renowned 這個字,意義與下列何者最為接近?
    (A) 受過訓練的
    (B) 有名的
    (C) 有經驗的
    (D) 有知識的

解析 (B) renowned 的意思是「著名的、有名的」。選項(A)(C)(D)都不是這個字的意思。

199. 哈金女士想對行程做什麼更改?
    (A) 將她的行程增加一天
    (B) 換一家飯店
    (C) 再加一場員工會議
    (D) 週末待在威爾特郡

解析 (A) 哈金女士想將回程日從星期五改為星期六,以便參加商業博覽會。選項(B)(C)(D)就商務語境是有可能的,但並非此處的正確答案。

200. 關於哈金女士,文中有何暗示?
    (A) 她未曾到過威爾特郡辦公室。
    (B) 她經常出差。
    (C) 她正在聘僱人員。
    (D) 她曾在威爾特郡工作。

解析 (A) 哈金女士在信中寫到「I'm really looking forward to finally having the chance to meet the Wiltshire team」,暗示了她以前沒到過威爾特郡辦公室。選項(B)和電子郵件的主題有關,但她沒有提及。選項(C)是她到商業博覽會可能會做的事,但她也沒有提及。選項(D)和正確答案相抵觸。

STOP 本測驗到此結束。如果你在時間結束前作答完畢,可以回頭檢查 Part 5、6、7 的答案。

EZ TALK

New TOEIC 新制多益聽力閱讀全題型攻略＋實戰模擬 6 回題庫大全

TOEIC Premium: 6 Practice Tests + Online Audio, 10th edition

作　　者：Lin Lougheed Ph.D.
譯　　者：丁宥榆
主　　編：潘亭軒
責任編輯：鄭雅方
審　　訂：Judd Piggott、洪欣
封面設計：兒日設計
版型設計：洪伊珊
內頁排版：簡單瑛設
行銷企劃：張爾芸

發 行 人：洪祺祥
副總經理：洪偉傑
副總編輯：曹仲堯
法律顧問：建大法律事務所
財務顧問：高威會計師事務所

出　　版：日月文化出版股份有限公司
製　　作：EZ 叢書館
地　　址：臺北市信義路三段 151 號 8 樓
電　　話：(02)2708-5509
傳　　真：(02)2708-6157
客服信箱：service@heliopolis.com.tw
網　　址：www.heliopolis.com.tw
郵撥帳號：19716071 日月文化出版股份有限公司

總 經 銷：聯合發行股份有限公司
電　　話：(02)2917-8022
傳　　真：(02)2915-7212
印　　刷：中原造像股份有限公司
初　　版：2025 年 8 月
定　　價：899 元
Ｉ Ｓ Ｂ Ｎ：978-626-7641-75-0

New TOEIC 新制多益聽力閱讀全題型攻略＋實戰模擬 6 回題庫大全 = TOEIC premium : 6 practice tests + online audio/Lin Lougheed 著；丁宥榆譯. -- 初版. -- 臺北市：日月文化出版股份有限公司, 2025.08
1264 面；　19x25.7 公分. -- (EZ talk)
譯自：TOEIC premium : 6 practice tests + online audio, 10th ed.
ISBN 978-626-7641-75-0（平裝）
1.CST: 多益測驗

805.1895　　　　　　　　　　114007746

This edition arranged with Barron's Educational Series in association with Biagi Literary Management through Andrew Nurnberg Associates International Limited.
Traditional Chinese copyright © 2025 by HELIOPOLIS CULTURE GROUP

◎版權所有 翻印必究
◎本書如有缺頁、破損、裝訂錯誤，請寄回本公司更換

本書所附音檔由 EZ Course 平台 (https://ezcourse.com.tw) 提供。購書讀者使用音檔，須註冊 EZ Course 會員，並同意平台服務條款及隱私權與安全政策，完成信箱認證後，前往「書籍音頻」頁面啟動免費訂閱程序。訂閱過程中，購書讀者需完成簡易書籍問答驗證，以確認購書資格與使用權限。完成後，即可免費線上收聽本書專屬音檔。

音檔為授權數位內容，僅限購書讀者本人使用。請勿擅自轉載、重製、散布或提供他人，違反使用規範者將依法追究。購書即表示購書讀者已了解並同意上述條件。詳細操作方式請見書中說明，或至 EZ Course 網站「書籍音頻操作指引」常見問答頁面查詢。